THE HARRY BOSCH NOVELS

By Michael Connelly

The Black Echo

The Black Ice

The Concrete Blonde

The Last Coyote

The Poet

Trunk Music

Blood Work

Angels Flight

Void Moon

A Darkness More than Night

Michael CONNELLY

THE HARRY BOSCH NOVELS

The Black Echo
The Black Ice
The Concrete Blonde

LITTLE, BROWN AND COMPANY

New York Boston

Little, Brown and Company
Time Warner Book Group
1271 Avenue of the Americas, New York, NY 10020
Visit our Web site at www.twbookmark.com

First Omnibus Edition, 2001

The characters and events in this book are fictitious.
Any similarity to real persons, living or dead, is coincidental
and not intended by the author.

Library of Congress Cataloging-in-Publication Data
Connelly, Michael.
The Harry Bosch novels / by Michael Connelly.
p. cm.
Contents: The black echo — The black ice — The concrete blonde.
ISBN 0-316-15497-0
1. Detective and mystery stories, American. 2. Bosch, Harry
(Fictitious character) — Fiction. 3. Police — California — Los
Angeles — Fiction. 4. Los Angeles (Calif.) — Fiction. I. Title.
PS 3553.O51165 A6 2001
813'.54 — dc21   2001029486

10 9 8 7 6 5 4

Q-FF
Printed in the United States of America

Contents

The
Black
Echo

*This is for W. Michael Connelly
and Mary McEvoy Connelly*

Acknowledgments

I would like to thank the following people for their help and support:

Many thanks to my agent, Philip Spitzer, and to my editor, Patricia Mulcahy, for all their hard work, enthusiasm and belief in this book.

Also, thanks to the many police officers who over the years have given me an insight into their jobs and lives. I also want to acknowledge Tom Mangold and John Pennycate, whose book *The Tunnels of Cu Chi* tells the real story of the tunnel rats of the Vietnam War.

Last, I would like to thank my family and friends for their encouragement and unqualified support. And, most of all, I am indebted to my wife, Linda, whose belief and inspiration never waned.

PART I

SUNDAY, MAY 20

The boy couldn't see in the dark, but he didn't need to. Experience and long practice told him it was good. Nice and even. Smooth strokes, moving his whole arm while gently rolling his wrist. Keep the marble moving. No runs. Beautiful.

He heard the hiss of the escaping air and could sense the roll of the marble. They were sensations that were comforting to him. The smell reminded him of the sock in his pocket and he thought about getting high. Maybe after, he decided. He didn't want to stop now, not until he had finished the tag with one uninterrupted stroke.

But then he stopped — when the sound of an engine was heard above the hiss of the spray can. He looked around but saw no light save for the moon's silvery white reflection on the reservoir and the dim bulb above the door of the pump house, which was midway across the dam.

But the sound didn't lie. There was an engine approaching. Sounded like a truck to the boy. And now he thought he could hear the crunching of tires on the gravel access road that skirted the reservoir. Coming closer. Almost three in the morning and someone was coming. Why? The boy stood up and threw the aerosol can over the fence toward the water. He heard it clunk down in the brush, short of the mark. He pulled the sock from his pocket and decided just one quick blow to give himself balls. He buried his nose in the sock and drew in heavily on the paint fumes. He rocked back on his heels, and his eyelids fluttered involuntarily. He threw the sock over the fence.

The boy stood his motorbike up and wheeled it across the road, back toward the tall grass and the bottlebrush and pine trees at the base of the hill. It was good cover, he thought, and he'd be able to see what was coming. The sound of the engine was louder now. He was sure it was just a few seconds away, but he didn't see the glow of headlights. This confused him. But it was too late to run. He put the motorbike down in the tall brown grass and stilled the free-spinning front wheel with his hand. Then he huddled down on the earth and waited for whatever and whoever was coming.

Harry Bosch could hear the helicopter up there, somewhere above the darkness, circling up in the light. Why didn't it land? Why didn't it bring help? Harry was moving through a smoky, dark tunnel and his batteries were dying. The beam of the flashlight grew weaker every yard he covered. He needed help. He needed to move faster. He needed to reach the end of the tunnel before the light was gone and he was alone in the black. He heard the chopper make one more pass. Why didn't it land? Where was the help he needed? When the drone of the blades fluttered away again, he felt the terror build and he moved faster, crawling on scraped and bloody knees, one hand holding the dim light up, the other pawing the ground to keep his balance. He did not look back, for he knew the enemy was behind him in the black mist. Unseen, but there. And closing in.

When the phone rang in the kitchen, Bosch immediately woke. He counted the rings, wondering if he had missed the first one or two, wondering if he had left the answering machine on.

He hadn't. The call was not picked up and the ringing didn't stop until after the required eight rounds. He absentmindedly wondered where that tradition had come from. Why not six rings? Why not ten? He rubbed his eyes and looked around. He was slumped in the living room chair again, the soft recliner that was the centerpiece of his meager furnishings. He thought of it as his watch chair. This was a misnomer, however, because he slept in the chair often, even when he wasn't on call.

Morning light cut through the crack in the curtains and slashed its mark across the bleached pine floor. He watched particles of dust floating lazily in the light near the sliding glass door. The lamp on the table next to him was on, and the TV against the wall, its sound very low, was broadcasting a Sunday-morning Jesus show. On the table next to the chair were the companions of insomnia: playing cards, magazines, and paperback mystery novels — these only lightly thumbed and then discarded. There was a crumpled pack of cigarettes on the table and three empty beer bottles — assorted brands that had once been members of six-packs of their own tribe. Bosch was fully dressed, right down to a rumpled tie held to his white shirt by a silver 187 tie tack.

He reached his hand down to his belt and then around back to the area below his kidney. He waited. When the electronic pager sounded he cut the annoying chirp off in a second. He pulled the device off his belt and looked at the number. He wasn't surprised. He pushed himself out of the chair, stretched, and popped the joints of his neck and back. He walked to the kitchen, where the phone was on the counter. He wrote "Sunday, 8:53 A.M." in a notebook he took from his jacket pocket before dialing. After two rings a voice said, "Los Angeles Police Department, Hollywood Division. This is Officer Pelch, how can I help you?"

Bosch said, "Somebody could die in the time it took to get all that out. Let me talk to the watch sergeant."

Bosch found a fresh pack of cigarettes in a kitchen cabinet and got his first smoke of the day going. He rinsed dust out of a glass and filled it with tap water, then took two aspirins out of a plastic bottle that was also in the cabinet. He was swallowing the second when a sergeant named Crowley finally picked up.

"What, did I catch you in church? I rang your house. No answer."

"Crowley, what have you got for me?"

"Well, I know we had you out last night on that TV thing. But you're still catching. You and your partner. All weekend. So, that means you got the DB up at Lake Hollywood. In a pipe up there. It's on the access road to the Mulholland Dam. You know it?"

"I know the place. What else?"

"Patrol's out. ME, SID notified. My people don't know what they got, except a DB. Stiff's about thirty feet into this pipe there. They don't want to go all the way in, mess up a possible crime scene, you know? I had 'em page your partner but he hasn't called in. No answer at his phone either. I thought maybe the two of you was together or something. Then I thought, nah, he ain't your style. And you ain't his."

"I'll get ahold of him. If they didn't go all the way in, how they know it's a DB and not just some guy sleeping it off?"

"Oh, they went in a bit, you know, and reached in with a stick or something and poked around at the guy pretty good. Stiff as a wedding night prick."

"They didn't want to mess up a crime scene but then they go poking around the body with a stick. That's wonderful. These guys get in after they raised the college requirement, or what?"

"Hey, Bosch, we get a call, we've got to check it out. Okay? You want for us to transfer all our body calls directly to the homicide table to check out? You guys'd go nuts inside a week."

Bosch crushed the cigarette butt in the stainless steel sink and looked out the kitchen window. Looking down the hill he could see one of the tourist trams moving between the huge beige sound studios in Universal City. A side of one of the block-long buildings was painted sky blue with wisps of white clouds; for filming exteriors when the natural L.A. exterior turned brown as wheat.

Bosch said, "How'd we get the call?"

"Anonymous to nine one one. A little after oh four hundred. Dispatcher said it came from a pay phone on the boulevard. Somebody out screwin' around, found the thing in the pipe. Wouldn't give a name. Said there was a stiff in the pipe, that's all. They'll have the tape down at the com center."

Bosch felt himself getting angry. He pulled the bottle of aspirin out of the cabinet and put it in his pocket. While thinking about the 0400 call, he opened the refrigerator and bent in. He saw nothing that interested him. He looked at his watch.

"Crowley, if the report came in at four A.M. why are you just getting to me now, nearly five hours later?"

"Look, Bosch, all we had was an anonymous call. That's it. Dispatcher said it was a kid, no less. I wasn't going to send one of my guys up that pipe in the middle of the night on information like that. Coulda been a prank. Coulda been an ambush. Coulda been anything, fer crissake. I waited till it got light out and things slowed down around here. Sent some of my guys over there at the end of shift. Speaking of end of shifts, I'm outta here. I've been waiting to hear from them and then from you. Anything else?"

Bosch felt like asking if it ever occurred to him that it would be dark in the pipe whether they went poking around at 0400 or 0800, but let it go. What was the use?

"Anything else?" Crowley said again.

Bosch couldn't think of anything, but Crowley filled the empty space.

"It's probly just some hype who croaked himself, Harry. No righteous one eighty-seven case. Happens all the time. Hell, you remember we pulled one out of that same pipe last year. . . . Er, well, that was before you came out to Hollywood. . . . So, see, what I'm saying is some guy, he goes into this same pipe — these transients, they sleep up there all the time — and he's a slammer but he shoots himself with a hot load and that's it. Checks out. 'Cept we didn't find him so fast that time, and with the sun and all beating on the pipe a couple days, he gets cooked in there. Roasted like a tom turkey. But it didn't smell as good."

Crowley laughed at his own joke. Bosch didn't. The watch sergeant continued.

"When we pulled this guy out, the spike was still in his arm. Same thing here. Just a bullshit job, a no-count case. You go out there, you'll be back home by noon, take a nap, maybe go catch the Dodgers. And then next weekend? Somebody else's turn in the barrel. You're off watch. And that's a three-day pass. You got Memorial Day weekend coming next week. So do me a favor. Just go out and see what they've got."

Bosch thought a moment and was about to hang up, then said, "Crowley, what did you mean you didn't find that other one so fast? What makes you think we found this one fast?"

"My guys out there, they say they can't smell a thing off this stiff other than a little piss. It must be fresh."

"Tell your guys I'll be there in fifteen minutes. Tell them not to fuck anymore with anything at my scene."

"They —"

Bosch knew Crowley was going to defend his men again but hung up before he had to hear it. He lit another cigarette as he went to the front door to get the *Times* off the step. He spread the twelve pounds of Sunday paper out on the kitchen counter, wondering how many trees died. He found the real estate supplement and paged through it until he saw a large display ad for Valley Pride Properties. He ran his finger down a list of Open Houses until he found one address and description marked Call Jerry. He dialed the number.

"Valley Pride Properties, can I help you?"

"Jerry Edgar, please."

A few seconds passed and Bosch heard a couple of transfer clicks before his partner got on the line.

"This is Jerry, may I help you?"

"Jed, we just got another call. Up at the Mulholland Dam. And you aren't wearing your pager."

"Shit," Edgar said, and there was silence. Bosch could almost hear him thinking, I've got three showings today. There was more silence and Bosch pictured his partner on the other end of the line in a $900 suit and a bankrupt frown. "What's the call?"

Bosch told him what little he knew.

"If you want me to take this one solo, I will," Bosch said. "If anything comes up with Ninety-eight, I'll be able to cover it. I'll tell him you're taking the TV thing and I'm doing the stiff in the pipe."

"Yeah, I know you would, but it's okay, I'm on my way. I'm just going to have to find someone to cover for my ass first."

They agreed to meet at the body, and Bosch hung up. He turned the answering machine on, took two packs of cigarettes from the cabinet and put them in his sport coat pocket. He reached into another cabinet and took out the nylon holster that held his gun, a Smith & Wesson 9mm — satin finished, stainless steel and loaded with eight rounds of XTPs. Bosch thought about the ad he had seen once in a police magazine. Extreme Terminal Performance. A bullet that expanded on impact to 1.5 times its width, reaching terminal depth in the body and leaving maximum wound channels. Whoever had written it had been right. Bosch had killed a man a year earlier with one shot from twenty feet. Went in under the right armpit, exited below the left nipple, shattering heart and lungs on its way. XTP. Maximum wound channels. He clipped the holster to his belt on the right side so he could reach across his body and take it with his left hand.

He went into the bathroom and brushed his teeth without toothpaste: he was out and had forgotten to go by the store. He dragged a wet comb through his hair and stared at his red-rimmed, forty-year-old eyes for a long moment. Then he studied the gray hairs that were steadily crowding out the brown in his curly hair. Even the mustache was going gray. He had begun seeing flecks of gray in the sink when he shaved. He touched a hand to his chin but decided not to shave. He left his house then without changing even his tie. He knew his client wouldn't mind.

Bosch found a space where there were no pigeon droppings and leaned his elbows on the railing that ran along the top of the Mulholland Dam. A cigarette dangled from his lips, and he looked through the cleft of the hills to the city below. The sky was gunpowder gray and the smog was a form-fitted shroud over Hollywood. A few of the far-off towers in downtown poked up through the poison, but the rest of the city was under the blanket. It looked like a ghost town.

There was a slight chemical odor on the warm breeze and after a while he pegged it. Malathion. He'd heard on the radio that the fruit fly helicopters had been up the night before spraying North Hollywood down through the Cahuenga Pass. He thought of his dream and remembered the chopper that did not land.

To his back was the blue-green expanse of the Hollywood reservoir, 60 million gallons of the city's drinking water trapped by the venerable old dam in a canyon between two of the Hollywood Hills. A six-foot band of dried clay ran the length of the shoreline, a reminder that L.A. was in its fourth year of drought. Farther up the reservoir bank was a ten-foot-high chain-link fence that girded the entire shoreline. Bosch had studied this barrier when he first arrived and wondered if the protection was for the people on one side of the fence or the water on the other.

Bosch was wearing a blue jumpsuit over his rumpled suit. His sweat had stained through the underarms and back of both layers of clothing. His hair was damp and his mustache drooped. He had been inside the pipe. He could feel the slight, warm tickle of a Santa Ana wind drying the sweat on the back of his neck. They had come early this year.

Harry was not a big man. He stood a few inches short of six feet and was built lean. The newspapers, when they described him, called him wiry. Beneath the jumpsuit his muscles were like nylon cords, strength concealed by economy of size. The gray that flecked his hair was more partial to the left side. His eyes were brown-black and seldom betrayed emotion or intention.

The pipe was located above ground and ran for fifty yards alongside the reservoir's access road. It was rusted inside and out, and was empty and unused except by those who sought its interior as a shelter or its exterior as a canvas for spray paint. Bosch had had no clue to its purpose until the reservoir caretaker had volunteered the information. The pipe was a mud break. Heavy rain, the caretaker said, could loosen earth and send mud sliding off the hillsides and into the reservoir. The three-foot-wide pipe, left over from some unknown district project or boondoggle, had been placed in a predicted slide area as the reservoir's first and only defense. The pipe was held in place by half-inch-thick iron rebar that looped over it and was embedded in concrete below.

Bosch had put on the jumpsuit before going into the pipe. The letters LAPD were printed in white across the back. After taking it out of the trunk of his car and stepping into it, he realized it was probably cleaner than the suit he was trying to protect. But he wore it anyway, because he had always worn it. He was a methodical, traditional, superstitious detective.

As he had crawled with flashlight in hand into the damp-smelling, claustrophobic cylinder, he felt his throat tighten and his heartbeat quicken. A familiar emptiness in his gut gripped him. Fear. But he snapped on the light and the darkness receded along with the uneasy feelings, and he set about his work.

Now he stood on the dam and smoked and thought about things. Crowley, the watch sergeant, had been right, the man in the pipe was certainly dead. But he had also been wrong. This would not be an easy one. Harry would not be home in time for an afternoon nap or to listen to the Dodgers on KABC. Things were wrong here. Harry wasn't ten feet inside the pipe before he knew that.

There were no tracks in the pipe. Or rather, there were no tracks that were of use. The bottom of the pipe was dusty with dried orange mud and cluttered with paper bags, empty wine bottles, cotton balls, used syringes, newspaper bedding — the debris of the homeless and addicted. Bosch had studied it all in the beam of the flashlight as he slowly made his way toward the body. And he had found no clear trail left by the dead man, who lay headfirst into the pipe. This was not right. If the dead man had crawled in of his own accord, there would be some indication of this. If he had been dragged in, there would be some sign of that, too. But there was nothing, and this deficiency was only the first of the things that troubled Bosch.

When he reached the body, he found the dead man's shirt — a black, open-collar crew shirt — pulled up over his head with his arms tangled inside. Bosch had seen enough dead people to know that literally nothing was impossible during the last breaths. He had worked a suicide in which a man who had shot himself in the head had then changed pants before dying, apparently because he did not want his body to be discovered soaked in human waste. But the shirt and the arms on the dead man in the pipe did not seem acceptable to Harry. It looked to Bosch as if the body had been dragged into the pipe by someone who had pulled the dead man by the collar.

Bosch had not disturbed the body or pulled the shirt away from the face. He noted that it was a white male. He detected no immediate indication of the fatal injury. After finishing his survey of the body, Bosch carefully moved over the corpse, his face coming within a half foot of it, and then continued through the pipe's remaining forty yards. He found no tracks and nothing else of evidentiary value. In twenty minutes he was back in the sunlight. He then sent a crime scene tech named Donovan in to chart the location of debris in the pipe and video the body in place. Donovan's face had betrayed his surprise at having to go into the pipe on a case he'd already written off as an OD. He had tickets to the Dodgers, Bosch figured.

After leaving the pipe to Donovan, Bosch had lit a cigarette and walked to the dam's railing to look down on the fouled city and brood.

At the railing he could hear the sound of traffic filtering up from the Hollywood Freeway. It almost sounded gentle from such a distance. Like a calm ocean. Down through the cleft of the canyon he saw blue swimming pools and Spanish tile roofs.

A woman in a white tank top and lime-green jogging shorts ran by him on the dam. A compact radio was clipped to her waistband, and a thin yellow wire carried sound to the earphones clamped to her head. She seemed to be in her own world, unaware of the grouping of police ahead of her until she reached the yellow crime scene tape stretched across the end of the dam. It told her to stop in two languages. She jogged in place for a few moments, her long blond hair clinging to sweat on her shoulders, and watched the police, who were mostly watching her. Then she turned and headed back past Bosch. His eyes followed her, and he noticed that when she went by the pump house she deviated her course to avoid something. He walked over and found glass on the pavement. He looked up and saw the broken bulb in the socket above the pump house door. He made a mental note to ask the caretaker if the bulb had been checked lately.

When Bosch returned to his spot at the railing a blur of movement from below drew his attention. He looked down and saw a coyote sniffing among the pine needles and trash that covered the earth below the trees in front of the dam. The animal was small and its coat was scruffy and completely missing some patches of hair. There were only a few of them left in the city's protected areas, left to scavenge among the debris of the human scavengers.

"They're pulling it out now," a voice said from behind.

Bosch turned and saw one of the uniforms that had been assigned to the crime scene. He nodded and followed him off the dam, under the yellow tape, and back to the pipe.

A cacophony of grunts and heavy gasps echoed from the mouth of the graffiti-scarred pipe. A shirtless man, with his heavily muscled back scratched and dirty, emerged backward, towing a sheet of heavy black plastic on top of which lay the body. The dead man was still face up with his head and arms mostly obscured in the wrapping of the black shirt. Bosch looked around for Donovan and saw him stowing a video recorder in the back of the blue crime scene van. Harry walked over.

"Now I'm going to need you to go back in. All the debris in there, newspapers, cans, bags, I saw some hypos, cotton, bottles, I need it all bagged."

"You got it," Donovan said. He waited a beat and added, "I'm not saying anything, but, Harry, I mean, you really think this is the real thing? Is it worth busting our balls on?"

"I guess we won't know until after the cut."

He started to walk away but stopped.

"Look, Donnie, I know it's Sunday and, uh, thanks for going back in."

"No problem. It's straight OT for me."

The shirtless man and a coroner's technician were sitting on their haunches, huddled over the body. They both wore white rubber gloves. The technician was Larry Sakai, a guy Bosch had known for years but had never liked. He had a plastic fishing-tackle box open on the ground next to him.

He took a scalpel from the box and made a one-inch-long cut into the side of the body, just above the left hip. No blood came from the slice. From the box he then removed a thermometer and attached it to the end of a curved probe. He stuck it into the incision, expertly though roughly turning it and driving it up into the liver.

The shirtless man grimaced, and Bosch noticed he had a blue tear tattooed at the outside corner of his right eye. It somehow seemed appropriate to Bosch. It was the most sympathy the dead man would get here.

"Time of death is going to be a pisser," Sakai said. He did not look up from his work. "That pipe, you know, with the heat rising, it's going to skew the temperature loss in the liver. Osito took a reading in there and it was eighty-one. Ten minutes later it was eighty-three. We don't have a fixed temp in the body or the pipe."

"So?" Bosch said.

"So I am not giving you anything here. I gotta take it back and do some calculating."

"You mean give it to somebody else who knows how to figure it?" Bosch asked.

"You'll get it when you come in for the autopsy, don't worry, man."

"Speaking of which, who's doing the cutting today?"

Sakai didn't answer. He was busy with the dead man's legs. He grabbed each shoe and manipulated the ankles. He moved his hands up the legs and reached beneath the thighs, lifting each leg and watching as it bent at the knee. He then pressed his hands down on the abdomen as if feeling for contraband. Lastly, he reached inside the shirt and tried to turn the dead man's head. It didn't move. Bosch knew rigor mortis worked its way from the head through the body and then into the extremities.

"This guy's neck is locked but good," Sakai said. "Stomach's getting there. But the extremities still have good movement."

He took a pencil from behind his ear and pressed the eraser end against the skin on the side of the torso. There was purplish blotching on the half of the body closest to the ground, as if the body were half full of red wine. It was post-mortem lividity. When the heart stops pumping, the blood seeks the low ground. When Sakai pressed the pencil against the dark skin, it did not blanch white, a sign the blood had fully clotted. The man had been dead for hours.

"The po-mo lividity is steady," Sakai said. "That and the rig makes me estimate that this dude's been dead maybe six to eight hours. That's going to have to hold you, Bosch, until we can work with the temps."

Sakai didn't look up as he said this. He and the one called Osito began pulling the pockets on the dead man's green fatigue pants inside out. They were empty, as were the large baggy pockets on the thighs. They rolled the body to one side to check the back pockets. As they did this, Bosch leaned down to look closely at the exposed back of the dead man. The skin was purplish with lividity and dirty. But he saw no scratches or marks that allowed him to conclude that the body had been dragged.

"Nothing in the pants, Bosch, no ID," Sakai said, still not looking up.

Then they began to gently pull the black shirt back over the head and onto the torso. The dead man had straggly hair that had more gray in it than the original black. His beard was unkempt and he looked to be about fifty, which made Bosch figure him at about forty. There was something in the breast pocket of the shirt and Sakai fished it out, looked at it a moment and then put it into a plastic bag held open by his partner.

"Bingo," Sakai said and handed the bag up to Bosch. "One set of works. Makes our jobs all a lot easier."

Sakai next peeled the dead man's cracked eyelids all the way open. The eyes were blue with a milky caul over them. Each pupil was constricted to about the size of a pencil lead. They stared vacantly up at Bosch, each pupil a small black void.

Sakai made some notes on a clipboard. He'd made his decision on this one. Then he pulled an ink pad and a print card from the tackle box by his side. He inked the fingers of the left hand and began pressing them on the card. Bosch admired how quickly and expertly he did this. But then Sakai stopped.

"Hey. Check it out."

Sakai gently moved the index finger. It was easily manipulated in any direction. The joint was cleanly broken, but there was no sign of swelling or hemorrhage.

"It looks post to me," Sakai said.

Bosch stooped to look closer. He took the dead man's hand away from Sakai and felt it with both his own, ungloved hands. He looked at Sakai and then at Osito.

"Bosch, don't start in," Sakai barked. "Don't be looking at him. He knows better. I trained him myself."

Bosch didn't remind Sakai that it was he who had been driving the ME wagon that dumped a body strapped to a wheeled stretcher onto the Ventura Freeway a few months back. During rush hour. The stretcher rolled down the Lankershim Boulevard exit and hit the back end of a car at a gas station. Because of the fiberglass partition in the cab, Sakai didn't know he had lost the body until he arrived at the morgue.

Bosch handed the dead man's hand back to the coroner's tech. Sakai turned to Osito and spoke a question in Spanish. Osito's small brown face became very serious and he shook his head no.

"He didn't even touch the guy's hands in there. So you better wait until the cut before you go saying something you aren't sure about."

Sakai finished transferring the fingerprints and then handed the card to Bosch.

"Bag the hands," Bosch said to him, though he didn't need to. "And the feet."

He stood back up and began waving the card to get the ink to dry. With his other hand he held up the plastic evidence bag Sakai had given him. In it a rubber band held together a hypodermic needle, a small vial that was half filled with what looked like dirty water, a wad of cotton and a pack of matches. It was a shooter's kit and it looked fairly new. The spike was clean, with no sign of corrosion. The cotton, Bosch guessed, had only been used as a strainer once or twice. There were tiny whitish-brown crystals in the fibers. By turning the bag he could look inside each side of the matchbook and see only two matches missing.

Donovan crawled out of the pipe at that moment. He was wearing a miner's helmet equipped with a flashlight. In one hand he carried several plastic bags, each containing a yellowed newspaper, or a food wrapper or a crushed beer can. In the other he carried a clipboard on which he had diagramed where each item had been found in the pipe. Spiderwebs hung off the sides of the helmet. Sweat was running down his face and staining the painter's breathing mask he wore over his mouth and nose. Bosch held up the bag containing the shooter's kit. Donovan stopped in his tracks.

"You find a stove in there?" Bosch asked.

"Shit, he's a hype?" Donovan said. "I knew it. What the fuck are we doin' all this for?"

Bosch didn't answer. He waited him out.

"Answer is yes, I found a Coke can," Donovan said.

The crime scene tech looked through the plastic bags in his hands and held one up to Bosch. It contained two halves of a Coke can. The can looked reasonably new and had been cut in half with a knife. The bottom half had been inverted and its concave surface used as a pan to cook heroin and water. A stove. Most hypes no longer used spoons. Carrying a spoon was probable cause for arrest. Cans were easy to come by, easy to handle and disposable.

"We need the kit and the stove printed as soon as we can," Bosch said. Donovan nodded and carried his burden of plastic bags toward the police van. Bosch turned his attention back to the ME's men.

"No knife on him, right?" Bosch said.

"Right," Sakai said. "Why?"

"I need a knife. Incomplete scene without a knife."

"So what. Guy's a hype. Hypes steal from hypes. His pals probably took it."

Sakai's gloved hands rolled up the sleeves of the dead man's shirt. This revealed a network of scar tissue on both arms. Old needle marks, craters left by abscesses and infections. In the crook of the left elbow was a fresh spike mark and a large yellow-and-purplish hemorrhage under the skin.

"Bingo," Sakai said. "I'd say this guy took a hot load in the arm and, phssst, that was it. Like I said, you got a hype case, Bosch. You'll have an early day. Go get a Dodger dog."

Bosch crouched down again to look closer.

"That's what everybody keeps telling me," he said.

And Sakai was probably right, he thought. But he didn't want to fold this one away yet. Too many things didn't fit. The missing tracks in the pipe. The shirt pulled over the head. The broken finger. No knife.

"How come all the tracks are old except the one?" he asked, more of himself than Sakai.

"Who knows?" Sakai answered anyway. "Maybe he'd been off it awhile and decided to jump back in. A hype's a hype. There aren't any reasons."

Staring at the tracks on the dead man's arms, Bosch noticed blue ink on the skin just below the sleeve that was bunched up on the left bicep. He couldn't see enough to make out what it said.

"Pull that up," he said and pointed.

Sakai worked the sleeve up to the shoulder, revealing a tattoo of blue and red ink. It was a cartoonish rat standing on hind legs with a rabid, toothy and vulgar grin. In one hand the rat held a pistol, in the other a booze bottle marked XXX. The blue writing above and below the cartoon was smeared by age and the spread of skin. Sakai tried to read it.

"Says 'Force' — no, 'First.' Says 'First Infantry.' This guy was army. The bottom part doesn't make — it's another language. 'Non . . . Gratum . . . Anum . . . Ro —' I can't make that out."

"Rodentum," Bosch said.

Sakai looked at him.

"Dog Latin," Bosch told him. "Not worth a rat's ass. He was a tunnel rat. Vietnam."

"Whatever," Sakai said. He took an appraising look at the body and the pipe. He said, "Well, he ended up in a tunnel, didn't he? Sort of."

Bosch reached his bare hand to the dead man's face and pushed the straggly black and gray hairs off the forehead and away from the vacant eyes. His doing this without gloves made the others stop what they were doing and watch this unusual, if not unsanitary, behavior. Bosch paid no notice. He stared at the face for a long moment, not saying anything, not hearing if anything was said. In the moment that he realized that he knew the face, just as he knew the tattoo, the vision of a young man flashed in his mind. Raw-boned and tan, hair buzzed short. Alive, not dead. He stood up and turned quickly away from the body.

Making such a quick, unexpected motion, he banged straight into Jerry Edgar, who had finally arrived and walked up to huddle over the body. They both took a step back, momentarily stunned. Bosch put a hand to his forehead. Edgar, who was much taller, did the same to his chin.

"Shit, Harry," Edgar said. "You all right?"

"Yeah. You?"

Edgar checked his hand for blood.

"Yeah. Sorry about that. What are you jumping up like that for?"

"I don't know."

Edgar looked over Harry's shoulder at the body and then followed his partner away from the pack.

"Sorry, Harry," Edgar said. "I sat there waiting an hour till somebody came out to cover me on my appointments. So tell me, what have we got?"

Edgar was still rubbing his jaw as he spoke.

"Not sure yet," Bosch said. "I want you to get in one of these patrol cars that has an MCT in it. One that works. See if you can get a sheet on a Meadows, Billy, er, make that William. DOB would be about 1950. We need to get an address from DMV."

"That's the stiff?"

Bosch nodded.

"Nothing, no address with his ID?"

"There is no ID. I made him. So check it out on the box. There should be some contact in the last few years. Hype stuff, at least, out of Van Nuys Division."

Edgar sauntered off toward the line of parked black-and-whites to find one with a mobile computer terminal mounted on the dashboard. Because he was a big man, his gait seemed slow, but Bosch knew from experience that Edgar was a hard man to keep pace with. Edgar was impeccably tailored in a brown suit with a thin chalk line. His hair was close cropped and his skin was almost as smooth and as black as an eggplant's. Bosch watched Edgar walk away and couldn't help but wonder if he had timed his arrival to be just late enough to avoid having to wrinkle his ensemble by stepping into a jumpsuit and crawling into the pipe.

Bosch went to the trunk of his car and got out the Polaroid camera. He then went back to the body, straddled it and stooped to take photographs of the face. Three would be enough, he decided, and he placed each card that was ejected from the camera on top of the pipe while the photo developed. He couldn't help but stare at the face, at the changes made by time. He thought of that face and the inebriated grin that creased it on the night that all of the First Infantry rats had come out of the tattoo parlor in Saigon. It had taken the burned-out Americans four hours, but they had all been made blood brothers by putting the same brand on their shoulders. Bosch remembered Meadows's joy in the companionship and fear they all shared.

Harry stepped away from the body while Sakai and Osito unfolded a black, heavy plastic bag with a zipper running up the center. Once the body bag was unfolded and opened, the coroner's men lifted Meadows and placed him inside.

"Looks like Rip Van-fucking-Winkle," Edgar said as he walked up.

Sakai zipped the bag up and Bosch saw a few of Meadows's curling gray hairs had been caught in the zipper. Meadows wouldn't mind. He had once told Bosch that he was destined for the inside of a body bag. He said everybody was.

Edgar held a small notepad in one hand, a gold Cross pen in the other.

"William Joseph Meadows, 7–21–50. That sound like him, Harry?"

"Yeah, that's him."

"Well, you were right, we have multiple contacts. But not just hype shit. We've got bank robbery, attempted robbery, possession of heroin. We got a loitering right here at the dam a year or so ago. And he did have a couple hype beefs. The one in Van Nuys you were talking about. What was he to you, a CI?"

"No. Get an address?"

"Lives up in the Valley. Sepulveda, up by the brewery. Tough neighborhood to sell a house in. So if he wasn't an informant, how'd you know this guy?"

"I didn't know him — at least recently. I knew him in a different life."

"What does that mean? When did you know the guy?"

"Last time I saw Billy Meadows was twenty years ago, or thereabouts. He was — it was in Saigon."

"Yeah, that'd make it about twenty years." Edgar walked over to the Polaroids and looked down at the three faces of Billy Meadows. "You know him good?"

"Not really. About as well as anybody got to know somebody there. You learned to trust people with your life, then when it's over you realize you didn't really even know most of them. I never saw him once I got back here. Talked to him once on the phone last year, that's all."

"How'd you make him?"

"I didn't, at first. Then I saw the tattoo on his arm. That brought the face back. I guess you remember guys like him. I do, at least."

"I guess . . ."

They let the silence sit there awhile. Bosch was trying to decide what to do, but could only wonder about the coincidence of being called to a death scene to find Meadows. Edgar broke the reverie.

"So you want to tell me what you've got that looks hinky here? Donovan over there looks like he's getting ready to shit his pants, all the work you're putting him through."

Bosch told Edgar about the problems, the absence of distinguishable tracks in the pipe, the shirt pulled over the head, the broken finger and that there was no knife.

"No knife?" his partner said.

"Needed something to cut the can in half to make a stove — if the stove was his."

"Could've brought the stove with him. Could have been that somebody went in there and took the knife after the guy was dead. If there was a knife."

"Yeah, could have been. No tracks to tell us anything."

"Well, we know from his sheet he was a blown-out junkie. Was he like that when you knew him?"

"To a degree. A user and seller."

"Well, there you go, longtime addict, you can't predict what they're going to do, when they're going to get off the shit or on it. They're lost people, Harry."

"He was off it, though — at least I thought he was. He's only got one fresh pop in his arm."

"Harry, you said you hadn't seen the guy since Saigon. How do you know whether he was off or on?"

"I hadn't seen him, but I talked to him. He called me once, last year sometime. July or August, I think. He'd been pulled in on another track marks beef by the hype car up in Van Nuys. Somehow, maybe reading newspapers or something — it was about the same time as the Dollmaker thing — he knew I was a cop, and he calls me up at Robbery-Homicide. He calls me from Van Nuys jail and asks if I could help him out. He would've only done, what, thirty days in county, but he was bottomed out, he said. And he, uh, just said he couldn't do the time this time, couldn't kick alone like that. . . ."

Bosch trailed off without finishing the story. After a long moment Edgar prompted him.

"And? . . . Come on, Harry, what'd you do?"

"And I believed him. I talked to the cop. I remember his name was Nuckles. Good name for a street cop, I thought. And then I called the VA up there in Sepulveda and I got him into a program. Nuckles went along with it. He's a vet, too. He got the city attorney to ask the judge for diversion. So anyway, the VA outpatient clinic took Meadows in. I checked about six weeks later and they said he'd completed, had kicked and was doing okay. I mean, that's what they told me. Said he was in the second level of maintenance. Talking to a shrink, group counseling. . . . I never talked to Meadows after that first call. He never called again, and I didn't try to look him up."

Edgar referred to his pad. Bosch could see the page he was looking at was blank.

"Look, Harry," Edgar said, "that was still almost a year ago. A long time for a hype, right? Who knows? He could have fallen off the wagon and kicked three times since then. That's not our worry here. The question is, what do you want to do with what we have here? What do you want to do about today?"

"Do you believe in coincidence?" Bosch asked.

"I don't know. I —"

"There are no coincidences."

"Harry, I don't know what you're talking about. But you know what I think? I don't see anything here that's screaming in my face. Guy crawls into the pipe, in the dark maybe he can't see what he's doing, he puts too much juice in his arm and croaks. That's it. Maybe somebody else was with him and smeared the tracks going out. Took his knife, too. Could be a hundred dif —"

"Sometimes they don't scream, Jerry. That's the problem here. It's Sunday. Everybody wants to go home. Play golf. Sell houses. Watch the ballgame. Nobody cares one way or the other. Just going through the motions. Don't you see that that's what they are counting on?"

"Who is 'they,' Harry?"

"Whoever did this."

He shut up for a minute. He was convincing no one, and that almost included himself. Playing to Edgar's sense of dedication was wrong. He'd be off the job as soon as he put in twenty. He'd then put a business card–sized ad in the union newsletter — "LAPD retired, will cut commission for brother officers" — and make a quarter million a year selling houses to cops or for cops in the San Fernando Valley or the Santa Clarita Valley or the Antelope Valley or whatever valley the bulldozers aimed at next.

"Why go in the pipe?" Bosch said then. "You said he lived up in the Valley. Sepulveda. Why come down here?"

"Harry, who knows? The guy was a junkie. Maybe his wife kicked him out. Maybe he croaked himself up there and his friends dragged his dead ass down here because they didn't want to be bothered with explaining it."

"That's still a crime."

"Yeah, that's a crime, but let me know when you find a DA that'll file it for you."

"His kit looked clean. New. The other tracks on his arm look old. I don't think he was slamming again. Not regularly. Something isn't right."

"Well, I don't know. . . . You know, AIDS and everything, they're supposed to keep a clean kit."

Bosch looked at his partner as if he didn't know him.

"Harry, listen to me, what I'm telling you is that he may have been your foxhole buddy twenty years ago but he was a junkie this year. You'll never be able to explain every action he took. I don't know about the kit or the tracks, but I do know that this does not look like one we should bust our humps on. This is a nine-to-fiver, weekends and holidays excluded."

Bosch gave up — for the moment.

"I'm going up to Sepulveda," he said. "Are you coming, or are you going back to your open house?"

"I'll do my job, Harry," Edgar said softly. "Just because we don't agree on something doesn't mean I'm not gonna do what I'm paid to do. It's never been that way, never will be. But if you don't like the way I do business, we'll go see Ninety-eight tomorrow morning and see about a switch."

Bosch was immediately sorry for the cheap shot, but didn't say so. He said, "Okay. You go on up there, see if anybody's home. I'll meet you after I sign off on the scene."

Edgar walked over to the pipe and took one of the Polaroid photos of Meadows. He slipped it into his coat pocket, then walked down the access road toward his car without saying another word to Bosch.

After Bosch took off his jumpsuit and folded it away in the trunk of his car, he watched Sakai and Osito slide the body roughly onto a stretcher and then into the back of a blue van. He started over, thinking about what would be the best way to get the autopsy done as a priority, meaning by at least the next day instead of four or five days later. He caught up with the coroner's tech as he was opening the driver's door.

"We're outta here, Bosch."

Bosch put his hand on the door, holding it from opening enough for Sakai to climb in.

"Who's doing the cutting today?"

"On this one? Nobody."

"Come on, Sakai. Who's on?"

"Sally. But he's not going near this one, Bosch."

"Look, I just went through this with my partner. Not you, too, okay?"

"Bosch, you look. You listen. I've been working since six last night and this is the seventh scene I've been to. We got drive-bys, floaters, a sex case. People are dying to meet us, Bosch. There is no rest for the weary, and that means no time for what you think might be a case. Listen to your partner for once. This one is going on the routine schedule. That means we'll get to it by Wednesday, maybe Thursday. I promise Friday at the latest. And tox results is at least a ten-day wait, anyway. You know that. So what's your goddam hurry?"

"Are. Tox results *are* at least a ten-day wait."

"Fuck off."

"Just tell Sally I need the prelim done today. I'll be by later."

"Christ, Bosch, listen to what I'm telling you. We've got bodies on gurneys stacked in the hall that we already know are one eighty-sevens and need to be cut. Salazar is not going to have time for what looks to me and everybody else around here except you like a hype case. Cut and dried, man. What am I going to say to him that's going to make him do the cut today?"

"Show him the finger. Tell him there were no tracks in the pipe. Think of something. Tell him the DB was a guy who knew needles too well to've OD'd."

Sakai put his head back against the van's side panel and laughed loudly. Then he shook his head as if a child had made a joke.

"And you know what he'll say to me? He'll say that it doesn't matter how long he'd been spiking. They all fuck up. Bosch, how many sixty-five-year-old junkies do you see around? None of them go the distance. The needle gets them all in the end. Just like this guy in the pipe."

Bosch turned and looked around to make sure none of the uniforms were watching and listening. Then he turned back to Sakai's face.

"Just tell him I'll be by there later," he said quietly. "If he doesn't find anything on the prelim, then fine, you can stick the body at the end of the line in the hall, or you can park it down at the gas station on Lankershim. I won't care then, Larry. But you tell him. It's his decision, not yours."

Bosch dropped his hand from the door and stepped back. Sakai got in the van and slammed the door. He started the engine and looked at Bosch through the window for a long moment before rolling it down.

"Bosch, you're a pain in the ass. Tomorrow morning. It's the best I can do. Today is no way."

"First cut of the day?"

"Just leave us alone today, okay?"

"First cut?"

"Yeah. Yeah. First cut."

"Sure, I'll leave you alone. See you tomorrow, then."

"Not me, man. I'll be sleeping."

Sakai rolled the window back up and the van moved away. Bosch stepped back to let it pass, and when it was gone he was left staring at the pipe. It was really for the first time then that he noticed the graffiti. Not that he hadn't seen that the exterior of the pipe was literally covered with painted messages, but this time he looked at the individual scrawls. Many were old, faded together — a tableau of letters spelling threats either long forgotten or since made good. There were slogans: Abandon LA. There were names: Ozone, Bomber, Stryker, many others. One of the fresher tags caught his eye. It was just three letters, about twelve feet from the end of the pipe — *Sha*. The three letters had been painted in one fluid motion. The top of the S was jagged and then contoured, giving the impression of a mouth. A gaping maw. There were no teeth but Bosch could sense them. It was as though the work wasn't completed. Still, it was good work, original and clean. He aimed the Polaroid at it and took a photo.

Bosch walked to the police van, putting the exposure in his pocket. Donovan was stowing his equipment on shelves and the evidence bags in wooden Napa Valley wine boxes.

"Did you find any burned matches in there?"

"Yeah, one fresh one," Donovan said. "Burned to the end. It was about ten feet in. It's there on the chart."

Bosch picked up a clipboard on which there was a piece of paper with a diagram of the pipe showing the body location and where the other material taken from the pipe had been. Bosch noticed that the match was found about fifteen feet from the body. Donovan then showed him the match, sitting at the bottom of its own plastic evidence bag. "I'll let you know if it matches the book in the guy's kit," he said. "If that's what you're thinking."

Bosch said, "What about the uniforms? What'd they find?"

"It's all there," Donovan said, pointing to a wooden bin in which there were still more plastic evidence bags. These contained debris picked up by patrol officers who had searched the area within a fifty-yard radius of the pipe. Each bag contained a description of the location where the object had been found. Bosch took each bag out and examined its contents. Most of it was junk that would have nothing to do with the body in the pipe. There were newspapers, clothing rags, a high-heeled shoe, a white sock with dried blue paint in it. A sniff rag.

Bosch picked up a bag containing the top to a can of spray paint. The next bag contained the spray paint can. The Krylon label said it was Ocean Blue. Bosch hefted the bag and could tell there was still paint in the can. He carried the bag to the pipe, opened it and, touching the nozzle with a pen, sprayed a line of blue next to the letters *Sha*. He sprayed too much. The paint ran down the curved side of the pipe and dripped onto the gravel. But Bosch could see the colors matched.

He thought about that for a moment. Why would a graffiti tagger throw half a can of paint away? He looked at the writing on the evidence bag. It had been found near the edge of the reservoir. Someone had attempted to throw the can into the lake but came up short. Again he thought, Why? He squatted next to the pipe and looked closely at the letters. He decided that whatever the message or name was, it wasn't finished. Something had happened that made the tagger stop what he was doing and throw the can, the top and his sniff sock over the fence. Was it the police? Bosch took out his notebook and wrote a reminder to call Crowley after midnight to see if any of his people had cruised the reservoir during the A.M. watch.

But what if it wasn't a cop that made the tagger throw the paint over the fence? What if the tagger had seen the body being delivered to the pipe? Bosch thought about what Crowley had said about an anonymous caller reporting the body. A kid, no less. Was it the tagger who called? Bosch took the can back to the SID truck and handed it to Donovan.

"Print this after the kit and the stove," he said. "I think it might belong to a witness."

"Will do," Donovan said.

Bosch drove down out of the hills and took the Barham Boulevard ramp onto the northbound Hollywood Freeway. After coming up through the Cahuenga Pass he went west on the Ventura Freeway and then north again on the San Diego Freeway. It took about twenty minutes to go the ten miles. It was Sunday and traffic was light. He exited on Roscoe and went east a couple of blocks into Meadows's neighborhood on Langdon.

Sepulveda, like most of the suburban communities within Los Angeles, had both good and bad neighborhoods. Bosch wasn't expecting trimmed lawns and curbs lined with Volvos on Meadows's street, and he wasn't disappointed. The apartments were at least a decade past being attractive. There were bars over the windows of the bottom units and graffiti on every garage door. The sharp smell of the brewery on Roscoe wafted into the neighborhood. The place smelled like a 4 A.M. bar.

Meadows had lived in a U-shaped apartment building that had been built in the 1950s, when the smell of hops wasn't yet in the air, gangbangers weren't on the street corner and there was still hope in the neighborhood. There was a pool in the center courtyard but it had long been filled in with sand and dirt. Now the courtyard consisted of a kidney-shaped plot of brown grass surrounded by dirty concrete. Meadows had lived in an upstairs corner apartment. Bosch could hear the steady drone of the freeway as he climbed the stairs and moved along the walkway that fronted the apartments. The door to 7B was unlocked and it opened into a small living room–dining room–kitchen. Edgar was leaning against a counter, writing in his notebook. He said, "Nice place, huh?"

"Yeah," Bosch said and looked around. "Nobody home?"

"Nah. I checked with a neighbor next door and she hadn't seen anybody around since the day before yesterday. Said the guy that lived here told her his name was Fields, not Meadows. Cute, huh? She said he lived all by himself. Been here about a year, kept to himself, mostly. That's all she knew."

"You show her the picture?"

"Yeah, she made him. Didn't like looking at a picture of a dead guy, though."

Bosch walked into a short hallway that led to a bathroom and a bedroom. He said, "You pick the door?"

"Nah — it was unlocked. No shit, I knock a couple times and I'm fixing to get my pouch outta the car and finesse the lock when, for the hell of it, I try the door."

"And it opens."

"It opens."

"You talk to the landlord?"

"Landlady's not around. Supposed to be, but maybe she went out to eat lunch or score some horse. I think everybody I seen around here is a spiker."

Bosch came back into the living room and looked around. There wasn't much. A couch covered with green vinyl was pushed against one wall, a stuffed chair was against the opposite wall with a small color television on the carpet next to it. There was a Formica-topped table with three chairs around it in the dining room. The fourth chair was by itself against the wall. Bosch looked at an old cigarette-scarred coffee table in front of the couch. On it were an overloaded ashtray and a crossword puzzle book. Playing cards were laid out in an unfinished game of solitaire. There was a *TV Guide*. Bosch had no idea if Meadows smoked but knew that no cigarettes had been found on the body. He made a mental note to check on it later.

Edgar said, "Harry, this place was turned. Not just the door being open and all, but, I mean, there are other things. The whole place has been searched. They did a halfway decent job, but you can tell. It was rushed. Go check out the bed and the closet, you'll see what I mean. I'm gonna give the landlady another try."

Edgar left and Bosch walked back through the living room to the bedroom. Along the way he noted the smell of urine. In the bedroom, he found a queen-sized bed without a backboard pushed against one wall. There was a greasy discoloration on the white wall at about the level where Meadows would have leaned his head while sitting up in bed. Opposite the bed an old six-drawer dresser was against the wall. A cheap rattan night table with a lamp on it stood next to the bed. Nothing else was in the room, not even a mirror.

Bosch studied the bed first. It was unmade, with pillows and sheets in a pile in the center. Bosch noticed that a corner of one of the sheets was folded between the mattress and the box spring, in the midsection of the left side of the bed. The bed would not have been made that way, obviously. Bosch pulled the corner out from under the mattress and let it hang loosely off the side of the bed. He lifted the mattress as if to search underneath it, then lowered it back into place. The corner of the sheet was back between the mattress and the box spring. Edgar was right.

He next opened the six bureau drawers. What clothes there were — underwear, white and dark socks and several T-shirts — were neatly folded and seemed undisturbed. When he closed the bottom left drawer he noticed that it slid unevenly and would not close all the way. He pulled it all the way out of the bureau. Then he pulled another drawer completely out of the dresser. Then the rest. When he had all the drawers out he checked the underside of each to see if something was or had been taped to it. He found nothing. He put them back in but kept changing their order until each one slid easily into place and closed completely. When he was done the drawers were in a different order. The right order. He was satisfied that someone had pulled the drawers out to search beneath and behind them, and had then put them back in the wrong order.

He went into the walk-in closet. He found only a quarter of the available space used. On the floor were two pairs of shoes, a pair of black Reebok running shoes that were dirty with sand and gray dust, and a pair of laced work boots that looked as though they had been recently cleaned and oiled. There was more of the gray dust from the shoes in the carpet. He crouched down and pinched some between his fingers. It seemed like concrete dust. He took a small evidence bag from his pocket and put some of the granules into it. Then he put the bag away and stood up. There were five shirts on hangers, a single white button-down oxford and four long-sleeved black pullovers, like the one Meadows had been wearing. On hangers next to the shirts were two pairs of well-faded jeans and two pairs of black pajamas or karate-style pants. The pockets on all four pairs of pants had been turned inside out. A plastic laundry basket on the floor contained dirty black pants, T-shirts, socks and a pair of boxer shorts.

Bosch walked out of the closet and left the bedroom. He stopped in the hallway bathroom and opened the medicine cabinet. There was a half-used tube of toothpaste, a bottle of aspirin and a single, empty insulin syringe box. When he closed the cabinet, he looked at himself and saw weariness in his eyes. He smoothed his hair.

Harry walked back to the living room and sat on the couch, in front of the unfinished solitaire hand. Edgar came in.

"Meadows rented the place last July first," he said. "The landlady's back. It was supposed to be a month-to-month lease but he paid for eleven months up front. Four bills a month. That's nearly five grand in cash he put down. Said she didn't ask him for references. She just took the money. He lived —"

"She said he paid for eleven months?" Bosch interrupted. "Was it a deal, pay for eleven, get the twelfth free?"

"Nah, I asked her about that and she said no, it was him. That's just the way he wanted to pay. Said he'd move out June first, this year. That's — what — ten days from now? She said he told her he moved out here on some kind of job, she thinks from Phoenix. Said he was some kind of shift supervisor for the tunnel dig on the subway project downtown. She got the impression that's all his job would take, eleven months, and then he'd go back to Phoenix."

Edgar was looking in his notebook, reviewing his conversation with the landlady.

"That's about it. She ID'd him off the Polaroid, too. She also knew him as Fields. Bill Fields. Said he kept odd hours, like he was on a night shift or something. Said she saw him last week coming home one morning, getting dropped off from a beige or tan Jeep. No license number because she wasn't looking. But she said he was all dirty, that's how she knew he was coming home from work."

They were silent for a few moments, both thinking.

Bosch finally said, "J. Edgar, I have a deal for you."

"You got a deal for me? Okay, let me hear it."

"You go home now or back to your open house or whatever. I'll take this from here. I'll go pull the tape at the com center, go back to the office and start the paper going. I'll see if Sakai made next-of-kin notification. I think, if I remember right, that Meadows was from Louisiana. Anyway, I've got the autopsy skedded for tomorrow at eight. I'll take that, too, on my way in.

"Now, your end is tomorrow you finish up last night's TV thing and take it over to the DA. Shouldn't be any problems with it."

"So you're taking the end that's dipped in shit and letting me skate. The transvestite-offs-transvestite case is as cut and dried as they come. No pun intended."

"Yeah. There's one thing I'd also want. On your way in from the Valley tomorrow, stop by the VA in Sepulveda and see if you can talk them into letting you see Meadows's file. Might have some names that could help. Like I said before, he was supposedly talking to a shrink in the outpatient care unit and in one of those circle jerks. Maybe one of those guys was spiking with him, knows what happened here. It's a long shot, I know. If they give you a hard time, give me a call and I'll work on a search warrant."

"Sounds like a deal. But I'm worried about you, Harry. I mean, you and I haven't been partners too long, and I know you probably want to work your way back downtown to Robbery-Homicide, but I don't see the percentage in busting your balls on this one. Yeah, this place has been turned over, but that isn't the question. The question is why. And on the face of things, nothing really stirs me. It looks to me like somebody dumped Meadows down at the reservoir after he croaked and searched his place to find his stash. If he had one."

"Probably that's the way it was," Bosch said after a few moments. "But a couple things still bother me. I want to puzzle with it a little more until I'm sure."

"Well, like I said, no problem with me. You're giving me the clean end of the stick."

"I think I'm going to look around a little more. You go ahead, and I'll see you tomorrow when I get back in from the cut."

"Okay, partner."

"And Jed?"

"Yeah?"

"It's got nothing to do with getting downtown again."

Bosch sat alone, thinking, and scanning the room for secrets. His eyes eventually came down on the cards spread out before him on the coffee table. Solitaire. He saw that all four aces were up. He picked up the deck of remaining cards and went through it, peeling off three cards at a time. In the course of going through he came across the two and three of spades and the two of hearts. The game hadn't stalled. It had been interrupted. And never finished.

He became restless. He looked down into the green glass ashtray and saw that all the butts were nonfiltered Camels. Was that Meadows's brand or his killer's? He got up and walked around the room. The faint smell of urine hit him again. He walked back into the bedroom. He opened the drawers of the bureau and stared at their contents once more. Nothing turned in his mind. He went to the window and looked out at the back end of another apartment building across an alley. There was a man with a supermarket cart in the alley. He was poking through a Dumpster with a stick. The cart was half full of aluminum cans. Bosch walked away and sat down on the bed and put his head back against the wall where the headboard should have been and the white paint was a dingy gray. The wall felt cool against his back.

"Tell me something," he whispered to no one.

Something had interrupted the card game and Meadows had died here, he believed. Then he was taken to the pipe. But why? Why not leave him? Bosch leaned his head back to the wall and looked straight across the room. It was at that moment that he noticed a nail in the wall. The nail was about three feet above the bureau and had been painted white along with the wall at some point a long time ago. That was why he hadn't noticed it before. He got up and went to look behind the bureau. In the three-inch space between it and the wall, he saw the edge of a fallen picture frame. With his shoulder, he pushed the heavy bureau away from the wall and picked up the frame. He stepped backward and sat on the edge of the bed studying it. The glass was cracked into an intricate spiderweb that had probably occurred when the frame fell. The damaged glass partially obscured an eight-by-ten black-and-white photograph. It was grainy and fading to a brownish yellow around the edges. The photo was more than twenty years old. Bosch knew this because between two cracks in the glass he saw his own, young face staring out and smiling.

Bosch turned the frame over and carefully bent back the tin prongs that kept the cardboard backing in place. As he was sliding the yellowed photo out, the glass finally gave way and the pieces dropped to the floor in shatters. He moved his feet away from the glass but didn't get up. He studied the photograph. There were no markings on front or back to tell where or when it had been taken. But he knew it must have been sometime in late 1969 or early 1970, because some of the men in the picture were dead after that.

There were seven of them in the photo. All tunnel rats. All shirtless and proudly displaying their T-shirt tan lines and tattoos, each man's dog tags taped together to keep them from jangling while they crawled through the tunnels. They had to have been in the Echo Sector of Cu Chi District, but Bosch could not tell or remember what village. The soldiers stood in a trench, positioned on both sides of a tunnel entrance no wider than the pipe in which Meadows would later be found dead. Bosch looked at himself and thought that his smile in the photograph was foolish. He was embarrassed by it now, in light of what was still to come after the moment was captured. Then he looked at Meadows in the photo and saw the thin smile and vacant stare. The others had always said Meadows would have a thousand-yard stare in an eight-by-eight room.

Bosch looked down at the glass between his feet and saw a pink piece of paper about the size of a baseball card. He picked it up by its edges and studied it. It was a pawn ticket from a shop downtown. The customer name on it was William Fields. It listed one item pawned: an antique bracelet, gold with jade inlay. The ticket was dated six weeks earlier. Fields had gotten $800 for the bracelet. Bosch slipped it into an evidence envelope from his pocket and stood up.

The trip downtown took an hour because of the traffic heading to Dodger Stadium. Bosch spent the time thinking about the apartment. It had been searched, but Edgar was right. It was a rush job. The pants pockets were the obvious tip. But the bureau drawers should've been put back in correctly, and the photo and the hidden pawn slip should not have been missed. What had been the hurry? He concluded it was because Meadows's body was in the apartment. It had to be moved.

Bosch exited on Broadway and headed south past Times Square to the pawnshop located in the Bradbury Building. Downtown L.A. was as quiet as Forest Lawn on most weekends, and he didn't expect to find the Happy Hocker open. He was curious and just wanted to drive by and take a look at the place before heading to the communications center. But when he drove past the storefront he saw a man outside with an aerosol can painting the word OPEN in black on a sheet of plywood. The board stood in place of the shop's front window. Bosch could see shards of glass on the dirty sidewalk below the plywood. He pulled to the curb. The spray painter was inside by the time he got to the door. He stepped through the beam of an electric eye, which sounded a bell from somewhere above all the musical instruments hanging from the ceiling.

"I'm not open, not Sundays," a man called from the back. He was standing behind a chrome cash register that was atop a glass counter.

"That's not what the sign you just painted says."

"Yes, but that is for tomorrow. People see boards over your windows they think you're out of business. I'm not out of business. I'm open for business, except for weekends. I just have a board out there for a few days. I painted OPEN so people will know, you see? Starting tomorrow."

"Do you own this business?" Bosch said as he pulled his ID case out and flipped open his badge. "This will only take a couple minutes."

"Oh, police. Why din't you say? I been waiting all day for you police."

Bosch looked around, confused, then put it together.

"You mean the window? I'm not here about that."

"What do you mean? The patrol police said to wait for detective police. I waited. I been here since five A.M. this morning."

Bosch looked around the shop. It was filled with the usual array of brass musical instruments, electronic junk, jewelry and collectibles. "Look, Mr. —"

"Obinna. Oscar Obinna pawnshops of Los Angeles and Culver City."

"Mr. Obinna, detectives don't roll on vandalism reports on weekends. I mean, they might not even be doing that during the week anymore."

"What vandalism? This was a breakthrough. Grand robbery."

"You mean a break-in? What was taken?"

Obinna gestured to two glass counter cases that flanked the cash register. The top plate in each case had been smashed into a thousand pieces. Bosch walked up closer and could see small items of jewelry, cheap-looking earrings and rings, nestled among the glass. But he also saw velvet-covered jewelry pedestals, mirrored plates and wood ring pegs where pieces should have been but weren't. He looked around and saw no other damage in the store.

"Mr. Obinna, I can call the duty detective and see if anyone is going to come out today, and if so when they will be here. But that is not what I've come for."

Bosch then pulled out the clear plastic envelope with the pawn ticket in it. He held it up for Obinna to see.

"Can I see this bracelet please?" The moment he said it he felt a bad premonition come over him. The pawnbroker, a small, round man with olive skin and dark hair noodled over a bare cranium, looked at Bosch incredulously, his dark bushy eyebrows knitted together.

"You're not going to take the report on my cases?"

"No sir, I'm investigating a murder. Can you please show me the bracelet pawned on this ticket? Then I will call the detective bureau and find out if anyone is coming today on your break-in. Thank you for your cooperation."

"Aygh! You people! I cooperate. I send my lists each week, even take pictures for your pawn men. Then all I ask for is one detective to investigate a robbery and I get a man who says his job is murder. I been waiting now since five A.M. in the morning."

"Give me your phone. I'll get somebody over."

Obinna took the receiver off a wall phone behind one of the damaged counters and handed it across. Bosch gave him the number to dial. While Bosch talked to the duty detective at Parker Center, the shopkeeper looked up the pawn ticket in a logbook. The duty detective, a woman Bosch knew had not been involved in a field investigation during her entire career with the Robbery-Homicide Division, asked Bosch how he had been, then told him that she had referred the pawnshop break-in to the local station even though she knew there would be no detectives there today. The local station was Central Division. Bosch walked around the counter and dialed the detective bureau there anyway. There was no answer. While the phone rang on unanswered, Bosch began a one-sided conversation.

"Yeah, this is Harry Bosch, Hollywood detectives, I'm just trying to check on the status of the break-in over at the Happy Hocker on Broadway. . . . He is. Do you know when? . . . Uh huh, uh huh. . . . Right, Obinna, O-B-I-N-N-A."

He looked over and Obinna nodded at the correct spelling.

"Yeah, he's here waiting. . . . Right . . . I'll tell him. Thank you."

He hung up the phone. Obinna looked at him, his bushy eyebrows arched.

"It's been a busy day, Mr. Obinna," Bosch said. "The detectives are out, but they'll get here. Shouldn't be too much longer. I gave the watch officer your name and told him to get 'em over here as soon as possible. Now, can I see the bracelet?"

"No."

Bosch dug a cigarette out of a package he pulled from his coat pocket. He knew what was coming before Obinna spread his arm across one of the damaged display cases.

"Your bracelet, it is gone," the pawnbroker said. "I looked it up here in my record. I see that I had it here in the case because it was a fine piece, very valuable to me. Now it is gone. We are both victims of the robber, yes?"

Obinna smiled, apparently happy to share his woe. Bosch looked into the glitter of sharp glass in the bottom of the case. He nodded and said, "Yes."

"You are a day late, detective. A shame."

"Did you say only these two cases were robbed?"

"Yes. A smash and grab. Quick. Quick."

"What time?"

"Police called me at four-thirty in the morning. That is the time of the alarm. I came at once. The alarm, when the window was smashed, the alarm went off. The officers found no one. They stayed until I came. Then I begin to wait for detectives that do not come. I cannot clean up my cases until they get here to investigate this crime."

Bosch was thinking of the time scheme. The body dumped sometime before the anonymous 911 call at 4 A.M. The pawnshop broken into about the same time. A bracelet pawned by the dead man taken. There are no coincidences, he told himself.

"You said something about pictures. Lists and pictures for the pawn detail?"

"Yes, LAPD, that is true. I turn over lists of everything I take in to the pawn detectives. It is the law. I cooperate fully."

Obinna nodded his head and frowned mournfully into the broken display case.

"What about the pictures?" Bosch said.

"Yes, pictures. These pawn detectives, they ask me to take pictures of my best acquisitions. Help them better identify for stolen merchandise. It is not the law, but I say sure, I cooperate fully. I buy the Polaroid kind of camera. I keep pictures if they want to come and look. They never do. It's bullshit."

"You have a picture of this bracelet?"

Obinna's eyebrows arched again as he considered the idea for the first time.

"I think," he said, and then he disappeared through a black curtain in a doorway behind the counter. He came out a few moments later with a shoe box full of Polaroid photos with yellow carbon slips paper-clipped to them. He rustled through the photos, occasionally pulling one out, raising his eyebrows, and then sliding it back into place. Finally, he found what he wanted.

"Here. There it is."

Bosch took the photo and studied it.

"Antique gold with carved jade, very nice," Obinna said. "I remember it, top line. No wonder the shitheel that broke through my window took it. Made in the 1930s, Mexico . . . I gave the man eight hundred dollars. I have not often paid such a price for a piece of jewelry. I remember, very big man, he came here with the ring for the Super Bowl. Nineteen eighty-three. Very nice. I gave him one thousand dollars. He did not come back for it."

He held out his left hand to display the oversized gold ring, which seemed even larger on his small finger.

"The guy who pawned the bracelet, you remember him as well?" Bosch asked.

Obinna looked puzzled. Bosch decided that watching his eyebrows was like watching two caterpillars charging each other. He took one of the Polaroids of Meadows out of his pocket and handed it to the pawnbroker. He studied it closely.

"The man is dead," Obinna said after a moment. The caterpillars seemed to quiver with fear. "The man looks dead."

"I don't need your help for that," Bosch said. "I want to know if he pawned the bracelet."

Obinna handed the photo back. He said, "I think yes."

"He ever come in here and pawn anything else, before or after the bracelet?"

"No. I think I'd remember him. I'll say no."

"I need to take this," Bosch said, holding up the Polaroid of the bracelet. "If you need it back, give me a call."

He put one of his business cards on the cash register. The card was one of the cheap kind, with his name and phone number handwritten on a line. As he walked to the front door, crossing under a row of banjos, Bosch looked at his watch. He turned to Obinna, who was looking through the box of Polaroids again.

"Mr. Obinna, the watch officer, he said to tell you that if the detectives didn't get here in a half hour, you should go home and they will be by in the morning."

Obinna looked at him without saying a word. The caterpillars charged and collided. Bosch looked up and saw himself in the polished brass elbow of a saxophone that hung overhead. A tenor. Then he turned and walked out the door, heading to the com center to pick up the tape.

The watch sergeant in the com center beneath City Hall let Bosch record the 911 call off one of the big reel-to-reels that never stop rolling and recording the cries of the city. The voice of the emergency operator was female and black. The caller was male and white. The caller sounded like a boy.

"Nine one one emergency. What are you reporting?"

"Uh, uh —"

"Can I help you? What are you reporting?"

"Uh, yeah, I'm reporting you have a dead guy in a pipe."

"You said you are reporting a dead body?"

"Yeah, that's right."

"What do you mean a pipe, sir?"

"He is in a pipe up by the dam."

"What dam is that?"

"Uh, you know, where they got the water reservoir and everything, the Hollywood sign."

"Is that the Mulholland Dam, sir? Above Hollywood?"

"Yeah, that's it. You got it. Mulholland. I couldn't remember the name."

"Where is the body?"

"They have a big old pipe up there. You know, the one that people sleep in. The dead guy is in the pipe. He's there."

"Do you know this person?"

"No, man, no way."

"Is he sleeping?"

"Shit, no." The boy laughed nervously. "He's dead."

"How are you sure?"

"I'm sure. I'm just telling you. If you don't want to —"

"What is your name, sir?"

"What is this? What do you need my name for? I just saw it. I didn't do it."

"How am I to know this is a legitimate call?"

"Check the pipe, you'll know. I don't know what else to tell you. What's my name got to do with anything?"

"For our records, sir. Can you give me your name?"

"Uh, no."

"Sir, will you stay there until an officer arrives?"

"No, I'm already gone. I'm not there, man. I'm down —"

"I know, sir. I have a readout here that says you are at a pay phone on Gower near Hollywood Boulevard. Will you wait for the officer?"

"How —? Never mind, I gotta go now. You check it out. The body is there. A dead guy."

"Sir, we would like to talk —"

The line was disconnected. Bosch put the cassette tape in his pocket and headed out of the com center the way he had come in.

It had been ten months since Harry Bosch had been on the third floor at Parker Center. He had worked in RHD — the Robbery-Homicide Division — for almost ten years, but never came back after his suspension and transfer from the Homicide Special squad to Hollywood detectives. On the day he got the word, his desk was cleared by two goons from Internal Affairs named Lewis and Clarke. They dumped his stuff on the homicide table at Hollywood Station, then left a message on his phone tape at home saying that's where he could find it. Now, ten months later, he was back on the hallowed floor of the department's elite detective squad, and he was glad it was Sunday. There would be no faces he knew. No reason to look away.

Room 321 was empty except for the weekend duty detective, whom Bosch didn't know. Harry pointed to the back of the room and said, "Bosch, Hollywood detectives. I have to use the box."

The duty man, a young guy with a haircut he had kept when he split the Marine Corps, had a gun catalog open on his desk. He looked back at the computers along the back wall as if to make sure they were still there and then back at Bosch.

"S'pose to use the one in your own division," he said.

Bosch walked by him. "I don't have the time to go out to Hollywood. I got an autopsy in twenty minutes," he lied.

"You know, I've heard of you, Bosch. Yeah. The TV show and all of that. You used to be on this floor. Used to."

The last line hung in the air like smog and Bosch tried to ignore it. As he went back to the computer terminals, he couldn't help but let his eyes wander over his old desk. He wondered who used it now. It was cluttered, and he noticed the cards on the Rolodex were crisp and unworn at the edges. New. Harry turned around and looked at the duty man, who was still watching him.

"This your desk when you aren't pulling Sundays?"

The kid smiled and nodded his head.

"You deserve it, kid. You're just right for the part. That hair, that stupid grin. You're going to go far."

"Just 'cause you got busted out of here for being a one-man army . . . Ah, fuck you, Bosch, you has-been."

Bosch pulled a chair on casters away from a desk and pushed it in front of the IBM PC sitting on a table against the rear wall. He hit the switch and in a few moments the amber-colored letters appeared on the screen: "Homicide Information Tracking Management Automated Network."

For a moment Bosch smiled at the department's unceasing need for acronyms. It seemed to him that every unit, task force and computer file had been christened with a name that gave its acronym the sound of eliteness. To the public, acronyms meant action, large numbers of manpower applied to vital problems. There was HITMAN, COBRA, CRASH, BADCATS, DARE. A hundred others. Somewhere in Parker Center there was someone who spent all day making up catchy acronyms, he believed. Computers had acronyms, even ideas had acronyms. If your special unit didn't have an acronym, then you weren't shit in this department.

Once he was in the HITMAN system, a template of case questions appeared on the screen and he filled in the blanks. He then typed in three search keys: "Mulholland Dam," "overdose" and "staged overdose." He then pushed the execute key. Half a minute later, the computer told him that a search of eight thousand homicide cases — about ten years' worth — stored on the computer's hard disk had come up with only six hits. Bosch called them up one by one. The first three were unsolved slayings of young women who were found dead on the dam in the early 1980s. Each was strangled. Bosch glanced quickly at the information and went on. The fourth case was a body found floating in the reservoir five years earlier. Cause of death was not drowning but otherwise unknown. The last two were drug overdoses, the first of which occurred during a picnic at the park above the reservoir. It looked pretty straightforward to Bosch and he went on. The last hit was a DB found in the pipe fourteen months earlier. Cause of death was later determined to be heart stoppage due to an overdose of tar heroin.

"Decedent known to frequent area of the dam and sleep in pipe," the computer readout said. "No further follow-up."

It was the death that Crowley, the Hollywood watch sergeant, had mentioned when he woke Bosch up that morning. Bosch pushed a key and printed out the information on the last death, though he didn't think it figured into his case. He signed off and shut down the computer, then he sat there a moment thinking. Without getting out of the chair he rolled over to another PC. He turned it on and fed his password in. He took the Polaroid out of his pocket, looked at the bracelet and typed in its description for a stolen property records search. This in itself was an art. He had to describe the bracelet the way he believed other cops would, cops who might be typing in descriptions of a whole inventory of jewelry taken in a robbery or burglary. He described the bracelet simply as "antique gold bracelet with carved jade dolphin design." He pressed the search key and in thirty seconds the computer screen said "No hit." He tried it again, typing "gold-and-jade bracelet" and then punching the search key. This time there were 436 hits. Too many. He needed to thin the herd. He typed "gold bracelet with jade fish" and pressed search. Six hits. That was more like it.

The computer said a gold bracelet with carved jade fish had turned up on four crime reports and two departmental bulletins that had been entered into the computer system since its development in 1983. Bosch knew that because of the immense duplication of records in any police department, all six entries could be and probably were from the same case or report of a missing or stolen bracelet. He called the abbreviated crime reports up on the computer screen and found that his suspicion was correct. The reports were generated by a single burglary in September at Sixth and Hill downtown. The victim was a woman named Harriet Beecham, age seventy-one, of Silver Lake. Bosch tried to place the location in his mind but could not think of what building or business was there. There was no summary of the crime on the computer; he would have to go to records and pull a hard copy. But there was a limited description of the gold-and-jade bracelet, and several other pieces of jewelry taken from Beecham. The bracelet Beecham reported lost could or could not have been the one that Meadows had pawned — the description was too vague. There were several supplementary report numbers given on the computer report and Bosch wrote them all down in his notebook. It seemed to him as he did this that Harriet Beecham's loss had generated an unusual amount of paper.

He next called up the information on the two bulletins. Both had come from the FBI, the first issued two weeks after Beecham had been burglarized. It was then reissued three months later when Beecham's jewelry had still not turned up. Bosch wrote down the bulletin number and turned off the computer. He went across the room to the robbery/commercial burglary section. On a steel shelf that ran along the back wall were dozens of black binders that held the bulletins and BOLOs from past years. Bosch took down the one marked September and began looking through it. He quickly realized that the bulletins were not in chronological order and weren't all issued in September. In fact, there was no order. He might have to look through all ten months since Beecham's burglary to find the bulletin he needed. He pulled an armful of the binders off the shelf and sat down at the burglary table. A few moments later he felt the presence of someone across the table from him.

"What do you want?" he said without looking up.

"What do I want?" the duty detective said. "I want to know what the fuck you are doing, Bosch. This isn't your place anymore. You can't just come in here like you're running the crew. Put that shit back on the shelf, and if you want to look through it come back down here tomorrow and ask, goddammit. And don't give me any bullshit about an autopsy. You've already been here a half hour."

Bosch looked up at him. He put his age at twenty-eight, maybe twenty-nine, even younger than Bosch had been when he had made it to Robbery-Homicide. Either standards had dropped or RHD wasn't what it was. Bosch knew it was actually both. He looked back down at the bulletin binder.

"I'm talking to you, asshole!" the detective boomed.

Bosch reached his foot up under the table and kicked the chair that was across from him. The chair shot out from the table and its backrest hit the detective in the crotch. He doubled over and made an *oomph* sound, grabbing the chair for support. Bosch knew he had his reputation going for him now. Harry Bosch: a loner, a fighter, a killer. C'mon kid, he was saying, do something.

But the young detective just stared at Bosch, his anger and humiliation in check. He was a cop who could pull the gun but maybe not the trigger. And once Bosch knew that, he knew the kid would walk away.

The young cop shook his head, waved his hands like he was saying Enough of this, and walked back to the duty desk.

"Go ahead, write me up, kid," Bosch said to his back.

"Fuck you," the kid feebly returned.

Bosch knew he had nothing to worry about. IAD wouldn't even look at an officer-on-officer beef without a corroborating witness or tape recording. One cop's word against another's was something they wouldn't touch in this department. Deep down, they knew a cop's word by itself was worthless. That was why Internal Affairs cops always worked in pairs.

An hour and seven cigarettes later, Bosch found it. A photocopy of another Polaroid of the gold-and-jade bracelet was part of a fifty-page packet of descriptions and photos of property lost in a burglary at WestLand National Bank at Sixth and Hill. Now Bosch was able to place the address in his mind, and he remembered the dark smoked glass of the building. He had never been inside the bank. A bank heist with jewelry taken, he thought. It didn't make much sense. He studied the list. Almost every item was a piece of jewelry and there was too much there for a walk-in robbery. Harriet Beecham alone was listed as having lost eight antique rings, four bracelets, four earrings. Besides that, these were listed as burglary losses, not robbery losses. He looked through the Be on Lookout package for any kind of crime summary, but didn't find any. Just a bureau contact: Special Agent E. D. Wish.

Then he noticed in a block on the BOLO sheet that there were three dates noted for the date of the crime. A burglary over a three-day span during the first week of September. Labor Day weekend, he realized. Downtown banks are closed three days. It had to have been a safe-deposit caper. A tunnel job? Bosch leaned back and thought about that. Why hadn't he remembered it? A heist like that would have played in the media for days. It would have been talked about in the department even longer. Then he realized he had been in Mexico on Labor Day, and for the next three weeks. The bank heist had occurred while he was serving the one-month suspension for the Dollmaker case. He leaned forward, picked up a phone and dialed.

"*Times*, Bremmer."

"It's Bosch. Still got you working Sundays, huh?"

"Two to ten, every Sunday, no parole. So, what's up? I haven't talked to you since, uh, your problem with the Dollmaker case. How you liking Hollywood Division?"

"It'll do. For a while, at least." He was speaking low so the duty detective would not overhear.

Bremmer said, "Like that, huh? Well, I heard you caught the stiff up at the dam this morning."

Joel Bremmer had covered the cop shop for the *Times* longer than most cops had been on the force, including Bosch. There was not much he didn't hear about the department, or couldn't find out with a phone call. A year ago he called Bosch for comment on his twenty-two-day suspension, no pay. Bremmer had heard about it before Bosch. Generally, the police department hated the *Times*, and the *Times* was never short in its criticism of the department. But in the middle of that was Bremmer, whom any cop could trust and many, like Bosch, did.

"Yeah, that's my case," Bosch said. "Right now, it's nothing much. But I need a favor. If it works out the way it's looking, then it will be something you'd want to know about."

Bosch knew he didn't have to bait him, but he wanted the reporter to know there might be something later.

"What do you need?" Bremmer said.

"As you know, I was out of town last Labor Day on my extended vacation, courtesy of IAD. So I missed this one. But there was —"

"The tunnel job? You're not going to ask about the tunnel job, are you? Over here in downtown? All the jewelry? Negotiable bonds, stock certificates, maybe drugs?"

Bosch heard the reporter's voice go up a notch in urgency. He had been right, it had been a tunnel and the story had played well. If Bremmer was this interested, then it was a substantial case. Still, Bosch was surprised he had not heard of it after coming back to work in October.

"Yeah, that's the one," he said. "I was gone then, so I missed it. Ever any arrests?"

"No, it's open. FBI's doing it, last I checked."

"I want to look at the clips on it tonight. Is that all right?"

"I'll make copies. When are you coming?"

"I'll head over in a little while."

"I take it this has got something to do with this morning's stiff?"

"It's looking that way. Maybe. I can't talk right now. And I know the fee-bees have the case. I'll go see them tomorrow. That's why I want to see the clips tonight."

"I'll be here."

After hanging up the phone, Bosch looked down at the FBI photocopy of the bracelet. There was no doubt it was the piece that had been pawned by Meadows and was in Obinna's Polaroid. The bracelet in the FBI photo was in place on a woman's liver-spotted wrist. Three small carved fish swimming on a wave of gold. Bosch guessed it was Harriet Beecham's seventy-one-year-old wrist and the photo had probably been taken for insurance purposes. He looked over at the duty detective, who was still leafing through the gun catalog. He coughed loudly like he had seen Nicholson do in a movie once and at the same time tore the BOLO sheet out of the binder. The kid detective looked over at Bosch and then went back to the guns and bullets.

As he folded the BOLO sheet into his pocket, Bosch's electronic pager went off. He picked up the phone and called Hollywood Station, expecting to be told there was another body waiting for him. It was a watch sergeant named Art Crocket, whom everyone called Davey, who took the call.

"Harry, you still out in the field?" he said.

"I'm at Parker Center. Had to check on a few things."

"Good, then you're already near the morgue. A tech over there name of Sakai called, said he needs to see you."

"See me?"

"He said to tell you that something came up and they're doing your cut today. Right now, matter of fact."

It took Bosch five minutes to get over to County-USC Hospital and fifteen minutes to find a parking spot. The medical examiner's office was located behind one of the medical center buildings that had been condemned after the '87 earthquake. It was a two-story yellow prefab without much architectural style or life. As Bosch was going through the glass doors where the living people entered and into the front lobby, he passed a sheriff's detective he had spent some time with while working the Night Stalker task force in the early eighties.

"Hey, Bernie," Bosch said and smiled.

"Hey, fuck you, Bosch," Bernie said. "The rest of us catch ones that count, too."

Bosch stopped there a moment to watch the detective walk into the parking lot. Then he went in and to the right, down a government-green corridor, passing through two sets of double doors — the smell getting worse each time. It was the smell of death and industrial-strength disinfectant. Death had the upper hand. Bosch stepped into the yellow-tiled scrub room. Larry Sakai was in there, putting a paper gown over his hospital scrubs. He already had on a paper mask and booties. Bosch took a set of the same out of cardboard boxes on a stainless steel counter and started putting them on.

"What's with Bernie Slaughter?" Bosch asked. "What happened in here to piss him off?"

"You're what happened, Bosch," Sakai said without looking at him. "He got a call out yesterday morning. Some sixteen-year-old shoots his best friend. Up in Lancaster. Looks like accidental but Bernie's waiting on us to check the bullet track and powder stippling. He wants to close it. I told him we'd get to it late today, so he came in. Only we aren't going to get to it at all today. 'Cause Sally's got a bug up his ass about doing yours. Don't ask me why. He just checked the stiff out when I brought it in and said we'd do it today. I told him we'd have to bump somebody, and he said bump Bernie. But I couldn't get him on the line in time to stop him from coming in. So that's why Bernie's pissed. You know he lives all the way down to Diamond Bar. Long ride in for nothing."

Bosch had the mask, gown and booties on and followed Sakai down the tiled hall to the autopsy suite. "Then maybe he ought to be pissed at Sally, not me," he said.

Sakai didn't answer. They walked to the first table, where Billy Meadows lay on his back, naked, his neck braced against a short cut of two by four wood. There were six of the stainless steel tables in the room. Each had gutters running alongside its edges and drain holes in the corners. There was a body on each. Dr. Jesus Salazar was huddled over Meadows's chest with his back to Bosch and Sakai.

"Afternoon, Harry, I've been waiting," Salazar said, still not looking. "Larry, I'm going to need slides on this."

The medical examiner straightened up and turned. In his rubber-gloved hand he held what looked like a square plug of flesh and pink muscle tissue. He placed it in a steel pan, the kind brownies are cooked in, and handed it to Sakai. "Give me verticals, one of the puncture track, then two on either side for comparison."

Sakai took the pan and left the room to go to the lab. Bosch saw that the plug of meat had been cut from Meadows's chest, about an inch above the left nipple.

"What'd you find?" Bosch asked.

"Not sure yet. We'll see. The question is, what did you find, Harry? My field tech told me you were demanding an autopsy on this case today. Why is that?"

"I told him I needed it today because I wanted to get it done tomorrow. I thought that was what we had agreed on, too."

"Yes, he told me so, but I got curious about it. I love a good mystery, Harry. What made you think this was hinky, as you detectives say?"

We don't say it anymore, Bosch thought. Once it's said in the movies and people like Salazar pick it up, it's ancient.

"Just some things didn't fit at the time," Bosch said. "There are more things now. From my end, it looks like a murder. No mystery."

"What things?"

Bosch got out his notebook and started flipping through the pages as he talked. He listed the things he had noticed wrong at the death scene: the broken finger, the lack of distinct tracks in the pipe, the shirt pulled over the head.

"He had a hype kit in his pocket and we found a stove in the pipe, but it doesn't look right. Looks like a plant to me. Looks to me like the pop that killed him is in the arm there. Those other scars on his arms are old. He hasn't been using his arms in years."

"You're right about that. Aside from the one recent puncture in the arm, the groin area is the only area where punctures are fresh. The inside thighs. An area usually used by people going to great lengths to hide their addiction. But then again, this could have just been his first time back on the arms. What else you got, Harry?"

"He smoked, I'm pretty sure. There was no pack of cigarettes with the body."

"Couldn't somebody have taken them off the body? Before it was discovered. A scavenger?"

"True. But why take the smokes and not the kit? There's also his apartment. Somebody searched the place."

"Could have been someone who knew him. Someone looking for his stash."

"True again." Bosch flipped through a few more pages in the notebook. "The kit on the body had whitish-brown crystals in the cotton. I've seen enough tar heroin to know it turns the straining cotton dark brown, sometimes black. So it looks like it was some fine stuff, probably overseas, that was put in his arm. That doesn't go with the way he was living. That's uptown stuff."

Salazar thought a moment before saying, "It's all a lot of supposition, Harry."

"The last thing, though, is — and I am just starting to work on this — he was involved in some kind of caper."

Bosch gave him a brief synopsis of what he knew about the bracelet, its theft from the bank vault and then from the pawnshop. Salazar's domain was the forensic detail of the case. But Bosch had always trusted Sally and found that it sometimes helped to bounce other details of a case off him. The two had met in 1974, when Bosch was a patrolman and Sally was a new assistant coroner. Bosch was assigned guard duty and crowd control on East Fifty-fourth in South-Central where a firefight with the Symbionese Liberation Army had left a house burned to the ground and five bodies in the smoking rubble. Sally was assigned to see if there was a sixth — Patty Hearst — somewhere in the char. The two of them spent three days there, and when Sally finally gave up, Bosch had won a bet that she was still alive. Somewhere.

When Bosch was finished with the story about the bracelet, it seemed to have mollified Sally's worries about the death of Billy Meadows not being a mystery. He seemed energized. He turned to a cart on which his cutting tools were piled and rolled it next to the autopsy table. He switched on a sound-activated tape recorder and picked up a scalpel and a pair of regular gardening shears. He said, "Well, let's get to work."

Bosch moved back a few steps to avoid any spatter and leaned against a counter on which there was a tray full of knives and saws and scalpels. He noticed that a sign taped to the side of the tray said: To Be Sharpened.

Salazar looked down at the body of Billy Meadows and began: "The body is that of a well-developed Caucasian male measuring sixty-nine inches in length, weighing one hundred sixty-five pounds and appearing generally consistent with the stated age of forty years. The body is cold and unembalmed with full rigor and posterior dependent fixed lividity."

Bosch watched him start but then noticed the plastic bag containing Meadows's clothes on the counter next to the tool pan. He pulled it over and opened it up. The smell of urine immediately assaulted his nostrils, and he thought for a moment of the living room at Meadows's apartment. He pulled on a pair of rubber gloves as Salazar continued to describe the body.

"The left index finger shows a palpable fracture without laceration or petechial contusion or hemorrhage."

Bosch glanced over his shoulder and saw that Salazar was wiggling the broken digit with the blunt end of the scalpel as he spoke to the tape recorder. He concluded his external description of the body by mentioning the skin punctures.

"There are hemorrhagic puncture wounds, hypodermic type, on the upper inside thighs and interior side of the left arm. The arm puncture exudes a bloody fluid and appears to be most recent. No scabbing. There is another puncture, in the upper left chest, which exudes a small amount of bloody fluid and appears to be slightly larger than that caused by hypodermic puncture."

Salazar put his hand over the tape recorder's mike and said to Bosch, "I'm having Sakai get slides of this chest puncture. It looks very interesting."

Bosch nodded and turned back to the counter and began spreading out Meadows's clothes. Behind him he heard Salazar using the shears to open up the dead man's chest.

The detective pulled each pocket out and looked at the lint. He turned the socks inside out and checked the inside lining of the pants and shirt. Nothing. He took a scalpel out of the To Be Sharpened pan and cut the stitches out of Meadows's leather belt and pulled it apart. Again nothing. Over his shoulder he heard Salazar saying, "The spleen weighs one hundred ninety grams. The capsule is intact and slightly wrinkled, and the parenchyma is pale purple and trabecular."

Bosch had heard it all hundreds of times before. Most of what a pathologist said into his tape recorder meant nothing to the detective who stood by. It was the bottom line the detective waited for. What killed the person on the cold steel table? How? Who?

"The gallbladder is thin walled," Salazar was saying. "It contains a few cc's of greenish bile with no stones."

Bosch shoved the clothes back into the plastic bag and sealed it. Then he dumped the leather work shoes Meadows had been wearing out of a second plastic bag. He noticed reddish-orange dust fall from inside the shoes. Another indication the body had been dragged into the pipe. The heels had scraped on the dried mud at the bottom of the pipe, drawing the dust inside the shoes.

Salazar said, "The bladder mucosa is intact, and there are only two ounces of pale yellow urine. The external genitalia and vagina are unremarkable."

Bosch turned around. Salazar had his hand on the tape recorder speaker. He said, "Coroner's humor. Just wanted to see if you were listening, Harry. You might have to testify to this one day. To back me up."

"I doubt it," Bosch said. "They don't like boring juries to death."

Salazar started the small circular saw that was used to open the skull. It sounded like a dentist's drill. Bosch turned back to the shoes. They were well oiled and cared for. The rubber soles showed only modest wear. Stuck in one of the deep grooves of the tread of the right shoe was a white stone. Bosch pried it out with the scalpel. It was a small chunk of cement. He thought of the white dust in the rug in Meadows's closet. He wondered if the dust or the chunk from the shoe tread could be matched to the concrete that had guarded the WestLand Bank's vault. But if the shoes were so well cared for, could the chunk have been in the tread for nine months since the vault break-in? It seemed unlikely. Perhaps it was from his work on the subway project. If he actually had such a job. Bosch slipped the chunk of cement into a small plastic envelope and put it in his pocket with the others he had collected throughout the day.

Salazar said, "Examination of the head and cranial contents reveals no trauma or underlying pathological disease conditions or congenital anomalies. Harry, I'm going to do the finger now."

Bosch put the shoes back in their plastic bag and returned to the autopsy table as Salazar placed an X ray of Meadows's left hand on a light window on the wall.

"See here, these fragments?" he said as he traced small, sharp white spots on the negative. There were three of them near the fractured joint. "If this was an old break, these would, over time, have moved into the joint. There is no scarring discernible on the X ray but I am going to take a look."

He went to the body and used a scalpel to make a T-incision in the skin on the top of the finger joint. He then folded the skin back and dug around with the scalpel in the pink meat, saying, "No . . . no . . . nothing. This was post, Harry. You think it could have been one of my people?"

"I don't know," Bosch said. "Doesn't look like it. Sakai said he and his sidekick were careful. I know I didn't do it. How come there's no damage to the skin?"

"That is an interesting point. I don't know. Somehow the finger was broken without the exterior being damaged. I can't answer that one. But it shouldn't have been too hard to do. Just grab the finger and yank down. Provided you have the stomach for it. Like so."

Salazar went around the table. He lifted Meadows's right hand and yanked the finger backward. He couldn't get the leverage needed and couldn't break the joint.

"Harder than I thought," he said. "Perhaps the digit was struck with a blunt object of some kind. One that did not blemish the skin."

When Sakai came in with the slides fifteen minutes later, the autopsy was completed and Salazar was sewing Meadows's chest closed with thick, waxed twine. He then used an overhead hose to spray debris off the body and wet down the hair. Sakai bound the legs together and the arms to the body with rope, to prevent them from moving during the different stages of rigor. Bosch noticed that the rope cut across the tattoo on Meadows's arm, across the rat's neck.

Using his thumb and forefinger, Salazar closed Meadows's eyes.

"Take him to the box," he said to Sakai. Then to Bosch, "Let's take a look at these slides. This seemed odd to me because the hole was bigger than your normal scag spike and its location, in the chest, was unusual.

"The puncture is clearly antemortem, possibly perimortem — there was only slight hemorrhaging. But the wound is not scabbed over. So we're talking shortly before, or even during death. Maybe the cause of death, Harry."

Salazar took the slides to a microscope that was on the counter at the back of the room. He chose one of the slides and put it on the viewing plate. He bent over to look and after half a minute finally said, "Interesting."

He then looked briefly at the other slides. When he was done, he put the first slide back on the viewing plate.

"Okay, basically, I removed a one-inch-square section of the chest where this puncture was located. I went into the chest about one and a half inches deep with the cut. The slide is a vertical dissection of the sample, showing the track of the perforation. Do you follow me?"

Bosch nodded.

"Good. It's kind of like slicing an apple open to expose the track of a worm. The slide traces the path of the perforation and any immediate impact or damage. Take a look."

Bosch bent to the eyepiece of the microscope. The slide showed a straight perforation about one inch deep, through the skin and into the muscle, tapering in width like a spike. The muscle's pink color changed to a dark brownish color around the deepest point of the penetration.

"What does it mean?" he asked.

"It means," said Salazar, "that the puncture was through the skin, through the fascia — that's the fibrous fat layer — and then directly into the pectoral muscle. You notice the deepening color of the muscle around the penetration?"

"Yes, I notice."

"Harry, that's because the muscle is burned there."

Bosch looked away from the microscope to Salazar. He thought he could make out the line of a thin smile beneath the pathologist's breathing mask.

"Burned?"

"A stun gun," the pathologist said. "Look for one that fires its electrode dart deep into the skin tissue. About three to four centimeters deep. Though in this case, it is likely the electrode was manually pressed deeper into the chest."

Bosch thought a moment. A stun gun would be virtually impossible to trace. Sakai came back into the room and leaned on the counter by the door, watching. Salazar collected three glass vials of blood and two containing yellowish liquid from the tool cart. There was also a small steel pan containing a brown lump of material that Bosch recognized from experience in this room as liver.

"Larry, here are the tox samples," Salazar said. Sakai took them and disappeared from the room again.

"You're talking about torture, electric shock," Bosch said.

"I would say it looks so," Salazar said. "Not enough to kill him, the trauma is too small. But possibly enough to get information from him. An electric charge can be very persuasive. I think there is ample history on that. With the electrode positioned in the subject's chest, he could probably feel the juice going right into his heart. He would have been paralyzed. He'd tell them what they wanted and then could only watch while they put a fatal dosage of heroin into his arm."

"Can we prove any of this?"

Salazar looked down at the tile floor and put his finger on his mask, and scratched his lip beneath it. Bosch was dying for a cigarette. He had been in the autopsy room nearly two hours.

"Prove any of it?" Salazar said. "Not medically. Tox tests will be done in a week. For the sake of argument, say they come back heroin overdose. How do we prove that someone else put it in his arm, not himself? Medically, we can't. But we can show that at the time of death or shortly before, there was a traumatic assault on the body in the form of electric shock. He was being tortured. After death there is the unexplained damage to the first digit of the left hand."

He rubbed the finger over his mask again and then concluded, "I could testify that this was a homicide. The totality of the medical evidence indicates death at the hands of others. But, for the moment, there is no cause. We wait for the tox studies to be completed and then we'll put our heads together again."

Bosch wrote a paraphrase of what Salazar had just said into his notebook. He would have to type it into his own reports.

"Of course," Salazar said, "proving any of this beyond a reasonable doubt to a jury is another matter. I would guess that, Harry, you have to find that bracelet and find out why it was worth torturing and killing a man for."

Bosch closed his notebook and started to pull off the paper gown.

The setting sun burned the sky pink and orange in the same bright hues as surfers' bathing suits. It was beautiful deception, Bosch thought, as he drove north on the Hollywood Freeway to home. Sunsets did that here. Made you forget it was the smog that made their colors so brilliant, that behind every pretty picture there could be an ugly story.

The sun hung like a ball of copper in the driver's-side window. He had the car radio tuned to a jazz station and Coltrane was playing "Soul Eyes." On the seat next to him was a file containing the newspaper clippings from Bremmer. The file was weighted down by a six-pack of Henry's. Bosch got off at Barham and then took Woodrow Wilson up into the hills above Studio City. His home was a wood-framed, one-bedroom cantilever not much bigger than a Beverly Hills garage. It hung out over the edge of the hill and was supported by three steel pylons at its midpoint. It was a scary place to be during earthquakes, daring Mother Nature to twang those beams and send the house down the hill like a sled. But the view was the trade-off. From the back porch Bosch could look northeast across Burbank and Glendale. He could see the purple-hued mountains past Pasadena and Altadena. Sometimes he could see the smoky loom-up and orange blaze of brush fires in the hills. At night the sound of the freeway below softened and the searchlights at Universal City swept the sky. Looking out on the Valley never failed to give Bosch a sense of power which he could not explain to himself. But he did know that it was one reason — the main reason — he bought the place and would never want to leave it.

Bosch had bought it eight years earlier, before the real estate boom got seriously endemic, with a down payment of $50,000. That left a mortgage of $1,400 a month, which he could easily afford because the only things he spent money on were food, booze and jazz.

The down payment money had come from a studio that gave it to him for the rights to use his name in a TV miniseries based on a string of murders of beauty shop owners in Los Angeles. Bosch and his partner during the investigation were portrayed by two midlevel TV actors. His partner took his fifty grand and his pension and moved to Ensenada. Bosch put his down on a house he wasn't sure could survive the next earthquake but that made him feel as though he were prince of the city.

Despite Bosch's resolve never to move, Jerry Edgar, his current partner and part-time real estate man, told him the house was now worth three times what he had paid for it. Whenever the subject of real estate came up, which was often, Edgar counseled Bosch to sell and trade up. Edgar wanted the listing. Bosch just wanted to stay where he was.

It was dark by the time he reached the hill house. He drank the first beer standing on the back porch, looking out at the blanket of lights below. He had a second bottle while sitting in his watch chair, the file closed on his lap. He hadn't eaten all day and the beer hit him quickly. He felt lethargic and yet jumpy, his body telling him it needed food. He got up and went to the kitchen and made a pressed turkey sandwich that he brought back to the chair with another beer.

When he was finished eating he brushed the sandwich crumbs off the file and opened it up. There had been four *Times* stories on the WestLand bank caper. He read them in the order of publication. The first was just a brief that had run on page 3 of the Metro section. The information had apparently been gathered on the Tuesday the break-in was discovered. At the time, the LAPD and the FBI weren't that interested in talking to the press or letting the public know what had happened.

AUTHORITIES PROBE BANK BREAK-IN

An undisclosed amount of property was stolen from the WestLand National Bank in downtown during the three-day holiday weekend, authorities said Tuesday.

The burglary, being investigated by the FBI and the Los Angeles Police Department, was discovered when managers of the bank located at the corner of Hill Street and Sixth Avenue arrived Tuesday and found the safe-deposit vault had been looted, FBI Special Agent John Rourke said.

Rourke said an estimate on the loss of property had not been made. But sources close to the investigation said more than $1 million worth of jewels and other valuables stored in the vault by customers of the bank was taken.

Rourke also declined to say how the burglars entered the vault but did say that the alarm system was not working properly. He declined to elaborate.

A spokesman for WestLand declined Tuesday to discuss the burglary. Authorities said there were no arrests or suspects.

Bosch wrote the name John Rourke in his notebook and went on to the next newspaper story, which was much longer. It had been published the day after the first and had been bannered across the top of the front page of the Metro section. It had a two-deck headline and was accompanied by a photograph of a man and woman standing in the safe-deposit vault looking down at a manhole-sized opening in the floor. Behind them was a pile of deposit boxes. Most of the small doors on the back wall were open. Bremmer's byline was on the story.

AT LEAST $2 MILLION TAKEN IN BANK TUNNEL JOB;
BANDITS HAD HOLIDAY WEEKEND TO DIG INTO VAULT

The article expanded on the first story, filling in the detail that the perpetrators had tunneled into the bank, digging an approximately 150-yard line from a city storm main that ran under Hill Street. The story said an explosive device had been used to make the final break through the floor of the vault. According to the FBI, the burglars probably were in the vault through most of the holiday weekend, drilling open the individual safe-deposit boxes. The entry tunnel from the stormwater main to the vault was believed to have been dug during seven to eight weeks before the heist.

Bosch made a note to ask the FBI how the tunnel had been dug. If heavy equipment was used, most banks' alarms, which measured sound as well as earth vibrations, would have picked up the ground movement and sounded. Also, he wondered, why hadn't the explosive device set off alarms?

He looked then at the third article, published the day after the second. This one wasn't written by Bremmer, though it still had been played on the front of Metro. It was a feature on the dozens of people lining up at the bank to see if their safe-deposit boxes were among those pried open and emptied. The FBI was escorting them into the vault and then taking their statements. Bosch scanned the story but saw the same thing over and over again: people angry or upset or both because they had lost items that they had placed in the vault because they believed it was safer than their homes. Near the bottom of the story Harriet Beecham was mentioned. She had been interviewed as she came out of the bank, and she told the reporter she had lost a lifetime's collection of valuables bought while traveling the world with her late husband, Harry. The story said Beecham was dabbing at her eyes with a lace handkerchief.

"I lost the rings he bought me in France, a bracelet of gold and jade from Mexico," Beecham said. "Whoever they were that did this, they took my memories."

Very melodramatic. Bosch wondered if the last quote had been made up by the reporter.

The fourth story in the file had been published a week later. By Bremmer, it was short and had been buried in the back of Metro, behind where they stuffed the Valley news. Bremmer reported that the WestLand investigation was being handled exclusively by the FBI. The LAPD provided initial backup, but as leads dried up, the case was left in the bureau's hands. Special Agent Rourke was quoted again in this story. He said agents were still on the case full-time but no progress had been made or suspects identified. None of the property taken from the vault, he said, had turned up.

Bosch closed the file. The case was too big for the bureau to slough off like a bank stickup. He wondered if Rourke had been telling the truth about the lack of suspects. He wondered if Meadows's name had ever come up. Two decades earlier Meadows had fought and sometimes lived in the tunnels beneath the villages of South Vietnam. Like all the tunnel fighters, he knew demolition work. But that was for bringing a tunnel down. Implosion. Could he have learned how to blow through the concrete-and-steel floor of a bank vault? Then Bosch realized that Meadows would not necessarily have needed to know how. He was sure the WestLand job had taken more than one person.

He got up and got another beer from the refrigerator. But before going back to the watch chair he detoured into the bedroom, where he pulled an old scrapbook out of the bottom drawer of the bureau. Back in the chair he drank down half the beer, then opened the book. There were bunches of photographs loose between the pages. He had meant to mount them but had never gotten around to it. He rarely even opened the book. The pages were yellowed and had gone to brown at the edges. They were brittle, much like the memories the photos evoked. He picked up each snapshot and examined it, at some point realizing that he had never mounted them on the pages because he liked the idea of holding each picture in his hands, feeling it.

The photographs were all taken in Vietnam. Like the picture found in Meadows's apartment, these were mostly in black and white. It was cheaper back then, getting black-and-white film developed in Saigon. Bosch was in some of the shots, but most were photos that he had taken with an old Leica his foster father had given him before he left. It was a peace gesture from the old man. He hadn't wanted Harry to go, and they had fought about it. So the camera was given. And accepted. But Bosch was not one to tell stories when he returned, and the snapshots were left spread through the pages of the scrapbook, never to be mounted, rarely to be looked at.

If there was a recurring theme of the photographs it was the smiling faces and the tunnels. In almost every shot, there were soldiers standing in defiant poses at the mouth of a hole they had probably just been in and conquered. To the outsider, the photos would appear strange, maybe fascinating. But to Bosch they were scary, like newspaper photos he had seen of people trapped in wrecked cars, waiting to be cut out by the firemen. The photos were of the smiling faces of young men who had dropped down into hell and come back to smile into the camera. Out of the blue and into the black is what they called going into a tunnel. Each one was a black echo. Nothing but death in there. But, still, they went.

Bosch turned a cracked page of the album and found Billy Meadows staring up at him. The photo had undoubtedly been taken a few minutes after the one Bosch had found at Meadows's apartment. The same group of soldiers. The same trench and tunnel. Echo Sector, Cu Chi District. But Bosch wasn't in this portrait because he had left the frame to snap the photo. His Leica had caught Meadows's vacant stare and stoned smile — his pale skin looked waxy but taut. He had captured the real Meadows, Bosch thought. He put the photo back in the page and turned to the next one. This one was of himself, no one else in the frame. He clearly remembered setting the camera down on a wooden table in a hootch and setting the timer. Then he moved into the frame. The camera had snapped as he was shirtless, the tattoo on his deeply tanned shoulder catching the falling sun through the window. Behind him, but out of focus, was the dark entrance to a tunnel lying uncovered on the straw floor of the hootch. The tunnel was blurred, forbidding darkness, like the ghastly mouth in Edvard Munch's painting *The Scream.*

It was a tunnel in the village they called Timbuk2, Bosch knew as he stared at the photo. His last tunnel. He was not smiling in the picture. His eyes were set in dark sockets. And neither was he smiling as he looked at it now. He held the photo in two hands, absentmindedly rubbing his thumbs up and down the borders. He stared at the photograph until fatigue and alcohol pulled him down into sleepy thought. Almost dreamlike. He remembered that last tunnel and he remembered Billy Meadows.

Three of them went in. Two of them came out.

The tunnel had been discovered during a routine sweep at a small village in E Sector. The village had no name on the recon maps, so the soldiers called it Timbuk2. The tunnels were turning up everywhere, so there weren't enough rats to go around. When the tunnel mouth was found under a rice basket in a hootch, the top sergeant didn't want to have to wait for a dust-off to land with fresh rats. He wanted to press on, but he knew he had to check the tunnel out. So the top made a decision like so many others in the war. He sent three of his own men in. Three virgins, scared as shit, maybe six weeks in country among them. The top told them not to go far, just set charges and come out. Do it fast, and cover each other's ass. The three green soldiers dutifully went down into the hole. Except a half-hour later, only two came out.

The two who made it out said that the three of them had separated. The tunnel branched into several directions and they split up. They were telling the top this when there was a rumble, and a huge cough of noise and smoke and dust belched from the tunnel mouth. The C-4 charges had detonated. The company loot came in then and said they wouldn't leave the zone without the missing man. The whole company waited a day for the smoke and dust to settle in the tunnel and then two tunnel rats were dropped during a dust-off — Harry Bosch and Billy Meadows. He didn't care if the missing soldier was dead, the lieutenant told them. Get him out. He wasn't going to leave one of his boys in that hole. "Go get 'im and bring 'im out here so we can get 'im a decent burial," the lieutenant said.

Meadows said, "We wouldn't leave any of our own in there, either."

Bosch and Meadows went down the hole then and found that the main entry led to a junction room where baskets of rice were stored and three other passageways began. Two of these had collapsed in the C-4 explosions. The third was still open. It was the one the missing soldier had taken. And that was the way they went.

They crawled through the darkness, Meadows in front, using their lights sparingly, until they reached a dead end. Meadows poked around the tunnel's dirt floor until he found the concealed door. He pried it open and they dropped down into another level of the labyrinth. Without saying a word, Meadows pointed one way and crawled off. Bosch knew he would go the other way. Each would be alone now, unless the VC were waiting ahead. Bosch's way was a winding passage that was as warm as a steam bath. The tunnel smelled damp and faintly like a latrine. He smelled the missing soldier before he saw him. He was dead, his body putrifying but sitting in the middle of the tunnel with his legs straight out and spread, the toes of his boots pointed upward. His body was propped against a stake planted in the floor of the tunnel. A piece of wire that cut an inch into his neck was wrapped around the stake and held him in place. Afraid of a booby trap, Bosch didn't touch him. He played the beam of his flashlight over the neck wound and followed the trail of dried blood down the front of the body. The dead man wore a green T-shirt with his name stenciled in white on the front. Al Crofton, it said beneath the blood. There were flies mired in the crusted blood on his chest, and for a moment Bosch wondered how they found their way so far down. He dipped the light to the dead soldier's crotch and saw that it, too, was black with dried blood. The pants were torn open and Crofton looked as though he had been mauled by a wild animal. Sweat began to sting Bosch's eyes and his breathing became louder, more hurried than he wanted it to be. He was immediately aware of this but was also aware that he could do nothing to stop it. Crofton's left hand was palm up on the ground next to his thigh. Bosch put the light on it and saw the bloody set of testicles. He stifled the urge to vomit but could not prevent himself from hyperventilating.

He cupped his hands over his mouth and tried to slow his gasping for air. It didn't work. He was losing it. He was panicking. He was twenty years old and he was scared. The walls of the tunnel were closing tighter on him. He rolled away from the body and dropped the light, its beam still focused on Crofton. Bosch kicked at the clay walls of the tunnel and curled into a fetal position. The sweat in his eyes was replaced by tears. At first they came silently, but soon his sobs racked his entire body and his noise seemed to echo in all directions in the darkness, right to where Charlie sat and waited. Right to hell.

PART II

MONDAY, MAY 21

Bosch came awake in his watch chair about 4 A.M. He had left the sliding glass door open to the porch, and the Santa Ana winds were billowing the curtains, ghostlike, out across the room. The warm wind and the dream had made him sweat. Then the wind had dried the moisture on his skin like a salty shell. He stepped out onto the porch and leaned against the wood railing, looking down at the lights of the Valley. The searchlights at Universal were long since retired for the night and there was no traffic sound from the freeway down in the pass. In the distance, maybe from Glendale, he heard the *whupping* sound of a helicopter. He searched and found the red light moving low in the basin. It wasn't circling and there was no searchlight. It wasn't a cop. He thought then that he could smell the slight scent of malathion, sharp and bitter, on the red wind.

He went back inside and closed the sliding glass door. He thought about bed but knew there would be no more sleep this night. It was often this way with Bosch. Sleep would come early in the night but not last. Or it would not come until the arriving sun softly cut the outline of the hills in the morning fog.

He had been to the sleep disorder clinic at the VA in Sepulveda but the shrinks couldn't help him. They told him he was in a cycle. He would have extended periods of deep sleep trances into which torturous dreams invaded. This would be followed by months of insomnia, the mind reacting defensively to the terrors that awaited in sleep. Your mind has repressed the anxiety you feel over your part in the war, the doctor told him. You must assuage these feelings in your waking hours before your sleep time can progress undisturbed. But the doctor didn't understand that what was done was done. There was no going back to repair what had happened. You can't patch a wounded soul with a Band-Aid.

He showered and shaved, afterward studying his face in the mirror and remembering how unkind time had been to Billy Meadows. Bosch's hair was turning to gray but it was full and curly. Other than the circles under his eyes, his face was unlined and handsome. He wiped the remaining shaving cream off and put on his beige summer suit with a light-blue button-down oxford. On a hanger in the closet he found a maroon tie with little gladiator helmets on it that was not unreasonably wrinkled or stained. He pegged it in place with the 187 tie pin, clipped his gun to his belt and then headed out into the predawn dark. He drove into downtown for an omelet, toast and coffee at the Pantry on Figueroa. Open twenty-four hours a day since before the Depression. A sign boasted that the place had not gone one minute in that time without a customer. Bosch looked around from the counter and saw that at the moment he was personally carrying the record on his shoulders. He was alone.

The coffee and cigarettes got Bosch ready for the day. After, he took the freeway back up to Hollywood, passing a frozen sea of cars already fighting to get downtown.

Hollywood Station was on Wilcox just a couple of blocks south of the Boulevard, where most of its business came from. He parked at the curb out front because he was only staying awhile and didn't want to get caught in the back lot traffic jam at the change of watch. As he walked through the small lobby he saw a woman with a blackened eye, who was crying and filling out a report with the desk officer. But down the hall to the left the detective bureau was quiet. The night man must have been out on a call or up in the Bridal Suite, a storage room on the second floor where there were two cots, first come, first served. The detective bureau's hustle and bustle seemed to be frozen in place. No one was there, but the long tables assigned to burglary, auto, juvenile, robbery and homicide were all awash in paperwork and clutter. The detectives came and went. The paper never changed.

Bosch went to the back of the bureau to start a pot of coffee. He glanced through a rear door and down the back hallway where the lockup benches and the jail were located. Halfway down the hall to the holding tank, a young white boy with blond dreadlocks sat handcuffed to a bench. A juvie, maybe seventeen at most, Bosch figured. It was against California law to put them in a holding tank with adults. Which was like saying it might be dangerous for coyotes to be put in a pen with Dobermans.

"What you looking at, fuckhead?" the boy called down the hall to Bosch.

Bosch didn't say anything. He dumped a bag of coffee into a paper filter. A uniform stuck his head out of the watch commander's office farther down the hall.

"I told you," the uniform yelled at the kid. "Once more and I'm going to go up a notch on the cuffs. Half hour and you won't feel your hands. Then how you going to wipe your ass in the john?"

"I guess I'll have to use your fuckin' face."

The uniform stepped into the hall and headed toward the kid, his hard black shoes making long, mean strides. Bosch shoved the filter bowl into the coffee machine and hit the brewing cycle switch. He walked away from the hallway door and over to the homicide table. He didn't want to see what happened with the kid. He dragged his chair away from his spot at the table and over to one of the community typewriters. The pertinent forms he needed were in slots on a rack on the wall above the machine. He rolled a blank crime scene report into the typewriter. Then he took his notebook out of his pocket and opened to the first page.

Two hours of typing and smoking and drinking bad coffee later, a bluish cloud hung near the ceiling lights over the homicide table and Bosch had completed the myriad forms that accompany a homicide investigation. He got up and made copies on the Xerox in the back hall. He noticed the dreadlock kid was gone. Then he got a new blue binder out of the office supplies closet — after finessing the door with his LAPD ID card — and hooked one set of the typed reports onto the three rings. The other set he hid in an old blue binder he kept in a file drawer and that was labeled with the name of an old unsolved case. When he was done, he reread his work. He liked the order the paperwork gave the case. On many previous cases he had made it a practice to reread the murder book each morning. It helped him draw out theories. The smell of the binder's new plastic reminded him of other cases and invigorated him. He was in the hunt again. The reports he had typed and placed in the murder book were not complete, though. On the Investigating Officer's Chronological Report he had left out several parts of his Sunday afternoon and evening. He neglected to type in the connection he had made between Meadows and the WestLand bank burglary. He also left out the visits to the pawnshop and to see Bremmer at the *Times*. There were no typed summaries of these interviews either. It was only Monday, day two. He wanted to wait until he had been to the FBI before committing any of that information to the official record. He wanted to know, exactly, what was going on first. It was a precaution he took on every case. He left the bureau before any of the other detectives had arrived for the day.

By nine Bosch had driven to Westwood and was on the seventeenth floor of the Federal Building on Wilshire Boulevard. The FBI waiting room was austere, the usual plastic-covered couches and scarred coffee table with old copies of the *FBI Bulletin* fanned across its fake wood-grain veneer. Bosch didn't bother to sit down or read. He stood before the sheer white curtains that covered the floor-to-ceiling windows and looked out at the panorama. The northern exposure offered a view that stretched from the Pacific eastward around the rim of the Santa Monica Mountains to Hollywood. The curtains served as a layer of fog over the smog. He stood with his nose almost touching the soft gauze fabric and looked down, across Wilshire, at the Veterans Administration Cemetery. Its white stones sprouted in the manicured grass like row after row of baby teeth. Near the cemetery's entrance a funeral was in progress, with a full honor guard at attention. But there wasn't much of a crowd of mourners. Farther north, at the top of a rise where there were no tombstones, Bosch could see several workers removing sod and using a backhoe to dig up a long slice of the earth. He checked their progress from time to time as he scanned the view, but he could not figure out what they were doing. The clearing was far too long and wide for a grave.

By ten-thirty the soldier's funeral was done but the cemetery workers were still toiling on the hill. And Bosch was still waiting at the curtain. A voice finally hit him from behind.

"All those graves. Such neat rows. I try never to look out the windows here."

He turned. She was tall and lithesome with brown wavy hair about to the shoulder with blond highlights. A nice tan and little makeup. She looked hard-shell and maybe a little weary for so early in the day, the way lady cops and hookers get. She wore a brown business suit and a white blouse with a chocolate-brown western bow. He detected the unsymmetrical curves of her hips beneath the jacket. She was carrying something small on the left side, maybe a Rugar, which was unusual. Bosch had always known female detectives to carry their weapons in their purses.

"That's the veterans cemetery," she said to him.

"I know."

He smiled, but not at that. It was that he had expected Special Agent E. D. Wish to be a man. No reason other than that was who most of the bureau agents assigned to the bank detail were. Women were part of the newer image of the bureau and weren't usually found in the heavy squads. It was a fraternity largely made up of dinosaurs and cast-outs, guys who couldn't or wouldn't cut it in the bureau's hard-charging focus on white-collar, espionage and drug investigations. The days of Melvin Purvis, G-man, were just about over. Bank robbery wasn't flashy anymore. Most bank robbers weren't professional thieves. They were hypes looking for a score that would keep them going for a week. Of course, stealing from a bank was still a federal crime. That was the only reason the bureau still bothered.

"Of course," she said. "You must know that. How can I help you, Detective Bosch? I'm Agent Wish."

They shook hands, but Wish made no movement toward the door she had come through. It had closed and the lock had snapped home. Bosch hesitated a moment and then said, "Well, I've been waiting all morning to see you. It's about the bank squad . . . One of your cases."

"Yes, that's what you told the receptionist. Sorry to have kept you, but we had no appointment and I had another pressing matter. I wish you had called first."

Bosch nodded his understanding, but again there was no movement toward inviting him in. This isn't working right, he thought.

"Do you have any coffee back there?" he said.

"Uh . . . yes, I believe we do. But can we make this quick? I'm really in the middle of something at the moment."

Who isn't, Bosch thought. She used a card key to open the door and then pulled it open and held it for him. Inside, she led him down a corridor where there were plastic signs on the walls next to the doors. The bureau didn't have the same affinity for acronyms as the police department. The signs were numbered — Group 1, Group 2 and so on. As they went along, he tried to place her accent. It had been slightly nasal but not like New York. Philadelphia, he decided, maybe New Jersey. Definitely not Southern California, never mind the tan that went with it.

"Black?" she said.

"Cream and sugar, please."

She turned and entered a room that was furnished as a small kitchen. There was a counter and cabinets, a four-cup coffeemaker, a microwave and a refrigerator. The place reminded Bosch of law offices he had been to to give depositions. Nice, neat, expensive. She handed him a Styrofoam cup of black coffee and signaled for him to put in his own cream and sugar. She wasn't having any. If it was an attempt to make him uncomfortable, it worked. Bosch felt like an imposition, not someone who brought good news, a break in a big case. He followed her back into the hallway and they went through the next doorway, which was marked Group 3. It was the bank robbery kidnap unit. The room was about the size of a convenience store. It was the first federal squad room Bosch had been in, and the comparison to his own office was depressing. The furniture here was newer than anything he had ever seen in any LAPD squad. There was actually carpet on the floor and a typewriter or computer at almost every desk. There were three rows of five desks and all of them but one were empty. A man in a gray suit sat at the first desk in the middle row, holding a phone to his ear. He didn't look up as Bosch and Wish walked in. Except for the background noise of a tactical channel coming from a scanner on a file cabinet in the back, the place could have passed for a real estate office.

Wish took a seat behind the first desk in the first row and gestured for Bosch to take the seat alongside it. This put him directly between Wish and Gray Suit on the phone. Bosch put his coffee down on her desk and began to figure right away that Gray Suit wasn't really on the phone, even though the guy kept saying "Uh huh, uh huh" or "Uh uh" every few moments or so. Wish opened a file drawer in her desk and pulled out a plastic bottle of water, some of which she poured into a paper cup.

"We had a two eleven at a savings and loan in Santa Monica, just about everybody's out on it," she explained as he scanned the almost empty room. "I was coordinating from here. That's why you had to wait out there. Sorry."

"No problem. Get him?"

"What makes you say it was a him?"

Bosch shrugged his shoulders. "Percentages."

"Well, it was two of them. One of each. And yes, we got them. They were in a stolen from Reseda reported yesterday. Female went in and took care of business. Male was the wheel. They took the 10 to the 405, then into LAX, where they left the car in front of a skycap at United. Then they took the escalator to the arrivals level, got on a shuttle bus to the Flyaway station in Van Nuys and then took a cab all the way back down to Venice. To a bank. We had an LAPD copter over them the whole time. They never looked up. When she went into the second bank we thought we were going to see another two eleven so we rushed her while she was waiting in line for a teller. Got him in the parking lot. Turns out she was just going to deposit the take from the first bank. An interbank transfer, the hard way. See some dumb people in this business, Detective Bosch. What can I do for you?"

"You can call me Harry."

"As I am doing what for you?"

"Interdepartmental cooperation," he said. "Kinda like you and our helicopter this morning."

Bosch drank some of his coffee and said, "Your name is on a BOLO I came across yesterday. Year-old case out of downtown. I'm interested in it. I work homicide out of Hollywood Div —"

"Yes, I know," Agent Wish interrupted.

"— ision."

"The receptionist showed me the card you gave. By the way, do you need it back?"

That was a cheap shot. He saw his sad-looking business card on her clean green blotter. It had been in his wallet for months and its corners were curled up at the edges. It was one of the generic cards the department gave detectives who worked out in the bureaus. It had the embossed police badge on it and the Hollywood Division phone number but no name. You could buy yourself an ink pad and order a stamp and sit at your desk at the beginning of each week and stamp out a couple dozen cards. Or you could just write your name on the line with a pen and not give out too many. Bosch had done the latter. Nothing the department could do could embarrass him anymore.

"No, you can keep it. By the way, you have one?"

In a quick, impatient motion, she opened the top middle drawer of the desk, took a card out of a little tray and put it down on the desk top next to the elbow Bosch had leaned there. He took another sip of coffee while glancing down at it. The E stood for Eleanor.

"So anyway you know who I am and where I come from," he began. "And I know a little bit about you. For instance, you investigated, or are investigating, a bank caper from last year in which the perps came in through the ground. A tunnel job. WestLand National."

He noticed her attention immediately pick up with that, and even thought he sensed Gray Suit's breathing catch. Bosch had a line in the right water.

"Your name is on the bulletins. I am investigating a homicide I believe is related to your case and I want to know . . . basically, I want to know what you've got. . . . Can we talk about suspects, possible suspects. . . . I think we might be looking for the same people. I think my guy might have been one of your perps."

Wish was quiet for a moment and played with a pencil she'd picked up off the blotter. She pushed Bosch's card around on the green square with the eraser end. Gray Suit was still acting like he was on the phone. Bosch glanced over at him and their eyes briefly connected. Bosch nodded and Gray Suit looked away. Bosch figured he was looking at the man whose comments had been in the newspaper articles. Special Agent John Rourke.

"You can do better than that, can't you, Detective Bosch?" Wish said. "I mean, you just walk in here and wave the flag of cooperation and you expect me to just open up our files."

She tapped the pencil three times on the desk and shook her head like she was disciplining a child.

"How about a name?" she said. "How about giving me some reason for the connection? We usually handle this kind of request through channels. We have liaisons that evaluate requests from other law enforcement agencies to share files and information. You know that. I think it might be best —"

Bosch pulled the FBI bulletin with the insurance photo of the bracelet out of his pocket. He unfolded it and laid it on the blotter. Then he took the pawnshop Polaroid out of the other pocket and also dropped that on the desk.

"WestLand National," he said, tapping a finger on the bulletin. "The bracelet was pawned six weeks ago in a downtown shop. My guy pawned it. Now he's dead."

She kept her eyes on the Polaroid bracelet and Bosch saw recognition there. The case had stayed that much with her.

"The name is William Meadows. Found him in a pipe yesterday morning, up at the Mulholland Dam."

Gray Suit ended his one-sided conversation. He said, "I appreciate the information. I have to go, we're wrapping up a two eleven. Uh huh. . . . Thank you. . . . You too, good-bye now."

Bosch didn't look at him. He watched Wish. He thought he sensed that she wanted to look over at Gray Suit. Her eyes darted that way but then quickly went back to the photograph. Something wasn't right, and Bosch decided to jump back into the silence.

"Why don't we skip the bullshit, Agent Wish? As far as I can tell, you've never recovered a single stock certificate, a single coin, a single jewel, a single gold-and-jade bracelet. You've got nothing. So screw the liaison stuff. I mean, what is this? My guy pawned the bracelet; he ended up dead. Why? We have parallel investigations here, don't you think? More likely, the same investigation."

Nothing.

"My guy was either given that bracelet by your perps or he stole it from them. Or possibly, he was one of them. So, maybe the bracelet wasn't supposed to turn up yet. Nothing else has. And he goes and breaks the rules and pawns the thing. They whack him, then go to the pawnshop and steal it back. Whatever. The thing is, we are looking for the same people. And I need a direction to start in."

She remained silent still, but Bosch sensed a decision coming. This time he waited her out.

"Tell me about him," she finally said.

He told her. About the anonymous call. About the body. About the apartment that had been searched. About finding the pawn stub hidden behind the photo. And then going to the pawnshop to find the bracelet stolen. He didn't say that he had known Meadows.

"Anything else taken from the pawnshop, or just this bracelet?" she asked when he was done.

"Of course. Yes. But just as a cover for the real thing they wanted. The bracelet. Way I see it, Meadows was killed because whoever killed him wanted the bracelet. He was tortured before he was murdered because they wanted to know where it was. They got what they needed, killed him, then went and got the bracelet. Mind if I smoke?"

"Yes, I do. What could be so important about one bracelet? This bracelet is only a drop in the bucket of what was taken, of what hasn't ever turned up."

Bosch had thought of that and didn't have an answer. He said, "I don't know."

"If he was tortured as you say, why was the pawn ticket there for you to find? And why did they have to break into the pawnshop? You're suggesting that he told them where the bracelet was but didn't give up the ticket?"

Bosch had thought about this, too. He said, "I don't know. Maybe he knew they wouldn't let him live. So he only gave them half of what they needed. He kept something back. It was a clue. He left the pawn stub behind as a clue."

Bosch thought about the scenario. He had first begun to put it together when rereading his notes and the reports he had typed. He decided it was time to play one more card.

"I knew Meadows twenty years ago."

"You knew this victim, Detective Bosch?" Her voice was louder now, accusatory. "Why didn't you say that when you first came in here? Since when does the LAPD allow its detectives to go around investigating the deaths of their friends?"

"I didn't say that. I said I knew him. Twenty years ago. And I didn't ask for the case. It was my turn in the bucket. I got the call out. It was . . .'"

He didn't want to say coincidence.

"This is all very interesting," Wish said. "It is also irregular. We — I'm not sure we can help you. I think —"

"Look, when I knew him, it was with the U.S. Army, First Infantry in Vietnam. Okay? We were both there. He was what they called a tunnel rat. Do you know what that means? . . . I was one too."

Wish said nothing. She was looking down at the bracelet again. Bosch had totally forgotten about Gray Suit.

"The Vietnamese had tunnels under their villages," Bosch said. "Some were a century old. The tunnels went from hootch to hootch, village to village, jungle to jungle. They were under some of our own camps, everywhere. And that was our job, the tunnel soldiers, to go down into those things. There was a whole other war under the ground."

Bosch realized that aside from a shrink and a circle group at the VA in Sepulveda he had never told anyone about the tunnels and what he did.

"And Meadows, he was good at it. As much as you could like going down into that blackness with just a flashlight and a .45, well, he did. Sometimes we'd go down and it would take hours, and sometimes it would take days. And Meadows, well, he was the only one I ever knew over there that wasn't scared of going down there. It was life above ground that scared him."

She didn't say anything. Bosch looked over at Gray Suit, who was writing on a yellow tablet Bosch couldn't read. Bosch heard someone report on the tac channel that he was transporting two prisoners to the Metro lockup.

"So now twenty years later you've got a tunnel caper and I've got a dead tunnel fighter. He was found in a pipe, a tunnel. He had property from your caper." Bosch felt around in his pockets for his cigarettes, then remembered she had said no. "We have to work together on this one. Right now."

He knew by her face it hadn't worked. He emptied his coffee cup, ready for the door. He didn't look at Wish now. He heard Gray Suit pick up the phone again and punch a number out. He stared down at the residue of sugar in the bottom of his cup. He hated sugar in his coffee.

"Detective Bosch," Wish began, "I am sorry you had to wait in the hall so long this morning. I am sorry this fellow soldier you knew, Meadows, is dead. Whether it was twenty years ago or not, I am. I have sympathy for him, and you, and what you may have had to go through. . . . But I am also sorry that I can't help you at the moment. I will have to follow established protocol and talk to my supervisor. I will get back to you. As soon as possible. That is all I can do at the moment."

Bosch dropped the cup into a trash can next to her desk and reached over to pick up the Polaroid and the bulletin page.

"Can we keep the photo here?" Agent Wish asked. "I need to show it to my supervisor."

Bosch kept the Polaroid. He got up and stepped in front of Gray Suit's desk. He held the Polaroid up to the man's face. "He's seen it," he said over his shoulder as he walked out of the office.

Deputy Chief Irvin Irving sat at his desk, bruxing his teeth and working the muscles of his jaw into hard rubber balls. He was disturbed. And this clenching and gnashing of teeth was his habit when disturbed or in solitary, contemplative moods. As a result, the musculature of his jaw had become the most pronounced feature of his face. When looked at head-on, Irving's jawline was actually wider than his ears, which were pinned flat against his shaven skull and had a winglike shape to them. The ears and the jaw gave Irving an intimidating if not odd visage. He looked like a flying jaw, as though his powerful molars could crush marbles. And Irving did all he could to promote this image of himself as a fearsome junkyard dog who might sink his teeth into a shoulder or leg and tear out a piece of meat the size of a softball. It was an image that had helped overcome his one impediment as a Los Angeles policeman — his silly name — and could only aid him in his long-planned ascendancy to the chief's office on the sixth floor. So he indulged the habit, even if it did cost him a new set of $2,000 molar implants every eighteen months.

Irving pulled his tie tight against his throat and ran his hand over his gleaming scalp. He reached to the intercom buzzer. Though he could have easily pushed the speaker button then and barked his command, he waited for his new adjutant's reply first. This was another of his habits.

"Yes, Chief?"

He loved hearing that. He smiled, then leaned forward until his great, wide jaw was inches from the intercom speaker. He was a man who did not trust that technology could do what it was supposed to do. He had to put his mouth to the speaker and shout.

"Mary, get me the jacket on Harry Bosch. It should be in the actives."

He spelled the first and last names for her.

"Right away, Chief."

Irving leaned back, smiled through clenched teeth but then thought he felt something out of alignment. He deftly ran his tongue over his left rear lower molar, searching for a defect in its smooth surface, maybe a slight fissure. Nothing. He opened the desk drawer and took out a small mirror. He opened his mouth and studied the back teeth. He put the mirror back and took out a pale blue Post-it pad and made a note to call for a dental checkup. He closed the drawer and remembered the time he had popped a fortune cookie into his mouth while dining with the city councilman from the Westside. The right rear lower molar had crumbled on the stale cookie. The junkyard dog decided to swallow the dental debris rather than expose the weakness to the councilman, whose confirmation vote he would someday need and expect. During the meal, he had brought to the councilman's attention the fact that his nephew, an LAPD motorman, was a closet homosexual. Irving mentioned that he was doing his best to protect the nephew and prevent his exposure. The department was as homophobic as a Nebraska church, and if the word leaked to the rank and file, Irving explained to the councilman, the officer could forget any hope for advancement. He could also expect brutal harassment from the rest of L.A.'s finest. Irving didn't need to mention the consequences if a scandal broke publicly. Even on the liberal Westside, it wouldn't help a councilman's mayoral ambitions.

Irving was smiling at the memory when Officer Mary Grosso knocked and then walked into the office with a one-inch-thick file in her hand. She placed it on Irving's glass-topped desk. There was nothing else on its gleaming surface, not even a phone.

"You were right, Chief. It was still in the actives files."

The deputy chief in charge of the Internal Affairs Division leaned forward and said, "Yes, I believe I did not have it transferred to archives because I had a feeling we had not seen the last of Detective Bosch. Let me see, that would be Lewis and Clarke, I believe."

He opened the file and read the notations on the inside of the jacket.

"Yes. Mary, will you have Lewis and Clarke come in, please."

"Chief, I saw them in the squad. They were getting ready for a BOR. I'm not sure which case."

"Well, Mary, they will have to cancel the Board of Rights — and please do not talk to me in abbreviations. I am a slow-moving, careful policeman. I do not like shortcuts. I do not like abbreviations. You will learn that. Now, tell Lewis and Clarke I want them to delay the hearing and report to me forthwith."

He flexed his jaw muscles and held them, hard as tennis balls, at their full width. Grosso scurried from the office. Irving relaxed and paged through the file, reacquainting himself with Harry Bosch. He noted Bosch's military record and his fast advance through the department. From patrol to detectives to the elite Robbery-Homicide Division in eight years. Then the fall: administrative transfer last year from Robbery-Homicide to Hollywood homicide.

Should have been fired, Irving lamented as he studied the entries on Bosch's career chronology.

Next, Irving scanned the evaluation report on a psychological given Bosch the year before to determine if he should be allowed to return to duty after killing an unarmed man. The department psychologist wrote:

> Through his war and police experiences, most notably including the aforementioned shooting resulting in fatality, the subject has to a high degree become desensitized to violence. He speaks in terms of violence or the aspect of violence being an accepted part of his day-to-day life, for all of his life. Therefore, it is unlikely that what transpired previously will act as a psychological deterrent should he again be placed in circumstances where he must act with deadly force in order to protect himself or others. I believe he will be able to act without delay. He will be able to pull the trigger. In fact, his conversation reveals no ill effects at all from the shooting, unless his sense of satisfaction with the outcome of the incident — the suspect's death — should be deemed inappropriate.

Irving closed the file and tapped it with a manicured nail. He then picked a strand of long brown hair — Officer Mary Grosso's, he presumed — off the glass desk top and dropped it into a wastebasket next to the desk. Harry Bosch was a problem, he thought. A good cop, a good detective — actually, Irving grudgingly admired his homicide work, particularly his affinity for serial slayers. But in the long run, the deputy chief believed, outsiders did not work well inside the system. Harry Bosch was an outsider, always would be. Not part of the LAPD Family. And now the worst had come to Irving's attention. Bosch had not only left the family but appeared to be engaged in activities that would hurt the family, embarrass the family. Irving decided that he would have to move swiftly and surely. He swiveled in his chair and looked out the window at City Hall across Los Angeles Street. Then his gaze dropped, as it always did, to the marble fountain in front of Parker Center, the memorial to officers killed in the line of duty. There was family, he thought. There was honor. He clenched his teeth powerfully, triumphantly. Just then the door opened.

Detectives Pierce Lewis and Don Clarke strode into the office and presented themselves. Neither spoke. They could have been brothers. They shared close-cropped brown hair, the arms-splayed build of weight lifters, conservative gray silk suits. Lewis's had a thin charcoal stripe, Clarke's maroon. Each man was built wide and low to the ground for better handling. Each had a slightly forward tilt to his body, as if he were wading out to sea, crashing through breakers with his face.

"Gentlemen," said Irving, "we have a problem — a priority problem — with an officer who has come across our threshold before. An officer you two worked with some degree of success before."

Lewis and Clarke glanced at each other and Clarke allowed himself a small, quick smile. He couldn't guess who it could be, but he liked going after repeaters. They were so desperate.

"Harry Bosch," Irving said. He waited a moment to let the name sink in, then said, "You need to take a little ride up to Hollywood Division. I want to open a one point eighty-one on him right away. Complainant will be the Federal Bureau of Investigation."

"FBI?" Lewis said. "What did he do with them?"

Irving corrected him for using the abbreviation for the bureau and told them to sit down in the two chairs in front of his desk. He spent the next ten minutes recounting the telephone call he had received minutes earlier from the bureau.

"The bureau says it is too coincidental," he concluded. "I concur. He may be dirty in this, and the bureau wants him off the Meadows case. At the very least, it appears he intervened to help this suspect, his former military comrade, avoid a jail term last year, possibly so he could accomplish this bank burglary. Whether Bosch knew this, or if there was further involvement in the crime, I do not know. But we are going to find out what Detective Bosch is up to."

Irving delayed here to drive home his point with a full jaw flex. Lewis and Clarke knew better than to interrupt. Irving then said, "This opportunity opens the door for the department to do what it was unable to accomplish before with Bosch. Eliminate him. You will report directly to me. Oh, and I want Bosch's supervisor, a Lieutenant Pounds, copied with your daily reports. On the quiet. But you will do more than copy me. I want telephonic reports twice daily, morning and evening."

"We're on our way," Lewis said as he stood up.

"Aim high, gentlemen, but be careful," Irving counseled them. "Detective Harry Bosch is no longer the celebrity he once was. But, nevertheless, do not let him slip away."

Bosch's embarrassment at being unceremoniously dismissed by Agent Wish had turned to anger and frustration as he rode down the elevator. It was like a physical presence in his chest that jumped into his throat as the stainless steel cell descended. He was alone, and when the pager on his belt started to chirp, he let it go on for its allotted fifteen seconds rather than turn it off. He swallowed his anger and embarrassment and formed it into resolve. As he stepped out of the elevator car, he looked down at the phone number on the pager's digital display. An 818 area code — the Valley, but he didn't recognize the number. He stepped to a pod of pay phones in the courtyard in front of the Federal Building and dialed the number. Ninety cents, an electronic voice said. Luckily he had the loose change. He dumped it in and the call was picked up on a half ring by Jerry Edgar.

"Harry," he began without a hello, "I'm still up here at the VA and I'm getting the runaround, man. They don't have any files on Meadows. They say I have to go through D.C. or I gotta get a warrant. I tell them I know there is a file, you know, on account of what you told me. I say, 'Look, if I was to get a search warrant, can you look and make sure you know where this file is?' And so they're lookin' for a while and what they finally come out saying is, yes, they had a file but it's gone. Guess who came and got it with a court order last year?"

"The FBI."

"You know something I don't know?"

"I haven't exactly been sitting on my ass. They say when the bureau took it or why?"

"They weren't told why. FBI agent just came in with the warrant and took it. Checked it out last September and hasn't brought it back since. Didn't give a reason. The Fucking-B-I doesn't have to."

Bosch was quiet while he thought about this. They knew all along. Wish knew about Meadows and the tunnels and everything else he had just told her. It had all been a show.

"Harry, you there?"

"Yeah, listen, did they show you a copy of the paperwork or know the name of the agent?"

"No, they couldn't find the subpoena receipt and nobody remembered the agent's name, except that she was a woman."

"Take this number where I'm at. Go back to them in records and ask for another file, just see if it's there. My file."

He gave Edgar the pay phone number, his date of birth, social security number and his full name, spelling out his real first name.

"Jesus, that's your first name?" Edgar said. "Harry for short. How'd your momma come up with that one?"

"She had a thing about fifteenth-century painters. It goes with the last name. Go check on the file, then call me back. I'll wait here."

"I can't even pronounce it, man."

"Rhymes with 'anonymous.'"

"Okay, I'll try that. Where you at, anyway?"

"A pay phone. Outside the FBI."

Bosch hung up before his partner could ask any questions. He lit a cigarette and leaned on the phone booth while watching a small group of people walking in a circle on the long green lawn in front of the building. They were holding up homemade signs and placards that protested a proposal to open new oil leases in Santa Monica Bay. He saw signs that said Just Say No to Oil and Isn't the Bay Polluted Enough? and United States of Exxon and so on.

He noticed a couple of TV news crews on the lawn filming the protest. That was the key, he thought. Exposure. As long as the media showed up and put it on the six o'clock news, the protest was a success. A sound-bite success. Bosch noticed that the group's apparent spokesman was being interviewed on camera by a woman he recognized from Channel 4. He also recognized the spokesman but he wasn't sure from where. After a few moments of watching the man's ease during the interview in front of the camera, Bosch placed him. The guy was a TV actor who used to play a drunk on a popular situation comedy that Bosch had seen once or twice. Though the guy still looked like a drunk, the show wasn't on anymore.

Bosch was on his second cigarette, leaning on the phone booth and beginning to feel the heat of the day, when he looked up at the glass doors of the building and saw Agent Eleanor Wish walking through. She was looking down and digging a hand through her purse and hadn't noticed him. Quickly and without analyzing why, he ducked behind the phones and, using them as a shield, moved around them as she walked by. It was sunglasses she had been looking for in the purse. Now she had them on as she walked past the protestors without even a glance in their direction. She headed up Veteran Avenue to Wilshire Boulevard. Bosch knew the federal garage was under the building. Wish was walking in the opposite direction. She was going somewhere nearby. The phone rang.

"Harry, they have your file, too. The FBI. What's going on?"

Edgar's voice was urgent and confused. He didn't like waves. He didn't like mysteries. He was a straight nine-to-five man.

"I don't know what's going on, they wouldn't tell me," Bosch replied. "You head into the office. We'll talk there. If you get there before me, I want you to make a call over to the subway project. Personnel. See if they had Meadows working there. Try under the name Fields, too. Then just do the paper on the TV stabbing. Like we said. Keep your end of our deal. I'll meet you there."

"Harry, you told me you knew this guy, Meadows. Maybe we should tell Ninety-eight it's a conflict, that we ought to turn the case over to RHD or somebody else on the table."

"We'll talk about it in a little while, Jed. Don't do anything or talk to anybody about it till I get there."

Bosch hung up the phone and walked off toward Wilshire. He could see Wish already had turned east toward Westwood Village. He closed the distance between them, crossed to the other side of the street and followed behind. He was careful not to get too close, so that his reflection would not be in the shop windows she was looking in as she walked. When she reached Westwood Boulevard she turned north and crossed Wilshire, coming to Bosch's side of the street. He ducked into a bank lobby. After a few moments he went back out on the sidewalk and she was gone. He looked both ways and then trotted up to the corner. He saw her a half block up Westwood, going into the village.

Wish slowed in front of some shop windows and came to a stop in front of a sporting goods store. Bosch could see female manikins in the window, dressed in lime-green running shorts and shirts. Last year's fad on sale today. Wish looked at the outfits for a few moments and then headed off, not stopping until she was in the theater district. She turned into Stratton's Bar & Grill.

Bosch, on the other side of the street, passed the restaurant without look-ing and went up to the next corner. He stood in front of the Bruin, below the old theater's marquee, and looked back. She hadn't come out. He wondered if there was a rear door. He looked at his watch. It was a little early for lunch but maybe she liked to beat the crowd. Maybe she liked to eat alone. He crossed the street to the other corner and stood below the canopy of the Fox Theater. He could see through the front window of Stratton's but didn't see her. He walked through the parking lot next to the restaurant and into the rear alley. He saw a public access door at the back. Had she seen him and used the restaurant to slip away? It had been a long while since he had been on a one-man tail, but he didn't think she had made him. He headed down the alley and went in the back door.

Eleanor Wish was sitting alone in the row of wooden booths along the restaurant's right wall. Like any careful cop she sat facing the front door, so she didn't see Bosch until he slid onto the bench across from her and picked up the menu she had already scanned and dropped on the table.

He said, "Never been here, anything good?"

"What is this?" she said, surprise clearly showing on her face.

"I don't know, I thought you might want some company."

"Did you follow me? You followed me."

"At least I'm being up front about it. You know, you made a mistake back at the office. You played it too cool. I walk in with the only lead you've had in nine months and you want to talk about liaisons and bullshit. Something wasn't right but I couldn't figure out what. Now I know."

"What are you talking about? Never mind, I don't want to know."

She made a move to slide out of the booth, but Bosch reached across the table and firmly put his hand on her wrist. Her skin was warm and moist from the walk over. She stopped and turned and smoked him with brown eyes so angry and hot they could have burned his name on a tombstone.

"Let go," she said, her voice tightly controlled but carrying enough of an edge to suggest she could lose it. He let go.

"Don't leave. Please." She lingered a moment and he worked quickly. He said, "It's all right. I understand the reasons for the whole thing, the cold reception back there, everything. I have to say it actually was good work, what you did. I can't hold it against you."

"Bosch, listen to me, I don't know what you are talking about. I think —"

"I know you already knew about Meadows, the tunnels, the whole thing. You pulled his military files, you pulled mine, you probably pulled files on every rat that made it out of that place alive. There had to have been some-thing in the WestLand job that connected to the tunnels back there."

She looked at him for a long moment and was about to speak, when a waitress approached with a pad and pencil.

"For now, just one coffee, black, and an Evian. Thank you," Bosch said before Wish or the waitress could speak. The waitress walked away, writing on the pad.

"I thought you were a cream-and-sugar cop," Wish said.

"Only when people try to guess what I am."

Her eyes seemed to soften then, but only a bit.

"Detective Bosch, look, I don't know how you know what you think you know, but I am not going to discuss the WestLand case. It is exactly as I said at the bureau. I can't do it. I am sorry. I really am."

Bosch said, "I guess maybe I should resent it, but I don't. It was a logical step in the investigation. I would've done the same. You take anybody who fit the profile — tunnel rat — and sift them through the evidence."

"You're not a suspect, Bosch, okay? So drop it."

"I know I'm not a suspect." He gave a short, forced burst of laughter. "I was serving a suspension down in Mexico and can prove it. But you already know that. So for me, fine, I'll drop it. But I need what you have on Meadows. You pulled his files back in September. You must have done a workup on him. Surveillance, known associates, background. Maybe . . . I bet you even pulled him in and talked to him. I need it all now — today, not in three, four weeks when some liaison puts a stamp on it."

The waitress came back with the coffee and water. Wish pulled her glass close but didn't drink.

"Detective Bosch, you are off the case. I'm sorry. I shouldn't be the one to tell you. But you're off. You go back to your office and you'll find out. We made a call after you left."

He was holding his coffee with two hands, elbows on the table. He carefully put the cup down on the saucer, in case his hands began to shake.

"What did you do?" Bosch asked.

"I'm sorry," Eleanor Wish said. "After you left, Rourke — the guy you shoved the picture in front of? — he called the number on your card and talked to a Lieutenant Pounds. He told him about your visit today and suggested there was a conflict, you investigating a friend's death. He said some other things and —"

"What other things?"

"Look, Bosch, I know about you. I'll admit we pulled your files, we checked you out. Hell, but to do that, all we had to do was read the newspapers back then. You and that Dollmaker thing. So I know what you have been through with the internal people, and this isn't going to help, but it was Rourke's decision. He —"

"What other things did he tell?"

"He told the truth. He said both your name and Meadows's had come up in our investigation. He said you both knew each other. He asked that you be taken off the case. So all of this doesn't matter."

Bosch looked off, out of the booth.

"I want to hear you answer," he said. "Am I a suspect?"

"No. At least you weren't until you walked in this morning. Now, I don't know. I'm trying to be honest. I mean, you have to look at this from our standpoint. One guy we looked at last year comes in and says he is investigating the murder of another guy we looked very hard at. This first guy says, 'Let me see your files.'"

She didn't have to tell him as much as she had. He knew this and knew she was probably going out on a limb saying anything at all. For all the shit he had just stepped in or been put in, Harry Bosch was beginning to like cold, hard Eleanor Wish.

"If you won't tell me about Meadows, tell me one thing about myself. You said I was looked at and then dropped. How'd you clear me? You go to Mexico?"

"That and other things." She looked at him a moment before going on. "You were cleared early on. At first we got excited. I mean, we look through the files of people with tunnel experience in Vietnam and there sitting on the top was the famous Harry Bosch, detective superstar, a couple books written about his cases. TV movie, a spinoff series. And the guy the newspapers just happened to have been filled with, the guy whose star crashed with a one-month suspension and transfer from the elite Robbery-Homicide Division to . . ." She hesitated.

"The sewer." He finished it for her.

She looked down into her glass and continued.

"So, right away Rourke started figuring that maybe that's how you spent your time, digging this tunnel into the bank. From hero to heel, this was your way to get back at society, something crazy like that. But when we backgrounded you and asked around quietly, we heard you went to Mexico for the month. We sent someone down to Ensenada and checked it out. You were clear. Around then we also had gotten your medical files from the VA up at Sepulveda — oh, that's it, that's who you checked with this morning, isn't it?"

He nodded. She continued.

"Anyway, in the medical there were the psychiatrist's reports . . . I'm sorry. This seems like such an invasion."

"I want to know."

"The therapy for PTS. I mean, you are completely functional. But you have infrequent manifestation of post-traumatic stress in forms of insomnia and other things, claustrophobia. A doctor even wrote once that you wouldn't go into a tunnel like that, never again. Anyway, we put a profile of you through our behavioral sciences lab in Quantico. They discounted you as a suspect, said it was unlikely that you would cross the line for something like financial gain."

She let all of that sink in for a few moments.

"Those VA files are old," Bosch said. "The whole story is old. I'm not going to sit here and present a case for why I should be a suspect. But that VA stuff is old. I haven't seen a shrink, VA or otherwise, in five years. And as far as that phobia shit goes, I went into a tunnel to look at Meadows yesterday. What do you think your shrinks in Quantico would write about that?"

He could feel his face turn red with embarrassment. He had said too much. But the more he tried to control and hide it, the more blood rushed into his face. The wide-hipped waitress chose that moment to come back and freshen his coffee.

"Ready to order?" she said.

"No," Wish said without taking her eyes off Bosch. "Not yet."

"Hon, we have a big lunch crowd come in here, and we're going to need the table for people what want to eat. I make my living off the hungry ones. Not the ones too angry to eat."

She walked away with Bosch thinking that waitresses were probably better observers of human behavior than most cops. Wish said, "I am sorry about all of this. You should have let me get up when I first wanted to."

The embarrassment was gone but the anger was still there. He wasn't looking out of the booth anymore. He was looking right at her.

"You think you know me from some papers in a file? You don't know me. Tell me what you know."

"I don't know you. I know about you," she said. She stopped a moment to gather her thoughts. "You are an institutional man, Detective Bosch. Your whole life. Youth shelters, foster homes, the army, then the police. Never leave the system. One flawed societal institution after another."

She sipped some water and seemed to be deciding whether to go on. She did. "Hieronymus Bosch. . . . The only thing your mother gave you was the name of a painter dead five hundred years. But I imagine the stuff you've seen would make the bizarre stuff of dreams he painted look like Disneyland. Your mother was alone. She had to give you up. You grew up in foster homes, youth halls. You survived that and you survived Vietnam and you survived the police department. So far, at least. But you are an outsider in an insider's job. You made it to RHD and worked the headline cases, but you were an outsider all along. You did things your way and eventually they busted you out for it."

She emptied her glass, seemingly to give Bosch time to stop her from continuing. He didn't.

"It only took one mistake," she said. "You killed a man last year. He was a killer himself but that didn't matter. According to the reports, you thought he was reaching under a pillow on the bed for a gun. Turned out he was reaching for his toupee. Almost laughable, but IAD found a witness who said she told you beforehand that the suspect kept his hair under the pillow. Since she was a street whore, her credibility was in question. It wasn't enough to bounce you, but it cost you your position. Now you work Hollywood, the place most people in the department call the sewer."

Her voice trailed off. She was finished. Bosch didn't say anything, and there was a long period of silence. The waitress cruised by the booth but knew better than to speak to them.

"When you get back to the office," he finally began, "you tell Rourke to make one more call. He got me off the case, he can get me back on."

"I can't do it. He won't do it."

"Yes, he'll do it, and tell him he has until tomorrow morning to do it."

"Or what? What can you do? I mean, let's be honest. With your record, you'll probably be suspended by tomorrow. As soon as Pounds got off the phone with Rourke he probably called IAD, if Rourke didn't do it himself."

"Doesn't matter. Tomorrow morning I hear something, or tell Rourke he'll be reading a story in the *Times* about how an FBI suspect in a major bank heist, a subject of FBI surveillance no less, was murdered right under the bureau's nose, taking with him the answers to the celebrated WestLand tunnel caper. All the facts might not be right or in the correct order, but it will be close enough. More important than that, it will be a good read. And it'll make waves all the way to D.C. It'll be embarrassing and it'll also be a warning to whoever did Meadows. You'll never get them then. And Rourke will always be known as the guy who let them get away."

She looked at him, shaking her head as if she were above this whole mess. "It's not my call. I'll have to go back to him and let him decide what to do. But if it was me, I'd call your bluff. And I will tell you straight out that's what I'll tell him to do."

"It's no bluff. You've checked me out, you know I'll go to the media and the media will listen to me and like it. Be smart. You tell him it's no bluff. I'll have nothing to lose by doing it. He'll have nothing to lose by bringing me in."

He began to slide out of the booth. He stopped and threw a couple of dollar bills on the table.

"You've got my file. You know where you can reach me."

"Yes, we do," she said, and then, "Hey, Bosch?"

He stopped and looked back at her.

"The street whore, was she telling the truth? About the pillow?"

"Don't they all?"

Bosch parked in the lot behind the station on Wilcox and smoked right up until he reached the rear door. He killed the butt on the ground and went in, leaving behind the odor of vomit that wafted from the mesh windows at the rear of the station holding tank. Jerry Edgar was pacing in the back hall waiting for him.

"Harry, we've got a forthwith from Ninety-eight."

"Yeah, what about?"

"I don't know, but he's been coming out of the glass box every ten minutes looking for you. You got your beeper and the Motorola turned off. And

I saw a couple of the IAD silks up from downtown go in there with him a while ago."

Bosch nodded without saying anything comforting to his partner.

"What's going on?" Edgar blurted. "If we've got a story, let's get it straight before we go in there. You've had experience with this shit, not me."

"I'm not sure what's going on. I think they're kicking us off the case. Me, at least." He was very nonchalant about the whole thing.

"Harry, they don't bring IAD in to do that. Something's on, and, man, I hope whatever you did, you didn't fuck me up, too."

Edgar immediately looked embarrassed.

"Sorry, Harry, I didn't mean it that way."

"Relax. Let's go see what the man wants."

Bosch headed toward the detective squad room. Edgar said he'd cut through the watch office and then come in from the front hall so it wouldn't look like they had collaborated on a story. When Bosch got to his desk, the first thing he noticed was that the blue murder book on the Meadows case was gone. But he also noticed that whoever had taken it had missed the cassette tape with the 911 call on it. Bosch picked up the cassette and put it in his coat pocket just as Ninety-eight's voice boomed out of the glass office at the head of the squad room. He yelled just one word: "Bosch!" The other detectives in the squad room looked around. Bosch got up and slowly walked toward the glass box, as the office of Lieutenant Harvey "Ninety-eight" Pounds was called. Through the windows he could see the backs of two suits sitting in there with Pounds. Bosch recognized them as the two IAD detectives who had handled the Dollmaker case. Lewis and Clarke.

Edgar came into the squad through the front hallway just as Bosch passed and they walked into the glass box together. Pounds sat dull-eyed behind his desk. The men from Internal Affairs did not move.

"First thing, no smoking, Bosch, you got that?" Pounds said. "In fact, the whole squad stunk like an ashtray this morning. I'm not even going to ask if it was you."

Department and city policy outlawed smoking in all community-shared offices such as squad rooms. It was okay to smoke in a private office if it was your office or if the office's occupant allowed visitors to smoke. Pounds was a reformed smoker and militant about it. Most of the thirty-two detectives he commanded smoked like junkies. When Ninety-eight wasn't around, many of them would go into his office for a quick fix, rather than have to go out to the parking lot, where they'd miss phone calls and where the smell of piss and puke migrated from the rear windows of the drunk tank. Pounds had taken to locking his office door, even on quick trips up the hall to the station commander's office, but anybody with a letter opener could pop the door in three seconds. The lieutenant was constantly returning and finding his office space fouled by smoke. He had two fans in the ten-by-ten room and a can of Glade on the desk. Since the frequency of the fouling had increased with the reassignment of Bosch from Parker Center to Hollywood detectives, Ninety-eight Pounds was convinced Bosch was the major offender. And he was right, but he had never caught Bosch in the act.

"Is that what this is about?" Bosch asked. "Smoking in the office?"

"Just sit down," Pounds snapped.

Bosch held his hands up to show there were no cigarettes between his fingers. Then he turned to the two men from Internal Affairs.

"Well, Jed, it looks like we might be off on a Lewis and Clarke expedition here. I haven't seen the great explorers on the move since they sent me on a no-expense-paid vacation to Mexico. Did some of their finest work on that one. Headlines, sound bites, the whole thing. The stars of Internal Affairs."

The two IAD cops' faces immediately reddened with anger.

"This time, you might do yourself a favor and keep your smart mouth shut," Clarke said. "You're in serious trouble, Bosch. You get it?"

"Yeah, I get it. Thanks for the tip. I got one for you, too. Go back to the leisure suit you used to wear before you became Irving's bendover. You know, the yellow thing that matched your teeth. The polyester does more for you than the silk. In fact, one of the guys out there in the bullpen mentioned that the ass end of that suit is getting shiny, all the work you do riding a desk."

"All right, all right," Pounds cut in. "Bosch, Edgar, sit down and shut up for a minute. This —"

"Lieutenant, I didn't say one thing," Edgar began. "I —"

"Shut up! Everybody! Shut up a minute," Pounds barked. "Jesus Christ! Edgar, for the record, these two are from Internal Affairs, if you didn't already know, Detectives Lewis and Clarke. What this is —"

"I want a lawyer," Bosch said.

"Me too, I guess," added Edgar.

"Oh, bullshit," Pounds said. "We are going to talk about this and get some things straight, and we aren't bringing any Police Protective League bullshit into it. If you want a lawyer, you get one later. Right now you are going to sit here, the both of you, and answer some questions. If not, Edgar, you are going to be bounced out of that eight-hundred-dollar suit and back into uniform, and Bosch, shit, Bosch, you'll probably go down for the count this time."

For a few moments there was silence in the small room, even though the tension among the five men threatened to shatter the windows. Pounds looked out at the squad room and saw about a dozen detectives acting as if they were working but who were actually trying to pick up whatever they could through the glass. Some had been attempting to read the lieutenant's lips. He got up and lowered a set of venetian blinds over the windows. He rarely did this. It was a signal to the squad that this was big. Even Edgar showed his concern, audibly exhaling. Pounds sat back down. He tapped a long fingernail on the blue plastic binder that lay closed on his desk.

"Okay, now let's get down to it," he began. "You two guys are off the Meadows case. That's number one. No questions, you're done. Now, from the top, you are going to tell us anything and everything."

At that, Lewis snapped open a briefcase and pulled out a cassette tape recorder. He turned it on and put it on Pounds's spotless desk.

Bosch had been partnered with Edgar only eight months. He didn't know him well enough to know how he would take this kind of bullying, or how far he could hold out against these bastards. But he did know him well enough to know he liked him and didn't want him to get jammed up. His only sin in this whole thing was that he had wanted Sunday afternoon off to sell houses.

"This is bullshit," Bosch said, pointing to the recorder.

"Turn that off," Pounds said to Lewis, pointing to the recorder, which was actually closer to him than to Lewis. The Internal Affairs detective stood up and picked up the recorder. He turned it off, hit the rewind button and replaced it on the desk.

After Lewis sat back down Pounds said, "Jesus Christ, Bosch, the FBI calls me today and tells me they've got you as a possible suspect in a goddam bank heist. They say this Meadows was a suspect in the same job, and by virtue of that you should now be considered a suspect in the Meadows kill. You think we aren't going to ask questions about that?"

Edgar was exhaling louder now. He was hearing this for the first time.

"Keep the tape off and we'll talk," Bosch said. Pounds contemplated that for a moment and said, "For now, no tape. Tell us."

"First off, Edgar doesn't know shit about this. We made a deal yesterday. I take the Meadows case and he goes home. He does the wrap-up on Spivey, the TV stabbed the night before. This FBI stuff, the bank job, he doesn't know for shit. Let him go."

Pounds seemed to make a point of not looking at Lewis or Clarke or Edgar. He'd make this decision on his own. It produced a slight glimmer of respect in Bosch, like a candle set out in the eye of a hurricane of incompetence. Pounds opened his desk drawer and pulled out an old wooden ruler. He fiddled with it with both hands. He finally looked at Edgar.

"That right, what Bosch says?"

Edgar nodded.

"You know it makes him look bad, like he was trying to keep the case for himself, conceal the connections from you?"

"He told me he knew Meadows. He was up front all the way. It was a Sunday. We weren't going to get anybody to come out and take it off us on account of him knowing the guy twenty years ago. Besides, most of the people who end up dead in Hollywood the police have known one way or the other. This stuff about the bank and all, he must've found out after I left. I'm finding it all out sitting here."

"Okay," Pounds said. "You got any of the paper on this one?"

Edgar shook his head.

"Okay, finish up what you've got on the — what did you call it? — Spivey, yeah, the Spivey case. I'm assigning you a new partner. I don't know who, but I'll let you know. Okay, go on, that's all."

Edgar let out one more audible breath and stood up.

Harvey "Ninety-eight" Pounds let things settle in the room for a few moments after Edgar left. Bosch wanted a cigarette badly, even to just hold one unlit in his mouth. But he wouldn't show them such a weakness.

"Okay, Bosch," Pounds said. "Anything you want to tell us about all this?"

"Yeah. It's bullshit."

Clarke smirked. Bosch paid no mind. But Pounds gave the IAD detective a withering look that further increased his stock of respect with Bosch.

"The FBI told me today I was no suspect," Bosch said. "They looked at me nine months ago because they looked at anybody around here who'd worked the tunnels in Vietnam. They found some connection to the tunnels back there. Simple as that. It was good work, they had to check out everybody. So they looked at me and went on. Hell, I was in Mexico — thanks to these two goons — when the bank thing went down. The FBI just —"

"Supposedly," Clarke said.

"Shove it, Clarke. You're just angling for a way to take your own vacation down there, at taxpayers' expense, checking it out. You can check with the bureau and save the money."

Bosch then turned back to Pounds and adjusted his chair so his back was to the IAD detectives. He spoke in a low voice to make it clear he was talking to Pounds, not them. "The bureau wants me off it because, one, I threw a curve at 'em when I showed up there today to ask about the bank caper. I mean, I was a name from the past, and they panicked and called you. And two, they want me off the case because they probably fucked it up when they let Meadows skate last year. They blew their one chance at him and don't want an outside department to come in and see that or to break the thing they couldn't break for nine months."

"No, Bosch, that's what's bullshit," Pounds said. "This morning I received a formal request from the assistant special agent in charge who runs their bank squad, a guy named —"

"Rourke."

"You know him. Well, he asked that —"

"I be removed from the Meadows case forthwith. He says I knew Meadows, who just happened to be the prime suspect in the bank job. He ends up dead and I'm on the case. Coincidence? Rourke thinks not. I'm not sure myself."

"That's what he said. So that's where we start. Tell us about Meadows, how you knew him, when you knew him, don't leave one thing out."

Bosch spent the next hour telling Pounds about Meadows, the tunnels, the time Meadows called after almost twenty years and how Bosch got him into VA Outreach in Sepulveda without ever seeing him. Just phone calls. At no time did Bosch address the IAD detectives or acknowledge that they were even in the room.

"I didn't make it a secret that I knew him," he said at the end. "I told Edgar. I walked right in and told the FBI. You think I would have done that if I was the one who did Meadows? Not even Lewis and Clarke are that dumb."

"Well, then, Jesus Christ, Bosch, why didn't you tell me?" Pounds boomed. "Why isn't it in the reports in this book? Why do I have to hear it from the FBI? Why does Internal Affairs have to hear it from the FBI?"

So Pounds hadn't made the call to IAD. Rourke had. Bosch wondered if Eleanor Wish had known that and had lied, or if Rourke called out the goons on his own. He hardly knew the woman — he didn't know the woman — but he found himself hoping she hadn't lied to him.

"I only started the reports this morning," Bosch said. "I was going to bring them up to date after seeing the FBI. Obviously, I didn't get the chance."

"Well, I'm saving you the time," Pounds said. "It's been turned over to the FBI."

"What has? The FBI has no jurisdiction over this. This is a murder case."

"Rourke said they believe the slaying is directly related to their ongoing investigation of the bank job. They will include this in their investigation. We will assign our own case officer through an interdepartmental liaison. If and when the time comes to charge someone with the murder, the appointed officer will take it to the DA for state charges."

"Christ, Pounds, there is something going on. Don't you see that?"

Pounds put the ruler back in the drawer and closed it.

"Yes, something is going on. But I don't see it your way," he said. "That's it, Bosch. That's an order. You are off. These two men want to talk to you and you are on a desk till Internal Affairs is finished with its investigation."

He was quiet a moment before beginning again in a solemn tone. A man unhappy with what he had to say.

"You know, you were sent out here to me last year and I could have put you anywhere. I could have put you on the goddam burglary table, handling fifty reports a week, just buried you in paper. But I didn't. I recognized your skills and put you on homicide, what I thought you wanted. They told me last year that you're good but you don't stay in the lines. Now I see they were right. How this will hurt me, I don't know. But I'm not worrying about what's best for you anymore. Now, you can either talk to these guys or not. I don't really care. But that's it. We're done, you and me. If somehow you ride this one out, you better see about getting a transfer, because you won't be on my homicide table anymore."

Pounds picked up the blue binder off his desk and stood up. As he headed out of the office he said, "I have to get somebody to take this over to the bureau. You men can have the office as long as you need it."

He closed the door and was gone. Bosch thought about it and decided he really couldn't fault Pounds for what he had said, or done. He took out a cigarette and lit it.

"Hey, no smoking, you heard the man," Lewis said.

"Fuck off," Bosch said.

"Bosch, you're dead," Clarke said. "We're going to toast your ass right this time. You aren't the hero you once were. No PR problems this time. Nobody's going to give a shit about what happens to you."

Then he stood up and turned the tape recorder back on. He recited the date, the names of the three men present and the Internal Affairs case number assigned to the investigation. Bosch realized the number was about seven hundred higher than the case number from the internal investigation nine months earlier that sent him to Hollywood. Nine months, and seven hundred other cops have been through the bullshit wringer, he thought. One day there will be no one left to do what it says on the side of every patrol car, to serve and protect.

"Detective Bosch" — Lewis took over then in a modulated, calm tone — "we would like to ask you questions regarding the investigation of the death of William Meadows. Will you tell us of any past association with or knowledge you had of the decedent."

"I refuse to answer any questions without an attorney present," Bosch said. "I cite my right to representation under California's Policeman's Bill of Rights."

"Detective Bosch, the department administration does not recognize that aspect of the Policeman's Bill of Rights. You are commanded to answer these questions, and if you do not you will be subject to suspension and possible dismissal. You —"

"Can you loosen these handcuffs, please?" Bosch said.

"What?" Lewis cried out, losing his calm, confident tone.

Clarke stood up and went to the tape recorder and bent over it.

"Detective Bosch is not handcuffed and there are two witnesses here who can attest to that fact," he said.

"Just the two that cuffed me," Bosch said. "And beat me. This is a direct violation of my civil rights. I request that a union rep and my attorney be present before we continue."

Clarke rewound the tape and turned the recorder off. His face was almost purple with anger as he carried it back to his partner's briefcase. It was a few moments before words came to either one of them.

Clarke said, "It's going to be a pleasure to do you, Bosch. We'll have the suspension papers on the chief's desk by the end of the day. You'll be assigned to a desk at Internal Affairs where we can keep an eye on you. We'll start with CUBO and work our way up from there, maybe even to murder. Either way, you're done in the department. You're over."

Bosch stood up and so did the two IAD detectives. Bosch took a last drag on his cigarette, dropped it on the floor in front of Clarke and stepped on it, grinding it into the polished linoleum. He knew they would clean it up rather than let Pounds know they had not controlled the interview or the interviewee. He stepped between them then, exhaled the smoke and walked out of the room without saying a word. Outside, he heard Clarke's barely controlled voice call out.

"You stay away from the case, Bosch!"

Avoiding the eyes that followed him, Bosch walked through the squad room and dropped into his seat at the homicide table. He looked across at Edgar, who was seated at his own space.

"You did good," Bosch said. "You should come out all right."

"What about you?"

"I'm off the case and those two assholes are going to put paper in on me. I've got the afternoon and that's about it before I get the ROD."

"God damn."

The deputy chief in charge of IAD had to sign off on all Relieved of Duty orders and temporary suspensions. Stiffer penalties had to be recommended to a police commission subcommittee for approval. Lewis and Clarke would go for a temporary ROD for conduct unbecoming an officer, or CUBO, as it was known. Then they'd work on something stiffer to take to the commission. If the deputy chief signed an ROD on Bosch, he would have to be notified according to union regs. That meant in person or in a tape-recorded phone conversation. Once notification was made, Bosch could be assigned to a desk at IAD in Parker Center or to his home until the conclusion of the investigation. But as they had just promised, Lewis and Clarke would go for assignment to IAD. That way they could put him on display like a trophy.

"You need anything from me on Spivey?" he asked Edgar.

"No. I'm set. I'm gonna start typing it up if I can get a machine."

"Did you happen to check like I asked on Meadows's job on the subway project?"

"Harry, you . . ." Edgar must have thought better of saying what he wanted to say. "Yeah, I checked it out. For what it's worth, they said they haven't had anyone named Meadows on the job. There is a Fields, but he's black and he was at work today. And Meadows probly wasn't working under any other name because they aren't running a midnight shift. The project is ahead of schedule, if you can believe that shit." Edgar then called out, "I got dibs on the Selectric."

"No way," called back an autos detective named Minkly. "I'm on deck with that one."

Edgar started looking around for another candidate. Late in the day, the typewriters in the office were like gold. There were a dozen machines for thirty-two detectives: that was if you included the manual jobs and the electrics with nervous tics like moving borders or jumpy space bars.

"Okay then," Edgar called out. "I got dibs after you, Mink." Then Edgar lowered his voice and turned to Bosch. "Who you think he'll put me with?"

"Pounds? I don't know." It was like guessing who your wife would marry after you punched the time clock for the last time. Bosch wasn't all that interested in speculating who would be partnered with Edgar. He said, "Listen, I have to do some things."

"Sure, Harry. You need any help, anything from me?"

Bosch shook his head and picked up the phone. He called his lawyer and left a message. It usually took three messages before the guy would call back, and Bosch made a note to call again. Then he turned his Rolodex, got a number and called the U.S. Armed Services Records Archive in St. Louis. He asked for a law enforcement clerk and got a woman named Jessie St. John. He put in a priority request for copies of all of Billy Meadows's military records. Three days, St. John said. He hung up thinking that he would never see the records. They'd come but he wouldn't be in this office, at this table, on this case. Next he called Donovan at SID and learned there had been no latent prints on the needle kit found in Meadows's shirt pocket and only smears on the can of spray paint. The light-brown crystals found in the straining cotton in the kit came back as 55 percent pure heroin, Asian blend. Bosch knew that most heroin dealt on the street and shot into the vein was about 15 percent pure. Most of it was tar heroin made by Mexicans. Somebody had given Meadows a very hot shot. In Harry's mind, that made the tox tests he was waiting for a formality. Meadows had been murdered.

Nothing else from the crime scene was of much use, except Donovan mentioned that the freshly burned match found in the pipe was not torn from the matchbook in Meadows's kit. Bosch gave Donovan the address of Meadows's apartment and asked him to send a team out to process it. He said to check the matches in an ashtray on the coffee table against the book in the kit. Then he hung up, wondering if Donovan would send somebody before word spread that Bosch was off the case or suspended.

The last call he made was to the coroner's office. Sakai said he had made next-of-kin notification. Meadows's mother was still alive and was reached in New Iberia, Louisiana. She had no money to send for him or bury him. She hadn't seen him in eighteen years. Billy Meadows would not be going home. L.A. County would have to bury him.

"What about the VA?" Bosch asked. "He was a veteran."

"Right. I'll check it out," Sakai said and hung up.

Bosch got up and took a small portable tape recorder from one of his drawers in the file cabinets. The bank of files ran along the wall behind the homicide table. He slipped the recorder into his coat pocket with the 911 tape and walked out of the squad room through the rear hallway. He went past the lockup benches and the jail, down to the CRASH office. The tiny office was more crowded than the detective bureau. Desks and files for five men and a woman were crammed into a room no bigger than a second bedroom in a Venice apartment. Down one wall of the room was a row of four-drawer file cabinets. On the opposite wall was the computer and teletype. In between were three sets of two desks pushed side by side. The back wall had the usual map of the city with black lines detailing the eighteen police divisions. Above the map were the Top 10: color eight-by-tens of the ten top assholes of the moment in Hollywood Division. Bosch noticed one was a morgue shot. The kid was dead but still made the list. Now that's an asshole, he thought. And above the photos, black plastic letters spelled out Community Resources Against Street Hoodlums.

Only Thelia King was in, sitting in front of the computer. That was what Bosch wanted. Also known as The King, which she hated, and Elvis, which she didn't mind, Thelia King was the CRASH computer jockey. If you wanted to trace a gang lineage or were just looking for a juvie floating somewhere around Hollywood, Elvis was the one to see. But Bosch was surprised she was alone. He looked at his watch. Just after two, too early for the gang troops to be on the street.

"Where's everybody at?"

"Hey, Bosch," she said, looking away from the screen. "Funerals. We got two different gangs, and I mean warring tribes, planting homeboys in the same cemetery today up in the Valley. They got all hands up there to make sure things stay cool."

"And so why aren't you out there with the boys?"

"Just got back from court. So, before you tell me why you are here, Harry, why don't you tell me what happened in Ninety-eight Pounds's office today?"

Bosch smiled. Word traveled faster through a police station than it did on the street. He gave her an abbreviated account of his time in the barrel and the expected battle with IAD.

"Bosch, you take things too seriously," she said. "Why don't you get yourself an outside gig? Something to keep yourself sane, moving in the flow. Like your partner. Too bad that sucker's married. He's making three times selling houses on the side what we make bustin' heads full-time. I need a gig like that."

Bosch nodded. But too much going with the flow is heading us into the sewer, he thought but didn't say. Sometimes he believed that he took things just right and everybody else didn't take them seriously enough. That was the problem. Everybody had an outside gig.

"What do you need?" she said. "I better do it now before they put your paper through. After that, you'll be a leper 'round here."

"Stay where you are," he said, and then he pulled over a chair and told her what he needed from the computer.

The CRASH computer had a program called GRIT, an acronym within an acronym, this one for Gang-Related Information Tracking. The program files contained the vitals on the 55,000 identified gang members and juvenile offenders in the city. The computer also tied in with the gang computer at the sheriff's department, which had about 30,000 of its own gangbangers on file. One part of the GRIT program was the moniker file. This stored references to offenders by their street names and could match them with real names, DOBs, addresses, and so on. All monikers that came to police attention through arrests or shake cards — field interrogation reports — were fed into the computer program. It was said the GRIT file had more than 90,000 monikers in it. You just needed to know which keys to push. And Elvis did.

Bosch gave her the three letters he had. "I don't know if that's the whole thing or a partial," he said. "I think it's a partial."

She typed in the commands to open the GRIT files, put in the letters S-H-A and hit the prompt key. It took about thirteen seconds. A frown creased Thelia King's ebony face. "Three hundred forty-three hits," she announced. "You might be hidin' out here a while, Hon."

He told her to eliminate the blacks and Latinos. The 911 tape sounded white to him. She pressed more keys, then the computer screen's amber letters recomposed the list.

"That's better, nineteen hits," King said.

There was no moniker that was just the three letters, Sha. There were five Shadows, four Shahs, two Sharkeys, two Sharkies and one each of Shark, Shabby, Shallow, Shank, Shabot and Shame. Bosch thought quickly about the graffiti he had seen on the pipe up at the dam. The jagged S, almost like a gaping mouth. The mouth of a shark?

"Pull up the variations on Shark," he said.

King hit a couple of keys and the top third of the screen filled with new amber letters. Shark was a Valley boy. Limited contact with police; he had gotten probation and graffiti clean-up after he was caught tagging bus benches along Ventura Boulevard in Tarzana. He was fifteen. It wasn't likely he would have been up at the dam at three o'clock on a Sunday morning, Bosch guessed. King pulled the first Sharkie up on the screen. He was currently in a Malibu fire camp for juvenile offenders. The second Sharkie was dead, killed in a gang war between the KGB — Kids Gone Bad — and the Vineland Boyz in 1989. His name had not yet been purged from the computer records.

When King called up the first Sharkey the screen filled with information and a blinking word at the bottom said "More." "Here's a regular trouble-maker," she said.

The computer report described Edward Niese, a male white, seventeen years of age, known to ride a yellow motorbike, tag number JVN138, and who had no known gang affiliation but used Sharkey as a graffiti tag. A frequent runaway from his mother's home in Chatsworth. Two screens of police contacts with Sharkey followed. Bosch could tell by the location of each arrest or questioning that this Sharkey was partial to Hollywood and

West Hollywood when he ran away. He scanned to the bottom of the second screen, where he saw a loitering arrest three months earlier at the Hollywood reservoir.

"This is him," he said. "Forget the last kid. Hard copy?"

She pushed keys to print the computer file and then pointed to the wall of file cabinets. He went over and opened the N drawer. He found a file on Edward Niese and pulled it. Inside was a color booking photo. Sharkey was blond and seemed small in the picture. He had the look of hurt and defiance that was as common as acne on teenagers' faces these days. But Bosch was struck by a familiarity about the face. He couldn't place it. He turned the photo over. It was dated two years earlier. King handed him the computer printout and he sat down at one of the empty desks to study it and the contents of the file.

The most serious offenses the boy who called himself Sharkey had committed — and been caught at — were shoplifting, vandalism, loitering and possession of marijuana and speed. He had been held once — twenty days — at Sylmar Juvenile Hall after one of the drug arrests but later released on home probation. All the other times he was popped he was immediately released to his mother. He was a chronic runaway from home and a throwaway from the system.

There was not much more in the file than was on the computer. A little elaboration on the arrests was all. Bosch shuffled through the papers until he found the report on the loitering charge. It went to pretrial intervention and was dismissed when Sharkey agreed to go home to his mother and stay there. That apparently didn't last long. There was a report that the mother had reported him missing to his probation officer two weeks later. According to these records, he had not been picked up yet.

Bosch read the investigating officer's summary on the loitering arrest. It said:

I/O interviewed Donald Smiley, a caretaker at the Mulholland Dam, who said at 7 A.M. this date he went into the pipe situated alongside the reservoir access road to clear it of debris. Smiley found the boy asleep on a bed made of newspapers. The boy was dirty and incoherent when roused. Subject appeared to be under the influence of narcotics. Police were called and I/O responded. The arrestee stated to I/O that he had been sleeping there regularly because his mother did not want him at home. I/O determined the subject was a reported runaway and took him into custody this date, suspicion of loitering.

Sharkey was a creature of habit, Bosch thought. He was arrested at the dam two months ago, but had gone back there to sleep Sunday morning. He looked through the rest of the papers in the file for indications of other habits that would help Bosch find him. From a three-by-five shake card, Bosch learned that Sharkey had been stopped and questioned but not arrested on Santa Monica Boulevard near West Hollywood in January. Sharkey was lacing up new Reeboks and the officer, believing he might have just lifted them, asked Sharkey to produce a receipt. He did and that would have been that. But when the boy pulled the receipt out of a leather pouch on his motorbike, the officer noticed a plastic bag in there and asked to see that as well. The bag contained ten photographs of Sharkey. He was naked in each and stood in different poses, fondling himself in some, his penis erect in others. The officer took the photos and destroyed them, but noted on the shake card that he would alert the sheriff's station in West Hollywood that Sharkey was hustling photos to homosexuals on Santa Monica Boulevard.

That was it. Bosch closed the file but kept the photo of Sharkey. He thanked Thelia King and left the small office. He was walking through the station's rear hallway, past the lockup benches, when he placed the familiarity in the photo. The hair was longer now and in dreadlocks, the defiance crowding out the hurt in the face, but Sharkey had been the kid who was cuffed to the juvie bench early that morning. Bosch felt sure of it. Thelia had missed it on the computer search because the arrest had not yet been logged in. Bosch cut into the watch commander's office, told the lieutenant what he was looking for and was led to a box labeled A.M. Watch. Bosch looked through the reports stacked in the box until he found the paperwork on Edward Niese.

Sharkey had been picked up at 4 A.M. loitering near a newsstand on Vine. A patrol officer thought he was hustling. After he grabbed him he ran a computer check and learned he was a runaway. Bosch checked the day's arrest sheet and learned the kid had been held until 9 A.M., when his probation officer came and got him. Bosch called the PO at Sylmar Juvenile Hall but learned that Sharkey had already been arraigned before a juvenile court referee and was released to the custody of his mother.

"And that's his biggest problem," the PO said. "He'll be gone by tonight, back on the street. I guarantee it. And I told the ref that, but he wasn't going to book the kid into the monkey house just 'cause he was caught loitering and his mother happens to be a telephone whore."

"A what?" Bosch asked.

"It should be in the file. Yeah, while Sharkey's on the street, dear old mom is at home telling guys on the phone how she's gonna piss in their mouths and put rubber bands on their dicks. Advertises in skin mags. She gets forty bucks for fifteen minutes. Takes MasterCard, Visa, puts 'em on hold while she checks on another line to make sure the number is valid and they got credit. Anyway, she's been doing it, near as I can tell, five years now. Edward's formative years were listening to this shit. I mean, no wonder the kid's a scammer and runner. What do you expect?"

"How long ago did he leave with her?"

"'Bout noon. You want to catch him there, you better go. You got the address?"

"Yeah."

"And Bosch, one thing: Don't be expecting no whore when you get there. His mom, she doesn't look like the part she plays on the phone, if you know what I mean. Her voice might do the job but her looks would scare a blind man."

Bosch thanked him for the warning and hung up. He took the 101 out to the Valley and then the 405 north to the 118 and west. He got off in Chatsworth and drove into the rocky bluffs at the top corner of the Valley. There was a condominium community built on what he knew was once a movie ranch. It had been one of the places Charlie Manson and his crew used to hide out. Parts of one member of that crew's body were supposedly still missing and buried around there someplace. It was near dusk when Bosch got there. People were off work and getting home. A lot of traffic on the development's thin roads. A lot of closing doors. A lot of calls to Sharkey's mother. Bosch was too late.

"I have no time to talk to more police," Veronica Niese said when she answered the door and looked at the badge. "As soon as I get him home he is out the door again. I don't know where he goes. You tell me. That's your job. I have three calls waiting, one long distance. I gotta go."

She was in her late forties, fat and wrinkled. She obviously wore a wig and the dilation of her eyes did not match. She had the dirty-socks smell of a speed addict. Her callers were better off with their fantasies, with just a voice with which to construct a body and face.

"Mrs. Niese, I'm not looking for your son for something he did. I need to talk to him because of something he saw. He could possibly be in danger."

"Oh, bullshit. I've heard that line before."

She closed the door and he just stood there. After a few moments he could hear her on the phone, and he thought it was a French accent but couldn't be sure. He could only make out a few of the sentences but they made him blush. He thought about Sharkey and realized he wasn't really a runaway, because there was nothing here to run away from. He left the doorstep and went back to the car. That would be it for the day. And he was out of time. Lewis and Clarke must have paper out on him by now. He'd be assigned to a desk at IAD by morning. He drove back to the station and signed out. Everyone was already gone and there were no messages on his desk, not even from his lawyer. On the way home he stopped by the Lucky and bought four bottles of beer, a couple from Mexico, a lager from England called Old Nick and a Henry's.

He expected to find a message from Lewis and Clarke on his phone tape when he got home. He wasn't wrong, but the message was not what he expected.

"I know you're there, so listen," said a voice Bosch recognized as Clarke's. "They can change their mind but they can't change ours. We'll see you around."

There were no other messages. He played Clarke's message over three times. Something had gone wrong for them. They must have been called off. Could his lame threat to the FBI to go to the media have worked? Even as he thought the question, he doubted the answer was yes. So then, what happened? He sat down in the watch chair and began drinking the beers, the Mexicans first, and looking through the war scrapbook he had forgotten to put away. When he had opened it Sunday night he had opened a dark memory. He now found himself entranced by it, the distance of time having faded the threat as well as the photos. Sometime after dark the phone rang and Harry picked it up before the tape machine.

"Well," said Lieutenant Harvey Pounds, "the FBI now thinks they might have been too harsh. They've reassessed and want you back in. You are to aid their investigation in any way they request. That comes down from administration, Parker Center."

Pounds's voice betrayed his astonishment at the reversal.

"What about IAD?" Bosch asked.

"Nothing filed on you. Like I said, the FBI is backing away, so is IAD. For now."

"So I am back in."

"You're back in. Not my choice. Just so you know, they went over me, because I told them to blow it out their collective asses. Something about this stinks, but I guess that will have to wait for later. For now, you are on detached assignment. You are working with them until further notice."

"What about Edgar?"

"Don't worry about Edgar. He's not your concern anymore."

"Pounds, you act like you did me a favor putting me on the homicide table when they kicked me out from Parker Center. I did you the favor, man. So if you're looking for apologies from me, you aren't getting any."

"Bosch, I'm not looking for anything from you. You fucked yourself. Only problem with that is that you may have fucked me in the process. If it was up to me, you wouldn't be near this case. You'd be checking pawnshop lists."

"But it isn't up to you, is it?"

He hung up before Pounds could reply. He stood there thinking for a few moments and his hand was still on the phone when it rang again.

"What?"

"Rough day, right?" Eleanor Wish said.

"I thought it was somebody else."

"Well, I guess you've heard."

"I heard."

"You'll be working with me."

"How come you called off the dogs?"

"Simple, we want to keep the investigation out of the papers."

"There's more to it."

She didn't say anything but she didn't hang up. Finally, he thought of something to say.

"Tomorrow, what do I do?"

"Come see me in the morning. We'll go from there."

Bosch hung up. He thought about her, and about how he didn't know what was going on. He didn't like it, but he couldn't walk away now. He went into the kitchen and took the bottle of Old Nick from the refrigerator.

Lewis stood with his back to the passing traffic, using his wide body to block the sound from intruding into the pay phone.

"He starts with the FBI — er, the bureau, tomorrow morning," Lewis said. "What do you want us to do?"

Irving didn't answer at first. Lewis envisioned him on the other end of the line, jaw worked into a clench. Popeye face, Lewis thought and smirked. Clarke walked over from the car then and whispered, "What's so funny? What did he say?"

Lewis batted him away and made a don't-bother-me face at his partner.

"Who was that?" Irving asked.

"It was Clarke, sir. He's just anxious to know our assignment."

"Did Lieutenant Pounds talk to the subject?"

"Yes sir," Lewis said, wondering if Irving was taping the call. "The lieutenant said the, uh, subject has been told he is to work with the F — the bureau. They are consolidating the murder and the bank investigations. He is working with Special Agent Eleanor Wish."

"What's his scam . . . ?" Irving said, though no reply was expected, or offered by Lewis. There was silence on the phone line for a while because Lewis knew better than to interrupt Irving's thoughts. He saw Clarke approaching the phone booth again and he waved him away and shook his head as if he were dealing with an impetuous child. The doorless phone booth was at the bottom of Woodrow Wilson Drive, next to the Barham Boulevard crossing over the Hollywood Freeway. Lewis heard the sound of a semi thunder by on the freeway and felt warm air blow into the booth. He looked up at the lights of the houses on the hillside and tried to pinpoint which one came from Bosch's stilt house. It was impossible to tell. The hill looked like a giant, fat Christmas tree with too many lights.

"He must have some kind of leverage on them," Irving finally said. "He's muscled his way into it. I'll tell you what your assignment is. You two stay on him. Not so he knows. But stay with him. He is up to something. Find out what. And build your one point eighty-one case along the way. The Federal Bureau of Investigation may have withdrawn its complaint, but we will not back off."

"What about Pounds, you still want him copied?"

"That is Lieutenant Pounds, Detective Lewis. And yes, copy him your daily surveillance log. That will be enough for him."

Irving hung up without another word.

"Very good, sir," Lewis said to the dead phone. He didn't want Clarke to know he had been slighted. "We'll stay with it. Thank you, sir. Good night."

Then he, too, hung up, privately embarrassed that his commander had not deemed it necessary to say good night to him. Clarke quickly walked up.

"So?"

"So we pick him up again tomorrow morning. Bring your piss bottle."

"That's it? Just surveillance?"

"At this time."

"Shit. I want to search that fucker's house. Break some stuff. He's probably got the shit from that heist sitting up there."

"If he was involved, I doubt he would be so stupid. We sit back for now. If he's dirty on this, we'll see."

"Oh, he's dirty. Don't worry."

"We'll see."

Sharkey sat on the concrete block wall that fronted a parking lot on Santa Monica Boulevard. He closely watched the lighted front of the 7-Eleven across the street, checking out who was coming and who was going. Mostly tourist trade and couples. No singles yet. None that fit the bill. The boy called Arson sauntered over and said, "This ain't going nowhere, budro."

Arson's hair was red and waxed into spiky flames. He wore black jeans and a dirty black T-shirt. He was smoking a Salem. He wasn't stoned but he was hungry. Sharkey looked at him and then past him to where the third boy, the one known as Mojo, sat on the ground near the bikes. Mojo was shorter and wider, with his black hair slicked back in a knob behind his head. Acne scars marked his face forever as sullen.

"Give it a few more minutes," Sharkey said.

"I want to eat, man," Arson said.

"Well, what do you think I'm trying to do? We all want to eat."

"Maybe we could see how Bettijane's doing," Mojo said. "She'll have made enough for us to eat."

Sharkey looked over at him and said, "You two go ahead. I'm staying till I score. I'm gonna eat."

As he said this he watched a maroon Jaguar XJ6 pull into the convenience store's lot.

"How about the guy in the pipe?" Arson asked. "You think they found him yet? We could go up there and check him out, see if there is any bread. I don't know why you didn't have the balls to do it last night, Shark."

"Hey, you go up there by yourself and check it out if you want," Sharkey said. "See who has balls then."

He hadn't told them that he had called 911 about the body. That would be harder for them to forgive than his fear of going into the pipe. A lone man got out of the Jaguar. He looked like late thirties, brush cut, baggy white slacks and shirt, sweater draped around his shoulders. Sharkey saw no one waiting in the car.

"Hey, check out the Jag," he said. The other two looked over at the store. "This is it. I'm going."

"We'll be here," Arson said.

Sharkey got off the wall and trotted across the boulevard. He watched the Jag's owner through the windows of the store. He had an ice cream in his hand and was looking at the magazine rack. His eyes were constantly on the prowl as he looked at the other men in the store. Sharkey was encouraged as he saw the man head toward the counter to pay for the ice cream. He squatted against the front of the store, the grille of the Jag four feet away.

When the man came out, Sharkey waited for their eyes to lock and the man to smile before he spoke up.

"Hey, mister?" he said as he got up. "I was wondering if you could do me a favor?"

The man looked around the parking lot before answering.

"Sure. What do you need?"

"Well, I was wondering if you might go in and get me a beer. I'll give you the money and all. I just want a beer. To relax, you know?"

The man hesitated. "I don't know . . . that would be illegal, wouldn't it? You're not twenty-one. I could get in trouble."

"Well," Sharkey said with a smile, "do you have any beer at home? Then you wouldn't have to be buying it. Just giving somebody a beer ain't no crime."

"Well. . . ."

"I wouldn't stay long. We could probably relax each other a little bit, you know?"

The man took another look around the parking lot. No one was watching. Sharkey thought he had him now.

"Okay," he said. "I can take you back here later if you want."

"Sure. That'd be cool."

They drove east on Santa Monica to Flores and then south a couple of blocks to a townhouse development. Sharkey never turned around or tried to look in the mirrors. They would be back there. He knew it. There was a security gate on the outside of the property which the man had a key for and pulled closed behind them. Then they went into his townhouse.

"My name is Jack," the man said. "What can I get you?"

"I'm Phil. Do you have any food? I'm kind of hungry, too." Sharkey looked around for the security intercom, and the button that would unlatch the gate. The apartment was mostly light-colored furniture on an off-white deep pile carpet. "Nice place."

"Thanks. Let me see what I have. If you want to wash your clothes, we can get that done, too, while you are here. I don't do this very often, you know. But when I can help someone I try."

Sharkey followed him into the kitchen. The security console was on the wall next to the phone. When Jack opened the refrigerator and bent down to look in, Sharkey pushed the button that opened the gate outside. Jack didn't notice.

"I have tuna fish. And I can make a salad. How long have you been on the street? I'm not going to call you Phil. If you don't want to tell me your real name, that's fine."

"Um, tuna fish would be good. Not too long."

"Are you clean?"

"Yeah, sure. I'm okay."

"We'll take precautions."

It was time. Sharkey stepped backward into the hall. Jack looked up from the refrigerator, a plastic bowl in his hand, his mouth slightly ajar. Sharkey thought there was a look of recognition in his face, like he knew what was about to happen. Sharkey twisted the dead bolt and opened the door. Arson and Mojo walked in.

"Hey, what is this?" Jack said, though there was no confidence in his voice. He rushed into the hall and Arson, who was the biggest of all four of them, hit him with a fist on the bridge of his nose. There was a sound like a pencil breaking, and the plastic bowl of tuna fish clumped to the ground. Then there was a lot of blood on the off-white carpet.

PART
III

TUESDAY, MAY 22

Eleanor Wish called again Tuesday morning while Harry Bosch was fiddling with his tie in front of the bathroom mirror. She said she wanted to meet at a coffee shop in Westwood before taking him into the bureau. He had already had two cups of coffee but said he'd be there. He hung up, fastened the top button on his white shirt and pulled the tie snugly to his neck. He couldn't remember the last time he had paid such attention to the details of his appearance.

When he got there, she was in one of the booths along the front windows. She had both hands on the water glass in front of her and looked content. There was a plate pushed off to the side that had the paper wrapping from a muffin on it. She gave him a short courtesy smile as he slid in and waved a hand at a waitress.

"Just coffee," Bosch said.

"You already ate?" Wish said when the waitress went away.

"Uh, no. But I'm fine."

"You don't eat much, I can tell."

Said more like a mother than a detective.

"So, who's going to tell me about it? You or Rourke?"

"Me."

The waitress put down a cup of coffee. Bosch could hear four salesmen in the next booth dickering over the table's breakfast bill. He took a small swallow of hot coffee.

"I would like the FBI's request for my help put on paper, signed by the senior special agent in charge of the Los Angeles office."

She hesitated a moment, put her glass down and looked directly at him for the first time. Her eyes were so dark they betrayed nothing about her. At their corners, he saw just the beginning of a gentle web of lines in the tan skin. At the line of her chin there was a small, white crescent scar, very old and almost unnoticeable. He wondered if the scar and the lines bothered her, as he believed they would most women. Her face seemed to him to have a slight sadness cast in it, as if a mystery carried inside had worked its way outside. Perhaps it was fatigue, he thought. Nevertheless, she was an attractive woman. He figured her age for early thirties.

"I think that can be arranged," she said. "Any other demands before we get to work?"

He smiled and shook his head no.

"You know, Bosch, I got your murder book yesterday and read through it last night. For what you had there, and for one day's work, it was very good work. Most other detectives, that body'd still be in the waiting line at the morgue and listed as probable accidental OD."

He said nothing.

"Where should we begin on it today?" she asked.

"I've got some things working that weren't in the book yet. Why don't you tell me about the bank burglary first? I need the background. All I know is what you put out to the papers and on the BOLOs. You bring me up, then I'll take it from there, tell you about Meadows."

The waitress came and checked his cup and her glass. Then Eleanor Wish told the story of the bank heist. Bosch thought of questions as she went along, but he tried to note them in his head to ask afterward. He sensed that she marveled at the story, the planning and execution of the caper. Whoever they were, the tunnelers, they had her respect. He found himself almost jealous.

"Beneath the streets of L.A.," she said, "there are more than four hundred miles of storm lines that are wide enough and tall enough to drive a car through. After that, you've got even more tributary lines. Eleven hundred more miles that you could walk or at least crawl through.

"This means anybody can go under and, if they know the way, get close to any building they want to in the city. And it is not that difficult to find the way. The plans for the whole network are public record, on file with the county recorder's office. Anyway, these guys used the drainage system to get to WestLand National."

He had already figured as much but didn't bother to say. She said the FBI believed there were at least three underground men and then at least one on top to act as lookout, provide other necessary functions. The topsider probably communicated with them by radio, except possibly near the end because of the danger that radio waves might set off the explosive detonators.

The underground men made their way through the drainage system on Honda all-terrain vehicles. There was a drive-in entrance to the storm sewer system at a wash in the Los Angeles River basin northeast of downtown. They drove in there, probably under cover of darkness, and following recorder's maps, made their way through the tunnel network to a spot under Wilshire Boulevard in downtown, about 30 feet below and 150 yards west of WestLand National. It was a two-mile trip.

An industrial drill with a twenty-four-inch circle bit, probably diamond-tipped, was attached to a generator on one of the ATVs and used to cut a hole through the six-inch concrete wall of the stormwater tunnel. From there the underground men began to dig.

"The actual break-in to the vault occurred on Labor Day weekend," Wish said. "We think they must have begun the tunnel three or four weeks earlier. They'd only work nights. Go in, dig some and be back out by dawn. The DWP has inspectors that routinely go through the system looking for cracks and other problems. They work days, so the perps probably didn't risk it."

"What about the hole they cut in the side, wouldn't the water and power people have seen that?" asked Bosch, who immediately became annoyed with himself for asking a question before she was done.

"No," she said. "These guys thought of everything. They had a piece of plywood cut in a circle twenty-four inches wide. They coated it with concrete — we found it there after. We think that when they left each morning, they put this in the hole, and then each time they'd caulk around the edges with more concrete. It would look like a pipeline from a storm drain that had been capped off. That's pretty common down there. I've been. You see capped lines all over the place. The twenty-four inches is a standard size. So this would have looked normal. It doesn't get noticed and the perps just come back the next night, go back in and dig a little farther toward the bank."

She said the tunnel was dug primarily with hand tools — shovels, picks, drills powered off the generator on the ATV. The tunnelers probably used flashlights but also candles. Some of them were found still burning in the tunnel after the robbery was discovered. They were propped in small indentations cut in the walls.

"That ring a bell?" Wish asked.

He nodded.

"We figure they made about ten to twenty feet of progress a night," she said. "We found two wheelbarrows in the tunnel, after. They had been cut in half and disassembled to fit through the twenty-four-inch hole and then strapped back together to be used during the digging. It must have been one or two of the perps' jobs to make runs back out of the tunnel and to dump the dirt and debris from the dig into the main drainage line. There is a steady flow of water on the floor of the line, and it would have washed the dirt away, eventually, to the river wash. We figure that on some nights their topside partner opened fire hydrants up on Hill to get more water flowing down there."

"So they had water down there, even in a drought."

"Even in a drought. . . ."

Wish said that when the thieves finally dug their way under the bank, they tapped into the bank's own underground electric and telephone lines. With downtown a ghost town on weekends, the bank branch was closed on Saturdays. So on Friday, after business hours, the thieves bypassed the alarms. One of the perps had to be a bellman. Not Meadows, he was probably the explosives man.

"The funny thing was, they didn't need a bellman," she said. "The vault's sensor alarm had repeatedly been going off all week. These guys, with their digging and their drills, must have been tripping the alarms. Four straight nights the cops are called out along with the manager. Sometimes three times in one night. They don't find anything and begin to think it's the alarm. The sound-and-movement sensor is off balance. So the manager calls the alarm company and they can't get anybody out until after the holiday weekend, you know, Labor Day. So this guy, the manager —"

"Turns the alarm off." Bosch finished for her.

"You got it. He decides he isn't going to get called out each night during the weekend. He's supposed to go down to the Springs to his time-share condo and play golf. He turns the alarms off. Of course, he no longer works for WestLand National."

Under the vault, the bandits used a water-cooled industrial drill, which was bolted upside down to the underside of the vault slab, to bore a two-and-a-half-inch hole through the five feet of concrete and steel. FBI crime scene analysts estimated that took five hours, and only if the drill didn't overheat. Water to cool it came from a tap into an underground water main. They used the bank's water.

"After they got the hole drilled, they packed it with C-4," she said. "Ran the wire down through their tunnel and out into the drainage tunnel. They popped it from there."

She said LAPD emergency-response records showed that at 9:14 A.M. on that Saturday, alarms were reported at a bank across the street from West-Land National and a jewelry store a half-block away.

"We figure that was the detonation time," Wish said. "Patrol was sent out, looked around and didn't find anything, decided the alarms were probably triggered by an earthquake tremor and left. Nobody bothered to check West-Land National. Its alarm hadn't made a peep. They didn't know that it had been turned off."

Once into the vault, they didn't leave, she said. They worked right through the three-day weekend, drilling the locks on the deposit boxes, pulling the drawers and emptying them.

"We found empty food cans, potato chip bags, freeze-dried food packets, you know, survival store stuff," Wish said. "It looks like they stayed there, maybe slept in shifts. In the tunnel there was a wide part, it was like a small room. Like a sleeping room, we think. We found the pattern from a sleeping bag impressed on the dirt floor. We also found impressions in the sand left by the stocks of M-16s — they brought automatic weapons with them. They weren't planning on surrendering if things went wrong."

She let him think about that a few moments and then continued. "We estimate they were in the vault sixty hours, maybe a few more. They drilled four hundred and sixty-four of the boxes. Out of seven fifty. If there were three of them, then that's about a hundred and fifty-five boxes each. Subtract about fifteen hours for rest and eating over the three days they were in there, and you've got each man drilling three, four boxes an hour."

They must have had a time limit, she said. Maybe three o'clock or thereabouts Tuesday morning. If they quit drilling by then, it gave them plenty of time to pack up and get out. They took the loot and their tools and backed out. The bank manager, with a fresh Palm Springs tan on his face, discovered the heist when he opened the vault for business Tuesday morning.

"That's it in a nutshell," she said. "Best thing I've seen or heard of since I've been in the job. Only a few mistakes. We've found out a lot about how they did it but not much about who did it. Meadows was as close as we ever got, and now he's dead. That photograph you showed me yesterday. Of the bracelet? You were right, it's the first thing that's ever turned up from one of those boxes that we know of."

"But now it's gone."

Bosch waited for her to say something but she was done.

"How'd they pick the boxes to drill?" he asked.

"It looks random. I have a video at the office I'll show you. But it looks like they said, 'You take that wall, I'll take this one, you take that one,' and so on. Some boxes right next to others that were drilled were left untouched. Why, I don't know. Didn't look like a pattern. Still, we had losses reported in ninety percent of the boxes they drilled. Mostly untraceable stuff. They chose well."

"How did you come up with three of them?"

"We figured it would take at least that many to drill that many boxes. Plus, that's how many ATVs there were."

She smiled and he bit. "Okay, how'd you know about the ATVs?"

"Well, there were tracks in the mud in the drainage line and we identified them from tires. We also found paint, blue paint, on the wall on one of the curves of the drainage line. One of them had slid on the mud and hit the wall. The paint lab in Quantico came up with the model year and make. We hit all the Honda dealers in Southern California until we came up with a purchase of three blue ATVs at a dealership in Tustin, four weeks before Labor Day. Guy paid cash and loaded them on a trailer. Gave a phony name and address."

"What was it?"

"The name? Frederic B. Isley, as in FBI. It would come up again. We once showed the salesman some six-packs that included Meadows's, yours and a few other people's photos but he couldn't make anybody as Isley."

She wiped her mouth on a napkin and dropped it on the table. He could see no lipstick on it.

"Well," she said, "I've had enough water for a week. Meet me back at the bureau and we'll go over what we've got and what you've got on the Meadows thing. Rourke and I think that is the way to go. We've exhausted all leads on the bank job, been banging against the wall. Maybe the Meadows case will bring us the break we need."

Wish picked up the tab, Bosch put down the tip.

They took their separate cars to the Federal Building. Bosch thought about her as he drove and not the case. He wanted to ask her about that little scar on her chin and not how she connected the WestLand tunnelers to Vietnam tunnel rats. He wanted to know what gave the sweet sad look to her face. He followed her car through a neighborhood of student apartments near UCLA and then across Wilshire Boulevard. They met at the elevator in the parking garage of the Federal Building.

"I think this will be best if you basically just deal with me," she said as they rode up alone. "Rourke — You and Rourke did not start off well and —"

"We didn't even start off," Bosch said.

"Well, if you would give him the chance you would see he is a good man. He did what he thought was right for the case."

The elevator doors spread apart on the seventeenth floor, and there was Rourke.

"There you two are," he said. He put his hand out to Bosch, who took it without much conviction. Rourke introduced himself.

"I was just going down for coffee and a roll," he said. "Care to join me?"

"Uh, John, we just came from a coffee shop," Wish said. "We'll meet you back up here."

Bosch and Wish were now outside the elevator and Rourke was inside. The assistant special agent in charge just nodded his head, and the door closed. Bosch and Wish headed into the office.

"He's a lot like you in a way — been through the war and all," she said. "Give him a try. You're not going to help things if you don't thaw out."

He let it go by. They walked down the hall to the Group 3 squad and Wish pointed to a desk behind hers. She said it was empty since the agent who used it had been transferred to Group 2, the porno squad. Bosch put his briefcase on the desk and sat down. He looked around the room. It was much more crowded than the day before. About a half-dozen agents were at desks and three more were in the back standing around a file cabinet where there was a box of donuts. He noticed a television and VCR on a rack in the back of the office. It hadn't been there the day before.

"You said something about a video," he said to Wish.

"Oh, yes. I'll get that set up and you can watch while I answer a few phone messages on other things."

She took a videotape out of a drawer in her desk and they walked to the back of the squad. The gang of three quietly moved away with their donuts, alarmed by the presence of an outsider. She set the tape up and left him there to watch alone.

The video, obviously shot with a hand-held camera, was a bouncy, unprofessional walk-through of the thieves' trail. It began in what Bosch surmised was the storm sewer, a square tunnel that curved away into a darkness the camera's strobe couldn't reach. Wish had been right, it was large. A truck could have driven down it. A small stream of water moved slowly down the center of the concrete floor. There was mold and algae on the floor and the lower part of the walls, and Bosch could almost smell the dampness. The camera panned down to the grayish-green floor. There were tire tracks in the slime. The next video scene was the entrance to the thieves' tunnel, a cleanly cut hole in the sewer wall. A pair of hands moved into the picture holding the plywood circle Wish said had been used to cover the hole during the day. The hands moved further into the screen, then a head of dark hair. It was Rourke. He was wearing a dark jumpsuit with white letters across the back. FBI. He held the plywood up to the hole. It was a perfect fit.

The video jumped then, and the scene was now from inside the thieves' tunnel. It was eerie for Bosch to watch, and brought back memories of the hand-dug tunnels he had crawled through in Vietnam. This tunnel curved to the right. Surreal lighting flickered from candles set every twenty feet or so in notches dug into the wall. After curving for what he judged was about sixty feet, the tunnel turned sharply to the left. It then followed a straightaway for almost a hundred feet, candles still flickering from the walls. The camera finally came to a dead end where there was a pile of concrete rubble, twisted pieces of steel rebar and plating. The camera panned up to a gaping hole in the ceiling of the tunnel. Light poured down from the vault above. Rourke stood up there in his jumpsuit, looking down at the camera. He dragged a finger across his neck and the picture cut again. This time the camera was inside the vault, a wide-angle shot of the entire room. As in the newspaper photo Bosch had seen, hundreds of safe-deposit box doors stood open. The boxes lay empty in piles on the floor. Two crime scene techs were dusting the doors for fingerprints. Eleanor Wish and another agent were looking up at the steel wall of box doors and writing in notebooks. The camera panned down to the floor and the hole to the tunnel below. Then the tape went black. He rewound it, brought it back and put it on her desk.

"Interesting," he said. "I saw a few things I had seen before. In the tunnels over there. But nothing that would have made me start looking at tunnel rats in particular. What was the lead to Meadows, people like me?"

"First off, there was the C-4," she said. "Alcohol, Tobacco, and Firearms sent a team out to go through the concrete and steel from the blast hole. There were trace elements of the explosive. The ATF guys ran some tests and came up with C-4. I'm sure you know it. It was used in Vietnam. Tunnel rats used it especially to implode tunnels. The thing is, you can get much better stuff now, with more compressed impact area, easier handling and detonation. It's even cheaper. Also less dangerous to handle and easier to get ahold of. So we figured — I mean the ATF lab guy figured — the reason C-4 was used was because the user was comfortable with it, had used it before. So right off we thought it would be a Vietnam-era vet.

"Another corollary to Vietnam was the booby traps. We think that before they went up into the vault to start drilling, they wired the tunnel to protect their rear. We sent an ATF dog through as a precaution, you know, to make sure there wasn't any more live C-4 lying around. The animal got a reading — indicated explosives — in two places in the tunnel. The midway point and at the entrance cut in the wall of the storm line. But there was nothing there anymore. The perps took it with them. But we found peg holes in the floor of the tunnel and snippets of steel wire at both spots — like the leftover stuff when you are cutting lengths with a wire cutter."

"Tripwires," Bosch said.

"Right. We're thinking they had the tunnel wired for intruders. If anybody had come in from behind to take them, the tunnel would have gone up. They'd've been buried under Hill Street. At least, the tunnelers took the explosives out with them when they left. Saved us stumbling across them."

"But an explosion like that probably would've killed the tunnelers along with the intruders," Bosch said.

"We know. These guys just weren't taking chances. They were heavily armed, fortified and ready to go down. Succeed or suicide. . . .

"Anyway, we didn't narrow it down specifically to tunnel rats possibly being involved until somebody caught something when we were going over the tire tracks in the main sewer line. The tracks were here and there, no complete trail. So it took us a couple days to track them from the tunnel back to the entrance at the river wash. It wasn't a straight shot. It's a labyrinth down there. You had to know your way. We figured these guys weren't sitting there on their ATVs with a flashlight and a map every night."

"Hansel and Gretel? They left crumbs along the way?"

"Sort of. The walls down there have a lot of paint on them. You know, DWP marks, so they know where they are, what line is going where, dates of inspection and so forth. With all the paint on them, some look like the side of a 7-Eleven in an East L.A. barrio. So we figured the perps marked the way. We walked the trail and looked for reoccurring marks. There was only one. Kind of a peace sign, without the circle. Just three quick slash marks."

He knew the mark. He'd used it himself in tunnels twenty years ago. Three quick slashes on a tunnel wall with a knife. It was the symbol they'd used to mark their way, so they could find the way out again.

Wish said, "One of the cops there that day — this was before LAPD turned the whole thing over to us — one of the robbery guys said he recognized it from Vietnam. He wasn't a tunnel rat. But he told us about them. That's how we connected it. From there, we went to the Department of Defense and the VA and got names. We got Meadows's. We got yours. Others."

"How many others?"

She pushed a six-inch stack of manila files across her desk.

"They're all here. Have a look if you want."

Rourke walked up then.

"Agent Wish has told me about the letter you requested," he said. "I have no problem with it. I roughed out something and we'll try to get Senior Special Agent Whitcomb to sign it sometime today."

When Bosch didn't say anything Rourke went on.

"We may have overreacted yesterday, but I hope I've set everything straight with your lieutenant and your Internal Affairs people." He gave a smile a politician would envy. "And by the way, I wanted to tell you I admire your record. Your military record. Myself, I served three tours. But I never went down into any of those ghastly tunnels. I was over there, though, till the very end. What a shame."

"What was the shame, that it ended?"

Rourke eyed him a long moment, and Bosch saw red spread across his face from the point where his dark eyebrows knitted together. Rourke was a very pale man with a sallow face that gave the impression he was sucking on a sourball. He was a few years older than Bosch. They were the same height but Rourke had more weight on his frame. To the bureau's traditional uniform of blue blazer and light-blue button-down shirt, he had added a red power tie.

"Look, detective, you don't have to like me, that's fine," Rourke said. "But, please, work with me on this. We want the same thing."

Bosch gave in for the time being.

"What is it that you want me to do? Tell me exactly. Am I just along for the ride or do you really want my work?"

"Bosch, you are supposedly a top-notch detective. Show us. Just follow your case. Like you said yesterday, you find who killed Meadows and we find who ripped off WestLand. So, yes, we want your best work. Proceed as you normally would but with Special Agent Wish as your partner."

Rourke walked away and out of the squad. Bosch figured he must have his own office somewhere off the quiet hallway. He turned to Wish's desk and picked up the stack of files. He said, "Okay then, let's go."

Wish signed out a bureau car and drove while Bosch looked through the stack of military files on his lap. He noticed his own was on top. He glanced at some of the others and recognized only Meadows's name.

"Where to?" Wish asked as she pulled out of the garage and took Veteran Avenue up to Wilshire.

"Hollywood," he said. "Is Rourke always such a stiff?"

She turned east and smiled one of those smiles that made Bosch wonder whether she and Rourke had something going on.

"When he wants," she said. "He's a good administrator, though. He runs the squad well. Always has been the leader type, I guess. I think he said he was in charge of a whole outfit or something when he was with the army. Over there in Saigon."

No way there was anything between them, he thought then. You don't defend your lover by calling him a good administrator. There was nothing there.

"He's in the wrong business for administrating," Bosch said. "Go up to Hollywood Boulevard, the neighborhood south of the Chinese theater."

It would take fifteen minutes to get there. He opened the top file — it was his own — and began looking through the papers. Between a set of psychiatric evaluation reports he found a black-and-white photo, almost like a mug shot, of a young man in uniform, his face unlined by age or experience.

"You looked good in a crew cut," Wish said, interrupting his thoughts. "Reminded me of my brother when I saw that."

Bosch looked at her but didn't say anything. He put the photo down and went back to roaming through the documents in the file, reading snatches of information about a stranger who was himself.

Wish said, "We were able to find nine men with Vietnam tunnel experience living in Southern California. We checked them all out. Meadows was the only one we really moved up to the level of suspect. He was a hype, had the criminal record. He also had a history of working in tunnels even after he came back from the war." She drove in silence for a few minutes while Bosch read. Then she said, "We watched him a whole month. After the burglary."

"What was he doing?"

"Nothing that we could tell. He might have been doing some dealing. We were never sure. He'd go down to Venice to buy balloons of tar about every three days. But it looked like it was for personal consumption. If he was selling, no customers ever came. No other visitors the whole month we watched. Hell, if we could prove he was selling, we would have popped him and then had something decent to scam him with when we talked about the bank job."

She was quiet again for a moment, then in a tone that Bosch thought was meant more to convince herself than him said, "He wasn't selling."

"I believe you," he said.

"You going to tell me what we're looking for in Hollywood?"

"We're looking for a wit. A possible witness. How was Meadows living during the month you watched? I mean, moneywise. How'd he get money to go down to Venice?"

"Near as we could tell, he was on welfare and had a VA disability check. That's it."

"Why did you call it off after a month?"

"We didn't have anything, and we weren't even sure he had anything to do with it. We —"

"Who pulled the plug?"

"Rourke did. He couldn't —"

"The administrator."

"Let me finish. He couldn't justify the cost of continued surveillance without any results. We were going on a hunch, nothing more. You're just looking at it from hindsight. But it had been almost two months since the robbery. There was nothing there that pointed to him. In fact, we were just going through the motions after a while. We thought whoever it really was, they were in Monaco or Argentina. Not scoring balloon hits of tar heroin on Venice beach and living in a tramp apartment in the Valley. At the time, Meadows didn't make sense. Rourke called the watch. But I concurred. I guess now we know we fucked up. Satisfied?"

Bosch didn't answer. He knew Rourke had been correct in calling the watch. Nowhere is hindsight better than in cop work. He changed the subject.

"Why that bank, did you ever think about that? Why WestLand National? Why not a Wells Fargo or a vault in a Beverly Hills bank? Probably more money in the banks over in the Hills anyway. You said these underground tunnels go all over the place."

"They do. I don't know the answer to that one. Maybe they picked a downtown bank because they wanted a full three days to open the boxes and they knew downtown banks aren't open Saturdays. Maybe only Meadows and his friends know the answer. What are we looking for in this neighborhood? There was nothing in your reports about a possible witness. Witness to what?"

They were in the neighborhood. The street was lined with run-down motels that had looked depressing the day they were finished being built. Bosch pointed out one of these, the Blue Chateau, and told her to park. It was as depressing as all the others on the street. Concrete block, early fifties design. Painted light blue with darker blue trim that was peeling. It was a two-story courtyard building with towels and clothes hanging out of almost every open window. It was a place where the interior would rival the exterior as an eyesore, Bosch knew. Where runaways crowded eight or ten to a room, the strongest getting the bed, the others the floor or the bathtub. There were places like this on many of the blocks near the Boulevard. There always had been and always would be.

As they sat in the fed car looking at the motel Bosch told her about the half-finished paint scrawl he had found on the pipe at the reservoir and the anonymous 911 caller. He told her he believed the voice went with the paint. Edward Niese, AKA Sharkey.

"These kids, the runaways, they form street cliques," Bosch said as he got out of the car. "Not exactly like gangs. It's not a turf thing. It's for protection and business. According to the CRASH files, Sharkey's crew has been hanging out at the Chateau here for the last couple of months."

As Bosch closed the car door, he noticed a car pull to the curb a half-block up the street. He took a quick glance at it but didn't recognize the car. He thought he could see two figures in it, but it was too far away for him to be sure, or to tell if it was Lewis and Clarke. He headed up a flagstone walkway to an entrance hallway below a broken neon sign for the motel office.

In the office Bosch could see an old man sitting behind a glass window with a slide tray at its base. The man was reading the day's green sheet from Santa Anita. He didn't pull his eyes away until Bosch and Wish were at the window.

"Yes, officers, what can I do for you?"

He was a worn-out old man whose eyes had quit caring about anything but the odds on three-year-olds. He knew cops before they flipped their buzzers. And he knew to give them what they wanted without much fuss.

"Kid named Sharkey," Bosch said. "What's the room?"

"Seven, but he's gone. I think. His motorbike usually sets there in the hall when he's around. There's no bike there. He's gone. Most probably."

"Most probably. Anybody else in seven?"

"Sure. Somebody's always around."

"First floor?"

"Yup."

"Back door or window?"

"Both. Sliding door on the back. Very expensive to replace."

The old man reached over to the key rack and took a key off a hook marked 7. He slid it into the tray beneath the window between him and Bosch.

Detective Pierce Lewis found a receipt from an automatic teller machine in his wallet and used it to pick his teeth. His mouth tasted as though there was still a piece of breakfast sausage in there somewhere. He slid the paper card in and out between his teeth until they felt clean. He made a smacking, unsatisfied sound with his mouth.

"What?" Detective Don Clarke said. He knew his partner's behavioral nuances. The teeth picking and lip smacking meant something was bothering him.

"I think he made us, is all," Lewis said after flipping the card out the window into the street. "That little look he threw down the street when they got out of the car. He was very quick, but I think he made us."

"He didn't make us. If he did, he woulda come charging down here to start up a commotion or something. That's how they do it. Make a commotion, file a lawsuit. He'd've had the Police Protective League up our ass by now. I'm telling you, cops are the last to notice a tail."

"Well . . . I guess," Lewis said.

He let it go for the moment. But he stayed worried. He didn't want to mess up this job. He'd had Bosch by the balls once before and the guy skated because Irving, that flying jaw, had pulled Lewis and Clarke back. But not this time, Lewis silently promised himself. This time he goes down.

"You taking notes?" he asked his partner. "What do you think they're doing in that dump?"

"Looking for something."

"You're shitting me. You really think so?"

"Jeez, who put the pencil up your ass today?"

Lewis looked away from the Chateau to Clarke, who had his hands folded on his lap and his seat back at a sixty-degree angle. With his mirrored glasses shielding his eyes, it was impossible to tell if he was awake or not.

"Are you taking notes or what?" Lewis said loudly.

"If you want notes, whyn't you takin' 'em?"

"Because I'm driving. That's always the deal. You don't want to drive, you gotta write and take the pictures. Now, write something down so we have something to show Irving. Otherwise he'll write up a one eighty-one on us and forget about Bosch."

"That's one *point* eighty-one. Let's not take shortcuts, even in our language."

"Fuck off."

Clarke snickered and took a notebook out of his inside coat pocket and a gold Cross pen from his shirt pocket. When Lewis was satisfied that notes were being taken and looked back at the motel, he saw a teenage boy with blond dreadlocks circle twice in the road on a yellow motorbike. The boy pulled up next to the car Lewis had just watched Bosch and the FBI woman get out of. The boy shaded his eyes and looked through the driver's-side window into the car.

"Now, what's this?" Lewis said.

"Some kid," Clarke said after looking up from his notes. "He's looking for a stereo to snatch. If he makes a move, what are we going to do? Blow the surveillance to save some asshole's tape deck?"

"We aren't going to do anything. And he's not going to make a move. He sees the Motorola two-way. He knows it's a cop car. He's backing away now."

The boy revved the bike and did another two circles in the street. As the bike circled, he kept his eyes on the front of the motel. He then cruised through the side parking lot and back out onto the street. He stopped behind an old Volkswagen bus that was parked at the curb and shielded him from the motel. He seemed to be watching the entrance to the Chateau through the windows of the beat-up old bus. He did not notice the two IAD men in the car parked a half-block behind him.

"Come on kid, get going," Clarke said. "I don't want to have to call out patrol on you. Fucking delinquent."

"Use the Nikon and get his picture," Lewis said. "You never know. Something might happen and we'll need it. And while you're at it, get the number off the motel sign. We'll have to call later and see what Bosch and the FBI girl were doing."

Lewis could have easily picked the camera up off the seat himself and taken the photos, but that would set a dangerous precedent that could harm the delicate balance of the rules of surveillance. The driver drives. The rider writes — and does all such related work.

Clarke dutifully picked up the camera, which was equipped with a telephoto lens, and took the photos of the boy on the bike.

"Get one with the bike's plate," Lewis said.

"I know what I am doing," Clarke said as he put the camera down.

"Did you get the motel number? We'll have to call."

"I got it. I'm writing it down. See? What's the big deal? Bosch is probly in there knocking off a piece. A nice federal piece. Maybe when we call we find out they rented a room."

Lewis watched to make sure Clarke wrote down the number on the surveillance log.

"And maybe we don't," Lewis said. "They just met and, anyway, I doubt he'd be so stupid. They've got to be in there looking for somebody. A wit maybe."

"But there was nothing about any witness in the murder book."

"He held it back. That's Bosch. That's how he works."

Clarke didn't say anything. Lewis looked back down the street to the Chateau. He then noticed that the kid was gone. There was no sign of the motorbike.

Bosch waited a minute to give Eleanor Wish time to get behind the Chateau to watch the sliding door on the back of room 7. He bent and held his ear to the door and thought he heard a rustling sound and an occasional word mumbled. There was someone in the room. When it was time, he knocked heavily on the door. He heard the sound of movement — fast steps on carpet — from the other side of the door, but no one answered. He knocked again and waited, then heard a girl's voice.

"Who is it?"

"Police," Bosch said. "We want to talk to Sharkey."

"He's not here."

"Then I guess we want to talk to you."

"I don't know where he is."

"Open the door, please."

He heard more noise, like someone banging into furniture. But nobody opened the door. Then he heard a rolling sound, a glass door sliding open. He put the key in the doorknob and opened the door in time to catch a glimpse of a man going through the back doorway and jumping off the porch to the ground. It wasn't Sharkey. He heard Wish's voice outside, ordering the man to stop.

Bosch took a quick inventory of the room. An entrance hall with closet to the left, bathroom to the right, both empty except for some clothes on the closet floor. Two large double beds pushed up against opposite walls, a dresser with a mirror on the wall above it, a yellow-brown carpet worn flat on the pathways around the beds and to the bathroom. The girl, blond-haired, small, maybe seventeen years old, sat on the front edge of one of the beds with a sheet around her. Bosch could see the outline of a nipple pressing out against the dingy, once-white cloth. The room smelled like cheap perfume and sweat.

"Bosch, you all right in there?" Wish called from outside. He could not see her because of a sheet hung like a curtain over the sliding door.

"Okay. You?"

"Okay. What have we got?"

Bosch walked to the sliding door and looked out. Wish stood behind a man who had his arms extended and his hands on the motel's back wall. He was about thirty, with the sallow skin of a man who just did a month in county lockup. His pants were open in the front. His plaid shirt was buttoned incorrectly. And he stared straight down to the ground with the bug-eyed look of a man who had no explanation but needed one badly. Bosch was momentarily struck by the man's apparent decision to button his shirt before his pants.

"He's clean," she said. "Looks a little winded, though."

"Looks like soliciting sex with a minor if you want to spend the time with it. Otherwise kick him loose."

He turned to the girl on the bed.

"No bullshit, how old are you and what did he pay? I'm not here to bust you."

She thought it over a moment. Bosch never took his eyes off hers.

"Almost seventeen," she said in a bored monotone. "He didn't pay me anything. He said he would, but he didn't get to that yet."

"Who's in charge of your crew, Sharkey? Didn't he ever tell you to get the money first?"

"Sharkey ain't always around. And how'd you get his name?"

"Heard it around. Where is he today?"

"I tol' you, I don't know."

The plaid-shirted man came into the room through the front door followed by Wish. His hands were cuffed behind him.

"I am going to book him. I want to. This is sick. She looks —"

"She told me she was eighteen," Plaid Shirt said.

Bosch walked up to him and pulled open his shirt with a finger. There was a blue eagle with its wings spreading across his chest. In its talons it carried a dagger and a Nazi swastika. Beneath that it said One Nation. Bosch knew that meant the Aryan Nation, the white supremacist prison gang. He let the shirt fall back into place.

"Hey, how long you been out?" he asked.

"Hey, come on, man," Plaid Shirt said. "This is bullshit. She pulled me in from the street. And let me at least button my goddam pants. This is bullshit."

"Give me my money, fucker," the girl said.

She jumped from the bed, the sheet falling to the floor, and lunged naked at the john's pants pockets.

"Get her off me, get her off," he called out as he squirmed to avoid her hands. "See, you see! She should be going, not me."

Bosch moved in and separated the two and pushed the girl back to the bed. He moved behind the man and said to Wish, "Give me your key."

She made no move, so he reached into his own pocket and got out his own cuff key. One size fits all. He unlocked the cuffs and walked Plaid Shirt over to the room's front door. He opened it and pushed him through. In the hallway the man stopped to button his pants, which gave Bosch the opportunity to put his foot on his butt and push. "Get out of here, short eyes," he said as the man stumbled down the hall. "This is your lucky day."

The girl was wrapped in the dirty sheet again when Bosch went back into the room. He looked at Wish and saw anger in her eyes. He knew it wasn't just for the man in the plaid shirt. Bosch looked at the girl and said, "Get your clothes, go into the bathroom and get dressed." When she didn't move, he said, "Now! Let's go!"

After she grabbed up some clothes from the floor next to the bed and walked to the bathroom, letting the sheet fall to the ground, Bosch turned to Wish.

"We've got too much else to do," he began. "You would have spent the rest of the afternoon getting her statement and booking that guy. In fact, it's a state beef, so I would've had to book him. And it's a flopper; can go felony or misdemeanor. And one look at that girl and the DA would have gone misdee if he filed it at all. It wasn't worth it. It's the life down here, Agent Wish."

She looked at him with smoldering eyes, the same eyes he had seen when he had gripped her wrist to keep her from leaving the restaurant.

"Bosch, I had decided it was worth it. Don't ever do that again."

They stood there trying to outstare each other until the girl came out of the bathroom. She wore faded jeans that were split at the knees and a black tank top. No shoes, and Bosch noticed her toenails were painted red. She sat on the bed without saying anything.

"We need to find Sharkey," Bosch said.

"About what? You got a cigarette?"

He pulled out a pack of cigarettes and shook one out for her. He gave her a match and she lit it herself.

"About what?" she said again.

"About Saturday night," Wish said curtly. "We do not want to arrest him. We do not want to hassle him. We only want to ask him a few questions."

"What about me?" the girl said.

"What about you?" Wish said.

"Are you going to hassle me?"

"You mean are we going to turn you over to Division of Youth Services, don't you?" Bosch looked at Wish to try to gauge a reaction. He got no reading. He said, "No, we won't call DYS if you help us. What's your name? Your real name."

"Bettijane Felker."

"All right, Bettijane, you don't know where Sharkey is? All we want to do is talk to him."

"All I know is that he's working."

"What do you mean? Where?"

"Boytown. He's probably taking care of business with Arson and Mojo."

"Those the other guys in the crew?"

"Right."

"Where in Boytown did they say they were going?"

"They didn't. They just go where the queers are, I guess. You know."

The girl either couldn't be more specific or wouldn't be. Bosch knew it didn't matter. He had the addresses from the shake cards and knew he'd find Sharkey somewhere on Santa Monica Boulevard.

"Thank you," he said to the girl and started heading toward the door. He was halfway down the hall before Wish came out of the room, walking after him at a brisk, angry pace. Before she said anything he stopped at a pay phone in the hallway by the office. He took out a small phone book he always carried, looked up the number for DYS and dialed. He was put on hold for two minutes before an operator transferred him to an automated tape line on which he reported the date and time and the location of Bettijane Felker, suspected runaway. He hung up wondering how many days it would be before they got the message and how many days after that it would be before they got to Bettijane.

They were all the way into West Hollywood on Santa Monica Boulevard and she was still hot. Bosch had tried to defend himself but realized there was no chance. So he sat there quietly and listened.

"It's a matter of trust, that's all," Wish said. "I don't care how long or short we work together. If you are going to keep up the one-man army stuff, there will never be the trust we need to succeed."

He stared at the mirror on the passenger's side, which he had adjusted so he could watch the car that had pulled away from the curb and followed them from the Blue Chateau. He was sure now it was Lewis and Clarke. He had seen Lewis's huge neck and crew cut behind the wheel when the car had pulled up within three car lengths at a traffic signal. He didn't tell Wish they were being followed. And if she had noticed the tail, she hadn't said so. She was too involved in other things. He sat there watching the tail car and listening to her complaints about how badly he had handled things.

Finally he said, "Meadows was found Sunday. Today is Tuesday. It is a fact of life in homicide that the odds, the likelihood, of solving a homicide grow longer as each day on the calendar flips by. And so, I'm sorry. I did not think it would help us to waste a day booking some asshole who was probably baited into a motel room by a hooker sixteen years old going on thirty. I also did not think it would be worth waiting for DYS to come out to pick up the girl because I would bet a paycheck that DYS already knows that girl and knows where she is, if they want her. In short, I wanted to get on with it, leave other people's jobs to other people and do my job. And that meant doing what we are doing now. Slow down up here at Ragtime. It's one of the spots I got off the shake cards."

"We both want to solve this, Bosch. So don't be so goddam condescending, as if you have this noble mission and I am just along for the ride. We are both on it. Don't forget it."

She slowed in front of the open-air café, where pairs of men sat in white wrought-iron chairs at glass-top tables, drinking ice tea with slices of orange hooked on the rim of beveled glasses. A few of the men looked at Bosch and then looked away uninterested. He scanned the dining area but didn't see Sharkey. As the car cruised past, he looked down the side alley and saw a couple of young men hanging around, but they were too old to be Sharkey.

They spent the next twenty minutes driving around gay bars and restaurants, keeping mostly on Santa Monica, but did not see the boy. Bosch watched as the Internal Affairs car kept pace, never more than a block back. Wish never said anything about them. But Bosch knew that law officers were usually the last to notice a surveillance because they were the last to ever think they might be followed. They were the hunters, not the prey.

Bosch wondered what Lewis and Clarke were doing. Did they expect that he would break some law or cop rule with an FBI agent in tow? He began to wonder if the two IAD detectives weren't just hotdogging on their own time. Maybe they wanted him to see them. Some kind of a psych-out. He told Wish to pull to a curb in front of Barnie's Beanery and he jumped out to use the pay phone near the old bar's screen door. He dialed the Internal Affairs nonpublic number, which he knew by heart, having had to call in twice a day when he was put on home duty the year before while they investigated him. A woman, the desk officer, answered the phone.

"Is Lewis or Clarke there?"

"No, sir, they're not. Can I take a message?"

"No thanks. Uh, this is Lieutenant Pounds, Hollywood detectives. Are they just out of the office? I need to check a point with them."

"I believe they are code seven till P.M. watch."

He hung up. They were off duty until four. They were scamming, or Bosch had simply kicked them too hard in the balls this time and now they were going after him on their own time. He got back in the car and told Wish he had checked his office for messages. It was as she merged the car back into traffic that he saw the yellow motorbike leaning on a parking meter about a half block from Barnie's. It was parked in front of a pancake restaurant.

"There," he said and pointed. "Go on by and I'll get the number. If it's his, we'll sit on it."

It was Sharkey's bike. Bosch matched the plate to his notes from the kid's CRASH file. But there was no sign of the boy. Wish drove around the block and parked in the same spot in front of Barnie's that they had been in before.

"So, we wait," she said. "For this kid you think might be a witness."

"Right. It's what I think. But two of us don't need to waste the time. You can leave me here if you want. I'll go in the beanery, order a pitcher of Henry's and a bowl of chili and watch from the window."

"That's all right. I'm staying."

Bosch settled back for a wait. He took out his cigarettes but she nailed him before he got one out of the pack.

"Have you heard of the draft risk assessment?" she asked.

"The what?"

"Secondhand cigarette smoke. It's deadly, Bosch. The EPA came out last month, officially. Said it's a carcinogen. Three thousand people are getting lung cancer a year from passive smoking, they call it. You are killing yourself and me. Please don't."

He put the cigarettes back in his coat pocket. They were quiet as they watched the bike, which was chain-locked to the parking meter. Bosch took a few glances at the side-view mirror but didn't see the IAD car. He glanced over at Wish, too, whenever he thought she wasn't looking. Santa Monica Boulevard steadily got crowded with cars as the apex of rush hour approached.

Wish kept her window closed to cut down on the carbon monoxide. It made the car very hot.

"Why do you keep staring at me?" she asked about an hour into the surveillance.

"At you? I didn't know that I was."

"You were. You are. You ever have a female partner before?"

"Nope. But that's not why I would be staring. If I was."

"Why then? If you were."

"I'd be trying to figure you out. You know, why you are here, doing this. I always thought, I mean at least I heard, that the bank squad over at the FBI was for dinosaurs and fuckups, the agents too old or too dumb to use a computer or trace some white-collar scumbag's assets through a paper trail. Then, here you are. On the heavy squad. You're no dinosaur, and something tells me you're no fuckup. Something tells me you're a prize, Eleanor."

She was quiet a moment, and Bosch thought he saw the trace of a smile play on her lips. Then it was gone, if it had been there at all.

"I guess that is a backhanded compliment," she said. "If it is, thank you. I have my reasons for choosing where I am with the bureau. And believe me, I do get to choose. As far as the others in the squad, I would not characterize any of them as you do. I think that attitude, which, by the way, seems to be shared by many of your fellow —"

"There's Sharkey," he said.

A boy with blond dreadlocks had come through a side alley between the pancake shop and a mini-mall. An older man stood with him. He wore a T-shirt that said The Gay 90s Are Back! Bosch and Wish stayed in the car and watched. Sharkey and the man exchanged a few words and then Sharkey took something from his pocket and handed it over. The man shuffled through what looked like a stack of playing cards. He took a couple of cards and gave the rest back. He then gave Sharkey a single green bill.

"What's he doing?" Wish asked.

"Buying baby pictures."

"What?"

"A pedophile."

The older man headed off down the sidewalk and Sharkey walked to his motorbike. He hunched over the chain and lock.

"Okay," Bosch said, and they got out of the car.

That would be enough for today, Sharkey thought. Time to kick. He lit a cigarette and bent over the seat of his motorbike to work the combination on the Master lock. His dreads flopped down past his eyes and he could smell some of the coconut stuff he had put in his hair the night before at the Jaguar guy's house. That was after Arson had broken the guy's nose and the blood got everywhere. He stood up and was about to wrap the chain around his waist when he saw them coming. Cops. They were too close. Too late to run. Trying to act like he hadn't yet seen them, he quickly made a mental list of everything in his pockets. The credit cards were gone, already sold. The money could have come from anywhere, some of it did. He was cool. The only thing they'd have would be the queer guy's identification if they had a lineup. Sharkey was surprised the guy had made a report. No one ever had before.

Sharkey smiled at the two approaching cops, and the man held up a tape recorder. A tape recorder? What was this? The man hit the play button and after a few seconds Sharkey recognized his own voice. Then he recognized where it had come from. This wasn't about the Jaguar guy. This was about the pipe.

Sharkey said, "So?"

"So," said the man, "we want you to tell us about it."

"Man, I didn't have anything to do with it. You ain't going to put that — Hey! You're the guy from the police station. Yeah, I saw you there the next night. Well, you ain't going to get me to say I did that shit up there."

"Take it down a notch, Sharkey," the man said. "We know you didn't do it. We just want to know what you saw, is all. Lock your bike up again. We'll bring you back."

The man gave his name and the woman's. Bosch and Wish. He said she was FBI, which really confused things. The boy hesitated, then stooped and locked the bike again.

Bosch said, "We just want to take a ride over to Wilcox to ask you some questions, maybe draw a picture."

"Of what?" Sharkey asked.

Bosch didn't answer; he just gestured with his hand to come along and then pointed up the block at a gray Caprice. It was the car Sharkey had seen in front of the Chateau. As they walked, Bosch kept his hand on Sharkey's shoulder. Sharkey wasn't as tall as Bosch yet, but they shared the same wiry build. The boy wore a tie-dyed shirt of purple and yellow shades. Black sunglasses hung around his neck on orange string. The boy put them on as they approached the Caprice.

"Okay, Sharkey," Bosch said at the car. "You know the procedure. We've got to search you before you go in the car. That way we won't have to cuff you for the ride. Put everything on the hood."

"Man, you said I was no suspect," Sharkey protested. "I don't have to do this."

"I told you, procedure. You get it all back. Except the pictures. We can't do that."

Sharkey looked first at Bosch and then Wish, then he started putting his hands in the pockets of his frayed jeans.

"Yeah, we know about the pictures," Bosch said.

The boy put $46.55 on the hood along with a pack of cigarettes and book of matches, a small penknife on a key chain and a deck of Polaroid photos. They were photos of Sharkey and the other guys in the crew. In each, the model was naked and in various stages of sexual arousal. As Bosch shuffled through them, Wish looked over his shoulder and then quickly looked away. She picked up the pack of cigarettes and looked through it, finding a single joint among the Kools.

"I guess we have to keep that, too," Bosch said.

They drove to the police station on Wilcox because it was rush hour and it would have taken them an hour to get to the Federal Building in Westwood. It was after six by the time they got into the detective bureau, and the place was deserted, everybody having gone home. Bosch took Sharkey into one of the eight-by-eight interview rooms. There was a small, cigarette-scarred table and three chairs in the room. A handmade sign on one wall said No Sniveling! He sat Sharkey down in the Slider — a wooden chair with its seat heavily waxed and a quarter-inch of wood cut off the bottom of the front two legs. The incline was not enough to notice, but enough that the people who sat in the chair could not get comfortable. They would lean back like most hard cases and slowly slide off the front. The only thing they could do was lean forward, right into the face of their interrogator. Bosch told the boy not to move, then stepped outside to plan a strategy with Wish, shutting the door. She opened the door after he closed it.

She said, "It's illegal to leave a juvenile in a closed room unattended."

Bosch closed the door again.

"He isn't complaining," he said. "We've got to talk. What's your feel for him? You want him, or you want me to take it?"

"I don't know," she said.

That settled it. That was a no. An initial interview with a witness, a reluctant witness at that, required a skillful blend of scamming, cajoling, demanding. If she didn't know, she didn't go.

"You're supposed to be the expert interrogator," she said in what seemed to Bosch to be a mocking voice. "According to your file. I don't know if that's using brains or brawn. But I'd like to see how it's done."

He nodded, ignoring the jab. He reached into his pocket for the boy's cigarettes and matches.

"Go in and give him these. I want to go check my desk for messages and set up a tape." When he saw the look on her face as she eyed the cigarettes, he added, "First rule of interrogation: make the subject think he is comfortable. Give 'im the cigarettes. Hold your breath if you don't like it."

He started to walk away but she said, "Bosch, what was he doing with those pictures?"

So that was what was bothering her, he thought. "Look. Five years ago a kid like him would have gone with that man and done who knows what. Nowadays, he sells him a picture instead. There are so many killers — diseases and otherwise — these kids are getting smart. It's safer to sell your Polaroids than to sell your flesh."

She opened the door to the interview room and went in. Bosch crossed the squad room and checked the chrome spike on his desk for messages. His lawyer had finally called back. So had Bremmer over at the *Times*, though he had left a pseudonym they had both agreed on earlier. Bosch didn't want anybody snooping around his desk to know the press had called.

Bosch left the messages on the spike, took out his ID card and went to the supply closet and slipped the lock. He opened a new ninety-minute cassette and popped it into the recorder on the bottom shelf of the closet. He turned on the machine and made sure the backup cassette was turning. He set it on record and watched to make sure both tapes were rolling. Then he went back down the hallway to the front desk and told a fat Explorer Scout who was sitting there to order a pizza to be delivered to the station. He gave the kid a ten and told him to bring it to the interview room with three Cokes when it came.

"What do you want on it?" the kid asked.

"What do you like?"

"Sausage and pepperoni. Hate anchovies."

"Make it anchovies."

Bosch walked back to the detective bureau. Wish and Sharkey were silent when he walked back into the small interview room, and he had the feeling they had not been talking much. Wish had no feel for the boy. She sat to Sharkey's right. Bosch took the seat on his left. The only window was a small square of mirrored glass in the door. People could look in but not out. Bosch decided to be up front with the boy from the start. He was a kid, but he was probably wiser than most of the men who had sat on the Slider before him. If he sensed deceit, he would start answering questions in one-syllable words.

"Sharkey, we are going to tape this because it might help us later to go over it," Bosch said. "Like I said, you are not a suspect, so you don't have to worry about what you say, unless of course you're going to say you did it."

"See what I mean?" the boy protested. "I knew you'd get around to saying that and putting on the tape. Shit, I been in one of these rooms before, you know."

"That's why we aren't bullshitting you. So let's say it once for the record. I'm Harry Bosch, LAPD, this is Eleanor Wish, FBI, and you are Edward Niese, AKA Sharkey. I want to start by —"

"What's this shit? Was that the president what got dragged in that pipe? What's the FBI doing here?"

"Sharkey!" Bosch said loudly. "Cool it. It's just an exchange program. Like when you used to go to school and the kids would come from France or someplace. Think like she's from France. She's just kinda watching and learning from the pros." He smiled and winked at Wish. Sharkey looked over at her and smiled a little, too. "First question, Sharkey, let's get it out of the way so we can get to the good stuff. Did you do the guy up at the dam?"

"Fuck no. I see —"

"Wait a minute, wait a minute," Wish broke in. She looked at Bosch. "Can we go outside a moment?"

Bosch got up and walked out. She followed, and this time she closed the interview room door.

"What are you doing?" he said.

"What are *you* doing? Are you going to read that kid his rights, or do you want to taint this interview from the start?"

"What are you talking about? He didn't do it. He isn't a suspect. I'm just asking him questions because I'm trying to establish an interrogation pattern."

"We don't know he isn't the killer. I think we should give him his rights."

"We read him his rights and he is going to think we think he's a suspect, not a witness. We do that and we might as well go in there and talk to the walls. He won't remember a thing."

She walked back into the interview room without another word. Bosch followed and picked up where he had left off, without saying anything about anybody's rights.

"You do the guy in the pipe, Sharkey?"

"No way, man. I seen him, that's all. He was already dead."

The boy looked to his right at Wish as he said this. Then he pulled himself up in his chair.

"Okay, Sharkey," Bosch said. "By the way, how old are you, where you from, tell me a couple of things like that."

"Almost eighteen, man, then I'm free," the boy said, looking at Bosch. "My mom lives up in Chatsworth, but I try not to live with — man, you already got all of this in one of your little notebooks."

"You a faggot, Sharkey?"

"No way, man," the boy said, staring hard at Bosch. "I sell them pictures, big fucking deal. I ain't one of 'em."

"You do more'n sell pictures to them? You roll a few when you get the chance? Bust 'em up, take their money. Who's going to file a complaint? Right?"

Now Sharkey looked back over to Wish and raised an open hand. "I don't do that shit. I thought we're talking about the dead guy."

"We are, Sharkey," Bosch said. "I just want to figure out who we're dealing with here, is all. Take it from the top. Tell us the story. I got pizza coming and there's more cigarettes. We got the time."

"It won't take any time. I din't see anything, except the body in there. I hope there's no anchovies."

He said this looking at Wish while pulling himself up in the chair. He had established a pattern in which he would look at Bosch when he was telling the truth, at Wish when he was shading it or outright lying. Scammers always play to the women, Bosch thought.

"Sharkey," Bosch said, "if you want we can take you up to Sylmar and have 'em hold you overnight. We can start again in the morning, maybe when you're memory's a little —"

"I'm worried about my bike back there, might get stole."

"Forget the bike," Bosch said, leaning into the boy's personal space. "We aren't spoiling you, Sharkey, you haven't told us anything yet. Start the story, then we'll worry about the bike."

"Okay, okay. I'll tell you everything."

The boy reached for his cigarettes on the table and Bosch pulled back and got out one of his own. The leaning in and out of his face was a technique Bosch had learned while spending what seemed like ten thousand hours in these little rooms. Lean in, invade that foot and a half that is all theirs, their own space. Lean back when you get what you want. It's subliminal. Most of what goes on in a police interrogation has nothing to do with what is said. It is interpretation, nuance. And sometimes what isn't said. He lit Sharkey's cigarette first. Wish leaned back in her chair as they exhaled the blue smoke.

"You wanna smoke, Agent Wish?" Bosch said.

She shook her head no.

Bosch looked at Sharkey and a knowing look passed between them. It said, You and me, sport. The boy smiled. Bosch nodded for him to start his story and he did. And it was a story.

"I go up there to crash sometimes," Sharkey said. "You know? When I don't find anybody to help me out with some motel money or nothing. Sometimes the room at my crew's motel is too crowded. I gotta get out. So I go up there, sleep in the pipe. It stays warm most the night. Not bad. So anyway, it was one of those nights. So I went up there —"

"What time was this?" Wish asked.

Bosch gave her a look that said, Cool it, ask the questions after the story is out. The kid had been going pretty good.

"Musta been pretty late," Sharkey answered. "Three, maybe four o'clock. I don't have a watch. And so I went up there. And I went in the pipe and I saw the guy that was dead. Just laying there. I climbed out and split. I wasn't going to stay in there with a dead guy. When I got down the hill I called you guys, nine one one."

He looked back from Wish to Bosch.

"That's it," he said. "Can I get a ride back to my bike?"

No one answered, so Sharkey lit another cigarette and pulled himself up in the chair.

"That's a nice story, Edward, but we need the whole thing," Bosch said. "We also need it right."

"Whaddaya mean?"

"I mean it sounds like it was made up by a moron, is what I mean. How'd you see the body in there?"

"I had a flashlight," he explained to Wish.

"No you didn't. You had matches, we found one." Bosch leaned forward until his face was only a foot from the boy's. "Sharkey, how do you think we knew it was you that called? You think the operator just recognized your voice? 'Oh, that's old Sharkey. He's a good kid, calling us about the body.' Think, Sharkey. You signed your name — or at least half of it on the pipe up there. We got your prints off a half a can of paint. And we know you only crawled halfway in the pipe. That's when you got scared and got out. You left tracks."

Sharkey stared forward, his eyes slightly lifted toward the mirrored window on the door.

"You knew the body was there before you went in. You saw somebody drag it into the pipe, Sharkey. Look at me now and tell me the real story."

"Look, I didn't see nobody's face. It was too dark, man," the boy said to Bosch. Eleanor let out a breath. Bosch felt like telling her that if she thought the boy was a waste of time she could leave.

"I was hiding," Sharkey said. "'Cause, see, at first I thought they were after me or something. I had nothin' to do with this. Why you dragging me down, man?"

"We got a man dead, Edward. We've got to find out why. We don't care about faces. That's fine. Tell us what you did see, and then you're no longer in it."

"That'll be it?"

"That'll be it."

Bosch leaned back then and lit his second cigarette.

"Well, yeah, I was up there and I wasn't too tired yet so I was doing my paint thing and I heard a car coming. Like holy shit. And what was weird was that I heard it before I saw it. 'Cause the guy has no lights on. So, man, I hauled ass and hid in the bushes on the hill right by there, you know, right by the pipe, right by where I hide my bike, you know, while I'm sleeping."

The boy was becoming more animated, using his hands and nodding his head and looking mostly at Bosch now.

"Shit, I thought those guys were coming for me, like somebody had called the cops on account of me being up there spraying a scrip or something. So like I hid. In fact, when they got there a guy gets out and says to the other guy he smells paint. But it turns out they didn't even see me. They just stopped by the pipe 'cause of the body. And only it wasn't a car, either. It was a Jeep."

"You get a license plate number?" Wish said.

"Let him tell it," Bosch said without looking at her.

"No, I didn't get a fuckin' plate. Shit, their lights were off and it was too dark. So anyway, there was three of them, if you count the dead guy. One guy gets out, he was the driver, and he pulls the dead guy right out of the back, from underneath a blanket or something. Opened a little back door those Jeeps got and drug the guy onto the ground. It was total horror, man. I could tell it was real, you know, a real dead body, just kinda by the way it fell on the ground. Like a dead guy. It made a noise like a body. Not like on TV. But what you'd expect, like, 'Oh no, that's a body he drug out of there,' or something. Then he drug it into the pipe. The other guy wouldn't help him. He stayed in the Jeep. So the first dude, he did it by hisself."

Sharkey took a deep drag on his cigarette and then killed it in the tin ashtray, which was already full of ash and old butts. He exhaled through his nose and looked at Bosch, who just nodded for him to continue. The boy pulled himself up in the seat.

"Um, I stayed there and the guy came out of the pipe after a minute. No longer than that. He looked around when he came out but didn't see me. He went over to a bush near where I was hiding and tore off a branch. Then he went back inside the pipe for a while. And I could hear him in there sweeping or something with the branch. Then he came out and they left. Oh, and uh, he started to back up and the reverse light went on, you know. He took it out of gear like real quick. Then I heard him say something about they couldn't go backward 'cause of the light. They might get seen. So then they went forward, you know, without lights. They drove down the road and across the dam and around the other side of the lake. When they went by that little house on the dam they bashed the light bulb. I saw it go out. I stayed hidden till I couldn't hear the engine anymore. Then I come out."

Sharkey stopped the story for a beat and Wish said, "I'm sorry, can we open the door, get some of this smoke out of here?"

Bosch reached over and pulled the door open without getting up or trying to hide his annoyance. "Go on, Sharkey," was all he said.

"So when they were gone I went over to the pipe and yelled in to the guy. You know, 'Hey, in there' and 'Are you all right,' stuff like that. But nobody answered. So I leaned my bike down on the ground so the light would go in there and I crawled in a little bit. I also lighted a match like you say. And I could see him in there and he looked dead and all. I was going to check but it was too creepy. I got out. I went down the hill and I called the cops. That's all I did, and that's the whole thing."

Bosch figured the boy was going to rob the body but got scared halfway in. That was okay though. The boy could keep that as his secret. Then he thought of the branch taken from the bush and used by the man Sharkey had seen to obliterate the tracks and drag marks in the pipe. He wondered why the uniform cops hadn't come across either the discarded branch or the broken bush during the crime scene search. But he didn't dwell on it long, because he knew the answer. Sloppiness. Laziness. It wasn't the first time things had been missed and wouldn't be the last.

"We're going to go check on that pizza," Bosch said, and he stood up. "We'll only be a couple of minutes."

Outside the interview room Bosch checked his anger and said, "My fault. We should have talked more about how we wanted to do it before we heard his story. I like to hear what they have to say first, then ask questions. It was my fault."

"No problem," Wish said curtly. "He doesn't seem that valuable anyway."

"Maybe." He thought a moment. "I was thinking of going back in and talking a little more to him, maybe bring an Identikit in. And if he doesn't get any better at remembering things we could hypnotize him."

Bosch had no way of knowing what her reaction to the last suggestion would be. He offered it in an offhand manner, half hoping it would slip by unnoticed. California courts had ruled that hypnotizing a witness taints that witness's later court testimony. If they hypnotized Sharkey, he could never be a witness in any court case that could arise from the Meadows investigation.

Wish frowned.

"I know," Bosch said. "We'd lose him in court. But we might never get to court with what he's given us now. You just said yourself he's not that valuable."

"I just don't know whether we should close the door on his usefulness now. So early in the investigation."

Bosch walked over to the interview room door and looked through the one-way glass at the boy. He was smoking another cigarette. He put it down on the ashtray and stood up. He looked at the door window, but Bosch knew he couldn't see out. The boy quickly and quietly switched his chair with the one Wish had been using. Bosch smiled and said, "He's a smart kid. There might be more there that we won't get unless we put him under. I think it's worth the chance."

"I didn't know you were one of LAPD's hypnotists. I must have missed that in your file."

"I'm sure there's a lot you missed," Bosch replied. After a few moments, he said, "I guess I'm one of the last around. After the supreme court shot it down the department quit training people. There was only one class of us. I was one of the youngest. Most of the others have retired."

"Anyway," she said, "I don't think we should do it yet. Let's talk to him some more, maybe wait a couple days before we waste him as a witness."

"Fine. But in a couple days who knows where a kid like Sharkey will be?"

"Oh, you're resourceful. You found him this time. You can do it again."

"You want to take a shot in there?"

"No, you're doing okay. As long as I can jump in now, whenever I think of something."

She smiled and he smiled and they went back into the interview room, which smelled of smoke and sweat. Bosch left the door open again to air it out. Wish didn't have to ask.

"No food?" Sharkey said.

"Still on the way," Bosch said.

Bosch and Wish took Sharkey through his story two more times, picking up small details along the way. They did it as a team. Partners, exchanging knowing looks, surreptitious nods, even smiles. A few times Bosch noticed Wish slipping in her chair and thought he saw a smile play on Sharkey's boyish face. When the pizza came he protested the anchovies but still ate three-quarters of the pie and downed two of the Cokes. Bosch and Wish passed.

Sharkey told them the Jeep that Meadows's body came in was dirty white or beige. He said there was a seal on the side door but he could not describe it. Perhaps this was so it would look like a DWP vehicle, Bosch thought. Maybe it was a DWP vehicle. Now he definitely wanted to hypnotize the boy, but he decided not to bring it up again. He'd wait for Wish to come around, to see that it had to be done.

Sharkey said the one who stayed behind in the Jeep as the body was dragged into the pipe didn't say a word the whole time the boy watched. This person was smaller than the driver. Sharkey described seeing only a slightly built form, a whisper of a silhouette against what little light there was from the moon above the reservoir perimeter's thick stand of pine.

"What did this other guy do?" Wish asked.

"Just watched, I guess. Like a lookout. He didn't even do the driving. I guess he was in charge or something."

The boy got a better look at the driver but not enough to describe a face, or to make a drawing with the facial templates in the Identikit that Bosch had brought into the interview room. The driver had dark hair and was white. Sharkey couldn't, or wouldn't, be any more exact in his description. He had worn matching dark shirt and pants, maybe overalls. Sharkey said that he also wore some kind of equipment belt or carpenter's apron. Its dark tool pockets hung empty at the hips and flapped like an apron at his waist. This was curious to Bosch, and he asked Sharkey several questions, coming at it from different angles but getting no better description.

After an hour they were finished. They left Sharkey in the smoky room while they conferred outside again. Wish said, "All we have to do now is find a Jeep with a blanket in the back. Do a microanalysis and match hairs. Only must be a couple million white or beige Jeeps in the state. You want me to put out a BOLO, or you want to handle it?"

"Look. Two hours ago we had nothing. Now we've got a lot. If you want, let me hypnotize the kid. Who knows, we might get a license plate, a better description of the driver, maybe he'll remember a name spoken or be able to describe the seal on the door."

Bosch held his hands out palms up. His offer was out, but she had already turned it down. And she did again.

"Not yet, Bosch. Let me talk to Rourke. Maybe tomorrow. I don't want to rush into that and possibly have it come back on us as a mistake. Okay?"

He nodded and dropped his hands.

"So what now?" she said.

"Well, the kid's eaten. Why don't we get him squared away and then you and I get something to eat? There's a place —"

"I can't," she said.

"— on Overland I know."

"I already have plans for tonight. I'm sorry. Maybe we can make it another night."

"Sure." He walked over to the interview room door and looked through the glass. Anything to avoid showing his face to her. He felt foolish for trying to move so quickly with her. He said, "If you have to get going, go ahead. I'll get him in a shelter or something for the night. We don't both have to waste our time with it."

"You sure?"

"Yeah. I'll take care of him. I'll get a patrol unit to take us. We'll get his bike on the way. I'll have 'em drop me by my car."

"That's nice. I mean about you getting his bike and taking care of him."

"Well, we made a deal with him, remember?"

"I remember. But you care about him. I watched how you handled him. You see some of yourself there?"

He turned away from the glass to look at her.

"No, not especially," he said. "He's just another wit that has to be interviewed. You think he's a little bastard now, wait another year, wait till he's nineteen or twenty, if he makes it. He'll be a monster then. Preying on people. This isn't the last time he'll be sitting in that room. He'll be in and out of there his whole life till he kills somebody or they kill him. It's Darwin's rules; survival of the fittest, and he's fit to survive. So no, I don't care about him. I'm putting him in a shelter because I want to know where he is in case we need him again. That's all."

"Nice speech, but I don't think so. I know a little bit about you, Bosch. You care, all right. The way you got him dinner and asked him —"

"Look, I don't care how many times you read my file. You think that means you know about me? I told you, that's bullshit."

He had come up close to her, until his face was only a foot from hers. But she looked away from him, down at her notebook, as if what she had written there might have something to do with what he was saying.

"Look," he said, "we can work this together, maybe even find out who killed Meadows if we get a few more breaks like the one with the kid today. But we won't really be partners and we won't really know each other. So maybe we shouldn't act like we do. Don't tell me about your little brother with a crew cut and how he looks the way I did, because you don't know how I was. A bunch of papers and pictures in a file don't say anything about me."

She closed the notebook and put it in her purse. Then she finally looked up at him. There was a knocking from inside the interview room. Sharkey was looking at himself in the mirrored window of the door. But they both ignored him and Wish just drilled Bosch with her eyes.

"You always get this way when a woman turns you down for dinner?" she asked calmly.

"That's got nothing to do with it and you know it."

"Sure. I know it." She started to walk away, then said, "Let's say nine A.M., we meet at the bureau again?"

He didn't answer and then she did walk away, toward the squad room door. Sharkey pounded on his door again, and Bosch looked over and saw the boy picking the acne on his face in the door's mirror. Wish turned once more before she was out of the room.

"I wasn't talking about my little brother," she said. "He was my big brother, actually. And I was talking about a long time ago. About the way he looked when I was a little girl and he was going away for a while, to Vietnam."

Bosch didn't look at her. He couldn't. He realized what was coming.

"I remember how he looked then," she said, "because it was the last time I saw him. It sticks with you. He was one of the ones that didn't come back."

She walked out.

Harry ate the last slice of pizza. It was cold and he hated anchovies and he felt he deserved it that way. Same for the Coke, which was warm. Afterward, he sat at the homicide table and made calls until he found an empty bed, rather, an empty space, in one of the no-questions-asked shelters near the Boulevard. At Home Street Home they didn't try to send runaways back to where they came from. They knew in most cases home was a worse nightmare than the streets. They just gave the children a safe place to sleep and then tried to send them off to any place but Hollywood.

He checked out an unmarked car and drove Sharkey to his motorbike. It would not fit in the trunk, so Bosch made a deal with the boy. Sharkey would ride the bike to the shelter and Bosch would follow. When the boy got there and got checked in, Bosch would give him back his money and wallet and cigarettes. But not the Polaroids and the joint. Those went into the trash. Sharkey didn't like it but he did it. Bosch told him to hang around the shelter a couple of days, though he knew the boy would probably split first thing in the morning.

"I found you once. If I need to, I can do it again," he said as the boy locked his bike up outside the home.

"I know, I know," Sharkey said.

It was an idle threat. Bosch knew that he had found Sharkey when the boy didn't know he was being looked for. It would be a different story if he wanted to hide. Bosch gave the boy one of his cheap business cards and told him to give a call if he thought of anything that would help.

"That would help you or me?" Sharkey asked.

Bosch didn't answer. He got back in the car and drove back to the station on Wilcox, watching the mirror for signs of a tail. He didn't see any. After checking the car in he went to his desk and picked up the FBI files. He went to the watch office, where the night lieutenant called one of his patrol units in to give Bosch a lift to the Federal Building. The patrol officer was a young cop with a quarter-inch hairdo. Asian. Bosch had heard around the station that he was called Gung Ho. They rode in silence the whole twenty minutes to the Federal Building.

Harry got home by nine. The red light on his phone machine was blinking but there was no message, just the sound of someone hanging up. He turned on the radio for the Dodgers game, but then he turned it off, tired of hearing people talk. He put CDs by Sonny Rollins, Frank Morgan, and Branford Marsalis into the stereo and listened to the saxophone instead. He spread the files out on the table in the dining room and turned the cap on a bottle of beer. Alcohol and jazz, he thought as he swallowed. Sleeping with your clothes on. You're a cliché cop, Bosch. An open book. And no different from the dozen other fools who must hit on her every day. Just stick to the business in front of you. And don't hope for anything else. He opened the file on Meadows, carefully reading every page, whereas before, in the car with Wish, he had only skimmed.

Meadows was an enigma to Bosch. A pillhead, a heroin user, but a soldier who had re-upped to stay in Vietnam. Even after they took him out of the tunnels, he stayed. In 1970, after two years in the tunnels, he was assigned to a military police unit attached to the American embassy in Saigon. Never saw enemy action again but stayed right up to the end. After the treaty and pullout of 1973, he got a discharge and stayed on again, this time as one of the civilian advisers attached to the embassy. Everybody was going home, but not Meadows. He didn't leave until April 30, 1975, the day of the fall of Saigon. He was on a helicopter and then a plane ferrying refugees out of the country, on their way to the United States. That was his last government assignment: security on the massive refugee transport to the Philippines and then to the States.

According to the records, Meadows stayed in Southern California after coming back. But his skills were limited to military police, tunnel killer, and drug dealer. There was an LAPD application in the file that was marked rejected. He failed the drug test. Next in the file was a National Criminal Intelligence Computer sheet that showed Meadows's record. His first arrest, for possession of heroin, was in 1978. Probation. The next year, he was popped again, this time for possession with intent to sell. He pleaded it out to simple possession and got eighteen months at Wayside Honor Rancho. He did ten of them. The next two years were marked by frequent arrests on marks beefs — fresh needle tracks being a misdemeanor good for sixty days in county lockup. It looked like Meadows was riding the revolving door at county until 1981, when he went away for some substantial time. It was for attempted robbery, a federal beef. The NCIC printout didn't say if it was bank robbery, but Bosch figured it had to be to bring the feds in. The sheet said Meadows was sentenced to four years at Lompoc and served two.

He wasn't out but a few months before he was picked up for a bank robbery. They must have had him cold. He pleaded guilty and took five years back to Lompoc. He would have been out in three but two years into the sentence he was busted in an escape attempt. He got five more years and was transferred to Terminal Island.

Meadows was paroled from TI in 1988. All those years in stir, Bosch thought. He never knew, never heard from him. What would he have done if he had heard? He thought about that for a moment. It probably changed Meadows more than the war. He was paroled to a halfway house for Vietnam vets. The place was called Charlie Company and was on a farm north of Ventura, about forty miles from Los Angeles. He stayed there nearly a year.

After that there were no further contacts, according to Meadows's sheet. The marks beef that had prompted Meadows to call Bosch a year earlier had never been processed. It wasn't on the sheet. No other known contact with police upon his release from prison.

There was another sheet in the package. This one was handwritten and Bosch guessed it was Wish's clean, legible hand. It was a work and home history. Gathered from records searches of Social Security and DMV records, the entries ran vertically down the left side of the paper. But there were gaps. Time periods unaccounted for. Meadows had worked for the Southern California Water District when he first came back from Vietnam. He was a pipeline inspector. He lost the job after four months for excessive tardiness and sick-outs. From there he must have tried his hand at dealing heroin, because the next lawful employment was not listed until after he got out of Wayside in 1979. He went to work for DWP as an underground inspector — storm drainage division. Lost the job six months later for the same reasons as with the water district. There were a few other sporadic employments. After he left Charlie Company he caught on with a gold mining company in the Santa Clarita Valley for a few months. Nothing else.

There were almost a dozen home addresses listed. Most of them were apartments in Hollywood. There was a house in San Pedro, prior to the 1979 bust. If he was dealing at the time, he was probably getting it at the port in Long Beach, Bosch thought. The San Pedro address would have been convenient.

Bosch also saw that he had lived in the Sepulveda apartment since leaving Charlie Company. There was nothing else in the file about the halfway house or what Meadows did there. Bosch found the name of Meadows's parole officer on the copies of his six-month evaluation reports. Daryl Slater, worked out of Van Nuys. Bosch wrote it down in the notebook. He also wrote down the address of Charlie Company. He then spread the arrests sheet, the work and home history, and the parole reports out in front of him. On a new piece of paper he began to write out a chronology beginning with Meadows's being sent to federal prison in 1981.

When he was done, many of the gaps were closed. Meadows served a total of six and a half years in the federal pen. He was paroled in early 1988, when he was sponsored by the Charlie Company program. He spent ten months in the program before moving to the apartment in Sepulveda. Parole reports showed he secured a job as a drill operator in the gold mine in the Santa Clarita Valley. He completed parole in February 1989 and he quit his job a day after his PO signed him off. No known employment since, according to the Social Security Administration. IRS said Meadows hadn't filed a return since 1988.

Bosch went into the kitchen and got a beer out and made a ham and cheese sandwich. He stood by the sink eating and drinking and trying to organize things about the case in his head. He believed that Meadows had been scheming from the time he walked out of TI, or at least Charlie Company. He'd had a plan. He worked legitimate jobs until he cleared parole, and then he quit and the plan was set into action. Bosch felt sure of it. And he felt that it was therefore likely that, at either the prison or the halfway house, Meadows had hooked up with the men who had burglarized the bank with him. And then killed him.

The doorbell rang. Bosch checked his watch and saw it was eleven o'clock. He walked to the door and looked through the peephole and saw Eleanor Wish staring at him. He stepped back, glanced at the mirror in the entrance hall and saw a man with dark, tired eyes looking back at him. He smoothed his hair and opened the door.

"Hello," she said. "Truce?"

"Truce. How'd you know where I — never mind. Come in."

She was wearing the same suit as earlier, hadn't been home yet. He saw her notice the files and paperwork on the card table.

"Working late," he said. "Just looking over some things in the file on Meadows."

"Good. Um, I happened to be out this way and I just wanted, I just came by to say that we . . . Well, it's been a rough week so far. For both of us. Maybe tomorrow we can start this partnership over."

"Yes," he said. "And, listen, I'm sorry for what I said earlier . . . and I'm sorry about your brother. You were trying to say something nice and I. . . . Can you stay a few minutes, have a beer?"

He went to the kitchen and got two fresh bottles. He handed her one and led her through the sliding door to the porch. It was cool out, but there was a warm wind occasionally blowing up the side of the dark canyon. Eleanor Wish looked out at the lights of the Valley. The spotlights from Universal City swept the sky in a repetitive pattern.

"This is very nice," she said. "I've never been in one of these. They're called cantilevers?"

"Yes."

"Must be scary during an earthquake."

"It's scary when the garbage truck drives by."

"So how'd you end up in a place like this?"

"Some people, the ones down there with the spotlights, gave me a bunch of money once to use my name and my so-called technical advice for a TV show.

So I didn't have anything else to do with it. When I was growing up in the Valley I always wondered what it would be like to live in one of these things. So I bought it. It used to belong to a movie writer. This is where he worked. It's pretty small, only one bedroom. But that's all I'll ever need, I guess."

She leaned on the railing and looked down the slope into the arroyo. In the dark there was only the dim outline of the live oak grove below. He also leaned over, and absentmindedly peeled bits of the gold foil label off his beer bottle and dropped them. The gold glinted in the darkness as it fluttered down out of sight.

"I have questions," he said. "I want to go up to Ventura."

"Can we talk about it tomorrow? I didn't come up to go over the files. I've been reading those files for almost a year now."

He nodded and stayed quiet, deciding to let her get to whatever it was that brought her. After some time she said, "You must be very angry about what we did to you, the investigation, us checking you out. Then what happened yesterday. I'm sorry."

She took a small sip from her bottle and Bosch realized he had never asked if she wanted a glass. He let her words hang out there in the dark for a few long moments.

"No," he finally said. "I'm not angry. The truth is, I don't really know what I am."

She turned and looked at him. "We thought you'd drop it when Rourke made trouble for you with your lieutenant. Sure, you knew Meadows, but that was a long time ago. That's what I don't get. It's not just another case for you. But why? There must be something more. Back in Vietnam? Why's it mean so much to you?"

"I guess I have reasons. Reasons that have nothing to do with the case."

"I believe you. But whether I believe you is not the point. I'm trying to know what's going on. I need to know."

"How's your beer?"

"It's fine. Tell me something, Detective Bosch."

He looked down and watched a little piece of the printed foil disappear in the black.

"I don't know," he said. "Actually I do know and I don't. I guess it goes back to the tunnels. Shared experience. It's nothing like he saved my life or I saved his. Not that easy. But I feel something is owed. No matter what he did or what kind of fuckup he became after. Maybe if I had done more than make a few calls for him last year. I don't know."

"Don't be silly," she said. "When he called you last year he was well into this caper. He was using you then. It's like he's using you now, even though he's dead."

He'd run out of label to peel. He turned around and leaned his back on the railing. He fumbled a cigarette out of his pocket with one hand, put it in his mouth but didn't light it.

"Meadows," he said and shook his head at the memory of the man. "Meadows was something else. . . . Back then, we were all just a bunch of kids, afraid of the dark. And those tunnels were so damn dark. But Meadows, he wasn't afraid. He'd volunteer and volunteer and volunteer. Out of the blue and into the black. That's what he said going on a tunnel mission was. We called it the black echo. It was like going to hell. You're down there and you could smell your own fear. It was like you were dead when you were down there."

They had gradually turned so that they were facing each other. He searched her face and saw what he thought was sympathy. He didn't know if that's what he wanted. He was long past that. But he didn't know what he wanted.

"So all of us scared little kids, we made a promise. Every time anybody went down into one of the tunnels we made a promise. The promise was that no matter what happened down there, nobody would be left behind. Didn't matter if you died down there, you wouldn't be left behind. Because they did things to you, you know. Like our own psych-ops. And it worked. Nobody wanted to be left behind, dead or alive. I read once in a book that it doesn't matter if you're lying beneath a marble tombstone on a hill or at the bottom of an oil sump, when you're dead you're dead.

"But whoever wrote that wasn't over there. When you're alive but you're that close to dying, you think about those things. And then it does matter. . . . And so we made the promise."

Bosch knew he hadn't explained a thing. He told her he was going to get another beer. She said she was fine. When he came back out she smiled at him and said nothing.

"Let me tell you a story about Meadows," he said. "See, the way they worked it was, they'd assign a couple, maybe three of us tunnel rats to go out with a company. So when they'd come across a tunnel, we'd zip on down, check it out, mine it, whatever."

He took a long pull on the fresh beer.

"And so once, this would have been in 1970, Meadows and me were tagging at the back of a patrol. We were in a VC stronghold and, man, it was just riddled with tunnels. Anyway, we were about three miles from a village called Nhuan Luc when we lost a point man. He got — I'm sorry, you probably don't want to hear this. With your brother and all."

"I do want to hear. Please."

"So this point got shot by a sniper who was in a spider hole. That was what they called the little entrances to a tunnel network. So somebody took out the sniper and then me and Meadows had to go down the hole to check it out. We went down, and right away we had to split up. This was a big network. I followed one line one way and he went the other. We had said we'd go for fifteen minutes, set charges with a twenty-minute delay, then head back, setting more along the way. . . . I remember I found a hospital down there. Four empty grass mats, a cabinet of supplies, all just sitting in the middle of this tunnel. I remember I thought, Jesus Christ, what's going to be around the bend, a drive-in movie or something? I mean these people had dug themselves in. . . . Anyway, there was a little altar in there and there was incense burning. Still burning. I knew then that they were still in there somewhere, the VC, and it scared me. I set a charge and hid it behind the altar, and then I started back as fast as I could. I set two more charges along the way, timing everything so it would all go off at once. So I get back to the drop-in point, you know, the original spider hole, and no Meadows. I waited a few minutes and it's getting close. You don't want to be down there when the C-4 goes. Some of those tunnels are a hundred years old. There was nothing I could do, so I climbed out. He wasn't up top either."

He stopped to drink some beer and think about the story. She watched intently but didn't prod him.

"A few minutes later my charges went off and the tunnel, at least the part I had been in, came down. Whoever was in there was dead and buried. We waited a couple hours for the smoke and dust to settle. We hooked a Mighty Mite fan up and blew air down the entry shaft, and then you could see smoke being pushed out and coming up out of the air vents and other spider holes all around the jungle.

"And when it was clear, me and another guy went in to find Meadows. We thought he was dead, but we had the promise; no matter what, we were going to get him out and send him home. But we didn't find him. Spent the rest of the day down there looking, but all we found were dead VC. Most of them had been shot, some had cut throats. All of them had ears slashed off. When we came up, the top told us we couldn't wait anymore. We had orders. We pulled out, and I had broken the promise."

Bosch was staring blankly out into the night, seeing only the story he was telling.

"Two days later, another company was in the village, Nhuan Luc, and somebody found a tunnel entrance in a hootch. They get their rats to check it out, and they aren't in that tunnel more than five minutes when they find Meadows. He was just sitting like Buddha in one of the passageways. Out of ammo. Talking gibberish. Not making sense, but he was okay. And when they tried to get him to come up with them, he didn't want to. They finally had to tie him up and put a rope on him and have the patrol up there pull him out. Up in the sunlight they saw he was wearing a necklace of human ears. Strung with his tags."

He finished the beer and walked in off the balcony. She followed him to the kitchen, where he got a fresh bottle. She put her half-finished bottle on the counter.

"So that's my story. That was Meadows. He went to Saigon for some R and R but he came back. He couldn't stay away from the tunnels. After that one, though, he was never the same. He told me that he just got mixed up and lost down there. He just kept going in the wrong direction, killing anything he came across. The word was that there were thirty-three ears on his neck-lace. And somebody asked me once why Meadows let one of the VC keep an ear. You know, accounting for the odd number. And I told him that Mead-ows let them all keep an ear."

She shook her head. He nodded his.

Bosch said, "I wish I had found him that time I went back in to look. I let him down."

They both stood for a while looking down at the kitchen floor. Bosch poured the rest of his beer down the sink.

"One question about Meadows's sheet and then no more business," he said. "He got jammed up at Lompoc on an escape attempt. Then sent to TI. You know anything about that?"

"Yes. And it was a tunnel. He was a trusty and he worked in the laundry. The gas dryers had underground vents going out of the building. He dug beneath one of them. No more than an hour a day. They said he had prob-ably been at it at least six months before it was discovered, when the sprinklers they use in the summer on the rec field softened the ground and there was a cave-in."

He nodded his head. He figured it had been a tunnel.

"The two others that were in on it," she said. "A drug dealer and a bank robber. They're still inside. There's no connection to this."

He nodded again.

"I think I should go now," she said. "We have a lot to do tomorrow."

"Yeah. I have a lot more questions."

"I'll try to answer them if I can."

She passed closely by him in the small space between the refrigerator and counter and moved out into the hallway. He could smell her hair as she went by. An apple scent, he thought. He noticed that she was looking at the print hanging on the wall opposite the mirror in the hallway. It was in three separate framed sections and was a print of a fifteenth-century painting called *The Garden of Delights*. The painter was a Dutchman.

"Hieronymus Bosch," she said as she studied the nightmarish landscape of the painting. "When I saw that was your full name I wondered if —"

"No relation," he said. "My mother, she just liked his stuff. I guess 'cause of the last name. She sent that print to me once. Said in the note that it reminded her of L.A. All the crazy people. My foster parents . . . they didn't like it, but I kept it for a lot of years. Had it hanging there as long as I've had this place."

"But you like to be called Harry."

"Yeah, I like Harry."

"Good night, Harry. Thanks for the beer."

"Good night, Eleanor. . . . Thanks for the company."

PART IV

WEDNESDAY, MAY 23

By 10 A.M. they were on the Ventura Freeway, which cuts across the bottom of the San Fernando Valley and out of the city. Bosch was driving and they were going against the grain of traffic, heading northwest, toward Ventura County, and leaving behind the blanket of smog that filled the Valley like dirty cream in a bowl.

They were heading to Charlie Company. The FBI had only done a cursory check on Meadows and the prison outreach program the year before. Wish said she had thought its importance was minimal because Meadows's stay had ended nearly a year before the tunnel caper. She said the bureau had requested a copy of Meadows's file but had not checked the names of other convicts who were part of the program at the same time as Meadows. Bosch thought this was a mistake. Meadows's work record indicated the bank caper was part of a long-range plan, he told Wish. The bank burglary might have been hatched at Charlie Company.

Before leaving, Bosch had called Meadows's parole officer, Daryl Slater, and was given a rundown on Charlie Company. Slater said the place was a vegetable farm owned and operated by an army colonel who was retired and born again. He contracted with the state and federal prisons to take early release cases, the only requirement being that they be Vietnam combat veterans. That wasn't too difficult a bill to fill, Slater said. As in every other state in the country, the prisons in California had high populations of Vietnam vets. Gordon Scales, the former colonel, didn't care what crimes the vets had been convicted of, Slater said. He just wanted to set them right again. The place had a staff of three, including Scales, and held no more than twenty-four men at a time. The average stay was nine months. They worked the vegetable fields from six to three, stopping only for lunch at noon. After the work day there was an hour-long session called soul talk, then dinner and TV. Another hour of religion before lights-out. Slater said Scales used his connections in the community to place the vets in jobs when they were ready for the outside world. In six years, Charlie Company had a recidivist record of only 11 percent. A figure so enviable that Scales got a favorable mention in a speech by the president during his last campaign swing through the state.

"The man's a hero," Slater said. "And not 'cause of the war. For what he did after. When you get a place like that, moving maybe thirty, forty cons through it a year, and only one in ten gets his ass in a jam again, then you are talking about a major success. Scales, he has the ear of the federal and state parole boards and half the wardens in this state."

"Does that mean he gets to pick who goes to Charlie Company?" Bosch asked.

"Maybe not pick, but give final approval to, yes," the PO said. "But the word on this guy is out. His name is known in every and any cellblock where you got a vet doing time. These guys come to him. They send letters, send Bibles, make phone calls, have lawyers get in contact. All to get Scales to sponsor them."

"Is that how Meadows got there?"

"Far as I know. He was already heading there when he was assigned to me. You'd have to call Terminal Island and have them check their files. Or talk to Scales."

Bosch filled Wish in on the conversation while they were on the road. Otherwise, it was a long ride and there were long periods of silence. Bosch spent much of the time wondering about the night before. Her visit. Why had she come? After they crossed into Ventura County his mind came back to the case, and he asked her some of the questions he had come up with the night before while reviewing the files.

"Why didn't they hit the main vault? At WestLand there were two vaults. Safe-deposit and then the bank's main vault, for the cash and the tellers' boxes. The crime scene reports said the design of both vaults was the same. The safe-deposit vault was bigger but the armoring in the floor was the same. So it would seem that Meadows and his partners could just as easily have tunneled to the main vault, gotten in and taken whatever was there and gotten out. No need to risk spending a whole weekend inside. No need to pry open safe-deposit boxes either."

"Maybe they didn't know they were the same. Maybe they assumed the main vault would be tougher."

"But we are assuming they had some knowledge of the safe-deposit vault's structure before they started on this. Why didn't they have the same knowledge of the other vault?"

"They couldn't recon the main vault. It's not open to the public. But we think one of them rented a box in the safe-deposit vault and went in to check it out. Used a phony name, of course. But, see, they could check out one vault and not the other. Maybe that's why."

Bosch nodded and said, "How much was in the main vault?"

"Don't know offhand. It should have been in the reports I gave you. If not, it's in the other files back at the bureau."

"More, though. Right? There was more cash in the main vault than what, the two or three million in property they got from the boxes."

"I think that is probably right."

"See what I'm saying? If they had hit the main vault the stuff would have been laying around in stacks and bags. Right there for the taking. It would have been easier. There probably would have been more money for less trouble."

"But, Harry, we know that from hindsight. Who knows what they knew going in? Maybe they thought there was more in the boxes. They gambled and lost."

"Or maybe they won."

She looked over at him.

"Maybe there was something there in the boxes that we don't even know about. That nobody reported missing. Something that made the safe-deposit vault the better target. Made it worth more than the main vault."

"If you're thinking drugs, the answer is no. We thought of that. We had the DEA bring around one of their dogs and he went through the broken boxes. Nothing. No trace of drugs. He then sniffed around the boxes the thieves hadn't gotten to and he got one hit. On one of the small ones."

She laughed for a moment and said, "So then we drilled this box the dog went nuts over and found five grams of coke in a bag. This poor guy who kept his coke stash at the bank got busted just because somebody happened to tunnel into the same vault."

Wish laughed again, but it seemed to be a little forced to Bosch. The story wasn't that funny. "Anyway," she said, "the case against the guy was kicked by an assistant U.S. attorney because he said it was a bad search. We violated the guy when we drilled his box without a warrant."

Bosch exited the freeway into the town of Ventura and headed north. "I still like the drug angle, despite the dog," he said after a quarter hour of silence. "They aren't infallible, those dogs. If the stuff was packed in there right and the thieves got it, there may not have been a trace. A couple of those boxes with coke in them and the caper starts being worth their while."

"Your next question will be about the customer lists, right?" she said.

"Right."

"Well, we did a lot of work on that. We checked everybody, right down to tracing purchases of things they said were in the boxes. We didn't find who did the job, but we probably saved the bank's insurance companies a couple million in paying for things that were reported stolen but never really existed."

He pulled into a gas station so he could take out a map book from under the seat and figure out the way to Charlie Company. She continued to defend the FBI investigation.

"The DEA looked at every name on the boxholder list and drew a blank. We ran the names through NCIC. We got a few hits but nothing serious, mostly old stuff." She gave another one of those short fake laughs. "One of the holders of one of the bigger boxes had a kiddy porn conviction from the seventies. Served a deuce at Soledad. Anyway, after the bank job he was contacted and he reported nothing was taken, said he had recently emptied his box. But they say these pedophiles can never part with their stuff, their photos and films, even letters written about kids. And there was no record at the bank of him going into the box in the two months before the burglary. So we figured that the box was for his collection. But, anyway, that had nothing to do with the job. Nothing we turned up did."

Bosch found the way on the map and pulled out of the service station. Charlie Company was in grove country. He thought about her story about the pedophile. Something about it bothered him. He rolled it around in his head but couldn't get to it. He let it drift and went on to another question.

"Why was nothing ever recovered? All that jewelry and bonds and stocks, and nothing ever turns up except for a single bracelet. Not even any of the other worthless things that were taken."

"They are sitting on it until they think they are clear," Wish said. "That's why Meadows was smoked. He went out of line and pawned the bracelet before he should have, maybe before everyone agreed they were clear. They found out he'd sold it. He wouldn't say where, so they buzzed him until he told them. Then they killed him."

"And by coincidence, I get the call."

"It happens."

"There is something in that story that doesn't work," Bosch said. "We start out with Meadows getting juiced, tortured, right? He tells them what they want, they put the hot load in his arm and they go get the bracelet from the pawnshop, okay?"

"Okay."

"But, see, it doesn't work. I've got the pawn slip. It was hidden. So he didn't give it to them, and they had to go break in the shop and take the bracelet, covering the scam by also taking a lot of other junk. So if he didn't give them the pawn slip, how'd they know where the bracelet was?"

"He told them, I guess," Wish said.

"I don't think so. I don't see him giving up one and not the other. He had nothing to gain from holding back the slip. If they got the name of the shop out of him, they would've gotten the slip."

"So, you're saying he died before he told them anything. And they already knew where the bracelet was pawned."

"Right. They worked him to get the ticket, but he wouldn't give it up, wouldn't break. They killed him. Then they dump the body and roll his place. But they still don't find the pawn stub. So they hit the pawnshop like third-rate burglars. The question is, if Meadows didn't tell them where he had sold the bracelet and they didn't find the stub, how did they know where it was?"

"Harry, this is speculation on top of speculation."

"That's what cops do."

"Well, I don't know. Could have been a lot of things. They could have had a tail on Meadows 'cause they didn't trust him and could have seen him go into the pawnshop. Could've been a lot of things."

"Could've been they had somebody, say a cop, who saw the bracelet on the monthly pawn sheets and told them. The sheets go to every police department in the county."

"I think that kind of speculation is reckless."

They were there. Bosch braked the car at a gravel entranceway below a wooden sign with a green eagle painted on it and the words Charlie Company. The gate was open and they drove down a gravel road with muddy irrigation ditches running along both sides. The road split the farmland, with tomatoes on the right and what smelled like peppers on the left. Up ahead there was a large aluminum-sided barn and a sprawling ranch-style house. Behind these Bosch could see a grove of avocado trees. They drove into a circular parking area in front of the ranch house and Bosch cut the engine.

A man wearing a white apron that was as clean as his shaven head came to the screen at the front door.

"Mr. Scales here?" Bosch asked.

"Colonel Scales, you mean? No, he is not. It's almost time for chow, though. He'll be coming in from the fields then."

The man did not invite them to come in out of the sun, and so Bosch and Wish went back and sat in the car. A few minutes later a dusty white pickup truck drove up. It had an eagle inside a large letter C painted on the driver's door. Three men got out of the cab and six more piled out of the back. They moved quickly toward the ranch house. They ranged in age from late thirties to late forties. They wore military green pants and white T-shirts soaked with sweat. No one wore a bandanna or sunglasses or had his sleeves rolled up. No one's hair was longer than a quarter inch. The white men were burned brown like stained wood. The driver, wearing the same uniform but at least ten years older than the rest, slowed to a stop and let the others go inside. As he approached, Bosch put him on the early side of his sixties, but a guy who was almost as solid as he had been in his twenties. His hair, what could be seen of it against his gleaming skull, was white and his skin was like walnut. He was wearing work gloves.

"Help you?" he asked.

"Colonel Scales?" Bosch said.

"That's right. You police?"

Bosch nodded and made introductions. Scales didn't seem too impressed, even with the FBI being mentioned.

"You remember about seven, eight months ago the FBI asked you for some information on a William Meadows, who spent some time here?" Wish asked.

"Sure I do. I remember every time you people call up or come around ask-

ing about one of my boys. I resent it, so I remember it. You want more information on Billy? Is he in some trouble?"

"Not anymore," Bosch said.

"What's that supposed to mean?" Scales said. "Sounds like you're saying
he's dead."

"You didn't know?" Bosch said.

"'Course I didn't. Tell me what happened to him."

Bosch thought he saw genuine surprise and then a flashing hint of sadness cross Scales's face. The news had hurt.

"He was found dead three days ago in L.A. A homicide. We think it is
related to a crime he took part in last year, that you may have heard about
from the FBI's previous contact."

"The tunnel thing? At that bank in L.A.?" he asked. "I know what I was
told by the FBI. That's it."

"That's fine," Wish said. "What we need from you is more complete information about who was here when Meadows was. We went over this ground
before, but we are rechecking, looking for anything that might help. Will
you cooperate with us?"

"I always cooperate with you people. I don't like it because half the time I
think you got your wires crossed. Most of my boys, when they leave here,
they don't get mixed up again. We have a good record here. If Meadows did
what you're saying he did, he is the rarity."

"We understand that," she said. "And this will be strictly confidential."

"O'right then, come into my office and you can ask your questions."

As they went through the front door Bosch saw two long tables in what
was probably once the ranch house's living room. About twenty men sat
before plates of what looked like chicken-fried steaks and mounds of vegetables. Not one looked at Eleanor Wish. That was because they were
silently saying grace, their heads down, eyes closed and hands folded. Bosch
could see tattoos on almost every arm. When they stopped their prayer a
chorus of forks struck home on the plates. A few of the men took the time
then to look at Eleanor approvingly. The man in the apron who had come to
the screen door earlier now stood in the doorway of the kitchen.

"Colonel, are you eating with the men today, sir?" he called.

Scales nodded and said, "I'll be through in a few minutes."

They went down a hallway and through the first door into an office that
was supposed to be a bedroom. It was crowded by a desk with a top the size
of a door. Scales pointed to two chairs in front of it and Bosch and Wish sat
down, while he took the upholstered job behind the desk.

"Now, I know exactly what I am required by law to give you and what I
don't have to even speak to you about. But I am inclined to do more, if it will
help and we have an understanding. Meadows — I sort of knew he would
end up as you say he did. I prayed to the Good Lord to guide him, but I knew.
I will help you. No one should take a life in a civilized world. No one at all."

"Colonel," Bosch began, "we appreciate your help. I want you to know, first off, that we know what kind of job you are doing here. We know you have the respect and encouragement of both state and federal authorities. But our investigation of Meadows's death leads us to conclude he was involved in a conspiracy with other men who had the same skills as he and —"

"You are saying they are vets," Scales cut in. He was filling a pipe with tobacco from a canister on the desk.

"Possibly. We have not identified them yet, so we don't know it for a fact. But if that is the case, there would seem a possibility that the players in the conspiracy may have met here. I stress the word 'may.' Therefore, there are two things we want from you. A look at any records you still have on Meadows and a list of every man that was here during the ten months he was."

Scales was tamping his pipe and seemingly paying no attention to what had just been said. Then he said, "No problem on his records — he's dead. On the other, I suppose I should call my lawyer just to make sure I can do that. We run a good program here. And vegetables and money from the state and the feds don't cover it. I get out the soapbox and make the rounds. We rely on the tithings of the community, civic organizations, things like that. Bad publicity will dry that money up faster than a Santa Ana wind. I help you, I risk that. The other risk is the loss in the faith of the men who come here for a new start. See, most of those men that were here back when Meadows was, they've gone on to new lives. They aren't criminals anymore. If I'm handing out their names to every cop that comes around, then that doesn't look too good for my program, does it?"

"Colonel Scales, we don't have time for lawyers to look this over," Bosch said. "We are on a murder case, sir. We need this information. You know we can get it if we go to the state and federal correctional departments, but that might take longer than your lawyer. We can also get it with a subpoena, but we thought mutual cooperation would be best. We are much more inclined to tread lightly if we have your cooperation."

Scales didn't move and again didn't seem to be listening. A curl of blue smoke swirled like a ghost out of his pipe bowl.

"I see," he finally said. "Then I'll just get those files, won't I?" He stood up then and went to a row of beige file cabinets that lined the wall behind his desk. He went to one drawer marked M-N-O and after a short search pulled out a thin manila file. He dropped it on his desk near Bosch. "That's the file on Meadows, there," he said. "Now let's see what else we can find here."

He went to the first drawer, which had no marking in the card slot on front. He looked through files without taking any out. Then he chose one and sat down with it.

"You are free to look through that file and I can copy anything you need from it," Scales said. "This one is my master flow chart of people through here. I can make you a list of any people Meadows could have met here. I assume you will need DOBs and PINs?"

"That would help, thank you," Wish said.

It took only fifteen minutes to look through Meadows's file. He had started a correspondence with Scales a year before his release from TI. He had the backing of a chaplain and an intake counselor who knew him because he had been assigned to maintenance at the prison's intake and placement office. In one of the letters Meadows had described the tunnels he had been into in Vietnam and how he had been drawn to their darkness.

"Most of the other guys were scared to go down there," he wrote. "I wanted to go. I didn't know why then, but I think now that I was testing my limits. But the fulfillment I received from it was false. I was as hollow as the ground we fought on. The fulfillment I now have is in Jesus Christ and knowing He is with me. If given the chance, and with His guidance, I can make the right choices this time and leave these bars forever behind. I want to go from hollow ground to hallowed ground."

"Tacky but sincere enough, I guess," Wish said.

Scales looked up from the desk, where he was writing names, birth dates and prison identification numbers on a sheet of yellow paper. "He was sincere," he said in a voice that suggested there was no other way about it. "When Billy Meadows left here, I thought, I believed, he was ready for the outside and that he had shed past alliances with drugs and crime. It becomes obvious that he fell back into that temptation. But I doubt you two will find what you are looking for here. I give you these names but they won't help you."

"We'll see," Bosch said. Scales went back to writing, and Bosch watched him. He was too consumed by his faith and loyalty to see he might have been used. Bosch believed Scales was a good man but one who might be too quick to see his beliefs and hopes in someone else, perhaps someone like Meadows.

"Colonel, what do you get out of all this?" Bosch asked.

This time he put his pen down, adjusted his pipe in his set jaw and folded his hands together on the desk. "It's not what I get. It's what the Lord gets." He picked up the pen again, but then another thought came to him. "You know, these boys were destroyed in many ways when they got back. I know, it's an old story and everybody's heard it, everybody's seen the movies. But these guys have had to live it. Thousands came back here and literally marched off to the prisons. One day I was reading about that and I wondered what if there hadn't been any war and these boys never went anywhere. They just stayed in Omaha and Los Angeles and Jacksonville and New Iberia and wherever. Would they still have ended up in prison? Would they be homeless, wandering mental cases? Drug addicts?

"For most of them, I doubt that. It was the war that did it to them, that sent them the wrong way." He took a long drag on the dead pipe. "So all I do, with the help of the earth and a few prayer books, is try to put back inside what the Vietnam experience took out. And I'm pretty good at it. So

I'm giving you this list, letting you take a look at that file there. But don't hurt what we've got here. You two have a natural suspicion of what goes on here, and that's fine. It's healthy for people in your position. But be careful with what is good here. Detective Bosch, you look the right age, were you over there?"

Bosch nodded and Scales said, "Then you know." He went back to finishing the list. Without looking up he said, "You two join us for lunch? Freshest vegetables in the county on our table."

They declined and stood up to go after Scales handed Bosch the list with the twenty-four names he had come up with. As Bosch turned to the office door he hesitated and said, "Colonel, do you mind me asking what other vehicles you have on the farm? I saw the pickup."

"We don't mind you asking, because we have nothing to hide. We got two more pickups like that, two John Deeres and a four-wheel-drive vehicle."

"What kind of four-wheel-drive vehicle?"

"It's a Jeep."

"And what color?"

"It's white. What's going on?"

"Just trying to clear up something. But I guess the Jeep would have the Charlie Company seal on the side, like the pickup?"

"That's right. All our vehicles are marked. When we go into Ventura we're proud of what we've accomplished. We want people to know where the vegetables are coming from."

Bosch didn't look at the names on the list until he was in the car. He didn't recognize any, but he noticed that Scales had written the letters PH after eight of the twenty-four names.

"What's that mean?" Wish asked as she leaned over and looked at the list also.

"Purple Heart," Bosch said. "One more way to say be careful, I guess."

"What about the Jeep?" she said. "He said it was white. It has a seal on the side."

"You saw how dirty the pickup was. A dirty white Jeep, it could have looked beige. If it's the right Jeep."

"He just doesn't seem right. Scales. He seems legit."

"Maybe he is. Maybe it's the people he lends his Jeep to. I didn't want to press it with him until we know more."

He started the car and they headed down the gravel road to the gate. Bosch rolled his window down. The sky was the color of bleached jeans and the air was invisible and clean and smelled like fresh green peppers. But not for long, Bosch thought. We go back into the nastiness now.

On the way back to the city Bosch cut off the Ventura Freeway and headed south through Malibu Canyon to the Pacific. It would take longer to get back, but the clean air was addictive. He wanted it for as long as possible.

"I want to see the list of the victims," he said after they had made their way through the winding canyon and the hazy blue surface of the ocean could be seen ahead. "This pedophile you mentioned earlier. Something about that story bothered me. Why would they take the guy's collection of kiddie porno?"

"Harry, come on, you are not going to suggest that was a reason, that these guys tunneled for weeks and then blasted into a bank vault to steal a collection of kiddie porn?"

"Of course not. But that's why it raises the question. Why'd they take the stuff?"

"Well, maybe they wanted it. Maybe one was a pedophile and he liked it. Who knows?"

"Or maybe it was all part of a cover. Take everything from every box they drilled to hide the fact that what they were really after was one box. You know, sort of blur the picture by hitting dozens of boxes. But all along the target was something in only one of the boxes. Same principle with the pawnshop break-in: take a lot of jewelry to cover they only wanted the bracelet.

"But with the vault, they wanted something that wouldn't be reported stolen afterward. Something that couldn't be reported stolen because it would get the owner into some kind of jam. Like with the pedophile. When his stuff got stolen what could he say? That's the sort of thing the tunnelers were after, but something more valuable. Something that would make hitting the safe-deposit vault more attractive than hitting the main vault.

"Something that would make killing Meadows a necessity when he endangered the whole caper by pawning the bracelet."

She was quiet. Bosch looked over at her, but behind her sunglasses she was unreadable.

"Sounds to me like you are talking about drugs again," she said after a while. "And the dog said no drugs. The DEA found no connections on our list of customers."

"Maybe drugs, maybe not. But that's why we should look at the box-holders again. I want to look at the list for myself. Want to see if anything rings a bell with it. The people who reported no losses, they are the ones that I want to start with."

"I'll get the list. We've got nothing else going anyway."

"Well, we've got these names from Scales to run down," Bosch said. "I was thinking that we'd pull mugs and take 'em to Sharkey."

"Worth a try, I guess. More like just going through the motions."

"I don't know. I think the kid is holding something. I think he maybe saw a face that night."

"I left a memo with Rourke about the hypnosis. He'll probably get back to us on that today or tomorrow."

They took the Pacific Coast Highway around the bay. The smog had been blown inland and it was clear enough to see Catalina Island out past the whitecaps. They stopped at Alice's Restaurant for lunch, and since it was late there was an open table by a window. Wish ordered an ice tea and Bosch had a beer.

"I used to come out to this pier when I was a kid," Bosch told her. "They'd take a busload of us out. Back then, they had a bait shop out on the end. I'd fish for yellowtail."

"Kids from DYS?"

"Yeah. Er, no. Back then it was called DPS. Department of Public Services. Few years back they finally realized they needed a whole department for the kids, so they came up with DYS."

She looked out the restaurant window and down along the pier. She smiled at his memories and he asked where hers were.

"All over," she said. "My father was in the military. Most I ever spent in one place was a couple years. So my memories aren't really of places. They're people."

"You and your brother were close?" Bosch said.

"Yes, with my father gone a lot. He was always there. Until he enlisted and went away for good."

Salads were put down on the table and they ate a little bit and small-talked a little bit and then sometime between when the waitress picked up the salad plates and put down the lunch plates she told her brother's story.

"Every week he'd write me from over there and every week he said he was scared, wanted to come home," she said. "It wasn't something he could say to our father or mother. But Michael wasn't the type. He should never have gone. He went because of our father. He couldn't let him down. He wasn't brave enough to say no to him, but he was brave enough to go over there. It doesn't make sense. Have you ever heard anything so dumb?"

Bosch didn't answer because he had heard similar stories, his own included. And she seemed to stop there. She either didn't know what had happened to her brother over there or didn't want to recount the details.

After a while she said, "Why'd you go?"

He knew the question was coming but in his whole life he had never been able to truthfully answer it, even to himself.

"I don't know. No choice, I guess. The institutional life, like you said before. I wasn't going to college. Never really thought about Canada. I think it would have been harder to go there than to just get drafted and go to Vietnam. Then in sixty-eight I sort of won the draft lottery. My number came up so low I knew I was going to go. So I thought I'd outsmart 'em by joining, thought I'd write my own ticket."

"And so?"

Bosch laughed a little in the same phony way she had laughed before. "I got in, went through basic and all the bullshit and when it came time to choose something, I picked the infantry. I still have never figured out why. They get you at that age, you know? You're invincible. Once I got over there I volunteered for a tunnel squad. It was kind of like that letter Meadows wrote to Scales. You want to see what you've got. You do things you'll never under-stand. You know what I mean?"

"I think so," she said. "What about Meadows? He had chances to leave and he never did, not till the very end. Why would anybody want to stay if they didn't have to?"

"There were a lot like that," Bosch said. "I guess it wasn't usual or unusual. Some just didn't want to leave that place. Meadows was one of them. It might have been a business decision, too."

"You mean drugs?"

"Well, I know he was using heroin while he was there. We know he was using and selling afterward when he got back here. So maybe when he was over there he got involved in moving it and he didn't want to leave a good thing. There is a lot that points to it. He was moved to Saigon after they took him out of the tunnels. Saigon would have been the place to be, especially with embassy clearance like he had as an MP. Saigon was sin city. Whores, hash, heroin, it was a free market. A lot of people jumped into it. Heroin would have made him some nice money, especially if he had a plan, a way to move some of the stuff back here."

She pushed pieces of red snapper she wasn't going to eat around on her plate with a fork.

"It's unfair," she said. "He didn't want to come back. Some boys wanted to come home but never got the chance."

"Yes. There was nothing fair about that place."

Bosch turned and looked out the window at the ocean. There were four surfers in bright wet suits riding on the swells.

"And after the war you joined the cops."

"Well, I kicked around a little and then joined the department. It seemed most of the vets I knew, like what Scales said today, were going into the police departments or the penitentiaries."

"I don't know, Harry. You seem like the loner type. A private eye, not a man who has to take orders from men he doesn't respect."

"There are no more private operators. Everybody takes orders. . . . But all this stuff about me is in the file. You know it all."

"Not everything about somebody can be put down on paper. Isn't that what you said?"

He smiled as a waitress cleared the table. He said, "What about you? What's your story with the bureau?"

"Pretty simple, really. Criminal justice major, accounting minor, recruited out of Penn State. Good pay, good benefits, women highly sought and val-ued. Nothing original."

"Why the bank detail? I thought the fast track was antiterrorism, white-collar stuff, maybe even drugs. But not the heavy squad."

"I did the white-collar stuff for five years. I was in D.C., too, the right place to be. The thing is, the emperor had no clothes. It was all deadly, deadly boring stuff." She smiled and shook her head. "I realized I just wanted to be a cop. So, that's what I became. I transferred to the first good street unit that had an opening. L.A. is the bank robbery capital of the country. When an opening came up here, I called in my markers and got the transfer. Call me a dinosaur, if you want."

"You are too beautiful for that."

Despite her dark tan, Bosch could tell the remark embarrassed her. It embarrassed him, too, just sort of slipping out like that.

"Sorry," he said.

"No. No, that was nice. Thank you."

"So, are you married, Eleanor?" he said and then he turned red, immediately regretting his lack of subtlety. She smiled at his embarrassment.

"I was. But it was a long time ago."

Bosch nodded. "You don't have anything . . . what about Rourke? You two seemed . . ."

"What? Are you kidding?"

"Sorry."

They laughed together then, and followed it with smiles and a long, comfortable silence.

After lunch they walked out on the pier to the spot where Bosch had once stood with rod and reel. There was no one fishing. Several of the buildings at the end of the pier were abandoned. There was a rainbow sheen on top of the water near one of the pylons. Bosch also noticed the surfers were gone. Maybe all the kids are in school, Bosch thought. Or maybe they don't fish here anymore. Maybe no fish make it this far into the poisoned bay.

"I haven't been here in a long time," he said to Eleanor. He leaned on the pier railing, his elbows on wood scarred by a thousand bait knives. "Things change."

It was midafternoon by the time they got back to the Federal Building. Wish ran the names and prisoner identification numbers Scales had given them through the NCIC and state department of justice computers and ordered mug shots photo-faxed from various prisons in the state. Bosch took the list of names and called U.S. military archives in St. Louis and asked for Jessie St. John, the same clerk he had dealt with on Monday. She said the file on William Meadows that Bosch had asked for was already on the way. Bosch didn't tell her he already had seen the FBI's copy of it. Instead, he talked her into calling up the new names he had on her computer and giving him the basic service biography of each man. He kept her past the end of shift at five o'clock in St. Louis, but she said she wanted to help.

By five o'clock L.A. time Bosch and Wish had twenty-four mug shots and brief criminal and military service sketches of the men to go with them. Nothing jumped off Wish's desk and hit either of them over the head. Fifteen of the men had served in Vietnam at some point during the period

Meadows was there. Eleven of these were U.S. Army. None were tunnel rats, though four were First Infantry along with Meadows on his first tour. There were two others who were MPOs in Saigon.

They focused on the NCIC records of the six soldiers who were First Infantry or military police. Only the MPOs had bank robbery records. Bosch shuffled through the mug shots and pulled those two out. He stared at the faces, half expecting to get confirmation from the hardened, disinterested looks they gave the camera. "I like these two," he said.

Their names were Art Franklin and Gene Delgado. They both had Los Angeles addresses. In Vietnam, they spent their tours in Saigon assigned to separate MP units. Not the embassy unit that Meadows was attached to. But, still, they were in the city. Both of them had been discharged in 1973. But as with Meadows, they stayed on in Vietnam as civilian military advisers. They were there until the end, April 1975. There was no question in Bosch's mind. All three men — Meadows, Franklin and Delgado — knew each other before they met at Charlie Company in Ventura County.

Stateside after 1975, Franklin got jammed up on a series of robberies in San Francisco and went away for five years. He went down on a federal rap of bank robbery in Oakland in 1984 and was at TI at the same time as Meadows. He was paroled to Charlie Company two months before Meadows left the program. Delgado was strictly a state offender; three pops for burglaries in L.A., for which he was able to get by on county lockup time, then an attempted bank robbery in Santa Ana in 1985. He was able to plead in state court under an agreement with federal prosecutors. He went up to Soledad, getting out in 1988 and arriving at Charlie Company three months ahead of Meadows. He left Charlie Company a day after Franklin arrived.

"One day," Wish said. "This means all three were together there at Charlie Company only one day."

Bosch looked at their photos and the accompanying descriptions. Franklin was the larger one. Six foot, 190, dark hair. Delgado was lean, five-six and 140. Dark hair, too. Bosch stared at the photos of the big man and the small man, and was thinking about the descriptions of the men in the Jeep that had dumped Meadows's body.

"Let's go see Sharkey," he said after a while.

He called Home Street Home and was told what he knew they were going to tell him: Sharkey was gone. Bosch tried the Blue Chateau and a tired old voice told him that Sharkey's crew had moved out at noon. His mother hung up on Bosch after she determined he was not a customer. It was near seven. Bosch told Wish they would have to go back to the street to find him. She said she'd drive. They spent the next two hours in West Hollywood, mostly in the Santa Monica Boulevard corridor. But there was no sign of Sharkey or his motorbike locked to a parking meter. They flagged down a few sheriff's cruisers and told them who they were looking for, but not even the extra eyes helped. They parked at the curb by the Oki Dog, and Bosch was thinking that maybe the boy had gone back to his mother's house and she had hung up the phone to protect him.

"You want to take a ride up to Chatsworth?" he asked.

"As much as I'd like to see this witch you told me Sharkey has for a mother, I was thinking more along the lines of calling it a day. We can find Sharkey tomorrow. How about that dinner we didn't have last night?"

Bosch wanted to get to Sharkey, but he also wanted to get to her. She was right, there was always tomorrow.

"Sounds good to me," he said. "Where you feel like going?"

"My place."

Eleanor Wish lived in a rent-controlled townhouse she subleased two blocks from the beach in Santa Monica. They parked at the curb in front, and as they went in she told Bosch that although she lived close by, if he wanted to actually see the ocean he had to walk out onto her bedroom balcony, lean over and look sharply to the right down Ocean Park Boulevard. A slice of the Pacific could then be seen between two condominium towers that guarded the shoreline. From that angle, she mentioned, he could also see into her next-door neighbor's bedroom. The neighbor was a has-been television actor turned small-time dope dealer who had a never-ending procession of women through the bedroom. It kind of took away from the view, she said. She told Bosch to have a seat in the living room while she got dinner started. "If you like jazz, I have a CD over there I just bought but haven't had time to listen to," she said.

He walked over to the stereo, which was stacked on shelves next to a set of bookcases, and picked up the new disk. It was Rollins's *Falling in Love with Jazz,* and inside Harry smiled because he had it at home. It was a warm connection. He opened the case, put the music on and began to look around the living room. There were pastel throw rugs and light-colored coverings on the furniture. Architectural books and home magazines were spread on a glass-topped coffee table in front of a light-blue couch. The place was very neat. A framed cross-stitch canvas on the wall next to the front door said Welcome To This Home. Small letters stitched in its corner said EDS 1970, and Bosch wondered about the last letter.

He made another one of those psychic connections with Eleanor Wish when he turned around and looked at the wall above the couch. Framed in black wood was a print of Edward Hopper's *Nighthawks.* Bosch didn't have the print at home but he was familiar with the painting and from time to time even thought about it when he was deep on a case or on a surveillance. He had seen the original in Chicago once and had stood in front of it studying it for nearly an hour. A quiet, shadowy man sits alone at the counter of a street-front diner. He looks across at another customer much like himself, but only the second man is with a woman. Somehow, Bosch identified with it, with that first man. I am the loner, he thought. I am the nighthawk. The print, with its stark dark hues and shadows, did not fit in this apartment, Bosch realized. Its darkness clashed with the pastels. Why did Eleanor have it? What did she see there?

He looked around the rest of the room. There was no TV. There was just the music on the stereo and the magazines on the table and the books on the lawyer's shelves against the wall across from the couch. He stepped over and looked through the glass panes and browsed the collection. The top two shelves were mostly high-brow book-of-the-month offerings descending into crime fiction by writers like Crumley and Willeford and others. He had read some of them. He opened the glass door and pulled out a book called *The Locked Door*. He'd heard of the book but had never seen it to buy. He opened the cover to see how old it was and he solved the mystery of the last letter on the needlework. On the first page, printed in ink, it said Eleanor D. Scarletti — 1979. She must have kept her husband's name after the divorce, Bosch thought. He put the book back and closed the case.

The books on the bottom two rows of the bookcase ranged from true crime to historical studies of the Vietnam War to FBI manuals. There was even an LAPD homicide investigation textbook. Many of these books Bosch had read. One of them he was even in. It was a book the *Times* reporter Bremmer had written about the so-called Beauty Shop Slasher. A guy named Harvard Kendal, the slasher killed seven women in one year in the San Fernando Valley. They were all beauty shop owners or employees. He cased the shops, followed the victims home and killed them by cutting their throats with a sharpened nail file. Bosch and his partner at the time connected Kendal through a license plate number the seventh victim had written on a pad in the salon the night before she was murdered. They never figured out why she had done it, but the detectives suspected she had seen Kendal watching the shop from his van. She wrote the tag number down as a precaution but then didn't take the precaution of not going home alone. Bosch and his partner traced the tag to Kendal and found out he had spent five years in Folsom for a series of beauty shop arsons near Oakland in the 1960s. They later discovered his mother had worked as a manicurist in a beauty shop when he was a boy. She had practiced her craft on young Kendal's nails, and the shrinks figured he never got over it. Bremmer had gotten a best-seller out of it. And when Universal made a movie of the week out of it, the studio paid Bosch and his partner for the use of their names and technical assistance. The money doubled when a cop series spun off the movie. His partner quit the department and moved to Ensenada. Bosch stayed on, investing his stake in the stilt house on the hill that looked down on the studio that paid him the money. Bosch always found an unexplainable symbiosis in that.

"I read that book before your name ever came up in this. It wasn't part of the research."

Eleanor had come out of the kitchen with two glasses of red wine. Harry smiled.

"I wasn't going to accuse you of anything," he said. "Besides, it isn't about me. It's about Kendal. The whole thing was luck, anyway. But they still made a book and TV show about it. Whatever it is in there, it smells good."

"You like pasta?"

"I like spaghetti."

"That's what we're having. I made a big pot of sauce Sunday. I love to spend an entire day in the kitchen, not thinking about anything else. I find it's good therapy for stress. And it lasts and lasts. All I have to do is warm it up and boil some noodles."

Bosch sipped his wine and looked around some more. He still hadn't sat down but was feeling very comfortable with her. A smile played across his face. He gestured toward the Hopper print. "I like it. But why something so dark?"

She looked at the print and crinkled her brow as if this were the first time she had considered it.

"I don't know," she said. "I've always liked that painting. Something there grabs me. The woman is with a man. So that isn't me. So I guess if it's anyone, it would be the man sitting with his coffee. All alone, kind of watching the two that are together."

"I saw it in Chicago once," Bosch said. "The original. I was out there on an extradition and had about an hour to kill until I could pick up the body. So I went into the Art Institute and it was there. I spent the whole hour looking at it. There's something about it — like you said. I can't remember the case or who I was bringing back here. But I remember that painting."

They sat at the table talking for nearly an hour after the food was gone. She told him more about her brother and her difficulty getting over the anger and loss. Eighteen years later she was still working it out, she said. Bosch told her that he was still working things out, too. He still dreamed of the tunnels from time to time, but more often he battled insomnia instead. He told her how mixed up he was when he got back, how thin the line was, the choice, between what he had done afterward and what Meadows did. It could have been different, he said, and she nodded, seeming to know that was true.

Later, she asked about the Dollmaker case and his fall from Robbery-Homicide. It was more than curiosity. He sensed that something important rode on what he told her. She was making a decision about him.

"I guess you know the basics," he began. "Somebody was strangling women, mostly prostitutes, then painting over their faces with makeup. Pancake, red lipstick, heavy rouge on the cheeks, sharp black eyeliner. The same thing every time. The bodies were bathed, too. But we never said it looked like he was making them into dolls. Some asshole — I think it was a guy named Sakai over at the coroner's — leaked that the makeup was the common denominator. Then this Dollmaker stuff started playing in the press. I think Channel 4 was the first to come up with that name. It took off from there. To me, it looked more like a mortician's work. But the truth is we weren't doing too good. We didn't have a handle on the guy until he was into double figures.

"Not much physical evidence. The victims were all dumped in random locations, all over the Westside. We knew from fiber evidence on a couple of the bodies that the guy probably wore a rug or some kind of hair disguise, fake beard or something. The women that were taken off the stroll, we were able to isolate times and places of their last trick. We went to the hourly motels and got nothing. So we figured the guy was picking them up in a car and then taking them somewhere else, maybe to his home or some kind of safe place he used as a killing pad. We started watching the Boulevard and other hot spots the pros work, and we must've busted up three hundred tricks before we got the break. This whore name of Dixie McQueen calls up the task force one morning, early, and says she just escaped from the Doll-maker and is there a reward if she gives him up. Well, we were getting calls like that every week. I mean, eleven murdered women and people are coming out of the woodwork with clues that aren't really clues. It's panic city."

"I remember," Wish said.

"But Dixie was different. I was working the late shift in the task force offices that day and I caught the call. I went and talked to her. She told me that this john she'd picked up on Hollywood near Spa Row, you know, near the Scientology mansion, took her to this garage apartment in Silver Lake. She said that while the guy was getting naked she wanted to use the toilet. So she goes in and while she's running the water she looks through the cabinet below the sink, probably to see if there is anything worth lifting. But she sees all these little bottles and compacts and all this women's stuff. She looks at it all and she just puts it all together. Just like that. Bingo; this has to be the guy. So she gets a case of total creeps and bails out. She comes out of the bathroom and the guy's in the bed. She just hauls ass through the front door.

"The thing is, we hadn't put out all the stuff about the makeup. Or, actually, the asshole that was the media leak didn't put out everything. See, we knew that the guy was keeping the victims' stuff. They were found with their purses but there were no cosmetics — you know, lipstick, compacts, things like that. So when Dixie told me about what was in the bathroom cabinet she got my attention. I knew she was legit.

"And that is the point where I screwed up. It was 3 A.M. by the time I was done talking to Dixie. Everybody on the task force had gone home and I was left there thinking that this guy might realize Dixie made him and clear out. So I went there alone. I mean, Dixie went with me to show me the place, but then she never left the car. Once we were there, I saw a light on above the garage, which was behind this rundown house off of Hyperion. I called for patrol backup, and while I'm waiting I see the guy's shadow going back and forth across the window. Something tells me he is getting ready to bug out and take all the stuff from the cabinet with him. And we had no evidence from the eleven bodies. We needed the stuff that was in the bathroom cabinet. The other consideration was, what if he has someone up there? You know, a replacement for Dixie. So I went up. Alone. You know the rest."

Wish said, "You went in without a warrant and shot him when he was reaching under the pillow on the bed. You later told the shooting team that you believed it was an emergency situation. There had been enough time for him to go out and get another prostitute. You said that gave you the authority to come through the door without a warrant. You said you fired because you believed the suspect was reaching for a weapon. It was one shot, upper torso from fifteen or twenty feet, if I remember the report. But the Dollmaker was alone, and under the pillow was only his toupee."

"Only his rug," Bosch said. He shook his head like a Monday-morning quarterback. "The shooting team cleared me. We connected him to two of the bodies through the hair from the toupee, and the makeup in the bathroom was traced to eight of the victims. There was no doubt. It was him. I was clear, but then the shooflies started in on it. A Lewis and Clarke expedition. They ran down Dixie and got her to sign a statement saying she told me beforehand that he put his hair under the pillow. I don't know what they used against her, but I can imagine. IAD's always had a hard-on for me. They don't like anybody who's not a hundred percent part of the family. Anyway, the next thing I know they are bringing departmental charges against me. They wanted to fire me and take Dixie to a grand jury to get criminal charges. It was like there was blood in the water and two fat white sharks."

He stopped there but Eleanor continued. "The IAD detectives misjudged things, though, Harry. They didn't realize that public opinion would be with you. You were known in the newspapers as the cop who broke the Beauty Shop Slasher and Dollmaker cases. A character in a TV show. They couldn't take you down without a lot of public scrutiny and embarrassment for the department."

"Someone reached down from above them and put a stop to the grand jury move," Bosch said. "They had to settle for a suspension and my demotion to Hollywood homicide."

Bosch had his fingers on the stem of his empty wine glass and was absentmindedly turning the glass on the table.

"Some settlement," he said after a while. "And those two IAD sharks are still swimming around out there, waiting for the kill."

They sat silently for a while then. He was waiting for her to ask the question she had asked once before. Had the whore lied? She never asked it, and after a while she just looked at him and smiled. And he felt as if he had just passed the test. She started gathering the plates off the table. Bosch helped her in the kitchen and when the work was done, they stood close, drying their hands on the same dish towel, and lightly kissed. Then, as if following the same secret signals, they pressed themselves against each other and kissed with the kind of hunger lonely people have.

"I want to stay," Bosch said after momentarily breaking away.

"I want you to stay," she said.

Arson's stoned eyes were shiny and reflected the neon night. He sucked hard on the Kool and held the precious smoke in. The cigarette had been dipped in PCP. A smile cracked across his face as the jet streams of smoke escaped his nostrils. He said, "You're the only shark I ever heard of being used as bait. Get it?"

He laughed and took another deep drag before handing the cigarette to Sharkey, who waved it away because he'd had enough. Mojo took it then.

"Yeah, I'm getting tired of this shit," Sharkey said. "You take a turn for once."

"Chill out, man, you're the only one can get away with it, man. Mojo and me, man, we just don't play the part good as you. Besides, we got our part. You ain't big enough to pound these faggots."

"Well, whyn't we do the 7-Eleven again?" Sharkey said. "I don't like this not knowing who it is. I like it at the 7-Eleven. We pick our meat, they don't pick me."

"No way," Mojo spoke up then. "We go back there, we don't know if that last guy reported it to the sheriffs or not. We have to stay clear a there awhile. They're probly watching the place from the same parking lot we did."

Sharkey knew they were right. He just thought that being out on Santa Monica on the queer stroll was getting too close to the real thing. Next thing, he guessed, the two dopers will not feel like charging in. They'll want him to go through with it, get the money that way. That was when he would split these guys, he knew.

"Okay," he said, stepping off the curb. "Don't fuck me up."

He started to cross the street. Arson yelled after him, "BMW or better!"

As if I need to be told, Sharkey thought. He walked a half block toward La Brea and then leaned against the door of a closed print shop. He was still a half block from Hot Rod's, an adult bookstore that offered twenty-five-cent all-male peeps. But he was close enough to catch the eye of somebody walking out. If the eye was looking. He looked back the other way and saw the glow of the joint in the darkness of the driveway where Arson and Mojo sat on their bikes.

Sharkey hadn't been standing there ten minutes when a car, a new Grand Am, pulled to the curb and the electric window glided down. Sharkey was going to blow this one off, remembering BMW or better, until he saw the glint of gold and stepped closer. His adrenaline kicked up a notch. The wrist the driver had draped over the steering wheel was adorned with a Rolex Presidential. If it was real, Arson knew where they could get $3,000 for it. A grand apiece, not to mention what else the meat might have at home or in his wallet. Sharkey looked the man over. The guy looked like a straight, a businessman. Dark hair, dark suit. Mid-forties, not too big. Sharkey might even be able to take him alone. The man smiled at Sharkey and said, "Hey, howya doin'?"

"Not bad. What's up?"

"Oh, I don't know. Just out for a ride. You want to take a ride?"

"Where to?"

"No place special. I know a place we can go. Be alone."

"You got a hundred dollars on you?"

"No, but I've got fifty dollars for night baseball."

"Pitching or catching?"

"I'm a pitcher. And I brought my own glove."

Sharkey hesitated and glanced toward the driveway where he had seen the glow from the Kool. It was gone now. They must be ready to move. He looked back at the watch.

"That's cool," he said, and got in the car.

The car headed west past the alley driveway. Sharkey held himself from looking, but he thought he heard the revving and popping sound of their bikes. They were following.

"Where we going?" he asked.

"Uh, I can't go home with you, my friend. But I know a place we can go. Nobody will bother us."

"Cool."

They stopped at the light at Flores, which made Sharkey think of the guy from the other night. They were near his place. Arson was hitting harder, it seemed. This would have to stop soon or they would kill someone. He hoped the man with the Rolex would give it up peaceably. There was no telling what those two would do. Stoked on PCP, they would be ready for battle and blood.

Suddenly the car lurched through the intersection. Sharkey noticed the light was still red.

"What's going on?" he said sharply.

"Nothing. I'm tired of waiting, is all."

Sharkey thought there would be nothing suspicious about looking back now. He turned and saw only cars waiting back at the intersection. No motorbikes. Those bastards, he thought. He felt a dampness beginning on his scalp and the first tremblings of fear. The car turned right after Barnie's Beanery and up the hill to Sunset. Then they went east to Highland and the man with the Rolex steered north again.

"Have we been together before?" the man asked. "You seem familiar. I don't know, maybe we've just seen each other around."

"No, I've never — I don't think so."

"Look at me."

"What?" Sharkey said, startled by the question and the man's sharp tone. "Why?"

"Look at me. You know me? Have you seen me before?"

"What is this, a credit card commercial? I said no, man."

The man turned the car off the street into the east parking lot of the Holly-wood Bowl. It was deserted. He drove quickly and without saying another word to the darkened north end. Sharkey thought, If this is your quiet little spot, then that ain't no real Rolex you got on your wrist, pal.

"Hey, what are we doing, man?" Sharkey said. He was thinking of a way to bail out of this. He was pretty sure Arson and Mojo, stoned as they were, were lost. He was alone with this guy and he wanted to scratch it.

"The bowl is closed," Rolex said. "But I got a key to the dressing rooms, see? We just take the tunnel under Cahuenga and then near where it comes up, there is a little walkway we take back around. There won't be anyone around. I work there. I know."

For a moment, Sharkey considered trying to take the guy alone, then decided he couldn't do it. Unless there was a way of taking him by surprise. He would see. The man turned the car engine off and opened his door. Sharkey opened his own door, got out and looked across the dark expanse of the empty parking lot. He was looking for the two lights of the motor-bikes, but there weren't any. I'll take this guy out on the other side, he decided. He would make his move. Either hit and run, or just run.

They headed toward the sign that said Pedestrian Expressway. There was a concrete outbuilding with an open doorway and then stairs. As they walked down the whitewashed steps, the man with the Rolex put his hand on Sharkey's shoulder and then clamped it on the back of his neck in a fatherly manner. Sharkey could feel the cold metal of the watch's wristband.

The man said, "You sure we don't know each other, Sharkey? Maybe seen each other?"

"No, man, I'm telling you, I haven't been with you."

They were about halfway through the tunnel when Sharkey realized he hadn't told the man his name.

PART V

THURSDAY, MAY 24

It had been a long time for him. And in Eleanor's bedroom, Harry Bosch was clumsy in the way of a man who is overly self-conscious and out of prac-tice. As with most first times he had had, it wasn't good. She directed him with her hands and whispers. And afterward he felt like apologizing but didn't. They held each other and lightly dozed, the smell of her hair in his face. The same apple scent he had encountered in his kitchen the night before. Bosch was infatuated with her and wanted to breathe the smell of her hair every minute. After a while he kissed her awake and they made love again. This time he needed no directions and she didn't need her hands. When they were done, Eleanor whispered to him, "Do you think you can be alone in this world and not be lonely?"

He didn't answer at first, and she said, "Are you alone or are you lonely, Harry Bosch?"

He thought about that for some time, while her fingers gently traced the tattoo on his shoulder.

"I don't know what I am," he finally whispered. "You get so used to things the way they are. And I've always been alone. I guess that makes me lonely. Until now."

They smiled in the dark and kissed, and soon he heard her deep, sleeping breaths. Much later, Bosch got up from the bed, pulled on his pants and went out on the balcony to smoke. On Ocean Park Boulevard there was no traffic and he could hear the ocean's noise from nearby. The lights were out in the apartment next door. They were out everywhere except on the street. He could see that the jacaranda trees along the sidewalk were shedding their flowers. They had fallen like a violet snow on the ground and the cars parked along the curb. Bosch leaned on the railing and blew smoke into the cool night wind.

When he was on his second cigarette he heard the door behind him slide open and then felt her hands come around his waist as she embraced him from behind.

"What's wrong, Harry?"

"Nothing, just thinking. You better watch out. Carcinogen alert. You ever heard of the draft risk easement?"

"Assessment, Harry, not easement. What are you thinking about? Is this how it is most nights for you?"

Bosch turned around in her arms and kissed her forehead. She was wearing a short robe of pink silk. He rubbed his thumb up and down the nape of her neck. "Almost no night is like this. I just couldn't sleep. I guess I was thinking about a lot of things."

"About us?" She kissed his chin.

"I guess."

"And?"

He brought his hand around to her face and traced the outline of her jaw with his fingers.

"I was wondering how you got this little scar here."

"Oh . . . that is from when I was a girl. My brother and I, we were riding on a bike and I was on the handlebars. And we went down this hill, it was called Highland Avenue — this was when we lived in Pennsylvania — and he lost control. The bike started weaving and I was so scared because I knew we were going to crash. And just as he really lost it and we were going down, he yelled, 'Ellie, you'll be all right!' Just like that. And because he had yelled that, he was right. I cut my chin but I didn't even cry. I always thought that was something, that he would try to yell something to me rather than worry about himself at a moment like that. But that was my brother."

Bosch dropped his hands from her face. He said, "I was also thinking that what happened between us was nice."

"I think so, too, Harry. Nice for a couple of nighthawks. Come back to bed now."

They went back in. Bosch first went into the bathroom and used his finger as a toothbrush and then crawled back under the sheet with her. The blue glow of a digital clock on the bedtable said 2:26 and Bosch closed his eyes.

When he opened them again the clock said 3:46 and there was an obnoxious chirping sound coming from somewhere in the room. He realized he was not in his own room. Then he remembered he was in Eleanor Wish's room. As he finally got oriented he saw her shadowy figure stooped next to the bed, her hands going through the pile of his clothes.

"Where is it?" she said. "I can't find it."

Bosch reached for his pants, traced his hands along the belt until he found the pager and turned it off without having to fumble with it. He had done it many times in the dark before.

"Jesus," she said. "That was rude."

Bosch swung his legs over the side of the bed, gathered the sheet around his waist and sat up. He yawned and then warned her that he was going to turn on the light. She said go ahead, and when the light came on it hit him like a diamond burst between his eyes. When his vision cleared, she was standing in front of him naked, looking down at the digital readout of the pager in his hand. Bosch finally looked down at the number but didn't recognize it. He wiped a hand across his face and rustled his hair. There was a telephone on the bedtable and he pulled it onto his lap. He dialed the number and then fumbled with his hands in his clothes for a cigarette, which he put in his mouth but didn't light.

Eleanor noticed her nakedness and walked over to a lounge chair to get her robe. After it was on she went into the bathroom and closed the door. Bosch heard water running. The other end of the line was picked up halfway through the first ring. Jerry Edgar didn't answer with a hello, just "Harry, where you at?"

"I'm not home. What is it?"

"This kid you were looking for, the one on the nine one one call, you found him, right?"

"Yeah, but we're looking for him again."

"Who's 'we' — you and the feebee woman?"

Eleanor came out of the bathroom and sat down on the edge of the bed next to him.

"Jerry, what are you calling me for?" Bosch asked. He was beginning to get a sinking feeling in his chest.

"What's the kid's name?"

Bosch was in a daze. It had been months since he had fallen so deeply asleep, only to be rousted out of it. He couldn't remember Sharkey's real name and he didn't want to ask Eleanor because Edgar might hear and then know they were together. Harry looked at Eleanor and when she began to speak, he touched his finger to her lips and shook his head.

"Is it Edward Niese?" Edgar spoke into the silence. "That the kid's name?"

The sinking feeling was gone. Bosch felt an invisible fist pressing up under his ribs and into the folds of his guts and heart.

"Right," he said. "That's the name."

"You gave him one of your business cards?"

"Right."

"Harry, you aren't looking for him anymore."

"Tell me about it."

"Come on out and see for yourself. I'm over at the bowl. Sharkey's in the pedestrian tunnel under Cahuenga. Park on the east side. You'll see the cars."

The Hollywood Bowl's east parking lot was supposed to be empty at 4:30 A.M. But as Bosch and Wish drove up Highland to the mouth of the Cahuenga Pass they saw that the north end of the lot was crowded with the usual grouping of official cars and vans that signal the violent, or at least unexpected, end of a life. There was yellow plastic crime scene tape strung in a square, boxing the entrance to the stairwell that went down to the pedestrian underpass. Bosch flashed his badge and gave his name to a uniform cop who was keeping the officers-on-the-scene list on a clipboard. He and Wish ducked under the tape and were met by the loud sound of an engine echoing from the mouth of the tunnel. Bosch knew by the sound that it was a generator making the juice for the crime scene lights. At the top step, before they began their descent, he turned to Eleanor and said, "You want to wait here? We don't both have to go."

"I'm a cop, for godsake," she said. "I've seen bodies before. You going to get protective of me now, Bosch? Tell you what. Want me to go down and you stay up here?"

Startled by her abrupt change in mood, Bosch didn't answer. He looked at her a moment longer, confused. He started down a few steps in front of her but stopped when he saw Edgar's large body come out of the tunnel and start up the steps. Edgar saw Bosch, and then Bosch saw his eyes go over his shoulder and take Eleanor Wish in.

"Hey, Harry," he said. "This your new partner? You must be getting along real fine already."

Bosch just stared at him. Eleanor was still three steps behind and probably hadn't heard the remark.

"Sorry, Harry," Edgar said just loud enough to be heard over the roar from the tunnel. "Out of line. Been a bad night. You should see who I got for a new partner, the useless fuck Ninety-eight Pounds stuck me with."

"I thought you were going to get —"

"Nope. Get this: Pounds put me with Porter from autos. The guy's a burned-out lush."

"I know. How'd you even get him out of bed for this?"

"He wasn't in bed. I had to track him down at the Parrot up in North Hollywood. It's one of them private bottle clubs. Porter gives me the number when we're first introduced as partners and tells me that's where he'll be most nights. Tells me he works a security detail there. But I called the off-duty assignments office at Parker Center to check it out and they got no record. I know the only thing he does there is booze. He must've been practically passed out when I called. The bartender said the pager on his belt went off but he didn't even hear it. Harry, I think the guy could blow a point two right now if we put a Breathalyzer on him."

Bosch nodded and frowned the required three seconds and then put Jerry Edgar's troubles aside. He felt Eleanor step down beside him and he introduced her to Edgar. They shook hands and smiled and Bosch said, "So, what have we got?"

"Well, we got these on the body," Edgar said, and he held up a clear plastic bag. There was a short stack of Polaroids in it. More nude shots of Sharkey. He hadn't wasted any time resupplying. Edgar turned the bag and there was Bosch's business card.

"It looks like the kid was a hustler down in Boytown," Edgar said, "but if you already pulled him in once you already know that. Anyway, I saw the card and figured he might be the kid from the nine one one call. If you want to come down and take a look, be my guest. We already processed the scene, so touch whatever you want. You can't hear yourself think in there, though. Sombody went through and knocked out every light in the tunnel. Haven't figured out whether that was the perp or the lights were knocked out before."

"Anyway, we had to set up our own. And our cables weren't long enough to put the generator up here. It's in there screaming like a five-horsepower baby."

He turned to head back into the tunnel but Bosch reached out and touched his shoulder.

"Jed, how'd you get the call on this?"

"Anonymous. It wasn't a nine one one line, so there's no tape or trace. Came in right to the Hollywood desk. Caller was a male, that's all the dip-shit, one of those fat Explorer kids who took it, could tell us."

Edgar turned back into the subway. Bosch and Wish followed. It was a long hallway that curved to the right. The floor was dirty concrete, its walls were white stucco with a heavy overlay of graffiti. Nothing like a dose of urban reality as you are leaving the symphony at the bowl, Bosch thought. The tunnel was dark except for the bright splash of light that bathed the crime scene about halfway in. There Bosch could see a human form sprawled on its back. Sharkey. He could see men standing and working in the light. Bosch walked with the fingers of his right hand trailing along the stuccoed wall. It steadied him. There was an old, damp smell in the tunnel that was mixed with the new odor of gasoline and exhaust from the generator. Bosch felt beads of sweat start to form on his scalp and under his shirt. His breathing was fast and shallow. They passed the generator thirty feet in and in another thirty feet or so Sharkey was lying on the tunnel floor under the brutal light of the strobes.

The boy's head was propped against the tunnel wall at an unnatural angle. He seemed smaller and younger than Bosch remembered him. His eyes were half open and had the familiar glaze of the unseeing on them. He wore a black T-shirt that said Guns N Roses on it, and it was matted with his blood. The pockets of his faded jeans were pulled out and empty. At his side stood a can of spray paint in a plastic evidence bag. On the wall above his head a painted inscription read RIP Sharkey. The paint had been applied with an inexperienced hand and too much had been used. Black paint had run down the wall in thin lines, some of them into Sharkey's hair.

When Edgar yelled, "You want to see it?" above the din of the generator Bosch knew that he meant the wound. Because Sharkey's head was angled forward, the throat wound was not visible. Only the blood. Bosch shook his head no.

Bosch noticed the blood splatter on the wall and floor about three feet from the body. Porter the lush was comparing the shapes of the drops with those on splatter cards on a steel ring. A crime scene tech named Roberge was also photographing the spots. The blood on the floor was in round spots. The wall splatter drops were elliptical. You didn't need splatter cards to know the kid had been killed right here in the tunnel.

"The way it's looking," Porter said loudly to no one in particular, "somebody comes up behind him here, cuts him and pushes him down against the wall there."

"You only got it half right, Porter," Edgar said. "How's somebody come up behind somebody in a tunnel like this? He was with somebody and they did him. It was no sneak job, Porter."

Porter put the splatter cards in his pocket and said, "Sorry, partner."

He didn't say anything else. He was fat and broken down the way many cops get when they stay on longer than they should. Porter could still wear a size 34 belt, but above it a tremendous gut bloomed outward like an awning. He wore a tweed sport coat with a frayed elbow. His face was gaunt and as pallid as a flour tortilla, behind a drinker's nose that was large, misshapen and painfully red.

Bosch lit a cigarette and put the burnt match in his pocket. He crouched down like a baseball catcher next to the body and lifted the bag containing the paint can and hefted it. It was almost full, and that confirmed what he already knew, already feared. It was he who had killed Sharkey. In a way, at least. Bosch had tracked him down and made him valuable, or potentially valuable, to the case. Someone could not allow this. Bosch squatted there, elbows on knees, holding cigarette to mouth, smoking and studying the body, making sure he would not forget it.

Meadows had been part of this thing — the circle of connected events that had gotten him killed. But not Sharkey. He was street trash and his death here probably saved someone else's life down the line. But he did not deserve this. In this circle he was an innocent. And that meant things were out of control and there were new rules — for both sides. Bosch signaled with his hand to Sharkey's neck and a coroner's investigator pulled the body away from the wall. Bosch put one hand down on the ground to balance himself and stared for a long time at the ravaged neck and throat. He did not want to forget a single detail. Sharkey's head lolled back, exposing the gaping neck wound. Bosch's eyes never wavered.

When Bosch finally looked up from the body, he noticed that Eleanor was no longer in the tunnel. He stood up and signaled Edgar to come outside to talk. Harry didn't want to have to shout over the sound of the generator. When they got out of the tunnel, he saw that Eleanor was sitting alone on the top step. They walked up past her, and Harry put his hand on her shoulder as he went by. He felt it go rigid at his touch.

When he and his old partner were reasonably away from the noise, Harry said, "So what do the techs have?"

"Not a damned thing," Edgar said. "If it was a gang thing, it's one of the cleanest I've ever seen. Not a single print or partial. The spray can is clean. No weapon. No wits."

"Sharkey had a crew, used to stay at a motel near the Boulevard until today, but he wasn't into gangs," Bosch said. "It's in the files. He was a scammer. You know, with the Polaroids, rolling homosexuals, stuff like that."

"You're saying he's in the gang files but he isn't in a gang?"

"Right."

Edgar nodded and said, "He still could've been taken down by somebody who thought he was a gangbanger."

Wish walked over to them then but said nothing.

"You know this isn't a gang thing, Jed," Bosch said.

"I do?"

"Yeah, you do. If it was, there wouldn't be a full can of paint in there. No gangbanger's going to leave something like that behind. Also, whoever painted the wall in there didn't have the touch. The paint ran. Whoever did it, didn't know about spraying a wall."

"Come here a sec," Edgar said.

Bosch looked at Eleanor and nodded that it was okay. He and Edgar walked away a few steps and stood near the crime scene tape.

"What did this kid tell you, and how come he was running around loose if he's part of the case?" he asked.

Bosch told him the basics of the story, that they didn't know if Sharkey was important to the case. But somebody apparently did or couldn't risk waiting to find out. As Bosch spoke he looked up over the hills and saw the first light of dawn outlining the tall palms at the top. Edgar took a step away and tilted his head up that way, too. But he wasn't looking at the sky. His eyes were closed. He eventually turned back to Bosch.

"Harry, you know what this weekend is?" he said. "It's Memorial Day weekend. It's the biggest three-day showing weekend of the year. Start of the summer season. Last year I sold four houses on this weekend, made almost as much as I made all year as a cop."

Bosch was confused by the sudden departure in the conversation. "What are you talking about?"

"What I'm talking about is . . . I'm not going to be busting my ass on this case. It isn't going to fuck up my weekend like the last one. So, what I'm saying is if you want it, I'll go to Pounds and tell him you and the FBI want to take it 'cause it goes with the one you are already working. Otherwise, I'm going to work it strictly as a nine-to-five."

"You tell Pounds whatever you want, Jed. It's not my call."

Bosch started back toward Eleanor, and Edgar said, "Just one thing. Who knew you had found the kid?"

Bosch stopped and looked at Eleanor. Without turning around, he said, "We took him off the street. We interviewed him over on Wilcox. The reports went to the bureau. What do you want me to say, Jed?"

"Nothing," Edgar said. "But, Harry, maybe you and the FBI there should have looked out for your witness a little better. Maybe saved me some time and that boy some life."

Bosch and Wish walked silently back to the car. Once inside Bosch said, "Who knew?"

"What do you mean?" she said.

"What he asked back there, who knew about Sharkey?"

She thought for a moment. Then said, "On my end, Rourke gets the daily summary reports, and he got the memo on hypnosis. The summaries go to records and are copied to the senior special agent. The tape from the interview that you gave me is locked in my desk. Nobody's heard that. It hasn't been transcribed. So, I guess anyone could have seen the summaries. But don't even think about that, Harry. Nobody . . . It can't be."

"Well, they knew we found the kid and he might be important. What's that tell you? They've got to have somebody on the inside."

"Harry, that's speculation. It could have been a lot of things. Like you told him, we picked him up on the street. Anybody could have been watching. His own friends, that girl, anybody could have put out the word that we were looking for Sharkey."

Bosch thought about Lewis and Clarke. They must have seen them pick up Sharkey. What part were they playing? Nothing made sense.

"Sharkey was a tough little bastard," he said. "You think he just went walking with somebody into that tunnel? I think he didn't have a choice. And to do that, it maybe took somebody with a badge."

"Or maybe somebody with money. You know he'd go with somebody if there was money in it."

She didn't start the car and they sat in it thinking. Bosch finally said, "Sharkey was a message."

"What?"

"A message to us. See? They leave my card with him. They call it in on a no-trace line. And they do him in a tunnel. They want us to know they did it. They want us to know they've got somebody inside. They're laughing at us."

She started the car. "Where to?"

"The bureau."

"Harry, be careful with that stuff about an inside man. If you go trying to sell that and it's not true, you could give your enemies all they need to bury you."

Enemies, Bosch thought. Who are my enemies this time?

"I got that kid killed," he said. "The least I am going to do is find who did it."

Bosch looked through the cotton curtains in the waiting room, down at the veterans cemetery, while Eleanor Wish unlocked the door to the bureau offices. The ground fog had not burned off the field of stones yet, and from above it looked like a thousand ghosts rising from their boxes at once. Bosch could see the dark gash dug into the crest of the hill at the north side of the cemetery but still could not make out what it was. It looked almost like a mass grave, a long gouge into the hill, a huge wound. The exposed soil was covered with black plastic sheets.

"You want coffee?" Wish said from behind him.

"Of course," he said. He pulled himself away from the curtains and followed her in. The bureau was empty. They went into the office kitchen and he watched as she dumped a packet of ground coffee into a filter basket and turned the machine on. They stood there silently, watching the coffee slowly drip into a round glass pot on the heating pad. Bosch lit a cigarette and tried only to think about the coffee that was coming. She waved the smoke away with a hand but didn't tell him to put it out.

When the coffee was ready, Bosch took it black and it hit his system like a shot. He filled up a second cup and carried both into the squad room. He lit a cigarette off the butt of the first when he got to his temporary desk.

"My last one," he promised when he saw her looking.

Eleanor poured herself a cup of water from a bottle she took from her file drawer.

"You ever run out of that stuff?" he asked.

She ignored the question. "Harry, we can't blame ourselves for Sharkey. If we're to blame, then we might as well offer every person we talk to protection. Should we go up and grab his mother and put her in witness protection? What about the girl in the motel room that knew him? See, it gets crazy. Sharkey was Sharkey. You live by the street, you die by the street."

Bosch didn't say anything at first. Then he said, "Let me see the names."

Wish pulled out the files on the WestLand case. She rifled through them and pulled out a computer printout several pages long and folded accordion-style. She tossed it on the desk in front of him.

"That's the master there," she said. "Everybody who had a box. There are notes written after some of the names, but they probably are not germane. Most of that was if we thought they were scamming insurance or not."

Bosch started unfolding the printout and realized it was one long list and five shorter lists marked A through E. He asked what they were, and she came around the desk and looked over his shoulder. He smelled the apple in her hair.

"Okay, the long list is like I said, everybody who had a box. It's an all-inclusive list. Then we did five breakouts, A through E. The first — that's A — is a breakout on boxes rented within the three months prior to the burglary. Then B, we did a breakout on boxholders who reported no loss at all in the burglary. Then C is the list of dead ends; boxholders who were actually dead or we couldn't find because of changes in addresses or they had given phony information to rent them.

"Then the fourth and fifth breakouts are matching lists from the first three. D is anybody who rented a box in the previous three months and also reported no loss. E is anybody on the dead-end list who was also on the three-month list. Understand?"

He did. The FBI's thinking had been that the vault had to have been cased by the thieves before the break-in and that was most likely accomplished by simply going into the bank and renting a box. That way they had legitimate access; the guy who rented the box could go inside the vault anytime he wanted during business hours and have a look around. So the list including anybody who rented a box within three months of the robbery stood a good chance of also including the scout.

Second, it was likely that this scout would not want to draw attention to himself after the robbery, so he might report nothing stolen from his box. So that would put him on the D list. But if he made no report at all or had given untraceable information on his box rental card, then his name would be on the E list.

There were only seven names on the D list and five on the E list. One of the E names was circled. Frederic B. Isley of Park La Brea, the name of the man who had bought three Honda ATVs in Tustin. The other names had check marks next to them.

"Remember?" Eleanor said. "I said that name would come up again."

Harry nodded.

"Isley," she said. "We think he was the scout. Rented the box nine weeks before the burglary. The bank records show he made a total of four visits to the vault during the next seven weeks. But after the break-in, he never came back, whoever he was. Never filed a report. And when we tried to contact him we found the address was phony."

"Get a description?"

"Not one that would do us any good. Small, dark and maybe handsome was about as good as the vault clerks could do. We thought this guy was the scout even before we found out about the ATVs. When a boxholder wants to see his box, the clerk takes him in, unlocks the little door and then escorts him to one of the viewing rooms. When he's done, they both take the box back and the customer initials his box card. Kind of like at a library. So, when we looked at this guy's card we saw the initials — FBI. You're a man who doesn't like coincidences. Neither did we. We think somebody was having fun with us. Later, it was confirmed when we tracked the ATVs to Tustin."

Harry sipped his coffee.

"Not much good it did us," she said. "Never found him. In the debris of the vault after the burglary we were able to find his box. We printed it and the door. Nothing. We showed the vault clerks some mugs — Meadows was in there — and they couldn't make anybody."

"We could go back to them now with Franklin and Delgado, see if one of them was this Isley."

"Yeah. We will. I'll be right back."

She got up and left and Bosch went back to drinking coffee and studying the list. He read every name and address on the list, but nothing jogged his memory aside from the handful of names of celebrities, politicians and the like that had safe-deposit boxes. Bosch was going over the list a second time when Eleanor came back. She was carrying a piece of paper, which she slid onto his desk.

"I checked Rourke's office. He already sent most of the paperwork I turned in over to records. But the hypnosis memo was still in his in box, so he must not have seen it yet. I took it back. It's useless now and it might be better if he didn't see it."

Harry glanced at the memo and then folded the page and put it in his pocket.

"Frankly," she said, "I don't think any of the paper was out in the open long enough . . . I mean, I just don't see it. And Rourke . . . he's a technocrat, not a killer. Like they said about you at behavioral sciences, he wouldn't cross the line for money."

Bosch looked at her and found himself wanting to say something to please her, to get her back on his side. He could think of nothing and could not understand this new coldness in her manner.

"Forget it," he said, and then, looking down at the lists, he added, "How far did you people check out these people who reported no losses?"

She looked down at the printouts where Bosch had circled list B. There were nineteen names on the list.

"We ran each name for criminal records," she began. "We did a telephone interview and later a face-to-face. If an agent got weird vibes or somebody's story didn't play well, then another agent would come by unannounced to do a follow-up interview. Kind of get another opinion. I was not part of that. We had a second crew who handled most of the field interviews. If there is a particular name there that you are interested in, I could pull the interview summaries."

"What about the Vietnamese names on the lists? I count thirty-four box-holders with Vietnamese names, four are on the no-loss list, one on the dead-end list."

"What about the Vietnamese? There is also probably a breakout, if you look for it, on Chinese, Korean, whites, blacks and Latinos. These were equal opportunity bandits."

"Yeah, but you came up with a connection to Vietnam in Meadows. Now we have Franklin and Delgado, possibly involved. All three were MPs in Vietnam. We've got Charlie Company, which may or may not have a part in this. So, after Meadows became a suspect and you started pulling military records of tunnel rats, did you do any further checking with the Vietnamese on this list?"

"No — well, yes. On the foreign nationals we ran their names through INS to see how long they'd been here, whether they were legal. But that was about it." She was quiet a moment. "I can see what you are getting at. It's a flaw in the way we handled it. See, we didn't develop Meadows as a possible suspect until a few weeks after the robbery. By then most of these people had already been interviewed. After we started looking at Meadows, I don't think we went back to see if any of the names on the list fit in with him. You think one of the Vietnamese could have somehow been part of this?"

"I don't know what I'm thinking. Just looking for connections. Coincidences that aren't coincidences."

Bosch took a notebook out of his coat pocket and started making a list of the names, DOBs and addresses of the Vietnamese boxholders. He put the four who reported no loss and the name from the dead-end list at the top of his own list. He had just finished the list and closed the notebook when Rourke walked into the squad room, his hair still wet from his morning shower. He was carrying a coffee mug that said Boss on the side of it. He saw Bosch and Wish and then looked at his watch.

"Getting an early start?"

"Our witness, he turned up dead," Wish said, no expression on her face.

"Jesus. Where? They get somebody?"

Wish shook her head and looked at Bosch with a face that warned him not to start anything. Rourke looked at him also.

"Does it relate to this?" he said. "Any evidence of that?"

"We think so," Bosch said.

"Jesus!"

"You said that," Bosch said.

"Should we take the case from LAPD, add it to the Meadows investigation?" He said this looking directly at Wish. Bosch was not part of the decision-making team here. She didn't answer, so Rourke added, "Should we have offered him protection?"

Bosch couldn't resist. "From who?"

A strand of wet hair dropped out of place and across Rourke's forehead. His face flushed deeply red.

"What the hell is that supposed to mean?"

"How'd you know LAPD had the case?"

"What?"

"You just asked if we should take the case from LAPD. How'd you know they had it? We didn't say."

"I just assumed. Bosch, I resent what that implies and I resent the hell out of you. Are you implying that I or someone — If you are saying there is a law enforcement leak on this case, then I will request an internal review today. But I'll tell you right now that if there was a leak it wasn't from the bureau."

"Then where the hell else could it have been? What happened to the reports we filed with you? Who saw them?"

Rourke shook his head.

"Harry, don't be ridiculous. I understand your feelings, but let's calm down and think for a minute. The witness was snatched off the street and interviewed at Hollywood Station, then dropped off at a public youth shelter.

"And, lastly, you're being followed around by your own department, Detective. I'm sorry, but even your own people apparently don't trust you."

Bosch's face grew dark. He felt betrayed in a sense. Rourke could only have known about the tail through Wish. She had made Lewis and Clarke. Why hadn't she said anything to him instead of Rourke? Bosch looked over at her but she was looking down at her desk. He looked back at Rourke, who was nodding his head as if it were on a spring.

"Yes, she made the tail on you the first day." Rourke looked around the empty squad room, obviously wishing he had a larger audience. He was moving his weight from one foot to the other now, like a boxer in his corner impatiently waiting for the next round to begin so he could deliver the knockout punch on a fading opponent. Wish continued to sit silently at her desk. And in that moment it seemed to Bosch to be a million years ago that they had held each other in her bed. Rourke said, "Maybe you should look at yourself and your own department before running around making reckless accusations."

Bosch said nothing. He just stood up and headed to the door.

"Harry, where are you going?" Eleanor called from her desk.

He turned around and looked at her a moment, then he kept walking.

Lewis and Clarke picked up Bosch's Caprice as soon as it came out of the federal garage. Clarke was driving. Lewis dutifully noted the time on the surveillance log.

He said, "He's got a bug up his ass, better move up on him some."

Bosch had turned west on Wilshire and was heading for the 405. Clarke increased his speed to stay with him in the morning rush hour traffic.

"I'd have a bug somewhere if I'd just lost my only witness," Clarke said. "If I'd gotten him killed."

"How you figure?"

"You saw it. He stuffed the kid in that shelter and went his merry way. I don't know what that kid saw or what he told them, but it was important enough for him to have to be eliminated. Bosch shoulda taken better care. Kept him under lock and key."

They went south on the 405. Bosch was ten cars ahead, now staying in the slow lane. The freeway was thick with a stinking, polluting mass of moving steel.

"I think he's going for the 10," Clarke said. "He's going into Santa Monica. Maybe back to her place, probably forgot his toothbrush. Or she's coming back to meet him for a nooner. You know what I say? I say we let him go and we go back to talk to Irving. I think we can build something on this witness thing. Maybe dereliction of duty. There is enough to get an administrative hearing. He'd at least get bounced out of homicide, and if Harry Bosch ain't allowed to be on the homicide table then he'll pick up and leave. One more notch on our barrel."

Lewis thought about his partner's idea. It wasn't bad. It could work. But he didn't want to pull off the surveillance without Irving's say-so.

"Keep with him," he said. "When he stops somewhere, I'll drop a quarter and see what Irving wants to do. When he buzzed me this morning about the kid, he seemed pretty stoked. Like things were getting good. So I don't want to pull off without his say-so."

"Whatever. Anyway, how'd Irving know about the kid getting snuffed so fast?"

"I don't know. Watch it here. He's taking the 10."

They followed the gray Caprice onto the Santa Monica Freeway. They were now going away from the working city, against the grain, and were in lighter traffic. But Bosch no longer was speeding. And he went past the Clover Field and Lincoln exits to Eleanor Wish's home, staying on the freeway until it curved through the tunnel and came out below the beach cliffs as the Pacific Coast Highway. He headed north along the coast, with the sun bright overhead and the Malibu mountains just opaque whispers ahead in the haze.

"Now what?" Clarke said.

"I don't know. Hang back some."

There wasn't much traffic on the PCH and they were having trouble keeping at least one car between them and Bosch's car at all times. Though Lewis still believed that most cops never bothered to check if they were being followed, today he was making an exception to that theory with Bosch. His witness had been murdered; he might instinctively think someone had been following him, or still was.

"Yeah, just hang back. We got all day and so does he."

Bosch's pace held steady for the next four miles, until he turned into a parking lot next to Alice's and the Malibu pier. Lewis and Clarke cruised by. After a half mile Clarke made an illegal U-turn and headed back. When they pulled into the parking lot, Bosch's car was still there but they didn't see him.

"The restaurant again?" Clarke said. "He must love the place."

"It's not even open this early."

They both began looking around in all directions. There were four other cars at the end of the lot, and the racks on top of them said they belonged to the cluster of surfers rising and falling on the seas south of the pier. Finally, Lewis saw Bosch and pointed. He was halfway to the end of the pier, walking, with his head down and his hair blowing a hundred different ways. Lewis looked around for the camera and realized it was still in the trunk. He took a pair of binoculars out of the glove compartment and trained them on Bosch's diminishing figure. He watched until Bosch reached the end of the wooden planking and leaned his elbows on the railing.

"What's he doing?" Clarke asked. "Let me see."

"You're driving. I'm watching. He's not doing anything anyway. Just leaning there."

"He's got to be doing something."

"He's thinking. Okay? . . . There. He's lighting a cigarette. Happy? He's doing something. . . . Wait a minute."

"What?"

"Shit. We should've had the camera ready."

"What's this 'we' shit? That's your job today. I'm driving. What's he doing?"

"He dropped something. Into the water."

Through the field glasses Lewis saw Bosch's body leaning limply on the railing. He was looking down into the water below. There was no one else on the pier as far as Lewis could see.

"What did he drop? Can you see?"

"How the fuck do I know what he dropped? I can't see the surface from here. Do you want for me to go out there and get one of the surfer boys to paddle over and see for us? I don't know what he dropped."

"Cool your jets. I was just asking. Now, can you remember the color of this object he dropped?"

"It looked white, like a ball. But it sort of floated."

"I thought you said you couldn't see the surface."

"I meant it floated down. I think it was a tissue or some kind of paper."

"What's he doing now?"

"Just standing there at the railing. He's looking down into the water."

"Crisis of conscience time. Maybe he'll jump and we can forget this whole damned thing."

Clarke giggled at his feeble joke. Lewis didn't.

"Yeah, right. I'm sure that's going to happen."

"Give me the glasses and go call in. See what Irving wants to do."

Lewis handed over the binoculars and got out. First, he went to the trunk, opened it and got out the Nikon. He attached a long lens and then took it around to the driver's window and handed it to Clarke.

"Get a picture of him out there, so we'll have something to show Irving."

Then Lewis trotted over to the restaurant to find a phone. He was back in less than three minutes. Bosch was still leaning on the rail at the end of the pier.

"Chief says under no circumstances are we to break off the tail," Lewis said. "He also said our reports sucked ass. He wants more detail, and more pictures. Did you get him?"

Clarke was too busy watching through the camera to answer. Lewis picked up the binoculars and looked. Bosch remained unmoving. Lewis couldn't figure it. What is he doing? Thinking? Why come all the way out here to think?

"Fucking Irving, that figures," Clarke suddenly said, dropping the camera into his lap to look at his partner. "And yeah, I got a few pictures of him. Enough to make Irving happy. But he's not doing anything. Just leaning there."

"Not anymore," Lewis said, still looking through the binoculars. "Start her up. It's showtime."

Bosch walked off the pier after dropping the crumpled hypnotism memo into the water. Like a flower cast on a spoiled sea, it held its own on the surface for a few brief moments and then sank out of sight. His resolve to find Meadows's killer was now stronger: now he sought justice for Sharkey as well. As he made his way on the old planking of the pier he saw the Plymouth that had been following him pull out of the restaurant lot. It's them, he thought. But no matter. He didn't care what they had seen, or thought they had seen. There were new rules now, and Bosch had plans for Lewis and Clarke.

He drove east on the 10 into downtown. He never bothered to check his mirror for the black car because he knew it would be there. He wanted it to be there.

When he got to Los Angeles Street, he parked in a no-parking zone in front of the U.S. Administration Building. On the third floor Bosch walked through one of the crowded waiting rooms of the Immigration and Naturalization Service. The place smelled like a jail — sweat, fear and desperation. A bored woman was sitting behind a sliding glass window working on the *Times* crossword. The window was closed. On the sill was a plastic paper-ticket dispenser like they use at a meat-market counter. After a few moments she looked up at Bosch. He was holding his badge up.

"Do you know a six-letter word for a man of constant sorrow and loneliness?" she asked after sliding the window open and then checking her nail for damage.

"Bosch."

"What?"

"Detective Harry Bosch. Buzz me in. I want to see Hector V."

"Have to check first," she said in a pouty way. She whispered something into the phone, then reached to Bosch's badge case and put her finger on the name on the ID card. Then she hung up.

"He says go on back." She buzzed the lock on the door next to the window. "He says you know the way."

Bosch shook Hector Villabona's hand in a cramped squad room much smaller than Bosch's own.

"I need a favor. I need some computer time."

"Let's do it."

That's what Bosch liked about Hector V. He never asked what or why before deciding. He was a let's-do-it type of guy. He didn't play bullshit games that Bosch had come to believe everybody in his profession played. Hector rolled his chair over to an IBM on a desk against the wall and entered his password. "You want to run names, right? How many?"

Bosch wasn't going to bullshit him, either. He showed him the list of thirty-four names. Hector whistled lowly and said, "Okay, we'll run them through, but these are Vietnamese. If their cases were not worked out of this office their files won't be here. I'll only have what's on the computer. Dates of entry, documentation, citizenship, whatever is on the computer. You know how it is, Harry."

Bosch did. But he also knew that Southern California was where most of the Vietnamese refugees made their homes after making the trip. Hector started typing in the names with two fingers, and twenty minutes later Bosch was looking at a printout from the computer.

"What are we looking for, Harry?" Hector said as he studied the list with him.

"I don't know. What do you see that is unusual?"

A few moments passed and Bosch thought Hector would say nothing was unusual. A dead end. But Bosch was wrong.

"Okay, on this one I think you will find he was connected."

The name was Ngo Van Binh. It meant nothing to Bosch other than it had come from the B list; Binh had reported nothing stolen from his safe-deposit box.

"Connected?"

"He had some kind of pull," Hector said. "Connected politically, I guess you would call it. See, his case number has the prefix GL. Those are files handled by our special cases bureau in D.C. Usually, SCB doesn't deal with people from the masses. Very political. Handles people like the shah and the Marcoses, Russian defectors if they are scientists or ballerinas. Stuff like that. Stuff I never see."

He nodded his head and put his finger on the printout.

"Okay, then we have the dates, they are too close. It happened too fast, which tells me this case was greased. I don't know this guy from Adam, but I know this guy knew people. Look at the date of entry, May 4, 1975. That's just four days after the guy left Vietnam. You figure the first day is getting to Manila and the last day is getting to the States. That leaves only two days in between in Manila for him to get approval and get his ticket punched for the mainland. And at that time, I mean, man, they were coming in by the boat-load to Manila. No way in two days unless it was greased. So what that means is this guy, this Binh, already had approval. He was connected. It's not that unusual, because a lot of people were. We got a lot of people out of there when the shit hit the fan. A lot of them were the elite. A lot of them just had money to pay to make them elite."

Bosch looked at the date Binh had left Vietnam. April 30, 1975. The same day Meadows left Vietnam for the last time. The day Saigon fell to the North Army.

"And this DOD?" Villabona said, pointing at another date. "Very short time to receive documentation. May 14. That's ten days after arrival this guy gets a visa. That's too fast for the average Joe. Or in this case, the average Ngo."

"So what do you think?"

"Hard to say. He could have been an operative. He could've just had enough money to get him on a helicopter. Lotta rumors still floating around from that time. People getting rich. Seats on military transports going for ten grand. No question visas going for more. Nothing ever confirmed."

"Can you pull the file on this guy?"

"Yeah. If I was in D.C."

Bosch just looked at him, and Hector finally said, "All GLs are there, Harry. That's where the people that people are connected to are. Get it?"

Bosch didn't say anything.

"Don't get mad, Harry. I'll see what I can do. I'll make a couple calls. You going to be around later?"

Bosch gave him the FBI's number but didn't say it was the FBI. Then they shook hands again and Bosch left. In the first-floor lobby he watched through the smoked-glass doors, looking for Lewis and Clarke. When he finally saw the black Plymouth turn the corner as the two IAD detectives finished another circuit of the block, Bosch walked through the doors and down the steps to his car. In his peripheral vision he saw the IAD car slow and turn into the curb while they waited for him to get in his car and drive off.

Bosch did as they wanted. Because it was what he wanted.

Woodrow Wilson Drive winds counterclockwise around and up the side of the Hollywood Hills, the cracked, patchwork asphalt never wide enough at any point for two cars to pass without a cautious slowing. Going up, the homes on the left crawl vertically up the hillside. They are the old money, solid and secure. Spanish tile and stucco. To the right, the newer houses fearlessly swing their wood frame rooms out over the brown brush arroyos and daisies in the canyon. They are balanced on stilts and hope and cling as tenuously to the edge of the hill as their owners do to their positions at the studios down below. Bosch's home was fourth from the end on the right side.

As he drove around the final bend, the house came into sight. He looked at the dark wood, the shoebox design, seeking a sign that it had somehow changed — as if the exterior of the house could tell him if something was wrong with the interior. He checked the rearview then and caught the front end of the black Plymouth nosing around the curve. Bosch pulled into the carport next to his house and got out. He went inside without looking back at the tail car.

He had gone to the pier to think about what Rourke had said. And in doing so he thought about the hang-up call that was on his phone tape. Now, he went to the kitchen and played back his messages. First there was the hang-up call, which had come in Tuesday, and then a message from Jerry Edgar in the predawn hours today, when Edgar had called looking for Bosch to get him out to the Hollywood Bowl. Bosch rewound the tape and listened to the hang-up call again, silently chastising himself for not having picked up on its significance the first time he heard it. Someone had called, listened to his taped message and then hung up after the first message beep. The hang-up was on the tape. Most people, if they didn't want to leave a message, would simply hang up as soon as they heard Bosch's tape-recorded voice saying he wasn't in. Or, if they thought he was home, would have called out his name after the beep. But this caller had listened to the tape and then didn't hang up until after the beep. Why? Bosch had missed it at first, but now thought the call had been a transmitter test.

He went to the closet by the door and took out a pair of binoculars. He went to the living room window and looked through a crack in the curtain for the black Plymouth. It was a half-block farther up the hill. Lewis and Clarke had driven by the house, turned around and parked at the curb, facing downhill and ready to continue the tail if Bosch came out. Through the binoculars Bosch could see Lewis behind the wheel, watching the house.

Clarke had his head back on the passenger seat and his eyes closed. Neither of them appeared to be wearing earphones. Still, Harry had to be sure. Without taking his eyes from the binoculars, he reached over to the front door and opened it a few inches and closed it. The men in the IAD car showed no reaction, no alert. Clarke's eyes remained closed. Lewis continued picking his teeth with a business card.

Bosch decided that if they had dropped a bug on him, it was transmitting to a remote. It was safer that way. Probably a sound-activated minireel hidden on the exterior of the house. They'd wait until he drove away and then one of them would jump out of the car and quickly collect the reel, replacing it with a fresh one. They could then catch up the tail on him before he got down the hill to the freeway. He walked away from the window and made a quick survey of the living room and kitchen. He studied the underside of tables and electric fixtures but he didn't find the bug and didn't expect to. The smart place, he knew, was the phone, which he was saving for last. It had a ready power source, and placement there would provide sound intake of the immediate interior of the house as well as any conversations that came in through the phone.

Bosch picked up the phone and with a small penknife that was attached to his key chain he popped the cover off the mouthpiece. There was nothing there that shouldn't be. Then he took the cover off the earpiece. It was there. Using the knife he carefully lifted out the speaker. Attached behind it by a small magnet was a small, flat, round transmitter about the size of a quarter. There were two wires attached to the device, which, he knew, was sound activated and called a T-9. One wire was wrapped around one of the phone's receiver wires, piggybacking power for the bug. The other wire went into the barrel of the handset. Bosch gingerly pulled it, and out came the backup energy source: a small, thin power pack containing a single AA battery. The bug ran off the phone's juice, but if the phone was disconnected from the wall, the battery could provide power for maybe another eight hours. Bosch disconnected the device from the phone and placed it on the table. It was now running off the battery. He just stared at it, thinking about what he was going to do. It was a standard police department wire. Pickup range, fifteen to twenty feet, designed to take in everything said in the room. The transmission range was minimal, maybe twenty-five yards at most, depending on how much metal was in the building.

Bosch went to the living room window again to look up the street. Lewis and Clarke still showed no sign of alert or that the bug had been discovered. Lewis was through picking his teeth.

Bosch turned on the stereo and put on a Wayne Shorter CD. He then went out a side door in the kitchen into the carport. He could not be seen from the IAD car. He found the tape recorder in the first place he looked; the junction box beneath the DWP electric meter on the back wall of the carport. The two-inch reels were turning to the sound of Shorter's saxophone. The

Nagra recorder, like the T-9, was wired to the house current but had a battery backup. Bosch disconnected it and brought it inside, where he set it on the table next to its counterpart.

Shorter was finishing "502 Blues." Bosch sat in the watch chair, lit a cigarette and looked at the device as he tried to form a plan. He reached over, rewound the tape and pushed the play button. The first thing he heard was his own voice saying he wasn't there, then Jerry Edgar's message about the Hollywood Bowl. Then the next sounds were the door opening and closing twice, then Wayne Shorter's sax. They had changed reels at least once since the test call had been made. Then he realized that Eleanor Wish's visit had been taped. He thought about that and wondered if the bug had picked up what had been said on the back porch. Bosch's stories about himself and Meadows. He grew angry thinking about the intrusion, the delicate moment stolen by the two men in the black Plymouth.

He shaved, showered and dressed in a fresh set of clothes, a tan summer suit with pink oxford shirt and blue tie. Then he went to the living room and loaded the bug and recorder into the pockets of his jacket. He took another look through the curtains with the field glasses: still no movement in the Internal Affairs car. He went out the side door again and carefully climbed down the embankment to the base of the first stilt, an iron I beam. He gingerly made his way across the incline beneath his house. He noticed along the way that the dried brush was sprinkled with pieces of gold foil, the beer label he had picked at and dropped from the porch when he was with Eleanor.

Once he got to the other side of his property, he picked his way across the hill, going under the next three stilt houses. After the third, he scrambled up the hillside and looked around the front corner into the street. He was now behind the black Plymouth. He picked the burrs off the cuffs of his pants and then walked casually into the road.

Bosch came up unnoticed on the passenger-side door. The window was down and just before he flung the door open he thought he could hear snoring coming from the car.

Clarke's mouth was open and his eyes still shut when Bosch leaned in through the open door and grabbed both men by their silk ties. Bosch put his right foot on the doorsill for leverage and pulled both men toward him. Though there were two of them, the advantage belonged to Bosch. Clarke was disoriented and Lewis had little more idea what was happening. Pulling them by their ties meant that any struggle or resistance tightened the ties around their necks, cutting off their air. They came out almost willingly, tumbling like dogs on leashes and landing next to a palm tree planted three feet from the sidewalk. Their faces were red and sputtering. Their hands went to their necks, clawing at the knots of their ties as they fought to get air back into their pipes. Bosch's hands went to their belts and yanked away the handcuffs. As the two IAD detectives were gulping air through their reopened throats Bosch managed to cuff Lewis's left hand to Clarke's right. Then, on the other side of the tree, he got Lewis's right into the other set of cuffs. But Clarke realized what Bosch was doing and tried to stand up and pull away. Bosch grabbed his tie again and gave it a sharp yank down. Clarke's head came forward and his face rammed the palm tree. He was momentarily stunned and Bosch slapped the last cuff on his wrist. Both IAD cops were wallowing on the ground then, locked to each other with the palm tree in the middle of the circle of their arms. Bosch unholstered their weapons, then stepped back to catch his own breath. He threw their guns onto the front seat of their car.

"You're dead," Clarke finally managed to croak through his swollen throat.

They worked their way up into standing positions, the palm tree between them. They looked like two grown men caught playing ring-around-the-rosy.

"Assaulting a fellow officer, two counts," Lewis said. "Conduct unbecoming. We can get you for a half-dozen other things now, Bosch." He coughed violently, spittle hitting Clarke's suit coat. "Unhook us and maybe we can forget this."

"No way. We aren't forgetting a fucking thing," Clarke said to his partner. "He's going down like a flaming asshole."

Bosch took the listening device out of his pocket and held it out on his palm for them to see. "Who's going down?" he asked.

Lewis looked at the bug, recognizing what it was, and said, "We don't know anything about that."

"Course not," Bosch said. He took the recorder out of his other pocket and held that out, too. "Sound-sensitive Nagras, that's what you guys use on all your jobs, legal or not, isn't it? Found it in my phone. Same time I notice that you two dummies have been following me all over the city. Don't suppose you guys also dropped the bug on me so you could listen as well as watch?"

Neither Lewis nor Clarke answered and Bosch didn't expect them to. He noticed a small drop of blood poised at the edge of one of Clarke's nostrils. A car driving on Woodrow Wilson slowed and Bosch pulled his badge and held it up. The car kept going. The two IAD detectives did not call for help, which made Bosch begin to feel he was safe. This would be his play. The department had taken such bad publicity for illegally bugging officers, civil rights leaders, even movie stars in the past, that these two were not going to make an issue of this. Saving their own hides came before skinning Bosch.

"You got a warrant saying you can drop a bug on me?"

"Listen to me, Bosch," Lewis said. "I told you, we —"

"I didn't think so. Have to have evidence of a crime to get a warrant. Least that's what I always heard. But Internal Affairs doesn't usually bother with details like that. You know what your assault case looks like, Clarke? While you two are taking me to the Board of Rights and getting me fired for dragging you out of the car and getting grass stains on your shiny asses, I'm going to be taking you two, your boss Irving, IAD, the police chief and the whole fucking city to federal court on a Fourth Amendment case. Illegal search and seizure. I'll throw in the mayor, too. How's that?"

Clarke spit on the grass at Bosch's feet. A drop of blood from his nose fell onto his white shirt. He said, "You can't prove that came from us, 'cause it didn't."

"Bosch, what do you want?" Lewis blurted out, his rage turning his face a darker red than it had been when his tie had been tightened like a noose around his neck. Bosch started walking in a slow circle around them, so they had to constantly turn their heads or bend around the palm trunk to watch him.

"What do I want? Well, as much as I despise you two, I don't really want to have to drag your asses into court. Dragging them across the sidewalk was enough. What I want —"

"Bosch, you ought to get your fuckin' head examined," Clarke burst out.

"Shut up, Clarke," Lewis said.

"You shut up," Clarke said back.

"Matter of fact, I have had it examined," Bosch said. "And I still would rather have mine than yours. You'd need a proctologist to check yours out."

He said this as he circled close behind Clarke. Then he moved out a few steps and continued to make the rounds. "I'll tell you what, I'm willing to let bygones be bygones on this. All you have to do is answer a few questions and we're square on this little mix-up. I'll cut you loose. After all, we're all part of the Family, right?"

"What questions, Bosch?" Lewis said. "What are you talking about?"

"When'd you start the tail?"

"Tuesday morning, we picked you up when you left the FBI," Lewis said.

"Don't tell him shit, man," Clarke said to his partner.

"He already knows."

Clarke looked at Lewis and shook his head like he couldn't believe what he was hearing.

"When'd you drop the bug in my phone?"

"Didn't," Lewis said.

"Bullshit. But never mind. You saw me interview the kid down in Boytown." It was a statement, not a question. Bosch wanted them to think he knew most of it and just needed the gaps filled in.

"Yeah," Lewis said. "That was our first day on it. So you made us. So fucking what?"

Harry saw Lewis pull his hand toward his coat pocket. He quickly moved in and got his hand in first. He pulled out a key ring that included a cuff key. He threw the keys into the car. Behind Lewis, he said, "Who'd you tell about it?"

"Tell?" Lewis said. "About the kid? Nobody. We didn't tell anybody, Bosch."

"You write up a daily surveillance log, don't you? You take pictures, don't you? I bet there's a camera in the backseat of that car. Unless you forgot and left it in the trunk."

"Course we do."

Bosch lit a cigarette and started walking again. "Where did it all go?"

It was a few moments before Lewis answered. Bosch saw him make eye contact with Clarke. "We turned in the first log and the film yesterday. Put it in the deputy chief's box. Like always. Don't even know if he looked at it yet. That's the only paper we've done so far. So, Bosch, take these cuffs off. This is embarrassing. People seein' us and all. We can still talk after."

Bosch walked up between them and blew smoke into the center of the huddle and told them the cuffs stayed on until the conversation was over. He then leaned close to Clarke's face and said, "Who else was copied?"

"With the surveillance report? Nobody was copied, Bosch," Lewis said. "That would violate department procedure."

Bosch laughed at that, shook his head. He knew they would not admit any illegality or violation of department policy. He started to walk away, back to his house.

"Wait a minute, wait a minute, Bosch," Lewis called out. "We copied the report to your lieutenant. All right? Come on back."

Bosch did and Lewis continued. "He wanted to be kept apprised. We had to do it. The DC, Irving, okayed it. We did what we were told."

"What did the report say about the kid?"

"Nothing. Just some kid is all. . . . Uh, 'Subject engaged juvenile in conversation. Juvenile was transported to Hollywood Station for formal interview,' something like that."

"Did you ID him in the report?"

"No name. We didn't even know his name. Honest, Bosch. We just watched you, that's all. Now uncuff us."

"What about Home Street Home? You watched me take him there. Was that in the report?"

"Yeah, on the log."

Bosch moved in close again. "Now here's the big question. If there is no complaint from the bureau anymore, why is IAD still on me? The FBI made the call to Pounds and withdrew the complaint. Then you guys act like you were called off but you weren't. Why?"

Lewis started to say something but Bosch cut him off. "I want Clarke to tell me. You're thinking too fast, Lewis."

Clarke didn't say a word.

"Clarke, the kid you saw me with ended up dead. Somebody did him because he talked to me. And the only people who knew he talked to me were you and your partner here. Something is going on here, and if I don't get the answers I need I'm just going to lay it all out, go public with it. You are going to find your own ass being investigated by Internal Affairs."

Clarke said his first two words in five minutes: "Fuck you."

Lewis jumped in then.

"Look, Bosch, I'll tell you. The FBI doesn't trust you. That's the thing. They said they brought you into the case, but they told us they weren't sure about you. They said you muscled onto the case and they were going to have to watch you, make sure you weren't pulling a scam. That's all. So we were told to drop back but stay on you. We did. That's all, man. Now cut us loose. I can hardly breathe, and my wrists are starting to hurt with these cuffs. You really put them on tight."

Bosch turned to Clarke. "Where's your cuff key?"

"Right front pocket," he said. He was cool about it, refusing to look at Bosch's face. Bosch walked around behind him and reached both hands around his waist. He pulled a key ring out of Clarke's pocket and then whispered in his ear, "Clarke, you ever go in my home again and I'll kill you."

Then he yanked the detective's pants and boxer shorts down to his ankles and started walking away. He threw the key ring into the car.

"You bastard!" Clarke yelled. "I'll kill you first, Bosch."

As long as he kept the bug and the Nagra, Bosch was reasonably certain Lewis and Clarke would not seek departmental charges against him. They had more to lose than he. A lawsuit and public scandal would cut their careers off at the stairway to the sixth floor. Bosch got in his car and drove back to the Federal Building.

Too many people knew about Sharkey or had the opportunity to know, he realized as he tried to assess the situation. There was no clear-cut way of flushing out the inside man. Lewis and Clarke had seen the boy and passed the information on to Irving and Pounds and who knew who else. Rourke and the FBI records clerk knew about him as well. And those names didn't even include the people on the street who might have seen Sharkey with Bosch, or had heard that Bosch was looking for him. Bosch knew that he would have to wait for things to develop.

At the Federal Building, the red-haired receptionist behind the glass window on the FBI floor made him wait while she called back to Group 3. He checked the cemetery again through the gauze curtains and saw several people working in the trench cut in the hill. They were lining the earth wound with blocks of black stone that reflected sharp white light points in the sun. And Bosch at last believed he knew what it was they were doing. The door lock buzzed behind him and Bosch headed back. It was twelve-thirty and the heavy squad was out, except for Eleanor Wish. She sat at her desk eating an egg salad sandwich, the kind they sold in plastic triangle-shaped boxes at every government building cafeteria he'd ever been in. The plastic bottle of water and a paper cup were on the desk. They exchanged small hellos. Bosch felt that things had changed between them, but he didn't know how much.

"You been here since this morning?" he asked.

She said she hadn't. She told him that she had taken the mugs of Franklin and Delgado to the vault clerks at WestLand National and one of the women positively identified Franklin as Frederic B. Isley, the holder of a box in the vault. The scout.

"It's enough for a warrant, but Franklin isn't around," she said. "Rourke sent a couple crews to the addresses DMV had on both him and Delgado. Called back in a little while ago. Either they've moved on or never lived in the places in the first place. Looks like they're in the wind."

"So, what's next?"

"I don't know. Rourke's talking about closing shop on it until we catch them. You'll probably get to go back to your homicide table. When we catch one of them, we'll bring you down to work on him about the Meadows murder."

"Sharkey's murder, too. Don't forget that."

"That, too."

Bosch nodded. It was over. The bureau was going to close it down.

"By the way, you got a message," she said. "Someone called for you, said his name was Hector. That was all."

Bosch sat down at the desk next to hers and dialed Hector Villabona's direct line. He picked up after two rings.

"It's Bosch."

"Hey, what're you doing with the bureau?" he asked. "I called the number you gave and somebody said it was the FBI."

"Yeah, it's a long story. I'll tell you later. Did you come up with anything?"

"Not much, Harry, and I'm not going to, either. I can't get the file. This guy Binh, whoever he is, he has got some connections. Like we figured. His file is still classified. I called a guy I know out there and asked him to send it out. He called me back and said no can do."

"Why would it still be classified?"

"Who knows, Harry? That's why it's still classified. So people won't find this shit out."

"Well, thanks. It's not looking that important anymore."

"If you have a source at State, somebody with access, they might have better luck than me. I'm just the token beaner in the bean-counting department. But, listen, there is one thing this guy I know kind of let slip."

"What?"

"Well, see, I gave him Binh's name, you know, and when he calls back he says, 'Sorry, Captain Binh's file is classified.' Just like that is how he said it. Captain, he called him. So this guy musta been a military guy. That's probably why they got him out of there and over here so fast. If he was military, they saved his ass for sure."

"Yeah," Bosch said, then he thanked Hector and hung up.

He turned to Eleanor and asked if she had any contacts in the State Department. She shook her head no. "Military intelligence, CIA, anything like that?" Bosch said. "Somebody with access to computer files."

She thought a moment and said, "Well, there is a guy on the State floor. I sort of know him from D.C. But what's going on, Harry?"

"Can you call him and tell him you need a favor?"

"He doesn't talk on the phone, not about business. We'll just have to go down there."

He stood up. Outside the office, while they waited for the elevator, Bosch told her about Binh, his rank, and the fact that he left Vietnam on the same day as Meadows. The elevator opened and they got on and she pushed seven. They were alone.

"You knew all along, that I was being tailed," Bosch said. "Internal Affairs."

"I saw them."

"But you knew before you saw them, didn't you?"

"Does it make a difference?"

"I think it does. Why didn't you tell me?"

She took a while. The elevator stopped.

"I don't know," she said. "I'm sorry. I didn't at first, and then when I wanted to tell you I couldn't. I thought it would spoil everything. I guess it did, anyway."

"Why didn't you at first, Eleanor? Because there was still a question about me?"

She looked into the stainless steel corner of the elevator. "In the beginning, yes, we weren't sure about you. I won't lie about that."

"What about after the beginning?"

The door opened on the seventh floor. Eleanor moved through it, saying, "You're still here, aren't you?"

Bosch stepped out after her. He took hold of her arm and stopped her. They stood there as two men in almost matching gray suits charged through the open elevator door.

"Yes, I'm still here, but you didn't tell me about them."

"Harry, can we talk about this later?"

"The thing is, they saw us with Sharkey."

"Yes, I thought so."

"Well, why didn't you say anything when I was talking about the inside man, when I was asking about who you told about the kid?"

"I don't know."

Bosch looked down at his feet. He felt like the only man on the planet who didn't understand what was going on.

"I talked to them," he said. "They claim they just watched us with the kid. They never followed up to see what it was about. Said they didn't have his ID. Sharkey's name wasn't in their reports."

"And do you believe them?"

"Never have before. But I don't see them involved in this. It just doesn't fit. They're just after me and they'll do anything to get me. But not take out a witness. That's crazy."

"Maybe they're feeding information to someone who is involved and they just don't realize it."

Bosch thought about Irving and Pounds again.

"A possibility. The point is, there is an inside man. Somewhere. We know this. And it might be from my side. It might be yours. So we have to be very careful, about who we talk to and what we're doing."

After a moment he looked straight into her eyes and said, "Do you believe me?"

It took her a long time, but she finally nodded her head. She said, "I can't think of any other way to explain what's happening."

Eleanor went up to a receptionist while Bosch hung back a bit. After a few minutes a young woman came out from a closed door and showed them down a couple of hallways and into a small office. No one was sitting behind the desk. They sat in two chairs facing the desk and waited.

"Who is this we're seeing?" Bosch whispered.

"I'll introduce you, and he can tell you what he wants you to know about him," she said.

Bosch was about to ask her what that meant when the door opened and a man strode in. He looked to be about fifty, with silvery hair that was carefully groomed and a strong build beneath the blue blazer. The man's gray eyes were as dull as day-old barbecue coals. He sat down and did not look at Bosch. He kept his eyes exclusively on Eleanor Wish.

"Ellie, good to see you again," he said. "How are you doing?"

She said she was doing fine, exchanged a few pleasantries and then got around to introducing Bosch. The man got up and reached across the desk to shake hands.

"Bob Ernst, assistant deputy, trade and development, nice to meet you. So this is an official visit then, not just dropping by to see an old friend?"

"Yes, I'm sorry, Bob, but we are working on something and need some help."

"Whatever I can do, Ellie," Ernst said. He was annoying Bosch, and Bosch had only known him a minute.

"Bob, we need to background somebody whose name has come up on a case we are working," Wish said. "I think you are in a position that you could get that information for us without a great deal of inconvenience or time."

"That's our problem," Bosch added. "It's a homicide case. We don't have a lot of time to go through normal channels. To wait for things from Washington."

"Foreign national?"

"Vietnamese," Bosch said.

"Came here when?"

"May 4, 1975."

"Ah, right after the fall. I see. Tell me, what kind of homicide would the FBI and the LAPD be working on together that involves such ancient history, and history in another country as well?"

"Bob," Eleanor began, "I think —"

"No, don't answer that," Ernst yelped. "I think you are right. It would be best if we compartmentalized the information."

Ernst went through the motions of straightening his blotter and the knickknacks on his desk. Nothing was really out of order to begin with.

"How soon you need the information?" he finally said.

"Now," Eleanor said.

"We'll wait," Harry said.

"You realize, of course, I may not come up with anything, especially on short notice?"

"Of course," Eleanor said.

"Give me the name."

Ernst slid a piece of paper across his blotter. Eleanor wrote Binh's name on it and slid it back. Ernst looked at it a moment and got up without ever touching the paper.

"I'll see what I can do," he said and left the room.

Bosch looked at Eleanor.

"'Ellie'?"

"Please, I don't allow anybody to call me that. That's why I don't take his calls and don't return them."

"You mean until now. You'll owe him now."

"If he finds something. And so will you."

"I guess I'll have to let him call me Ellie."

She didn't smile.

"How'd you meet this guy, anyway?"

She didn't answer.

Bosch said, "He's probably listening to us right now."

He looked around the room, though obviously any listening devices would be hidden. He took out his cigarettes when he saw a black ashtray on the desk.

"Please, don't smoke," Eleanor said.

"Just a half."

"I met him once when we were both in Washington. I don't even remember what for now. He was assistant something-or-other with State back then, too. We had a couple of drinks. That's all. Sometime after that, he transferred out here. When he saw me in the elevator here and found out I was transferred, he started calling."

"CIA all the way, right? Or something close."

"More or less. I think. It doesn't matter if he gets what we need."

"More or less. I knew shitheads like him in the war. No matter how much he tells us today, there will be something more. Guys like that, information is their currency. They never give up everything. Like he said, they compartmentalize everything. They'll get you killed before they tell it all."

"Can we stop talking now?"

"Sure . . . Ellie."

Bosch passed the time smoking and looking at the empty walls. The guy didn't make much of an effort to make it look like a real office. No flag in the corner. Not even a picture of the president. Ernst was back in twenty minutes, and by then Bosch was on his second half-cigarette. As the assistant deputy for trade and development strode to his desk empty-handed, he said, "Detective, would you mind not smoking? I find it very bothersome in a closed room like this."

Bosch stubbed the butt out in the small black bowl on the corner of his desk.

"Sorry," he said. "I saw the ashtray. I thought —"

"It's not an ashtray, Detective," Ernst said in a somber tone. "That is a rice bowl, three centuries old. I brought it home with me after my stationing in Vietnam."

"You were working on trade and development then, too?"

"Excuse me, Bob, did you find anything?" Eleanor interjected. "On the name?"

It took Ernst a long moment to break his stare away from Bosch.

"I found very little, but what I did find may be useful. This man, Binh, is a former Saigon police officer. A captain. . . . Bosch, are you a veteran of the altercation?"

"You mean the war? Yes."

"Of course you are," Ernst said. "Then tell me, does this information mean anything to you?"

"Not a lot. I was in the bush most of my time. Didn't see much of Saigon except the Yankee bars and tattoo parlors. The guy was a police captain, should it mean something to me?"

"I suppose not. So let me tell you. As a captain, Binh ran the police department's vice unit."

Bosch thought about that and said, "Okay, he was probably as corrupt as everything else that went with that war."

"I don't suppose, coming from in the bush, you know much about the system, the way things worked in Saigon?" Ernst asked.

"Why don't you tell us about it? Sounds like that was your department. Mine was just trying to keep alive."

Ernst ignored the shot. He chose to ignore Bosch as well. He looked only at Eleanor as he spoke.

"It operated quite simply, really," he said. "If you dealt in substances, in flesh, gambling, anything on the black market, you were required to pay a local tariff, a tithe to the house, so to speak. That payment kept the local police away. It practically guaranteed your business would not be interrupted — within certain bounds. Your only worry then was the U.S. military police. Of course, they could be paid off as well, I suppose. There was always that rumor. Anyway, this system went on for years, from the very beginning until after the American withdrawal, until, I imagine, April 30, 1975, the day Saigon fell."

Eleanor nodded and waited for him to go on.

"The major American military involvement lasted longer than a decade, before that there was the French. We are talking many, many years of foreign intervention."

"Millions," Bosch said.

"What's that?"

"You are talking about millions of dollars in payoffs."

"Yes, absolutely. Tens of millions when added up over the years."

"And where does Captain Binh fit in?" Eleanor asked.

"You see," Ernst said, "our information at the time was that the corruption within the Saigon police department was orchestrated or controlled by a triad called the Devil's Three. You paid them or you did not do business. It was that simple.

"Coincidentally, or rather not coincidentally, the Saigon police had three captains whose domain corresponded, so to speak, quite nicely with the domain of the triad. One captain in charge of vice. One narcotics. One for patrol. Our information is that these three captains were, in fact, the triad."

"You keep saying 'Our information.' Is that trade and development's information? Where are you getting this?"

Ernst made a movement to straighten things on the top of his desk again and then stared coldly at Bosch. "Detective, you come to me for information. If you want to know where the source is, then you have made a mistake. You've come to the wrong person. You can believe what I tell you or not. It is of no consequence to me."

The two men locked eyes but said nothing else.

"What happened to them?" Eleanor asked. "The members of the triad."

Ernst pulled his eyes away from Bosch and said, "What happened is that after the United States pulled military forces in 1973 the triad's source of revenue was largely gone. But like any responsible business entity they saw it coming and looked to replace it. And our intelligence at the time was that they shifted their position considerably. In the early seventies they moved from the role of providing protection to narcotics operations in Saigon to actually becoming part of those operations. Through political and military contacts and, of course, police enforcement they solidified themselves as the brokers for all brown heroin that came out of the highlands and was moved to the United States."

"But it didn't last," Bosch said.

"Oh, no. Of course not. When Saigon fell in April 1975, they had to get out. They had made millions, an estimated fifteen to eighteen million American dollars each. It would mean nothing in the new Ho Chi Minh City and they wouldn't be alive to enjoy it anyway. The triad had to get out or they'd face the firing squads of the North Vietnamese Army. And they had to get out with their money. . . ."

"So, how'd they do it?" Bosch said.

"It was dirty money. Money that no Vietnamese police captain could or should have. I suppose they could have wired it to Zurich, but you have to remember you are dealing with the Vietnamese culture. Born of turmoil and distrust. War. These people did not even trust banks in their homeland. And besides it wasn't money anymore."

"What?" Eleanor said, puzzled.

"They had been converting all along. Do you know what eighteen million dollars looks like? Would probably fill a room. So they found a way to shrink it. At least, that's what we believe."

"Precious gems," Bosch said.

"Diamonds," Ernst said. "It is said eighteen million dollars' worth of the right diamonds would easily fit in two shoe boxes."

"And into a safe-deposit box," Bosch said.

"That could be, but, please, I don't want to know what I don't need to know."

"Binh was one of the captains," Bosch said. "Who were the other two?"

"I am told one of them was named Van Nguyen. And he is believed to be dead. He never left Vietnam. Killed by the other two, or maybe the North Vietnamese Army. But he never got out. That was confirmed by our agents in Ho Chi Minh after the fall. The other two did. They came here. And both had passes, arranged through connections and money, I suppose. I can't help you there. . . . There was Binh, who it seems you have found, and the other was Nguyen Tran. He came with Binh. Where they went and what they did here, I can't help you with. It's been fifteen years. Once they came across they were no longer our concern."

"Why would you allow them to come across?"

"Who says we did? You have to realize, Detective Bosch, that much of this information was put together after the fact."

Ernst stood up then. That was all the information he would decompartmentalize for today.

Bosch didn't want to go back up to the bureau. The information from Ernst was amphetamine in his blood. He wanted to walk. He wanted to talk, to storm. When they got in the elevator he pushed the button for the lobby and told Eleanor they were going outside. The bureau was like a fishbowl. He wanted a big room.

In any investigation, it had always seemed to Bosch, information would come slowly, like sand dropping steadily through the cinched middle of an hourglass. At some point, there was more information in the bottom of the glass. And then the sand in the top seemed to drop faster, until it was cascading through the hole. They were at that point with Meadows, the bank burglary, the whole thing. Things were coming together.

They went out through the front lobby and onto the green lawn where there were eight U.S. flags and a California state flag flapping lazily on poles posted in a semicircle. There were no protestors on this day. The air was warm and unseasonably humid.

"Do we have to walk out here?" Eleanor asked. "I would rather be upstairs, where we'd be near the phones. You could have a coffee."

"I want to smoke."

They walked north toward Wilshire Boulevard.

Bosch said, "It's 1975. Saigon is about to go down the sewer. Police Captain Binh pays people to get him and his share of diamonds out. Who he pays, we don't know. But we do know that he gets VIP treatment all the way. Most people took boats out, he flew. Four days from Saigon to the States. He is accompanied by an American civilian adviser to help smooth things. That's Meadows. He —"

"He may have been accompanied," she said. "You forgot the word 'may' there."

"We're not in court. I'm saying it the way I see it might've been, okay? Afterward, if you don't like it, you say it your way."

She raised her arms in a hands-off kind of way and Bosch continued.

"So, Meadows and Binh are together. Nineteen seventy-five. Meadows is working refugee security or something. See, he's getting out of there, too. He may or may not have known Binh from his old sideline, dealing heroin. The chances are he did. He was probably, in effect, working for Binh. Now, he may or may not have known what Binh was carrying with him to the States. Chances are he at least had an idea."

Bosch stopped to organize his thoughts and Eleanor reluctantly took over.

"Binh takes with him his cultural dislike or distrust for putting his money in the hands of bankers. He has an additional problem, too. His money is not kosher. It is undeclared, unknown and illegal for him to have. He can't declare it or make a normal deposit because this would be noticed and then have to be explained. So, he keeps this sizable fortune in the next best thing: a safe-deposit vault. Where are we going?"

Bosch didn't answer. He was too consumed by his thoughts. They were at Wilshire. When the walk sign flashed above the crosswalk they went with the flow of bodies. On the other side of the street they turned west, walking along the hedges that bordered the veterans cemetery. Bosch took over the story.

"Okay, so Binh's got his share in the safe-deposit box. He starts the great American dream as a refugee. Only he's a rich refugee. Meantime, Meadows comes back after the war, can't get into the groove of real life, can't beat his habit, and starts capering to feed it. But things aren't as easy as in Saigon. He gets caught, spends some time in stir. He gets out, goes back, gets out, then finally starts blocking some real time on federal raps on a couple of bank jobs."

There was an opening in the hedge and a brick walkway. Bosch followed it and they stood looking at the expanse of the cemetery, the rows of carved stones a weather-polished white against the sea of grass. The tall hedge buffered the sound from the street. It was suddenly very peaceful.

"It's like a park," Bosch said.

"It's a graveyard," she whispered. "Let's go."

"You don't have to whisper. Let's walk around. It's quiet."

Eleanor hesitated but then trailed him as he followed the bricks beneath an oak tree that shaded the graves of a grouping of World War I veterans. She caught up and continued the dialogue.

"So we have Meadows in TI. Somehow, he hears about this place Charlie Company. He gets the ear of the ex-soldier-slash-minister who operates the place, gets his backing and gets early release from TI. Now, at Charlie Company, he connects with two old war buddies. Or so we assume. Delgado and Franklin. Except there is only one day that all three of them are at Charlie Company at the same time. Just one day. Are you telling me they hatched this whole thing on that one day?"

"I don't know," Bosch said. "Could've been, but I doubt it. It might have been planned later, after they made that recontact at the farm. The important thing is that we have them together, or in close proximity, in Saigon, 1975. Now we have them together again at Charlie Company. After that, Meadows graduates, takes a few cover jobs until he finishes parole. Then he quits and disappears from view."

"Until?"

"Until the WestLand burglary. They go in, they hit the boxes until they find Binh's box. Or maybe they already knew which one was his. They must have followed him to plan the job and find out where he kept whatever was left of his share of the diamonds. We need to go back to the vault records and see if this Frederic B. Isley ever visited at the same time as Binh. I bet we find that he did. He saw which box was Binh's because he was in the vault with him at the same time.

"Then during the vault break-in, they hit his box and then all the others, taking everything as camouflage. The genius of it was that they knew Binh couldn't report what was taken from him because it did not exist, legally. They knew this. It was perfect. And what made it that way is them taking all the other stuff, to cover for the real target. The diamonds."

"The perfect crime," she said, "until Meadows pawned the bracelet with the jade dolphins on it. That gets him killed. Which brings us back to the question we had a few days ago. Why? And another thing that makes no sense: why, if he had helped loot the vault, was Meadows living in that dump? He was a rich man not acting like a rich man."

Bosch walked in silence for a while. It was the question he had been formulating an answer to since halfway through the meeting with Ernst. He thought about Meadows's eleven-month lease, paid in advance. If he were alive, he would be moving out next week. As they walked through the garden of white stone, it all seemed to fit together. There was no sand left in the top of the hourglass. He finally spoke.

"Because the perfect crime was only half over. By pawning the bracelet, he was giving it away too soon. So he had to go, and they had to get that bracelet back."

She stopped and looked at him. They were standing on the access road next to the World War II section. Bosch saw that the roots of another old oak had pushed some of the weathered stones out of alignment. They looked like teeth waiting for an orthodontist's hands.

"Explain that to me, what you just said," Eleanor said.

"They hit several of the boxes to cover that all they really wanted was what was in Binh's box. Okay?"

She nodded. They still weren't walking.

"Okay. So in order to keep that cover, what would be the thing to do? Get rid of the stuff from all the other boxes so it would never turn up again. And I don't mean fence it. I mean get rid of it, destroy it, sink it, bury it for good, somewhere it would never be found. Because the minute the first piece of jewelry or old coin or stock certificate turns up and the police find out about it, then they've got a lead and they'll come looking."

"So you think Meadows was killed because he pawned the bracelet?" she said.

"Not quite because of that. There is some other current moving through all of this. Why, if Meadows had a share of Binh's diamonds, would he even bother with a bracelet worth a few thousand bucks? Why would he live the way he lived? Doesn't make sense."

"You're losing me, Harry."

"I'm losing myself. But look at it this way for a minute. Say they — Meadows and the others — knew where both Binh and the other police captain, Nguyen Tran, were, and where each of them had stashed what was left of the diamonds they had brought over here. Say there were two banks and the diamonds were in two safe-deposit boxes. And say they were going to hit them both. So first they rip off Binh's bank. And now they are going for Tran's."

She nodded that she was following along. Bosch felt excitement building.

"Okay. So these things take time to plan, to put the strategy together, to plan it for a time the bank is closed three days in a row because that's how much time they need to open enough boxes to make it look real. And then there is the time needed to dig the tunnel."

He'd forgotten to light a cigarette. He realized now and put one in his mouth, but started talking again before lighting it.

"You with me?"

She nodded. He lit the cigarette.

"Okay, then what would be the best thing to do after you have hit the first bank but before the second one is taken down? You lie low and you don't give a goddam hint away. You get rid of all the stuff taken as cover, all the stuff from the other boxes. You keep nothing. And you sit on the diamonds from Binh's box. You can't start to fence them, because it might draw attention to you and spoil the second hit. In fact, Binh probably had feelers out, looking for the diamonds. I mean, over the years, he was probably cashing them in piecemeal and was familiar with the gem-fencing network. So, they had to watch out for him, too."

"So Meadows broke the rules," she said. "He held something back. The bracelet. His partners found out and whacked him. Then they broke into the pawnshop and stole the bracelet back." She shook her head, admiring the plan. "The thing would still be perfect if he hadn't done that."

Bosch nodded. They stood there looking at each other and then around at the grounds of the cemetery. Bosch dropped his cigarette and stepped on it. At the same moment they looked up the hill and saw the black walls of the Vietnam Veterans Memorial.

"What's that doing there?" she asked.

"I don't know. It's a replica. Half size. Fake marble. I think they move it around the country, in case somebody who wants to see it can't make it to D.C."

Eleanor's breath caught sharply and she turned to him.

"Harry, this Monday is Memorial Day."

"I know. Banks closed two days, some three. We've got to find Tran."

She turned to head back to the bureau. He took a last look at the memorial. The long sheath of false marble with all the names carved into it was embedded in the side of the hill. A man in a gray uniform was sweeping the walkway in front of it. There was a pile of violet flowers from a jacaranda tree.

Harry and Eleanor were silent until they were out of the cemetery and walking back across Wilshire toward the Federal Building. She asked a question Bosch had been turning over in his mind and studying but had no good answer for.

"Why now? Why so long? It's been fifteen years."

"I don't know. Just might be the right time, that's all. People, things, unseen forces, sort of come together from time to time. That's what I believe. Who knows? Maybe Meadows forgot all about Binh and just saw him one day on the street and it all came to him. The perfect plan. Maybe it was someone else's plan or it really was hatched on that one day the three of them were together at Charlie Company. The whys you never really know. You just need the hows and the whos."

"You know, Harry, if they're out there, or I should say, under there, digging a new tunnel, then we have less than two days to find them. We have to put some crews underground and look for them."

He thought that putting a crew in the city's tunnels looking for a possible entrance to a bandit tunnel was a long shot. She had told him there were more than 1,500 miles of tunnels under L.A. alone. They might not find the bandits' tunnel if they had a month. The key would be Tran. Find the last police captain, then find his bank. There you find the bandits. And the killers of Billy Meadows. And Sharkey.

He said, "Do you think Binh would give Tran to us?"

"He didn't report his fortune was taken from the vault, so he doesn't seem like the type that's going to tell us about Tran."

"Right. I think we should try finding him ourselves before we go to Binh. Let's make Binh the last resort."

"I'll start on the computer."

"Right."

The FBI computer and the computer networks it could access did not divulge the location of Nguyen Tran. Bosch and Wish found no mention of him in DMV, INS, IRS or Social Security files. There was nothing in the fictitious name filings in the Los Angeles County recorder's office, no mention of him in DWP records or the voter or property tax rolls. Bosch called Hector Villabona and confirmed that Tran entered the United States on the same day as Binh, but there was no further record. After three hours of staring at the amber letters on the computer screen, Eleanor turned it off.

"Nothing," she said. "He's using another name. But he hasn't legally changed it, at least in this county. Nobody has the guy."

They sat there dejected and quiet. Bosch took the last swallow of coffee from a Styrofoam cup. It was after five and the squad room was deserted. Rourke had gone home, after being informed of the latest developments and deciding not to send anyone into the tunnels.

"You know how many miles of underground flood-control tunnels there are in L.A.?" he had asked. "It's like a freeway system down there. These guys, if they are really down there, could be anywhere. We would be stumbling around in the dark. They'll have the advantage and one of us could get hurt."

Bosch and Wish knew he was right. They gave him no argument and set to work finding Tran. And they had failed.

"So now we go to Binh," Bosch said after finishing his coffee.

"You think he'll cooperate?" she said. "He'll know that if we want Tran, then we must know about their past. About the diamonds."

"I don't know what he'll do," he said. "I'll go see him tomorrow. You hungry?"

"We'll go see him tomorrow," she corrected and smiled. "And yes, I'm hungry. Let's get out of here."

They ate at a grill on Broadway in Santa Monica. Eleanor picked the place, and since it was near her apartment Bosch's spirits were high and he was relaxed. There was a trio playing in the corner on a wooden stage, but the place's brick walls made the sound harsh and mostly unnotable. Afterward, Harry and Eleanor sat in a comfortable silence while nursing espressos. There was a warmness between them that Bosch felt but couldn't explain to himself. He didn't know this woman who sat across from him. One look at those hard brown eyes told him that. He wanted to get behind them. They had made love, but he wanted to be in love. He wanted her.

Always seeming to know his thoughts, she asked, "Are you coming home with me tonight?"

Lewis and Clarke were on the second level of the parking garage across the street and down a half block from the Broadway Bar & Grill. Lewis was out of the car and crouched at the guardrail, watching through the camera. Its foot-long lens was steadied on a tripod and pointed at the front door of the restaurant, a hundred yards away. He was hoping the lights over the door, by the valet's stand, would be enough. He had high-speed film in the camera, but the blinking red dot in the viewfinder was telling him not to take the shot. There still wasn't enough light. He decided he would try anyway. He wanted a hand shot.

"You're not going to get it," Clarke said from behind him. "Not in this light."

"Let me do my work. If I don't get it, I don't get it. Who cares?"

"Irving."

"Well, fuck him. He tells us he wants more documentation. He'll get it. I'm only trying to do what the man says."

"We should try to go down there by that deli, get a closer —"

Clarke shut up and turned around at the sound of footsteps. Lewis kept his eye to the camera, waiting for the shot at the restaurant. The steps belonged to a man in a blue security uniform.

"Can I ask you what you guys are doing?" the guard asked.

Clarke badged him and said, "We're on the job."

The guard, a young black man, stepped closer to look at the badge and ID and raised his hand to hold it steady. Clarke jerked it up out of his reach.

"Don't touch it, bro. Nobody touches my badge."

"That says LAPD. You all check in with Santa Monica PD? They know you're out here?"

"Who the fuck cares? Just leave us alone."

Clarke turned around. When the guard didn't leave, he turned back and said, "Son, you need something?"

"This garage is my beat, Detective Clarke. I can be wherever I want to be."

"You can get the fuck outta here. I can —"

Clarke heard the camera shutter close and the sound of the automatic wind. He turned to Lewis, who stood up smiling.

"I got it — a hand shot," Lewis said as he stood up. "They're on the move, let's go."

Lewis collapsed the telescope legs of the tripod and quickly got in the passenger seat of the gray Caprice they had traded the black Plymouth for.

"See ya, bro," Clarke said to the guard. He got in behind the wheel.

The car backed out, forcing the security guard to jump out of the way. Clarke looked in the rearview mirror smiling as he drove toward the exit ramp. He saw the guard talking into a hand-held radio.

"Talk all you want, buddy boy," he said.

The IAD car pulled up to the exit booth. Clarke handed the parking stub and two dollars to the man in the booth. He took it but didn't lift the black-and-white-striped pipe that served as a gate.

"Benson said I have to hold you guys here," the man in the booth said.

"What? Who the fuck is Benson?" Clarke said.

"He's the security. He said hold it here a minute."

Just then, both IAD officers saw Bosch and Wish drive by the garage, heading up to Fourth Street. They were going to lose them. Clarke held out his badge to the booth attendant.

"We're on the job. Open that goddam gate. Now!"

"He'll be along. I gotta do what he say. Else I'll lose my job."

"You open that gate or you're going to lose it, peckerwood," Clarke yelled.

He put his foot down and revved the engine to show he meant to drive through it.

"Why you think we got a pipe 'stead a flimsy piece a wood. You go ahead. That pipe'll take out your windshield, mister. You do what you want, but he's coming right along."

In the rearview, Clarke saw the security guard walking down the ramp. Clarke's face was becoming blotchy red with anger. He felt Lewis's hand on his arm.

"Cool it, partner," Lewis said. "They were holding hands when they came out of the restaurant. We won't lose them. They're only going to her place. I'll bet you a week's driving that we'll pick 'em up there."

Clarke shook his hand off and let out a long breath; that seemed to bring a more placid tone to his face. He said, "I don't care. I don't fucking like this shit one bit."

On Ocean Park Boulevard Bosch found a parking space across from Eleanor's building. He pulled in but made no move to get out of the car. He looked at her, still feeling the glow of a few minutes before but unsure where they were going with this. She seemed to know this, maybe even feel it herself. She put her hand on top of his and leaned over to kiss him. She whispered, "Come in with me."

He got out and came around to her side. She was already out and he closed the door. They rounded the front end of the car and then stood next to it, waiting for an approaching car to pass by. The car's high beams were on and Bosch turned away and looked at Eleanor. So it was she who first noticed the high beams drift toward them.

"Harry?"

"What?"

"Harry!"

Then Bosch turned back to the approaching car and saw the lights — actually four beams from two sets of square side-by-side headlights — bearing down on them. In the few seconds that were left Bosch clearly came to the conclusion that the car was not drifting their way but rather driving at them. There was no time, yet time seemed to go into suspension. In what seemed to him to be slow motion, Bosch turned to his right, to Eleanor. But she needed no help. In unison, they leapt onto the hood of Bosch's car. He was rolling over her and they were both tumbling toward the sidewalk when his car lurched violently and there was a high-pitched keening sound of tearing metal. Bosch saw a shower of blue sparks pass in his peripheral vision. Then he landed on top of Eleanor on the thin strip of sod that was between the curb and the sidewalk. They were safe, Bosch could sense. Scared, but safe for the moment.

He came up, gun out and steadied by both hands. The car that had come after them was not stopping. It was already fifty yards east, heading away and picking up speed. Bosch fired one round that he thought ricocheted off the rear window, the bullet too weak at that distance to penetrate the glass. He heard Eleanor's gun fire twice at his side, but saw no damage to the hit-and-run car.

Without a word they both piled into Bosch's car through the passenger door. Bosch held his breath while he turned the key, but the engine started and the car squealed away from the curb. Bosch rocked the steering wheel from side to side as he picked up speed. The suspension felt a little loose. He had no idea what the extent of the damage was. When he tried to check the side-view mirror he saw it was gone. When he turned on the lights, only the passenger-side beam worked.

The hit-and-run car was at least five blocks ahead, near the crest where Ocean Park Boulevard rises and then drops from sight. The lights on the speeding car went out just as it dropped over the hill out of sight. He was heading for Bundy Drive, Bosch thought. From there a short jog to the 10. And from there he would be gone and they'd never catch him. Bosch grabbed the radio and called in an Officer Needs Assistance. But he could not provide a description of the car, only the direction of the chase.

"He's going for the freeway, Harry," Eleanor yelled. "Are you okay?"

"Yeah. Are you? Did you get a make?"

"I'm fine. Scared is all. No make. American, I think. Uh, square head-lights. No color, just dark. I didn't see the color. We won't catch him if he makes the freeway."

They were heading east on Ocean Park, parallel to the 10, which was about eight blocks to the north. They approached the top of the crest, and Bosch cut off the one working headlight. As they came over, he saw the unlit form of the hit-and-run car passing through the lighted intersection at Lincoln. Yeah, he was going for Bundy. At Lincoln, Bosch took a left and floored the gas pedal. He put the lights back on. And as the car's speed increased there was a thumping sound. The front left tire and alignment were damaged.

"Where are you going?" Eleanor shouted.

"I'm going for the freeway first."

Bosch had no sooner said that than the freeway entrance signs came up and the car made a wide, arcing right turn onto the ramp. The tire held up. They sped down the ramp into the traffic.

"How'll we know?" Eleanor shouted. The noise from the tire was very loud now, almost a continual throbbing.

"I don't know. Look for the square lights."

In one minute they were coming up on the Bundy entrance, but Bosch had no idea whether they had beaten the other car or if it was already well ahead of them. A car was coming up the ramp and into the merging lane. The car was white and foreign.

"I don't think so," Eleanor called.

Bosch gunned it to the floor again and moved ahead. His heart was pounding almost as fast as the tire, half with the excitement of the chase, half with the excitement of still being alive and not broken on the street in front of Eleanor's apartment. He was gripping the steering wheel at the ten and two o'clock positions, urging the car on as if he held the reins of a galloping horse. They were moving through sparse traffic at ninety miles an hour, both of them looking at the front ends of the cars they passed, searching for the four square lights or a damaged right side.

A half-minute later, Bosch's knuckles as white as bones wrapped around the wheel, they came upon a maroon Ford going at least seventy in the slow lane. Bosch swung out from behind and passed alongside. Eleanor had her gun in her hands but was holding it below the window so it could not be seen from outside the car. The white male driver didn't even look over or register notice. As they pulled ahead, Eleanor shouted, "Square lights, side by side."

"Is it the car?" Bosch called back excitedly.

"I can't — I don't know. Can't see the right side for damage. It could be. The guy isn't showing anything."

They were three-quarters of a car length ahead now. Bosch grabbed the portable pull-over light off the transmission hump on the floor and swung it out the window onto the roof. He switched on the revolving blue light and slowly began to angle the Ford onto the shoulder. Eleanor put her hand out the window and signaled the car over. The driver began to comply. Bosch braked sharply and let the other car shoot by onto the shoulder, then Bosch swung his car onto the shoulder behind it. When both had stopped alongside a sound barrier wall Bosch realized he had a big problem. He put on the high beams, but still only the passenger-side headlight responded. The car in front was too close to the wall for Bosch and Wish to see if the right side was damaged. Meantime, the driver sat in his car, mostly shrouded in darkness.

"Shit," Bosch said. "Okay. Don't come up till I say it's clear, okay?"

"Got it," she said.

Bosch had to throw his weight hard against the door to open it. He came out of the car, gun in one hand and flashlight in the other. He held the light out away from his body and trained its beam on the driver of the car ahead. The roar of passing traffic in his ears, Bosch started to shout, but a diesel horn drowned him out and a blast of wind from the passing semi shoved him forward. Bosch tried again, shouting for the driver to stick both hands out the side window where Bosch could see them. Nothing. Bosch shouted the order again. After a long moment, with Bosch poised off the left rear fender of the maroon car, the driver finally complied. Bosch ran the flash beam through the back window and saw no other occupants. He ran up and put the light on the driver and ordered him to step out slowly.

"What is this?" the man protested. He was small, with pale skin, reddish hair and a transparent mustache. He opened the car door and stepped out with his hands up. He was wearing a white button-down shirt and beige pants held up by suspenders. He looked out into the passing field of cars, almost as if beckoning for a witness to this commuter's nightmare.

"Can I see a badge?" he stammered. Bosch rushed forward, spun him around and slammed his body into the side of his car, his head and shoulders over its roof. With one hand on the back of the man's neck, holding him down, and the other holding the gun to his ear, Bosch shouted to Eleanor that it was clear.

"Check the front side."

The man beneath Bosch let out a moaning sound, like a scared animal, and Bosch could feel him shaking. His neck felt clammy. Bosch never took his eyes off him to see where Eleanor was. Suddenly her voice was right behind him.

"Let him go," she said. "It's not him. There's no damage. We've got the wrong car."

PART VI

They were interviewed by the Santa Monica police, the California Highway Patrol, LAPD and the FBI. A DUI unit had been called to give Bosch a sobriety test. He passed. And by 2 A.M. he sat in an interview room at the West Los Angeles bureau, bone-tired and wondering if the Coast Guard or IRS would be next. He and Eleanor had been separated and he hadn't seen her since they had arrived three hours earlier. It bothered him that he could not be with her to protect her from the interrogators. Lieutenant Harvey "Ninety-eight" Pounds came into the room then and told Bosch they were finished for the night. Bosch could tell that Ninety-eight was angry, and it wasn't just because he had been rousted from home.

"What kind of cop doesn't get the make of the car that tries to run him down?" he asked.

Bosch was used to the second-guessing tone to the questions. It had been that way all night.

"Like I told every one of those guys before you, I was a little busy at the time. I was trying to save my ass."

"And this guy you pull over," Pounds cut in. "Jesus, Bosch, you rough him up on the side of the freeway. Every asshole with a car phone is dialing nine one one reporting kidnap, murder, who knows what else. Couldn't you have tried to get a look at the right side of his car before you pulled him over?"

"It was impossible. All of this is covered in the report we typed up, Lieutenant. I've gone over it, seems like ten times already."

Pounds acted as though he didn't hear. "And he's a lawyer no less."

"So what?" Bosch said, now losing his patience. "We apologized. It was a mistake. The car looked the same. And if he is going to sue anybody it will be the FBI. They've got deeper pockets. So don't worry about it."

"No, he'll sue us both. He's already talking about it, fer crissake. And this is not the time to try to be funny, Bosch."

"It's also not the time to be worried about what we did or didn't do right. None of the suits that have come in here to interview me have seemed to care that somebody might be trying to kill us. They just want to know how far away I was when I fired and whether I endangered bystanders and why I pulled that car over without probable cause. Well, fuck it, man. Somebody is out to kill my partner and me. Excuse me if I'm not feeling particularly sorry for the lawyer who got his suspenders twisted."

Pounds was ready for that argument.

"Bosch, for all we have evidence of, it could have just been a drunk. And what do you mean 'partner'? You are on a day-to-day loan to this investigation. And after tonight, I think the loan is going to be withdrawn. You've spent five solid days on this case, and from what I understand from Rourke, you've got nothing."

"It was no drunk, Pounds. We were a target. And I don't care what Rourke says we have, I'm going to clear this one. And if you'd quit undermining the effort, believe in your own people for once and maybe get those Internal Affairs assholes off me, you might be in line for a piece of the honors when it happens."

Pounds's eyebrows arched like roller coasters.

"Yeah, I know about Lewis and Clarke," Bosch said. "And I know their paper was being copied to you. I guess they didn't tell you about the little talk we had? I caught 'em snoozing outside my house."

It was clear from his expression that Pounds had not heard. Lewis and Clarke were staying low and Bosch would not get jammed up over what he had done to them. He began to wonder where the two IAD detectives had been when he and Eleanor had almost been run down.

Meanwhile, Pounds remained silent for a long time. He was a fish swimming around the bait Bosch had cast, seeming to know there was a hook in it but thinking there might be a way to get the bait without the hook. Finally he told Bosch to give him a rundown on the week's investigation. He was on the hook now. Bosch ran the case down for him, and though Pounds never spoke once during the next twenty minutes Bosch could tell by his roller-coasting eyebrows whenever he heard something that Rourke had neglected to bring up.

When the story was finished, there was no more talk from Pounds of Bosch's being withdrawn from the case. Nevertheless, Bosch felt very tired of the whole thing. He wanted to sleep, but Pounds still had questions.

"If the FBI isn't putting people into the tunnels, should we?" he asked.

Bosch could see he was thinking in terms of being in on the bust, if there was one. If he put LAPD people into the drainage tunnels, the FBI wouldn't be able to crowd the department out when the credit for the bust came. Pounds would receive a slap on the back from the chief if he could defend against such a maneuver.

But Bosch had come to believe that Rourke's reasoning was sound and correct. A tunnel crew would stand a good chance of stumbling into the thieves and maybe getting killed.

"No," Bosch told Pounds. "Let's first see if we can get a fix on Tran and where he keeps his stash. For all we know, it might not even be a bank."

Pounds stood up, having heard enough. He said Bosch was free to go. As the lieutenant headed to the interview room door he said, "Bosch, I don't think you'll have any problems with this incident tonight. It sounds to me like you did what you could. The lawyer got his feathers ruffled but he'll settle down. Or just settle."

Bosch didn't say anything or smile at his meager joke.

"One thing," Pounds continued. "The fact that this happened in front of Agent Wish's home is a bit troubling because it has the appearance of impropriety. Just a hint, no? You were just walking her to the door, weren't you?"

"I don't really care how it appeared, Lieutenant," Bosch answered. "I was off duty."

Pounds looked at Bosch a moment, shook his head as if Bosch had ignored his outstretched hand, and then went through the door of the small room.

Bosch found Eleanor sitting by herself in an interview room next to his. Her eyes were closed and she had her head propped on her hands, her elbows up on the scarred wooden table. Her eyes opened as he walked in. She smiled and he immediately felt healed of fatigue, frustration and anger. It was a smile a child gives another when they've gotten away with something on the adults.

"All done?" she said.

"Yeah. You?"

"Been done more than an hour. You are the one they wanted to grill."

"As usual. Rourke has left?"

"Yeah, he split. Said he wants me to check in with him every other hour tomorrow. After what happened tonight, he thinks he hasn't kept a tight enough rein on this."

"Or you."

"Yeah. It looks like there is some of that, too. He wanted to know what we were doing at my place. I told him you were just walking me to my door."

Bosch sat down wearily at the other side of the table and dug a finger into a cigarette pack in search of the last one. He put it in his mouth but didn't light it.

"Besides being titillated or jealous of what we might have been doing, who does Rourke think tried to take us out?" he asked. "A drunk driver, like my people seem to think?"

"He did mention the drunk driver theory. He also asked whether I have a jealous ex-boyfriend. Other than that, there doesn't seem to be a great amount of concern that it might have something to do with our case."

"I hadn't thought of the ex-boyfriend angle. What did you tell him?"

"You're as conniving as he is," she said, flashing her brilliant smile. "I told him it wasn't any of his business."

"Good going. Is it mine?"

"The answer is no." She let him hang over the cliff a few seconds, then added, "That is, no jealous ex-boyfriends. So, can we leave now and get to where we were" — she looked at her watch — "about four hours ago?"

Bosch was awake in Eleanor Wish's bed long before dawn light crept around the curtain drawn across the sliding glass door. Unable to defeat insomnia, he finally got up and took a shower in the downstairs bathroom. After, he looked through her kitchen cabinets and refrigerator and began to put together a breakfast of coffee, eggs and cinnamon raisin bagels. He couldn't find any bacon.

When he heard the shower upstairs go off, he carried a glass of orange juice up and found her in front of the bathroom mirror. She was naked and braiding her hair, which she'd divided into three thick hanks. He was entranced by her and watched as she expertly maneuvered her hair into a French braid. She then accepted the juice and a long kiss from Bosch. She put on her short robe and they went downstairs to eat.

After, Harry opened the kitchen door and stood just outside it while he smoked a cigarette.

"You know," he said, "I'm just happy nothing happened."

"You mean last night on the street?"

"Yeah. To you. I don't know how I'd've handled it. I know we just met and all, but . . . uh, I care. You know?"

"Me too."

Bosch had taken a shower, but his clothes were as fresh as the ashtray in a used car. After a while he said he had to leave, to go by his house and change. Eleanor said she would go into the bureau and check for fallout from last night's activities and get whatever was on file about Binh. They agreed to meet at Hollywood Station, on Wilcox, because it was closest to Binh's business, and Bosch needed to turn in his damaged car, anyway. She walked him to the door and they kissed as if she were seeing him off to a day at the office at the accounting firm.

When Bosch got to his house, he found no messages on the phone machine and no sign that the place had been entered. He shaved and changed clothes and then headed down the hill through Nichols Canyon and then over to Wilcox. He was at his desk, updating the Investigating Officer's Chronological Report forms, when Eleanor came in at ten. The squad room was full and most of the detectives who were male stopped what they were doing to check her out. She had an uncomfortable smile on her face when she sat down in the steel chair next to the homicide table.

"Anything wrong?"

"I just think I would rather walk through Biscailuz," she said, referring to the sheriff's jail downtown.

"Oh. Yeah, these guys can leer better than most flashers. You want a glass of water?"

"No. I'm fine. Ready?"

"Let's do it."

They took Bosch's new car, which was actually at least three years old and had seventy-seven thousand miles on it. The station fleet manager, a permanent desk assignee since he'd had four fingers blown off by a pipe bomb he stupidly picked up one Halloween, said it was the best he could do. Budget restraints had halted the replacement of cars, though repairing the old ones actually cost the department more. At least, Bosch learned after starting the car, the air conditioner worked reasonably well. There was a light Santa Ana condition kicking up and the forecast was for an unseasonably warm holiday weekend.

Eleanor's research on Binh showed he had an office and business on Vermont near Wilshire. There were more Korean-run shops in the area than Vietnamese, but they coexisted. As near as Wish had been able to find out, Binh controlled a number of businesses that imported cheap clothing and electronic and video merchandise from the Orient and then moved it through Southern California and Mexico. Many of the items turistas thought they were getting on the cheap in Mexico and then bringing back to the States had already been here. It all seemed successful on paper, though it was small-time. Still, it was enough to make Bosch question if Binh even needed the diamonds. Or ever had any.

Binh owned the building his office and discount video equipment store was based in. It was a 1930s auto showroom that had been converted years before Binh had ever seen it. Unreinforced concrete block fronted with wide picture windows and guaranteed to come down in a decent shaker. But for someone who had made it out of Vietnam the way Binh had, earthquakes were probably viewed as a minor inconvenience, not a risk.

After they found an empty parking space across the street from Ben's Electronics, Bosch told Eleanor he wanted her to handle the questioning, at least at first. Bosch said he figured that Binh might be more inclined to talk to the feds than to the locals. They decided on a plan to small-talk him and then ask about Tran. Bosch didn't tell her that he also had a second plan in mind.

"Doesn't exactly look like the kind of place run by a guy with a box full of diamonds in a bank vault," Bosch said as they got out of the car.

"That is *had* in the bank," she said. "And remember, he couldn't flaunt that stuff. He had to be like every other Joe Immigrant. The appearance of living day to day. The diamonds, if there were any, were the collateral for this place, for his American success story. But it had to look like he made it from scratch."

"Wait a second," Bosch said as they got to the other side of the street. He told Eleanor he had forgotten to ask Jerry Edgar to fill in on a court appearance for him that afternoon. He pointed to a pay phone at a service station next to Binh's building and trotted over. Eleanor stayed behind, looking in the windows of the store.

Bosch called Edgar but didn't say anything about a court appearance.

"Jed, I need a favor. You won't even have to get up."

Edgar hesitated, as Bosch thought he would.

"What do you need?"

"You aren't supposed to say it like that. You're supposed to say, 'Sure, Harry, what do you need?'"

"Come on, Harry, we both know we're under the glass. We've got to be careful. Tell me what you need. I'll tell you if I can do it."

"All I want you to do is buzz me in ten minutes. I need to get out of a meeting. Just buzz me, and when I call in, just put the phone down for a couple minutes. And if I don't call in, buzz me again in five minutes. That's it."

"That's all you need? Just the buzz?"

"Right. Ten minutes from now."

"Okay, Harry," Edgar said, relief in his voice. "Hey, I heard about your thing last night. That was close. And word around here is that it wasn't no drunk driver. You watch your ass."

"Always. What's going on with Sharkey?"

"Nothing. I ran down his crew like you told me. Two of 'em told me they were with him that night. I think they were rolling faggots. They said they lost sight of him after he got in a car. That was a couple hours before the desk got the call that he was in the tunnel up at the bowl. I figure whoever was in that car did him."

"Description?"

"The car? Not very good. Dark color, American sedan. Something new. That's about it."

"What kind of headlights?"

"Well, I showed 'em the car book and they picked different taillights. One guy's got round, the other says rectangle. But on the headlights. They both said they —"

"Square, side-by-side squares."

"Right. Hey, Harry, you thinking this is the car that came down on you and the FBI woman? Jesus! We ought to get together on this."

"Later. Maybe later. Meantime, buzz me in ten minutes."

"Ten minutes, right."

Bosch hung up and went back to Eleanor, who was looking through the plate-glass window at the ghetto blasters on display. They entered the store, shook off two salesmen, walked around a stack of boxed camcorders on sale for $500 each and told a woman standing at a cash register station in the back that they were there to see Binh. The woman stared blankly at them until Eleanor showed her badge and federal ID card.

"You wait here," the woman said and then disappeared through a door located behind the cash counter. There was a small mirrored window in the door that reminded Bosch of the interview room back at Wilcox. He looked at his watch. He had eight minutes.

The man who emerged from the door behind the cash register looked to be about sixty years old. He had white hair. He was short but Bosch could tell he had once been physically powerful for his size. Built wide and low to the ground, he now was softened by an easier life than he had had in his native land. He wore silver-framed glasses with a pink tint and an open-collar shirt and golf slacks. His breast pocket sagged with the weight of almost a dozen pens and a clip-on pocket flashlight. Ngo Van Binh was low key all the way.

"Mr. Binh? My name is Eleanor Wish. I am from the FBI. This is Detective Bosch, LAPD. We'd like to ask you a few questions."

"Yes," he said, the stern expression on his face unchanging.

"It's about the break-in at the bank where you had a safe-deposit box."

"I reported no loss, my deposit box had sentimental occupants only."

Diamonds ranked fairly high up there on the sentimental range, Bosch thought. "Mr. Binh, can we go back to your office and talk privately?" he said instead.

"Yes, but I suffered no loss. You look. It is in the reports."

Eleanor held her hand out, urging Binh to lead the way. They followed him through the door with the mirror window and into a warehouselike storage room. There were hundreds of boxes of electronic appliances on steel shelves going to the ceiling. They passed through into a smaller room that was a repair or assembly shop. There was a woman sitting at a tool bench with a bowl of soup held to her mouth. She did not look up as they passed. There were two doors at the back of the shop, and the procession went through one into Binh's office. It was here that Binh shed his peasant trappings. The office was large and plush, with a desk and two chairs to the right and a dark leather L-shaped couch to the left. The couch was at the edge of an Oriental rug that featured a three-headed dragon poised to strike. The couch faced two walls of shelves filled by books and stereo and video equipment, much finer than what Bosch had seen out front. We should have braced him at his home, Bosch thought. Seen how he lived, not how he worked.

Bosch quickly scanned the room and saw a white telephone on the desk. It would be perfect. It was an antique, the kind where the handset was cradled above a rotary dial. Binh moved toward his desk but Bosch quickly spoke up.

"Mr. Binh? Would it be okay if we sat over here on the couch? We'd like to keep this as informal as possible. We sit at desks all day, to tell you the truth."

Binh shrugged his shoulders as though it made no difference to him, that they were inconveniencing him no matter where they sat. It was a distinctly American gesture, and Bosch believed his seeming difficulty with English was a front used to better insulate him. Binh sat down on one side of the L-shaped couch and Eleanor and Bosch took the other. "Nice office," Bosch said and looked around. He saw no other phone in the room.

Binh nodded. He offered no tea or coffee, no small talk. He just said, "What do you want, please?"

Bosch looked at Eleanor.

She said, "Mr. Binh, we are just retracing our steps. You reported no financial loss in the vault break-in. We —"

"That is right. No loss."

"That is correct. What did you keep in the box?"

"Nothing."

"Nothing?"

"Papers and such, no value. I told this to everyone already."

"Yes, we know. We are sorry to bother you again. But the case remains open and we have to go back and see if we missed anything. Could you tell me in specific detail what papers you lost? It might help us, if we make a recovery of property and can identify who it belongs to."

Eleanor took a small notebook and pen out of her purse. Binh looked at his two visitors as if he could not possibly see how his information could help. Bosch said, "You'd be surprised sometimes what little things can —"

His pager tone sounded and Bosch pulled the device off his belt and looked at the number display. He stood up and looked around, as if he was just noticing the room for the first time. He wondered if he was overdoing it.

"Mr. Binh, can I use your phone? It'll be local."

Binh nodded, and Bosch walked to the front of the desk, leaned over and picked up the handset. He made a show of checking the pager number again, then dialed Edgar's number. He remained standing with his back to Eleanor and Binh. He looked up at the wall, as if studying the silk tapestry that hung there. He heard Binh begin to describe to Eleanor the immigration and citizenship papers that had been taken from his safe-deposit box. Bosch put the pager in his coat pocket and came out with the small pocketknife, the T-9 phone bug and the small battery he had disconnected from his own phone.

"This is Bosch, who paged me?" he said into the phone when Edgar picked up. After Edgar put the phone down, he said, "I'll hold a few minutes, but tell him I'm in the middle of an interview. What's so important?"

With his back still to the couch and Binh still talking, Bosch turned slightly to the right and cocked his head as if he were holding the phone to his left ear, where Binh could not see it. Bosch brought the handset down to stomach level, used the knife to pop off the earpiece cover — clearing his throat as he did this — and then pulled out the audio receiver. With one hand he connected the bug to its battery — he had practiced doing it earlier while waiting for the new car in the fleet yard at Wilcox. Then he used his fingers to shove the bug and battery into the barrel of the handset. He put the receiver back in and snapped on the cover, coughing loudly to camouflage any sound.

"Okay," Bosch said into the phone. "Well, tell him I'll call back when I am through here. Thanks, man."

He put the phone back on the desk while returning the knife to his pocket. He went back to the couch, where Eleanor was writing in a notebook. When she was finished she looked at Bosch and Bosch knew without any sign that now the interview would shift into a new direction.

"Mr. Binh," she said. "Are you sure that is all you had in the box?"

"Yes, sure, why do you ask me so much?"

"Mr. Binh, we know who you are and the circumstances of your coming to this country. We know you were a police officer."

"Yes, so? What's it mean?"

"We also know other things —"

"We know," Bosch cut in, "you were very highly paid as a police officer in Saigon, Mr. Binh. We know that for some of your work you were paid in diamonds."

"What does this mean, what he says?" Binh said, looking at Eleanor and gesturing with his hand to Bosch. He was lapsing into the defense of language barrier. He seemed to know less English as the interview went on.

"It means what he says," she answered. "We know about the diamonds you brought here from Vietnam, Captain Binh. We know you kept them in the safe-deposit box. We believe the diamonds were the motivation for the vault break-in."

The news didn't shake him, he may have already considered as much. He did not move. He said, "This not true."

"Mr. Binh, we've got your package," Bosch said. "We know all about you. We know what you were in Saigon, what you did. We know what you took with you when you came here. I don't know what you are into now — it all looks legit, but we don't really care. What we do care about is who ripped off that bank. And they ripped it off because of you. They took the collateral for all this and everything else you've got. Now, I don't think we are telling you something that you probably haven't figured out or thought about on your own. In fact, you might have even thought your old partner Nguyen Tran was behind it because he knew what you had and maybe where it was. Not a bad guess, but we don't think so. In fact, we think he is next on the list."

Not a crack formed on the stone that was Binh's face.

"Mr. Binh, we want to talk to Tran," Bosch said. "Where is he?"

Binh looked down through the coffee table in front of him to the three-headed dragon on the rug beneath it. He put his hands together on his lap, shook his head and said, "Who is this Tran?"

Eleanor glared at Bosch and tried to salvage what rapport she had had with the man before he butted in.

"Captain Binh, we're not interested in taking any action against you. We simply want to stop another vault break-in before it happens. Can you help us, please?"

Binh didn't answer. He looked down at his hands.

"Look, Binh, I don't know what you've got going on this," Bosch said. "You might have people out there trying to find the same people we are, I don't know. But I'm telling you right now, you are out of it. So tell us where Tran is."

"I don't know this man."

"We are your only hope. We have to get to Tran. The people that ripped you off, they are in the tunnels again. Right now. If we don't get to Tran this weekend, there won't be anything left for you or him."

Binh remained a stone, as Bosch expected. Eleanor stood up.

"Think about it, Mr. Binh," she said.

"We're running out of time, and so is your old partner," Bosch said as they headed for the door.

After walking through the showroom door Bosch looked both ways for traffic and ran across Vermont to the car. Eleanor walked it, anger making her strides stiff and jerky. Bosch got in and reached to the floor behind the front seat for the Nagra. He turned it on and set the recording speed at its fastest level. He didn't think the wait would be long. He hoped all the electronic equipment in the store would not skew the reception. Eleanor got in the passenger side and started to complain.

"That was magnificent," she said. "We'll never get anything out of that guy now. He's just going to call up Tran and — what the hell is that?"

"Something I picked up from the shooflies. They dropped a bug in my phone. Oldest trick in the IAD book."

"And you just put it in . . ." She pointed across the street and Bosch nodded.

"Bosch, do you realize what could happen to us, what this means? I'm going back in there and getting —"

She opened the car door but he reached across and pulled it closed.

"You don't want to do that. This is our only way to get to Tran. Binh wasn't going to tell us, no matter how we handled the interview, and deep down behind those angry eyes you know it. So it's this or nothing. Binh warns Tran and we never know where he is, or we use this to maybe find him. Maybe. We'll probably know soon enough."

Eleanor looked straight forward and shook her head.

"Bosch, this could mean our jobs. How could you do this without consulting me?"

"For that reason. It could mean *my* job. You didn't know."

"I'd never prove it. The whole thing looks like a setup. I keep him occupied while you do your little charade on the phone."

"It was a setup, only you didn't know. Besides, Binh and Tran are not the targets of our investigation. We are not gathering evidence against them, just from them. This will never go in a report. And if he finds the bug, he can't prove I put it there. There was no register number. I looked. The suits weren't stupid enough to make it traceable. We're clear. You're clear. Don't worry."

"Harry, that is hardly reassur —"

The red light on the Nagra flicked on. Someone was using Binh's phone. Bosch checked to make sure the tape was rolling.

"Eleanor, you make the call," Bosch said, holding the recorder up on the palm of his hand. "Turn it off if you want. Your choice."

She turned and looked at the recorder, then at Bosch. Just then the dialing stopped and it was silent in the car. A phone began to ring at the other end of Binh's call. She turned away. Someone answered the phone. A few words were exchanged in Vietnamese and then more silence. Then a new voice was on the line and a conversation began, also in Vietnamese. Bosch could tell one of the voices belonged to Binh. The other sounded like a man about Binh's age. It was Binh and Tran, together again. Eleanor shook her head and forced a short laugh.

"Brilliant, Harry, now who do we get to translate? We aren't letting anyone else know about this. We can't risk it."

"I don't want to translate it." He turned the receiver off and rewound the tape. "Get out your little pad and pen."

Bosch adjusted the recorder to its slowest speed and hit the play button. When the dialing started, it was slow enough that Bosch could count the clicks. Bosch called the numbers out to Eleanor, who wrote them down. They had the number Binh had dialed.

The phone number was a 714 area code. Orange County. Bosch switched the receiver on; the telephone conversation between Binh and the unknown man was continuing. He turned it off and picked up the radio microphone. He gave a dispatcher the phone number and asked for the name and address that went with it. It would take a few minutes while someone looked it up in a reverse directory. Meantime, Bosch started the car and headed south toward Interstate 10. He had already connected with the 5 and was heading into Orange County when the dispatcher got back to him.

The phone number belonged to a business called the Tan Phu Pagoda in Westminster. Bosch looked over at Eleanor, who looked away.

"Little Saigon," he said.

Bosch and Wish got to the Tan Phu Pagoda from Binh's business in an hour. The pagoda was a shopping plaza on Bolsa Avenue where no sign was printed in English. The building was off-white stucco with glass fronts on the half-dozen shops that lined the parking lot. Each was a small establishment that sold mostly unneeded junk like electronic equipment or T-shirts. There were competing Vietnamese restaurants on either end. Next to one of the restaurants was a glass door that led to an office or business without a front display window. Though neither Bosch nor Wish could decipher the words on the door, they immediately figured it was the entrance to the shopping center office.

"We need to get in there and confirm that's Tran's place, see if he's there and if there are other exits," Bosch said.

"We don't even know what he looks like," Wish reminded him.

He thought a moment. If Tran wasn't using his real name, it would tip him off to go in asking for him.

"I've got an idea," Wish said. "Find a pay phone. Then I'll go in the office. You dial the number you got off the tape and when I'm in there I'll see if it rings. If I hear a phone we have the right place. I'll also try to scope out Tran and the exits."

"Phones might be ringing in there every ten seconds," Bosch said. "It might be a boiler room or a sweatshop. How will you know it's me?"

She was silent a moment.

"Chances are they don't speak English, or at least not well," she said. "So you ask whoever answers to speak English or get someone who can. When you get someone who understands, say something that will get a reaction I'll be able to see."

"You mean if the phone rings in a place where you will see."

She shrugged, her eyes showing him she was tired of his shooting down every suggestion she made. "Look, it's the only thing we can do. Come on, there's a phone, we don't have a lot of time."

He drove out of the parking lot and a quarter block down to a pay phone out front of a liquor store. Wish walked back to the Tan Phu Pagoda and Bosch watched until she reached the door of the office. He dropped a quarter in the phone and dialed the number he had written on his pad in front of Binh's. The line was busy. He looked back at the office door. Wish was gone from view. He dropped the quarter and dialed again. Busy. He did it in quick succession two more times before he got a ring. He was thinking that he had probably dialed the wrong number, when the call was answered.

"Tan Phu," a male voice said. Young, Asian, probably early twenties, Bosch thought. Not Tran.

"Tan Phu?" Bosch asked.

"Yes, please."

Bosch could not think of what to do. He whistled into the phone. The comeback was a staccato verbal attack of which Bosch could not understand a single word or sound. Then the phone at the other end was slammed down. Bosch walked back to the car and drove back toward the shopping plaza and into the narrow parking lot. He was cruising through it slowly when Wish appeared at the glass door with a man. An Asian. Like Binh, he had gray hair and had the aura; unspoken power, unflexed muscle. He held the door open for Eleanor and nodded to her as she said thanks. He watched her walk off and then disappeared inside again.

"Harry," she said as she got in the car, "what did you say to the guy on the phone?"

"Not a word. So it was that office?"

"Yeah. I think that was our Mr. Tran who held the door for me. Nice guy."

"So what did you do to become such great pals?"

"I told him I was a real estate lady. When I went in I asked to see the boss. Then Mr. Gray Hair came out of a back office. He said his name was Jimmie Bok. I said I represented Japanese investors and asked if he was interested in taking an offer on the shopping center. He said no. He said, in very fine English, 'I buy, I don't sell.' Then he escorted me out. But I think that was Tran. Something about him."

"Yeah, I saw it," Bosch said. Then he picked up the radio and asked dispatch to run the name Jimmie Bok on the NCIC and DMV computers.

Eleanor described the inside of the office. A central reception area, a hallway running behind it with four doors, including one at the rear that looked like an exit, judging by the double lock. No women. At least four men other than Bok. Two of them looked like hired muscle. They stood up from the reception room couch when Bok walked out of the middle door in the hallway.

Bosch drove out of the lot and around the block. He cut up the alley that ran behind the shopping plaza. He stopped when he had driven far enough to see a gold stretch Mercedes parked next to a rear door to the complex. There was a double lock on the door.

"That's got to be his wheels," Wish said.

They decided they would watch the car. Bosch drove on by it to the end of the alley and parked behind a Dumpster. Then he realized it was full of garbage from the restaurant. He backed out and drove out of the alley completely. He parked on the side street so that by looking out the passenger side of the car, they both could see the rear end of the Mercedes. Bosch could also look at Eleanor at the same time.

"So, I guess we wait," she said.

"Guess so. No way of telling whether he'll do anything after Binh's warning. Maybe he did something after Binh got ripped off last year and we're just spinning our wheels."

Bosch got a radio callback from the dispatcher: Jimmie Bok had a clean driving record. He lived in Beverly Hills and he had no criminal record. Nothing else.

"I'm going back to the phone," Eleanor announced. Bosch looked at her. "I have to check in. I'll tell Rourke we're set up on this guy and see if he can't shake someone loose to maybe call some banks and run his name. To see if he is a customer. I'd also like to run him on the property computer. He said, 'I buy, I don't sell.' I'd like to know what he buys."

"Fire a shot if you need me," Bosch said, and she smiled as she opened the door.

"You want something to eat?" she asked. "I'm thinking about getting take-out for lunch from one of those restaurants up front."

"Just coffee," he said. He hadn't eaten Vietnamese food in twenty years. He watched her walk around to the front of the center.

About ten minutes after she was gone, as Bosch watched the Mercedes, he saw a car pass by the other end of the alley. He immediately made it as a police sedan. A white Ford LTD without wheel covers, just the cheap hubcaps that revealed the matching white wheels. It had been too far away for him to see who was in it. He alternately looked at the Mercedes and then at the rearview mirror to see if the LTD was coming around the block. But in five minutes, he never saw it.

Wish was back ten minutes after that. She was carrying a grease-stained brown bag from which she pulled one coffee and two goldfish cartons. Steamed rice and crab boh, she said. He passed on her offer and rolled his window down. He sipped the coffee she handed to him and grimaced.

"Tastes like it was made in Saigon and shipped over," he said. "Did you get Rourke?"

"Yeah. He's going to get somebody to check Bok out and page me if they come up with anything. He wants to know, on a radio patch-through, the minute the Mercedes starts moving."

Two hours passed easily as they small-talked and watched the gold Mercedes. Eventually Bosch announced that he was going to break camp and drive around the block just to change the pace. What he didn't say was that he was bored and his butt was falling asleep and that he wanted to look for the white LTD.

"Do you think maybe we should call to see if he's still there, and then hang up if he gets on?" she said.

"If Binh gave him the warning, a call like that might shake him up, make him think something is going on, make him more cautious."

He drove the car up to the corner and along the front of the shopping plaza. Nothing unusual caught his eye. He went around the block and parked in the same spot again. He had not seen the LTD.

As soon as they were back in position, Wish's pager sounded and she got out to go to the phone again. Bosch concentrated on the gold Mercedes and forgot about the LTD for the time being. But after Eleanor was gone twenty minutes he began to get nervous. It was after 3 P.M. and Bok/Tran had not left as they expected he would. Something didn't seem right. But what? Bosch looked up at the front corner of the shopping center, studying it and waiting for Eleanor to make the turn around the stucco siding. He heard a sound, like a muffled impact. Two or three of them. Shots? He thought of Eleanor, and his heart was pushed by a fist up into his throat. Or had the sound been car doors closing? He looked at the Mercedes but could only see the trunk and taillights. He saw no one around the car. Back at the front corner; no Eleanor. Then back at the Mercedes, and he saw the brake lights go on. Bok was leaving. Bosch started the car and drove up to the corner, his rear tires spitting gravel as he gunned it forward. At the corner he saw Eleanor walking along the sidewalk toward him. He honked the horn and signaled for her to hurry. Eleanor trotted to the car and was just getting in when the Mercedes appeared in Bosch's rearview mirror and turned out of the alley toward them.

"Get down," he said and pulled Eleanor down on the seat.

The Mercedes floated by and turned onto Bolsa. He released his grip on her neck. "What the hell do you think you're doing?" she demanded as she came up.

Bosch pointed at the Mercedes, which was heading away. "They were coming by. You would've been made because you went in the office today. What took you so long?"

"They had to track down Rourke. He wasn't in his office."

Harry pulled out and started following the Mercedes from a distance of about two blocks. After a long moment composing herself, Eleanor said, "Is he by himself?"

"I don't know. I didn't see him get in. I was looking up at the corner for you. I think I heard more than one car door close. I'm sure I did."

"But you don't know if Tran was one of them who got in?"

"Right. Don't know. But it's getting late. I figure it's gotta be him."

Bosch realized then that he might have fallen for the oldest ruse in the surveillance book. Bok, or Tran, or whoever he was, could have simply sent one of his minions in the hundred-thousand-dollar car to draw away the tail.

"What do you think, go back?" he said.

Wish didn't answer until he looked over at her. "No," she said. "Go with what we got. Don't second-guess yourself. You're right about the time. A lot of banks close at five before a holiday weekend. He had to get going. He was warned by Binh. I think it's him."

Bosch felt better. The Mercedes turned west and then north again on the Golden State Freeway toward Los Angeles. The traffic crept slowly into downtown, and then the gold car went west on the Santa Monica Freeway, exiting on Robertson at twenty minutes before five. They were heading into Beverly Hills. Wilshire Boulevard was lined with banks from downtown to the ocean. As the Mercedes turned west, Bosch felt they had to be close. Tran would keep his treasure at a bank near his home, he thought. The gamble had been right. He relaxed a bit and finally got around to asking Eleanor what Rourke had said when she called in.

"He confirmed through the Orange County clerk's office that Jimmie Bok is Nguyen Tran. They had a fictitious name filing. He changed his name nine years ago. We should've checked Orange County. I forgot about Little Saigon.

"Also," she said, "if this guy Tran had diamonds, he might have used them all up already. Property recs show he owns two more shopping centers like that one back there. In Monterey Park and Diamond Bar."

Bosch told himself it was still possible. The diamonds could be the collateral for the real estate empire. Just like with Binh. He kept his eyes on the Mercedes, only a block ahead now because rush hour was in full force and he didn't want to get cut off. He watched the black windows of the car move along the rich street, and he told himself it was heading to the diamonds.

"And I saved the best for last," Wish announced then. "Mr. Bok, also known as Mr. Tran, controls his many holdings through a corporation. The title of said corporation, according to the records check by Special Agent Rourke, is none other than Diamond Holdings, Incorporated."

They passed Rodeo Drive and were in the heart of the commercial district. The buildings lining Wilshire took on more stateliness, as if they knew they had more money and class in them. Traffic slowed to a crawl in some areas, and Bosch got as close as two car lengths behind the Mercedes, not wanting to lose the car on a missed light. They were almost to Santa Monica Boulevard and Bosch was beginning to figure they were headed to Century City. Bosch looked at his watch. It was four-fifty. "If this guy is going to a bank in Century City, I don't think he's going to make it."

Just then the Mercedes made a right turn into a parking garage. Bosch slowed to the curb and without saying a word Wish jumped out and walked into the garage. Bosch took the next right and went around the block. Cars were pouring out of office parking lots and garages, cutting in front of him again and again. When he finally got around, Eleanor was standing at the curb at the same spot where she had jumped out. He pulled up and she leaned into the window.

"Park it," she said, and she pointed across the street and down half a block. There was a rounded structure that was built out to the street from the first floor of a high-rise office building. The walls of the semicircle were glass. And inside this huge glass room Bosch saw the polished steel door of a vault. A sign outside the building said Beverly Hills Safe & Lock. He looked at Eleanor and she was smiling.

"Was Tran in the car?" he asked.

"Of course. You don't make mistakes like that."

He smiled back. Then he saw a space open up at a meter just ahead. He drove up and parked.

"Since we started thinking there would be a second vault hit, my whole orientation was banks," Eleanor Wish said. "You know, Harry? Maybe a savings and loan. But I drive by this place a couple times a week. At least. I never considered it."

They had walked down Wilshire and were standing across the street from Beverly Hills Safe & Lock. She was actually standing behind him and peeking at the place over his shoulder. Tran, or Bok as he was now known, had seen her earlier, and they couldn't risk his spotting her here. The sidewalk was clogged with office types that were pouring through the revolving glass doors of the buildings, heading to parking garages and trying to get even a five-minute jump on the traffic, on the holiday weekend.

"It fits though," Bosch said. "He comes here, doesn't trust banks, like your friend at State was talking about. So he finds a vault without a bank. Here it is. But even better. As long as you have the money to pay, these places don't need to know who you are. No federal banking regulations because it isn't a bank. You can rent a box and only identify yourself with a letter or a number code."

Beverly Hills Safe & Lock had all the appearances of a bank but was far from it. There were no savings or checking accounts. No loan department, no tellers. What it offered was what it showed in the front window. Its polished steel vault. It was a business that protected valuables, not money. In a town like Beverly Hills, this was a precious commodity. The rich and famous kept their jewels here. Their furs. Their prenuptial agreements.

And it all sat out there in the open. Behind glass. The business was the bottom floor of the fourteen-story J. C. Stock Building, a structure unnotable save for the glass vault room that protruded in a half circle from the first-floor facade. The entrance to Beverly Hills Safe & Lock was on the side of the building at Rincon Street, where Mexicans in short yellow jackets stood ready to valet a client's car.

After Bosch had dropped Eleanor off and gone around the block, she had watched Tran and two bodyguards get out of the gold Mercedes and walk to the safe and lock. If they thought they might be followed, they hadn't shown it. They never looked behind them. One of the bodyguards carried a steel briefcase.

Eleanor said, "I think I made at least one of the bodyguards as carrying. The other's coat was too baggy. Is that him? Yeah, there he is."

Tran was being escorted by a man in a dark-blue banker's suit into the vault room. A bodyguard trailed behind with the steel briefcase. Bosch saw the heavy man's eyes sweep the sidewalk outside until Tran and Banker's Suit disappeared through the vault's open door. The man with the briefcase waited. Bosch and Wish also waited, and watched. It was about three minutes before Tran came out, followed by the suit, who carried a metal safe-deposit box about the size of a woman's shoe box. The bodyguard took up the rear, and the three men walked out of the glass room, out of sight.

"Nice, personal service," Wish said. "Beverly Hills all the way. He's probably taking it into a private sitting room to make the transfer."

"Think you can get ahold of Rourke and get a crew over here to follow Tran when he leaves?" Bosch asked. "Use a landline. We have to stay off the air in case the people underground have someone up top listening to our frequencies."

"I take it we're staying here with the vault?" she asked, and Bosch nodded.

She thought a moment and said, "I'll make the call. He'll be glad to know we found the place. We'll be able to put the tunnel crew down."

She looked about, saw a pay phone next to a bus stop on the next corner and made a move to walk that way. Bosch held her arm.

"I'm going to go inside, see what's up. Remember, they know you, so stay out of sight until they're gone."

"What if they split before reinforcements come?"

"I'm staying with that vault. I don't care about Tran. You want the keys? You can take the car and tail him."

"No, I'll stay with the vault. With you."

She turned and headed toward the phone. Bosch crossed Wilshire and went in the safe and lock, passing an armed security guard who had been walking toward the door with a key ring in his hand.

"Closing up, sir," said the guard, who had the swagger and gruffness of an ex-cop.

"I'll only be a minute," Bosch said without stopping.

Banker's Suit, who had led Tran into the vault, was one of three young, fair-haired men sitting at antique desks on the plush gray carpet in the reception area. He glanced up from some papers on his desk, sized up Bosch's appearance and said to the younger of the other two, "Mr. Grant, would you like to help this gentleman."

Though his unspoken answer was no, the one called Grant stood up, came around his desk and with the best phony smile in his arsenal approached Bosch.

"Yes, sir?" the man said. "Thinking of opening a vault account with us?"

Bosch was about to ask a question when the man stuck out his hand and said, "James Grant, ask me anything. Though we are running a little short of time. We are closing for the weekend in a few minutes."

Grant drew up his coat sleeve to check his watch to confirm closing time.

"Harvey Pounds," Bosch said, taking his hand. "How did you know I don't already have a vault account?"

"Security, Mr. Pounds. We sell security. I know every vault client on sight. So do Mr. Avery and Mr. Bernard." He turned slightly and nodded at Banker's Suit and the other salesman, who solemnly nodded back.

"Not open weekends?" Bosch asked, trying to sound disappointed.

Grant smiled. "No, sir. We find our clients are the type of people who have well-planned schedules, well-planned lives. They reserve the weekend for pleasures, not errands like these others you see. Scurrying to the banks, the ATMs. Our clients are a measure above that, Mr. Pounds. And so are we. You can appreciate that."

There was a sneer in his voice when he said this. But Grant was right. The place was as slick as a corporate law office, with the same hours and the same self-important front men.

Bosch took an expansive look around. In an alcove to the right where there was a row of eight doors he saw Tran's two bodyguards standing on each side of the third door. Bosch nodded at Grant and smiled.

"Well, I see you have guards all over the place. That's the kind of security I'm looking for, Mr. Grant."

"I beg your pardon, Mr. Pounds, those men are merely waiting for a client who is in one of the private offices. But I assure you our security provision can't be compromised. Are you looking for a vault with us, sir?"

The man had more creepy charm than an evangelist. Bosch disliked him and his attitude.

"Security, Mr. Grant, I am looking for security. I want to lease a vault but I need to be assured of the security, from both outside and inside problems, if you know what I mean."

"Of course, Mr. Pounds, but do you have any idea of the cost of our service, the security we provide?"

"Don't know and don't care, Mr. Grant. See, the money is not the object. The peace of mind is. Agreed? Last week my next-door neighbor, I'm talking about just three doors down from the former president, had a burglary. The alarm was no obstacle to them. They took very valuable things. I don't want to wait for that to happen to me. No place is safe these days."

"Truly a shame, Mr. Pounds," Grant said, an unbridled note of excitement in his voice. "I didn't realize it was getting that way in Bel Air. But I couldn't agree more with your plan of action. Have a seat at my desk and we can talk. Would you like coffee, perhaps some brandy? It is near the cocktail hour, of course. Just one of the little services we provide that a banking institution cannot."

Grant laughed then, silently, with his head nodding up and down. Bosch declined the offer and the salesman sat down, pulling his chair in behind him. "Now, let me tell you the basics of how we work. We are completely nonregulated by any government agency. I think your neighbor would be happy about that."

He winked at Bosch, who said, "Neighbor?"

"The former president, of course." Bosch nodded and Grant proceeded. "We provide a long list of security services, both here and for your home, even an armed security escort if needed. We are the complete security consultant. We —"

"What about the safe-deposit vault?" Bosch cut in. He knew Tran would be coming out of the private office at any moment. He wanted to be in the vault by then.

"Yes, of course, the vault. As you saw, it is on display to the world. The glass circle, as we call it, is perhaps our most brilliant security ploy. Who would attempt to breach it? It is on display twenty-four hours a day. Right on Wilshire Boulevard. Genius?"

Grant's smile was wide with triumph. He nodded slightly in an effort to prompt agreement from his audience.

"What about from underneath?" Bosch asked, and the man's mouth dropped back into a straight line.

"Mr. Pounds, you can't expect me to outline our structural security measures, but rest assured the vault is impregnable. Between you, me and the lamppost, you won't find a bank vault in this town with as much concrete and steel in the floor, in the walls, in the ceiling of that vault. And the electrical? You couldn't — if you excuse the expression — break wind in the circle room without setting off the sound, motion and heat sensors."

"May I see it?"

"The vault?"

"Of course."

"Of course."

Grant adjusted his jacket and ushered Bosch toward the vault. A glass wall and a mantrap separated the semicircular vault room from the rest of Beverly Hills Safe & Lock. Grant waved his hand at the glass and said, "Double-plated tempered glass. Vibration alarm tape between the sheets of glass to make tampering impossible. You'll find this on the exterior windows as well. Basically, the vault room is sealed in two plys of three-quarter-inch glass."

Using his hand again like a model pointing out prizes on a game show, Grant indicated a boxlike device beside the door to the mantrap. It was about the size of an office water fountain, and a circle of white plastic was inlaid on top. On the circle was the black outline of a hand, its fingers splayed.

"To get in the vault room, your hand must be on file. The bone structure. Let me show you."

He placed his right hand on the black silhouette. The device began to hum and the white plastic inlay was lit from inside the machine. A bar of light swept below the plastic and Grant's hand, as if it were a Xerox machine.

"X ray," Grant said. "More positive than fingerprints, and the computer can process it in six seconds."

In six seconds the machine emitted a short beep and the electronic lock on the first door of the trap snapped open. "You see, your hand becomes your signature here, Mr. Pounds. No need for names. You give your box a code and you put the bone structure of your hand on file with us. Six seconds of your time is all we need."

Behind him Bosch heard a voice he recognized as belonging to Banker's Suit, the one called Avery. "Ah, Mr. Long, are we finished?"

Bosch glanced around to see Tran emerging from the alcove. Now he was the one who carried the briefcase. And one of the bodyguards carried the safe-deposit box. The other big man looked right at Bosch. Bosch turned back to Grant and said, "Can we go in?"

He followed Grant into the mantrap. The door closed behind them. They were in a glass-and-white-steel room about twice the size of a telephone booth. There was a second door at the end. Behind it stood another uniformed guard.

"This is just a detail we borrowed from the L.A. County Jail," Grant said. "This door in front of us cannot open unless the one behind us is closed and locked. Maury, our armed guard, makes a final visual check and opens the last door. You see, we have the human and electronic touch here, Mr. Pounds." He nodded to Maury, who unlocked and opened the last door of the trap. Bosch and Grant walked out into the vault room. Bosch didn't bother to mention that he had just successfully circumvented the elaborate security obstacles by playing on Grant's greed and pitching a story with a Bel Air address.

"And now into the vault," Grant said, holding his hand out like a congenial host.

The vault was larger than Bosch had envisioned. It was not wide but it extended far back into the J. C. Stock Building. There were safe-deposit boxes along both side walls and in a steel structure running down the center of the vault. The two began walking down the aisle to the left as Grant explained that the center boxes were for larger storage needs. Bosch could see that the doors were much larger than those on the side walls. Some were big enough to walk through. Grant saw Bosch staring at these and smiled.

"Furs," he said. "Minks. We do very good business storing expensive furs, gowns, what have you. The ladies of Beverly Hills keep them here in the off season. Tremendous insurance savings, not to mention the peace of mind."

Bosch tuned out the sales pitch and watched as Tran walked into the vault, trailed by Avery. Tran still had the briefcase, and Bosch noticed a thin band of polished steel on his wrist. He was handcuffed to the briefcase. Bosch's adrenaline kicked in at a higher notch. Avery stepped up to an open box door marked 237 and slid the deposit box in. He closed the door and used a key in one of the two locks on the door. Tran stepped up and put his own key in the other lock and turned it. He then nodded to Avery and both men walked out, Tran never having looked at Bosch.

Once Tran was gone, Bosch announced that he had seen enough of the vault and headed out also. He walked to the double-plated glass and looked out on Wilshire Boulevard and watched Tran, flanked by the two massive guards, making his way to the parking garage where the Mercedes was parked. No one followed them. Bosch looked around but didn't see Eleanor.

"Is something wrong, Mr. Pounds?" Grant said from behind him.

"Yes," Bosch said. He reached into his coat pocket and brought out his badge wallet. He held it up over his shoulder so Grant could see it from behind. "You better get me the manager of this place. And don't call me Mr. Pounds anymore."

Lewis stood at a pay phone in front of a twenty-four-hour diner called Darling's. He was around the corner and about a block from Beverly Hills Safe & Lock. It had been more than a minute since Officer Mary Grosso had answered the call and said she would get Deputy Chief Irving on the line.

Lewis was thinking that if the man wanted hourly updates — by landline, no less — then the least he could do was take the damn call promptly. He switched the phone to his other ear and dug in his coat pocket for something to pick his teeth with. His wrist was sore where it chafed against the pocket. But thinking about being handcuffed by Bosch only made him angry, so he tried to concentrate on the investigation. He had no idea what was going on, what Bosch and the FBI woman were up to. But Irving was convinced there was a caper on, and so was Clarke. If so, Lewis promised himself at the pay phone, he would be the one who would squeeze the cuffs on Bosch's wrists.

An old tramp with scary eyes and white hair shuffled up to the pay phone next to the one Lewis was at and checked the change slot. It was empty. He reached a finger toward the slot of the phone Lewis was using, but the IAD detective batted it away.

"Anything there, it's mine, pop," Lewis said.

Undeterred, the tramp said, "You got a quarter so I can get something to eat?"

"Fuck off," Lewis said.

"What?" a voice said.

"What?" Lewis said, and then realized the voice had come from the phone. It was Irving. "Oh, not you, sir. I didn't realize you were — uh, I was talking, uh, I'm having a problem here with someone. I —"

"You speak like that with a citizen?"

Lewis reached a hand into his pants pocket and pulled out a dollar bill. He handed it to the white-haired man and shooed him away.

"Detective Lewis, are you there?"

"Yes, Chief. Sorry. I've taken care of the situation now. I wanted to report. There has been an important development."

He hoped this last would draw Irving's attention away from the earlier indiscretion.

Irving said, "Tell me what you have. Do you still have Bosch in sight?"

Lewis exhaled sharply, relieved.

"Yes," he said, "Detective Clarke is continuing surveillance while I make this report."

"All right, then give it to me. It is Friday evening, Detective, I would like to get home at a reasonable hour."

Lewis spent the next fifteen minutes updating Irving on Bosch's tail of the gold Mercedes from Orange County to the Beverly Hills Safe & Lock. He said the tail was terminated at the safe and lock, which appeared to have been the intended destination.

"What are they doing now, Bosch and the bureau woman?"

"They are still in there. It looks like they are interviewing the manager. Something's going on. It was like they didn't know where they were going but once they got to this place, they knew this was it."

"Was what?"

"That's it. I don't know. Whatever it is they are up to. I think the guy they followed made a deposit. There is a vault, a large vault in the front window of the place."

"Yes, I know where you are talking about."

Irving did not speak for a long period, and Lewis, his report completed, knew better than to interrupt. He started daydreaming about cuffing Bosch's hands behind his back and walking him past a battery of television cameras. He heard Irving clear his throat.

"I don't know their plan," the deputy chief said. "But I want you to stay with them. If they don't go home tonight, neither do you. Understood?"

"Yes, sir."

"If they allowed the Mercedes Benz to go on, then it must be the vault they wanted to find. They will place the vault under surveillance. And you, in turn, will continue to keep them under surveillance."

"Yes, Chief," Lewis said, though he was still lost.

Irving spent the next ten minutes giving his detective instructions and his theory of what was happening with Beverly Hills Safe & Lock. Lewis pulled out a pad and pen and took some quick notes. At the end of the one-sided dialogue, Irving entrusted Lewis with his home telephone number and said, "Don't move in without my prior approval. You can call me at the number at any time, day or night. Understood?"

"Yes, sir," Lewis said urgently.

Irving hung up without saying another word.

Bosch waited in the reception area without telling Grant or the other salesmen what was going on until Wish arrived. They stood behind their fancy desks with their mouths open. When Eleanor came to the door it was locked. She knocked and held up her badge. The guard let her in and she walked into the reception area.

As the salesman named Avery opened his mouth to say something, Bosch said, "This is FBI Agent Eleanor Wish. She is with me. We are going to step into one of your client offices for a private conversation. Just take a minute. If there is a head man here, we'd like to speak to him as soon as we come out."

Grant, still flustered, just pointed to the second door in the alcove. Bosch went in the third door and Wish followed. He closed the door on all three of the salesmen's eyes and locked it.

"So, what have we got? I don't know what to tell them," he whispered as he looked around the desk and two chairs in the room for a scrap of paper or anything else Tran might have mistakenly left behind. There was nothing. He opened the drawers of the mahogany desk. There were pens and pencils and envelopes and a stack of bond paper. Nothing else. There was a fax machine on a table against the wall opposite the door but it was not turned on.

"We watch and wait," she said, speaking very quickly. "Rourke says he is putting together a tunnel crew. They'll go in and have a look around. They're going to get with DWP first to see exactly what's down there. They should be able to figure what the best spot for a tunnel would be and then they'll go from there. Harry, you really think this is it?"

He nodded. He wanted to smile but didn't. Her excitement was contagious.

"Did he get a tail on Tran in time?" he asked. "By the way, here they know him as Mr. Long."

There was a knocking on the door and someone's voice saying, "Excuse me. Excuse me." Bosch and Wish ignored it.

"Tran, Bok, now Long," Wish said. "I don't know about the tail. Rourke said he was going to try. I gave him the plate and told him where the Mercedes was parked. Guess we'll find out later. He said he'd also send over a crew to work the surveillance with us. We are going to have a surveillance meeting in the garage across the street at eight o'clock. What did they say here?"

"I haven't told them what's going on yet."

There was another knock, this one louder.

"Well, then, let's go see the head man."

The owner and chief operating officer of Beverly Hills Safe & Lock turned out to be Avery's father, Martin B. Avery III. He was of the same stock as many of his customers and wanted everybody to know it. He had a private office at the rear of the alcove. Behind his desk was a collection of framed photographs attesting to the fact that he was not just another chiseler feeding off the rich. He was one of them. There was Avery III with a couple of presidents, a movie mogul or two, and English royalty. One photo was of Avery and the Prince of Wales in full polo regalia, though Avery appeared too thick around the middle and loose in the jowls to be much of a horseman.

Bosch and Wish summarized the situation for him and he was immediately skeptical. He said his vault was impregnable. They told him to save the sales pitch and asked to see design and operation plans for the vault. Avery III flipped his $60 blotter over, and there was the vault schematic taped to the back. It was clear that Avery III and his blow-cut salesmen were overselling the vault. Starting from its outermost skin and going inward, it was one-inch steel plating followed by a foot of rebarred concrete followed by another inch of steel. The vault was thicker on the bottom and top, where there was another two-foot layer of concrete. As with all vaults, the most impressive thing was the thick steel door, but that was for show. Just like the hand X ray and the mantrap. Only a show. Bosch knew that if the tunnel bandits were really down below, they would have little trouble coming up for air.

Avery III said that there had been a vault alarm on each of the past two nights, including two alarms on Thursday night. Each time he was called at home by the Beverly Hills police. He in turn called his son, Avery IV, and dispatched him to meet the officers. The officers and the heir then entered the business and reset the alarm after finding nothing amiss.

"We had no idea that there might be someone in the sewers below us," Avery III said. He said it like the word sewers was wholly beneath his usage. "Hard to believe, hard to believe."

Bosch asked more detailed questions about the vault's operation and security devices. Not realizing its significance, Avery III mentioned matter-of-factly that unlike conventional bank vaults his vault had a time-lock override. He had a code he could enter into the computer lock which would purge the time-lock coordinates. He was able to open the vault door anytime.

"We must accede to our client's needs," he explained. "If a Beverly Hills lady should call on a Sunday because she needs her tiara for the charity ball, I want to be able to get that tiara for her. You see, it is the service we sell."

"Do all your clients know about that weekend service?" Wish asked.

"Of course not," Avery III said. "Only a select few. You see, we charge a hefty fee. We must bring in a security guard to do it."

"How long does it take to do the override and swing the door open?" Bosch asked.

"Not long. I tap in the override code on the keypad next to the vault door and it is done in a matter of seconds. You then set the vault unlock code in, then turn the wheel and the door opens under its own weight. Thirty seconds, perhaps a minute, perhaps less."

Not fast enough, Bosch thought. Tran's box was located near the front of the vault. That's where the bandits would be working. They would see and probably hear the vault door being opened. No element of surprise.

An hour later, Bosch and Wish were back in his car. They had moved to the second level of the parking garage across Wilshire and east a half block from Beverly Hills Safe & Lock. From there they had an open view of the vault room. After they had left Avery III and taken the surveillance position, they had watched as Avery IV and Grant swung the huge stainless steel vault door closed. They turned the wheel and typed on the computer keypad, locking it. Then the lights inside the business went out, all except those in the glass vault room. Those always stayed on to display the very symbol of the security they offered.

"You think they'll come through tonight?" Wish asked.

"Hard to say. Without Meadows, they're down a man. They might be behind schedule."

They had told Avery III to go home and be ready for a callout. The owner had agreed but remained skeptical of the whole scenario Bosch and Wish had spun for him.

"We are going to have to get them from underground," Bosch said, his hands holding the steering wheel as if he were driving. "We'd never get that door open fast enough."

Bosch idly looked to his left, up Wilshire. He saw a white LTD with police wheels parked at the curb a block away. It was parked next to a fire hydrant and there were two figures in it. He still had company.

Bosch and Wish stood next to his car, which was parked on the second level of the garage facing the retainer wall at the south end. The garage had been virtually empty for more than an hour, but the drab concrete enclosure smelled of exhaust fumes and burning brakes. Bosch was sure the brakes smell was from his car. The stop-and-go tail from Little Saigon had taken its toll on the replacement car. From their position they could look across Wilshire and west a half block to the vault showroom of Beverly Hills Safe & Lock. Farther down Wilshire the sky was pink and the setting sun a deep orange. Evening lights were coming on in the city and traffic was thinning out. Bosch looked east up Wilshire and could see the white LTD parked at the curb, its occupants shadows behind the tinted windshield.

At eight o'clock a procession of three cars, the last a Beverly Hills patrol car, came up the ramp and cut across the empty parking spaces to where Bosch and Wish stood at the wall.

"Well, if our perps have their lookout in any of these high rises and they saw this little parade, you can bet he is pulling them out now," Bosch said.

Rourke and four other men got out of the two unmarked cars. Bosch could tell by the suits that three of them were agents. The fourth man's suit was a little too worn, its pockets baggy like Bosch's. He carried a cardboard tube. Harry figured him for the DWP supe Wish had said was coming. Three Beverly Hills uniforms, one with captain's bars on his collar, got out of the patrol car. The captain was also carrying a rolled tube of paper.

Everybody converged at Bosch's car and used its hood as the meeting table. Rourke made some quick introductions. The three from BHPD were there because the operation was in their jurisdiction. Interdepartmental courtesy, Rourke said. They were also on hand because Beverly Hills Safe & Lock had filed a design plan with the local police department's commercial security division. They would only observe the meeting, Rourke said, and be called on later if their department was needed for backup. Two of the FBI agents, Hanlon and Houck, would work the overnight surveillance with Bosch and Wish. Rourke wanted a view of Beverly Hills Safe & Lock from at least two angles. The third agent was the FBI's SWAT coordinator. And the last man was Ed Gearson, a DWP underground facilities supervisor.

"Okay, let's set the battle plans," Rourke announced at the end of the introductions. He took the cardboard tube from Gearson without asking and slid out a rolled blueprint. "This is a DWP schematic print for this area. It has all the utility lines, the tunnels and culverts. It tells us exactly what is down there."

He unfurled the grayish map with smeared blue lines on it across the hood. The three Beverly Hills cops anchored the other end with their hands.

It was getting dark in the garage and the SWAT man, an agent named Heller, held a penlight with a surprisingly wide and bright beam over the drawing. Rourke took a pen out of his shirt pocket, pulled on it until it telescoped into a pointer.

"Okay, we are . . . right . . ." Before he could find the spot Gearson reached his arm into the light and put a finger on the map. Rourke brought his pen point over to the spot. "Yes, right here," he said and gave Gearson a don't-fuck-with-me look. The DWP man's shoulders seemed to stoop a little more in his threadbare jacket.

Everyone around the car leaned in closer over the hood to study the location. "Beverly Hills Safe & Lock is here," Rourke said. "The actual vault is here. Can we see your blueprint, Captain Orozco?"

Orozco, who was built like an inverted pyramid, broad shoulders over thin hips, unrolled his drawing across the top of the DWP print. It was a copy of the drawing Avery III had shown Bosch and Wish earlier.

"Three thousand square feet of vault space," said Orozco, indicating the vault area with his hand. "Small private boxes along the sides and free-standing closets down the middle. If they are under there, they could come up through the floor anywhere along these two aisles. So we are talking about a range of about sixty feet in which they could come through the floor."

"Now, Captain," Rourke said, "if you pick that up and we look back at the DWP chart, we can place that breakthrough zone right here." With a Day-Glo yellow underliner he outlined the floor of the vault on the utility map. "Using that as a guide, we can see the subterranean structures that offer the closest proximity. What do you think, Mr. Gearson?"

Gearson leaned over the car hood another few inches and studied the utility map. Bosch also leaned in. He saw thick lines he assumed indicated major east-west drainage lines. The kind the tunnelers would seek. He noticed that they corresponded to major surface streets: Wilshire, Olympic, Pico. Gearson pointed out the Wilshire line, saying it ran thirty feet below ground and was large enough to drive a truck through. With his finger, the DWP man traced the Wilshire line east ten blocks to Robertson, a major north-south stormwater line. From that intersection, he said, it was just a mile south to an open drainage culvert that ran alongside the Santa Monica Freeway. The opening at the culvert was as big as a garage door and blocked only by a gate with a padlock on it.

"I'd say that's where they could've come in," Gearson said. "Like following surface streets. You take the Robertson line up to Wilshire. Take a left and you're practically here by your yellow line. The vault. But I don't think they'd dig a tunnel off the Wilshire line."

"No?" Rourke said. "How so?"

"Too busy is how so," Gearson said, sensing he was the man with the answers as nine faces peered at him from around the car hood. "We got DWP people underground all the time in these main lines. Checking for cracks, blockages, problems of any sort. And Wilshire's the main drag down there, east and west. Just like up top. If somebody knocked a hole in the wall it'd get noticed. See?"

"What if they were able to conceal the hole?"

"You're talking about like they did a year or so ago in that burglary downtown. Yeah, that might work again, maybe somewhere else, but there is a good chance on the Wilshire line that it'd be seen. We look for that sort of thing now. And, like I said, there's a lot of traffic on the Wilshire line."

There was silence as they took time to consider this. The engines of the cars ticked away the heat.

"Then where would they dig, Mr. Gearson, to get into this vault?" Rourke finally said.

"We got all manner of linkups down there. Don't think us guys don't think of this from time to time when we're working down there. You know, the perfect crime and all that. I've hashed stuff like this around, especially when I read about that last one in the papers. I think if you are saying that's the vault they want to get into, then they'd still do just like I said: come up Robertson and then over on the Wilshire line. But then I think they'd move down one of the service tunnels to sort of stay out of sight. The service tunnels are three to five feet wide. They're round. Plenty of room to work and move equipment. They hook up the main artery lines to the street storm drains and the utility systems in the buildings along here."

He put his hand back into the light and traced the smaller lines he was talking about on the DWP map.

"If they did this right," he said, "what they did was get in the gate down by the freeway and drive their equipment and all up to Wilshire and then over to your target area. They unload their stuff, hide it in one of these service tunnels, as we call 'em, and then take their vehicle back out. They hike back in on foot and set to work in the service tunnel. Hell, they could be working in there five, six weeks before we might have occasion to go up that particular line."

Bosch still thought it sounded too simple.

"What about these other storm lines?" he asked, indicating Olympic and Pico on the map. There was a crosshatch pattern of the smaller service tunnels running from these lines north toward the vault. "What about using one of these and coming up behind the vault?"

Gearson scratched his bottom lip with a finger and said, "That's fine. There's that too. But the thing is, these lines aren't going to get you as close to the vault as these Wilshire offshoots. See what I mean? Why would they dig a hundred-yard tunnel when they could dig a hundred-footer here?"

Gearson liked holding court, the idea of knowing more than the silk suits and uniforms around him. Having finished his speech, he rocked back on his heels, a satisfied look on his face. Bosch knew the man was probably correct on every detail.

"What about earth displacement?" Bosch asked him. "These guys are digging a tunnel through dirt and rock, concrete. Where do they get rid of it? How?"

"Bosch, Mr. Gearson is not a detective," Rourke said. "I doubt that he knows every nuance of —"

"Easy," Gearson said. "The floors of the main lines like Wilshire and Robertson are graded three degrees to center. There is always water running down the center, even most days during a drought. It might not be raining up top but water flows, you know. You'd be surprised how much. Either it's runoff from the reservoirs or commercial use or both. Your fire department gets a call, where you think the water goes when they are done puttin' the fire out? So what I am saying is, if they had enough water they could use it to move the displaced earth or whatever you want to call it."

"It's got to be tons." Hanlon spoke for the first time.

"But it's not several tons at once. You said they took days to dig this. You spread it out over days and the runoff could handle it. Now, if they are in one of the service tunnels they'd have to figure a way to get water through there, down to your main line. I'd check your fire hydrants in the area. You got one leaking or had a report of somebody opening one up, that'd be your boys."

One of the uniforms leaned to Orozco's ear and said something. Orozco leaned over the hood and raised his finger above the map. Then he poked it down on a blue line. "We had a hydrant vandalized here two nights ago."

"Somebody opened it up," the uniform who had whispered to the captain said, "and used a bolt cutter to cut the chain that holds the cap. They took the cap with them, and it took the fire department an hour to get out here with a replacement."

"That would be a lot of water," Gearson said. "That would have taken care of some of your earth displacement."

He looked at Bosch and smiled. And Bosch smiled back. He liked when pieces of the puzzle began to fit.

"Before that, let's see, Saturday night it was, we had an arson," Orozco said. "A little boutique in behind the Stock Building off Rincon."

Gearson looked at the spot Orozco pointed to on the blueprint as being the location of the boutique. He put his own finger on the fire hydrant location. "The water from both of those things would have gone into three street catches, here, here and here," he said, moving his hand deftly over the gray paper. "These two drain to this line. The other drains here."

The investigators looked at the two drainage lines. One ran parallel to Wilshire, behind the J. C. Stock Building. The other ran perpendicular to Wilshire, a straight offshoot, and next to the building.

"Either one and we're still looking at, what, a hundred-foot tunnel?" Wish said.

"At least," Gearson said. "If they had a straight shot. They might've hit ground utilities or hard rock and had to divert some. Doubt any tunnel down there could be a straight shot."

The SWAT expert tugged Rourke's cuff and the two walked away from the crowd for a whispered conversation. Bosch looked at Wish and softly said, "They're not going to go in."

"What do you mean?"

"This isn't Vietnam. Nobody has to go down there. If Franklin and Delgado and anybody else are down there in one of these lines, there's no way to go in safely and unannounced. They hold all the advantages. They'd know we're coming."

She studied his face but didn't say anything.

"It would be the wrong move," Bosch said. "We know they're armed and probably have trips set up. We know they're killers."

Rourke came back to the gathering around the car hood and asked Gearson to wait in one of the bureau cars while he finished up with the investigators. The DWP man walked to the car with his head down, disappointed he was no longer part of the plan.

"We're not going in after them," Rourke said after Gearson shut the car door. "Too dangerous. They have weapons, explosives. We have no element of surprise. It adds up to heavy casualties for us. . . . So, we trap them. We let things take their course and then we will be there waiting, safely, when they come out. Then we'll have surprise on our side.

"Tonight SWAT will make a recon run through the Wilshire line — we'll get some DWP uniforms from Gearson — and look for their entry point. Then we'll set up and wait in whatever's the best location. Whatever's safest from our standpoint."

There was a beat of silence, punctuated by a horn from the street, before Orozco protested.

"Wait a minute, wait a minute." He waited until every face was on his. Except Rourke's. He didn't look at Orozco at all.

"We can't be talking about sitting out here with our thumbs up our asses and letting these people blast their way into that vault," Orozco said. "To let them go in and pry open a couple hundred boxes and then just back out. My obligation is to protect the property of the citizens of Beverly Hills, who probably happen to constitute ninety percent of that business's customers. I'm not going along with this."

Rourke collapsed his pen pointer, put it in the inside pocket of his coat and then spoke. He still did not look at Orozco.

"Orozco, your exception can be noted for the record, but we're not asking you to go along with this," Rourke said. Bosch noticed that along with failing to address Orozco by his rank, Rourke had dropped all pretense of courtesy.

"This is a federal operation," Rourke continued. "You are here as a professional courtesy. Besides, if my thinking is correct, they will open one deposit box only. When they find it empty they will cancel the operation and leave the vault."

Orozco was lost. His face showed it. Bosch could see he obviously had not been given many details of the investigation. He felt sorry for him, hung out to dry by Rourke.

"There are things we can't discuss at this point," Rourke said. "But we believe their target is only one box. We have reason to believe it is now empty. When the perps break into the vault and open that particular box and find it is empty, we believe they will back out in a hurry. Our job now is to be ready for that."

Bosch wondered about Rourke's supposition. Would the thieves back out? Or would they think they had the wrong box and keep drilling, looking for Tran's diamonds? Or would they loot the other boxes in hope of stealing property valuable enough to make the tunnel caper worth it? Bosch didn't know. He certainly wasn't as sure as Rourke, but then he knew the FBI agent might just be posturing to get Orozco out of the way.

"What if they don't back out?" Bosch asked. "What if they keep drilling?"

"Then we all have a long weekend ahead of us," Rourke said, "because we are going to wait them out."

"Either way, you're going to put that place out of business," Orozco said, pointing in the direction of the Stock Building. "Once it is known that somebody blew a hole through the vault they've got sitting out there in the big window, there will be no public confidence. Nobody will put their property in there."

Rourke just stared at him. The captain's plea was falling on deaf ears.

"If you can catch them after they break in, why not before?" Orozco said. "Why don't we open up that place, run a siren, make some noise, even sit a patrol car out front? Do something to let 'em know we are here and we know about them. That'll scare 'em out before they break in. We catch them, we save the business. We don't, we still save the business and we get them another day."

"Captain," Rourke said, the false congeniality back, "if you let them know we are here, you take away our one advantage — surprise — and invite a firefight in the tunnels and perhaps up on the street in which they will not care who is hurt, who is killed. That's including themselves and perhaps innocent bystanders. Then, how do we explain to the public and even ourselves that we did it this way because we wanted to try to save a business?"

Rourke waited a beat to let his words sink in, then said, "You see, Captain, I am not going to hedge on safety on this operation. I can't. These men that are down there, they don't scare. They kill. Two people that we know about, including a witness. And that's only this week. No way are we going to let them get away. No fucking way."

Orozco leaned across the hood and rolled his blueprint up. As he snapped a rubber band around it, he said, "Gentlemen, don't fuck up. If you do, my department and I will not hold back our criticism or the details of what was discussed at this meeting. Good night."

He turned and walked back to the patrol car. The two uniforms followed without being told to. Everybody else just watched. When the patrol car drove down the ramp, Rourke said, "Well, you heard the man. We can't fuck this up. Anybody else want to suggest something?"

"What about putting people in the vault now and waiting for them to come up?" Bosch said. He hadn't really considered it but threw it out as it came to him.

"No," the SWAT man said. "You put people in the vault and they are in a corner. No options. No way out. I wouldn't even ask my men for volunteers."

"They could be injured by the blast," Rourke added. "No telling where or when the perps will come up."

Bosch nodded. They were right.

"Can we open the vault and go in, once we know they have come up?" one of the agents said. Bosch couldn't remember now whether he was Hanlon or Houck.

"Yes, there's a way to take the door off the time lock," Wish said. "We'd need to get Avery, the owner, back out here."

"From what Avery said, it looks like that would take too long," Bosch said. "Too slow. Avery can take it off time lock and open it, but it's a two-ton door that swings open on its own weight. At best, it would take a half minute to get it open. Maybe less, but they'd still have the drop on us, the people inside. Same risk as coming at them through the tunnels."

"What about a flash bang?" one of the agents said. "We open the vault door just a bit and throw in a flash grenade. Then we go in and take them."

Rourke and the SWAT man shook their heads in unison.

"For two reasons," the SWAT man said. "If they wire the tunnel as we assume they will, the flash could detonate the charges. We could see Wilshire Boulevard out there drop thirty feet, and we don't want that. Think of the paperwork."

When no one smiled, he continued. "Secondly, that's a glass room we are talking about. Our position in there would be very vulnerable. If they have a lookout, we're dead. We think they go with radio silence when they've got the explosives out. But what if they don't and this lookout lets them know we're out there. They might be ready to toss something out at *us* while we're tossing something in."

Rourke added his own thoughts. "Never mind the lookout. We put a SWAT team in that glass room and they can watch it on TV. We'll have every station in L.A. with a camera out on the sidewalk and traffic backed up to Santa Monica. It'd be a circus. So forget that. SWAT will get with Gearson, do the recon and get the exits down by the freeway covered. We wait for them underneath and we take 'em on *our* terms. That's it."

The SWAT man nodded and Rourke continued. "Starting tonight we'll have twenty-four-hour surveillance topside on the vault. I want Wish, Bosch, on the vault side of the building. Hanlon, Houck, on Rincon Street so you can see the door. If it looks or sounds like it is going down, I want to be alerted and I will alert SWAT to stand by. Use landlines if possible. We don't know if they are monitoring our freeks. You people on the surveillance will have to work out a code to use on the radio. Everybody got that?"

"What if there is an alarm?" Bosch asked. "There have been three so far this week."

Rourke thought a moment and said, "Handle it routinely. Meet the call-out manager, Avery or whoever, at the door and reset the alarm and send him on his way. I'll get back to Orozco and tell him to send his patrols on the alarms but we'll handle things."

"Avery will get the callouts," Wish said. "He already knows what we think is going to happen here. What if he wants to open the vault, take a look around?"

"Don't let him. It's that simple. It's his vault but his life would be endangered. We can prevent it."

Rourke looked around at the faces. There were no more questions.

"Then that's it. I want people in position in ninety minutes. That gives you all-nighters time to eat, piss and get coffee. Wish, give me status reports, landline, at midnight and oh six hundred. Got it?"

"Got it."

Rourke and the SWAT man got in the car where Gearson was waiting and drove down the ramp. Bosch, Wish, Hanlon, and Houck then worked out a radio code to use. They decided to switch the streets in the surveillance area with the names of streets downtown. The idea was if anyone was listening to the simplex 5 public safety frequency, they would think they were hearing reports on a surveillance at Broadway and First Street in downtown instead of Wilshire and Rincon in Beverly Hills. They also decided to refer to the vault room as a pawnshop while on the radio. That done, the two sets of investigators split up and agreed to check in at the start of the surveillance. As Hanlon and Houck's car headed toward the ramp, Bosch, alone with Wish for the first time since the plans were set, asked what she thought.

"I don't know. I don't like the idea of letting them go into the vault and then run around loose down there after. I wonder if the SWAT team can really cover everything."

"I guess we'll find out."

A car came up the ramp and drove toward them. The lights blinded Bosch, and for a moment he thought of the car that had come at them the night before. But then the car swerved and came to a stop. It was Hanlon and Houck. The passenger window was rolled down and Houck held a thick manila envelope out the window.

"Mail call, Harry," the agent said. "Forgot we were supposed to give this to you. Somebody from your office dropped it by the bureau today, said you were waiting for it but hadn't been by Wilcox to get it."

Bosch took the envelope and held it out away from his body. Houck noticed the discomfort on his face.

"The guy's name was Edgar, a black guy, said you used to be partners," Houck said. "Said it had been sitting in your mailbox two days and he thought it might be important. Said he was showing somebody a house out in Westwood and decided to drop it by while he was in the area. That sound legit to you?"

Bosch nodded and the two agents drove away again. The heavy envelope was sealed but the return address was the U.S. Armed Services Records Archive in St. Louis. He tore off the end of the envelope and looked inside. There was a thick file of papers.

"What is it?" Wish asked.

"It's Meadows's package. I forgot I ordered it. Did it Monday, before I knew you guys were on the case. Anyway, I've already seen this stuff."

He tossed the envelope through the open window of the car onto the backseat.

"Hungry?" she asked him.

"I want some coffee at least."

"I know a place."

Bosch was sipping steaming black coffee from a plastic cup he had taken from the restaurant, an Italian place on Pico behind Century City. He was in the car, back in place on the second floor of the parking garage across Wilshire from the vault. Wish opened the door and got in after making her midnight check-in call to Rourke.

"They found the Jeep."

"Where?"

"Rourke says SWAT did the reconnaissance ride through the Wilshire storm sewer but found no sign of intruders or a tunnel entry. Looks like Gearson was right. They're tucked in one of the smaller tributary lines. Anyway, the SWAT guys then went down to the drainage wash by the freeway to set the trap. They were deploying at three exit positions from the tunnels when they came across the Jeep. Rourke said there's a car pool parking lot down by the freeway. There's a beige Jeep parked with a covered trailer attached. It's theirs. The three blue ATVs are in the trailer."

"Is he getting a warrant?"

"Yeah, he's got somebody trying to find a judge now. So they'll have it. But they aren't going to go near it until they take down the operation. In case their plan is for someone to come out and get the ATVs. Or somebody already outside is going to show up and drive 'em in."

Bosch nodded and sipped. It was the smart way to go. He remembered he had a cigarette going in the ashtray and tossed it out the open window.

As if guessing what he would be thinking, she said, "Rourke said that from what they could see there was no blanket in the back of the Jeep. But if it's the Jeep Meadows's body was carried to the reservoir in, there still should be fiber evidence."

"What about the seal that Sharkey saw on the door?"

"Rourke said there was no seal. But there could have been one and they just took it off when they were leaving the Jeep out there."

"Yeah," Bosch said. After a few moments of thought, he said, "Does it bother you how everything is just coming together so well?"

"Should it?"

Bosch shrugged his shoulders. He looked up Wilshire. The curb in front of the fireplug was empty. Since they had come back from dinner Bosch hadn't seen the white LTD, which he'd been sure was an IAD car. He didn't know if Lewis and Clarke were around or had called it a night.

"Harry, good detective work pays off with cases that come together," Eleanor told him. "I mean, we aren't out of the dark on this by a long shot. But I think we finally have a measure of control. Damned sight better than we were three days ago. So why the worry when a few things finally start coming together?"

"Three days ago Sharkey was still alive."

"Well, while you're taking the blame for that, why don't you add every-body else who has ever made a choice and gotten themselves killed. You can't change those things, Harry. And you're not supposed to be a martyr."

"What do you mean, choice? Sharkey didn't make any choice."

"Yes, he did. When he chose the streets, he knew he might die on the streets."

"You don't believe that. He was a kid."

"I believe that shit happens. I believe that the best you can do in this job is come out even. Some people win and some lose. Hopefully, half the time it is the good guys who win. That's us, Harry."

Bosch drank his cup dry and they sat in silence for a while after that. They had a clear view of the vault sitting at the center of the glass room like a throne. Out there in the open, polished and shiny under the bright ceiling lights, it said "Take me" to the world, he thought. And somebody would. We're going to let them.

Wish picked up the radio handset, keyed the transmit button twice and said, "Broadway One to First, do you guys copy?"

"We copy, Broadway. Anything?" It was Houck's voice on the comeback. There was a lot of static, as the radio waves ricocheted off the tall buildings in the area.

"Only checking. What's your position?"

"We are due south of the front door of the pawnshop. A clear view of nothing going on."

"We're east. Can see the —" She clicked off the mike and looked at Bosch. "We forgot a code for the vault. Got any ideas?"

Bosch shook his head no, but then said, "Saxophone. I've seen saxophones hanging in pawnshop windows. Musical instruments, lots of them."

She clicked the mike open again. "Sorry, First Street, had technical difficulty. We are east of the pawnshop, have the piano in the window in sight. No activity inside."

"Stay awake."

"That's a K. Broadway out."

Bosch smiled and shook his head.

"What?" she said. "What?"

"I've seen lots of musical instruments in pawnshops, but I don't know about a piano. Who is going to take a piano to a pawnshop? You'd need a truck. We've blown our cover now."

He picked up the radio mike, but without clicking the transmit button, and said, "Uh, First Street, check that. It's not a piano in the window. That's an accordion. Our mistake."

She slugged him on the shoulder and told him to never mind the piano. They settled into an easy silence. Surveillance jobs were the bane of most detectives' existence. But in his fifteen years on the job Bosch had never minded a single stakeout. In fact, many times he enjoyed them when he was with good company. He defined good company not by the conversation but by the lack of it. When there was no need to talk to feel comfortable, that was the right company. Bosch thought about the case and watched the traffic pass by the vault. He recapped the events as they had occurred, in order, from start to present. Revisiting scenes, listening to the dialogue over again. He found that often this reaccounting helped him make the next choice or step. What he mulled over now, poking at it like a loose tooth with his tongue, was the hit-and-run. The car that had come at them the night before. Why? What did they know at that point that made them so dangerous? It seemed to be a foolish move to kill a cop and a federal agent. Why was it undertaken? His mind then drifted to the night they had spent together after all the questions were asked by all the supervisors. Eleanor was spooked. More so than he. As he had held her in her bed, he felt as though he were calming a frightened animal. Holding and caressing her as she breathed into his neck. They had not made love. Just held each other. It had somehow seemed more intimate.

"Are you thinking about last night?" she asked then.

"How did you know?"

"A guess. Any ideas?"

"Well, I think it was nice. I think we —"

"I'm talking about who tried to kill us last night."

"Oh. No, no ideas. I was thinking about the after."

"Oh. . . . You know, I didn't thank you, Harry, for being with me like that, not expecting anything."

"I should thank you."

"You're sweet."

They drifted into their own thoughts again. Leaning against the door with his head against the side window, Bosch rarely took his eyes off the vault. Traffic on Wilshire was light but steady. People heading to or from the clubs over on Santa Monica Boulevard or around Rodeo Drive. There was probably a premiere at nearby Academy Hall. It seemed to Bosch that every limousine in L.A. was working Wilshire this night. Stretch cars of all makes and colors cruised by, one by one. They moved so smoothly they seemed to float. They were beautiful, and intriguing with their black windows. Like exotic women in sunglasses. A car built just for this city, Bosch thought.

"Has Meadows been buried?"

The question surprised him. He wondered what tumble of thought led to it. "No," he answered. "Monday, over at the veterans cemetery."

"A Memorial Day funeral, sounds kind of fitting. So his life of crime did not disqualify him from being placed in such sacred ground?"

"No. He did his time over there in Vietnam. They've saved a space for him. There's probably one there for me, too. Why did you ask?"

"I don't know. Just thinking is all. Will you go?"

"If I'm not sitting here watching this vault."

"That will be nice of you. I know he meant something to you. At one point in your life."

He let it drop, but then she said, "Harry, tell me about the black echo. What you said the other day. What did you mean?"

For the first time he looked away from the vault and at Eleanor. Her face was in darkness, but headlights from a passing car lit the interior of the car for a moment and he could see her eyes on his. He looked back at the vault.

"There isn't anything really to tell. It's just what we called one of the intangibles."

"Intangibles?"

"There was no name for it, so we made up a name. It was the darkness, the damp emptiness you'd feel when you were down there alone in those tunnels. It was like you were in a place where you felt dead and buried in the dark. But you were alive. And you were scared. Your own breath kind of echoed in the darkness, loud enough to give you away. Or so you thought. I don't know. It's hard to explain. Just . . . the black echo."

She let some time slide between them before she said, "I think your going to the funeral is nice."

"Is something wrong?"

"What do you mean?"

"What I said. The way you're talking. You haven't seemed right since last night. Like something — I don't know, forget it."

"I don't know, either, Harry. You know, after the adrenaline wore off, I guess I kind of just got scared. Made me start thinking about things."

Bosch nodded his head but didn't say anything. His mind drifted and he remembered a time in the Triangle when a company that had taken heavy casualties from sniper fire stumbled onto the entrance to a tunnel complex. Bosch, Meadows and a couple of other rats named Jarvis and Hanrahan were dropped at a nearby LZ and escorted to the hole. The first thing they did was drop a couple of LZ flares, a blue one and a red one, into the hole and blow the smoke in with a Mighty Mite fan, to find the other entrances in the jungle. Pretty soon ribbons of smoke started curling out of the ground at a couple dozen spots for two hundred yards in all directions. The smoke was coming up through the spider holes the snipers used as firing positions or to move in and out of the tunnels. There were so many of them, the jungle was turning purple from the smoke. Meadows was stoned. He popped a cassette into the portable tape player he always carried and started blasting Hendrix's "Purple Haze" into the tunnel. It was one of Bosch's most vivid memories, aside from his dreams, of the war.

He never liked rock and roll after that. The jolting energy of the music reminded him too much of the war.

"Did you ever go see the memorial?" Eleanor asked.

She didn't have to say which one. There was only the one, in Washington. But then he remembered the long black replica he had watched them installing at the cemetery by the Federal Building.

"No," he said after a while. "I've never seen it."

After the air in the jungle cleared and the Hendrix tape was done, the four of them had gone into the tunnel while the rest of the company sat on backpacks and chowed and waited. An hour later, only Bosch and Meadows had come back. Meadows carried with him three NVA scalps. He held them up for the troops above ground and yelled, "You're looking at the baddest blood brother in the black echo." And so came the name. Later, they found Jarvis and Hanrahan in the tunnels. They had fallen into punji traps. They were dead.

Eleanor said, "I visited it when I was living in D.C. I couldn't make myself go to the dedication in eighty-two. But a lot of years later I finally got the courage. I wanted to see my brother's name. I thought maybe it would help me sort things out, you know, about what happened with him."

"And did it?"

"No. Made it worse. It made me angry. It left me with this need for justice, if that makes sense. I wanted justice for my brother."

The silence filled the car again and Bosch poured more coffee into his cup. He was beginning to feel the onset of caffeine jitters but couldn't stop. He was addicted. He watched a couple of drunks who were stumbling down the street stop in front of the window before the vault. One of the men threw his hands up as if trying to gain a measure of the vault's huge door. After a while they moved on. He thought of the rage Eleanor must have felt because of her brother. The helplessness. He thought of his own rage. He knew the same feelings, maybe not to the same degree but from a different perspective. Anybody who was touched by the war knew some part of those feelings. He had never worked it out completely and wasn't sure he wanted to. The anger and sadness gave him something that was better than complete emptiness. Is that what Meadows felt? He wondered. The emptiness. Is that what bounced him from job to job and needle to needle until he was finally and fatally used up on this last mission? Bosch decided that he would go to Meadows's funeral, that he owed him that much.

"You know what you were telling me the other day about that guy, the Dollmaker killer?" Eleanor asked.

"What about it?"

"IAD, they tried to make a case that you executed him?"

"Yes, I told you. They tried. But it wasn't there. All they got me on was suspension for procedure violations."

"Well, I just wanted to say that even if they were right, they were wrong. That would have been justice in my book. You knew what would happen with a guy like that. Look at the Night Stalker. He'll never get the gas. Or it'll take twenty years."

Bosch felt uncomfortable. He had only thought of his motives and actions in the Dollmaker case when alone. He never spoke aloud about it. He didn't know where she was going with this.

She said, "I know if it was true you could never admit it, but I think you either consciously or subconsciously made a decision. You went for justice for all those women, his victims. Maybe even for your mother."

Shocked, Bosch turned to her and was about to ask how she knew about his mother and how she had come to think of her relation to the Dollmaker. Then he remembered the files again. It was probably in there somewhere. When he had applied to the department, he had to say on the forms if he or any close relatives had ever been the victim of a crime. He had been orphaned at eleven, he wrote, when his mother was found strangled in an alley off Hollywood Boulevard. He didn't need to write what she did for a living. The location and crime said enough.

When he recovered his cool, Bosch asked Eleanor what her point was.

"No point," she said. "I just . . . respect that. If it were me, I would have liked to have done the same thing, I think. I hope I would have been brave enough."

He looked over at her, the darkness shielding both their faces. It was late now and no car lights drifted by to show them to each other.

"You go ahead and take the first shift sleeping," he said. "I drank too much coffee."

She didn't answer. He offered to get out a blanket he had put in the trunk, but she declined.

"Did you ever hear what J. Edgar Hoover said about justice?" she asked.

"He probably said a lot, but I don't recall any of it offhand."

"He said that justice is incidental to law and order. I think he was right."

She said nothing else and after a while he could hear her breathing turn deeper and longer. When the rare car drove by he would look over at her face as the light washed across it. She slept like a child, with her head leaning against her hands. Bosch cracked the window and lit a cigarette. He smoked and wondered if he could or would fall in love with her, and she with him. He was thrilled and disquieted by the thought, all at the same time.

PART VII

SATURDAY, MAY 26

Gray dawn came up over the street and filled the car with weak light. The morning also brought with it a gentle drizzle that wet the street and put a smear of condensation on the lower half of the windows of Beverly Hills Safe & Lock. It was the first rain of any kind in months that Bosch could remember. Wish slept and he watched the vault: overhead lights still glowed on the chrome-and-brushed-steel finish. It was past six o'clock, but Bosch had forgotten the check-in call to Rourke and let Eleanor sleep. In fact, during the night he had never wakened her so that he could take a turn sleeping. He just never got tired. Houck checked in on the radio at three-thirty to make sure someone was awake. After that there were no disturbances and no activity in the vault room. For the rest of the night Bosch thought alternately of Eleanor Wish and the vault he watched.

He reached for the cup on the dashboard and checked for even a cold gulp of coffee, but it was empty. He dropped the empty over the seat to the floor. As he did this, he noticed the package from St. Louis on the backseat. He reached back and grabbed the manila envelope. He pulled out the thick sheaf of papers and idly looked through them while glancing up at the vault every few seconds.

Most of Meadows's military records he had already seen. But he quickly noticed that there were several that had not been in the FBI jacket Wish had given him. This was a more complete record. There was a photostat of his draft report notice and medical exam. There were also medical records from Saigon. He had been treated twice for syphilis, once for acute stress reaction.

Paging through the package, he stopped when his eyes fell on a copy of a two-page letter from a Louisiana congressman named Noone. Curious, Bosch began to read. It was dated 1973 and was addressed to Meadows at the embassy in Saigon. The letter, bearing the official congressional seal, thanked Meadows for his hospitality and help during the congressman's recent fact-finding visit. Noone noted that it had been a pleasant surprise to find a fellow New Iberian in the strange country. Bosch wondered how much of a coincidence it had been. Meadows had probably been assigned to security for the congressman so they would hit it off and the legislator would go back to Washington with a high opinion of personnel and morale in Southeast Asia. There are no coincidences.

The second page of the letter congratulated Meadows on a fine career and referred to the good reports Noone had received from Meadows's commanding officer. Bosch read on. Meadows's involvement in stopping an illegal entry into the embassy hotel during the congressman's stay was mentioned; a Lieutenant Rourke had furnished details of Meadows's heroics to the congressman's staff. Bosch felt a trembling below his heart, as if the blood was draining from it. The letter finished with some small talk about the home parish. There was the large, flowing signature of the congressman and a typed notation in the bottom left margin:

cc: U.S. Army, Records Division, Washington, D.C.
   Lt. John H. Rourke, U.S. Embassy, Saigon, V.N.
   The Daily Iberian; attention news editor

Bosch stared at the second page for a long time without moving or breathing. He actually thought he felt the beginning sensation of nausea and wiped his hand across his forehead. He tried to think if he had ever heard Rourke's middle name or initial. He couldn't remember. But it didn't matter. There was no doubt. No coincidences.

Eleanor's pager sounded, startling them both like a shot. She sat forward and began fumbling with her purse until she found the pager and shut off the noise.

"Oh, God, what time is it?" she said, still disoriented.

He said it was six-twenty and only then remembered that they were supposed to have checked in with Rourke on a landline twenty minutes earlier. He slid the letter back into the stack of papers and put them back in the envelope. He threw it back on the backseat.

"I've got to call in," Wish said.

"Hey, take a couple of minutes to wake up," Bosch replied quickly. "I'll call in. I've got to find a restroom anyway, and I'll get some coffee and water."

He opened the door and stepped out before she could protest the plan. She said, "Harry, why did you let me sleep?"

"I don't know. What's his number?"

"I should call him."

"Let me. Give me the number."

She gave it to him and Bosch walked around the corner and a short distance to the twenty-four-hour diner called Darling's. He was in a daze the whole way, ignoring the panhandlers who had come out with the sun, trying to fathom that it was Rourke who was the inside man. What was he doing? There was a part of this that was missing and Bosch couldn't figure it. If Rourke was the insider, then why would he allow them to set up surveillance on the vault? Did he want his people caught? He saw the pay phones out front of the restaurant.

"You're late," Rourke said after picking up on half a ring.

"We forgot."

"Bosch? Where's Wish? She's supposed to make the call."

"Don't worry about it, Rourke. She's watching the vault like she's supposed to. What are you doing?"

"I've been waiting to hear from you people before I headed in. Did you two fall asleep or what? What is happening there?"

"Nothing is happening. But you already know that, don't you?"

There was a silence during which an old panhandler walked up to the booth and asked Bosch for money. Bosch put his hand on the man's chest and firmly pushed him away.

"You still there, Rourke?" he said into the phone.

"What was that supposed to mean? How do I know what's going on there when you people don't call in like you're supposed to? And you with the veiled references all the time. Bosch, I don't get you."

"Let me ask you something. Did you really put people down at the tunnel exits, or was that blueprint and your pointer and the SWAT guy all for show?"

"Put Wish on the line. I don't know what you're saying."

"Sorry, she can't come to the phone at the moment."

"Bosch, I'm calling you in. Something is wrong. You've been out all night on this. I think you should — no, I'll get a couple of fresh people out there. I'm going to have to call your lieutenant and —"

"You knew Meadows."

"What?"

"What I said. You knew him. I have his file, man. His *complete* file. Not the edited version you gave Wish to give me. You were his CO at the embassy in Saigon. I know."

More silence. Then, "I was CO to a lot of people, Bosch. I didn't know them all."

Bosch shook his head.

"That's weak, Lieutenant Rourke. Really weak. That was worse than just admitting it. I tell you what, I'll see you around."

Bosch hung up the phone and went into Darling's, where he ordered two coffees and two mineral waters. He stood by the cash register, waiting for the girl to put the order together, and looking out the window. He was thinking only of Rourke.

The girl came up to the cash register with the order in a cardboard carry-out box. He paid and tipped her and went back out to the pay phone.

Bosch called Rourke's number again with no plan other than to see if he was on the phone or had left. He hung up after ten rings. Then he called the LAPD dispatch center and told an operator to call FBI dispatch and ask if they had a SWAT callout working in the Wilshire area in or near Beverly Hills and if they needed any help. While he waited he tried to put his mind inside Rourke's caper. He opened up one of the coffees and sipped it.

The dispatcher came back on the line with a confirmation that FBI did have a SWAT surveillance in the Wilshire district. No backup was requested. Bosch thanked her and hung up. Now he thought he knew what Rourke was doing. It had to be that there were no men about to break into the vault. The setup on the vault was just that, a setup. The vault was a decoy. Bosch thought about how he had let Tran go his way after following him to the vault. What he had done was flush the second captain out, with his diamonds, so Rourke could have at him. Bosch had simply played into his hands.

When Bosch got back to the car he saw that Eleanor was looking through Meadows's files. She hadn't gotten to the congressman's letter yet.

"Where have you been?" she said good-naturedly.

"Rourke had a lot of questions." He took the Meadows file out of her hands and said, "There is something I want you to see here. Where did you get the file on Meadows that you showed me?"

"I don't know. Rourke got it. Why?"

He found the letter and handed it to her without saying anything.

"What is this? Nineteen seventy-three?"

"Read it. This is Meadows's file, the one I had copied and sent from St. Louis. There is no letter like this one in the file Rourke gave you to give me. He sanitized it. Read, you'll see why."

He glanced over at the vault door. Nothing was happening and he didn't expect anything to be. Then he watched her as she read. She raised an eyebrow as she scanned both pages, not seeing the name.

"Yes, so he was some kind of a hero, it says. I don't —" Her eyes widened as she got to the bottom. "Copied to Lieutenant John Rourke."

"Uh huh. You also missed the first reference."

He pointed to the sentence that named Rourke as Meadows's CO.

"The inside man. What do you think we should do?"

"I don't know. Are you sure? This doesn't prove anything."

"If it was a coincidence, he should have said he knew the guy, cleared it up. Like me. I came in. He didn't because he didn't want the connection known. I called him on it when we were on the phone. He lied. He didn't know we had this."

"Now he knows you know?"

"Yeah. I don't know what he thinks I know. I hung up on him. The question is, what do we do about it? We're probably spinning our wheels here. The whole thing's a charade. Nobody's going into that vault. They probably took Tran down after he checked his diamonds out and left. We led him right to slaughter."

Then he realized that maybe the white LTD belonged to the robbers, not Lewis and Clarke. They had followed Bosch and Wish to Tran.

"Wait a minute," Eleanor said. "I don't know. What about the alarms all week? The fire hydrant and the arson? It has to be happening like we thought."

"I don't know. Nothing is making sense right now. Maybe Rourke is leading his people into a trap. Or a slaughter."

They both stared ahead at the vault. The rain had slacked off, the sun was completely up now and it set the steel door aglow. Eleanor finally spoke.

"I think we have to get some help. We have Hanlon and Houck sitting on the other side of the bank, and SWAT, unless that was part of Rourke's charade."

Bosch told her he had checked on the SWAT surveillance and learned that it actually was in place.

"Then what is Rourke doing?" she said.

"Pushing all the buttons."

They kicked it around for a few minutes and decided to call Orozco at Beverly Hills police. First, Eleanor checked in with Hanlon and Houck. Bosch wanted to keep them in place.

"You guys awake over there?" she said into the Motorola.

"That's a ten-four, barely. I feel like that guy stuck in his car in the overpass after the earthquake up in Oakland. What's up, anything?"

"No, just checking. How's the front door?"

"Not a knock all night."

She signed off and there was a moment of silence before Bosch turned to get out of the car, to call Orozco. He stopped and looked back at her.

"You know, he died," he said.

"Who died?"

"The guy that was in that overpass."

Just then there was a thump that slightly shook the car. Not as much a sound as a vibration, an impact, not unlike the first jolt of an earthquake. There was no following vibration. But after one or two seconds an alarm sounded. The ringing came loud and clear from the Beverly Hills Safe & Lock Company. Bosch sat bolt upright, staring into the vault room. There was no visible sign of intrusion. Almost immediately, the radio crackled with Hanlon's voice.

"We've got a bell. What's our plan of action?"

Neither Bosch nor Wish answered the radio call at first. They just sat staring at the vault, dumbfounded. Rourke had let his people walk right into a trap. Or so it seemed.

"Son of a bitch," Bosch said. "They're in."

Bosch said, "Tell Hanlon and Houck to stay cool until we get orders."

"And who is going to give the orders?" Eleanor asked.

Bosch didn't answer. He was thinking of what was going on in the vault. Why would Rourke lead his people into a setup?

"He must not have been able to warn them, tell them that the diamonds aren't there and that we're up here," he said. "I mean, twenty-four hours ago we didn't know about this place or what was going on. Maybe by the time we got onto it, it was too late. They were too far in."

"So they are just proceeding as planned," Eleanor said.

"They'll pop Tran's box first, if they've done their homework and know which one it is. They'll find it empty, and then what do they do? Split, or open more boxes until they get enough stuff to make the whole thing worth their while?"

"I think they split," she answered. "I think when they open Tran's box and find no diamonds, they figure something is going down and get the hell out of there."

"Then we won't have much time. My guess is they will get stuff ready in the vault but they won't actually drill the box until after we've reset the alarm and cleared the scene. We can delay the resetting a bit, but too long and they might get suspicious and clear out, looking and ready for our people in the tunnels."

He got out of the car and looked back at Eleanor.

"Get on the radio. Tell those guys to stay put, then get a message to your SWAT people. Tell them we think we've got people in the vault."

"They'll want to know why Rourke isn't telling them."

"Think of something. Tell them you don't know where Rourke is."

"Where are you going?"

"To meet the patrol callout for the alarm. I'll have them call Orozco out here."

He slammed the door shut and walked down the garage ramp. Eleanor made the radio calls.

As Bosch approached Beverly Hills Safe & Lock he took his badge wallet out, folded it backward and hooked it in the breast pocket of his coat. He turned the corner around the glass vault room and jogged to the front steps just as a Beverly Hills patrol car pulled up, lights flashing but no siren. Two patrolmen got out, sliding their sticks out of the PVC pipe holders on the doors and then into the rings on their belts. Bosch introduced himself, told them what he was doing and asked them to get a message through to

Captain Orozco as soon as possible. One of the cops said the manager, a guy named Avery, was being called out to reset the alarm while the cops checked the place out. All routine. They said they were getting to know the guy, it was the third alarm they had been called to here this week. They also said they already had orders to report any calls to this address to Orozco at his home, no matter the hour.

"You mean these callouts, they weren't false alarms?" said the one named Onaga.

"We aren't sure," Bosch said. "But we want to handle this like it is a false alarm. The manager gets called out and together you reset the alarm and everybody goes on their way. Okay? Just nice and relaxed. Nothing unusual."

"Good enough," said the other cop. The copper plate over his pocket said Johnstone. Holding his nightstick in place on his belt, he trotted back to their cruiser to make the call to Orozco.

"Here's our Mr. Avery now," Onaga said.

A white Cadillac floated to a stop at the curb behind the Beverly Hills car. Avery III, who was wearing a pink sport shirt and madras slacks, got out and walked up. He recognized Bosch and greeted him by name.

"Has there been a break-in?"

"Mr. Avery, we think something might be going on here, we don't know. We need time to check it out. What we want for you to do is open up the office, take a walk around like you usually do, like you did when the alarms went off earlier this week. Then reset the alarm and lock up again."

"That's it? What if —"

"Mr. Avery, what we want you to do is get in your car and drive away like you usually do, like you're going home. But I want you to go around the corner to Darling's. Go in and have a coffee. I'll either come by to tell you what is happening or send for you. I want you to relax. We can handle whatever comes up here. We have other people checking it out, but for the sake of appearances, we want to make it seem that we are passing this off as another false alarm."

"I see," Avery said, digging a key ring from his pocket. He walked to the front door and opened it. "And by the way, that is not the vault alarm that is ringing. It is the exterior alarm, set off by vibrations on the windows of the vault room. I can tell. It's a different tone, you see."

Bosch figured the tunnelers had disabled the vault alarm system, not realizing the exterior alarm was a separate system.

Onaga and Avery went in, with Bosch trailing behind. As Harry stood in the entryway looking for smoke and not seeing any, sniffing for cordite but not smelling any, Johnstone came in. Bosch put his hands to his lips to warn the officer against yelling above the sound of the alarm. Johnstone nodded, cupped his hand to Bosch's ear and told him that Orozco would be there in twenty minutes tops. He lived up in the Valley. Bosch nodded and hoped it would be soon enough.

The alarm shut off and Avery and Onaga came out of Avery's office into the lobby, where Johnstone and Bosch waited. Onaga looked at Bosch and shook his head, indicating nothing amiss.

"Do you usually check the vault room?" Bosch asked.

"We just look around," Avery said. He proceeded to the X-ray machine, switched it on and explained it took fifty seconds to warm up. They passed the time without talking. Finally, Avery put his hand on the reader. It read it and approved the bone structure and the lock on the first door of the mantrap snapped open.

"Since I don't have my man inside the vault room, I have to override the lock on the second door," Avery said. "Gentlemen, if you don't mind not looking once we are in."

The four of them moved into the tiny mantrap and Avery pushed a set of numbers on the combination lock on the second door. It snapped open and they moved into the vault room. There was nothing to see but steel and glass. Bosch stood near the vault door and listened but heard nothing. He walked to the glass wall and looked up Wilshire. He could see that Eleanor was back in the car on the second floor of the garage. He turned his attention to Avery, who walked up to his side as if to look out the window himself but instead huddled into a conspiratorial posture.

"Remember, I can open the vault," he said in a low whisper.

Bosch looked at him and shook his head, then said, "No. I don't want to do that. Too dangerous. Let's get out of here."

Avery had a perplexed look on his face, but Bosch walked away. Five minutes later Beverly Hills Safe & Lock was cleared and locked down. The two cops went back out on patrol and Avery left. Bosch walked back to the garage. The street was busier now, and the noise of the day had begun. The garage was filling with cars and the stink of exhaust. Inside the car, Wish told him that Hanlon, Houck, and SWAT were in holding positions. He told her Orozco was on the way.

Bosch wondered how long it would take before the men in the tunnel believed it was safe to start drilling. Orozco was still ten minutes away. It was a long time.

"So what do we do when he gets here?" she said.

"His town, his call," he said. "We just lay it out for him and do whatever he wants to do. We tell him we have one fucked-up operation going here and we don't know who to trust. Not the guy in charge of it, at least."

They sat in silence for a minute or two after that. Bosch smoked a cigarette and Eleanor didn't say anything about it. She seemed lost in her own thoughts, a puzzled look on her face. They both nervously checked their watches every thirty seconds or so.

Lewis waited until the white Cadillac he tailed had turned north off Wilshire. As soon as the car was out of sight of Beverly Hills Safe & Lock,

Lewis picked the blue emergency light up off the floor and put it on the dashboard. He flicked it on, but the driver of the Cadillac was already pulling to the side of the road in front of Darling's. Lewis got out of his car and walked up to the Caddy; he was met halfway by Avery.

"What is going on, officer?" Avery said.

"Detective," Lewis said and he opened his badge wallet. "Internal Affairs, LAPD. I need to ask you a few questions, sir. We are conducting an investigation of the man, Detective Harry Bosch, who you were just speaking with at Beverly Hills Safe & Lock."

"What do you mean 'we'?"

"I left my partner on Wilshire so he can keep an eye on your business. But what I would like is for you to step into my car so we can talk for a few minutes. Something is going on and I need to know what."

"That Detective Bosch — hey, how do I know you are for real?"

"How do you know he is? The thing is, we have had Detective Bosch under surveillance for a week, sir, and we know he is engaged in activities that could be, if not illegal, embarrassing to the department. We aren't sure what at this juncture. That's why we need you, sir. Would you step into the car, please?"

Avery took two tentative steps toward the IAD car and then seemed to decide, What the heck. He moved quickly to the passenger side and got in. Avery identified himself as the owner of Beverly Hills Safe & Lock and briefly told Lewis what had been said during his two encounters with Bosch and Wish. Lewis listened without commenting, then opened the car door. "Wait here, please. I'll be right back."

Lewis walked briskly up to Wilshire; he stood on the corner a few moments apparently looking for someone, then made an elaborate show of checking his watch. He came back to the car and slid in behind the wheel. On Wilshire, Clarke was waiting in the alcove of a store entrance and watching the vault. He caught sight of Lewis's signal and strolled casually to the car.

As Clarke climbed into the backseat, Lewis said, "Mr. Avery here says that Bosch told him to go to Darling's and wait, said there may be people in the vault. Come up from underground."

"Did Bosch say what he would be doing?" Clarke asked.

"Not a word," Avery said.

Everyone was silent, thinking. Lewis couldn't figure it. If Bosch was dirty, what was he doing? He thought some more on this and realized that if Bosch was involved in ripping off the vault, he was in a perfect situation by being the man calling the shots on the outside. He could confuse the coverage on the burglary. He could send all the manpower to the wrong place while his people in the vault went safely the opposite way.

"He's got everybody by the short hairs," Lewis said, more to himself than to the other two men in the car.

"Who, Bosch?" Clarke asked.

"He is running the caper. Nothing we can do but watch. We can't get in that vault. We can't go underground without knowing where we are going. He's already got the bureau's SWAT team tied up down by the freeway. They're waiting for burglars that aren't coming, goddammit."

"Wait a minute, wait a minute," Avery said. "The vault. You can get in it."

Lewis turned fully around in his seat to look at Avery. The vault owner told them that federal banking regulations didn't apply to Beverly Hills Safe & Lock because it wasn't a bank, and how he had the computer code that would open the vault.

"Did you tell this to Bosch?" Lewis asked.

"Yesterday and today."

"Did he already know?"

"No. He seemed surprised. He asked detailed questions on how long it would take to open the vault, what I had to do, things like that. Then today, when we had the alarm, I asked him if we should open it. He said no. Just said to get out of there."

"Damn," Lewis said excitedly. "I better call Irving."

He leapt from the car and trotted to the pay phones in front of Darling's. He dialed Irving at home and got no answer. He dialed the office and only got the duty officer. He had the officer page Irving with the pay phone number. He then waited for five minutes, pacing in front of the phone and worrying about the time going by. The phone never rang. He used the one next to it to call the duty officer back to make sure Irving had been paged. He had. Lewis decided he couldn't wait. He would have to make this call himself and it would be he who would become the hero. He left the bank of phones and went back to the car.

"What'd he say?" Clarke asked.

"We go in," Lewis said. He started the car.

The police radio keyed twice and then Hanlon's voice came on.

"Hey, Broadway, we have visitors over here on First."

Bosch grabbed up the radio.

"What have you got, First? Nothing showing on Broadway."

"We've got three white males going in on our side. Using a key. Looks like one is the man that was here earlier with you. Old guy. Plaid pants."

Avery. Bosch held the microphone up to his mouth and hesitated, not sure what to say. "Now what?" he said to Eleanor. Like Bosch, she was staring down the street at the vault room, but there was no sign of the visitors. She said nothing.

"Uh, First," Bosch said into the mike. "Did you see any vehicle?"

"None seen," Hanlon's voice came back. "They just walked out of the alley on our side. Must have parked there. Want us to take a look?"

"No, hold there a minute."

"They are now inside, no longer in visual contact. Advise, please."

He turned to Wish and raised his eyebrows. Who could it be?

"Ask for descriptions of the two with Avery," she said.

He did.

"White males," Hanlon began. "Number one and two in suits, worn and wrinkled. White shirts. Both early thirties. One with red hair, stocky build, five-eight, one-eighty. The other, dark-brown hair, thinner. I don't know, I'd say these guys were cops."

"Heckle and Jeckle?" Eleanor said.

"Lewis and Clarke. It's gotta be them."

"What are they doing in there?"

Bosch didn't know. Wish took the radio from him.

"First?"

The radio clicked.

"Reason to believe the two subjects in suits are Los Angeles police officers. Stand by."

"There they are," Bosch said, as three figures moved into the glare in the vault room. He opened the glove compartment and grabbed a pair of binoculars.

"What are they doing?" Wish asked as he focused.

"Avery is at the keypad next to the vault. I think he is opening the damned thing."

Through the binoculars, Bosch saw Avery step away from the computer board and move to the chrome wheel on the vault door. He saw Lewis turn slightly and glance up the street in the direction of the parking garage. Was there a slight trace of a smile there? Bosch thought he saw it. Then through the binoculars he saw Lewis draw his weapon from an underarm holster. Clarke did likewise and Avery started turning the wheel, the captain steering the Titanic.

"Those dumb assholes, they are opening it!"

Bosch leapt out of the car and started running down the ramp. He unholstered his gun and held it up as he ran. He glanced along Wilshire and saw an opening in the sporadic traffic. He bounded across the street, Wish just a short distance behind him.

Bosch was still twenty-five yards away and knew he would be too late. Avery had stopped turning the vault wheel, and Bosch could see him pull back with all his weight. The door began slowly to move open. Bosch heard Eleanor's voice behind him.

"No!" she yelled. "Avery, no!"

But Bosch knew the double glass made the vault room silent. Avery couldn't hear her, and Lewis and Clarke wouldn't have stopped what they were doing even if they could hear.

What happened was like a movie to Bosch. An old movie on a TV set with the sound turned down. The slowly opening vault door, with its widening band of blackness inside, gave the picture an ethereal, almost underwater quality, a slow-motion inevitability. Bosch felt as if he were on a moving sidewalk going the wrong way, running but getting no closer. He kept his eyes on the vault door. The black margin opening wider. Then Lewis's body moved into Bosch's line of sight and toward the opening vault. Almost immediately, propelled by some unseen force, Lewis jerked backward. His hands flew up and his gun hit the ceiling and then fell soundlessly to the floor. As he backpedaled from the vault, his back and head ripped open and blood and brain spattered the glass wall behind him. As Lewis was hurled away from the vault door, Bosch could see the muzzle flash from the darkness inside. And then spiderwebs of cracks crazed the double glass as bullets struck silently. Lewis backstepped into a panel of the weakened glass and crashed through onto the sidewalk three feet below.

The vault was half open now and the shooter had freer range. The barrage of machine-gun fire turned toward Clarke, who stood unprotected, his mouth open in shock. Bosch could hear the shots now. He saw Clarke attempt to jump away from the line of fire. But it wasn't worth the effort. He, too, was thrown backward by the force of bullets impacting. His body slammed into Avery and both men fell to the polished marble floor in a heap.

The gunfire from the vault ended.

Bosch jumped through the opening where the wall of glass had been and slid on his chest across the marble and glass dust. In the same instant he looked into the vault and saw the blur of a man dropping through the floor. The movement made a swirl in the concrete dust and smoke that hung inside the vault. Like a magician, the man just disappeared in the mist. Then, from the darkness farther inside, a second man moved into the view framed by the doorway. He sidestepped to the hole, swinging an M-16 assault rifle in a covering, side-to-side sweep. Bosch recognized him as Art Franklin, one of the Charlie Company graduates.

When the black hole of the M-16 came his way, Bosch leveled his gun with both hands, wrists on the cold floor, and fired. Franklin fired at the same time. His shots went high, and Bosch heard more glass shattering behind him. Bosch fired two more rounds into the vault. He heard one ping off the steel door. The other caught Franklin in the upper right chest, knocking him to the floor on his back. But in one quick motion, the injured man rolled and went headfirst through the floor. Bosch kept his gun on the doorway to the vault, waiting for anybody else. But there was nothing, only the sound of Clarke and Avery, gagging and moaning on the floor to his left. Bosch stood up but kept the gun trained on the vault. Eleanor climbed into the room then, her Beretta in hand. In marksman crouches, Bosch and Wish approached the vault from either side of the door. There was a light control next to the computer keypad on the steel wall right of the door. Bosch hit the switch and the interior vault was flooded with light. He nodded to her and Wish went in first. Then he followed. It was empty.

Bosch came out and quickly went to Clarke and Avery, who were still tangled on the floor. Avery was saying, "Dear God, Dear God." Clarke had both hands clamped to his own throat and was gasping for air, his face turning so red that for one bizarre moment it looked to Bosch as if he were strangling himself. He was lying across Avery's midsection and his blood was over both of them.

"Eleanor," Bosch shouted. "Get backup and ambulances. Tell SWAT that they're coming. At least two. Automatic weapons."

He pulled Clarke off Avery and by grabbing the shoulders of his jacket, dragged him out of the line of fire from the vault. The IAD detective had taken a round in the lower neck. Blood was seeping from between his fingers and there were small blood-tinted bubbles at the corners of his mouth. He had blood in his chest cavity. He was shaking and going into shock. He was dying. Harry turned back to Avery, who had blood on his chest and neck and a brownish-yellow piece of wet sponge on his cheek. A piece of Lewis's brain.

"Avery, you hit?"

"Yes, uh . . . uh, uh, I think . . . I don't know," he managed in a strangled voice.

Bosch knelt next to him and quickly scanned his body and bloody clothes. He wasn't hit and Harry told him so. Bosch went back to where the double-glazed window had been and looked down at Lewis on his back on the sidewalk. He was dead. The bullets, having caught him in a rising arc, had stitched their way up his body. There were entry wounds on his right hip, stomach, left chest, and left of center of his forehead. He had been dead before he hit the glass. His eyes were open, staring at nothing.

Wish came in from the lobby then.

"Backup on the way," she said.

Her face was red and she was breathing almost as hard as Avery. She seemed barely in control of the movement of her eyes, which flitted about the room.

"When backup gets here," Bosch said, "tell them if they go into the tunnels that there is an officer friendly down there. I want you to tell your SWAT people that, too."

"What are you talking about?"

"I'm going down. I hit one, I don't know how bad. It was Franklin. Another went down ahead of him. Delgado. But I want the good guys to know I'm down there. Tell 'em I'm in a suit. The two I chased down there were in black fatigues."

He opened his gun and took out the three spent cartridges and reloaded with bullets from his pocket. A siren was sounding in the distance. He heard a sharp pounding and looked through the glass wall and the lobby to see Hanlon pounding the heel of his gun on the glass front door. From that angle the FBI agent could not see that the glass wall of the vault room had been shattered. Bosch motioned him to come around.

"Wait a minute," Wish said. "You can't do this. Harry, they have automatic weapons. Wait till the backup is here and we come up with a plan."

He moved to the vault door, saying, "They already have a head start. I gotta go. Make sure you tell them I'm down there."

He stepped past her into the vault, hitting the light switch as he went. He looked over the edge of the blast hole. The drop was about eight feet. There were chunks of broken concrete and rebar at the bottom. He could see blood in the rubble, and a flashlight.

There was too much light. If they were waiting down there for him he would be a sitting duck. He backed out and around behind the vault door. He put his shoulder against it and slowly began to push the huge slab of steel closed.

Bosch could hear several sirens approaching now. Looking out into the street he saw an ambulance and two police cars coming down Wilshire. The unmarked car with Houck in it screeched to a halt in front and he came out with handgun drawn. The door was halfway closed and finally moving under its own force. Bosch slipped around it and back into the vault. He stood there over the blast hole as the door slowly closed and the light dimmed. He realized he had poised at such a moment many times before. It was always at the edge, at the entrance, that the moment was most thrilling and frightening to him. He would be at his most vulnerable at the moment he dropped into the hole. If Franklin or Delgado was down there waiting for him, they had him.

"Harry," he heard Wish call to him, though he couldn't understand how her voice made it through the now paper-thin opening. "Harry, be careful. There may be more than two."

Her voice echoed in the steel room. He looked down into the hole and got his bearings. When he heard the vault door clink shut and there was only blackness, he jumped.

As he came down in the rubble Bosch crouched and fired a shot from his Smith & Wesson into the blackness and then hurled himself flat against the bottom of the tunnel. It was a war trick. Shoot before they shoot you. But nobody was waiting for him. There was no return fire. No sound, except the faraway sound of running footsteps on the marble floor above and outside the vault. He realized he should have warned Eleanor, told her the first shot would be his.

He held his lighter out away from his body and snapped it on. Another war trick. Then he picked up the flashlight, turned it on and looked around. He saw that he had fired his shot into a dead end. The tunnel the thieves had dug to the vault went the other way. West, not east as they had thought when they looked over the blueprints the night before. That meant they had not come from the storm line Gearson had guessed they would. Not from Wilshire, but maybe Olympic or Pico to the south, or Santa Monica to the north. Bosch realized that the DWP man and all the rest of the agents and cops had been skillfully led astray by Rourke. Nothing would be as they had planned or thought. Harry was on his own. He focused the beam down the tunnel's black throat. It sloped down and then up, giving him only about thirty feet of visibility. The tunnel went west. The SWAT team was waiting to the south and east. They were waiting for nobody.

Holding the flashlight off to the right, away from his body, he began to crawl down the passageway. The tunnel was no taller than three and a half feet, top to bottom, and maybe three feet wide. He moved slowly, holding his gun in the same hand he used to crawl with. There was the smell of cordite in the air, and bluish smoke hung in the beam of the flashlight. Purple Haze, Bosch thought. He felt himself perspiring freely, from the heat and the fear. Every ten feet he stopped to wipe sweat out of his eyes with the sleeve of his jacket. He didn't take the jacket off because he didn't want to differ from the description given to the people who would follow him in. He didn't want to be killed by friendly fire.

The tunnel alternately curved left and then right for fifty yards, causing Bosch to become confused about his direction. At one point it dipped below a utility pipeline. And at times he could hear the rumble of traffic, making the tunnel sound like it was breathing. Every thirty feet burned a candle placed in a notch dug into the tunnel wall. In the sandy, chunky rubble at the bottom of the tunnel he looked for trip-wires but found a trail of blood.

After a few minutes of slow travel, he turned the flashlight off and sank back on his calves to rest and try to control the sound of his breathing. But he could not seem to get enough air into his lungs. He closed his eyes for a few moments, and when he opened them he realized there was a pale light coming from the curve ahead. The light was too steady to be from a candle. He started moving slowly, keeping the flashlight off. When he made his way around the bend, the tunnel widened. It was a room. Tall enough to stand in and wide enough to live in, he thought, during the dig.

The light came from a kerosene lantern sitting on top of an Igloo cooler in the corner of the underground room. There were also two bedrolls and a portable Coleman gas stove. There was a portable chemical toilet. He saw two gas masks and also two backpacks with food and equipment in them. And there were plastic bags full of trash. It was the camp room, like the one Eleanor had assumed was used during the dig into the WestLand vault. Bosch looked at all the equipment and thought of Eleanor's warning about there possibly being more than two. But she had been wrong. Just two of everything.

The tunnel continued on the other side of the camp room, where there was another three-foot-wide hole. Bosch turned the lantern flame off so he wouldn't be backlit and crawled into the passageway. There were no candles in the walls here. He used the flashlight intermittently, turning it on to get his bearings and then crawling a short distance in the dark. Occasionally, he stopped, held his breath and listened. But the sound of traffic seemed farther away. And he heard nothing else. About fifty feet past the camp room the tunnel reached a dead end, but Bosch saw a circular outline on the floor. It was a plywood circle covered with a layer of dirt. Twenty years earlier he would have called it a rathole. He backed away, crouched down and studied the circle. He saw no indication it was a trap. In fact, he did not expect one. If the tunnelers had rigged the opening, it would have been to guard against entry, not exit. The explosives would be on this side of the circle. Nevertheless, he took his key-chain knife out and carefully ran its edge around the circle, then lifted it up a half inch. He pointed the light into the crack and saw no wires or attachments to the underside of the plywood. He then flipped it up. There were no shots. He crawled to the edge of the hole and saw another tunnel below. He dropped his arm and the flashlight through the hole and flicked on the beam. He swept it around and braced for the inevitable gunfire. Again, none came. He saw that the lower passageway was perfectly round. It was smooth concrete with black algae and a trickle of water at the bottom of its curve. It was a stormwater drainage culvert.

He dropped through the hole and immediately lost his footing on the slime and slipped onto his back. He propped himself up and with the flashlight began looking for a trail in the black slime. There was no blood, but in the algae there were scrape marks that could have been made with shoes digging for purchase. The trickle of water moved in the same direction as the scrape marks. Bosch went that way.

By now, he had lost his sense of direction, but he believed that he was heading north. He turned off the beam and moved slowly for twenty feet before flicking it on again. When he did so, he saw that the trail was confirmed. A smeared handprint of blood was at about three o'clock on the curved wall of the pipe. Two feet farther and at five o'clock there was another. Franklin was losing blood and strength quickly, he guessed. He had stopped here to check the wound. He would not be too much farther ahead.

Slowly, trying to lower the noise of his breathing, Bosch moved forward. The pipe smelled like a wet towel and the air was damp enough to put a film on his skin. The sound of traffic rumbled from somewhere nearby. There was the sound of sirens. He felt the pipe was on a gradual downward slope that kept the trickle of water moving. He was going deeper underground. There were cuts on his knees that bled and stung as he slipped and scraped along the bottom.

After maybe a hundred feet Bosch stopped and put on the beam, still holding it out to the side of his body and ready with the gun in his other hand. There was more blood on the curving wall ahead. When he switched off the flashlight, he noticed that the darkness changed farther ahead. There was light with a gray-dawn quality to it. He could tell that the pipeline ended, or rather, connected with a passageway where there was dim light. He realized then that he could hear water. A lot of water compared to what was running between his knees. It sounded like there was a river channel up ahead.

He moved slowly and quietly to the edge of the dim light. The pipeline he crouched in was a porthole on the side of a long hallway. He was in the tributary. Across the floor of the huge hallway, silvery black water moved. It was an underground canal. Looking at it, Bosch could not tell if the water was three inches or three feet deep.

Squatting at the edge, he first listened for sounds other than lapping water. Hearing nothing, he slowly extended his upper body forward to look down the hallway. The water was flowing to his left. He first looked that way and could see the dim outline of the concrete passageway curving gradually to the right. There was shadowy light filtering down at intervals from holes in the ceiling. He guessed that this light came from drain holes drilled in manholes thirty feet above. This was a main line, as Ed Gearson would say. Which one it was Bosch didn't know and no longer cared. There was no blueprint for him to follow, to tell him what to do.

He turned to look upstream and immediately pulled his head back into his pipe like a turtle. There was a dark form against the inside wall of the passage. And Bosch had seen two orange eyes glowing in the darkness, looking right at him.

Bosch didn't move and barely breathed for a whole minute. Stinging sweat dripped into his eyes. He closed them but heard nothing but the sound of the black water. Then slowly he moved back to the edge until he could see the dark form again. It hadn't moved. Two eyes, like the alien eyes of someone who looks into the flash in a snapshot, stared back at Bosch. He edged the flashlight around the corner and hit the switch. In the beam he saw Franklin slumped against the wall; his M-16 was strapped around his chest, but his hands had fallen away from it into the water. The end of the barrel dipped to the water also. Franklin wore a mask that Bosch took a few seconds to realize was not a mask. He wore NVGs — night-vision goggles.

"Franklin, it's over," Bosch called. "I'm police. Give it up."

There was no reply and Bosch didn't expect one. He glanced up and down the main line one more time and then jumped down into the water. The water just covered his ankles. He kept his gun and the light on the still figure but didn't believe he would need the weapon. Franklin was dead. Bosch saw that blood still seeped from a chest wound and down the front of his black T-shirt. Then it mixed into the water and was carried away. Bosch checked the man's neck for a pulse and found none. He holstered his gun and lifted the M-16 over the dead man's head. Then he pulled the night goggles off the corpse and put them on.

He looked one way down the long hallway and then the other. It was like looking at an old black-and-white TV. But the whites and grays had an amber tint. It would take some getting used to, but he could see his way better with the goggles and he kept them on.

Next he checked the supply pockets on the thighs of Franklin's black fatigue pants. He found a sopping wet package of cigarettes and matches.

There was an extra clip of bullets, which Bosch put in his jacket pocket, and a folded piece of wet paper on which blue ink was bleeding through and blurring. He carefully unfolded it and could tell that it had been a hand-drawn map. No names identifying anything. Just smeared blue lines. There was a square box near the center, which Bosch took to represent the vault. The blue lines were the drainage tunnels. He turned the map around in his hand, but the pattern did not seem familiar. A line running along the front of the box was the heaviest drawn. He figured that might be Wilshire or Olympic. Lines that intersected this were the cross streets, Robertson, Doheny, Rexford and others. There was a crosshatching of more lines continuing to the side of the page. Then a circle with an X through it. The exit point.

Bosch decided the map was useless, for he didn't know where he was or what direction he had taken. He dropped it into the water and watched it float off. In that moment he decided that he would follow the current. As good a choice as any.

Bosch splashed through the water, moving with the current, in a direction he thought was west. The black water curled against the wall in orange-tinted eddies. The water was above his ankles and filled his shoes, making his steps plodding and unsteady.

He thought about how Rourke had played it so well. It didn't matter if the Jeep and the ATVs had been found down by the freeway. That was all a decoy, a setup. Rourke and his bandits had shown the obvious, then done the opposite. Rourke had talked everybody into believing it while setting the battle plans the night before. The SWAT team was waiting down there with a reception no one would attend.

He looked for signs of a trail in the passageway but found nothing. The water took all chance of that away with it. There were painted markings on the walls, even gang graffiti, but each scribble could have been there for years. He looked at it all but recognized none as a signal or direction. This time, Hansel and Gretel didn't leave a trail.

The traffic sounds grew louder now, and there was more light. Bosch flipped up the NVGs and saw shadowy cones of bluish light filtering down every hundred feet or so from manholes and drains. After a while he came to an underground intersection, and as the water from his line collided and splashed with water moving in the other channel, Bosch crept along the side wall and slowly looked around the corner. He saw and heard no one. He had no clue as to which way to go. Delgado could have gone in any of three different directions. Bosch decided to follow the new passageway to the right because it would take him, he believed, farther away from the SWAT setup.

He had taken no more than three steps into the new tunnel when he heard a loud whisper from ahead.

"Artie, you going to make it? Come on, hurry. Artie!"

Bosch froze. It came from about twenty yards dead ahead. But he couldn't see anyone. He knew that it had been the NVGs he wore — the orange eyes — that had prevented him from walking into an ambush. But the cover wouldn't last long. If he got much closer, Delgado would know that he wasn't Franklin.

"Artie!" the voice called hoarsely again. "Come on!"

"Coming," Bosch whispered. He took one step forward and felt instinctively that it hadn't worked. Delgado would know. He dove forward, bringing the M-16 up as he went down.

Bosch saw a whirl of movement ahead and to the left, then saw a muzzle flash. The sound of gunfire was deafening in the concrete tunnel. Bosch returned fire and kept his finger tight on the trigger until he heard the injector go dry of bullets. His ears were ringing, but he could tell that Delgado, or whoever was up there, had stopped also. Bosch heard him snap a new clip into his weapon, then running footsteps on a dry floor. Delgado was moving away, in another passageway ahead. Harry jumped up and followed, pulling the empty clip out of his borrowed gun and replacing it with the backup as he went.

In twenty-five yards he came to a tributary pipeline. It was about five feet in diameter and Bosch had to take a step up to move into it. There was black algae rimming the bottom but no running water. Lying in the scum was the empty clip from an M-16.

Bosch had the right tunnel, but he no longer heard Delgado's footsteps. He began moving in the pipe quickly. There was a slight incline and in about thirty seconds he reached a lighted junction room thirty feet below a grated drain. On the other side of this room the pipeline continued. Bosch had no choice but to follow, this time with the pipe running on a gradual decline. He went another fifty yards before he could see that the line he was in emptied into a larger passage — a main line. He could hear water running up ahead.

Bosch realized too late that he was moving too fast to stop. As he lost his footing and slid on the algae toward the opening, it became clear to him that he had followed Delgado into a trap. Bosch dug his heels into the black slime in a worthless effort to stop himself. Instead, he went feet first, arms flailing for balance, into the new passageway.

It seemed odd to him, but he felt the bullet tear into his right shoulder before he heard the gunfire. It felt as though a hook on a rope had swung down from above, embedded in his right shoulder and then yanked him backward off his feet and down.

He let go of the gun and fell what seemed to him to be a hundred feet. But, of course, it wasn't. The floor of the passageway with its two inches of water came up like a wall of water and hit him in the back of the head. The goggles flew off and he watched, idly and detached, as sparks arced above him and bullets bit into the wall and ricocheted away.

When he came to it felt like he had been out for hours, but he quickly realized it was only a few seconds. The sound of the gunfire still echoed down the tunnel. He smelled cordite. He heard running steps again. Running away, he thought. He hoped.

Bosch rolled in the darkness and water and spread his hands out to find the M-16 and the goggles. He gave up after a while and tried to draw his own gun. The holster was empty. He sat up and pushed himself against the wall. He realized his right hand was numb. The bullet had hit him in the ball of the shoulder, and his arm hummed with dull pain from the point of impact down to the dead hand. He could feel blood running under his shirt and down his chest and arm. It was a warm counterpoint to the cool water swirling around his legs and balls.

He became aware that he was gasping for air and tried to regulate his intake. He was going into shock and he knew it. There was nothing he could do.

The sound of the steps, the running away, stopped then. Bosch held his breath and listened. Why had he stopped? He was home free. Bosch scissored his legs along the floor of the tunnel, still looking for one of the weapons. There was nothing there, and it was too dark to see where they had fallen. The flashlight was gone as well.

There was a voice then, too far away and too muffled to be distinguished or understood, but someone was talking. And then there was a second voice. Two men. Bosch tried to make out what was said but couldn't. The second voice suddenly grew shrill, then there was a shot, and then another. Too much time had elapsed between shots, Bosch thought. That wasn't the M-16.

As he thought about the significance of this, he heard the sound of steps in water again. After a while, he could tell the steps were coming through the darkness toward him.

There was nothing hurried about the steps that came through the water toward Bosch. Slow, even, methodical, like a bride coming down the aisle. Bosch sat slumped against the wall and again swished his legs along the watery, slimy floor in hopes of locating one of the weapons. They were gone. He was weak and tired, defenseless. The humming pain in his arm had moved up a notch to a throb. His right hand was still useless, and he was pressing his left against the torn flesh of his shoulder. He was shaking badly now, his body in shock, and he knew he would soon pass into unconsciousness and not wake up.

Now Bosch could see the beam of a small light moving toward him in the tunnel. He stared fixedly at it with his mouth dropped open. Some of his muscle controls were already shutting down. In a few moments the sloshing steps stopped in front of him and the light hung there above his face like a sun. It was just a penlight but it was still too bright; he couldn't see behind it. Just the same, he knew whose face would be back there, whose hand held the light and what was in the other.

"Tell me," he said in a hoarse whisper. He hadn't realized how parched his throat had become. "That and your little pointer a matched set?"

Rourke lowered the beam until it pointed to the floor. Bosch looked around and saw the M-16 and his own gun side by side in the water next to the opposite wall. Too far to reach. He noticed that Rourke, dressed in a black jumpsuit tucked into rubber boots, held another M-16 pointed at him.

"You killed Delgado," Bosch said. A statement, not a question.

Rourke didn't speak. He hefted the gun in his hand.

"You going to kill a cop now, that the idea?"

"It's the only way I'll come out of this. The way it will look is Delgado gets you first with this." He held the M-16 up. "Then I get him. I come out a hero."

Bosch didn't know whether to say anything about Wish. It would put her in danger. But it might also save his life.

"Forget it, Rourke," he finally said. "Wish knows. I told her. There's a letter in Meadows's file. It ties you in. She's probably already told everybody up there. Give it up now and get me some help. It will go better for you if you get me out of here. I'm going into shock, man."

Bosch wasn't sure but he thought he saw a slight change in Rourke's face, his eyes. They stayed open, but it was as if they had stopped seeing, as if the only thing he was seeing was what was inside. Then they were back, looking at Bosch without sympathy, just contempt. Bosch braced his heels in the slime and tried to push himself up the wall into a standing position. But he had moved only a few inches when Rourke leaned over and easily pushed him back down.

"Stay there, don't fuckin' move. You think I'm going to take you out of here? I figure you cost us five, maybe six million, from what Tran had in his box. Had to be that much. But I'll never know now. You fucked up the perfect crime. You aren't getting out of here."

Bosch dropped his head until his chin was on his chest. His eyes were rolling up into their lids. He wanted to sleep now but he was fighting it. He groaned but said nothing.

"You were the only thing left to chance in the whole goddam plan. And what happens? The one chance something will happen, it does. You're Murphy's fuckin' Law, man, in the flesh."

Bosch managed to look up at Rourke. It was a terrible struggle. After, his good arm fell away from the shoulder wound. There was no more strength left to hold it there.

"What?" he managed to say. "Wh-wha . . . do you mean? . . . Chance?"

"What I mean is coincidence. You getting the callout on Meadows. That wasn't part of the plan, Bosch. You believe that shit? I wonder what the odds are. I mean, Meadows is put in a pipe we knew he had crashed in before.

We're hoping maybe he won't be found for a couple of days and then maybe it takes two, three days for somebody to make the ID off the prints. Meantime, he gets written off as an OD, a no-count. The guy's got a hype card in the files. Why not?

"But what happens? This kid reports the body right off the fucking bat" — he shook his head, the persecuted man — "and who gets the call, a dipshit dick who actually knew the fucking stiff and ID's him in about two seconds. An asshole buddy from the tunnels of Viet-fucking-nam. I don't believe this shit myself.

"You messed everything up with that, Bosch. Even your own miserable life . . . Hey, still with me?"

Bosch felt his head raise, the gun barrel under his chin.

"Still with me?" Rourke said again, and then he poked the barrel into Bosch's right shoulder. It sent a shock wave of red neon pain searing down his arm and through his chest, right down to his balls. He groaned and gasped for air, then took a slow-motion swing with his left hand at the gun. It wasn't enough. He only got air. He swallowed back vomit and felt beads of sweat running through his damp hair.

"You don't look so good, buddy," Rourke said. "I'm thinking maybe I won't have to do this after all. Maybe my man Delgado did it right with the first shot."

The pain had brought Bosch back. It pulsed through him, leaving him alert, albeit temporarily. He could already feel himself fading. Rourke continued to lean over him, and he looked up and noticed the flaps hanging from the chest and waist of the FBI agent's jumpsuit. Pockets. He was wearing the jumpsuit inside out. Something clicked in Bosch's brain. He remembered Sharkey saying he saw an empty tool belt around the waist of the man who pulled the body into the pipe at the reservoir. That was Rourke. He wore the jumpsuit inside out that night, too. Because it said FBI on the back. He didn't want to risk that that would be seen. It was a bit of information that was useless now, but for some reason it pleased Bosch to be able to put it in place in the puzzle.

"What are you smiling at, dead man?" Rourke asked.

"Fuck you."

Rourke raised his foot and kicked at Bosch's shoulder but Bosch was ready for it. He grabbed the heel with his left hand and pushed upward and out. Rourke's other foot gave way on the slick bed of algae and slipped out from under him. He went down on his back with a splash. But he didn't drop the gun as Bosch had hoped. That was it. That was all there was. Bosch made a halfhearted effort to grab the weapon, but Rourke easily peeled his fingers off the barrel and pushed him back against the wall. Bosch leaned to his side and vomited into the water. He felt a new flow of blood coming from his shoulder, running down his arm. That had been his play. There was nothing else.

Rourke got up out of the water. He moved in close and put the barrel of the gun against Bosch's forehead. "You know, Meadows used to tell me about all that black echo stuff. All that bullshit. Well, Harry, here you are. This is it."

"Why'd he die?" Bosch whispered. "Meadows. Why?"

Rourke stepped back and looked up and down the tunnel before speaking.

"You know why. He was a fuckup over there, he was a fuckup here. That's why he died." Rourke seemed to be reviewing a memory in his mind and he shook his head disgustedly. "It was all perfect except for him. He held back the bracelet. Little jade dolphins on gold."

Rourke stared off into the darkness of the tunnel. A wistful look played on his face. "That's all it took," he said. "See, the plan relied on complete adherence for success. Meadows, goddammit — he didn't do that."

He shook his head, still angry at the dead man, and was quiet. It was at that moment that Bosch thought he could hear the sound of steps somewhere off in the distance. He wasn't sure if he had heard it or if it was what he hoped to hear. He moved his left leg in the water. Not enough to cause Rourke to pull the trigger, but enough to make the water slosh and to cover the sound of the steps. If they were even there.

"He kept the bracelet," Bosch said. "That was it?"

"That was enough," Rourke said angrily. "Nothing was to turn up. Don't you see? That was the beauty of the thing. Nothing would turn up. We'd get rid of everything except the diamonds. And those we'd keep until we were done with both jobs. But that fool couldn't wait until the second job was completed. He palms that cheap bracelet and pawns it to score dope.

"I saw it on the pawn reports. Yeah, after the WestLand job, we went to LAPD and asked them to send over their monthly pawn lists so we could check 'em out, too. We started to get 'em at the bureau. The only reason I made the bracelet and your pawn guys didn't was I was looking for it. The pawn detail has to look for a thousand things. I only looked for that one thing.

"I knew somebody had held it back. There was a lot reported stolen from that first vault that wasn't in the shit we took out of there. Insurance scammers. But the dolphin bracelet I knew was legit. That old lady . . . crying. The story behind it with her husband and all that sentimental value shit. Interviewed her myself. And I knew she wasn't scamming. So I knew one of my tunnel people had held the bracelet back."

Keep him talking, Bosch thought. He keeps talking and you'll end up walking. Out of here. Out of here. Someone's coming, my arm's humming. He laughed in his delirium and that made him vomit again. Rourke just went on.

"I bet on Meadows right from the start. Once on the needle . . . you know how that goes. So when the bracelet turned up he was the first one I went to."

Rourke drifted off then, and Bosch made more water noise with his legs. The water now seemed warm to him and it was the blood that ran down his side that was cold.

Rourke finally said, "You know, I really don't know whether to kiss you or kill you, Bosch. You cost us millions on this job, but then again my share of the first one sure has gone up now that three of my guys are dead. Probably even out in the end."

Bosch did not think he could stay awake much longer. He felt tired, helpless and resigned. The alertness had run out of him. Even now when he managed to reach his hand up and throw it against his torn shoulder, there was no pain. He couldn't get it back. He lapsed into contemplation of the water moving slowly around his legs. It felt so warm and he felt so cold. He wanted to lie down and pull it over him like a blanket. He wanted to sleep in it. But from somewhere a voice told him to hang in. He thought of Clarke clutching his throat. The blood. He looked at the beam of light in Rourke's hand and tried one more time.

"Why so long?" he asked in a voice no louder than a whisper. "All these years. Tran and Binh. Why now?"

"No answer, Bosch. Things just come together sometimes. Like Halley's comet. It comes around every seventy-two or whatever years. Things come together. I helped them bring their diamonds across. Set the whole thing up for them. I was paid well and never thought otherwise. And then one day the seed planted all those years ago came out of the ground, man. It was there for the taking and, man, we took it. I took it! That's why now."

A gloating smile played across Rourke's face. He brought the muzzle of the weapon back to a point in front of Bosch's face. All Bosch could do was watch.

"I'm out of time, Bosch, and so are you."

Rourke braced the gun with both hands and spread his feet to the width of his shoulders. At that final moment Bosch closed his eyes. He cleared his mind of all thought but of the water. So warm, like a blanket. He heard two gunshots, echoing like thunder through the concrete tunnel. He fought to open his eyes and saw Rourke leaning against the other wall, both his hands up in the air. One held the M-16, the other the penlight. The gun dropped and clattered into the water, then the penlight. It bobbed on the surface, its bulb still on. It cast a swirling pattern on the roof and walls of the tunnel as it slowly moved away with the current.

Rourke never said a word. He slowly sagged down the wall, staring off to his right — the direction Bosch thought the shots had come from — and leaving a smear of blood that followed him down. In the dimming light, Bosch could see surprise on his face and then a look of resolve in his eyes. Pretty soon he sat like Bosch against the wall, the water moving around his legs, his dead eyes no longer staring at anything.

Things went out of focus for Bosch then. He wanted to ask a question but couldn't form the words. There was another light in the tunnel and he thought he heard a voice, a woman's voice, telling him everything was okay. Then he thought he saw Eleanor Wish's face, floating in and out of focus. And then it sank away into inky blackness. That blackness was finally all he saw.

PART VIII

SUNDAY, MAY 27

Bosch dreamed of the jungle. Meadows was there, and all the soldiers from Harry's photo album. They stood around the hole at the bottom of a leaf-covered trench. Above them a gray mist clung to the top of the jungle canopy. The air was still and warm. Bosch took photographs of the other rats with his camera. Meadows was going into the ground, he said. Out of the blue and into the black. He looked at Bosch through the camera and said, "Remember the promise, Hieronymus."

"Rhymes with anonymous," Bosch said.

But before he could tell him not to go, Meadows promptly jumped feet first into the hole and disappeared. Bosch rushed to the edge and looked down but saw nothing, just darkness like ink. Faces came into focus, then slipped back into the blackness. There was Meadows and Rourke and Lewis and Clarke. From behind him, he heard a voice he recognized but couldn't place with a face.

"Harry, c'mon, man. I need to talk to you."

Then Bosch became aware of a deep pain in his shoulder, throbbing from elbow to neck. Someone was tapping his left hand, lightly patting it. He opened his eyes. It was Jerry Edgar.

"Yeah, that's it," Edgar said. "I don't have much time. This guy on the door says they'll be here anytime now. Plus he's due to go off watch. I wanted to try to talk to you before the brass did. Would've been by yesterday but this place was crawling with silk. Besides, I heard you were out most of the day. Too delirious."

Bosch just stared at him.

"On these things," Edgar said, "I've always heard it's best to say you can't remember a thing. Let them put it whatever way they want. I mean, when you catch a round, there's no way they can say you're lying about remembering. The mind shuts down, man, when there is traumatic insult to the body. I've read that."

By now Bosch realized he was in a hospital room and he began to look about. He noticed five or six vases of flowers, and the room smelled putridly sweet. He also noticed he had restraining belts across his chest and waist.

"You're at MLK, Harry. Um, doctors say you'll be all right. They still have some work to do on your arm, though." Edgar lowered his voice to a whisper. "I snuck in. Think the nurses have a change of shift or something. Cop on the door, he's over from Wilshire patrol, let me in 'cause he's selling and he musta heard that's my gig. I told him I'd take his listing for two points if he gave me five minutes in here."

Bosch still hadn't spoken. He wasn't sure he could. He felt like he was floating on a layer of air. He had trouble concentrating on Edgar's words. What did he mean about points? And why was he at Martin Luther King-Drew Medical Center near Watts? Last he remembered, he had been in Beverly Hills. In the tunnel. UCLA Med Center or Cedars would have been closer.

"Anyway," Edgar was saying, "I'm just trying to let you know what's going on as much as possible before the silks get here and try to fuck you over. Rourke is dead. Lewis is dead. Clarke is bad, he's on the machine, and I heard they were just keeping him going for parts. As soon as they line up people that need 'em, they'll pull the plug. How'd you like to end up with that asshole's heart or eyeball or something? Anyway, like I said, you should come out of this all right. Either way, with that arm, you can get your eighty percent, no questions asked. Line of duty. You're a made man."

He smiled at Bosch, who just looked at him blankly. Harry's throat was dry and cracked when he finally tried to speak.

"MLK?"

It came out a little weak but okay. Edgar poured a cup of water from a pitcher on the bedside table and handed it to him. Bosch unbuckled the restraints, sat himself up to drink it and immediately felt a wave of nausea hit him. Edgar didn't notice.

"It's a gun-and-knife club, man. This is where they take the gangbangers after the drive-bys. No better place to go with a gunshot in the county, leastwise those yuppie doctors over at UCLA. They train military doctors here. So they'll be ready for war casualties. They brought you in on a chopper."

"What time is it?"

"It's a little after seven, Sunday morning. You lost a day."

Then Bosch remembered Eleanor. Was she the one in the tunnel at the end? What had happened? Edgar seemed to read him. Everybody had been doing that lately.

"Your lady partner is fine. She and you are in the spotlight, man, heroes."

Heroes. Bosch thought about that. After a while, Edgar said, "I gotta book on out of here. If they know I talked to you first, I'll get shipped out to Newton."

Bosch nodded. Most cops wouldn't mind Newton Division. Nonstop action in Shootin' Newton. But not Jerry Edgar, real estate agent.

"Who's coming?"

"Usual crew, I guess. IAD, Officer Involved Shooting team, the FBI is in on the act. Bev Hills, too. I think everybody's still figurin' out what the fuck happened down there. And they only got you and Wish to tell 'em. They probly want to make sure you two have the same story. That's why I'm saying, tell 'em you don't remember dick. You're shot, man. You are an injured officer. Line of duty. It's your right not to remember what happened."

"What do you know about what happened?"

"The department isn't saying shit. No scut going around on this at all. When I heard it went down I went out to the scene and Pounds was already there. He saw me and ordered me back. Fuckin' Ninety-eight, he wouldn't say shit. So I only know what's in the press. The usual load of bullshit. TV last night didn't know shit. The *Times* this morning doesn't have much, either. The department and the bureau, they look like they joined up to make everybody a valiant soldier."

"Everybody?"

"Yeah. Rourke, Lewis, Clarke — they all went down in the line of duty."

"Wish said that stuff?"

"No. She's not in the story. I mean, she isn't quoted. I 'spect they're keeping her kind of under wraps till the investigation is over."

"What's the official line?"

"The *Times* says the department says Lewis and Clarke and you were part of the FBI surveillance at that vault. Now I know that's a lie 'cause you'd never let those clowns near one of your operations. Besides, they're IAD. I think the *Times* knows something about it stinks, too. That Bremmer guy you know was calling me yesterday, seeing what I heard. But I didn't talk. My name gets in the paper on this and I'll get worse than Newton. If there is such a place."

"Yeah," Bosch said. He looked away from his old partner and became immediately depressed. It seemed to make his arm throb all the harder.

"Look, Harry," Edgar said after a half minute. "I better get out of here. I don't know when they'll be coming, but they will be, man. You take care and do like I told you. Amnesia. Then take the eighty percent line-of-duty disability and fuck 'em."

Edgar pointed a finger to his temple and nodded his head. Harry nodded absently and then Edgar left. Bosch could see a uniformed officer sitting on a chair outside the door.

After a while Bosch picked up the phone that was attached to the railing alongside his bed. He couldn't get a dial tone, so he pushed the nurse call button and a few minutes later a nurse came in and told him the phone was shut off, as per LAPD orders. He asked for a newspaper and she shook her head. Same thing.

He became even more depressed. He knew that both LAPD and the FBI faced huge public relations problems with what had happened, but he couldn't see how it could be covered up. Too many agencies. Too many people. They could never keep a lid on it. Could they be stupid enough to try?

He loosened the strap across his chest and tried to sit all the way up. It made him dizzy, and his arm screamed to be left alone. He felt nausea overtake him and reached for a stainless steel pan on the bed table. The feeling subsided. But it jogged loose a memory of being in the tunnel with Rourke the morning before. He began remembering pieces of Rourke's conversation. He tried to fit the new information with what he had already known. Then he wondered about the diamonds — the cache from the WestLand job — and whether they had been found. Where? As much as he had grown to admire the engineering of the caper, he could not bring himself to admire its maker. Rourke.

Bosch felt fatigue overcome him like a cloud crossing the sun. He dropped back against the pillow. And the last thing he thought of before dozing off was what Rourke had said in the tunnel. The part about getting a larger share because Meadows, Franklin and Delgado were dead. It was then, as he slid into the black jungle hole that Meadows had jumped into before, that Bosch realized the full meaning of what Rourke had said.

The man in the visitor's chair wore an $800 pinstripe suit, gold cuff links and an onyx pinky ring. But it was no disguise.

"IAD, right?" Bosch said and yawned. "Wake up from a dream to a nightmare."

The man started. He hadn't seen Bosch open his eyes. He stood up and left the hospital room without saying a word. Bosch yawned again and looked around for a clock. There was none. He loosened the chest belt again and tried to sit up. This time he was much better. No dizziness. No sickness. He looked over at the floral arrangements on the windowsill and the bureau. He thought that their number might have grown while he was asleep. He wondered if any of them were from Eleanor. Had she come by to see him? They probably wouldn't let her.

In another minute, Pinstripe came back in, carrying a tape recorder and leading a procession that included four other suits. One was Lieutenant Bill Haley, head of the LAPD Officer Involved Shooting squad, and one was Deputy Chief Irvin Irving, head of IAD. Bosch figured the other two for FBI men.

"If I'd known I had so many suits waiting for me, I would have set an alarm," Bosch said. "But they didn't give me an alarm clock, or a phone that works or a TV or a newspaper."

"Bosch, you know who I am," Irving said and threw a hand toward the others. "And you know Haley. This is Agent Stone and this is Agent Folsom, FBI."

Irving looked at Pinstripe and nodded toward the bed table. The man stepped forward and placed the recorder on the table, put a finger on the record button and looked back at Irving. Bosch looked at him and said, "You don't rate an introduction?"

Pinstripe ignored him and so did everybody else.

"Bosch, I want to do this quickly and without any of your brand of humor," Irving said. He flexed his massive jaw muscles and nodded at Pinstripe. The recorder was turned on. Irving dryly spoke the date, day and time. It was 11:30 A.M. Bosch had only been asleep a few hours. But he felt much stronger than when Edgar had visited.

Irving then added the names of those present in the room, this time giving a name to Pinstripe. Clifford Galvin, Jr. Same name, minus the junior part, as one of the department's other deputy chiefs. Junior was being groomed and doomed, Bosch thought. He was on the fast track, under Irving's wing.

"Let's do it from the top," Irving said. "Detective Bosch, you start by telling us everything about this deal since the moment you climbed in."

"You got a couple days?"

Irving walked over to the recorder and hit the pause button.

"Bosch," he said, "we all know what a smart guy you are, but we are not going to hear it today. I stop the tape only this once. If I do it again, I will have your badge in a glass block by Tuesday morning. And that's only because of the holiday tomorrow. And never mind any line-of-duty pension. I will see you get eighty percent of nothing."

He was referring to the department practice of forbidding a retiring cop to keep his badge. The chief and the city council didn't like the idea of some of the city's former finest floating around the city with buzzers to show off. Shakedowns, free meals, free flops, it was a scandal they could see coming a hundred miles away. So if you wanted to take your badge with you, you could: set nicely in a Lucite block with a decorative clock. It was about a foot square. Too big to fit in the pocket.

Irving nodded and Junior pushed the button again. Bosch told it like it had been, leaving out nothing and stopping only when Junior needed to turn the tape over. The suits asked him questions from time to time but mostly just let him tell it. Irving wanted to know what Bosch had dropped from the Malibu pier. Bosch almost didn't even remember. Nobody took notes. They just watched him tell it. He finally finished the tale an hour and a half after starting. Irving looked at Junior then and nodded. Junior stopped the tape.

When they had no more questions, Bosch asked his.

"What did you find at Rourke's place?"

"That's not your business," Irving said.

"The hell it isn't. It's part of a murder investigation. Rourke was the murderer. He admitted it to me."

"Your investigation has been reassigned."

Bosch said nothing as the anger pushed its way into his throat. He looked around the room and noticed that none of the others, even Junior, would look at him.

Irving said, "Now, before I would go around shooting my mouth off about fellow law enforcement officers killed in the line of duty, I would make sure I knew the facts. And I would make sure that I had the evidence supporting those facts. We don't want any rumors being spread about good men."

Bosch couldn't hold back.

"You think you people will pull this off? What about your two goons? How are you going to explain that? First they put the bug in my phone, then they blunder into a fucking surveillance and get themselves shot. And you want to make them heroes. Who are you kidding?"

"Detective Bosch, it already has been explained. That is not your worry. It is also not your role to contradict the public statements of the department or the bureau on this matter. That, Detective, is an order. If you talk to the press about this, it will be the last time you do as a Los Angeles police detective."

Now it was Bosch who could not look at them. He stared at the flowers on the table and said, "Then why the tape, the statement, all the suits here with you? What's the point when you don't want to know the truth?"

"We want the truth, Detective. You are confusing that with what we choose to tell the public. But out of the public eye I guarantee and the Federal Bureau of Investigation guarantees that we will complete your investigation and take appropriate action where fitting."

"That's pathetic."

"And so are you, Detective. So are you." Irving leaned over the bed with his face close enough that Bosch could smell his sour breath. "This is one of those rare times when you hold your future in your own hands, Detective Bosch. You do what is right, maybe you find yourself back at Robbery-Homicide. Or you can pick up that phone — yes, I am going to have the nurse turn it on — and call your pals at that rag over on Spring Street. But if you do that, you better ask them if there are any career opportunities there for a former homicide detective."

The five of them then left, leaving Bosch alone with his anger. He sat up and was ready to take a swing with his good arm at a vase of daisies on the bedside table, when the door opened and Irving came back in. Alone. No tape recorder.

"Detective Bosch, this is unofficial. I told the others I forgot to give you this."

He pulled a greeting card out of his coat pocket and propped it upright on the windowsill. On the front was a busty policewoman with her uniform blouse unbuttoned to the navel. She was rapping her nightstick in her hand impatiently. A bubble from her mouth said Get Well Soon or. . . . Bosch would have to read the inside to get the punch line.

"I didn't forget. I just wanted to say something private." He stood mute at the foot of the bed until Bosch nodded. "You are good at what you do, Detective Bosch. Anybody knows that. But that doesn't mean you are a good police officer. You refuse to be part of the Family. And that's not good. And, meantime, you see, I have this department to protect. To me, that's the most important job in the world. And one of the best ways to do that is to control public opinion. Keep everybody happy. So if it means putting out a couple of nice press releases and putting on a couple of big funerals with the mayor and the TV cameras and all the brass there, that's what we are going to do. The protection of the department is more important than the fact that two dumb cops made a mistake.

"Same goes for the Federal Bureau of Investigation. They will grind you up before they publicly flog themselves with Rourke. So what I am telling you is that rule one is you have to go along to get along."

"That's bullshit and you know it."

"No, I do not know it. Deep down neither do you. Let me ask you something. Why is it, you think, that Lewis and Clarke were pulled back on the investigation of the Dollmaker shooting? Who do you think reined them in?"

When Bosch didn't say anything Irving nodded. "You see, we had to make a decision. Would it be better to see one of our detectives dragged through the papers and brought up on criminal charges, or for him to be quietly demoted and transferred?" He let that hang there a few seconds before continuing. "Another thing. Lewis and Clarke came to me last week with the story about what you did to them. Cuffing them to that tree. Very brutal, that was. But they were as happy as a couple of high school cheerleaders after an evening with the football team. They had you by the balls and were ready to put the paper in right then. They —"

"They had me, but I had them."

"No. That's what I'm telling you. They came to me with this story about the bug in the phone, what you told them. But the thing is, they didn't drop the bug in your phone, like you thought. I checked it out. That is what I am telling you. They had you."

"Then who —" Bosch stopped right there. He knew the answer.

"I told them to hold back a few days. To watch, see what happened. Something was going on. Those two men were always hard to bridle when it came to you. They overstepped when they decided to stop that fellow Avery and then told him to take them back to the vault. They paid the price."

"What about the FBI, what do they say about the bug?"

"I don't know and I'm not asking. If I did, they would say, 'What bug?' You know that."

Bosch nodded and was immediately tired of the man. A thought was pushing into his head that he didn't want to allow in. He looked away from Irving to the window. Irving told him once more to think of the department before he did anything, then walked out. When he was sure Irving had made his way down the hall, Bosch lashed out with his left arm and sent the vase of daisies tumbling into the corner of the room. The vase was plastic and didn't break. The damage was just spilled water and flowers. Galvin Junior's ferret face momentarily poked in and then out of the room. He said nothing, but it tipped Bosch that the IAD man was posted outside in the hall. Was that for his protection? Or for the department's? Bosch didn't know. He didn't know anything anymore.

Bosch pushed away an untouched tray containing an institutional meal of turkey loaf with flour gravy, corn, yams, a hard roll that was supposed to be soft, and strawberry shortcake with flat whipped cream.

"You eat that, you might never get out of here."

He looked up. It was Eleanor. She stood in the open door, smiling. He smiled back. He couldn't help himself.

"I know."

"How are you, Harry?"

"Okay. I'll be okay. Might not be able to do chin-ups anymore, but I'll survive with that. How are you, Eleanor?"

"I'm fine," she said, and her smile just slayed him. "They put you through the Veg-O-Matic today?"

"Oh, yeah. Sliced and diced. The best and the brightest of my fine department — a couple of your pals, too — had me on the ropes all morning. There's a chair on this side."

She circled the bed but continued standing next to the chair. She looked around and a slight frown creased her brow, as if she knew this room and therefore knew something wasn't right.

"They got me, too. Last night. They wouldn't let me come see you till they were through with you. Orders. Didn't want us going together on the story. But I guess our stories came out all right. At least they didn't pull me back in after they talked to you today. Told me that was it."

"They find the diamonds?"

"Not that I've heard, but they aren't telling me much anymore. They've got two crews working it today, but I'm out of it. I'm on a desk till it cools off and the shooting team finishes up. They're still probably at Rourke's place looking."

"What about Tran and Binh, they cooperate?"

"No. They aren't saying one word. I know that from a friend who was on the interrogation. They don't know anything about any diamonds. Probably got their own people together in a posse. They'll be out on the treasure hunt, too."

"Where do you think the treasure is?"

"I don't have any idea. This whole thing, Harry, it's kind of thrown me. I don't know what I think about things anymore."

That included how she thought about him, he knew. He didn't say anything and after a while the silence became uneasy.

"What happened, Eleanor? Irving told me Lewis and Clarke intercepted Avery. But that's all I know. I don't understand."

"They watched us watch the vault all night. They must've gotten it into their heads that we were lookouts. If you start with the assumption that you were a bad cop, like they did, then you might come to the same conclusion. So when they see you turn Avery away and send the two uniforms home, they figure they know your game. They grab Avery at Darling's and he tells them about your visit the day before, and all the alarms this week, and then he lets it slip that you didn't want him to open the vault."

"And they said, 'You mean you can open the vault?' and the next thing is they are sneaking down the alley."

"Yeah. They had an idea about being heroes. Catching the bad cops and the robbers all at once. Nice plan until the payoff."

"Poor dumb jerks."

"Poor dumb jerks."

The silence came back then and Eleanor didn't wait for it to settle.

"Well, I just wanted to see how you were doing."

He nodded.

"And . . . and to tell you —"

Here it is, he thought, the kiss good-bye.

"— I've decided to quit. I'm going to leave the bureau."

"What about. . . . What will you do?"

"I don't know. But I'm going to leave here, Harry. I have some money so I'll travel awhile and then see what I want to do."

"Eleanor, why?"

"I don't — it's hard for me to explain. But everything that happened. Everything about the job has turned to shit. And I don't think I can go back and work in that squad room again after what has happened."

"Will you come back to L.A.?"

She looked down at her hands and then around the room again.

"I don't know. Harry, I'm sorry. It seemed like — I don't know, I'm very confused about things right now."

"What things?"

"I don't know. Us. What's happened. Everything."

Silence filled the room again and it seemed so loud that Bosch hoped a nurse or even Galvin Junior would stick a head in to see if everything was all right. He needed a cigarette badly. He realized it was the first time today that he had thought about smoking. Eleanor looked down at her feet now, and he looked over at his untouched food. He picked up the roll and started to toss it up and down in his hand like a baseball. After a while Eleanor's eyes made their third trip around the room without seeing whatever it was she was looking for. Bosch couldn't figure it out.

"Didn't you get the flowers I sent?"

"Flowers?"

"Yes, I sent daisies. Like the ones growing on the hill below your house. I don't see any in here."

Daisies, Bosch thought. The vase he had knocked against the wall. Where are my goddam cigarettes, he wanted to yell.

"They'll probably come later. They only make deliveries up here once a day."

She frowned.

"You know," Bosch said, "if Rourke knew we'd found the second vault and were watching it, and if he knew that we watched Tran go in and clear his box, why didn't he get his people out? That really bothers me about this whole thing. Why'd he go through with it?"

She shook her head slowly. "I don't know. Maybe . . . well, I've been thinking that maybe he wanted them to go down. He knew those guys, maybe he knew it would work out that they'd go down shooting, that without them he'd get to keep all the diamonds from the first vault."

"Yeah. But you know, I've been remembering things all day. About when we were down there. It's been coming back, and I remember that he didn't say he'd get it all. He said something about his share being bigger now with Meadows and the other two dead. He still used the word 'share,' like there was still someone else to split it with."

She raised her eyebrows. "Maybe, but it's just semantics, Harry."

"Maybe."

"I've got to go. You know how long they'll keep you?"

"Haven't been told, but I think tomorrow I'll take myself out. Thinking about going to Meadows's funeral over at veterans."

"A Memorial Day funeral. Sounds appropriate to me."

"Want to go with me?"

"Mmmm, no. I don't think I want anything more to do with Mr. Meadows. . . . But I'll be at the bureau tomorrow. Clearing out my desk and writing up status sheets on the cases I'll have to pass to other agents. You could come by if you'd like. I'll brew you some fresh coffee like before. But, you know, I don't really think they are going to let you out so fast, Harry. Not with a bullet wound. You need to rest. You need to heal some."

"Sure," Bosch said. He knew she was saying good-bye to him.

"Okay, then, maybe I'll see you."

She leaned over and kissed him good-bye, and he knew it was good-bye to everything about them. She was almost out the door before he opened his eyes.

"One last thing," he said, and she turned at the door and looked back at him. "How'd you find me, Eleanor? You know, in the tunnels with Rourke."

She hesitated and her eyebrows went up again.

"Well, I went down with Hanlon. But when we got out of the hand-dug tunnel we split up. He went one way in that first line and I went the other. I picked the winner. I found the blood. Then I found Franklin. Dead. And after that I was a little lucky. I heard the shots and then the voices. Mostly Rourke's voice. I followed that. Why did you think of that now?"

"I don't know. It just sort of came up. You saved my life."

They looked at each other. Her hand was on the door handle and it was open just enough so that Bosch could look past her and see Galvin Junior still there, sitting in a chair in the hallway.

"All I can say is thanks."

She made a shushing sound, dismissing his gratitude.

"You don't have to say anything."

"Don't quit."

He saw the crack in the door disappear, Junior with it. She stood there silently.

"Don't leave."

"I must. I'll see you, Harry."

She pulled the door all the way open now.

"Good-bye," she said, and then she was gone.

Bosch remained motionless on the hospital bed for the better part of an hour. He was thinking about two people: Eleanor Wish and John Rourke. For a long time he closed his eyes and dwelt on the look on Rourke's face as he crumpled and went down into the black water. I'd be surprised, too, Bosch thought, but there was also something else there, something he couldn't exactly identify. Some kind of knowing look of recognition and resolution — not of his dying, but of another, secret knowledge.

After a while he got up and took a few tentative steps alongside his bed. His body felt weak, yet all the sleep in the last thirty-six hours had made him restless. After he got his bearings and his shoulder made a slightly painful adjustment to gravity, he began to pace back and forth alongside the bed. He was wearing pale green hospital pajamas, not one of the opened-back smocks that he would have found humiliating. He padded around the room in bare feet, stopping to read the cards that had come with the flowers. The protective league had sent one of the vases. The others came from a couple of cops he knew but wasn't particularly close to, the widow of an old partner, his union lawyer and another old partner who lived in Ensenada.

He walked away from the flowers and went to the door. He opened it a crack and saw Galvin Junior still sitting there, reading a police equipment catalog. Bosch pulled the door all the way open. Galvin's head jerked up and he slapped the magazine closed and slipped it into a briefcase at his feet. He didn't say anything.

"So, Clifford — I hope I can call you that — what are you doing here? Am I supposed to be in danger?"

The younger cop didn't say anything. Bosch glanced up and down the hall and saw that it was empty all the way down to the nurses' station about fifty feet away. He looked at his door and noticed he was in room 313.

"Detective, please go back in your room," Galvin finally said. "I am only here to keep the press out of your room. The deputy chief thinks they will probably try to get in to get an interview with you, and my job is to prevent that, to prevent you from being disturbed."

"What if they use the sneaky method of just"— Bosch made a show of looking up and down the hall to make sure no one would hear —"using the telephone?"

Galvin exhaled loudly and continued not to look at Bosch. "The nurses are screening incoming calls. Only family, and I am told you don't have family, so no calls."

"How'd that lady FBI agent get by you?"

"She was cleared by Irving. Go back into your room, please."

"Certainly."

Bosch sat on his bed and tried to go over the case again in his mind. But the more he turned the parts of it over the more he got an anxious feeling that sitting on a bed in a hospital room was wasting time. He felt he was onto something, a breakthrough in the logic of the case. A detective's job was to walk down the trail of evidence, examine each piece and take it with him. At the end of the trail, what he had in his basket made or lost the case. Bosch had a full basket, but he began to believe there were pieces missing. What had he missed? What had Rourke told him at the end? Not so much in his words but his meaning. And the look on his face. Surprise. But surprise at what? Was he shocked at the bullet? Or shocked by where, and who, it came from? It could have been both, Bosch decided, and either way, what did it mean?

Rourke's reference to his share growing larger because of the deaths of Meadows, Franklin and Delgado continued to bother him. He tried to put himself in Rourke's position. If all his partners were dead and he was suddenly the sole beneficiary of the first vault caper, would he say, "My share has gone up," or would he simply say, "It's all mine"? Bosch's gut feeling was he would say the latter, unless there was still someone else sharing in the pot.

He decided he had to do something. He had to get out of this room. He was not under house arrest, but he knew that if he left Galvin was there to follow and report to Irving. He checked the phone and found that it had been turned on as Irving promised. No calls in, but Harry could call out.

He got up and checked the closet. His clothes were there, what was left of them. Shoes, socks and pants, that was it. The pants had abrasion marks on the knees but had been cleaned and pressed by the hospital. His sport coat and shirt had probably been taken off with scissors in the ER and either thrown away or put in an evidence bag. He grabbed all the clothing and got dressed, tucking his pajama top into his pants when he was done. He looked cloddish, but it would do until he got some clothes on the outside.

The pain in his shoulder was least when he held his arm up in front of his chest, so he began to put his belt around his shoulders to use it as a sling. But deciding that would make him too noticeable going out of the hospital, he put the belt back through the loops of his pants. He checked the drawer of the nightstand and found his wallet and badge, but no gun.

When he was ready, he picked up the phone on the bedside table, dialed the operator and asked for the third-floor nursing station. A woman's voice said hello and Bosch identified himself as Deputy Chief Irvin Irving. "Can you get Detective Galvin, my man on the chair down the hall, to come to the phone? I need to speak with him."

Bosch put the phone down on the bed and walked softly to the door. He opened it just wide enough to see Galvin sitting on the chair reading the catalog again. Bosch heard the nurse's voice calling him to the phone, and Galvin got up. Bosch waited about ten seconds before looking down the hall. Galvin was still walking toward the nurses' station. Bosch stepped out of the room and began walking quietly the opposite way.

After ten yards there was an intersection of hallways and Bosch took a left. He came to an elevator with a sign above it that said Hospital Personnel Only and he punched the button. When it came, it was a stainless steel and fake wood-grain affair with another set of doors at the back, big enough for at least two beds to be wheeled in. He pushed the first-floor button and the door closed. His treatment for the bullet wound had ended.

The elevator dropped Bosch off in the emergency room. He walked through and out into the night. On the way to Hollywood Station in a cab, he had the driver stop at his bank, where he got money out of an ATM, and then at a Sav-On drugstore, where he bought a cheap sport shirt, a carton of cigarettes, a lighter since he couldn't handle matches, and some cotton, fresh bandages and a sling. The sling was navy blue. It would be perfect for a funeral.

He paid the cabdriver at the station on Wilcox and went in through the front door, where he knew there was less chance that he would be recognized or spoken to. There was a rookie he didn't know on the front desk with the same pimple-faced Explorer Scout who had brought the pizza to Sharkey. Bosch held up his badge and passed by without saying a word. The detective bureau was dark and deserted, as it was on most Sunday nights, even in Hollywood. Bosch had a desk light clamped to his spot at the homicide table. He turned it on rather than using the bureau's ceiling lights, which might draw curious patrol officers down the hall from the watch commander's office. Harry didn't feel like answering questions, even the well-meaning ones from the uniform troops.

He first went to the back of the room and started a pot of coffee. Then he went into one of the interview rooms to change into his new shirt. His shoulder sent arrows of searing pain through his chest and down his arm as he pulled the hospital shirt off. He sat down in one of the chairs and examined the bandage for signs of a blood leak. There was none. Carefully, and much less painfully, he slipped the new shirt on — it was extra large. There was a small drawing of a mountain, sun, and seascape on the left breast and the words City of Angels. Bosch covered that when he put on the sling and adjusted it so that it held his arm tightly against his chest.

The coffee was ready when he was finished changing. He carried a steaming cup to the homicide table, lit a cigarette and pulled the murder book and other files on the Meadows case out of a file drawer. He looked at the pile and didn't know where to start or what he was looking for. He began reading through it all, hoping something would hit him as being wrong. He was looking for anything, a new name, a discrepancy in somebody's statement, something that had been discarded earlier as unimportant but would look different to him now.

He quickly scanned his own reports because most of the information he could still recall. Then he reread Meadows's military file. It was the slimmer version, the FBI handout. He had no idea what had happened to the more detailed records he had received from St. Louis and had left in the car when he went running toward the vault the morning before. He realized then that he had no idea where that car was, either.

Bosch drew a blank on the military file. While he was looking down at the miscellaneous paperwork in the back of the binder, the ceiling lights came on and an old beat cop named Pederson came in. He was heading toward one of the typewriters with an arrest report in his hand and didn't notice Bosch until he had sat down. He looked around when he smelled the cigarettes and coffee and saw the detective with the sling.

"Harry, how goes it? They let you out quick. Word around here was that you were righteously fucked up."

"Just a scratch, Peds. You get it worse from the fingernails of the he-shes you pull in every Saturday night. Least with a bullet you don't have to worry about the AIDS shit."

"You're telling me." Pederson instinctively massaged his neck where he still had scars from scratches inflicted by a transvestite hooker infected with the HIV virus. The old beat cop had sweated out two years of testing every three months but didn't get the virus. It was a story that was nightmarish legend in the division and probably the single reason the average occupancy in the TV and prostitute tanks at the station jail had dropped by half since then. Nobody wanted to arrest them anymore, unless it was for murder.

"Anyway," Pederson said, "sorry it went to shit out there, Harry. I heard the second cop went code seven a little while ago. Two cops and a feebee down in one shootout. Not to mention you gettin' your arm all fucked up. Probably some kind of a record for this town. Mind if I have a cup?"

Bosch gestured to the coffeepot. He hadn't heard that Clarke had died. Code seven. Out of service, for good. He still couldn't bring himself to feel sorry for the two IAD cops, and that made him feel sorry for himself. Made him feel like the hardening of the heart was now complete. He no longer had compassion for anybody, not even poor dumb jerks who screwed up and got themselves killed.

"They don't tell you shit around here," Pederson was saying as he poured, "but when I read those names in the paper I said, 'Whoah, I know them guys.' Lewis and Clarke. They were IAD, not on any bank detail. They called them two the great explorers. Always digging around, looking to fuck somebody up. I think everybody knows that's who they were but the TV and the *Times*. Anyway, that sure was curious, you know, what they were doing there."

Bosch wasn't going to bite on that. Pederson and the other cops would have to find out from another source what really went down at Beverly Hills Safe & Lock. In fact, he began to wonder if Pederson really had an arrest report to type up. Or had the rookie at the front desk spread the word that Bosch was in the bureau and the old beat cop been sent back to pump him?

Pederson had hair whiter than chalk and was considered an old cop but was actually only a few years older than Bosch. He had walked or driven the Boulevard beat for twenty years on night watch, and that was enough to turn a man's hair white early. Bosch liked Pederson. He was a silo of information about the street. There was rarely a murder on the Boulevard that went by without Bosch's checking with him to see what his informants were saying. And he almost always came through.

"Yeah, it's curious," Bosch said. He added nothing else.

"You doing paper from your shooting?" Pederson asked after settling himself in front of a typewriter. When Bosch didn't answer he added, "You got any more of those cigarettes?"

Bosch got up and carried a whole pack over to Pederson. He put them down on the typewriter in front of the beat cop and told him they were his. Pederson got the message. Nothing personal, but Bosch wasn't going to talk about the shoot-out, especially about what a couple of IAD cops were doing there.

Pederson got to work on the typewriter after that, and Bosch went back to his murder book. He finished reading through it without a single forty-watt bulb lighting up in his head. He sat there with the typewriter clacking in the background and smoked and tried to think of what else there was to do. There was nothing. He was at the wall.

He decided to call his home and check the tape machine. He picked up his phone, then thought better of using it and hung up. On the off chance his desk phone wasn't a private line, he walked around to Jerry Edgar's spot at the table and used his line. He got his answering machine, punched in a code and listened as it played a dozen messages. The first nine were from cops and some old friends wishing him a speedy recovery. The last three, the most recent messages, were from the doctor who had been treating him, Irving and Pounds.

"Mr. Bosch, this is Dr. McKenna. I consider it very unwise and unsafe for you to have left the hospital environment. You are risking further damage to your body. If you get this message, would you please return to the hospital. We are holding the bed. I can no longer treat you or consider you my patient if you do not return. Please. Thank you."

Irving and Pounds were not as worried about Bosch's health.

Irving's message said, "I do not know where you are or what you are doing, but it better be that you just do not like hospital food. Think about what I told you, Detective Bosch. Do not make a mistake we will both be sorry for."

Irving hadn't bothered to identify himself but didn't have to. Neither did Pounds. His message was the last. It was the chorus.

"Bosch, call me at home as soon as you get this. I have received word that you left the hospital and we need to talk. Bosch, you are not, repeat, not, to continue any line of investigation relating to the shootings on Saturday. Call me."

Bosch hung up. He wasn't going to call any of them. Not yet. While sitting at Edgar's spot he noticed a scratch pad on the table on which the name Veronica Niese was written. Sharkey's mother. There was also a phone number. Edgar must have called her to notify her about her son's death. Bosch thought of her answering the call, expecting it to be another one of her jerkoff customers, and instead it was Jerry Edgar calling to say her son was dead.

His thought of the boy reminded Bosch of the interview. He had not had the tape transcribed yet. He decided to listen to it, and went back to his place at the table. He pulled his tape recorder out of a drawer. The tape was gone. He remembered he had given it to Eleanor. He went to the supply closet, try-ing to calculate whether the interview would still be on the backup tape. The backup automatically rewound when it reached its end and then started tap-ing over itself. Depending on how often the taping system in the interview room had been used since Tuesday's session with Sharkey, the Q-and-A with the boy might still be intact on the backup tape.

Bosch popped the cassette out of the recorder and brought it back to his table. He put it in his own portable, put on a set of earphones and rewound the tape to its beginning. He reviewed it by playing it for a few seconds until he could tell whether it was his voice or Sharkey's or Eleanor's, and then fast-forwarding for about ten seconds. He repeated this process for several min-utes before he finally hit the Sharkey interview in the last half of the tape.

Once he found it, he rewound the tape a bit so he could hear the inter-view from the start. He rewound too far and ended up listening to half a minute of another interview concluding. Then he heard Sharkey's voice.

"What are you looking at?"

"I don't know." It was Eleanor. "I was wondering if you knew me. You seem familiar. I didn't realize I was staring."

"What? Why should I know you? I never did no federal shit, man. I don't know —"

"Never mind. You looked familiar to me, that's all. I was wondering if you recognized me. Why don't we wait until Detective Bosch comes in."

"Yeah, okay. Cool."

There was silence on the tape then. Listening to it, Bosch was confused. Then he realized that what he had just heard had been said before he went into the interview room.

What had she been doing? The silence on the tape ended and Bosch heard his own voice.

"Sharkey, we are going to tape this because it might help us later to go over it. Like I said, you are not a suspect so you —"

Bosch stopped the tape and rewound it to the exchange between the boy and Eleanor. He listened to it again and then again. Each time it felt as if he had been punched in the heart. His hands were sweating and his fingers slipped on the buttons of the recorder. He finally pulled the earphones off and flung them onto the table.

"Damn it," he said.

Pederson stopped typing and looked over.

PART
IX

MONDAY, MAY 28
MEMORIAL DAY OBSERVED

By the time Bosch got to the veterans cemetery in Westwood, it was just after midnight.

He had checked a new car out of the Wilcox fleet garage and then driven by Eleanor Wish's apartment. There were no lights on and he felt like a teenager checking on the girlfriend who dumped him. Even though he was alone he was embarrassed. He didn't know what he would have done if there had been a light. He headed back east toward the cemetery, thinking about Eleanor and how she had betrayed him in love and business, all at the same time.

He started with the supposition that Eleanor had asked Sharkey if he recognized her because it was she who had been in the Jeep that delivered Meadows's body to the reservoir. She had been looking for a sign that the boy realized this and recognized her. But he didn't. Sharkey went on — after Bosch joined the interview — to say he had seen two people who he thought were men. He said the smaller of the two stayed in the Jeep's passenger seat and didn't help with the body at all. It seemed to Bosch that the boy's mistake should have insured his life. But he knew that it had been he who had then doomed Sharkey when he suggested hypnotizing him. Eleanor had passed that on to Rourke, who knew he couldn't risk it.

Next was the question of why. The money was the ultimate answer, but Bosch could not comfortably attribute this motive to Eleanor. There was something more. The others involved — Meadows, Franklin, Delgado and Rourke — all shared the common bond of Vietnam as well as direct knowledge of the two targets, Binh and Tran. How did Eleanor fit into this? Bosch thought about her brother, killed in Vietnam. Was he the connection? He remembered that she had said his name was Michael, but she hadn't mentioned how or when he was killed. Bosch hadn't let her. Now he regretted having stopped her when she apparently wanted to talk about him. She had mentioned the memorial in Washington and how it had changed her. What could she have seen that would do that? What could the wall have told her that she didn't already know?

He drove into the cemetery off Sepulveda Boulevard and up to the great black iron gates that stood closed across the gravel entrance road. Bosch got out and walked up, but they were locked with a chain and padlock. He looked through the black bars and saw a small stone-block house about thirty yards up the gravel road. He saw the pale blue glow of TV light against a curtained window. Bosch went back to the car and flipped the siren. He let it wail until a light came on behind the curtain. The cemetery attendant came out a few moments later and walked toward the gate with a flashlight, while Bosch got his badge case out and held it open through the bars. The man wore dark pants and a light-blue shirt with a tin badge on it.

"You police?" he asked.

Bosch felt like saying no, Amway. Instead, he said, "LAPD. I wonder if you can open 'er up for me."

The attendant put the flashlight on his badge and ID. In the light Bosch could see the white whiskers on the man's face and smell the slight scent of bourbon and sweat.

"What's the problem, officer?"

"Detective. I'm on a homicide investigation, Mr. . . . ?"

"Kester. Homicide? We got plenty dead people here, but these cases are closed, I guess you could say."

"Mr. Kester, I don't have time to go through all the details but what I need to do is take a look at the Vietnam memorial, the replica that is on display here for the holiday weekend."

"What's wrong with your arm, and where's your partner? Don't you guys travel in twos?"

"I was hurt, Mr. Kester. My partner is working on another part of the investigation. You watch too much TV in that little room of yours. That's TV cops stuff."

Bosch said this last part with a smile, but he was already getting tired of the old security guard. Kester turned and looked at the cemetery house and then back at Bosch.

"You seen the TV light, right? I figured that one. Uh, this is federal property and I don't know if I can open it up without —"

"Look, Kester, I know you're civil service and they haven't fired anyone since maybe Truman was president. But if you give me a bad time on this, I'm going to give you a bad time. I'll put a drinking-on-the-job beef in on you Tuesday morning. First thing. Now let's do it. Open it up and I won't bother you. I just need to take a look at the wall."

Bosch rattled the chain. Kester stared dull-eyed at the lock and then fished a ring of keys off his belt and opened the gate.

"Sorry," Bosch said.

"I still don't think this is proper," Kester said angrily. "What's that black stone got to do with a homicide anyway?"

"Maybe everything," Bosch said. He started walking back to his car but then turned around, remembering something he had read about the memorial. "There's a book. It tells where the names are on the wall. You can look them up. Is that up there at the wall?"

Kester had a puzzled look on his face that Bosch could see even in the dark. He said, "Don't know about any book. All I know is that the U.S. Park Service people brought that thing in here, set it up. Took a bulldozer to clear a spot on the hill. They got some guy that stays with it during proper visiting hours. He's the one you'll have to ask about books. And don't ask me where he is. I don't even know his name. You gonna be a while or should I leave it unlocked?"

"Better lock it up. I'll come get you when I'm leaving."

He drove the car through the gate after the old man pulled it open, then up to a gravel parking area near the hill. Bosch could see the dark shine of the wall in the gash carved out of the rise. There were no lights and the area was deserted. He took a flashlight off the car seat and headed up the slope.

He first swung the light around to get an idea of the wall's size. It was about sixty feet long, tapering at each end. Then he walked up close enough to read the names. An unexpected feeling came over him. A dread. He did not want to see these names, he realized. There would be too many that he knew. And what was worse was that he might come across names he didn't expect, that belonged to men he didn't know were here. He swept the beam around and saw a wooden lectern, its top canted and ledged to hold a book, like a church Bible stand. But when he walked over, he found nothing on the stand. The park service people must have taken the directory with them for safekeeping. Bosch turned and looked back at the wall, its far end tapering off into darkness. He checked his cigarettes and saw he had nearly a whole pack. He admitted to himself that he had expected it would be this way. He would have to read every name. He knew it before he came. He lit a cigarette and put the beam on the first panel of the wall.

It was four hours before he saw a name he recognized. It wasn't Michael Scarletti. It was Darius Coleman, a boy Bosch had known from First Infantry. Coleman was the first guy Bosch had known, really known, to get blown away. Everybody had called him Cake. He had a knife-cut tattoo on his forearm that said Cake. And he was killed by friendly fire when a twenty-two-year-old lieutenant called in the wrong chart coordinates for an air strike in the Triangle.

Bosch reached to the wall and ran his fingers along the letters in the dead soldier's name. He had seen people do that on TV and in movies. He pictured Cake with a reefer tucked behind his ear, sitting on his pack and eating chocolate cake out of a can. He was always trading for everybody's cake. The reefer made him crave the chocolate.

Harry moved on to other names after that, stopping only to light cigarettes, until he had none left. In nearly four more hours he had come across three dozen more names belonging to soldiers he had known and knew were dead. There were no surprise names, and so his fear in that regard was unfounded. But despair came from something else. A small picture of a man in uniform was wedged into the thin crack between the false marble panels of the memorial. The man offered his full, proud smile to the world. Now he was a name on the wall. Bosch held the photo in his hand and turned it over. It said: "George, we miss your smile. All our love, Mom and Teri."

Bosch carefully put the photo back into the crack, feeling like an intruder on something very private. He thought about George, a man he never knew, and grew sad for no reason he could explain to himself. After a while, he moved on.

At the end, after 58,132 names, there was one he had not seen. Michael Scarletti. It was what he had expected. Bosch looked up at the sky. It was turning orange in the east and he could feel a slight breeze coming out of the northwest. To the south the Federal Building loomed above the cemetery tree line like a giant dark tombstone. Bosch was lost. He didn't know why he was here or whether what he had found meant a damned thing. Was Michael Scarletti still alive? Had he ever existed? What Eleanor had said about her trip to the memorial had seemed so real and true. How could any of this make sense? The beam of the flashlight was weak and dying. He turned it off.

Bosch napped a couple of hours in his car at the cemetery. When he woke the sun was high in the sky, and for the first time he noticed that the cemetery lawns were awash in flags, each grave marked by a small plastic Old Glory on a wooden stick. He started the car and slowly made his way along the thin cemetery roads, looking for the spot where Meadows would be buried.

It wasn't hard to find. Nestled on the side of one of the roads that wound into the northeast section of the cemetery were four vans with microwave antennas. There was a grouping of other cars as well. The media. Bosch hadn't expected all of the TV cameras and the reporters. But once he saw this crowd he realized that he had forgotten that holidays were slow news days. And the tunnel caper, as it had been dubbed by the media, was still a hot item. The video vampires would need fresh footage for the evening's broadcasts.

He decided to stay in the car, and watched as the short ceremony at Meadows's gray casket was filmed in quadruplicate. It was presided over by a rumpled minister who probably came from one of the downtown missions. There were no real mourners except for a few professionals from the VFW. A three-man honor guard also stood at attention.

When it was over, the minister pushed the brake pedal with his foot and the casket slowly descended. The cameras came in tight on this. And then, afterward, the news teams broke off in different directions to film stand-up reports at locations around the gravesite. They were spread out in a semi-circle. This way, each reporter would look as if he or she had been at the funeral exclusively. Bosch recognized a few as people who had shoved microphones in his face before. Then he noticed that one of the men he had thought was one of the professional mourners was actually Bremmer. The *Times* reporter walked away from the grave and was heading to one of the cars parked along the access road. Bosch waited until Bremmer was almost next to his car before he rolled down the window and called to him.

"Harry, I thought you were in the hospital or something."

"I thought I'd come by. But I didn't know it was going to be a circus. Don't you people have anything better to do?"

"Hey, I'm not with them. That's a pig fuck."

"What?"

"TV reporters. That's what they call one of these gangbangs. So, what are you doing here? I didn't think you'd be out so soon."

"I escaped. Why don't you get in and take a ride." Then indicating the TV reporters with his hand, Bosch said, "They might see me here and charge over and trample us."

Bremmer walked around and got in the car. Bosch took the driveway to the west section of the cemetery. He parked under the shade of a sprawling oak tree, from which they could see the Vietnam memorial. There were several people milling about, mostly men, mostly alone. They all looked at the black stone quietly. A couple of the men wore old fatigue jackets, the sleeves cut off.

"You seen the papers or TV yet on this thing?" Bremmer asked.

"Not yet. But I heard what was put out."

"And?"

"Bullshit. Most of it, at least."

"Can you tell me?"

"Not that it gets back to me."

Bremmer nodded. They had known each other a long time. Bosch did not have to ask for promises and Bremmer did not have to go over the differences between off-the-record statements, background statements and statements not for attribution. They had a trust built on prior credibility, going both ways.

"Three things you should check," Bosch said. "Nobody's asked about Lewis and Clarke. They weren't part of my surveillance. They were working for Irving over at IAD. So once you get that established, put the heat on them to explain what they were doing."

"What were they doing?"

"That you'll have to get somewhere else. I know you have other sources in the department."

Bremmer was writing in a long, thin spiral notebook, the kind that always gave reporters away. He was nodding as he wrote.

"Second, find out about Rourke's funeral. It will probably be out of state somewhere. Someplace far enough away that the media back here won't bother to send anybody. But send somebody anyway. Somebody with a camera. He'll probably be the only one there. Just like today's planting. That should tell you something."

Bremmer looked up from his notebook. "You mean no hero's funeral? You're saying Rourke was part of this thing, or he just fucked it up? Christ, the bureau — and we, the media — are making the guy out to be John Wayne reincarnated."

"Yeah, well, you gave him life after death. You can take it away, I guess."

Bosch just looked at him a moment, contemplating how much he should tell, what was safe for him to tell. For just a moment he felt so outraged he wanted to tell Bremmer everything he knew, and the hell with what would happen and what Irving had said. But he didn't. Control came back.

"What's the third thing?" Bremmer asked.

"Get the military records of Meadows, Rourke, Franklin and Delgado. That will tie it up for you. They were in Vietnam, same time, same unit. That's where this whole thing starts. When you get that far, call me and I'll try to fill in what you don't have."

Then all at once Bosch grew tired of the charade being orchestrated by his department and the FBI. The thought of the boy, Sharkey, kept coming to mind. Flat on his back, his head cocked at that odd, sickening angle. The blood. They were going to mop that one up like it didn't matter.

"There's a fourth thing," he said. "There was a kid."

When the story about Sharkey was finished, Bosch started the car and drove Bremmer back down the driveway to his own car. The TV reporters had cleared out of the cemetery and a man in a small front loader was pushing dirt into Meadows's grave. Another man leaned on a shovel nearby and watched.

"I'll probably need a job after your story comes out," Bosch said while watching the gravediggers.

"You won't be in it as an attribution. Plus, when I get the military records, they'll speak for themselves. I'll be able to scam the department's public information officers into confirming some of this other stuff, make it look like it came from them. And then near the bottom of the story, I'll say, 'Detective Harry Bosch declined comment.' How's that?"

"I'll probably need a job after your story comes out."

Bremmer just looked at the detective for a long moment.

"Are you going over to the grave?"

"I might. After you leave me alone."

"I'm leaving." He opened the car door and got out, then leaned back in. "Thanks, Harry. This is going to be a good one. Heads are going to bounce."

Bosch looked at the reporter and sadly shook his head. "No they aren't," he said.

Bremmer stared uneasily and Bosch dismissed him with his hand. The reporter closed the door and went to his own car. Bosch had no misconceived notion about Bremmer. The reporter was not guided by any genuine sense of outrage or by his role as a watchdog for the public. All he wanted was a story no other reporter had. Bremmer was thinking of that, and maybe the book that would come after, and the TV movie, and the money and ego-feeding fame. That was what motivated him, not the outrage that had made Bosch tell him the story. Bosch knew this and accepted it. It was the way things worked.

"Heads never bounce," he said to himself.

He watched the gravediggers finish their job. After a while he got out and walked over. There was one small bouquet of flowers next to the flag stuck in the soft orange ground. The flowers were from the VFW. Bosch stared at the scene and didn't know what he should feel. Maybe some kind of sentimental affection or remorse. Meadows was underground for good this time. Bosch didn't feel a thing. After a while he looked up from the grave and toward the Federal Building. He started walking in that direction. He felt like a ghost, coming from the grave for justice. Or maybe just vengeance.

If she was surprised it was Bosch who had pressed the door buzzer, Eleanor Wish didn't show it. Harry had flipped his badge to the guard on the first floor and been waved to the elevator. There was no receptionist working on the holiday, so he had pressed the night bell. It was Eleanor who opened the door. She wore faded jeans and a white blouse. There was no gun on her belt.

"I thought you might come, Harry. Were you at the funeral?"

He nodded but made no move toward the door she held open. She looked at him a long moment, her eyebrows arched in that lovely questioning look she had. "Well, are you going to come in or stand out there all day?"

"I was thinking we would take a walk. Talk alone."

"I have to get my keycard so I can come back in." She made a move to go back in and then stopped. "I doubt you heard this, because they haven't put the word out. But they found the diamonds."

"What?"

"Yes. They traced Rourke to some public storage lockers in Huntington Beach. They found receipts somewhere. They got the court order this morning and just opened them. I've been listening to the scanner. They're saying hundreds of diamonds. They'll have to get an appraiser. We were right,

Harry. Diamonds. You were right. They also found all the other stuff — in a second locker. Rourke hadn't gotten rid of it. The boxholders will get their stuff back. There's going to be a press conference, but I doubt they will be saying whose lockers they were."

He just nodded, and she disappeared through the door. Bosch wandered over to the elevators and pushed the button while waiting for her. She had her purse with her when she came out. It made him conscious of not having a gun. And it privately embarrassed him that he momentarily thought that was a concern. They didn't speak on the way down, not until they were out of the building and on the sidewalk, heading toward Wilshire. Bosch had been weighing his words, wondering if the finding of the diamonds meant anything. She seemed to be waiting for him to begin but uncomfortable in the silence.

"I like the blue sling," she finally said. "How do you feel, anyway? I'm surprised they let you out of there so soon."

"I just left. I feel fine." He stopped to put a cigarette in his mouth. He had bought a pack from a machine in the lobby. He lit it with the lighter.

"You know," she said, "this would be a good time to quit those. Make a new start."

He ignored the suggestion and breathed the smoke in deeply.

"Eleanor, tell me about your brother."

"My brother? I told you."

"I know. I want to hear again. About what happened to him and what happened when you visited the wall in Washington. You said it changed things for you. Why did it change things for you?"

They were at Wilshire. Bosch pointed across the street and they crossed toward the cemetery. "I left my car over here. I'll drive you back."

"I don't like cemeteries. I told you."

"Who does?"

They walked through the opening in the hedge and the sound of traffic was quieted. Before them was the expanse of green lawn, white stones and American flags.

"My story's the same as a thousand others," she said. "My brother went over there and didn't come back. That's all. And then, you know, going to the memorial, well, it filled me with a lot of different feelings."

"Anger?"

"Yes, there was that."

"Outrage?"

"Yes, I guess. I don't know. It was very personal. What's going on, Harry? What has this got to do with . . . with anything?"

They were on the gravel drive that ran alongside the rows of white stone. Bosch was leading her toward the replica.

"You said your father was career military. Did you get the details of what happened to your brother?"

"He did, but he and my mother never really said anything to me. About details. I mean, they just said he was coming home soon, and I had gotten a letter from him saying he was coming. Then, like the next week, you know, they said he had been killed. He didn't make it home after all. Harry, you are making me feel . . . What do you want? I don't understand this."

"Sure you do, Eleanor."

She stopped and just looked down at the ground. Bosch saw the color in her face change to a lighter shade of pale. And her expression became one of resignation. It was subtle, but it was there. Like the faces of mothers and wives he had seen while making next-of-kin notification. You didn't have to tell them somebody was dead. They opened the door; they knew the score. And now Eleanor's face showed that she knew Bosch had her secret. She lifted her eyes and looked off, away from him. Her gaze settled on the black memorial gleaming in the sun at the top of the rise.

"That's it, isn't it? You brought me here to see that."

"I guess I could ask you to show me where your brother's name is. But we both know it's not on there."

"No . . . it's not."

She was transfixed by the sight of the memorial. Bosch could see in her face that the hard-shell resistance was gone. The secret wanted to come out.

"So, tell me about it," he said.

"I did have a brother, and he died. I never lied to you, Harry. I never actually said he was killed over there. I said he never came back, and he didn't. That is true. But he died here in L.A. On his way home. It was 1973."

She seemed to go off on a memory. Then she came back.

"Amazing. I mean, to make it through that war and then to not make the trip home. It doesn't make sense. He had a two-day layover in L.A. on the way back to D.C. to the hero's welcome we were going to have for him. There was a nice safe job, arranged through Father at the Pentagon. Only they found him in a brothel in Hollywood. The spike was still in his arm. Heroin."

She looked up at Bosch's face and then looked away.

"That's the way it looked, but that wasn't the way it was. It was ruled an OD, but he was murdered. Just like Meadows so many years later. But my brother was written off the way Meadows was supposed to have been written off."

Bosch thought she might be beginning to cry. He needed to keep her on track, telling the story.

"What's going on, Eleanor? What's it got to do with Meadows?"

"Nothing," she said, and looked back along the trail they had walked.

Now she was lying. He knew there was something. He had the dreadful feeling in his gut that the whole thing revolved around her. He thought of the daisies she had sent to his hospital room. The music they had played at her apartment. The way she had found him in the tunnel. Too many coincidences.

"Everything," he said, "it was all part of your plan."

"No, Harry."

"Eleanor, how did you know there are daisies growing on the hill below my house?"

"I saw them when I —"

"You visited me at night. Remember? You couldn't see anything below the porch." He let that sink in a little. "You had been there before, Eleanor. When I was taking care of Sharkey. And then the visit later that night, that wasn't a visit. That was a test. Like the hang-up phone call. That was you. Because it was you who put the bug in my phone. This whole thing was. . . . Why don't you just tell me?"

She nodded without looking at him. He could not take his eyes off her. She composed herself and began.

"Did you ever have one thing that was at your center, was the very seed of your existence? Everybody has one unalterable truth at their core. For me, it was my brother. My brother and his sacrifice. That's how I dealt with his death. By making it and him larger than life. Making him a hero. It was the seed that I protected and nurtured. I built a hard shell around it and watered it with my adoration, and as it grew it became a bigger part of me. It grew into the tree that shaded my life. Then, all of a sudden, one day it was gone. The truth was false. The tree was chopped down, Harry. No more shade. Just the blinding sun."

She was quiet a moment and Bosch studied her. She seemed all at once to be so fragile he wanted to rush her to a chair before she collapsed. She cupped one elbow with her hand and held the other hand to her lips. It dawned on him what she was saying.

"You didn't know, did you?" Bosch said. "Your parents . . . nobody told you the truth."

She nodded. "I grew up thinking he was the hero my mother and father told me he was. They shielded me. They lied. But how could they know that one day a monument would be made and they would put every name on it. . . . Every name but my brother's."

She stopped, but this time he waited her out.

"One day a few years ago I went to the memorial. And I thought there was some kind of mistake. There was a book there, an index of the names, and I looked and he wasn't listed. No Michael Scarletti. I yelled at the parks people. 'How could you just leave someone's name out of the book?' And so I spent the rest of the day reading the names on the wall. All of them. I was going to show them how wrong they were. But . . . he wasn't there, either. I couldn't — Do you know what it's like to spend almost fifteen years of your life believing something, to build your beliefs around one single, shining fact, and have . . . to find that all that time it actually was like cancer growing inside?"

Bosch smeared the tears on her cheeks with his hand. He leaned his face close to hers.

"So what did you do, Eleanor?"

The fist against her lips squeezed tighter, her knuckles as bloodless as a corpse's. Bosch noticed a park bench farther down the walkway and he took her by the shoulder and directed her there.

"This whole thing," he said after they were sitting. "I don't understand, Eleanor. This whole thing. You were the — You wanted some kind of revenge against —"

"Justice. Not revenge, not vengeance."

"Is there a difference?"

She didn't answer.

"Tell me what you did."

"I confronted my parents. And they finally told me about L.A. I went through all my things from him and I found a letter, his last letter. I still had it in my things at my parents' house but I'd forgotten it. It's here."

She opened her purse and pulled out her wallet. Bosch could see the rubber grips and the handle of her gun in the purse. She opened her wallet and pulled out a twice-folded piece of lined notebook paper. She delicately unfolded it and held it open for him to read. He didn't touch it.

Ellie,

I'm getting so short here I can practically taste the soft-shell crabs. I should be home in two weeks or so. First I have to stop off in Los Angeles to make some money. Ha Ha! I have a plan (but don't tell the OM). I'm supposed to drop off a "diplomatic" package in L.A. But there might be a way to do something better with it. When I get back, maybe we can go up to the Poconos again before I have to go back to work for the "war machine." I know what you think about what I'm doing but I can't tell the OM no. We'll see how it goes. One thing's for sure, I'm glad to be leaving this place. I've been in the bush for six weeks before getting some R & R here in Saigon. I don't want to go back, so I'm having them treat me for dysentery. (Ask the OM what that is! Ha Ha.) All I had to do was eat some of the restaurant food in this town and got the symptoms. Anyway, that's all for now. I'm safe and I'll be home soon. So get those crab traps out of the shed.
Love,
Michael

She folded the letter carefully and put it away.

"The OM?" Bosch asked.

"The Old Man."

"Right."

Her composure was coming back. Her face was taking on the hard look Bosch had seen the first day he met her. Her eyes dropped from his face to his chest and his arm in the blue sling.

"I'm not wired, Eleanor," he said. "I'm here for myself. I want to know for myself."

"That's not what I was looking at," she said. "I knew you wouldn't be wired. I was thinking of your arm. Harry, if there is anything that you believe about me now, that you can believe, believe me when I say no one was supposed to get hurt.

"No one. . . . Everybody was to lose. But that was all. After that day — at the memorial, I looked and I searched and I found out what happened to my brother. I used Ernst at State, I used the Pentagon, my father, I used whatever I could and I found out about my brother."

She searched his eyes but he tried not to reveal the thoughts behind them. "And?"

"And it was like Ernst told us. Toward the end of the war, the three captains, the triad, were taking an active part in the transport of heroin to the States. One conduit was Rourke and his crew at the embassy, the military police. That included Meadows, Delgado and Franklin. They would find short-timers in the bars in Saigon and proposition them: a few thousand dollars to take a sealed diplomatic package through customs. Nothing to it. They could arrange for them to receive temporary courier status, put them on a plane, and somebody would be waiting for the package in L.A. My brother was one of those that accepted. . . . But Michael had a plan. It didn't take a genius to figure out what they were carrying. And so he must have thought he could get over here and make a better deal with somebody else. I don't know how far he thought it out or had it set up. But it didn't matter. They found him and they killed him."

"They?"

"I don't know who. People working for the captains. For Rourke. It was perfect. He was killed in a way that the army, his family, just about everybody, would want to keep quiet. So it was quickly tidied up and that was that."

Bosch sat next to her as she told the rest of the story and did not interrupt until it was done, until it had come out of her like a demon.

She said the first one she found was Rourke. He was, to her astonishment, in the bureau. She called in her markers and transferred from D.C. out to his crew. She had a different last name than her brother had. Rourke didn't know who she was. After that, Meadows, Franklin and Delgado were located easily enough in prisons. They weren't going anywhere.

"Rourke was the key," she said. "I went to work on him. I guess you could say I seduced him with the plan."

Bosch felt something tear loose inside, some final feeling for her.

"I clearly insinuated that I wanted to make a score. I knew he would go for it because he'd been corrupt for years. And he was greedy. One night he told me about the diamonds, how he had helped these two guys out of Saigon with boxes full of diamonds. It was Tran and Binh. From there, it was easy to plan the whole thing. Rourke recruited the other three and pulled some strings, anonymously, to get them early releases into Charlie Company. It was a perfect plan and Rourke actually thought it was his. That's what made it perfect. In the end, I was going to disappear with the treasure. Binh and Tran would be robbed of the fortune they had spent their lives collecting and hoarding, and the other four would taste the biggest score of their lives and have it taken away. It would be the best way of hurting them the most. But no one outside the circle of guilt was to get hurt. . . . Things just happened."

"Meadows took the bracelet," Bosch said.

"Yes. Meadows took the bracelet. I saw it on the pawn lists that got sent over from LAPD. It was routine, but I panicked. Those lists go to every burglary unit in the county. I thought it would get noticed by somebody, Meadows would be pulled in and spill the story. I told Rourke. And he panicked, too. He waited until they were pretty much done with the second tunnel, and then he and the two others confronted Meadows. I wasn't there."

Her eyes were fixed on a point far away. There was no emotion in her voice anymore. It was just a flat line. Bosch didn't have to prompt her. The rest just came out.

"I wasn't there," she said again. "Rourke called me. He told me that, you know, Meadows died without giving up the pawn ticket. He said he'd made it look like an overdose. The bastard actually said that he knew people who had done it before, a long time ago, and gotten away with it. You see? He was talking about my brother. When he said that, I knew I was doing the right thing . . .

"Anyway, he needed my help. They had searched Meadows's place and couldn't find the pawn stub. That meant Delgado and Franklin were going to break into the shop and get the bracelet back. But Rourke wanted my help with Meadows. The body. He didn't know what to do with it."

She said she knew from Meadows's record that he had been busted for loitering at the reservoir. It wasn't difficult for her to convince Rourke it was a good place to leave the body.

"But I also knew that the reservoir was Hollywood Division, that if you didn't get the call you would at least hear about it and probably take an interest after Meadows was ID'd. See, I knew about you and Meadows. And now I knew Rourke was out of control. You were the safety valve, in case I needed to bring the whole thing down. I couldn't let Rourke get away with it again."

She swept her gaze across the stones and absentmindedly raised a hand and dropped it in her lap, a small show of resignation.

"After we put his body in the Jeep and covered it with the blanket, Rourke went back in to make a last sweep of the place. I stayed outside. There was a tire iron in the back. I took it and hit his fingers with it. Meadows's fingers. It was so somebody would see it was murder. I remember the sound so clearly. The bone. So loud I thought Rourke might even have heard. . . ."

"What about Sharkey?" Bosch asked.

"Sharkey," she said wistfully, as if she were trying the name out for the first time.

"After the interview, I told Rourke that Sharkey didn't see our faces at the dam. He even thought I was a man, sitting in the Jeep. But I made a mistake. I mentioned how we discussed hypnotizing him. Even though I stopped you and trusted that you wouldn't do it without me, Rourke didn't trust you. So he did what he did with Sharkey. After we were called out there and I saw him I . . ."

She didn't finish but Bosch wanted to know everything.

"You what?"

"Later, I confronted Rourke and told him I was bringing the whole thing down because he was out of control, killing innocent people. He told me there was no way to stop it. Franklin and Delgado were in the tunnel and out of reach. They turned the radios off when they brought the C-4 in. It's too unstable. He said there was no stopping it without more spilled blood. Then the next night you and I were almost run down. That was Rourke, I'm sure."

She said that the two of them played an unspoken game of mutual distrust and suspicion after that. The burglary of Beverly Hills Safe & Lock continued as planned, and Rourke steered Bosch and everybody else away from going underground to stop it. He had to let Franklin and Delgado go through with it, even though there were no diamonds left in Tran's box. Rourke could not risk going underground to warn them, either.

Eleanor finally ended the game when she followed Bosch down into the tunnel and killed Rourke, his eyes staring at her as he slid down into the black water.

"And that's the whole story," she said quietly.

"My car is over this way," Bosch said as he stood up from the bench. "I'll take you back now."

They found his car on the driveway, and Bosch noticed her eyes linger on the fresh soil on Meadows's grave before she got in. He wondered if she had watched from the Federal Building as the casket was put in the ground. As he drove toward the exit, Harry said, "Why couldn't you let it go? What happened to your brother was another time, another place. Why didn't you let it go?"

"You don't know how many times I've asked that and how many times I didn't know the answer. I still don't."

They were at the light at Wilshire and Bosch was wondering what he was going to do. And once again she read him, she sensed his indecision.

"Are you going to take me in now, Harry? You might have a hard time proving your case. Everybody's dead. It could look like you were part of it, too. You going to risk that?"

He didn't say anything. The light changed and he drove down to the Federal Building, pulling to the curb near the garden of flags.

She said, "If it means anything to you at all, what happened between you and me, it wasn't part of any plan. I know you won't ever know if that's the truth, but I wanted to say —"

"Don't," he said. "Don't say a thing about it."

A few uneasy moments of silence passed between them.

"You're just letting me go here?"

"I think it would be best for you, Eleanor, if you turned yourself in. Go get a lawyer and then come in. Tell them you didn't have anything to do with the murders. Tell them the story about your brother. They are reasonable people and they'll want to keep it low profile, avoid the scandal. The U.S. attorney will probably let you plead to something short of murder. The bureau will go along."

"And what if I don't turn myself in? You will tell them?"

"No. Like you said, I'm too much a part of it. They'd never go with what I'd tell them."

He thought a long moment. He didn't want to say what he was going to say next unless he was sure he meant it. And could, and would, do it.

"No, I won't tell them. . . . But if I don't hear in a few days that you went in, I will tell Binh. And I'll tell Tran. I won't need to prove it to them. I'll just tell them the story with enough facts that they'll know it is true. Then, you know what they'll do? They'll act like they don't know what the hell I'm talking about and they'll tell me to get out. And then they'll come after you, Eleanor, looking for the same kind of justice you got for your brother."

"You would do that, Harry?"

"I said I would. I'll give you two days to go in. Then I tell them the story."

She looked at him, and the pained expression on her face asked why.

Harry said, "Somebody has to answer for Sharkey."

She turned away, put her hand on the door handle and looked out the car window at the flags flapping in the Santa Ana breeze. She didn't look back at him when she said, "So, I guess I was wrong about you."

"If you mean the Dollmaker case, the answer is yes, you were wrong about me."

She looked back at him with a wan smile as she opened the door. She quickly leaned over and kissed him on the cheek. She said, "Good-bye, Harry Bosch."

Then she was out of the car, standing in the wind and looking in at him. She hesitated and then closed the door. As Harry drove away he glanced once in the mirror and saw her still at the curb. She stood there looking down like someone who had dropped something in the gutter. After that, he didn't look back.

Epilogue

The morning after Memorial Day, Harry Bosch checked back into MLK, where he was severely chastised by his doctor, who seemed, to Harry at least, to take a perverse pleasure in ripping the home-applied bandages away from his shoulder and then using a stinging saline solution to rinse the wound. He spent two days resting and then was wheeled into the OR for surgery to reattach muscles that had been torn from bone by the bullet.

On the second day of his recovery from surgery, a nurse's aide dropped off a day-old *Los Angeles Times* for him to while away a few hours with. Bremmer's story was on the front page, and it accompanied a photograph of a priest standing before a lonely casket at a cemetery in Syracuse, New York. It was FBI Special Agent John Rourke's casket. Bosch could tell from the photo that more mourners — albeit members of the media — had been at Meadows's funeral. But Bosch tossed the front section aside after scanning the first few paragraphs of the story and realizing it wasn't about Eleanor. He turned to the sports.

The next day, he had a visitor. Lieutenant Harvey Pounds told Bosch that when he was recovered, he would report back to Hollywood homicide. Pounds said that neither of them had any choice in the matter. The order came from the sixth floor at Parker Center. The lieutenant didn't have much else to say, and didn't mention the newspaper article at all. Harry took the news with a smile and a nod, not wanting to show a hint of what he felt or thought.

"Of course, this is all contingent on you being able to pass a departmental physical when you're released by your physicians here," Pounds added.

"Of course," Bosch said.

"You know, Bosch, some officers would want the disability, retire at eighty percent pay. You could get a job in the private sector and do very nicely. You'd deserve it."

Ah, Harry thought, there is the reason for the visit.

"Is that what the department wants me to do, Lieutenant?" he asked. "Are you the messenger?"

"Of course not. The department wants you to do what you want, Harry. I'm just looking at the advantages of the situation. You know, just something to think about. I understand private investigation is the growth market of the nineties. No trust anymore, you know? Nowadays people are secretly getting complete backgrounds — medical, financial, romantic — on the people they are going to marry."

"That doesn't sound like my kind of work."

"You'll take the homicide table, then?"

"Soon as I pass the physical."

He had another visitor the next day. This one was expected. She was a prosecutor from the U.S. attorney's office. Her name was Chavez and she wanted to know about the night Sharkey was killed. Eleanor Wish had come in, Bosch knew then.

He told the prosecutor that he had been with Eleanor, confirming her alibi. Chavez said she just had to check to be sure, before they started talking a deal. She asked a few other questions about the case, then got up from the visitor's chair to go.

"What's going to happen to her?" Bosch asked.

"I can't discuss that, Detective."

"Off the record?"

"Off the record, she's obviously going to have to go away, but it probably won't be long. The climate is right for this to be handled very quietly. She came forward, she brought competent counsel and it appears she was not directly responsible for the deaths involved. If you ask me, she'll get out of this very lucky. She'll plead and do maybe thirty months tops up at Tehachapi."

Bosch nodded and Chavez was gone.

Harry, too, was gone the next day, sent home for six weeks' recuperative leave before reporting back to the station on Wilcox. When he arrived at the house on Woodrow Wilson he found a yellow slip of paper in his mailbox. He took it to the post office and exchanged it for a wide, flat package in brown paper. He didn't open it until he was home. It was from Eleanor Wish, though it did not say so: it was just something he knew. After tearing away the paper and bubbled plastic liner, he found a framed print of Hopper's *Nighthawks*. It was the piece he had seen above her couch that first night he was with her.

Bosch hung the print in the hallway near his front door, and from time to time he would stop and study it when he came in, particularly from a weary day or night on the job. The painting never failed to fascinate him, or to evoke memories of Eleanor Wish. The darkness. The stark loneliness. The man sitting alone, his face turned to the shadows. I am that man, Harry Bosch would think each time he looked.

The
Black
Ice

This is for
Linda McCaleb Connelly

1

The smoke carried up from the Cahuenga Pass and flattened beneath a layer of cool crossing air. From where Harry Bosch watched, the smoke looked like a gray anvil rising up the pass. The late afternoon sun gave the gray a pinkish tint at its highest point, tapering down to deep black at its root, which was a brushfire moving up the hillside on the east side of the cut. He switched his scanner to the Los Angeles County mutual aid frequency and listened as firefighter battalion chiefs reported to a command post that nine houses were already gone on one street and those on the next street were in the path. The fire was moving toward the open hillsides of Griffith Park, where it might make a run for hours before being controlled. Harry could hear the desperation in the voices of the men on the scanner.

Bosch watched the squadron of helicopters, like dragonflies from this distance, dodging in and out of the smoke, dropping their payloads of water and pink fire retardant on burning homes and trees. It reminded him of the dustoffs in Vietnam. The noise. The uncertain bobbing and weaving of the overburdened craft. He saw the water crushing through flaming roofs and steam immediately rising.

He looked away from the fire and down into the dried brush that carpeted the hillside and surrounded the pylons that held his own home to the hillside on the west side of the pass. He saw daisies and wildflowers in the chaparral below. But not the coyote he had seen in recent weeks hunting in the arroyo below his house. He had thrown down pieces of chicken to the scavenger on occasion, but the animal never accepted the food while Bosch watched. Only after Bosch went back in off the porch would the animal creep out and take the offerings. Harry had christened the coyote *Timido*. Sometimes late at night he heard the coyote's howl echoing up the pass.

He looked back out at the fire just as there was a loud explosion and a concentrated ball of black smoke rotated up within the gray anvil. There was excited chatter on the scanner and a battalion chief reported that a propane tank from a barbecue had ignited.

Harry watched the darker smoke dissipate in the larger cloud and then switched the scanner back to the LAPD tactical frequencies. He was on call. Christmas duty. He listened for a half minute but heard nothing other than routine radio traffic. It appeared to be a quiet Christmas in Hollywood.

He looked at his watch and took the scanner inside. He pulled the pan out of the oven and slid his Christmas dinner, a roasted breast of chicken, onto a plate. Next he took the lid off a pot of steamed rice and peas and dumped a large portion onto the plate. He took his meal out to the table in the dining room, where there was already a glass of red wine waiting, next to the three cards that had come in the mail earlier in the week but that he had left unopened. He had Coltrane's arrangement of "Song of the Underground Railroad" on the CD player.

As he ate and drank he opened the cards, studied them briefly and thought of their senders. This was the ritual of a man who was alone, he knew, but it didn't bother him. He'd spent many Christmases alone.

The first card was from a former partner who had retired on book and movie money and moved to Ensenada. It said what Anderson's cards always said: "Harry, when you coming down?" The next one was also from Mexico, from the guide Harry had spent six weeks living and fishing and practicing Spanish with the previous summer in Bahia San Felipe. Bosch had been recovering from a bullet wound in the shoulder. The sun and sea air helped him mend. In his holiday greeting, written in Spanish, Jorge Barrera also invited Bosch's return.

The last card Bosch opened slowly and carefully, also knowing who it was from before seeing the signature. It was postmarked Tehachapi. And so he knew. It was handprinted on off-white paper from the prison's recycling mill and the Nativity scene was slightly smeared. It was from a woman he had spent one night with but thought about on more nights than he could remember. She, too, wanted him to visit. But they both knew he never would.

He sipped some wine and lit a cigarette. Coltrane was now into the live recording of "Spiritual" captured at the Village Vanguard in New York when Harry was just a kid. But then the radio scanner — still playing softly on a table next to the television — caught his attention. Police scanners had played for so long as the background music of his life that he could ignore the chatter, concentrate on the sound of a saxophone, and still pick up the words and codes that were unusual. What he heard was a voice saying, "One-K-Twelve, Staff Two needs your twenty."

Bosch got up and walked over to the scanner, as if looking at it would make its broadcast more clear. He waited ten seconds for a reply to the request. Twenty seconds.

"Staff Two, location is the Hideaway, Western south of Franklin. Room seven. Uh, Staff Two should bring a mask."

Bosch waited for more but that was it. The location given, Western and Franklin, was within Hollywood Division's boundaries. One-K-Twelve was a radio designation for a homicide detective out of the downtown headquarters' Parker Center. The Robbery-Homicide Division. And Staff Two was the designation for an assistant chief of police. There were only three ACs in the department and Bosch was unsure which one was Staff Two. But it didn't matter. The question was, what would one of the highest-ranking men in the department be rolling out for on Christmas night?

The second question bothered Harry even more. If RHD was already on the call, why hadn't he — the on-call detective in Hollywood Division — been notified first? He went to the kitchen, dumped his plate in the sink, dialed the station on Wilcox and asked for the watch commander. A lieutenant named Kleinman picked up. Bosch didn't know him. He was new, a transfer out of Foothill Division.

"What's going on?" Bosch asked. "I'm hearing on the scanner about a body at Western and Franklin and nobody's told me a thing. And that's funny 'cause I'm on call out today."

"Don't worry 'bout it," Kleinman said. "The hats have got it all squared away."

Kleinman must be an oldtimer, Bosch figured. He hadn't heard that expression in years. Members of RHD wore straw bowlers in the 1940s. In the fifties it was gray fedoras. Hats went out of style after that — uniformed officers called RHD detectives "suits" now, not "hats" — but not homicide special cops. They still thought they were the tops, up there high like a cat's ass. Bosch hated that arrogance even when he'd been one of them. One good thing about working Hollywood, the city's sewer. Nobody had any airs. It was police work, plain and simple.

"What's the call?" Bosch asked.

Kleinman hesitated a few seconds and then said, "We've got a body in a motel room on Franklin. It's looking suicide. But RHD is going to take it — I mean, they've already taken it. We're out of it. That's from on high, Bosch."

Bosch said nothing. He thought a moment. RHD coming out on a Christmas suicide. It didn't make much — then it flashed to him.

Calexico Moore.

"How old is this thing?" he asked. "I heard them tell Staff Two to bring a mask."

"It's ripe. They said it'd be a real potato head. Problem is, there isn't much head left. Looks like he smoked both barrels of a shotgun. At least, that's what I'm picking up on the RHD freek."

Bosch's scanner did not pick up the RHD frequency. That was why he had not heard any of the early radio traffic on the call. The suits had apparently switched freeks only to notify Staff Two's driver of the address. If not for that, Bosch would not have heard about the call until the following morning when he came into the station. This angered him but he kept his voice steady. He wanted to get what he could from Kleinman.

"It's Moore, isn't it?"

"Looks like it," Kleinman said. "His shield is on the bureau there. Wallet. But like I said, nobody's going to make a visual ID from the body. So nothing is for sure."

"How did this all go down?"

"Look, Bosch, I'm busy here, you know what I mean? This doesn't concern you. RHD has it."

"No, you're wrong, man. It does concern me. I should've gotten first call from you. I want to know how it went down so I understand why I didn't."

"Awright, Bosch, it went like this. We get a call out from the owner of the dump says he's got a stiff in the bathroom of room seven. We send a unit out and they call back and say, yeah, we got the stiff. But they called back on a land line — no radio — 'cause they saw the badge and the wallet on the bureau and knew it was Moore. Or, at least, thought it was him. We'll see. Anyway, I called Captain Grupa at home and he called the AC. The hats were called in and you were not. That's the way it goes. So if you have a beef, it's with Grupa or maybe the AC, not me. I'm clean."

Bosch didn't say anything. He knew that sometimes when he was quiet, the person he needed information from would eventually fill the silence.

"It's out of our hands now," Kleinman said. "Shit, the TV and *Times* are out there. *Daily News*. They figure it's Moore, like everybody else. It's a big mess. You'd think the fire up on the hill would be enough to keep them occupied. No way. They're out there lined up on Western. I gotta send another car over for media control. So, Bosch, you should be happy you aren't involved. It's Christmas, for Chrissake."

But that wasn't good enough. Bosch should have been called and then it should have been his decision when to call out RHD. Someone had taken him out of the process altogether and that still burned him. He said good-bye and lit another cigarette. He got his gun out of the cabinet above the sink and hooked it to the belt on his blue jeans. Then he put on a light-tan sport coat over the Army green sweater he was wearing.

It was dark outside now and through the sliding glass door he could see the fire line across the pass. It burned brightly on the black silhouette of the hill. It was a crooked devil's grin moving to the crest.

From out in the darkness below his house he heard the coyote. Howling at the rising moon or the fire, or maybe just at himself for being alone and in the dark.

2

Bosch drove down out of the hills into Hollywood, traveling mostly on deserted streets until he reached the Boulevard. On the sidewalks there were the usual groupings of runaways and transients. There were strolling prostitutes — he saw one with a red Santa hat on. Business is business, even on

Christmas night. There were elegantly made up women sitting on bus benches who were not really women and not really waiting for buses. The tinsel and Chistmas lights strung across the Boulevard at each intersection added a surreal touch to the neon glitz and grime. Like a whore with too much makeup, he thought — if there was such a thing.

But it wasn't the scene that depressed Bosch. It was Cal Moore. Bosch had been expecting this for nearly a week, since the moment he heard that Moore had failed to show up for roll call. For most of the cops at Hollywood Division it wasn't a question of whether Moore was dead. It was just a question of how long before his body turned up.

Moore had been a sergeant heading up the division's street narcotics unit. It was a night job and his unit worked the Boulevard exclusively. It was known in the division that Moore had separated from his wife and replaced her with whiskey. Bosch had found that out firsthand the one time he had spent time with the narc. He had also learned that there might be something more than just marital problems and early burnout plaguing him. Moore had spoken obliquely of Internal Affairs and a personnel investigation.

It all added up to a heavy dose of Christmas depression. As soon as Bosch heard they were starting a search for Cal Moore, he knew. The man was dead.

And so did everyone else in the department, though nobody said this out loud. Not even the media said it. At first the department tried to handle it quietly. Discreet questions at Moore's apartment in Los Feliz. A few helicopter runs over the nearby hills in Griffith Park. But then a TV reporter was tipped and all the other stations and the newspapers followed the story for the ride. The media dutifully reported on the progress of the search for the missing cop, Moore's photograph was pinned to the bulletin board in the Parker Center press room and the weight of the department made the standard pleas to the public. It was drama. Or, at least, it was good video; horseback searches, air searches, the police chief holding up the photo of the darkly handsome and serious-looking sergeant. But nobody said they were looking for a dead man.

Bosch stopped the car for the light at Vine and watched a man wearing a sandwich board cross the street. His stride was quick and jerky and his knees continuously popped the cardboard sign up in the air. Bosch saw there was a satellite photograph of Mars pasted on the board with a large section of it circled. Written in large letters below was REPENT! THE FACE OF THE LORD WATCHES US! Bosch had seen the same photograph on the cover of a tabloid while standing in line at a Lucky store, but the tabloid had claimed that the face was that of Elvis.

The light changed and he continued on toward Western. He thought of Moore. Outside of one evening spent drinking with him at a jazz bar near the Boulevard, he had not had much interaction with Moore. When Bosch had been transferred to Hollywood Division from RHD the year before, there had been hesitant handshakes and glad-to-know-yous from everyone in the division. But people generally kept their distance. It was understandable, since he had been rolled out of RHD on an IAD beef, and Bosch didn't mind. Moore was one of those who didn't go out of his way to do much more than nod when they passed in the hall or saw each other at staff meetings. Which was also understandable since the homicide table where Bosch worked was in the first-floor detective bureau and Moore's squad, the Hollywood BANG — short for Boulevard Anti-Narcotics Group — was on the second floor of the station. Still, there had been the one encounter. For Bosch it had been a meeting to pick up some background information for a case he was working. For Moore it had been an opportunity to have many beers and many whiskeys.

Moore's BANG squad had the kind of slick, media-grabbing name the department favored but in reality was just five cops working out of a converted storage room and roaming Hollywood Boulevard at night, dragging in anybody with a joint or better in his pocket. BANG was a numbers squad, created to make as many arrests as possible in order to help justify requests for more manpower, equipment and, most of all, overtime in the following year's budget. It did not matter that the DA's office handed out probation deals on most of the cases and kicked the rest. What mattered were those arrest statistics. And if Channel 2 or 4 or a *Times* reporter from the Westside insert wanted to ride along one night and do a story on the BANG squad, all the better. There were numbers squads in every division.

At Western Bosch turned north and ahead he could see the flashing blue and yellow lights of the patrol cars and the lightning-bright strobes of TV cameras. In Hollywood such a display usually signaled the violent end of a life or the premiere of a movie. But Bosch knew nothing premiered in this part of town except thirteen-year-old hookers.

Bosch pulled to the curb a half block from the Hideaway and lit a cigarette. Some things about Hollywood never changed. They just came up with new names for them. The place had been a run-down dump thirty years ago when it was called the El Rio. It was a run-down dump now. Bosch had never been there but he had grown up in Hollywood and remembered. He had stayed in enough places like it. With his mother. When she was still alive.

The Hideaway was a 1940s-era courtyard motel that during the day would be nicely shaded by a large banyan tree which stood in its center. At night, the motel's fourteen rooms receded into a darkness only the glow of red neon invaded. Harry noticed that the E in the sign announcing MONTHLY RATES was out.

When he was a boy and the Hideaway was the El Rio, the area was already in decay. But there wasn't as much neon and the buildings, if not the people, looked fresher, less grim. There had been a Streamline Moderne office building that looked like an ocean liner docked next to the motel. It had set sail a long time ago and another mini-mall was there now.

Looking at the Hideaway from his parked car, Harry knew it was a sorry place to stay the night. A sorrier place to die. He got out and headed over.

Yellow crime scene tape was strung across the mouth of the courtyard and was manned by uniformed officers. At one end of the tape bright lights from TV cameras focused on a group of men in suits. The one with the gleaming, shaven scalp was doing all the talking. As Bosch approached, he realized that the lights were blinding them. They could not see past the interviewers. He quickly showed his badge to one of the uniforms, signed his name on the Crime Scene Attendance Log the cop held on a clipboard and slipped under the tape.

The door to room 7 was open and light from inside spilled out. The sound of an electric harp also wafted from the room and that told Bosch that Art Donovan had caught the case. The crime scene tech always brought a portable radio with him. And it was always tuned to The Wave, a new-age music channel. Donovan said the music brought a soothing calm to a scene where people had killed or been killed.

Harry walked through the door, holding a handkerchief over his mouth and nose. It didn't help. The odor that was like no other assaulted him as soon as he passed the threshold. He saw Donovan on his knees dusting fingerprint powder onto the dials of the air-conditioner unit in the wall below the room's front, and only, window.

"Cheers," Donovan said. He was wearing a painter's mask to guard against the odor and the intake of the black powder. "In the bathroom."

Bosch took a look around, quickly, since it was likely he would be told to leave as soon as the suits discovered him. The room's queen-sized bed was made with a faded pink coverlet. There was a single chair with a newspaper on it. Bosch walked over and noted that it was the *Times*, dated six days earlier. There was a bureau and mirror combination to the side of the bed. On top of it was an ashtray with a single butt pressed into it after being half smoked. There was also a .38 Special in a nylon boot holster, a wallet and a badge case. These last three had been dusted with the black fingerprint powder. There was no note on the bureau — the place Harry would've expected it to be.

"No note," he said, more to himself than Donovan.

"Nope. Nothing in the bathroom, either. Have a look. That is, if you don't mind losing your Christmas dinner."

Harry looked down the short hallway that went to the rear off the left side of the bed. The bathroom door was on the right and he felt reluctance as he approached. He believed there wasn't a cop alive who hadn't thought at least once of turning his own hand cold.

He stopped at the threshold. The body sat on the dingy white floor tile, its back propped against the tub. The first thing to register on Bosch was the boots. Gray snakeskins with bulldog heels. Moore had worn them the night they had met for drinks. One boot was still on the right foot and he could see the manufacturer's symbol, an S like a snake, on the worn rubber heel. The left boot was off and stood upright next to the wall. The exposed foot, which was in a sock, had been wrapped in a plastic evidence bag. The sock had once been white, Bosch guessed. But now it was grayish and the limb was slightly bloated.

On the floor next to the door jamb was a twenty-gauge shotgun with side-by-side barrels. The stock was splintered along the bottom edge. A four-inch-long sliver of wood lay on the tile and had been circled with a blue crayon by Donovan or one of the detectives.

Bosch had no time to deliberate on these facts. He just tried to take it all in. He raised his eyes the length of the body. Moore was wearing jeans and a sweatshirt. His hands were dropped at his sides. His skin was gray wax. The fingers thick with putrefaction, the forearms bulging like Popeye's. Bosch saw a misshapen tattoo on the right arm, a devil's grinning face below a halo.

The body was slumped back against the tub and it almost appeared that Moore had rolled his head back as if to dip it into the tub, maybe to wash his hair. But Bosch realized it only looked that way because most of the head was simply not there. It had been destroyed by the force of the double-barrel blast. The light blue tiles that enclosed the tub area were awash in dried blood. The brown drip trails all went down into the tub. Some of the tiles were cracked where shotgun pellets had struck.

Bosch felt the presence of someone behind him. He turned into the stare of Assistant Chief Irvin Irving. Irving was wearing no mask and holding no rag to his mouth and nose.

"Evening, Chief."

Irving nodded and said, "What brings you here, Detective?"

Bosch had seen enough to be able to put together what had happened. He stepped away from the threshold, moved around Irving and walked toward the front door. Irving followed. They passed two men from the medical examiner's office who were wearing matching blue jumpsuits. Outside the room Harry threw his handkerchief into a trash can brought to the scene by the cops. He lit a cigarette and noticed that Irving was carrying a manila file in his hand.

"I picked it up on my scanner," Bosch said. "Thought I'd come out since I'm supposed to be on call tonight. It's my division, it's supposed to be my call."

"Yes, well, when it was established who was in the room, I decided to move the case to Robbery-Homicide Division immediately. Captain Grupa contacted me. I made the decision."

"So it's already been established that's Moore in there?"

"Not quite." He held up the manila file. "I ran by records and pulled his prints. They will be the final factor, of course. There is also the dental — if there is enough left. But all other appearances lead to that conclusion. Whoever's in there checked in under the name Rodrigo Moya, which was the alias Moore used in BANG. And there's a Mustang parked behind the motel that was rented under that name. At the moment, I don't think there is much doubt here among the collective investigative team."

Bosch nodded. He had dealt with Irving before, when the older man was a deputy chief in command of the Internal Affairs Division. Now he was an AC, one of the top three men in the department, and his purview had been extended to include IAD, narcotics intelligence and investigation, and all detective services. Harry momentarily debated whether he should risk pushing the point about not getting the first call.

"I should have been called," he said anyway. "It's my case. You took it away before I even had it."

"Well, Detective, it was mine to take and give away, wouldn't you agree? There is no need to get upset. Call it streamlining. You know Robbery-Homicide handles all officer deaths. You would have had to pass it to them eventually. This saves time. There is no ulterior motive here other than expediency. That's the body of an officer in there. We owe it to him and his family, no matter what the circumstances of his death are, to move quickly and professionally."

Bosch nodded again and looked around. He saw an RHD detective named Sheehan in a doorway below the MONTHLY RAT s sign near the front of the motel. He was questioning a man of about sixty who was wearing a sleeveless T-shirt despite the evening chill and chewing a sodden cigar stump. The manager.

"Did you know him?" Irving asked.

"Moore? No, not really. I mean, yes, I knew him. We worked the same division, so we knew each other. He was on night shift mostly, working the streets. We didn't have much contact . . ."

Bosch did not know why in that moment he decided to lie. He wondered if Irving had read it in his voice. He changed the subject.

"So, it's suicide — is that what you told the reporters?"

"I did not tell the reporters a thing. I talked to them, yes. But I said nothing about the identity of the body in this room. And will not, until it is officially confirmed. You and I can stand here and say we are pretty sure that is Calexico Moore in there but I won't give that to them until we've done every test, dotted every i on the death certificate."

He slapped the manila file hard on his thigh.

"This is why I pulled his personnel file. To expedite. The prints will go with the body to the medical examiner." Irving looked back toward the door of the motel room. "But you were inside, Detective Bosch, you tell me."

Bosch thought a moment. Is this guy interested, or is he just pulling my chain? This was the first time he had dealt with Irving outside of the adversarial situation of an Internal Affairs investigation. He decided to take a chance.

"Looks like he sits down on the floor by the tub, takes off his boot and pulls both triggers with his toe. I mean, I assume it was both barrels, judging by the damage. He pulls the triggers with his toe, the recoil throws the shotgun into the door jamb, splintering off a piece of the stock. His head goes the other way. Onto the wall and into the tub. Suicide."

"There you go," Irving said. "Now I can tell Detective Sheehan that you concur. Just as if you had gotten the first callout. No reason for anybody to feel left out."

"That's not the point, Chief."

"What is the point, Detective? That you can't go along to get along? That you do not accept the command decisions of this department? I am losing my patience with you, Detective. Something I had hoped would never happen to me again."

Irving was standing too close to Bosch, his wintergreen breath puffing right in his face. It made Bosch feel pinned down by the man and he wondered if it was done on purpose. He stepped back and said, "But no note."

"No note yet. We still have some things to check."

Bosch wondered what. Moore's apartment and office would have been checked when he first turned up missing. Same with his wife's home. What was left? Could Moore have mailed a note to somebody? It would have arrived by now.

"When did it happen?"

"Hopefully, we'll get an idea from the autopsy tomorrow morning. But I am guessing he did it shortly after he checked in. Six days ago. In his first interview, the manager said Moore checked in six days ago and hadn't been seen outside the room since. This jibes with the condition of the room, the condition of the body, the date on the newspaper."

The autopsy was tomorrow morning. That told Bosch that Irving had this one greased. It usually took three days to get an autopsy done. And the Christmas holiday would back things up even further.

Irving seemed to know what he was thinking.

"The acting chief medical examiner has agreed to do it tomorrow morning. I explained there would be speculation in the media that would not be fair to the man's wife or the department. She agreed to cooperate. After all, the acting chief wants to become the permanent chief. She knows the value of cooperation."

Bosch didn't say anything.

"So we will know then. But nobody, the manager included, saw Sergeant Moore after he checked in six days ago. He left specific instructions that he was absolutely not to be disturbed. I think he went ahead and did it shortly after checking in."

"So why didn't they find him sooner?"

"He paid for a month in advance. He demanded no disturbances. A place like this, they don't offer daily maid service anyway. The manager thought he was a drunk who was either going to go on a binge or try to dry out. Either way, a place like this, the manager can't be choosey. A month, that's $600. He took the money.

"And they made good on their promise not to go to room seven until today, when the manager's wife noticed that Mr. Moya's car — the Mustang — had been broken into last night. That and, of course, they were curious. They knocked on his door to tell him but he didn't answer. They used a passkey. The smell told them what was happening as soon as they opened the door."

Irving said that Moore/Moya had set the air-conditioner on its highest and coldest level to slow decomposition and keep the odor contained in the room. Wet towels had been laid across the floor at the bottom of the front door to further seal the room.

"Nobody heard the shot?" Bosch asked.

"Not that we found. The manager's wife is nearly deaf and he says he didn't hear anything. They live in the last room on the other side. We've got stores on one side, an office building on the other. They all close at night. Alley behind. We are going through the registry and will try to track other guests that were here the first few days Moore was. But the manager says he never rented the rooms on either side of Moore's. He figured Moore might get loud if he was detoxing cold turkey.

"And, Detective, it is a busy street — bus stop right out front. It could have been that nobody heard a thing. Or if they heard it, didn't know what it was."

After some thought, Bosch said, "I don't get renting the place for a month. I mean, why? If the guy was going to off himself, why try to hide it for so long? Why not do it and let them find your body, end of story?"

"That's a tough one," Irving said. "Near as I can figure it, he wanted to cut his wife a break."

Bosch raised his eyebrows. He didn't get it.

"They were separated," Irving said. "Maybe he didn't want to put this on her during the holidays. So he tried to hold up the news a couple weeks, maybe a month."

That seemed pretty thin to Bosch but he had no better explanation just then. He could think of nothing else to ask at that moment. Irving changed the subject, signaling that Bosch's visit to the crime scene was over.

"So, Detective, how is the shoulder?"

"It's fine."

"I heard you went down to Mexico to polish your Spanish while you mended."

Bosch didn't reply. He wasn't interested in this banter. He wanted to tell Irving that he didn't buy the scene, even with all the evidence and explanations that had been gathered. But he couldn't say why, and until he could, he would be better off keeping quiet.

Irving was saying, "I have never thought that enough of our officers — the non-Latins, of course — make a good enough effort to learn the second language of this city. I want to see the whole depart —"

"Got a note," Donovan called from the room.

Irving broke away from Bosch without another word and headed to the door. Sheehan followed him into the room along with a suit Bosch recognized as an Internal Affairs detective named John Chastain. Harry hesitated a moment before following them in.

One of the ME techs was standing in the hallway near the bathroom door with the others gathered around him. Bosch wished he hadn't thrown away his handkerchief. He kept the cigarette in his mouth and breathed in deeply.

"Right rear pocket," the tech said. "There's putrefaction but you can make it out. It was folded over twice so the inside surface is pretty clean."

Irving backed out of the hallway holding a plastic evidence bag up and looking at the small piece of paper inside it. The others crowded around him. Except for Bosch.

The paper was gray like Moore's skin. Bosch thought he could see one line of blue writing on the paper. Irving looked over at him as if seeing him for the first time.

"Bosch, you will have to go."

Harry wanted to ask what the note said but knew he would be rejected. He saw a satisfied smirk on Chastain's face.

At the yellow tape he stopped to light another cigarette. He heard the clicking of high heels and turned to see one of the reporters, a blonde he recognized from Channel 2, coming at him with a wireless microphone in her hand and a model's phoney smile on her face. She moved in on him in a well-practiced and quick maneuver. But before she could speak Harry said, "No comment. I'm not on the case."

"Can't you just —"

"No comment."

The smile dropped off her face as quick as a guillotine's blade. She turned away angrily. But within a moment her heels were clicking sharply again as she moved with her cameraman into position for the A-shot, the one her report would lead with. The body was coming out. The strobes flared and the six cameramen formed a gauntlet. The two medical examiner's men, pushing the covered body on a gurney, passed through it on the way to the waiting blue van. Harry noticed that a grim-faced Irving, walking stoically erect, trailed behind — but not far enough behind to be left out of the video frame. After all, any appearance on the nightly news was better than none, especially for a man with an eye on the chief's office.

After that, the crime scene began to break up. Everybody was leaving. The reporters, cops, everybody. Bosch ducked under the yellow tape and was looking around for Donovan or Sheehan when Irving came up on him.

"Detective, on second thought, there is something I need you to do that will help expedite matters. Detective Sheehan has to finish securing the scene here. But I want to beat the media to Moore's wife. Can you handle next-of-kin notification? Of course, nothing is definite but I want his wife to know what is happening."

Bosch had made such a show of indignation earlier, he couldn't back away now. He wanted part of the case; he got it.

"Give me the address," he said.

A few minutes later Irving was gone and the uniforms were pulling down the yellow tape. Bosch saw Donovan heading to his van, carrying the shotgun, which was wrapped in plastic, and several smaller evidence bags.

Harry used the van's bumper to tie his shoe while Donovan stowed the evidence bags in a wooden box that had once carried Napa Valley wine.

"What do you want, Harry? I just found out you weren't supposed to be here."

"That was before. This is now. I just got put on the case. I got next-of-kin duty."

"Some case to be put on."

"Yeah, well, you take what they give. What did he say?"

"Who?"

"Moore."

"Look, Harry, this is —"

"Look, Donnie, Irving gave me next of kin. I think that cuts me in. I just want to know what he said. I knew this guy, okay? It won't go anywhere else."

Donovan exhaled heavily, reached into the box and began sorting through the evidence bags.

"Really didn't say much at all. Nothing that profound."

He turned on a flashlight and put the beam on the bag with the note in it. Just one line.

I found out who I was

3

The address Irving had given him was in Canyon Country, nearly an hour's drive north of Hollywood. Bosch took the Hollywood Freeway north, then connected with the Golden State and took it through the dark cleft of the Santa Susanna Mountains. Traffic was sparse. Most people were inside their homes eating roasted turkey and dressing, he guessed. Bosch thought of Cal Moore and what he did and what he left behind.

I found out who I was.

Bosch had no clue to what the dead cop had meant by the one line scratched on a small piece of paper and placed in the back pocket. Harry's single experience with Moore was all he had to go on. And what was that? A couple of hours drinking beer and whiskey with a morose and cynical cop. There was no way to know what had happened in the meantime. To know how the shell that protected him had corroded.

He thought back on his meeting with Moore. It had been only a few weeks before and it had been business, but Moore's problems managed to come up. They met on a Tuesday night at the Catalina Bar & Grill. Moore was working but the Catalina was just a half block south of the Boulevard. Harry was waiting at the bar in the back corner. They never charged cops the cover.

Moore slid onto the next stool and ordered a shot and a Henry's, the same as Bosch had on the bar in front of him. He was wearing jeans and a sweatshirt that hung loose over his belt. Standard undercover attire and he looked at home in it. The thighs of the jeans were worn gray. The sleeves of the sweatshirt were cut off and peeking from below the frayed fringe of the right arm was the face of a devil tattooed in blue ink. Moore was handsome in a rugged way, but he was at least three days past needing a shave and he had a look about him, an unsteadiness — like a hostage released after long captivity and torment. In the Catalina crowd he stood out like a garbage man at a wedding. Harry noticed that the narc hooked gray snakeskin boots on the side rungs of the stool. They were bulldoggers, the boots favored by rodeo ropers because the heels angled forward to give better traction when taking down a roped calf. Harry knew street narcs called them "dustbusters" because they served the same purpose when they were taking down a suspect high on angel dust.

They smoked and drank and small-talked at first, trying to establish connections and boundaries. Bosch noticed that the name Calexico truly represented Moore's mixed heritage. Dark complexioned, with hair black as ink, thin hips and wide shoulders, Moore's dark, ethnic image was contradicted by his eyes. They were the eyes of a California surfer, green like anti-freeze. And there was not a trace of Mexico in his voice.

"There's a border town named Calexico. Right across from Mexicali. Ever been there?"

"I was born there. That's how come I got the name."

"I've never been."

"Don't worry, you haven't missed much. Just a border town like all the rest. I still go on down every now and then."

"Family?"

"Nah, not anymore."

Moore signaled the bartender for another round, then lit a cigarette off the one he had smoked down to the filter.

"I thought you had something to ask about," he said.

"Yeah, I do. I gotta case."

The drinks arrived and Moore threw his shot back in one smooth movement. He had ordered another before the bartender had finished writing on the tab.

Bosch began to outline his case. He had caught it a few weeks earlier and so far had gotten nowhere. The body of a thirty-year-old male, later identified through fingerprints as James Kappalanni of Oahu, Hawaii, was dumped beneath the Hollywood Freeway crossing over Gower Street. He had been strangled with an eighteen-inch length of baling wire with wooden dowels at the ends, the better to grip the wire with after it had been wrapped around somebody's neck. Very neat and efficient job. Kappallani's face was the bluish gray color of an oyster. The blue Hawaiian, the acting chief medical examiner had called him when she did the autopsy. By then Bosch knew through NCIC and DOJ computer runs that in life he had also been known as Jimmy Kapps, and that he had a drug record that printed out about as long as the wire somebody had used to take his life.

"So it wasn't too big a surprise when the ME cut him open and found forty-two rubbers in his gut," Bosch said.

"What was in them?"

"This Hawaiian shit called glass. A derivative of ice, I am told. I remember when ice was a fad a few years back. Anyway, this Jimmy Kapps was a courier. He was carrying this glass inside his stomach, had probably just gotten off the plane from Honolulu when he walks into the baling wire.

"I hear this glass is expensive stuff and the market for it is extremely competitive. I guess I'm looking for some background, maybe shake an idea loose here. 'Cause I've got nothing on this. No ideas on who did Jimmy Kapps."

"Who told you about glass?"

"Major narcs downtown. Not much help."

"Nobody really knows shit, that's why. They tell you about black ice?"

"A little. That's the competition, they said. Comes from the Mexicans. That's about all they said."

Moore looked around for the bartender, who was down at the other end of the bar and seemed to be purposely ignoring them.

"It's all relatively new," he said. "Basically, black ice and glass are the same thing. Same results. Glass comes from Hawaii. And black ice comes from Mexico. The drug of the twenty-first century, I guess you'd call it. If I was a salesman I'd say it covers all the demographics. Basically, somebody took coke, heroin and PCP and rocked 'em all up together. A powerful little rock. It's supposed to do everything. It's got a crack high but the heroin also gives it legs. I'm talking about hours, not minutes. Then it's got just a pinch of dust, the PCP, to give it a kick toward the end of the ride. Man, once it really takes hold on the streets, they get a major market going, then, shit, forget about it, there'll be nothing but a bunch of zombies walking around."

Bosch said nothing. Much of this he already knew but Moore was going good and he didn't want to knock him off track with a question. He lit a cigarette and waited.

"Started in Hawaii," Moore said. "Oahu. They were making ice over there. Just plain ice, they called it. That's rocking up PCP and coke. Very profitable. Then it evolved. They added heroin. Good stuff, too. Asian white. Now they call it glass. I guess that was their motto or something; smooth as glass.

"But in this business there is no lock on anything. There is only price and profit."

He held up both hands to signify the importance of these two factors.

"The Hawaiians had a good thing but they had trouble getting it to the mainland. You got boats and you got planes and these can be regulated to a good degree. Or, at least, to some degree. I mean, they can be checked and watched. So they end up with couriers like this Kapps who swallow the shit and fly it over. But even that is harder than it seems. First of all, you got a limited quantity that you can move. What, forty-two balloons in this guy? What was that, about a hundred grams? That's not much for the trouble. Plus you got the DEA, they got people in the planes, airports. They're looking for people like Kapps. They call them 'rubber smugglers.' They've got a whole shakedown profile. You know, a list of what to look for. People sweating but with dry lips, licking their lips — the anti-diarrhetic does that. That Kaopectate shit. The rubber smugglers swig that shit like it's Pepsi. It gives them away.

"Anyway, what I am saying is that the Mexicans got it a whole helluva lot easier. Geography is on their side. They have boats and planes and they also have a two-thousand-mile border that is almost nonexistent as a form of control and interdiction. They say the feds stop one pound of coke for every ten that gets by them. Well, when it comes to black ice, they aren't even getting an ounce at the border. I know of not one single black ice bust at the border."

He paused to light a cigarette. Bosch saw a tremor in his hand as he held the match.

"What the Mexicans did was steal the recipe. They started replicating glass. Only they're using homegrown brown heroin, including the tar. That's the pasty shit at the bottom of the cooking barrel. Lot of impurities in it, turns it black. That's how they come up with calling it black ice. They make it cheaper, they move it cheaper and they sell it cheaper. They've 'bout put the Hawaiians out of the business. And it's their own fucking product."

Moore seemed to conclude there.

Harry asked, "Have you heard anything about the Mexicans taking down the Hawaiian couriers, maybe trying to corner the market that way?"

"Not up here, at least. See, you gotta remember, the Mexicans make the shit. But they ain't the ones necessarily selling it on the street. You're talking several levels removed when you get down to the street."

"But they still have to be calling the shots."

"True. That's true."

"So who put down Jimmy Kapps?"

"Got me, Bosch. This is the first I've heard about it."

"Your team ever make any arrests of black ice dealers? Shake anybody down?"

"A few, but you're talking about the lowest rungs on the ladder. White boys. Rock dealers on the Boulevard are usually white boys. It's easier for them to do business. Now, that doesn't mean it isn't Mexicans givin' it to them. It also doesn't mean it ain't South-Central gangs givin' it. So the arrests we've made probably wouldn't help you any."

He banged his empty beer mug on the bar until the bartender looked up and was signaled for another round. Moore seemed to be getting morose and Bosch hadn't gotten much help from him.

"I need to go further up the ladder. Can you get me anything? I don't have shit on this and it's three weeks old. I've got to come up with something or drop it and move on."

Moore was looking straight ahead at the bottles that lined the rear wall of the bar.

"Look, I'll see what I can do," he said. "But you gotta remember, we don't spend time on black ice. Coke and dust, some reefer, that's what we deal in day in and day out. Not the exotics. We're a numbers squad, man. But I've got a connection at DEA. I'll talk to him."

Bosch looked at his watch. It was near midnight and he wanted to go. He watched Moore light a cigarette though he still had one burning in the crowded ashtray. Harry still had a full beer and shot in front of him but stood up and began digging in his pockets for money.

"Thanks, man," he said. "See what you can do and let me know."

"Sure," Moore said. After a beat he said, "Hey, Bosch?"

"What?"

"I know about you. You know, . . . what's been said around the station. I know you've been in the bucket. I wonder, did you ever come up against an IAD suit name of Chastain?"

Bosch thought a moment. John Chastain was one of the best. In IAD, complaints were classified at the end as sustained, unsustained or unfounded. He was known as "Sustained" Chastain.

"I've heard of him," he said. "He's a three, runs one of the tables."

"Yeah, I know he's a detective third grade. Shit, everybody knows that. What I mean is, did he . . . is he one of them that came after you?"

"No, it was always somebody else."

Moore nodded. He reached over and took the shot that had been in front of Bosch. He emptied it, then said, "Chastain, from what you've heard, do you think he is good at what he does? Or is he just another suit with a shine on his ass?"

"I guess it depends on what you mean by good. But, no, I don't think any of them are good. Job like that, they can't be. But give 'em the chance, any one of them will burn you down and bag your ashes."

Bosch was torn between wanting to ask what was going on and not wanting to step into it. Moore said nothing. He was giving Bosch the choice. Harry decided to keep out of it.

He said, "If they've got a hard-on for you, there isn't much you can do. Call the union and get a lawyer. Do what he says and don't give the suits anything you don't have to."

Moore nodded silently once more. Harry put down two twenty-dollar bills that he hoped would cover the tab and still leave something for the bartender. Then he walked out.

He never saw Moore again.

Bosch connected with the Antelope Valley Freeway and headed northeast. On the Sand Canyon overpass he looked across the freeway and saw a white TV van heading south. There was a large 9 painted on its side. It meant Moore's wife would already know by the time Bosch arrived. And Bosch felt a slight twinge of guilt at that, mixed with relief that he would not be the one breaking the news.

The thought made him realize that he did not know the widow's name. Irving had given him only an address, apparently assuming Bosch knew her name. As he turned off the freeway onto the Sierra Highway, he tried to recall the newspaper stories he had read during the week. They had carried her name.

But it didn't come to him. He remembered that she was a teacher — an English teacher, he thought — at a high school in the Valley. He remembered that the reports said they had no children. And he remembered that she had been separated a few months from her husband. But the name, her name, eluded him.

He turned on to Del Prado, watched the numbers painted on the curbs and then finally pulled to a stop in front of the house that had once been Cal Moore's home.

It was a common ranch-style home, the kind minted by the hundreds in the planned communities that fed the freeways to overflow each morning. It looked large, like maybe four bedrooms, and Bosch thought that was odd for a childless couple. Maybe there had been plans at one time.

The light above the front door was not on. No one was expected. No one was wanted. Still, in the moonlight and shadow, Bosch could see the front lawn and knew that the mower was at least a month past due. The tall grass surrounded the post of the white Ritenbaugh Realty sign that was planted near the sidewalk.

There were no cars in the driveway and the garage door was closed, its two windows dark empty sockets. A single dim light shone from behind the curtained picture window next to the front door. He wondered what she would be like and if she would feel guilt or anger. Or both.

He threw his cigarette into the street and then got out and stepped on it. Then he headed past the sad-looking For Sale sign to the door.

4

〰〰〰

The mat on the porch below the front door said WELCOME but it was worn and nobody had bothered to shake the dust off it in some time. Bosch noticed all of this because he kept his head down after knocking. He knew that looking at anything would be better than looking at this woman.

Her voice answered after his second knock.

"Go away. No comment."

Bosch had to smile, thinking how he had used that one himself tonight.

"Hello, Mrs. Moore? I'm not a reporter. I'm with the L.A. police."

The door came open a few inches and her face was there, backlit and hidden in shadow. Bosch could see the chain lock stretching across the opening. Harry was ready with his badge case already out and opened.

"Yes?"

"Mrs. Moore?"

"Yes?"

"I am Harry Bosch. Um, I'm a detective, LAPD. And I've been sent out — could I come in? I need . . . to ask you a few questions and inform you of some, uh, developments in —"

"You're late. I've had Channel 4 and 5 and 9 already out here. When you knocked I figured you were somebody else. Two or seven. I can't think who else."

"Can I come in, Mrs. Moore?"

He put his badge wallet away. She closed the door and he heard the chain slide out of its track. The door came open and she signaled him in with her arm. He stepped into an entryway of rust-colored Mexican tile. There was a round mirror on the wall and he saw her in it, closing and locking the door. He saw she held tissue in one hand.

"Will this take long?" she asked.

He said no and she led him to the living room, where she took a seat on an overstuffed chair covered in brown leather. It looked very comfortable and it was next to the fireplace. She motioned him toward a couch that faced the fireplace. This was where the guests always sat. The fireplace had the glowing remnants of a dying fire. On the table next to where she sat he saw a box of tissues and a stack of papers. More like reports or maybe scripts; some were in plastic covers.

"Book reports," she said, having noticed his gaze. "I assigned books to my students with the reports due before the Christmas vacation. It was going to be my first Christmas alone and I guess I wanted to make sure I had something to keep me busy."

Bosch nodded. He looked around the rest of the room. In his job, he learned a lot about people from their rooms, the way they lived. Often the people could no longer tell him themselves. So he learned from his observations and believed that he was good at it.

The room in which they sat was sparse. Not much furniture. It didn't look like a lot of entertaining of friends or family happened here. There was a large bookshelf at one end of the room that was filled by hardback novels and oversized art books. No TV. No sign of children. It was a place for quiet work or fireside talks.

But no more.

In the corner opposite the fireplace was a five-foot Christmas tree with white lights and red balls, a few homemade ornaments that looked as if they might have been passed down through generations. He liked the idea that she had put up the tree by herself. She had continued her life and its routines amidst the ruins of her marriage. She had put the tree up for herself. It made him feel her strength. She had a hard shell of hurt and maybe loneliness but there was a sense of strength, too. The tree said she was the kind of woman who would survive this, would make it through. On her own. He wished he could remember her name.

"Before you start," she said, "can I ask you something?"

The light from the reading lamp next to her chair was low wattage but he could clearly see the intensity of her brown eyes.

"Sure."

"Did you do that on purpose? Let the reporters come up here first so you wouldn't have to do the dirty work? That's what my husband used to call it. Telling families. He called it the dirty work and he said the detectives always tried to get out of it."

Bosch felt his face grow warm. There was a clock on the fireplace mantel that now seemed to be ticking very loudly in the silence. He managed to say, "I was told only a short time ago to come here. I had a little trouble finding it. I —"

He stopped. She knew.

"I'm sorry. I guess you're right. I took my time."

"It's okay. I shouldn't put you on the spot. It must be a terrible job."

Bosch wished he had a fedora like the ones the detectives in the old movies always had; that way he could hold it in his hands and fiddle with it and let his fingers trace its brim, give him something to do. He looked at her closely now and saw the quality of damaged beauty about her. Mid-thirties, he guessed, with brown hair and blonde highlights, she seemed agile, like a runner. Clearly defined jawline above the taut muscles of her neck. She had not used makeup to try to hide the lightly etched lines that curved under her eyes. She wore blue jeans and a baggy white sweatshirt that he thought might have been her husband's once. Bosch wondered how much of Calexico Moore she still carried in her heart.

Harry actually admired her for taking the shot at him about the dirty work. He knew he deserved it. In the three minutes he had known her he thought she reminded him of someone but he wasn't sure who. Someone from his past maybe. There was a quiet tenderness there beside her strength. He kept bringing his eyes back to hers. They were magnets.

"Anyway, I'm Detective Harry Bosch," he began again, hoping she might introduce herself.

"Yes, I've heard of you. I remember the newspaper articles. And I'm sure my husband spoke of you — I think it was when they sent you out to Hollywood Division. Couple years ago. He said before that one of the studios had paid you a lot of money to use your name and do a TV movie about a case. He said you bought one of those houses on stilts up in the hills."

Bosch nodded reluctantly and changed the subject.

"I don't know what the reporters told you, Mrs. Moore, but I have been sent out to tell you that it appears your husband has been found and he is dead. I am sorry to have had to tell you this. I —"

"I knew and you knew and every cop in town knew it would come to this. I didn't talk to the reporters. I didn't need to. I told them no comment. When that many of them come to your house on Christmas night, you know it's because of bad news."

He nodded and looked down at the imaginary hat in his hands.

"So, are you going to tell me? Was it an official suicide? Did he use a gun?"

Bosch nodded and said, "It looks like it but nothing is definite un —"

"Until the autopsy. I know, I know. I'm a cop's wife. Was, I mean. I know what you can say and can't say. You people can't even be straight with me. Until then there are always secrets to keep to yourselves."

He saw the hard edge enter her eyes, the anger.

"That's not true, Mrs. Moore. I'm just trying to soften the im —"

"Detective Bosch, if you want to tell me something, just tell me."

"Yes, Mrs. Moore, it was with a gun. If you want the details, I can give you the details. Your husband, if it was your husband, took his face off with a shotgun. Gone completely. So, we have to make sure it was him and we have to make sure he did it himself, before we can say anything for sure. We are not trying to keep secrets. We just don't have all the answers yet."

She leaned back in her chair, away from light. In the veil of shadows Bosch saw the look on her face. The hardness and anger in her eyes had softened. Her shoulders seemed to untighten. He felt ashamed.

"I'm sorry," he said. "I don't know why I told you that. I should have just —"

"That's okay. I guess I deserved it. . . . I apologize, too."

She looked at him then without anger in her eyes. He had broken through the shell. He could see that she needed to be with someone. The house was too big and too dark to be alone in right now. All the Christmas trees and book reports in the world couldn't change that. But there was more than that making Bosch want to stay. He found that he was instinctively attracted to her. For Bosch it had never been an attraction of an opposite but the reverse of that myth. He had always seen something of himself in the women who attracted him. Why it was this way, he never understood. It was just there. And now this woman whose name he didn't even know was there and he was being drawn to her. Maybe it was a reflection of himself and his own needs, but it was there and he had seen it. It hooked him and made him want to know what had etched the circles beneath such sharp eyes. Like himself, he knew, she carried her scars on the inside, buried deep, each one a mystery. She was like him. He knew.

"I'm sorry but I don't know your name. The deputy chief just gave me the address and said go."

She smiled at his predicament.

"It's Sylvia."

He nodded.

"Sylvia. Um, is that coffee I smell by any chance?"

"Yes. Would you like a cup?"

"That would be great, if it's not too much trouble."

"Not at all."

She got up and as she passed in front of him so did his doubts.

"Listen, I'm sorry. Maybe I should go. You have a lot to think about and I'm intruding here. I've —"

"Please stay. I could use the company."

She didn't wait for an answer. The fire made a popping sound as the flames found the last pocket of air. He watched her head toward the kitchen. He waited a beat, took another look around the room and stood up and headed toward the lighted doorway of the kitchen.

"Black is fine."

"Of course. You're a cop."

"You don't like them much, do you. Cops."

"Well, let's just say I don't have a very good record with them."

Her back was to him and she put two mugs on the counter and poured coffee from a glass pot. He leaned against the doorway next to the refrigerator. He was unsure what to say, whether to press on with business or not.

"You have a nice home."

"No. It's a nice house, not a home. We're selling it. I guess I should say I'm selling it now."

She still hadn't turned around.

"You know you can't blame yourself for whatever he did."

It was a meager offering and he knew it.

"Easier said than done."

"Yeah."

There was a long moment of silence then before Bosch decided to get on with it.

"There was a note."

She stopped what she was doing but still did not turn.

"'I found out who I was.' That's all he said."

She didn't say anything. One of the mugs was still empty.

"Does it mean anything to you?"

She finally turned to him. In the bright kitchen light he could see the salty tracks that tears had left on her face. It made him feel inadequate, that he was nothing and could do nothing to help heal her.

"I don't know. My husband . . . he was caught on the past."

"What do you mean?"

"He was just — he was always going back. He liked the past better than the present or the hope of the future. He liked to go back to the time he was growing up. He liked . . . He couldn't let things go."

He watched tears slide into the grooves below her eyes. She turned back to the counter and finished pouring the coffee.

"What happened to him?" he asked.

"What happens to anybody?" For a while after that she didn't speak, then said, "I don't know. He wanted to go back. He had a need for something back there."

Everybody has a need for their past, Bosch thought. Sometimes it pulls harder on you than the future. She dried her eyes with tissue and then turned and gave him a mug. He sipped it before speaking.

"Once he told me he lived in a castle," she said. "That's what he called it, at least."

"In Calexico?" he asked.

"Yes, but it was for a short while. I don't know what happened. He never told me a lot about that part of his life. It was his father. At some point, he wasn't wanted anymore by his father. He and his mother had to leave Calexico — the castle, or whatever it was — and she took him back across the border with her. He liked to say he was from Calexico but he really grew up in Mexicali. I don't know if you've ever been there."

"Just to drive through. Never stopped."

"That's the general idea. Don't stop. But he grew up there."

She stopped and he waited her out. She was looking down at her coffee, an attractive woman who looked weary of this. She had not yet seen that this was a beginning for her as well as an end.

"It was something he never got over. The abandonment. He often went back there to Calexico. I didn't go but I know he did. Alone. I think he was watching his father. Maybe seeing what could have been. I don't know. He kept pictures from when he was growing up. Sometimes at night when he thought I was asleep, he'd take them out and look at them."

"Is he still alive, the father?"

She handed him a mug of coffee.

"I don't know. He rarely spoke of his father and when he did he said his father was dead. But I don't know if that was metaphorically dead or that he actually was dead. He was dead as far as Cal went. That was what mattered. It was a very private thing with Cal. He still felt the rejection, all these years later. I could not get him to talk about it. Or, when he would, he would just lie, say the old man meant nothing and that he didn't care. But he did. I could tell. After a while, after years, I have to say that I stopped trying to talk with him about it. And he would never bring it up. He'd just go down there — sometimes for a weekend, sometimes a day. He'd never talk about it when he came back."

"Do you have the photos?"

"No, he took them when he left. He'd never leave them."

Bosch sipped some coffee to give himself time to think.

"It seems," he said, "I don't know, it seems like . . . could this have had anything to do with . . ."

"I don't know. All I can tell you is that it had a lot to do with us. It was an obsession with him. It was more important to him than me. It's what ended it for us."

"What was he trying to find?"

"I don't know. In the last few years he shut me out. And I have to say that after a while I shut him out. That's how it ended."

Bosch nodded and looked away from her eyes. What else could he do? Sometimes his job took him too far inside people's lives and all he could do was stand there and nod. He was asking questions he felt guilty asking because he had no right to the answers. He was just the messenger boy here. He wasn't supposed to find out why somebody would hold a double-barrel shotgun up to his face and pull the triggers.

Still, the mystery of Cal Moore and the pain on her face wouldn't let him go. She was captivating in a way that went beyond her physical beauty. She was attractive, yes, but the hurt in her face, the tears and yet the strength in her eyes tugged at him. The thought that occurred to him was that she did not deserve this. How could Cal Moore have fucked up so badly?

He looked back at her.

"There was another thing he told me once. Uh, I've had some experience with the IAD, uh, that's Internal —"

"I know what it is."

"Yes, well, he asked me for some advice. Asked me about if I knew somebody that was asking questions about him. Name of Chastain. Did Cal tell you about this? What it was about?"

"No, he didn't."

Her demeanor was changing. Bosch could actually see the anger welling up from inside again. Her eyes were very sharp. He had struck a nerve.

"But you knew about it, right?"

"Chastain came here once. He thought I would cooperate with whatever it was he was doing. He said I made a complaint about my husband, which was a lie. He wanted to go through the house and I told him to leave. I don't want to talk about this."

"When did Chastain come?"

"I don't know. Couple months ago."

"You warned Cal?"

She hesitated and then nodded.

Then Cal came to the Catalina and asked me for advice, Harry realized.

"You sure you don't know what it was about?"

"We were separated by then. We didn't talk. It was over between us. All I did was tell Cal that this man had come and that he had lied about who made the complaint. Cal said that was all they do. Lie. He said don't worry about it."

Harry finished his coffee but held the mug in his hand. She had known her husband had somehow fallen, had betrayed their future with his past, but she had stayed loyal. She had warned him about Chastain. Bosch couldn't fault her for that. He could only like her better.

"What are you doing here?" she asked.

"What?"

"If you are investigating my husband's death, I would assume you already know about IAD. You are either lying to me, too, or don't know. If that's the case, what are you doing here?"

He put the mug down on the counter. It gave him a few extra seconds.

"I was sent out by the assistant chief to tell you what was —"

"The dirty work."

"Right. I got stuck with the dirty work. But like I said, I sort of knew your husband and . . ."

"I don't think it's a mystery you can solve, Detective Bosch."

He nodded — the old standby.

"I teach English and lit at Grant High in the Valley," she said. "I assign my students a lot of books written about L.A. so they can get a feel for the history and character of their community. Lord knows, few of them were born here. Anyway, one of the books I assign is *The Long Goodbye*. It's about a detective."

"I've read it."

"There is a line. I know it by heart. 'There is no trap so deadly as the trap you set for yourself.' Whenever I read that I think of my husband. And me."

She started to cry again. Silently, never taking her eyes off Bosch. This time he didn't nod. He saw the need in her eyes and crossed the room and put his hand on her shoulder. It felt awkward, but then she moved into him and leaned her head against his chest. He let her keep crying until she pulled away.

An hour later, Bosch was home. He picked up the half-filled glass of wine and the bottle that had been sitting on the table since dinner. He went out on the back porch and sat and drank and thought about things until early into the morning hours. The glow of the fire across the pass was gone. But now something burned within himself.

Calexico Moore had apparently answered a question that all people carry deep within themselves — that Harry Bosch, too, had longed to answer. *I found out who I was.*

And it had killed him. It was a thought that pushed a fist into Bosch's guts, into the most secret folds of his heart.

5

Thursday, the morning after Christmas, was one of those days the postcard photographers pray for. There was no hint of smog in the sky. The fire in the hills had burned out and the smoke had long been blown over the hills by Pacific breezes. In its stead the Los Angeles basin basked under a blue sky and puffy cumulus clouds.

Bosch decided to take the long way down out of the hills, driving on Woodrow Wilson until it crossed Mulholland and then taking the winding route through Nichols Canyon. He loved the views of the hills covered with blue wisteria and violet ice plants, topped with aging million-dollar homes that gave the city its aura of fading glory. As he drove he thought of the night before and how it had made him feel to comfort Sylvia Moore. It made him feel like a cop in a Rockwell painting. Like he had made a difference.

Once he was out of the hills he took Genesee to Sunset and then cut over to Wilcox. He parked behind the station and walked past the fenced windows of the drunk tank into the detective bureau. The gloom in the squad room was thicker than cigarette smoke in a porno theater. The other detectives sat at their tables with their heads down, most talking quietly on the phone or with their faces buried in the paperwork that haunted their lives with its never-ceasing flow.

Harry sat down at the homicide table and looked across at Jerry Edgar, his some-of-the-time partner. There were no permanently assigned partners anymore. The bureau was shorthanded and there was a departmental hiring and promotion freeze because of budget cuts. They were down to five detectives on the homicide table. The bureau commander, Lieutenant Harvey "Ninety-eight" Pounds, managed this by working detectives solo except on key cases, dangerous assignments or when making arrests. Bosch liked working on his own, anyway, but most of the other detectives complained about it.

"What's going on?" Bosch asked Edgar. "Moore?"

Edgar nodded. They were alone at the table. Shelby Dunne and Karen Moshito usually came in after nine and Lucius Porter was lucky if he was sober enough to get in by ten.

"Little while ago Ninety-eight came out of the box and said they got the fingerprint match. It was Moore. He blew his own shit away."

They were silent for a few minutes after that. Harry scanned the paperwork on his desk but couldn't help thinking about Moore. He imagined Irving or Sheehan or maybe even Chastain calling Sylvia Moore to tell her the identification was confirmed. Harry could see his slim connection to the case disappearing like smoke. Without having to turn, he realized someone was standing behind him. He looked around to see Pounds looking down at him.

"Harry, c'mon in."

An invitation to the glass box. He looked at Edgar, who raised his eyes in a who-knows gesture. Harry got up and followed the lieutenant into his office at the head of the squad room. It was a small room with windows on three sides that enabled Pounds to look out on his charges but limit his actual contact with them. He didn't have to hear them or smell them or know them. The blinds that were often used to cut off his sight of them were open this morning.

"Sit down, Harry. I don't have to tell you not to smoke. Have a good Christmas?"

Bosch just looked at him. He was uncomfortable with this guy calling him Harry and asking him about Christmas. He hesitantly sat down.

"What's up?" he said.

"Let's not get hostile, Harry. I'm the one who should be hostile. I just heard you spent a good part of Christmas night at that dump motel, the Hideaway, where nobody in this world would want to be and where Robbery-Homicide happened to be conducting an investigation."

"I was on call," Bosch said. "And I should have been called out to the scene. I went by to see what was going on. Turned out, Irving needed me, anyway."

"That's fine, Harry, if you leave it at that. I have been told to tell you not to get any ideas about the Moore case."

"What's that supposed to mean?"

"Just what it sounds like it means."

"Look, if you —"

"Never mind, never mind." Pounds raised his hands in a calming gesture, then pinched the bridge of his nose, signifying the onset of a headache. He opened the center drawer of his desk and took out a small tin of aspirin. He took two without water.

"Enough said, okay?" Pounds said. "I'm not — I don't need to get into —"

Pounds made a choking sound and jumped up from his desk. He moved past Bosch and out of the box to the water fountain near the entrance to the bureau. Bosch didn't even watch him. He just sat in his chair. Pounds was back in a few moments and continued.

"Excuse me. Anyway, what I was saying was that I don't need an argument with you every time I bring you in here. I really think you have to work through this problem you have with dealing with the command structure of this department. You take it to extremes."

Bosch could still see chalky white aspirin caking at the corners of his mouth. Pounds cleared his throat again.

"I was just passing on an aside in your best —"

"Why doesn't Irving pass it on himself?"

"I didn't say — look, Bosch, forget it. Just forget it. You've been told and that's that. If you have any ideas about last night, about Moore, drop them. It's being handled."

"I am sure it is."

The warning delivered, Bosch stood up. He wanted to throw this guy through his glass wall but would settle for a cigarette out behind the drunk tank.

"Siddown," Pounds said. "That's not why I brought you in."

Bosch sat down again and quietly waited. He watched Pounds try to compose himself. He opened the drawer again and pulled out a wood ruler, which he absentmindedly manipulated in his hands while he began to talk.

"Harry, you know how many homicides we've caught in the division this year?"

The question came from left field. Harry wondered what Pounds was up to. He knew he had handled eleven cases himself, but he had been out of the rotation for six weeks during the summer while in Mexico recovering from the bullet wound. He figured the homicide squad for about seventy cases in the year. He said, "I have no idea."

"Well, I'm going to tell you," Pounds said. "Right now we are at sixty-six homicides for the year to date. And, of course, we've still got five days to go. Probably, we'll pick up another. I'm thinking, at least one. New Year's Eve is always trouble. We'll pro —"

"So what about it? I remember we had fifty-nine last year. Murder is going up. What else is new?"

"What is new is that the number of cases we have cleared is going down. It is less than half that number. Thirty-two out of sixty-six cases have been cleared. Now, a good number of those cases have been cleared by you. I have you with eleven cases. Seven have been cleared by arrest or other. We have warrants out on two others. Of the two you have open, one is idle pending developments and you are actively pursuing the James Kappalanni matter. Correct?"

Bosch nodded. He didn't like the way this was going but wasn't sure why.

"The problem is the overall record," Pounds said. "When taken in its entirety, . . . well, it's a pitiful record of success."

Pounds slapped the ruler hard into his palm and shook his head. An idea was forming in Harry's mind about what this was about, but still there was a part missing. He wasn't sure exactly what Pounds was up to.

"Think of it," Pounds continued. "All those victims — and their families! — for whom justice eludes. And then, and then, think how badly the public's confidence in us, in this department, will erode when the L.A. Times trumpets across their Metro page that more than half the killers in Hollywood Division walk away from their crimes?"

"I don't think we have to worry about public confidence going down," Bosch said. "I don't think it can."

Pounds rubbed the bridge of his nose again and quietly said, "This is not the time for your unique cynical view of the job, Bosch. Don't bring your arrogance in here. I can take you off that table and put you on autos or maybe juvies any time I want to make the move. Get me? I'd gladly take the heat when you took a beef to the union."

"Then where's your homicide clearance rate going to be? What's it going to say in the Metro section then? Two thirds of the killers in Hollywood walk?"

Pounds put the ruler back in the drawer and closed it. Bosch thought there was a thin smile on his face and he began to believe he had just talked his way into a trap. Pounds then opened another drawer and brought a blue binder up onto the desk. It was the type used to keep record of a murder investigation but Bosch saw few pages inside it.

"Point well taken," Pounds said. "Which brings us to the point of this meeting. See, we're talking about statistics, Harry. We clear one more case and we're at the halfway mark. Instead of saying more than half get away, we can say half of the killers are caught. If we clear two more, we can say *more* than half are cleared. Get me?"

Pounds nodded when Bosch said nothing. He made a show of straightening the binder on his desk, then he looked directly at Bosch.

"Lucius Porter won't be back," he said. "Talked to him this morning. He is going stress-related. Said he is getting a doctor lined up."

Pounds reached into the drawer and pulled up another blue murder book. Then another. Bosch could see what was happening now.

"And I hope he has a good one lined up," Pounds was saying as he added the fifth and sixth binders to the pile. "Because last I checked this department doesn't consider cirrhosis of the liver a stress-related malady. Porter's a lush, simple as that. And it's not fair that he claim a stress disability and take early retirement because he can't handle his booze. We're going to bust him at the administrative hearing. I don't care if he has Mother Theresa as his lawyer. We'll bust him."

He tapped his finger on top of the pile of blue binders. "I've looked through these cases — he has eight open cases — and it's just pathetic. I've copied the chronologies and I'm going to verify them. I'll bet dollars to doughnuts they are replete with fraudulent entries. He was sitting on a stool somewhere, his head on the bar, when he says he was interviewing wits or doing the legwork."

Pounds shook his head sadly.

"You know, we lost our checks and balances when we stopped partnering our investigators. There was nobody to watch this guy. Now I'm sitting here with eight open investigations that were as slipshod as anything I've ever seen. For all I know, each one could've been cleared."

And whose idea was it to make detectives work solo, Bosch wanted to say but didn't. Instead, he said, "You ever hear the story about when Porter was in uniform about ten years back? He and his partner stopped one time to write up a citation for some shitbag they saw sitting on a curb drinking in public. Porter was driving. It was routine — just a misdee writeup — so he stayed behind the wheel. He's sitting there when the shitbag stands up and caps his partner in the face. Standing there, both hands on his cite book, takes it right between the eyes and Porter sat there watching."

Pounds looked exasperated.

"I know that story, Bosch," Pounds said. "They re-enact it for every class of recruits that goes through the academy. A lesson in what not to do, how not to fuck up. But it's ancient history. If he wanted a stress-out, he should've taken it then."

"That's the point, man. He didn't take it then when he could have. He tried to make it through. Maybe he tried for ten years and then he just went down in the flood of all the shit in the world. What do you want him to do? Take the same out Cal Moore took? You get a star in your file for saving the city the pension?"

Pounds did not speak for a few seconds, then said, "Very eloquent, Bosch, but in the long run it is none of your business what happens to Porter. I should not have brought it up. But I did so you would understand what I have to say now."

He went through his housekeeping trick of making sure all the corners were aligned on the stack of blue binders. Then he pushed the stack across the desk toward Bosch.

"You are taking Porter's caseload. I want you to shelve the Kappalanni matter for a few days. You're not getting anywhere at the moment. Put it down until after the first and dive into this.

"I want you to take Porter's eight open cases and study them. Do it quickly. I want you to look for the one you think you can do something with quickly and then hit it with everything you've got for the next five days — until New Year's Day. Work the weekend, I'll approve the overtime. If you need one of the others on the table to double up with you, no problem. But put somebody in jail, Harry. Go get me an arrest. I — we need to clear one more case to get to that halfway mark. The deadline is midnight, New Year's Eve."

Bosch just looked at him over the stack of binders. He had the full measure of this man now. Pounds wasn't a cop anymore. He was a bureaucrat. He was nothing. He saw crime, the spilling of blood, the suffering of humans, as statistical entries in a log. And at the end of the year the log told him how well he did. Not people. Not the voice from within. It was the kind of impersonal arrogance that poisoned much of the department and isolated it from the city, its people. No wonder Porter wanted out. No wonder Cal Moore pulled his own plug. Harry stood up and picked up the stack of binders and stared at Pounds with a look that said, I know you. Pounds turned his eyes away.

At the door, Bosch said, "You know, if you bust Porter down, he'll just get sent back here to the table. Then where will you be? Next year how many cases will there still be open?"

Pounds's eyebrows went up as he considered this.

"If you let him go, you'll get a replacement. A lot of sharp people on the other tables. Meehan over on the juvenile table is good. You bring him over to our table and I bet you'll see your stats go up. But if you go ahead and bust Porter and bring him back, we might be doing this again next year."

Pounds waited a moment, to make sure Bosch was done, before speaking.

"What is it with you, Bosch? When it comes to investigations Porter couldn't carry your lunch. Yet you're standing there trying to save his ass. What's the point?"

"There is no point, Lieutenant. I guess that's the point. Get me?"

He carried the binders to his spot at the table and dropped them on the floor next to his chair. Edgar looked at him. So did Dunne and Moshito, who had recently arrived.

"Don't ask," Harry said.

He sat down and looked at the pile at his feet and didn't want to have anything to do with it. What he wanted was a cigarette but there was no smoking in the squad room, at least while Pounds was around. He looked up a number in his Rolodex and dialed. The call was not picked up until the seventh ring.

"What now?"

"Lou?"

"Who is it?"

"Bosch."

"Oh, yeah, Harry. Sorry, I didn't know who was calling. What's going on? You hear I'm going for a stress-out?"

"Yeah. That's why I'm calling. I got your cases — Pounds gave 'em to me — and, uh, I want to try to turn one real quick, like by the end of the week. I was wondering if you had any idea — you think you might know which one I should hit? I'm starting from scratch."

There was a long silence on the phone.

"Harry, shit," he finally said and for the first time Bosch realized he might already be drunk. "Aw, damn. I didn't think that cocksucker would dump it all on you. I, uh, Harry . . . Harry, I didn't do too good on . . ."

"Hey, Lou. It's no biggee, you know? My decks were cleared. I'm just looking for a place to start. If you can't point me, that's okay. I'll just look through the stuff."

He waited and realized the others at the table had been listening to him and not even acting like they weren't.

"Fuck it," Porter said. "I, aw fuck it, I don't know, Harry. I — I haven't been on it, you know what I mean. I been kinda fallin' apart here. You hear about Moore? Shit, I saw the news last night. I . . ."

"Yeah, it's too bad. Listen, Lou, don't worry about it, okay? I'll look through the stuff. I got the murder books here and I'll look through 'em."

Nothing.

"Lou?"

"Okay, Harry. Give me a call back if you want. Maybe later I'll think of something. Right now I'm not too fucking good."

Bosch thought a few moments before saying anything else. In his mind he pictured Porter on the other end of the line standing in total darkness. Alone.

"Listen," he said in a low voice. "You better . . . you have to watch out for Pounds on your application. He might ask the suits to check you out, you know what I mean, put a couple of guys on you. You gotta stay out of the bars. He might try to bust your application. Understand?"

After a while Porter said he understood. Bosch hung up then and looked at the others at the table. The squad room always seemed loud until he had to make phone calls he didn't want anyone to hear. He got out a cigarette.

"Ninety-eight dumped Porter's whole caseload on you?" Edgar asked.

"That's right. That's me, the bureau garbage man."

"Yeah, then what's that make us, chopped liver?"

Bosch smiled. He could tell Edgar didn't know whether to be happy he avoided the assignment or mad because he was passed over.

"Well, Jed, if you want, I'll hustle back into the box and tell Ninety-eight that you're volunteering to split this up with me. I'm sure the pencil-pushing prick will —"

He stopped because Edgar had kicked him under the table. He turned in his seat and saw Pounds coming up from behind. His face was red. He had probably heard the last exchange.

"Bosch, you're not going to smoke that disgusting thing in here, are you?"

"No, Lieutenant, I was just on my way out back."

He pushed his chair back and walked out to the back parking lot to smoke. The backdoor of the drunk tank was unlocked and open. The Christmas-night drunks had already been loaded into the jail bus and hauled to arraignment court to make their pleas. A trustee in gray overalls was spraying the floor of the tank with a hose. Harry knew the concrete floor of the tank had been graded on a slight incline as an aid in this daily cleansing. He watched the dirty water slosh out the door and into the parking lot where it flowed to a sewer drain. There was vomit and blood in the water and the smell from the tank was terrible. But Harry stood his ground. This was his place.

When he was done he threw his cigarette butt into the water and watched the flow take it to the drain.

6

It felt like the detective bureau had become a fishbowl and he was the only one in the water. He had to get away from the curious eyes that were watching him. Bosch picked up the stack of blue binders and walked out the backdoor into the parking lot. Then he quickly walked back into the station through the watch office door, went down a short hallway past the lockup and up a staircase to the second-floor storage room. It was called the Bridal Suite because of the cots in the back corner. An unofficial official cooping station. There was an old cafeteria table up there and a phone. And it was quiet. It was all he needed.

The room was empty today. Bosch put the stack of binders down and cleared a dented bumper marked with an evidence tag off the table. He leaned it against a stack of file boxes next to a broken surfboard that had also been tagged as evidence. Then he got down to work.

Harry stared at the foot-high stack of binders. Pounds said the division had sixty-six homicides so far in the year. Figuring the rotation and including Harry's two-month absence while recovering from the bullet wound, Porter had probably caught fourteen of the cases. With eight still open, that meant he had cleared six others. It wasn't a bad record, considering the transient nature of homicide in Hollywood. Nationwide, the vast majority of murder victims know their killer. They are the people they eat with, drink with, sleep with, live with. But Hollywood was different. There were no norms. There were only deviations, aberrations. Strangers killed strangers here. Reasons were not a requirement. The victims turned up in alleys, on freeway shoulders, along the brushy hillsides in Griffith Park, in bags dropped like garbage into restaurant Dumpsters. One of Harry's open files was the discovery of a body in parts — one on each of the fire escape landings of a six-story hotel on Gower. That one didn't raise too many eyebrows in the bureau. The joke going around was that it was a lucky thing that the victim hadn't stayed at the Holiday Inn. It was fifteen stories.

The bottom line was that in Hollywood a monster could move smoothly in the flow of humanity. Just one more car on the crowded freeway. And some would always be caught and some would always be untraceable, unless you counted the blood they left behind.

Porter had gone six and eight before punching out. It was a record that wouldn't get him any commendations but, still, it meant six more monsters were out of the flow. Bosch realized he could balance Porter's books if he could clear one of the eight open cases. The broken-down cop would at least go out with an even record.

Bosch didn't care about Pounds and his desire to clear one more case by midnight on New Year's Eve. He felt no allegiance to Pounds and believed the annual tabulating, charting and analysing of lives sacrificed added up to nothing. He decided that if he was to do this job, he would do it for Porter. Fuck Pounds.

He pushed the binders to the back of the table so he would have room to work. He decided to quickly scan each murder book and separate them into two piles. One stack of possible quick turns, another for the cases he did not think he could do anything with in a short time.

He reviewed them in chronological order, starting with a Valentine's Day strangulation of a priest in a stall at a bathhouse on Santa Monica. By the time he was done two hours had passed and Harry had only two of the blue binders in his stack of possibilities. One was a month old. A woman was pulled from a bus stop bench on Las Palmas into the darkened entranceway of a closed Hollywood memorabilia store and raped and stabbed. The other was the eight-day-old discovery of the body of a man behind a twenty-four-hour diner on Sunset near the Directors Guild building. The victim had been beaten to death.

Bosch focused on these two because they were the most recent cases and experience had instilled in him a firm belief that cases become exponentially more difficult to clear with each day that passes. Whoever strangled the priest was as good as gold. Harry knew the percentages showed that the killer had gotten away.

Bosch also saw that the two most recent cases could quickly be cleared if he caught a break. If he could identify the man found behind the restaurant, then that information could lead to his family, friends and associates and most likely to a motive and maybe a killer. Or, if he could trace the stabbing victim's movement back to where she was before going to the bus stop, he might be able to learn where and how the killer saw her.

It was a toss-up and Bosch decided to read each case file thoroughly before deciding. But going with the percentages he decided to read the freshest case first. The body found behind the restaurant was the warmest trail.

On first glance, the murder book was notable for what it did not contain. Porter had not picked up a finished, typed copy of the autopsy protocol. So Bosch had to rely on the Investigator's Summary reports and Porter's own autopsy notes, which simply said the victim had been beaten to death with a "blunt object" — policespeak, meaning just about anything.

The victim, estimated to be about fifty-five years old, was referred to as Juan Doe #67. This because he was believed to be Latin and was the sixty-seventh unidentified Latin man found dead in Los Angeles County during the year. There was no money on the body, no wallet and no belongings other than the clothing — all of it manufactured in Mexico. The only identification key was a tattoo on the upper left chest. It was a monocolor outline of what appeared to be a ghost. There was a Polaroid snapshot of it in the file. Bosch studied this for several moments, deciding the blue line drawing of a Casper-like ghost was very old. The ink was faded and blurred. Juan Doe #67 had gotten the tattoo as a young man.

The crime scene report Porter had filled out said the body had been found at 1:44 A.M. on December 18 by an off-duty police officer, identified only by his badge number, going in for an early breakfast or late dinner when he saw the body lying next to the Dumpster near the kitchen door of the Egg and I Diner.

R/O #1101 had recently reported code seven and parked behind the location with the intention of entering to eat. Victim was viewed on the eastern side of the dumpster. Body was laying in a supine position, head to the north and feet to the south. Extensive injuries were readily noticeable and R/O notified the watch commander that a homicide callout was necessary. R/O saw no other individuals in the vicinity of the dumpster before or after the body was located.

Bosch looked through the binder for a summary filed by the reporting officer but there was none. He next reviewed the other photos in the binder. These were of the body in place, before the techs had moved it to the morgue.

Bosch could see the victim's scalp had been rent open by one vicious blow. There were also wounds on the face and dried black blood on the neck and all over the once-white T-shirt the man was wearing. The dead man's hands lay open at his sides. In close-ups of the hands, Bosch saw two fingers on the right hand bent backward in compound fractures — classic defense wounds. Aside from the wounds, Bosch noted the rough and scarred hands and the ropey muscles that went up the arms. He had been a worker of some kind. What had he been doing in the alley behind the diner at one o'clock in the morning?

Next in the binder were witness statements taken from employees at the Egg and I. They were all men, which seemed wrong to Bosch because he had eaten at the Egg and I on several early mornings and remembered that there were always waitresses working the tables. Porter had apparently decided they were unimportant and concentrated only on the kitchen help. Each of the men interviewed said he did not recall seeing the victim in life or death.

Porter had scribbled a star on the top of one of the statements. It was from a fry cook who had reported to work at 1 A.M. and had walked right past the east side of the Dumpster and through the kitchen door. He had seen no body on the ground and was sure he would have seen one if there had been one to see when he made his entrance.

That had helped Porter set the timing of the slaying to sometime during the forty-four-minute window between the arrivals of the fry cook and the police officer who found the body.

Next in the file were printouts from LAPD, National Crime Index, California Department of Justice, and Immigration and Naturalization Service computer runs on the victim's fingerprints. All four were negative. No matches. Juan Doe #67 remained unidentified.

At the back of the binder were notes Porter had taken during the autopsy, which had not been conducted until Tuesday, Christmas Eve, because of the usual backlog of cases at the coroner's office. Bosch realized that it might have been Porter's last official duty to watch one more body be cut up. He didn't come back to work after the holiday.

Perhaps Porter knew he would not return, for his notes were sparse, just a single page with a few thoughts jotted down. Some of them Bosch could not read. Other notes he could understand but they were meaningless. But near the bottom of the page Porter had circled a notation that said, "TOD — 12 to 6 P.M."

Bosch knew the notation meant that, based on the rate of decrease in liver temperature and other appearances of the body, the time of death was likely to have been between noon and 6 P.M., but no later than 6 P.M.

This did not make sense, Bosch thought at first. That put the time of death at least seven and a half hours before the discovery of the body. It also did not jibe with the fry cook not seeing any body by the Dumpster at 1 A.M.

These contradictions were the reason Porter had circled the notation. It meant Juan Doe #67 had not been killed behind the diner. It meant he was killed somewhere else, nearly half a day earlier, and then dumped behind the diner.

He took a notebook out of his pocket and began to make a list of people he wanted to talk to. First on the list was the doctor who had performed the autopsy; Harry needed to get the completed autopsy protocol. Then he noted Porter down for a more detailed interview. After that he wrote the fry cook's name on the list because Porter's notes only said the cook did not see a body on the ground while going to work. There was nothing about whether the cook saw anybody else or anything unusual in the alley. He also made a note to check with the waitresses who had been on duty that morning.

To complete his list, Bosch had to pick up the phone and call the watch commander's office.

"I want to talk to eleven-oh-one," Bosch said. "Can you look it up on the board there and tell me who that is?"

It was Kleinman again. He said, "Very funny, smart guy."

"What?" Bosch said, but at that moment it struck him. "Is it Cal Moore?"

"Was Cal Moore. Was."

Harry hung up the phone as several thoughts crowded into his brain at once. Juan Doe #67 had been found on the day before Moore checked into the Hideaway. He tried to piece out what this could mean. Moore stumbles onto a body in an alley early one morning. The next day he checks into a motel, turns up the air-conditioner and puts two barrels of double-ought buckshot into his face. The message he leaves behind is as simple as it is mysterious.

I found out who I was

Bosch lit a cigarette and crossed #1101 off his list, but he continued to center his thoughts on this latest piece of information. He felt impatient, bothered. He fidgeted in the chair, then stood up and began to walk in a circle around the table. He worked Porter into the framework this development provided and ran through it several times. Each time it was the same: Porter gets the call out on the Juan Doe #67 case. He obviously would have had to talk to Moore at the scene. The next day Moore disappears. The next week Moore is found dead, and then the next day Porter announces he is getting a doctor and is pulling the pin. Too many coincidences.

He picked up the phone and called the homicide table. Edgar answered and Harry asked him to reach across the table and check his Rolodex for Porter's home number. Edgar gave it to him and said, "Harry, where you at?"

"Why, Ninety-eight looking for me?"

"Nah. One of the guys from Moore's unit called a few minutes ago. Said he was looking for you."

"Yeah, why?"

"Hey, Harry, I'm only passing on the message, not doing your job for you."

"Okay, okay. Which one called?"

"Rickard. He just asked me to tell you they had something for you. I gave him your pager number 'cause I didn't know if you were coming back any-time soon. So, where you at?"

"Nowhere."

He hung up and dialed Porter's house. The phone rang ten times. Harry hung up and lit another cigarette. He didn't know what to think about all of this. Could Moore have simply stumbled onto the body as it said in the report? Could he have dumped it there? Bosch had no clues.

"Nowhere," he said aloud to the room full of storage boxes.

He picked up the phone again and dialed the medical examiner's office. He gave his name and asked to be connected to Dr. Corazón, the acting chief. Harry refused to say what the call was about to the operator. The phone was dead for nearly a minute before Corazón picked up.

"I'm in the middle of something here," she said.

"Merry Christmas to you, too."

"Sorry."

"It's the Moore cut?"

"Yes, but I can't talk about it. What do you need, Harry?"

"I just inherited a case and there's no autopsy in the file. I'm trying to find out who did it so I can get a copy."

"Harry, you don't need to ask for the acting chief to track that. You could ask any of the investigators I have sitting around here on their asses."

"Yeah, but they aren't as sweet to me as you."

"Okay, hurry up, what's the name?"

"Juan Doe #67. Date of death was the eighteenth. The cut was the twenty-fourth."

She said nothing and Bosch assumed she was checking a scheduling chart.

"Yeah," she said after a half minute. "The twenty-fourth. That was Salazar and he's gone now. Vacation. That was his last autopsy until next month. He went to Australia. It's summer there."

"Shit."

"Don't fret, Harry. I have the package right here. Sally expected Lou Porter would be by to pick it up today. But Lou never came. How'd you inherit it?"

"Lou pulled the pin."

"Jeez, that was kind of quick. What's his — hold on —"

She didn't wait for him to say he would. This time she was gone more than a minute. When she came back, her voice had a higher pitch to it.

"Harry, I really've got to go. Tell you what, wanna meet me after work? By then I'll've had some time to reach through this and I'll tell you what we've got. I just remembered that there is something kind of interesting here. Salazar came to me for a referral approval."

"Referral to what?"

"An entomologist — a bug doctor — over at UCLA. Sally found bugs."

Bosch already knew that maggots would not have bred in a body dead twelve hours at the most. And Salazar would not have needed an entomologist to identify them anyway.

"Bugs," he said.

"Yeah. In the stomach content analysis and nasal swabs. But I don't have time at the moment to discuss this. I've got four impatient men in the autopsy suite waiting for me. And only one of 'em is dead."

"I guess that would make the live ones Irving, Sheehan and Chastain, the three musketeers."

She laughed and said, "You got it."

"Okay. When and where do you want to meet?"

He looked at his watch. It was almost three.

"Maybe around six?" she said. "That would give me time to finish here and look through this package on your Juan Doe."

"Should I come there?"

His pager began to chirp. He cut it off with a well-practiced move with his right hand to his belt.

"No, let's see," she said. "Can you meet me at the Red Wind? We can wait out the rush hour."

"I'll be there," Harry said.

After hanging up he checked the number on his pager, recognized it as a pay phone exchange and dialed it.

"Bosch?" a voice said.

"Right."

"Rickard. I worked with Cal Moore. The BANG unit?"

"Right."

"I got something for you."

Bosch didn't say anything. He felt the hairs on the top of his hands and forearms begin to tingle. He tried to place the name Rickard with a face but couldn't. The narcs kept such odd hours and were a breed unto themselves. He didn't know who Rickard was.

"Or, I should say, Cal left something for you," Rickard spoke into the silence. "You wanna meet? I don't want this to go down in the station."

"Why not?"

"I've got my reasons. We can talk about that when I see you."

"Where's that gonna be?"

"You know a place on Sunset, the Egg and I? It's a diner. Decent food. The hypes don't hang out here."

"I know it."

"Good. We're in the last booth in the back, right before the kitchen door. The table with the only black guy in the place. That's me. There's parking in the back. In the alley."

"I know. Who's 'we'?"

"Cal's whole crew is here."

"That where you guys always hang out?"

"Yeah, before we hit the street. See ya soon."

The restaurant's sign had been changed since the last time he had been there. It was now the *All-American* Egg and I, which meant it had probably been sold to foreigners. Bosch got out of his Caprice and walked through the back alley, looking at the spot where Juan Doe #67 had been dumped. Right outside the backdoor of a diner frequented by the local narc crew. His thoughts on the implications of this were interrupted by the panhandlers in the alley who came up to him shaking their cups. Bosch ignored them but their presence served to remind him of another shortcoming in Porter's meager investigation. There had been nothing in the reports about vagrants in the alley being interviewed as possible witnesses. It would probably be impossible to track them down now.

Inside the restaurant, he saw four young men, one of them black, in a rear booth. They were sitting silently with their faces turned down to the empty coffee cups in front of them. Harry noticed a closed manila file on the table as he pulled a chair away from an empty table and sat at the end of the booth.

"I'm Bosch."

"Tom Rickard," the black one said. He put out his hand and then introduced the other three as Finks, Montirez and Fedaredo.

"We got tired of being around the office," Rickard said. "Cal used to like this place."

Bosch just nodded and looked down at the file. He saw the name written on the tab was Humberto Zorrillo. It meant nothing to him. Rickard slid the file across the table to him.

"What is it?" Harry asked, not yet touching it.

"Probably the last thing he worked on," Rickard said. "We were going to give it over to RHD but thought what the hell, he was working it up for you. And those boys down there at Parker are just trying to drag him through the shit. Ain't going to help with that."

"What do you mean?"

"I mean they can't let it be that the man killed himself. They hafta dissect his life and figure out exactly why he did this and why he done that. The man fucking killed himself. What else is there to say about it?"

"You don't want to know why?"

"I already know why, man. The job. It will get us all in the end. I mean, I know why."

Bosch just nodded again. The other three narcs still hadn't said anything.

"I'm just letting off steam," Rickard said. "Been one of those days. Longest fucking day of my life."

"Where was this?" Harry asked, pointing to the file. "Didn't RHD already go through his desk?"

"Yeah, they did. But that file wasn't in it. See, Cal left it in one of the BANG cars — one of those undercover pieces of shit we use. In the pocket behind the front seat. We never noticed it during the week he was missing because today was the first time any of us rode in the back of the car. We usually take two cars out on operations. But today we all jumped in one for a cruise on the Boulevard after we came in and heard the news. I saw it shoved down into the pocket. It's got a little note inside. Says to give it to you. We knew he was working on something for you 'cause of that night he peeled off early to go meet with you at the Catalina."

Bosch still hadn't opened the file. Just looking at it gave him an uneasy feeling.

"He told me that night at the Catalina that the shoeflies were on him. You guys know why?"

"No, man, we don't know what was going down. We just know they were around. Like flies on shit. IAD went through his desk before RHD. They took files, his phone book, even took the fucking typewriter off the desk. That was the only one we had. But what it was about, we don't know. The guy had a lot of years in and it burns my ass that they were gunning for him. That's what I meant before about the job doing him in. It'll get all of us."

"What about outside the job? His past. His wife said —"

"I don't want to hear about that shit. She's the one who put the suits on him. Made up some story when he walked out and dropped the dime on him. She just wanted to bring him down, you ask me."

"How do you know it was her?"

"Cal told us, man. Said the shoeflies might come around asking questions. Told us it came from her."

Bosch wondered who had been lying, Moore to his partners or Sylvia to himself. He thought about her for a moment and couldn't see it, couldn't see her dropping the dime. But he didn't press it with the four narcs. He finally reached down and picked up the file. Then he left.

He was too curious to wait. He knew that he should not even have the file. That he should pick up a phone and call Frankie Sheehan at RHD. But he unconsciously took a quick look around the car to make sure he was alone and began to read. There was a yellow Post-it note on the first page.

Give to Harry Bosch.

It was not signed or dated. It was stuck to a sheet of paper with five green Field Interview cards held to it with a paper clip. Harry detached the FI cards and shuffled through them. Five different names, all males. Each had been stopped by members of the BANG unit in October or November. They were questioned and released. Each card held little more information than a description, home address, driver license number, and date and location of the shakedown. The names meant nothing to Bosch.

He looked at the sheet the cards had been attached to. It was marked INTERNAL MEMO and had a subheading that said BANG Intelligence Report #144. It was dated November 1 and had a FILED stamp mark on it that was dated two days after that.

In the course of gathering intelligence on narcotics activities in Reporting District 12 officers Moore, Rickard, Finks, Fedaredo and Montirez have conducted numerous field interrogations of suspects believed to be involved in drug sales in the area of Hollywood Boulevard. In recent weeks it has come to these officers' attention the fact that individuals were involved in the sale of a drug known as "black ice" which is a narcotic combining heroin, cocaine and PCP in rock form. The demand for this drug remains low on the street at this time but its popularity is expected to increase.

Officers assigned to this unit believe several transient-type individuals are engaged in the street level sale of "black ice." Five suspects have been identified through investigation but no arrests have followed. The street sales network is believed to be directed by an individual whose identity is not known to officers at this time.

Informants and users of "black ice" have revealed that the predominant form of the drug sold at street level in the reporting zone comes from Mexico, rather than Hawaii where ice originated — refer to DEA advisory 502 — and still is imported to the mainland in large quantities.

Reporting officers will contact DEA for intelligence on sources of this narcotic and will continue to monitor activities in RD12.

Sgt. C. V. Moore #1101

Bosch reread the report. It was a cover-your-ass paper. It said nothing and meant nothing. It had no value but could be produced to show a superior that you were aware of a problem and had been taking steps to attack it. Moore must have realized that black ice was becoming more than a rarity on the street and wanted to file a report to shield himself against future repercussions.

Next in the file was an arrest report dated November 9 of a man named Marvin Dance for possession of a controlled substance. The report said Dance was arrested by BANG officers on Ivar after they watched him make a delivery of black ice to a street dealer. BANG unit officers Rickard and Finks had set up on Dance on Ivar north of the Boulevard. The suspect was sitting in a parked car and the narcs watched as another man walked up and got in.

The report said Dance took something out of his mouth and handed it to the other man, who then got out of the car and walked on. The two officers split up and Finks followed the walker until he was out of Dance's sight, then stopped him and seized an eightball — eight individually wrapped grams of black ice in a balloon. Rickard kept a watch on Dance, who remained in the car waiting for the next dealer to come for the product. After Finks radioed that he had made his bust, Rickard moved in to take down Dance.

But Dance swallowed whatever else was in his mouth. While he sat cuffed on the sidewalk, Rickard searched the car and found no drugs. But in a crumpled McDonald's cup in the gutter by the car door, the narc found six more balloons, each containing an eightball.

Dance was arrested for sales and possession with intent to sell. The report said the suspect refused to talk to the arresting officers about the drugs other than to say the McDonald's cup was not his. He didn't ask for a lawyer but one arrived at the station within an hour and informed the officers that it would be unconstitutional for them to take his client to a hospital to have his stomach pumped or to search his client's feces when the time came for him to use the bathroom. Moore, who got involved in processing the arrest at the station, checked with the on-call DA and was told the lawyer was right.

Dance was released on $125,000 bail two hours after his arrest. Bosch thought this was curious. The report said time of arrest was 11:42 P.M. That meant that in two hours in the middle of the night, Dance had come up with a lawyer, bail bondsman and the ten percent cash — $12,500 — needed to make bail.

And no charges were ever filed against Dance. The next page of the file was a rejection slip from the DA's office. The filing deputy who reviewed the case determined that there was insufficient evidence linking Dance to the McDonald's cup that was in the gutter three feet from the car.

So, no possession charge. Next, the sales charge was scuttled because the narcs saw no money change hands when Dance gave the eightball to the man who had gotten in the car. His name was Glenn Druzon. He was seventeen years old and had refused to testify that he had received the balloon from Dance. In fact, the rejection report said, he was ready to testify that he had the balloon with him before he got into the car with Dance. If called he would testify that he had tried to sell it to Dance but Dance was not interested.

The case against Dance was kicked. Druzon was charged with possession and later put on juvenile probation.

Bosch looked away from the reports and down the alley. He could see the circular copper-and-glass Directors Guild building rising at the end. He could just see the top of the Marlboro Man billboard that had been on Sunset for as long as he could remember. He lit a cigarette.

He looked at the DA reject form again. Clipped to it was a mug shot of the blond-haired Dance smirking at the lens. Bosch knew that what had happened was the routine way in which many, if not most, street cases go. The small fish, the bottom feeders, get hooked up. The bigger fish break the line and swim away. The cops knew that all they could do was disrupt things, never rid the streets of the problem. Take one dealer down and somebody takes his place. Or an attorney on retainer springs him and then a DA with a four-drawer caseload cuts him loose. It was one of the reasons why Bosch stayed in homicide. Sometimes he thought it was the only crime that really counted.

But even that was changing.

Harry took the mug shot and put it in his pocket, then closed the file for the time being. He was bothered by the Dance arrest. He wondered what connection Calexico Moore had seen between Dance and Jimmy Kapps that had prompted him to put it in the file for Bosch.

Bosch took a small notebook out of his inside coat pocket and began to make a chronological list. He wrote:

> Nov. 9 Dance arrested
> Nov. 13 Jimmy Kapps dead
> Dec. 4 Moore, Bosch meet

Bosch closed the notebook. He knew he had to go back into the diner to ask Rickard a question. But first he reopened the file. There was only one page left, another unit intelligence report. This one was a summary of a briefing Moore had gotten from a DEA agent assigned to Los Angeles. This was dated December 11, meaning it had been put together by Moore a week after he and Bosch had met at the Catalina.

Harry tried to figure how this played with everything else and what, if anything, it meant. At their meeting Moore had withheld information, but afterward had gone to the DEA to request information. It was as if he were playing both sides of the fence. Or, possibly, Moore was trying to hotdog Bosch's case, trying to put it together on his own.

Bosch began reading the report slowly, unconsciously bending the top corners of the file with his fingers.

Information provided this date by DEA asst. special agent in charge Rene Corvo, Los Angeles bureau operations indicates origin of black ice is primarily Baja California. Target 44Q3 Humberto Zorrillo (11/11/54) believed operating a clandestine lab in the Mexicali zone that is producing Mexican ice for distribution in the U.S. Subject lives on a 6,000-acre bull ranch SW Mexicali. State Judicial Police has not moved against Zorrillo for political reasons. Mode of transport used by this operation is unknown. Air surveillance shows no airstrip on ranch property. It is DEA opinion based on experience that the operation uses vehicle routes through Calexico or possibly San Ysidro, however, no shipments intercepted at those crossings at this time. It is believed that subject enjoys support and cooperation of officers with the SJP. He is widely known and revered as a hero in the barrios of SW Mexicali. Subject's support is based in part on generous donations of jobs, med supplies, barrio dwellings and cook camps in the poor neighborhoods he grew up in. Some of the residents in SW neighborhoods refer to Zorrillo as El Papa de Mexicali. Additionally, Zorrillo's rancho remains under heavy guard 24-hours. El Papa — The Pope — is rarely seen outside of the rancho. Exception is weekly trips to observe bulls bred on the ranch at bullrings in Baja. SJP authorities advise at this time that their cooperation in any DEA action that focuses on Zorrillo would be impossible.

Sgt. C. V. Moore #1101

Bosch stared for a few moments at the file after closing it. He had a jumble of differing thoughts. He was a man who didn't believe in coincidences, and so he had to wonder about how Cal Moore's presence had come to throw a shadow across everything on his own plate. He looked at his watch and saw it would soon be time to get going to meet Teresa Corazón. But, finally, all the movement in his mind could not distract him from the thought that was pushing through: Frankie Sheehan at RHD should have the information in the Zorrillo file. Bosch had worked with Sheehan at RHD. He was a good man and a good investigator. If he was conducting a legitimate investigation, he should have the file. If he wasn't, then it didn't matter.

He got out of the car and headed back to the diner. This time he walked in through the kitchen door on the alley. The BANG crew was still there, the four young narcs sitting as quietly as if they were in the back room at a funeral home. Bosch's chair was still there, too. He sat down again.

"What's up?" Rickard said.

"You read this, right? Tell me about the Dance bust."

"What's to tell?" Rickard said. "We kick ass, the DA kicks the case. What's new? It's a different drug, man, but it's the same old thing."

"What made you set up on Dance? How'd you know he was making deliveries there?"

"Heard it around."

"Look, it's important. It involves Moore."

"How?"

"I can't tell you now. You have to trust me until I put a few things together. Just tell me who got the tip. That's what it was, right?"

Rickard seemed to weigh the choices he had.

"Yeah, it was a tip. It was my snitch."

"Who was it?"

"Look, man, I can't —"

"Jimmy Kapps. It was Jimmy Kapps, wasn't it?"

Rickard hesitated again and that confirmed it for Bosch. It angered him that he was finding this out almost by accident and only after a cop's death. But the picture was clearing. Kapps snitches off Dance as a means of knocking out some of the competition. Then he flies back to Hawaii, picks up a bellyful of balloons and comes back. But Dance isn't in lockup anymore and Jimmy Kapps gets taken down before he can sell even one of his balloons.

"Why the fuck didn't you come talk to me when you heard Kapps got put down? I've been trying to get a line on this and all the —"

"What're you talking about, Bosch? Moore met you that night on the Kapps thing. He . . ."

It became apparent to everybody at the table that Moore had not told Bosch everything he knew that night at the Catalina. The silence fell heavy on them. If they hadn't known it before, they knew it now: Moore had been up to something. Bosch finally spoke.

"Did Moore know your snitch was Kapps?"

Rickard hesitated once more, but then nodded.

Bosch stood up and slid the file across the table to a spot in front of Rickard.

"I don't want this. You call Frank Sheehan at RHD and tell him you just found it. It's up to you but I wouldn't say that you let me look at it first. And I won't, either."

Harry made a move to step away from the table but then stopped.

"One other thing. This guy Dance, any of you seen him around?"

"Not since the bust," Fedaredo said.

The other three shook their heads.

"If you can dig him up, let me know. You got my number."

Outside the diner's kitchen door Bosch looked again at the spot in the alley where Moore had found Juan Doe #67. Supposedly. He didn't know what to believe about Moore anymore. But he couldn't help but wonder what the connection was between the Juan Doe and Dance and Kapps, if there was a connection at all. He knew the key was to find out who the man with the worker's hands and muscles had been. Then he would find the killer.

8

At Parker Center, Harry walked past the memorial sculpture in front and into the lobby where he had to badge the officer at the front counter to get in. The department was too big and impersonal. The cops at the counter would recognize no one below the rank of commander.

The lobby was crowded with people coming and going. Some were in uniform, some in suits, some with VISITOR stickers on their shirts and the wide-eyed look of citizens venturing into the maze for the first time. Harry had come to regard Parker Center as a bureaucratic labyrinth that hindered rather than eased the job of the cop on the street. It was eight floors with fiefdoms on every hallway on every floor. Each was jealously guarded by commanders and deputy chiefs and assistant chiefs. And each group had its suspicions about the others. Each was a society within the great society.

Bosch had been a master of the maze during his eight years in Robbery-Homicide. And then he crashed and burned under the weight of an Internal Affairs investigation into his shooting of an unarmed suspect in a series of killings. Bosch had fired as the man reached under a pillow in his killing pad for what Harry thought was a gun. But there was no gun. Beneath the pillow was a toupee. It was almost laughable, except for the man who took the bullet. Other RHD investigators tied him to eleven killings. His body was shipped in a cardboard box to a crematorium. Bosch was shipped out to Hollywood Division.

The elevator was crowded and smelled like stale breath. He got out on the fourth floor and walked into the Scientific Investigations Division offices. The secretary had already left. Harry leaned over the countertop and reached the button that buzzed open the half door. He walked through the ballistics lab and into the squad room. Donovan was still there, sitting at his desk.

"How'd you get in here?"

"Let myself in."

"Harry, don't do that. You can't go around breaching security like that."

Bosch nodded his contrition.

"What do you want?" Donovan asked. "I don't have any of your cases."

"Sure you do."

"What one?"

"Cal Moore."

"Bullshit."

"Look, I've got a part of it, okay? I just have a few questions. You can answer them if you want. If you don't, that's fine, too."

"What've you got?"

"I'm running down some things that came up on a couple cases I'm working and they run right across Cal Moore's trail. And so I just . . . I just want to be sure about Moore. You know what I mean?"

"No, I don't know what you mean."

Bosch pulled a chair away from another desk and sat down. They were alone in the squad room but Bosch spoke low and slow, hoping to draw the SID tech in.

"Just for my own knowledge I need to be sure. What I am wondering is, can you tell me if all the stuff checked out."

"Checked out to what?"

"Come on, man. Was it him and was there anybody else in that room?"

There was a long silence and then Donovan cleared his throat. He finally said, "What do you mean, you're working cases that cross his trail?"

Fair enough question, Bosch thought. There was a small window of opportunity there.

"I got a dead drug dealer. I had asked Moore to do some checking on the case. Then, I got a dead body, a Juan Doe, in an alley off Sunset. Moore's the one who found the body. The next day he checks into that dump and does the number with the shotgun. Or so it looks. I just want some reassurances it's the way it looks. I heard they got an ID over at the morgue."

"So what makes you think these two cases are connected with Moore's thing?"

"I don't think anything right now. I'm just trying to eliminate possibilities. Maybe it's all the coincidences. I don't know."

"Well," Donovan said. "I don't know what they got over at the ME's, but I got lifts in the room that belonged to him. Moore was in that room. I just got finished with it. Took me all day."

"How come?"

"The DOJ computer was down all morning. Couldn't get prints. I went up to personnel to get Moore's prints from his package and they told me Irving had already raided it. He took the prints out and took 'em over to the coroner. You know, you're not supposed to do that, but who's gonna tell him, get on his shit list. So I had to wait for the Justice computer to come back on line. Got his prints off of that after lunch and just finished with it a little while ago. That was Moore in the room."

"Where were the prints?"

"Hang on."

Donovan rolled back his chair to a set of file cabinets and unlocked a drawer with a key from his pocket. While he was leafing through the files, Bosch lit a cigarette. Donovan finally pulled out a file and then rolled his chair back to his desk.

"Put that shit out, Harry. I hate that shit."

Bosch dropped the cigarette to the linoleum, stepped on it and then kicked the butt under Donovan's desk. Donovan began reviewing some pages he had pulled from a file. Bosch could see that each one showed a top-view drawing of the motel room where Moore's body was found.

"Okay, then," Donovan said. "The prints in the room came back to Moore. All of them. I did the comp —"

"You said that."

"I'm getting to it, I'm getting to it. Let's see, we have a thumb — fourteen points — on the stock of the weapon. That, I guess, was the bell ringer, the fourteen."

Harry knew that only five matching points in a fingerprint comparison were needed for an identification to be accepted in court. A fourteen-point match of a print on a gun was almost as good as having a photo of the person holding the gun.

"Then, we . . . let's see . . . we had four three-pointers on the barrels of the weapon. I think these kind of got smudged when it kicked out of his hands. So we got nothing real clear there."

"What about the triggers?"

"Nope. Nothing there. He pulled the triggers with his toe and he was still wearing a sock, remember?"

"What about the rest of the place? I saw you dusting the air-conditioner."

"Yeah, but I didn't get anything there on the dial. We thought he turned the air up, you know, to control decomp. But the dial was clean. It's plastic with a rough surface, so I don't think it would have held anything for us."

"What else?"

Donovan looked back down at his charts.

"I got a lift off his badge — index and thumb, five and seven points respectively. The badge was on the bureau with the wallet. But nothing on the wallet. Only smears. On the gun on the bureau I only got a bunch of smears but a clear thumb on the cartridge.

"Then, let's see, I got the whole hand just about, a palm, thumb and three fingers on the left cabinet door under the bathroom sink. I figure he must've put his hand on it to steady himself when he was getting on the floor there. What a way to go, man."

"Yeah. That's it?"

"Yeah. Er, no. On the newspaper — there was a newspaper on the chair, I got a big match there. Thumb again and three fingers."

"And the shells?"

"Only smudges. Couldn't get anything on the shells."

"What about the note?"

"Nothing on it."

"Somebody check the handwriting?"

"Well, actually, it was printing. But Sheehan had it checked by somebody in suspicious documents. He said it matched. Few months back Moore moved out on his wife and took a place in Los Feliz called The Fountains. He filled out a change-of-address form. It was there in the personnel file Irving grabbed. Anyway, the change-of-address card was printed, too. There were a lot of commonalities with the note. You know, 'Found' and 'Fountains.'"

"What about the shotgun? Anybody trace the serial?"

"The number had been filed and acid-burned. No trace. You know, Harry, I shouldn't be saying so much. I think we should just . . ."

He didn't finish the sentence. He turned his chair back to the file cabinet and began to put his charts away.

"I'm almost done, man. What about a projectile pattern? Did you do one?"

Donovan closed and locked the file drawer and turned back around.

"Started to. Haven't finished. But you're talking side-by-side barrels, double-ought shells. That's an immediate spread pattern. I'd say he could have done it from six inches away and gotten that kind of damage. No mystery there."

Bosch nodded and looked at his watch, then stood up.

"One last thing."

"Might as well. I've already told you enough to put my ass in a permanent sling. You going to be careful with what I've told you?"

"Course I am. Last thing. Outstanding prints. How many lifts you get that you haven't matched to Moore?"

"Not a one. I was wondering if anybody would care about that."

Bosch sat back down. This made no sense. Bosch knew that a motel room was like a working girl. Every customer leaves a little something, his mark, behind. It didn't matter if the rooms were made up and reasonably cleaned between renters. There was always something, a telltale sign. Harry could not accept that every surface Donovan had checked had been clean except for those where Moore's prints were found.

"What do you mean nobody cared?"

"I mean nobody said shit. I told Sheehan and that IAD stiff that's been following him around. They acted like it didn't mean a thing to them. You know? It was like 'big deal, so there were no other prints.' I guess they never did a motel-room stiff before. Shit, I thought I'd be collecting prints in there last night 'til midnight. But all I got were the ones I just told you about. That was the goddamned cleanest motel room I've ever printed. I mean, I even put on the laser. Didn't see a thing but wipe marks where the room had been cleaned up. And if you ask me, Harry, that wasn't the kinda place the management cared too much about cleanliness."

"You told Sheehan this, right?"

"Yeah, I told him when I got done. I was thinking, you know, it being Christmas night that they were going to say I was full of shit and just trying to get home to the family. But I told 'em and they just said, fine, that'll be all, good night, Merry Christmas. I left. Fuck it."

Bosch thought about Sheehan and Chastain and Irving. Sheehan was a competent investigator. But with those two hovering over him, he could have made a mistake. They had gone into the motel room one hundred percent sure it was a suicide. Bosch would have done the same. They even found a note. After that they would have probably had to find a knife in Moore's back to change their minds. The lack of other prints in the room, no serial number on the shotgun. These were things that should've been enough to cut the percentage of their assuredness back to fifty-fifty. But they hadn't made a dent in their assumption. Harry began to wonder about the autopsy results, if they would back the suicide conclusion.

He stood up once more, thanked Donovan for the information and left.

He took the stairs down to the third floor and walked into the RHD suite. Most of the desks lined in three rows were empty, as it was after five o'clock. Sheehan's was among those that were deserted in the Homicide Special bullpen. A few of the detectives still there glanced up at him but then looked away. Bosch was of no interest to them. He was a symbol of what could happen, of how easily one could fall.

"Sheehan still around?" he asked the duty detective who sat at the front desk and handled the phone lines, incoming reports and all the other shitwork.

"Gone for the day," she said without looking up from a staff vacation schedule she was filling out. "Called from the ME's office a few minutes ago and said he was code seven until the A.M."

"There a desk I can use for a few minutes? I have to make some phone calls."

He hated to ask for such permission, having worked in this room for eight years.

"Just pick one," she said. She still didn't look up.

Bosch sat down at a desk that was reasonably clear of clutter. He called the Hollywood homicide table, hoping there would still be someone there. Karen Moshito answered and Bosch asked if he had any messages.

"Just one. Somebody named Sylvia. No last name given."

He took the number down, feeling his pulse quicken.

"Did you hear about Moore?" Moshito asked.

"You mean the ID? Yeah, I heard."

"No. The cut is screwed up. Radio news says the autopsy is inconclusive. I never heard of a shotgun in the face being inconclusive."

"When did this come out?"

"I just heard it on KFWB at five."

Bosch hung up and tried Porter's number once more. Again there was no answer and no tape recording picked up. Harry wondered if the broken-down cop was there and just not answering. He imagined Porter sitting with a bottle in the corner of a dark room, afraid to answer the door or the phone.

He looked at the number he had written down for Sylvia Moore. He wondered if she had heard about the autopsy. That was probably it. She picked up after three rings.

"Mrs. Moore?"

"It's Sylvia."

"This is Harry Bosch."

"I know."

She didn't say anything further.

"How are you holding up?"

"I think I'm okay. I . . . I called because I just want to thank you. For the way you were last night. With me."

"Oh, well, you didn't — it was . . ."

"You know that book I told you about last night?"

The Long Goodbye?"

"There's another line in it I was thinking about. 'A white knight for me is as rare as a fat postman.' I guess nowadays there are a lot of fat postmen." She laughed very softly, almost like her crying. "But not too many white knights. You were last night."

Bosch didn't know what to say and just tried to envision her on the other end of the silence.

"That's very nice of you to say. But I don't know if I deserve it. Sometimes I don't think the things I have to do make me much of a knight."

They moved on to small talk for a few moments and then said good-bye. He hung up and sat still for a moment, staring at the phone and thinking about things said and unsaid. There was something there. A connection. Something more than her husband's death. More than just a case. There was a connection between them.

He turned the pages of the notebook back to the chronological chart he had made earlier.

Nov.   9 Dance arrested
Nov. 13 Jimmy Kapps dead
Dec.   4 Moore, Bosch meet

He now started to add other dates and facts, even some that did not seem to fit into the picture at the moment. But his overriding feeling was that his cases were linked and the link was Calexico Moore. He didn't stop to consider the chart as a whole until he was finished. Then he studied it, finding that it gave some context to the thoughts that had jumbled in his head in the last two days.

Nov.   1 BANG cya memo on black ice
Nov.   9 Rickard gets tip — from Jimmy Kapps
Nov.   9 Dance arrested, case kicked
Nov. 13 Jimmy Kapps dead
Dec.   4 Moore, Bosch meet — Moore holds back
Dec. 11 Moore receives DEA briefing
Dec. 18 Moore finds body — Juan Doe #67
Dec. 18 Porter assigned Juan Doe case
Dec. 19 Moore checks in, Hideaway — suicide?
Dec. 24 Juan Doe #67 autopsy — bugs?
Dec. 25 Moore's body found
Dec. 26 Porter pulls pin
Dec. 26 Moore autopsy — inconclusive?

But he couldn't study it too long without thinking of Sylvia Moore.

9

≋

Bosch took Los Angeles Street to Second and then up to the Red Wind. In front of St. Vibiana's he saw an entourage of bedraggled, homeless men leaving the church. They had spent the day sleeping in the pews and were now heading to the Union Street mission for dinner. As he passed the *Times* building he looked up at the clock and saw it was exactly six. He turned on KFWB for the news. The Moore autopsy was the second story, after a report on how the mayor had become the latest victim in a wave of kamikazi AIDS protests. He was hit with a balloon full of pig blood on the white stone steps of City Hall. A group called Cool AIDS took credit.

"In other news, an autopsy on the body of Police Sergeant Calexico Moore was inconclusive in confirming that the narcotics officer took his own life, according to the Los Angeles County coroner's office. Meanwhile, police have officially classified the death as suicide. The thirty-eight-year-old officer's body was found Christmas Day in a Hollywood motel room. He had been dead of a shotgun blast for about a week, authorities said. A suicide note was found at the scene but the contents have not been released. Moore will be buried Monday."

Bosch turned the radio off. The news report had obviously come from a press release. He wondered what was meant by the autopsy results being inconclusive. That was the only grain of real news in the whole report.

After parking at the curb in front of the Red Wind he went inside but did not see Teresa Corazón. He went into the restroom and splashed water on his face. He needed a shave. He dried himself with a paper towel and tried to smooth his mustache and curly hair with his hand. He loosened his tie, then stood there a long moment staring at his reflection. He saw the kind of man not many people approached unless they had to.

He got a package of cigarettes from the machine by the restroom door and looked around again but still didn't see her. He went to the bar and ordered an Anchor and then took it to an empty table by the front door. The Wind was becoming crowded with the after-work crowd. People in business suits and dresses. There were a lot of combinations of older men with younger women. Harry recognized several reporters from the *Times*. He began to think Teresa had picked a bad place to meet, if she intended to show up at all. With today's autopsy story, she might be noticed by the reporters. He drained the beer bottle and left the bar.

He was standing in the chilled evening air on the front sidewalk, looking down the street into the Second Street tunnel, when he heard a horn honk and a car pulled to a stop in front of him. The electric window glided down. It was Teresa.

"Harry, wait inside. I'll just find a place to park. Sorry I'm late."

Bosch leaned into the window.

"I don't know. Lot of reporters in there. I heard on the radio about the Moore autopsy. I don't know if you want to risk getting hassled."

He could see reasons for it and against it. Getting her name in the paper improved her chances of changing acting chief ME to permanent chief. But the wrong thing said or a misquote could just as easily change acting to interim or, worse yet, former.

"Where can we go?" she asked.

Harry opened the door and got in.

"Are you hungry? We can go down to Gorky's or the Pantry."

"Yeah. Is Gorky's still open? I want some soup."

It took them fifteen minutes to wend their way through eight blocks of downtown traffic and to find a parking space. Inside Gorky's they ordered mugs of home-brewed Russian beer and Teresa had the chicken-rice soup.

"Long day, huh?" he offered.

"Oh, yeah. No lunch. Was in the suite for five hours."

Bosch needed to hear about the Moore autopsy but knew he could not just blurt out a question. He would have to make her want to tell it.

"How was Christmas? You and your husband get together?"

"Not even close. It just didn't work. He never could deal with what I do and now that I have a shot at chief ME, he resents it even more. He left Christmas Eve. I spent Christmas alone. I was going to call my lawyer today to tell her to resume filing but I was too busy."

"Should've called me. I spent Christmas with a coyote."

"Ahh. Is Timido still around?"

"Yeah, he still comes around every now and then. There was a fire across the pass. I think it spooked him."

"Yeah, I read about that. You were lucky."

Bosch nodded. He and Teresa Corazón had had an on-and-off relationship for four months, each meeting sparked with this kind of surface intimacy. But it was a relationship of convenience, firmly grounded on physical, not emotional, needs and never igniting into deep passion for either of them. She had separated earlier in the year from her husband, a UCLA Medical School professor, and had apparently singled Harry out for her affections. But Bosch knew he was a secondary diversion. Their liaisons were sporadic, usually weeks apart, and Harry was content to allow Teresa to initiate each one.

He watched her bring her head down to blow onto a spoonful of soup and then sip it. He saw slices of carrot floating in the bowl. She had brown ringlets that fell to her shoulders. She held some of the tresses back with her hand as she blew on another spoonful and then sipped. Her skin was a deep natural brown and there was an exotic, elliptical shape to her face accentuated by high cheekbones. She wore red lipstick on full lips and there was just a whisper of fine white peach fuzz on her cheeks. He knew she was in her mid-thirties but he had never asked exactly how old. Lastly, he noticed her fingernails. Unpolished and clipped short, so as not to puncture the rubber gloves that were the tools of her trade.

As he drank the heavy beer from its heavy stein, he wondered if this was the start of another liaison or whether she really had come to tell him of something significant in the autopsy results of Juan Doe #67.

"So now I need a date for New Year's Eve," she said, looking up from the soup. "What are you staring at?"

"Just watching you. You need a date, you got one. I read in the paper that Frank Morgan's playing at the Catalina."

"Who's he and what does he play?"

"You'll see. You'll like him."

"It was a dumb question anyway. If he's someone you like, then he plays the saxophone."

Harry smiled, more to himself than her. He was happy to know he had a date. Being alone on New Year's Eve bothered him more than Christmas, Thanksgiving, any of the other days. New Year's Eve was a night for jazz, and the saxophone could cut you in half if you were alone.

She smiled and said, "Harry, you're so easy when it comes to lonely women."

He thought of Sylvia Moore, remembering her sad smile.

"So," Teresa said, seeming to sense that he was drifting away. "I bet you want to know about the bugs inside Juan Doe #67."

"Finish your soup first."

"Nope, that's okay. It doesn't bother me. I always get hungry, in fact, after a long day chopping up bodies."

She smiled. She said things like that often, as if daring him not to like what she did for a living. He knew she was still hooked by her husband. It didn't matter what she said. He understood.

"Well, I hope you don't miss the knives when they make you permanent chief. You'll be cutting budgets then."

"No, I'd be a hands-on chief. I'd handle the specials. Like today. But after today, I don't know if they'll ever make me permanent."

Harry sensed that now he was the one who had shaken a bad feeling loose and sent her traveling with it. Now might be the right time.

"You want to talk about it?"

"No. I mean I do, but I can't. I trust you, Harry, but I think I have to keep this close for the time being."

He nodded and let it go, but he intended to come back to it later and find out what had gone wrong on the Moore autopsy. He took his notebook out of his coat pocket and put it on the table.

"Okay, then, tell me about Juan Doe #67."

She pushed the soup bowl to the side of the table and pulled a leather briefcase onto her lap. She pulled out a thin manila file and opened it in front of her.

"Okay. This is a copy so you can keep it when I'm done explaining. I went over the notes and everything else Salazar had on this. I guess you know, cause of death was multiple blunt-force trauma to the head. Crushing blows to the frontal, parietal, sphenoid and supraorbital."

As she described these injuries she touched the top of her forehead, the back of her head, her left temple and rim of her left eye. She did not look up from the paperwork.

"Any one of these was fatal. There were other defensive wounds which you can look at later. Um, he extracted wood splinters from two of the head injuries. Looks like you are talking about something like a baseball bat, but not as wide, I think. Tremendous crushing blows, so I think we are talking about something with some leverage. Not a stick. Bigger. A pick handle, shovel, something like — possibly a pool cue. But most likely something unfinished. Like I said, Sally pulled splinters out of the wounds. I'm not sure a pool cue with a sanded and lacquered finish would leave splinters."

She studied the notes a moment.

"The other thing — I don't know if Porter told you this, but this body most likely was dumped in that location. Time of death is at least six hours before discovery. Judging by the traffic in that alley and to the rear door of the restaurant, that body could not have gone unnoticed there for six hours. It had to have been dumped."

"Yeah, that was in his notes."

"Good."

She started turning through the pages. Briefly looking at the autopsy photos and putting them to the side.

"Okay, here it is. Tox results aren't back yet but the colors of the blood and liver indicate there will be nothing there. I'm just guessing — or, rather, Sally is just guessing, so don't hold us to that."

Harry nodded. He hadn't taken any notes yet. He lit a cigarette and she didn't seem to mind. She had never protested before, though once when he was attending an autopsy she walked in from the adjoining suite and showed him a lung from a forty-year-old, three-pack-a-day man. It looked like an old black loafer that had been run over by a truck.

"But as you know is routine," she continued, "we took swabs and did the analysis on the stomach contents. First, in the earwax we found a kind of brown dust. We combed some of it out of the hair, and got some from the fingernails, too."

Bosch thought of tar heroin, an ingredient in black ice.

"Heroin?"

"Good guess, but no."

"Just brown dust."

Bosch was writing in his notebook now.

"Yeah, we put it on some slides and blew it up and as near as we can tell it's wheat. Wheat dust. It's — it apparently is pulverized wheat."

"Like cereal? He had cereal in his ears and hair?"

A waiter in a white shirt and black tie with a brush mustache and his best dour Russian look came to the table to ask if they wanted anything else. He looked at the stack of photos next to Teresa. On top was one of Juan Doe #67 naked on a stainless steel table. Teresa quickly covered it with the file and Harry ordered two more beers. The man walked slowly away from the table.

"You mean some kind of wheat cereal?" Bosch asked again. "Like the dust at the bottom of the box or something?"

"Not exactly. Keep that thought, though, and let me move on. It will all tie up."

He waved her on.

"On the nasal swabs and stomach content, two things came up that are very interesting. It's kind of why I like what I do, despite other people not liking it for me." She looked up from the file and smiled at him. "Anyway, in the stomach contents, Salazar identified coffee and masticated rice, chicken, bell pepper, various spices and pig intestine. To make a long story short, it was chorizo — Mexican sausage. The intestine used as sausage casing leads me to believe it was some kind of homemade sausage, not manufactured product. He had eaten this shortly before death. There had been almost no breakdown in the stomach yet. He may've even been eating when he was assaulted. I mean, the throat and mouth were clear but there was still debris in the teeth.

"And by the way, they were all original teeth. No dental work at all — ever. You getting the picture that this man was not from around here?"

Bosch nodded, remembering Porter's notes said all of Juan Doe #67's clothing was made in Mexico. He was writing in the notebook.

She said, "There was also this in the stomach."

She slid a Polaroid photograph across the table. It was of a pinkish insect with one wing missing and the other broken. It looked wet, as indeed it would be, considering where it had been found. It lay on a glass culture dish next to a dime. The dime was about ten times the size of the bug.

Harry noticed the waiter standing about ten feet away with two mugs of beer. The man held the mugs up and raised his eyebrows. Bosch signaled that it was safe to approach. The waiter put the glasses down, stole a glance at the bug photo and then moved quickly away. Harry slid the photo back to Teresa.

"So what is it?"

"*Trypetid*," she said, and she smiled.

"Shoot, I was about to guess that," he said.

She laughed at the lame joke.

"It's a fruit fly, Harry. Mediterranean variety. The little bug that lays big waste to the California citrus industry? Salazar came to me to send it out on referral because we had no idea what it was. I had an investigator take it over to UCLA to an entomologist Gary suggested. He identified it for us."

Gary, Bosch knew, was her estranged, soon to be ex-husband. He nodded at what she was telling him but was not seeing the significance of the find.

She said, "We go on to the nasal swabs. Okay, there was more wheat dust and then we found this."

She slid another photo across the table. This was also a photo of a culture dish with a dime in it. There was also a small pinkish-brown line near the dime. This was much smaller than the fly in the first photo, but Bosch could tell it was also some kind of insect.

"And this?" he asked.

"Same thing, my entomologist tells me. Only this is a youngun. This is a larva."

She folded her fingers together and pointed her elbows out. She smiled and waited.

"You love this, don't you?" he said. He drafted off a quarter of his beer. "Okay, you got me. What's it all mean?"

"Well, you have a basic understanding of the fruit fly right? It chews up the citrus crop, can bring the entire industry to its knees, umpty-ump millions lost, no orange juice in the morning, et cetera, et cetera, the decline of civilization as we know it. Right?"

He nodded and she went on, talking very quickly.

"Okay, we seem to have an annual medfly infestation here. I'm sure you've seen the quarantine signs on the freeways or heard the helicopters spraying malathion at night."

"They make me dream of Vietnam," Harry said.

"You must have also seen or read about the movement against malathion spraying. Some people say it poisons people as well as these bugs. They want it stopped. So, what's a Department of Agriculture to do? Well, one thing is step up the other procedure they use to get these bugs.

"The USDA and state Medfly Eradication Project release billions of sterile medflies all across southern California. Millions every week. See, the idea is that when the ones that are already out there mate, they'll do it with sterile partners and eventually the infestation will die out because less and less are reproduced. It's mathematical, Harry. End of problem — if they can saturate the region with enough sterile flies."

She stopped there but Bosch still didn't get it.

"Geez, this is all really fantastic, Teresa. But does it get to a point eventually or are we just —"

"I'm getting there. I'm getting there. Just listen. You are a detective. Detectives are supposed to listen. You once told me that solving murders was getting people to talk and just listening to them. Well, I'm telling it."

He held his hands up. She went on.

"The flies released by the USDA are dyed when they are in the larval stage. Dyed pink, so they can keep track of them or quickly separate the sterile ones from the nonsterile ones when they check those little traps they have in orange trees all over the place. After the larvae are dyed pink, they are irradiated to make them sterile. Then they get released."

Harry nodded. It was beginning to sound interesting.

"My entomologist examined the two samples taken from Juan Doe #67 and this is what he found." She referred to some notes in the file. "The adult fly obtained from the deceased's stomach was both dyed and sterilized, female. Okay, nothing unusual about that. Like I said, they release something like three hundred million of these a week — billions over the year — and so it would seem probable that one might be accidentally swallowed by our man if he was anywhere in, say, southern California."

"That narrows it down," Bosch said. "What about the other sample?"

"The larva is different." She smiled again. "Dr. Braxton, that's the bug doctor, said the larval specimen was dyed pink as to USDA specifications. But it had not yet been irradiated — sterilized — when it went up our Juan Doe's nose."

She unfolded her hands and put them down at her sides. Her factual report was concluded. Now it was time to speculate and she was giving him the first shot.

"So inside his body he has two dyed flies, one sterilized and one not sterilized," Bosch said. "That would lead me to conclude that shortly before his death, our boy was at the location where these flies are sterilized. Millions of flies around. One or two could have gotten in his food. He could have breathed one in through the nose. Anything like that."

She nodded.

"What about the wheat dust? In the ears and hair."

"The wheat dust is the food, Harry. Braxton said that is the food used in the breeding process."

He said, "So I need to find where they make, where they breed, these sterile flies. They might have a line on Juan Doe. Sounds like he was a breeder or something."

She smiled and said, "Why don't you ask me where they breed them."

"Where do they do it, Teresa?"

"Well, the trick is to breed them where they are already a part of the natural insect population or environment and therefore not a problem in case some happen to slip out the door before getting their dose of radiation.

"And, so, the USDA contracts with breeders in only two places; Hawaii and Mexico. In Hawaii there are three breeding contractors on Oahu. In Mexico there is a breeder down near Zihuatenejo and the largest of all five is located near —"

"Mexicali."

"Harry! How did you know? Did you already know all of this and let me —"

"It was just a guess. It fits with something else I've been working on."

She looked at him oddly and for a moment he was sorry he had spoiled her fun. He drained his beer mug and looked around for the squeamish waiter.

10

She drove him back to get his car near the Red Wind and then followed him out of downtown and up to his home in the hills. She lived in a condo in Hancock Park, which was closer, but she said she had been spending too much time there lately and wanted a chance to see or hear the coyote. He knew her real reason was that it would be easier for her to extricate herself from his place than to ask him to leave hers.

Bosch didn't mind, though. The truth was, he felt uncomfortable at her place. It reminded him too much of what L.A. was coming to. It was a fifth-floor loft with a view of downtown in a historic residence building called the Warfield. The exterior of the building was still as beautiful as the day in 1911 it was completed by George Allan Hancock. Beaux Arts architecture with a blue-gray terra-cotta facade. George hadn't spared the oil money and from the street the Warfield, with its fleurs-de-lys and cartouches, showed it. But it was the interior — the current interior, that is — that Bosch found objectionable. The place had been bought a few years back by a Japanese firm and completely gutted, then retrofitted, renovated and revamped. The walls in each apartment were knocked down and each place was nothing but a long, sterile room with fake wood floors, stainless-steel counters and track lighting. Just a pretty shell, Bosch thought. He had a feeling George would've thought the same.

At Harry's house they talked while he lit the hibachi on the porch and put an orange roughy filet on the grill. He had bought it Christmas Eve and it was still fresh and large enough to split. Teresa told him the County Commission would probably informally decide before New Year's on a permanent chief medical examiner. He wished her good luck but privately wasn't sure he meant it. It was a political appointment and she would have to toe the line. Why get into that box? He changed the subject.

"So, if this guy, this Juan Doe, was down in Mexicali — near where they make these fruit flies — how do you think his body got all the way up here?"

"That's not my department," Teresa said.

She was at the railing, staring out over the Valley. There were a million lights glinting in the crisp, cool air. She was wearing his jacket over her shoulders. Harry glazed the fish with a pineapple barbecue sauce and then turned it over.

"It's warm over here by the fire," he said. He dawdled a bit over the filet and then said, "I think what it was is that maybe they didn't want anybody checking around that USDA contractor's business. You know? They didn't want that body connected to that place. So they take the guy's body far away."

"Yeah, but all the way to L.A.?"

"Maybe they were . . . well, I don't know. That is pretty far away."

They were both silent with their thoughts for a few moments. Bosch could hear and smell the pineapple sizzling as it dripped on the coals. He said, "How do you smuggle a dead body across the border?"

"Oh, I think they've smuggled larger things than that across, don't you?"

He nodded.

"Ever been down there, Harry, to Mexicali?"

"Just to drive through on my way to Bahia San Felipe, where I went fishing last summer. I never stopped. You?"

"Never."

"You know the name of the town just across the border? On our side?"

"Uh uh."

"Calexico."

"You're kidding? Is that where —"

"Yup."

The fish was done. He forked it onto a plate, put the cover on the grill and they went inside. He served it with Spanish rice he made with Pico Pico. He opened a bottle of red wine and poured two glasses. Blood of the gods. He didn't have any white. As he put everything on the table he saw a smile on her face.

"Thought I was a TV dinner guy, didn't you?"

"Crossed my mind. This is very nice."

They clicked glasses and ate quietly. She complimented him on the meal but he knew the fish was a little too dry. They descended into small talk again. The whole time he was looking for the opening to ask her about the Moore autopsy. It didn't come until they were finished.

"What will you do now?" she asked after putting her napkin on the table.

"Guess I'll clear the table and see if —"

"No. You know what I mean. About the Juan Doe case."

"I'm not sure. I want to talk to Porter again. And I'll probably look up the USDA. I'd like to know more about how those flies get here from Mexico."

She nodded and said, "Let me know if you want to talk to the entomologist. I can arrange that."

He watched her as she once again got the far-off stare that had been intruding all night.

"What about you?" he asked. "What will you do now?"

"About what?"

"About the problems with the Moore autopsy."

"That obvious, huh?"

He got up and cleared the plates away. She didn't move from the table. He sat back down and emptied the bottle into the glasses. He decided he would have to give her something in order for her to feel comfortable giving him something in return.

"Listen to me, Teresa. I think you and I should talk about things. I think we have two investigations, probably three investigations, here, that may all be part of the same thing. Like different spokes on the same wheel."

She brought her eyes up, confused. "What cases? What are you talking about?"

"I know that all of what I'm about to say is outside your venue but I think you need to know it to help make your decision. I've been watching you all night and I can tell you have a problem and don't know what to do."

He hesitated, giving her a chance to stop him. She didn't. He told her about Marvin Dance's arrest and its relation to the Jimmy Kapps murder.

"When I found out Kapps had been bringing ice over from Hawaii, I went to Cal Moore to ask about black ice. You know, the competition. I wanted to know where it comes from, where you get it, who's selling it, anything that would help me get a picture of who might've put down Jimmy Kapps. Anyway, the point is I thought Moore shined me on, said he knew nothing, but today I find out he was putting together a file on black ice. He was gathering string on my case. He held stuff back from me, but at the same time was putting something together on this when he disappeared. I got the file today. There was a note. It said 'Give to Harry Bosch' on it."

"What was in it? The file."

"A lot. Including an intelligence report, says the main source of black ice is probably a ranch down in Mexicali."

She stared at him but said nothing.

"Which brings us to our Juan Doe. Porter bails out and the case comes to me today. I am reading through the file and I'll give you one guess who it was that found the body and then disappeared the next day."

"Shit," she said.

"Exactly. Cal Moore. What this means I don't know. But he is the reporting officer on the body. The next day he is in the wind. The next week he is found in a motel room, a supposed suicide. And then the next day — after the discovery of Moore has been in the papers and on TV — Porter calls up and says, 'Guess what, guys, I quit.' Does all of this sound aboveboard to you?"

She abruptly stood up and walked to the sliding door to the porch. She stared through the glass out across the pass.

"Those bastards," she said. "They just want to drop the whole thing. Because it might embarrass somebody."

Bosch walked up behind her.

"You have to tell somebody about it. Tell me."

"No. I can't. You tell me everything."

"I've told you. There isn't much else and it's all a jumble. The file didn't have much, other than that the DEA told Moore that black ice is coming up from Mexicali. That's how I guessed about the fruit fly contractor. And then there's Moore. He grew up in Calexico and Mexicali. You see? There are too many coincidences here that I don't think are coincidences."

She still faced the door and he was talking to her back, but he saw the reflection of her worried face in the glass. He could smell her perfume.

"The important thing about the file is that Moore didn't keep it in his office or his apartment. It was in a place where someone from IAD or RHD wouldn't find it. And when the guys on his crew found it, there was the note that said to give it to me. You understand?"

The confused look in the glass answered for her. She turned and moved into the living room, sitting on the cushioned chair and running her hands through her hair. Harry stayed standing and paced on the wood floor in front of her.

"Why would he write a note saying give the file to me? It wouldn't have been a note to himself. He already knew he was putting the file together for me. So, the note was for someone else. And what does that tell us? That he either knew when he wrote it that he was going to kill himself. Or he —"

"Knew he was going to be killed," she said.

Bosch nodded. "Or, at least, he knew he had gotten into something too deep. That he was in trouble. In danger."

"Jesus," she said.

Harry approached and handed her her wineglass. He bent down close to her face.

"You have to tell me about the autopsy. Something's wrong. I heard that bullshit press release they put out. Inconclusive. What is that shit? Since when can't you tell if a shotgun blast to the face killed somebody or not?

"So tell me, Teresa. We can figure out what to do."

She shrugged her shoulders and shook her head, but Harry knew she was going to tell.

"They told me because I wasn't a hundred percent — Harry, you can't reveal where you got this information. You can't."

"It won't get back to you. If I have to, I will use it to help us, but it won't get back to you. That's my promise."

"They told me not to discuss it with anyone because I couldn't be completely sure. The assistant chief, Irving, that arrogant prick knew just where to stick it in. Talking about the County Commission deciding soon about my position. Saying they would be looking for a chief ME who knew discretion. Saying what friends he had on the commission. I'd like to take a scalpel —"

"Never mind all of that. What was it you weren't one hundred percent sure about?"

She drained her wineglass. Then the story came out. She told him that the autopsy had proceeded as routine, other than the fact that in addition to the two case detectives observing it, Sheehan and Chastain from IAD, was assistant police chief Irving. She said a lab technician was also on hand to make the fingerprint comparisons.

"The decomposition was extensive," Teresa said. "I had to take the fingertips off and spray them with a chemical hardening agent. Collins, that's my lab tech, was able to take prints after that. He made the comparison right there because Irving had brought exemplars. It was a match. It was Moore."

"What about the teeth?"

"Dental was tough. There wasn't much left that hadn't been fragged. We made a comparison between a partial incisor found in the tub and some dental records Irving came up with. Moore had had a root canal and it was there. That was a match, too."

She said she began the autopsy after confirming the identity and immediately concluded the obvious: that damage from the double-barrel-shotgun blast was massive and fatal. Instantly. But it was while examining the material that had separated from the body that she began to question whether she could rule Moore's death a suicide.

"The force of the blast resulted in complete cranial displacement," she said. "And, of course, the autopsy protocol calls for examination of all vital organs, including the brain.

"Problem was the brain was mostly unmassed due to the wide projectile pattern. I believe I was told the pellets came from a double-barrel, side-by-side configuration. I could see that. The projectile pattern was very wide. Nevertheless, a large portion of the frontal lobe and corresponding skull fragment were left largely intact, though it had been separated.

"You know what I mean? The diagram said this had been charted in the bathtub. Is this . . . too much? I know you knew him."

"Not that well. Go on."

"So I examined this piece, not really expecting anything more than what I was seeing earlier. But I was wrong. There was hemorrhagic demarcation in the lobe along the skull lining."

She took a hit off his wineglass and breathed heavily, as if casting out a demon.

"And so, you see Harry, that was a big fucking problem."

"Tell me why."

"You sound like Irving. 'Tell me why. Tell me why.' Well, it should be obvious. For two reasons. First of all you don't have that much hemorrhage on instant death like that. There is not much bleeding in the brain lining when the brain has been literally disconnected from the body in a split second. But while there is some room for some debate on that — I'll give that to Irving — there is no debate whatsoever on the second reason. This hemorrhaging was clearly indicative of a contre-coup injury to the head. No doubt in my mind at all."

Harry quickly reviewed the physics he had learned over the ten years he had been watching autopsies. Contre-coup brain injury is damage that occurs to the side of the brain opposite the insult. The brain, in effect, was a Jell-O mold inside the skull. A jarring blow to the left side often did its worst damage to the right side because the force of impact pushed the Jell-O against the right side of the skull. Harry knew that for Moore to have the hemorrhage Teresa described to the front of the brain, he would have to be struck from behind. A shotgun blast to the face would not have done it.

"Is there any way . . . ," he trailed off, unclear of what he wanted to ask. He suddenly became aware of his body's pangs for a cigarette and smacked the end of a fresh pack on his palm.

"What happened?" he asked as he opened it.

"Well, when I started explaining, Irving got all uptight and kept asking, 'Are you sure? Is that a hundred percent accurate? Aren't we jumping the gun?' and on and on like that. I think it was pretty clear. He didn't want this to be anything other than a suicide. The minute I raised a doubt he started talking about jumping to conclusions and the need to move slowly. He said the department could be embarrassed by what an investigation could lead to if we did not proceed slowly and cautiously and correctly. Those were his words. Asshole."

"Let sleeping dogs lie," Bosch said.

"Right. So I just flat-out told them I was not going to rule it a suicide. And then . . . then they talked me out of ruling it a homicide. So that's where the inconclusive comes from. A compromise. For now. It makes me feel like I am guilty of something. Those bastards."

"They're just going to drop it," Bosch said.

He couldn't figure it out. The reluctance had to be because of the IAD investigation. Whatever Moore was into, Irving must believe it either led him to kill himself or got him killed. And either way Irving didn't want to open that box without knowing first what was in it. Maybe he never wanted to know. That told Bosch one thing: he was on his own. No matter what he came up with, turning it over to Irving and RHD would get it buried. So if Bosch went on with it, he was freelancing.

"Do they know that Moore was working on something for you?" Teresa asked.

"By now they do, but they probably didn't when they were with you. Probably won't make any difference."

"What about the Juan Doe case? About him finding the body."

"I don't know what they know on that."

"What will you do?"

"I don't know. I don't know anything. What will you do?"

She was silent for a long time, then she got up and walked to him. She leaned into him and kissed him on the lips. She whispered, "Let's forget about all of this for a while."

He conceded to her in their lovemaking, letting her lead and direct him, use his body the way she wanted. They had been together often enough so that they were comfortable and knew each other's ways. They were beyond the stages of curiosity or embarrassment. At the end, she was straddled over him as he leaned back, propped on pillows, against the headboard. Her head snapped back and her clipped nails dug painlessly into his chest. She made no sound at all.

In the darkness he looked up and saw the glint of silver dripping from her ears. He reached up and touched the earrings and then ran his hands down her throat, over her shoulders and breasts. Her skin was warm and damp. Her slow methodical motion drew him further into the void where everything else in the world could not go.

When they were both resting, she still huddled on top of him, a sense of guilt came over him. He thought of Sylvia Moore. A woman he had met only the night before, how could she intrude on this? But she had. He wondered where the guilt came from. Maybe it was for what was still ahead of them.

He thought he heard the short, high-pitched bark of the coyote in the distance behind the house. Teresa raised her head off his chest and then they heard the animal's lonesome baying.

"Timido," he heard her say quietly.

Harry felt the guilt pass over him again. He thought of Teresa. Had he tricked her into telling him? He didn't think so. Maybe, again, it was guilt over what he had not yet done. What he knew he would do with the information she had given.

She seemed to know his thoughts were away from her. Perhaps a change in his heartbeat, a slight tensing in his muscles.

"Nothing," she said.

"What?"

"You asked what I was going to do. Nothing. I'm not going to get involved in this bullshit any further. If they want to bury it, let them bury it."

Harry knew then that she would make a good permanent chief medical examiner for the county of Los Angeles.

He felt himself falling away from her in the dark.

Teresa rolled off him and sat on the edge of the bed, looking out the window at the three-quarter moon. They had left the curtain open. The coyote howled once more. Bosch thought he could hear a dog answering somewhere in the distance.

"Are you like him?" she asked.

"Who?"

"Timido. Alone out there in the dark world."

"Sometimes. Everybody is sometimes."

"Yes, but you like it, don't you?"

"Not always."

"Not always . . ."

He thought about what to say. The wrong word and she'd be gone.

"I'm sorry if I'm distant," he tried. "There's a lot of things . . ."

He didn't finish. There was no excuse.

"You do like living up here in this little, lonely house, with the coyote as your only friend, don't you?"

He didn't answer. The face of Sylvia Moore inexplicably came back into his mind. But this time he felt no guilt. He liked seeing her there.

"I have to go," Teresa said. "Long day tomorrow."

He watched her walk naked into the bathroom, picking her purse up off the night table as she went. He listened as the shower ran. He imagined her in there, cleaning all traces of him off and out of her and then splashing on the all-purpose perfume she always carried in her purse to cover up any smells left on her from her job.

He rolled to the side of the bed to the pile of his clothes on the floor and got out his phone book. He dialed while the water still ran. The voice that answered was dulled with sleep. It was near midnight.

"You don't know who this is and I never talked to you."

There was silence while Harry's voice registered.

"Okay, okay. Got it. I understand."

"There's a problem on the Cal Moore autopsy."

"Shit, I know that, man. Inconclusive. You don't have to wake me up to —"

"No, you don't understand. You are confusing the autopsy with the press release on the autopsy. Two different things. Understand now?"

"Yeah . . . I think I do. So, what's the problem?"

"The assistant chief of police and the acting chief ME don't agree. One says suicide, the other homicide. Can't have both. I guess that's what you call inconclusive in a press release."

There was a low whistling sound in the phone.

"This is good. But why would the cops want to bury a homicide, especially one of their own? I mean, suicide makes the department look like shit as it is. Why bury a murder unless it means there's something —"

"Right," Bosch said and he hung up the phone.

A minute later the shower was turned off and Teresa came out, drying herself with a towel. She was totally unabashed about her nakedness with him and Harry found he missed that shyness. It had eventually left all the women he became involved with before they eventually left him.

He pulled on blue jeans and a T-shirt while she dressed. Neither spoke. She looked at him with a thin smile and then he walked her out to her car.

"So, we still have a date for New Year's Eve?" she asked after he opened the car door for her.

"Of course," he said, though he knew she would call with an excuse to cancel it.

She leaned up and kissed him on the lips, then slipped into the driver's seat.

"Good-bye, Teresa," he said, but she had already closed the door.

It was midnight when he came back inside. The place smelled of her perfume. And his own guilt. He put Frank Morgan's *Mood Indigo* on the CD player and stood there in the living room without moving, just listening to the phrasing on the first solo, a song called "Lullaby." Bosch thought he knew nothing truer than the sound of a saxophone.

11

Sleep was not a possibility. Bosch knew this. He stood on the porch looking down on the carpet of lights and let the chill air harden his skin and his resolve. For the first time in months he felt invigorated. He was in the hunt again. He let everything about the cases pass through his mind and made a mental list of people he had to see and things he had to do.

On top was Lucius Porter, the broken-down detective whose pullout was too timely, too coincidental to be coincidental. Harry realized he was becoming angry just thinking about Porter. And embarrassed. Embarrassed at having stuck his neck out for him with Pounds.

He went to his notebook and then dialed Porter's number one more time. He was not expecting an answer and he wasn't disappointed. Porter had at least been reliable in that respect. He checked the address he had written down earlier and headed out.

Driving down out of the hills he did not pass another car until he reached Cahuenga. He headed north and got on the Hollywood Freeway at Barham. The freeway was crowded but not so that traffic was slow. The cars moved northward at a steady clip, a sleekly moving ribbon of lights. Out over Studio City, Bosch could see a police helicopter circling, a shaft of white light cast downward on a crime scene somewhere. It almost seemed as if the beam was a leash that held the circling craft from flying high and away.

He loved the city most at night. The night hid many of the sorrows. It silenced the city yet brought deep undercurrents to the surface. It was in this dark slipstream that he believed he moved most freely. Behind the cover of shadows. Like a rider in a limousine, he looked out but no one looked in.

There was a random feel to the dark, the quirkiness of chance played out in the blue neon night. So many ways to live. And to die. You could be riding in the back of a studio's black limo, or just as easily the back of the coroner's blue van. The sound of applause was the same as the buzz of a bullet spinning past your ear in the dark. That randomness. That was L.A.

There was flash fire and flash flood, earthquake, mudslide. There was the drive-by shooter and the crack-stoked burglar. The drunk driver and the always curving road ahead. There were killer cops and cop killers. There was the husband of the woman you were sleeping with. And there was the woman. At any moment on any night there were people being raped, violated, maimed. Murdered and loved. There was always a baby at his mother's breast. And, sometimes, a baby alone in a Dumpster.

Somewhere.

Harry exited on Vanowen in North Hollywood and went east toward Burbank. Then he turned north again into a neighborhood of rundown apartments. Bosch could tell by the gang graffiti it was a mostly Latino neighborhood. He knew Porter had lived here for years. It was all he could afford after paying alimony and for his booze.

He turned into the Happy Valley Trailer Park and found Porter's double-wide at the end of Greenbriar Lane. The trailer was dark, not even a light on above the door, and there was no car under the aluminum-roofed carport. Bosch sat in his car smoking a cigarette and watching for a while. He heard mariachi music wafting into the neighborhood from one of the Mexican clubs over on Lankershim. Soon it was drowned out by a jet that lumbered by overhead on its way to Burbank Airport. He reached into the glove compartment for a leather pouch containing his flashlight and picks and got out.

After the third knock went unanswered, Harry opened the pouch. Breaking into Porter's place did not give him pause. Porter was a player in this game, not an innocent. To Bosch's mind, Porter had forfeited protection of his privacy when he had not been straight with him, when he hadn't mentioned that Moore had been the one who found Juan Doe #67's body. Now Bosch was going to find Porter and ask him about that.

He took out the miniature flashlight, turned it on and then held it in his mouth as he stooped down and worked a pick and tiny pressure wrench into the lock. It took him only a few minutes to push the pins and open the door.

A sour odor greeted Bosch when he entered. He recognized it as the smell of a drunk's sweat. He called Porter's name but got no answer.

He turned on the lights as he moved through the rooms. There were empty glasses on nearly every horizontal surface. The bed was unmade and the sheets were a dingy white. Amidst the glasses on the night table was an ashtray overloaded with butts. There was also a statue of a saint Bosch could not identify. In the bathroom off the bedroom, the bathtub was filthy, a toothbrush was on the floor and in the wastebasket there was an empty bottle of whiskey, a brand either so expensive or so cheap that Harry had never heard of it. But he suspected it was the latter.

In the kitchen, there was another empty bottle in the trash can. There were also dirty dishes piled on the counters and sink. He opened the refrigerator and saw only a jar of mustard and an egg carton. Porter's place was very much like its owner. It showed a marginal life, if it could be called that at all.

Back in the living room Bosch picked a framed photograph up off a table next to a yellow couch. It was a woman. Not too attractive, except to Porter maybe. An ex-wife he couldn't get over. Maybe. Harry put the photo back down and the phone rang.

He traced the noise to the bedroom. The phone was on the floor next to the bed. He picked up on the seventh ring, waited a moment and in a voice designed to appear jerked from sleep said, "Huh?"

"Porter?"

"Yeah."

The line went dead. It hadn't worked. But had Bosch recognized the voice? Pounds? No, not Pounds. Only one word spoken. But, still, the accent was there. Spanish, he thought. He filed it away in his mind and got up off the bed. Another plane crossed above and the trailer shuddered. He went back into the living room where he made a half-hearted search of a one-drawer desk, though he knew that no matter what he found it wouldn't solve the immediate problem: where was Porter?

Bosch turned all the lights off and relocked the front door as he left. He decided to start in North Hollywood and work his way south toward downtown. In every police division there was a handful of bars that carried a heavy clientele of cops. Then after two, when they closed, there were the all-night bottle clubs. Mostly they were dark pits where men came to drink hard and quietly, as if their lives depended on it. They were havens from the street, places to go to forget and forgive yourself. It was at one of these Bosch believed he would find Porter.

He began with a place on Kittridge called the Parrot. But the bartender, a one-time cop himself, said he hadn't seen Porter since Christmas Eve. Next, he went to the 502 on Lankershim and then Saint's on Cahuenga. They knew Porter in these places but he hadn't been at either tonight.

It went like that until two. By then, Bosch had worked his way down into Hollywood. He was sitting in his car in front of the Bullet, trying to think of nearby bottle-club locations, when his pager went off. He checked the number and didn't recognize it. He went back into the Bullet to use the pay phone. The lights in the bar came on after he dialed. Last call was over.

"Bosch?"

"Yeah."

"It's Rickard. Bad time?"

"Nah. I'm at the Bullet."

"Hell, man, then you're close by."

"For what? You got Dance?"

"Nah, not quite. I'm at a rave behind Cahuenga and south of the boulevard. Couldn't sleep so I thought I'd do some hunting. No Dance but I got my eye on one of his old salesmen. One of the ones that was on the shake cards in the file. Name's Kerwin Tyge."

Bosch thought a moment. He remembered the name. He was one of the juvies the BANG team had stopped and checked out, tried to scare off the street. His name was on one of the file cards in the ice file Moore had left behind.

"What's a rave?"

"An underground. They got a warehouse off this alley. A fly-by-night party. Digital music. They'll run all night, 'til about six. Next week it will be somewhere else."

"How'd you find it?"

"They're easy to find. The record stores on Melrose put out the phone numbers. You call the number, get on the list. Twenty bucks to get in. Get stoned and dance 'til dawn."

"He selling black ice?"

"Nah, he's selling sherms out front."

A sherm was a cigarette dipped in liquid PCP. Went for twenty bucks a dip and would leave its smoker dusted all night. Tyge apparently was no longer working for Dance.

"I figure we can make a righteous bust," Rickard said. "After that, we might squeeze Dance out of his ass. I think Dance has blown, but the kid might know where. It's up to you. I don't know how important Dance is to you."

"Where do you want me?" Bosch asked.

"Come west on the Boulevard and just when you pass Cahuenga come south at the very next alley. The one that comes down behind the porno shops. It's dark but you'll see the blue neon arrow. That's the place. I'm about a half block north in a red piece-of-shit Camaro. Nevada plates. I'll be waiting. Hafta figure out a scam or something to grab him with the shit."

"You know where the dip is?"

"Yeah. He's got it in a beer bottle in the gutter. Keeps going in and out. Brings his clients outside. I'll think of something by the time you get here."

Bosch hung up and went back out to the car. It took him fifteen minutes to get there because of all the cruisers on the Boulevard. In the alley he parked illegally behind the red Camaro. He could see Rickard sitting low in the driver's seat.

"Top of the morning to ya," the narc said when Bosch slipped into the Camaro's passenger seat.

"Same. Our boy still around?"

"Oh, yeah. Seems like he's having a good night, too. He's selling shermans like they're the last thing on earth. Too bad we gotta spoil his fun."

Bosch looked down the dark alley. In the intervals of blue light cast by a blinking neon arrow he could see a grouping of people in dark clothes in front of a door in the brick siding of the warehouse. Occasionally, the door would open and someone would go in or come out. He could hear the music when the door was open. Loud, techno-rock, a driving bass that seemed to shake the street. As his eyes adjusted, he saw that the people outside were drinking and smoking, cooling off after dancing. A few of them held blown-up balloons. They would lean on the hoods of the cars near the door, suck from the balloon and pass it on as if it were a joint.

"The balloons are full of nitrous oxide," Rickard said.

"Laughing gas?"

"Right. They sell it at these raves for five bucks a balloon. They can make a couple of grand off one tank stolen from a hospital or dentist."

A girl fell off a car hood and her balloon of gas shot away into the dark. Others helped her up. Bosch could hear their shrieks of laughter.

"That legal?"

"It's a flopper. It's legal to process — a lot of legit uses for it. But it's a misdee to consume recreationally. We don't even bother with it, though. Somebody wants to suck on it and fall down and split their head open, have at it, I say. Why should — there he is now."

The slight figure of a teenager walked through the warehouse door and over to the cars parked along the alley.

"Watch him go down," Rickard said.

The figure disappeared behind a car, dropping down.

"See, he's making a dip. Now he'll wait a few minutes 'til it dries a little and his customer comes out. Then he'll make the deal."

"Want to go get him?"

"No. We take him with just the one sherm, that's nothing. That's personal possession. They won't even keep him overnight in the drunk tank. We need him with his dip if we wanna squeeze him good."

"So what do we do?"

"You just get back in your car. I want you to go back around on Cahuenga and come up the alley the other way. I think you can get in closer. Park it and then try to work your way up to be my backup. I'll come down from this end. I got some old clothes in the trunk. Undercover shit. I got a plan."

Bosch then went back to the Caprice, turned it around and drove out of the alley. He drove around the block and came up from the south side. He found a spot in front of a Dumpster and stopped. When he saw the hunched-over figure of Rickard moving down the alley, Harry got out and started moving. They were closing in on the warehouse door from both sides. But while Bosch remained in the shadows, Rickard — now wearing a grease-stained sweatshirt and carrying a bag of laundry — was walking down the center of the alley, singing. Because of the noise from the warehouse Bosch wasn't sure but he thought it was Percy Sledge's "When a Man Loves a Woman," delivered in a drunken slur.

Rickard had the undivided attention of the people standing outside the warehouse door. A couple of the stoned girls cheered his singing. The distraction allowed Bosch to move within four cars of the door and about three cars from the spot where Tyge had his dip.

As he passed the spot, Rickard stopped his song in mid-chorus and acted as if he had just spotted a treasure. He ducked between the two parked cars and came up with the beer bottle in hand. He was about to place it in his bag when the boy moved quickly between the cars and grabbed the bottle. Rickard refused to let go and spun so that the boy's back was now to Bosch. Harry started moving.

"It's mine, man," Rickard yelled.

"I put it there, bro. Let it go before it spills."

"Go get your own, man. This here's mine."

"Let it go!"

"You sure it's yours?"

"It's mine!"

Bosch hit the boy forcefully from behind. He let go of the bottle and doubled over the trunk of the car. Bosch kept him pinned there, pushing his forearm against the boy's neck. The bottle stayed in Rickard's hand. None of it spilled.

"Well, if you say so, I guess it's yours," the narc said. "And I guess that makes you under arrest."

Bosch pulled his cuffs off his belt and hooked the boy up and then pulled him off the trunk. Some of the others were gathering around now.

"Fuck off, people," Rickard said loudly. "Go back inside and sniff your laughing gas. Go get deaf. This here don't concern you unless you want to go along with this boy to the shit can."

He bent down to Tyge's ear and said, "Right, *bro?*"

When nobody in the crowd moved, Rickard took a menacing step toward them and they scattered. A couple of the girls ran back into the warehouse. The music drowned out Rickard's laugh. He then turned around and grabbed Tyge by the arm.

"Let's go. Harry, let's take your wheels."

They drove in silence for a while toward the station on Wilcox. They hadn't discussed it earlier but Harry was going to let Rickard make the play. Rickard was riding in the back with the boy. In the mirror, Harry saw he had greasy, unkempt brown hair that fell to his shoulders. About five years earlier he should have had braces put on his teeth but one look at him and Bosch could tell he came from a home where things like that were not a consideration. He had a gold earring and an uninterested look on his face. But the teeth were what got to Bosch. Crooked and protruding, they more than anything else showed the desperation of his life.

"How old are you now, Kerwin?" Rickard said. "And don't bother lying. We got a file on you at the station. I can check."

"Eighteen. And you can wipe your ass with the file. I don't give a shit."

"Wooo!" Rickard yelped. "Eighteen. Looks like we got ourselves an A-dult here, Harry. No holding hands all the way to the juvie hall. We'll go put this kid in seven thousand, see how quick he starts keeping house with one of the heavies."

Seven thousand was what most cops and criminals called the county adult detention center, on account of the phone number for inmate information, 555-7000. The jail was downtown and it was four floors of noise and hate and violence sitting atop the county sheriff's headquarters. Somebody was stabbed there every day. Somebody raped every hour. And nothing was ever done about it. Nobody cared, unless you were the one getting raped or stabbed. The sheriff's deputies who ran the place called it an NHI detail. No Humans Involved. Bosch knew if they were going to squeeze this kid that Rickard had picked the right way to go.

"We got you bagged and tagged, Kerwin," Rickard said. "There's at least two ounces in here. Got you cold for possession with intent to sell, dude. You're gone."

"Fuck you."

The kid drew each word out with sarcasm. He was going to go down fighting. Bosch noticed that Rickard was holding the green beer bottle outside the window so the fumes wouldn't fill the car and give them headaches.

"That's not nice, Kerwin. Especially, when the man driving here is willing to do a deal. . . . Now if it was me, I'd just let you make your deals with the brothers in seven thousand. Couple days in there and you'll be shaving your legs and walking 'round in pink underwear they dipped in the Hawaiian Punch."

"Fuck off, pig. Just get me to a phone."

They were on Sunset, coming up to Wilcox. Almost there and Rickard hadn't even gotten around to what they wanted. It didn't look as if the kid was going to deal, no matter what they wanted.

"You'll get a phone when we feel like giving you a phone. You're tough now, white boy, but it don't last. Everybody gets broken down inside. You'll see. Unless you want to help us out. We just want to talk to your pal Dance."

Bosch turned onto Wilcox. The station was two blocks away. The kid said nothing and Rickard let the silence go for a block before giving another try.

"What do you say, kid? Give an address. I'll dump this shit right now. Don't be one of those fools who think seven thousand makes them the man. Like it's some fucking rite of passage. It ain't, kid. It's just the end of the line. That what you want?"

"I want you to die."

Bosch pulled into the driveway that led to the station's rear parking lot. They would have to process the arrest here first, book the evidence, then take the kid downtown. Harry knew they would have to go through with it. The kid wasn't talking. They had to show him that they weren't bluffing.

12

Bosch didn't get back to his search for Porter until four in the morning. By then he had had two cups of coffee in the station and was holding his third. He was back in the Caprice, alone and roaming the city.

Rickard had agreed to ferry Kerwin Tyge downtown. The kid had never talked. His shell of hardened rejection, cop hate and misguided pride never cracked. At the station, it had become a mission for Rickard to break the kid. He renewed the threats, the questions, with a zeal that Bosch found disturbing. He finally told Rickard that it was over. He told the narc to book the kid and they'd try again later. After stepping out of the interview room, the two decided to meet at seven thousand at 2 P.M. That would give the kid about a ten-hour taste of the big house, enough time to make a decision.

Now Bosch was cruising the bottle clubs, the after-hour joints where "members" brought their own bottles and were charged for the setups. The setups, of course, were a ripoff, and some clubs even charged a membership fee. But some people just couldn't drink at home alone. And some people didn't have much of a home.

At a stoplight on Sunset at Western, a blur passed the car on the right and a figure lunged over the passenger side of the hood. Bosch instinctively drew his left hand up to his belt and almost dropped his coffee but then realized the man had begun to rub a newspaper on the windshield. Half past four in the morning and a homeless man was cleaning his windshield. Badly. The man's efforts only smudged the glass. Bosch pulled a dollar out of his pocket and handed it out the window to the man when he came around to do the driver's side. He waved him away.

"Don't worry about it, partner," he said and the man silently walked away.

Bosch headed off, hitting bottle clubs in Echo Park near the police academy and then Chinatown. No sign of Porter. He crossed over the Hollywood Freeway into downtown, thinking of the kid as he passed the county lockup. He'd be on seven, the narco module, where the inhabitants were generally less hostile. He'd probably be okay.

He saw the big blue trucks pulling out of the garage on the Spring Street side of the *Times* building, heading off with another morning's cargo of news. He tried a couple of bottle clubs near Parker Center, then one near skid row. He was scratching bottom now, getting near the end of the line and running out of places to check.

The last place he stopped was Poe's, which was centrally located on Third Avenue near skid row, the *Los Angeles Times,* St. Vibiana's and the glass bank towers of the financial district, where alcoholics were manufactured wholesale. Poe's did a good business in the morning hours before downtown came alive with hustle and greed.

Poe's was on the first floor of a prewar brick walkup that had been tagged for demolition by the Community Redevelopment Agency. It had not been earthquake-proofed and retrofitting it would cost more than the building was worth. The CRA had bought it and was going to knock it down to put up condos that would draw live-in residents downtown. But the whole thing was on hold. Another city agency, the Office of Preservation, wanted the Poe building, as it was informally known, granted landmark status and was suing to stop the demolition. So far they had held up the plan four years. Poe's was still open. The four floors above it were abandoned.

Inside, the place was a black hole with a long, warped bar and no tables. Poe's wasn't a place to sit in a booth with friends. It was a place to drink alone. A place for executive suicides who needed courage, broken cops who couldn't cope with the loneliness they built into their lives, writers who could no longer write and priests who could no longer forgive even their own sins. It was a place to drink mean, as long as you still had the green. It cost you five bucks for a stool at the bar and a dollar for a glass of ice to go with your bottle of whiskey. A soda setup was three bucks but most of these people took their medicine straight up. It was cheaper that way and more to the point. It was said that Poe's was not named after the writer but for the general philosophy of its clientele: Piss On Everything.

Even though it was dark outside, stepping into Poe's was like walking into a cave. For a moment, Bosch was reminded of that first moment after dropping into a VC tunnel in Vietnam. He stood utterly still by the door until his eyes focused in the dim light and he saw the red leather padding on the bar. The place smelled worse than Porter's trailer. The bartender, in a wrinkled white shirt and unbuttoned black vest, stood to the right, backed by the rows of liquor bottles, each with the bottle owner's name attached on a piece of masking tape. A red stem of neon ran along the booze shelf, behind the bottles, and gave them an eerie glow.

From the darkness to Bosch's left, he heard, "Shit, Harry, whaddaya doing? You looking for me?"

He turned and there was Porter at the other end of the bar, sitting so he could see whoever came in before they could see him. Harry walked over. He saw a shot glass in front of Porter along with a half-filled water glass and a third-filled bottle of bourbon. There was a twenty and three ones fanned out on the bar as well and a package of Camels. Bosch felt anger rising in his throat as he approached and came up on Porter's back.

"Yeah, I'm looking for you."

"Whassup?"

Bosch knew he had to do what he had to do before any sympathy could crack through his anger. He yanked Porter's sport coat down over his shoulders so his arms were caught at his sides. A cigarette dropped out of his hand to the floor. Bosch reached around and pulled the gun out of his shoulder holster and put it on the bar.

"What're you still carrying for, Lou? You pulled the pin, remember? What, you scared of something?"

"Harry, what's going on? Why are you doing this?"

The bartender started walking down behind the bar to the aid of his club member but Bosch fixed him with a cold stare, held up his hand like a traffic cop and said, "Cool it. It's private."

"Damned right. It's a private club and you ain't a member."

"It's okay, Tommy," Porter spoke up. "I know him. I'll take care of it."

A couple of men who had been sitting a few stools from Porter got up and moved to the other end of the bar with their bottles and drinks. A couple of other drunks were already down there watching. But nobody left, not with booze still in their jars and it not quite being six o'clock yet. There would be no place else to go. Bars wouldn't open until seven and the hour or so until then could last a lifetime. No, they weren't going anywhere. This crew would sit there and watch a man murdered if they had to.

"Harry, c'mon," Porter said. "Cool it yourself. We can talk."

"Can we? Can we? Why didn't you talk when I called the other day? How about Moore? Did you have a talk with Cal Moore?"

"Look, Harry —"

Bosch spun him around off the stool and face first into the wood-paneled wall. He came easier than Harry had thought he would and hit the wall hard. His nose made a sound like an ice-cream cone hitting the sidewalk. Bosch leaned his back against Porter's back, pinning him face first against the wall.

"Don't 'Look, Harry' me, Porter. I stood up for you, man, 'cause I thought you were . . . I thought you were worth it. Now I know, Porter. I was wrong. You quit on the Juan Doe. I want to know why. I want to know what's going on."

Porter's voice was muffled by the wall and his own blood. He said, "Harry, shit, I think you broke my nose. I'm bleeding."

"Don't worry about it. What about Moore? I know he reported the body."

Porter made some kind of wet snorting sound but Bosch just pushed him harder. The man stunk of sour body odor, booze and cigarettes, and Bosch wondered how long he had been sitting in Poe's, watching the door.

"I'm calling the police now," the bartender yelled. He stood holding the phone out so Bosch would see it was a real threat, which of course it wasn't. The bartender knew if he dialed that phone every stool in the bar would be left spinning as the drunks filed out. There would be no one left to scam on the change or to leave quarters for his cup.

Using his body to keep Porter pinned to the wall, Bosch pulled out his badge wallet and held it up. "I am the police. Mind your own fucking business."

The bartender shook his head as if to say what is this fine business coming to, and put the phone back next to the cash register. The announcement that Bosch was a police officer resulted in about half the other customers jerking their drinks down and leaving. There were probably warrants out for everybody in the place, Bosch thought.

Porter was starting to mumble and Bosch thought he might be crying again, like on the phone Thursday morning.

"Harry, I — I didn't think I was doing . . . I had —"

Bosch bounced harder against his back and heard Porter's forehead hit the wall.

"Don't start that shit with me, Porter. You were takin' care of yourself. That's what you were doing. And —"

"I'm sick. I'm gonna be sick."

"— and right now, believe it or not, right now the only one that really cares about you is me. You fuck, you just tell me what you did. Just tell me what you did and we're square. It goes nowhere else. You go for your stress out and I never see your face again."

Bosch could hear his wet breathing against the wall. It was almost as if he could hear him thinking.

"You sure, Harry?"

"You don't have a choice. You don't start talking, you end up with no job, no pension."

"He, uh — I just . . . there's blood on my shirt. It's roon."

Bosch pushed harder against him.

"Okay, okay, okay. I'll tell ya, I'll tell . . . I just did him a favor, thas all, and he ended up deader'n shit. When I heard, I, uh, I couldn't come back in, see. I didn't know what happened. I mean, I mean, they — somebody could be looking for me. I got scared, Harry. I'm scared. I been sitting in bars since I talked to you yesterday. I stink like shit. And now all this blood. I need a napkin. I think they're after me."

Bosch took his weight off him but held one hand pressed against his back so he would not go anywhere. He reached back to the bar and took a handful of cocktail napkins off a stack near a bowl of matches. He held them over Porter's shoulder and the broken cop worked his hand loose from his jacket and took them. He turned his head away from the wall to press the napkin to his swelling nose. Harry saw tears on his face and looked away.

The door to the bar opened then and dawn's early gray light shot into the bar. A man stood there, apparently adjusting to the darkness of the bar as Bosch had done. Bosch saw he was dark complexioned with ink-black hair. Three tattooed tears dripped down his cheek from the corner of his left eye. Harry knew he was no banker or lawyer who needed a double-scotch breakfast to start the day. He was some kind of player, maybe finishing a night collecting for the Italians or Mexicans and needing something to smooth out the edges. The man's eyes finally fell on Bosch and Porter, then to Porter's gun, which was still on the bar. The man sized up the situation and calmly and wordlessly backed out through the door.

"Fucking great," the bartender yelled. "Would you get the hell out of here. I'm losing customers. The both of you, get the fuck out."

There was a sign that said Toilet and an arrow pointing down a darkened hallway to Bosch's left. He pushed Porter that way. They turned a corner and went into the men's room, which smelled worse than Porter. There was a mop in a bucket of gray water in the corner, but the cracked tile floor was dirtier than the water. He pushed Porter toward the sink.

"Clean yourself up," Bosch said. "What was the favor? You said you did something for Moore. Tell me about it."

Porter was looking at his blurred reflection in a piece of stainless steel that was probably put in when the management got tired of replacing broken mirrors.

"It won't stop bleeding, Harry. I think it's broke."

"Forget your nose. Tell me what you did."

"I, uh — look, all he did was tell me that he knew some people that would appreciate it if the stiff behind the restaurant didn't get ID'd for a while. Just string it out, he said, for a week or two. Christ, there was no ID on the body, anyway. He said I could do the computer runs on the prints cause he knew they wouldn't bring a match. He said just take my time with it and that these people, the ones he knew, would take care of me. He said I'd get a nice Christmas present. So, I, you know, I went through the motions last week. I wouldn't have gotten anywhere with it, anyway. You know, you saw the file. No ID, no wits, no nothing. The guy'd been dead at least six hours before he got dumped there."

"So what spooked you? What happened Christmas?"

Porter blew his nose into a bouquet of paper towels and this brought more tears to his eyes.

"Yeah, it's broke. I'm not getting any air through. I gotta go to a clinic, get it set. Anyway . . . well, nothing happened Christmas. That's the thing. I mean, Moore'd been missing for almost a week and I was getting pretty nervous about the whole thing. On Christmas Moore didn't come, nobody did. Then when I'm walking home from the Lucky my neighbor in the trailer next door says to me about how real sorry she was about that dead cop they found. I said thanks and went inside and put on the radio. I hear it's Moore and that scares me shitless, Harry. It did."

Porter soaked a handful of towels and began stroking his bloodstained shirt in a manner that Bosch thought made him look more pathetic than he was. Bosch saw his empty shoulder holster and remembered he had left the gun on the bar. He was reluctant to go back and get it while Porter was talking.

"See, I knew Moore wasn't no suicide. I don't care what they're putting out at Parker. I know he didn't do himself like that. He was into something. So, I decided, that was enough. I called the union and got a lawyer. I'm outta here, Harry. I'm gonna get cleaned up and go to Vegas, maybe get in with casino security. Millie's out there with my boy. I wanna be close by."

Right, Bosch thought. And always be looking over your shoulder. He said, "You're bleeding again. Wash your face. I'm going to get some coffee. I'm taking you out of here."

Bosch moved through the door but Porter stopped him.

"Harry, you going to take care of me on this?"

Bosch looked at his damaged face a long moment before saying, "Yeah, I'll do what I can."

He walked back out to the bar and signaled the bartender, who was standing all the way down at the other end smoking a cigarette. The man, about fifty, with faded blue tattoos webbing both forearms like extra veins, took his time coming over. By then Bosch had a ten-dollar bill on the bar.

"Give me a couple coffees to go. Black. Put a lot of sugar in one of them."

"'Bout time you got outta here." The bartender nodded at the ten-dollar bill. "And I'm taking out for the napkins, too. They're not for cops who go round beat'n' on people. That oughta 'bout cover it. You can just leave that on the bar."

He poured coffee that looked like it had been sitting in the glass pot since Christmas into foam cups. Bosch went to Porter's spot at the bar and gathered up the Smith thirty-eight and the twenty-three dollars. He moved back to his ten-dollar bill and lit a cigarette.

Not realizing Bosch was now watching, the bartender poured a gagging amount of sugar into both coffees. Bosch let it slide. After snapping plastic covers on the cups, the bartender brought them over to Bosch and tapped one of the tops, a smile that would make a woman frigid on his face.

"This is the one with no — hey, what is this shit?"

The ten Bosch had put down on the bar was now a one. Bosch blew smoke in the bartender's face as he took the coffees and said, "That's for the coffee. You can shove the napkins."

"Just get the fuck out of here," the bartender said. Then he turned and started walking down to the other end of the bar, where several of the patrons were impatiently holding their empty glasses up. They needed more ice to chill their plasma.

Bosch pushed the door to the restroom open with his foot but didn't see Porter. He pushed the door to the only stall open and he wasn't there either. Harry left the room and quickly pushed through the women's restroom door. No Porter. He followed the hallway around another corner and saw a door marked Exit. He saw drops of blood on the floor. Regretting his play with the bartender and wondering if he'd be able to track Porter by calling hospitals and clinics, he hit the door's push bar with his hip. It opened only an inch or so. There was something on the other side holding it closed.

Bosch put the coffees down on the floor and put his whole weight on the door. It slowly moved open as the blockage gave way. He squeezed through and saw a Dumpster had been shoved against the door. He was standing in an alley behind Poe's and the morning light, flowing down the alley from the east, was blinding.

There was an abandoned Toyota, its wheels, hood and one door gone, sitting dead in the alley. There were more Dumpsters and the wind was blowing trash around in a swirl. And there was no sign of Porter.

13

Bosch sat at the counter at the Original Pantry drinking coffee, picking at a plate of eggs and bacon, and waiting for a second wind to come. He hadn't bothered with trying to follow Porter. He knew that there would be no chance. Knowing Bosch wanted him, even a broken-down cop like Porter would know enough to stay away from the likely places Harry would look. He would stay in the wind.

Harry had his notebook out and opened to the chronological chart he had constructed the day before. But he could not concentrate on it. He was too depressed. Depressed that Porter had run from him, that he hadn't trusted him. Depressed that it seemed clear that Moore's death was connected to the darkness that was out there at the outer edge of every cop's vision. Moore had crossed over. And it had killed him.

I found out who I was.

The note bothered him, too. If Moore wasn't a suicide, where did it come from? It made him think about what Sylvia Moore had said about the past, about how her husband had been snared in a trap he had set for himself. He then thought of calling her to tell her what he had learned but discarded the idea for the time being. He did not have the answers to questions she would surely ask. Why was Calexico Moore murdered? Who did it?

It was just after eight o'clock. Bosch left money on the counter and walked out. Outside two homeless men shook cups in front of him and he acted like they weren't even there. He drove over to Parker Center and got into the lot early enough to get a parking space. He first checked the Robbery-Homicide Division offices on the third floor but Sheehan wasn't in yet. Next he went up to the fourth to Fugitives, to pick up where Porter would have if he hadn't made his deal with Moore. Fugitives also handled missing-persons reports and Bosch always thought there was something symbiotic about that. Most missing persons were fugitives from something, some part of their lives.

A missing-persons detective named Capetillo asked Bosch what he needed and Harry asked to see the male Latin missings for the last ten days. Capetillo led him to his desk and told him to have a seat while he went to the files. Harry looked around and his eyes fell on a framed photo of the portly detective posed with a woman and two young girls. A family man. Taped to the wall above the desk was a bullfight poster advertising the lineup for a fight two years earlier at Tijuana's Bullring by the Sea. The names of the six matadors were listed down the right side. The entire left side of the poster was a reproduction of a painting of a matador turning with a charging bull, leading the horns away with the flowing red cape. The caption inscribed below the painting said "El Arte de la Muleta."

"The classic veronica."

Bosch turned. It was Capetillo and he was holding a thin file in one hand.

"Excuse me?" Bosch asked.

"The veronica. Do you know anything about the *corrida de toros*? The bull-fights?"

"Never been."

"Magnificent. I go at least four times a year. Nothing compares to it. Football, basketball, nothing. The veronica is that move. He slyly leads the horns away. In Mexico the bullfight is called the brave festival, you know."

Bosch looked at the file in the detective's hand. Capetillo opened it and handed Bosch a thin stack of papers.

"That's all we have in the last ten days," Capetillo said. "Your Mexicans, Chicanos, a lot don't report their missings to police. A cultural thing. Most just don't trust the cops. Lot of times when people don't turn up, they just figure they went south. A lot of people are here illegally. They won't call the cops."

Bosch made it through the stack in five minutes. None of the reports fit the description of Juan Doe #67.

"What about telexes, inquiries from Mexico?"

"Now that's something different. We keep official correspondence separate. I could look. Why don't you tell me what you're pushing."

"I'm pushing a hunch. I have a body with no identification. I think the man may have come from down there, maybe Mexicali. This is a guess more than anything else."

"Hang tight," Capetillo said and he left the cubicle again.

Bosch studied the poster again, noticing how the matador's face betrayed no sign of indecision or fear, only concentration on the horns of death. The bullfighter's eyes were flat and dead like a shark's. Capetillo was back quickly.

"Nice hunch. I have three reports received in the last two weeks. They all concern men that sound like your guy, but one more than the others. I think we got lucky."

He handed a single piece of paper to Bosch and said, "This one came from the consulate on Olvera Street yesterday."

It was a photocopy of a telex to the consulate by a State Judicial Police officer named Carlos Aguila. Bosch studied the letter, which was written in English

Seeking information regarding the disappearance of Fernal Gutierrez-Llosa, 55, day laborer, Mexicali. Whereabouts unknown. Last sighting: 12/17 — Mexicali.

Description: 5-foot-8, 145 pounds. Brown eyes, brown hair, some gray. Tattoo right upper chest (blue ink ghost symbol — City of Lost Souls barrio).

Contact: Carlos Aguila, 57-20-13, Mexicali, B.C.

Bosch reread the page. There wasn't much there but it was enough. Fernal Gutierrez-Llosa disappeared in Mexicali on the seventeenth and early the next morning the body of Juan Doe #67 was found in Los Angeles. Bosch looked quickly at the other two pages Capetillo had but they dealt with men who were too young to be Juan Doe #67. He went back to the first sheet. The tattoo was the clincher.

"I think this is it," he said. "Can I get a copy?"

"Of course. You want me to call down there? See if they can send some prints up?"

"Nah, not yet. I want to check a few other things out." Actually, he wanted to limit Capetillo's involvement to just the help he had given.

"There's one thing," Bosch said. "You know what this City of Lost Souls description means? This reference to the tattoo."

"Yeah. Basically, the tattoo is a barrio symbol. Fernal Gutierrez-Llosa resided in the barrio Ciudad de los Personas Perdidos — City of Lost Souls. Many of the barrio dwellers down there do this. Mark themselves. It's similar to graffiti up here. Only down there, they mark themselves and not the frigging walls as much. The police down there know what tattoos symbolize what barrios. It is fairly common in Mexicali. When you contact Aguila he can tell you. Maybe he can send you a photo, if you need it."

Bosch was silent for a moment as he pretended to reread the consulate paper. City of Lost Souls, he thought. A ghost. He tumbled this piece of information in his mind the way a boy who has found a baseball turns it in his hands to study the seams for wear. He was reminded of the tattoo on Moore's arm. The devil with a halo. Was that from a Mexicali barrio?

"You say the cops there keep track of these tattoos?"

"That's right. It's one of the few decent jobs they do."

"How d'you mean?"

"I mean, have you ever been down there? On a detail? It's third world, man. The police, uh, apparatus, I guess you'd call it, is very primitive by our standards. Fact, it would not surprise me if they have no fingerprints on this man to send you. I'm surprised they even sent anything to the consul here in the first place. This Aguila, he must've had a hunch like you."

Bosch took one last look at the poster on the wall, thanked Capetillo for his help and the copy of the consulate's telex and then left the office.

He got on an elevator to go down and saw Sheehan already on it. The car was crowded and Sheehan was at the back, behind the pile. They didn't talk until they got off on three.

"Hey, Frankie," Bosch said. "Didn't get a chance to talk to you Christmas night."

"What're you doing here, Harry?"

"I'm waiting for you. You must be running late, or do you check in on the fifth floor nowadays?"

That was a little poke at Sheehan. The IAD squads were on the fifth floor. It was also to let Sheehan know that Harry had an idea of what was going on with the Moore case. Since Sheehan was going down, he had come from either the fifth or sixth floors. That was either IAD or Irving's office. Or maybe both.

"Don't fuck with me, Bosch. Reason I haven't been in is I've been busy this morning, thanks to the games you like to play."

"What do you mean?"

"Don't worry about it. Look, I don't like you being seen with me in here, anyway. Irving gave me specific instructions about you. You are not in this investigation. You helped out the other night but it ended there."

They were in the hallway outside the RHD offices. Bosch didn't like the sound of Sheehan's tone. He had never known Frankie to bow his head to the brass like this.

"C'mon, Frankie, let's go get a cup. You can tell me what's bugging you."

"Nothing's bugging me, man. You forget, I worked with you. I know how you get your teeth on something and won't let go. Well, I'm telling you where things stand. You were there the night we found him. It ended there. Go back to Hollywood."

Bosch took a step toward him and lowered his voice. He said, "But we both know it didn't end there, Frankie. And it's not going to end there. So if you feel you gotta do it, go tell Irving I said it's so."

Sheehan stared at him for a few seconds and then Bosch saw the resolve fade away.

"Awright, Harry, c'mon in. I'm going to be kicking myself for this later."

They walked to Sheehan's desk and Bosch pulled a chair from another desk alongside it. Sheehan took off his coat and put it on a hanger on a rack next to the desk. After he sat down, adjusted his shoulder holster and folded his arms, he said:

"Know where I've been all morning? The ME's, trying to work out a deal to keep a lid on this a few hours. Seems overnight we sprang a leak and already this morning Irving's getting calls that we are sitting on a homicide of one of our own officers. You wouldn't know anything about this, would you?"

Harry said, "Only thing I know is I've been thinking about the scene out at the motel and the autopsy being inconclusive, like they say, and I'm not thinking suicide anymore."

"You're not thinking anything. You're not on it. Remember? And what about this?"

He opened a drawer and brought a file up. It was the Zorrillo file Rickard had shown him the day before.

"Don't bother telling me you haven't seen this before. Because then I might take it over to SID and have 'em run prints on it. I'd bet my wife's diaphragm I'd find yours."

"You'd lose, Frankie."

"Then I'd have more kids. But I wouldn't lose, Harry."

Bosch waited a beat for him to settle down.

"All this huffin' and puffin' at me tells me one thing: you don't see a suicide, either. So quit with the bullshit."

"You're right. I don't. But I got an assistant chief sitting on my ass and he's gotten the bright idea of sticking me with an IAD suit on this. So it's like I got both my feet in buckets of shit before I even start off."

"You saying they don't want this to go anywhere?"

"No, I am not saying that."

"What are they going to tell the *Times*?"

"Press conference this afternoon. Irving's going to give it to everybody. He'll say we are looking at the possibility — the *possibility* — of homicide. Fuck giving it to the *Times*. Who said it was the *Times* making the noise anyway?"

"Lucky, I guess."

"Yeah, be careful, Bosch. You slip like that with Irving and he'll fry your ass. He'd love to, with your record and all the history going back with you. I already have to figure out about this file. You told Irving you didn't know the guy and now we have a file that shows he was doing some digging for you."

Bosch realized he had forgotten to remove the Post-it tag Moore had placed on the file.

"Tell Irving whatever you want. Think I care?" Bosch looked down at the file. "What do you think?"

"About this file? I think nothing out loud."

"C'mon, Frankie, I ask Moore to look around on this dope killing and he ends up in a motel with his head in the tub in small pieces. It was a very smooth job, right down to not a single lift belonging to anybody else being found in that room."

"So what if it was smooth and there's no other prints? In my book some guys deserve what they got coming, you know?"

There was the break in Sheehan's defense. Whether intentional or not, he was telling Bosch that Moore had crossed.

"I need more than that," he said in a very low voice. "You got the weight on you but I don't. I'm a free agent and I'm going to put it together. Moore might've crossed, yeah, but nobody should've put him down on the tiles like that. We both know that. Besides, there are other bodies."

Harry could see this had grabbed Sheehan's attention.

"We can trade," Bosch said quietly.

Sheehan stood up and said, "Yeah, let's go get that coffee."

Five minutes later they were at a table in the second-floor cafeteria and Bosch was telling him about Jimmy Kapps and Juan Doe #67. He outlined the connections between Moore and Juan Doe, Juan Doe and Mexicali, Mexicali and Humberto Zorillo, Zorillo and black ice, black ice and Jimmy Kapps. On and on it went. Sheehan asked no questions and took no notes until Harry was done.

"So what do you think?" he asked then.

"I think what you think," Bosch said. "That Moore had crossed. Maybe he was fronting up here for Zorillo, the ice man, and got so deep he couldn't get out. I don't know how it all ties up yet but I still have some ideas I am playing with. I'm thinking a number of things. Maybe he wanted out and the ice man whacked him. Maybe he was working that file, going to give me something, and they whacked him."

"Possibilities."

"There's also the possibility that word of the IAD investigation your partner Chastain was conducting got around, and they saw Moore as a danger and whacked him."

Sheehan hesitated. It was the moment of truth. If he discussed the IAD investigation he would be breaking enough departmental regs to get shipped permanently out of RHD. Like Harry.

"I could get busted for talking about that," Sheehan said. "Could end up like you, out there in the cesspool."

"It's all a cesspool, man. Doesn't matter if you're on the bottom or the top. You're still swimming in shit."

Sheehan took a sip of his coffee.

"IAD had taken a report, this was about two months ago, that Moore was some way involved in the traffic on the Boulevard. Possibly offering protection, possibly a deeper involvement. The source was not clear on that."

"Two months ago?" Bosch asked. "Didn't they get anything? I mean, Moore was still working the street all this time. Wasn't there enough to at least put him on a desk?"

"Look, you've got to remember that Irving put Chastain with me on this. But I'm not with Chastain. He doesn't do much talking to me. All he would tell me was the investigation was in its infancy when Moore disappeared. He had no proof substantiating or discrediting the claim."

"You know how hard he worked it?"

"I assume very hard. He's IAD. He's always looking for a badge to pull. And this looked like more than just departmental charges. This would have gone to the DA. So I assume he had a hard-on for it. He just didn't get anything. Moore must've been very good."

Not good enough, Bosch thought. Obviously.

"Who was the source?"

"You don't need that."

"You know I do. If I'm going to be a free agent on this I have to know what's what."

Sheehan hesitated but didn't make a good show of it.

"It was anonymous — a letter. But Chastain said it was the wife. That's what he figured. She turned him in."

"How's he so sure?"

"The details of the letter, whatever they were, Chastain said they would only be known by someone close to him. He told me it wasn't unusual. It often comes from the spouse. But he said that a lot of times it's bogus. A wife or husband will report something totally false, you know, if they are going through a divorce or something, just to fuck the other up with work. So, he spent a lot of time just seeing if that was the case here. 'Cause Moore and his wife were splitting up. He said she never admitted it but he was sure she sent it. He just never got very far with substantiating what was in it."

Bosch thought of Sylvia. He was sure they were wrong.

"Did you talk to the wife, tell her the ID was confirmed?"

"No, Irving did that last night."

"He tell her about the autopsy, 'bout it not being suicide?"

"I don't know about that. See, I don't get to sit down with Irving like you with me here and ask him everything that comes into my head."

Bosch was wearing out his welcome.

"Just a few more, Frankie. Did Chastain focus on black ice?"

"No. When we got this file of yours yesterday, he about shit his pants. I got the feeling he was hearing about all that side of it for the first time. I kind of enjoyed that, Harry. If there was anything to enjoy about any of this."

"Well, now, you can tell him all the rest I told you."

"No chance. This conversation didn't take place. I gotta try to put it all together like it was my own before I hand anything over to him."

Bosch was thinking quickly. What else was there to ask?

"What about the note? That's the part that doesn't fit now. If it was no suicide then where's this note come from?"

"Yeah, that's the problem. That's why we gave the coroner such a hard time. Far as we can guess, he either had it all along in his back pocket or whoever did him made him write it. I don't know."

"Yeah." Bosch thought a moment. "Would you write a note like that if somebody was about to put you down on the floor?"

"I don't know, man. People do things you'd never expect when they've got the gun on them. They always've got hope that things might turn out all right. That's the way I see it."

Bosch nodded. But he didn't know if he agreed or not.

"I gotta go," Sheehan said. "Let me know what comes up."

Bosch nodded and Sheehan left him there with two cups of coffee on the table. A few moments later Sheehan was back.

"You know, I never told you, it was too bad about what happened with you. We could use you back here, Harry. I've always thought that."

Bosch looked up at him.

"Yeah, Frankie. Thanks."

14

The Medfly Eradication Project Center was at the edge of East L.A., on San Fernando Road not far from County–USC Med Center, which housed the morgue. Bosch was tempted to drop by to see Teresa but he figured he should give her time to cool. He also figured that decision was cowardly but he didn't change it. He just kept driving.

The project center was a former county psychiatric ward which had been abandoned to that cause years earlier when Supreme Court rulings made it virtually impossible for the government — in the form of the police — to take the mentally ill off the streets and hold them for observation and public safety. The San Fernando Road ward was closed as the country consolidated its psych centers.

It had been used since for a variety of purposes, including a set for a slasher movie about a haunted nuthouse and even a temporary morgue when an earthquake damaged the facility at County–USC a few years back. Bodies had been stored in two refrigerated trucks in the parking lot. Because of the emergency situation, county administrators had to get the first trucks they could get their hands on. Painted on the side of one of them had been the words "Live Maine Lobsters!" Bosch remembered reading about it in the "Only in L.A." column in the *Times*.

There was a check-in post at the entry manned by a state police officer. Bosch rolled down the window, badged him and asked who the head medfly eradicator was. He was directed to a parking space and an entrance to the administration suite.

The door to the suite still said No Unescorted Patients on it. Bosch went through and down a hallway, nodding to and passing another state officer. He came to a secretary's desk where he identified himself again to the woman sitting there and asked to see the entomologist in charge. She made a quick phone call to someone and then escorted Harry into a nearby office, introducing him to a man named Roland Edson. The secretary hovered near the door with a shocked look on her face until Edson finally told her that would be all.

When they were alone in the office, Edson said, "I kill flies for a living, not people, Detective. Is this a serious visit?"

Edson laughed hard and Bosch forced a smile to be polite. Edson was a small man in a short-sleeved white shirt and pale green tie. His bald scalp had been freckled by the sun and was scarred by misjudgments. He wore thick, rimless glasses that magnified his eyes and made him somewhat resemble his quarry. Behind his back his subordinates probably called him "The Fly."

Bosch explained that he was working a homicide case and could not tell Edson a lot of the background because the investigation was of a highly confidential nature. He warned him that other investigators might be back with more questions. He asked for some general information about the breeding and transport of sterile fruit flies into the state, hoping that the appeal for expert advice would get the bureaucrat to open up.

Edson responded by giving him much of the same information Teresa Corazón had already provided, but Bosch acted as if it was all new to him and took notes.

"Here's the specimen here, Detective," Edson said, holding up a paperweight. It was a glass block in which a fruit fly had been perpetually cast, like a prehistoric ant caught in amber.

Bosch nodded and steered the interview specifically toward Mexicali. The entomologist said the breeding contractor there was a company called Enviro-Breed. He said EnviroBreed shipped an average of thirty million flies to the eradication center each week.

"How do they get here?" Bosch asked.

"In the pupal stage, of course."

"Of course. But my question is how?"

"This is the stage in which the insect is nonfeeding, immobile. It is what we call the transformation stage between larva and imago — adult. This works out quite well because it is an ideal point for transport. They come in incubators, if you will. Environment boxes, we call them. And then, of course, shortly after they get here metamorphosis is completed and they are ready to be released as adults."

"So when they get here, they have already been dyed and irradiated?"

"That is correct. I said that."

"And they are in the pupal stage, not larva?"

"Larvae is the plural, Detective, but, yes, that is essentially correct. I said that, also."

Bosch was beginning to think Edson was essentially an officious prick. He was sure they definitely called him The Fly around here.

"Okay," Harry said. "So what if, here in L.A., I found a larvae, I mean a larva, that was dyed but not irradiated? Is that possible?"

Edson was silent a moment. He didn't want to speak too soon and be wrong. Bosch was getting the idea that he was the type of guy who watched "Jeopardy" on the tube each night and barked out the answers ahead of the contestants even if he was alone.

"Well, Detective, any given scenario is possible. I would, however, say the example you just gave is highly unlikely. As I said, our suppliers send the pupae packages through an irradiation machine before they are shipped here. In these packages we often find larvae mixed with the pupae because it would generally be impossible to completely separate the two. But these larvae samplings have been through the same irradiation as the pupae. So, no, I don't see it."

"So if I had a person who on their body carried a single pupa that had been dyed but not irradiated, that person would not have come from here, right?"

"Yes, that would be my answer."

"Would?"

"Yes, Detective, that *is* my answer."

"Then where would this person have come from?"

Edson gave it some thought first. He used the eraser end of a pencil he had been fiddling with to press his glasses up on the bridge of his nose.

"I take it this person is dead, you having introduced yourself as a homicide detective and obviously being unable to ask the person this question yourself."

"You should be on 'Jeopardy,' Mr. Edson."

"It's Doctor. Anyway, I couldn't begin to guess where the person would have picked up this specimen you speak of."

"He could have been from one of the breeders you mentioned, down in Mexico or over in Hawaii, couldn't he?"

"Yes, that's a possibility. One of them."

"And what's another?"

"Well, Mr. Bosch, you saw the security we have around here. Frankly, there are some people who are not happy with what we are doing. Some extremists believe nature should take its course. If the medfly comes to southern California, who are we to try to eradicate it? Some people believe we have no business being in this business. There have been threats from some groups. Anonymous, but nevertheless, threats to breed nonsterile medflies and release them, causing a massive infestation. Now, if I were going to do that, I might dye them to obfuscate my opponent."

Edson was pleased with himself on that one. But Bosch didn't buy it. It did not fit with the facts. But he nodded, indicating to Edson that he would give it some consideration and thought. Then he said, "Tell me, how do these deliveries from the breeders get here? For example, how do they get here from the place down in Mexicali you deal with?"

Edson said that at the breeding facility thousands of pupae were packed into plastic tubes resembling six-foot-long sausages. The tubes were then strung in cartons complete with incubators and humidifiers. The environment boxes were sealed at the EnviroBreed lab under the scrutiny of a USDA inspector and then trucked across the border and north to Los Angeles. The deliveries from EnviroBreed came two to three times a week, depending on availability of supply.

"The cartons are not inspected at the border?" Bosch asked.

"They are inspected but not opened. It could endanger the product if the cartons were opened. Each carton contains a carefully controlled environment, you understand. But as I said, the cartons are sealed under the eye of government inspectors, and each carton is reinspected upon the breaking of such seals at the eradication center to make sure there has been no tampering. Um, at the border, the Border Patrol checks the seal numbers and cartons against the driver's bill of lading and our separate notification of transport crossing. It's very thorough, Detective Bosch. The system was all hashed out at the highest levels."

Bosch said nothing for a while. He wasn't going to debate the security of the system, but he wondered who designed it at the highest levels, the scientists or the Border Patrol.

"If I was to go down there, to Mexicali, could you get me into Enviro-Breed?"

"Impossible," Edson said quickly. "You have to remember these are private contractors. We get all our bred flies from privately owned facilities. Though we have a state USDA inspector at each facility and state entomologists, such as myself, make routine visits, we cannot order them to open their doors to an inquiry by police or anyone, for that matter, without showing notice of an infraction of our contract.

"In other words, Detective Bosch, tell me what they did and I will tell you if I can get you in there."

Bosch didn't answer. He wanted to tell Edson as little as possible. He changed the subject.

"These environment boxes that the bug tubes come in, how big are they?" he asked.

"Oh, they're a pretty decent size. We generally use a forklift when unloading deliveries."

"Can you show me one?"

Edson looked at his watch and said, "I suppose that is possible. I don't know what has come in, if anything."

Bosch stood up to force the issue. Edson finally did, too. He led Harry out of the office and down another hallway past more offices and labs that had once been the holding pens for the insane, the addicted and the abandoned. Harry recalled that once while a patrolman he had walked down this same hallway escorting a woman he had arrested on Mount Fleming, where she was climbing the steel frame behind the first O of the Hollywood sign. She had a nylon cord with her, already tied into a noose at one end. A few years later he read in the newspaper that after getting out of Patton State Hospital she had gone back to the sign and done the job he had interrupted.

"Must be tough," Edson said. "Working homicides."

Bosch said what he always said when people said that to him.

"Sometimes it's not so bad. At least the victims I deal with are out of their misery."

Edson didn't say anything else. The hall ended at a heavy steel door, which he pushed open. They walked out onto a loading dock that was inside a large hangarlike building. About thirty feet away, there were a half dozen or so workers, all Latinos, placing white plastic boxes on wheeled dollies and then pulling them through a set of double doors on the other side of the unloading area. Bosch noted that each of the boxes was just about the size of a coffin.

The boxes were first being removed from a white van with a mini-forklift. On the side of the van the word "EnviroBreed" was painted in blue. The driver's door was open and a white man stood watching the work. Another white man with a clipboard was at the end of the truck, bending down to check numbers on the seals of each of the boxes and then making notes on the clipboard.

"We're in luck," Edson said. "A delivery in process. The environment boxes are taken into our lab where the M&M process, that's what we call metamorphosis around here, is completed."

Edson pointed through the open garage doors to a row of six orange pickup trucks parked outside in the lot.

"The mature flies are placed in covered buckets and we use our fleet to take them to the attack areas. They are released by hand. Right now the attack zone is about one hundred square miles. We are dropping fifty million sterile flies a week. More if we can get them. Ultimately, the steriles will overwhelm the wild fly population and breed it out of existence."

There was a note of triumph in the entomologist's voice.

"Would you like to speak with the EnviroBreed driver?" Edson said. "I am sure he would be ha —"

"No," Bosch said. "I just wanted to see how it is done. I'd appreciate it, Doctor, if you kept my visit confidential."

As he said this, Bosch noticed the EnviroBreed driver was looking right at him. The man's face was deeply lined and tanned and his hair was white. He wore a straw plantation hat and smoked a brown cigarette. Bosch returned the stare, knowing full well that he had been made. He thought he saw a slight smile on the driver's face, then the man finally broke away his stare and went back to watching the unloading process.

"Then is there anything else I can do for you, Detective," Edson said.

"No, Doc. Thanks for your cooperation."

"I'm sure you know your way out."

Edson turned and went back in through the steel door. Harry put a cigarette in his mouth but left it unlit. He waved a nattering of flies, probably pink medflies, he thought, away from his face, went down the loading-dock stairs and walked out through the garage door.

Driving back toward downtown, Bosch decided to get it over with and face Teresa. He pulled into the County–USC parking lot and spent ten minutes looking for a spot big enough to put the Caprice in. He finally found one in the back where the lot is on a rise overlooking the old railroad yard. He sat in the car for a few moments thinking about what to say and smoking and looking down at all the rusted boxcars and iron tracks. He saw a group of *cholos* in their oversized white T-shirts and baggy pants making their way through the yard. The one carrying a spray can dropped back from the others and along one of the old boxcars sprayed a scrip. It was in Spanish but Bosch understood it. It was the gang's imprimatur, its philosophy:

LAUGH NOW CRY LATER

He watched them until they had moved behind another line of boxcars. He got out and went into the morgue through the rear door, where the deliveries are made. A security guard nodded after seeing his badge.

Today was a good day inside. The smell of disinfectant had the upper hand over the odor of death. Harry walked past the doors to refrigeration rooms one and two and then through a door to a set of stairs that led up to the second-floor administration offices.

Bosch asked the secretary in the chief medical examiner's office if Dr. Corazón could see him. The woman, whose pale skin and pinkish hair made her resemble some of the clients around the place, spoke quietly on the phone and then told him to go in. Teresa was standing behind her desk, looking out the window. She had the same view Bosch had of the railroad yard and may have even seen him coming. But from the second floor, she also had a view that spanned the area from the towers of downtown to Mt Washington. Bosch noticed how clear the towers were in the distance. It was a good day outside as well.

"I'm not talking to you," Teresa announced without turning around.

"C'mon."

"I'm not."

"Then why'd you let me in?"

"To tell you I am not talking to you and that I am very angry and that you have probably compromised my position as chief medical examiner."

"C'mon, Teresa. I hear you have a press conference later today. It will work out."

He couldn't think of anything else to say. She turned around and leaned back against the windowsill. She looked at him with eyes that could've carved his name on a tombstone. He could smell her perfume all the way across the room.

"And, of course, I have you to thank for that."

"Not me. I heard Irving called the press con —"

"Don't fuck with me, Harry. We both know what you did with what I told you. And we both know that little shit Irving automatically thinks I did it. I now have to consider myself seriously fucked as far as the permanent job goes. Take a good look around the office, Harry. Last time you'll ever see me here."

Bosch had always noticed how many of the professional women he encountered, mostly cops and lawyers, turned profane when arguing. He wondered if they felt it might put them on the same level as the men they were battling.

"It will work out," he said.

"What are you talking about? All he has to do is tell a few commissioners that I leaked information from a confidential, uncompleted investigation to the press and that will eliminate me completely from consideration."

"Listen, he can't be sure it was you and he'll probably think it was me. Bremmer, the *Times* guy who stirred this all up, we go back some. Irving will know. So quit worrying about it. I came to see if you want to have lunch or something."

Wrong move. He saw her face turn red with pure anger.

"Lunch or something? Are you kidding? Are you — you just told me we are the two likely suspects on this leak and you want me to sit with you in a restaurant? Do you know what could —"

"Hey, Teresa, have a nice press conference," Bosch cut in. He turned around and headed to the door.

On the way into downtown, his pager went off and Bosch noticed the number was Ninety-eight's direct line. He must be worried about his statistics, Harry thought. He decided to ignore the page. He also turned the Motorola radio in the car off.

He stopped at a *mariscos* truck parked on Alvarado and ordered two shrimp tacos. They were served on corn tortillas, Baja style, and Bosch savored the heavy cilantro in the salsa.

A few yards from the truck stood a man reciting scripture verses from memory. On top of his head was a cup of water that nestled comfortably in his seventies-style Afro and did not spill. He reached up for the cup and took a drink from time to time but never stopped bouncing from book to book of the New Testament. Before each quote, he gave his listeners the chapter and verse numbers as a reference. At his feet was a glass fishbowl half full of coins. When he was done eating, Bosch ordered a Coke to go and then dropped the change into the fishbowl. He got a "God bless you" back.

15

The Hall of Justice took up an entire block across from the criminal courts building. The first six floors housed the sheriff's department and the top four the county jail. Anyone could tell this from the outside. Not just because of the bars behind the windows, but because the top four floors looked like an abandoned, burned-out shell. As if all the hate and anger held in those un-air-conditioned cells had turned to fire and smoke and stained the windows and concrete balustrades forever black.

It was a turn-of-the-century building and its stone-block construction gave it an ominous fortresslike appearance. It was one of the only buildings in downtown that still had human elevator operators. An old black woman sat on a padded stool in the corner of each of the wood-paneled cubicles and pulled the doors open and worked the wheel that leveled the elevator with each floor it stopped at.

"Seven thousand," Bosch said to the operator as he stepped on. It had been some time since he had been in the Hall and he could not remember her name. But he knew she had been working the elevators here since before Harry was a cop. All of the operators had. She opened the door on the sixth floor where Bosch saw Rickard as soon as he stepped out. The narc was standing at the glass window at the check-in counter, putting his badge case into a slide drawer.

"Here you go," Bosch said and quickly put his badge in the drawer.

"He's with me," Rickard said into the microphone.

The deputy behind the glass exchanged the badges for two visitor clearance badges and slid them out. Bosch and Rickard clipped them to their shirts. Bosch noticed they were cleared to visit the High Power block on the tenth floor. High Power was where the most dangerous criminal suspects were placed while awaiting trial or to be shipped out to state prisons following guilty verdicts.

They began walking down a hall to the jail elevator.

"You got the kid in High Power?" Bosch asked.

"Yeah. I know a guy. Told him one day, that's all we needed. The kid's going to be shitless. He's going to tell you everything he knows about Dance."

They took the security elevator up, this one operated by a deputy. Bosch figured it had to be the worst job in law enforcement. When the door opened on ten they were met by another deputy, who checked their badges and had them sign in. Then they moved through two sets of sliding steel doors to an attorneys' visiting area, which consisted of a long table with benches running down both sides of it. There was also a foot-high divider running lengthwise down the table. At the far end of the table a female attorney sat on one side, leaning toward the divider and whispering to a client, who cupped his ears with his hands to hear better. The muscles on the inmate's arms bulged and stretched the sleeves of his shirt. He was a monster.

On the wall behind them was a sign that read NO TOUCHING, KISSING, REACHING ACROSS THE DIVIDER. There was also another deputy at the far end, leaning against the wall, his own massive arms folded, and watching the lawyer and her client.

As they waited for the deputies to bring out Tyge, Bosch became aware of the noise. Through the barred door behind the visiting table he could hear a hundred voices competing and echoing in a metallic din. There were steel doors banging somewhere and occasionally an unintelligible shout.

A deputy walked up to the barred door and said, "It'll be a few minutes, fellas. We have to get him out of medical."

The deputy was gone before either of them could ask what happened. Bosch didn't even know the kid but felt his stomach tighten. He looked over at Rickard and saw he was smiling.

"We'll see how things have changed now," the narc cop said.

Bosch didn't understand the delight Rickard seemed to take in this. For Bosch, it was the low end of the job, dealing with desperate people and using desperate tactics. He was here because he had to be. It was his case. But he didn't get it with Rickard.

"So, how come you're doing this? What do you want?"

Rickard looked over at him.

"What do I want? I want to know what's going on. I think you're the only one that might know. So if I can help out, I'll help out. If it costs this kid his asshole, then that's the cost. But what I want to know from you is what is happening here. What did Cal do and what's going to be done about it?"

Bosch leaned back and tried to think for a few moments about what to say. He heard the monster at the end of the table start to raise his voice, something about not accepting the offer. The deputy took a step toward him, dropping his arms to his sides. The inmate went quiet. The deputy's sleeves were rolled up tight to reveal his impressive biceps. On his bulging left forearm Bosch could see the "CL," tattoo, almost like a brand on his white skin. Harry knew that, publicly, deputies who had the tattoo claimed the letters stood for Club Lynwood, after the sheriff's station in the gang-infested L.A. suburb. But he knew the letters also stood for *chango luchador*, monkey fighter. The deputy was a gang member himself, albeit one sanctioned to carry weapons and paid by the county.

Bosch looked away. He wished he could light a cigarette but the county had passed a no-smoking code, even in the jail. It had nearly caused an inmate riot.

"Look," he said to Rickard, "I don't know what to tell you about Moore. I'm working on it but I'm not, you know what I mean? Thing is, it runs across two cases I do have. So, it's unavoidable. If this kid can give me Dance, then it's a help. I could look at Dance for my two cases, maybe even Moore's. But I don't know that. I do know, and they will go public with this today, that Moore looks like a homicide. What they won't go public with is that he crossed. That's why IAD was sniffing around. He crossed."

"Can't be," Rickard said, but there was no conviction in it. "I'd've known."

"You can't know people that well, man. Everybody's got a private room."

"So what's Parker Center going to do?"

"I don't know. I don't think they know what to do. I think they wanted to let it go as suicide. But the ME started making waves, so they'll call it homicide. But I don't think they are going to put the dirty laundry basket out there on Spring Street for every reporter in town to pick through."

"Well, they better get their shit together. I'm not going to stand by. I don't care if he crossed, man. I've seen him do things. He was a good cop. I've seen him go into a gallery and take out four dealers without a backup. I've seen him step between a pimp and his property and take the punch meant for her, pop his teeth right onto the sidewalk. I been with him when he blew nine stoplights trying to get a wretched old hype to the hospital before he went out on a heroin overdose.

"Those aren't things a cop on the pad does. So what I'm saying is that if he crossed, then I think he was trying to cross back and that's why somebody did him."

He stopped then and Bosch didn't interrupt the silence. They both knew that once you cross, you can never come back. Bosch could hear footsteps coming toward the bars.

Rickard said, "They better show me something down there at Parker, not let this thing go. Or I'll show them something."

Bosch wanted to say something but the deputy was at the door with Tyge. He looked like he had aged ten years in the last ten hours. Now he had a distance in his eyes that reminded Bosch of men he had seen and known in Vietnam. There was also a bruise high on his left cheekbone.

The door was slid open by means of unseen electronics and the boy/man walked to the bench after the deputy pointed the way. He sat down tentatively and seemed purposely to keep his eyes away from Rickard.

"How's it hanging, Kerwin?" Rickard asked.

Now the boy looked at Rickard and his eyes made Bosch's stomach knot. He remembered the first night he had spent in McLaren Youth Hall as a boy.

The pure fear and screaming loneliness. And there he had been surrounded by kids, most of them nonviolent. This boy had been surrounded for the last twelve hours by wild animals. Bosch felt ashamed to be part of this but said nothing. It was Rickard's show.

"Look, my man, I know you're probably having a not-so-fun time in there. That's why we came by, t'see if you changed your mind any about what we discussed last night."

Rickard was speaking very low so the monster at the end would not hear.

When the boy said nothing, gave no indication that he even heard, Rickard pressed on.

"Kerwin, you want out of here? Here's your man. Mr. Harry Bosch. He'll let me drop the whole thing, even though it was a righteous bust, if you talk to us about this cat Dance. Here, look-it here."

Rickard unfolded a piece of white paper from his shirt pocket. It was a standard case-filing form from the district attorney's office.

"Man, I have forty-eight hours to file a case on you. 'Cause of the weekend, that's puts it over 'til Monday. This here is the paperwork about you. I haven't done nothing with it 'cause I wanted to check with you one more time to see if you wanted to help yourself out. If you don't, then I'll go file it and this will be your home for the next — probably you're looking at a year with good time."

Rickard waited and nothing happened.

"A year. What do you think you'll be like after a year back in there, Kerwin?"

The boy looked down for a moment and then the tears rolled down his cheeks.

"Go to hell," he managed to say in a strangled voice.

Bosch already was there. He would remember this one for a long time. He realized that he was clenching his teeth and tried to relax his jaw. He couldn't.

Rickard leaned forward to say something to the boy but Bosch put his hand on his shoulder to stop him.

"Fuck it," Bosch said. "Cut him loose."

"What?"

"We're dropping it."

"The fuck you talking about?"

The boy looked over at Bosch, an expression of skepticism on his face. But it was no act with Bosch. He felt sick at what they had done.

"Look," Rickard said. "We got two ounces of PCP off this asshole. He's mine. If he don't want to help out, then too fucking bad. He goes back into the zoo."

"No, he doesn't." And then Bosch leaned close to Rickard so the deputy behind the boy could not hear. "No, he doesn't, Rickard. We're taking him out. Now do it, or I'm going to fuck you up."

"What did you say?"

"I'll go to the fifth floor with it. This boy should've never been up here with that charge. That's on you, Rickard. I'll make the complaint. Your connection in here will get burned too. You want that? Just because you couldn't get this kid to talk?"

"You think IAD's going to give a shit about a little punk pusher?"

"No. But they'll give a shit about bagging you. They'll love you. You'll come out walking slower than this boy."

Harry leaned back away from him. Nobody said anything for a few moments and Bosch could see Rickard thinking it through, trying to decide if it was a bluff.

"A guy like you, going to IAD. I can't see it."

"That's the risk you take."

Rickard looked down at the paper in his hand and then slowly crumpled it.

"Okay, my man, but you better put me on the list."

"What list?"

"The one you got of people you have to watch your back with."

Bosch stood up and so did Rickard.

"We're cutting him loose," Rickard said to the guard.

Bosch pointed to the boy and said, "I want an escort with this man until he is out of there, got it?"

The deputy nodded. The boy said nothing.

It took an hour to get him out. After Rickard signed the appropriate papers and they got their badges back, they waited wordlessly by the glass window on the seventh floor.

Bosch was disgusted with himself. He had lost sight of the art. Solving cases was simply getting people to talk to you. Not forcing them to talk. He had forgotten that this time.

"You can go if you want," he said to Rickard.

"As soon as he walks out that door and you've got him, I'm gone. Want nothing to do with him. But I want to see him leave with you, Bosch. In case any of this comes back on me."

"Yeah, that's smart."

"Yes, it is."

"But you still've got a lot to learn, Rickard. Everything isn't black and white. Not everybody has to be ground into the sidewalk. You take a kid like that and —"

"Spare me the lesson, Bosch. I might have a lot to learn but it won't be from you. You're a class A fuckup. Think the only thing you could teach me is how to climb down the ladder. No thanks."

"Sure," Bosch said and walked to the other side of the room where there was a bench. He sat down and fifteen minutes later the boy came out. He walked between Rickard and Bosch to the elevator. Outside the Hall of Justice, Rickard headed off to his car after simply saying to Bosch, "Fuck you."

"Right," Bosch said.

He stood on the sidewalk, lit a cigarette and offered one to the boy. He declined.

"I'm not telling you anything," the boy said.

"I know. That's cool. You want me to take you anywhere? A real doctor? A lift back to Hollywood?"

"Hollywood's fine."

They walked to Bosch's car, which was parked two blocks away at Parker Center and he took Third Street toward Hollywood. They were halfway there before either one spoke.

"You have a place? Where do you want me to drop you?"

"Anywhere."

"No place?"

"No."

"Family?"

"Nope."

"What will you do?"

"Whatever."

Harry turned north on Western. They were silent for another fifteen minutes or so, until Bosch pulled to a stop in front of the Hideaway.

"What's this?"

"Sit tight. I'll only be a minute."

Inside the office, the manager tried to rent Bosch room seven but Harry flipped him his badge and told him try again. The manager, who was still wearing a dingy sleeveless T-shirt, gave him the key to room thirteen. He went back to the car and got in and gave the boy the key. He also took out his wallet.

"You've got a room in there for a week," Bosch said. "For what it's worth, which you probably don't think is much, my advice is that you think about things and then get as far away from this town as you can. There are better places to live than this."

The boy looked at the key in his hand. Bosch then handed him all the money he had, which was only $43.

"What, you give me a room and money and you think I'm going to talk to you? I've seen TV, man. The whole thing was a hoax, you and that guy."

"Don't misunderstand, kid. I'm doing this because it's something that I need to do. It doesn't mean I think what you do for a living is okay. I don't. If I ever see you out on the street again I'm going to come down on you. It's a pretty fucking desperate chance but it's a chance just the same. Do with it what you want. You can go. It's no hoax."

The boy opened the car door and got out. He looked back in at Bosch.

"Then why're you doing it?"

"I don't know. I guess 'cause you told him to go to hell. I should've said that and I didn't. I gotta go."

The boy looked at him a moment before speaking.

"You know, man, Dance's gone. I don't know why you're all worried about him."

"Look, kid, I didn't do —"

"I know."

Harry just looked at him.

"He left, man. Left town. He said our source split and so he went down to see if he could get the thing going again. You know, he wants to step up and be the source, now."

"Down?"

"He said Mexico, but that's all I know. He's gone. That's why I was doing sherms."

The boy closed the door and disappeared into the courtyard of the motel. Bosch sat there thinking and Rickard's question came back to him. Where would the boy be in a year? Then he thought of himself staying in rundown motels so many years ago. Bosch had made it through. Had survived. There was always the chance. He restarted the car and pulled out.

16

Talking to the kid sealed it. Bosch knew he was going to Mexico. All the spokes on the wheel pointed to the hub. The hub was Mexicali. But, then, he'd known that all along.

He drove to the station on Wilcox, trying to determine a strategy. He knew he would have to contact Aguila, the State Judicial Police officer who had sent the letter identifying Juan Doe #67 to the consulate. He would also have to contact the DEA, which had provided the intelligence report to Moore. He would have to get the trip cleared by Pounds, but he knew that might end it right there. He would have to work around that.

In the bureau, the homicide table was empty. It was after four on a Friday, and a holiday week as well. With no new cases, the detectives would clear out as soon as possible to go home to families and lives outside the cop-shop. Harry could see Pounds in his glass booth; his head was down and he was writing on a piece of paper, using his ruler to keep his sentences on a straight line.

Bosch sat down and checked through a pile of pink message slips at his spot. Nothing needing an immediate return. There were two from Bremmer at the *Times* but he had left the name Jon Marcus — a code they had once worked out so it would not become known that the reporter was calling for Bosch. There were a couple from DAs who were prosecuting cases Harry had worked and needed information or the location of evidence. There was a message that Teresa had called but he looked at the time on the note and saw that he had seen her since then. He guessed that she had called to tell him she wasn't talking to him.

There was no message from Porter and no message from Sylvia Moore. He took out the copy of the inquiry from Mexicali that the missing-persons detective, Capetillo, had given him and dialed the number Carlos Aguila had provided. The number was a general exchange for the SJP office. His Spanish was unconfident despite his recent refresher, and it took Bosch five minutes of explanations before he was connected to the investigations unit and asked once again for Aguila. He didn't get him. Instead, he got a captain who spoke English and explained that Aguila was not in the office but would return later and would also be working Saturday. Bosch knew that the cops in Mexico worked six-day weeks.

"Can I be of help?" the captain asked.

Bosch explained that he was investigating a homicide and was answering the inquiry Aguila had sent to the consulate in Los Angeles. The description was similar to the body he had. The captain explained that he was familiar with the case, that he had taken the report before handing the case to Aguila. Bosch asked whether there were fingerprints available to confirm the identification but the captain said there were none. Chalk one up for Capetillo, Bosch thought.

"Perhaps you have a photograph from your morgue of this man that you could send to us," the captain said. "We could make identification from the family of Mr. Gutierrez-Llosa."

"Yes. I have photos. The letter said Gutierrez-Llosa was a laborer?"

"Yes. He found day work at the circle where employers come to find workers. Beneath the statue of Benito Juarez."

"Do you know if he worked at a place, a business called EnviroBreed? It does business with the state of California."

There was a long silence before the Mexican replied.

"I am sorry. I do not know of his work history. I have taken notes and will discuss this with Investigator Aguila upon his return. If you send the photographs we will act promptly on securing positive identification. I will personally expedite this matter and contact you."

Now Bosch let silence fill the phone connection.

"Captain, I didn't get your name."

"Gustavo Grena, director of investigations, Mexicali."

"Captain Grena, please tell Aguila that he will have the photos tomorrow."

"That soon?"

"Yes. Tell him I'm bringing them down myself."

"Investigator Bosch, this is not necessary. I believe —"

"Don't worry, Captain Grena," Bosch cut him off. "Tell him I will be there by early afternoon, no later."

"As you wish."

Bosch thanked him and hung up. He looked up and saw Pounds staring at him through the glass in his office. The lieutenant raised his thumb and his eyebrows in an inquiring, pleading way. Bosch looked away.

A laborer, Bosch thought. Fernal Gutierrez-Llosa was a day laborer who got jobs at the circle, whatever that was. How did a day laborer fit? Perhaps he was a mule who brought black ice across the border. And perhaps he had not been a part of the smuggling operation at all. Perhaps he had done nothing to warrant his death other than to be somewhere he should not have been, seen something he should not have seen.

What Bosch had were just parts of the whole. What he needed was the glue that would correctly hold them together. When he had first received his gold shield he had a partner on the robbery table in Van Nuys who told him that facts weren't the most important part of an investigation, the glue was. He said the glue was made of instinct, imagination, sometimes guesswork and most times just plain luck.

Two nights earlier Bosch had looked at the facts that lay inside a run-down motel room and from them extrapolated a cop's suicide. He now knew he'd been wrong. He considered the facts again, along with everything else he had collected, and this time he saw a cop's murder as one of several connected murders. If Mexicali was the hub of the wheel with so many spokes, then Moore was the bolt that held the wheel on.

He took out his notebook and looked up the name of the DEA agent who was listed on the intelligence report Moore had put in the Zorrillo file. He then got the DEA's local number out of his Rolodex and dialed it. The man who answered asked who was calling when Bosch asked for Corvo.

"Tell him it's the ghost of Calexico Moore."

One minute later a voice said, "Who's this?"

"Corvo?"

"Look, you want to talk, give me an ID. Otherwise I hang up."

Bosch identified himself.

"What's with the ruse, man?"

"Never mind. I want to meet."

"You haven't given me a reason yet."

"You want a reason? Okay. Tomorrow morning, I'm going to Mexicali. I'm going after Zorrillo. I could use some help from somebody who knows his shit. I thought you might want to talk first. Being that you were Cal Moore's source."

"Who says I even knew the guy?"

"You took my call, didn't you? You also were passing DEA intelligence to him. He told me."

"Bosch, I spent seven years under. You trying to bluff me? Uh-uh. Try some of the eightball dealers on Hollywood Boulevard. They might buy your line."

"Look, man, at seven o'clock I'll be at the Code Seven, in the back bar. After that, I'll be heading south. It's your choice. If I see you, I see you."

"And if I decide to show up, how will I know you?"

"Don't worry. I'll know you. You'll be the guy who still thinks he's under-cover."

When he hung up, Harry looked up and saw Pounds hovering near the homicide table, standing there reading the latest CAP report, another sore subject for the division's statisticians. Crimes Against Persons, meaning all crimes of violence, were growing at a rate faster than the overall crime rate. That meant not only was crime going up but the criminals were becoming meaner, more prone to violence. Bosch noticed the white dust on the upper part of the lieutenant's pants. It was there often and was cause for great comical debate and derision in the squad room. Some of the dicks said he was probably blowing coke up his nose and was just sloppy about it. This was especially humorous because Pounds was one of the department's born-agains. Others said the mystery dust was from sugar doughnuts that he secretly scarfed down in the glass booth after closing the blinds so no one would see. Bosch, though, figured it out once he identified the odor that was always about Pounds. Harry believed the lieutenant had the habit of putting baby powder on in the morning before he put on his shirt and tie — but after putting on his pants.

Pounds looked away from his report and said in a phoney matter-of-fact voice, "So how's it looking? Getting anywhere with the cases?"

Bosch smiled reassuringly and nodded but said nothing. He'd make Pounds work for it.

"Well, what's up?"

"Oh, some things. Have you heard from Porter today?"

"Porter? No, why? Forget about him, Bosch. He's a mutt. He can't help you. What have you got? You haven't filed any updates. I just went through the box. Nothing from you there."

"I've been busy, Lieutenant. I got something going on Jimmy Kapps and I got an ID and possible death scene on Porter's last case. The one dumped in the alley off Sunset last week. I'm close to knowing who and why. Maybe tomorrow on both of them. I'm going to work through the weekend if that's okay with you."

"Excellent. By all means, take the time you need. I'll fill the overtime authorization out today."

"Thanks."

"But why juggle the cases? Why don't you pick the one you think is easier to complete? We need to clear a case."

"I think the cases are related, that's why."

"Are you —" Then Pounds held up his hand, signaling Bosch not to speak. "Better come into my office for this."

After sitting down behind his glass-topped desk, Pounds immediately picked up his ruler and began manipulating it in his hand.

"Okay, Harry, what's going on?"

Bosch was going to wing it. He tried to make his voice sound as though he had hard evidence to back everything he was saying. Truth was it was all a lot of speculation and not a lot of glue. He sat down in the chair in front of the lieutenant's desk. He could smell the baby powder on the other man.

"Jimmy Kapps was a payback. Found out yesterday that he set up a bust on a competitor named Dance. He was putting black ice out on the street. Jimmy apparently didn't like that 'cause he's trying to make Hawaiian ice the growth market. So he snitched Dance off to the BANG guys. Only after Dance got taken down, the DA kicked the case. A bad bust. He walked. Four days later Kapps gets the whack."

"Okay, okay," Pounds said. "Sounds good. Dance is your suspect then?"

"Until I come up with something better. He's in the wind."

"Okay, now how does this tie in with the Juan Doe case?"

"The DEA says the black ice that Dance was putting out comes from Mexicali. I got a tentative ID from the state police down there. Looks like our Juan Doe was a guy named Gutierrez-Llosa. He was from Mexicali."

"A mule?"

"Possibly. Couple things don't fit with that. The state police down there carried him as a day laborer."

"Maybe he went for the big money. A lot of them do."

"Maybe."

"And you think he got whacked back, a payback for Kapps?"

"Maybe."

Pounds nodded. So far so good, Bosch thought. They were both silent for a few moments. Pounds finally cleared his throat.

"That's quite a lot of work for two days, Harry. Very good. Now where do you go from here?"

"I want to go after Dance and get the Juan Doe ID confirmed . . ." He trailed off. He wasn't sure how much to give Pounds. He knew he was going to keep his trip to Mexicali out of it.

"You said Dance is in the wind."

"I'm told that by a source. I'm not sure. I plan to go looking this weekend."

"Fine."

Bosch decided to open the door a little further.

"There's more to it, if you want to hear it. It's about Cal Moore."

Pounds put the ruler down on the desk, folded his arms and leaned back. His posture signaled caution. They were stepping into an area where careers could be permanently damaged.

"Aren't we getting on thin ice, here? The Moore case is not ours."

"And I don't want it, Lieutenant. I've got these two. But it keeps coming up. If you don't want to know, fine. I can deal with it."

"No, no, I want you to tell me. I just don't like this kind of . . . uh, entanglement. That's all."

"Yeah, entanglement is a good word. Anyway, like I said, it was the BANG crew that made the Dance bust. Moore wasn't there until after it went down, but it was his crew.

"After that, you have Moore finding the body on the Juan Doe case."

"Cal Moore found the body?" Pounds said. "I didn't see that in Porter's book."

"He's in there by badge number. Anyway, he was the one that found the body dumped there. So you've got his presence around both of these cases. Then, the day after he finds Juan Doe in the alley he checks into that motel and gets his brains splattered in the bathtub. I suppose you've heard RHD now says it was no suicide."

Pounds nodded. But he had a paralysed look on his face. He had thought he was going to get a summary of a couple of case investigations. Not this.

"Somebody whacked him, too," Bosch continued. "So now you have three cases. You have Kapps, then Juan Doe, then Moore. And you have Dance in the wind."

Bosch knew he had said enough. He could now sit back and watch Pounds's mind go to work. He knew that the lieutenant knew that he should probably pick up the phone and call Irving to ask for assistance or at least direction. But Pounds knew that a call like that would result in RHD taking jurisdiction over the Kapps and Juan Doe cases. And the RHD dicks would take their sweet-ass time about it. Pounds wouldn't see any of the cases closed out for weeks.

"What about Porter? What's he say about all of this?"

Bosch had been doing his best to keep Porter clear. He didn't know why. Porter had fallen and had lied, but somewhere inside Bosch still felt something. Maybe it was that last question. *Harry, you going to take care of me on this?*

"I haven't found Porter," Bosch lied. "No answer on his phone. But I don't think he'd had much time to put all of this together."

Pounds shook his head disdainfully.

"Of course not. He probably was on a drunk."

Bosch didn't say anything. It was in Pounds's court now.

"Listen, Harry, you're not . . . you're being straight with me here, right? I can't afford to have you running around like a loose cannon. I've got it all, right?"

Bosch knew that what he meant was he wanted to know how badly he could be fucked if this went to shit.

Bosch said, "You know what I know. There are two cases, probably three, including Moore, out there to be cleared. You want 'em cleared in six, eight weeks, then I'll write up the paper and you can ship it to Parker Center. If you want to get them cleared by the first like you said, then let me have the four days."

Pounds was staring off somewhere above Bosch's head and using the ruler to scratch himself behind the ear. He was making a decision.

"Okay," he finally said. "Take the weekend and see what you can do. We'll see where things stand Monday. We might have to call in RHD then. Meantime, I want to hear from you tomorrow and Sunday. I want to know your movements, what's happening, what progress has been made."

"You got it," Bosch said. He stood up and turned to leave. He noticed that above the door was a small crucifix. He wondered if that had been what Pounds had been staring at. Most said he was a political born-again. There were a lot in the department. They all joined a church up in the Valley because one of the assistant chiefs was a lay preacher there. Bosch guessed they all went there Sunday mornings and gathered around him, told him what a great guy he was.

"I'll talk to you tomorrow, then," Pounds said from behind.

"Right. Tomorrow."

A short while after that, Pounds locked his office and went home. Bosch hung around the office alone, drinking coffee and smoking and waiting for the six o'clock news. There was a small black-and-white television on top of the file cabinet behind the autos table. He turned it on and played with the rabbit ears until he got a reasonably clear picture. A couple of the uniforms walked down from the watch office to watch.

Cal Moore had finally made the top of the news. Channel 2 led with a report on the press conference at Parker Center in which Assistant Chief Irvin Irving revealed new developments. The tape showed Irving at a cluster of microphones. Teresa stood behind him. Irving credited her with finding new evidence during the autopsy that pointed to homicide. Irving said a full-scale homicide investigation was underway. The report ended with a photograph of Moore and a voiceover from the reporter.

"Investigators now have the task, and they say the personal obligation, to dig deep into the life of Sergeant Calexico Moore to determine what it was that led him to the beat-up motel room where someone executed him. Sources tell me the investigators do not have much to start with, but they do start with a debt of thanks to the acting chief medical examiner, who discovered a murder that had been written off . . . as a cop's lonely suicide."

The camera zoomed in closer on Moore's face here and the reporter ended it, "And so, the mystery begins . . ."

Bosch turned the TV off after the report. The uniforms went back down the hall and he went back to his spot at the homicide table and sat down. The picture they had shown of Moore had been taken a few years back, Harry guessed. His face was younger, the eyes clearer. There was no portent of a hidden life.

Thinking about it brought to mind the other photographs, the ones Sylvia Moore had said her husband had collected over his life and looked at from time to time. What else had he saved from the past? Bosch didn't have one photo of his mother. He hadn't known his father until the old man was on his deathbed. What baggage did Cal Moore carry with him?

It was time for him to head for the Code Seven. But before heading out to the car, Harry walked down the hall to the watch office. He picked up the clipboard that hung on the wall next to the wanted flyers and carried the station's duty roster clipped to it. He doubted that it would have been updated in the last week and he was correct. He found Moore's name and address in Los Feliz on the page listing sergeants. He copied the address into his notebook and then headed out.

17

Bosch dragged deeply on a cigarette and then dropped the butt into the gutter. He hesitated before pulling the billy club that was the door handle of the Code Seven. He stared across First Street to the grass square that flanked City Hall and was called Freedom Park. Beneath the sodium lights he saw the bodies of homeless men and women sprawled asleep in the grass around the war memorial. They looked like casualties on a battlefield, the unburied dead.

He went inside, walked through the front restaurant and then parted the black curtains that hid the entrance to the bar like a judge's robes. The place was crowded with lawyers and cops and blue with cigarette smoke. They had all come to wait out the rush hour and either gotten too comfortable or too drunk. Harry went down to the end of the bar where the stools were empty and ordered a beer and a shot. It was seven on the dot according to the Miller clock over the bar. He scanned the room in the mirror behind the bar but saw nobody he could assume was the DEA agent Corvo. He lit another cigarette and decided he would give it until eight.

The moment he decided that he looked back in the mirror and saw a short, dark man with a full black beard split the curtain and hesitate as his eyes focused in the dim bar. He wore blue jeans and a pullover shirt. Bosch saw the pager on his belt and the bulge the gun made under his shirt. The man looked around until their eyes met in the mirror and Harry nodded once. Corvo came over and took the stool next to him.

"So you made me," Corvo said.

"And you made me. I guess we both need to go back to the academy. You want a beer?"

"Look, Bosch, before you start getting friendly on me, I gotta tell you I don't know about this. I don't know what this is about. I haven't decided whether to talk to you."

Harry took his cigarette from the ashtray and looked at Corvo in the mirror.

"I haven't decided if Certs is a breath mint or a candy."

Corvo slid back off his stool.

"Have a good one."

"C'mon Corvo, have a beer, why don't you? Relax, man."

"I checked you out before I came over. The line on you is that you're just another head case. You're on the fast track to nowhere. RHD to Hollywood, the next stop probably riding shotgun in a Wells Fargo truck."

"No, the next stop is Mexicali. And I can go down there blind, maybe walk in on whatever you got going with Zorrillo, or you can help me and yourself by telling me what's what."

"What's what is that you aren't going to do anything down there. I leave here I pick up the phone and your trip is over."

"I leave here and I'm gone, on my way. Too late to stop. Have a seat. If I've been an asshole, I'm sorry. It's the way I am sometimes. But I need you guys and you guys need me."

Corvo still didn't sit down.

"Bosch, what are you gonna do? Go down to the ranch, put the pope over your shoulder and carry him back up here? That it?"

"Something like that."

"Shit."

"Actually, I don't know what I'm going to do. I'm just going to play it as it comes. Maybe I never see the pope, maybe I do. You want to risk it?"

Corvo slid back onto the stool and signaled the bartender. He ordered the same as Bosch. In the mirror Bosch noticed a long, thick scar cutting through the right side of Corvo's beard. If he had grown the beard to cover the purplish-pink slug on his cheek, it hadn't worked. Then again, maybe he didn't want it to. Most DEA agents Bosch knew or had worked with had a macho swagger about them. A scar couldn't hurt. It was a life of bluffing and bluster. Scars were worn like badges of courage. But Bosch wondered if the guy could do much undercover work with such a recognizable physical anomaly.

After the bartender put down the drinks, Corvo threw back the shot like a man used to it.

"So," he said. "What are you really going down there for? And why should I trust you the least bit?"

Bosch thought about it for a few moments.

"Because I can give you Zorrillo."

"Shit."

Bosch didn't say anything. He had to give Corvo his due, had to let him run out his string. After he was done posturing they would get down to business. Bosch thought at the moment that the one thing the movies and TV shows didn't get wrong or overexaggerate was the relationship of jealousy and distrust that existed between local and federal cops. One side always thought it was better, wiser, more qualified. Usually, the side that thought that was wrong.

"Okay," Corvo said. "I'll bite. What have you got?"

"Before I get into it. I have one question. Who are you, man? I mean, you're up here in L.A. Why are you the one in Moore's files? How come you're the expert on Zorrillo?"

"That's about ten questions. The basic answer to all of them is I'm a control agent on an investigation in Mexicali that is being jointly worked by Mexico City and L.A. offices. We are equidistant; we are splitting the case. I'm not telling you anything else until I know you're worth talking to. Talk."

Bosch told him about Jimmy Kapps, Juan Doe and the ties between their deaths and Dance and Moore and the Zorrillo operation. Lastly, he said that he had information that Dance had gone to Mexico, probably Mexicali, after Moore was murdered.

Corvo drained his beer glass and said, "Tell me something, because it's a big fucking hole in your scenario. How come you think this Juan Doe was whacked out down there? And then, how come his body was taken all the way up here? Doesn't make sense to me."

"The autopsy puts his death six to eight hours before Moore found it, or said he found it up here. There were things about the autopsy that tie it to Mexicali, to a specific location in Mexicali. I think they wanted to get it out of Mexicali to make sure it was not connected to that location. It got sent to L.A. because there was already a truck heading this way. It was convenient."

"You're talking jigsaws, Bosch. What location are we talking about?"

"We aren't talking. That's the problem. I'm talking. You haven't said shit. But I'm here to trade. I know your record. You guys haven't taken down one of Zorrillo's shipments. I can give you Zorrillo's pipeline. What can you give me?"

Corvo laughed and shot a peace sign at the bartender. He brought two more beers.

"Know something? I like you. Believe it or not. I did check you out but I do like what I know of you. But something tells me you don't have shit worth trading for."

"You ever check out a place down there called EnviroBreed?"

Corvo looked down at the beer placed in front of him and seemed to be composing his thoughts. Bosch had to prompt him.

"Yes or no?"

"EnviroBreed is a plant down there. They make these sterile fruit flies to set loose around here. It's a government contractor. They have to breed the bugs down there 'cause —"

"I know all of that. How come you know?"

"The only reason is that I was involved in setting plans on our operation down there. We wanted a ground Observation Point on the target's ranch. We went into the industrial parks that border the ranch to look for candidates. EnviroBreed was obvious. American-managed. It was a government contractor. We went to see if we could set up an OP, maybe on the roof or an office or something. The ranch property starts just across the street."

"But they said no."

"No, actually, they said yes. We said no."

"How come?"

"Radiation. Bugs — they got those damned flies buzzing all over the god-damn place. But most of all the view was obscured. We went up on the roof and we could see the ranch all right but the barn and stables — the whole bull-breeding facility — was in line between EnviroBreed and the main ranch facilities. We couldn't use the place. We told the guy there, thanks but no thanks."

"What was your cover? Or did you just come out and say DEA?"

"Nah, we cooked something up. Said we were from the National Weather Service on a project tracking desert and mountain wind systems. Some bullshit like that. The guy bought it."

"Right."

Corvo wiped his mouth with the back of his hand.

"So, how does EnviroBreed figure into it from this end?"

"My Juan Doe. He had those bugs you were talking about in his body. I think he was probably killed there."

Corvo turned so he was looking directly at Bosch. Harry continued to watch him in the mirror behind the bar.

"Okay, Bosch, let's say you've got my attention. Go ahead and spin the tale."

Bosch said he believed that EnviroBreed, which he didn't even know was across from Zorrillo's ranch until Corvo told him, was part of the black ice pipeline. He told Corvo the rest of his theory: that Fernal Gutierrez-Llosa was a day laborer who either hired on as a mule and didn't make the grade or had worked at the bug breeding plant and seen something he should not have seen or done something he should not have done. Either way, he was beaten to death, his body put in one of the white environment boxes and taken with a shipment of fruit flies to Los Angeles. His body was then dumped in Hollywood and reported by Moore, who probably handled everything on this end.

"They had to get the body out of there because they couldn't bring an investigation into the plant. There is something there. At least, something that was worth killing an old man for."

Corvo had his arm up on the bar and his face in the palm of his hand. He said, "What did he see?"

"I don't know. I do know that EnviroBreed has a deal with the feds not to have their shipments across the border bothered with. Opening those boxes could damage the goods."

"Who have you told this to?"

"Nobody."

"Nobody? You have told no one about EnviroBreed?"

"I've made some inquiries. I haven't told anyone the story I just told you."

"Who have you made inquiries with? You called the SJP?"

"Yeah. They put out a letter to the consulate on the old man. That's how I put it together. I still have to make a formal ID of the body when I'm down there."

"Yeah, but did you bring up EnviroBreed?"

"I asked if they ever heard of him working at EnviroBreed."

Corvo spun back toward the bar with an exasperated sigh.

"Who did you talk to there?"

"A captain named Grena."

"I don't know him. But you've probably spoiled your lead. You just don't go to the locals with this sort of thing. They pick up the phone, tell Zorrillo what you just said and then pick up a bonus at the end of the month."

"Maybe it's spoiled, maybe it isn't. Grena brushed me off and may think that's it. At least I didn't go walking into the bug place and ask to set up a weather station."

Neither spoke. Each one thinking about what the other had said so far.

"I'm going to get down on this right away," Corvo said after a while. "You have to promise me you won't go fucking around with it when you get down there."

"I'm not promising anything. And so far I've done all the giving here. You haven't said shit."

"What do you want to know?"

"About Zorrillo."

"All you really gotta know is that we've wanted his ass for a long time."

This time Bosch signaled for two more beers. He lit a cigarette and saw the smoke blur his reflection in the mirror.

"Only thing you have to know about Zorrillo is that he is one smart fucker and, like I said, it wouldn't surprise me in the least if he already knows you're coming. Fuckin' SJP. We only deal with the *federales*. Even them you can trust about as much as an ex-wife."

Bosch nodded meaningfully, just hoping Corvo would continue.

"If he doesn't know now, he'll know before you get there. So you've got to watch your ass. And the best way of doing that is not to go. With you, I know, that isn't an option. The second best way is to skip the SJP altogether. You can't trust 'em. The pope has people inside there. Okay?"

Bosch nodded at him in the mirror. He decided to stop nodding all the time.

"Now, I know everything I just said went in your ears and out your asshole," Corvo said. "So what I'm willing to do is put you with a guy down there, work it from there. Name's Ramos. You go down, say your howdy-dos with the local SJPs, act like everything is nice, and then hook up with Ramos."

"If this EnviroBreed thing pans out and you make a move on Zorrillo, I want to be there."

"You will. Just hang with Ramos. Okay?"

Bosch thought it over a few moments and said, "Yeah. Now tell me about Zorrillo. You keep going off on other shit."

"Zorrillo's been around a long time. We've got intelligence on him going back to the seventies at least. A career doper. One of the bounces on the trampoline, I'd guess you'd call him."

Bosch had heard the term before but was confident Corvo would get around to explaining it anyway.

"Black ice is just his latest thing. He was a *marijuanito* when he was a kid. Pulled out of the barrio by someone like himself today. He took backpacks of grass over the fence when he was twelve, made the truck runs when he was older and just worked his way up. By the eighties, when we had most of our efforts concentrated on Florida, the Colombians contracted with the Mexicans. They flew cocaine to Mexico and the Mexicans took it across the border, using the same old pot trails. Mexicali across to Calexico was one of them. They called the route the Trampoline. The shit bounces from Colombia to Mexico and then up to the states.

"And Zorrillo became a rich man. From the barrio to that nice big ranch with his own personal *guardia* and half the cops in Baja on his payroll. And the cycle started over. He pulled most of his people out of the slums. He never forgot the barrio and it never forgot him. A lot of loyalty. That's when he got the name El Papa. So once we shifted our resources a little bit to address the cocaine situation in Mexico, the pope moved on to heroin. He had tar labs in the nearby barrios. Always had volunteers to mule it across. For one trip he'd pay one of those poor suckers down there more than they'd make in five years doing anything else."

Bosch thought of the temptation, that much money for what amounted to so little risk. Even those who were caught spent little time in jail.

"It was a natural transition to go from tar heroin to black ice. Zorrillo's an entrepreneur. Obviously, this is a drug that is in its infancy as far as awareness in the drug culture goes. But we think he is the country's main supplier. We've got black ice showing up all over the place. New York, Seattle, Chicago, all your large cities. Whatever operation you stumbled over in L.A., that was just a drop in the bucket. One of many. We think he's still running straight heroin with his barrio mules but the ice is his growth product. It's the future and he knows it. He's shifting more and more of his operation into it and he's going to drive Hawaiians out. His overhead is so low, his stuff is selling twenty bucks a cap below the going rate for Hawaiian ice, or glass, or whatever they call it this week. And Zorrillo's stuff is better. He's putting the Hawaiians out of business on the mainland. Then when the demand for this thing really starts to escalate — conceivably as fast as crack did in the mid-eighties — he'll bump the price and have a virtual monopoly until the others catch up with him.

"Zorrillo's kinda like one of those fishing boats with the ten-mile net behind it. He's circling around and he's going to pull that sucker closed on all the fish."

"An entrepreneur," Bosch said, just to be saying something.

"Yeah, that's what I'd call him. You remember a couple years ago the Border Patrol found the tunnel in Arizona? Went from a warehouse on one side of the border to a warehouse on the other? In Nogales? Well, we think that he was an investor in that. One of them at least. It was probably his idea."

"But the bottom line is you've never touched him."

"Nope. Whenever we'd get close, somebody'd end up dead. I guess you'd say he's a violent sort of entrepreneur."

Bosch envisioned Moore's body in the dingy motel bathroom. Had he been planning to make a move, to go against Zorrillo?

"Zorrillo's tied in with the *eMe*," Corvo said. "Word is he can have anybody anywhere whacked out. Supposedly back in the seventies there was all kinds of slaughter going on for control of the pot trails. Zorrillo emerged on top. It was like a gang war, barrio against barrio. He has since united all of them but back then, his was the dominant clan. Saints and Sinners. A lot of the *eMe* came out of that."

The *eMe* was the Mexican Mafia, a Latino gang with control over inmates in most of Mexico's and California's prisons. Bosch knew little about them and had had few cases that involved members. He did know that allegiance to the group was strictly enforced. Infractions were punishable by death.

"How do you know all of that?" he asked.

"Informants over the years. The ones that lived to talk about it. We've got a whole history on our friend the pope. I even know he's got a velvet painting of Elvis in his office at the ranch."

"Did his barrio have a sign?"

"What do you mean, a sign?"

"A symbol."

"It's the devil. With a halo."

Bosch emptied his beer and looked around the bar. He saw a deputy district attorney he knew was part of a team that rubber-stamped investigations of police shootings. He was sitting alone at a table with a martini. There were a few cops Bosch recognized huddled at other tables. They all were smoking, dinosaurs all. Harry wanted to leave, to go somewhere he could think about this information. The devil with a halo. Moore had it tattooed on his arm. He had come from the same place as Zorrillo. Harry could feel his adrenaline kicking up a notch.

"How will I get together with Ramos down there?"

"He'll come to you. Where're you staying?"

"I don't know."

"Stay at the De Anza, in Calexico. It's safer on our side of the border. Water's better for you, too."

"Okay. I'll be there."

"Another thing is, you can't take a weapon across. I mean, it's easy enough to do. You flash your badge at the crossing and nobody's going to check your trunk. But if something happens down there, the first thing that will be checked is whether you checked your gun in at the police station in Calexico."

He nodded meaningfully at Bosch.

"They have a gun locker at Calexico PD where they check weapons for crossing cops. They keep a log, you get a receipt. Professional courtesy. So check a weapon. Don't take it across and then think you can say you left it up here at home. Check it in down there. Get it on the log. Then you don't have a problem. *Comprende?* It's like having an alibi for your gun in case something happens."

Bosch nodded. He knew what Corvo was telling him.

Corvo took out his wallet and gave Bosch a business card.

"Call anytime and if I'm not in the office they will locate me. Just tell the operator it's you. I'll leave your name and word that you are to be put through."

Corvo's speech pattern had changed. He was talking faster. Bosch guessed this was because he was excited about the EnviroBreed tip. The DEA agent was anxious to get on it. Harry studied him in the mirror. The scar on his cheek seemed darker now, as if it had changed color with his mood. Corvo looked at him in the mirror.

"Knife fight," he said, fingering the scar. "Zihuatenajo. I was under, working a case. Carrying my piece in my boot. Guy got me here before I could get to the boot. Down there they don't have hospitals for shit. They did a bad job on it and I ended up with this. I couldn't go under anymore. Too recognizable."

Bosch could tell he liked telling the story. He was stoked with bravado as he told it. It was probably the one time he had come close to his own end. Bosch knew what Corvo was waiting for him to ask. He asked anyway.

"And the guy who did it? What did he get?"

"A state burial. I put him down once I got to my piece."

Corvo had found a way to make killing a man who brought a knife to a gunfight sound heroic. At least to his own ears. He probably told the story a lot, every time he caught someone new looking at the scar. Bosch nodded respectfully and slipped off his stool and put money on the bar.

"Remember our deal. You don't move on Zorrillo without me. Make sure you tell Ramos."

"Oh, we've got a deal," Corvo said. "But I'm not guaranteeing it will happen when you're down there. We aren't going to rush anything. Besides, we've lost Zorrillo. Temporarily, I'm sure."

"What are you talking about, you've lost him?"

"I mean we haven't had a bona fide sighting in about ten days or so. We think he's there on the ranch, though. He's just laying low, changing his routine."

"Routine?"

"The pope is a man who likes to be seen. He likes to taunt us. Usually, he rides the ranch in a Jeep, hunting coyotes, shooting his Uzi, admiring his bulls. There is one bull in particular, a champion that once killed a matador. El Temblar, he is called. Zorrillo often goes out to watch this bull. It's like him, I guess. Very proud.

"Anyway, Zorrillo has not been seen on the ranch or the Plaza de Toros, which was his Sunday custom. He hasn't been seen cruising the barrios, reminding himself of where he came from. He's a well-known figure in them all. He gets off on this pope of Mexicali shit."

Bosch tried to imagine Zorrillo's life. A celebrity in a town that celebrated nothing. He lit a cigarette. He wanted to get out of there.

"So when was the last bona fide?"

"If he is still there, he hasn't come out of the compound since December fifteenth. That was a Sunday. He was at the plaza watching his bulls. That's the last bona fide. After that, we have some informants who move that up to the eighteenth. They say they saw him at the compound, dicking around outside. But that's it. He's either split or he is laying low, like I said."

"Maybe because he ordered a cop blown away."

Corvo nodded.

Bosch left alone after that. Corvo said he was going to use the pay phone. Harry stepped out of the bar, felt the brisk night air and took the last drag on his cigarette. He saw movement in the darkness of the park across the street. Then one of the crazies moved into the cone of light beneath a streetlight. It was a black man, high-stepping and making jerking movements with his arms. He made a crisp turn and began moving back into the darkness. He was a trombone player in a marching band in a world somewhere else.

18

The apartment building where Cal Moore had lived was a three-story affair that stuck out on Franklin about the same way cabs do at the airport. It was one of the many stuccoed, post–World War II jobs that lined the streets in that area. It was called The Fountains but they had been filled in with dirt and made into planters. It was about a block from the mansion that was headquarters for the Church of Scientology and the complex's white neon sign threw an eerie glow down to where Bosch was standing on the curb. It was near ten o'clock, so he wasn't worried about anyone offering him a personality test. He stood there smoking and studying the apartment building for a half hour before finally deciding to go ahead with the break-in.

It was a security building but it really wasn't. Bosch slipped the lock on the front gate with a butter knife he kept with his picks in the glove compartment of the Caprice. The next door, the one leading to the lobby, he didn't have to worry about. It needed to be oiled and showed this by not snapping all the way closed. Bosch went through the door, checked a listing of tenants and found Moore's name listed next to number seven, on the third floor.

Moore's place was at the end of a hallway that split the center of the floor. At the door, Harry saw the police evidence sticker had been placed across the jamb. He cut it with the small pen knife attached to his key chain and then knelt down to look at the lock. There were two other apartments on the hallway. He heard no TV sound or talking coming from either. The lighting in the hall was good, so he didn't need the flashlight. Moore had a standard pin tumbler dead bolt on the door. Using a curved tension hook and saw-tooth comb, he turned the lock in less than two minutes.

With his handkerchief-wrapped hand on the knob ready to open the door, he wondered again how prudent he was in coming here. If Irving or Pounds found out, he'd be back on the street in blue before the first of the year. He looked down the hall behind him once more and opened the door. He had to go in. Nobody else seemed to care what had happened to Cal Moore and that was fine. But Bosch did care for some reason. He thought maybe he would find that reason here.

Once inside the apartment, he closed and relocked the door. He stood there, a couple of feet inside, letting his eyes adjust. The place smelled musty and was dark, except for the bluish-white glow of the Scientology light that leaked through the sheer curtains over the living room window. Bosch walked into the room and switched on the lamp on an end table next to an old misshapen sofa. The light revealed that the place had come furnished in the same decor it had maybe twenty years ago. The navy blue carpet was worn flat as Astroturf in pathways from the couch to the kitchen and to the hallway that went off to the right.

He moved farther in and took quick glances in the kitchen and the bedroom and the bathroom. He was struck by the emptiness of the place. There was nothing personal here. No pictures on the walls, no notes on the refrigerator; no jacket hung over the back of a chair. There wasn't even a dish in the sink. Moore had lived here but it was almost as if he hadn't existed.

He didn't know what he was looking for, so he started in the kitchen. He opened cabinets and drawers. He found a box of cereal, a can of coffee and a three-quarters-empty bottle of Early Times. In another cabinet he found an unopened bottle of sweet rum with a Mexican label. Inside the bottle was a stalk of sugar cane. There was some silverware and cooking tools in the drawers, several books of matches from Hollywood area bars like Ports and the Bullet.

The freezer was empty, except for two trays of ice. On the top shelf in the refrigerator section below there was a jar of mustard, a half-finished package of now-rancid bologna and a lone can of Budweiser, its plastic six-pack collar still choking it. On the lower shelf on the door was a two-pound bag of Domino sugar.

Harry studied the sugar. It was unopened. Then he thought, What the hell, I've come this far. He took it out and opened it and slowly poured it into the sink. It looked like sugar to him. It tasted like sugar to him. There was nothing else in the bag. He turned on the hot water and watched as the white mound was washed down the drain.

He left the bag on the counter and went into the bathroom. There was a toothbrush in the holder, shaving equipment behind the mirror. Nothing else.

In the bedroom Bosch first went into the walk-in closet. An assortment of clothes was on hangers and more filled a plastic laundry basket on the floor. On the shelf there was a green plaid suitcase and a white box with the word "Snakes" printed on it. Bosch first dumped the basket over and checked the pockets of the dirty shirts and pants. They were empty. He picked through the hanging clothes until he reached the back of the closet and found Moore's dress uniform wrapped in plastic. Once you left patrol, there was really only one reason to save it. To be buried in. Bosch thought saving it was a bad omen, a lack of confidence. As required by the department, he kept one uniform, to be worn in time of civil crisis such as a major earthquake or riot. But he had dumped his dress blues ten years ago.

He brought down the suitcase; it was empty and smelled musty. It had not been used for some time. He pulled down the boot box but could tell it was empty before he opened it. There was some tissue paper inside it.

Bosch put it back up on the shelf, remembering how he had seen Moore's one boot standing upright on the tile in the bathroom at the Hideaway. He wondered if Moore's killer had had difficulty pulling it off to complete the suicide scene. Or had he ordered Moore to take it off first? Probably not. The blow to the back of the head that Teresa found meant Moore probably hadn't known what hit him. Bosch envisioned the killer, his identity cloaked in shadow, coming up from behind and swinging the stock of the shotgun against the back of Moore's head. Moore goes down. The killer pulls off the boot, drags him into his bathroom, props him against the tub and pulls both triggers. Wipe off the triggers, press the dead man's thumb against the stock and rub his hands on the barrels to make convincing smears. Then set the boot upright on the tile. Add the splinter from the stock and the scene was set. Suicide.

The queen-sized bed was unmade. On the night table was a couple of dollars in change and a small framed photograph of Moore and his wife. Bosch bent over and studied it without touching it. Sylvia was smiling and appeared to be sitting in a restaurant, or perhaps at a banquet table at a wedding. She was beautiful in the picture and her husband was looking at her as if he knew it.

"You fucked up, Cal," Harry said to no one.

He moved to the bureau, which was so old and scarred by cigarettes and knife-cut initials that the Salvation Army might even reject it. In the top drawer were a comb and a cherrywood picture frame lying face down. Bosch picked up the frame and saw that it was empty. He considered this for a few moments. The frame had a floral design carved into it. It would have been expensive and obviously did not come with the apartment. Moore had brought it with him. Why was it empty? He would have liked to be able to ask Sheehan if he or anybody else had taken a photograph from the apartment as part of the investigation. But he couldn't without revealing he had been here.

The next drawer contained underwear and socks and a stack of folded T-shirts, nothing else. There were more clothes in the third drawer, all having been neatly folded at a laundry. Beneath a stack of shirts was a skin magazine which announced on the cover that nude photos of a leading Hollywood actress were provided inside. Bosch leafed through the magazine, more out of curiosity than belief there would be a clue inside. He was sure the magazine had been pawed over by every dick and blue suit who had been in the apartment during the investigation into Moore's disappearance.

He put the magazine back after seeing that the photos of the actress were dark, grainy shots in which it could just barely be determined that she was barebreasted. He assumed they were from an early movie, made before she had enough clout to control the exploitation of her body. He imagined the disappointment of the men who bought the magazine only to discover those shots were the payoff on the cover's lurid promise. He imagined the actress's anger and embarrassment. And he wondered what they did for Cal Moore. A vision of Sylvia Moore flashed in his head. He shoved the magazine under the shirts and closed the drawer.

The last drawer of the bureau contained two things, a folded pair of faded blue jeans and a white paper bag that was crumpled and soft with age and contained a thick stack of photographs. It was what he had come for. Bosch instinctively knew this when he picked the bag up. He took it out of the bedroom, hitting the switch turning off the ceiling light as he went through the door.

Sitting on the couch next to the light, he lit a cigarette and pulled the stack of photos from the bag. Immediately he recognized that most of them were faded and old. These photographs somehow seemed more private and invasive than even those in the skin mag. They were pictures that documented Cal Moore's unhappy history.

The photos seemed to be in some kind of chronological order. Bosch could tell this because they moved from faded black and white to color. Other benchmarks, like clothing and cars, also seemed to prove this.

The first photo was a black-and-white shot of a young Latina in what looked like a white nurse's uniform. She was dark and lovely and wore a girlish smile and a look of mild surprise as she stood next to a swimming pool, her arms behind her back. Bosch saw the edge of a round object behind her and then realized she was holding a servant tray behind her back. She had not wanted to be photographed with the tray. She wasn't a nurse. She was a maid. A servant.

There were other photographs of her in the stack, extending over several years. Age was kind to her but it still exacted its toll. She retained an exotic beauty but worry lines formed and her eyes lost some of their warmth. In some of the photographs Bosch leafed through, she held a baby, then she posed with a little boy. Bosch looked closely and even with the print being black and white he could see that the boy with dark hair and complexion had light-colored eyes. Green eyes, Bosch thought. It was Calexico Moore and his mother.

In one of the photos the woman and the small boy stood in front of a large white house with a Spanish-tile roof. It looked like a Mediterranean villa. Rising behind the mother and boy, but unclear because of the focus, was a tower. Two darkly blurred windows, like empty eyes, were near the top. Bosch thought about what Moore had said to his wife about growing up in a castle. This was it.

In another of the photos the boy stood rigidly next to a man, an Anglo with blond hair and darkly tanned skin. They stood next to the sleek form of a late-fifties Thunderbird. The man held one hand on the hood and one on the boy's head. They were his possessions, the photo seemed to say. The man squinted into the camera.

But Bosch could see his eyes. They were the same green eyes of his son. The man's hair was thinning on top and by comparing photos of the boy with his mother taken at about the same time, Bosch guessed that Moore's father had been at least fifteen years older than his mother. The photo of the father and son was worn around the edges from handling. Much more worn than any of the others in the stack.

The next grouping of photos changed the venue. They were pictures from what was probably Mexicali. There were fewer photos to document a longer period of time. The boy was growing by leaps and the backgrounds of the photos had a third-world quality to them. They were shot in the barrio. More often than not there were crowds of people in the background, all Mexicans, all having that slight look of desperation and hope Bosch had seen in the ghettos of L.A.

And now there was another boy. He was the same age or slightly older. He seemed stronger, tougher. He was in many of the same frames with Cal. A brother maybe, Bosch thought.

It was in this grouping of photos that the mother began to show clearly the advance of age. The girl who hid the servant's tray was gone. A mother used to the harshness of life had replaced her. The photos now took on a haunting quality. It bothered Harry to study them because he believed that he understood the hold the pictures had on Moore.

The last black-and-white photo showed the two boys, shirtless and sitting back to back on a picnic table, laughing at a joke preserved forever in time. Calexico was a young teenager with a guileless smile on his face. The other boy, maybe a year or two older, looked like trouble. He had a hard, sullen look in his eyes. In the picture Cal had his right arm cocked and was making a muscle for the photographer. Bosch saw the tattoo was already there. The devil with a halo. Saints and Sinners.

In the photos after that, the other boy never appeared again. These were color shots taken in Los Angeles. Bosch recognized City Hall shooting up in the background of one of them and the fountain in Echo Park in another. Moore and his mother had come to the United States. Whoever the other boy was, he had been left behind.

Toward the end of the stack, the mother dropped out of the photos as well. Harry wondered if that meant she was dead. The final two pictures were of Moore as an adult. The first was his graduation from the police academy. There was a shot of a class of newly sworn officers gathered on the grass outside what was later renamed the Daryl F. Gates Auditorium. They were throwing their hats into the air. Bosch picked Moore out of the crowd. He had his arm around the shoulder of another probee and there was genuine joy in his face.

And the last photo was of Moore in dress uniform pulling a young Sylvia close in a smiling cheek-to-cheek embrace. Her skin was smoother then, her eyes brighter and her hair longer and fuller. But she was still very much the same as now, still a beautiful woman.

He pushed the photographs back into the bag and put it on the couch next to him. He looked at the bag and was curious why the photos had never been mounted in an album or put on display. They were just glimpses of a lifetime kept in a bag and ready to go.

But he knew the reason. At his home he had stacks of his own pictures that he would never mount in a book, that he felt the need to hold when he looked at them. They were more than pictures of another time. They were parts of a life, a life that could not go forward without knowing and understanding what was behind.

Bosch reached up to the lamp and turned it off. He smoked another cigarette, the glow of its tip floating in the dark. He thought about Mexico and Calexico Moore.

"You fucked up," he whispered again.

He had told himself he had to come here to get a feel for Moore. That was how he had sold it to himself. But sitting there in the dark he knew there was more to it. He knew he had come because he wanted to understand a life's course that could not be explained. The only one with all the answers to all of the questions was Cal Moore. And he was gone.

He looked at the white neon glow on the curtains across the room and they looked like ghosts to him. It made him think of the worn photo of the father and son, fading to white. He thought of his own father, a man he never knew and did not meet until he was on his death bed. By then it had been too late for Bosch to change his own life's course.

He heard a key hit the dead bolt on the other side of the front door. He was up, with his gun out, moving quickly across the room to the hallway. He went into the bedroom first but then went back into the hall and into the bathroom because it afforded a better view of the living room. He dropped his cigarette into the toilet and heard it hiss as it died.

He heard the front door open and then a few seconds of silence. Then a light went on in the living room and he stepped back into the dark recesses of his hiding spot. In the medicine cabinet mirror he saw Sylvia Moore standing in the middle of the living room looking around as if it was her first time in the apartment. Her eyes fell on the white bag on the couch and she picked it up. Bosch watched her as she looked through the photographs. She lingered over the last one. It was the one of her. She held her hand to her cheek as if charting the changes of time.

When she was done, she put the photographs back in the bag and placed it back on the couch. She then started for the hallway and Bosch moved further back, silently stepping into the bathtub. Now a light came from the bedroom and he heard the closet door open. Hangers scraping on the bar. Bosch holstered his gun and then stepped out of the tub and the bathroom and into the hallway.

"Mrs. Moore? Sylvia?" he called from the hall, unsure how to get her attention without scaring her.

"Who's that?" came the high-pitched, frightened reply.

"It's me, Detective Bosch. It's okay."

She came out of the bedroom closet then, the fright wide in her eyes. She carried the hanger with her dead husband's dress uniform on it.

"Jesus, you scared me. What are you doing here?"

"I was going to ask you the same thing."

She held the uniform up in front of her as if Bosch had walked in on her while she was undressed. She took one step back toward the bedroom door.

"You followed me?" she said. "What's going on?"

"No, I didn't follow you. I was already here."

"In the dark?"

"Yes. I was thinking. When I heard somebody opening the door I went into the bathroom. Then when I saw it was you, I didn't know how to come out without scaring you. Sorry. You scared me. I scared you."

She nodded once, seeming to accept his explanation. She was wearing a light blue denim shirt and unbleached blue jeans. Her hair was tied behind her head and she wore earrings made of a pinkish crystal. Her left ear had a second earring. It was a silver crescent moon with a star hooked on its bottom point. She put on a polite smile. Bosch became aware that he had not shaved in a day.

"Did you think it was the killer?" she said when he said nothing else. "Kind of like coming back to the scene of the crime?"

"Maybe. Something like that . . . Actually, no, I don't know what I thought. This isn't the scene of the crime, anyway."

He nodded toward the uniform she carried.

"I have to take this by McEvoy Brothers tomorrow."

She must have read the frown on his face.

"It's a closed-casket service. Obviously. But I think he would've liked it this way, wearing the dress blues. Mr. McEvoy asked me if I had it."

Harry nodded. They were still in the hallway. He backed out into the living room and she followed.

"What do you hear from the department? How are they going to handle it? The funeral, I mean."

"Who knows? But as of now, they are saying he went down in the line of duty."

"So he's going to get the show."

"I think so."

A hero's farewell, Bosch thought. The department wasn't into self-flagellation. It wasn't going to announce to the world that a bad cop was put down by the bad people he had done bad things for. Not unless it had to. And not when it could throw a hero's funeral at the media and then sit back and watch sympathetic stories on seven different channels that night. The department needed all the sympathy it could get.

He also realized that a line-of-duty death meant the widow would get full pension rights. If Sylvia Moore wore a black dress, dabbed at her eyes with a tissue at appropriate times and kept her mouth shut, she'd get her husband's paycheck for the rest of her life. Not a bad deal. Either way. If Sylvia was the one who tipped IAD, she now stood to lose the pension if she pressed it or went public. The department could claim Cal had been killed because of his extracurricular activities. No pension. Bosch was sure this didn't have to be explained to her.

"So when's the funeral?" he asked.

"It's Monday at one. At the San Fernando Mission Chapel. The burial is at Oakwood, up in Chatsworth."

Well, Bosch thought, if they are going to put on the show, that's the place to do it. A couple hundred motor cops coming in in procession on curving Valley Circle Boulevard always made a good front-page photo.

"Mrs. Moore, why did you come here at" — he looked at his watch; it was 10:45 — "so late to get your husband's dress blues?"

"Call me Sylvia."

"Sure."

"To tell you the truth, I don't know why now. I haven't been sleeping — I mean at all — since it . . . since he was found. I don't know. I just felt like taking a drive. I just got the key to the place today, anyway."

"Who gave it to you?"

"Assistant Chief Irving. He came by, said they were through with the apartment and if there was anything I wanted I could take it. Trouble is, there isn't. I had hoped I'd never see this place. Then the man at the funeral home called and said he needed the dress uniform if I had it. Here I am."

Bosch picked the bag of photographs up off the couch and held it out to her.

"What about these? Do you want them?"

"I don't think so."

"Ever see them before?"

"I think some of them. At least, some of them seemed familiar. Some of them I know I never saw."

"Why do you think that is? A man keeps photographs his whole life and never shows some of them to his wife?"

"I don't know."

"Strange." He opened the bag and while he was looking through the photos said, "What happened to his mother, do you know?"

"She died. Before I knew him. Had a tumor in her head. He was about twenty, he said."

"What about his father?"

"He told me he was dead. But I told you, I don't know if that was true. Because he never said how or when. When I asked, he said he didn't want to talk about it. We never did."

Bosch held up the photo of the two boys on the picnic table.

"Who's this?"

She stepped close to him and looked at the photo. He studied her face. He saw flecks of green in her brown eyes. There was a light scent of perfume.

"I don't know who it is. A friend, I guess."

"He didn't have a brother?"

"Not one he ever told me about. He told me when we got married, he said I was his only family. He said . . . said he was alone except for me."

Now Bosch looked at the photo.

"Kinda looks like him to me."

She didn't say anything.

"What about the tattoo?"

"What about it?"

"He ever tell you where he got it, what it means?"

"He told me he got it in the village he grew up in. He was a boy. Actually, it was a barrio. I guess. They called it Saints and Sinners. That's what the tattoo means. Saints and Sinners. He said that was because the people that lived there didn't know which they were, which they would be."

He thought of the note found in Cal Moore's back pocket. *I found out who I was.* He wondered if she realized the significance of this in terms of the place he grew up. Where each young boy had to find out who he was. A saint or a sinner.

Sylvia interrupted his thoughts.

"You know, you didn't really say why you were already here. Sitting in the dark thinking. You had to come here to do that?"

"I came to look around, I guess. I was trying to shake something loose, get a feel for your husband. That sound stupid?"

"Not to me."

"Good."

"And did you? Did you shake something loose?"

"I don't know yet. Sometimes it takes a little while."

"You know, I asked Irving about you. He said you weren't on the case. He said you only came out the other night because the other detectives had their hands full with the reporters and . . . and the body."

Like a schoolboy, Bosch felt a tingling of excitement. She had asked about him. It didn't matter that now she knew he was freelancing on the case, she had made inquiries about him.

"Well," he said, "that's true, to a degree. Technically, I am not on the case. But I have other cases that are believed to be tied in with the death of your husband."

Her eyes never left his. He could see she wanted to ask what cases but she was a cop's wife. She knew the rules. In that moment he was sure she did not deserve what she had been handed. None of it.

He said, "It really wasn't you, was it? The tip to IAD. The letter."

She shook her head no.

"But they won't believe you. They think you started the whole thing."

"I didn't."

"What did Irving say? When he gave you the key to this place."

"Told me that if I wanted the money, the pension, I should let it go. Not get any ideas. As if I did. As if I cared anymore. I don't. I knew that Cal went wrong. I don't know what he did, I just knew he did it. A wife knows without being told. And that as much as anything else ended it between us. But I didn't send any letter like that. I was a cop's wife to the end. I told Irving and the guy who came before him that they had it wrong. But they didn't care. They just wanted Cal."

"You told me before it was Chastain who came?"

"It was him."

"What exactly did he want? You said something about he wanted to look inside the house."

"He held up the letter and said he knew I wrote it. He said I might as well tell him everything. Well, I told him I didn't write it and I told him to get out. But at first he wouldn't leave."

"What did he say he wanted, specifically?"

"He — I don't really remember it all. He wanted bank account statements and he wanted to know what properties we had. He thought I was sitting there waiting for him to come so I could give him my husband. He said he wanted the typewriter and I told him we didn't even have one. I pushed him out and closed the door."

He nodded and tried to compute these facts into those he already had. It was too much of a whirlwind.

"You don't remember anything about what the letter said?"

"I didn't really get the chance to read it. He didn't show it to me to read because he thought — and he and the others still believe — that it came from me. So I only read a little before he put it back in his briefcase. It said something about Cal being a front for a Mexican. It said he was giving protection. It said something along the lines that he had made a Faustian pact. You know what this is, right? A deal with the devil."

Bosch nodded. He was reminded that she was a teacher. He also realized that they had been standing in the living room for at least ten minutes. But he made no move to sit down. He feared that any sudden movement would break the spell, send her out the door and away from him.

"Well," she said. "I don't know if I would have gotten so allegorical if I had written it, but essentially that letter was correct. I mean, I didn't know what he had done but I knew something happened. I could see it was killing him inside.

"Once — this was before he left — I finally asked him what was happening and he just said he had made a mistake and he would try to correct it himself. He wouldn't talk about it with me. He shut me out."

She sat down on the edge of an upholstered chair, holding the dress blues on her lap. The chair was an awful green color and there were cigarette burns on its right arm. Bosch sat down on the couch next to the bag of photos.

She said, "Irving and Chastain. They don't believe me. They just nod their heads when I tell them. They say the letter had too many intimate details. It had to be me. Meanwhile, I guess somebody is happy out there. Their little letter brought him down."

Bosch thought of Kapps and wondered if he could have known enough details about Moore to have written the letter. He had set up Dance. Maybe he had tried to set up Moore first. It seemed unlikely. Maybe the letter had come from Dance because he wanted to move up the ladder and Moore was in the way.

Harry thought of the coffee can he had seen in the kitchen cabinet and wondered if he should ask her if she wanted some. He didn't want the time with her to end. He wanted to smoke but didn't want to risk having her ask him not to.

"Do you want any coffee? There is some in the kitchen I could make."

She looked toward the kitchen as if its location or cleanliness had a role in her answer. Then she said no, she wasn't planning to stay that long.

"I am going to Mexico tomorrow," Bosch said.

"Mexicali?"

"Yes."

"It's the other cases?"

"Yes."

Then he told her about them. About black ice and Jimmy Kapps and Juan Doe #67. And he told her of the ties to both her husband and Mexicali. It was there he hoped to unravel the whirlwind.

He finished the story by saying, "As you can tell, people like Irving, they want this to go by. They don't really care who killed Cal because he had crossed. They write him off like a bad debt. They are not going to pursue it because they don't want it to blow up in their faces. You understand what I'm saying?"

"I was a cop's wife, remember?"

"Right. So you know. The thing about this is I care. Your husband was putting a file together for me. A file on black ice. It makes me think like maybe he was trying to do something good. He might have been trying to do the impossible. To cross back. It might've been what got him killed. And if it is, then I'm not letting it go by."

They were quiet a long time after that. Her face looked pained but her eyes remained sharp and dry. She pulled the suit up higher on her lap. Bosch could hear a police helicopter circling somewhere in the distance. It wouldn't be L.A. without police helicopters and spotlights circling at night.

"Black ice," she said after a while in a whispery voice.

"What about it?"

"It's funny, that's all." She was quiet a few moments and seemed to look around the room, realizing this was the place her husband had come to after leaving her. "Black ice. I grew up in the Bay Area — San Francisco mostly — and that was something we always were told to watch out for. But, you know, it was the other black ice we were told about."

She looked at him then and must have read his confusion.

"In the winter, on those days when it really gets cold after a rain. When the rain freezes on the road, that's black ice. It's there on the road, on the black asphalt, but you can't see it. I remember my father teaching me to drive and he was always saying, 'Watch out for the black ice, girl. You don't see the danger until you are in it. Then it's too late. You're sliding out of control.'"

She smiled at the memory and said, "Anyway, that was the black ice I knew. At least while I was growing up. Just like coke used to be a soda. The meaning of things can change on you."

He just looked at her. He wanted to hold her again, touch the softness of her cheek with his own.

"Didn't your father ever tell you to watch out for the black ice?" she asked.

"I didn't know him. I sorta taught myself to drive."

She nodded and didn't say anything but didn't look away.

"It took me about three cars to learn. By the time I finally got it down, nobody would dare lend me a car. Nobody ever told me about the black ice, either."

"Well, I did."

"Thank you."

"Are you hung up on the past, too, Harry?"

He didn't answer.

"I guess we all are. What's that saying? Through studying the past we learn our future. Something like that. You seem to me to be a man still studying, maybe."

Her eyes seemed to look into him. They were eyes with great knowledge. And he realized that for all of his desires the other night, she did not need to be held or healed of pain. In fact, she was the healer. How could Cal Moore have run from this?

He changed the subject, not knowing why, only that he must push the attention away from himself.

"There's a picture frame in the bedroom. Carved cherrywood. But no picture. You remember it?"

"I'll have to look."

She stood, leaving her husband's suit on the chair, and moved into the bedroom. She looked at the frame in the top drawer of the bureau a long time before saying she didn't recognize it. She didn't look at Bosch until after she said this.

They stood there next to the bed looking at each other in silence. Bosch finally raised his hand, then hesitated. She took a step closer to him and that was the sign that his touch was wanted. He caressed her cheek, the way she had done it herself when she had studied the photograph earlier and thought she was alone. Then he dropped his hand down the side of her throat and around the back of her neck.

They stared at each other. Then she came closer and brought her mouth up to his. Her hand came to his neck and pulled him to her and they kissed. She held him and pressed herself against him in a way that revealed her need. He saw her eyes were closed now and at that moment Bosch realized she was his reflection in a mirror of hunger and loneliness.

They made love on her husband's unmade bed, neither of them paying mind to where they were or what this would mean the next day or week or year. Bosch kept his eyes closed, wanting to concentrate on other senses — her smell and taste and touch.

Afterward, he pulled himself back, so that his head lay on her chest between her freckled breasts. She had her hands in his hair and was drawing her fingers through the curls. He could hear her heart beating in rhythm with his.

19

It was after one A.M. by the time Bosch turned the Caprice onto Woodrow Wilson and began the long, winding ascent to his house. He saw the spotlights tracing eights on the low-lying clouds over Universal City. On the road he had to navigate his way around cars double-parked outside holiday parties and a discarded Christmas tree, a few strands of lonely tinsel still clinging to its branches, that had blown into his path. On the seat next to him were the lone Budweiser from Cal Moore's refrigerator and Lucius Porter's gun.

All his life he believed he was slumming toward something good. That there was meaning. In the youth shelter, the foster homes, the Army and Vietnam, and now the department, he always carried the feeling that he was struggling toward some kind of resolution and knowledge of purpose. That there was something good in him or about him. It was the waiting that was so hard. The waiting often left a hollow feeling in his soul. And he believed people could see this, that they knew when they looked at him that he was empty. He had learned to fill that hollowness with isolation and work. Sometimes drink and the sound of the jazz saxophone. But never people. He never let anyone in all the way.

And now he thought he had seen Sylvia Moore's eyes. Her true eyes, and he had to wonder if she was the one who could fill him.

"I want to see you," he had said when they separated outside The Fountains.

"Yes," was all she said. She touched his cheek with her hand and got into her car.

Now Bosch thought about what that one word and the accompanying touch could mean. He was happy. And that was something new.

As he rounded the last curve, slowing for a car with its brights on to pass, he thought of the way she had looked at the picture frame for so long before saying she did not recognize it. Had she lied? What were the chances that Cal Moore would have bought such an expensive frame after moving into a dump like that? Not good, was the answer.

By the time he pulled the Caprice into the carport, he was full of confusing feelings. What had been in the picture? What difference did it make that she had held that back? If she did. Still sitting in the car, he opened the beer and drank it down quickly, some of it spilling onto his neck. He would sleep tonight, he knew.

Inside, he went to the kitchen, put Porter's gun in a cabinet and checked the phone machine. There were no messages. No call from Porter saying why he had run. No call from Pounds asking how it was going. No call from Irving saying he knew what Bosch was up to.

After two nights with little sleep, Bosch looked forward to his bed as he did on few other nights. It was most often this way, part of a routine he kept. Nights of fleeting rest or nightmares followed by a single night when exhaustion finally drove him down hard into a dark sleep.

As he gathered the covers and pillows about him, he noticed there was still the trace of Teresa Corazón's powdery perfume on them. He closed his eyes and thought about her for a moment. But soon her image was pushed out of his mind by Sylvia Moore's face. Not the photo from the bag or the night stand, but the real face. Weary but strong, her eyes focused on Bosch's own.

The dream was like others Harry had had. He was in the dark place. A cavernous blackness enveloped him and his breath echoed in the dark. He sensed, or rather, he knew in the way he had knowledge of place in all his dreams that the darkness ended ahead and he must go there. But this time he was not alone. That was what was different. He was with Sylvia, and they huddled in the black, their sweat stinging their eyes. Harry held her and she held him. And they did not speak.

They broke from each other's embrace and began to move through the darkness. There was dim light ahead and Harry headed that way. His left hand was extended in front of him, his Smith & Wesson in its grasp. His right hand was behind him, holding hers and leading her along. And as they came into the light Calexico Moore was waiting there with the shotgun. He was not hidden, but he stood partially silhouetted by the light that poured into the passage. His green eyes were in shadow. And he smiled. Then he raised the shotgun.

"Who fucked up?" he said.

The roar was deafening in the blackness. Bosch saw Moore's hands fly loose from the shotgun and up away from his body like tethered birds trying to take flight. He back-stepped wildly into the darkness and was gone. Not fallen, but disappeared. Gone. Only the light at the end of the passage remained in his wake. In one hand Harry still gripped Sylvia's hand. In the other, the smoking gun.

He opened his eyes then.

Bosch sat up on the bed. He saw pale light leaking around the edges of the curtains on the windows facing east. The dream had seemed so short, but he realized because of the light he had slept until morning. He held his wrist up to the light and checked his watch. He had no alarm clock because he never needed one. It was six o'clock. He rubbed his face in his palms and tried to reconstruct the dream. This was unusual for him. A counselor at the sleep dysfunction lab at the VA had once told him to write down what he remembered from his dreams. It was an exercise, she said, to try to inform the conscious mind what the subconscious side was saying. For months he kept a notebook and pen by the bed and dutifully recorded his morning memories.

But Bosch had found it did him no good. No matter how well he understood the source of his nightmares, he could not eliminate them from his sleep. He had dropped out of the sleep deprivation counseling program years ago.

Now, he could not recapture the dream. Sylvia's face disappeared in the mist. Harry realized he had been sweating heavily. He got up and pulled the bed sheets off and dumped them in a basket in the closet. He went to the kitchen and started a pot of coffee. He showered, shaved and dressed in blue jeans, a green corduroy shirt and a black sport coat. Driving clothes. He went back to the kitchen and filled his Thermos with black coffee.

The first thing he took out to the car was his gun. He removed the rug that lined the trunk and then lifted out the spare tire and the jack that were stowed beneath it. He placed the Smith & Wesson, which he had taken from his holster and wrapped in an oilcloth, in the wheel well and put the spare tire back on top of it. He put the rug back in place and laid the jack down along the rear of the trunk. Next he put his briefcase in and a duffel bag containing a few days' changes of clothes. It all looked passable, though he doubted anyone would even look.

He went back inside and got his other gun out of the hallway closet. It was a forty-four with grips and safety configured for a right-handed shooter. The cylinder also opened on the left side. Bosch couldn't use it because he was left-handed. But he had kept it for six years because it had been given to him as a gift by a man whose daughter had been raped and murdered. Bosch had winged the killer during a brief shootout during his capture near the Sepulveda Dam in Van Nuys. He lived and was now serving life without parole. But that hadn't been enough for the father. After the trial he gave Bosch the gun and Bosch accepted it because not to take it would have been to disavow the man's pain. His message to Harry was clear; next time do the job right. Shoot to kill. Harry took the gun. And he could have taken it to a gunsmith and had it reconfigured for left-hand use, but to do that would be to acknowledge the father had been right. Harry wasn't sure he was ready to do that.

The gun had sat on a shelf in the closet for six years. Now he took it down, checked its action to make sure it was still operable, and loaded it. He put it in his holster and was ready to go.

On his way out, he grabbed his Thermos in the kitchen and bent over the phone machine to record a new message.

"It's Bosch. I will be in Mexico for the weekend. If you want to leave a message, hang on. If it's important and you want to try to reach me, I'll be at the De Anza Hotel in Calexico."

It was still before seven as he headed down the hill. He took the Hollywood Freeway until it skirted around downtown, the office towers opaque behind the early morning mixture of fog and smog. He took the transition road to the San Bernardino Freeway and headed east, out of the city. It was 250 miles to the border town of Calexico and its sister city of Mexicali, just on the other side of the fence. Harry would be there before noon. He poured himself a cup of coffee without spilling any and began to enjoy the drive.

The smog from L.A. didn't clear until Bosch was past the Yucaipa turnoff in Riverside County. After that the sky turned as blue as the oceans on the maps he had next to him on the seat. It was a windless day. As he passed the windmill farm near Palm Springs the blades of the hundreds of electric generators stood motionless in the morning desert mist. It was eerie, like a cemetery, and Harry's eyes didn't linger.

Bosch drove through the plush desert communities of Palm Springs and Rancho Mirage without stopping, passing streets named after golfing presidents and celebrities. As he passed Bob Hope Drive, Bosch recalled the time he saw the comedian in Vietnam. He had just come in from thirteen days of clearing Charlie's tunnels in the Cu Chi province and thought the evening of watching Hope was hilarious. Years later he had seen a clip of the same show on a television retrospective on the comedian. This time, the performance made him feel sad. After Rancho Mirage, he caught Route 86 and was heading directly south.

The open road always presented a quiet thrill to Bosch. The feeling of going someplace new coupled with the unknown. He believed he did some of his best thinking while driving the open road. He now reviewed his search of Moore's apartment and tried to look for hidden meanings or messages. The ragged furniture, the empty suitcase, the lonely skin mag, the empty frame. Moore left behind a puzzling presence. He thought of the bag of photos again. Sylvia had changed her mind and taken it. Bosch wished he had borrowed the photo of the two boys, and the one of the father and son.

Bosch had no photographs of his own father. He had told Sylvia that he hadn't known him, but that had been only partially true. He had grown up not knowing and not, at least outwardly, caring who he was. But when he returned from the war he came back with a sense of urgency to know about his origins. It led him to seek out his father after twenty years of not even knowing his name.

Harry had been raised in a series of youth shelters and foster homes after authorities took him from his mother's custody. In the dormitories at McClaren or San Fernando or the other halls, he was comforted by his mother's steady visits, except during the times she was in jail. She told him they couldn't send him to a foster home without her consent. She had a good lawyer, she said, trying to get him back.

On the day the housemother at McClaren told him the visits were over because his mother was dead, he took the news unlike most boys of eleven. Outwardly, he showed nothing. He nodded that he understood and then walked away. But that day during the swimming period, he dove to the bottom of the deep end and screamed so loud and long that he was sure the noise was breaking through the surface and would draw the attention of the lifeguard. After each breath on top, he would go back down. He screamed and cried until he was so exhausted he could only cling to the pool's ladder, its cold steel tubes the arms that comforted him. Somehow he wished he could have been there. That was all. He somehow wanted to have protected her.

He was termed ATA after that. Available to Adopt. He began to move through a procession of foster homes where he was made to feel as though he was on tryout. When expectations were not met, it was on to the next house and the next pair of judges. He was once sent back to McClaren because of his habit of eating with his mouth open. And once before he was sent to a home in the Valley, the Choosers, as they were called by the ATAs, took Harry and several other thirteen-year-olds out to the rec field to throw a baseball around. Harry was the one chosen. He soon realized it was not because he exhibited the sterling virtues of boyhood. It was because the man had been looking for a lefthander. His plan was to develop a pitcher and lefthanders were the premium. After two months of daily workouts, pitching lessons and oral education on pitching strategies, Harry ran away from the home. It was six weeks before the cops later picked him up on Hollywood Boulevard. He was sent back to McClaren to await the next set of Choosers. You always had to stand up straight and smile when the Choosers came through the dorm.

He began his search for his father at the county recorder's office. The 1950 birth records of Hieronymus Bosch at Queen of Angels Hospital listed his mother as Margerie Philips Lowe and his father's name as his own: Hieronymus Bosch. But Harry, of course, knew this was not the case. His mother had once told him he was the namesake of an artist whose work she admired. She said the painter's five-hundred-year-old paintings were apt portraits of present L.A., a nightmarish landscape of predators and victims. She told him she would tell him his true father's name when the time was right. She was found dead in an alley off Hollywood Boulevard before that time came.

Harry hired a lawyer to petition the presiding judge of the juvenile dependency court to allow him to examine his own custody records. The request was granted and Bosch spent several days in the county Hall of Records archive. The voluminous documents given to him chronicled the unsuccessful lengths his mother had gone to keep custody of him. Bosch found it spiritually reassuring, but nowhere in the files was the name of the father. Bosch was at a dead end but wrote down the name of the lawyer who had filed all the papers in his mother's quest. J. Michael Haller. In writing it down, Bosch realized he knew the name. Mickey Haller had been one of L.A.'s premier criminal defense attorneys. He had handled one of the Manson girls. In the late fifties he had won an acquittal for the so-called Highwayman, a highway patrol officer accused of raping seven women he had stopped for speeding on lonely stretches of the Golden State. What was J. Michael Haller doing on a child custody case?

On nothing more than a hunch, Bosch went to the Criminal Courts Building and ordered all of his mother's cases from archives. In sorting through them, he found that in addition to the custody battle Haller had represented Margerie P. Lowe on six loitering arrests between 1948 and 1961. That was well into Haller's time as a top trial lawyer.

In his gut, Harry knew then.

The receptionist in the five-name law office on the top floor of a Pershing Square tower told Bosch that Haller had retired recently because of a medical condition. The phone book didn't list his residence but the roll of registered voters did. Haller was a Democrat and he lived on Canon Drive in Beverly Hills. Bosch would always remember the rosebushes that lined the walkway to his father's mansion. They were perfect roses.

The maid who answered the door said Mr. Haller was not seeing visitors. Bosch told the woman to tell Mr. Haller it was Margerie Lowe's son come to pay his respects. Ten minutes later he was led past members of the lawyer's family. All of them standing in the hallway with strange looks on their faces. The old man had told them to leave his room and send Bosch in alone. Standing at the bedside, Harry figured him for maybe ninety pounds now, and he didn't need to ask what was wrong because he could tell cancer was eating away at him from the inside out.

"I guess I know why you've come," he rasped.

"I just wanted to . . . I don't know."

He stood there in silence for quite a time, watching how it wore the man out just to keep his eyes open. There was a tube from a box on the bedside that ran under the covers. The box beeped every once in a while as it pumped pain-killing morphine into the dying man's blood. The old man studied him silently.

"I don't want anything from you," Bosch finally said. "I don't know, I think I just wanted to let you know I made it by okay. I'm all right. In case you ever worried."

"You have been to the war?"

"Yes. I'm done with that."

"My son — my other son, he . . . I kept him away from that. . . . What will you do now?"

"I don't know."

After some more silence the old man seemed to nod. He said, "You are called Harry. Your mother told me that. She told me a lot about you. . . . But I could never. . . . Do you understand? Different times. And after it went by so long, I couldn't. . . . I couldn't reverse things."

Bosch just nodded. He hadn't come to cause the man any more pain. More silence passed and he heard the labored breathing.

"Harry Haller," the old man whispered then, a broken smile on the thin, peeling lips burned by chemotherapy. "That could have been you. Did you ever read Hesse?"

Bosch didn't understand but nodded again. There was a beep sound. He watched for a minute until the dosage seemed to take some effect. The old man's eyes closed and he sighed.

"I better get going," Harry said. "You take care."

He touched the man's frail, bluish hand. It gripped his fingers tightly, almost desperately, and then let go. As he stepped to the door, he heard the old man's rasp.

"I'm sorry, what did you say?"

"I said I did. I did worry about you."

There was a tear running down the side of the old man's face, into his white hair. Bosch nodded again and two weeks later he stood on a hill above the Good Shepherd section at Forest Lawn and watched them put the father he never knew in the ground. During the ceremony, he saw a grouping that he suspected was his half brother and three half sisters. The half brother, probably born a few years ahead of Bosch, was watching Harry during the ceremony. At the end, Bosch turned and walked away.

Near ten o'clock Bosch stopped at a roadside diner called El Oasis Verde and ate huevos rancheros. His table was at a window that looked out at the blue-white sheath called the Salton Sea and then farther east to the Chocolate Mountains. Bosch silently reveled in the beauty and the openness of the scene. When he was done, and the waitress had refilled his Thermos, he walked out into the dirt parking lot and leaned against the fender of the Caprice to breathe the cool, clean air and look again.

The half brother was now a top defense lawyer and Harry was a cop. There was a strange congruence to that that Bosch found acceptable. They had never spoken and probably never would.

He continued south as 86 ran along the flats between the Salton Sea and the Santa Rosa Mountains. It was agricultural land that steadily dropped below sea level. The Imperial Valley. Much of it was cut in huge squares by irrigation ditches and his drive was accompanied by the smell of fertilizer and fresh vegetables. Flatbed trucks, loaded with crates of lettuce or spinach or cilantro, occasionally pulled off the farm roads in front of him and slowed him down. But Harry didn't mind and waited patiently to pass.

Near a town called Vallecito, Bosch pulled to the side of the road to watch a squad of low-flying aircraft come screaming over a mountain that rose to the southwest. They crossed 86 and flew out over the Salton. Bosch knew nothing about identifying war aircraft in the modern era. These jets had evolved into faster and sleeker machines than those he remembered from Vietnam. But they had flown low enough for him to clearly see that beneath each craft's wings hung the hardware of war. He watched the three jets bank and come about in a tight triangle pattern and retrace their path back to the mountain. After they crossed above him, Harry looked down at his maps and found blocks marked off to the southwest as closed to the public. It was the U.S. Naval Gunnery Range at Superstition Mountain. The map said it was a live bombing area. Keep out.

Bosch felt a dull vibration rock the car slightly and then the following rumble. He looked up from the map and thought he could make out the plume of smoke beginning to rise from the base of Superstition. Then he felt and heard another bomb hit. Then another.

As the jets, the silvery skin of each reflecting a diamond of sunlight, passed overhead again to begin another run, Bosch pulled back onto the road behind a flatbed truck with two teenagers in the back. They were Mexican field-workers with weary eyes that seemed already knowledgeable about the long, hard life ahead of them. They were about the same age as the two boys on the picnic table in the photo that had been in the white bag. They stared at Bosch with indifference.

In a few moments it was clear to pass the slow-moving truck. Bosch heard other explosions from Superstition Mountain as he moved away. He went on to pass more farms and mom-and-pop restaurants. He passed a sugar mill where a line painted at the top of its huge silo marked sea level.

The summer after he had talked to his father Bosch had picked up the books by Hesse. He was curious about what the old man had meant. He found it in the second book he read. Harry Haller was a character in it. A disillusioned loner, a man of no real identity, Harry Haller was the steppenwolf.

That August Bosch joined the cops.

He believed he felt the land rising. The farmland gave way to brown brush and there were dust devils rising in the open land. His ears popped as he ascended. And he knew the border was nearing long before he passed the green sign that told him Calexico was twenty miles away.

20

Calexico was like most border towns: dusty and built low to the ground, its main street a garish collision of neon and plastic signage, the inevitable golden arches being the recognizable if not comforting icon amid the drive-through Mexican auto insurance offices and souvenir shops.

In town, Route 86 connected with 111 and dropped straight down to the border crossroad. Traffic was backed up about five blocks from the exhaust-stained concrete auto terminal manned by the Mexican *federales*. It looked like the five o'clock lineup at the Broadway entrance to the 101 in L.A. Before he got caught up in it, Bosch turned east on Fifth Street. He passed the De Anza Hotel and drove two blocks to the police station. It was a one-story concrete-block affair that was painted the same yellow as the tablets lawyers used. From the signs out front, Bosch learned it was also Town Hall. It was also the town fire station. It was also the historical society. He found a parking space in front.

As he opened the door of the dirty Caprice he heard singing from the park across the street. On a picnic bench five Mexican men sat drinking Budweisers. A sixth man, wearing a black cowboy shirt with white embroidery and a straw Stetson, stood facing them, playing a guitar and singing in Spanish. The song was sung slowly and Harry had no trouble translating.

> *I don't know how to love you*
> *I don't even know how to embrace you*
> *Because what never leaves me*
> *Is this pain that hurts me so*

The singer's plaintive voice carried strongly across the park and Bosch thought the song was beautiful. He leaned against his car and smoked until the singer was done.

> *The kisses that you gave me my love*
> *Are the ones that are killing me*
> *But my tears are now drying*
> *With my pistol and my heart*
> *And here as always I spend my life*
> *With the pistol and the heart*

At the song's end, the men at the picnic table gave the singer a cheer and a toast.

Inside the glass door marked Police was a sour-smelling room no larger than the back of a pickup truck. On the left was a Coke machine, straight ahead was a door with an electronic bolt, and on the right was a thick glass window with a slide tray beneath it. A uniformed officer sat behind the glass. Behind him, a woman sat at a radio-dispatch console. On the other side of the console was a wall of square-foot-sized lockers.

"You can't smoke in there, sir," the uniform said.

He wore mirrored sunglasses and was overweight. The plate over his breast pocket said his name was Gruber. Bosch stepped back to the door and flicked the butt out into the parking lot.

"You know, it's a hundred-dollar fine for littering in Calexico, sir," Gruber said.

Harry held up his open badge and I.D. wallet.

"You can bill me," he said. "I need to check a gun."

Gruber smiled curtly, revealing his receding, purplish gums.

"I chew tobacco myself. Then you don't have that problem."

"I can tell."

Gruber frowned and had to think about that a moment before saying, "Well, let's have it. Man says he wants to check a gun has to turn the gun in to be checked."

He turned back to the dispatcher to see if she thought that he now had the upper hand. She showed no response. Bosch noticed the strain Gruber's gut was putting on the buttons of his uniform. He pulled the forty-four out of his holster and put it in the slide tray.

"Foe-dee foe," Gruber announced and he lifted the gun out and examined it. "You want to keep it in the holster?"

Bosch hadn't thought about that. He needed the holster. Otherwise he'd have to jam the Smith in his waistband and he'd probably lose it if he ended up having to do any running.

"Nah," he said. "Just checking the gun."

Gruber winked and took it over to the lockers, opened one up and put the gun inside. After he closed it, he locked it, took the key out and came back to the window.

"Let me see the I.D. again. I have to write up a receipt."

Bosch dropped his badge wallet into the tray and watched as Gruber slowly wrote out a receipt in duplicate. It seemed that the officer had to look from the I.D. card to what he was writing every two letters.

"How'd you get a name like that?"

"You can just write Harry for short."

"It's no problem. I can write it. Just don't ask me to say it. Looks like it rhymes with anonymous."

He finished and put the receipts into the tray and told Harry to sign them both. Harry used his own pen.

"Lookee there, a lefty signing for a right-handed gun," Gruber said. "Somethin' you don't see 'round here too often."

He winked at Bosch again. Bosch just looked at him.

"Just talking is all," Gruber said.

Harry dropped one of the receipts into the tray and Gruber exchanged it for the locker key. It was numbered.

"Don't lose it now," Gruber said.

As he walked back to the Caprice he saw that the men were still at the picnic table in the park but there was no more singing. He got into the Caprice and put the locker key in the ashtray. He never used it for smoking. He noticed an old man with white hair unlocking the door below the historical society sign. Bosch backed out and headed over to the De Anza.

It was a three-story, Spanish-style building with a satellite dish on the roof. Bosch parked in the brick drive up in front. His plan was to check in, drop his bags in his room, wash his face and then make the border crossing into Mexicali. The man behind the front desk wore a white shirt and brown bow tie to match his brown vest. He could not have been much older than twenty. A plastic tag on the vest identified him as Miguel, assistant front desk manager.

Bosch said he wanted a room, filled out a registration card and handed it back. Miguel said, "Oh, yes, Mr. Bosch, we have messages for you."

He turned to a basket file and pulled out three pink message forms. Two were from Pounds, one from Irving. Bosch looked at the times and noticed all three calls had come in during the last two hours. First Pounds, then Irving, then Pounds again.

"Wait a minute," he said to Miguel. "Is there a phone?"

"Around the corner, sir, to your right."

Bosch stood there with the phone in his hand wondering what to do. Something was up, or both of them wouldn't have tried to reach him. Something had made one or both of them call his house and they heard the taped message. What could have happened? Using his PacBell card he called the Hollywood homicide table, hoping someone was in and that he might learn what was going on. Jerry Edgar answered the call on the first ring.

"Jed, what's up? I've got phone calls from the weight coming out my ass."

There was a long silence. Too long.

"Jed?"

"Harry, where you at?"

"I'm down south, man."

"Where down south?"

"What is it, Jed?"

"Wherever you're at, Pounds is trying to recall you. He said if anybody talks to you, t'tell you to get your ass back here. He said —"

"Why? What's going on?"

"It's Porter, man. They found him this morning up at Sunshine Canyon. Somebody wrapped a wire 'round his neck so tight that it was the size of a watchband."

"Jesus." Bosch pulled out his cigarettes. "Jesus."

"Yeah."

"What was he doing up there? Sunshine, that's the landfill up in Foothill Division, right?"

"Shit, Harry, he was dumped there."

Of course. Bosch should have realized that. Of course. He wasn't thinking right.

"Right. Right. What happened?"

"What happened was that they found his body out there this morning. A rag picker come across it. He was covered in garbage and shit. But RHD traced some of the stuff. They got receipts from some restaurants. They got the name of the hauler the restaurants use and they've got it traced to a particular truck and a particular route. It's a downtown run. Was made yesterday morning. Hollywood's working it with them. I'm fixing to go start canvassing on the route. We'll find the Dumpster he came from and go from there."

Bosch thought of the Dumpster behind Poe's. Porter hadn't run out on him. He had probably been garroted and dragged out while Bosch was having his say with the bartender. Then he remembered the man with the tattooed tears. How had he missed it? He had probably stood ten feet from Porter's killer.

"I didn't go out to the scene but I hear he'd been worked over before they did him," Edgar said. "His face was busted up. Nose broke, stuff like that. A lot of blood, I hear. Man, what a pitiful way to go."

It wouldn't be long before they came into Poe's with photos of Porter. The bartender would remember the face and would gladly describe Bosch as the man who had come in, said he was a cop, and attacked Porter. Bosch wondered if he should tell Edgar now and save a lot of legwork. A survival instinct flared inside him and he decided to say nothing about Poe's.

"Why do Pounds and Irving want me?"

"Don't know. All I know is first Moore gets it, then Porter. Think maybe they're closing ranks or something. I think they want everybody in where it's nice and safe. Word going 'round here is that those two cases are one. Word is those boys had some kinda deal going. Irving's already doubled them up. He's running a joint op on both of them. Moore and Porter."

Bosch didn't say anything. He was trying to think. This put a new spin on everything.

"Listen to me, Jed. You haven't heard from me. We didn't talk. Understand?"

Edgar hesitated before saying, "You sure you want to play it that way?"

"Yeah. For now. I'll be talking to you."

"Watch your back."

Watch out for the black ice, Bosch thought as he hung up and stood there for a minute, leaning against the wall. Porter. How had this happened? He instinctively moved his arm against his hip but felt no reassurance. The holster was empty.

He had a choice now: go forward to Mexicali or go back to L.A. He knew if he went back it would mean the end of his involvement in the case. Irving would cut him out like a bad spot on a banana.

Therefore, he realized, he actually had no choice. He had to go on. Bosch pulled a twenty-dollar bill out of his pocket and went back to the front desk. He slid the bill across to Miguel.

"Yes, sir?"

"I'd like to cancel my room, Miguel."

"No problem. There is no charge. You never got the room."

"No, that's for you, Miguel. I have a slight problem. I don't want anybody to know I was here. Understand?"

Miguel was young but he was wise. He told Bosch his request was no problem. He pulled the bill off the counter and tucked it into a pocket inside his vest. Harry then slid the phone messages across.

"If they call again, I never showed up to get these, right?"

"That's right, sir."

In a few minutes he was in line for the crossing at the border. He noticed how the U.S. Customs and Border Patrol building where incoming traffic was handled dwarfed its Mexican counterpart. The message was clear; leaving this country was not a difficulty; coming in, though, was another matter entirely. When it was Bosch's turn at the gate he held his badge wallet open and out the window. When the Mexican officer took it, Harry then handed him the Calexico P.D. receipt.

"Your business?" the officer asked. He wore a faded uniform that had been Army green once. His hat was sweat-stained along the band.

"Official. I have a meeting at the Plaza Justicia."

"Ah. You know the way?"

Bosch held up one of the maps from the seat and nodded. The officer then looked at the pink receipt.

"You are unarmed?" he said as he read the paper. "You leave your forty-four behind, huh?"

"That's what it says."

The officer smiled and Bosch thought he could see disbelief in his eyes. The officer nodded and waved his car on. The Caprice immediately became engulfed in a torrent of automobiles that were moving on a wide avenue with no painted lines denoting lanes. At times there were six rows of moving vehicles and sometimes there were four or five. The cars made the transitions smoothly. Harry heard no horns and the traffic flowed quickly. He had gone nearly a mile before a red light halted traffic and he was able to consult his maps for the first time.

He determined he was on Calzado Lopez Mateos, which eventually led to the justice center in the southern part of the city. The light changed and the traffic began moving again. Bosch relaxed a little and looked around as he drove, careful to keep an eye on the changing lane configuration. The boulevard was lined with old shops and industrial businesses. Their pastel-painted facades had been darkened by exhaust fumes from the passing river of metal and it was all quite depressing to Bosch. Several large Chevrolet school buses with multicolor paint jobs moved on the road but they weren't enough to bring much cheer to the scene. The boulevard curved hard to the south and then rounded a circular intersection with a monument at its center, a golden man upon a rearing stallion. He noticed several men, many wearing straw cowboy hats, standing in the circle or leaning against the base of the monument. They stared into the sea of traffic. Day laborers waiting for work. Bosch checked the map and saw that the spot was called Benito Juarez Circle.

In another minute Bosch came upon a complex of three large buildings with groupings of antennas and satellite dishes on top of each. A sign near the roadway announced AYUNTAMIENTO DE MEXICALI.

He pulled into a parking lot. There were no parking meters or attendant's booth. He found a spot and parked. While he sat in the car, studying the complex, he couldn't help but feel as though he were running from something, or someone. The death of Porter shook him. He had been right there. It made him wonder how he had escaped and why the killer had not tried to take him as well. One obvious explanation was that the killer did not want to risk taking on two targets at once. But another explanation was that the killer was simply following orders, a hired assassin instructed to take down Porter. Bosch had the feeling that if that were so, the order had come from here in Mexicali.

Each of the three buildings in the complex fronted one side of a triangular plaza. They were of modern design with brown-and-pink sandstone facades. All the windows on the third floor of one of the buildings were covered from the inside with newspaper. To block the setting sun, Bosch assumed. It gave the building a shabby look. Above the main entranceway to this building chrome letters said POLICIA JUDICIAL DEL ESTADO DE BAJA CALIFORNIA. He got out of the car with his Juan Doe #67 file, locked the car door, and headed that way.

Walking through the plaza, Bosch saw several dozen people and many vendors selling food and crafts, but mostly food. On the front steps of the police building several young girls approached him with hands out, trying to sell him chewing gum or wristbands made of colorful threads. He said no thanks. As he opened the door to the lobby a short woman balancing a tray on her shoulder that contained six pies almost collided with him.

Inside, the waiting room contained four rows of plastic chairs that faced a counter on which a uniformed officer leaned. Almost every chair was taken and every person watched the uniform intently. He was wearing mirrored glasses and reading a newspaper.

Bosch approached him and told him in Spanish that he had an appointment with Investigator Carlos Aguila. He opened his badge case and placed it on the counter. The man behind it did not seem impressed. But he slowly reached under the counter and brought up a phone. It was an old rotary job, much older than the building they were in, and it seemed to take him an hour to dial the number.

After a moment, the desk officer began speaking rapid-fire Spanish into the phone. Harry could make out only a few words. Captain. Gringo. Yes. LAPD. Investigator. He also thought he heard the desk man say Charlie Chan. The desk officer listened for a few moments and then hung up. Without looking at Bosch he jerked his thumb toward the door behind him and went back to his newspaper. Harry walked around the counter and through the door into a hallway that extended both right and left with many doors each way. He stepped back into the waiting room, tapped the desk officer on the shoulder and asked which way.

"To the end, last door," the officer said in English and pointed to the hallway to the left.

Bosch followed the directions and came to a large room where several men milled around standing and others sat on couches. There were bicycles leaning on the walls where there was not a couch. There was a lone desk, at which a young woman sat typing while a man apparently dictated to her. Harry noticed the man had a Barretta 9mm wedged in the waistband of his double-knit pants. He then noticed that some of the other men wore guns in holsters or also in their waistbands. This was the detective bureau. The chatter in the room stopped when Bosch walked in. He asked the man closest to him for Carlos Aguila. This caused another man to call through a doorway at the back of the room. Again, it was too fast but Bosch heard the word Chan and tried to think what it meant in Spanish. The man who had yelled then jerked his thumb toward the door and Bosch went that way. He heard quiet laughter behind him but didn't turn around.

The door led to a small office with a single desk. Behind it a man with gray hair and tired eyes sat smoking a cigarette. A Mexican newspaper, a glass ashtray and a telephone were the only items on the desk. A man with mirrored aviator glasses — what else was new? — sat in a chair against the far wall and studied Bosch. Unless he was sleeping.

"Buenos dias," the older man said. In English he said, "I am Captain Gustavo Grena and you are Detective Harry Bosch. We spoke yesterday."

Bosch reached across the desk and shook his hand. Grena then indicated the man in the mirrors.

"And Investigator Aguila is who you have come to see. What have you brought from your investigation in Los Angeles?"

Aguila, the officer who had sent the inquiry to the Los Angeles consulate, was a small man with dark hair and light skin. His forehead and nose were burned red by the sun but Bosch could see his white chest through the open collar of his shirt. He wore jeans and black leather boots. He nodded to Bosch but made no effort to shake his hand.

There was no chair to sit down on so Harry walked up close to the desk and placed the file down. He opened it and took out morgue Polaroids of Juan Doe #67's face and the chest tattoo. He handed them to Grena, who studied them a moment and then put them down.

"You also look for a man, then? The killer, perhaps?" Grena asked.

"There is a possibility that he was killed here and his body taken to Los Angeles. If that is so, then your department should look for the killer, perhaps."

Grena put a puzzled look on his face.

"I don't understand," he said. "Why? Why would this happen? I am sure you must be mistaken, Detective Bosch."

Bosch shook his shoulders. He wasn't going to press it. Yet.

"Well, I'd like to at least get the identification confirmed and then go from there."

"Very well," Grena said. "I leave you with Investigator Aguila. But I have to inform you, the business you mentioned on the phone yesterday, EnviroBreed,

I have personally interviewed the manager and he has assured me that your Juan Doe did not work there. I have saved you that much time."

Grena nodded as if to say his efforts were no inconvenience at all. Think nothing of it.

"How can they be sure when we don't have the ID yet?"

Grena dragged on his cigarette to give him time to think about that one. He said, "I provided the name Fernal Gutierrez-Llosa to him. No such employee at any time. This is an American contractor, we must be careful. . . . You see, we do not wish to step on the toes of the international trade."

Grena stood up, dropped his cigarette in the ash tray and nodded to Aguila. Then he left the office. Bosch looked at the mirrored glasses and wondered if Aguila had understood a word of what had just been said.

"Don't worry about the Spanish," Aguila said after Grena was gone. "I speak your language."

21

Bosch insisted that he drive, saying he did not want to leave the Caprice — it wasn't his, he explained — in the parking lot. What he didn't explain was that he wanted to be near his gun, which was still in the trunk. On their way through the plaza, they waved away the children with their hands out.

In the car, Bosch said, "How're we going to make the ID without prints?"

Aguila picked the file up off the seat.

"His friends and wife will look at the photos."

"We going to his house? I can lift prints, take 'em back to L.A. to have someone take a look. It would confirm it."

"It is not a house, Detective Bosch. It is a shack."

Bosch nodded and started the car. Aguila directed him farther south to Boulevard Lazaro Cardenas on which they headed west for a short while before turning south again on Avenida Canto Rodado.

"We go to the barrio," Aguila said. "It is know as Ciudad de los Personas Perdidos. City of Lost Souls."

"That's what the tattoo means, right? The ghost? Lost Souls?"

"Yes, that is correct."

Bosch thought a moment before asking, "How far is it from Lost Souls barrio to Saints and Sinners?"

"It is also in the southwest sector. Not far from Lost Souls. I will show it to you if you wish."

"Yeah, maybe."

"Is there a reason you ask?"

Bosch thought of Corvo's admonition not to trust the local police.

"Just curious," he said. "It's another case."

He immediately felt guilty at not being truthful with Aguila. He was a cop and Bosch felt he deserved the benefit of the doubt. But not according to Corvo. They drove in silence for a while after that. They were moving away from the city and the comfort of buildings and traffic. The commercial businesses and the shops and restaurants gave way to more shacks and cardboard shanties. Harry saw a refrigerator box near the side of the road that was somebody's home. The people they passed, sitting on rusted engine blocks, oil drums, stared at the car with hollow eyes. Bosch tried to keep his eyes on the dusty road.

"They called you Charlie Chan back there, how come?"

He asked primarily because he was nervous and thought conversation might distract him from his uneasiness and the unpleasantness of the journey they were making.

"Yes," Aguila said. "It is because I am Chinese."

Bosch turned and looked at him. From the side, he could look behind the mirrors and see the slight rounding of the eyes. It was there.

"Partly, I should say. One of my grandfathers. There is a large Chinese-Mexican community in Mexicali, Detective Bosch."

"Oh."

"Mexicali was created around 1900 by the Colorado River Land Company. They owned a huge stretch of land on both sides of the border, and they needed cheap labor to pick their cotton, their vegetables," Aguila said. "They established Mexicali. Across the border from Calexico. Like mirror images, I suppose, at least according to plan. They brought in ten thousand Chinese, all men, and they had a town. A company town."

Bosch nodded. He had never heard the story but found it interesting. He had seen many Chinese restaurants and signs on his drive through the city but did not recall seeing many Asians.

"They all stayed — the Chinese?" he asked.

"Most of them, yes. But like I said, ten thousand Chinamen. No women. The company wouldn't allow it. Thought it would take away from the work. Later, some women came. But most of the time the men married into Mexican families. The blood was mixed. But as you probably have seen, much of the culture was preserved. We will enjoy some Chinese food at siesta, okay?"

"Sure, okay."

"Police work has largely remained the domain of the traditional Mexicans. There are not many like me in the State Judicial Police. For this reason I am called Charlie Chan. I am considered an outsider by the others."

"I think I know how you feel."

"You will reach a point, Detective Bosch, where you will be able to trust me. I am comfortable waiting to discuss this other case you mentioned."

Bosch nodded and felt embarrassed and tried to concentrate on his driving. Soon Aguila directed him onto a narrow, unpaved road that cut through the heart of a barrio. There were flat-roofed concrete-block buildings with blankets hung in open doorways. Additions to these buildings were constructed of plywood and sheets of aluminum. There was trash and other debris scattered about. Haggard, gaunt-looking men milled around and stared at the Caprice with California plates as it went by.

"Pull to the building with the painted star," Aguila instructed.

Bosch saw the star. It was hand-painted on the block wall of one of the sad structures. Above the star was painted Personas Perdidos. Scrawled beneath it were the words Honorable Alcade y Sheriff.

Bosch parked the Caprice in front of the hovel and waited for instructions.

"He is neither a mayor or sheriff, if that's what you may be thinking," Aguila said. "Arnolfo Munoz de la Cruz is simply what you would call a peacekeeper here. To a place of disorder he brings order. Or tries. He is the sheriff of the City of Lost Souls. He brought the missing man to our attention. This is where Fernal Gutierrez-Llosa lived."

Bosch got out, carrying the Juan Doe file with him. As he walked around the front of the car, he again rubbed his hand against his jacket, where it hung over his holster. It was a subconscious move he made every time he got out of the car and was on the job. But this time, when the comforting feel of the gun beneath was not there, he became acutely aware that he was an unarmed stranger in a strange land. He could not retrieve his Smith from the trunk while in the presence of Aguila. At least not until he knew him better.

Aguila rang a clay bell that hung near the doorway of the structure. There was no door, just a blanket that was draped over a wood slat hammered across the top of the passage. A voice inside called, "Abierto," and they went inside.

Munoz was a small man, deeply tanned and with gray hair tied in a knot behind his head. He wore no shirt, which exposed the sheriff's star tattooed on the right side of his chest, the ghost on the left. He looked at Aguila and then at Bosch, staring curiously at him. Aguila introduced Bosch and told Munoz why they had come. He spoke slowly enough so that Bosch could understand. Aguila told the old man that he needed to take a look at some photographs. This confused Munoz — until Bosch slipped the morgue shots out of the file and he saw that the photographs were of a dead man.

"Is it Fernal Gutierrez-Llosa?" Aguila inquired after the man had studied the photographs long enough.

"It is him."

Munoz now looked away. Bosch looked around for the first time. The one-room shack was very much like a large prison cell. Just the necessities. A bed. A box of clothes. A towel hung over the back of an old chair. A candle and a mug with a toothbrush in it on top of a cardboard box next to the bed. It had a squalid smell and he felt embarrassed that he had intruded.

"Where was his place?" he asked Aguila in English.

Aguila looked at Munoz and said, "I am sorry for the loss of your friend, Mr. Munoz. It will be my duty to inform his wife. Do you know if she is here?"

Munoz nodded and said the woman was at her dwelling.

"Would you like to come with us to help?"

Munoz nodded again, picked a white shirt up off the bed and put it on. Then he went to the door, parted the curtain over the opening and held it for them.

Bosch first went to the trunk of the Caprice and got the print kit from his briefcase. Then they walked farther down the dusty street until they came to a plywood shack with a canvas canopy in front of it. Aguila touched Bosch on the elbow.

"Señor Munoz and I will deal with the woman. We will bring her out here. You go in and collect the fingerprints you need and do whatever else you need to do."

Munoz called out the name Marita and a few moments later a small woman peeked through the white plastic shower curtain hung across the doorway. When she saw Munoz and Aguila she came out. Bosch could tell by her face that she already knew the news that the men were there to deliver. Women were always that way. Harry thought of the first night he had seen Sylvia Moore. She knew. They all knew. Bosch handed the file to Aguila, in case the woman demanded to see the photos, and ducked into the room the woman and the Juan Doe had shared.

It was a room with spare furnishings. No surprise there. A queen-sized mattress lay on top of a wooden pallet. There was a single chair on one side of it and on the other a bureau had been made out of a wood and cardboard shipping crate. A few articles of clothing hung inside the box. The back wall of the room was a large piece of uncut aluminum with the Tecate beer trademark printed on it. Wood-slat shelves went across this, holding coffee cans, a cigar box and other small items.

Bosch could hear the woman crying quietly outside the shack and Munoz trying to console her. He looked around the room quickly, trying to decide which was a likely spot to lift prints. He was unsure if he even needed to do this. The woman's tears seemed to confirm the identity.

He walked to the shelves and used a fingernail to flip open the cigar box. It contained a dirty comb, a few pesos and a set of dominoes.

"Carlos?" he called out.

Aguila stuck his head in past the shower curtian.

"Ask if she has handled this box lately. It looks like it was her husband's stuff. If it's his, I'll try some lifts on it."

He heard the questioning in Spanish outside and the woman said she did not touch the box ever because it was her husband's. Using his nails Harry put the box on top of the makeshift bureau. He opened the print kit and took out a small spray bottle, a vial of black powder, a sable-hair brush, a wide roll of clear tape and a stack of 3 × 5 cards. He laid all of these out on the bed and set to work.

He picked up the spray bottle and pumped four sprays of ninhydrin mist over the box. After the mist settled, he took out a cigarette, lit it and then moved the still-burning match along the edge of the box about two inches from the surface. The heat brought up the ridges of several fingerprints in the ninhydrin. Bosch bent over the table and studied them, looking for complete examples. There were two. He uncapped the vial of black powder and lightly brushed some onto the prints, clearly defining the ridges and bifurcations. He then unrolled a short length of tape, held it down on one of the prints and lifted it. He pressed the tape against a white 3 × 5 card. He did it again with the other print. He had two good prints to take back with him.

Aguila came into the room then.

"Did you get a print?"

"A couple. Hopefully they are his and not hers. Doesn't seem to matter much. Sounded like she made an ID, too. She look at the pictures?"

Aguila nodded and said, "She insisted. Did you search the room?"

"For what?"

"I do not know."

"I looked around. Not much here."

"Did you take fingerprints from the coffee cans?"

Bosch looked at the shelves. There were three old Maxwell House cans. He said, "Nah, I figured her prints are on them. I don't want to have to print her to clear her for comparisons. It's not worth putting her through that."

Aguila nodded but then looked puzzled.

"Why would a poor man and his wife have three cans of coffee?"

It was a good point. Bosch went to the shelves and took down one can. It rattled and when he opened it he found a handful of pesos inside the can. The next one he pulled down was about a third full of coffee. The last one was the lightest. Inside he found papers, a baptismal certificate for Gutierrez-Llosa and a marriage license. The couple had been married thirty-two years. It depressed him to think about it. There was also a Polaroid photo of Gutierrez-Llosa and Bosch could see it was Juan Doe #67. Identity confirmed. And there was a Polaroid of his wife. And lastly, there was a stack of check stubs held together in a rubber band. Bosch looked through these, finding them all for small amounts of money from several businesses — the financial records of a day laborer. The businesses that didn't pay their day laborers in cash paid with checks. The last two in the stack were receipts for sixteen dollars each for checks issued by EnviroBreed Inc. Bosch put the check stubs into his pocket and told Aguila he was ready to go.

While Aguila expressed condolences again to the new widow, Bosch went to the trunk of the car to put away the fingerprint kit and the cards with the lifts he had taken. He looked over the trunk lid and saw Aguila still standing with Munoz and the woman. Harry quickly lifted up the rug on the right side of the trunk, pulled up the spare tire and grabbed his Smith. He put the gun in his holster and slid it around on his waist so that the gun would be on his back. It was under his jacket but an eye looking for such things could see it. However, Bosch was no longer worried about Aguila. He got in the car and waited. Aguila got in a few moments later.

Bosch watched the widow and the sheriff in the rear view mirror as they drove away.

"What will happen with her now?" he asked Aguila.

"You don't want to know, Detective Bosch. Her life was difficult before. Now, her hardships will only multiply. I believe she cries for herself as much as her lost husband. And rightly so."

Bosch drove in silence until they were out of Lost Souls and back on the main road.

"That was clever, what you did back there," he said after a while. "With the coffee cans."

Aguila didn't say anything. He didn't have to. Bosch knew he had been in there before and had seen the EnviroBreed stubs. Grena was scamming and Aguila didn't like it or approve of it or maybe he was just unhappy because he hadn't been cut in on the deal. Whatever the reason, he was pointing Bosch in the right direction. Aguila wanted Bosch to find the stubs. He wanted Bosch to know Grena was a liar.

"Did you go to EnviroBreed, check it out on your own?"

"No," Aguila said. "This would be reported to my captain. I could not go there after he had made the appropriate inquiry. EnviroBreed is involved in international business. It holds contracts with government agencies in the United States. You must understand, it is a . . ."

"Delicate situation?"

"Yes, this is true."

"I'm familiar with those. I understand. You can't buck Grena but I can. Where is EnviroBreed?"

"Not far from here. To the southwest, where the land is mostly flat until it rises into the Sierra de los Cucapah. There are many industrial concerns there and large ranches."

"And how close is it between EnviroBreed and the ranch owned by the pope?"

"The pope?"

"Zorrillo. The pope of Mexicali. I thought you wanted to know about the other case I'm working."

They drove a little bit in silence. Bosch looked over and saw that Aguila's face had clouded. Even with the mirrors, Bosch could see this. His mention of Zorrillo probably confirmed a suspicion the Mexican detective had held since Grena had tried to derail the investigation. Bosch already knew from Corvo that EnviroBreed was just across the highway from the ranch. His question was merely one more test of Aguila.

It was a while before Aguila finally answered.

"The ranch and EnviroBreed are very close, I'm afraid."

"Good. Show me."

22

≈≈≈

"Let me ask you a question," Bosch said. "How come you sent that inquiry to the consul's office? I mean, you don't have missing persons down here. Somebody turns up missing, they crossed the border but you don't send out inquiries. What made you think this was different?"

They were heading toward the range of mountains that rose high above a layer of light brown smog from the city. They were going southwest on Avenida Val Verde and were moving through an area where ranch lands extended to the west and industrial parks lined the roadway to the east.

"The woman convinced me," Aguila said. "She came to the plaza with the sheriff and made the report. Grena gave me the investigation and her words convinced me that Gutierrez-Llosa would not cross the border willingly — without her. So I went to the circle."

Aguila said the circle below the golden statue of Benito Juarez on Calzado Lopez Mateos was where men went to wait for work. Other day laborers interviewed at the circle said the EnviroBreed vans came two or three times a week to hire workers. The men who had worked at the bug-breeding plant had described it as difficult work. They made food paste for the breeding process and loaded heavy incubation cartons into the vans. Flies constantly flew in their mouths and eyes. Many who had worked there said they never went back, choosing to wait for other employers to stop at the circle.

But not Gutierrez-Llosa. Others at the circle had reported seeing him get into the EnviroBreed van. Compared to the other laborers, he was an old man. He did not have much choice in employers.

Aguila said that when he learned the product made at EnviroBreed was shipped across the border, he sent out missing-person notices to consulates in southern California. Among his theories was that the old man had been killed in an accident at the plant and his body hidden to avoid an inquiry that could halt production. Aguila believed this was a common occurrence in the industrial sectors of the city.

"A death investigation, even accidental death, can be very expensive," Aguila said.

"La mordida."

"Yes, the bite."

Aguila explained that his investigation stopped when he discussed his findings with Grena. The captain said he would handle the EnviroBreed inquiry and later reported it to be a dead end. And that was where it stood until Bosch called with news of the body.

"Sounds like Grena got his bite."

Aguila did not answer this. They began to pass a ranch protected by a chain metal fence topped with razor wire. Bosch looked through it to the Sierra de los Cucapah and saw nothing in the vast expanse between the road and mountains. But soon they passed a break in the fence, an entrance to the ranch where there was a pickup truck parked lengthwise across the roadway. Two men were sitting in the cab and they looked at Bosch and he looked at them as he drove by.

"That's it, isn't it?" he said. "That's Zorrillo's ranch."

"Yes. The entrance."

"Zorrillo's name never came up before you heard it from me?"

"Not until you said it."

Aguila offered no other comment. In a minute they were coming up to some buildings inside the ranch's fence line but close to the road. Bosch could see a concrete barnlike structure with a garage door that was closed. There were corrals on either side of it and in these he saw a half dozen bulls in single pens. He saw no one around.

"He breeds bulls for the ring," Aguila said.

"I heard that. Lot of money in that around here, huh?"

"All from the seed of one prized bull. El Temblar. A very famous animal in Mexicali. The bull that killed Meson, the famous torero. He lives here now and roams the ranch at his will, taking the heifers as he wishes. A champion animal."

"The Tremble?" he said.

"Yes. It is said that man and earth tremble when the beast charges. That is the legend. The death of Meson a decade ago is very well known. A story recalled each Sunday at the plaza."

"And the Tremble just runs around in there loose? Like a watchdog or something. A bulldog."

"Sometimes people stand at the fence waiting for a glimpse of the great animal. The bulls his seed produces are considered the most game in all of Baja. Pull over here."

Bosch turned onto the shoulder. He noticed Aguila was looking across the street at a line of warehouses and businesses. Some had signs on them. Most in English. They were companies that used cheap Mexican labor and paid low taxes to make products for the United States. There were furniture manufacturers, tile makers, circuit board factories.

"See the Mexitec Furniture building?" Aguila said. "The second structure down, with no sign, that is EnviroBreed."

It was a white building, and Aguila was right. No sign or other indication of what went on there. It was surrounded by a ten-foot fence topped with razor wire. Signs on the fence warned in two languages that it was electrified and there were dogs inside of it. Bosch didn't see any dogs and decided they were probably only put in the yard at night. He did see two cameras on the front corners of the building and several cars parked inside the compound. He saw no EnviroBreed vans but the two garage doors at the front of the building were closed.

Bosch had to press a button, state his business and hold his badge up to a remote camera before the fence gate automatically rolled open. He parked next to a maroon Lincoln with California tags and they walked across the dusty unpaved lot to the door marked Office. He brushed his hand against the back of his hip and felt the gun under his jacket. A small measure of comfort. The door was opened as he reached for the doorknob and a man wearing a Stetson to shade his acne-scarred and sun-hardened face stepped out lighting a cigarette. He was an Anglo and Bosch thought he might have been the van driver he had seen at the eradication center in L.A.

"Last door on the left," the man said. "He's waiting."

"Who's he?"

"Him."

The man in the Stetson smiled and Bosch thought his face might crack. Bosch and Aguila stepped through the door into a wood-paneled hallway. It went straight back with a small reception desk on the left followed by three doors. At the end of the hall there was a fourth door. A young Mexican woman sat at the reception desk and stared at them silently. Bosch nodded and they headed back. The first door they passed was closed and letters on it said USDA. The next two doors had no letters. The one at the end of the hall had a sign that said:

DANGER — RADIATION   NO UNAUTHORIZED ADMITTANCE

Harry saw a hook next to the door that had goggles and breathing masks hanging on it. He opened the last door on the left and they stepped into a small anteroom with a secretary's desk but no secretary.

"In here, please," a voice said from the next room.

Bosch and Aguila stepped into a large office that was weighted in the center by a huge steel desk. A man in a light blue guayaberra shirt sat behind it.

He was writing something in a ledger book and there was a Styrofoam cup of steaming coffee on the desk. Enough light came through the jalousie window behind him so that he didn't need a desk light. He looked about fifty years old, with gray hair that showed streaks of old black dye. He also was a gringo.

The man said nothing and continued writing. Bosch looked around and saw the four-picture closed-circuit television console on a low shelf against the wall next to the desk. He saw the black-and-white images from the gate and front corners. The fourth image was very dark and was an interior look at what Harry assumed was the cargo-loading room. He saw a white van with its rear doors open, two or three men loading large white boxes into it.

"Yes?" the man said. He still hadn't looked up.

"Quite a lot of security for flies."

Now he looked up. "Excuse me?"

"Didn't know they were so valuable."

"What can I do for you?" He threw his pen down on the desk to signal that the wheels of international commerce were grinding to a halt because of Bosch.

"Harry Bosch, Los Angeles po —"

"You said that at the gate. What can I do for you?"

"I am here to talk about one of your employees."

"Name?" He picked up the pen again and went back to work on the ledger.

"You know something? I would think that if a cop had come three hundred miles, crossed the border, just to ask you a few questions, then it might rate a little interest. But not with you. That bothers me."

The pen went down harder this time and bounced off the desk into the trash can next to it.

"Officer, I don't care whether it bothers you or not. I have a shipment of perishable material I must get on the road by four o'clock. I can't afford to show the interest you seem to think you rate. Now, if you want to give me the employee's name — that is, if he was an employee — I will answer what I can."

"What do you mean 'was an employee'?"

"What?"

"You said, 'was,' just then."

"So?"

"So, what's it mean?"

"You said — you're the one who came in here with these questions. I —"

"And your name is?"

"What?"

"What is your name?"

The man stopped, thoroughly confused, and drank from the cup. He said, "You know, mister, you have no authority here."

"You said, 'even if the guy was an employee,' and I never said anything about 'was.' Makes me think, you already know we are talking about an individual that was. Who is dead now."

"I just assumed, okay. A cop comes all the way down from L.A., I just assumed we were talking about a dead guy. Don't try to put words — you can't come in here with that badge that isn't worth the tin it's made of once you cross that border and start pushing me. I don't have —"

"You want some authority? This is Carlos Aguila of the State Judicial Police here. You can consider that he is asking the same questions as me."

Aguila nodded but said nothing.

"That's not the point," the man behind the desk said. "The point is this typical bullshit American imperialism you bring with you. I find it very distasteful. My name is Charles Ely. I am proprietor of EnviroBreed. I do not know anything about the man you said worked here."

"I didn't tell you his name."

"It doesn't matter. You understand now? You made a mistake. You played this game wrong."

Bosch took the morgue photo of Gutierrez-Llosa out of his pocket and slid it across the desk. Ely did not touch the photo but looked down at it. He showed no reaction that Bosch could see. Then Bosch put down the pay stubs. Same thing. No reaction.

"Name is Fernal Gutierrez-Llosa," Bosch said. "A day laborer. I need to know when he worked here last, what he was doing."

Ely retrieved his pen from the trash can and flicked the photo back toward Bosch with it.

"Afraid I can't help. Day laborers we don't carry records on. We pay them with 'pay to bearer' checks at the end of each day. Different people all the time. I wouldn't know this man from Adam. And I believe we already answered questions about this man. From the SJP. A Captain Grena. I guess I will have to call him now to see why that wasn't sufficient."

Bosch wanted to ask whether he meant the payoff Ely had given Grena or the information wasn't sufficient. But he held back because it would come back on Aguila. Instead he said, "You do that, Mr. Ely. Meantime, somebody else around here might remember this man. I am going to take a look around."

Ely became immediately agitated. "No, sir, you are not going to have free range of this facility. Portions of this building are used to irradiate material and are considered dangerous and off limits to all but certified personnel. Other areas are subject to USDA monitoring and quarantine and we cannot allow anyone access. Again, you have no authority here."

"Who owns EnviroBreed, Ely?" Bosch asked.

Ely seemed startled by the change in subject.

"Who?" he sputtered.

"Who is the man, Ely?"

"I don't have to answer that. You have no —"

"The man across the street? Is the pope the man?"

Ely stood up and pointed at the door.

"I don't know what you are talking about but you're leaving. And I will be contacting both the SJP and the American and Mexican authorities. We will see if this is how they want police from Los Angeles to operate on foreign soil."

Bosch and Aguila moved back into the hall and closed the door. Harry stood there for a moment and listened for the sound of a telephone or steps. He heard nothing and then turned to the door at the end of the hall. He tried it but it was locked.

In front of the door marked USDA, he leaned his head forward and listened but heard nothing. He opened the door without knocking and a man with bureaucrat written all over him looked up from behind a small wooden desk. The room was about a quarter the size of Ely's suite. The man wore a short-sleeved white shirt with a thin blue tie. He had close-cropped gray hair, a mustache that looked like the end of a toothbrush and small, dead eyes that looked out from behind bifocals that squeezed against his pudgy pink temples. The plastic ink guard in his pocket had his name printed on the flap: Jerry Dinsmore. He had a half-eaten bean burrito on his desk, sitting on oil-stained paper.

"Can I help you?" he said with a mouthful.

Bosch and Aguila moved into the room.

Bosch showed him his ID and let him have a good look at it. Then he put the morgue photo on the desk, next to the burrito. Dinsmore looked at it and folded up the paper around his half-finished meal and put it in a drawer.

"Recognize him?" Bosch said. "Just a routine check. Infectious disease alert. Guy took it with him up to L.A. and croaked. We are retracing him so we can get anybody who had contact inoculated. We still got plenty of time. We hope."

Dinsmore was chewing his food much slower now. He looked down at the Polaroid and then up over his glasses at Bosch.

"Was he one of the men who worked around here?"

"We think so. We are checking with all the regular employees. We thought you might recognize him. It depends on how close you got as far as whether you need to be quarantined."

"Well, I never get close to the laborers. I'm in the clear. But what is the disease that you are talking about? I don't see why LAPD is — this man looks like he was beaten."

"I'm sorry, Mr. Dinsmore, that's confidential until we determine if you are at risk. If you are, well, then we have to put our cards on the table. Now, how do you mean you never get close to the laborers? Are you not the inspection officer for this facility?"

Bosch expected Ely to burst in any moment.

"I am the inspector but I am only interested in the finished product. I inspect samples directly from the travel cases. Then I seal the cases. This is done in the shipping room. You have to remember, this is a private facility and consequently I do not have free reign of the breeding or sterilization labs. Therefore, I do not interface with the workers."

"You just said, 'samples.' So that means you don't look in all of the boxes."

"Wrong. I don't look in all of the larvae cylinders in each of the transport cases, but I do inspect and seal the cases. I don't see what this has to do with this man. He didn't —"

"I don't see it, either. Never mind. You're in the clear."

Dinsmore's small eyes widened slightly. Bosch winked at him to further confuse him. He wondered if Dinsmore was part of what was going on here or whether, like a mole, he was in the dark. He told him to go back to his burrito and then he and Aguila stepped back into the hall. Just at that moment the door at the end of the hall opened and through it stepped Ely. He pulled a breathing mask and goggles off his face and charged down the hall, coffee slopping over the sides of the Styrofoam cup.

"I want you two out of here unless you have a court order."

He was right up to Bosch now and anger was etching red lines on his face. It was the act he might have used to intimidate others but Bosch was not impressed. He looked down into the shorter man's coffee cup and smiled as a small piece of the puzzle slipped into place. The stomach contents of Juan Doe #67 had included coffee. That was how he had swallowed the medfly which had brought Bosch here. Ely followed his eyes down and saw the medfly floating on the surface of the hot liquid.

"Fuckin' flies," he said.

"You know," Bosch said, "I'll probably get that court order."

He couldn't think of anything else to say and didn't want to leave Ely with the satisfaction of throwing him out. He and Aguila headed for the exit.

"Don't count on it," Ely said. "This is Mexico. You aren't jackshit here."

23

Bosch stood at the window of his third-floor room in the Hotel Colorado on Calzado Justo Sierra and looked out at what he could see of Mexicali. To his left the view was obscured by the other wing of the hotel. But looking out to the right he saw the streets were clogged with cars and the colorful buses he had seen earlier. He could hear a mariachi band playing somewhere. There was the smell of frying grease in the air from a nearby restaurant. And the sky above the ramshackle city was purple and red in the day's dying light. In the distance he could see the buildings of the justice center and, near them to the right, the rounded shape of a stadium. Plaza de los Toros.

He had called Corvo in Los Angeles two hours earlier, left his number and location, and was waiting for a call back from his man in Mexicali, Ramos. He walked away from the window and looked at the phone. He knew it was time to make the rest of the calls but he hesitated. He grabbed a beer out of the tin ice bucket on the bureau and opened it. He drank a quarter of it and sat on the bed next to the phone.

There were three messages on the phone tape at his home, all of them from Pounds saying the same thing: "Call me."

But he didn't. Instead, he called the homicide table first. It was Saturday night but the chances were it would still be all hands on deck because of Porter. Jerry Edgar answered.

"What's the situation?"

"Shit, man, you gotta come in." He was speaking in a very low voice. "Everybody's looking for you. RHD's got the lead on this thing so I don't know exactly what's happening. I'm just one of the gofers. But, I think uh, . . . I don't know, man."

"What? Say it."

"It's like they think you either did Porter or you might be next. It's hard to gauge what the fuck they're doing or thinking."

"Who's there?"

"Everybody. This is the command post. Irving's in there in the box with Ninety-eight now."

Bosch knew he couldn't let it go on much further. He had to call in. He might have already damaged himself beyond repair.

"Okay," he said. "I'm going to call them. I have to make one other call first. Thanks."

Bosch hung up and dialed another number, hoping he had remembered it correctly and that she would be home. It was near seven and he thought maybe she had gone out for dinner, but then she picked up on the sixth ring.

"It's Bosch. A bad time?"

"What do you want?" Teresa said. "Where are you? Everybody's looking for you, you know."

"I heard. But I'm outta town. I was just calling 'cause I heard they found my friend Lucius Porter."

"Yeah, they did. Sorry. I just got back from the cut."

"Yeah, I figured you'd do it."

And then silence before she said, "Harry, why do I get the feeling you want — that you aren't calling just because he was your friend?"

"Well . . ."

"Oh, shit, here we go again, right?"

"No. I just wanted to know how he got it is all. He was a friend. I worked with him. Never mind."

"I don't know why I let you do this to me. Shit. Mexican necktie, Harry. There, you happy? Got all you need now?"

"Garrote?"

"Yes. Steel baling wire, wrapped at the ends around two wooden pegs. I'm sure you've seen it before. Do I get to read this in the *Times* tomorrow, too?"

He was silent until he was sure she was done. He looked from the bed to the open window and saw the daylight was now completely gone. The sky was a deep red wine. He thought of the man at Poe's. Three tears.

"Did you do a compar —"

"Comparison to the Jimmy Kapps case? Yes. We're way ahead of you, but it won't be done for a few days."

"How come?"

"Because it takes that long to do wood-fiber testing between the dowel pegs and alloy-content analysis on the baling wire. We did do a cut analysis on the wire, though. It looks very good."

"Meaning?"

"Meaning it looks like the wire on the garrote used to kill Porter was cut from the same length of wire used to kill Kapps. The ends match. It's not one hundred percent because similar pliers will leave similar cut tracings. So we are doing the metal-alloy comparison. We'll know in a few days."

She seemed so matter-of-fact about it all. He was surprised she was still angry with him. The television reports of the night before seemed to be in her favor. He didn't know what to say. He had gone from being at ease in bed with her to being nervous on the phone with her.

"Thanks, Teresa," he finally said. "I'll see you."

"Harry?" she said before he could hang up.

"Yeah?"

"When you get back, I don't think you should call me again. I think we should keep it professional. If we see each other in the suite, then that's fine. But let's leave it there."

He didn't say anything.

"Okay?"

"Sure."

They hung up. Bosch sat without moving for several minutes. Finally, he picked the phone up again and dialed the direct line into the glass box. Pounds picked up immediately.

"It's Bosch."

"Where are you?"

"Mexicali. You left messages?"

"I called the hotel on your tape. They said you never checked in."

"I decided to stay on the other side of the border."

"Never mind the bullshit. Porter is dead."

"What!" Bosch tried his best to make it seem real. "What happened? I just saw him yesterday. He —"

"Never mind the bullshit, Bosch. What are you doing down there?"

"You told me to go where the case followed. It led here."

"I never told you to go to Mexico." He was yelling. "I want you back here ten minutes ago. This does not look good for you. We have a bartender that so help me Christ is ready to put your dick in the dirt on this. He — hang on."

"Bosch," a new voice on the line said. "Assistant Chief Irving here. What is your location?"

"I'm in Mexicali."

"I want you in my office at oh eight hundred tomorrow."

Bosch didn't hesitate. He knew he could not show any weakness.

"Can't do that, Chief. I have some unfinished business here that'll probably take me through tomorrow at least."

"We are talking about a fellow officer's murder here, Detective. I don't know if you realize this, but you could be in danger yourself."

"I know what I am doing. It's a fellow officer's murder that brings me here. Remember? Or doesn't Moore matter?"

Irving ignored that.

"You are refusing my direct order to return?"

"Look, Chief, I don't care what some bartender is telling you, you know I wasn't the doer."

"I never said that. But your conversation already reveals that you know more about this than you should if you were not involved."

"All I'm saying is that the answer to a lot of questions — about Moore, Porter and the rest — are down here. It's all down here. I'm staying."

"Detective Bosch, I was wrong about you. I gave you a lot of rope this time because I thought I detected a change in you. I see now that I was wrong. You fooled me again. You —"

"Chief, I am doing my —"

"Don't interrupt me! You may be unwilling to follow my explicit commands to return but don't you interrupt me. I am telling you that you don't want to return, fine. Don't. But you might as well never return, Bosch. Think about that. What you had before won't be waiting when you get back."

After Irving hung up Bosch picked a second bottle of Tecate from the bucket and lit a cigarette at the window. He didn't care about Irving's threats. Not that much, at least. He'd probably draw a suspension, maybe five days max. He could handle that. But Irving wouldn't move Bosch. Where could he send him? There weren't very many places lower than Hollywood. Instead, Bosch thought about Porter. He had been able to put it off, put it out of his mind. But now he had to think about Porter. Strangled with baling wire, left in a Dumpster. Poor bastard. But something in Bosch refused to let him grant the dead cop sympathy. Nothing about it touched his heart the way he thought it would, or should. It was a pitiful end of life. But he felt no pity. Porter had made fatal mistakes. Bosch promised himself that he would not and that he would go on.

He tried to focus on Zorrillo. Harry was sure that it was the pope who was manipulating things, who had sent the assassin to clean up the loose ends. If it was likely the same man had killed both Kapps and Porter, it was then easy to add Moore in as a victim as well. And possibly even Fernal Gutierrez-Llosa. The man with three tears. Did that leave Dance off the hook? Bosch doubted it. It might have taken Dance to lure Moore to the Hideaway. His thoughts reassured him that he was doing the right thing staying. The answers were here, not in L.A.

He went to his briefcase on the bureau and took out the mug shot of Dance that had been in the file Moore had put together. He looked at the practiced sulk of a young man who still had a boyish face and bleached blond hair. Now he wanted to move up the ladder and had come south of the border to make his case. Bosch realized that if Dance was in Mexicali he would not blend in easily. He'd have to have help.

The knock on the door startled him. Bosch quietly put down the bottle and took the gun off the night table. Through the peephole he saw a man of about thirty with dark hair and a thick mustache. He was not the room service waiter who had brought the beer.

"Si?"

"Bosch. It's Ramos."

Bosch opened the door on the chain and asked for some identification.

"Are you kidding? I don't carry ID around here. Let me in. Corvo sent me."

"How do I know?"

"Because you called L.A. Operations two hours ago and left your address. I tell you, I really get fucking paranoid having to explain all of this while standing out in the hallway."

Bosch closed the door, flipped off the chain and reopened it. He kept the gun in his hand but down at his side. Ramos walked past him into the room. He walked up to the window and looked out, then he walked away and began pacing near the bed. He said, "Smells like shit out there. Somebody cooking tortillas or some shit. Got any more brew? And by the way, the *federales* catch you with that piece and you might have trouble trying to get back across. How come you didn't stay in Calexico like Corvo told you to, man?"

If he had been anyone other than a cop, Bosch would have figured he was coked to the eyelids. But he decided it was probably something else, something he didn't know about yet, that made Ramos seem wired. Bosch picked up the phone and ordered a six-pack from room service, never taking his eyes off the man in his room. After he hung up, he put the gun in his waistband and sat down in the chair by the window.

"I didn't want to deal with the lines at the border," he said in answer to one of Ramos's many questions.

"You didn't want to put your trust in Corvo is what you mean. I don't blame you. Not that I don't trust him. I do. But I can see the need to want to go your own way. They got better food over here, anyway. But Calexico, there's a wild little town. It's one of those places, you never know what kind of shit is going down. You hit that place the wrong way and you go into a slide, man. I like it better over here myself. Did you eat?"

For a moment, Bosch thought about what Sylvia Moore had said about the black ice. Ramos was still pacing the room and Bosch noticed he had two electronic pagers on his belt. The agent was hyped on something. Bosch was sure of it.

"I already ate," Bosch said and moved his chair near the window because the room had taken on the tang of the agent's body odor.

"I know the best Chinese food in two countries. We could pop over for —"

"Hey! Ramos, sit down. You're making me nervous. Just sit down and tell me what's going on."

Ramos looked around himself as if seeing the room for the first time. He dragged a chair away from the wall near the door and straddled it backward in the middle of the room.

"What's going on, man, is that we are not too impressed with the shit you pulled at EnviroBreed today."

Bosch was surprised the DEA knew so much so fast but tried not to show it.

"That was not cool at all," Ramos was saying. "So I came here to tell you to quit the one-man show. Corvo told me that was your bag, but I didn't expect to see it so soon."

"What's the problem?" Bosch said. "It was my lead. From what Corvo said, you people didn't know shit about that place. I went in there to shake 'em up a little bit. That's all."

"These people don't shake, Bosch. That's what I am saying. Now look, enough said. I just wanted to say my little piece and to see what you have going besides the bug place. What I'm asking is, what are you doing here?"

Before Bosch could answer there was a loud knock on the door and the DEA agent jumped off the chair, coming down in a crouched position.

"It's room service," Bosch said. "What's wrong with you?"

"Always get this way before we jam."

Bosch got up looking curiously at the DEA agent and went to the door. Through the peephole he saw the same man who had delivered the first two beers. He opened the door, paid for the delivery and gave Ramos a bottle from the new bucket.

Ramos chugged half the bottle before sitting back down. Bosch took a beer back to his seat.

"What do you mean by 'before we jam'?"

"Well," Ramos said after another swallow. "The stuff you gave Corvo was good info. But then you canceled that out by cowboying it over there today. You nearly fucked things up."

"You said that. What did you find out?"

"EnviroBreed. We ran down the info and it's a direct hit. We traced owner-ship through a bunch of blinds to a Gilberto Ornelas. That's a known alias for a guy named Fernando Ibarra, one of Zorrillo's lieutenants. We are work-ing with the *federales* on getting search approvals. They are cooperating on this one. This new attorney general they got down here is clean and mean. He's working with us. So it's going to be a major jam, if we get the approval."

"When will you know?"

"Any time. One last piece has to fall."

"What's that?"

"If he's moving black ice across the border in EnviroBreed shipments, then how is he getting it from the ranch to the bug house? See, we've been watching the ranch and would've seen it. And we're pretty sure it's not man-ufactured at EnviroBreed. Too small, too many people around, too close to the road, et cetera, et cetera. All our intelligence says it's made on the ranch. Underground, in a bunker. We got aerials that show the heat patterns from the ventilation. Anyway, the question is then, how's he get it across the street to EnviroBreed?"

Bosch thought about what Corvo had said at the Code 7. That Zorrillo was suspected of helping to finance the tunnel that went under the border at Nogales.

"He doesn't take it across the street. He takes it under."

"Exactly," Ramos said. "We are working our informants on it right now. We get it confirmed, we get our approval from the attorney general and we go in. We hit the ranch and EnviroBreed simultaneously. Joint operation. The AG sends the federal militia. We send CLET."

Bosch hated all the acronyms law enforcement agencies cling to but asked what CLET was anyway.

"Clandestine Laboratory Enforcement Team. These guys are fuckin' ninjas."

Bosch thought this information over. He didn't understand why it was happening so quickly. Ramos was leaving something out. There had to be new intelligence on Zorrillo.

"You've seen him, haven't you? Zorrillo. Or somebody has."

"You got it. And that other little white squirrel you came down looking for. Dance."

"Where? When?"

"We have a CI inside the fence who saw the both of them outside the main compound shooting at targets this morning. And then we —"

"How close was he? The informant."

"Close enough. Not close enough to say 'Howdy do, Mr. Pope' but close enough to make the ID."

Ramos cackled loudly and got up to get another beer. He threw a bottle to Bosch, who wasn't yet done with his first.

"Where had he been?" Bosch asked.

"Christ, who knows? Only thing I care about is that he is back and he is going to be there when the CLETs come through the door. And by the way, you better not bring that gun with you or the *federales* will hook you up, too. They are giving a special weapons privilege to the CLETs but that is it. The AG is going to sign it — God, I hope this guy never gets bought off or assassinated. Anyway, like I'm saying, if they want you to have a gun, they'll give you something from their own armory."

"And how am I going to know when it goes down?"

Ramos was still standing. He jerked his head back and poured down half the bottle of beer. His odor had totally filled the room. Bosch held his bottle up near his mouth and nose so he'd smell the beer instead of the DEA agent.

"We'll let you know," Ramos said. "Take this and wait."

He tossed Bosch one of the pagers off his belt.

"You put that on and I'll give you a buzz when we are ready to rock. It will be soon. At least before New Year's, I'm hoping. We gotta move on this. There is no telling how long the target is going to stay in place this time."

He finished the beer and put the bottle on the table. He didn't pick up another. The meeting was done.

"What about my partner?" Bosch asked.

"Who, the Mex? Forget it. He's state. You can't tell him about this, Bosch. The pope has the SJP and the other locals wired. It's a given. Don't trust anybody over there, don't tell anybody over there. Just wear the pager like I said and wait for the beep. Go to the bullfights. Hang by the pool or something. Hell, man, look at yourself. You could use the color."

"I know Aguila better than I know you."

"Did you know he works for a man who is a regular guest of Zorrillo's at the bullfights each Sunday?"

"No," Bosch said. He thought of Grena.

"Did you know that to become a detective in the SJP, the promotion is bought for an average of two thousand dollars, not based on any skill in investigative technique?"

"No."

"I know you didn't. But that's the way it is here. You've got to understand that. Trust no one. You may be working with the last honest cop in Mexicali, but why bet your life on it?"

Bosch nodded and said, "One more thing, I want to come in tomorrow and check your mug books. You have Zorrillo's people?"

"Most of them. What do you want?"

"I'm looking for a guy with three tattooed tears. He's Zorrillo's hit man. He hit another cop yesterday in L.A."

"Jesus! Okay, in the morning, call me at this number. We'll set it up. If you make an ID we'll get the word to the AG. It'll help us get the search approval."

He gave Bosch a card with a phone number on it, nothing else. Then he was gone. Harry put the chain back on the lock.

24

Bosch sat on the bed with his beer, thinking about the reappearance of Zorrillo. He wondered where he had been and why he had left the safety of his ranch in the first place. Harry poked at the idea that maybe Zorrillo had been in L.A. and that it had taken his presence there to lure Moore to the motel room where he was put down on the bathroom floor. Maybe Zorrillo was the only one Moore would have gone there for.

The sharp sound of squealing brakes and crashing metal shot through the window. Before he even got up he heard voices arguing in the street below. The words grew harsher until they were threats being yelled so fast Bosch could not understand them. He went to the window and saw two men standing chests out beside two cars. One had rear-ended the other.

As he turned away he detected a small flash of blue light to his left. Before he had time to look, the bottle in his hand shattered and beer and glass exploded in all directions. He instinctively took a step back and launched himself over the bed and down onto the floor. He braced himself for more shots but none came. His heartbeat rapidly increased and he felt the familiar rush of mental clarity that comes only in situations of life and death. He crawled along the floor to the table and pulled the lamp plug out of the wall, dropping the room in darkness. As he reached up to the table for his gun, he heard the two cars speeding away in the street. A beautiful setup, he thought, but they missed.

He moved beneath the window opening and then stood up while pressing his back to the wall. All the while he was realizing how stupid he had been to literally pose in the window. He looked through the opening into the darkness where he believed he had seen the muzzle flash. There was no one there. Several of the windows of the other rooms were open and it was impossible to pinpoint where the shot had come from. Bosch looked back into his room and saw the headboard of the bed splintered at the spot where the bullet had impacted. By imagining a line from the impact point though the position he had held the bottle and then out the window, he focused on an open but dark window on the fifth floor of the other wing. He saw no movement there other than the curtain swaying gently with the breeze. Finally, he put his gun in his waistband and left the room, his clothes smelling of beer and with small slivers of glass embedded in his shirt and pricking his skin. He knew he had at least two slight glass cuts. One on his neck and one on his right hand, which had been holding the bottle. He held his cut hand to his neck wound as he walked.

He had judged that the open window belonged to the fourth room on the fifth floor. He now had his gun out and pointed in front of him as he moved slowly down the fifth-floor hallway. He was debating whether he should kick the door open but found the decision academic. A cool breeze from the open window flowed out through the open door of room 504.

The room was dark and Bosch knew he would be silhouetted by the lighted hallway. So he hit the room's entrance-light switch as he moved quickly through the doorway. He covered the room with his Smith and found it empty. The smell of burned gunpowder hung in the air. Harry looked out the window and followed the imaginary line down to his own third-floor room's window. It had been an easy shot. It was then that he heard the screeching of tires and saw the taillights of a large sedan pull out of the hotel parking lot and then speed away.

Bosch put the gun in his waistband and pulled his shirt out over it. He looked quickly around the room to see if the shooter had left anything behind him. The glint of copper from the fold of the bedspread where it was tucked beneath the pillows caught his eye. He pulled the bedspread out straight and lying there was a shell casing that had been ejected from a thirty-two rifle. He got an envelope out of the desk drawer and scooped the shell inside it.

As he left room 504 and walked down the hallway, no one looked out a door, no house detectives came running and no approaching sirens blared in the distance. No one had heard a thing, except maybe a bottle breaking. Bosch knew that the thirty-two fired at him had had a silencer screwed to the end of its barrel. Whoever it had been, he had taken his time and waited for the one shot. But he had missed. Had that been intentional? He decided it wasn't, to make a shot that close but intend to miss was too chancy. He had simply been lucky. His turn from the window at the last moment had probably saved his life.

Bosch headed back to his room to dig the slug out of the wall, bandage his wounds and check out. Along the way he started running when he realized he had to warn Aguila.

Back in his room, he quickly dug through his wallet for the piece of paper on which Aguila had written his address and phone number. Aguila picked up almost immediately.

"Bueno."

"It's Bosch. Someone just took a shot at me."

"Yes. Where? Are you injured?"

"I am okay. In my room. They shot through the window. I'm calling to warn you."

"Yes?"

"We were together today, Carlos. I don't know if it's just me or the both of us. Are you okay?"

"Yes, I am."

Bosch realized he didn't know if Aguila had a family or was alone. In fact, he realized, he knew the man's ancestry but little else.

"What will you do?" Aguila asked.

"I don't know. I'm leaving here . . ."

"Come here, then."

"Okay, yes . . . No. Can you come here? I won't be here but I want you to come and find out whatever you can about the person who rented room 504. That's where the shot came from. You can get the information easier than me."

"I am leaving now."

"We'll meet at your place. I have something to do first."

A moon like the smile of the Cheshire cat hung over the top of the ugly silhouette of the industrial park on Val Verde. It was ten o'clock. Bosch sat in his car in front of the Mexitec furniture factory. He was about two hundred yards from EnviroBreed and he was waiting for the last car to leave the bug plant. It was a maroon Lincoln that he suspected was Ely's. On the seat next to him was a bag containing the items he had bought earlier. The smell of the roasted pork was filling the car and he rolled down the window.

As he watched the EnviroBreed lot, he was still breathing hard and the adrenaline continued to course through his arteries like amphetamine. He was sweating, though the evening air was quite cool. He thought of Moore and Porter and the others. Not me, he thought. Not me.

At 10:15 he saw the door to EnviroBreed open and a man came out, accompanied by the blur of two black figures. Ely. Dogs. The dark shapes bobbed up and down at his waist as he walked. Ely then scattered something in the lot but the dogs stayed by his side. He then slapped his hip and yelled, "Chow!" and the dogs scattered and chased each other to varying points in the lot where they fought over whatever it was Ely had thrown.

Ely got in the Lincoln. After a few moments Bosch saw the taillights flare and the car backed away from its space at the front of the lot. Bosch watched as the headlights traced a circle in the lot and then led the car to the gate. The gate slowly rolled open and the car slipped through. Then the driver hesitated on the fringe of the roadway, though it was clear to pull out. He waited until the gate had trundled closed, the dogs safely inside the fenced compound, and then pulled away. Bosch slipped down in his seat, even though the Lincoln had headed the other way, north toward the border.

Bosch waited a few minutes and watched. Nothing moved anywhere. No cars. No people. He didn't expect there to be any DEA surveillance because they would pull back when planning a raid, so as not to tip their hand. He hoped they would, at least. He got out with the bag, his flashlight and his lock picks. Then he leaned back into the car and pulled out the rubber floor mats, which he rolled up and put under his arm.

Bosch's take on EnviroBreed's security measures, from when he had been there during the day, were that they were strictly aimed at deterring entry, not sounding an alert once security had been bridged. Dogs and cameras, a twelve-foot fence topped with electrified razor wire. But inside the plant Bosch had seen no tape on the windows in Ely's office, no electric eyes, not even an alarm key pad inside the front door.

This was because an alarm brought police. The breeders wanted to keep people out of the bug plant, but not if it drew the attention of authorities. It didn't matter if those authorities could be easily corrupted and paid to look the other way. It was just good business not to involve them. So, no alarms. This, of course, did not mean an alert would not be sent somewhere else — such as the ranch across the street — if a break-in occurred. But that was the risk Bosch was taking.

Bosch cut down the side of the Mexitec factory to an alley that ran behind the buildings that fronted Val Verde. He walked to the rear of EnviroBreed and waited for the dogs.

They came around quickly but silently. They were sleek black Dobermans and they moved right up to the fence. One made a low, guttural sound and the other followed suit. Bosch walked along the fence line, looking up at the razor wire. The dogs walked along with him, saliva dripping from their lagging tongues. Bosch saw the pen they were caged in during the day in the back. There was a wheelbarrow leaning up against the rear wall of the building and nothing else.

Except the dogs. Bosch crouched to the ground in the alley and opened up the bag. First he took out and opened the plastic bottle of Sueño Mas. Then he opened the wrapped paper bundle of roast pork he had bought at the Chinese takeout near the hotel. The meat was almost cold now. He took a chunk about the size of a baby's fist and pressed three of the extra-strength sleeping pills into it. He squeezed it in his hand and then lofted it over the fence. The dogs raced to it and one took a position over it but did not touch it. Bosch repeated the process and threw another piece over. The other dog stood over it.

They sniffed at the pork and looked at Bosch, sniffed some more. They looked around to see if their master might be nearby to help with a decision. Finding no help, they looked at each other. One dog finally picked his chunk up in its teeth and then dropped it. They both looked at Bosch and he yelled "Chow!"

The dogs did nothing. Bosch yelled the command a few more times but nothing changed. Then he noticed they were watching his right hand. He understood. He slapped his hand on his hip and issued the command again. The dogs ate the pork.

Bosch quickly made two more drug-laden snacks and threw them over the fence. They were eaten quickly. Bosch started pacing alongside the fence in the alley. The dogs stayed with him. He went back and forth twice, hoping the exercise would hurry their digestion. Harry ignored them for a while and looked up at the spiral of thin steel that ran along the top of the fence. He studied the glint it gave off in the moonlight. He also saw the electrical circuits spaced every twelve feet along the top and thought he heard a soft buzzing sound. The wire would tear a climber up and fry him before he got one leg over. But he was going to try.

He had to duck behind a Dumpster in the alley when he saw lights and a car came slowly down the alley. When it got closer he saw that it was a police car. He froze with momentary fear of how he would explain himself. He realized he had left the rolled car mats in the alley by the fence. The car slowed even more as it went by the EnviroBreed fence. The driver made a kissing sound at the dogs who still stood by the fence. The car moved on and Bosch came out of hiding.

The Dobermans stood on their side of the fence watching him for nearly an hour before one dropped into a sitting position and the other quickly did the same. The leader then worked its front paws forward until it was lying down. The follower did likewise. Bosch watched as their heads, almost in unison, bowed and then dropped onto their outstretched front legs. He saw urine forming in a puddle next to one of them. Both dogs kept their eyes open. When he took the last chunk of pork out of the wrapper and tossed it over the fence, he saw one of the dogs strain to raise his head and follow the arc of the falling food. But then the head dropped back down. Neither dog went for the offering. Bosch laced his fingers in the fence in front of the dogs and shook it, the steel making a whining sound, but the animals paid little attention.

It was time. Bosch crumpled the grease-stained paper and threw it in the Dumpster. He took a pair of work gloves out of the bag and put them on. Then he unfurled the front floor mat and held it by one end in his left hand. He took a high grip on the fence with his right, raised his right foot as high as he could and pointed his shoe into one of the diamond-shaped openings in the fence. He took a deep breath and in one move pulled himself up the fence, using his left hand and arm to swing the rubber mat up and over the top, so that it hung down over the spiral of razor wire like a saddle. He repeated the maneuver with the rear mat. They hung there side by side, their weight pressing the spiral of razor wire down.

It took him less than a minute to get to the top and gingerly swing one leg over the saddle and then pull the other over. The electric buzz was louder on top and he carefully moved his hand grips until he was able to drop down next to the still forms of the dogs. He took the small penlight from his pick set and put it on the dogs. Their eyes were open and dilated, their breathing heavy. He stood a moment watching their bodies rise and fall on the same beat, then he moved the light around on the ground until he found the uneaten piece of pork. He threw it over the fence, down the alley. Then, gripping the dogs by the collars, he dragged their bodies into their pen and latched the gate. The dogs were no longer a threat.

Bosch ran quietly up the side of the building and looked around the corner to make sure the parking lot was still empty. Then he came back down the side to the window of Ely's office.

He studied the window, double-checking to be sure he was correct about there being no alarm. He ran the light along all four sides of the louvered window and saw no wires, no vibration tape, no sign of an alarm. He opened the blade on his knife and pried back one of the metal strips that held the bottom pane of glass in place. He carefully slid the pane out of the window and leaned it against the wall. He moved the light through the opening and swung its beam around inside. The room was empty. He saw Ely's desk and other furnishings. The panel of four video tubes was black. The cameras were off.

After taking five glass sections out of the window and stacking them neatly against the outside wall, there was enough room for him to hoist himself up and crawl into the office.

The top of the desk was clear of paperwork and other clutter. The glass paperweight took the beam from the penlight and shot prism colors around the room. Bosch tried the drawers of the desk but found them locked. He opened them with a hook pick but found nothing of interest. There was a ledger in one drawer but it seemed to pertain to incoming breeding supplies.

He directed the light into the wastebasket on the floor inside the desk well and saw several crumpled pieces of paper. He emptied the basket on the floor. He reopened each piece of trash and then recrumpled it and dropped it back into the basket as he determined it was meaningless.

But not all of it was trash. He found one piece of crumpled paper that had several scribbles on it, including one that said:

Colorado   504

What to do with this? he thought. The paper was evidence of the effort to kill Bosch. But Bosch had discovered it during an illegal search. It was worthless unless found later during a legitimate search. The question was, when would that be? If Bosch left the crumpled paper in the trash can, there was a good chance the can would be emptied and the evidence lost.

He crumpled the paper back up and then took a long piece of tape off the dispenser on the desk. He attached one piece to the paper ball, which he then put in the trash can, pressing the other end of the tape down on the bottom of the can. Now, he hoped, if the can was emptied the crumpled paper would remain attached and inside the can. And maybe the person who emptied the can wouldn't notice.

He moved out of the office into the hall. By the lab door he took goggles and a breathing mask off the hook and put them on. The door had a common three-pin lock and he picked it quickly.

The doorway opened into blackness. He waited a beat and then moved into it. There was a cloying, sickly sweet smell to the place. It was humid. He moved the flashlight beam around what looked like the shipping room. He heard a fly buzzing in his ear and another insect was nattering around his masked face. He waved them off and moved farther through the room.

At the other end of the room, he passed through a set of double doors and into a room where the humidity was oppressive. It was lit by red bulbs that were spaced above rows of fiberglass bug bins. The warm air surrounded him. He felt a squadron of flies bumping and buzzing around his mask and forehead. Again, he waved them away. He moved to one of the bins and put his light into it. There was a brownish-pink mass of insect larvae moving like a slow-motion sea under the light.

He then cast the light about the room and saw a rack containing several tools and a small, stationary cement mixer that he guessed was what the day laborers used to mix the food paste for the bugs. Several shovels, rakes and brooms hung on pegs in a row at the back of the room. There were pallets containing large bags of pulverized wheat and sugar, and smaller bags of yeast. The markings on the bags were all in Spanish. He guessed this could be called the kitchen.

He played the light over the tools and noticed that one of the shovels stood out because it had a new handle. The wood was clean and light, while all of the other tools had handles that had darkened over time with dirt and human sweat.

Looking at the new handle Bosch knew that Fernal Gutierrez-Llosa had been killed here, beaten so hard with a shovel that it broke or became so blood-stained it had to be replaced. What had he seen that required his death? What had the simple day laborer done? Bosch swung the light around again until it came upon another set of doors at the far side of the room. On these a sign said:

DANGER! RADIATION! KEEP OUT!
PELIGRO! RADIACION!

He used his picks once again to open the door. He flashed the light around and saw no other doors. This was the terminus of the building. It was the largest of the three rooms in the complex and was divided in two by a partition with a small window in it. A sign on the partition said in English only:

PROTECTION MUST BE WORN

Bosch stepped around the partition and saw that this space was largely taken up by a large boxlike machine. Attached was a conveyor belt that carried trays into one side of the machine and then out the other side, where the trays would be dumped into bins like the ones he saw in the other room. There were more warning signs on the machine. This was where the larvae were sterilized by radiation.

He moved around to the other side of the room and saw large steel worktables with cabinets overhead. These were not locked and inside he saw boxes of supplies: plastic gloves and the sausagelike casings the larvae were shipped in, batteries and heat sensors. This was the room where the larvae were packed into casings and placed in the environment boxes. The end of the line. There was nothing else here that seemed significant.

Bosch stepped backward toward the door. He turned the flash off and there was only the small red glow from the surveillance camera mounted in the corner near the ceiling. What have I missed, he asked himself. What is left?

He put the light back on and walked back around the partition to the radiation machine. All of the signs in the building were designed to keep people away from this spot. This would be where the secret was. He focused on the floor-to-ceiling stacks of the wide steel trays used for moving larvae. He put his shoulder against one of the stacks and began to slide it on the floor. Beneath was only concrete. He tried the next stack and looked down and saw the edge of a trapdoor.

The tunnel.

But at that moment it hit him. The red light on the surveillance camera. The video panel in Ely's office had been off. And earlier, when Bosch had visited, he had noticed that the only interior view Ely had on video was of the shipping room.

It meant someone else was watching this room. He looked at his watch, trying to estimate how long he had been in the room. Two minutes? Three minutes? If they were coming from the ranch, he had little time. He looked down at the outline of the door in the floor and then up at the red eye in the darkness.

But he couldn't take the chance that no one was watching. He quickly pushed the stack back over the door in the floor and moved out of the third room. He retraced his path through the complex, hooking the mask and goggles on the peg by Ely's office. Then he went through the office and out the window. He quickly put the glass panes back in place, bending the metal strips back with his fingers.

The dogs were still lying in the same spot, their bodies pumping with each breath. Bosch hesitated but then decided to drag them out in case the monitor at the end of the camera's cable line was not being watched and he hadn't been seen. He grabbed them by the collars and dragged them out of the pen. He heard one try to growl but it sounded more like a whine. The other did likewise.

He hit the fence on the run, climbed it quickly but then forced himself to go slow over the floor mats. When he was at the top he thought he heard the sound of an engine above the sound of the electric buzz. As he was about to drop over, he jerked the mats up off the razor wire and dropped down with them into the alley.

He checked his pockets to make sure he had not dropped the picks or flashlight. Or his keys. His gun was still in its holster. He had everything. There was the sound of a vehicle now, maybe more than one. He definitely had been seen. As he ran down the alley toward Mexitec, he heard someone shouting "*Pedro y Pablo! Pedro y Pablo!*" The dogs, he realized. Peter and Paul were the dogs.

He crawled into his car and sat crouched in the front seat watching Enviro-Breed. There were two cars in the front lot and three men that he could see. They were holding guns and standing beneath the spotlight over the front door. Then a fourth man came around the corner, speaking in Spanish. He had found the dogs. Something about the man looked familiar but it was too dark and Bosch was too far away to be able to see any tattoo tears. They opened the door and, like cops with their guns up, they went inside the building. That was Bosch's cue. He started the Caprice and pulled out onto the road. As he sped away he realized he was once again shaking with the release of tension, the high of a good scare. Sweat was running down out of his hair and drying in the cool night air on his neck.

He lit a cigarette and threw the match out of the window. He laughed nervously into the wind.

25

≈≈≈

On Sunday morning Bosch called the number Ramos had given him from a pay phone at a restaurant called Casa de Mandarin in downtown Mexicali. He gave his name and number, hung up and lit a cigarette. Two minutes later the phone rang and it was Ramos.

"Qué pasa, amigo?"

"Nothing. I want to look at the mugs you got, remember?"

"Right. Right. Tell you what. I'll pick you up on my way in. Give me a half hour."

"I checked out."

"Leaving, are you?"

"No, I just checked out. I usually do that when somebody tries to kill me."

"What?"

"Somebody with a rifle, Ramos. I'll tell you about it. Anyway, I'm in the wind at the moment. You want to pick me up, I'm at the Mandarin in downtown."

"Half an hour. I want to hear about this."

They hung up and Bosch went back to his table, where Aguila was still finishing breakfast. They had both ordered scrambled eggs with salsa and chopped cilantro, fried dumplings on the side. The food was very good and Bosch had eaten quickly. He always did after a sleepless night.

The night before, after he drove laughing from EnviroBreed, they had met at Aguila's small house near the airport and the Mexican detective reported on his findings at the hotel. The desk clerk could offer little description of the man who rented 504 other than to say he had three tears tattooed on his cheek below the left eye.

Aguila had not asked where Bosch had been, seeming to know that an answer would not be given. Instead he offered Harry the couch in his sparsely furnished house. Harry accepted but didn't sleep. He just spent the night watching the window and thinking about things until bluish gray light pushed through the thin white curtains.

Much of the time Lucius Porter had been in his thoughts. He envisioned the detective's body on the cold steel table, naked and waxy, Teresa Corazón opening him up with the shears. He thought of the pinprick-sized blood hemorrhages she would find in the corneas of his eyes, the confirmation of strangulation. And he thought of the times he had been in the suite with Porter, watching others be cut up and the gutters on the table filling with their debris. Now it was Lucius on the table, a piece of wood under his neck, propping his head back into position for the bone saw. Just before dawn Harry's thoughts became confused with fatigue and in his mind he suddenly saw it was himself on the steel table, Teresa nearby, readying her equipment for the cut.

He had sat up then and reached for his cigarettes. And he made a vow to himself that it would never be himself on that table. Not that way.

"Drug enforcement?" Aguila asked as he pushed his plate away.

"Huh?"

Aguila nodded to the pager on his belt. He had just noticed it.

"Yeah. They wanted me to wear it."

Bosch believed he had to trust this man and that he had earned that trust. He didn't care what Ramos had said. Or Corvo. All his life Bosch had lived and worked in society's institutions. But he hoped he had escaped institutional thinking, that he made his own decisions. He would tell Aguila what was happening when the time was right.

"I'm going over there this morning, look at some mugs and stuff. Let's get together later."

Aguila agreed and said he would go to the Justice Plaza to complete paperwork on the confirmation of Fernal Gutierrez-Llosa's death. Bosch wanted to tell him about the shovel with the new handle he had seen in EnviroBreed but thought better of it. He planned to tell only one person about the break-in.

Bosch drank coffee and Aguila drank tea for a while without speaking. Bosch finally asked, "Have you ever seen Zorrillo? In person?"

"At a distance, yes."

"Where was that? The bullfights?"

"Yes, at the Plaza de los Toros. El Papa often attends to see his bulls. But he has a box in the shade reserved each week for him. I have afforded only seats on the sun side of the arena. This is the reason for the distance from which I have viewed him."

"He pulls for the bulls, huh?"

"Excuse me?"

"He goes to see his bulls win? Not the fighters?"

"No. He goes to see that his bulls die honorably."

Bosch wasn't sure what that meant but let it go.

"I want to go today. Can we get in? I want to sit in a box near the pope's."

"I don't know. These are expensive. Sometimes they cannot sell them. Even so, they keep them locked . . ."

"How much?"

"You would need at least two hundred dollars American, I'm afraid. It is very expensive."

Bosch took out his wallet and counted out $210. He left a ten on the table for the breakfast and pushed the rest across the faded green tablecloth to Aguila. It occurred to him it was more money than Aguila made in a six-day week on the job. He wished he had not been so quick to make a decision that would have taken Aguila hours of careful consideration.

"Get us a box near the pope."

"You must understand, there will be many men with him. He will be —"

"I just want a look at him, is all. Just get us the box."

They left the restaurant then and Aguila said he would walk to the Justice Plaza, a couple blocks away. After he left, Harry stood in front of the restaurant waiting for Ramos. He looked at his watch and saw it was eight o'clock. He was supposed to be in Irving's office at Parker Center. He wondered if the assistant chief had initiated disciplinary action against him yet. Bosch would probably be put on a desk as soon as he got back into town.

Unless . . . unless he brought back the whole package in his back pocket. That was the only way he would have any leverage with Irving. He knew he had to come out of Mexico with everything tied together.

It dawned on him that it was stupid to be standing like a target on the sidewalk in front of the restaurant. He stepped back inside and watched for Ramos through the front door. The waitress approached him and bowed effusively several times and walked away. It must've been the three-dollar tip, he thought.

It took Ramos nearly an hour to get there. Bosch decided he didn't want to be without a car so he told the agent he would follow him. They drove north on Lopez Mateos. At the circle around the statue of Juarez they went east, into a neighborhood of unmarked warehouses. They went down an alley and parked behind a building that had been tagged dozens of times with graffiti. Ramos looked furtively around after he got out of the beat-up Chevy Camaro with Mexican plates he was driving.

"Welcome to our humble federal office," he said.

Inside, it was Sunday morning quiet. No one else was there. Ramos put on the overhead lights and Bosch saw several rows of desks and file cabinets.

Toward the back were two weapons storage lockers and a two-ton Cincinnati safe for storing evidence.

"Okay, let me see what we got while you tell me about last night. You are sure somebody tried to do you, right?"

"Only way to be surer was if I got hit."

The Band-Aid Bosch had used on his neck was covered by his collar. There was another on his right palm, which also was not very noticeable.

Bosch told Ramos about the hotel shooting, leaving out no detail, including that he had recovered a shell from room 504.

"What about the slug? Recoverable?"

"I assume it's still in the headboard. I didn't hang around long enough to check."

"No, I bet you went running to warn your pal, the Mexican. Bosch, I am telling you to wise up. He may be a good guy but you don't know him. He mighta been the one that set the whole thing up."

"Actually, Ramos, I did warn him. But then I left and did what you wanted me to do."

"What're you talking about?"

"EnviroBreed. I went in last night."

"What? Are you crazy, Bosch? I didn't tell you to —"

"C'mon, man, don't fuck with me. You told me all that shit last night so I would know what was needed to get the search okayed. Don't bullshit me. We're alone here. I know that's what you wanted and I got it. Put me down as a CI."

Ramos was pacing in front of the file cabinets. He was making a good show of it.

"Look, Bosch, I have to clear any confidential informant I use with my supe. So that's not going to fly. I can't —"

"Make it fly."

"Bosch, I —"

"Do you want to know what I found there or should we just drop it?"

That quieted the DEA agent for a few moments.

"Do you have your ninjas, the — what did you call them, the clits, in town yet?

"CLETs, Bosch. And, yeah, they came in last night."

"Good. You're going to have to get going. I was seen."

Bosch watched the agent's face grow dark. He shook his head and dropped down into a chair.

"Fuck! How do you know?"

"There was a camera. I didn't see it until it was too late. I got out of there but some people came looking. I wasn't identifiable. I was wearing a mask. But, still, they know somebody was inside."

"Okay, Bosch, you aren't leaving me many options. What did you see?"

There it was. Ramos was acknowledging the illegal search. He was sanctioning it. Bosch would not have it come back on him now. He told the agent about the trapdoor hidden beneath the stack of bug trays in the radiation room.

"You didn't open it?"

"Didn't have time. But I wouldn't have done it anyway. I worked tunnels in Vietnam. Every trapdoor was just that, a trap. The people that came after I got out of there came by car, not through the tunnel. That tells you right there that there might be a rig in the tunnel."

He then told Ramos that his application for a search warrant or approval or whatever they called them in Mexico should include requests to seize all tools and debris from trash cans.

"Why?"

"Because the stuff you will find will help me make one of the murder cases I came down here for. There is also evidence of a conspiracy to murder a law enforcement officer — me."

Ramos nodded and didn't ask for further explanation. He wasn't interested. He got up and went to a file cabinet and pulled out two large black binders.

Bosch sat down at an empty desk and Ramos put the binders down in front of him.

"These are KOs — known operatives — associated with Humberto Zorrillo. We have some bio info on some of them. Others, it's just surveillance stuff. We might not even have a name."

Bosch opened the first binder and looked at the picture on top. It was a fuzzy eight-by-ten blow-up of a surveillance shot. Ramos said it was Zorrillo and Bosch had guessed as much. Dark hair, beard, intense stare through dark eyes. Bosch had seen the face before. Younger, no beard, a smile instead of the long, empty gaze. It was the grown-up face of the boy who had been in the pictures with Calexico Moore.

"What do you know about him?" Bosch asked Ramos. "You know anything about his family?"

"None that we know of. Not that we looked real hard. We don't give a shit where he came from, just what he's doing now and where he's going."

Bosch turned the plastic page and began looking at the mugs and surveillance shots. Ramos went back to his desk, rolled a piece of paper into a typewriter and began typing.

"I'm working up a CI statement here. I'll get it by somehow."

About two-thirds through the first book Bosch found the man with three tears. There were several photos of him — mugs and surveillance — from all angles and over several years. Bosch saw his face change as the tears were added from a smiling wiseass to a hardened con. The brief biographical data said his name was Osvaldo Arpis Rafaelillo and that he was born in 1952. They said his three stays in the *penitenciaro* were for murder as a juvenile, murder as an adult and drug possession. He had spent half his life in prisons. The data described him as a lifelong associate of Zorrillo's.

"Here, I got him," Bosch said.

Ramos came over. He recognized the man also.

"You're saying he was up in L.A. whacking out cops?"

"Yeah. At least one. I think he might have done the job on the first one, too. I think he also took down a courier for the competition. A Hawaiian named Jimmy Kapps. He and one of the cops were strangled the same way."

"Mexican necktie, right?"

"Right."

"And the laborer? The one you think got it at the bug house?"

"He could've done them all. I don't know."

"This guy goes way back. Arpis. Yeah, he just got out of the *penta* a year or so ago. He's a stone-cold killer, Bosch. One of the pope's main men. An enforcer. In fact, people 'round here call him 'Alvin Karpis,' you know, after that killer with the machine gun in the thirties? The Ma Barker gang? Arpis was put away for a couple hits but they say that doesn't do him service. He's really down for more than you can count."

Bosch stared at the photos and said, "That's all you got on him? This stuff here?"

"There's more around someplace but that's all you have to know. Most of it is just he said/she said informant stuff. The main story about Al Karpis is that when Zorrillo first made his move to the top, this guy was a one-man front line doing the heavy stuff. Every time Zorrillo had a piece of work to do, he'd turn to his buddy Arpis from the barrio. He'd get the job done. And like I said, they only bagged him a couple times. He probably paid his way out of the rest."

Bosch began writing some of the information from the bio in a notebook. Ramos kept talking.

"Those two, they came from a barrio south of here. Some —"

"Saints and Sinners."

"Yeah, Saints and Sinners. Some of the local cops, the ones I trust about as far as I can throw 'em, said Arpis had a real taste for killing. In the barrio they had a saying. *Quien eres?* Means who are you? It was a challenge. It means what side are you on, you know? Are you with us or against us? Saint or Sinner? And when Zorrillo rose to power, he had Arpis taking out the people that were against them. The locals said that after they whacked somebody, they'd spread the word around the barrio. *El descubrio quien era.* Means —"

"He found out who he was."

"Right. It was good PR, made the natives fall in behind him. Supposedly they really got into it. Got to the point they were leaving messages with the body. You know? They'd kill a guy and write out 'He found out who he was,' or whatever and leave it pinned to his shirt."

Bosch said nothing and wrote nothing. Another piece of the puzzle dropped into place.

"Sometimes you still see it on graffiti around the barrio," Ramos said. "It's part of the folklore surrounding Zorrillo. It's part of what makes him the pope."

Harry finally closed his notebook and stood up.

"I got what I need."

"All right. Be careful out there, Bosch. Nothing that says they won't try again, especially if Arpis is on the job. You just want to hang out here today? It's safe."

"Nah, I'll be okay." He nodded and took a step toward the door. He touched the pager on his belt. "I will get a call?"

"Yeah, you're in. Corvo's coming down for the show so I gotta make sure you're there. Where you gonna be later today?"

"I don't know. I think I'm going to make like a tourist. Go to the historical society, take in a bullfight."

"Just be cool. You'll get a call."

"I better."

He walked out to the Caprice thinking only about the note that had been found in Cal Moore's back pocket.

I found out who I was.

26

It took Bosch thirty minutes to get across the border. The line of cars extended nearly half a mile back from the drab brown Border Patrol port of entry. While waiting and measuring his progress in one or two car-length movements, he ran out of change and one-dollar bills as an army of peasants came to his window holding up their palms or selling cheap bric-a-brac and food. Many of them washed the windshield unbidden with their dirty rags and held up their hands for coins. Each progressive washing smeared the glass more until Bosch had to put on the wipers and use the car's own spray. When he finally made it to the checkpoint, the BP inspector in mirrored shades just waved him through after seeing his badge. He said, "Hose up there on the right if you want to wash the shit off your windshield."

A few minutes later he pulled into one of the parking spaces in front of the Calexico Town Hall. Bosch parked and looked out across the park while smoking a cigarette. There were no troubadours today. The park was almost empty. He got out and headed toward the door marked Calexico Historical Society, not sure what he was looking for. He had the afternoon to spend and all he knew was that he believed there was a deeper line running through Cal Moore's death — from his decision to cross to the note in his back pocket to the photo of him with Zorrillo so many years ago. Bosch wanted to find out what happened to the house he had called a castle and the man he had posed with, the one with the hair white as a sheet.

The glass door was locked and Bosch saw that the society didn't open until one on Sundays. He looked at his watch and saw he still had fifteen minutes to wait. He cupped his hands to the glass and looked in and saw no one inside the tiny space that included two desks, a wall of books and a couple of glass display cases.

He stepped away from the door and thought about using the time to get something to eat. He decided it was too early. Instead, he walked down to the police station and got a Coke from the machine in the minilobby. He nodded at the officer behind the glass window. It wasn't Gruber today.

While he stood leaning against the front wall, drinking the soda and watching the park, Harry saw an old man with a latticework of thin white hair on the sides of his head unlock the door to the historical society. He was a few minutes early, but Bosch headed down the walk and followed him in.

"Open?" he said.

"Might as well be," the old man said. "I'm here. Anything in particular I can help you with?"

Bosch walked into the center of the room and explained he was unsure what he wanted.

"I'm sort of tracing the background of a friend and I believe his father was a historical figure. In Calexico, I mean. I want to find their house if it's still standing, find out what I can about the old man."

"What's this fellow's name?"

"I don't know. Actually, I just know his last name was Moore."

"Hell, boy, that name don't much narrow it down. Moore's one of the big names around here. Big family. Brothers, cousins all over the place. Tell you what, let me —"

"You have pictures? You know, books with photos of the Moores? I've seen pictures of the father. I could pick —"

"Yeah, that's what I'm saying, let me set you up here with a couple things. We'll find your Moore. I'm kinda curious now myself. What're you doing this for your friend for, anyway?"

"Trying to trace the family tree. Put it all together for him."

A few minutes later the old man had him sitting at the other desk with three books in front of him. They were leather-bound and smelled of dust. They were the size of yearbooks and they wove photographic and written history together on every page. Randomly opening one of the books, he looked at a black-and-white photo of the De Anza Hotel under construction.

Then he started them in order. The first was called *Calexico and Mexicali: Seventy-five Years on the Border* and as he scanned the words and photos on the pages, Bosch picked up a brief history of the two towns and the men who built them. The story was the same one Aguila had told him, but from the white man's perspective. The volume he read described the horrible poverty in Tapai, China, and told how the men facing it gladly came to Baja California to seek their fortunes. It didn't say anything about cheap labor.

In the 1920s and 1930s Calexico was a boomtown, a company town, with the Colorado River Land Company's managers the lords of all they surveyed. The book said many of these men built opulent homes and estates on bluffs rising on the outskirts of town. As Bosch read he repeatedly saw the names of three Moore brothers: Anderson, Cecil and Morgan. There were other Moores listed as well, but the brothers were always described in terms of importance and had high-level titles in the company.

While leafing through a chapter called "A Dirt Road Town Paves Its Streets in Gold," Bosch saw the man he was interested in. He was Cecil Moore. There, amidst the description of the riches the cotton brought to Calexico, was a photograph of a man with prematurely white hair standing in front of a Mediterranean-style home the size of a school. It was the man in the photo Moore had kept in the crumpled white bag. And rising like a steeple on the left-hand side of the home was a tower with two arched windows side by side at its uppermost point. The tower gave the house the appearance of a Spanish castle. It was Cal Moore's childhood home.

"This is the man and this is the place," Bosch said, taking the book over to the old man.

"Cecil Moore," the man said.

"Is he still around?"

"No, none of those brothers are. He was the last to go, though. Last year about this time, went in his sleep, Cecil did. I think you're mistaken though."

"Why's that?"

"Cecil had no children."

Bosch nodded.

"Maybe you're right. What about this place. That gone, too?"

"You're not working on any family tree, are you now?"

"No. I'm a cop. I came from L.A. I'm tracing down a story somebody told me about this man. Will you help me?"

The old man looked at him and Bosch regretted not being truthful with him in the first place.

"I don't know what it's got to do with Los Angeles but go ahead, what else you want to know?"

"Is this place with the tower still there?"

"Yes, Castillo de los Ojos is still there. Castle of the Eyes. Gets its name from those two windows up in the tower. When they were lit at night, it was said that they were eyes that looked out on all of Calexico."

"Where is it?"

"It's on a road called Coyote Trail west of town. You take 98 out there past Pinto Wash to an area called Crucifixion Thorn. Turn onto Anza Road — like the hotel here in town. That'll take you to Coyote Trail. The castle's at the end of the road. You can't miss it."

"Who lives there now?"

"I don't think anyone does. He left it to the city, you know. But the city couldn't handle the upkeep on a place like that. They sold it — I believe the man came down from Los Angeles, matter of fact. But as far as I know he never moved in. It's a pity. I was hoping to have maybe made a museum out of it."

Bosch thanked him and left to head out to Crucifixion Thorn. He had no idea whether Castillo de los Ojos was anything more than a dead rich man's estate with no bearing on his case. But he had nothing else going and his impulse was to keep moving forward.

State road 98 was a two-lane blacktop that stretched west from Calexico-town proper, running alongside the border, into farmland delineated into a huge grid by irrigation ditches. As he drove, he smelled green pepper and cilantro. And he realized after running alongside a field planted in cotton that this wide expanse was all once the Company's huge acreage.

Ahead, the land rose into hills and he could see Calexico Moore's boy-hood home long before he was near. Castillo de los Ojos. The two arched windows were dark and hollow eyes against the peach-colored stone face of the tower rising from a promontory on the horizon.

Bosch crossed a bridge over a dry bed that he assumed was Pinto Wash, though there was no sign on the road. Glancing down into the dusty bed as he passed, Harry saw a lime-green Chevy Blazer parked below. He caught just a glimpse of a man behind the wheel with binoculars held to his eyes. Border Patrol. The driver was using the bed's low spot as a blind from which he could watch the border for crossers.

The wash marked the end of the farmland. Almost immediately the earth began to rise into brown-brush hills. There was a turnout in the road by a stand of eucalyptus and oak trees that were still in the windless morning. This time there was a sign marking the location:

CRUCIFIXION THORN NATURAL AREA
Danger Abandoned Mines

Bosch remembered seeing a reference in the books at the historical society to the turn-of-the-century gold mines that pockmarked the border zone. Fortunes had been found and lost by speculators. The hills had been heavy with bandits. Then the Company came and brought order.

He lit a cigarette and studied the tower, which was much closer now and rose from behind a walled compound. The stillness of the scene and the tower windows, like soulless eyes, somehow seemed morbid. The tower was not alone on the hill, though. He could see the barrel-tile roofs of other homes. But something about the tower rising singularly above them with its empty glass eyes seemed lonely. Dead.

Anza Road came up in another half mile. He turned north and the single-lane road curved and bumped and rose along the circumference of the hill. To his right he could look down on the farmland basin extending below. He turned left onto a road marked Coyote Trail and was soon passing large haciendas on sprawlng estates. He could see only the second floors of most of them because of the walls that surrounded almost every property.

Coyote Trail ended in a circle that went around an ancient oak tree with branches that would shade the turnaround in the summer. Castillo de los Ojos was here at the end of the road.

From the street, an eight-foot-high stone wall eclipsed all but the tower. Only through a black wrought-iron gate was there a fuller view. Bosch pulled onto the driveway and up to the gate. Heavy steel chain and lock kept it closed. He got out, looked through the bars and saw that the parking circle in front of the house was empty. The curtains inside every front window were pulled closed.

On the wall next to the gate were a mailbox and an intercom. He pushed the ringer but got no response. He wasn't sure what he would have said if someone had answered. He opened the mailbox and found that empty too.

Bosch left his car where it was and walked back down Coyote Trail to the nearest house. This was one of the few without a wall. But there was a white picket fence and an intercom at the gate. And this time when he rang the buzzer, he got a response.

"Yes?" a woman's voice asked.

"Yes, ma'am, police. I was wondering if I can ask a few questions about your neighbor's house."

"Which neighbor?"

The voice was very old.

"The castle."

"Nobody lives there. Mr. Moore died some time ago."

"I know that, ma'am. I was wondering if I could come in and talk to you a moment. I have identification."

There was a delay before he heard a curt "Very well" over the speaker and the gate lock buzzed.

The woman insisted that he hold his ID up to a small window set in the door. He saw her in there, white-haired and decrepit, straining to see it from a wheelchair. She finally opened up.

"Why do they send a Los Angeles police officer?"

"Ma'am, I'm working on a Los Angeles case. It involves a man who used to live in the castle. As a boy, long ago."

She looked up at him through squinting eyes, as if she was trying to see past a memory.

"Are you talking about Calexico Moore?"

"Yes. You knew him?"

"Is he hurt?"

Bosch hesitated, then said, "I'm afraid he's dead."

"Up there in Los Angeles?"

"Yes. He was a police officer. I think it had something to do with his life down here. That's why I came out here. I don't really know what to ask . . . He didn't live here long. But you remember him, yes?"

"He didn't live here long but that doesn't mean I never saw him again. Quite the contrary. I saw him regularly over the years. He'd ride his bicycle or he'd drive a car and come and sit out there on the road and just watch that place. One time I had Marta bring him out a sandwich and a lemonade."

He assumed Marta was the maid. These estates came with them.

"He'd just watch and remember, I guess," the old woman was saying. "Terrible thing that Cecil did to him. He's probably paying for it now, that Cecil."

"What do you mean, 'terrible'?"

"Sending the boy and his mother away like that. I don't think he ever spoke to that boy or the woman again after that. But I'd see the boy and I'd see him as a man, come out here to look at the place. People 'round here say that's why Cecil put that wall up. Did that twenty years ago. They say it's because he got tired of seeing Calexico in the street. That was Cecil's way of doing things. You don't like what you see out your window, you put up a wall. But I'd still see young Cal from time to time. One time I took a cold drink out to him myself. I wasn't in this chair then. He was sitting in a car, and I asked him, 'Why do you come out here all the time?' and he just said, 'Aunt Mary, I like to remember.' That's what he said."

"Aunt Mary?"

"Yes. I thought that was why you came here. My Anderson and Cecil were brothers, God rest their souls."

Bosch nodded and waited a respectful five seconds before speaking.

"The man at the museum in town said Cecil had no children."

"'Course he said that. Cecil kept it a secret from the public. Big secret. He didn't want the company name blemished."

"Calexico's mother was the maid?"

"Yes, she — it sounds like you know all of this already."

"Just a few parts. What happened? Why did he send her and the boy away?"

She hesitated before answering, as if to compose a story that was more than thirty years old.

"After she became pregnant, she lived there — he made her — and she had the baby there. Afterward, four or five years, he discovered she had lied to him. One day he had some of his men follow her across when she went to Mexicali to visit her mother. There was no mother. Just a husband and another son, this one older than Calexico. That was when he sent them away. His own blood he sent away."

Bosch thought about this for a long moment. The woman was staring off at the past.

"When was the last time you saw Calexico?"

"Oh, let me see, must have been years now. He eventually stopped coming around."

"Do you think he knew of his father's death?"

"He wasn't at the funeral, not that I blame him."

"I was told Cecil Moore left the property to the city."

"Yes, he died alone and he left everything to the city, not a thing to Calexico or any of the ex-wives and mistresses. Cecil Moore was a mean man, even in death. Of course the city couldn't do anything with that place. Too big and expensive to keep up. Calexico isn't a boomtown like it once was and can't keep a place like that. There was a thought that it would be used as a historical museum. But you couldn't fill a closet with the history of this town. Never mind the museum. The city sold the place. I heard, for more than a million. Maybe they'll operate in the black for a few years."

"Who bought it?"

"I don't know. But they never moved in. They got a caretaker comes around. I saw lights on over there last week. But, nope, nobody's ever moved in as far as I know. It must be an investment. In what I don't know. We're sitting out here in the middle of nowhere."

"One last question. Was there ever anybody else with Moore when he would watch the place?"

"Always alone. That poor boy was always out there alone."

On the way back into town Bosch thought about Moore's lonely vigils outside the house of his father. He wondered if his longings were for the house and its memories or the father who had sent him away. Or both.

Bosch's mind touched his memory of his brief meeting with his own father. A sick old man on his death bed. Bosch had forgiven him for every second he had been robbed. He knew he had to or he would face the rest of his life wasting his pain on it.

27

The line of traffic to go back into Mexico was longer and slower than the day before. Bosch figured this was because of the bullfight, which drew people from the entire region. It was a Sunday evening tradition as popular here as Raiders football was in L.A.

Bosch was two cars from the Mexican border officer when he realized he still had the Smith in its holster on his back. It was too late to do anything about it. When he got to the man, he simply said, "Bullfight," and was waved on through.

The sky was clear over Mexicali and the air cool. It looked like it would be perfect weather. Harry felt the tingle of anticipation in his throat. It was for two things: seeing the ritual of the fight and maybe seeing Zorrillo, the man whose name and lore had surrounded his last three days so thoroughly that Bosch found himself buying into his myth. He just wanted to see the pope in his own element. With his bulls. With his people.

Bosch took a pair of surveillance binoculars out of the glove compartment after parking at the Justice Plaza. The arena was only three blocks away and he figured they'd walk. After showing ID to the front-desk officer and being approved to go back, he found Aguila sitting behind the lone desk in the investigators' squadroom. He had several handwritten reports in front of him.

"Did you get the tickets?"

"Yes, I have them. We have a box on the sun side. This will not be a problem because the boxes get little sun."

"Is it close to the pope?"

"Almost directly across — if he is there today."

"Yeah, if. We'll see. You done?"

"Yes, I have completed the reports on the Fernal Gutierrez-Llosa investigation. Until a suspect is charged."

"Which will probably never happen down here."

"This is correct. . . . I believe we should go now."

Bosch held up the binoculars.

"I'm ready."

"You will be so close you will not need those."

"These aren't for looking at bulls."

As they walked toward the arena they moved into a steady stream of people heading the same way. Many of them carried little square pillows on which they would sit in the arena. They passed several young children holding armfuls of pillows and selling them for a dollar each.

After entering the gate, Bosch and Aguila descended a set of concrete stairs to an underground level where Aguila presented their box tickets to an usher. They were then led through a catacomblike passageway that curved as it followed the circumference of the ring. There were small wooden doors marked with numbers on their left.

The usher opened a door with the number seven on it and they went into a room no larger than a jail cell. Its floor, walls and ceiling were all unpainted concrete. The vaulted ceiling sloped downward from the back to a six-foot-wide opening that looked out into the ring. They were directly on the outer ring where matadors, toreros and other players in the fights stood and waited. Bosch could smell the dirt ring, its horse and bull odors, its blood. There were six steel chairs folded and leaning against the rear wall. They opened two and sat down after Aguila thanked the usher and closed and locked the door.

"This is like a pillbox," Bosch said as he looked through the window slot into the boxes across the ring. He did not see Zorrillo.

"What is a pillbox?"

"Never mind," Bosch said, realizing he had never been in one, either. "It's like a jail cell."

"Perhaps," Aguila said.

Bosch realized he had insulted him. These were the best seats in the house.

"Carlos, this is great. We'll see everything from here."

It was also loud in the concrete box and in addition to the smells from the ring there was the pervasive odor of spilled beer. The little room seemed to reverberate with a thousand steps as the stadium above them filled. A band played from seats high up in the stadium. Bosch looked out into the ring and saw the toreros being introduced. He felt the growing excitement of the crowd and the echo in the room grew louder with the cheers as the matadors bowed.

"I can smoke in here, right?" Bosch asked.

"Yes," Aguila said as he stood. *"Cervesa?"*

"I like that Tecate if they have it."

"Of course. Lock the door. I will knock."

Aguila nodded and left the room. Harry locked the door and wondered if he was doing it to protect himself, or simply to keep uninvited observers out of the box. He realized once he was alone that he did not feel protected in the fortresslike surroundings. It was not like a pillbox after all.

He held the binoculars up and viewed the openings into the other boxes across the ring. Most of these were still empty and he did not see anyone among those already in place who he believed was Zorrillo. But he noticed that many of these boxes were customized. He could see shelves of liquor bottles or tapestries on the back walls, padded chairs. These were the shaded boxes of the regulars. Soon Aguila knocked and Bosch let him in with the beers. And the spectacle began.

The first two fights were uneventful and uninspired. Aguila called them sloppy. The matadors were heartily booed by those in the arena when their final sword thrusts into each bull's neck failed to kill and each fight became a prolonged, bloody display that had little resemblance to art or a test of bravery.

In the third fight, the arena came alive and the noise thundered in the box where Bosch and Aguila sat when a bull black as pitch — except for the whitish Z branded on its back — charged violently into the side of one of the picadors' horses. The tremendous power of the beast pushed the horse's padded skirt up to the rider's thigh. The horseman drove his iron-pointed lance down into the bull's back and leaned his weight on it. But this seemed only to enrage the beast further. The animal found new strength and made another violent lunge into the horse. The confrontation was only thirty feet from Bosch, but still he lifted the binoculars for a closer look. In what was like a slow-motion tableau captured in the scope of the binoculars' frame, he saw the horse rear against its master's rein and the picador topple off into the dust. The bull continued its charge, its horns impaling the padded skirt and the horse went over on top of the picador.

The crowd became even louder, cheering wildly, as the banderilleros flooded the ring, waving capes and drawing the bull's attention from the fallen horse and rider. Others helped the picador to his feet and he limped to the ring gate. He then shrugged their hands away, refusing any further help. His face was slick with sweat and red with embarrassment and the cheers of the arena had a jeering quality. With the binoculars, Bosch felt as though he was standing next to the man. A pillow came down from the stands and glanced off the man's shoulder. He did not look up, for to do that would be to invite more.

The bull had won this crowd and in a few minutes they respectfully cheered its death. A matador's sword deeply embedded in its neck, the animal's front legs buckled and its huge weight collapsed. A torero, a man who was older than all the other players, quickly moved in with a short dagger and stabbed it into the base of the bull's skull. Instant death after the prolonged torment. Bosch watched the man wipe the blade on the dead animal's black coat and then walk away, replacing the dagger in a sheath strapped to his vest.

Three mules in harness were brought into the ring, a rope was looped around the black bull's horns and the body was dragged around in a circle and then out. Bosch saw a red rose fall from above and hit the dead beast as it made a flattened path in the ring's dirt floor.

Harry studied the man with the dagger. Applying the coup de grâce seemed to be his only role in each fight. Bosch couldn't decide if his job was administering mercy or more cruelty. The man was older; his black hair was streaked with gray and his face had a worn, impassive look. He had soulless eyes in a face of worn brown stone. Bosch thought of the man with three tear drops on his face. Arpis. What look did he have when he choked the life out of Porter, when he held the shotgun up to Moore's face and pulled the trigger?

"The bull was very brave and beautiful," Aguila said. He had said little through the first three fights other than to pronounce the skills of the matadors as expert or sloppy, good or bad.

"I guess Zorrillo would have been very proud," Bosch said, "if he had been here."

It was true, Zorrillo had not come. Bosch had found himself checking the empty box Aguila had pointed out but it had remained empty. Now, with one fight to go, it seemed unlikely that the man who bred the bulls for this day's fights would arrive.

"Do you wish to leave, Harry?"

"No. I want to watch."

"Good, then. This match will be the finest and most artful. Silvestri is Mexicali's greatest matador. Another *cervesa*?"

"Yeah. I'll get this one. What do you —"

"No. It is my duty, a small means of repaying."

"Whatever," Bosch said.

"Lock the door."

He did. Then he looked at his ticket, on which the names of the bullfighters were printed. Cristobal Silvestri. Aguila had said he was the most artful and bravest fighter he had ever seen. A cheer went up from the crowd as the bull, another huge black monster, charged into the ring to confront his killers. The toreros began moving about him with green and blue capes opening like flowers. Bosch was struck by the ritual and pageantry of the bullfights, even the sloppy ones. It was not a sport, he was sure of this. But it was something. A test. A test of skills and, yes, bravery, resolve. He believed that if he had the opportunity he would want to go often to this arena to be a witness.

There was a knock on the door and Bosch got up to let Aguila in. But when he opened the door there were two men waiting. One he did not recognize. The other he did but it took him a few moments to place him. It was Grena, the captain of investigations. From what little he could see past their two figures, there was no sign of Aguila.

"Señor Bosch, may we come in?"

Bosch stepped back but only Grena entered. The other man turned his back as if to guard the doorway. Grena closed and locked it.

"So we won't be disturbed, yes?" he said as he scanned the room. He did this at length, as if it were the size of a basketball court and needed careful study in determining there was no one else present.

"It is my custom to come for the last fight, Señor Bosch. Particularly, you see, when Silvestri is in the ring. A great champion. I hope you will enjoy this."

Bosch nodded and casually looked out into the ring. The bull was still lively and moving about the ring while the toreros sidestepped and waited for it to slow.

"Carlos Aguila? He has gone?"

"*Cervesa*. But you probably already know that, Captain. So why don't you tell me what's up?"

"What is 'up'? How do you mean?"

"I mean what do you want, Captain. What are you doing here?"

"Ah, *si*, you want to watch our little pageant and do not wish to be bothered by business. Get to the point, is the way it is said, I believe."

"Yeah, that works."

There was a cheer and both men looked out into the ring. Silvestri had entered and was stalking the bull. He wore a white-and-gold suit of lights and he walked in a regal manner, his back straight and his head canted downward, as he sternly studied his adversary. The bull was still game as it charged about the ring, whipping the blue and yellow banderillas stuck in its neck from side to side.

Bosch pulled his attention back to Grena. The police captain was wearing a black jacket of soft leather, its right cuff barely covering his Rolex.

"My point is I want to know what you are doing, Señor Bosch. You don't come down here for bullfights. So why are you here? I am told identification of Señor Gutierrez-Llosa has been made. Why do you stay? Why do you bother Carlos Aguila with your time?"

Bosch was not going to tell this man anything but he did not want to endanger Aguila. Bosch would be leaving eventually, but not Aguila.

"I am leaving in the morning. My work is completed."

"Then you should leave tonight, eh? An early start?"

"Maybe."

Grena nodded.

"You see, I have had an inquiry from a Lieutenant Pounds of the LAPD. He is very anxious at your return. He asked me to tell you this personally. Why is that?"

Bosch looked at him and shook his head.

"I don't know. You would have to ask him."

There was a long silence during which Grena's attention was drawn to the ring again. Bosch looked that way, too, just in time to see Silvestri leading the charging bull past him with his cape.

Grena looked at him for a long time and then smiled, probably the way Ted Bundy had smiled at the girls on campus.

"You know the art of the cape?"

Bosch didn't answer and the two just stared at each other. A thin smile continued to play across the captain's dark face.

"*El arte de la muleta*," Grena finally said. "It is deception. It is the art of survival. The matador uses the cape to fool death, to make death go where he is not. But he must be brave. He must risk himself over the horns of death. The closer death comes, the braver he becomes. Never for a moment can he show fear. Never show fear. To do so is to lose. It is to die. This is the art, my friend."

He nodded and Bosch just stared at him.

Grena smiled broadly now and turned to the door. He opened it and the other man was still there. As he turned to reclose the door he looked at Bosch and said, "Have a good trip, Detective Harry Bosch. Tonight, eh?"

Bosch said nothing and the door was closed. He sat there for a moment but his attention was drawn by the cheers to the ring. Silvestri had dropped to one knee in the center of the ring and had lured the bull to a charge. He remained stoically fixed in position until the beast was on him. He then moved the cape away from his body in a smooth flow. The bull rushed by within inches and Silvestri was untouched. It was beautiful and the cheers rose from the stadium. The unlocked door to the box opened and Aguila stepped in.

"Grena, what did he want?"

Bosch didn't answer. He held the binoculars up and checked Zorrillo's box. The pope wasn't there but now Grena was, staring back at him with the same thin smile on his lips.

Silvestri felled the bull with a single thrust of his sword, the blade diving deep between its shoulders and slicing through the heart. Instant death. Bosch looked over at the man with the dagger and thought he saw a trace of disappointment on his hardened face. His work wasn't needed.

The cheering for Silvestri's expert kill was deafening. And it did not let up as the matador made a circuit around the ring, his arms up to receive the applause. Roses, pillows, women's high-heeled shoes showered down into the ring. The bullfighter beamed in the adulation. The noise was so loud that it was quite some time before Bosch realized that the pager on his belt was sounding its call to him.

28

At nine o'clock Bosch and Aguila turned off Avenida Cristobal Colon onto a perimeter road that skirted Rodolfo Sanchez Taboada Aeropuerto Internacional. The roadway passed several old quonset-hut hangars and then a larger grouping of newer structures. On one of these was a sign that said Aero Carga. The huge bay doors had been spread a few feet and the opening was lit from the inside. It was their destination, a DEA front. Bosch pulled into the lot in front and parked near several other cars. He noticed that most of them had California plates.

As soon as he stepped out of the Caprice he was approached by four DEA types in blue plastic windbreakers. He showed his ID and evidently passed muster after one of them consulted a clipboard.

"And you?" the clipboard man said to Aguila.

"He's with me," Bosch said.

"We have you down as a solo entry, Detective Bosch. Now we have a problem."

"I guess I forgot to RSVP that I'd bring a date," Bosch said.

"It's not very funny, Detective Bosch."

"Of course not. But he's my partner. He stays with me."

Clipboard had a distressed look on his face. He was an Anglo with a ruddy complexion and hair that had been bleached almost white by the sun. He looked as though he had been watching the border a long time. He turned to look back at the hangar, as if hoping for direction on how to handle this. On the back of his windbreaker Bosch saw the large yellow *DEA* letters.

"Better get Ramos," Bosch said. "If my partner goes, I go. Then where's the integrity of the operation's security?"

He looked over at Aguila, who was standing stiffly with the three other agents around him like bouncers ready to toss somebody out of a nightclub on the Sunset Strip.

"Think about it," Bosch continued. "Anybody who's come this far has to go the distance. Otherwise, you got someone outside the circle. Out there and unaccounted for. Go ask Ramos."

Clipboard hesitated again, then told everybody to stay cool and took a radio from the pocket of his jacket. He radioed to someone called Staff Leader that there was a problem in the lot. Then everybody stood around for a few moments in silence. Bosch looked over at Aguila and when their eyes met he winked. Then he saw Ramos and Corvo, the agent from L.A., walking briskly toward them.

"What's this shit, Bosch," Ramos started before he got to the car. "Do you know what you've done? You've compromised the whole fucking operation. I gave explicit instru —"

"He's my partner on this, Ramos. He knows what I know. We are together on this. If he's out, then so am I. And when we leave, I go across the border. To L.A. I don't know where he goes. How will that hold with your theory on who can be trusted?"

In the light from the hangar, Bosch could see the pulse beating in an artery on Ramos's neck.

"See," Bosch said, "if you let him leave, you are trusting him. So, if you trust him, you might as well let him stay."

"Fuck you, Bosch."

Corvo put his hand on Ramos's arm and stepped forward.

"Bosch, if he fucks up or this operation in any way becomes compromised, I will make it known. You know what I mean? It'll be known in L.A. that you brought this guy in."

He made a signal across the car to the others and they stepped away from Aguila. The moonlight reflected on Corvo's face and Bosch saw the scar that split his beard on the right side. He wondered how many times the DEA agent would be telling the story of the knife fight tonight.

"And another thing," Ramos threw in. "He goes in naked. We only have one more vest. That's for your ass, Bosch. So if he gets hit, it's on you."

"Right," Bosch said. "I get it. No matter what goes wrong, it's my ass. I got it. I also have a vest in my trunk. He can use yours. I like my own."

"Briefing's at twenty-two hundred," Ramos said as he walked back toward the hangar.

Corvo followed and Bosch and Aguila fell in behind him. The other agents brought up the rear. Inside the cavernous hangar Bosch saw there were three black helicopters sitting side by side in the bay area. There were several men, most in black jumpsuits, milling about and drinking coffee from white cups. Two of the helicopters were wide-bodied personnel transport craft. Bosch recognized them. They were UH-1Ns. Hueys. The distinctive whop-whop of their rotors would forever be the sound of Vietnam to him. The third craft was smaller and sleeker. It looked like a craft manufactured for commercial use, like a news or police chopper, but it had been converted into a gunship. Bosch recognized the gun turret mounted on the right side of the copter's body. Beneath the cockpit another mount held an array of equipment, including a spotlight and night-vision sensor. The men in the black jumpsuits were stripping the white numbers and letters off the tail sections of the craft. They were preparing for a total blackout, a night assault.

Bosch noticed Corvo come up next to him.

"We call it the Lynx," he said, nodding to the smallest of the three craft. "Mostly use 'em in Central and South America ops, but we snagged this one on its way down. It's for night work. You've got total night vision set up — infrared, heat-pattern displays. It will be the in-air command post tonight."

Bosch just nodded. He was not as impressed with the hardware as Corvo was. The DEA supervisor seemed more animated than during their meeting at the Code 7. His dark eyes were darting around the hangar, taking it all in. Bosch realized that he probably missed fieldwork. He was stuck in L.A. while guys like Ramos got to play the war games.

"And that's where you're going to be, you and your partner," Corvo said, nodding at the Lynx. "With me. Nice and safe. Observers."

"You in charge of this show, or is Ramos?"

"I'm in charge."

"Hope so." Then, looking at the war chopper, Bosch said, "Tell me something, Corvo, we want Zorrillo alive, right?"

"That's right."

"Okay, then, when we get him, what's the plan? He's a Mexican citizen. You can't take him over the border. You just going to give him to the Mexicans? He'll be running the penitentiary they put him in within a month. That is, if they put him in a pen."

It was a problem every cop in southern California had come up against. Mexico refused to extradite its citizens to the United States for crimes committed there. But it would prosecute them at home. The problem was that it was well known that the country's biggest drug dealers turned penitentiary stays into hotel visits. Women, drugs, alcohol and other comforts could be had as long as the money was paid. One story was that a convicted drug lord had actually taken over the warden's office and residence at a prison in Juarez. He had paid the warden $100,000 for the privilege, about four times what the warden made in a year. Now the warden was an inmate at the prison.

"I know what you're saying," Corvo said. "But don't worry about it. We got a plan for that. Only things you have to worry about are your own ass and your partner's. You better watch him good. And you better get some coffee. It's going to be a long night."

Bosch rejoined Aguila, who was standing at the workbench where the coffee had been set up. They nodded at some of the agents who were milling about the bench but the gestures were rarely returned. They were the invited uninvited. From where they stood, they could see into a suite of offices off the aircraft bays. There were several Mexicans in green uniforms sitting at desks and tables, drinking coffee and waiting.

"Militia," Aguila said. "From Mexico City. Is there no one in Mexicali that the DEA trusts?"

"Well, after tonight, they'll trust you."

Bosch lit a cigarette to go with the coffee and took an expansive look around the hangar.

"What do you think?" he said to Aguila.

"I think the pope of Mexicali is going to have a wake-up call tonight."

"Looks that way."

They moved away from the coffee bench to let others have at it and leaned against a nearby counter to watch the raid equipment being prepared. Bosch looked over toward the back of the hangar and saw Ramos standing with a group of men wearing bulky black jumpsuits. Harry walked over and saw that the men were wearing Nomex fire-retardant suits beneath the jumpsuits. Some of them were smearing bootblack around their eyes and then pulling on black ski masks. The CLET squad. They couldn't wait to get in the air, to get going. Bosch could almost smell their adrenaline.

There were twelve of them. They were reaching into black trunks and laying out the equipment they would need for the night's mission. Bosch saw Kevlar helmets and vests, sound-disorientation grenades. Holstered already on one man's hip was a 9mm P-226 with an extended magazine. That would just be for backup, he guessed. He could see the barrel of a long gun protruding from one of the trunks. Ramos noticed him then and reached into the trunk and brought the weapon over. There was a strange leer spreading on his face.

"Check this shit out," Ramos said. "Colt only makes 'em for the DEA, man. The RO636. It's a suppressed version of the standard nine submachine. Uses one-forty-seven-grain subsonic hollow points. You know what one of them will do? It'll go through three bodies before it even thinks about slowing down.

"It's got a suppressed silencer. Means no muzzle flash. These guys are always jumping labs. You get ether fumes and the muzzle flash could set it off. Boom — you land about two blocks away. But not with these. No muzzle flash. It's beautiful. I wish I was going in with one of these tonight."

Ramos was holding and ogling the weapon like a mother with her first baby.

"You were in Vietnam, weren't you, Bosch?" Ramos asked.

Bosch just nodded.

"I could tell. Something about you. I always can tell." Ramos handed the gun back to its owner. There was still an odd smile on his face. "I was too young for Nam and too old for Iraq. Ain't that a pisser?"

The raid briefing did not start until nearly ten-thirty. Ramos and Corvo gathered all the agents, the militia officers and Bosch and Aguila in front of a large bulletin board on which a blowup of an aerial photo of Zorrillo's ranch had been tacked. Bosch could see that the ranch contained vast areas of open, unused land. The pope had found security in space. To the west of his property were the Cucapah Mountains, a natural boundary, while in the other directions he had created a buffer zone of thousands of acres of scrubland.

Ramos and Corvo stood on either side of the bulletin board and Ramos conducted the meeting. By using a yardstick as a pointer he delineated the boundaries of the ranch and identified what he called the population center — a large, walled compound that included a hacienda, ranch house and adjoining bunker-type building. He then circled the breeding corrals and barn located about a mile from the population center along the perimeter of the ranch that fronted Val Verde Highway. He also pointed out the Enviro-Breed compound across the highway.

Next, Ramos tacked up another blowup, this one detailing about a quarter of the ranch — ranging from the population center to the breeding center/EnviroBreed compound area. This shot was close enough that tiny figures could be seen on the roofs of the bunker building. In the scrubland behind the buildings there were black figures against the light brown and green earth. The bulls. Bosch wondered which one of them was El Temblar. He could hear one of the militia officers translating the meeting for a group of the guardsmen gathered around him.

"Okay, these photos are about thirty hours old," Ramos said. "We had NASA do a fly-over in a U-thirty-four. We also had them shoot heat resonance strips and that's where this gets good. The reds you see are the hot spots."

He tacked a new blowup next to the other. This was a computer-generated graphic that had red squares — the buildings — against a sea of blues and greens. There were small dots of red outside the square and Bosch assumed these were the bulls.

"These photos were taken at the same second yesterday," Ramos said. "By jumping back and forth between the graphic and the live shot we can pinpoint certain anomalies. These squares become the buildings and most of these smaller red blotches become the bulls."

He used the yardstick to refer back and forth between the two blowups. Bosch realized that there were more red spots on the graphic than there were bulls on the photo.

"Now these marks do not correspond with animals on the photo," Ramos said. "What they do correspond with is the feed boxes."

With Corvo's help they pinned up two more enlargements. These were the closest shots so far. Bosch could clearly make out the tin roof of a small shed. There was a black steer standing near it. In the corresponding graphic, both the steer and the shed were bright red.

"These basically are little shelters to keep rain off the hay and feed for the livestock. NASA says these shelters would emit some residual heat that the resonance photos would pick up. But NASA said it clearly would not be what we are seeing here. So, what we think this means is that these feed boxes are decoys. We think they are exhaust vents for an underground complex. We believe there is some kind of entrance somewhere in the population center structures that leads to the underground lab back here."

He let it sink in for a few moments. Nobody asked any questions.

"Also," he said, "there is a — we have information from a confidential informant that there is a tunnel system. We believe it runs from the breeding center here to this complex — a business called EnviroBreed — here. We believe it has allowed Zorrillo to circumvent surveillance and is one of the possible means of moving product from the ranch to the border."

Ramos went on to detail the raid. The plan was to strike at midnight. The Mexican militia would have a two-part responsibility. A single unmarked car would be sent to the ranch gate, swerving as if driven by a drunk on the gravel road. Using this ruse, the three guardsmen in the car would take custody of the two gate sentries. After that, half of the remaining militia would move down the ranch road to the population center while the other half would advance to the EnviroBreed compound, surround it and await developments on the ranch.

"The success of the operation largely relies on the two men on the gate being taken before issuing a warning to the PC," Corvo said. His first words during the briefing. "If we fail that, we lose the element of surprise."

After the ground attack was underway, the three air squads would come. The two transport craft would put down on the north and east sides of the PC to drop the CLET team. The CLETs would perform initial entry to all structures. The third helicopter, the Lynx, would remain airborne and act as a flying command post.

Lastly, Ramos said, the ranch had two rovers, two-man Jeep patrols. Ramos said they followed no set patrol or pattern and they would be impossible to pinpoint until the raid began.

"They are the wild cards," Ramos said. "That is what we have a mobile air command for. They warn us when the Jeeps are spotted coming in or the Lynx will just take them out."

Ramos was pacing back and forth in front of the bulletin board, swinging the yardstick. Bosch could tell he liked this, the feeling of being in charge of something. Maybe it made up for Vietnam or Iraq.

"Okay, gentlemen, I've got a few more things here," Ramos said as he pinned another photo up. "Our target is the ranch. We have search warrants for drugs. If we find manufacturing apparatus we are gold. If we find narcotics we are gold. But the thing we really want is this man here."

The photo was a blowup from the mug book Bosch had looked at that morning.

"This is our main man," Ramos said. "Humberto Zorrillo. The pope of Mexicali. If we don't get him, this whole operation goes down the tubes. He's the mastermind. He's the one we want.

"It might interest you to know that in addition to his activities related to narcotics, he is a suspect in the killing of two L.A. cops, not to mention a couple other killings up there in the last month or so. This is a man who doesn't think twice about it. If he doesn't do it himself, he has plenty of people working for him who will. He's dangerous. Anybody we encounter on the ranch has to be considered armed and dangerous. Questions?"

One of the militia asked a question in Spanish.

"Good question," Ramos replied. "We are not going into EnviroBreed initially because of two reasons. One, our prime target is the ranch and we would have to initially deploy more resources to EnviroBreed if we were to make simultaneous entry to the compound and the ranch. Secondly, our CI indicates the tunnel on that side may be rigged. Booby-trapped. We don't want to chance it. When we get the ranch secured, we'll go in then or we'll follow the tunnel over."

He waited for more questions. There were none. The men in front of him were shifting their weight from foot to foot or chewing their nails or flicking their thumbs on their knees. The adrenaline rush was just beginning to kick. Bosch had seen it before, in Vietnam and since. So he approached his own rising excitement with an uneasy sense of dread.

"All right then!" Ramos yelled. "I want everybody locked and loaded in one hour. At midnight we jam!"

The gathering broke up with some adolescent howls from the younger agents. Bosch moved toward Ramos as he was taking the photos off the board.

"Sounds like a plan, man."

"Yeah. Just hope it goes down close to the way we said it. They never go down exactly right."

"Right. Corvo told me you've got another plan. The one to get Zorrillo across the border."

"Yeah, we've got something cooked up."

"You gonna tell me?"

He turned around from the board, all the photos in a nice stack in his hands.

"Yeah, I'll tell you. You'll like this, Bosch, since it will get him up to L.A. to face trial on your guys. What's going to happen is that after the little fuck is captured he will resist arrest and injure himself. Probably facial injuries and they are going to look worse than they really are. But we will want to get him immediate medical attention. The DEA will offer the use of one of the helicopters. The commander of the militia unit will gratefully accept. But, you see, the pilot will become confused and mistake the lights of Imperial County Memorial Hospital on the other side of the border with the Mexicali General Clinic, which is just on this side of the border. When the chopper lands at the wrong hospital and Zorrillo gets off on the wrong side of the border, he will be subject to arrest and the American justice system. Tough break for him. We might have to put a notice of reprimand in the pilot's personnel file."

Ramos had that leering smile on his face again. He winked at Bosch and then walked away.

29

The Lynx was crossing over the carpet of Mexicali's lights, heading southwest toward the dark shape of the Cucapah Mountains. The ride was smoother and quieter than anything he remembered from Vietnam or his dreams after.

Bosch was in the rear compartment huddled next to the left window. The cold night air was somehow getting in through a vent somewhere. Aguila was on the seat next to him. And in the forward compartment were Corvo and the pilot. Corvo was Air Leader, handling communications and directions on the ranch assault. Ramos was Ground One, in charge on the surface. Looking into the forward compartment, Bosch could see the dim reflection of the cockpit's green dials on the visor of Corvo's helmet.

The helmets of all four of the men in the chopper were connected through electronic umbilical cords to a center console port. The helmets had air-to-ground and on-board radio two-way and night-vision capabilities.

After they had flown for fifteen minutes the lights through the windows became fewer. Without the glare of the brightness from below, Harry could make out the silhouette of one of the other helicopters about two hundred yards to the left side. The other black ship would be on the right side. They were flying in formation.

"ETA two minutes," a voice said in his ear. The pilot.

Bosch took the Kevlar vest he held in his lap and slipped it underneath him, onto the seat. A protection against ground fire. He saw Aguila do the same thing with the DEA loaner.

The Lynx began a sharp descent and the voice in his ears said, "Here we go." Bosch snapped the night vision apparatus down and looked into the lenses. The earth moved quickly below, a yellow river of scrub brush and little else. They passed over a road and then a turnoff. The helicopter banked in the direction of the turn. He saw a car, a pickup truck and a Jeep stopped on the road and then several other vehicles moving on the dirt road, yellow clouds of dust billowing behind them. The militia was in and speeding toward the population center. The battle had been engaged.

"Looks like our friends have already taken care of one of the patrol Jeeps," Corvo's voice said in Bosch's earpiece.

"That's a ten-four," came a returning voice, apparently from one of the other choppers.

The Lynx overtook the militia vehicles. Bosch was staring at open road in the night-vision scope. The craft's descent continued and then leveled off at what Bosch estimated was an elevation of about three hundred yards. In the yellow vision field he could now see the hacienda and the front of the bunker. He saw the other two helicopters, looking like black dragonflies, set down on their assigned sides of the house. Then he felt the Lynx pull up slightly as if hovering on an air pocket.

"One down!" a voice shouted in the headset.

"Two down!" came another.

Men in black began spilling from the side doors of the landed craft. One group of six went immediately to the front of the hacienda. The six-man group from the other helicopter moved toward the bunker building. Militia cars now began pulling into the field of view. Bosch saw more figures leap from the helicopters. That would be Ramos and the backup.

It all appeared surrealistic in the scope to Bosch. The yellow tint. The tiny figures. It seemed like a badly filmed and edited movie.

"Switching to ground com," Corvo said.

Bosch heard the click as the frequencies were switched. Almost immediately he began to pick up radio chatter and the heavy breathing of men running. Then there was a loud banging sound, but Bosch could tell it was not weapon fire. It was the ram used to open the door. Over the air there were now panicked shouts of *"Policia!* DEA!" Corvo's voice cut through a momentary lull in the shouting.

"Ground One, talk to me. What have we got? Let's talk to the mothership."

There was some static and then Ramos's voice came back.

"We have entry at Point A. We have — I'm going —"

Ramos was cut off. Point A was the hacienda. The plan had been to hit the hacienda and the bunker, Point B, at once.

"Ground Two, do we have entry yet at Point B?" Corvo asked.

No answer. It was a few long moments of silence and then Ramos came back up on the air.

"Air Leader, can't tell on Ground Two at this time. Target team has approached entry point and we —"

Before the transmission was cut off, Bosch heard the unmistakable sound of automatic gunfire. He felt adrenaline begin to flood his body. Yet he could do nothing but sit and listen to the dead radio air and watch the murky yellow night vision display. He saw what he believed were muzzle flashes from the front of the bunker. Then Ramos came back up on the air.

"We're hot! We're hot!"

The helicopter lurched as the pilot took them up higher. As the craft rose, the night scope offered a larger view of the scene below. The entire PC became visible. Now Bosch could see figures on the roof of the bunker, moving toward the front of the structure. He pushed the switch on the side of his helmet and said into the mouthpiece, "Corvo, they've got people on the roof. Warn them."

"Stay off!" Corvo shouted. Then to below, he radioed, "Ground Two, Ground Two, you have weapons on the roof of the bunker. Count two positions approaching northside, copy?"

Bosch could hear no shooting over the sound of the rotor but he could see the muzzle flash from automatic weapons from two locations at the front of the bunker. He saw sporadic flashes from the vehicles but the militia was pinned down. He heard a radio transmission open and heard the sound of fire but then it was closed and no one had spoken.

"Ground Two, copy?" Corvo said into the voice. There was just the initial strain of panic in his voice. There was no reply. "Ground Two, do you copy?"

A hard-breathing voice came back. "Ground Two. Yeah. We're pinned down in the Point B entry. We're in a crossfire here. Would like some help."

"Ground One, report," Corvo barked.

There was a long moment of silence. Then Ramos came on the air. His words were partially obscured by gunfire.

"Here. We've . . . the house, . . . have three suspects down. No others present. Looks like they're . . . fucking bunker."

"Get to the bunker. Two needs backup."

"— that way."

Bosch noticed how the voices on the radio were higher and more urgent. The code words and formal language had been stripped away. Fear did that. He had seen it in the war. He'd seen it on the streets when he was in uniform. Fear, though always unspoken, nevertheless stripped men of their carefully orchestrated poses. The adrenaline roars and the throat gurgles with fear like a backed-up drain. Sheer desire for survival takes over. It sharpens the mind, pares away all the bullshit. A once-modulated reference to Point B becomes the almost hysterical expletive.

From four hundred yards up and looking down through the night scope, Bosch could also see the flaw in the plan. The DEA agents had hoped to outrun the militia in their helicopters, charge the population center and secure things before the ground troops arrived. But that hadn't happened. The militia was there and now one of the CLET groups was pinned down between the militia and the people in the bunker.

There was a sudden increase in the shooting from the bunker. Bosch could tell this by the flaring of repeated muzzle flashes. Then on the scope he saw a Jeep suddenly begin speeding from the back of the bunker. It smashed through a gate in the wall that surrounded the compound and began moving across the scrubland in a southeasterly direction. Bosch pushed his transmit button again.

"Corvo, we have a runner. Jeep heading southeast."

"Have to let him go for now. It's going to shit down there and I can't move anybody. Stay off the fucking line."

The Jeep was now well out of the scope's field of vision. He flipped the lenses up off his face and looked out the window. There was nothing. Only darkness. The Jeep was running without lights. He thought of the barn and stables out near the highway. That was where the runner was going.

"Ramos," Corvo said over the radio. "Do you want lights?"

No return.

"Ground One? . . . Ground Two, do you want lights?"

". . . ights would be good but you'd be a sit . . . ," the Ground Two voice said. "Better hold it a few until we . . . eaned up."

"That's a copy. Ramos are you copying?"

There was no answer.

The shooting ended quickly after that. The pope's guardians put down their weapons after apparently determining that their odds of survival in a prolonged firefight were not good.

"Air Leader, give us that light now," Ramos radioed from below, the tone of his voice back to being calmly modulated and confident.

Three powerful beams from the belly of the Lynx then illuminated the ground below. Men with hands laced together on the tops of their heads were walking out of the bunker and into the hands of the militia. There were at least a dozen. Bosch saw one of the CLETs drag a body out of the bunker and leave it on the ground outside.

"We're secure down here," Ramos radioed.

Corvo signaled with his thumb to the pilot and the craft began to descend. Bosch felt tension drift out of him as they went down. In thirty seconds they were on the ground next to one of the other helicopters.

In the yard in front of the bunker, the prisoners were kneeling while some of the militia officers used plastic disposable handcuffs to bind their wrists. Others were making a stack of confiscated weapons. There were a couple of Uzis and AK-47s but mostly shotguns and M-16s. Ramos was standing with the militia captain, who had his radio to his ear.

Bosch did not see a recognizable face among the prisoners. He left Aguila and went to Ramos.

"Where's Zorrillo?"

Ramos held up his hand in a do-not-disturb gesture and didn't answer. He was looking at the captain. Corvo walked up then, too. There was a report over the captain's radio and then he looked at Ramos and said, "*Nada.*"

"Okay, nothing's happening at EnviroBreed," Ramos said. "Nobody in or out since this went down here. The militia is maintaining a watch over there."

Ramos saw Corvo and in a lower voice, meant just for him, said, "We've got a problem. We've lost one."

"Yeah, we saw him," Bosch said. "He was in the Jeep and headed southeast out of —"

He stopped when he realized what Ramos had meant.

"Who'd we lose?" Corvo asked.

"Kirth, one of the CLETs. But that's not the whole problem."

Bosch stepped back from the two men. He knew he had no place in this.

"What the fuck do you mean?" Corvo said.

"Come on, I'll show you."

The two agents headed off around the hacienda. Bosch trailed at a discreet distance behind. A covered porch ran the length of the rear of the house. Ramos crossed it to an open door. A CLET agent, his mask pulled up to expose his blood- and sweat-streaked face, was on the floor three feet inside the door. It looked to Bosch like four rounds: two in the upper chest, just above the vest, and two in the neck. A nice tight pattern, all of them through-and-through wounds. Blood was still leaking out from beneath the body into a pool. The dead agent's eyes and mouth were open. He had died quickly.

Bosch could see the problem. It was friendly fire. Kirth had been hit with fire from one of the 636s. The wounds were too big, too devastating and bunched too close together to have come from the weapons stacked near the prisoners.

"Looks like he came running out this back door when he heard the shooting," Ramos was saying. "Ground Two was already in a crossfire. Someone from Two's unit must have opened on the door, hit Kirth here."

"God damn it!" Corvo yelled. Then in a lower voice, he said, "All right, come over here, Ramos."

They huddled together and this time Bosch could not hear what was said but didn't have to. He knew what they would do. Careers were at stake here.

"Got it," Ramos said, returning to a normal voice and breaking away from Corvo.

"Good," Corvo said. "When you are done with that, I want you to get to a secure line and call L.A. Operations. We are going to need Public Info Officers down here and up there to work on this ASAP. The media is going to be crawling all over this. From all over."

"You got it."

Corvo started to go into the house but came back.

"Another thing, keep the Mexicans away from this."

He meant the militia. Ramos nodded and then Corvo stalked off. Ramos looked over at Bosch standing in the shadows of the porch. A silent acknowledgement passed between them. Bosch knew that the media would be told that Kirth had been fatally wounded by Zorrillo's men. Nobody would say anything about friendly fire.

"You got a problem?" Ramos said.

"I don't have a problem with anything."

"Good. Then I'm not going to have to worry about you. Right, Bosch?"

Bosch stepped to the door.

"Ramos, where's Zorrillo?"

"We're still searching. Still a lot of space in these buildings to cover. All I can tell you is we've cleared the hacienda and he isn't here. Only three inside are dead and he ain't one of them. So no one's talking. But your cop killer's in there, Bosch. The man with the tears."

Bosch silently stepped around Ramos and the body and into the hacienda. He was careful not to step into the blood. As he passed, he looked down into the dead man's eyes. They were already filming and looked like chips of dirty ice.

He followed a hallway to the front of the house, where he heard voices from a doorway at the bottom of the stairs in the front entry. As he approached he could see the room beyond was an office. There was a large polished wood desk, its center drawer open. Behind the desk was a wall of bookshelves.

Inside the room were Corvo and one of the CLET agents. And two bodies. One was on the floor next to an overturned couch. The other was in a chair near the room's only window, off to the right of the desk.

"C'mon in here, Bosch," Corvo said. "We can probably use your expertise here."

The body in the chair held Bosch's attention. The man's expensive black leather jacket was open, revealing a gun still holstered on the belt. It was Grena, though this was not easy at first to tell because a bullet fired into the police captain's right temple had obliterated much of the face when it exited beneath the left eye. Blood had flowed down both shoulders and ruined the jacket.

Bosch pulled his eyes away and looked at the man on the floor. One leg was over the back of the couch, which had been knocked backwards. He had at least five holes in his chest that Bosch could make out in the blood. The three teardrops tattooed on the cheek were also unmistakable. Arpis. The man he had seen at Poe's. There was a chrome-plated forty-five on the floor next to his right leg.

"That your man?" Corvo asked.

"One of 'em, yeah."

"Good. Don't have to worry about him, then."

"The other one is SJP. He's a captain named Grena."

"Yeah, I just pulled the ID out of his pocket. He also had six grand in his wallet. Not bad, since SJP captains make about three hundred bucks a week. Take a look over here."

He moved to the other side of the desk. Bosch followed and saw that the rug had been folded back, exposing a floor safe about the size of a hotel refrigerator. Its thick steel door was propped open and the interior was empty.

"This is how it was found when the CLETs came in. What do you think? These stiffs don't look too old. I think we got here just a little late for the show, huh?"

Bosch studied the scene for a few moments.

"Hard to say. Looks like the end of a business deal. Maybe Grena got greedy. Asked for more than he deserved. Maybe he was making some kind of play with Zorrillo, some kind of scam, and it went to shit. I saw him a few hours ago at the bullfight."

"Yeah, what did he say? That he was heading over to the pope's for a shot?"

Corvo didn't laugh and neither did Bosch.

"No, he just told me to get out of town."

"So, who shot him?"

"Looks like a forty-five to me. Just guessing. That would make Arpis over here a likely candidate."

"Then who shot Arpis?"

"Got me. But if I was guessing, it looks like Zorrillo or whoever was behind the desk pulls a gun out of the drawer there and starts popping him right here in front of the desk. He goes backwards and over the couch."

"Why would he shoot him?"

"I don't know. Maybe Zorrillo didn't like what he did to Grena. Maybe Zorrillo was starting to get scared of him. Maybe Arpis made the same play Grena did. Could've been a lot of things. We'll never know. I thought Ramos said it was three bodies."

"Across the hall."

Bosch crossed the hall into a long and wide living room. It had deep-pile, white shag carpet and a white piano. There was a painting of Elvis on the wall above a white leather couch. The rug was stained with blood from the third man, who was lying in front of the couch. It was Dance. Bosch recognized him from the mug shot even with the bullet wound in his forehead and the blond hair now dyed black. The practiced sulk had been replaced on his face with a look of wonder. His eyes were open and almost seemed to be looking up at the hole in his forehead.

Corvo walked in behind him.

"What do you think?"

"I think it looks like the pope had to get out of here in a hurry. And he didn't want to leave these three behind to talk about it. . . . Shit, I don't know, Corvo."

Corvo raised the hand-held radio to his mouth.

"Search teams," he said. "Status."

"Search Leader here. We've got the underground lab. Entrance is through the bunker structure. It's major. We have product sitting in the drying pans. Multiweight. We're home. We're gold."

"What about the priority suspect?"

"Negative at this time. No suspects in the lab."

"Shit," Corvo said after signing off. He rubbed the edge of the Motorola against the scar on his cheek as he thought about what to do next.

"The Jeep," Bosch said. "We have to go after it."

"If he's heading to EnviroBreed, the militia is there waiting. At the moment, I can't cut people loose to go running around the ranch. It's six thousand fucking acres."

"I'll go."

"Wait a minute, Bosch. This is not your action."

"Fuck it, Corvo. I'm going."

30

Bosch came out of the house looking in the dim light for Aguila and finally saw him standing near the prisoners and the militia. Bosch realized he probably felt more like an outsider here than Harry did himself.

"I am going after the Jeep we saw. I think it was Zorrillo."

"I am ready," the Mexican said.

Before they could move Corvo came running up. But it was not to stop them.

"Bosch, I've got Ramos in the chopper. It's all I can spare."

The silence that followed was punctuated by the sound from the other side of the hacienda of the helicopter's rotor beginning to turn.

"Go!" Corvo yelled. "Or he'll go without you."

They ran around the building and climbed back into their spots in the Lynx. Ramos was in the cockpit with the pilot. The craft abruptly lifted off and Bosch forgot about the seatbelt. He was too busy putting on his helmet and night-vision equipment.

There was nothing in the scope yet. No Jeep. No runner. They were heading southwest from the ranch's population center. As he watched the yellow land go by in the night-vision lenses, Harry realized he still hadn't informed Aguila of his captain's demise. When we are done here, he decided.

In two minutes they came upon the Jeep. It was parked in a copse of euca-lyptus trees and tall brush. A tumbleweed as big as a truck had blown up against it or been put up against it as a meager disguise. The vehicle was about fifty yards from the corrals and barn. The pilot put on the spots and the Lynx began circling. There was no sign of the driver, the runner. Zorrillo. Looking between the front seats, Bosch saw Ramos give the pilot the thumbs down sign and the craft began its descent. The lights were cut off and until Harry's eyes adjusted, it felt like they were dropping through the depths of a black hole.

He finally felt the impact of the ground and his muscles relaxed slightly. He heard the engine cut and there was just the chirping and whupping sound of the free-turning rotor winding down. Through the window Bosch could see the western side of the barn. There were no doors or windows on this exposure and he was thinking that they could approach with reasonable cover when he heard Ramos yell.

"What the — hold on!"

There was a hard impact and the helicopter lurched violently and began sliding. Bosch looked out his window and could only see that they were being pushed sideways. The Jeep. Someone had been hidden in the Jeep. The Lynx's landing rails finally caught on something in the earth and the craft tipped over. Bosch covered his face and ducked when he saw the still spinning rotor start biting into the ground and splintering. Then he felt Aguila's weight crash down on him and heard yelling in the cockpit that he could not decipher.

The helicopter rocked in this position for only a few seconds before there was another loud impact, this time from the front. Bosch heard tearing metal and shattering glass and gunfire.

Then it was gone. Bosch could feel the vibration in the ground dissipating as the Jeep sped away.

"I think I got him!" Ramos yelled. "Did you see that?"

All Bosch could think of was their vulnerability. The next hit would prob-ably be from behind where they could not see to shoot. He tried to reach his Smith but his arms were trapped under Aguila. The Mexican detective finally began to crawl off him and they both tentatively moved into crouches in the now sideways compartment. Bosch reached up and tried the door, which was now above them. It slid about halfway open before catching on some-thing, a torn piece of metal. They took off their helmets and Bosch went out first. Then Aguila handed him the bullet-proof vests. Bosch didn't know why but took them. Aguila followed him out.

The smell of fuel was in the air. They moved to the crushed front of the helicopter where Ramos, gun in one hand, was trying to slide through the hole where the front window used to be.

"Help him," Bosch said. "I'll cover."

He pulled his gun and turned in a full circle but saw no one. Then he saw the Jeep, parked where he had seen it from the air, the tumbleweed still pressed against it. This made no sense to Bosch. Unless —

"The pilot is trapped," Aguila said.

Harry looked into the cockpit. Ramos was shining a flashlight on the pilot, whose blond mustache was inked with blood. There was a deep slash on the bridge of his nose. His eyes were wide and Bosch could see the flight control apparatus was crushed in on his legs.

"Where's the radio?" Bosch said. "We've got to get help out here."

Ramos stuck his upper body back through the cockpit window and came back out with the hand-held radio.

"Corvo, Corvo, come up, we've got an emergency here." While waiting for a response, Ramos said to Bosch, "Do you believe this shit? That fucking monster comes outta nowhere. I didn't know what the —"

"What's happening?" Corvo's voice came back on the radio.

"We've got a situation here. We need a medevac out here. Tools. The Lynx is wrecked. Corcoran is pinned inside. Has injuries."

"— cation of the crash?"

"It's not a crash, man. A goddamn bull attacked it on the ground. It's wrecked and we can't get Corcoran out. Our location is one hundred yards northeast of the breeding center, the barn."

"Stay there. Help's on the way."

Ramos clipped the radio to his belt, held the flashlight under his arm and reloaded his handgun.

"Let's each take a side of a triangle, the chopper in the middle and watch for this thing. I know I hit it but it didn't show a thing."

"No," Bosch said. "Ramos, you and Aguila take sides of it and wait for help. I'm going to clear the barn. Zorrillo's getting —"

"No, no, no, we don't do it like that, Bosch. You aren't calling any of the shots here. We wait here and when help —"

He stopped in midsentence and made a full turn. Then Bosch realized he heard it, too. Or, rather, felt it. A rhythmic vibration in the ground, growing stronger. It was impossible to place the direction. He watched Ramos turn in circles with the flashlight. He heard Aguila say, "El Temblar."

"What?" Ramos yelled. "What?"

And then the bull appeared at the edge of vision. A huge black beast, it came at them undeterred by their number. This was his turf to defend. The bull seemed to Bosch in that moment to have come from within the darkness, an apparition of death, its head down and jagged horns up. It was less than thirty feet away when it locked on a specific target. Bosch.

In one hand he held the Smith. In the other the vest, with the word POLICE on it in reflective yellow tape. In the seconds he had left he realized the tape had caught the beast's attention and singled him out. He also came to the conclusion that his gun was useless. He could not fell the animal with bullets. It was too big and powerful. It would take a perfect shot on a moving target. Wounding it, as Ramos had, would not stop it.

He dropped the gun and held the vest up.

Bosch heard yelling and shooting from his right side. It was Ramos. But the bull stayed on him. As it came closer he swept the vest to his right, its yellow letters catching the light of the moon. He let it go as the animal closed in. The bull, like a blur of black in darkness, hit the vest before it left his hand. Bosch tried to jump out of the way but one of the massive shoulders of the animal brushed him and sent him tumbling.

From the ground he looked up to see the animal cut to its left like a gifted athlete and close in on Ramos. The agent was still firing and Bosch could see the reflection of the moon off the shells as they were ejected from his gun. But the bullets did not stop the beast's charge. They did not even slow it. Bosch heard the gun's ejector go dry and Ramos was pulling the trigger on an empty chamber. His last cry was unintelligible. The bull hit him low in the legs and then raised its brutish and bloodied neck up, ejecting him into the air. Ramos seemed to tumble in slow motion before coming down head-first and unmoving.

The bull tried to stop its charge but momentum and damage from bullets finally left it unable to control its huge weight. Its head dipped and it cartwheeled onto its back. It righted itself and prepared for another charge. Bosch crawled to his gun, picked it up and aimed. But the animal's front legs faltered and it went down. Then it slowly turned onto its side and lay unmoving, save for the hesitant rise and fall of its chest. Then that stopped, too.

Aguila and Bosch took off for Ramos at the same time. They huddled over him but did not move him. He was on his back and his eyes were still open and caked with dirt. His head lolled at an unnatural angle. His neck appeared to have been cleanly broken in the fall. In the distance they could hear the sound of one of the Hueys flying their way. Bosch stood up and could see its spotlight sweeping over the scrubland, looking for them.

"I'm going to the tunnel," Bosch said. "When they land, come in with backup."

"No," Aguila said. "I'm going with you."

He said it in a way that invited no debate. He leaned down and took the radio off Ramos's belt and picked up the flashlight. He gave the radio to Bosch.

"Tell them we are both going."

Bosch radioed Corvo.

"Where's Ramos?"

"We just lost Ramos. Me and Aguila are going to the tunnel. Alert the militia at EnviroBreed that we are coming through. We don't want to get shot."

He turned the radio off before Corvo could reply and dropped it on the ground next to the dead DEA agent. The other helicopter was almost on them now. They ran to the barn, their weapons held up and ready, and moved slowly around the outside until they were at the front and could see the bay door had been slid open. Wide enough for a man to pass through.

They went through and crouched in the darkness. Aguila began to sweep the flashlight's beam around. It was a cavernous barn with stalls running along both sides to the back. There were crates used for trucking bulls to arenas stacked in the back along with towers made of bales of hay. Bosch saw a line of overhead lights running down the center of the building. He looked around and found the switch near the bay door.

Once the interior was lighted they moved down the aisle between the rows of stalls, Bosch taking the right and Aguila the left. The stalls were all empty, the bulls set free to roam the ranch. It was when they reached the back that they saw the opening to the tunnel.

A forklift was parked in the corner, holding a pallet of hay bales four feet off the ground. There was a four-foot-wide hole in the concrete floor where the pallet had sat. Zorrillo, or whoever the runner had been, had used the forklift to lift the pallet but there had been no one to drop it back down to hide his escape.

Bosch crouched down and moved to the edge of the hole and looked down. He saw a ladder leading about twelve feet down to a lighted passageway. He looked up at Aguila.

"Ready?"

The Mexican nodded.

Bosch went first. He climbed a few steps down the ladder and then dropped the rest of the way, bringing up his gun and ready to shoot. But there was no one in the tunnel as far as he could see. It wasn't even like a tunnel. It was more of a hallway. It was tall enough to stand in and an electrical conduit ran along the ceiling feeding lights in steel cages every twenty feet. There was a slight curve to the left and so he could not see where it ended. He moved into the passageway and Aguila dropped down behind him.

"Okay," Bosch whispered. "Let's stay to the right. If there is shooting, I'll go low and you go high."

Aguila nodded and they began to move quickly through the tunnel. Bosch, trying to figure his bearings, believed they were heading east and slightly north. They covered the ground to the curve quickly and then pressed themselves hard against the wall as they moved into the second leg of the passage.

Bosch realized that the bend in the passage was too wide for them to still be on line with EnviroBreed. He stared down the last segment of the tunnel and saw that it was clear. He could see the exit ladder maybe fifty yards ahead. And he knew they were going somewhere other than EnviroBreed. He wished he hadn't left the radio with Ramos's body.

"Shit," Harry whispered.

"What?" Aguila whispered back.

"Nothing. C'mon."

They began to move again, covering the first twenty-five yards quickly and then slowing to a cautious and quieter approach to the exit ladder. Aguila switched to the right wall and they came upon the opening at the same time, both with guns extended upward, sweat getting in their eyes.

There was no light from the opening above them. Bosch took the flashlight from Aguila and put its beam through the hole. He could see exposed wooden rafters of a low ceiling in the room above. No one looked down at them. No one shot at them. No one did a thing. Harry listened for any sound but heard nothing. He nodded to Aguila to cover and holstered his gun. He started climbing the ladder, one hand holding the flashlight.

He was scared. In Vietnam, leaving one of Charlie's tunnels always meant the end of fear. It was like being born again; you were leaving the darkness for safety and the hands of comrades. Out of the black and into the blue. But not this time; this time was the opposite.

When he reached the top, before rising through the opening, he flashed the beam around again but saw nothing. Then, like a turtle, he slowly moved his head out of the opening. The first thing he noticed in the beam was the sawdust everywhere on the floor. He climbed farther out, taking in the rest of the surroundings. It was some kind of storage room. There were steel shelves stocked with saw blades, boxes of sanding belts for industrial machinery. There were some hand tools and carpentry saws. One group of shelves were stacked with wooden dowel pegs, with different sizes on different shelves. Bosch immediately thought of the pegs attached to the baling wire that had been used to kill Kapps and Porter.

He moved fully into the room now and signaled to Aguila that it was safe to come up. Then Harry approached the storage room's door.

It was unlocked and it opened into a huge warehouse with lines of machinery and work benches on one side and the completed product — unfinished furniture, tables, chairs, chests of drawers — stacked on the other. Light came from a single bulb that hung from a cross support beam. It was the night-light. Aguila came up behind him then. They were in Mexitec, Bosch knew.

At the far end of the warehouse were sets of double doors. One of these was open and they moved to it quickly. It led to a loading-dock area that was off the back alley Bosch had walked through the night before. There was a puddle at the bottom of the parking bay and he saw wet tire tracks leading into the alley. There was no one in sight. Zorrillo was long gone.

"Two tunnels," Bosch said, unable to hide the dejection in his voice.

"Two tunnels," Corvo said. "Ramos's informant fucked us."

Bosch and Aguila were sitting on chairs of unfinished pine watching Corvo pacing and looking like shit, like a man in charge of an operation that had lost two men, a helicopter and its main target. It had been nearly two hours since they had come up through the tunnel.

"How d'you mean?" Bosch asked.

"I mean the CI had to have known about the second tunnel. How's he know about one and not the other? He set us up. He left Zorrillo the escape route. If I knew who he was I'd charge him with accessory in the death of a federal agent."

"You don't know?"

"Ramos didn't register this one with me. Hadn't gotten around to it."

Bosch breathed a little easier.

"I can't fucking believe this," Corvo was saying. "I might as well never go back. I'm done, man. Done. . . . Least you got your cop killer, Bosch. I got a shit sandwich."

"Have you put out a Telex?" Bosch said to change the subject.

"Already out. To all stations, all law enforcement agencies. But it doesn't matter. He's long gone. He'll probably go to the interior, lie low for a year and then start over. Right where he left off. Probably Michoacan, maybe farther down."

"Maybe he went north," Bosch said.

"No way he'd try to cross. He knows if we get him up there, he'll never see daylight again. He went south, where's he's safe."

There were several other agents in the factory with clipboards, cataloging and searching. They had found a machine that hollowed out table legs so that they could be filled with contraband, recapped and sent across the border. Earlier they had found the second tunnel opening in the barn and followed it through to EnviroBreed. There had been no explosives on the trapdoor and they had gone in. The place was empty except for the two dogs outside. They killed them.

The operation had closed down a major smuggling network. Agents had left for Calexico to arrest the head of EnviroBreed, Ely. There were fourteen arrests made on the ranch. Others would follow. But all of that wasn't enough for Corvo or anybody. Not when agents were dead and Zorrillo was in the wind. Corvo had been wrong if he thought Bosch would be satisfied that Arpis was dead. Bosch wanted Zorrillo, too. He was the man who had called the hits.

Bosch got up so he wouldn't have to witness the agent's anguish anymore. He had enough of his own. Aguila must have felt the same. He, too, stood and began to walk listlessly around the machines and the furniture. Basically, they were waiting for one of the militia cars to take them back to the airport to Bosch's car. The DEA would be here until well after sunup. But Bosch and Aguila were finished.

Harry watched Aguila go back into the storage room and approach the tunnel entrance. He had told him about Grena and the Mexican had simply nodded. He hadn't shown a thing. Now Aguila dropped to his haunches and seemed to be studying the floor, as if the sawdust were a spread of tea leaves in which he could read Zorrillo's location.

After a few moments, he said, "The pope has new boots."

Bosch walked over and Aguila pointed to the footprints in the sawdust. There was one that was not from Aguila's or Bosch's shoes. It was very clear in the dust and Harry recognized the elongated heel of a bulldog boot. Inside it was the letter "S" formed by a curving snake. The edges of the print were sharp in the dust, the head of the snake clearly imprinted.

Aguila had been right. The pope had new boots.

31

All the way to the border crossing, Bosch contemplated how it had been done, how all the parts now seemed to fit, and how it might have gone unnoticed if not for Aguila noticing the footprint. He thought about the Snakes box in the closet of the apartment in Los Feliz. A clue so obvious, yet he had missed it. He had seen only what he wanted to see.

It was still early, just the first hint of dawn's light was fighting its way up the eastern horizon, and there was not yet much of a line at the crossing. Nobody was cleaning windshields. Nobody was selling junk. Nobody was there at all. Bosch badged the bored-looking Border Patrol agent and was waved through.

He needed a phone and some caffeine. He drove two minutes to the Calexico Town Hall, got a Coke from the machine in the police department's cramped lobby and took it out to the pay phone on the front wall. He looked at his watch and knew she would be at home, probably awake and getting ready for work.

He lit a cigarette and dialed, charging the call to his own PacTel card. While he waited for it to go through he looked across the street into the fog. He saw the shapes of sleeping figures under blankets scattered about the park. The ground fog gave the images a ghostly, lonely resonance.

Teresa picked up after two rings. She sounded like she had been awake already.

"Hi."

"Harry? What is it?"

"Sorry to wake you up."

"You didn't. What's the matter?"

"Are you getting dressed up to go to Moore's funeral today?"

"Yes. What is this? You called me at ten minutes before six to ask —"

"That isn't Moore they'll be putting in the ground."

There was a long silence during which Bosch looked into the park and saw a man standing there, a blanket wrapped around his shoulders, staring back at him in the fog. Harry looked away.

"What are you saying? Harry, are you all right?"

"I'm tired but never better. What I'm saying is he's still alive. Moore. I just missed him this morning."

"Are you still in Mexico?"

"At the border."

"That doesn't make sense. What you said. There were matches made on the latents, we got dental, and his own wife ID'd a photograph of the tattoo on the body. His identification was confirmed."

"It's all bullshit. He set it up."

"Why, Harry, are you calling me now and telling me this?"

"I want you to help me, Teresa. I can't go to Irving. Only you. You help me and you'll help yourself. If I'm right."

"That's a big if, Harry."

Bosch looked back into the park and the man in the blanket was gone.

"Just tell me how it could be possible," she said. "Convince me."

Bosch was silent a moment, like a lawyer composing himself before a cross-examination. He knew that every word he spoke now had to stand the test of her scrutiny or he would lose her.

"Besides the prints and dental, Sheehan told me they also matched his handwriting to the I-found-out-who-I-was note. He said they compared it to a change-of-address card Moore had put in his personnel file a few months ago after he and his wife separated."

He took a deep drag on the cigarette and she thought he had finished.

"So? I don't see — what about it?"

"One of the concessions the protective league won a few years back during contract negotiations was guaranteed access to your personnel file. So cops could check if there were beefs on their record, commendations, letters of complaint, anything like that. So Moore had access to his P-file. He went into Personnel a few months back and asked for it because he had just moved and needed to update it with his new address."

Bosch held it there a moment, to compose the rest of it in his mind.

"Okay, okay," she said.

"The P-files also contain print cards. Moore had access to the print card Irving took to you on the day of the autopsy. That was the card your tech used to identify the prints. You see? While Moore had the file, he could have switched his card for someone else's. Then you used the bogus card to identify his body. But, see, it wasn't his body. It was the other person's."

"Who?"

"I think it was a man from down here named Humberto Zorrillo."

"This seems too farfetched. There were other IDs. I remember that day in the suite. What's his name, Sheehan, he got a call from SID saying they matched prints in the motel room to Moore. They used a different set than we did. It's a double-blind confirmation, Harry. Then we have the tattoo. And the dental. How do you explain all of that?"

"Look, Teresa, listen to me. It all can be explained. It all works. The dental? You told me you only found one usable fragment, part of a root canal. That meant no root was left. It was a dead tooth so you could not tell how long it had been out, only that it matched his dentist's charts. That's fine, but one of Moore's crew told me he once saw Moore get punched during a Boulevard brawl and he lost a tooth. That could've been it, I don't know."

"Okay, what about the prints in the room? Explain that?"

"Easy. Those were his prints. Donovan, the SID guy, told me he pulled prints from the Department of Justice computer. Those would have been Moore's real prints. That meant he was really in the room. It doesn't mean it's his body. Normally, one set of exemplars — the ones from the DOJ computer — would be used to do all the match work, but Irving screwed it up by going to the P-file. And that's the beauty of Moore's plan. He knew Irving or someone in the department would do it this way. He could count on it because he knew the department would put a rush on the autopsy, the ID, everything, because it was a fellow officer. It's been done before and he knew they would do it for him."

"Donovan never did a cross-match between our prints and the set he pulled?"

"Nope, because it wasn't the routine. He might've gotten around to it later when he thought about it. But things were happening too fast on this case."

"Shit," she said. He knew he was winning her over. "What about the tattoo?"

"It's a barrio insignia. A lot of people could have had them. I think Zorrillo had one."

"Who is he?"

"He grew up with Moore down here. They might be brothers, I don't know. Anyway, Zorrillo became the local drug kingpin. Moore went to L.A. and became a cop. But somehow Moore was working for him up there. The story goes on from there. The DEA raided Zorrillo's ranch last night. He got away. But I don't think it was Zorrillo. It was Moore."

"You saw him?"

"I didn't need to."

"Is anyone looking for him?"

"The DEA is looking. They're concentrating in interior Mexico. Then again, they're looking for Zorrillo. Moore may never turn up again."

"It all seems . . . You're saying Moore killed Zorrillo and then traded places with him?"

"Yeah. Somehow he got Zorrillo to L.A. They meet at the Hideaway and Moore puts him down — the trauma to the back of the head you found. He puts his boots and clothes on the body. Then he blows the face away with the shotgun. He makes sure to leave some of his own prints around to make Donovan bite and puts the note in the back pocket.

"I think the note worked on a number of levels. It was taken as a suicide note at first. Authenticating the handwriting helped add to the identification. On another level, I think it was something personal between Moore and Zorrillo. Goes back to the barrio. 'Who are you?' 'I found out who I was.' That part of it is a long story."

They were both silent for a while, rethinking all of what Bosch had just said. He knew there were still a lot of loose ends. A lot of deception.

"Why all the killings?" she asked. "Porter and Juan Doe, what did they have to do with anything?"

This is where he had few answers.

"I don't know. They were somehow in the way, I guess. Zorrillo had Jimmy Kapps killed because he was an informant. I think Moore was the one who told Zorrillo. After that Juan Doe — his name, by the way, is Gutierrez-Llosa — gets beaten to death down here and taken up there. I don't know why. Then Moore pops Zorrillo and takes his place. Why he had to do Porter, I don't know. I guess he thought Lou might figure it out."

"That's so cold."

"Yeah."

"How could it happen?" she asked then, more to herself than Bosch. "They are about to bury him, this drug dealer . . . full honors, the mayor and chief there. The media."

"And you'll know the truth."

She thought about that for a long time before asking the next question.

"Why did he do it?"

"I don't know. We're talking about different lives. The cop and the drug dealer. But there must've been something still between them, that bond — whatever it is — from the barrio. And somehow one day the cop crosses over, starts watching out for the dealer on the streets of L.A. Who knows what made him do it. Maybe money, maybe just something he had lost a long time ago when he was a kid."

"What do you mean?"

"I don't know. I'm still thinking."

"If they were that close, why did he kill him?"

"I guess we'll have to ask him. If we ever find him. Maybe he — maybe like you said it was just to take Zorrillo's place. All that money. Or maybe it was guilt. He got in too far and he needed a way to end it. . . . Moore was — or is — hung up on the past. His wife said that. Maybe he was trying to recapture something, go back. I don't know yet."

There was silence on the line again. Bosch took a last drag on his cigarette.

"The plan seems almost perfect," he said. "He leaves a body behind in circumstances he knew would make the department not want to come looking."

"But you did, Harry."

"Yeah."

And here I am, he thought. He knew what he had to do now. He had to finish it. He could see the ghostly figures of several people in the park now. They were waking to another day of desperation.

"Why did you call me, Harry? What do you want me to do?"

"I called because I have to trust someone. I could only think of you, Teresa."

"Then what do you want me to do?"

"You have access to the DOJ prints in your office, right?"

"That's how we make most of our IDs. That's how we will make all of them after this. I have Irving by the balls now."

"Do you still have the print card he brought over for the autopsy?"

"Um, I don't know. But I'm sure the techs made a copy of it to keep with the body. You want me to do the cross-check?"

"Yeah, do a cross and you'll see they don't match."

"You're so sure."

"Yeah. I'm sure but you might as well confirm it."

"Then what?"

"Then, I guess, I'll see you at the funeral. I've got one more stop to make and then I'm heading up."

"What stop?"

"I want to check out a castle. It's part of the long story. I'll tell you later."

"You don't want to try to stop the funeral?"

Harry thought a few moments before answering. He thought of Sylvia Moore and the mystery she still held for him. Then he thought about the idea of a drug lord getting a cop's farewell.

"No, I don't want to stop it. Do you?"

"No way."

He knew her reasons were far different from his. But he didn't care about that. Teresa was well on her way to winning her assignment as permanent chief medical examiner. If Irving got in her way now, he'd end up looking like one of the customers in the autopsy suite. In that case, more power to her, he thought.

"I'll see you in a little bit," he said.

"Be careful, Harry."

Bosch hung up and lit another cigarette. The morning sun was up now and beginning to burn the ground fog off the park. People were moving around over there. He thought he heard a woman laughing. But at the moment he felt very much alone in the world.

32

Bosch pulled his car up to the front gate at the end of Coyote Trail and saw that the circular driveway in front of Castillo de los Ojos was still empty. But the thick chain that had secured the two halves of the iron gate the day before hung loose and the lock was open. Moore was here.

Harry left his car there, blocking the exit, and slipped through the gate on foot. He ran across the brown lawn in a crouched, uneasy trot, mindful that the windows of the tower looked down at him like the dark accusing eyes of a giant. He pressed himself against the stucco surface of the wall next to the front door. He was breathing heavily and sweating, though the morning air was still quite cool.

The knob was locked. He stood there unmoving for a long period, listening for something but hearing nothing. Finally, he ducked below the line of windows that fronted the first floor and moved around the house to the side of the four-bay garage. There was another door here and it, too, was locked.

Bosch recognized the rear of the house from the photographs that had been in Moore's bag. He saw the sliding doors running along the pool deck. One door was open and the wind buffeted the white curtain. It flapped like a hand beckoning him to come in.

The open door led to a large living room. It was full of ghosts — furniture covered by musty white sheets. Nothing else. He moved to his left, silently passing through the kitchen and opening a door to the garage. There was one car, which was covered by more sheets, and a pale green panel van. It said MEXITEC on the side. Bosch touched the van's hood and found it still warm. Through the windshield he saw a sawed-off shotgun lying across the passenger seat. He opened the unlocked door and took the weapon out. As quietly as he could, he cracked it open and saw both barrels were loaded with double-ought shells. He closed the weapon, holstered his own, and carried it with him.

He pulled the sheet off the front end of the other car and recognized it as the Thunderbird he had seen in the father-and-son photo in Moore's bag. Looking at the car, Bosch wondered how far back you have to go to trace the reason for a person's choices in life. He didn't know the answer about Moore. He didn't know the answer about himself.

He went back to the living room and stopped and listened. There was nothing. The house seemed still, empty, and it smelled dusty, like time spent slowly and painfully in wait for something or someone not coming. All the rooms were full of ghosts. He was considering the shape of a shrouded fan chair when he heard the noise. From above, like the sound of a shoe dropping on a wood floor.

He moved toward the front and in the entry area he saw the wide stone staircase. Bosch moved up the steps. The noise from above was not repeated.

On the second floor he went down a carpeted hallway, looking through the doors to four bedrooms and two bathrooms but finding each room empty.

He went back to the stairs and up into the tower. The lone door at the top landing was open and Harry heard no sound. He crouched and moved slowly into the opening, the sawed-off leading the way like a water finder's divining rod.

Moore was there. Standing with his back to the door and looking at himself in the mirror. The mirror was on the back of a closet door which was open slightly, angling the glass so that it did not catch Harry's reflection. He watched Moore unseen for a few moments, then looked around. There was a bed in the center of the room with an open suitcase on it. Next to it was a gym bag that was zipped closed and already appeared to be packed. Moore still had not moved. He was intently staring at the reflection of his face. He had a full beard now, and his eyes were brown. He wore faded blue jeans, new snakeskin boots, a black T-shirt and a black leather jacket with matching gloves. He was Melrose Avenue cool. From a distance he could easily pass for the pope of Mexicali.

Bosch saw the wood grips and chrome handle of an automatic tucked into Moore's belt.

"You going to say something, Harry? Or just stare."

Without moving his hands or head, Moore shifted his weight to the left and then he and Bosch were staring at each other in the mirror.

"Picked up a new pair of boots before you put Zorrillo down, didn't you?"

Now Moore turned completely to face him. But he didn't say anything.

"Keep your hands out front like that," Bosch said.

"Whatever you say, Harry. You know, I kinda thought that if somebody came, you'd be the one."

"You wanted somebody to come, didn't you?"

"Some days I did. Some days I didn't."

Bosch moved into the room and then took a step sideways so he was directly facing Moore.

"New contacts, beard. You look like the pope — from a distance. But how'd you convince his lieutenants, his *guardia*. They were just going to stand back and let you move in and take his place?"

"Money convinced them. They'd probably let you move in there if you had the bread, Harry. See, anything is negotiable when you have your hands on the purse strings. And I did."

Moore nodded slightly toward the duffel bag on the bed.

"How about you? I have money. Not much. About a hundred and ten grand there."

"I figured you'd be running away with a fortune."

"Oh, I am. I am. What's in the bag is just what I have on hand. You caught me a little short. But I can get you more. It's in the banks."

"Guess you've been practicing Zorrillo's signature as well as his looks."

Moore didn't answer.

"Who was he?"

"Who?"

"You know who."

"Half brother. Different fathers."

"This place. This is what it was all about, wasn't it? It's the castle you lived in before you were sent away."

"Something like that. Decided to buy it after he was gone. But it's falling apart on me. It's so hard to take care of something you love these days. Everything is a chore."

Bosch tried to study him. He looked tired of it all.

"What happened back at the ranch?" Bosch asked.

"You mean the three bodies? Yes, well, I guess you could say justice happened. Grena was a leech who had been sucking Zorrillo for years. Arpis detached him, you could say."

"Then who detached Arpis and Dance?"

"I did that, Harry."

He said it without hesitation and the words froze Bosch. Moore was a cop. He knew never to confess. You didn't talk until there was a lawyer by your side, a plea bargain in place, and a deal that was signed.

Harry adjusted his sweating hands on the sawed-off. He took a step forward and listened for any other sound in the house. There was only silence until Moore spoke again.

"I'm not going back, Harry. I guess you know that."

He said it matter-of-factly, as if it was a given, something that had been decided a long time ago.

"How'd you get Zorrillo up to L.A., and then into that motel room? How'd you get his prints for the personnel file?"

"You want me to tell you, Harry? Then what?"

Moore looked down at the gym bag briefly.

"Then nothing. We're going back to L.A. You haven't been advised — nothing you can say now can be used against you. It's just you and me here."

"The prints were easy. I was making him IDs. He had three or four so he could come across when he liked. One time he told me he wanted a passport and full wallet spread. I told him I needed prints. Took 'em myself."

"And the motel?"

"Like I said, he crossed over all the time. He'd go through the tunnel and the DEA would be out there sitting on the ranch thinking he was still inside.

He liked to come up to see the Lakers, sit down on court level near that blonde actress who likes to get on TV. Anyway, he was up there and I told him I wanted to meet. He came."

"And you put him down and took his place. . . . What about the old man, the laborer? What did he do?"

"He was just in the wrong place. Zorrillo told me he was there when he came up through the floor on the last trip. He wasn't supposed to be in that room. But I guess he couldn't read the signs. Zorrillo said he couldn't take the chance he'd tell someone about the tunnel."

"Why'd you dump him in the alley? Why didn't you just bury him out in Joshua Tree. Someplace he'd never be found."

"The desert would've been good but I didn't dump him, Bosch. Don't you see? They were controlling me. They brought him up here and dumped him there. Arpis did. That night I get a call from Zorrillo telling me to meet him at the Egg and I. He says park in the alley. I did and there was the body. I wasn't going to move the fucking thing. I called it in. You see it was one more way for him to keep his hold on me. And I went along. Porter caught the case and I made a deal with him to take it slow."

Bosch didn't say anything. He was trying to envision the sequence Moore had just described.

"This is getting boring, man. You going to try to cuff me, take me in, be the hero?"

"Why couldn't you let it go?" Bosch asked.

"What?"

"This place. Your father. The whole thing. You should have let the past go."

"I was robbed of my life, man. He kicked us right out. My mother — How do you let go of a past like that? Fuck you, Bosch. You don't know."

Bosch said nothing. But he knew he was allowing this to go on too long. Moore was taking control of the situation.

"When I heard he was dead, it did something," Moore said. "I don't know. I decided I wanted this place and I went to see my brother. That was my mistake. Things started small but they never stopped. Soon I was running the show for him up there. I had to get out from under it. There was only one way."

"It was the wrong way."

"Don't bother, Bosch. I know the song."

Bosch was sure Moore had told the story the way he believed it. But it was clear to Bosch he had fully embraced the devil. He had found out who he was.

"Why me?" Bosch asked.

"Why you what?"

"Why did you leave the file for me? If you hadn't done that, I wouldn't be here. You'd be in the clear."

"Bosch, you were my backup. You don't see? I needed something in case the suicide play didn't work. I figured you'd get that file and take it from there. I knew with just a little misdirection you would sound the alarm. Murder. Thing is, I never thought you'd get this far. I thought Irving and the rest of them would crush you because they wouldn't want to know what it was all about. They'd just want the whole thing to die with me."

"And Porter."

"Yeah, well, Porter was weak. He's probably better off now, anyway."

"And me? Would I be better off if Arpis had hit me with the bullet in the hotel room?"

"Bosch, you were getting too close. Had to take the shot."

Harry had nothing more to say or ask. Moore seemed to sense that they were at a final point. He tried one more time.

"Bosch, in that bag I have account numbers. They're yours."

"Not interested, Moore. We're going back."

Moore laughed at that notion.

"Do you really think anybody up there gives a rat's ass about all of this?"

Bosch said nothing.

"In the department?" Moore said. "No fucking way they care. They don't want to know about something like this. Bad for business, man. But, see, you — you're not in the department, Bosch. You're in it but not of it. See what I'm saying? There's the problem. There's — you take me back, man, and they're gonna look at you as being just as bad as me. Because you'll be pulling this wagon full of shit behind you.

"I think you're the only one who cares about it, Bosch. I really think you are. So just take the money and go."

"What about your wife? You think she cares?"

That stopped him, for a few moments, at least.

"Sylvia," he said. "I don't know. I lost her a long time ago. I don't know if she cares about this or not. I don't care anymore myself."

Bosch watched him, looking for the truth.

"Water under the bridge," Moore said. "So take the money. I can get more to you later."

"I can't take the money. I think you know that."

"Yeah, I guess I know that. But I think you know I can't go back with you, either. So where's that leave us?"

Bosch shifted his weight on to his left side, the butt of the shotgun against his hip. There was a long moment of silence during which he thought about himself and his own motives. Why hadn't he told Moore to take the gun out of his pants and drop it?

In a smooth, quick motion, Moore reached across his body with his right hand and pulled the gun out of his waistband. He was bringing the barrel around toward Bosch when Harry's finger closed over the shotgun's triggers. The double-barrel blast was deafening in the room. Moore took the brunt of it in the face. Through the smoke Bosch saw his body jerk backward into the air. His hands flew up toward the ceiling and he landed on the bed. His handgun fired but it was a stray shot, shattering one of the panes of the arched windows. The gun dropped onto the floor.

Pieces of blackened wadding from the shells floated down and landed in the blood of the faceless man. There was a heavy smell of burned gunpowder on the air and Bosch felt a slight mist on his face that he also knew by smell was blood.

He stood still for more than a minute, then he looked over and saw himself in the mirror. He quickly looked away.

He walked over to the bed and unzipped the duffel bag. There were stacks and stacks of money inside it, most of it in one-hundred-dollar bills. There was also a wallet and passport. He opened them and found they identified Moore as Henry Maze, age forty, of Pasadena. There were two loose photos held in the passport.

The first was a Polaroid that he guessed had come from the white bag. It was a photo of Moore and his wife in their early twenties. They were sitting on a couch, maybe at a party. Sylvia was not looking at the camera. She was looking at him. And Bosch knew why he had chosen this photo to take. The loving look on her face was beautiful. The second photo was an old black and white with discoloration around the edges, indicating it had come from a frame. It showed Cal Moore and Humberto Zorrillo as boys. They were playfully wrestling, both shirtless and laughing. Their skin was bronze, blemished only by the tattoos. Each boy had the Saints and Sinners tattoo on his arm.

He dropped the wallet and passport back into the duffel bag but put the two photos in his coat pocket. He walked over to the window with the broken pane and looked out onto Coyote Trail and the lowlands leading to the border. No police cars were coming. No Border Patrol. No one had even called for an ambulance. The thick walls of the castle had held the sound of the man dying inside.

The sun was high in the sky and he could feel its warmth through the triangular opening in the broken glass.

33

Bosch did not begin to feel whole again until he reached the smogged outskirts of L.A. He was back in the nastiness again but he knew that it was here that he would heal. He skirted downtown on the freeway and headed up through

Cahuenga Pass. Midday traffic was light. Looking up at the hills he saw the charred path of the Christmas-night fire. But he even took some comfort in that. He knew that the heat of the fire would have cracked open the seeds of the wildflowers and by spring the hillside would be a riot of colors. The chaparral would follow and soon there would be no scar on the land at all.

It was after one. He was going to be too late for Moore's funeral mass at the San Fernando Mission. So he drove through the Valley to the cemetery. The burial of Calexico Moore, killed in the line of duty, was to be at Eternal Valley in Chatsworth, the police chief, the mayor and the media presiding. Bosch smiled as he drove. We gather here to honor and bury a drug dealer.

He got there before the motorcade but the media were already set up on a bluff near the entrance road. Men in black suits, white shirts and black ties, with funeral bands around their left arms, were in the cemetery drive and signaled him to a parking area. He sat in the car, using the rearview mirror to put on a tie. He was unshaven and looked crumpled but didn't care.

The plot was near a stand of oak trees. One of the armbands had pointed the way. Harry walked across the lawn, stepping around plots, the wind blowing his hair in all directions. He took a position a good distance away from the green funeral canopy and accompanying bank of flowers and leaned against one of the trees. He smoked a cigarette while he watched cars start to arrive. A few had beaten the procession. But then he heard the approaching sound of the helicopters — the police air unit that flew above the hearse and the media choppers that started circling the cemetery like flies. Then the first motorcycles cut through the cemetery gate and Bosch watched as the TV cameras on the bluff followed the long line in. There must have been two hundred cycles, Bosch guessed. The best day to run a red light, break the speed limit or make an illegal U-turn in the city was on a cop's funeral day. Nobody was left minding the store.

The hearse and attendant limousine followed the cycles. Then came the rest of the cars and pretty soon people were parking all over the place and walking across the cemetery from all directions toward the plot. Bosch watched one of the armbands help Sylvia Moore out of the limo. She had been riding alone. Though he was maybe fifty yards away, Harry could tell she looked lovely. She wore a simple black dress and the wind gusted hard against it, pressing the material against her and showing her figure. She had to hold a black barrette in place in her hair. She wore black gloves and black sunglasses. Red lipstick. He couldn't take his eyes off her.

The armband led her to a row of folding chairs beneath the canopy and alongside the hole that had been expertly dug into the earth. Along the way, her head turned slightly and Bosch believed she was looking at him but was not sure because the glasses hid her eyes and her face showed no sign. After she was seated, the pallbearers, composed of Rickard, the rest of Moore's narcotics unit, and a few others Bosch didn't know, brought the grayish-silver steel casket.

"So, you made it back," a voice said from behind.

Bosch turned to see Teresa Corazón walking up behind him.

"Yeah, just got in."

"You could use a shave."

"And a few other things. How's it going, Teresa?"

"Never better."

"Good to hear. What happened this morning after we talked?"

"About what you expected. We pulled DOJ prints on Moore and compared them to what Irving had given us. No match. Two different people. That isn't Moore in the silver bullet over there."

Bosch nodded. Of course, by now he didn't need her confirmation. He had his own. He thought of Moore's faceless body lying on the bed.

"What are you going to do with it?" he asked.

"I've already done it."

"What?"

"I had a little discussion with Assistant Chief Irving before the funeral mass. Wish you could have seen his face."

"But he didn't stop the funeral."

"He's playing the percentages, I guess. Chances are Moore, if he knows what's good for him, won't ever show up again. So he is hoping that all it costs him is a recommendation on the medical examiner's office. He volunteered to do it. I didn't even have to explain his position to him."

"I hope you enjoy the job, Teresa. You're in the belly of the beast now."

"I will, Harry. And thanks for calling me this morning."

"Does he know how you came up with all of this? Did you tell him I called?"

"No. But I'm not sure I had to."

She was right. Irving would know Bosch was in the middle of this somehow. He looked past Teresa to look at Sylvia again. She was sitting quietly. The chairs on either side of her empty. No one was going to come near her.

"I'm going over to the group," Teresa said. "I told Dick Ebart I would meet him here. He wants to set up a date to call for the commission's full vote."

Bosch nodded. Ebart was a county commissioner of twenty-five years in office and closing in on seventy years old. He was her informal sponsor for the job.

"Harry, I still want to keep things on just a professional basis. I appreciate what you did for me today. But I want to keep things at a distance, for a while at least."

He nodded and watched her walk toward the gathering, her footing unsteady in high heels on the cemetery turf. For a moment Bosch envisioned her in a carnal coupling with the aged commissioner whose photos in the newspaper were most notable because of his drooping, crepe-paper neck. He was repulsed by the image and by himself for imagining it. He blanked it out of his mind and watched Teresa mingling in the crowd, shaking hands and becoming the politician she would now have to be. He felt a sense of sadness for her.

The service was a few minutes away and people were still arriving. In the crowd he picked up the gleaming head of Assistant Chief Irvin Irving. He was in full uniform, carrying his hat under his arm. He was standing with the chief of police and one of the mayor's front men. The mayor was apparently late as usual. Irving then saw Bosch, broke away and started walking toward him. He seemed to be taking in the vista of the mountains as he walked. He didn't look at Bosch until he was next to him under the oak tree.

"Detective."

"Chief."

"When did you get in?"

"Just now."

"Could use a shave."

"Yeah, I know."

"So what do we do? What do we do?"

The way he said it was almost wistful and Bosch didn't know whether Irving wanted an answer from him or not.

"You know, Detective, yesterday when you did not come to my office as ordered, I opened a one-point-eighty-one on you."

"I figured you would, Chief. Am I suspended?"

"No action taken at the moment. I'm a fair man. I wanted to speak with you first. You spoke with the acting chief medical examiner this morning?"

Bosch wasn't going to lie to him. He thought this time he held all of the high cards.

"Yes. I wanted her to compare some fingerprints."

"What happened down there in Mexico to make you want to do that?"

"Nothing I care to talk about, Chief. I'm sure it will all be on the news."

"I'm not talking about that ill-fated raid undertaken by the DEA. I am talking about Moore. Bosch, I need to know if I need to walk over there and stop this funeral."

Bosch watched a blue vein pop high on Irving's shaven skull. It pulsed and then died.

"I can't help you there, Chief. It's not my call. We've got company."

Irving turned around to look back toward the gathering. Lieutenant Harvey Pounds, also in dress uniform, was walking toward them, probably wanting to find out how many cases he could close from Bosch's investigation. But Irving held up a hand like a traffic cop and Pounds abruptly stopped, turned and walked away.

"The point I am trying to make with you, Detective Bosch, is that it appears we are about to bury and eulogize a Mexican drug lord while a corrupt police officer is running around loose. Do you have any idea what embarrass — Damn it! I can't believe I just spoke those words out loud. I cannot believe I spoke those words to you."

"Don't trust me much, do you, Chief?"

"In matters like these, I do not trust anyone."

"Well, don't worry about it."

"I am not worried about who I can and cannot trust."

"I mean about burying a drug lord while a corrupt cop is running around loose. Don't worry about it."

Irving studied him, his eyes narrowing, as if he might be able to peer through Bosch's own eyes, into his thoughts.

"Are you kidding me? Don't worry about it? This is a potential embarrassment to this city and this department of unimaginable proportions. This could —"

"Look, man, I am telling you to forget about it. Understand? I am trying to help you out here."

Irving studied him again for a long moment. He shifted his weight to the other foot. The vein on his scalp pulsed with new life. Bosch knew it would not sit well with him, to have someone like Harry Bosch keeping such a secret. Teresa Corazón he could deal with because they both played on the same field. But Bosch was different. Harry rather enjoyed the moment, though the long silence was getting old.

"I checked with the DEA on that fiasco down there. They said this man they believe to be Zorrillo escaped. They don't know where he is."

It was a half-assed effort to get Bosch to open up. It didn't work.

"They never will know."

Irving said nothing to this but Bosch knew better than to interrupt his silence. He was working up to something. Harry let him work, watching as the assistant chief's massive jaw muscles bunched into hard pads.

"Bosch, I want to know right now if there is a problem on this. Even a potential problem. Because I have to know in the next three minutes whether to walk over there in front of the chief and the mayor and all of those cameras and put a stop to this."

"What's the DEA doing now?"

"What can they do? They are watching the airports, contacting local authorities. Putting his photo and description out. There is not a lot they can do. He is gone. At least, they say. I want to know if he is going to stay gone."

Bosch nodded and said, "They're never going to find the man they are looking for, Chief."

"Convince me, Bosch."

"Can't do that."

"And why not?"

"Trust goes two ways. So does the lack of trust."

Irving seemed to consider this and Bosch thought he saw an almost imperceptible nod.

Bosch said, "The man they are looking for, who they believe to be Zorrillo, is in the wind and he isn't coming back. That's all you need to know."

Bosch thought of the body on the bed at Castillo de los Ojos. The face was already gone. Another two weeks and the flesh would go. No fingerprints. No identification, other than the bogus credentials in the wallet. The tattoo would stay intact for a while. But there were plenty who had that tattoo, including the fugitive Zorrillo.

He had left the money there, too. An added precaution, enough there maybe to convince the first finder not to bother calling the authorities. Just take the money and run.

Using a handkerchief, he had wiped the shotgun of his prints and left it. He locked the house, wrapped the chain through the black bars of the gate and closed the hasp on the lock, careful to wipe each surface. Then he had headed home to L.A.

"The DEA, are they putting a nice spin on things yet?" he asked Irving.

"They're working on it," Irving said. "I am told the smuggling network has been closed down. They have ascertained that the drug called black ice was manufactured on the ranch, taken through tunnels to two nearby businesses, then moved across the border. The shipment would make a detour, probably in Calexico, where it would be removed and the delivery van would go on. Both businesses have been seized. One of them, a contractor with the state to provide sterile medflies, will probably prove embarrassing."

"EnviroBreed."

"Yes. By tomorrow they will finish comparisons between the bills of lading shown by drivers at the border and the receipt of cargo records at the eradication center here in Los Angeles. I am told these documents were altered or forged. In other words more sealed boxes passed through the border than were received at the center."

"Inside help."

"Most likely. The on-site inspector for the USDA was either dumb or corrupt. I don't know which is worse."

Irving brushed some imaginary impurity off the shoulder of his uniform. It could not be hair or dandruff, since he had neither. He turned away from Bosch to face the coffin and the thick gathering of officers around it. The ceremony was about to begin. He squared his shoulders and without turning back, he said, "I don't know what to think, Bosch. I don't know whether you have me or not."

Bosch didn't answer. That would be one Irving would have to worry about.

"Just remember," Irving said. "You have just as much to lose as the department. More. The department can always come back, always recover. It might take a good long time but it always comes back. The same can't be said for the individual who gets tarred with the brush of scandal."

Bosch smiled in a sad way. Never leave a thing uncovered. That was Irving. His parting shot was a threat, a threat that if Bosch ever used his knowledge against the department, he, too, would go down. Irving would personally see to it.

"Are you afraid?" Bosch asked.

"Afraid of what, Detective?"

"Of everything. Of me. Yourself. That it won't hold together. That I might be wrong. Everything, man. Aren't you afraid of everything?"

"The only thing that I fear are people without a conscience. Who act without thinking their actions through. I don't think you are like that."

Bosch just shook his head.

"So let's get down to it, Detective. I have to rejoin the chief and I see the mayor has arrived. What is it you want, provided it is within my authority to provide?"

"I wouldn't take anything from you," Bosch said very quietly. "That's what you just don't seem to get."

Irving finally turned around to face him again.

"You are right, Bosch. I really don't understand you. Why risk everything for nothing? You see? It raises my concerns about you all over again. You don't play for the team. You play for yourself."

Bosch looked steadily at Irving and didn't smile, though he wanted to. Irving had paid him a fine compliment, though the assistant chief would never realize it.

"What happened down there had nothing to do with the department," he said. "If I did anything at all, I did it for somebody and something else."

Irving stared back blankly, his jaw flexing as he ground his teeth. There was a crooked smile below the gleaming skull. It was then that Bosch recognized the similarity to the tattoos on the arms of Moore and Zorrillo. The devil's mask. He watched as Irving's eyes lit on something and he nodded knowingly. He looked back at Sylvia and then returned his gaze to Bosch.

"A noble man, is that it? All of this to insure a widow's pension?"

Bosch didn't answer. He wondered if it was a guess or Irving knew something. He couldn't tell.

"How do you know she wasn't part of it?" Irving said.

"I know."

"But how can you be sure? How can you take the chance?"

"The same way you're sure. The letter."

"What about it?"

Bosch had done nothing but think about Moore on his way back. He had had four hours of driving on the open road to put it together. He thought he had it.

"Moore wrote the letter himself," he began. "He informed on himself, you could say. He had this plan. The letter was the start. He wrote it."

He stopped to light a cigarette. Irving didn't say a word. He just waited for the story.

"For reasons that I guess go back to when he was a boy, Moore fucked up. He crossed and after he was already on the other side he realized there is no crossing back. But he couldn't go on, he had to get out. Somehow.

"His plan was to start the IAD investigation with that letter. He put just enough in the letter so Chastain would be convinced there was something to it, but not enough that Chastain would be able to find anything. The letter would just serve to cloud his name, put him under suspicion. He had been in the department long enough to know how it would go. He'd seen the way IAD and people like Chastain operate. The letter set the stage, made the water murky enough so that when he turned up dead at the motel the department, meaning you, wouldn't want to look too closely at it. You're an open book, Chief. He knew you'd move quickly and efficiently to protect the department first, find out what really happened second. So he sent the letter. He used you, Chief. He used me, too."

Irving turned toward the grave site. The ceremony was about to begin. He turned back to Bosch.

"Go ahead, Detective. Quickly, please."

"Layer after layer. Remember, you told me he had rented that room for a month. That was the first layer. If he hadn't been discovered for a month decomp would've taken care of things. There would have been no skin left to print. That would leave only the latents he left in the room and he'd've been home free."

"But he was found a few weeks early," Irving helpfully interjected.

"Yeah. That brings us to the second layer. You. Moore had been a cop a long time. He knew what you would do. He knew you'd go to personnel and grab his package."

"That's a big gamble, Bosch."

"You ask me, it was a better-than-even bet. Christmas night, when I saw you there with the file, I knew what it was before you said. So I can see Moore taking the gamble and switching the print cards. Like I said, he was gambling it would never come to that anyway. You were the second layer."

"And you? You were the third?"

"Yeah, the way I figure it. He used me as a sort of last backup. In case the suicide didn't wash, he wanted somebody who'd look at it and see a reason for Moore to have been murdered. That was me. I did that. He left the file for me and I went for it, thought he'd been killed over it. It was all a deflection. He just didn't want anybody looking too closely at who was actually on the tile floor in the motel. He just wanted some time."

"But you went too far, Bosch. He never planned on that."

"I guess not."

Bosch thought about his meeting with Moore in the tower. He still hadn't decided whether Moore had been expecting him, even waiting for him. Waiting for Harry to come kill him. He didn't think he'd ever know. That was Calexico Moore's last mystery.

"Time for what?" Irving asked.

"What?"

"You said he just wanted some time."

"I think he wanted time to go down there, take Zorrillo's place and then take the money and run. I don't think he wanted to be the pope forever. He just wanted to live in a castle again."

"What?"

"It's nothing."

They were silent a moment before Bosch finished up.

"Most of this I know you already have, Chief."

"I do?"

"Yeah, you do. I think you figured it out after Chastain told you that Moore sent the letter himself."

"And how did Detective Chastain know that?"

He wasn't going to give Bosch anything. That was okay, though. Harry found that telling the story helped clarify it. It was like holding it up to inspect for holes.

"After he got the letter, Chastain thought it was the wife who sent it. He went to her house and she denied it. He asked for her typewriter because he was going to make sure and she slammed the door in his face. But she didn't do it before saying she didn't even have a typewriter. So then, after Moore turns up dead, Chastain starts thinking about things and takes the machine out of Moore's office at the station. My guess is he matched the keys to the letter. From that point, it wouldn't be difficult to figure out the letter came from either Moore or somebody in the BANG squad. My guess is that Chastain interviewed them this week and concluded they hadn't done it. The letter was typed by Moore."

Irving didn't confirm any of it but didn't have to. Bosch knew. It all fit.

"Moore had a good plan, Chief. He played us like cheater's solitaire. He knew every card in the deck before it was turned over."

"Except for one," Irving said. "You. He didn't think you'd come looking."

Bosch didn't reply. He looked over at Sylvia again. She was innocent. And she would be safe. He noticed Irving turn his gaze on her, too.

"She's clear," Bosch said. "You know it. I know it. If you make trouble for her, I'll make trouble for you."

It wasn't a threat. It was an offer. A deal. Irving considered it a moment and nodded his head once. A blunt agreement.

"Did you speak to him down there, Bosch?"

Harry knew he meant Moore and he knew he couldn't answer.

"What did you do down there?"

After a few moments of silence Irving turned and walked as upright as a Nazi back to the rows of chairs holding the VIPs and top brass of the department. He took a seat his adjutant had been saving in the row behind Sylvia Moore. He never looked back at Bosch once.

34

Through the entire service Bosch had watched her from his position next to the oak tree. Sylvia Moore rarely raised her head, even to watch the line of cadets fire blanks into the sky or when the air squad flew over, the helicopters arranged in the missing-man formation. One time he thought she glanced over at him, or at least in his direction, but he couldn't be sure. He thought of her as being stoic. And he thought of her as being beautiful.

When it was over and the casket was in the hole and the people were moving away, she stayed seated and Bosch saw her wave away an offer from Irving to be escorted back to the limousine. The assistant chief sauntered off, smoothing his collar against his neck. Finally, when the area around the burial site was clear, she stood up, glanced once down into the hole, and then started walking toward Bosch. Her steps were punctuated by the slamming of car doors all across the cemetery. She took the sunglasses off as she came.

"You took my advice," she said.

This immediately confused him. He looked down at his clothes and then back at her. What advice? She read him and answered.

"The black ice, remember? You have to be careful. You're here, so I assume you were."

"Yes, I was careful."

He saw that her eyes were very clear and she seemed even stronger than the last time they had encountered each other. They were eyes that would not forget a kindness. Or a slight.

"I know there is more than what they have told me. Maybe you will tell me sometime?"

He nodded and she nodded. There was a moment of silence as they looked at each other that was neither long or short. It seemed to Bosch to be a perfect moment. The wind gusted and broke the spell. Some of her hair broke loose from the barrette and she pushed it back with her hand.

"I would like that," she said.

"Whenever you want," he said. "Maybe you'll tell me a few things, too."

"Such as?"

"That picture that was missing from the picture frame. You knew what it was, but you didn't tell me."

She smiled as if to say he had focused his attention on something unnecessary and trivial.

"It was just a picture of him and his friend from the barrio. There were other pictures in the bag."

"It was important but you didn't say anything."

She looked down at the grass.

"I just didn't want to talk or think about it anymore."

"But you did, didn't you?"

"Of course. That's what happens. The things you don't want to know or remember or think about come back to haunt you."

They were quiet for a moment.

"You know, don't you?" he finally said.

"That that wasn't my husband buried there? I had an idea, yes. I knew there was more than what people were telling me. Not you, especially. The others."

He nodded and the silence grew long but not uncomfortable. She turned slightly and looked over at the driver standing next to the limo, waiting. There was nobody left in the cemetery.

"There is something I hope you will tell me," she said. "Either now or sometime. If you can, I mean. . . . Um, is he . . . is there a chance he will be back?"

Bosch looked at her and slowly shook his head. He studied her eyes for reaction. Sadness or fear, even complicity. There was none. She looked down at her gloved hands, which grasped each other in front of her dress.

"My driver . . . ," she said, not finishing the thought.

She tried a polite smile and for the hundredth time he asked himself what had been wrong with Calexico Moore. She took a step forward and touched her hand to his cheek. It felt warm, even through the silk glove, and he could smell perfume on her wrist. Something very light. Not really a smell. A scent.

"I guess I should go," she said.

He nodded and she backed away.

"Thank you," she said.

He nodded. He didn't know what he was being thanked for but all he could do was nod.

"Will you call? Maybe we could . . . I don't know. I —"

"I will call."

Now she nodded and turned to walk back to the black limousine. He hesitated and then spoke up.

"You like jazz? The saxophone?"

She stopped and turned back to him. There was sharpness in her eyes. That need for touch. It was so clear he could feel it cut him. He thought maybe it was his own reflection.

"Especially the solos," she said. "The ones that are lonely and sad. I love those."

"There is . . . is tomorrow night too soon?"

"It's New Year's Eve."

"I know. I was thinking . . . I guess it might not be the right time. The other night — that was . . . I don't know."

She walked back to him and put her hand on his neck and pulled his face down to hers. He went willingly. They kissed for a long time and Bosch kept his eyes closed. When she let him go he didn't look to see if anyone was watching. He didn't care.

"What is a right time?" she asked.

He had no answer.

"I'll be waiting for you."

He smiled and she smiled.

She turned for the last time and walked to the car, her high heels clicking on the asphalt once she left the carpet of grass. Bosch leaned back against the tree and watched the driver open the door for her. Then he lit a cigarette and watched as the sleek black machine carried her out through the gate and left him alone with the dead.

The
Concrete
Blonde

This is for Susan, Paul and Jamie,
Bob and Marlen, Ellen, Jane and Damian

The house in Silverlake was dark, its windows as empty as a dead man's eyes. It was an old California Craftsman with a full front porch and two dormer windows set on the long slope of the roof. But no light shone behind the glass, not even from above the doorway. Instead, the house cast a foreboding darkness about it that not even the glow from the streetlight could penetrate. A man could be standing there on the porch and Bosch knew he probably wouldn't be able to see him.

"You sure this is it?" he asked her.

"Not the house," she said. "Behind it. The garage. Pull up so you can see down the drive."

Bosch tapped the gas pedal and the Caprice moved forward and crossed the entrance to the driveway.

"There," she said.

Bosch stopped the car. There was a garage behind the house with an apartment above it. Wooden staircase up the side, light over the door. Two windows, lights on inside.

"Okay," Bosch said.

They stared at the garage for several moments. Bosch didn't know what he expected to see. Maybe nothing. The whore's perfume was filling the car and he rolled his window down. He didn't know whether to trust her claim or not. The one thing he knew he couldn't do was call for backup. He hadn't brought a rover with him and the car was not equipped with a phone.

"What are you going to — there he goes!" she said urgently.

Bosch had seen it, the shadow of a figure crossing behind the smaller window. The bathroom, he guessed.

"He's in the bathroom," she said. "That's where I saw all the stuff."

Bosch looked away from the window and at her.

"What stuff?"

"I, uh, checked the cabinet. You know, when I was in there. Just looking to see what he had. A girl has to be careful. And I saw all the stuff. Makeup shit. You know, mascara, lipsticks, compacts and stuff. That's how I figured it was him. He used all that stuff to paint 'em when he was done, you know, killing them."

"Why didn't you tell me that on the phone?"

"You didn't ask."

He saw the figure pass behind the curtains of the other window. Bosch's mind was racing now, his heart jacking up into its overdrive mode.

"How long ago was this that you ran out of there?"

"Shit, I don't know. I hadda walk down to Franklin just to find a fucking ride over to the Boulevard. I was with the ride 'bout ten minutes. So I don't know."

"Guess. It's important."

"I don't know. It's been more than an hour."

Shit, Bosch thought. She stopped to turn a trick before she called the task force number. Showed a lot of genuine concern there. Now there could be a replacement up there and I'm sitting out here watching.

He gunned the car up the street and found a space in front of a hydrant. He turned off the engine but left the keys in the ignition. After he jumped out he stuck his head back in through the open window.

"Listen, I'm going up there. You stay here. If you hear shots, or if I'm not back here in ten minutes, you start knocking on doors and get some cops out here. Tell them an officer needs assistance. There's a clock on the dash. Ten minutes."

"Ten minutes, baby. You go be the hero now. But I'm getting that reward."

Bosch pulled his gun as he hurried down the driveway. The stairs up the side of the garage were old and warped. He took them three at a time, as quietly as he could. But still it felt as if he were shouting his arrival to the world. At the top, he raised the gun and broke the bare bulb that was in place over the door. Then, he leaned back into the darkness, against the outside railing. He raised his left leg and put all his weight and momentum into his heel. He struck the door above the knob.

The door swung open with a loud crack. In a crouch, Bosch moved through the threshold in the standard combat stance. Right away he saw the man across the room, standing on the other side of a bed. The man was naked and not only bald but completely hairless. His vision locked on the man's eyes and he saw the look of terror quickly fill them. Bosch yelled, his voice high and taut.

"COPS! DON'T FUCKING MOVE!"

The man froze, but only for a beat, and then began bending down, his right arm reaching for the pillow. He hesitated once and then continued the movement. Bosch couldn't believe it. What the fuck was he doing? Time went into suspension. The adrenaline pounding through his body gave his vision a slow-motion clarity. Bosch knew the man was either reaching for the pillow for something to cover himself with, or he was —

The hand swept under the pillow.

"DON'T DO IT!"

The hand was closing on something beneath the pillow. The man had never taken his eyes off Bosch. Then Bosch realized it wasn't terror in his eyes. It was something else. Anger? Hate? The hand was coming out from beneath the pillow now.

"NO!"

Bosch fired one shot, his gun kicking up in his two-handed grasp. The naked man jerked upright and backward. He hit the wood-paneled wall behind him, then bounced forward and fell across the bed thrashing and gagging. Bosch quickly moved into the room and to the bed.

The man's left hand was reaching again for the pillow. Bosch brought his left leg up and knelt on his back, pinning him to the bed. He pulled the cuffs off his belt and grabbed the groping left hand and cuffed it. Then the right. Behind the back. The naked man was gagging and moaning.

"I can't — I can't," he said, but his statement was lost in a bloody coughing fit.

"You can't do what I told you," Bosch said. "I told you not to move!"

Just die, man, Bosch thought but didn't say. It will be easier for all of us.

He moved around the bed to the pillow. He lifted it, stared at what was beneath it for a few moments and then dropped it. He closed his eyes for a moment.

"Goddammit!" he called at the back of the naked man's head. "What were you doing? I had a fucking gun and you, you reach — I told you not to move!"

Bosch came around the bed so he could see the man's face. Blood was emptying from his mouth onto the dingy white sheet. Bosch knew his bullet had hit the lungs. The naked man was the dying man now.

"You didn't have to die," Bosch said to him.

Then the man was dead.

Bosch looked around the room. There was no one else. No replacement for the whore who had run. He had been wrong on that guess. He went into the bathroom and opened the cabinet beneath the sink. The makeup was there, as the whore had said. Bosch recognized some of the brand names. Max Factor, L'Oréal, Cover Girl, Revlon. It all seemed to fit.

He looked back through the bathroom door at the corpse on the bed. There was still the smell of gunpowder in the air. He lit a cigarette and it was so quiet in the place that he could hear the crisp tobacco burn as he dragged the soothing smoke into his lungs.

There was no phone in the apartment. Bosch sat on a chair in the kitchenette and waited. Staring across the room at the body, he realized that his heart was still pounding rapidly and that he felt lightheaded. He also realized that he felt nothing — not sympathy or guilt or sorrow — for the man on the bed. Nothing at all.

Instead, he tried to concentrate on the sound of the siren that was now sounding in the distance and coming closer. After a while, he was able to discern that it was more than one siren. It was many.

1

≈≈≈

There are no benches in the hallways of the U.S. District Courthouse in downtown Los Angeles. No place to sit. Anybody who slides down the wall to sit on the cold marble floor will get rousted by the first deputy marshal who walks by. And the marshals are always out in the halls, walking by.

The lack of hospitality exists because the federal government does not want its courthouse to give even the appearance that justice may be slow, or nonexistent. It does not want people lining the halls on benches, or on the floor, waiting with weary eyes for the courtroom doors to open and their cases or the cases of their jailed loved ones to be called. There is enough of that going on across Spring Street in the County Criminal Courts building. Every day the benches in the hallways of every floor are clogged with those who wait. Mostly they are women and children, their husbands or fathers or lovers held in lockup. Mostly they are black or brown. Mostly the benches look like crowded life rafts — women and children first — with people pressed together and cast adrift, waiting, always waiting, to be found. Boat people, the courthouse smartasses call them.

Harry Bosch thought about these differences as he smoked a cigarette and stood on the front steps of the federal courthouse. That was another thing. No smoking in the hallways inside. So he had to take the escalator down and come outside during the trial's breaks. Outside there was a sand-filled ash can behind the concrete base of the statue of the blindfolded woman holding up the scales of justice. Bosch looked up at the statue; he could never remember her name. The Lady of Justice. Something Greek, he thought but wasn't sure. He went back to the folded newspaper in his hands and reread the story.

Lately, in the mornings, he would read only the Sports section, concentrating his full attention on the pages in the back where box scores and statistics were carefully charted and updated each day. He somehow found the columns of numbers and percentages comforting. They were clear and concise, an absolute order in a disordered world. Having knowledge of who had hit the most home runs for the Dodgers made him feel that he was still connected in some way to the city, and to his life.

But today he had left the Sports section folded and tucked into his briefcase, which was under his chair in the courtroom. The *Los Angeles Times*'s Metro section was in his hands now. He had carefully folded the section into quarters, the way he had seen drivers on the freeway do it so they could read while they drove, and the story on the trial was on the bottom corner of the section's front page. He once again read the story and once again felt his face grow hot as he read about himself.

TRIAL ON POLICE "TOUPEE" SHOOTING TO BEGIN
BY JOEL BREMMER, TIMES STAFF WRITER

As an unusual civil rights trial gets underway today, a Los Angeles police detective stands accused of having used excessive force four years ago when he shot and killed a purported serial killer he believed was reaching for a gun. The alleged killer was actually reaching for his toupee.

Los Angeles Police Detective Harry Bosch, 43, is being sued in U.S. District Court by the widow of Norman Church, an aerospace worker Bosch shot to death at the climax of the investigation into the so-called Dollmaker killings.

For nearly a year before the shooting, police had sought a serial killer so named by the media because he used makeup to paint the faces of his 11 victims. The highly publicized manhunt was marked by the killer's sending of poems and notes to Bosch and the *Times*.

After Church was killed, police announced they had unequivocal evidence proving that the mechanical engineer was the killer.

Bosch was suspended and later transferred from the homicide special unit of the LAPD Robbery-Homicide Division to the Hollywood Division homicide squad. In making the demotion, police stressed that Bosch was disciplined for procedural errors, such as his failure to call for a backup to the Silverlake apartment where the fatal shooting took place.

Police administrators maintained that the Church killing was a "good" shooting — department terminology meaning not improper.

Since Church's death precluded a trial, much of the evidence gathered by police has never been provided publicly under oath. That will likely change with the federal trial. A week-long jury selection process is expected to be completed today with the opening statements of the attorneys to follow.

Bosch had to refold the paper to continue reading the story on an inside page. He was momentarily distracted by seeing his own picture, which was on the inside page. It was an old photo and looked not unlike a mug shot. It was the same one that was on his department ID card. Bosch was more annoyed by the photo than the story. It was an invasion of his privacy to put his picture out like that. He tried to concentrate on the story.

Bosch is being defended by the City Attorney's Office because he was acting in the line of duty when the shooting occurred. If any judgment is won by the plaintiff, the city taxpayers, not Bosch, will pay.

Church's wife, Deborah, is being represented by civil rights attorney Honey Chandler, who specializes in police abuse cases. In an interview last week, Chandler said she will seek to prove to the jury that Bosch acted in such a reckless manner that a fatal shooting of Church was inevitable.

"Detective Bosch was cowboying and a man ended up dead," Chandler said. "I don't know if he was merely reckless or if there is something more sinister here, but we will find out in the trial."

That was the line that Bosch had read and reread at least six times since getting the paper during the first break. Sinister. What did she mean by that? He had tried not to let it bother him, knowing that Chandler would not be above using a newspaper interview for a psych-ops outing but, still, it felt like a warning shot. It let him know more was to come.

Chandler said she also plans to question the police evidence that Church was the Dollmaker. She said Church, the father of two daughters, was not the serial killer police sought and that they labeled him as such to cover up Bosch's misdeed.

"Detective Bosch killed an innocent man in cold blood," Chandler said. "What we are doing with this civil rights suit is what the police department and the district attorney's office refused to do: bring forward the truth and provide justice for Norman Church's family."

Bosch and Asst. City Atty. Rodney Belk, who is defending him, declined comment for this story. Along with Bosch, those expected to testify in the one- to two-week case include —

"Spare change, pal?"

Bosch looked up from the paper into the grimy but familiar face of the homeless man who had staked out the front of the courthouse as his turf. Bosch had seen him out here every day during the week of jury selection, making his change-and-cigarette rounds. The man wore a threadbare tweed jacket over two sweaters and corduroy pants. He carried a plastic bag of belongings and a Big Gulp cup to shake in front of people when he asked for change. He also always carried with him a yellow legal pad with scribbling all over it.

Bosch instinctively patted his pockets and shrugged. He had no change.

"I'd take a dollar, you know."

"Don't have a spare dollar."

The homeless man dismissed him and looked into the ash can. Yellowed cigarette butts grew from the sand like a crop of cancer. He put his yellow pad under his arm and began to pick through the offerings, taking those that still had a quarter inch or more of tobacco to smoke. Every now and then he would find a nearly whole cigarette and make a clicking sound with his mouth to show his approval. He put the harvest from the ash can in the Big Gulp cup.

Happy with his findings, the man stepped back from the ash can and looked up at the statue. He looked back at Bosch and winked, then began to rock his hips in a lewd mimicry of a sexual act.

"How 'bout my girl here?" he said.

The man then kissed his hand and reached up and patted the statue.

Before Bosch could think of something to say, the pager on his belt began to chirp. The homeless man stepped back another two steps and raised his free hand as if to ward off some unknown evil. Bosch saw the look of deranged panic spread on his face. It was the look of a man whose brain synapses were spread too far apart, the connections dulled. The man turned and scurried away, out toward Spring Street, with his cup of used cigarettes.

Bosch watched him until he was gone and then pulled the pager off his belt. He recognized the number on the display. It was Lieutenant Harvey "Ninety-eight" Pounds's direct line at the Hollywood station. He put what was left of his cigarette into the sand and went back into the courthouse. There was a bank of pay phones at the top of the escalator, near the second-floor courtrooms.

"Harry, what's happening there?" Pounds asked.

"The usual. Just waiting around. We got a jury, so now the lawyers are in with the judge, talking about openers. Belk said I didn't have to sit in on that, so I'm just hanging around."

He looked at his watch. It was ten to twelve.

"They'll be breaking for lunch soon," he added.

"Good. I need you."

Bosch didn't reply. Pounds had promised he would be off the case rotation until the trial was over. A week more, maybe two, at the most. It was a promise Pounds had no choice but to make. He knew that Bosch couldn't handle catching a homicide investigation while in federal court four days a week.

"What's going on? I thought I was off the list."

"You are. But we may have a problem. It concerns you."

Bosch hesitated again. Dealing with Pounds was like that. Harry would trust a street snitch before he'd trust Pounds. There was always the spoken motive and the hidden motive. It seemed that this time the lieutenant was doing one of his routine dances. Speaking in elliptical phrases, trying to get Bosch to bite on the hook.

"A problem?" Bosch finally asked. A good noncommittal reply.

"Well, I take it you saw the paper today — the *Times* story about your case?"

"Yeah, I was just reading it."

"Well, we got another note."

"A note? What are you talking about?"

"I'm talking about somebody dropping a note at the front desk. Addressed to you. And damn if it doesn't sound like those notes you got from the Dollmaker back when all of that was going on."

Bosch could tell Pounds was enjoying this, the stretching it out.

"If it was addressed to me, how do you know about it?"

"It wasn't mailed. No envelope. It was just one page, folded over. Had your name on the fold. Somebody left it at the front desk. Somebody there read it, you can figure it from there."

"What does it say?"

"Well, you're not going to like this, Harry, the timing is god-awful, but the note says, it says basically that you got the wrong guy. That the Dollmaker is still out there. The writer says he's the real Dollmaker and that the body count continues. Says you killed the wrong guy."

"It's bullshit. The Dollmaker's letters were carried in the paper, in Bremmer's book on the case. Anybody could pick up the style and write a note. You —"

"You take me for a moron, Bosch? I know anybody could've written this. But so did the writer know that. So to prove his point he included a little treasure map, I'd guess you'd call it. Directions to another victim's body."

A long silence filled the line while Bosch thought and Pounds waited.

"And so?" Bosch finally said.

"And so I sent Edgar out to the location this morning. You remember Bing's, on Western?"

"Bing's? Yeah, south of the Boulevard. Bing's. A pool hall. Didn't that place go down in the riots last year?"

"Right," Pounds said. "Complete burnout. They looted and torched the place. Just the slab and three walls left standing. There's a city demolition order against it but the owner hasn't acted yet. Anyway, that's the spot, according to this note we got. Note says she was buried under the floor slab. Edgar went out there with a city crew, jackhammers, the works. . . ."

Pounds was dragging it out. What a petty asshole, Bosch thought. This time he would wait longer. And when the silence grew nervously long, Pounds finally spoke.

"He found a body. Just like the note said he would. Beneath the concrete. He found a body. That's —"

"How old is it?"

"Don't know yet. But it's old. That's why I'm calling. I need you to go out there during the lunch break and see what you can make of this. You know, is it legit as a Dollmaker victim or is some other wacko jerking us off? You're the expert. You could go out there when the judge breaks for lunch. I'll meet you there. And you'll be back in time for openers."

Bosch felt numb. He already needed another cigarette. He tried to place all of what Pounds had just said into some semblance of order. The Dollmaker — Norman Church — had been dead four years now. There had been no mistake. Bosch knew that night. He still knew it in his guts today. Church was the Dollmaker.

"So this note just appeared at the desk?"

"Desk sergeant found it on the front counter about four hours ago. Nobody saw anybody leave it. You know, a lot of people come through the front in the mornings. Plus we had change of shift. I had Meehan go up and talk to the desk uniforms. Nobody remembers jack shit about it until they found it."

"Shit. Read it to me."

"Can't. SID has it. Doubt there will be any lifts, but we have to go through the motions. I'll get a copy and have it with me at the scene, okay?"

Bosch didn't answer.

"I know what you're thinking," Pounds said. "But let's hold our horses till we see what is out there. No reason to worry yet. Might be some stunt cooked up by that lawyer, Chandler. Wouldn't put it past her. She's the type, she'd do anything to nail another LAPD scalp to the wall. Likes seeing her name in the paper."

"What about the media? They heard about this yet?"

"We've gotten a few calls about a body being found. They must've gotten it off the coroner's dispatch freek. We've been staying off the air. Anyway, nobody knows about the note or the Dollmaker tie-in. They just know there's a body. The idea of it being found under the floor of one of the riot burnouts is sexy, I guess.

"Anyway, we have to keep the Dollmaker part under our hat for the time being. Unless, of course, whoever wrote it also sent copies out to the media. If he did that, we'll hear about it by the end of the day."

"How could he bury her under the slab of a pool hall?"

"The whole building wasn't a pool hall. There were storage rooms in the back. Before it was Bing's it was a studio prop house. After Bing's took the front, they rented out sections in the back for storage. This is all from Edgar, he got the owner out there. The killer must've had one of the rooms, broke through the existing slab and put this girl's body in there. Anyway, it all got burned down in the riots. But the fire didn't hurt the slab. This poor girl's body has been down in there through all of that. Edgar said it looks like a mummy or something."

Bosch saw the door to courtroom 4 open and members of the Church family came out followed by their lawyer. They were breaking for lunch. Deborah Church and her two teenaged daughters did not look at him. But Honey Chandler, known by most cops and others in the federal courts building as Money Chandler, stared at him with killer eyes as she passed. They were as dark as burnt mahogany and set against a tanned face with a strong jawline. She was an attractive woman with smooth gold hair. Her figure was hidden in the stiff lines of her blue suit. Bosch could feel the animosity from the group wash over him like a wave.

"Bosch, you still there?" Pounds asked.

"Yeah. It looks like we just broke for lunch."

"Good. Then head over there and I'll meet you. I can't believe I'm actually saying this, but I hope it's just another wacko. For your sake, it might be best."

"Right."

As Bosch was hanging up he heard Pounds's voice and brought the phone back to his ear.

"One more thing. If the media shows up out there, leave them to me. However this turns out, you shouldn't be formally involved in this new case because of the litigation stemming from the old. We are just having you out there as an expert witness, so to speak."

"Right."

"See you there."

2

Bosch took Wilshire out of downtown and cut up to Third after he made it through what was left of MacArthur Park. Turning north on Western he could see up on the left the grouping of patrol cars, detective cars and the crime-scene and coroner's vans. In the distance the HOLLYWOOD sign hung over the northern view, its letters barely legible in the smog.

Bing's was three blackened walls cradling a pile of charred debris. No roof, but the uniforms had hung a blue plastic tarp over the top of the rear wall and strung it to the chain-link fence that ran along the front of the property. Bosch knew it hadn't been done because the investigators wanted shade where they worked. He leaned forward and looked up through the windshield. He saw them up there, circling. The city's carrion birds: the media helicopters.

As Bosch pulled to a stop at the curb he saw a couple of city workers standing next to an equipment truck. They had sick looks on their faces and dragged hard and deep on cigarettes. Their jackhammers were on the ground near the back of the truck. They were waiting — hoping — that their work here was done.

On the other side of their truck Pounds was standing next to the coroner's blue van. It looked as though he was composing himself, and Bosch saw that he shared the same sick expression with the civilians. Though Pounds was commander of Hollywood detectives, including the homicide table, he had never actually worked homicide himself. Like many of the department's administrators, his climb up the ladder was based on test scores and brown-nosing, not experience. It always pleased Bosch to see someone like Pounds get a dose of what real cops dealt with every day.

Bosch looked at his watch before getting out of his Caprice. He had one hour before he had to be back in court for openers.

"Harry," Pounds said as he walked up. "Glad you made it."

"Always glad to check out another body, Lieutenant."

Bosch slipped off his suit coat and put it inside his car on the seat. Then he moved to the trunk and got out a baggy blue jumpsuit and put it on over his clothes. It would be hot, but he didn't want to come back into court covered with dirt and dust.

"Good idea," Pounds said. "Wish I had brought my stuff."

But Bosch knew he didn't have any stuff. Pounds ventured to a crime scene only when there was a good chance TV would show up and he could give a sound bite. And it was only TV he was interested in. Not print media. You had to make sense for more than two sentences in a row with a newspaper reporter. And then your words became attached to a piece of paper and were there all the next day and possibly forever to haunt you. It wasn't good department politics to talk to the print media. TV was a more fleeting and less dangerous thrill.

Bosch headed toward the blue tarp. Beneath it he saw the usual gathering of investigators. They stood next to a pile of broken concrete and along the edge of a trench dug into the concrete pad that had been the building's foundation. Bosch looked up as one of the TV helicopters made a low fly-over. They wouldn't get much usable video with the tarp hiding the scene. They were probably dispatching ground crews now.

There was still a lot of debris in the building's shell. Charred ceiling beams and timber, broken concrete block and other rubble. Pounds caught up with Bosch and they began carefully stepping through to the gathering beneath the tarp.

"They'll bulldoze this and make another parking lot," Pounds said. "That's all the riots gave the city. About a thousand new parking lots. You want to park in South Central these days, no problem. You want a bottle of soda or to put gas in your car, then you got a problem. They burned every place down. You drive through the South Side before Christmas? They got Christmas tree lots every block, all the open space down there. I still don't understand why those people burned their own neighborhoods."

Bosch knew that the fact people like Pounds didn't understand why "those people" did what they did was one reason they did it, and would have to do it again someday. Bosch looked at it as a cycle. Every twenty-five years or so the city had its soul torched by the fires of reality. But then it drove on. Quickly, without looking back. Like a hit-and-run.

Suddenly Pounds went down after slipping on the loose rubble. He stopped his fall with his hands and jumped up quickly, embarrassed.

"Damn it!" he cried out, and then, though Bosch hadn't asked, he added, "I'm okay. I'm okay."

He quickly used his hand to carefully smooth back the strands of hair that had slipped off his balding cranium. He didn't realize that he was smearing black char from his hand across his forehead as he did this and Bosch didn't tell him.

They finally picked their way to the gathering. Bosch walked toward his former partner, Jerry Edgar, who stood with a couple of investigators Harry knew and two women he didn't. The women wore green jumpsuits, the uniform of the coroner's body movers. Minimum-wage earners who were dispatched from death scene to death scene in the blue van, picking up the bodies and taking them to the ice box.

"Whereyat, Harry?" Edgar said.

"Right here."

Edgar had just been to New Orleans for the blues festival and had somehow come back with the greeting. He said it so often it had become annoying. Edgar was the only one in the detective bureau who didn't realize this.

Edgar was the standout amidst the group. He was not wearing a jumpsuit like Bosch — in fact, he never did because they wrinkled his Nordstrom suits — and somehow had managed to make his way into the crime scene area without getting so much as a trace of dust on the pants cuffs of his gray double-breasted suit. The real estate market — Edgar's onetime lucrative outside gig — had been in the shithouse for three years but Edgar still managed to be the sharpest dresser in the division. Bosch looked at Edgar's pale blue silk tie, knotted tightly at the black detective's throat, and guessed that it might have cost more than his own shirt and tie combined.

Bosch looked away and nodded to Art Donovan, the SID crime scene tech, but said nothing else to the others. He was following protocol. As at any murder scene a carefully orchestrated and incestuous caste system was in effect. The detectives did most of the talking amongst themselves or to the SID tech. The uniforms didn't speak unless spoken to. The body movers, the lowest on the totem pole, spoke to no one except the coroner's tech. The coroner's tech said little to the cops. He despised them because in his view they were whiners — always needing this or that, the autopsy done, the tox tests done, all of it done by yesterday.

Bosch looked into the trench they stood above. The jackhammer crew had broken through the slab and dug a hole about eight feet long and four feet deep. They had then excavated sideways into a large formation of concrete that extended three feet below the surface of the slab. There was a hollow in the stone. Bosch dropped to a crouch so he could look closer and saw that the concrete hollow was the outline of a woman's body. It was as if it were a mold into which plaster could be poured to make a cast, maybe to manufacture a mannikin. But it was empty inside.

"Where's the body?" Bosch asked.

"They took what was left out already," Edgar said. "It's in the bag in the truck. We're trying to figure out how to get this piece of the slab outta here in one piece."

Bosch looked silently into the hollow for a few moments before standing back up and making his way back out from beneath the tarp. Larry Sakai, the coroner's investigator, followed him to the coroner's van and unlocked and opened the back door. Inside the van it was sweltering and the smell of Sakai's breath was stronger than the odor of industrial disinfectant.

"I figured they'd call you out here," Sakai said.

"Oh, yeah? Why's that?"

"'Cause it looks like the fuckin' Dollmaker, man."

Bosch said nothing, so as not to give Sakai any indication of confirmation. Sakai had worked some of the Dollmaker cases four years earlier. Bosch suspected he was responsible for the name the media attached to the serial killer. Someone had leaked details of the killer's repeated use of makeup on the bodies to one of the anchors at Channel 4. The anchor christened the killer the Dollmaker. After that, the killer was called that by everybody, even the cops.

But Bosch always hated that name. It said something about the victims as well as the killer. It depersonalized them, made it easier for the Dollmaker stories that were broadcast to be entertaining instead of horrifying.

Bosch looked around the van. There were two gurneys and two bodies. One filled the black bag completely, the unseen corpse having been heavy in life or bloated in death. He turned to the other bag, the remains inside barely filling it. He knew this was the body taken from the concrete.

"Yeah, this one," Sakai said. "This other's a stabbing up on Lankershim. North Hollywood's working it. We were coming in when we got the dispatch on this one."

That explained how the media caught on so quickly, Bosch knew. The coroner's dispatch frequency played in every newsroom in the city.

He studied the smaller body bag a moment and without waiting for Sakai to do it he yanked open the zipper on the heavy black plastic. It unleashed a sharp, musty smell that was not as bad as it could have been had they found the body sooner. Sakai pulled the bag open and Bosch looked at the remains of a human body. The skin was dark and like leather stretched taut over the bones. Bosch was not repulsed because he was used to it and had the ability to become detached from such scenes. He sometimes believed that looking at bodies was his life's work. He had ID'd his mother's body for the cops when he wasn't yet twelve years old, he had seen countless dead in Vietnam, and in nearly twenty years with the cops the bodies had become too many to put a number to. It had left him, most times, as detached from what he saw as a camera. As detached, he knew, as a psychopath.

The woman in the bag had been small, Bosch could tell. But the deterioration of tissue and shrinkage made the body seem even smaller than it had certainly been in life. What was left of the hair was shoulder length and looked as if it had been bleached blonde. Bosch could see the powdery remains of makeup on the skin of the face. His eyes were drawn to the breasts because they were shockingly large in comparison to the rest of the shrunken corpse. They were full and rounded and the skin was stretched taut across them. It somehow seemed to be the most grotesque feature of the corpse because it was not as it should have been.

"Implants," Sakai said. "They don't decompose. Could probably take 'em out and resell them to the next stupid chick that wants 'em. We could start a recycling program."

Bosch didn't say anything. He was suddenly depressed at the thought of the woman — whoever she was — doing that to her body to somehow make herself more appealing, and then to end up this way. Had she only succeeded, he wondered, in making herself appealing to her killer?

Sakai interrupted his thoughts.

"If the Dollmaker did this, that means she's been in the concrete at least four years, right? So if that's the case, decomp isn't that bad for that length of time. Still got the hair, eyes, some internal tissues. We'll be able to work with it. Last week, I picked up a piece of work, a hiker they found out in Soledad Canyon. They figure it was a guy went missing last summer. Now he was nothing but bones. 'Course out in the open like that, you got the animals. You know they come in through the ass. It's the softest entry and the animals —"

"I know, Sakai. Let's stay on this one."

"Anyway, with this woman, the concrete apparently slowed things down for us. Sure didn't stop it, but slowed it down. It must've been like an airtight tomb in there."

"You people going to be able to establish just how long she's been dead?"

"Probably not from the body. We get her ID'd, then you people might find out when she went missing. That'll be the way."

Bosch looked at the fingers. They were dark sticks almost as thin as pencils. "What about prints?"

"We'll get 'em, but not from those."

Bosch looked over and saw Sakai smiling.

"What? She left them in the concrete?"

Sakai's glee was smashed like a fly. Bosch had ruined his surprise.

"Yeah, that's right. She left an impression, you could say. We're going to get prints, maybe even a mold of her face, if we can get what's left of that slab out of there. Whoever mixed this concrete used too much water. Made it very fine. That's a break for us. We'll get the prints."

Bosch leaned over the gurney to study the knotted strip of leather that was wrapped around the corpse's neck. It was thin black leather and he could see the manufacturer's seam along the edges. It was a strap cut away from a purse. Like all the others. He bent closer and the cadaver's smell filled his nose and mouth. The circumference of the leather strap around the neck was small, maybe about the size of a wine bottle. Small enough to be fatal. He could see where it had cut into the now darkened skin and choked away life. He looked at the knot. A slipknot pulled tight on the right side with the left hand. Like all the others. Church had been left-handed.

There was one more thing to check. The signature, as they had called it.

"No clothes? Shoes?"

"Nothing. Like the others, remember?"

"Open it all the way. I want to see the rest."

Sakai pulled the zipper on the black bag down all the way to the feet. Bosch was unsure if Sakai knew of the signature but was not going to bring it up. He leaned over the corpse and looked down, acting as if he was studying everything when he was only interested in the toenails. The toes were shriveled, black and cracked. The nails were cracked, too, and completely missing from a few toes. But Bosch saw the paint on the toes that were intact. Hot pink dulled by decomposition fluids, dust and age. And on the large toe on the right foot he saw the signature. What was still left of it to be seen. A tiny white cross had been carefully painted on the nail. The Dollmaker's sign. It had been there on all the bodies.

Bosch could feel his heart pounding loudly. He looked around the van's interior and began to feel claustrophobic. The first sense of paranoia was poking into his brain. His mind began churning through the possibilities. If this body matched every known specification of a Dollmaker kill, then Church was the killer. If Church was this woman's killer and is now dead himself, then who left the note at the Hollywood station front desk?

He straightened up and took in the body as a whole for the first time. Naked and shrunken, forgotten. He wondered if there were others out there in the concrete, waiting to be discovered.

"Close it," he said to Sakai.

"It's him, isn't it? The Dollmaker."

Bosch didn't answer. He climbed out of the van, pulled the zipper on his jumpsuit down a bit to let in some air.

"Hey, Bosch," Sakai called from inside the van. "I'm just curious. How'd you guys find this? If the Dollmaker is dead, who told you where to look?"

Bosch didn't answer that one either. He walked slowly back underneath the tarp. It looked like the others still hadn't figured out what to do about removing the concrete the body had been found in. Edgar was standing around trying not to get dirty. Bosch signaled to him and Pounds and they gathered together at a spot to the left of the trench, where they could talk without being overheard.

"Well?" Pounds asked. "What've we got?"

"It looks like Church's work," Bosch said.

"Shit," Edgar said.

"How can you be sure?" Pounds asked.

"From what I can see, it matches every detail followed by the Dollmaker. Including the signature. It's there."

"The signature?" Edgar asked.

"The white cross on the toe. We held that back during the investigation, cut deals with all the reporters not to put it out."

"What about a copycat?" Edgar offered hopefully.

"Could be. The white cross was never made public until after we closed the case. After that, Bremmer over at the *Times* wrote that book about the case. It was mentioned."

"So we have a copycat," Pounds pronounced.

"It all depends on when she died," Bosch said. "His book came out a year after Church was dead. If she got killed after that, you probably got a copycat. If she got put in that concrete before, then I don't know . . ."

"Shit," said Edgar.

Bosch thought a moment before speaking again.

"We could be dealing with one of a lot of different things. There's the copycat. Or maybe Church had a partner and we never saw it. Or maybe . . . I popped the wrong guy. Maybe whoever wrote this note we got is telling the truth."

That hung out there in the momentary silence like dogshit on the sidewalk. Everybody walks carefully around it without looking too closely at it.

"Where's the note?" Bosch finally said to Pounds.

"In my car. I'll get it. What do you mean, he may have had a partner?"

"I mean, say Church did do this, then where'd the note come from, since he is dead? It would obviously have to be someone who knew he did it and where he had hidden the body. If that's the case, who is this second person? A partner? Did Church have a killing partner we never knew about?"

"Remember the Hillside Strangler?" Edgar asked. "Turned out it was stranglers. Plural. Two cousins with the same taste for killing young women."

Pounds took a step back and shook his head as if to ward off a potentially career-threatening case.

"What about Chandler, the lawyer?" Pounds said. "Say Church's wife knows where he buried bodies, literally. She tells Chandler and Chandler hatches this scheme. She writes a note like the Dollmaker and drops it off at the station. It's guaranteed to fuck up your case."

Bosch replayed that one in his mind. It seemed to work, then he saw the fault lines. He saw that they ran through all the scenarios.

"But why would Church bury some bodies and not others? The shrink who advised the task force back then said there was a purpose to his displaying of the victims. He was an exhibitionist. Toward the end, after the seventh victim, he started dropping the notes to us and the newspaper. It doesn't make sense that he'd leave some of the bodies to be found and some buried in concrete."

"True," Pounds said.

"I like the copycat," Edgar said.

"But why copy someone's whole profile, right down to the signature, and then bury the body?" Bosch asked.

He wasn't really asking them. It was a question he'd have to answer himself. They stood there in silence for a long moment, each man beginning to see that the most plausible possibility might be that the Dollmaker was still alive.

"Whoever did it, why the note?" Pounds said. He seemed very agitated. "Why would he drop us the note? He'd gotten away."

"Because he wants attention," Bosch said. "Like the Dollmaker got. Like this trial is going to get."

The silence came back then for a long moment.

"The key," Bosch finally said, "is ID'ing her, finding out how long she's been in the concrete. We'll know then what we've got."

"So what do we do?" Edgar said.

"I'll tell you what we do," Pounds said. "We don't say a damned thing about this to anyone. Not yet. Not until we are absolutely sure of what we've got. We wait on the autopsy and the ID. We find out how long this girl's been dead and what she was doing when she disappeared. We'll make — I'll make a call on which way we go after that.

"Meantime, say nothing. If this is misconstrued, it could be very damaging to the department. I see some of the media is already here, so I'll handle them. No one else is to talk. We clear?"

Bosch and Edgar nodded and Pounds went off, slowly moving through the debris toward a knot of reporters and cameramen who stood behind the yellow tape the uniforms had put up.

Bosch and Edgar stood silent for a few moments, watching him go.

"I hope he knows what the hell he is saying," Edgar said.

"Does inspire a lot of confidence, doesn't he?" Bosch replied.

"Oh, yeah."

Bosch walked back over to the trench and Edgar followed.

"What are you going to do about the impression she left in the concrete?"

"The jackhammers don't think it's movable. They said whoever mixed the concrete she was put in didn't follow the directions too well. Used too much water and small-grain sand. It's like plaster of paris. We try to lift the whole thing out in one piece it will crumble under its own weight."

"So?"

"Donovan's mixing plaster. He's going to make a mold of the face. On the hand — we only got the left, the right side crumbled when we dug in. Donovan's going to try using rubber silicone. He says it's the best chance of pulling out a mold with prints."

Bosch nodded. For a few moments he watched Pounds talking to the reporters and saw the first thing worth smiling about all day. Pounds was on camera but apparently none of the reporters had told him about the dirt smeared across his forehead. He lit a cigarette and turned his attention back to Edgar.

"So, this area here was all storage rooms for rent?" he asked.

"That's right. The owner of the property was here a little while ago. Said that all this area back in here was partitioned storage. Individual rooms. The

Dollmaker — er, the killer, whoever the fuck it was — could've had one of the rooms and had his privacy to do what he wanted. The only problem would be the noise he made breaking up the original flooring. But it could've been night work. Owner said most people didn't come back into the storage area at night. People who rented the rooms got a key to an exterior door off the alley. The perp could've come in and done the whole job in one night."

The next question was obvious, so Edgar answered before Bosch asked.

"The owner can't give us the name of the renter. Not for sure, at least. The records went up in the fire. His insurance company made settlements with most people that filed claims and we'll get those names. But he said there were a few who never made a claim after the riots. He just never heard from them again. He can't remember all the names, but if one was our guy then it was probably an alias anyway. Leastwise, if I was going to rent a room and dig through the floor to bury a body, you wouldn't find me giving no real name."

Bosch nodded and looked at his watch. He had to get going soon. He realized that he was hungry but probably wouldn't get the chance to eat. Bosch looked down at the excavation and noticed the delineation of color between the old and newer concrete. The old slab was almost white. The concrete the woman had been encased in was a dark gray. He noticed a small piece of red paper protruding from a gray chunk at the bottom of the trench. He dropped down into the excavation and picked the chunk up. It was about the size of a softball. He pounded it on the old slab until it broke apart in his hand. The paper was part of a crumpled and empty Marlboro cigarette package. Edgar pulled a plastic evidence bag from his suit pocket and held it open for Bosch to drop the discovery in.

"It's got to've been put in with the body," he said. "Good catch."

Bosch climbed out of the trench and looked at his watch again. It was time to go.

"Let me know if you get the ID," he said to Edgar.

He dumped his jumpsuit back in the trunk and lit a fresh cigarette. He stood next to his Caprice and watched Pounds, who was wrapping up his skillfully planned impromptu press conference. Harry could tell by the cameras and the expensive clothes that most of the reporters were from TV. He saw Bremmer, the *Times* guy, standing at the edge of the pack. Bosch hadn't seen him in a while and noticed he had put on weight and a beard. Bosch knew that Bremmer was standing on the periphery of the circle waiting for the TV questions to end so he could hit Pounds with something solid that would take some thought to answer.

Bosch smoked and waited for five minutes before Pounds was done. He was risking being late for court but he wanted to see the note. When Pounds was finally done with the reporters he signaled Bosch to follow him to his car. Bosch got in the passenger side and Pounds handed him a photocopy.

Harry studied the note for a long time. It was written in the recognizable printed scrawl. The analyst in Suspicious Documents had called the printing

Philadelphia block style and had concluded that its right-to-left slant was the result of its being the work of an untrained hand; possibly a left-handed person printing with his right hand.

Newspaper says the trial's just begun
A verdict to return on the Dollmaker's run
A bullet from Bosch fired straight and true
But the dolls should know me work's not through

On Western is the spot where my heart doth sings
When I think o the dolly laid beneath at Bing's
Too bad, good Bosch, a bullet of bad aim
Years gone past, and I'm still in the game

Bosch knew style could be copied but something about the poem ground into him. It was like the others. The same bad schoolboy rhymes, the same semiliterate attempt at high-flown language. He felt confusion and a tugging in his chest.

It's him, he thought. It's him.

3

"Ladies and gentlemen," U.S. District Judge Alva Keyes intoned as he eyed the jury, "we begin the trial with what we call opening statements by the attorneys. Mind you, these are not to be construed by you as evidence. These are more or less blueprints — road maps, if you will, of the route each attorney wants to take with his or her case. You do not consider them evidence. They may make some highfalutin allegations, but just because they say it doesn't make it true. After all, they're lawyers."

This brought a polite titter of laughter from the jury and the rest of courtroom 4. With his southern accent, it sounded as if the judge had said lie-yers, which added to the glee. Even Money Chandler smiled. Bosch looked around from his seat at the defense table and saw that the public seats in the huge wood-paneled courtroom with twenty-foot ceilings were about half full. In the front row on the plaintiff's side were eight people who were Norman Church's family members and friends, not counting his widow, who sat up at the plaintiff's table with Chandler.

There were also about a half dozen courthouse hangers-on, old men with nothing better to do but watch the drama in other people's lives. Plus an assortment of law clerks and students who probably wanted to watch the great Honey Chandler do her thing, and a group of reporters with their pens poised over their pads. Openers always made a story — because, as the judge had said, the lawyers could say anything they wanted. After today, Bosch knew, the reporters would drop in from time to time but there probably wouldn't be many other stories until closing statements and a verdict.

Unless something unusual happened.

Bosch looked directly behind him. There was nobody in the benches back there. He knew Sylvia Moore would not be there. They had agreed on that before. He didn't want her seeing this. He had told her it was just a formality, part of the cop's burden to be sued for doing his job. He knew the real reason he didn't want her here was because he had no control over this situation. He had to sit there at the defense table and let people take their best shots. Anything could come up and probably would. He didn't want her watching that.

He wondered now if the jury would see the empty seats behind him in the spectators gallery and think that maybe he was guilty because no one had come to show support.

When the murmur of laughter died down he looked back at the judge. Judge Keyes was impressive up there on the bench. He was a big man who wore the black robe well, his thick forearms and big hands folded in front of his barrel chest, giving a sense of reserved power. His balding and sun-reddened head was large and seemed perfectly round, trimmed around the edges with gray hair and suggesting the organized storage of a massive amount of legal knowledge and perspective. He was a transplanted southerner who had specialized in civil rights cases as a lawyer and had made a name for himself by suing the LAPD for its disproportionate number of cases in which black citizens died after being put in chokeholds by officers. He had been appointed to the federal bench by President Jimmy Carter, right before he was sent back to Georgia. Judge Keyes had been ruling the roost in courtroom 4 ever since.

Bosch's lawyer, deputy city attorney Rod Belk, had fought like hell during pretrial stages to have the judge disqualified on procedural ground and to get another judge assigned to the case. Preferably a judge without a background as a guardian of civil rights. But he had failed.

However, Bosch was not as upset by this as Belk. He realized that Judge Keyes was cut from the same legal cloth as plaintiff's attorney Honey Chandler — suspicious of police, even hateful at times — but Bosch sensed that beyond that he was ultimately a fair man. And that's all Bosch thought he needed to come out okay. A fair shot at the system. After all, he knew in his heart his actions at the apartment in Silverlake were correct. He had done the right thing.

"It will be up to you," the judge was saying to the jury, "to decide if what the lawyers say is proven during trial. Remember that. Now, Ms. Chandler, you go first."

Honey Chandler nodded at him and stood up. She moved to the lectern that stood between the plaintiff's and the defense tables. Judge Keyes had set the strict guidelines earlier. In his courtroom, there was no moving about, no approaching the witness stand or jury box by lawyers. Anything said out loud by a lawyer was said from the lectern between the tables. Knowing the judge's strict demand for compliance to his guidelines, Chandler even asked his permission before turning the heavy mahogany altar at an angle so she would face the jury while speaking. The judge sternly nodded his approval.

"Good afternoon," she began. "The judge is quite right when he tells you that this statement is nothing more than a road map."

Good strategy, Bosch thought from the cellar of cynicism from which he viewed this whole case. Pander to the judge with your first sentence. He watched Chandler as she referred to the yellow legal pad she had put down on the lectern. Bosch noticed that over the top button of her blouse was a large pin with a round black onyx stone set in it. It was flat and as dead as a shark's eye. She had her hair pulled severely back and braided in a no-nonsense style behind her head. But one tress of hair had come loose and it helped affect the image of a woman not preoccupied with her looks but totally focused on the law, on the case, on the heinous miscarriage of justice perpetrated by the defendant. Bosch believed she probably pulled the hair loose on purpose.

As he watched her start, Bosch remembered the thud he had felt in his chest when he heard she was the lawyer for Church's wife. To him, it was far more disturbing than learning Judge Keyes had been assigned the trial. She was that good. That was why they called her Money.

"I would like to take you down the road a piece," Chandler said and Bosch wondered if she was even developing a southern accent now. "I just want to highlight what our case is about and what we believe the evidence will prove. It is a civil rights case. It involves the fatal shooting of a man named Norman Church at the hands of the police."

She paused here. Not to look at her yellow pad but for effect, to gather all attention to what she would say next. Bosch looked over at the jury. Five women and seven men. Three blacks, three Latinos, one Asian and five whites. They were looking at Chandler with rapt attention.

"This case," Chandler said, "is about a police officer who wasn't satisfied with his job and the vast powers it gave him. This officer also wanted your job. And he wanted Judge Keyes's job. And he wanted the state's job of administering the verdicts and sentences set down by judges and juries. He wanted it all. This case is about Detective Harry Bosch, who you see sitting at the defendant's table."

She pointed at Bosch while drawing out the word dee-fend-ant. Belk immediately stood up and objected.

"Miss Chandler does not need to point my client out to the jury or make sarcastic vocalizations. Yes, we are at the defense table. That's because this is a civil case and in this country anybody can sue anybody, even the family of a —"

"Objection, Your Honor," Chandler shouted. "He is using his objection to further try to destroy the reputation of Mr. Church, who was never convicted of anything because —"

"Enough!" Judge Keyes thundered. "Objection sustained. Ms. Chandler, we don't need to point. We all know who we are. We also do not need inflammatory accent being placed on any words. Words are beautiful and ugly, all on their own. Let them stand for themselves. As for Mr. Belk, I find it acutely annoying when opposing counsel interrupts opening statements or closing arguments. You will have your turn, sir. I would suggest that you not object during Ms. Chandler's statement unless an egregious trespass on your client has occurred. I do not consider pointing at him worth the objection."

"Thank you, Your Honor," Belk and Chandler said in unison.

"Proceed, Ms. Chandler. As I said in chambers this morning, I want opening statements done by the end of the day and I have another matter at four."

"Thank you, Your Honor," she said again. Then, turning back to the jury, she said, "Ladies and gentlemen, we all need our police. We all look up to our police. Most of them — the vast majority of them — do a thankless job and do it well. The police department is an indispensable part of our society. What would we do if we could not count on police officers to serve and protect us? But that is not what this trial is about. I want you to remember that as the trial progresses. This is about what we would do if one member of that police force broke away from the rules and regulations, the policies that govern that police force. What we are talking about is called a rogue cop. And the evidence will show that Harry Bosch is a rogue cop, a man who one night four years ago decided to be judge, jury and executioner. He shot a man that he thought was a killer. A heinous serial killer, yes, but at the moment the defendant chose to pull out his gun and fire on Mr. Norman Church there was no legal evidence of that.

"Now, you are going to hear from the defense all manner of supposed evidence that police said they found that connected Mr. Church to these killings, but remember during the trial where this evidence came from — the police themselves — and when it was found — after Mr. Church had been executed. I think we will show that this supposed evidence is questionable at best. Tainted, at best. And, in effect, you will have to decide if Mr. Church, a married man with two young children and a well-paying job at an aircraft factory, was indeed this killer, the so-called Dollmaker, or simply was made the fall guy, the scapegoat, by a police department covering up the sin of one of its own. The brutal, unwarranted and unnecessary execution of an unarmed man."

She continued on, speaking at length about the code of silence known to exist in the department, the force's long history of brutality, the Rodney King beating and the riots. Somehow, according to Honey Chandler, these were all black flowers on a plant grown from a seed that was Harry Bosch's killing of Norman Church. Bosch heard her go on but wasn't really listening anymore. He kept his eyes open and occasionally made eye contact with a juror, but he was off on his own. This was his own defense. The lawyers, the jurors and the judge were going to take a week, maybe longer, to dissect what he had thought and done in less than five seconds. To be able to sit in the courtroom for this he was going to have to be able to go off on his own.

In his private reverie he thought of Church's face. At the end, in the apartment over the garage on Hyperion Street. They had locked eyes. The eyes Bosch had seen were killer's eyes, as dark as the stone at Chandler's throat.

". . . even if he was reaching for a gun, would that matter?" Chandler was saying. "A man had kicked the door open. A man with a gun. Who could blame someone for reaching, according to police, for a weapon for protection. The fact that he was reaching for something seemingly as laughable as a hairpiece makes this episode all the more repugnant. He was killed in cold blood. Our society cannot accept that."

Bosch tuned her out again and thought of the new victim, entombed for what was likely years in a concrete floor. He wondered if a missing-person report was ever taken, if there was a mother or father or husband or child wondering all this time about her. After returning from the scene he had started to tell Belk about the discovery. He asked the lawyer to ask Judge Keyes for a continuance, to delay the trial until the new death could be sorted out. But Belk had cut him off, telling him that the less he knew the better. Belk seemed so frightened of the implications of the new discovery that he determined that the best tack was to do the opposite of what Bosch suggested. He wanted to hurry the trial through before news of the discovery and its possible connection to the Dollmaker became public.

Chandler was now near the end of the one-hour allotment for her opener. She had gone on at length about the police department's shooting policy and Bosch thought she might have lost the grip she had on the jury in the beginning. For a while she had even lost Belk, who sat next to Bosch paging through his own yellow pad and rehearsing his opener in his head.

Belk was a large man — almost eighty pounds overweight, Bosch guessed — and prone to sweating, even in the overly cooled courtroom. Bosch had often wondered during the jury selection if the sweating was Belk's response to the burden of weight he carried or the burden of trying a case against Chandler and before Judge Keyes. Belk couldn't be over thirty, Bosch guessed. Maybe five years max out of a middle-range law school and in over his head going up against Chandler.

The word "justice" brought Bosch's attention back. He knew that Chandler had turned it up a notch and was coming down the backstretch when she started using the word in almost every sentence. In civil court, justice and money were interchangeable because they meant the same thing.

"Justice for Norman Church was fleeting. It lasted all of a few seconds. Justice was the time it took Detective Bosch to kick open the door, point his satin-finished 9mm Smith & Wesson and pull the trigger. Justice was one shot. The bullet Detective Bosch chose to execute Mr. Church with was called an XTP. That is short for extreme terminal performance. It's a bullet that expands to 1.5 times its width on impact and takes out huge portions of tissue and organ in its path. It took out Mr. Church's heart. That was justice."

Bosch noticed that many of the jurors were not looking at Chandler but at the plaintiff's table. By leaning forward slightly he could see past the lectern and saw that the widow, Deborah Church, was dabbing tears on her cheeks with a tissue. She was a bell-shaped woman with short dark hair and small pale blue eyes. She had been the epitome of the suburban housewife and mother until the morning Bosch killed her husband and the cops showed up at her house with their search warrant and the reporters showed up with their questions. Bosch had actually felt sorry for her, even counted her as a victim, until she hired Money Chandler and started calling him a murderer.

"The evidence will show, ladies and gentlemen, that Detective Bosch is a product of his department," Chandler said. "A callous, arrogant machine that dispensed justice as he saw it on his own. You will be asked if this is what you want from your police department. You will be asked to right a wrong, to provide justice for a family whose father and husband was taken.

"In closing, I would like to quote to you from a German philosopher named Friedrich Nietzsche, who wrote something a century ago that I think is germane to what we are doing today. He said, 'Whoever fights monsters should see to it that in the process he does not become a monster. And when you look into the abyss, the abyss also looks into you. . . .'

"Ladies and gentlemen, that is what this case is about. Detective Harry Bosch has not only looked into the abyss, but on the night Norman Church was murdered it looked into him. The darkness engulfed him and Detective Bosch fell. He became that which he served to fight. A monster. I think you will find that the evidence will lead you to no other conclusion. Thank you."

Chandler sat down and patted her hand in a "there, there" gesture on Deborah Church's arm. Bosch, of course, knew this was done for the jury's sake, not the widow's.

The judge looked up at the brass hands of the clock built into the mahogany paneling above the courtroom door and declared a fifteen-minute recess before Belk would take the lectern. As he stood for the jury, Bosch noticed one of Church's daughters staring at him from the front row of the spectators section. He guessed she was about thirteen. The older one, Nancy. He quickly looked away and then felt guilty. He wondered if anyone in the jury saw this.

Belk said he needed the break time alone to go over his statement to the jury. Bosch felt like going up to the snack bar on the sixth floor because he still had not eaten, but it was likely a few of the jurors would go there, or worse yet, members of Church's family. Instead, he took the escalator down to the lobby and went out to the ash can in front of the building. He lit a cigarette and leaned back against the base of the statue. He realized that he was clammy with sweat beneath his suit. Chandler's hour-long opener had seemed like an eternity — an eternity with the eyes of the world on him. He knew the suit wouldn't last the week and he would have to make sure his other one was clean. Thinking about such minor details finally helped relax him.

He had already put one butt out in the sand and was on his second smoke when the steel-and-glass door to the courthouse opened. Honey Chandler had used her back to push open the heavy door and therefore hadn't seen him. She turned as she came through the door, her head bent down as she lit a cigarette with a gold lighter. As she straightened and exhaled she saw him. She walked toward the ash can, ready to bury the fresh cigarette.

"It's okay," Bosch said. "It's the only one around as far as I know."

"It is, but I don't think it does either of us good to have to face each other outside of court."

He shrugged and didn't say anything. It was her move, she could leave if she wanted to. She took another drag on the cigarette.

"Just a half. I have to get back in anyway."

He nodded and looked out toward Spring Street. In front of the county courthouse he saw a line of people waiting to go in through the metal detectors. More boat people, he thought. He saw the homeless man coming up the pavement to make his afternoon check of the ash can. The man suddenly turned around and walked back out to Spring and away. He looked back once uneasily over his shoulder as he went.

"He knows me."

Bosch looked back at Chandler.

"He knows you?"

"He used to be a lawyer. I knew him then. Tom something-or-other. I can't remember at the — Faraday, that's it. I guess he didn't want me to see him that way. But everybody around here knows about him. He's the reminder of what can happen when things go terribly wrong."

"What happened?"

"It's a long story. Maybe your lawyer will tell you. Can I ask you something?"

Bosch didn't answer.

"Why didn't the city settle this case? Rodney King, the riots. It's the worst time in the world to take a police case to trial. I don't think Bulk — that's what I call him, because I know he calls me Money. I don't think he's got a hold on this one. And you'll be the one hung out to dry."

Bosch thought a moment before answering.

"It's off the record, Detective Bosch," she said. "I'm just making conversation."

"I told him not to settle. I told him if he wanted to settle, I'd go out and pay for my own lawyer."

"That sure of yourself, huh?" She paused to inhale on her cigarette. "Well, we'll see, I guess."

"I guess."

"You know it's nothing personal."

He knew she would get around to saying that. The biggest lie in the game. "Maybe not for you."

"Oh, it is for you? You shoot an unarmed man and then you take it personally when his wife objects, when she sues you?"

"Your client's husband used to cut the strap off the purses of his victims, tie it in a slipknot around their neck and then slowly but steadily strangle them while he was raping them. He preferred leather straps. He didn't seem to care about what women he did this to. Just the leather."

She didn't even flinch. He hadn't expected her to.

"That's *late* husband. My client's late husband. And the only thing that is for sure in this case, that is provable, is that you killed him."

"Yeah, and I'd do it again."

"I know, Detective Bosch. That's why we're here."

She pursed her lips in a frozen kiss which sharply set the line of her jaw. Her hair caught the glint of the afternoon sun. She angrily stubbed her cigarette out in the sand and then went back inside. She swung the door open as if it were made of balsa wood.

4

Bosch pulled into the rear parking lot of the Hollywood station on Wilcox shortly before four. Belk had used only ten minutes of his allotted hour for his opening statement and Judge Keyes had recessed early, saying he wanted to start testimony on a separate day from openers so the jury would not confuse evidentiary testimony with the lawyers' words.

Bosch had felt uneasy with Belk's short discourse in front of the jurors but Belk had told him there was nothing to worry about. He walked in through the back door near the tank and took the rear hallway to the detective bureau. By four the bureau is usually deserted. It was that way when Bosch walked in, except for Jerry Edgar, who was parked in front of one of the IBMs typing on a form Bosch recognized as a 51 — an Investigating Officer's Chronological Record. He looked up and saw Bosch approaching.

"Whereyat, Harry?"

"Right here."

"Got done early, I see. Don't tell me, directed verdict. The judge threw Money Chandler out on her ass."

"I wish."

"Yeah, I know."

"What do you have so far?"

Edgar said there was nothing so far. No identification yet. Bosch sat down at his desk and loosened his tie. Pounds's office was dark so it was safe to light a cigarette. His mind trailed off into thinking about the trial and Money Chandler. She had captured the jury for most of her argument. She had, in effect, called Bosch a murderer, hitting with a gut-level, emotional charge. Belk had responded with a dissertation on the law and a police officer's right to use deadly force when danger was near. Even if it turned out there was no danger, no gun beneath the pillow, Belk said, Church's own actions created the climate of danger that allowed Bosch to act as he did.

Finally, Belk had countered Chandler's Nietzsche by quoting *The Art of War* by Sun Tzu. Belk said Bosch had entered the "Dying Ground" when he kicked Church's apartment door open. At that point he had to fight or perish, shoot or be shot. Second-guessing his actions afterward was unjust.

Sitting across from Edgar now, Bosch acknowledged to himself that it hadn't worked. Belk had been boring while Chandler had been interesting, and convincing. They were starting in the hole. He noticed Edgar had stopped talking and Harry had not registered anything he had said.

"What about prints?" he asked.

"Harry, you listening to me? I just said we finished with the rubber silicone about an hour ago. Donovan got prints off the hand. He said they look good, came up in the rubber pretty well. He'll start the DOJ run tonight and probably by morning we'll have the similars. It will probably take him the rest of the morning to go through them. But, at least, they're not letting this one drown in the backup. Pounds gave it a priority status."

"Good, let me know what comes out. I'll be in and out all week, I guess."

"Harry, don't worry, I'll let you know what we've got. But try to stay cool. Look, you got the right guy? You got any doubt about that?"

"Not before today."

"Then don't worry. Might is right. Money Chandler can blow the judge and the whole jury, it's not going to change that."

"Right is might."

"What?"

"Nothing."

Bosch thought about what Edgar had said about Chandler. It was interesting how often a threat from a woman, even a professional woman, was reduced by cops to a sexual threat. He believed that most cops might be like Edgar, thinking there was something about Chandler's sexuality that gave her an edge. They would not admit that she was damn good at her job, whereas the fat city attorney defending Bosch wasn't.

Bosch stood up and went back to the file cabinets. He unlocked one of his drawers and dug into the back to pull out two of the blue binders that were called murder books. Both were heavy, about three inches thick. On the spine of the first it said BIOS. The other was labeled DOCS. They were from the Dollmaker case.

"Who's testifying tomorrow?" Edgar called from across the squad room.

"I don't know the order. The judge wouldn't make her say. But she's got me subpoenaed, also Lloyd and Irving. She's got Amado, the ME coordinator, and even Bremmer. They all gotta show up and then she'll say which ones she'll put on tomorrow and which ones later."

"The *Times* isn't going to let Bremmer testify. They always fight that shit."

"Yeah, but he isn't subpoenaed as a *Times* reporter. He wrote that book about the case. So she served paper on him as the author. Judge Keyes already ruled he doesn't have the same reporter's-shield rights. *Times* lawyers may show up to argue but the judge already made the ruling. Bremmer testifies."

"See what I mean, she's probably already been back in chambers with that old guy. Anyway, it's no matter, Bremmer can't hurt you. That book made you out like the hero who saved the day."

"I guess."

"Harry, come here and take a look at this."

Edgar got up from his typing station and went over to the file cabinets. He gingerly slid a cardboard box off the top and put it down on the homicide table. It was about the size of a hatbox.

"Gotta be careful. Donovan says it should set overnight."

He lifted off the top of the box and there was a woman's face set in white plaster. The face was turned slightly so that its right side was fully sculpted in the plaster. Most of the lower left side, the jawline, was missing. The eyes were closed, the mouth slightly open and irregular. The hairline was almost unnoticeable. The face seemed swollen by the right eye. It was like a classical frieze Bosch had seen in a cemetery or a museum somewhere. But it wasn't beautiful. It was a death mask.

"Looks like the guy popped her on the eye. It swelled up."

Bosch nodded but didn't speak. There was something unnerving about looking at the face in the box, more so than looking at an actual dead body. He didn't know why. Edgar finally put the top back on the box and carefully put it back on top of the file cabinet.

"What are you going to do with it?"

"Not sure. If we don't get anything from the prints it might be our only way of getting an ID. There's an anthropologist at Cal State Northridge that contracts with the coroner to make facial recreations. Usually, he's working from a skeleton, a skull. I'll take this to him and see if he can maybe finish the face, put a blonde wig on it or something. He can paint the plaster, too, give it a skin color. I don't know, it's probably just pissing in the wind but I figure it's worth a try."

Edgar returned to the typewriter and Bosch sat down in front of the murder books. He opened the binder marked BIOS but then sat there and watched Edgar for a few moments. He did not know whether he should admire Edgar's hustle on the case or not. They had been partners once and Bosch had essentially spent a year training him to be a homicide investigator. But he was never sure how much of it took. Edgar was always going off to look at real estate, taking two-hour lunches to go to closings. He never seemed to understand that the homicide squad wasn't a job. It was a mission. As surely as murder was an art for some who committed it, homicide investigation was an art for those on the mission. And it chose you, you didn't choose it.

With that in mind it was hard for Bosch to accept that Edgar was busting ass on the case for the right reasons.

"What're you looking at?" Edgar asked without looking up from the IBM or stopping his typing.

"Nothing. I was just thinking about stuff."

"Harry, don't worry. It's going to work out."

Bosch dumped his cigarette butt in a Styrofoam cup of dead coffee and lit another.

"Did the priority Pounds put on the case open up the OT?"

"Absolutely," Edgar said, smiling. "You're looking at a man who has his head fully in the overtime trough."

At least he was honest about it, Bosch thought. Content that his original take on Edgar was still intact, Bosch went back to the murder book and ran his fingers along the edge of the thick sheaf of reports on its three rings. There were eleven divider tabs, each marked with a name of one of the Dollmaker's victims. He began leafing from section to section, looking at the crime scene photographs from each killing and the biographical data of each victim.

The women had all come from similar backgrounds; street prostitutes, the higher-class escort outfits, strippers, porno actresses who did outcall work on the side. The Dollmaker had moved comfortably along the underside of the city. He had found his victims with the same ease that they had gone into the darkness with him. There was a pattern in that, Bosch remembered the task force's psychologist had said.

But looking at the frozen faces of death in the photographs, Bosch remembered that the task force had never gotten a fix on common physical aspects of the victims. There were blondes and brunettes. Heavy-set women and frail drug addicts. There were six white women, two Latinas, two Asians and a black woman. No pattern. The Dollmaker had been indiscriminate in that respect, his only identifiable pattern being that he sought only women on the edge — that place where choices are limited and they go easily with a stranger. The psychologist had said each of the women was like an injured fish, sending off an invisible signal that inevitably drew the shark.

"She was white, right?" he asked Edgar.

Edgar stopped typing.

"Yeah, that's what the coroner said."

"They already did the cut? Who?"

"No, the autopsy's tomorrow or the next day but Corazón took a look when we brought it in. She guessed that the stiff had been white. Why?"

"Nothing. Blonde?"

"Yeah, at least when she died. Bleached. If you're going to ask if I checked missing persons on a white blonde chick who went into the wind four years ago, fuck you, Harry. I can use the OT but that description wouldn't narrow it down to but three, four hundred. I ain't going to wade into that when I'll probably pull a name on the prints tomorrow. Waste of time."

"Yeah, I know. I just wish . . ."

"You just wish you had some answers. We all do. But things take time sometimes, my man."

Edgar started typing again and Harry looked down into the binder. But he couldn't help but think about the face in the box. No name, no occupation. They knew nothing about her. But something about the plaster cast told him she had somehow fit into the Dollmaker's pattern. There was a hardness there that had nothing to do with the plaster. She had come from the edge.

"Anything else found in the concrete after I left?"

Edgar stopped typing, exhaled loudly and shook his head.

"How do you mean, like the cigarette package?"

"With the other ones the Dollmaker left their purses. He'd cut the straps off to strangle them, but when he dumped the bodies we always found the purses and clothes nearby. Only thing missing was their makeup. He always kept their makeup."

"Not this time — at least in the concrete. Pounds left a uniform on the site while they finished tearing it up. Nothing else was found. That stuff might've been stashed in the storage room and got burned up or looted. Harry, what're you thinking, copycat?"

"I guess."

"Yeah, me too."

Bosch nodded and told Edgar he was sorry he kept interrupting. He went back to studying the reports. After a few minutes Edgar rolled the form out of the typewriter and brought it back to the homicide table. He snapped it into a new binder with the thin stack of paperwork from the day's case and put it into a file cabinet behind his chair. He then went through his daily ritual of calling his wife while straightening up the blotter, the message spike and the message pad at his place. He told her he had to make a quick stop on his way home. Listening to the conversation made Bosch think of Sylvia Moore and some of the domestic rituals that had become ingrained for them.

"I'm outta here, Harry," Edgar said after hanging up.

Bosch nodded.

"So how come you're hanging around?"

"I don't know. I'm just reading through this stuff so I'll know what I'm saying when I testify."

That was a lie. He didn't need the murder books to refresh his memory of the Dollmaker.

"I hope you tear Money Chandler up."

"She'll probably rip me. She's good."

"Well, I gotta hit it. I'll see you."

"Hey, remember, if you get a name tomorrow, give me a beep or something."

After Edgar was gone Bosch looked at his watch — it was five — and turned on the TV that sat on top of the file cabinet next to the box with the face in it. While he was waiting for the story on the body he picked up his phone and dialed Sylvia's house.

"I'm not going to make it out there tonight."

"Harry, what's wrong? How did the opening statements go?"

"It's not the trial. It's another case. A body was found today, looks a lot like the Dollmaker did it. We got a note at the station. Basically said I killed the wrong guy. That the Dollmaker, the real one, is still out there."

"Can it be true?"

"I don't know. There had been no doubt before today."

"How could —"

"Wait a minute, the story's on the news. Channel 2."

"I'll put it on."

They watched on separate TVs but connected by phone as the story was reported on the early news show. The anchor reported nothing about the Dollmaker. There was an aerial shot of the scene and then a sound bite of Pounds saying that little was known, that an anonymous tip had led police to the body. Harry and Sylvia both laughed when they saw Pounds's char-smeared forehead. It felt good to Bosch to laugh. After the report Sylvia turned serious.

"So, he didn't tell the media."

"Well, we have to make sure. We have to figure out what's going on first. It was either him or a copycat . . . or maybe he had a partner we didn't know about."

"When will you know which direction to go?"

It was a nice way of asking when he'd know if he had killed an innocent man.

"I don't know, probably tomorrow. Autopsy will tell us some things. But the ID will tell us when she died."

"Harry, it wasn't the Dollmaker. Don't you worry."

"Thanks, Sylvia."

Her unequivocal loyalty was beautiful, he thought. He then immediately felt guilty because he had never been totally open with her about all the things that concerned them. He had been the one who held back.

"You still haven't said how it went in court today or why you aren't coming out here like you said you would."

"It's this new case they found today. I am involved . . . and I want to do some thinking on it."

"You can think anywhere, Harry."

"You know what I mean."

"Yes, I do. And court?"

"It went fine, I guess. We only had openers. Testimony starts tomorrow. But this new case . . . It's sort of hanging over everything."

He switched the channels as he spoke but he had missed reports on the new body discovery on the other channels.

"Well, what's your lawyer say about it?"

"Nothing. He doesn't want to know about it."

"What a shit."

"He just wants to get through the case quickly, hope that if the Dollmaker or a partner is still running around out there, that we don't confirm it until the trial is over."

"But, Harry, that is unethical. Even if it is evidence in the plaintiff's favor, doesn't he have to bring it forward?"

"Yes, if he knows about it. That's just it. He doesn't want to know about it. That makes him safe."

"When will it be your turn to testify? I want to be there. I can take a personal day and be there."

"No. Don't worry. It's all a formality. I don't want you to know any more about this story than you do already."

"Why? It's your story."

"No it's not. It's his."

He hung up after telling her he'd call her the next day. Afterward, he looked at the phone on the table in front of him for a long time. He and Sylvia Moore had been spending three or four nights a week together for nearly a year. Though Sylvia had been the one who spoke of changing the arrangement and even had her house for sale, Bosch had never wanted to touch the question for fear that it might disturb the fragile balance and comfort he felt with her.

He wondered now if he was doing just that, disturbing the balance. He had lied to her. He was involved in the new case to some degree, but he was done for the day and was going home. He had lied because he felt the need to be alone. With his thoughts. With the Dollmaker.

He flipped through the second binder to the back where there were clear plastic Ziploc pouches for holding documentary evidence. In these were copies of the Dollmaker's previous letters. There were three of them. The killer had begun sending them after the media firestorm started and he had been christened with the name Dollmaker. One had gone to Bosch, prior to the eleventh killing — the last. The other two had gone to Bremmer at the *Times* after the seventh and eleventh killings. Harry now studied the photocopy of the envelope that was addressed to him in a printed script of block letters. Then he looked at the poem on the folded page. It also had been printed in the same oddly slanted block script. He read the words he already knew by heart.

> *I feel compelled to forewarn and forsake.*
> *T'night I'm out for a snack — my lust partake.*
> *Another doll for the shelf, as it were't.*
> *She breathes her last — just as I squirt.*

> *A little late mommy and daddy weeple*
> *A fine young miss 'neath my steeple.*
> *As I tight the purse strings 'fore preparing the wash.*
> *I hear the last gasp — a sound like Boschhhhh!*

Bosch closed the binders and put them in his briefcase. He turned off the TV and headed out to the back parking lot. He held the station door for two uniform cops who were wrestling with a handcuffed drunk. The drunk threw a kick out at him but Harry stepped outside of its reach.

He pointed the Caprice north and took Outpost Road up to Mulholland, which he then took to Woodrow Wilson. After pulling into the carport, he sat with his hands on the wheel for a long time. He thought about the letters and the signature the Dollmaker had left on each victim's body, the cross painted on the toenail. After Church was dead they figured out what it had meant. The cross had been the steeple. The steeple of a Church.

5

In the morning, Bosch sat on the rear deck of his house and watched the sun come up over the Cahuenga Pass. It burned away the morning fog and bathed the wildflowers on the hillside that had burned the winter before. He watched and smoked and drank coffee until the sound of traffic on the Hollywood Freeway became one uninterrupted hiss from the pass below.

He dressed in his dark blue suit with a white shirt that had a button-down collar. As he put on a maroon tie dotted with gold gladiator helmets in front of the bedroom mirror, he wondered about how he must appear to the jurors. He had noticed the day before that when he made eye contact with any of the twelve, they were always the first to look away. What did that mean? He would have liked to ask Belk what it meant but he did not like Belk and knew he would feel uncomfortable asking his opinion on anything.

Using the same hole poked through it before, he secured the tie in place with his silver tie tack that said "187" — the California penal code for murder. He used a plastic comb to put his brown-and-gray hair, still wet from the shower, in place and then combed his mustache. He put Visine drops in his eyes and then leaned close to the glass to study them. Red-rimmed from little sleep, the irises as dark as ice on asphalt. Why do they look away from me, he wondered again. He thought about how Chandler had described him the day before. And he knew why.

He was heading to the door, briefcase in hand, when it opened before he got there. Sylvia stepped in while pulling her key out of the lock.

"Hi," she said when she saw him. "I hoped I'd catch you."

She smiled. She was wearing khaki pants and a pink shirt with a button-down collar. He knew she did not wear dresses on Tuesday and Thursday because those were her assigned days as a schoolyard rover. Sometimes she had to run after students. Sometimes she had to break up fights. The sun coming through the porch door turned her dark blonde hair gold.

"Catch me at what?"

She came to him smiling still and they kissed.

"I know I'm making you late. I'm late, too. But I just wanted to come and say good luck today. Not that you need it."

He held on to her, smelling her hair. It had been nearly a year since they met, but Bosch still held to her sometimes with the fear that she might abruptly turn and leave, declare her attraction to him a mistake. Perhaps he was still a substitute for the husband she'd lost, a cop like Harry, a narcotics detective whose apparent suicide Bosch had investigated.

Their relationship had progressed to a point of complete comfortableness but in recent weeks he had felt a sense of inertia begin to set in. She had, too, and had even talked about it. She said the problem was he could not drop his guard completely and he knew this was true. Bosch had spent a lifetime alone, but not necessarily lonely. He had secrets, many of them buried too deep to give up to her. Not so soon.

"Thanks for coming by," he said, pulling back and looking down into her face to see the light still there. She had gotten a fleck of lipstick on one of her front teeth. "You be careful in the yard today, huh?"

"Yes." Then she frowned. "I know what you said, but I want to come and watch court — at least one day. I want to be there for you, Harry."

"You don't have to be there to be there. Know what I mean?"

She nodded but he knew his answer didn't satisfy her. They dropped it and small-talked for a few minutes more, making plans to get together that night for dinner. Bosch said he would come to her place in Bouquet Canyon. They kissed again and headed out, he to court and she to the high school, both places fraught with danger.

There was always an adrenaline rush at the start of each day as the courtroom fell silent and they waited for the judge to open his door and step up to the bench. It was 9:10 and still no sign of the judge, which was unusual because he had been a stickler for promptness during the week of jury selection. Bosch looked around and saw several reporters, maybe more than the day before. He found this curious since opening arguments were always such a draw.

Belk leaned toward Bosch and whispered, "Keyes is probably in there reading the *Times* story. Did you see it?"

Running late because of Sylvia, Bosch had had no time to read the paper. He'd left it on the mat at the front door.

"What'd it say?"

The paneled door opened and the judge came out before Belk could answer.

"Hold the jury, Miss Rivera," the judge said to his clerk. He dropped his girth into his padded chair, surveyed the courtroom and said, "Counsel, any matters for discussion before we bring the jury in? Ms. Chandler?"

"Yes, Your Honor," Chandler said as she walked to the lectern.

Today she had on the gray suit. She had been alternating among three suits since jury selection began. Belk had told Bosch that this was because she didn't want to give the jurors the idea that she was wealthy. He said women lawyers could lose women jurors over something like that.

"Your Honor, the plaintiff asks for sanctions against Detective Bosch and Mr. Belk."

She held up the folded Metro section of the *Times*. Bosch could see the story had caught the bottom right corner, same as the story the day before. The headline said CONCRETE BLONDE TIED TO DOLLMAKER. Belk stood but did not say anything, for once observing the judge's strict decorum of noninterruption.

"Sanctions for what, Ms. Chandler?" the judge asked.

"Your Honor, the discovery of this body yesterday has a tremendous evidentiary impact on this case. As an officer of the court, it was incumbent upon Mr. Belk to bring this information forward. Under Rule 11 of discovery, defendant's attorney must —"

"Your Honor," Belk interrupted, "I was not informed of this development until last night. My intention was to bring the matter forward this morning. She is —"

"Hold it right there, Mr. Belk. One at a time in my courtroom. Seems you need a daily reminder of that. Ms. Chandler, I read that story you are referring to and though Detective Bosch was mentioned because of this case, he was not quoted. And Mr. Belk has rather rudely pointed out that he knew nothing about this until after court yesterday. Frankly, I don't see a sanctionable offense here. Unless you've got a card you haven't played."

She did.

"Your Honor, Detective Bosch was well aware of this development, whether quoted or not. He was at the scene during yesterday's lunch break."

"Your Honor?" Belk tried timidly.

Judge Keyes turned but looked at Bosch, not Belk.

"That right, Detective Bosch, what she says?"

Bosch looked at Belk for a moment and then up at the judge. Fucking Belk, he thought. His lie had left Bosch holding the bag.

"I was there, Your Honor. When I got back here for the afternoon session, there was no time to tell Mr. Belk about the discovery. I told him after court last night. I didn't see the paper yet this morning and I don't know what it says, but nothing has been confirmed about this body in regard to the Dollmaker or anyone else. There isn't even an ID yet."

"Your Honor," Chandler said, "Detective Bosch has conveniently forgotten that we had a fifteen-minute break during the afternoon session. I should think that was ample time for the detective to fill in his attorney on such important information."

The judge looked at Bosch.

"I wanted to tell him during the break but Mr. Belk said he needed the time to prepare his opening statement."

The judge eyed him closely for several seconds without saying anything. Bosch could tell the judge knew he was pushing the edge of the envelope of truth. Judge Keyes seemed to be making some kind of decision.

"Well, Ms. Chandler," he finally said. "I don't rightly see the conspiracy that you do here. I'm going to let this go with a warning to all parties; withholding evidence is the most heinous crime you can commit in my courtroom. If you do it and I catch ya, you're gonna wish you never took the LSAT. Now, do we want to talk about this new development?"

"Your Honor," Belk said quickly. He moved to the lectern. "In light of this discovery less than twenty-four hours ago, I move for a continuance so that this situation can be thoroughly investigated so that it can be determined exactly what it means to this case."

Now he finally asks, Bosch thought. He knew there was no way he'd get a delay now.

"Uh, huh," Judge Keyes said. "What do you think about that, Ms. Chandler?"

"No delay, Your Honor. This family has waited four years for this trial. I think any further delay would be perpetuating the crime. Besides, who does Mr. Belk propose investigate this matter, Detective Bosch?"

"I am sure the defense counselor would be satisfied with the LAPD handling the investigation," the judge said.

"But I wouldn't."

"I know you wouldn't, Ms. Chandler, but that's not your concern. You said yourself yesterday that the wide majority of police in this city are good, competent people. You'll just have to live by your own words. . . . But I am going to deny the request for a continuation. We've started a trial and we're not going to stop. The police can and should investigate this matter and keep the court informed but I'm not going to stand by. This case will continue until such time that these events need to be addressed again. Anything else? I've got a jury waiting."

"What about the story in the newspaper?" Belk asked.

"What about it?"

"Your Honor, I'd like the jury to be polled to see if anyone read it. Also, they should be warned again not to read the papers or watch the TV news tonight. All of the channels will likely follow the *Times*."

"I instructed jurors yesterday not to read the paper or watch the news but I plan to poll them anyway about this very story. Let's see what they say and then, depending on what we hear, we can clear 'em out again if you want to talk about a mistrial."

"I don't want a mistrial," Chandler said. "That's what the defendant wants. That'll just delay this another two months. This family has already waited four years for justice. They —"

"Well, let's just see what the jury says. Sorry to interrupt, Ms. Chandler."

"Your Honor, may I be heard on sanctions?" Belk said.

"I don't think you need to be, Mr. Belk. I denied her motion for sanctions. What more's to be said?"

"I know that, Your Honor. I would like to ask for sanctions against Miss Chandler. She has defamed me by alleging this cover-up of the evidence and I —"

"Mr. Belk, sit down. I'll tell you both right now; quit with the extracurricular sparring because it doesn't get you anywhere with me. No sanctions either way. One last time, any other matters?"

"Yes, Your Honor," Chandler said.

She had one more card. From beneath her legal pad she pulled out a document and walked it up to the clerk, who handed it to the judge. Chandler then returned to the lectern.

"Your Honor, that is a subpoena I have prepared for the police department that I would like reflected in the record. I am asking that a copy of the note referred to in the *Times* article, the note written by the Dollmaker and received yesterday, be released to me as part of discovery."

Belk jumped to his feet.

"Hold on, Mr. Belk," the judge admonished. "Let her finish."

"Your Honor, it is evidence in this case. It should be turned over immediately."

Judge Keyes gave Belk the nod and the deputy city attorney lumbered to the lectern, Chandler having to back up to give him room.

"Your Honor, this note is in no way evidence in this case. It has not been verified as having come from anybody. However, it is evidence in a murder case unattached to this proceeding. And it is not the LAPD's practice to parade its evidence out in an open court while there is a suspect still at large. I ask that you deny her request."

Judge Keyes clasped his hands together and thought a moment.

"Tell you what, Mr. Belk. You get a copy of the note and bring it in here. I'll take a look and then decide if it will be entered in evidence. That's all. Ms. Rivera, call in the jury please, we're losing the morning."

After the jury was in the box and everybody in court sat down, Judge Keyes asked who had seen any news stories relating to the case. No one in the box raised a hand. Bosch knew that if any one of them had seen the story, they wouldn't admit to it anyway. To do so would be to invite certain dismissal from the jury — a ticket straight back to the jury assembly room where the minutes tick by like hours.

"Very well," the judge said. "Call your first witness, Ms. Chandler."

Terry Lloyd took the witness stand like a man who was as familiar with it as the recliner chair he got drunk in every night in front of the TV set. He even adjusted the microphone in front of him without any help from the clerk. Lloyd had a drinker's badge of a nose and unusually dark brown hair for a man of his age, which was pushing sixty. That was because it was obvious to everyone who looked at him, except maybe himself, that he wore a rug. Chandler went through some preliminary questions, establishing that he was a lieutenant in the LAPD's elite Robbery-Homicide Division.

"During a period beginning four and a half years ago were you placed in charge of a task force of detectives attempting to identify a serial killer?"

"Yes I was."

"Can you tell the jury how that came about and functioned?"

"It was put together after the same killer was identified as the perpetrator in five killings. We were unofficially known in the department as the Westside Strangler Task Force. After the media got wind of it, the killer became known as the Dollmaker — because he used the victims' own makeup to paint their faces like dolls. I had eighteen detectives assigned to the task force. We broke them up into two squads, A and B. Squad A worked a day shift, B took the nights. We investigated the killings as they occurred and followed the call-in leads. After it hit the media, we were getting maybe a hundred calls a week — people saying this guy or that guy was the Dollmaker. We had to check them all out."

"The task force, no matter what it was called, was not successful, is that correct?"

"No, ma'am, that is wrong. We were successful. We got the killer."

"And who was that?"

"Norman Church was the killer."

"Was he identified as such before or after he was killed?"

"After. He was good for all of them."

"And good for the department, too?"

"I don't follow."

"It was good for the department that you were able to connect him to the murders. Otherwise you'd —"

"Ask questions, Ms. Chandler," the judge interrupted.

"Sorry, Your Honor. Lieutenant Lloyd, the man you say was the killer, Norman Church, was not killed himself until there were at least six more murders following the establishment of the task force, is that correct?"

"Correct."

"Allowing at least six more women to be strangled. How is that considered successful by the department?"

"We didn't allow anything. We did the best we could to track down this perpetrator. We eventually did. That made us successful. Very successful, in my book."

"In your book. Tell me, Lieutenant Lloyd, had the name Norman Church come up at any time in the investigation before the night he was shot to death while unarmed by Detective Bosch? Any reference at all?"

"No, it hadn't. But we connected —"

"Just answer the question I ask, Lieutenant. Thank you."

Chandler referred to her yellow pad on the lectern. Bosch noticed that Belk was alternately taking notes on one pad in front of him and writing down questions on another.

"Okay, Lieutenant," Chandler said, "your task force did not catch up with a supposed perpetrator, as you call it, until six deaths after you started. Would it be fair to say you and your detectives were under severe pressure to catch him, to close this case?"

"We were under pressure, yes."

"From who? Who was pressuring you, Lieutenant Lloyd?"

"Well, we had the papers, TV. The department was on me."

"How so? The department, I mean. Did you have meetings with your supervisors?"

"I had daily meetings with the RHD captain and weeklies — every Monday — with the police chief."

"What did they tell you about solving the case?"

"They said get the thing solved. People were dying. I didn't need to be told that but they did anyway."

"And did you communicate that to the task force detectives?"

"Of course. But they didn't need to be told it either. These guys were looking at the bodies every time one showed up. It was hard. They wanted this guy bad. They didn't need to read it in the papers or hear it from the chief or even me, for that matter."

Lloyd seemed to be getting off on his cop-as-a-lonely-hunter tangent. Bosch could see that he didn't realize he had walked into Chandler's trap. She was going to argue at the end of the trial that Bosch and the cops were under such pressure to find a killer that Bosch killed Church and then they fabricated his ties to the killings. The fall-guy theory. Harry wished he could call time out and tell Lloyd to shut the hell up.

"So everyone on the task force knew there was pressure to find a killer?"

"Not a killer. *The* killer. Yes, there was pressure. It's part of the job."

"What was Detective Bosch's role on the task force?"

"He was my B squad supervisor. He worked the night shift. He was a detective third grade so he kind of ran things when I wasn't there, which was often. Primarily, I was a floater but I usually worked the day shift with squad A."

"Do you recall saying to Detective Bosch, 'We've gotta get this guy,' words to that effect?"

"Not specifically. But I said words to that effect at squad meetings. He was there. But that was our goal, nothing wrong with that. We had to get this guy. Same situation, I'd say it again."

Bosch began to feel that Lloyd was paying him back for having stolen the show, closing the case without him. His answers no longer appeared to be grounded in congenial stupidity but in malice. Bosch bent close to Belk and whispered, "He's fucking me because he didn't get to shoot Church himself."

Belk put his finger to his lips, signaling Harry to be quiet. He then went back to writing on one of his two pads.

"Have you ever heard of the FBI's Behavioral Science Division?" Chandler asked.

"Yes, I have."

"What do they do?"

"They study serial killers among other things. Come up with psychological profiles, victim profiles, give advice, things like that."

"You had eleven murders, what advice did the FBI's Behavioral Science Division give you?"

"None."

"Why was that? Were they stumped?"

"No, we didn't call on them."

"Ah, and why didn't you call them?"

"Well, ma'am, we believed we had a handle on it. We had worked up profiles ourselves and we didn't think the FBI could help us much. The forensic psychologist helping us, Dr. Locke from USC, had once been an adviser to the FBI on sex crimes. We had his experience and the department's staff psychiatrist helping out. We believed we were in good shape in that department."

"Did the FBI offer their help?"

Lloyd hesitated here. It seemed he was finally understanding where she was headed.

"Uh, yes, somebody called after the case was making a lot of press. They wanted to get in on it. I told them we were fine, that no help was needed."

"Do you regret that decision now?"

"No. I don't think the FBI could've done any better than us. They usually come in on cases being handled by smaller departments or cases making a big media splash."

"And you don't think that's fair, correct?"

"What?"

"Bigfooting, I think it's called. You didn't want the FBI coming in and taking over, right?"

"No. It was like I said, we were okay without them."

"Isn't it true that the LAPD and the FBI have a long-standing history of jealousies and competitiveness that has resulted in the two agencies rarely communicating or working together?"

"No, I don't buy that."

It didn't matter if he bought it. Bosch knew she was making her points with the jury. Whether *they* bought it was the only thing that mattered.

"Your task force came up with a suspect profile, correct?"

"Yes. I believe I just mentioned that."

She asked Judge Keyes if she could approach the witness with a document she said was plaintiff's exhibit 1A. She handed it to the clerk, who handed it to Lloyd.

"What is that, Lieutenant?"

"This is a composite drawing and the psychological profile we came up with after, I think, the seventh killing."

"How did you come up with the drawing of the suspect?"

"Between the seventh and eighth victims, we had an intended victim who managed to survive. She was able to get away from the man and call the police. Working with this survivor, we came up with the drawing."

"Okay, are you familiar with the facial appearance of Norman Church?"

"Not to a great extent. I saw him after he was dead."

Chandler asked to approach again and submitted plaintiff's 2A, a collage of several photographs of Church taped to a piece of cardboard. She gave Lloyd a few moments to study them.

"Do you see any resemblance between the composite drawing and the photographs of Mr. Church?"

Lloyd hesitated and then said, "Our killer was known to wear disguises and our witness — the victim who got away — was a drug user. She was a porno actress. She wasn't reliable."

"Your Honor, can you instruct the witness to answer the questions that are asked?"

The judge did so.

"No," Lloyd said, his head bowed after being chastised. "No resemblance."

"Okay," Chandler said, "going back to the profile you have there. Where did that come from?"

"Primarily from Dr. Locke at USC and Dr. Shafer, an LAPD staff psychiatrist. I think they consulted with some others before writing it up."

"Can you read that first paragraph?"

"Yes. It says, 'Subject is believed to be a white male, twenty-five to thirty-five years old with minimal college education. He is a physically strong man though may not be large in appearance. He lives alone, alienated from family and friends. He is reacting to a deep-rooted hatred of women suggesting an abusive mother or female guardian. His painting of the faces of his victims with makeup is his attempt to remake women into an image that pleases him, that smiles at him. They become dolls, not threats.' Do you want me to read the part that outlines the repetitive traits of the killings?"

"No, that is not necessary. You were involved in the investigation of Mr. Church after he was killed by Bosch, correct?"

"Correct."

"List for the jury all of the traits in the suspect profile that your task force found that matched Mr. Church."

Lloyd looked down at the paper in his hands for a long time without speaking.

"I'll help you get started, Lieutenant," Chandler said. "He was a white male, correct?"

"Yes."

"What else is similar? Did he live alone?"

"No."

"He actually had a wife and two daughters, correct?"

"Yes."

"Was he between twenty-five and thirty-five years old?"

"No."

"Actually, he was thirty-nine years old, correct?"

"Yes."

"Did he have a minimal education?"

"No."

"Actually, he had a master's degree in mechanical engineering, didn't he?"

"Then what was he doing there in that room?" Lloyd said angrily. "Why was the makeup from the victims there? Why —"

"Answer the question asked of you, Lieutenant," Judge Keyes interjected. "Don't go asking questions. That isn't your job here."

"Sorry, Your Honor," Lloyd said. "Yes, he had a master's degree. I'm not sure exactly what it was for."

"You mentioned the makeup in your nonresponsive answer a moment ago," Chandler said. "What did you mean?"

"In the garage apartment where Church was killed. Makeup that belonged to nine of the victims was found in a cabinet in the bathroom. It tied him directly to those cases. Nine of eleven — it was convincing."

"Who found the makeup in there?"

"Harry Bosch did."

"When he went there alone and killed him."

"Is that a question?"

"No, Lieutenant. I withdraw it."

She paused to let the jury think about that while she flipped through her yellow pages.

"Lieutenant Lloyd, tell us about that night. What happened?"

Lloyd told the story as it had been described dozens of times before. On TV, in newspapers, in Bremmer's book. It was midnight, squad B was going off shift when the task force hot line rang and Bosch took the call, the last of the night. A street prostitute named Dixie McQueen said she had just escaped from the Dollmaker. Bosch went alone because the others on squad B had gone home and he figured it might be another dead end. He picked the woman up at Hollywood and Western and followed her directions into Silverlake. On Hyperion she convinced Bosch she had escaped from the Dollmaker and pointed to the lighted windows of an apartment over a garage. Bosch went up alone. A few moments later Norman Church was dead.

"He kicked open the door?" Chandler asked.

"Yes. There was the thought that maybe he had gone and gotten somebody to take the prostitute's place."

"Did he shout that he was police?"

"Yes."

"How do you know?"

"He said so."

"Any witnesses hear it?"

"No."

"What about Miss McQueen, the prostitute?"

"No. Bosch had kept her in the car parked on the street in case there was trouble."

"So what you're saying is we have Detective Bosch's word that he feared there might be another victim, that he identified himself and that Mr. Church made a threatening move toward the pillow."

"Yes," Lloyd said reluctantly.

"I notice, Lieutenant Lloyd, that you wear a toupee yourself."

There was some muffled laughter from the back. Bosch turned and saw that the media contingent was steadily growing. He saw Bremmer sitting in the gallery now.

"Yes," Lloyd said. His face had turned red to match his nose.

"Have you ever put your toupee under your pillow? Is that the proper care for it?"

"No."

"Nothing further, Your Honor."

Judge Keyes looked at the clock at the wall and then at Belk.

"What do you think, Mr. Belk? Break for lunch now so you won't be interrupted?"

"I only have one question."

"Oh, then by all means, ask it."

Belk took his pad to the lectern and leaned to the microphone.

"Lieutenant Lloyd, from all of your knowledge about this case, do you have any doubt whatsoever that Norman Church was the Dollmaker?"

"None at all. None . . . at . . . all."

After the jury filed out, Bosch leaned to Belk's ear and urgently whispered, "What was that? She tore him up and you asked only one question. What about all the other things that tied Church to the case?"

Belk held up his hand to calm Bosch and then spoke calmly.

"Because you are going to testify about all of that. This case is about you, Harry. We either win it or lose it with you."

6

The Code Seven had closed its dining room during the recession and somebody put a salad and pizza bar in the space to serve the office workers from the civic center. The Seven's barroom was still open but the dining room had been the last place within walking distance of Parker Center that Bosch had liked to eat at. So during the lunch break he got his car out of the lot at Parker and drove over to the garment district to eat at Gorky's. The Russian restaurant served breakfast all day and he ordered the eggs, bacon and potatoes special and took it to a table where someone had left behind a copy of the *Times*.

The concrete blonde story had Bremmer's byline on it. It combined quotes from the opening arguments in the trial with the discovery of the body and its possible connection to the case. The story also reported that police sources revealed that Detective Harry Bosch had received a note from someone claiming to be the real Dollmaker.

There was obviously a leak in Hollywood Division but Bosch knew it would be impossible to trace the person down. The note had been found at the front desk and any number of uniform officers could have known about it and leaked the word to Bremmer. After all, Bremmer was a good friend to have. Bosch had even leaked information to him in the past and on occasion found Bremmer to be quite useful.

Citing the unnamed sources, the story said police investigators had not concluded whether the note was legitimate or if the discovery of the body was connected to the Dollmaker case which ended four years earlier.

The only other point of interest in the story for Bosch was the short history on the Bing's Billiards building. It had been burned on the second night of the riots, no arrests ever made. Arson investigators said the separations between the storage units were not bearing walls, meaning trying to stop the flames was like trying to hold water in a cup made of toilet paper. From ignition to full involvement of flames was only eighteen minutes. Most of the storage units were rented by movie industry people and some valuable studio props were either looted or lost in the fire. The building was a total loss. The investigators traced the origin to the billiard hall. A pool table had been set on fire and it went from there.

Bosch put the paper down and began thinking about Lloyd's testimony. He remembered what Belk had said, that the case rode on himself. Chandler must know this as well. She would be waiting for him, ready to make Lloyd's outing seem like a joy ride in comparison. He grudgingly had to admit to himself that he respected her skill, her toughness. It made him remember something and he got up to use the pay phone out front. He was surprised to find Edgar was at the homicide table and not out eating lunch.

"Any luck on the ID?" Bosch asked.

"No, man, the prints didn't check. No matches at all. She didn't have a record. We're still trying other sources, adult entertainment licenses, stuff like that."

"Shit."

"Well, we got something else cooking. Remember that CSUN anthropology professor I was telling you about? Well, he's been here all morning with a student, painting the plaster face and getting it ready. I got the press coming in at three to show it off. Rojas went out to buy a blonde wig we'll stick on it. If we get good play on the tube we might crack loose an ID."

"Sounds like a plan."

"Yeah. How's court? The shit hit the fan in the *Times* today. That guy Bremmer has some sources."

"Court's fine. Let me ask you something. After you left the scene yesterday and went back to the station, where was Pounds?"

"Pounds? He was — we got back at the same time. Why?"

"When did he leave?"

"A little while later. Right before you got here."

"Was he on the phone in his office?"

"I think he made a few calls. I wasn't really watching. What's going on, you think he's Bremmer's source?"

"One last question. Did he close the door when he was on the phone?"

Bosch knew Pounds was paranoid. He always kept the door to his office open and the blinds on the glass partitions up so he could see and hear what was happening in the squad room. If he ever closed either or both, the troops outside knew something was up.

"Well, now that you mention it, I think he did have the door closed a little while. What is it?"

"Bremmer I'm not worried about. But somebody was talking to Money Chandler. In court this morning she knew I had been called out to the scene yesterday. That wasn't in the *Times*. Somebody told her."

Edgar was silent a moment before replying.

"Yeah, but why would Pounds talk to her?"

"I don't know."

"Maybe Bremmer. He could have told her, even though it wasn't in his story."

"The story says she couldn't be reached for comment. It's got to be somebody else. A leak. Probably the same person talked to Bremmer and Chandler. Somebody who wants to fuck me up."

Edgar didn't say anything and Bosch let it go for now.

"I better head back to court."

"Hey, how'd Lloyd do? I heard on KFWB he was the first wit."

"He did about as expected."

"Shit. Who's next?"

"I don't know. She has Irving and Locke, the shrink, on subpoena. My guess is, it will be Irving. He'll pick up where Lloyd left off."

"Well, good luck. By the way, if you're looking for something to do. This press gig I'm holding will hit the TV news tonight. I'll be here waiting by the phones. If you want to answer a few, I could use the help."

Bosch thought briefly about his plan for dinner with Sylvia. She'd understand.

"Yeah, I'll be there."

The afternoon testimony was largely uneventful. Chandler's strategy, it seemed to Bosch, was to build a two-part question into the jury's eventual deliberation, giving her clients two shots at the prize. One would be the wrong-man theory, which held that Bosch had flat-out killed an innocent man. The second question would be the use of force. Even if the jury determined that Norman Church, family man, was the Dollmaker, serial killer, they would have to decide whether Bosch's actions were appropriate.

Chandler called her client, Deborah Church, to the witness stand right after lunch. She gave a tearful account of a wonderful life with a wonderful husband who fawned over everybody; his daughters, his wife, his mother and mother-in-law. No misogynistic aberrations here. No sign of childhood abuse. The widow held a box of Kleenex in her hand as she testified, going to a new tissue every other question.

She wore the traditional black dress of a widow. Bosch remembered how appealing Sylvia had been when he saw her at her husband's funeral dressed in black. Deborah Church looked downright scary. It was as if she reveled in her role here. The widow of the fallen innocent. The real victim. Chandler had coached her well.

It was a good show, but it was too good to be true and Chandler knew it. Rather than leave the bad things to be drawn out on cross-examination, she finally got around to asking Deborah Church how, her marriage being so wonderful, her husband was in that garage apartment — which was rented under an alias — when Bosch kicked the door open.

"We had been having some difficulty." She stopped to dab an eye with a tissue. "Norman was going through a lot of stress — he had a lot of responsibility in the aircraft design department. He needed to expend it and so he took the apartment. He said it was to be alone. To think. I didn't know about this woman he brought there. I think it was probably his first time doing something like that. He was a naive man. I think she saw this. She took his money and then set him up by calling the police on him and giving the crazy story that he was the Dollmaker. There was a reward, you know."

Bosch wrote a note on a pad he kept in front of him and slid it over to Belk, who read it and then jotted something down on his own pad.

"What about all of the makeup found there, Mrs. Church?" Chandler asked. "Can you explain that?"

"All I know is that I would have known if my husband was that monster. I would have known. If there was makeup found there, it was put there by somebody else. Maybe after he was already dead."

Bosch believed he could feel the eyes of the courtroom burning into him as the widow accused him of planting evidence after murdering her husband.

After that, Chandler moved her questioning on to safer topics like Norman Church's relationship with his daughters and then ended her direct examination with a weeper.

"Did he love his daughters?"

"Very much so," Mrs. Church said as a new production of tears rolled down her cheeks. This time she did not wipe them away with a tissue. She let the jury watch them roll down her face into the folds of her double chin.

After giving her a few moments to compose herself, Belk got up and took his place at the lectern.

"Again, Your Honor, I will be brief. Mrs. Church, I want to make this very clear to the jury. Did you say in your testimony that you knew about your husband's apartment but didn't know about any women he may or may not have brought there?"

"Yes, that is correct."

Belk looked at his pad.

"Did you not tell detectives on the night of the shooting that you had never heard of any apartment? Didn't you emphatically deny that your husband even had such an apartment?"

Deborah Church didn't answer.

"I can arrange to have a tape of your first interview played in court if it will help refresh your —"

"Yes, I said that. I lied."

"You lied? Why would you lie to the police?"

"Because a policeman had just killed my husband. I didn't — I couldn't deal with them."

"The truth is you told the truth that night, correct, Mrs. Church? You never knew about any apartment."

"No, that's not true. I knew about it."

"Had you and your husband talked about it?"

"Yes, we discussed it."

"You approved of it?"

"Yes . . . , reluctantly. It was my hope he would stay at home and we could work this stress out together."

"Okay, Mrs. Church, then if you knew of the apartment, had discussed it and given your approval, reluctantly or not, why then did your husband rent it under a false name?"

She didn't answer. Belk had nailed her. Bosch thought he saw the widow glance in Chandler's direction. He looked at the lawyer but she made no move, no change in facial expression to help her client.

"I guess," the widow finally said, "that was one of the questions you could have asked him if Mr. Bosch had not murdered him in cold blood."

Without Belk's prompting, Judge Keyes said, "The jury will disregard that last characterization. Mrs. Church, you know better than that."

"I'm sorry, Your Honor."

"Nothing further," Belk said as he left the lectern.

The judge called a ten-minute recess.

During the break, Bosch went out to the ash can. Money Chandler didn't come out but the homeless man made a pass. Bosch offered him a whole cigarette, which he took and put in his shirt pocket. He was unshaven again and the slight look of dementia was still in his eyes.

"Your name is Faraday," Bosch said, as if speaking to a child.

"Yeah, what about it, Lieutenant?"

Bosch smiled. He had been made by a bum. All except for the rank.

"Nothing about it. I just heard that's what it was. I also heard you were a lawyer once."

"I still am. I'm just not practicing."

He turned and watched a jail bus go by on Spring, heading to the courthouse. It was full of angry faces looking out through the black wire windows.

Somebody by one of the back windows made Bosch as a cop, too, and stuck his middle index finger up through the wire. Bosch smiled back at him.

"My name was Thomas Faraday. But now I prefer Tommy Faraway."

"What happened to make you stop practicing law?"

Tommy looked back at him with milky eyes.

"Justice is what happened. Thanks for the smoke." He walked away then, cup in hand, and headed toward City Hall. Maybe that was his turf, too.

After the break, Chandler called a lab analyst from the coroner's office named Victor Amado. He was a very small and bookish-looking man with eyes that shifted from the judge to the jury as he walked to the witness chair. He was balding badly, though he seemed to be no more than twenty-eight. Bosch remembered that four years earlier he had all his hair and members of the task force referred to him as The Kid. He knew Belk was going to call Amado as a witness if Chandler didn't.

Belk leaned over and whispered that Chandler was following a good guy–bad guy pattern by alternating police witnesses with her sympathetic witnesses.

"She'll probably put one of the daughters up there after Amado," he said. "As a strategy, it is completely unoriginal."

Bosch didn't mention that Belk's trust-us-we're-the-cops defense had been around as long as the civil suit.

Amado testified in painstaking detail about how he had been given all of the bottles and compacts containing makeup that were found in Church's Hyperion apartment and had then traced them to specific victims of the Dollmaker. He said he had come up with nine separate lots or groupings of makeup — mascara, blush, eyeliner, lipstick, etc. Each lot was connected through chemical analysis to samples taken from the faces of the victims. This was further corroborated by detectives who interviewed relatives and friends to determine what brands the victims were known to use. It all matched up, Amado said. And in one instance, he added, an eyelash found on a mascara brush in Church's bathroom cabinet was identified as having come from the second victim.

"What about the two victims no matching makeup was found for?" Chandler asked.

"That was a mystery. We never found their makeup."

"In fact, with the exception of the eyelash that was allegedly found and matched to victim number two, you can't be one hundred percent sure that the makeup police did supposedly find in the apartment came from the victims, correct?"

"This stuff is mass produced and sold around the world. So there is a lot of it out there, but I would guess that the chances of nine different exact combinations of makeup being found like that by mere coincidence are astronomical."

"I didn't ask you to guess, Mr. Amado. Please answer the question I asked."

After flinching at being dressed down, Amado said, "The answer is we can't be one hundred percent sure, that is correct."

"Okay, now tell the jury about the DNA testing you did that connected Norman Church to the eleven killings."

"There wasn't any done. There —"

"Just answer the question, Mr. Amado. What about serology tests, connecting Mr. Church to the crimes?"

"There were none."

"Then it was the makeup comparison that was the clincher — the linchpin in the determination that Mr. Church was the Dollmaker?"

"Well, it was for me. I don't know about the detectives. My report said —"

"I'm sure for the detectives it was the bullet that killed him that was the clincher."

"Objection," Belk yelled angrily as he stood. "Your Honor, she can't —"

"Ms. Chandler," Judge Keyes boomed. "I have warned you both about exactly this sort of thing. Why would you go and say something you know full well is prejudicial and out of order?"

"I apologize, Your Honor."

"Well, it's a little late for apologies. We'll discuss this matter after the jury goes home for the day."

The judge then instructed the jurors to disregard her comment. But Bosch knew it had been a carefully thought out gambit by Chandler. The jurors would now see her even more as the underdog. Even the judge was against her — which he really wasn't. And they might be distracted, thinking about what just happened, when Belk stepped up to repair Amado's testimony.

"Nothing further, Your Honor," Chandler said.

"Mr. Belk," the judge said.

Don't say just a few questions again, Bosch thought as his lawyer moved to the lectern.

"Just a few questions, Mr. Amado," Belk said. "Plaintiff's counsel mentioned DNA and serology tests and you said they had not been done. Why is that?"

"Well, because there was nothing to test. No semen was ever recovered from any of the bodies. The killer had used a condom. Without samples to attempt to match to Mr. Church's DNA or blood, there was not much point in running tests. We would have the victims' but nothing to compare it to."

Belk drew a line with his pen through a question written on his pad.

"If there was no recovery of semen or sperm, how do you know these women were raped or even had engaged in consensual sexual activity?"

"The autopsies of all eleven of the victims showed vaginal bruising, much more than is considered usual or even possible from consensual sex. On two of the victims there was even tearing in the vaginal wall. The victims were brutally raped, in my estimation."

"But these women came from walks of life where sexual activity was common and frequent, even 'rough sex', if you will. Two of them performed in pornographic videos. How can you be sure they were sexually assaulted against their will?"

"The bruising was such that it would have been very painful, especially for the two with vaginal tears. Hemorrhaging was considered perimortem, meaning at the time of death. The deputy coroners who performed these autopsies unanimously concluded these women were raped."

Belk drew another line on his pad, flipped the page and came up with a new question. He was doing well with Amado, Bosch thought. Better than Money had. It may have been a mistake for her to have called him as a witness.

"How do you know that the killer used a condom?" Belk asked. "Couldn't these women have been raped with an object and that account for the lack of semen?"

"That could have happened and it could account for some of the damage. But there was clear evidence in five of the cases that they had had sex with a man wearing a condom."

"And what was that?"

"We did rape kits. There was —"

"Hold it a second, Mr. Amado. What is a rape kit?"

"It's a protocol for collecting evidence from bodies of people that may have been the victims of rape. In the case of a woman, we take vaginal and anal swabs, we comb the pubic area looking for foreign pubic hair, procedures such as that. We also take samples of blood and hair from the victim in case there is a call for comparison to evidence found on a suspect. It's collected together in an evidence kit."

"Okay. Before I interrupted there, you were going to tell us about the evidence found in five of the victims that was indicative of sex with a man who wore a condom."

"Yes, we did the rape kits each time we got a Dollmaker victim. And there was a foreign substance found in vaginal samplings in five of the victims. It was the same material in each of the women."

"What was it, Mr. Amado?"

"It was identified as a condom lubricant."

"Was this material something that could be identified to a specific brand and style of condom?"

Looking at Belk, Bosch could see the heavy man was chomping at the bit. Amado was answering each question slowly and each time Bosch could see that Belk could barely wait for the answer before plowing ahead with a new question. Belk was on a roll.

"Yes," Amado said. "We identified the product. It was from a Trojan-Enz lubricated condom with special receptacle end."

Looking at the court reporter, Amado said, "That's spelled E-N-Z."

"And that was the same for all five samples received from the five bodies?" Belk asked.

"Yes it was."

"I am going to ask you a hypothetical question. Assuming that the attacker of eleven women used the same brand of lubricated condom, how could you account for lubrication being found in the vaginal sampling of only five victims?"

"I believe that a number of factors could be involved. Such as the intensity of the victim's struggle. But essentially it would be just a matter of how much of the lubricant came off the condom and stayed in the vagina."

"When police officers brought you the various containers of makeup from the Hyperion apartment rented by Norman Church for analysis, did they bring anything else?"

"Yes they did."

"What was that?"

"A box of Trojan-Enz lubricated condoms with special receptacle ends."

"How many condoms did the box hold?"

"Twelve separately packaged condoms."

"How many were still in the box when the police delivered it to you?"

"There were three left."

"Nothing further."

Belk returned to the defense table with a triumphant spring in his walk.

"A moment, Your Honor," Chandler said.

Bosch watched her open a fat file full of police documents. She leafed through the pages and took out a short stack of documents held together with a paper clip. She read the top one quickly and then held it up to leaf through the rest. Bosch could see the top one was the protocol list from a rape kit. She was reading the protocols from all eleven victims.

Belk leaned over to him and whispered, "She's about to step into some deep shit. I was going to bring this up later, during your testimony."

"Ms. Chandler?" the judge intoned.

She jumped up.

"Yes, Your Honor, I'm ready. I have a quick redirect of Mr. Amado."

She brought the stack of protocols with her to the lectern, read the last two and then looked at the coroner's analyst.

"Mr. Amado, you mentioned that part of the rape kit consisted of combing for foreign pubic hairs, do I have that right?"

"Yes."

"Can you explain that procedure a little more?"

"Well, basically, the comb is passed through the pubic hair of the victim and it collects unattached hairs. Oftentimes, this unattached hair is from the victim's attacker, or possibly other sexual partners."

"How's it get there?"

Amado's face flushed to a crimson hue.

"Well, uh, it — uh, during sex . . . there is I guess what you call friction between the bodies?"

"I am asking the questions, Mr. Amado. You are answering."

There was quiet tittering from the gallery seats. Bosch felt embarrassed for Amado and thought that his own face might be turning red.

"Yes, well, there is friction," Amado said. "And this causes some transference. Loose pubic hair from one person can be transferred to that of the other."

"I see," Chandler said. "Now, you as coordinator of the Dollmaker evidence from the coroner's office were familiar with the rape kits of all eleven victims, correct?"

"Yes."

"With how many of the victims did the findings include foreign pubic hair?"

Bosch understood what was happening now and realized that Belk was right. Chandler was walking into the buzz saw.

"All of them," Amado answered.

Bosch saw Deborah Church raise her head and look sharply at Chandler at the lectern. Then she looked over at Bosch and their eyes met. She quickly looked away but Bosch knew. She, too, knew what was about to happen. Because she, too, knew her late husband the way Bosch had on that last night. She knew what he looked like naked.

"Ah, all of them," Chandler said. "Now, can you tell the jury how many of these pubic hairs found on these women were analyzed and identified as having been from the body of Norman Church?"

"None of them were from Norman Church."

"Thank you."

Belk was up and moving to the lectern before Chandler had time to remove her pad and the rape kit protocols. Bosch watched her sit down and saw the widow Church lean to her and desperately begin whispering. Bosch saw Chandler's eyes go dead. She held up her hand to tell the widow she had said enough and then leaned back and exhaled.

"Now, let's clear something up first," Belk said. "Mr. Amado, you said you found pubic hairs on all of the eleven victims. Were these hairs all from the same man?"

"No. We found a multitude of samples. In most cases, what looked like hair from possibly two or three men on each victim."

"What did you attribute this to?"

"Their lifestyle. We knew these were women with multiple sexual partners."

"Did you analyze these samples to determine if there were common hairs? In other words, whether hair from one man was found on each of the victims."

"No, we did not. There was a huge amount of evidence collected in these cases and manpower dictated that we focus on evidence that would help identify a killer. Because we had so many different samples, it was determined that this was evidence that would be held and then used to link or clear a suspect, once that suspect was in custody."

"I see, well, then once Norman Church had been killed and was identified as the Dollmaker, did you then match any of the hairs from the victims to him?"

"We did not."

"And why is that?"

"Because Mr. Church had shaved his body hair. There was no pubic hair to match."

"Why would he have done that?"

Chandler objected on the grounds that Amado could not answer for Church and the judge sustained it. But Bosch knew it didn't matter. Everybody in the courtroom knew why Church had shaved himself — so he wouldn't leave pubic hairs behind as evidence.

Bosch looked at the jury and he saw two of the women writing in the notebooks the marshals had given them to help them keep track of important testimony. He wanted to buy Belk — and Amado — a beer.

7

It looked like a cake in a box, one of those novelty things custom-made to look like Marilyn Monroe or something. The anthropologist had painted on a beige skin tone and red lipstick to go with blue eyes. It looked like frosting to Bosch. A wavy blonde wig was added. He stood in the squad room looking down at the plaster image, wondering if it really looked like anybody at all.

"Five minutes till show time," Edgar said.

He was sitting in his chair, which was turned toward the TV on the file cabinets. He was holding the channel changer. His blue suit coat was hung neatly on a hanger, which was hooked on the coatrack at the end of the table. Bosch took his jacket off and hung it on one of the coatrack pegs. He checked his slot in the message box and sat down at his spot at the homicide table. There had been a call from Sylvia, nothing else important. He dialed her number as the Channel 4 news began. He knew enough about the news priorities in this town to know the report on the concrete blonde wouldn't be a lead story.

"Harry, we're gonna need that line clear once they show it," Edgar said.

"I'll only be a minute. They won't show it for a while. If they show it at all."

"They'll show it. I made secret deals with all of them. They all think they'll be getting the exclusive if we get an ID. They all want to get a boo-hoo story with the parents."

"You're playing with fire, man. You make a promise like that and then they find out you fucked them around —"

Sylvia picked up the phone.

"Hey, it's me."

"Hi, where are you?"

"The office. We have to watch the phones a while. They're putting the face of the victim from yesterday's case on TV tonight."

"How was court?"

"It's the plaintiff's case at the moment. But I think we scored a couple punches."

"I read the *Times* today at lunch."

"Yeah, well, they got about half of it right."

"Are you coming out? Like you said."

"Well, eventually. Not right now. I've got to help answer phones on this and then it's depending on what we get. If we're skunked I'll be out early."

He noticed he had lowered his voice so Edgar wouldn't hear his conversation.

"And if you get something good?"

"We'll see."

An indrawn breath, then silence. Harry waited.

"You've been saying 'we'll see' too much, Harry. We've talked about this. Sometimes —"

"I know that."

"— I think that you just want to be left alone. Stay in your little house on the hill and keep the whole world out. Including me."

"Not you. You know that."

"Sometimes, I don't. I don't feel like I know it right now. You push me away just at the time when you need me — somebody — to be close."

He had no answer. He thought of her there on the other end. She was probably sitting on the stool in the kitchen. She had probably already begun making a dinner for both of them. Or maybe she was getting used to his ways and had waited for the call.

"Look, I'm sorry," he said. "You know how it is. What are you doing about dinner?"

"Nothing, and I'm not going to do anything, either,"

Edgar made a low, quick whistle. Harry looked up at the TV and saw it was showing the painted face of the victim. The TV was on Channel 7 now. The camera showed a long close-up of the face. It looked all right on the tube. At least, it didn't look much like a cake. The screen flashed the detective bureau's two public numbers.

"They're showing it now," Bosch said to Sylvia. "I need to keep this line clear. Let me call you back later, when I know something."

"Sure," she said coldly and hung up.

Edgar had the TV on 4 now and they were showing the face. He then flipped to 2 and caught the last few seconds of their report on it. They had even interviewed the anthropologist.

"Slow news day," Bosch said.

"Shit," Edgar replied. "We're banging on all cylinders now. All we —"

The phone rang and he grabbed it up.

"No, it just went out," he said after listening for a few moments. "Yeah, yeah, I will. Okay."

He hung up and shook his head.

"Pounds?" Bosch asked.

"Yeah. Thinks we're going to have her name ten seconds after the broadcast went out. Christ, whadda nitwit."

The next three calls were pranks, all testifying to the glaring lack of originality and the mental health of the TV viewing audience. All three callers said "Your mother!" or words to that effect and hung up laughing. About twenty minutes later Edgar got a call and started taking notes. The phone rang again and Bosch took it.

"This is Detective Bosch, who am I speaking with?"

"Is this being taped?"

"No, it's not. Who is this?"

"Never mind, just thought you'd like to know the girl's name is Maggie. Maggie something or other. It's Latin. I seen her on videos."

"What videos? MTV?"

"No, Sherlock. Adult videos. She fucked on film. She was good. She could put a rubber on a prick with her mouth."

The line went dead. Bosch wrote a couple of notes down on the pad he had in front of him. Latin? He didn't think the way the face had been painted gave any indication that the victim was a Latina.

Edgar hung up then and said his caller had said her name was Becky, that she had lived in Studio City a few years back.

"What'd you get?"

"I got a Maggie. No last name. Possibly a Latin last name. He said she was in porno."

"That would fit, except she don't look Mexican to me."

"I know."

The phone rang again. Edgar picked up and listened a few moments and then hung up.

"Another one that recognizes my mom."

Bosch took the next one.

"I just wanted to tell you that the girl they were showing on TV was in porno," the voice said.

"How do you know she was in porno?"

"I can tell by that thing they showed on TV. I rented a tape. Only once. She was in it."

Only once, Bosch thought, but he remembered. Yeah, sure.

"You know her name?"

The other phone rang and Edgar picked it up.

"I don't know names, man," Bosch's caller said. "They all use fake ones anyway."

"What was the name of the tape?"

"Can't remember. I was, uh, intoxicated when I saw it. Like I said, it was the only time."

"Look, I'm not taking your confession. You got anything else?"

"No, smartass, I don't."

"Who is this?"

"I don't have to say."

"Look, we're trying to find a killer here. What was the name of the place you rented it?"

"I'm not telling you, you might be able to get my name from them. Doesn't matter, they have those tapes all over, every adult place."

"How would you know if you only rented one once?"

The caller hung up.

Bosch stayed another hour. By the end they had five calls saying the painted face belonged to a porno starlet. Only one of the callers said her name was Maggie, the other four men saying they didn't pay much attention to names. There was one call naming her Becky of Studio City, and one saying she was a stripper who had worked for a while at the Booby Trap on La Brea. One man who called said the face belonged to his missing wife, but Bosch learned through further questioning that she had been missing only two months. The concrete blonde had been dead too long. The hope and desperation in the caller's voice seemed genuine to Bosch, and he didn't know whether he was telling the man good news by explaining that it could not be his wife or bad news because he was left in the void again.

There were three callers who gave vague descriptions of a woman they thought might be the concrete blonde, but after a few questions into each conversation Bosch and Edgar identified the callers as cop geeks, people who got a thrill from talking to the police.

The most unusual call was from a Beverly Hills psychic who mentioned that she had placed her hand on the TV screen while it showed the face and felt the dead woman's spirit cry out to her.

"What did it cry?" Bosch asked patiently.

"Praise."

"Praise for what?"

"Jesus our savior, I would assume but I don't know. That was all I received. I might receive more if I could touch the actual plaster cast of the —"

"Well, did this spirit that was giving praise identify itself? See, that's what we're doing here. We're more interested in a name than cries of praise."

"Someday you will believe but by then you will be lost."

She hung up on him.

At seven-thirty Bosch told Edgar he was splitting.

"How 'bout you? You going to hang out for the eleven o'clock news?"

"Yeah, I'll be here but I can handle it. If I get a lot of calls I'll pull one of the dipshits off the desk."

Stock that OT, Bosch thought.

"What's next?" he asked.

"I don't know. What do you think?"

"Well, aside from all the calls saying it's your mother, this porno thing seems to be the way to go."

"Leave my blessed mother out of it. How you think I can check the porno?"

"Administrative Vice. Guy over there, a detective-three, name of Ray Mora, he works porno. He's the best. He also was on the Dollmaker task force. Call him and see if he can come take a look at the face. He might've known her. Tell him we had one call saying her name was Maggie."

"Will do. It fits with the Dollmaker, doesn't it? The porno, I mean."

"Yeah, it fits." He thought about this a moment, then added, "Two of the other victims were in the business. The one that got away from him was, too."

"The lucky one — she still in it?"

"Last I heard. But she might be dead now for all I know."

"Still doesn't mean anything, Harry."

"What?"

"The porno. Still doesn't mean it was the Dollmaker. The real one, I mean."

Bosch just nodded. He had an idea about something to do on his way home. He went out to his Caprice and got the Polaroid camera out of the trunk. In the squad room, he took two shots of the face in the box and put them in his coat pocket after they developed.

Edgar watched this and asked, "What're you going to do?"

"Might stop at that adult supermarket in the Valley on my way up to Sylvia's."

"Don't get caught in one of those little rooms with your dick out."

"Thanks for the tip. Let me know what Mora says."

Bosch worked his way on surface streets up to the Hollywood Freeway. He went north and then exited on Lankershim, which took him into North Hollywood in the San Fernando Valley. He had all four windows down and the air was cool as it buffeted him from all directions. He smoked a cigarette, flicking the ashes into the wind. There was some techno-funk jazz on KAJZ so he turned the radio off and just drove.

The Valley was the city's bedroom community in more ways than the obvious. It was also home to the nation's pornography industry. The commercial-industrial districts of Van Nuys, Canoga Park, Northridge and Chatsworth housed hundreds of porno production outfits, distributors and warehouses. Modeling agencies in Sherman Oaks provided ninety percent of the women and men who performed in front of the cameras. And, consequently, the Valley was also one of the largest retail outlets for the material. It was made here, it was sold here — through video mail-order businesses also nestled in the warehouses with the production outfits, and places like X Marks the Spot on Lankershim Boulevard.

Bosch pulled into the lot in front of the huge store and appraised it for a few moments. It had formerly been a Pic N Pay supermarket, but the front plate-glass windows had been walled up. Under the red neon X Marks the Spot sign, the front wall was whitewashed and painted with black figures of naked and overly buxom female figures, like the metallic silhouettes Bosch saw all the time on the mudflaps of trucks on the freeway. The men who put those on their trucks were probably the same guys this place catered to, Bosch figured.

X Marks the Spot was owned by a man named Harold Barnes, who was a front for the Chicago Outfit. It grossed more than a million dollars a year — on the books. Probably another one under the counter. Bosch knew all of this from Mora of Ad-Vice, whom he had partnered with on some nights while they both were on the task force four years earlier.

Bosch watched a man of about twenty-five get out of his Toyota, walk quickly to the solid wood front door, and slip in like a secret agent. He followed. The front half of the former supermarket was dedicated to retail — the sale and rental of videos, magazines and other assorted adult-oriented and mostly rubber products. The rear was split between private "encounter" rooms and private video booths. The entry to this area was through a curtained doorway. Bosch could hear heavy-metal rock music coming from back there mixed with the canned-sounding cries of phony passion coming from the video booths.

To his left was a glass counter with two men behind it. One was a big man, there to keep the peace; the other was smaller, older, there to take the money. Bosch knew by the way they looked at him and the skin stretched tight around their eyes that they had made him as soon as he had come in. He walked over and put one of the Polaroids on the counter.

"I am trying to ID her. Heard she worked in video, do you recognize her?"

The small guy leaned forward and looked while the other guy didn't move.

"Looks like a fucking cake, man," the small guy said. "I don't know any cakes. I eat cakes."

He looked back at the big guy and they exchanged clever smiles.

"So you don't recognize her. What about you?"

"I say what he says," the big guy said. "I eat cakes, too."

This time they laughed out loud and probably had to restrain themselves from exchanging a high five. The small guy's eyes sparkled behind rose-tinted glasses.

"Okay," Bosch said. "Then I'll just look around. Thanks."

The big guy stepped forward and said, "Just keep your gun covered, man, we don't want to excite the patrons."

The big guy's eyes were dull and he set out a five-foot zone of body odor. A duster, Bosch thought. He wondered why the small guy didn't fire his ass.

"No more excited than they are," Bosch said.

He turned from the counter to the two walls of shelves that were lined with hundreds of video boxes for sale or rent. There were a dozen men, including the secret agent, looking. Appraising the scene and the number of video boxes, Bosch somehow was reminded of how he once had read all the names on the Vietnam War Memorial wall while on a case. It had taken several hours.

The video wall proved to be less time consuming. Skipping the gay and black performer videos he scanned each box for a face like the concrete blonde's or the name Maggie. The videos were in alphabetical order and it took him nearly an hour to get to the T's. A face on the box of a video called *Tails from the Crypt* caught his eye. There was a nude woman lying in a coffin on the front. She was blonde and had an upturned nose like the plaster face in the box. He turned the box over and there was another photo of the actress, on her hands and knees with a man pressed up behind her. Her mouth was slightly open and her face was turned back toward her sex partner.

It was her, Bosch knew. He looked at the credits and saw that the name fit. He took the empty video box to the counter.

"'Bout time," said the small guy. "We don't allow loitering here. The cops give us a hard time on that."

"I want to rent this."

"Can't, it's already rented. See, the box is empty."

"She in anything else you know of?"

The small guy took the box and looked at the photographs.

"Magna Cum Loudly, yeah. I don't know. She was just getting started and then dropped out. Probably married a rich guy, lots of them do."

The big guy stepped over to look at the box and Bosch stepped back, out of his odor zone.

"I'm sure they do," he said. "What else was she in?"

"Well," the small guy said, "she had just made her way out of the loops and then, pfffft, she's gone. *Tails* was her first top billing. She did a fabulous two-way in *Whore of the Roses* and that's what got her started. Before that it was just the loops."

Bosch went back to the W's and found the box for *Whore of the Roses*. It also was empty and there were no photos of Magna Cum Loudly on it. Her name was last billing on the credits. He went back to the small guy and pointed to the *Tails from the Crypt* box.

"What about the box, then? I'll buy it."

"We can't sell you just the box because then how do we display the video when it comes back? We don't sell many boxes here. Guys want stills, they buy magazines."

"What's the price of the whole video? I'll buy it. When the renter brings it back you can hold it for me and I'll come pick it up. How much?"

"Well, *Tails* is popular. We're going with a $39.95 price tag but for you, Officer, I'll give our law enforcement discount. Fifty bucks."

Bosch said nothing to that. He had the cash and paid it.

"I want a receipt."

After the purchase was completed, the small guy put the video box in a brown paper bag.

"You know," he said, "Maggie Cum Loudly is still on a couple of our loops in the back. You might want to check it out."

He smiled and pointed to a sign on the wall behind him.

"We have a no-exchange policy, by the way."

Bosch smiled back.

"I'll check it out."

"Hey, by the way, what name you want us to hold this video under when it comes back in?"

"Carlo Pinzi."

It was the name of the Outfit's L.A. capo.

"Very fucking funny, Mr. Pinzi, we'll do that."

Bosch went through the curtain into the back rooms and was almost immediately met by a woman wearing high heels, a black G-string and an ice-cream man's coin changer on a belt, nothing else. Her large silicone-perfected breasts were dotted by unusually small nipples. Her dyed blonde hair was short and she had too much makeup around her glassy brown eyes. She looked like she was either nineteen or thirty-five.

"Do you want a private encounter or change for the video booths?" she asked.

Bosch took out his now thin fold of cash and gave her two dollars for quarters.

"Can I keep a dollar for myself? I don't get paid nothin', just tips."

Bosch gave her another dollar and took his eight quarters to one of the small curtained booths where the occupied light wasn't on.

"Let me know if you need anything in there," the woman in the G-string called after him.

She was either too stoned or too stupid or both not to have made him as a cop. Bosch waved her away and pulled the curtain shut behind him. The space he had was about the size of a phone booth. There was a glass viewing window through which he could see a video screen. Displayed on the screen was a directory of twelve different videos he could select from. It was all video now, though they were still called loops, after the 16mm film loops that ran over and over again in the first peep machines.

There was no chair but there was a small shelf with an ashtray and a Kleenex box on it. Used tissues were littered on the floor and the booth smelled like the industrial disinfectant they used in the coroner's vans. He put all eight quarters in the coin slot and the video picture came on.

It was two women on a bed kissing and massaging each other. It took Bosch only a few seconds to eliminate them as possibly being the girl on the video box. He began pushing the channel button and the picture jumped from coupling to coupling — heterosexual, homosexual, bisexual — his eyes lingering only long enough to determine whether the woman he was looking for was there.

She was on the ninth loop. He recognized her from the video box he had bought. Seeing her in motion also helped convince him that the woman who used the name Magna Cum Loudly was the concrete blonde. In the video she lay on a couch on her back, biting one of her fingers while a man knelt between her legs on the floor and rhythmically ground his hips into hers.

Knowing this woman was dead, had died violently, and standing there watching her submit to another kind of violence affected him in a way he was unsure he even understood. Guilt and sorrow welled up as he watched. Like most cops, he had spent a stint in vice. He had also seen some of the films of the two other adult film actresses who were killed by the Dollmaker. But this was the first time this uneasiness had hit him.

On the video, the actress took the finger out of her mouth and began to moan loudly, living up to her billing. Bosch fumbled with the sound knob and turned it down. But he could still hear her, her moans turned into shouts, from videos in other booths. Other men were watching the same show. It made Bosch feel creepy knowing the video had drawn the interest of different men for different reasons.

The curtain behind him rustled and he heard someone move behind him into the booth. At the same moment he felt a hand move up his thigh to his crotch. He reached into his jacket for his gun as he turned but then saw it was the coin changer.

"What can I do for you, darling?" she cooed.

He pushed her arm away from him.

"You can start by getting out of here."

"C'mon, lover, why look at it on TV when you can be doing it? Twenty bucks. I can't go lower. I have to split it with the management."

She was pressed against him now and Bosch couldn't tell if it was his breath or hers that was lousy with cigarettes. Her breasts were hard and she was pushing them against his chest. Then suddenly she froze. She had felt the gun. Their eyes held each other for a moment.

"That's right," Bosch said. "If you don't want to go for a ride to the cage, get out of here."

"No problem, Officer," she said.

She parted the curtain and was gone. Just then the screen went back to the directory. Bosch's two dollars were up.

As he walked out, he heard Magna Cum Loudly yelling in false joy from the other booths.

8

On the ride on the freeway to the next valley, he tried to imagine that life. He wondered what hope she might still have had and still nurtured and protected like a candle in the rain, even as she lay there on her back with distant eyes turned toward the stranger inside her. Hope must have been the only thing she had left. Bosch knew that hope was the lifeblood of the heart. Without it there was nothing, only darkness.

He wondered how the two lives — killer's and victim's — had crossed. Maybe the seed of lust and murderous desire had been planted by the same loop Bosch had just seen. Maybe the killer had rented the video Bosch had just paid fifty dollars for. Could it have been Church? Or was there another out there? The box, Bosch thought, and pulled off at the next exit, Van Nuys Boulevard in Pacoima.

He pulled to the curb and took the video box out of the brown paper bag the small guy had provided. He turned the light on in the car and studied every surface of the box, reading every word. But there was no copyright date that would have told him when the tape was made, whether it had been made before or after Church's death.

He got back on the Golden State, which took him north into the Santa Clarita Valley. After exiting on Bouquet Canyon Road he wound his way through a series of residential streets, past a seemingly endless line of California custom homes. On Del Prado, he pulled to the curb in front of the house with the Ritenbaugh Realty sign out front.

Sylvia had been trying to sell the house for more than a year, without luck. When he thought about it, Bosch was relieved. It kept him from facing a decision about what he and Sylvia would do next.

Sylvia opened the door before he reached it.

"Hey."

"Hey."

"What do you have?"

"Oh, it's something from work. I've gotta make a couple calls in a while. Did you eat?"

He bent down and kissed her and moved inside. She had on the gray T-shirt dress she liked to wear around the house after work. Her hair was loose and down to her shoulders, the blonde highlights catching the light from the living room.

"Had a salad. You?"

"Not yet. I'll fix a sandwich or something. I'm sorry about this. With the trial and now this new case, it's . . . well, you know."

"It's okay. I just miss you. I'm sorry about how I acted on the phone."

She kissed him and held him. He felt at home with her. That was the best thing. That feeling. He had never had it before and he would forget it at times when he was away from her. But as soon as he was back with her it was there.

She took him by the hand into the kitchen and told him to sit down while she made him a sandwich. He watched her put a pan on the stove and turn on the gas. Then she put four strips of bacon in the pan. While they cooked, she sliced a tomato and an avocado and laid out a bed of lettuce. He got up, took a beer from the fridge and kissed her on the back of the neck. He stepped back, annoyed that the memory of the woman grabbing him in the booth intruded on the moment. Why had that happened?

"What's the matter?"

"Nothing."

She put two slices of sunflower bread into the toaster and took the bacon out of the pan. A few minutes later she put the sandwich in front of him at the table and sat down.

"Who do you have to call?"

"Jerry Edgar, maybe a guy at Ad-Vice."

"Ad-Vice? She was porno? This new victim?"

Sylvia had once been married to a cop and she made leaps of thought like a cop. Bosch liked that about her.

"Think so. I have a line on her. But I've got court, so I want to give it to them."

She nodded. He never had to tell her not to ask too much. She always knew just when to stop.

"How was school today?"

"Fine. Eat your sandwich. I want you to hurry up and make your calls because I want us to forget about court and school and your investigation. I want us to open some wine, light some candles and get in bed."

He smiled at her.

They had fallen into such a relaxed life together. The candles were always her signal, her way of initiating their lovemaking. Sitting there, Bosch realized he had no signals. She initiated it almost every time. He wondered what that meant about him. He worried that maybe theirs was a relationship solely founded on secrets and hidden faces. He hoped not.

"Are you sure nothing's wrong?" she asked. "You're really spaced."

"I'm fine. This is good. Thank you."

"Penny called tonight. She's got two people interested, so she's going to have an open house on Sunday."

He nodded, still eating.

"Maybe we could go somewhere for the day. I don't want to be here when she brings them through. We could even leave Saturday and go overnight somewhere. You could get away from all of this. Maybe Lone Pine would be good."

"That sounds good. But let's see what happens."

After she left the kitchen for the bedroom, Bosch called the bureau and Edgar picked up. Bosch deepened his voice and said, "Yeah, you know that thing you showed on TV. The one that gots no name?"

"Yes, can you help us?"

"Sure can."

Bosch covered his mouth with his hand to hold back the laughter. He realized he hadn't thought of a good punch line. His mind raced as he tried to decide what it should be.

"Well, who is it, sir?" Edgar said impatiently.

"It — it's — it's . . ."

"It's who?"

"It's Harve Pounds in drag!"

Bosch burst out laughing and Edgar easily guessed who it was. It was stupid, not even funny, but they both laughed.

"Bosch, what do you want?"

It took him some time to stop laughing. He finally said, "Just checking in. Did you call Ray Mora?"

"Nah, I called over to Ad-Vice and they said he wasn't working tonight. I was going to talk to him tomorrow. How'd you do?"

"I think I've got a name. I'll give Mora a call at home so he can pull what they have on her first thing."

He told Edgar the name and heard the other detective laugh.

"Well, at least it's original. How — what makes you think it's her?"

Bosch answered in a low voice in case his voice was carrying to the bedroom.

"I saw a loop and I have a box from a video with her picture on it. It looks like the plaster face you got. A little off on the wig. But I think it's her. I'll drop the box off on your desk on my way into court tomorrow."

"Cool."

"Maybe Mora can get an early start on getting her real name and prints over to you. She probably had an adult entertainment license. All right if I call him?"

"That's cool. You know him."

They hung up. Bosch didn't have a home number for Mora. He called Detective Services and gave his name and badge number and asked to be put through. It took about five minutes and then Mora answered after three rings. He seemed out of breath.

"It's Bosch, you gotta minute?"

"Bosch, yeah, Bosch, what's up, man?"

"How's business?"

"Still sucks."

He laughed at what Bosch guessed was an insider's joke.

"Actually, it goes further down all the time — no pun intended. Video ruined it, Bosch. Made it too big. The industry got big, the quality got small. Nobody cares about quality anymore."

Mora was talking more like a supporter of the porno industry than a watchdog.

"I miss the days when it was in those smoky theaters on Cahuenga and Highland. We had a better handle on things then. At least, I did. So how's court? I hear you guys caught another one that looks like the Dollmaker. What's going on with that? How could —"

"That's why I'm calling. I've got a name — I think she was from your side of the tracks. The victim."

"Give it to me."

"Magna Cum Loudly. Maybe known as Maggie, too."

"Yeah, I've heard that one. She was around a while ago and then, you're right, she disappeared or dropped out."

Bosch waited for more. He thought he heard a voice in the background — in person or on TV and Mora told him to hold on a minute. He couldn't make out what had been said or whether it was a man or a woman. It made him wonder what Mora had been doing when he called. There were rumors floating around the department about Mora having gotten too close to the subject he was expert in. It was a common cop malady. Still, he knew Mora had successfully fended off any attempts to transfer him in the early years of his assignment. Now, he had so much expertise, it would be ridiculous to move him. It would be like taking Orel Hershiser off the Dodgers pitching staff and putting him in the outfield. He was good at what he did. He had to be left there.

"Um, Harry, I don't know. I think she was around a couple years ago. What I'm saying is, if it's her, then it couldn't have been Church. You know what I'm saying? I don't know how that plays with what you've got working on this."

"Don't worry about it, Ray. If Church didn't do her, somebody else did. We still gotta get him."

"Right. So I'll get on it. By the way, how'd you make her?"

Bosch told him about his visit to X Marks the Spot.

"Yeah, I know them guys. The big one, that's Carlo Pinzi the capo's nephew, Jimmie Pinzi. They call him Jimmie Pins. He may act big and dumb but he's really the little guy Pinkie's boss. Watches over the place for his uncle. The little one's called Pinkie on account of those glasses he wears. Pinkie and Pins. It's all an act. Anyway, they charged you about forty beans too many for that video."

"That's what I guessed. Oh, and I was going to ask you, there's no copyright on the video box. Would that be on the video or is there any way I can figure out when this was made?"

"Usually they don't put the copyright on the box. Customers want fresh meat. So the players figure the customer sees a copyright on the box that's a couple years old, then they'll buy something else. It's a fast business. Perishable goods. So no dates. Sometimes they're not even on the video cartridge. Anyway, I've got catalogs at the office going back twelve years. I can find a date, no problem."

"Thanks, Ray. I might not make it by. A guy from the homicide table, Jerry Edgar, might come by to see you. I got court."

"That's fine, Harry."

Bosch had nothing else to ask and was about to say good-bye when Mora spoke in the silence.

"You know, I think about it a lot."

"What?"

"The task force. I wish I hadn't taken off early that night and I was there with you. Who knows, maybe we'd have gotten this guy alive."

"Yeah."

"Be no trial then — I mean, for you."

Bosch was silent as he looked at the picture on the back of video box. The woman's face turned to the side, just like the plaster face. It was her. He felt sure of it.

"Ray, with only this name — Magna Cum Loudly — can you still get a real name, get prints?"

"Sure can. No matter what anybody thinks of the product, there is legit stuff and illegit stuff out there. This girl Maggie looks like she had graduated to the legit world. She was out of loops and that shit and was in mainstream adult video. That means she probably had an agent, had an adult entertainment license. They gotta get 'em to prove they're eighteen. So her license will have her real name on it. I can go through them and find her — they got their pictures on them. Might take me a couple hours but I can find her."

"Okay, good, will you do that in the morning and, if Edgar doesn't come by, get the prints to him at Hollywood homicide?"

"Jerry Edgar. I'll do it."

Neither spoke for a few moments as they thought about what they were doing.

"Hey, Harry?"

"Yeah."

"The paper said that there was a new note, that true?"

"Yeah."

"Is it legit? Did we fuck up?"

"I don't know yet, Ray, but I appreciate you saying 'we.' A lot of people just want to point at me."

"Yeah, listen, I ought to tell you, I got subpoenaed today by that Money bitch."

It didn't surprise Bosch, since Mora had been on the Dollmaker task force.

"Don't worry about it. She's probably papered everybody who was on the task force."

"Okay."

"But try to keep this new stuff under your hat if you can."

"As long as I can."

"She's got to know what to ask before she can ask it. I'm just looking for some time to work with this, see what it means."

"No problem, man. You and I both know the right guy went down. No doubt about that, Harry."

But saying it out loud like that put a doubt to it, Bosch knew. Mora was wondering the same things Bosch was.

"You need me to drop this video box off tomorrow so you know what she looks like before flipping through the files?"

"No, like I said, we've got all sorts of catalogs. I'll just look up *Tails from the Crypt* and get it from there. If that don't work I'll go through the agency books."

They hung up and Bosch lit a cigarette, though Sylvia didn't like him doing it in the house. It wasn't that she had a problem with his smoking but she thought potential buyers might be turned off if they thought it had been a smoker's house. He sat there alone for several minutes, peeling the label off the empty beer bottle and thinking about how quickly things could change. Believe something for four years and then find out you might be wrong.

He brought a bottle of Buehler zinfandel and two glasses into the bedroom. Sylvia was in bed with the covers pulled up to her naked shoulders. She had a lamp on and was reading a book called *Never Let Them See You Cry*. Bosch walked to her side of the bed and sat down next to her. He poured out two glasses, they tapped them together and sipped.

"To victory in court," she said.

"Sounds good to me."

They kissed.

"Were you smoking out there again?"

"Sorry."

"Was it bad news? The calls?"

"No. Just bullshit."

"You want to talk?"

"Not now."

He went into the bathroom with his glass and took a quick shower. The wine, which had been beautiful, tasted terrible after he brushed his teeth. When he came out, the reading light was out and the book put away. There were candles burning on both night tables and the bureau. They were in silver votive candle holders with crescent moons and stars cut out on the sides. The flickering flames threw blurry, moving patterns on the walls and curtains and in the mirror, like a silent cacophony.

She lay propped on three pillows, the covers off. He stood naked at the foot of the bed for a few moments and they smiled at each other. She was beautiful to him, her body tan and almost girlish. She was thin, with small breasts and a small, flat stomach. Her chest was freckled from too many summer days at the beach while growing up.

He was eight years older and knew he looked it, but he was not ashamed of his physical appearance. At forty-three, he still had a flat stomach and his body was still ropey with muscles — muscles not created on machines but by lifting the day-to-day weight of his life, his mission. His body hair was curiously going to gray at a much faster pace than the hair on his head. Sylvia often would kid him about this, accusing him of having dyed his hair, of having a vanity they both knew he did not have.

When he climbed onto the bed next to her she ran her fingers over his Vietnam tattoo and the scars a bullet had left on his right shoulder a few years earlier. She traced the surgery zipper the way she did every time they were together here.

"I love you, Harry," she said.

He rolled onto her and kissed her deeply, letting her taste of red wine and the feel of her warm skin take him away from worry and the images of violent ends. He was in the temple of home, he thought but did not say. I love you, he thought but did not say.

9

For everything that had gone well for Bosch on Tuesday, the following morning provided a fresh undoing. The first disaster occurred in Judge Keyes's chambers, where he convened lawyers and clients after studying the note from the alleged Dollmaker in private for a half hour. His private reading had come after Belk had argued for an hour against the inclusion of the note in the trial.

"I have read the note and considered the arguments," he said. "I cannot see how this letter, note, poem, whatever, can possibly be withheld from this jury. It is so on point to the thrust of Ms. Chandler's case that it is the point. I'm not making any judgment on whether it's for real or from some crackpot, that will be for the jury to figure out. If they can. But because the investigation is still underway is no reason to withhold this. I am granting the subpoena and, Ms. Chandler, you can introduce this at the appropriate time, provided you've put down the proper foundation. No pun intended. Mr. Belk, your exception to this ruling will be noted for the record."

"Your Honor?" Belk tried.

"No, we'll have no more argument on it. Let's move on out to court."

"Your Honor! We don't know who wrote this. How can you allow it into evidence when we don't have the slightest idea where it came from or who sent it?"

"I know the ruling is a disappointment, so I'm allowing you some leeway as far as not coming down on you for that showing of your apparent disrespect for the wishes of this court. I said no more argument, Mr. Belk, so I'll go over this only one time. The fact that this note of unknown origin led directly to the discovery of a body bearing all the similarities of a Dollmaker victim is in itself a verification of some authenticity. This is no prank, Mr. Belk. No joke. There is something here. And the jury is going to see it. Let's go. Everybody out."

Court had no sooner been called into session than the next debacle occurred. Belk, perhaps dazed by his defeat in chambers, waltzed into a trap Chandler had deftly set for him.

Her first witness of the day was a man named Wieczorek, who testified that he knew Norman Church quite well and was sure he had not committed the eleven murders attributed to him. Wieczorek and Church had worked together for twelve years in the design lab, he said. Wieczorek was in his fifties, with white hair trimmed so short his pink scalp showed through.

"What makes you so confident in your belief that Norman was not a killer?" Chandler asked.

"Well, for one thing, I know for a fact he didn't kill one of those girls, the eleventh, because he was with me the whole time she was getting . . . whatever. He was with me. Then the police kill him and pin eleven murders on him. Well, I figure, if I know he didn't kill one of those girls, then they are probably lying about the rest. The whole thing is a cover-up for them killing —"

"Thank you, Mr. Wieczorek," Chandler said.

"Just saying what I think."

Belk stood and objected anyway, going to the lectern and whining that the entire answer was speculation. The judge agreed but the damage was done. Belk strode back to his chair and Bosch watched him leaf through a thick transcript of a deposition taken of Wieczorek a few months earlier.

Chandler asked a few more questions about where the witness and Church were on the night the eleventh victim was murdered and Wieczorek

answered that they were at his own apartment with seven other men holding a bachelor party for a fellow employee from the lab.

"How long was Norman Church at your apartment?"

"The whole time of the party. I'd say from nine o'clock on. We finished up
after two in the morning. The police said that girl, the eleventh one, went to
some hotel at one and got herself killed. Norman was with me at one
o'clock in the morning."

"Could he have slipped away for an hour or so without you realizing it?"

"No way. You're in a room with eight guys and you know if one mysteri-
ously disappears for a half hour."

Chandler thanked him and sat down. Belk leaned to Bosch and whispered,
"I wonder what he's going to do with the new asshole I'm going to tear him."

He got up armed with the deposition transcript and lumbered to the
lectern as if he were lugging an elephant rifle. Wieczorek, who wore thick
glasses that magnified his eyes, watched him suspiciously.

"Mr. Wieczorek, do you remember me? Remember the deposition I took
of you a few months back?"

Belk held the transcript up, as a reminder.

"I remember you," Wieczorek said.

"Ninety-five pages, Mr. Wieczorek. Nowhere in this transcript is there any
mention of any bachelor party. Why is that?"

"I guess because you didn't ask."

"But you didn't bring it up, did you? The police are saying your best
buddy murdered eleven women, you supposedly know that's a lie, but you
don't say a thing, is that right?"

"Yeah, that's right."

"Care to tell us why?"

"Far as I was concerned, you were part of it. I only answered what I was
asked. I wasn't volunteering shi — uh, nothing."

"Let me ask you, did you ever tell the police this? Back then, back when
Church was killed and all the headlines said he killed eleven women? Ever
pick up the phone one time and tell them they got the wrong guy?"

"No. At the time I didn't know. It was only when I read a book that came
out on the case a couple years ago and there were details in there about
when that last girl got killed. Then I knew he was with me during that whole
time. I called the police and asked for the task force and they said it was dis-
banded long ago. I left a message for that fellow the book said was in charge,
Lloyd, I think it was, and he never called me."

Belk exhaled into the lectern's microphone, creating a loud sigh that indicated his weariness in dealing with this moron.

"So, if I can recap, you are telling this jury that two years after the
murders, when this book came out, you read it and immediately realized
you had an ironclad alibi for your dead friend. Am I missing anything, Mr.
Wieczorek?"

"Uh, just the part about suddenly realizing. It wasn't sudden."

"Then what was it?"

"Well, when I read the date — September 28 — it set me to thinking and I just remembered that the bachelor party was on September 28 that year and Norman was there at my house all that time. So then I verified it and called Norman's wife to tell her he wasn't what they said he was."

"You verified it? With the others at the party?"

"No, didn't have to."

"Then how, Mr. Wieczorek?" Belk asked in an exasperated tone.

"I looked at the video I had of that night. It had the date and time down in the corner of the frame."

Bosch saw Belk's face turn a lighter shade of pale. The lawyer looked at the judge, then down at his pad, then back up at the judge. Bosch felt his heart sink. Belk had broken the same cardinal rule Chandler had broken the day before. He had asked a question for which he didn't already know the answer.

It didn't take a lawyer to know that since it was Belk who had drawn out mention of the videotape, Chandler was now free to explore it, to move to introduce the videotape as evidence. It had been a clever trap. Because it was new evidence from Wieczorek, not contained in his deposition, Chandler would have had to inform Belk earlier if she planned to draw it out on direct examination. Instead, she had skillfully allowed Belk to blunder in and draw it out. He now stood there defenseless, hearing it for the first time along with the jurors.

"Nothing further," Belk said and returned to his seat with his head down. He immediately pulled one of the law books on the table onto his lap and began paging through it.

Chandler went to the lectern for redirect.

"Mr. Wieczorek, this tape you mentioned to Mr. Belk, do you still have it?"

"Sure, brought it with me."

Chandler then moved to have the tape shown to the jury. Judge Keyes looked at Belk, who lumbered slowly to the lectern.

"Your Honor," Belk managed to say, "can defense have a ten-minute recess to research case law?"

The judge glanced at the clock.

"It's a little early, isn't it, Mr. Belk? We just started."

"Your Honor," Chandler said. "The plaintiff has no objection. I'll need time to set up the video equipment."

"Very well," the judge said. "Ten minutes for counsel. The jury can take a fifteen-minute break and then report back to the assembly room."

While they stood for the jury, Belk was flipping pages in the heavy law book. And when it was time to sit down, Bosch pulled his chair close to his lawyer's.

"Not now," Belk said. "I've got ten minutes."

"You fucked up."

"No, we fucked up. We are a team. Remember that."

Bosch left his teammate there while he went out to smoke a cigarette. When he got to the statue, Chandler was already there. He lit a smoke anyway and kept his distance. She looked at him and smirked. Bosch spoke.

"You tricked him, didn't you?"

"Tricked him with the truth."

"Is it?"

"Oh, yeah."

She put a half-smoked cigarette in the sand of the ash can and said, "I better get back in there and get the equipment set up."

She smirked again. Bosch wondered if she was that good or it was Belk who was that bad.

Belk lost his half-hour argument to keep the tape from being introduced. He said that since it was not brought up during deposition, it was new evidence which the plaintiff could not submit at so late a date. Judge Keyes denied his claim, pointing out what everyone knew, that it had been Belk who had brought the tape to light.

After the jury was brought back in, Chandler asked Wieczorek several questions about the tape and where it had been for the last four years. After Judge Keyes dismissed one more objection from Belk, she rolled a TV/VCR combination to a position in front of the jury box and put in the tape, which Wieczorek had retrieved from a friend sitting in the gallery. Bosch and Belk had to stand up and move into the gallery seats to get a view of the TV screen.

As he made the move, Harry saw Bremmer from the *Times* sitting in one of the back rows. He gave a small nod to Bosch. Harry wondered if he was there to cover the trial or because he was subpoenaed.

The tape was long and boring but was not continuous. It was stopped and started during the evening of the bachelor party but the digital readout in the lower right corner kept the time and date. If it was correct, it was true that Church had an alibi for the last killing attributed to him.

It was dizzying for Bosch to watch. There was Church, no toupee, bald as a baby, drinking beer and laughing with his friends. The man Bosch had killed, toasting a friend's marriage, looking like the All American nerd that Bosch knew he had not been.

The tape lasted ninety minutes, climaxing with a visit from a telegram stripper who sang a song to the groom-to-be, dropping lingerie on his head as she removed each piece. In the video, Church seemed embarrassed to be seeing this, his eye more on the groom than on the woman.

Bosch pulled his eyes from the screen to watch the jury and he could see the tape was devastating to his defense. He looked away.

After the tape was finished, Chandler had a few more questions for Wieczorek. They were questions Belk would have asked but she was beating him to the punch.

"How is the date and time set on the video frame?"

"Well, when you buy it, you set it. Then the battery keeps it going. Never had to fiddle with it after I bought it."

"But if you wanted to, you could put in any date you wanted, anytime you wanted, correct?"

"I s'pose."

"So, say you were going to take a video of a friend to be used later as an alibi, could you set the date back, say a year, and then take the video?"

"Sure."

"Could you put a date on an already existing video?"

"No. You can't superimpose a date over an existing video. Doesn't work that way."

"So, in this case, how could you do it? How could you make a phony alibi for Norman Church?"

Belk stood up and objected on the grounds that Wieczorek's answer would be speculation, but Judge Keyes overruled him, saying the witness had expertise with his own camera.

"Well, you couldn't do that now 'cause Norman's dead," Wieczorek said.

"So what you are saying is that in order to make a phony tape you would have to have conspired with Mr. Church to make it before he was killed by Mr. Bosch, correct?"

"Yes. We'd have to have known that somewhere down the line he'd need this tape and he'd have to've told me what date to set it on and so on and so forth. It's all pretty farfetched, especially because you can pull the newspapers from that year and find the wedding announcement that says my friend got married September thirtieth. That'll show you that his bachelor party had to have been the twenty-eighth or thereabouts. It's not a phony."

Judge Keyes agreed with Belk's objection to the last sentence as being nonresponsive to the question and told the jury to disregard it. Bosch knew they didn't need to have heard it. They all knew the tape wasn't a phony. He did, too. He felt clammy and sick. Something had gone wrong but he didn't know what. He wanted to get up and walk out but he knew that to do so would be an admission of guilt so loud the walls would shake as if during an earthquake.

"One last question," Chandler said. Her face had become flushed as she rode this one to victory. "Did you ever know Norman Church to wear a hairpiece of any kind?"

"Never. I knew him a lot of years and I never saw or heard of such a thing."

Judge Keyes turned the witness back over to Belk, who lumbered to the lectern without his yellow pad. He was apparently too flustered by this turnabout to remember to say, "Just a few questions." Instead he got right to his meager damage-control effort.

"You say you read a book about the Dollmaker case and then discovered this tape's date matched one of the killings, is that right?"

"That's right."

"Did you look into finding alibis for the other ten murders?"

"No, I didn't."

"So. Mr. Wieczorek, you have nothing to offer in terms of defending your longtime friend against these other cases a task force of numerous officers connected to him?"

"The tape put the lie to all of 'em. Your task —"

"You're not answering the question."

"Yes I am, you show the lie on one of the cases, it puts a lie to the whole shooting match, you ask me."

"We're not asking you, Mr. Wieczorek. Now, uh, you said you never saw Norman Church wear a hairpiece, correct?"

"That's what I said, yes."

"Did you know he kept that apartment, using a false name?"

"No, I did not."

"There was a lot you didn't know about your friend, wasn't there?"

"I suppose."

"Do you suppose it is possible that just as he had that apartment without you knowing, that he occasionally wore a hairpiece without you knowing?"

"I suppose."

"Now, if Mr. Church was the killer police claim him to be, and used disguises as police said the killer did, wouldn't it be —"

"Objection," Chandler said.

"— expected that there would be something such —"

"Objection!"

"— as a toupee in the apartment?"

Judge Keyes sustained Chandler's objection to Belk's question as seeking a speculative answer, and chastised Belk for continuing the question after the objection was lodged. Belk took the berating and said he had no further questions. He sat down, sweat lines gliding out of his hairline and running down his temples.

"Best you could do," Bosch whispered.

Belk ignored it, took out a handkerchief and wiped his face.

After accepting the videotape as evidence, the judge broke for lunch. After the jury was out of the courtroom a handful of reporters quickly moved up to Chandler. Bosch watched this and knew it was the final arbiter of how things were going. The media always gravitated to the winners, the perceived winners, the eventual winners. It's always easier to ask them questions.

"Better start thinking of something, Bosch," Belk said. "We could have settled this six months ago for fifty grand. Way things are going, that would have been nothing."

Bosch turned and looked at him. They were at the railing behind the defense table.

"You believe it, don't you? The whole thing. I killed him, then we planted everything that connected him to it."

"Doesn't matter what I believe, Bosch."

"Fuck you, Belk."

"Like I said, you better start thinking of something."

He pushed his wide girth through the gate and headed out of the courtroom. Bremmer and another reporter approached him but he waved them away. Bosch followed him out a few moments later and also brushed the reporters off. But Bremmer kept stride with him as he took the hallway to the escalator.

"Listen, man, my ass is on the line here, too. I wrote a book about the guy and if it was the wrong guy, I want to know."

Bosch stopped and Bremmer almost bumped into him. He looked closely at the reporter. He was about thirty-five, overweight, with brown, thinning hair. Like many men, he made up for this by growing a thick beard, which only served to make him look older. Bosch noticed that the reporter's sweat had stained the underarms of his shirt. But body odor wasn't his problem; cigarette breath was.

"Look, you think it's the wrong guy, then write another book and get another hundred thousand advance. What do you care if it's the wrong guy or not?"

"I have a reputation in this town, Harry."

"So did I. What are you going to write tomorrow?"

"I have to write what's going down in there."

"And you're also testifying? Is that ethical, Bremmer?"

"I'm not testifying. She released me from the subpoena yesterday. I just had to sign a stipulation."

"To what?"

"That said that to the best of my knowledge the book I wrote contained true and accurate information. The source of that information was almost wholly from police sources and police and other public records."

"Speaking of sources, who told you about the note for yesterday's story?"

"Harry, I can't reveal that. Look at how many times I've kept you confidential as a source. You know I can never reveal sources."

"Yeah, I know that. I also know somebody is setting me up."

Bosch stepped onto the escalator and went down.

10

Administrative Vice is located on the third floor of the Central Division station in downtown. Bosch got there in ten minutes and found Ray Mora behind his desk in the squad room, with the telephone held to his ear. Open on his desk was a magazine with color photographs of a couple engaged in sex. The girl in the photos looked very young. Mora was glancing at the photos and turning the pages while listening to the caller. He nodded to Bosch and pointed to a seat in front of his desk.

"Well, that was all I was checking," Mora said into the phone. "Just trying to put a line in the water. Ask around and let me know what you come up with."

Then there was more listening. Bosch looked at the vice cop. He was about Harry's size, with deep bronze skin and brown eyes. His straight brown hair was trimmed short and he had no facial hair. Like most vice cops, he affected a casual appearance. Blue jeans and black polo shirt, open at the neck. If Bosch could see under the desk he knew he'd find cowboy boots. Bosch could see a gold medallion hanging high on his chest. Imprinted on it was a dove, its wings open, the symbol of the Holy Spirit.

"You think you can get me the shoot location?"

Silence. Mora finished with the magazine, wrote something on the front cover and picked up another and began paging through it.

Bosch noticed the Adult Film Performers Guild calendar taped to the side of a vertical file on his desk. There was a photo of a porn star named Delta Bush lounging nude above the days of the week. She had become well known in recent years because she was linked romantically in the gossip tabs to a mainline movie star. On the desk below the calendar was a religious statue Bosch identified as the Infant of Prague.

He knew this because one of his foster mothers had given him a similar statue when he was a boy and was being sent back to McClaren. He hadn't been what the fosters had in mind. Giving him the statue and saying good-bye, the woman had explained to him that the infant was known as the Little King, the saint who took special care to hear the prayers of children. Bosch wondered if Mora knew that story, or if the statue was there as some kind of joke.

"All I'm saying is try," Mora said into the phone. "Get me the shoot. Then you'll be in line for the snitch fund . . . Yeah, yeah. Later."

He hung up.

"Hey, Harry, whereyat?"

"Edgar's been here, huh?"

"Just left a little while ago. He talk to you?"

"No."

Mora noticed Bosch looking at the spread on the page he had the magazine open to. It was two women kneeling in front of a man. He put a yellow Post-it on the page and closed it.

"Lord, I gotta look through all this shit. Got a tip that this publisher is using underage models. You know how I check?"

Bosch shook his head.

"It's not the face or the tits. It's ankles, Harry."

"Ankles."

"Yeah, ankles. Something about them. They are just smoother on younger chicks. I can usually tell, over or under eighteen, by the ankles. Then, of course, I go out and confirm with birth certificates, DLs, etc. It's crazy but it works."

"Good for you. What did you tell Edgar?"

The phone rang. Mora picked up, said his name and listened a few moments.

"I can't talk now. I have to get back to you. Whereyat?"

He hung up after making a note.

"Sorry. I gave Edgar the ID. Maggie Cum Loudly. I had prints, photos, the whole thing. I got some stills of her in action, if you want to see."

He pushed his chair back toward a file cabinet but Bosch told him never mind with the stills.

"Whatever. Anyway, Edgar has it all. Took prints to the coroner's I think, to confirm the ID. Chick's name was Rebecca Kaminski. Becky Kaminski. Be twenty-three if she were alive today. Formerly of Chicago before she came on out to sin city for fame and fortune. What a waste, huh? She was a fine young piece, God bless her."

Bosch felt uncomfortable with Mora. But this was not new. When they had worked the task force together, Harry had never had the feeling that the killings meant much to the vice detective. Didn't make much of a dent. Mora was just putting in his time, lending his help where it was needed. He definitely was good in his area of expertise, but it didn't seem to matter to him whether the Dollmaker was stopped or not.

Mora had a strange way of mingling gutter talk and Jesus talk. At first Bosch had thought he was simply playing the born-again line that was popular in the department a few years earlier, but he was never sure. He once saw Mora cross himself and say a silent prayer at one of the Dollmaker murder scenes. Because of the uneasiness Bosch felt, he had had little contact with Mora since the Norman Church shooting and the breakup of the task force. Mora went back to Ad-Vice and Bosch was shipped to Hollywood. Occasionally the two would see each other in the courthouse or at the Seven or the Red Wind. But even at the bars, they were usually with different groups and sat apart, taking turns sending beers back and forth.

"Harry, she was definitely among the living until at least two years ago. That flick you came across, *Tails from the Crypt*, it was made two years ago. Means Church definitely didn't do her. . . . Probably whoever sent the note did. I don't know if that is good or bad news for you."

"I don't either."

Church had a rock-solid alibi for the Kaminski killing; he was dead. With that added to the apparent alibi Wieczorek's video-tape provided Church for the eleventh killing, Bosch's sense of paranoia was turning to panic. For four years there had been no doubt for him about what he had done.

"So how's the trial going, anyway?" Mora asked.

"Don't ask. Can I use your phone?"

Bosch dialed Edgar's pager number and then punched in Mora's phone number. After he hung up to wait for the call back, he didn't know what else to say.

"The trial's a trial. You still supposed to testify?"

"I guess. I'm on for tomorrow. I don't know what she wants from me. I wasn't even there the night you took that bastard down."

"Well, you were on the task force with me. That's good enough to drag you into it."

"Well, we'll —"

The phone rang and Mora picked it up. He then passed it to Bosch.

"Whereyat, Harry?"

"I'm here with Mora. He filled me in. Anything on the prints?"

"Not yet. I missed my man at SID. Musta gone to lunch. So I left the prints there. Should have a confirmation later today. But I'm not waiting on it."

"Where are you now?"

"Missing Persons. Trying to see if this girl ever got reported missing, now that I have a name to go with the body."

"You gonna be there a while?"

"Just started. We're looking through hard copies. They only went to computer eighteen months ago."

"I'll be over."

"You got your trial, man."

"I have some time."

Bosch felt that he had to keep moving, to keep thinking. It was the only way to keep from examining the horror building in his mind, the possibility he had taken down the wrong man. He drove back to Parker Center and took the stairs down to the first subterranean level. Missing Persons was a small office inside the Fugitives section. Edgar was sitting on a desk, looking through a stack of white forms. Bosch recognized these as cases that were not even investigated after the reports had been made. They would have been in files if there had been any follow-up.

"Nothing so far, Harry," Edgar said. He then introduced Bosch to Detective Morgan Randolph, who was sitting at a nearby desk. Randolph gave Bosch a stack of reports and he spent the next fifteen minutes looking through the pages, each one an individual story of someone's pain that had fallen on the deaf ears of the department.

"Harry, on the description, look for a tattoo above the ass," Edgar said.

"How do you know?"

"Mora had some photos of Magna Cum Loudly. In action, as Mora says. And there's a tattoo — it's Yosemite Sam, you know, the cartoon? — to the left of the dimple over the left side of her ass."

"Well, did you find that on the body?"

"Didn't notice it 'cause of the severe skin discoloration. But I didn't really look at the backside, either."

"What's going on with that? I thought you said the cut was going to be done yesterday."

"Yeah, that's what they said, but I called over and they're still backed up from the weekend. They haven't even prepped it yet. I called Sakai a little while ago and he's going to take a look in the freezer after lunch. Check on the tattoo."

Bosch looked back at his stack. The recurrent theme was the young ages of the missing people. L.A. was a drain which drew a steady stream of the nation's runaways. But there were many who disappeared from here as well.

Bosch finished his stack without seeing the name Rebecca Kaminski, her alias, or anyone that matched her description. He looked at his watch and knew he had to get back to court. He took another stack off Randolph's desk anyway and began to wade through it. As he searched, he listened to the banter between Edgar and Randolph. It was clear that they had known each other before this day's meeting. Edgar called him Morg. Bosch figured they might've known each other from the Black Peace Officers Association.

He found nothing in the second stack.

"I gotta go. I'm gonna be late."

"Okay, man. I'll let you know what we find."

"And the prints, too, okay?"

"You got it."

Court was already in session when Bosch got to courtroom 4. He quietly opened the gate, went through and took his seat next to Belk. The judge eyed him disdainfully but said nothing. Bosch looked up to see Assistant Chief Irvin Irving in the witness seat. Money Chandler was at the lectern.

"Good going," Belk whispered to him. "Late for your own trial."

Bosch ignored him and watched as Chandler began asking Irving general questions about his background and years on the force. They were preliminary questions; Bosch knew he couldn't have missed much.

"Look," Belk whispered next. "If you don't care about this, at least pretend you do for the jury's sake. I know we are only talking about taxpayers' money here, but act like it's going to be your own money they will be deciding to give."

"I got tied up. It won't happen again. You know, I'm trying to figure out this case. Maybe that doesn't matter to you, since you've already decided."

He leaned back in his chair to get away from Belk. He was reminded that he had not eaten lunch by a sharp signal of resentment from his stomach. He tried to concentrate on the testimony.

"As assistant chief, what does your command include?" Chandler asked Irving.

"I am presently the commanding officer of all detective services."

"At the time of the Dollmaker investigation, you were one rank below. A deputy chief, correct?"

"Yes."

"As such you were in charge of the Internal Affairs Division, correct?"

"Yes. IAD and Operations Bureau, which basically means I was in charge of managing and allocating the department's personnel."

"What is the mission of the IAD, as it is known?"

"To police the police. We investigate all citizen complaints, all interior complaints of misconduct."

"Do you investigate police shootings?"

"Not per se. There is an Officer Involved Shooting team that handles the initial investigation. After that, if there is an allegation of misconduct or any impropriety, it is forwarded to IAD for follow-up."

"Yes, and what do you recall of the IAD investigation of the shooting of Norman Church by Detective Harry Bosch?"

"I recall all of it."

"Why was it referred to IAD?"

"The shooting team determined that Detective Bosch had not followed procedures. The shooting itself was within departmental policy but some of his actions prior to the gunfire were not."

"Can you be more specific?"

"Yes. Basically, he went there alone. He went to this man's apartment without backup, placing himself in danger. It ended in the shooting."

"It's called cowboying it, isn't it?"

"I've heard the phrase. I don't use it."

"But does it fit?"

"I wouldn't know."

"You wouldn't know. Chief, would you know if Mr. Church would be alive today if Detective Bosch had not created this situation by playing cow —"

"Objection!" Belk shrieked.

But before he could walk to the lectern to argue, Judge Keyes sustained the objection and told Chandler to avoid speculative questions.

"Yes, Your Honor," she said pleasantly. "Chief, basically what you have testified to is that Detective Bosch set in motion a series of events that ultimately ended with an unarmed man being killed, am I right?"

"That is incorrect. The investigation found no substantive indication or evidence that Detective Bosch deliberately set this scenario in motion. It was spur of the moment. He was checking out a lead. When it looked good, he should have called for backup. But he didn't. He went in. He identified himself and Mr. Church made the furtive move. And here we are. That is not to say that the outcome would have been different had there been a backup. I mean, anybody who would disobey an order from a police officer holding a gun would probably do it with two officers holding guns."

Chandler successfully had the last sentence of the answer struck from the record.

"To come to the conclusion that Detective Bosch did not intentionally set the situation into motion, did your investigators study all facets of the shooting?"

"Yes, indeed."

"How about Detective Bosch, was he studied?"

"Unquestionably. He was rigorously questioned about his actions."

"And about his motives?"

"His motives?"

"Chief, did you or any of your investigators know that Detective Bosch's mother was slain in Hollywood about thirty years ago by a killer who was never arrested? That prior to that, she had a record for multiple arrests for loitering?"

Bosch felt his skin go hot, as if klieg lights had been turned on him, and that everyone in the courtroom was staring at him. He was sure they were. But he looked only at Irving, who stared silently ahead, a palsied look on his face, the capillaries on either side of his nose flaring. When Irving didn't answer, Chandler prompted him.

"Did you know, Chief? It is referenced in Detective Bosch's personnel file. When he applied to the force, he had to say if he had ever been the victim of a crime. He lost his mother, he wrote."

Finally, Irving said, "No, I did not know."

"I believe that loitering was a euphemism for prostitution in the 1950s, when Los Angeles was engaged in a denial of crime problems such as rampant prostitution on Hollywood Boulevard, is that correct?"

"I don't recall that."

Chandler asked to approach the witness and handed Irving a thin stack of papers. She gave him nearly a minute to read through them. He furrowed his brow as he read and Bosch could not see his eyes. The muscles of his cheeks bunched together below his temples.

"What is that, Chief Irving?" Chandler asked.

"It is what we call a due diligence report detailing the investigation of a homicide. It is dated November 3, 1962."

"What is a due diligence report?"

"Every unsolved case is looked at annually — we call it due diligence — until such time that we feel the prognosis for bringing the case to a successful conclusion is hopeless."

"What is the victim's name and circumstances of her death?"

"Marjorie Phillips Lowe. She was raped and strangled, October 31, 1961. Her body was found in an alley behind Hollywood Boulevard between Vista and Gower."

"What is the investigator's conclusion, Chief Irving?"

"It says that at this time, which was a year after the crime, there are no workable leads and prognosis for successful conclusion of the case is deemed hopeless."

"Thank you. Now, one more thing, is there a box on the cover form listing next of kin?"

"Yes, it identifies the next of kin as Hieronymus Bosch. Next to that in brackets it says 'Harry.' A box marked 'son' has been checked off."

Chandler referred to her yellow pad for a few moments to let this information soak into the jury. It was so quiet Bosch could actually hear Chandler's pen scratching on the pad as she made a notation.

"Now," she said, "Chief Irving, would knowing about Detective Bosch's mother have caused you to take a closer look at this shooting?"

After a long moment of silence, he said, "I can't say."

"He shot a man suspected of doing almost the exact same thing that had happened to his mother — his mother's slaying being unsolved. Are you saying you don't know if that would have been germane to your investigation?"

"I, yes . . . I don't know at this time."

Bosch wanted to put his head down on the table. He had noticed that even Belk had stopped scribbling notes and was just watching the interchange between Irving and Chandler. Bosch tried to shake off the anger he felt and concentrate on how Chandler had obtained the information. He realized she had probably gotten the P-file in a discovery motion. But the details of the crime and his mother's background would not be in it. She had most likely procured the due diligence report from the archives warehouse on a Freedom of Information petition.

He realized he had missed several questions to Irving. He began watching and listening again. He wished he had a lawyer like Money Chandler.

"Chief, did you or any IAD detectives go to the scene of the shooting?"

"No, we did not."

"So your information about what happened came from members of the shooting team, who in turn got their information from the shooter, Detective Bosch, correct?"

"Essentially, yes."

"You have no personal knowledge of the evidentiary layout: the toupee under the pillow, the cosmetics beneath the sink in the bathroom?"

"Correct. I was not there."

"Do you believe all of that was there as I just stated?"

"Yes, I do."

"Why?"

"It was all there in the reports — reports from several different officers."

"But all originating with the information from Detective Bosch, correct?"

"To a degree. There were investigators swarming that place. Bosch didn't tell them what to write."

"Before, as you say, they swarmed the place, how long was Bosch there alone?"

"I don't know."

"Is that piece of information on any report that you know of?"

"I'm not sure."

"Isn't it true, Chief, that you wanted to fire Bosch and refer this shooting to the district attorney's office for the filing of criminal charges against him?"

"No, that is wrong. The DA looked at it and passed. It's routine. They said it was within policy, too."

Well, score one for me, Bosch thought. It was the first misstep he had seen her take with Irving.

"What happened to the woman who gave Bosch this tip? Her name was McQueen. I believe she was a prostitute."

"She died about a year later. Hepatitis."

"At the time of her death was she part of an ongoing investigation of Detective Bosch and this shooting?"

"Not that I am aware of and I was in charge of IAD at the time."

"What about the two IAD detectives who investigated the shooting? Lewis and Clarke, I believe their names were. Didn't they continue their investigation of Bosch long after the shooting had been determined officially to be within policy?"

Irving took a while to answer. He was probably leery of being led to slaughter again.

"If they conducted such an ongoing investigation it was without my knowledge or approval."

"Where are those detectives now?"

"They are also dead. Both killed in the line of duty a couple years ago."

"As the commander of IAD wasn't it your practice to initiate covert investigations of problem officers that you had marked for dismissal? Wasn't Detective Bosch one of those officers?"

"The answer to both questions is no. Unequivocally, no."

"And what happened to Detective Bosch for his violation of procedures during the shooting of the unarmed Norman Church?"

"He was suspended for one deployment period and transferred within detective services to Hollywood Division."

"In English, that means he was suspended for a month and demoted from the elite Robbery-Homicide squad to the Hollywood Division, correct?"

"You could say it that way."

Chandler flipped a page up on her pad.

"Chief, if there were no cosmetics in the bathroom and no evidence that Norman Church was anything other than a lonely man who had taken a prostitute to his apartment, would Harry Bosch still be on the force? Would he have been prosecuted for killing this man?"

"I'm not sure I understand the question."

"I'm asking, sir, did the alleged evidence tying Mr. Church to the killings that was allegedly found in his apartment save Detective Bosch? Did it not only save his job but save him from criminal prosecution?"

Belk stood up and objected, then walked to the lectern.

"She is asking him to speculate again, Your Honor. He can't tell what would have happened given an elaborate set of circumstances that didn't exist."

Judge Keyes clasped his hands together in front of him and leaned back thinking. Then he abruptly leaned forward to the microphone.

"Ms. Chandler is laying the groundwork to make a case that the evidence in the apartment was fabricated. I'm not saying whether she has adequately done this or not, but since that is her mission I think the question is answerable. I'm going to allow it."

After some thought, Irving finally said, "I can't answer that. I don't know what would have happened."

11

Bosch was able to smoke two cigarettes during the ten-minute recess that followed the end of Irving's testimony. On redirect Belk had asked only a few questions, trying to rebuild a fallen house with a hammer but no nails. The damage was done.

Chandler had so far used the day to skillfully plant the seeds of doubt about both Church and Bosch. The alibi for the eleventh killing opened the door to Church's possible innocence. And now she had subscribed a motive to Bosch's action: revenge for a murder more than thirty years old. By the end of the trial the seeds would be in full bloom.

He thought about what Chandler had said about his mother. Could she have been right? Bosch had never consciously considered it. It was always there — the idea of revenge — flickering in some part of his mind with the distant memories of his mother. But he had never taken it out and examined it. Why had he gone out there alone that night? Why hadn't he called one of the others back in — Mora or any of the investigators in his command?

Bosch had always told himself and others it was because he doubted the whore's story. But now, he knew, it was his own story he was beginning to doubt.

Bosch was so deep in these thoughts that he did not notice Chandler had come through the door until the flare of her lighter caught his eye. He turned and stared at her.

"I won't stay long," she said. "Just a half."

"I don't care."

He was almost done with the second cigarette.

"Who's next?"

"Locke."

The USC psychologist. Bosch nodded, though he immediately saw this as a break from her good guy–bad guy pattern. Unless she counted Locke as a good guy.

"Well, you're doing good," Bosch said. "But I guess you don't need me to tell you that."

"No, I don't."

"You may even win — you probably will win, but ultimately you're wrong about me."

"Am I? . . . Do you even know?"

"Yeah, I know. I know."

"I have to go."

She stubbed the cigarette out. It was less than half smoked. It would be a prize for Tommy Faraway.

Dr. John Locke was a gray-bearded, bald and bespectacled man who looked as though he could have used a pipe to complete the picture of university professor and researcher of sexual behavior. He testified that he had offered his expertise to the Dollmaker task force after reading about the killings in the newspapers. He helped an LAPD psychiatrist draw up the first profiles of the suspect.

"Tell the jury about your expertise," Chandler asked.

"Well, I am the director of the Psychohormonal Research Laboratory at USC. I am founder of that unit as well. I have conducted wide-ranging studies of sexual practice, paraphilia and psychosexual dynamics."

"What is a paraphilia, doctor? In language we will all understand, please."

"Well, in layman's terms, paraphilia are what are commonly referred to by the general public as sexual perversions — sexual behavior generally considered unacceptable by society."

"Such as strangling your sex partner?"

"Yes, that would be one of them, big time."

There was a polite murmur of humor in the courtroom and Locke smiled. He seemed very at ease on the witness stand, Bosch thought.

"Have you written scholarly articles or books about these subjects you mentioned?"

"Yes, I have contributed numerous articles to research publications. I've written seven books on various subjects, sexual development of children, prepubescent paraphilia, studies of sadomasochism — the whole bondage thing, pornography, prostitution. My last book was on childhood development histories of deviant murderers."

"So you've been around the block."

"Only as a researcher."

Locke smiled again and Bosch could see the jury warming to him. All twenty-four eyes were on the sex doctor.

"Your last book, the one on the murderers, what was it called?"

"*Black Hearts: Cracking the Erotic Mold of Murder.*"

Chandler took a moment to look at her notes.

"What do you mean by 'erotic mold'?"

"Well, Ms. Chandler, if I could digress a moment, I think I should fill in some background."

She nodded her go-ahead.

"There are generally two fields, or two schools of thought, when it comes to the study of sexual paraphilia. I am what you call a psychoanalyst, and psychoanalysts believe that the root of paraphilia in an individual comes from hostilities nurtured in childhood. In other words, sexual perversions — in fact, even normal erotic interests — are formed in early childhood and then manifest in expressions as the individual becomes an adult.

"On the other hand, behaviorists view paraphilia as learned behaviors. An example being, molestation in the home of a child may trigger similar behavior by him as an adult. The two schools, for lack of a better word, are not that divergent. They are actually quite closer than psychoanalysts and behaviorists usually like to admit."

He nodded and folded his hands together, seeming to have forgotten the original question.

"You were going to tell us about erotic molds," Chandler prompted.

"Oh yes, I'm sorry, I lost the train there. Uh, the erotic mold is the description I use to cover the whole shebang of psychosexual desires that go into an individual's ideal erotic scene. You see, everybody has an ideal erotic scene. This could include the ideal physical attributes of a lover, the location, the type of sex act, the smell, taste, touch, music, whatever. Everything, all the ingredients that go into this individual achieving the ultimate erotic scene. A leading authority on this, out of Johns Hopkins University, calls it a 'lovemap.' It is sort of a guide to the ultimate scene."

"Okay, now in your book, you applied it to sexual murderers."

"Yes, with five subjects — all convicted of murder involving a sexual motivation or practice — I attempted to trace each man's erotic mold. To crack it open and trace the parts back to development in childhood. These men had damaged molds, so to speak. I wanted to find where the damage took place."

"How did you pick your subjects?"

Belk stood up and made an objection and moved to the lectern.

"Your Honor, as fascinating as all of this is, I don't believe it is on point to this case. I will stipulate Dr. Locke's expertise in this field. I don't think we have to go through the history of five other murderers. We are here in trial on a case about a murderer who is not even mentioned in Dr. Locke's book. I am familiar with the book. Norman Church is not in it."

"Ms. Chandler?" Judge Keyes said.

"Your Honor, Mr. Belk is correct about the book. It's about sadistic sex killers. Norman Church is not in it. But its significance to this case will be clear in the next set of questions. I think Mr. Belk realizes this and that is the reason for his objection."

"Well, Mr. Belk, I think the time for an objection was probably about ten minutes ago. We are well into this line of questioning and I think we need to see it through now. Besides, you are correct about it being rather fascinating. Go on, Ms. Chandler. The objection is overruled."

Belk dropped back into his chair and whispered to Bosch, "He's gotta be banging her." It was said just loud enough that Chandler might have heard him, but not the judge. If she did, she showed nothing.

"Thank you, Your Honor," she said. "Dr. Locke, Mr. Belk and I were correct when we said that Norman Church was not one of the subjects of your study, were we not?"

"Yes, that is correct."

"When did the book come out?"

"Just last year."

"That would be three years after the end of the Dollmaker case?"

"Yes."

"Well, having been part of the Dollmaker task force and obviously becoming familiar with the crimes, why didn't you include Norman Church in your study? It would seem to be an obvious choice."

"It would seem that way but it wasn't. First of all, Norman Church was dead. I wanted subjects that were alive and cooperative. But incarcerated, of course. I wanted people that I could interview."

"But of the five subjects you wrote about, only four are alive. What about the fifth, a man named Alan Karps, who was executed in Texas before you even began your book? Why not Norman Church?"

"Because, Ms. Chandler, Karps had spent much of his adult life in institutions. There were voluminous public records on his treatment and psychiatric study. With Church there was nothing. He had never been in trouble before. He was an anomaly."

Chandler looked down at her yellow pad and flipped a page, letting the point she just scored hang in the quiet courtroom like a cloud of cigarette smoke.

"But you did at least make preliminary inquiries about Church, didn't you?"

Locke hesitated before answering.

"Yes, I made a very preliminary inquiry. It amounted to contacting his family and asking his wife if she would grant me an interview. She turned me down. Since the man himself was dead and there were no records about him — other than the actual details of the murders, which I was already familiar with — I didn't pursue it. I went with Karps in Texas."

Bosch watched Chandler cross several questions off on her legal pad and then flip several pages to a new set. He guessed that she was changing tack.

She said, "While you were working with the task force you drew up a psychological profile of the killer, correct?"

"Yes," Locke said slowly. He adjusted himself in the chair, straightening up for what he knew was coming.

"What was that based on?"

"An analysis of the crime scenes and method of homicide filtered through what little we know about the deviant mind. I came up with common attributes that I thought might be part of our suspect's makeup — no pun intended."

No one in the courtroom laughed. Bosch looked around and saw that the spectator rows were becoming crowded. This must be the best show in the building, he thought. Maybe all of downtown.

"You were not very successful, were you? If Norman Church was the Dollmaker, that is."

"No, not very successful. But that happens. It's a lot of guesswork. Rather than a testimonial to my failure, it is more a testimonial to how little we know about people. This man's behavior did not make so much as a blip on anybody's radar screen — not counting, of course, the women he killed — until the night he was shot."

"You speak as if it is a given that Norman Church was the killer, the Dollmaker. Do you know that to be true based on indisputable facts?"

"Well, I know it to be true because it is what the police told me."

"If you take it backwards, doctor. If you start with what you know about Norman Church now and leave out what the police have told you about the supposed evidence, would you ever believe him capable of what he has been accused of?"

Belk was about to stand up to object but Bosch strongly put his hand on his arm and held him down. Belk turned and looked angrily at him but by then Locke was answering.

"I wouldn't be able to count him in or out as a suspect. We don't know enough about him. We don't know enough about the human mind in general. All I know is, anybody is capable of anything. I could be a sexual killer. Even you, Ms. Chandler. We all have an erotic mold and for most of us, it is quite normal. For some it may be a bit unusual but still only playful. For the others, on the extreme, who find they can only reach erotic excitement and fulfillment through administering pain, even killing their partners, it is buried deep and dark."

Chandler was looking down at her pad and writing when he finished. When she didn't ask another question immediately, he continued unbidden.

"Unfortunately, the black heart is not worn on the sleeve. The victims who see it usually don't live to talk about it."

"Thank you, Doctor," Chandler said. "I have nothing further."

Belk plowed in without any preliminary softball questions, a look of concentration on his wide florid face that Bosch had not seen previously.

"Doctor, these men with these so-called paraphilia, what do they look like?"

"Like anybody. There is no look that gives them away."

"Yes, and are they always on the prowl? You know, looking to indulge their aberrant fantasies by acting them out?"

"No, actually, studies have shown that these people obviously know they have aberrant tastes and they work to keep them in check. Those brave enough to come forward with their problems often lead completely normal lives with the aid of chemical and psychological therapy. Those that don't are periodically overcome by the compulsion to act out, and they may follow these urges and commit a crime.

"Psychosexually motivated serial killers often exhibit patterns that are quite repetitive, so that police tracking them can almost predict within a few days or a week when they will strike. This is because the buildup of stress, the compulsion to act, will follow a pattern. Often, what you have are decreasing intervals — the overpowering urge comes back sooner and sooner each time."

Belk was leaning over the lectern, his weight firmly against it.

"I see, but between these moments of compulsion when the acts take place, does this man seem to have a normal life or, you know, is he standing in the corner, slobbering? Or whatever?"

"No, nothing like that — at least, until the intervals become so short that they literally don't exist. Then you might have someone out there always on the prowl, as you said. But between the intervals there is normalcy. The aberrant sexual act — rape, strangulation, voyeurism, anything — will provide the subject with the memory to construct fantasy. He will be able to use the act to fantasize and stimulate arousal during masturbation or normal sex."

"Do you mean that he will sort of replay the murder in his mind so that he can become sexually aroused for having normal sexual intercourse with, say, his wife?"

Chandler objected and Belk had to rephrase the question so it was not leading Locke.

"Yes, he will replay the aberrant act in his mind so that he can accomplish the act that is socially acceptable."

"So in doing so, a wife, for example, might not even know of her husband's real desires, correct?"

"That is correct. It has happened often."

"And a person such as this could carry on at work and with friends and not reveal this side of himself, correct?"

"Again, that is correct. There is ample evidence of this in the case histories of sexual sadists who kill. Ted Bundy led a well-documented double life. Randy Kraft, killer of dozens of hitchhikers here in Southern California. I could name many, many more. You see, this is the very reason they kill so many victims before being caught, and then it is usually only because of a small mistake."

"Like with Norman Church?"

"Yes."

"As you testified earlier, you could not find or gather enough information about Norman Church's early development and behavior to include him in your book. Does that fact dissuade you from belief that he was the killer police claim him to be?"

"Not in the least. As I said, these desires can be easily cloaked in normal behavior. These people know they have desires that are not accepted by society. Believe me, they take pains to hide them. Mr. Church was not the only subject I considered for the book and then discarded for lack of valuable information. I did preliminary studies of at least three other serial killers who were either dead or uncooperative and dropped them as well because of the lack of public record or background on them."

"You mentioned earlier that the roots of these problems are planted in childhood. How?"

"I should have said 'may,' the roots may be planted in childhood. It is a difficult science and nothing is known for sure. Getting to your question, if I had a definite answer I guess I wouldn't have a job. But what psychoanalysts such as myself believe is that the paraphilia can come through emotional or physical trauma or both. It basically is a synthesis of these, possibly some biological determinants and social learning. It is hard to pinpoint, but we believe it happens very early, generally five to eight years of age. One of the fellows in my book was molested by an uncle at age three. My thesis, or belief or whatever you want to call it, is that this trauma set him on the trail toward becoming a murderer of homosexuals. In most of these killings he emasculated his victims."

The courtroom had become so quiet during Locke's testimony that Bosch heard the slight bump of one of the rear doors opening. He glanced back and saw Jerry Edgar taking a seat in the rear row. Edgar nodded at Harry, who looked up at the clock. It was 4:15; the trial would be recessed for the day in fifteen minutes. Bosch figured Edgar was on his way back from the autopsy.

"Would the childhood trauma that's at the root of a person's criminal activities as an adult need to be so overt? In other words, as traumatic as molestation?"

"Not necessarily. It could be rooted in more traditional emotional stress placed on a child. The awesome pressure to succeed in a parent's eyes, coupled with other things. It is hard to discuss this in a hypothetical context because there are so many dimensions of human sexuality."

Belk followed up with a few more general questions about Locke's studies before ending. Chandler asked a couple more questions on redirect but Bosch had lost interest. He knew that Edgar would not have come to the courtroom unless he had something important. Twice he glanced back at the clock on the wall and twice he looked at his watch. Finally, when Belk said he had nothing further on cross, Judge Keyes called it a day.

Bosch watched Locke step down and head out through the gate and toward the door. A couple of the reporters followed him. Then the jury stood and filed out.

Belk turned to Bosch as they watched and said, "Better be ready tomorrow. My guess is that it's going to be your turn in the sun."

"What've you got, Jerry?" Bosch asked when he caught up with Edgar in the hallway leading to the escalator.

"Your car over at Parker Center?"

"Yeah."

"I'm there, too. Let's walk that way."

They got on the escalator but didn't talk because it was crowded with spectators from the courtroom. Out on the sidewalk, when they were alone, Edgar pulled a folded white form out of his coat pocket and handed it to Bosch.

"All right, we got it confirmed. The prints Mora dug up on Rebecca Kaminski match the hand mold we made on the concrete blonde. I also just came from the autopsy and the tattoo is there, above the ass. Yosemite Sam."

Bosch unfolded the paper. It was a photocopy of a standard missing person report.

"That's a copy of the report on Rebecca Kaminski, also known as Magna Cum Loudly. Missing twenty-two months and three days."

Bosch was looking at the report.

"Doesn't look like any doubt to me," he said.

"Nope, no doubt. It was her. The autopsy also confirms manual strangulation as the cause. The knot pulled tight on the right side. Most likely a lefty."

They walked without talking for half a block. Bosch was surprised by how warm it was for so late in the day. Finally, Edgar spoke.

"So, obviously, we've got it confirmed; this may look like one of Church's dolls but there's no way in the world he did it unless he came back from the dead . . .

"So I did some checking at the bookstore over by Union Station. Bremmer's book, *The Dollmaker*, with all the details a copycat would need. was published in hardback seventeen months after you put Church in the dirt. Becky Kaminski goes missing about four months after the book came out. So our killer could've bought the book and then used it as a sort of blueprint on what to do to make it look like that Dollmaker."

Edgar looked over at him and smiled.

"You're in the clear, Harry."

Bosch nodded, but didn't smile. Edgar didn't know about the videotape.

They walked down Temple to Los Angeles Street. Bosch didn't notice the people around him, the homeless shaking their cups on the corners. He almost crossed Los Angeles in front of traffic until Edgar put a hand on his arm. While waiting for the walk sign, he looked down and scanned the report again. It was bare bones. Rebecca Kaminski had simply gone out on a "date" and not returned. She was meeting the unnamed man at the Hyatt on Sunset. That was it. No follow-up, no additional information. The report had been made by a man named Tom Cerrone, who was identified in the report as Kaminski's roommate in Studio City. The light changed and they walked across Los Angeles Street and then right toward Parker Center.

"You going to talk to this Cerrone guy, the roommate?" he asked Edgar.

"I don't know. Probably get around to it. I'm more interested in what you think about all of this, Harry. Where do we go from here? Bremmer's book was a fuckin' bestseller. Anybody who read it is a suspect."

Bosch said nothing until they got to the parking lot and stopped near the entrance booth before separating. Bosch looked down at the report in his hands and then up at Edgar.

"Can I keep this? I might take a run by the guy."

"Be my guest. . . . Another thing you should know, Harry."

Edgar reached in his inside coat pocket and pulled out another piece of paper. This one was yellow and Bosch knew it was a subpoena.

"I got served at the coroner's office. I don't know how she knew I was there."

"When d'you have to be in court?"

"Tomorrow at ten. I had nothing to do with the Dollmaker task force so we both know what she's going to ask about. The concrete blonde."

12

Bosch threw his cigarette into the fountain that was part of the memorial to officers killed in the line of duty and walked through the glass doors into Parker Center. He badged one of the cops behind the front desk and walked around to the elevators. There was a red line painted on the black tile floor. That was the route visitors were told to take if they were going to the Police Commission hearing room. There was also a yellow line for Internal Affairs and a blue for applicants who wanted to become cops. It was a tradition for cops standing around waiting for elevators to stand on the yellow line, thereby making any citizens who were going to IAD — usually to file complaints — walk around them. This maneuver was usually accompanied by a baleful stare from cop to citizen.

Every time Bosch waited for an elevator he remembered the prank he had been partially responsible for while still in the academy. He and another cadet had come into Parker Center at four one morning, drunk and hiding paint brushes and cans of black and yellow paint in their windbreakers. In a quick and daring operation, his partner had used the black paint to obliterate the yellow line on the tile floor while Bosch painted a new yellow line which went past the elevators, down the hall, into a men's room and right to a urinal. The prank had given them near legendary status in their class, even among the instructors.

He got off the elevator on the third floor and walked back to the Robbery-Homicide Division. The place was empty. Most RHD cops worked a strict seven-to-three shift. That way the job didn't get in the way of all the moonlighting gigs they had lined up. RHD dicks were the cream of the department. They got all the best gigs. Chauffeuring visiting Saudi princes, security work for studio bosses, body-guarding Vegas high rollers — LVPD did not allow its people to moonlight, so the high-paying jobs fell to LAPD.

When Bosch had first been promoted to RHD there were still a few detective-threes around who had worked bodyguard duty for Howard Hughes. They had spoken of the experience as if that was what the RHD job was all about, a means to an end, a way to get a job working for some deranged billionaire who didn't need any bodyguards because he never went anywhere.

Bosch walked to the rear of the room and turned on one of the computers. He lit a cigarette while the tube warmed up and took the report Edgar had given him out of his coat pocket. The report was nothing. It had never been looked at, acted on, cared about.

He noticed it was a walk-in — Tom Cerrone had come into the North Hollywood Division station and made the report at the front desk. That meant it had probably been written up by a probationary rookie or a burned-out vet who didn't give a shit. In either case, it was not taken for what it was: a cover-your-ass report.

Cerrone said he was Kaminski's roommate. According to the brief summary, two days before the report was made she had told Cerrone she was going on a blind date, meeting an unnamed man at the Hyatt on the Sunset Strip and that she hoped the guy wasn't a creep. She never came back. Cerrone got worried and went to the cops. The report was taken, passed through North Hollywood detectives where it didn't make a blip on anyone's screen and then sent to Missing Persons in downtown where four detectives are charged with finding the sixty people reported missing on average each week in the city.

In reality, the report was put in a stack of others like it and was not looked at again until Edgar and his pal, Morg, found it. None of this bothered Bosch, though anyone who spent two minutes reading the report should have known that Cerrone wasn't what he said he was. But Bosch figured Kaminski was dead and in the concrete long before the report was made. So there was nothing anyone could have done anyway.

He punched the name Thomas Cerrone into the computer and ran a search on the California Department of Justice information network. As he expected, he got a hit. The computer file on Cerrone, who was forty years old, showed he had been popped nine times in as many years for soliciting for prostitution and twice for pandering.

He was a pimp, Bosch knew. Kaminski's pimp. Harry noticed that Cerrone was on thirty-six months' probation for his last conviction. He got out his black telephone book and rolled his chair over to a desk with a phone. He dialed the after-hours number for the county probation department and gave the clerk who answered Cerrone's name and DOJ number. She gave back Cerrone's current address. The pimp had come down in the world, from Studio City to Van Nuys, since Kaminski had gone to the Hyatt and not come back.

After hanging up, he thought of calling Sylvia and wondered if he should tell her it was likely he would be called by Chandler to testify the next day. He was unsure if he wanted her to be there, to see him cornered on the witness stand by Money Chandler. He decided not to call.

Cerrone's home address was an apartment on Sepulveda Boulevard in an area where prostitutes were not too discreet about how they got their customers. It was still daylight and Bosch counted four young women spread apart over a two-block stretch. They wore halter tops and short shorts. They held their thumb out like hitchhikers when cars went by. But it was clear they were only interested in a ride around the corner to a parking lot where they could take care of business.

Bosch parked at the curb across from the Van-Aire Apartments, where Cerrone had told his probation officer he was living. A couple of the numbers from the address had fallen off the front wall but it was readable because the smog had left the rest of the wall a dingy beige. The place needed new paint, new screens, some plastering to fill in the cracks in the facade and probably new tenants.

Actually, it needed to be knocked down. Start over, Bosch thought as he crossed the street. Cerrone's name was on the residents list next to the front security door but no one answered the buzzer at apartment six. Bosch lit a cigarette and decided to hang around for a while. He counted twenty-four units on the residents list. It was six o'clock. People would be coming home for dinner. Someone would come along.

He walked away from the door and back out to the curb. There was graffiti on the sidewalk, all of it in black paint. The monikers of the local homeboys. There was also a scrip painted in block letters that asked, R U THE NEX RODDY KING? He wondered how someone could misspell a name that had been heard and printed so many times.

A woman and two young children came to the steel-grated door from the other side. Bosch timed his approach so that he was at the door just as she opened it.

"Have you seen Tommy Cerrone around?" he asked as he passed her.

She was too busy with the children to answer. Bosch walked into the courtyard to get his bearings and to look for a door with a six on it — Cerrone's apartment. There was graffiti on the concrete floor of the courtyard, a gang insignia Bosch couldn't make out. He found number six on the first floor toward the back. There was a rusted-out hibachi grill on the ground next to the door. There was also a child's bike with training wheels parked under the front window.

The bike didn't fit. Bosch tried to look in but the curtains were drawn, leaving only a three-inch band of darkness he could not see beyond. He knocked on the door and as was his practice, stepped to the side. A Mexican woman with what looked like an eight-month pregnancy beneath her faded pink bathrobe answered the door. Behind the small woman Bosch could see a young boy sitting on the living room floor in front of a black-and-white TV tuned to a Spanish language channel.

"Hola," Bosch said. "Señor Tom Cerrone aquí?"

The woman stared at him with frightened eyes. She seemed to close in on herself, as if to get smaller before him. Her arms moved up from her side and closed over her swollen belly.

"No migra," Bosch said. "Policía. Tomás Cerrone. Aquí?"

She shook her head no and began to close the door. Bosch put his hand out to stop it. Struggling with his Spanish he asked if she knew Cerrone and where he was. She said he only came once a week to collect the mail and the rent. She moved back a step and gestured to the card table where there was a small stack of mail. Bosch could see an American Express bill on top. Gold Card.

"Teléfono? Necesidad urgente?"

She looked down from his eyes and her hesitation told him she had a number.

"Por favor?"

She told him to wait and she left the doorway. While she was gone the boy sitting ten feet inside the door turned from the TV — Bosch could see it was some kind of game show — and looked at him. Bosch felt uncomfortable. He looked away, into the courtyard. When he looked back the boy was smiling. He had his hand up and was pointing a finger at Bosch. He made a shooting sound and giggled. Then the mother was back at the door with a piece of paper. There was a local phone number on it, that was all.

Bosch copied it down in a small notebook he carried and then told her he would take the mail. The woman turned and looked at the card table as if the answer to what she should do was sitting on it with the mail. Bosch told her it would be okay and she finally lifted the stack and handed it to him. The frightened look was in her eyes again.

He stepped back and was going to walk away when he stopped and looked back at her. He asked how much the rent was and she told him it was one hundred dollars a week. Bosch nodded and walked away.

Out on the street he walked down to a pay phone that was in front of the next apartment complex. He called the downtown communications center, gave the operator the phone number he had just gotten and said he needed an address. While he waited he thought about the pregnant woman and wondered why she stayed. Could things be worse back in the Mexican town she came from? For some, he knew, the journey here was so difficult that returning was out of the question.

As he was flipping through Cerrone's mail, one of the hitchhikers walked up to him. She wore an orange tank top over her surgically augmented breasts. Her cutoff jeans were cut so high above the thighs that the white pockets hung out below. In one of the pockets he could see the distinctive shape of a condom package. She had the gaunt, tired look of a strawberry — a woman who would do anything, anytime, anywhere to keep crack in her pipe. Factoring in her deteriorated appearance, he put her age at no more than twenty. To Bosch's surprise, she said, "Hey, darling, looking for a date?"

He smiled and said, "You're going to have to be more careful than that, you want to stay out of the cage."

"Oh, shit," she said and turned to walk away.

"Wait a minute. Wait a minute. Don't I know you? Yeah, I know you. It's . . . what's your name, girl?"

"Look, man, I'm not talking to you and I'm not blowing you, so I gotta go."

"Wait. Wait. I don't want anything. I just thought, you know, that we'd met. Aren't you one of Tommy Cerrone's girls? Yeah, that's where I met you."

The name put a slight stutter in her step. Bosch let the phone dangle by its cord and caught up to her. She stopped.

"Look, I'm not with Tommy anymore, okay? I gotta go to work."

She turned from him and put her thumb out as a wave of southbound traffic started by.

"Wait a minute, just tell me something. Tell me where Tommy is these days. I need to get with him on something."

"On what? I don't know where he is."

"A girl. You remember Becky? Couple years ago. Blonde, liked red lipstick, had a set like yours. She mighta used the name Maggie. I want to find her and she was working for Tom. You remember her?"

"I wasn't even around then. And I haven't seen Tommy in four months. And you are full of shit."

She walked off and Bosch called after her, "Twenty bucks."

She stopped and came back.

"For what?"

"An address. I'm not bullshitting. I want to talk to him."

"Well, give it."

He took the money out of his wallet and gave it to her. It occurred to him that Van Nuys Vice might be watching him from somewhere around here and wondering why he was giving a hooker a twenty.

"Try the Grandview," she said. "I don't know the number or anything but it's on the top floor. You can't tell'm I sent ya. He'll fuck me up."

She walked away putting the money in one of the flapping pockets. He didn't have to ask her where the Grandview was. He watched her cut in between two apartment buildings and disappear, probably going to get a rock. He wondered if she had told the truth and why he could find it in himself to give her money but not the woman in apartment six. The police operator had hung up by the time he got back to the pay phone.

Bosch redialed and asked for her and she gave him the address that went with the phone number he'd gotten. Suite P-1, the Grandview Apartments, on Sepulveda in Sherman Oaks. He had just wasted twenty bucks on crack cocaine. He hung up.

In the car, he finished looking through the mail. Half of it was junk mail, the rest credit card bills and mailers from Republican candidates. There was also a postcard invitation to an Adult Film Performers Guild awards banquet in Reseda the following week.

Bosch opened the American Express bill. The illegality of this did not concern him in the least. Cerrone was a criminal who was lying to his probation officer. There would be no complaint from him. The pimp owed American Express $1855.05 this month. The bill was two pages, and Bosch noticed two billings for airline flights to Las Vegas and three billings from Victoria's

Secret. Bosch was familiar with Victoria's Secret, having studied the mail-order lingerie catalog at Sylvia's on occasion. In one month, Cerrone had ordered nearly $400 in lingerie by mail. The money paid by the poor woman who rented the apartment Cerrone was using as a front for a proba-tion address was basically subsidizing the lingerie bills of Cerrone's whores. It angered Bosch, but it gave him an idea.

The Grandview Apartments were the ultimate California ideal. Built along-side a shopping mall, the building afforded its tenants the ability to walk directly from their apartment into the mall, thereby cutting out the hereto-fore required middle ground for all Southern California culture and interac-tion: the car. Bosch parked in the mall's garage and entered the outer lobby through the rear entrance. It was an Italian marble affair with a grand piano in its center that was playing by itself. Bosch recognized the song as a Cab Calloway standard, "Everybody That Comes to My Place Has to Eat."

There was a directory and a phone on the wall by the security door that led to the elevators. The name next to P-1 was Kuntz. Bosch took it to be an inside joke. He lifted the phone and pushed the button. A woman answered and he said, "UPS. Gotta package."

"Uh," she said. "From who?"

"Um, it says, I can't read the writing — looks like Victor's secretary or something."

"Oh," she said and he heard her giggle. "Do I have to sign?"

"Yes, ma'am, I need a signature."

Rather than buzz him in, she said she would come down. Bosch stood at the glass door for two minutes waiting before he realized the scam wouldn't work. He was standing there in a suit and had no package in his hand. He turned his back to the elevator just as the polished chrome doors began to part.

He took a step toward the piano and looked down as if he was fascinated by it and didn't notice the elevator's arrival. From behind him he heard the security door start to open and he turned around.

"Are you UPS?"

She was blonde and stunning even in her blue jeans and pale blue Oxford shirt. Their eyes met and right away Bosch knew she knew it was a scam. She immediately tried to close the door but Bosch got there in time and pushed his way through.

"What are you doing? I —"

Bosch clamped a hand over her mouth because he thought she was about to scream. Covering half her face accentuated the fright in her eyes. She didn't seem as stunning to Bosch anymore.

"It's okay. I'm not going to hurt you, I just want to talk to Tommy. Let's go up."

He slowly pulled his hand back and she didn't scream.

"Tommy's not there," she said in a whisper, as if to signal her cooperation.

"Then we can wait."

He gently pushed her toward the elevator and punched the button.

She was right. Cerrone wasn't there. But Bosch didn't have to wait long. He had barely had time to check on the opulent furnishings of the two-bedroom, two-bath and loft apartment with private roof garden when the man arrived.

Cerrone stepped through the front door, *Racing Forum* in hand, just as Bosch stepped into the living room from the balcony that overlooked Sepulveda and the crowded Ventura Freeway.

Cerrone initially smiled at Bosch but then the face became blank. This often happened to Bosch with crooks. He believed it was because the crooks often thought they recognized him. And it was true they probably did. Bosch's picture had been in the paper and on TV several times in the last few years, including once this week. Harry believed that most crooks who read the papers or watched the news looked closely at the pictures of the cops. They probably thought it gave them an added advantage, someone to look out for. But instead it bred familiarity. Cerrone had smiled as though Bosch was a long-lost friend, then he realized it was probably the enemy, a cop.

"That's right," Bosch said.

"Tommy, he made me bring him up," the girl said. "He called on the —"

"Shut up," Cerrone barked. Then, to Bosch, he said, "If you had a warrant, you wouldn't be here alone. No warrant, get the fuck out."

"Very observant," Bosch said. "Sit down. I have questions."

"Fuck you and the questions you rode in on. Get out."

Bosch sat down on a black leather couch and took out his cigarettes.

"Tom, if I go, it's to go see your PO and see about getting you revoked for this address scam you're playing. The probation department frowns on cons telling them they live one place when they actually live somewhere else. Especially when one's a dump and one's the Grandview."

Cerrone threw the *Forum* across the room at the girl. "See?" he said. "See the shit you got me in?"

She seemed to know better than to say anything. Cerrone folded his arms and stood in the living room but he wasn't going to sit down. He was a well-built guy gone to fat. Too many afternoons at Hollywood or Del Mar, sipping cocktails and watching the ponies.

"Look, what do you want?"

"I want to know about Becky Kaminski."

Cerrone looked puzzled.

"You remember, Maggie Cum Loudly, the blonde with the tits you probably had her enlarge. You were bringing her up through the video business, doin' some outcall work on the side, and then she disappeared on you."

"What about her? That was a long time ago."

"Twenty-two months and three days, I am told."

"So what? She turned up and is saying some shit about me, it don't matter. Take it to court, man. We'll see —"

Bosch jumped up off the couch and slapped him hard across the face, then pushed him over a black leather chair onto the floor. Cerrone's eyes immediately went to the girl's, which told Bosch that he had complete control of the situation. The power of humiliation sometimes was more awesome than a gun held to the head. Cerrone's face was a bright red all over.

Bosch's hand stung. He bent over the fallen man and said, "She didn't turn up and you know it. She's dead and you knew it when you made the missing person report. You were just covering your ass. I want to know how you knew."

"Look, man, I didn't have any —"

"But you knew she wasn't coming back. How?"

"I just had a hunch. She didn't turn up for a couple days."

"Guys like you don't go to the police on hunches. Guys like you, they get their place broken into, they don't even call the cops. Like I said, you were just covering your ass. You didn't want to get blamed 'cause you knew she wasn't coming back alive."

"Awright, awright, it was more than a hunch. Okay? It was the guy. I never saw him but his voice and some of the things he said. It was familiar, you know? Then after I sent her and she didn't come back, it dawned on me. I remembered him. I had sent him somebody else once and she ended up dead."

"Who?"

"Holly Lere. I can't remember her real name."

Bosch could. Holly Lere was the porno name of Nicole Knapp. The seventh victim of the Dollmaker. He sat back down on the couch and put a cigarette in his mouth.

"Tommy," the girl said, "he's smoking."

"Shut the fuck up," he said to her.

"Well, you said no smoking in here except on the bal —"

"Shut the fuck up!"

"Nicole Knapp," Bosch said.

"Yeah, that's it."

"You knew the cops said the Dollmaker got her?"

"Yeah, and I always thought that until Becky disappeared and I remembered this guy and what he said."

"But you didn't tell anybody. You didn't call the cops."

"It's like you said, man, guys like me, we don't call."

Bosch nodded.

"What did he say? The caller, what was it he said?"

"He said, 'I have a special need tonight.' Both times. Just like that. He said the same thing both times. And his voice was weird. It was like he was talking through clenched teeth or something."

"And you sent her to that."

"I didn't put it together until after she didn't come back. Look, man, I made a report. I told the cops the hotel she went to and they never did nothing. I'm not the only one to blame. Shit, the cops said that guy was caught, that he was dead. I thought it was safe."

"Safe for you, or the girls you put out on the street?"

"Look, you think I would've sent her if I knew? I had a lot invested in her, man."

"I'm sure you did."

Bosch looked over at the blonde and wondered how long it would be before she looked like the one he had given the twenty to on the street. His guess was that Cerrone's girls all ended up used up and on the street with their thumb out, or they ended up dead. He looked back at Cerrone.

"Did Rebecca smoke?"

"What?"

"Smoke. Did she smoke? You lived with her, you should know."

"No, she didn't smoke. It's a disgusting habit."

Cerrone looked over at the blonde and glared. Bosch dropped his cigarette on the white rug and ground it out as he stood up. He headed toward the door but stopped after he opened it.

"Cerrone, the woman in that dump your mail goes to?"

"What about her?"

"She doesn't pay rent anymore."

"What are you talking about?"

He climbed up from the floor, regaining a measure of his pride.

"I'm talking about her not paying you rent anymore. I'm going to check on her from time to time. If she's paying rent, your PO gets a call and your scam gets blown. Probation gets revoked and you do your time. It's tough to run an outcall business from county lockup. Only two phones on each floor and the brothers control who uses them and for how long. I guess you'd have to cut them in."

Cerrone just stared at him, anger thumping in his temples.

"And she better still be there when I check," Bosch said. "If I hear she went back to Mexico, I blame you and make the call. If I hear she bought a fucking condo, I make the call. She just better be there."

"That's extortion," Cerrone said.

"No, asshole, that's justice."

He left the door open. Out in the hallway waiting for the elevator, he once again heard Cerrone yell, "Shut the fuck up!"

13

The last vestiges of the evening rush hour made it a slow run up to Sylvia's. She was sitting at the dining room table in faded blue jeans and a Grant High T-shirt, reading book reports, when he came in. One of the eleventh-grade English classes she taught down in the Valley at Grant was called Los Angeles in Literature. She had told him she developed the class so the students might come to know their city better. Most of them came from other places, other countries. She had once told him that the students in one of her classes accounted for eleven different native languages.

He put his hand on the back of her neck and bent down to kiss her. He noticed the reports were on Nathanael West's *Day of the Locust*.

"Ever read it?" she asked.

"Long time ago. Some English teacher in high school made us read it. She was crazy."

She elbowed him in the thigh.

"All right, wise guy. I try to rotate the tough ones with the easy ones. I assigned them *The Big Sleep*."

"That's probably what they thought this one should've been called."

"Aren't you the life of the party today. Something good happen?"

"Actually, no. Everything is turning to shit out there. But in here . . . it's different."

She got up and they embraced. He ran his hand up and down her back the way he knew she liked.

"What's happening on the case?"

"Nothing. Everything. I might be going into the mud puddle. Wonder if I can get a job after this as a private eye. Like Marlowe."

She pushed away.

"What are you talking about?"

"I'm not sure. Something. I have to work on it tonight. I'll take the kitchen table. You can stay out here with the locusts."

"It's your turn to cook."

"Then, I'm going to hire the colonel."

"Shit."

"Hey, that's not a good thing for an English teacher to say. What's the matter with the colonel?"

"He's been dead for years. Never mind. It's okay."

She smiled at him. This ritual occurred often. When it was his turn to cook he usually took her out. He could see she was disappointed by the prospect of fried chicken to go. But there was too much going on, too much to think about.

She had a face that made him want to confess everything bad he had ever done. Yet he knew he could not. She knew it, too.

"I humiliated a man today."

"What? Why?"

"Because he humiliates women."

"All men do that, Harry. What did you do to him?"

"Knocked him down in front of his woman."

"He probably needed it."

"I don't want you to come to court tomorrow. I'm probably going to be called by Chandler to testify but I don't want you there. It's going to be bad."

She was silent for a moment.

"Why do you do this, Harry? Tell me all these things that you do but keep the rest a secret? In some ways we are so intimate and in others . . . You tell me about the men you knock down but not about you. What do I know about you, your past? I want us to get to that, Harry. We have to or we'll end up humiliating each other. That's how it ended for me before."

Bosch nodded and looked down. He didn't know what to say. He was too burdened by other thoughts to get into this now.

"You want the extra crispy?" he finally asked.

"Fine."

She went back to her book reports and he went out to get dinner.

After they were done eating and she went back to the dining room table, he opened his briefcase on the kitchen table and took out the blue murder books. He had a bottle of Henry Weinhard's on the table but no cigarette. He wouldn't smoke inside. At least not while she was awake.

He unsnapped the first binder and laid out the sections on each of the eleven victims across the table. He stood up with the bottle so he could look down and take them all in at once. Each section was fronted by a photograph of the victim's remains, as they were found. There were eleven of these photos in front of him. He did some thinking on the cases and then went into the bedroom and checked the suit he had worn the day before. The Polaroid of the concrete blonde was still in the pocket.

He brought it back to the kitchen and laid it on the table with the others. Number twelve. It was a horrible gallery of broken, abused bodies, their garish makeup showing false smiles below dead eyes. Their bodies were naked, exposed to the harsh light of the police photographer.

Bosch drained the bottle and kept staring. Reading the names and the dates of the deaths. Looking at the faces. All of them lost angels in the city of night. He didn't notice Sylvia come in until it was too late.

"My God," she said in a whisper as she saw the photos. She took a step backward. She was holding one of her students' papers in her hand. Her other hand had come up to her mouth.

"I'm sorry, Sylvia," Bosch said. "I should've warned you not to come in."

"Those are the women?"

He nodded.

"What are you doing?"

"I'm not sure. Trying to make something happen, I guess. I thought if I looked at them all again I might get an idea, figure out what's happening."

"But how can you look at those? You were just standing there looking."

"Because I have to."

She looked down at the paper in her hand.

"What is it?" he asked.

"Nothing. Uh, one of my students wrote something. I was going to read it to you."

"Go ahead."

He stepped over to the wall and turned off the light that hung over the table. The photos and Bosch became shrouded in darkness. Sylvia stood in the light cast from the dining room through the kitchen entrance.

"Go ahead."

She held up the paper and said, "It's a girl. She wrote, 'West foreshadowed the end of Los Angeles's halcyon moment. He saw the city of angels becoming a city of despair, a place where hopes get crushed under the weight of the mad crowd. His book was the warning.'"

She looked up.

"She goes on but that was the part I wanted to read. She's only a tenth-grader taking advanced classes but she seemed to grasp something so strong there."

He admired her lack of cynicism. Bosch's first thought was that the kid had plagiarized — where'd she get a word like halcyon? But Sylvia saw past that. She saw the beauty in things. He saw the darkness.

"It's good," he said.

"She's African-American. She comes up on the bus. She's one of the smartest I have and I worry about her on the bus. She said the trip is seventy-five minutes each way and that is the time when she reads the assignments I give. But I worry about her. She seems so sensitive. Maybe too much so."

"Give her time and she'll grow a callous on her heart. Everybody does."

"No, not everybody, Harry. That's what I worry about with her."

She looked at him there in the darkness for a long moment.

"I'm sorry I intruded."

"You never intrude on me, Sylvia. I am sorry I brought this home. I can leave if you want, take it to my place."

"No, Harry, I want you here. You want me to put on some coffee?"

"No, I'm fine."

She went back to the living room and he turned the light back on. He looked over the gallery again. Though they looked the same in death because of the makeup applied by each one's killer, the women fell into numerous physical categories according to race, size, coloring, and so on.

Locke had told the task force that this meant that the killer was simply an opportunistic predator. Not concerned with body type, only the acquisition of a victim which he could then place into his erotic program. He did not care if they were black or white as long as he could snatch them with as little notice as possible. He was a bottom feeder. He moved on a level where the women he encountered were victims long before he got to them. They were women who had already given up their bodies to the unloving hands and eyes of strangers. They were out there waiting for him. The question, Bosch now knew, was whether the Dollmaker was still out there, too.

He sat down and from the pocket of the binder he pulled a map of West L.A. Its creases cracked and split in some sections as he unfolded it and put it down on top of the photos. The round black stickers that represented locations where bodies had been found were still in place. The victim's name and date of discovery were written next to each black dot. Geographically, the task force had found no significance until after Church was dead. The bodies were found in locations stretching from Silverlake to Malibu. The Dollmaker littered the entire Westside. Still, for the most part, the bodies were clustered in Silverlake and Hollywood, with only one found in Malibu and one in West Hollywood.

The concrete blonde was found farther south in Hollywood than any of the previous bodies. She was also the only one that had been buried. Locke had said location of disposal was probably a choice of convenience. After Church was dead this seemed true. Four of the bodies had been dumped within a mile of his Silverlake apartment. Another four were in eastern Hollywood, not a long drive, either.

The dates had done nothing for the investigation. No pattern. Initially there was a decreasing-interval pattern between discoveries of victims, then it began to vary widely. The Dollmaker would go five weeks between strikes, then two weeks, then three. Nothing to make of this; the detectives on the task force simply let it go.

Bosch moved on. He began reading the background packets that had been drawn up on each victim. Most of these were short — two to three pages about their sad lives. One of the women who worked Hollywood Boulevard at night was going to beautician school by day. Another had been sending money to Chihuahua, Mexico, where her parents believed she had a good job as a tour guide at the famous Disneyland. There were odd matches between some of the victims, but nothing that ever amounted to anything.

Three of the Boulevard whores went to the same doctor for weekly clap shots. Members of the task force put him under surveillance for three weeks. But one night while they were watching him, the real Dollmaker picked up a prostitute on Sunset and her body was found in Silverlake the next morning.

Two of the other women also shared a doctor. The same Beverly Hills plastic surgeon had performed breast-implant surgery on them. The task force had rallied on this discovery, for a plastic surgeon remakes images, similarly after a fashion to the way the Dollmaker used makeup. The plastic man, as he was called by the cops, was also placed under surveillance. But he never made a suspicious move and seemed to be the picture of domestic bliss with a wife whose physical features he had sculpted to his own liking. They were still watching him when Bosch took the telephone tip that led to the shooting of Norman Church.

As far as Bosch knew, neither doctor ever knew he had been watched. In the book Bremmer wrote, they were identified by pseudonyms.

Nearly two-thirds through the background packets, as he read about Nicole Knapp, the seventh victim, Bosch saw the pattern within the pattern. He had somehow missed it before. All of them had. The task force, Locke, the media. They had put all the victims into the same classification. A whore is a whore is a whore. But there were differences. Some were streetwalkers, some were higher up the scale as escorts. Within these two groups, some were also dancers; one was a telegram stripper. And two made livings in the pornography trade — as had the latest victim, Becky Kaminski — while taking outcall hooking assignments on the side.

Bosch took the packets and photos of Nicole Knapp, the seventh victim, and Shirleen Kemp, the eleventh victim, off the table. These were the two porn actresses, known on video as Holly Lere and Heather Cumhither, respectively.

He then paged through one of the binders until he found the package on the lone survivor, the woman who had gotten away. She, too, was a porn actress who took outcall sex jobs. Her name was Georgia Stern. Her video name was Velvet Box. She had gone to the Hollywood Star Motel to meet a date arranged through the outcall service she advertised in the local sex tabloids. After she arrived, her client asked her to undress. She turned her back to do this, offering a show of modesty in case that was a turn-on for the client. She then saw the leather strap of her purse come over her head and he began choking her from behind. She fought, as probably all the victims had, but she was able to get free by driving an elbow into her attacker's ribs, then turning and delivering a kick to his genitals.

She ran naked from the room, all thought of modesty long gone. By the time police went back in, the attacker was gone. It was three days before the reports on the incident filtered their way to the task force. By then the hotel room had been used dozens of times — the Hollywood Star offered hourly rates — and it was useless as far as gathering physical evidence went.

Reading the reports on it now, Bosch realized why the composite drawing that Georgia Stern had helped a police artist sketch was so different from the appearance of Norman Church.

It had been a different man.

An hour later, he turned one of the binders to the last page, where he had kept a listing of phone numbers and addresses of the principals involved in the investigation. He went to the wall phone and dialed the home of Dr. John Locke. He hoped the psychologist had not changed his number in four years.

Locke picked up after five rings.

"Sorry, Dr. Locke, I know it's getting late. It's Harry Bosch."

"Harry, how are you? I am sorry we didn't get to talk today. It was not the best circumstance for you, I'm sure, but I —"

"Yes, Doctor, listen, something's come up. It's related to the Dollmaker. I have some things I want to show you and talk about. Would it be possible for me to come there?"

There was a lengthy silence before Locke answered.

"Would that be about this new case I've read about in the paper?"

"Yes, that and some other things."

"Well, let's see, it's nearly ten o'clock. Are you sure this can't wait until tomorrow morning?"

"I am in court tomorrow morning, Doctor. All day. It's important. I'd really appreciate your time. I'll be there before eleven and be out before twelve."

When Locke didn't say anything, Harry wondered if the soft-spoken doctor was afraid of him or just didn't want a killer cop in his home.

"Besides," Bosch said into the silence, "I think you'll find it interesting."

"Very well," Locke said.

After getting the address, Harry packed all the paperwork back into the two binders. Sylvia came into the kitchen after hesitating at the doorway until she was sure the photos were packed away.

"I heard you talking. Are you going to his place tonight?"

"Yeah, right now. In Laurel Canyon."

"What's going on?"

He stopped his hurried movement. He had both binders stacked under his right arm.

"I . . . well, we missed something. The task force. We messed up. I think all along there were two, but I didn't see it until now."

"Two killers?"

"I think so. I want to ask Locke about it."

"Are you coming back tonight?"

"I don't know. It will be late. I was thinking about just going to my place. Check my messages, get some fresh clothes."

"This weekend is not looking good, is it?"

"What — oh, yeah, Lone Pine, yeah. Well, uh, I —"

"Don't worry about it. But I may want to hang out at your place while they have the open house here."

"Sure."

She walked him to the door and opened it. She told him to be careful and to call her the next day. He said he would. At the threshold he hesitated. He said, "You know, you were right."

"About what?"

"What you said about men."

14

Laurel Canyon is a winding cut through the Santa Monica Mountains that connects Studio City with Hollywood and the Sunset Strip. On the south side, where the road drops below Mulholland Drive and the fast four lanes thin to two crumbling invitations to a head-on collision, the canyon becomes funky L.A., where forty-year-old Hollywood bungalows sit next to multilevel glass contemporaries that sit next to gingerbread houses. Harry Houdini built a castle in here among the steep hillsides. Jim Morrison lived in a clapboard house near the little market that still serves as the canyon's only commercial outpost.

The canyon was a place where the new rich — rock stars, writers, film actors and drug dealers — came to live. They braved the mudslides and the monumental traffic tie-ups just to call Laurel Canyon home. Locke lived on Lookout Mountain Drive, a steep upward grade off Laurel Canyon Boulevard that made Bosch's department-issue Caprice work extra hard. The address he was looking for could not be missed because it blinked in blue neon from the front wall of Locke's house. Harry pulled to the curb behind a multicolor Volkswagen van that was at least twenty-five years old. Laurel Canyon was like that, a time warp.

Bosch got out, dropped his cigarette in the street and stepped on it. It was very quiet and dark. He heard the Caprice's engine ticking away its heat, the smell of burning oil wafting from the undercarriage. He reached in through the open window and grabbed the two binders.

It had taken most of an hour to get to Locke's and during that time Bosch had been able to refine his thoughts on the discovery of the pattern within a pattern. He also realized along the way that there was a key way of attempting to confirm it.

Locke answered with a glass of red wine in his hand. He was barefoot and wearing blue jeans and a surgeon's green shirt. Hanging from a leather thong around his neck was a large pink crystal.

"Good evening, Detective Bosch. Please come in."

He led the way through an entry hall to a large living room/dining room area with a wall of French doors that opened onto a brick patio surrounding a lighted blue pool. Bosch noticed the pinkish carpet was dirty and worn but otherwise the place was not bad for a college sex professor and author. He noticed the water of the pool was choppy, as if someone had been swimming recently. He thought he smelled a trace of stale marijuana smoke.

"Beautiful place," Bosch said. "You know we're almost neighbors. I live on the other side of the hill. On Woodrow Wilson."

"Oh, really? How come it took you so long to get here?"

"Well, actually, I didn't come from home. I was at a friend's place up in Bouquet Canyon."

"Ah, a girlfriend, that explains the forty-five-minute wait."

"Sorry to hold you up, Doctor. Why don't we get on with this so I don't keep you any longer than necessary."

"Yes, please."

He signaled Bosch to put the binders down on the dining room table. He didn't ask if Harry wanted a glass of wine, an ashtray or even a pair of swimming trunks.

"I'm sorry to intrude," Harry offered. "I'll be quick."

"Yes, you said that. I'm sorry this came up now myself. Testifying put me back a day on my research and writing schedule and I was trying to recoup tonight."

Bosch noticed his hair wasn't wet. Maybe he had been working while someone else had been in the pool.

Locke took a seat at the dining room table and Bosch told the story of the concrete blonde investigation in exact chronological order after starting by showing him the copy of the new note left at the station on Monday.

While telling the details of the latest death, Bosch saw Locke's eyes brighten with interest. When he was done, the psychologist folded his arms and closed his eyes and said, "Let me think about this before we go on."

He sat perfectly still. Bosch wasn't sure what to make of it. After twenty seconds went by, he finally said, "If you're going to think, I'm going to borrow your phone."

"In the kitchen," Locke said without opening his eyes.

Bosch got Amado's phone number from the task force list in the binder and called him. He could tell he had awakened the coroner's analyst.

After identifying himself, Bosch said, "Sorry to wake you. But things are happening very quickly on this new Dollmaker case. Did you read about it in the paper?"

"Yeah. But they said it wasn't known for sure if it was the Dollmaker."

"Right. That's what I'm working on. I have a question."

"Go ahead."

"You testified yesterday about the rape kits taken from each victim. Where are they now? The evidence, I mean."

There was a long silence before Amado said, "They're probably still in evidence storage. The coroner's policy is to keep evidence seven years after resolution of a case. You know, in case of appeals or something. Now, since your perp is dead, there would be no reason to keep the stuff even that long. But it takes an order from the medical examiner to clear out an evidence locker. The chances are the ME at the time would not have thought or remembered to do this after you, uh, killed Church. It's too big of a bureaucracy to run that well. My guess is the kits would still be there. The evidence custodian would only request a disposal order after seven years."

"Okay," Bosch said, excitement evident in his voice. "What about the condition? Would it still be usable as evidence? And for analysis?"

"Should be no deterioration, I would think."

"How full's your plate?"

"It's always full. But you've got me hooked here. What's up?"

"I need someone to pull the kits from victims seven and eleven. That's Nicole Knapp and Shirleen Kemp. Got it? Seven and eleven, like the store."

"I got it. Seven eleven. Then what?"

"Cross-reference the pubic combs. Look for the same foreign hair in both places, on both women. How long will it take?"

"Three, four days. We have to send that to the DOJ lab. I can put a rush on it, maybe get it sooner. Can I ask you something? Why are we doing this?"

"I think there was someone else besides Church. A copycat. He did seven, eleven and the one this week. And I'm thinking he might not have been smart enough to shave himself like Church. If you find similar hair in the combs, I think that will clinch it."

"Well, I can tell you something right off that is interesting about those two. Seven and eleven."

Bosch waited.

"I reviewed everything before I testified, so it's still fresh, you know? Remember I testified that two of the victims had extreme damage, vaginal tears? Well, it was those two, seven and eleven."

Bosch thought about this for a few moments. From out in the dining room he heard Locke say, "Harry?"

"Be right there," he called out. To Amado, he said, "That's interesting."

"It means this second guy, whoever he is, he's rougher trade than Church. Those two women were hurt the most."

Something came together in Bosch's mind then. Something that had not seemed right about Amado's testimony the day before. Now it was clear.

"The condoms," he said.

"What about them?"

"You testified that it was a box of twelve, only three left."

"That's right! Nine used. You subtract victims seven and eleven from the list and you have nine victims. It fits, Harry. Okay, first thing tomorrow, I'm on this. Give me three days, max."

They hung up and Bosch wondered if Amado would get any sleep tonight.

Locke had replenished his wineglass but still did not ask Bosch if he wanted a glass when he returned to the dining room. Bosch sat down across the table from him.

"I'm ready to go on," Locke said.

"Let's do it."

"You're saying that the body found this week exhibited every known detail ascribed to the Dollmaker?"

"Right."

"Except now we have a new method of disposal. A private disposal as opposed to the public challenge of the others. It's all very interesting. What else?"

"Well, from trial testimony I think we can eliminate Church as the perp in the eleventh killing. A wit produced a tape in —"

"A wit?"

"A witness. In court. He was a friend of Church's. He came in with a video that showed Church at a party at the time number eleven got abducted. The tape is convincing."

Locke nodded his head and was silent. At least he didn't close his eyes, Bosch thought. The psychologist thoughtfully rubbed the graying whiskers on his chin, which made Bosch do the same thing.

"Then there is number seven," Bosch said.

He told Locke about the information he got from Cerrone, about the voice the pimp had recognized.

"Voice identification wouldn't pass as evidence but say for the sake of argument he is right. That connects the concrete blonde to our seventh victim. The videotape eliminates Church from the eleventh case. Amado, the guy from the coroner's office, I don't know if you remember him, he says numbers seven and eleven had similar injuries, injuries that stood out if compared with those of the others.

"Another thing I just remembered is the makeup. After Church was dead they found the makeup in the Hyperion apartment, remember? They matched it to nine of the victims. The two victims there was no makeup for were —"

"Seven and eleven."

"Right. So what we have are multiple ties between these two cases — seven and eleven. Then you have a tangential connection to number twelve, this week's victim, based on the pimp recognizing the customer's voice. The connection gets stronger if you look at the lifestyles of the three women. All were in porno, all worked outcall."

"I see the pattern within the pattern," Locke said.

"Gets better. Now, we add in our lone survivor, she was also in porno and did outcall work."

"And she described an attacker who looked nothing like Church."

"Exactly. That's because I don't think it was Church. I think the three, plus the survivor, make up one set of victims of one killer. The remaining nine are another set with another killer. Church."

Locke got up and began pacing back and forth on one side of the dining room table. He kept his hand to his chin.

"Anything else?"

Bosch opened one of the binders and took out the map and a folded piece of paper on which he had earlier written a series of dates. He carefully unfolded the map and spread it on the table. He leaned in and over it.

"Okay, look. Let's call the nine Group A and the three Group B. On the map I have circled the locations where Group A victims were found. You see, if you take the Group B victims out of the picture, you have a nice geographic concentration. Group B vics were found in Malibu, West Hollywood, South Hollywood. But the A list was concentrated here in eastern Hollywood and Silverlake."

Bosch ran his finger in a circle on the map, showing the dumping zone Church had used.

"And here in almost the center of this zone is Hyperion Street — Church's killing pad."

He straightened up and dropped the folded paper on the map.

"Now here is a list of dates of the eleven killings originally attributed to Church. You see there is an interval pattern at the start — thirty days, thirty-two days, twenty-eight, thirty-one, thirty-one. But then the pattern goes to hell. Remember that? How it confused us back then?

"Yes, I do."

"We have twelve days, then sixteen, then twenty-seven, thirty and eleven. The pattern disintegrates into no pattern. But now separate the dates of Group A and Group B."

Bosch unfolded the paper. There were two columns of dates. Locke leaned over the table into the light to study the columns. Bosch could see a thin line, a scar, on the top of his bald and freckled crown.

"On Group A we now have a pattern," Bosch continued. "A clearly discernable pattern of intervals. We have thirty days, thirty-two, twenty-eight, thirty-one, thirty-one, twenty-eight, twenty-seven and thirty. On Group B we have eighty-four days between the two killings."

"Better stress management."

"What?"

"The intervals between the acting out of these fantasies is dictated by the buildup of stress. I testified about this. The better the actor handles it, the longer the interval between killings. The second killer has better stress management. Or, at least, had it back then."

Bosch watched him pace the room. He took out a cigarette and lit it. Locke said nothing.

"What I want to know is, is this possible?" Bosch asked. "I mean, is there any precedent for this that you know of?"

"Of course, it's possible. The black heart does not beat alone. You don't even have to look outside the boundaries of your own jurisdiction to find ample evidence it is possible. Look at the Hillside Stranglers. There was even a book written about them called *Two of a Kind*.

"Look at the similarities in the method of operation employed by the Nightstalker and the Sunset Strip Strangler in the early eighties. The short answer is, yes, it's possible."

"I know about those cases but this is different. I worked some of those and I know this is different. The Hillside Stranglers worked together. They were cousins. The other two were similar but there were major differences. Here, someone came along and copied the other exactly. So closely that we missed it and he got away."

"Two killers working independently of each other but using exactly the same methodology."

"Right."

"Again, I say anything is possible. Another example: remember in the eighties there was the Freeway Killer in Orange and LA counties?"

Bosch nodded. He had never worked those cases so he knew little about them.

"Well, one day they got lucky and caught a Vietnam vet named William Bonin. They tied him to a handful of the cases and believed he was good for the rest. He went to death row but the killings kept happening. They kept right on happening until a highway patrol officer pulled over a guy named Randy Kraft who was driving down the freeway with a body in his car. Kraft and Bonin didn't know each other but for a while they secretly shared the nom de plume 'The Freeway Killer'. Each working independently of the other, out there killing. And being mistaken for the same person."

That sounded close to the theory Bosch was working with. Locke continued talking, no longer bothered by the late-night intrusion.

"Do you know, there is a guard on death row at San Quentin whom I know from doing research up there. He told me there are four serial killers, including Kraft and Bonin, waiting for the gas. And, well, the four of them play cards every day. Bridge. Among them, they've got fifty-nine convictions for murder. And they play bridge. Anyway, the point is, he says Kraft and Bonin think so much alike that as a team they are almost never beaten."

Bosch started refolding the map. Without looking up, he said, "Kraft and Bonin, did they kill their victims the same way? The exact same way?"

"Not exactly. But my point is that there could be two. But the follower in this case is smarter. He knew exactly what to do to have all the police go the other way, to put it on Church. Then, when Church was dead and no longer available for use as camouflage, the follower went underground, so to speak."

Bosch looked up at him and a thought suddenly struck him that spun everything he knew into a new light. It was like the cue ball hitting a rack of eight, colors shooting off in all directions. But he didn't say anything. This new thought was too dangerous to bring up. Instead he asked Locke a question.

"But even when this follower went underground, he kept the same program as the Dollmaker," Bosch said. "Why do it, if no one was going to see it? Remember, with the Dollmaker we believed his leaving of the bodies in public locations, their faces painted, was part of the erotic program. Part of his turn-on. But why did the second killer do it — follow the same program — if the body was never intended to be found?"

Locke put both hands on the table to brace his weight and thought a moment. Bosch thought he heard a sound from the patio. He looked through the open French doors and saw only the darkness of the steep hillside rising above the illuminated pool. Its kidney-shaped surface was calm now. He looked at his watch. It was midnight.

"It's a good question," Locke said. "I don't know the answer. Maybe the acolyte knew that eventually the body would be revealed, that he himself might want to reveal it. You see, we probably have to assume now that it was the follower who sent the notes to you and the newspaper four years ago. It shows the exhibitionistic portion of his program. Church apparently didn't find the same need to torment his hunters."

"The follower got off on tweaking us."

"Exactly. What he was doing was having his fun, taunting his trackers and all the while the blame for the murders he committed went to the real Dollmaker. Follow?"

"Yes."

"Okay, so what happened? The real Dollmaker, Mr. Church, is killed by you. The follower no longer has a cover. So what he does is, he continues his work — his killing — but now he buries the victim, hides her under concrete."

"You're saying he still follows the whole erotic program with the makeup and everything but then buries her so no one will see her?"

"So no one will know. Yes, he follows the program because that is what turned him on in the first place. But he can no longer afford to discard the bodies publicly because that would reveal his secret."

"So then, why the note? Why send a note to the police this week that opens him to exposure?"

Locke paced around the dining room table thinking.

"Confidence," he finally said. "The follower has become strong over the past four years. He thinks he is invincible. It is a common trait in the disassembling phase of a psychopath. A state of confidence and invulnerability rises as, in actuality, the psychopath is making more and more mistakes. Disassembling. Becoming vulnerable to discovery."

"So because he has gotten away with his actions for four years, he thinks he is clear and is so untouchable that he sends another note to tweak us?"

"Exactly, but that is only one factor. Another is pride, authorship. This big trial on the Dollmaker has begun and he wants to steal some of the attention. You must understand, he craves attention for his acts. After all, it was the follower, not Church who sent the letters earlier. So being prideful and feeling above the reach of the police — I guess, godlike is the way to describe his sense of himself — he writes the note this week."

"Catch me if you can."

"Yes, one of the oldest games around. . . . And lastly, he might have sent the note because he is still angry with you."

"Me?"

Bosch was surprised. He had never considered this.

"Yes, you took Church away. You ruined his perfect cover. I don't imagine the note and its mention in the press has helped your court case any, has it?"

"No. It might sink me."

"Yes, so maybe this is the follower's way of repaying you. His revenge."

Bosch thought about all of this for a moment. He could almost feel the adrenaline surging through his body. It was after midnight but he wasn't the least bit tired. He had a focus now. He was no longer lost in the void.

"You think there are more out there, don't you?" he asked.

"You mean women in concrete, or similar confinement? Yes, unfortunately, I do. Four years is a long time. Many others are out there, I'm afraid."

"How do I find him?"

"I'm not sure. My work has usually come at the end. After they're caught. After they're dead."

Bosch nodded, closed the binders and put them under his arm.

"There is one thing, though," Locke said. "Look at his pool of victims. Who are they? How does he get to them? The three who are dead and the survivor, they all were in the porno industry, you said."

Bosch put the binders back down on the table. He lit another cigarette.

"Yes, they all did outcall work, too," he said.

"Yes. So while Church was the opportunistic killer, taking victims of any size, age or race, the follower was more specific in his tastes."

Bosch recalled the porno victims quickly.

"Right, the follower's victims were white, young, blonde and large-breasted."

"That is a clear pattern. Did these women advertise their outcall services in the adult-related media?"

"I know two of them did, and the survivor. The latest victim did outcall but I'm not sure how she advertised."

"Did the three who did advertise include photographs of themselves in the copy?"

Bosch could specifically remember only Holly Lere's ad, and it did not include her photo. Just her stage name, a phone drop and a guarantee of lewd pleasure.

"I don't think so. The one I remember didn't. But her porno name was in the ad. So anyone familiar with her work in video would know her physical appearance and attributes."

"Very good. We are already creating a profile of the follower. He is someone who uses adult videos to choose the women for his erotic program. He then contacts them through ads in the adult media by seeing either their names or photos in the advertisements. Have I helped you, Detective Bosch?"

"Absolutely. Thanks for the time. And keep this under your hat. I'm not sure we want to go public with this yet."

Bosch picked up the binders again and headed toward the door but Locke stopped him.

"We haven't finished, you know."

Bosch turned around.

"How do you mean?" he asked, though he knew.

"You haven't spoken about the aspect of this that is most troubling. The question of how our follower learned the killer's routine. The task force did not divulge every detail of the Dollmaker's program to the media. Not back then. Details were held back so the loonies who confessed would not know exactly what to confess to. It was a safeguard. The task force could quickly eliminate the bogus confessions."

"So?"

"So the question is, how did the follower know?"

"I don't —"

"Yes, you do. The book Mr. Bremmer wrote made those details available to the world. That, of course, could account for the concrete blonde. . . . But not, as I am sure you have realized, for victims seven and eleven."

Locke was right. It was what Bosch had realized earlier. He avoided thinking about it because he dreaded the implications.

Locke said, "The answer is that the follower was somehow privy to the details. The details are what triggered his action. You have to remember that what we are dealing with here is someone who very likely was already in the midst of some great internal struggle when he stumbled onto an erotic program that matched his own needs. This man already had problems, whether they had manifested in his committing crimes or not. He was a sick puppy, Harry, and he saw the Dollmaker's erotic mold and realized, That's me. That's what I want, what I need for fulfillment. He then adopted the

Dollmaker's program and acted on it, to the very last detail. The question is, how did he stumble onto it? And the answer is, he was given access."

For a moment they just looked at each other, then Bosch spoke.

"You're talking about a cop. Someone on the task force. That can't be. I was there. We all wanted this guy to go down. Nobody was . . . getting off on this, man."

"Possibly a member of the task force, Harry, only possibly. But remember, the circle of those who knew about the program was much larger than just the task force. You have medical examiners, investigators, beat cops, photographers, reporters, paramedics, the passersby who found the bodies — many people who had access to details the follower obviously knew about."

Bosch tried to pull together a quick profile in his mind. Locke read him.

"It would have to be someone in or around the investigation, Harry. Not necessarily a vital part or a continuous part. But someone who intersected with the investigation at a point that would allow him to gain knowledge of the full program. More than what was publicly known at the time."

Bosch said nothing until Locke prompted him.

"What else, Harry? Narrow it down."

"Left-handed."

"Possibly but not necessarily. Church was left-handed. The follower may only have used the left hand to make the perfect copy of Church's crimes."

"That's right but then there are the notes. Suspicious docs said they believed it was a left-handed writer. They weren't one hundred percent. They never are."

"Okay, then, possibly left-handed. What else?"

Bosch thought for a moment.

"Maybe a smoker. There was a package found in the concrete. Kaminski, the victim, didn't smoke."

"Okay, that's good. These are the things you need to think about to narrow it down. It's in the details, Harry, I'm sure of it."

A cool wind came down the hillside and in through the French doors and chilled Bosch. It was time to go, to be alone with this.

"Thanks again," he said as he started once more for the door.

"What will you do?" Locke called after him.

"I don't know yet."

"Harry?"

Bosch stopped at the threshold and looked back at Locke, the pool glowing eerily in the darkness behind him.

"The follower, he may be the smartest to come along in a long time."

"Because he's a cop?"

"Because he probably knows everything about the case that you know."

It was cold in the Caprice. At night the canyons always carried a dark chill. Bosch turned the car around and it floated quietly down Lookout Mountain to Laurel Canyon. He took a right and drove to the canyon market, where he bought a six-pack of Anchor Steam. Then he took his beer and his questions back up the hill to Mulholland.

He drove to Woodrow Wilson Drive and then down to his small house that stood on cantilevers and looked out across the Cahuenga Pass. He had left no lights on inside because with Sylvia in his life he never knew how long he would go without being here.

He opened the first beer as soon as the Caprice was parked at the curb in front. A car slowly went by and left him in the dark. He watched one of the beams from the spotlights at Universal City cut across the clouds over the house. Another one chased after it a few seconds later. The beer felt and tasted good going down his throat. But it felt heavy in his stomach and Bosch stopped drinking. He put the bottle back in its carton.

But it wasn't the beer, he knew, that was really bothering him. It was Ray Mora. Of all the people who were close enough to the case to know the details of the program, Mora was the one who jabbed at Bosch's gut. The follower's three victims were porno actresses. And that was Mora's gig. He probably knew them all. The question that was now beginning to push its way into Bosch's mind was, did he kill them all? It bothered him to even think about it, but he knew he had to. Mora was a logical starting point when Bosch considered Locke's advice. The vice cop stood out in Bosch's mind as someone who easily intersected both worlds: the porn trade and the Dollmaker's. Was it just coincidence or enough to classify Mora as an actual suspect? Bosch wasn't sure. He knew he had to proceed as cautiously with an innocent man as he would with a guilty man.

Inside, the place smelled musty. He went directly to the rear sliding door and opened it. He stood there for a moment listening to the hissing sound of traffic coming up from the freeway at the bottom of the pass. The sound never died. No matter what time, what day, there was always traffic down there, blood coursing through the veins of the city.

The light on the answering machine was blinking the number three. Bosch hit rewind and lit a cigarette. The first voice was Sylvia's: "I just want to say good-night, sweetheart. I love you and be careful."

Jerry Edgar was next: "Harry, it's Edgar. Wanted to let you know, I'm off it. Irving called me at home and told me to turn everything I've got over to RHD in the morning. To a Lieutenant Rollenberger. Take care, buddy. And watch six."

Watch six, Bosch thought. Watch your back. He hadn't heard that one since Vietnam. And he knew Edgar had never been there.

"It's Ray," the last voice on the tape said. "I've been thinking about this concrete blonde job and have a few ideas you might be interested in. Call me in the morning and we'll talk."

15

"I want a continuance."

"What?"

"You have to get the trial delayed. Tell the judge."

"What the fuck are you talking about, Bosch?"

Bosch and Belk were sitting at the defense table, waiting for the Thursday morning court session to begin. They were speaking in loud whispers and Bosch thought that when Belk cursed, it came off as sounding too contrived, as if he were a sixth-grader trying to fit in with the eighth-graders.

"I am talking about that witness yesterday, Wieczorek, he was right."

"About what?"

"The alibi, Belk. The alibi on the eleventh victim. It's legit. Church didn't —"

"Wait a minute," Belk yelped. Then in a low whisper he said, "If you are about to confess to me that you killed the wrong guy, I don't want to hear it, Bosch. Not now. It's too late."

He turned back to his legal tablet.

"Belk, listen goddammit, I'm not confessing anything. I got the right guy. But we missed something. Another guy. There were two killers. Church is good for nine — the nine we tied up on the makeup comparisons. The other two, and the one we found in the concrete this week, were done by somebody else. You have to stop this thing until we figure out what exactly is going on. If it comes out in court it will tip the second killer, the follower, to how close we are to him."

Belk threw his pen down on the pad and it bounced off the table. He didn't get up to get it.

"I'm going to tell you what's going on, Bosch. We are not stopping anything. Even if I wanted to, I probably couldn't — the judge is in her pants. All she needs to do is object and no sale, no delay. So I'm not even going to bring it up. You have to understand something, Bosch, this is a trial. This is the controlling factor of your universe right now. You don't control it. You can't expect the trial to recess every time you need to change your story . . ."

"You finished?"

"Yes, I'm finished."

"Belk, I understand everything you just said. But we have to protect the investigation. There is another guy out there killing people. And if Chandler puts me or Edgar up there and starts asking questions, the killer is going to read about it and know everything we've got. We'll never get him then. You want that?"

"Bosch, my duty is to win this case. If in doing that, it compromises your —"

"Yeah, but don't you want to know the truth, Belk? I think we're close. Delay it until next week and by then we'll have it together. We'll be able to come in here and blow Money Chandler out of the water."

Bosch leaned back, away from him. He was tired of fighting him.

"Bosch, how long you been a cop?" Belk asked without looking at him. "Twenty years?"

That was close. But Bosch didn't answer. He knew what was coming.

"And you're going to sit there and talk to me about truth? When was the last time you saw a truthful police report? When was the last time that you put down the unadulterated truth in a search warrant application? Don't tell me about truth. You want truth, go see a priest or something. I don't know where to go, but don't come in here. After twenty on the job you should know, the truth has got nothing to do with what goes on in here. Neither does justice. Just words in a law book I read in my previous life."

Belk turned away and took another pen out of his shirt pocket.

"Okay, Belk, you're the man. But I'm going to tell you how it's going to look when it comes out. It's going to come out in bits and pieces and it will look bad. That's Chandler's specialty. It will look like I hit the wrong guy."

Belk was ignoring him, writing on his yellow pad.

"You fool, she is going to stick it into us so deep it's going to come out the other side. You keep writing her off as having the judge's hand on her ass, but we both know that's how you deal with the fact that you couldn't carry her lunch. For the last time, get a delay."

Belk stood up and walked around the table to pick up the fallen pen. After straightening up, he adjusted his tie and his cuffs and sat back down. He leaned over his pad and without looking at Bosch said, "You're just afraid of her, aren't you, Bosch? Don't want to be on the stand with the cunt asking questions. Questions that might expose you for what you are: a cop who likes killing people."

Now he turned and looked at Bosch.

"Well, it's too late. Your time has come and there is no backing away. No delays. Show time."

Harry stood up and bent over the fat man.

"Fuck you, Belk. I'm going outside."

"That's nice," Belk said. "You know, you guys are all the same. You blow some guy away and then come in here and think that just because you wear that badge that you have some kind of a divine right to do whatever you want. That badge is the biggest power trip going."

Bosch went out to the bank of phones and called Edgar. He picked up on the homicide table after one ring.

"I got your message last night."

"Yeah, well, that's all there is. I'm gone. RHD came up this morning and took my file. Saw them snoopin' around your spot, too, but they didn't take anything."

"Who came?"

"Sheehan and Opelt. You know 'em?"

"Yeah, they're okay. You coming over here on the subpoena?"

"Yeah, I gotta be there by ten."

Bosch saw the door to courtroom 4 open and the deputy marshal leaned out and signaled to him.

"I gotta go."

Back in the courtroom, Chandler was at the lectern and the judge was speaking. The jury was not in the box yet.

"What about the other subpoenas?" the judge asked.

"Your Honor, my office is in the process of notifying those people this morning, releasing them."

"Very well, then. Mr. Belk, ready to proceed?"

As Bosch came through the gate Belk passed him on the way to the lectern without even looking at him.

"Your Honor, since this is unexpected, I would ask for a half-hour recess so I can consult with my client. We would be ready to proceed after that."

"Very well, we're going to do exactly that. Recess for a half hour. I'll see all parties back here then. And Mr. Bosch? I expect you to be in your place there, the next time I come out ready to begin. I don't like sending marshals up and down the halls when the defendant knows where he ought to be and when he ought to be there."

Bosch said nothing.

"Sorry, Your Honor," Belk said for him.

They stood as the judge left the bench and Belk said, "Let's go down the hall to one of the lawyer-client conference rooms."

"What happened?"

"Let's go down the hall."

As he was going through the courtroom door, Bremmer was coming in, holding his notebook and pen.

"Hey, what's happening?"

"I don't know," Bosch said. "Half-hour recess."

"Harry, I have to talk to you."

"Later."

"It's important."

At the end of the hall near the lavatories there were several small attorney conference rooms, all about the size of the interrogation rooms at the Hollywood station. Bosch and Belk went into one and took chairs on either side of a gray table.

"What happened?" Bosch asked.

"Your heroine rested."

"Chandler rested without calling me?"

This seemed to make no sense to Bosch.

"What's she doing?" he asked.

"She's being extremely shrewd. It's a very smart move."

"Why?"

"Look at the case. She is in very good shape. If it ended today and went to the jury, who would win? She would. See, she knows you have to get on the stand and defend what you did. Like I told you the other day, we win or lose with you. You either take the ball and ram it down her throat or you fumble it. She knows that and if she was to call you, she would ask the questions first, then I would come in with the fungoes — the easy ones that you'd hit out of the park.

"Now she's reversing that. My choice is to not call you and lose the case, or to call you and essentially give her the best shot at you. Very shrewd."

"So what are we going to do?"

"Call you."

"What about the delay?"

"What delay?"

Bosch nodded. There was no changing it. There would be no delay. He realized he had handled it badly. He had approached Belk the wrong way. He should have tried to make Belk believe it had been his own idea to go for a delay. Then it would have worked. Instead, Bosch was beginning to feel the jitters — that uneasy feeling that came with approaching the unknown. He felt the way he did before he climbed down into a VC tunnel for the first time in Vietnam. It was fear, he knew, blossoming like a black rose in the pit of his chest.

"We've got twenty-five minutes," Belk said. "Let's forget about delays and try to work out how we want your testimony to go. I am going to lead you down the path. The jury will follow. But remember, you have to take it slow or you will lose them. Okay?"

"We got twenty minutes," Bosch corrected him. "I need to go out for a smoke before I sit up there on the stand."

Belk pressed on as if he hadn't heard.

"Remember, Bosch, there could be millions of dollars at stake here. It may not be your money but it may be your career."

"What career?"

Bremmer was hanging around the door to the conference room when Bosch came out twenty minutes later.

"Get it all?" Harry asked.

He walked by him and headed toward the escalator. Bremmer followed.

"No, man, I wasn't listening. I'm just waiting for you. Listen, what's going on with the new case? Edgar won't tell me shit. Did you get an ID or what?"

"Yeah, we ID'd her."

"Who was it?"

"Not my case, man. I can't give it out. Besides, I give it to you and you'll run to Money Chandler with it, right?"

Bremmer stopped walking beside him.

"What? What are you talking about?"

Then he scurried up to Bosch's side and whispered.

"Listen, Harry, you're one of my main sources. I wouldn't screw you like that. If she's getting inside shit, look for somebody else."

Bosch felt bad about accusing the reporter. He'd had no evidence.

"You sure? I'm mistaken about this, right?"

"Absolutely. You're too valuable to me. I wouldn't do it."

"Okay, then."

That was as close as he'd come to an apology.

"So what can you tell me about the ID?"

"Nothing. It's still not my case. Try RHD."

"RHD has it? They took it from Edgar?"

Bosch got on the escalator and looked back at him. He nodded as he went down. Bremmer didn't follow.

Money Chandler was already on the steps smoking when Bosch came out. He lit a cigarette and looked back at her.

"Surprise, surprise," he said.

"What?"

"Resting."

"Only a surprise to Bulk," she said. "Any other lawyer would have seen it coming. I almost feel sorry for you, Bosch. Almost, but not quite. In a civil rights case, the chances of a win are always a long shot. But going up against the city attorney's office always kind of levels the playing field. These guys like Bulk, they couldn't make it on the outside. . . . If he had to win in order to eat, your lawyer would be a thin man. He needs that steady paycheck from the city coming in, win or lose."

What she said, of course, was correct. But it was old news. Bosch smiled. He didn't know how to act. A part of himself liked her. She was wrong about him, but somehow he liked her. Maybe it was her tenacity, because her anger — though misdirected — was so pure.

Maybe it was because she wasn't afraid to talk to him outside of court. He had seen how Belk studiously avoided coming in contact with Church's family. Before getting up during recesses, he would sit at the defendant's table until he was sure they were all safely down the hall and on the escalator. But Chandler didn't play that kind of game. She was an up-front player.

Bosch guessed that this was what it was like when two boxers touched gloves before the bell. He changed the subject.

"I talked to Tommy Faraday out here the other day. He's Tommy Faraway now. I asked him what happened but he didn't say. He just said justice happened, whatever that means."

She blew a long stream of blue smoke out but didn't say anything for a while. Bosch looked at his watch. They had three minutes.

"You remember the Galton case?" she said. "It was a civil rights case, an excessive force."

Bosch thought about it. The name was familiar but it was difficult to place in the blend of excessive force cases he had heard or known about over the years.

"It was a dog case, right?"

"Yes. André Galton. This was before Rodney King, back when the wide majority of people in this city did not believe that their police engaged in horrible abuses as a matter of routine. Galton was black and driving with an expired tag through the hills of Studio City when a cop decided to pull him over.

"He had done nothing wrong, wasn't wanted, just had the tag one month overdue. But he ran. Great mystery of life, he ran. He got all the way up to Mulholland and ditched the car at one of those pull-offs where people look out at the view. Then he jumped out and climbed down the incline. There was nowhere to go down there but he wouldn't come back up and the cops wouldn't go down — too dangerous, they claimed at the trial."

Bosch remembered the story now but he let her tell it. Her indignation was so pure and stripped of lawyerly pose that he just wanted to hear her tell it.

"So they sent a dog down," she said. "Galton lost both testicles and had permanent nerve damage to the right leg. He could walk but he had to kind of drag it behind him. . . ."

"Enter Tommy Faraday," Bosch prompted.

"Yeah, he took the case. It was dead bang. Galton had done nothing wrong but to run. The response of the police certainly did not meet the offense. Any jury would see this. And the city attorney's office knew this. In fact, I think it was Bulk's case. They offered half a million to settle and Faraday passed. He thought he'd get a minimum three times that in trial, so he passed.

"And like I said, this was in the old days. Civil rights lawyers call it BK, that's short for Before King. A jury listened to four days of evidence and found for the cops in thirty minutes. Galton got nothing but a dead leg and a dead dick out of the whole thing. He came out here afterward and went to that hedge right there. He had hidden a gun — wrapped it in plastic and buried it there. He came over to the statue here and put the gun in his mouth. Faraday was coming through the door just then and saw it happen. Blood all over the statue, everywhere."

Bosch didn't say anything. He remembered the case very clearly now. He looked up at the City Hall tower and watched the gulls circling above it. He always wondered what drew them there. It was miles from the ocean but there were always seabirds on top of City Hall. Chandler kept talking.

"Two things I've always been curious about," she said. "One, why did Galton run? And, two, why did he hide the gun? And I think the answers are both the same. He had no faith in justice, in the system. No hope. He had done nothing wrong but he ran because he was a black man in a white neighborhood and he had heard the stories all his life about what white cops do to black men in that position. His lawyer told him he had a dead-bang case, but he brought a gun to the courthouse because he had heard all his life about what jurors decide when it's a black man's word against the cops."

Bosch looked at his watch. It was time to go in but he did not want to walk away from her.

"So that's why Tommy said justice happened," she said. "That was justice for André Galton. Faraday referred all his cases to other lawyers after that. I took a few. And he never set foot in a courtroom again."

She stubbed out what was left of her cigarette.

"End of story," she said.

"I'm sure the civil rights lawyers tell that one a lot," Bosch said. "And now you put me and Church into that, is that it? I'm like the guy who sent the dog down the hill after Galton?"

"There are degrees, Detective Bosch. Even if Church was the monster you claim, he didn't have to die. If the system turns away from the abuses inflicted on the guilty, then who can be next but the innocents? You see, that's why I have to do what I'm going to do to you in there. For the innocents."

"Well, good luck," he said.

He put his own cigarette out.

"I won't need it," she said.

Bosch followed her gaze to the statue above the spot where Galton had killed himself. Chandler looked at it as if the blood were still there.

"That's justice," she said, nodding at the statue. "She doesn't hear you. She doesn't see you. She can't feel you and won't speak to you. Justice, Detective Bosch, is just a concrete blonde."

16

The courtroom seemed as silent as a dead man's heart while Bosch walked behind the plaintiff and defendant tables and in front of the jury box to get to the witness stand. After taking the oath he gave his full name and the clerk asked him to spell it.

"H-I-E-R-O-N-Y-M-U-S B-O-S-C-H."

Then the judge turned it over to Belk.

"Tell us a little bit about yourself, Detective Bosch, about your career."

"I've been a police officer nearly twenty years. I currently am assigned to the homicide table at Hollywood Division. Before that —"

"Why do they call it a table?"

Jesus, Bosch thought.

"Because it's like a table. It is six small desks pushed together to make a long table, three detectives on each side. It's always called a table."

"Okay, go on."

"Before this assignment I spent eight years in Robbery-Homicide Division's Homicide Special squad. Before that I was a detective on the homicide table in North Hollywood and robbery and burglary tables in Van Nuys. I was on patrol about five years, mostly in the Hollywood and Wilshire divisions."

Belk slowly led him through his career up until the time he was on the Dollmaker task force. The questioning was slow and boring — even to Bosch, and it was his life. Every now and then he would look at the jurors when he answered a question and only a few seemed to be looking at him or paying attention. Bosch felt nervous and his palms were damp. He had testified in court at least a hundred times. But never like this, in his own defense. He felt hot though he knew the courtroom was overly cool.

"Now where was the task force physically located?"

"We used a second-floor storage room at the Hollywood station. It was an evidence and file storage room. We temporarily moved that stuff out into a rented trailer and used the room. We also had a room at Parker Center. The night shift, which I was on, generally worked out of Hollywood."

"You were closer to the source, correct?"

"We thought so, yes. Most of the victims were taken from Hollywood streets. Many were later found in the area."

"So you wanted to be able to act quickly on tips and leads and being right there in the center of things helped you do that, correct?"

"Correct."

"On the night you got the call from the woman named Dixie McQueen, how did you get that call?"

"She called in on nine one one and when the dispatcher realized what she was talking about, the call was transferred out to the task force in Hollywood."

"Who answered it?"

"I did."

"Why is that? I thought you testified you were the supervisor of the night shift. Didn't they have people answering phones?"

"Yes, we had people, but this call came in late. Everybody had left for the night. I was only there because I was bringing the Chronological Investigation Record up to date — we had to turn it in at the end of each week. I was the only one there. I answered."

"When you went to meet this woman, why didn't you call for a backup?"

"She hadn't told me enough over the phone to convince me there was anything to it. We were getting dozens of calls a day. None of them amounted to anything. I have to admit I went to take her report not believing it would amount to anything."

"Well, if you thought that, Detective, why did you go to her? Why not just take her information over the phone?"

"The main reason was that she said she didn't know the address she had been to with this man, but could show me the place if I drove her down Hyperion. Also, there seemed to be something genuine about her complaint, you know? It seemed that something had definitely scared her. I was about to head home so I thought I would just check it out on the way."

"Tell us what happened after you got to Hyperion."

"When we got there we could see lights on in the apartment over the garage. We even saw a shadow pass across one of the windows. So we knew the guy was still there. That's when Miss McQueen told me about the makeup she saw in the cabinet under the sink."

"What did that mean to you?"

"A lot. It immediately got my attention because we had never said in the press that the killer was keeping the victims' makeup. It had leaked that he was painting their faces but not that he also kept their makeup. So when she told me she had seen this collection of makeup, it all clicked. It gave what she said some immediate legitimacy."

Bosch drank some water from a paper cup the marshal had filled for him earlier.

"Okay, what did you do next?" Belk said.

"It occurred to me that in the time it had taken her to call me and for me to pick her up and get back to Hyperion, he could have gone out and gotten another victim. So I knew there was a good chance there was another woman up there in danger. I went up. I ran up."

"Why didn't you call for backup?"

"First of all, I did not believe there was time to wait even five minutes for backup. If he had another woman in there, five minutes could mean her life. Secondly, I did not have a rover with me. I couldn't make the call even if I wanted to —"

"A rover?"

"A portable radio. Detectives usually take them on assignment. Problem is, there are not enough of them to go around. And since I was going home I didn't want to take one because I wasn't coming back until the next evening shift. That would mean one less rover available during the next day."

"So you couldn't radio for backup. What about a phone?"

"It was a residential neighborhood. I could drive out and find a pay phone or knock on somebody's door. It was about one A.M. and I didn't think people would open their doors quickly to a single man claiming to be a police officer. Everything was a question of time. I didn't believe I had any. I had to go up by myself."

"What happened?"

"Believing someone was in imminent danger, I went through the door without knocking. I was holding my gun out."

"Kicked it open?"

"Yes."

"What did you see?"

"First of all, I announced myself. I yelled, 'Police.' I moved a few steps into the room — it was a studio apartment — and I saw the man later identified as Church standing next to the bed. It was a foldout bed from a couch."

"What was he doing?"

"He was standing there naked, next to the bed."

"Did you see anyone else?"

"No."

"What next?"

"I yelled something along the lines of 'Freeze' or 'Don't move' and took another step into the room. At first he didn't move. Then he suddenly reached down to the bed and his hand swept under the pillow. I yelled, 'No,' but he continued the movement. I could see his arm move as if his hand had grasped something and he started bringing the hand out. I fired one time. It killed him."

"How far away from him would you say you were?"

"I was twenty feet away. It was one big room. We were at opposite sides of it."

"And did he die instantly?"

"Very quickly. He dropped across the bed. The autopsy later showed the bullet entered under the right arm — the one he was reaching under the pillow with — and crossed through the chest. It hit his heart and both lungs."

"After he was down, what did you do?"

"I went to the bed and checked to see if he was alive. He was still alive at that point, so I handcuffed him. He died a few moments later. I lifted the pillow. There was no gun."

"What was there?"

Looking directly at Chandler, Bosch said, "Great mystery of life, he had been reaching for a toupee."

Chandler had her head down and was busy writing but she stopped and looked up at him and their eyes locked momentarily until she said, "Objection, Your Honor."

The judge agreed to strike Bosch's comment about the mystery of life. Belk asked a few more questions about the shooting scene and then moved on to the investigation of Church.

"You were no longer part of that, correct?"

"No, as is routine I was assigned desk duty while my actions in the shooting were investigated."

"Well, were you made aware of the results of the task force's investigation into Church's background?"

"Generally. Because I had a stake in the outcome, I was kept informed."

"What did you learn?"

"That the makeup found in the bathroom cabinet was tied to nine of the victims."

"Did you ever have any doubts yourself or hear of any doubts from other investigators as to whether Norman Church was responsible for the deaths of those women?"

"For those nine? No, no doubts at all. Ever."

"Well, Detective Bosch, you heard Mr. Wieczorek testify about being with Mr. Church on the night the eleventh victim, Shirleen Kemp, was killed. You saw the videotape presented as evidence. Didn't that raise any doubts?"

"It does about that case. But Shirleen Kemp was not among the nine whose makeup was found in Church's apartment. There is no doubt in my mind or in anybody's on the task force that Church killed those nine women."

Chandler objected to Bosch speaking for the rest of the task force and the judge sustained it. Belk changed the subject, not wanting to venture any further into the area of victims seven and eleven. His strategy was to avoid any reference to a second killer, leaving that to Chandler to take a swing at on cross-examination, if she wanted to.

"You were disciplined for not going in with backup. Do you feel the department handled the matter correctly?"

"No."

"How so?"

"As I explained, I did not believe I had a choice in what I did. If I had to do it again — even knowing I would be transferred as a result — I would do the same thing. I would have to. If there had been another woman in there, another victim, and I had saved her, I probably would have been promoted."

When Belk didn't immediately ask a follow-up question, Bosch continued.

"I believe the transfer was a political necessity. The bottom line was, I shot an unarmed man. It did not matter that the man I shot was a serial killer, a monster. Besides, I was carrying baggage from —"

"That will be fine —"

"Run-ins with —"

"Detective Bosch."

Bosch stopped. He had made his point.

"So what you are saying is you don't have any regrets about what happened in the apartment, correct?"

"No, that's not correct."

This apparently surprised Belk. He looked down at his notes. He had asked a question he expected a different reply to. But he realized he had to follow through.

"What do you regret?"

"That Church made that move. He drew the fire. There was nothing I could do but respond. I wanted to stop the killings. I didn't want to kill him to do that. But that's the way it turned out. It was his play."

Belk showed his relief by breathing heavily into the microphone before saying he had no further questions.

Judge Keyes said there would be a ten-minute break before cross-examination began. Bosch returned to the defense table, where Belk whispered that he thought they had done well. Bosch didn't respond.

"I think everything is going to ride on her cross. If you can get through it without heavy damage I think we've got it."

"What about when she brings up the follower, introduces the note?"

"I don't see how she can. If she does, she'll be flying blind."

"No, she won't. She's got a source in the department. Someone fed her stuff about the note."

"I'll ask for a sidebar conference if it gets to that point."

That wasn't very encouraging. Bosch looked at the clock, trying to gauge whether he had time for a smoke. He didn't think so and got up and went back to the witness stand. He passed behind Chandler, who was writing on a legal pad.

"Great mystery of life," she said without looking up.

"Yeah," Bosch said without looking back at her.

As he sat and waited, he saw Bremmer come in, followed by the guy from the *Daily News* and a couple of wire service reporters. Somebody had put out the word that the top act was about to begin. Cameras were not allowed in federal court, so one of the stations had sent a sketch artist over.

From the witness seat, Bosch watched Chandler working. He guessed she was writing out questions for him. Deborah Church sat next to her with her hands folded on the table, her eyes averted from Bosch. A minute later the door to the jury room opened and the jurors filed into the box. Then the judge came out. Bosch took a deep breath and got ready as Chandler walked to the lectern with her yellow pad.

"Mr. Bosch," she began, "how many people have you killed?"

Belk immediately objected and asked for a sidebar. The attorneys and the court reporter moved to the side of the bench and whispered for five minutes. Bosch only heard bits and pieces, most of it from Belk, who was loudest. At one point he argued that one shooting only was in dispute — the Church slaying — and all others were irrelevant. He heard Chandler say that the information was relevant because it illustrated the mind-set of the defendant. Bosch couldn't hear the judge's response but after the attorneys and reporter were back in place, the judge said, "The defendant will answer the question."

"I can't," Bosch replied.

"Detective Bosch, the court is ordering you to answer."

"I can't answer it, Judge. I don't know how many people I've killed."

"You served in combat in Vietnam?" Chandler asked.

"Yes."

"What were your duties?"

"Tunnel rat. I went into the enemy's tunnels. Sometimes this resulted in direct confrontation. Sometimes I used explosives to destroy tunnel complexes. It's impossible for me to know how many people were in them."

"Okay, Detective, since you finished your duties with the armed services and became a police officer, how many people have you killed?"

"Three, including Norman Church."

"Can you tell us about the two incidents not involving Mr. Church? In general."

"Yes, one was before Church, the other after. The first time I killed someone it was during a murder investigation. I went to question a man I thought was a witness. Turned out he was the killer. When I knocked on the door, he fired a shot through it. Missed me. I kicked the door open and went in. I heard him running toward the rear of the house. I followed him to the yard, where he was climbing over a fence. As he was about to go over, he twisted around to take another shot at me. I fired first and he went down.

"The second time, this was after Church, I was involved in a murder and robbery investigation with the FBI. There was a shoot-out between two suspects and myself and my partner at the time, an FBI agent. I killed one of the suspects."

"So in those two cases, the men you killed were armed?"

"That is correct."

"Three shootings involving deaths, that is quite a lot, even for a twenty-year veteran, isn't it?"

Bosch waited a beat for Belk to make an objection but the fat man was too busy writing on his tablet. He had missed it.

"Um, I know twenty-year cops who have never even had to draw their guns, and I know some that have been involved in as many as seven deaths. It's a matter of what kind of cases you draw, it's a matter of luck."

"Good luck or bad luck?"

This time Belk objected and the judge sustained it. Chandler quickly went on.

"After you killed Mr. Church while he was unarmed, did you feel badly about it?"

"Not really. Not until I got sued and heard you were the lawyer."

There was laughter in the courtroom and even Honey Chandler smiled. After he had quieted the room with a sharp rebuke from his gavel, the judge instructed Bosch to keep his answers on point and to refrain from personal asides.

"No bad feelings," Bosch said. "Like I said before, I would rather have taken Church alive than dead. But I wanted to take him off the street, either way."

"But you set the whole thing up, tactically, so that it had to end in his permanent removal, didn't you?"

"No, I didn't. Nothing was set up. Things just happened."

Bosch knew better than to show any anger toward her. Rather than make angry denouncements, the rule of thumb was to answer each question as if he was dealing with a person who was simply mistaken.

"You were, however, satisfied that Mr. Church had been killed while unarmed, nude, totally defenseless?"

"Satisfaction doesn't enter into it."

"Your Honor," Chandler said. "May I approach the witness with an exhibit? It's marked plaintiff's 3A."

She handed copies of a piece of paper to Belk and the judge's clerk, who handed it over the bench to the judge. While the judge was reading it, Belk went to the lectern and objected.

"Your Honor, if this is offered as impeachment, I don't see how it is valid. These are the words of a psychiatrist, not my client."

Chandler moved to the microphone and said, "Judge, if you look in the section marked Summary, the last paragraph is what I would like to be read by the witness. You will also notice that the defendant signed the statement at the bottom."

Judge Keyes read some more, wiped his mouth with the back of his hand and said, "I'll accept it. You may show it to the witness."

Chandler brought another copy up to Bosch and placed it in front of him without looking at him. Then she walked back to the lectern.

"Can you tell us what that is, Detective Bosch?"

"It's a confidential psychological release form. Supposedly confidential, I guess I should say."

"Yes, and what does it relate to?"

"My release allowing me to return to duty after the Church shooting. It is routine to be interviewed by the department's psychiatrist after being involved in a shooting. Then he clears you to return to duty."

"You must know him well."

"Excuse me?"

"Ms. Chandler, that's not necessary," Judge Keyes said before Belk got up.

"No, Your Honor. Strike that. You were cleared to return to duty — to your new assignment in Hollywood — after the interview, correct?"

"Correct."

"Isn't it true that this is really nothing more than a rubber-stamp process? The psychiatrist never holds an officer back from returning on psychiatric grounds?"

"No on the first question. I don't know on the second."

"Well, let me turn it around. Have you ever heard of an officer being held back by the psychiatric interview?"

"No, I haven't. They're supposed to be confidential so I doubt I would hear anything anyway."

"Will you please read the last paragraph of the summary section on the report in front of you?"

"Yes."

He picked up the paper and began reading. Silently.

"Out loud, Detective Bosch," she said in an exasperated tone. "I thought that was implicit in the question."

"Sorry. It says: 'Through his war and police experiences, most notably including the aforementioned shooting resulting in fatality, the subject has to a high degree become desensitized to violence. He speaks in terms of violence or the aspect of violence being an accepted part of his day-to-day life, for all of his life. Therefore, it is unlikely that what transpired previously will act as a psychological deterrent should he again be placed in circumstances where he must act with deadly force in order to protect himself or others. I believe he will be able to act without delay. He will be able to pull the trigger. In fact, his conversation reveals no ill effects at all from the shooting, unless his sense of satisfaction with the outcome of the incident — the suspect's death — should be deemed inappropriate.'"

Bosch put the paper down. He noticed the entire jury was looking at him now. He had no idea whether the report was highly damaging or helpful to his cause.

"The subject of that report is you, correct?" Chandler asked.

"Yes, it's me."

"You just testified that there was no satisfaction, but the report by the psychiatrist said you did feel a sense of satisfaction with the outcome of the incident. Which is right?"

"Those are his words on the report, not mine. I don't think I would have said that."

"What would you have said?"

"I don't know. Not that."

"Then why did you sign the release form?"

"I signed it because I wanted to get back to work. If I was going to argue with him about what words he used, I was never going to get back to work."

"Tell me, Detective, did the psychiatrist who examined you and made that report know about your mother?"

Bosch hesitated.

"I don't know," he finally answered. "I didn't tell him. I don't know if he would have had the information previously."

He could hardly concentrate on his words, for his mind was scrambling.

"What happened to your mother?"

He looked directly at Chandler for a long moment before answering. She didn't look away.

"As was testified to earlier, she was killed. I was eleven. It happened in Hollywood."

"And no one was ever arrested, correct?"

"That is correct. Can we go on to something else? This has already been testified about."

Bosch looked over at Belk who got the point and stood up and objected to Chandler's repetitive line of questioning.

"Detective Bosch, do you want a break?" Judge Keyes asked. "To sort of calm down a little?"

"No, Judge, I'm fine."

"Well, I'm sorry. I can't restrict proper cross-examination. The objection is overruled."

The judge nodded to Chandler.

"I'm sorry to ask such personal questions, but, after she was gone, did your father raise you?"

"You're not sorry. You —"

"Detective Bosch!" the judge boomed. "We cannot have this. You must answer the questions asked of you. Say nothing else. Just answer the questions."

"No. I never knew my father. I was put in the youth hall and then foster homes."

"Any brothers or sisters?"

"No."

"So the man who strangled your mother not only took the one closest to you, he destroyed much of your life at that point?"

"I'd say so."

"Did the crime have something to do with your becoming a policeman?"

Bosch found he could no longer look at the jury. He knew his face had turned red. And he felt as if he were dying under a magnifying glass.

"I don't know. I never really analyzed myself to that extent."

"Did it have something to do with the satisfaction you felt in killing Mr. Church?"

"As I said before, if there was any satisfaction — you keep using that word — it was that I was satisfied with closing the case. To use your word, the man was a monster. He was a killer. I was satisfied we stopped him, wouldn't you be?"

"You're answering the questions, Detective Bosch," Chandler said. "The question I now have is, did you stop the killings? All of them?"

Belk jumped up and asked for a sidebar conference. The judge said to the jurors, "We're going to take that break now after all. We'll call you back when we're ready."

17

Belk asked for a discussion of his objection to Chandler's question out of earshot of the press, so the judge convened a hearing in his chambers. The hearing included the judge, Chandler, Belk, Bosch, the court reporter and the court clerk. They had to drag a couple of chairs in from the courtroom, then they all took places around the judge's huge desk. It was dark mahogany and looked like a box a small foreign car could have come in.

The first thing the judge did was light a cigarette. When Bosch saw Chandler follow suit, he did the same. The judge pushed the ashtray on his desk to the corner so they all could get at it.

"So, Mr. Belk, it's your party," the judge said.

"Your Honor, I am concerned with the direction Miss Chandler is taking this."

"Call her Ms. Chandler, Mr. Belk. You know she prefers it. As far as which way she's going, how can you tell from one question?"

It was obvious to Bosch that Belk may have objected too soon. It was unclear how much information Chandler had, aside from the note. But Bosch thought Belk's tap-dancing around the problem was a waste of time.

"Judge," he said. "If I answer that last question it will compromise an ongoing investigation."

The judge leaned back in his padded leather chair.

"How so?" he asked.

"We believe there is another killer," Bosch said. "The body found this week was identified yesterday and it has been determined that she could not have been killed by Church. She was alive up until two years ago. The —"

"The method used by the killer was identical to that of the real Dollmaker," Belk interjected. "The police believe there is a follower, someone who knew how Church killed and followed the same pattern. There is evidence to suggest the follower was responsible for the seventh and eleventh victims previously attributed to Church."

Bosch said, "The follower would have to be someone close to the original investigation, someone who knew the details."

Belk said, "If you allow her to open this line of questioning, it will be reported by the media and it will tip off the follower. He will know how close he is to being revealed."

The judge was silent as he considered all of this for a moment.

"That all sounds real interesting and I wish you all the best of luck catching this follower, as you call him," he finally said. "But the problem you have, Mr. Belk, is that you haven't given me any legal reason to stop your client from answering the question Ms. Chandler put to him. No one wants to compromise an investigation. But you put your client on the stand."

"That's if there is a second killer," Chandler said. "It's obvious there was only one killer and it wasn't Church. They've come up with this elaborate —"

"Ms. Chandler," the judge interrupted. "That's for the jury to decide. Save your argument for them. Mr. Belk, the problem is this is your witness. You called him and you've left him open to this line of questioning. I don't know what to tell you. I'm certainly not going to clear the media out of there. Off the record here, Miss Penny."

The judge watched the court reporter lift her fingers from the keys.

"Mr. Belk, you're fucked — 'scuse the language, ladies. He's gonna answer the question and the one after that and the one after that. Okay, we're back on."

The reporter put her fingers back on the keys.

"Your Honor, this can't —"

"I've made my ruling, Mr. Belk. Anything else?"

Belk then surprised Bosch.

"We would like a continuance."

"What?"

"Your Honor, plaintiff opposes," Chandler said.

"I know you do," the judge said. "What are you talking about, Mr. Belk?"

"Your Honor, you have to put the trial on hiatus. Until at least next week. It will give the investigation time to possibly come to some fruition."

"Some fruition? Forget it, Belk. You're in the middle of a trial, my friend."

Belk stood and leaned across the great wide desk.

"Your Honor, I request an emergency stay of these proceedings while we take the matter on appeal to the ninth district."

"You can appeal anything you like, Mr. Belk, but there is no stay. We're in trial here."

There was silence as everyone looked at Belk.

"What if I refuse to answer?" Bosch asked.

Judge Keyes looked at him a long moment and said, "Then I'll hold you in contempt. Then I'll ask you to answer again and if you refuse again I will put you in jail. Then when your attorney here asks for bail while he appeals, I will say no bail. All of this will take place out there in front of the jury and the media folks. And I will place no restrictions on what Ms. Chandler does or doesn't say to the reporters in the hallway. So, what I am saying is, you can try to be some kind of hero and not answer, but the story will get to the media anyway. It's like I said a few minutes ago to Mr. Belk when we were off the rec —"

"You can't do this," Belk suddenly erupted. "It, it — it's not right. You have to protect this investigation. You —"

"Son, don't you ever tell me what I have to do," the judge said very slowly and sternly. He seemed to grow in stature while Belk shrank back away from him. "Only thing I have to do is ensure there is a fair trial on this matter. You are asking me to sit on information that could be vital to the plaintiff's case. You are also trying to intimidate me and that is one thing I don't take to. I'm no county judge that needs your nod every time an election comes 'round. I'm appointed for life. We're off here."

Miss Penny stopped typing. Bosch almost didn't want to see Belk's slaughter. The deputy city attorney's head was bowed and he had assumed the posture of the doomed. The back of his neck was turned up and ready to receive the axe.

"So my advice here is that you get your fat ass out there and start working on how the hell you're going to salvage this on redirect. Because in five minutes Detective Bosch is going to answer that question or he's going to be handing his gun and his badge and his belt and shoelaces over to a marshal at the federal lockup. We're back on. Hearing adjourned."

Judge Keyes brought his arm down and ground his cigarette into the ashtray. He never took his eyes off Belk.

As the procession made its way back into the courtroom, Bosch moved up closely behind Chandler. He glanced back to make sure the judge had turned to go to the bench and then said in a low voice, "If you're getting your information from inside the department, I'm going to burn your source down when I find him."

She didn't miss a stride. She didn't even turn back when she said, "You mean, if you're not already ashes."

Bosch took his place at the witness stand and the jury was brought back in. The judge told Chandler to continue.

"Rather than have the reporter find the last question, let me just rephrase it. After you killed Mr. Church, did the so called Dollmaker killings stop?"

Bosch hesitated, thinking. He looked out into the spectator section and saw that there were more reporters now — or at least people he thought were reporters. They all sat together.

He also saw Sylvia, sitting in the back row by herself. She offered a small smile to him which he did not return. He wondered how long she had been out there.

"Detective Bosch?" the judge prompted.

"I can't answer the question without compromising an ongoing investigation," Bosch finally said.

"Detective Bosch, we just went over this," the judge said angrily. "Answer the question."

Bosch knew that his refusal and jailing would not stop the story from getting out. Chandler would tell all the reporters as the judge had given her the okay to do. So putting himself in jail, he knew, only stopped him from chasing the follower. He decided to answer. He carefully composed a statement while stalling by taking a long, slow drink of water from the paper cup.

"Norman Church obviously stopped killing people after he was dead. But there was somebody — there is somebody else still out there. A killer who uses the same methods as Norman Church."

"Thank you, Mr. Bosch. And when did you come to that conclusion?"

"This week, when another body was found."

"Who was that victim?"

"A woman named Rebecca Kaminski. She had been missing two years."

"The details of her death matched the murders of the other Dollmaker victims?"

"Exactly, except for one thing."

"And that was what?"

"She had been entombed in concrete. Hidden. Norman Church always discarded his victims in public places."

"No other differences?"

"Not that I know of at the moment."

"Yet, because she died two years after Norman Church was killed by you, there is no way possible that he is responsible."

"Correct."

"Because he was dead he has the perfect alibi, doesn't he?"

"Correct."

"How was the body found?"

"As I said, it had been buried in concrete."

"And what led police to the spot where it was buried?"

"We received a note with directions."

Chandler then offered a copy of the note as plaintiff's exhibit 4A and Judge Keyes accepted it after overruling an objection by Belk. Chandler then handed a copy to Bosch to identify and read.

"Out loud this time," she said before he could start. "For the jury."

Bosch felt eerie reading the words of the follower out loud in the quiet courtroom. After a beat of silence when he was done, Chandler began again.

" 'I'm still in the game,' he writes. What does that mean?"

"It means he is trying to take credit for all of the killings. He wants attention."

"Could that be because he committed all of the murders?"

"No, because Norman Church committed nine of them. The evidence found in Church's apartment irrefutably links him to those nine. There is no doubt."

"Who found this evidence?"

Bosch said, "Me."

"So, then, isn't there a lot of doubt, Detective Bosch? Isn't this idea of a second killer who uses the exact same method preposterous?"

"No, it's not preposterous. It is happening. I did not kill the wrong man."

"Isn't it the truth that this talk of a copycat killer, a follower, is all an elaborate charade for covering up the fact that you did exactly that, killed the wrong man? An innocent, unarmed man who had done nothing worse than hire a prostitute with his wife's tacit approval?"

"No, it's not. Norman Church killed —"

"Thank you, Mr. Bosch."

"— a lot of women. He was a monster."

"Like the one who killed your mother?"

He unconsciously looked out into the audience, saw Sylvia and then looked away. He tried to compose himself, slow his breathing. He was not going to let Chandler tear him open.

"I would say yes. They were probably similar. Both monsters."

"That's why you killed him, wasn't it? The toupee wasn't under the pillow. You killed him in cold blood because you saw your mother's killer."

"No. You are wrong. Don't you think if I was going to make up a story I could come up with something better than a toupee? There was a kitchenette, knives in the drawer. Why would I plant —"

"Hold it, hold it, hold it," Judge Keyes barked. "Now, we've gone off the tracks here. Ms. Chandler, you started making statements instead of asking questions and, Detective Bosch, you did the same thing instead of answering. Let's start over."

"Yes, Your Honor," Chandler said. "Isn't it true, Detective Bosch, that the whole thing — this pinning all the murders on Norman Church — was an elaborate cover-up that is now unraveling with the discovery of the woman in the concrete this week?"

"No, it is not true. Nothing is unraveling. Church was a killer and he deserved what he got."

Bosch mentally flinched and closed his eyes as soon as the words were out of his mouth. She had done it. He opened his eyes and looked at Chandler. Her eyes seemed flat and blank, emotionless.

Softly, she said, "You say he deserved what he got. When were you appointed judge, jury and executioner?"

Bosch drank more water from the cup.

"What I meant was that it was his play. Whatever happened to him, he was ultimately responsible. You put something in play like that and you have to accept the consequences."

"Like Rodney King deserved what he got?"

"Objection!" Belk shouted.

"Like André Galton deserved what he got?"

"Objection!"

"Sustained, sustained," the judge said. "All right now, Ms. Chandler, you —"

"They're not the same."

"Detective Bosch, I sustained the objections. That means don't answer."

"No further questions at this time, Your Honor," Chandler said.

Bosch watched her walk to the plaintiff's table and drop her tablet onto the wooden surface. The loose strand of hair was there at the back of her neck. He was sure now that even that detail was part of her carefully planned and orchestrated performance during the trial. After she sat down, Deborah Church reached over and squeezed her arm. Chandler didn't smile or make any gesture in return.

Belk did what he could to repair the damage on redirect examination, asking more details about the heinous nature of the crimes, and the shooting and investigation of Church. But it seemed as if no one was listening. The courtroom had been sucked into a vacuum created by Chandler's cross-examination.

Belk was apparently so ineffective that Chandler didn't bother to ask anything on recross and Bosch was excused from the witness seat. He felt as if the walk back to the defense table covered at least a mile.

"Next witness, Mr. Belk?" the judge asked.

"Your Honor, can I have a few minutes?"

"Surely."

Belk turned to Bosch and whispered, "We're going to rest, you have a problem with that?"

"I don't know."

"There is no one else to call, unless you want to get other members of the task force over here. They'll say the same thing you did and get the same treatment from Chandler. I'd rather leave that alone."

"What about bringing Locke back? He'll back me up on everything I said about the follower."

"Too risky. He is a psychologist, for everything we get him to say is a possibility, she'll also get him to concede it is possibly not. He hasn't been deposed on this matter and we won't know for sure what he would say. Besides, I think we need to stay off the second killer. It's confusing the jury and we —"

"Mr. Belk," the judge said. "We're waiting."

Belk stood up and said, "Your Honor, the defense rests."

The judge stared a long moment at Belk before turning to the jury and telling them they were excused for the day because the lawyers would need the afternoon to prepare closing arguments and he would need time to prepare jury instructions.

After the jury filed out, Chandler went to the lectern. She asked for a directed verdict in favor of the plaintiff, which the judge denied. Belk did the same thing, asking for a verdict in favor of the defendant. In a seemingly sarcastic tone, the judge told him to sit down.

Bosch met Sylvia in the hallway outside after the crowded courtroom took several minutes to empty. There was a large gathering of reporters around the two lawyers and Bosch took her arm and moved her down the hall.

"I told you not to come here, Sylvia."

"I know, but I felt I had to come. I wanted you to know that I support you no matter what. Harry, I know things about you the jury will never know. No matter how she tries to portray you, I know you. Don't forget that."

She was wearing a black dress with a silvery-white pattern that Bosch liked. She looked very beautiful.

"I, uh, I — how long were you here?"

"For most of it. I'm glad I came. I know it was rough, but I saw the goodness of what you are come through all the harshness of what you sometimes have to do."

He just looked at her a moment.

"Be optimistic, Harry."

"The stuff about my mother . . ."

"Yes, I heard it. It hurt me that this is where I learned about it. Harry, where are we if there are those kinds of secrets between us? How many times do I have to tell you that it is endangering what we have?"

"Look," he said, "I can't do this right now. Deal with this and you, us — it's too much for right now. It's not the right place. Let's talk about it later. You're right, Sylvia, but I, uh, I just can't . . . talk. I —"

She reached up and straightened his tie and then smoothed it on his chest.

"It's okay," she said. "What will you do now?"

"Follow the case. Whether officially or not, I have to follow this. I have to find the second man, the second killer."

She just looked at him for a few moments and he knew she had probably hoped for a different answer.

"I'm sorry. It's not something I can put off. Things are happening."

"I'm going to go in to school then. So I don't lose the whole day. Will you be up to the house tonight?"

"I'll try."

"Okay, see you, Harry. Be optimistic."

He smiled and she leaned into him and kissed him on the cheek. Then she walked off toward the escalator.

Bosch was watching her go when Bremmer came up.

"You want to talk about this? That was some interesting testimony in there."

"I said all I'm saying on the stand."

"Nothing else?"

"Nope."

"What about what she says? That the second killer is really the first and that Church didn't kill anybody."

"What do you expect her to say? It's bullshit. Just remember, what I said in the courtroom was under oath. What she says out here isn't. It's bullshit, Bremmer. Don't fall for it."

"Look, Harry, I have to write this. You know? It's my job. You going to understand that? No hard feelings?"

"No hard feelings, Bremmer. Everybody has got their job to do. Now I'm going to go do mine, okay?"

He walked off toward the escalator. Outside at the statue, he lit a cigarette and gave one to Tommy Faraway, who had been sifting through the ash can.

"What's happening, Lieutenant?" the homeless man asked.

"Justice is happening."

18

Bosch drove over to Central Division and found an open parking space at the front curb. For a while, he sat in his car looking at two trustees from the lockup washing the painted enamel mural that stretched along the front wall of the bunkerlike station. It was a depiction of a nirvana where black and white and brown children played together and smiled at friendly police officers. It was a depiction of a place where the children still had hope. In angry black spray paint along the bottom of the mural someone had written, "This is a damnable lie!"

Bosch wondered whether someone from the neighborhood or a cop had done it. He smoked two cigarettes and tried to clear his mind of what had happened in the courtroom. He felt strangely at peace with the idea that some of his secrets had been revealed. But he held little hope for the outcome of the trial. He had moved into a feeling of resignation, an acceptance that the jury would find against him, that the twisted delivery of evidence in the case would convince them that he had acted, if not like the monster Chandler had described, then at least in an undesirable and reckless manner. They would never know what it was like to have to make such decisions as he had made in so fleeting a moment.

It was the same old story that every cop knew. The citizens want their police to protect them, to keep the plague from their eyes, from their doors. But those same John Q.'s are the first to stare wide-eyed and point the finger of outrage when they see close up exactly what the job they've given the cops entails. Bosch wasn't a hardliner. He didn't condone the actions taken by police in the André Galton cases and the Rodney King cases. But he understood those actions and knew that his own actions ultimately shared a common root.

Through political opportunism and ineptitude, the city had allowed the department to languish for years as an understaffed and underequipped paramilitary organization. Infected with political bacteria itself, the department was top-heavy with managers while the ranks below were so thin that the dog soldiers on the street rarely had the time or inclination to step out of their protective machines, their cars, to meet the people they served. They only ventured out to deal with the dirtbags and, consequently, Bosch knew, it had created a police culture in which everybody not in blue was seen as a dirtbag and was treated as such. Everybody. You ended up with your André Galtons and your Rodney Kings. You ended up with a riot the dog soldiers couldn't control. You ended up with a mural on a station house wall that was a damnable lie.

He badged his way past the front desk and took the stairs up to the Administrative Vice offices. At the door to the squad room he stood for a half minute and watched Ray Mora sitting at his desk on the other side of the room. It looked as if Mora was writing a report, rather than typing it. That probably meant it was a Daily Activity Report, which required little attention — just a few lines — and wasn't worth the time it took to get up and find a working typewriter.

Bosch noticed that Mora wrote with his right hand. But he knew this did not eliminate the vice cop as possibly being the follower. The follower knew the details and would have known about pulling the ligature around his victim's neck from the left side, thereby emulating the Dollmaker. Just as he knew about painting the white cross on the toe.

Mora looked up and saw him.

"What're you doing over there, Harry?"

"Didn't want to interrupt."

Bosch walked over.

"What, interrupt a day report? Are you kidding?"

"Thought it might be something important."

"It's important for me to get my paycheck. That's about it."

Bosch dragged a chair away from an empty desk and pulled it up and sat down. He noticed the statue of the Infant of Prague had been moved. Turned, actually. Its face was no longer looking at the nakedness of the actress on the porn calendar. Bosch looked at Mora and realized he was not sure how to proceed here.

"You left a message last night."

"Yeah, I was thinking . . ."

"About what?"

"Well, we know Church didn't kill Maggie Cum Loudly because of the timing, right? He was already dead when she got her ass dropped in the concrete."

"That's right."

"So, we've gotta copycat."

"Right again."

"So I was thinking: what if the copycat who did her started earlier?"

Bosch felt his throat start to tighten. He tried not to show Mora anything. Just gave him the deadpan look.

"Earlier?"

"Yeah. What if the two other porno chicks who were killed were actually done by the copycat? Who says he had to start after Church was dead?"

Bosch felt the full chill now. If Mora was the follower, was he so confident that he would risk laying the whole pattern out for Bosch? Or could his hunch — after all, that's all it was, a guess — be completely out of line? Regardless, it felt creepy sitting with Mora, his desk covered by magazines with sex acts depicted on the covers, the calendar girl leering from the vertical file. The statue's clay face turned away. Bosch realized that Delta Bush, the actress on the calendar Mora had displayed, was blonde-haired and buxom. She fit the pattern. Was that why Mora had put up the calendar?

"You know, Ray," he said, after composing his voice into a monotone, "I've been thinking the same thing. It fits better that way, all the evidence, I mean, if the follower did all three of them . . . What made you think of it?"

Mora put the report he was working on away in a desk drawer and leaned onto his desk. Subconsciously he brought his left hand up and pulled the Holy Spirit medal from his open collar. He rubbed it between his thumb and forefinger as he leaned back in his seat again, elbows on the arm rests.

He dropped the medal and said, "Well, I remembered something is what I did. It was a tip that I got right before you nailed Church. See, I dropped it when you dropped Church."

"You're talking about four years ago."

"Yeah. We all thought that was it, end of case, when you got Church."

"Get to it, Ray, what'd you remember?"

"Yeah, right, well, I remember a couple days, maybe a week before you got Church, I was given one of the call-in tips. It was given to me 'cause I was the resident expert on porno and it was a porno chick who called it in. She used the name Gallery. That's it, just Gallery. She was in the bottom-line stuff. Loops, live shows, peep booths, nine hundred phone call stuff. And she was just beginning to move up, get her name on some video boxes.

"Anyway, she called the task force — this was right before you nailed Church — and said there was a Tom that'd been making the rounds of the sets up in the Valley. You know, watching the action, hanging out with the producers, but he wasn't like the other Toms."

"I don't know what you mean. Toms?"

"That's short for Peeping Tom. That's what the girls call these guys who hang out on the sets. Usually they're friendly with the producer or they've kicked in part of the budget. They throw a grand to the producer and he lets the guy hang around and watch 'em shoot. It's pretty common. These shoots draw a lot of people for whom seeing it on video isn't enough. They want to be right up there and see it live."

"All right, so what about this guy?"

"Well, Harry, look, there's really only one reason these people hang around the sets. They're hitting on the chicks between takes. I mean, these guys wanna get laid. Or they want to make flicks themselves. They want to break in. And that was the thing with this guy. He wasn't hitting on anybody. He was just hanging around. She — this is Gallery — said she never saw this dude make the move on anybody. He talked to some of the girls but never left with any of them."

"And that's what made him weird? He didn't want to get laid?"

Mora raised his hands and shrugged like he knew it sounded weak.

"Yeah, basically. But listen, Gallery worked shoots with both Heather Cumhither and Holly Lere, the two Dollmaker victims, and she said it was on those shoots that she saw this Tom. That's why she called."

Now the story had Bosch's attention. But he didn't know what to make of it. Mora could be simply trying to deflect attention, to send Bosch down the wrong trail.

"She didn't have a name on the guy?"

"No, that was the problem. That was why I didn't jump all over it. I had a backlog of tips I was assigned and she calls in with this one without a name. I would have gotten to it eventually, but a few days later you put Church's dick in the dirt and that was that."

"You let it go."

"Yeah, dropped it like a bag of shit."

Bosch waited. He knew Mora would go on. He had more to say. There had to be more.

"So the thing is, when I looked up the card on Magna Cum Loudly for you yesterday, I recognized some of her early titles. She worked with Gallery in some of her early work. That's what made me remember the tip. So just stringing along on a hunch, I try to look Gallery up, ask around with some people in the business I know, and it turns out Gallery dropped out of the scene three years ago. Just like that. I mean, I know a top producer with the Adult Film Association and he told me she dropped out right in the middle of one of his shoots. Never said a word to anyone. And no one ever heard from her again. The producer, he remembered it pretty clearly 'cause it cost him a lot of money to reshoot the flick. There would've been no continuity if he just dumped in another actress to take her place."

Bosch was surprised that continuity was even a factor in such films. He and Mora were both silent a moment, thinking about the story, before Bosch finally spoke.

"So, you're thinking she might be in the ground somewhere? Gallery, I'm talking about. In concrete like the one we found this week."

"Yeah, that's exactly what I'm thinking. People in the industry — I mean, they are not your mainstream people, so there are plenty of disappearing acts. I remember this one broad, she dropped out, next thing I know I see her in *People* magazine. One of those stories about some celebrity fund-raiser and she's on the arm of what's his name, guy has his own TV show about the guy in charge of a kennel. Noah's Bark. I can't think of —"

"Ray, I don't give —"

"Okay, okay, anyway the point is, these chicks drop in and out of the biz all the time. Not unusual. They aren't the smartest people in the first place. They just get it in their mind to do something else. Maybe they meet a guy who they think is going to keep them in cocaine and caviar, be their sugar daddy, like that Noah's Bark asshole, and they never show up for work again — until they find out they were wrong. As a group, they don't look much past the next line of blow.

"Y'ask me, what they're all looking for is Daddy. They all got knocked around when they were a kid and this is some fucked-up way of showing they're worth something to Daddy. Least I read that somewhere. Prob'ly bullshit like everything else."

Bosch didn't need the psychology lesson.

"C'mon Ray, I'm in court and I'm trying to run down this case. Get to the point. What about Gallery?"

"What I'm saying is that with Gallery the situation's unusual 'cause it's been almost three years and she never came back. See, they always come back. Even if they've fucked over a producer so bad he had to do reshoots, they always come back. They start at the bottom — loops, fluffing — and work their way back up."

"Fluffing?"

"A fluff is off-camera talent, you could say. Girls who keep the acts up and ready to perform while they're getting cameras ready, moving lights, changing angles. Things like that, if you know what I mean."

"Yeah, I know what you mean."

Bosch was depressed after hearing about the business for ten minutes. He looked at Mora, who had been in Ad-Vice for as long as Bosch could remember.

"What about the survivor? You ever check with her on this tip?"

"Never got around to it. Like I said, I dropped it when you dropped Church. Thought we were done with the whole thing."

"Yeah, so did I."

Bosch took out a small pocket notebook and wrote down a few notes from the conversation.

"Did you save any notes from this? From back then?"

"Nope, they're gone. The original tip sheet is probably in the main task force files. But it won't say more than I just told you."

Bosch nodded. Mora was probably right.

"What did this Gallery look like?"

"Blonde, nice set — definitely Beverly Hills plastic. I think I got a picture here."

He rolled his chair to the file cabinets behind him and dug through one of the drawers, then rolled back with a file. From it he pulled an 8 × 10 color publicity shot. It was a blonde woman posed at the edge of the ocean. She was nude. She had shaved her pubic area. Bosch handed the photo back to Mora and felt embarrassed, as if they were two boys in the schoolyard telling secrets about one of the girls. He thought he saw a slight smile on Mora's face and wondered if the vice cop found humor in his discomfort or it was something else.

"Hell of a job you've got."

"Yeah, well, somebody's gotta do it."

Bosch studied him a moment. He decided to take a chance, to try to figure out what made Mora hang on to the job.

"Yeah, but why you, Ray? You've been doing this a long time."

"I guess I'm a watchdog, Bosch. The Supreme Court says this stuff is legal to a point. That makes me one of the pointmen. It's gotta be monitored. It's gotta be kept clean, no joke intended. That means these people've gotta be licensed, of legal age, and nobody's forced to do something they don't want to do. I spend a lot of days looking through this trash, looking for the stuff even the Supreme Court couldn't take. Trouble is, community standards. L.A. doesn't have any, Bosch. Hasn't been a successful obscenity prosecution here in years. I've made some underage cases. But I'm still looking for my first obscenity jacket."

He stopped a moment before saying, "Most cops do a year in Ad-Vice and then transfer out. That's all they can take. This is my seventh year, man. I can't tell you why. I guess because there's no shortage of surprises."

"Yeah, but year after year of this shit. How can you take it?"

Mora's eyes dropped to the statue on the desk.

"I'm provided for. Don't worry about me." He waited another beat and said, "I've got no family. No wife anymore. Who's going to complain about what I do, anyway?"

Bosch knew from their work on the task force that Mora had volunteered for the B squad, to work nights, because his wife had just left him. He had told Bosch that he found it hardest to get through the nights. Bosch now wondered if Mora's ex-wife was blonde and, if she was, what it would mean.

"Look, Ray, I've been thinking the same things, about this follower. And she fits, you know? Gallery. The three vics and the survivor were all blondes. Church wasn't choosey but the follower apparently is."

"Hey, you're right," Mora said, looking at the photo of Gallery. "I hadn't thought about that."

"Anyway, this four-year-old tip is as good a place to start as any. There also might be other women, other victims. What've you got going?"

Mora smiled and said, "Harry, doesn't matter what I got going. It's dogshit compared to this. I gotta vacation next week but I don't leave till Monday. Till then, I'm on it."

"You mentioned the adult association. Is that —"

"Adult Film Association, yeah. It's run out of a lawyer's office in Sherman Oaks."

"Yeah, you tight with anybody there?"

"I know the chief counsel. He's interested in keeping the biz clean, so he's a cooperative individual."

"Can you talk to him, ask around, try to find out if anybody else dropped out like Gallery? They'd have to be blonde and built."

"You want to know how many other victims we might have."

"That's right."

"I'll get on it."

"What about the agents and the performers guild?"

Bosch nodded at the calendar with Delta Bush on it.

"I'll hit them, too. Two agents handle ninety percent of the casting in this business. They'd be the place to start."

"What about outcall? Do all of the women do it?"

"Not the top ranks of performers. But the ones below that, yeah, they pretty much go the outcall route. See, the top performers, they spend ten percent of the time making movies and the rest out on the road dancing. They go from strip club to strip club, make a lot of money. They can make a hundred grand a year dancing. Most people think they're getting a bundle to do the nasty on video. That's wrong. It's the dancing. Then if you go below that level, to the performers either going up or coming down, they're the ones you find doing outcall work in addition to the movies and the dancing. A lot of money there, too. These chicks will pull down a grand a night for outcall work."

"Do they work with pimps, what?"

"Yeah, some got management but it's not a requirement. It's not like the street, where a girl needs her pimp to protect her from the bad johns and other whores. In outcall, all you need is an answering service. Chick puts her ad and her picture in the X press and the calls come in. Most have rules. They won't go to anybody's house, strictly hotel work. They can control the class of clientele they keep by the expense of the hotel. Good way to keep the riff-raff out."

Bosch thought about Rebecca Kaminski and how she had gone to the Hyatt on Sunset. A nice place, but the riff-raff got in.

Apparently thinking the same thing, Mora said, "It doesn't always work, though."

"Obviously."

"So, I'll see what I can come up with, okay? But off the top of my head, I don't think there will be many. If there was a bunch of women doing the sudden and permanent disappearing act like Gallery did, I think I would've gotten wind of it."

"You got my beeper number?"

Mora wrote it down and Bosch headed out of the office.

He was heading across the lobby past the front desk when the pager on his belt sounded. He checked the number and saw it was a 485 exchange. He assumed Mora had forgotten to tell him something. He took the stairs back up to the second floor and ducked back into the Ad-Vice squad room.

Mora was there, holding the photo of Gallery and staring at it in a contemplative manner. He looked up then and saw Bosch.

"Did you just beep me?"

"Me? No."

"Oh, I just thought you were trying to catch me before I left. I'm gonna use one of the phones."

"You're welcome to 'em, Harry."

Bosch walked to an empty desk and dialed the number from the pager. He saw Mora slide the photo into the file. He put the file into a briefcase that was on the floor next to his chair.

A male voice answered the call after two rings.

"Chief Irvin Irving's office, this is Lieutenant Felder, how can I help you?"

19

As with all three of the department's assistant chiefs, Irving had his own private conference room at Parker Center. It was furnished with a large, round, Formica-topped table and six chairs, a potted plant and a counter that ran along the rear wall. There were no windows. The room could be entered through a door from Irving's adjutant's office or from the sixth floor's main hallway. Bosch was the last one to arrive at the summit meeting called by Irving, taking the last chair. In the others sat the assistant chief, followed counterclockwise by Edgar and three men from Robbery-Homicide Division. Two of them Bosch knew, detectives Frankie Sheehan and Mike Opelt. They had also been attached to the Dollmaker task force four years earlier.

The third man from RHD Bosch knew by name and reputation only. Lieutenant Hans Rollenberger. He had been promoted to RHD sometime after Bosch had been demoted out of it. But friends like Sheehan kept Bosch informed. They told him Rollenberger was another cookie-cutter bureaucrat who avoided controversial and career-threatening decisions the way people avoid panhandlers on the sidewalk, pretending not to see or hear them. He was a climber and, therefore, he couldn't be trusted. In RHD, the troops already referred to him as "Hans Off," because that was the kind of commander he was. Morale in RHD, the unit every detective in the police department aspired to, was probably the lowest since the day the Rodney King video hit the TV.

"Sit down, Detective Bosch," Irving said cordially. "I think you know everybody."

Before Bosch could answer, Rollenberger sprang from his chair and offered his hand.

"Lieutenant Hans Rollenberger."

Bosch shook it, then they both sat down. Bosch noticed a large stack of files at the center of the table and immediately recognized them as the Doll-maker task force case files. The murder books Bosch had were his own personal files. What was piled on the table was the entire main file, probably pulled out of the archives warehouse.

"We're sitting down to see what we can do about this problem that's come up with the Dollmaker case," Irving said. "I have — as Detective Edgar has probably told you, I am swinging this case over to RHD. I am prepared to have Lieutenant Rollenberger put as many people on it as needed. I have also arranged for the loan of Detective Edgar to the case and you, as soon as you are free from the trial. I want results quickly. This is already turning into a public relations nightmare with what I understand was revealed during testimony today in your trial."

"Yeah, well, sorry about that. I was under oath."

"I understand that. The problem was you were testifying to things only you knew about. I had my adjutant sit in and he informed us of your, uh, theory on what has happened with this new case. Last night, I made the decision to have RHD handle the matter. After hearing the sense of your testimony today, I want to task-force this and get it going.

"Now, I want you to bring us up to speed on exactly what is going on, what you think, what you know. Then, we will plan from there."

They all looked at Bosch for a moment and he was unsure where to begin. Sheehan stepped in with a question. It was a signal that he believed Irving was playing on the level on this one, that Bosch could feel safe.

"Edgar says it's a copycat. That there is no problem with Church?"

"That's right," Bosch answered. "Church was the man. But he was good for nine of the victims, not eleven. He spawned a follower halfway through his run and we didn't see it."

"Tell it," Irving said.

He did. It took Bosch forty-five minutes to tell it. Sheehan and Opelt asked several questions as he went. The only thing or person he did not mention was Mora.

At the end, Irving said, "When you ran this follower theory by Locke, did he say it's possible?"

"Yes. With him I think he thinks anything is possible. But he was useful. He made it pretty clear for me. I want to keep him informed. He's good to bounce stuff off of."

"I understand there's a leak. Could it be Locke?"

Shaking his head, Bosch said, "I didn't go to him until last night and Chandler has known things from the start. She knew I was out at the scene the first day. Today she seemed to know the direction we are going, that there is a follower. She's got a good source keeping her informed. And Bremmer over at the *Times,* who knows. He's got a lot of sources."

"Okay," Irving said. "Well, aside from Dr. Locke being the exception, nothing in this room leaves this room. No one talks to anyone. You two" — he looked at Bosch and Edgar — "don't even tell your supervisors at Hollywood what you're doing."

Without naming Pounds, Irving was postulating his suspicion that Pounds could be a leak. Edgar and Bosch nodded in agreement.

"Now" — Irving looked at Bosch — "where do we go from here?"

Without hesitation, Bosch said, "We have to retrace the investigation. Like I told you, Locke said it was someone who had intimate access to the case. Who knew every detail and then copied them. It was a perfect cover. For a while, at least."

"You're talking about a cop," Rollenberger said, his first words since the briefing began.

"Maybe. But there are other possibilities. The suspect pool is actually pretty large. You got the cops, people who found the bodies, the coroner's staff, passersby at the crime scenes, reporters, lot of people."

"Shit," Opelt said. "We're going to need more people."

"Don't worry about that," Irving said. "I'll get more. How do we narrow it down?"

Bosch said, "When we look at the victims we learn things about the killer. The victims and the survivor generally fall into the same archetype. Blonde, well built, worked in porno and did outcall work on the side. Locke thinks that is how the follower picked his victims. He saw them in videos, then found the means of contacting them in the outcall ads in the local adult newspapers."

"It's like he went shopping for victims," Sheehan said.

"Yeah."

"What else?" Irving said.

"Not a lot. Locke said the follower is very smart, much more so than Church was. But that he could be disassembling, as he calls it. Coming apart. That's why he sent the note. Nobody would've ever known but then he sent the note. He's moved into a phase where he wants the attention that the Dollmaker had. He got jealous that this trial threw attention on Church."

"What about other victims?" Sheehan asked. "Ones we don't know about yet? It's been four years."

"Yeah, I'm working on that. Locke says there's gotta be others."

"Shit," Opelt said. "We need more people."

Everyone was quiet while they thought about this.

"What about the FBI, shouldn't we contact their behavioral science people?" Rollenberger asked.

Everyone looked at Hans Off as if he were the kid who came to the sand-lot football game wearing white pants.

"Fuck them," Sheehan said.

"We seem to have a handle on this — initially, at least," Irving said.

"What else do we know about the follower?" Rollenberger said, hoping to immediately deflect attention from his miscue. "Do we have any physical evidence that can give us any insight into him?"

"Well, we need to track down the survivor," Bosch said. "She gave a composite drawing that everyone dismissed after I nailed Church. But now we know her drawing was probably of the follower. We need to find her and see if there is anything else that she has, that she can still remember, that will help."

As he said this Sheehan dug through the stack of files on the table and found the composite. It was very generic and didn't look like anyone Bosch recognized, least of all Mora.

"We have to assume he wore disguises, same as Church, so the composite might not help. But she might remember something else, something about the suspect's manners that might let us know if it was a cop.

"Also, I'm having Amado at the coroner's office compare the rape kits between the two victims we now attribute to the follower. There's a good chance the follower may have made a mistake here."

"Explain," Irving said.

"The follower did everything the Dollmaker did, right?"

"Right," Rollenberger said.

"Wrong. He only did what was known at the time about the Dollmaker. What we knew. What we didn't know was that Church had been smart. He had shaved his body so he would not leave trace hair evidence behind. We didn't know that until after he was dead, so neither did the follower. And by then he had already done two of the victims."

"So there is a chance those two rape kits hold physical evidence to our guy," Irving said.

"Right. I'm having Amado cross-check between the two kits. He should know something by Monday."

"That's very good, Detective Bosch."

Irving looked at Bosch and their eyes met. It was as if the assistant chief was sending him a message and taking one at the same time.

"We'll see," Bosch said.

"Other than that, that's all we've got, right?" Rollenberger said.

"Right."

"No."

It was Edgar, who up until now had been silent. Everyone looked at him.

"In the concrete we found — actually, Harry found it — a cigarette pack. It went in when the concrete was wet. So there's a good chance they were the follower's. Marlboro regulars. Soft pack."

"They also could have been the vic's, right?" Rollenberger asked.

"No," Bosch said. "I talked to her manager last night. He said she didn't smoke. The smokes were in all likelihood the follower's."

Sheehan smiled at Bosch and Bosch smiled back. Sheehan held his hands together as if waiting for handcuffs.

"Here I am boys," he said. "That's my brand."

"Mine, too," Bosch said. "But I've got you beat. I'm left-handed, too. I better get an alibi working."

The men at the table smiled. Bosch dropped his smile when he suddenly thought of something but knew he could not say anything yet. He looked at the files stacked at the center of the table.

"Shit, every cop smokes Marlboros or Camels," Opelt said.

"It's a dirty habit," Irving said.

"I agree," said Rollenberger, a little too quickly.

It brought silence back to the table.

"Who's your suspect?"

It was Irving who asked it. He was looking at Bosch again with those eyes Harry couldn't decipher. The question shocked Bosch. Irving knew. Somehow he knew. Harry didn't answer.

"Detective, it is clear you've had a handle on what's going on for a day. You've also been on this case from the start. I think you've got someone in mind. Tell us. We need to start somewhere."

Bosch hesitated again but finally said, "I'm not sure . . . and I don't want . . ."

"To ruin someone's career if you're wrong? To set the dogs on a possibly innocent man? That's understood. But we can't have you pursuing this on your own. Haven't you learned anything from this trial? I believe 'cowboying' was the term Money Chandler used to describe it."

They were all looking at him. He was thinking of Mora. The vice cop was strange but was he that strange? Over the years Bosch had often been investigated by the department and did not want to bring that kind of weight down on the wrong person.

"Detective?" Irving prompted. "Even if all you have is a hunch, then you must tell us. Investigations start with hunches. You want to protect one person but what are we going to do? We are about to go out and investigate cops. What difference is it if we start with this person or come to him in time? Either way we will get to him. Give us the name."

Bosch thought about everything Irving had said. He wondered what his own motive was. Was he protecting Mora or simply keeping him for himself? He thought a few more moments and finally said, "Give me five minutes alone in here with the files. If there is something there that I think is there, then I'll tell you."

"Gentlemen," Irving said, "let's go get some coffee."

After the room was cleared, Bosch looked at the files for nearly a minute without moving. He felt confused. He wasn't sure whether he wanted to find something that would convince him Mora was the follower or convince him he was not. He thought about what Chandler had said to the jury about monsters and the black abyss where they dwell. Whoever fights monsters, he thought, should not think too hard about it.

He lit a cigarette and pulled the stack close to him and began looking for two files. The chronologies file was near the top. It was thin. It was basically a quick guide to important dates in the investigation. He found the task force personnel file at the bottom of the stack. It was thicker than the first he pulled out because it contained the weekly shifts schedule for the detectives assigned to the task force and the overtime approval forms. As the detective-three in charge of the B squad, Bosch had been in charge of keeping the personnel file up to date.

From the chronologies file, Bosch quickly looked up the times and dates that the first two porno actresses were murdered and other pertinent information about the way they were lured to their death. Then he looked up the same information about the lone survivor. He wrote it all down in order on a page of his pocket notebook.

> — June 17, 11 P.M.
> Georgia Stern aka Velvet Box
> survivor
>
> — July 6, 11:30 P.M.
> Nicole Knapp aka Holly Lere
> W. Hollywood
>
> — Sept. 28, 4 A.M.
> Shirleen Kemp aka Heather Cumhither
> Malibu

Bosch opened the personnel file and pulled the shift schedules for the weeks the women were attacked or murdered. June seventeenth, the night Georgia Stern was attacked, was a Sunday, which was the B squad's night off. Mora could've done it, but so could anyone else who was on the squad.

On the Knapp case, Bosch got a hit and his fingers trembled a little as he held the schedule for the week of July 1. His adrenaline was moving faster now. July sixth, the day Knapp was sent on an outcall request at 9 P.M. and was found dead on the sidewalk on Sweetzer in West Hollywood at 11:30 P.M., was a Friday. Mora was on the schedule to be working the three-to-midnight shift with the B squad, but there next to his name in Bosch's own writing was the word "sick."

Bosch quickly pulled out the schedule for the week of September twenty-second. The nude body of Shirleen Kemp had been found at the side of the Pacific Coast Highway in Malibu at four in the morning on Friday, September twenty-eighth. He realized that wasn't enough information and looked for the file that contained the investigation of her death.

He quickly read through the file and learned that Kemp had a phone service that had logged a call for her services at the Malibu Inn at 12:55 A.M. When detectives went there they learned from phone records that at 12:55 A.M. a call had been placed by the occupant of room 311. The front desk staff could not provide a good description of the man in 311 and the identification he gave proved to be false. He had paid in cash. The one thing the desk people could say with absolute accuracy was that he checked in at 12:35 A.M. Each registration card was punched with the time. The man had called for Heather Cumhither twenty minutes after he checked in.

Bosch referred back to the work schedule. On the Thursday night before Kemp was murdered, Mora had worked. But he had apparently come in and left early. He had signed in at 2:40 P.M. and out at 11:45 P.M.

That gave him fifty minutes to get from the Hollywood station to the Malibu Inn and checked into room 311 at 12:35 A.M., Friday. Bosch knew that it could be done. Traffic would be light on the PCH that late at night.

It could be Mora.

He noticed that the cigarette he had set on the edge of the table had burned down to the butt and it had discolored the Formica edge. He quickly dropped the cigarette into a pot containing a ficus plant in the corner of the room and turned the table around so the burn mark was positioned at the spot where Rollenberger had been sitting. He waved one of the files in the air to disperse the smoke and then opened the door to Irving's office.

"Raymond Mora."

Irving had said the name out loud apparently to see how it sounded. He said nothing else when Bosch was finished telling what he knew. Bosch watched him and waited for more but the assistant chief only sniffed at the air, identified the cigarette smoke and frowned.

"Another thing," Bosch said. "Locke wasn't the only one I talked to about the follower. Mora knows just about everything I just told you. He was on the task force and we went to him this week for help on the ID of the concrete blonde. I was over at Ad-Vice when you paged me. He had called me last night."

"What did he want?" Irving asked.

"He wanted to let me know that he thought the follower might've done the two porno queens from the original eleven. He said it had just come to him, that maybe the follower had started way back then."

"Shit," Sheehan said, "this guy is playing with us. If he —"

"What did you tell him?" Irving interrupted.

"I told him I was thinking that, too. And I asked him to check with his sources to see if he could find out if there were other women who disappeared or dropped out of the business like Becky Kaminski did."

"You asked him to go to work on this?" Rollenberger said, his eyebrows arched in astonishment and outrage.

"I had to. It was the obvious thing for me to ask him. If I didn't, he'd know I was suspicious."

"He's right," Irving said.

Rollenberger's chest seemed to deflate a little bit. He couldn't get anything right.

"Yes, now I see," he dutifully responded. "Good work."

"We're going to need more people," Opelt said, since everybody was being so agreeable.

"I want to begin surveillance on him by tomorrow morning," Irving said. "We're going to need at least three teams. Sheehan and Opelt will be one. Bosch, you're involved in court and Edgar, I want you working on tracking down the survivor, so you two are out. Lieutenant Rollenberger, who else can you spare?"

"Well, Yde is sitting around since Buchert is on vacation. And Mayfield and Rutherford are in court on the same case. I can shake one of them loose to pair with Yde. That's all I've got, unless you want to pull back on some ongoing —"

"No, I don't want that. Get Yde and Mayfield in on this. I'll go to Lieutenant Hilliard and see what she can spare from the Valley. She's had three teams on the catering truck case for a month and they're at the wall. I'll take a team off of that."

"Very good, sir," Rollenberger said.

Sheehan looked at Harry and made a face like he was going to puke with this guy in charge. Bosch held back his smile. There was always this giddiness that detectives felt when they received their marching orders and were about to go out into the hunt.

"Opelt, Sheehan, I want you on Mora tomorrow morning at eight," Irving said. "Lieutenant, I want you to set up a meeting with the new people tomorrow morning. Bring them up to date on what we have and have one team take over surveillance from Opelt and Sheehan at four P.M. They stay with Mora until lights out. If overtime is needed, I'm authorizing it. The other pair will take the surveillance at eight A.M. Saturday and Opelt and Sheehan will take it back at four. Rotate like that. The night-shift watchers have to stay with him until they are sure he is in his home in bed for the night. I want no mistakes. If this guy pulls off something while we're watching him, we can all kiss our careers good-bye."

"Chief?"

"Yes, Bosch."

"There is no guarantee that he is going to do something. Locke said he thinks the follower has a lot of control. He doesn't think he is out there hunting every night. He thinks he controls the urge and lives pretty normally, then strikes at irregular intervals."

"There is no guarantee that we'll even be watching the right man, Detective Bosch, but I want to watch him anyway. I am sitting here hoping we are dreadfully wrong about Detective Mora. But the things you have said here are convincing in a circumstantial way. Nothing near being usable in court. So we watch him and hope if it's him we'll see the sign before he hurts anybody else. My —"

"I agree, sir," Rollenberger said.

"Don't interrupt me, Lieutenant. My forte is neither detective work nor psychoanalysis, but something tells me that whoever the follower is, he's feeling the pressure. Sure, he brought it on himself with that note. And he may think this is a cat-and-mouse game he can master. Nevertheless, he is feeling the pressure. And one thing I know, just from being a cop, when the pressure is on these people, the edge-dwellers I call them, then they react. Sometimes they crack, sometimes they act out. So what I am saying is, knowing what I know about this case, I want Mora covered if he even walks outside to get the mail."

They sat there in silence. Even Rollenberger, who seemed cowed by his misstep in interrupting Irving.

"Okay, then, we have our assignments. Sheehan, Opelt, surveillance. Bosch, you are freelancing until you get done with the trial. Edgar, you have the survivor and when you have the time do some checking on Mora. Nothing that will get back to him."

"He's divorced," Bosch offered. "Got divorced right before the Dollmaker task force was put together."

"All right, there's your start. Go to court, pull his divorce. Who knows, we might get lucky. Maybe his wife dropped him because he liked making her up like a doll. Things have been hard enough on this case, we could use a break like that."

Irving looked around the table at each man's face.

"The potential for embarrassment to the department on this case is huge. But I don't want anybody holding back. Let the stones fall where they will. . . . Okay, then, everybody has their assignments. Go to it. Everyone is excused with the exception of Detective Bosch."

As the others filed out of the room, Bosch thought Rollenberger's face showed his disappointment at not getting a chance for a private ass-kissing conference with Irving.

After the door closed, Irving was quiet for a few moments as he composed what he wanted to say. Throughout most of Bosch's career as a detective, Irving had been a nemesis of sorts, always trying to control him and bring him into the fold. Bosch had always resisted. Nothing personal, it just wasn't Bosch's gig.

But now Bosch sensed a softening in Irving. In the way he had treated Bosch during the meeting, in the way he testified earlier in the week. He could have hung Bosch out to dry but didn't. Yet, it wasn't something Bosch could or would acknowledge. So he sat there silently and waited.

"Good work on this, Detective. Especially with the trial and everything going on."

Bosch nodded but knew that wasn't what this was about.

"Uh, that's why I held you here. The trial. I wanted to — let's see, how do I say this . . . I wanted to tell you, and excuse the language, but I don't give a flying fuck what that jury decides or how much money they give those people. That jury has no idea what it's like to be out there on the edge. To have to make the decisions that may cost or save lives. You can't take a week to accurately examine and judge the decision you had to make in a second."

Bosch was trying to think of something to say and the silence seemed to drag on too long.

"Anyway," Irving finally said, "I guess it's taken me four years to come to that conclusion. But better late than never."

"Hey, I could use you for closing arguments tomorrow."

Irving's face cringed, the muscular jaws flexing as if he had just taken a mouthful of cold sauerkraut.

"Don't get me started on that, either. I mean, what is this city doing? The city attorney's office is nothing but a school. A law school for trial lawyers. And the taxpayers pay the tuition. We get these greenhorn, uh, uh, preppies, who don't know the first thing about trial law. They learn from the mistakes they make in court when it counts — for us. And when they finally get good and know what the hell they're doing, they quit and then they're the lawyers suing us!"

Bosch had never seen Irving so animated. It was as if he had taken off the starched public persona he always wore like a uniform. Harry was entranced.

"Sorry about that," Irving said. "I get carried away. Anyway, good luck with this jury but don't let it worry you."

Bosch said nothing.

"You know, Bosch, it only takes a half-hour meeting with Lieutenant Rollenberger in the room for me to want to take a good look at myself and this department and where it's headed. He's not the LAPD I joined or you joined. He's a good manager, yes, and so am I, at least I think so. But we can't forget we're cops . . ."

Bosch didn't know what to say, or if he should say anything. It seemed that Irving was almost rambling now. As if there was something he wanted to say, but was looking for anything else to say instead.

"Hans Rollenberger. What a name, huh? I can guess, the detectives in his crew must call him 'Hans Off,' am I right?"

"Sometimes."

"Yes, well, I guess that's expected. He — uh, you know, Harry, I've got thirty-eight years in the department."

Bosch just nodded. This was getting weird. Irving had never even called him by his first name before.

"And, uh, I worked Hollywood patrol for a lot of years right out of the academy. . . . That question Money Chandler asked me about your mother. That really came out of the blue and I'm sorry about that, Harry, sorry for your loss."

"It was a long time ago." Bosch waited a beat. Irving was looking down at his hands, which were clasped on the table. "If that's it, I think I'll —"

"Yes, that's basically it, but, you know, what I wanted to tell you is that I was there that day."

"What day?"

"That day that your mother — I was the RO."

"The reporting officer?"

"Yes, I was the one that found her. I was walking a foot beat on the Boulevard and I ducked into that alley off of Gower. I usually hit it once a day and, uh, I found her. . . . When Chandler showed me those reports I recognized the case right away. She didn't know my badge number — it was there on the report — or she would've known I was the one who found her. Chandler would've had some kind of a field day with that, I guess . . ."

This was hard for Bosch to sit through. Now he was glad Irving wasn't looking at him. He knew, or thought he knew, what it was that Irving wasn't saying. If he had worked the Boulevard foot beat, then he had known Bosch's mother before she was dead.

Irving glanced up at him and then looked away, toward the corner of the room. His eyes fell on the ficus plant.

"Somebody put a cigarette butt in my pot," he said. "That yours, Harry?"

20

Bosch was lighting a cigarette as he used his shoulder to push through one of the glass doors at the entrance to Parker Center. Irving had jolted him with his small-world story. Bosch had always figured he'd run into somebody in the department who knew her or knew the case. Never did Irving fit into that scenario.

As he walked through the south lot to the Caprice he noticed Jerry Edgar standing at the corner of Los Angeles and First waiting for the cross light. Bosch looked at his watch and saw it was 5:10, quitting time. He thought Edgar was probably walking up to the Code Seven or the Red Wind for a draft before fighting the freeway. He thought that wasn't a bad idea. Sheehan and Opelt were probably already sitting on stools at one of the bars.

By the time Bosch got to the corner, Edgar had a block-and-a-half lead on him and was walking up First toward the Seven. Bosch picked up the pace. For the first time in a long time, he felt the actual mental craving for alcohol. For just a while he wanted to forget Church and Mora and Chandler and his own secrets and what Irving had told him in the conference room.

But then Edgar walked right on by the billy club that served as the door handle at the Seven without even giving it a glance. He crossed Spring and walked alongside the *Times* building toward Broadway. Then it's the Red Wind, Bosch thought.

The Wind was okay as far as a watering hole went. They had Weinhard's by the bottle instead of on draft, so the place lost points there. Another minus was that the yuppies from the *Times* newsroom favored the place and it often was more crowded with reporters than cops. The big plus, however, was that on Thursdays and Fridays they had a quartet come in and play sets from six to ten. They were mostly retired club men who weren't too tight, but it was as good a way as any to miss the rush hour.

He watched Edgar cross Broadway and stay on First instead of taking a left to go down to the Wind. Bosch slowed his pace a bit so Edgar could renew his block-and-a-half lead. He lit another cigarette and felt uneasy about the prospect of following the other detective but did it anyway. There was a bad feeling beginning to nag at him.

Edgar turned left on Hill and ducked into the first door on the east side, across from the new subway entrance. The door he went through was to the Hung Jury, a bar that was off the lobby of the Fuentes Legal Center, an eight-story office building solely occupied by attorney offices. Mostly, the tenants were defense and litigation attorneys who had chosen the nondescript if not ugly building because of its main selling point; it was only a half block from the county courts building, a block from the criminal courts building and a block and a half from the federal building.

Bosch knew all of this because Belk had told him all about it on the day the two of them had come to the Fuentes Legal Center to find Honey Chandler's office. Bosch had been subpoenaed to give a deposition in the Norman Church case.

The uneasy feeling turned into a hollow in his gut as he passed the door to the Hung Jury and went into the main lobby of the Fuentes Center. He knew the layout of the bar, having dropped in for a beer and a shot after the deposition with Chandler, and he knew there was an entrance off the building's lobby. He pushed through the lobby entrance door now and stepped into an alcove where there were two pay phones and the doors to the restrooms. He moved up to the corner and carefully looked into the bar area.

A juke box Bosch couldn't see was playing Sinatra's "Summer Wind," a barmaid with a puffy wig and bills wrapped through her fingers — tens, fives, ones — was delivering a batch of martinis to a four top of lawyers sitting near the front entrance and the bartender was leaning over the dimly lit bar smoking a cigarette and reading the *Hollywood Reporter*. Probably an actor or a screenwriter when he wasn't tending bar, Bosch thought. Maybe a talent scout. Who in this town wasn't?

When the bartender leaned forward to stub out his smoke in an ashtray, Bosch saw Edgar sitting at the far end of the bar with a draft beer in front of him. A match flared in the darkness next to him and Bosch watched Honey Chandler light a smoke and then drop her match into an ashtray next to what looked like a Bloody Mary.

Bosch moved back into the alcove, out of sight.

He waited next to an old plywood shack that was built on the sidewalk at Hill and First and served as a news and magazine stand. It had been closed and boarded for the night. As it grew dark and the streetlights came on, Bosch spent his time fending off panhandlers and passing prostitutes looking for one last businessman's special before heading from downtown into Hollywood for the evening — and the rougher — trade.

By the time he saw Edgar come out of the Hung Jury, Bosch had a nice little pile of cigarette butts on the sidewalk at his feet. He flicked the one he had going into the street and stepped back alongside the news stand so Edgar wouldn't notice him. Bosch saw no sign of Chandler and assumed that she had left the bar through the other door and gone down to the garage and her car. Edgar probably had wisely declined a ride over to the Parker Center lot.

As Edgar passed the stand Bosch stepped out behind him.

"Jerry, whereyat?"

Edgar jumped as if an ice cube had been pressed against his neck and whipped around.

"Harry? What're you — hey, you wanna grab a drink? That's what I was looking to do."

Bosch let him stand there and squirm for a few seconds before saying, "You already had your drink."

"What do you mean?"

Bosch took a step toward him. Edgar looked genuinely scared.

"You know what I mean. A beer for you, right? Bloody Mary for the lady."

"Listen, Harry, look, I —"

"Don't call me that. Don't ever call me Harry again. Understand? You want to talk to me, call me Bosch. That's what the people who aren't my friends call me, the people I don't trust. Just call me that."

"Can I explain? Har — uh, I'd like the chance to explain."

"What's to explain? You fucked me over. Nothing to explain about that. What'd you tell her tonight? You just run down everything we just talked about in Irving's office? I don't think she needs it, pal. The damage is already done."

"No. She left a long time ago. I was in there most of the time alone thinking about how to get out of this. I didn't tell her shit about today's meeting. Harry, I didn't —"

Bosch took one more step and in a quick motion brought his hand up, palm out, and hit Edgar in the chest, knocking him backward.

"I said don't call me that!" he yelled. "You fuck! You — we worked together, man. I taught you . . . I'm in that courtroom getting fucked in the ass and I find out you're the guy, you're the goddamn leak."

"I'm sorry. I —"

"What about Bremmer? You the one who told him about the note? Is that where you're going for a drink now? Going to meet Bremmer? Well, don't let me stop you."

"No, man, I haven't talked to Bremmer. Look, I made a mistake, okay? I'm sorry. She screwed me, too. It was like blackmail. I couldn't — I tried to get out of it but she had me by the shorthairs. You gotta believe me, man."

Bosch looked at him for a long moment. It was fully dark now but he thought he saw that Edgar's eyes were shiny in the glow of the streetlights. Maybe he was holding back tears. But what were they tears for, Bosch wondered. For the loss of the relationship they had? Or were they tears of fear? Bosch felt the surge of his power over Edgar. And Edgar knew he had it.

In a low and very even voice Bosch said, "I want to know everything. You are going to tell me what you did."

The quartet at the Wind was on a break. They sat at a table in the back. It was a dark, wood-paneled room like hundreds of others in the city. A red leatherette pad ran along the edge of the cigarette-scarred bar and the barmaids wore black uniforms and white aprons and they all had too much red lipstick on their thin lips. Bosch ordered a double shot of Jack Black straight up and a bottle of Weinhard's. He also gave the barmaid money for a pack of cigarettes. Edgar, who now wore the face of a man whose life had run out on him, ordered Jack Black, water back.

"It's the damn recession," Edgar began before Bosch asked a question. "Real estate is in the toilet. I had to drop that gig and we had the mortgage and, you know how it is, man, Brenda had gotten used to a cert —"

"Fuck that. You think I want to hear about how you sell me out because your wife has to drive a Chevy instead of a BMW? Fuck you. You —"

"It's not like that. I —"

"Shut up. I'm talking. You're going to —"

They both shut up while the barmaid put the drinks and cigarettes down. Bosch put a twenty on her tray. He never took his dark, angry eyes off Edgar.

"Now, skip the bullshit and tell me what you did."

Edgar threw back his shot and washed it down with water before starting.

"Uh, you see, uh, it was late Monday afternoon, this was after we'd been out to the scene at Bing's and I was back at the office. And I got a call at the office and it was Chandler. She knew something was up. I don't know how she knew, but she knew about the note we got and the body being found. She musta gotten tipped by Bremmer or something. She started asking questions, you know, 'Was it confirmed as the Dollmaker?' Things like that. I put her off. No comment . . ."

"And then?"

"Then, well, she offered me something. I'm two back on the mortgage and Brenda doesn't even know."

"What'd I tell you? I don't want to hear your sad story, Edgar. I'm telling you, I don't have any sympathy for that. You tell it and it will only make me madder."

"All right, all right. She offered me money. I said I'd think about it. She said if I wanted to deal to meet her at the Hung Jury that night. . . . You won't let me say why, but I had reasons and so I went. Yeah, I went."

"Yeah, and you fucked yourself up," Bosch said, hoping to knock down the defiant tone that had crept into Edgar's voice.

He had finished the last of his Jack Black and signaled the barmaid but she didn't see him. The musicians were taking their places behind their instruments. The front man was a saxophone player and Bosch wished he was here under other circumstances.

"What did you give her?"

"Just what we knew that day. But she already had just about everything already. I told her you said it looked like the Dollmaker. It wasn't a lot, Ha — and most of it was in the paper the next day, anyway. And I wasn't Bremmer's source on that. You have to believe me."

"You told her I came out there? To the scene?"

"Yeah, I told her. What was the big secret about that?"

Bosch thought about all of this for a few minutes. He watched the band start up with a Billy Strayhorn number called "Lush Life." Their table was far enough away from the quartet that it wasn't too loud. Harry's eyes scanned the rest of the bar to see if anyone else was into it and he saw Bremmer sitting at the bar nursing a beer. He was with a group of what looked like reporter types. One of the other men even had one of those long, skinny notebooks that reporters always carry sticking out of his back pocket.

"Speaking of Bremmer, there he is. Maybe he wants to check a detail or two with you after we're done."

"Harry, it's not me."

Bosch let him get away with the Harry that time. He was getting tired and depressed with this scene. He wanted to get it over with and get out of there, go see Sylvia.

"How many times did you talk to her?"

"Every night."

"She turned it on you, didn't she? You had to go see her."

"I was stupid. I needed the money. Once I met her the first night she had me by the balls. She said she wanted updates on the investigation or she'd tell you I was the leak, she'd inform IAD. Fuck, she never even paid me."

"What happened tonight to make her split early?"

"She said the case was over, going to closing arguments tomorrow, so it didn't matter what was happening in the case. She cut me loose."

"But it won't end there. You know that, don't you? Whenever she needs a plate run, an address from DMV, a witness's unlisted number, she's going to call you. She's got you, man."

"I know. I'll have to deal with it."

"All for what? What was the price, that first night?"

"I wanted one goddamn mortgage payment. . . . Can't sell the fuckin' house, can't make the mortgage, I don't know what I'm going to do."

"What about me? Aren't you worried about what I'm going to do?"

"Yes. Yes, I am."

Bosch looked back at the quartet. They were staying with a Strayhorn set and were on to "Blood Count." There was a journeyman quality to the sax man's work. He stayed on point and his phrasing was clean.

"What are you going to do?" Edgar asked.

Bosch didn't have to think, he already knew. He didn't take his eyes from the sax man as he spoke.

"Nothing."

"Nothing?"

"It's what you are going to do. I can't work with you anymore, man. I know we got this thing with Irving but that's it, that's the end. After this is over you go to Pounds and tell him you want to transfer out of Hollywood."

"But there aren't openings in homicide anywhere else. I looked at the board, you know how rarely they come."

"I didn't say anything about homicide. I just said you're going to ask for a transfer. You ask for the first thing open, understand? I don't care if you end up on autos in the Seventy-seventh, you take the first thing you can get."

Now he looked at Edgar, whose mouth was slightly open, and said, "That's the price you pay."

"But homicide is what I do, you know that. It's where it's at."

"And you're not where it's at anymore. This isn't negotiable. Unless you want to take your chances with IAD. But either you go to Pounds or I go to them. I can't work with you anymore. That's it."

He looked back at the band. Edgar was silent and after a few moments Bosch told him to leave.

"You go first. I can't walk with you back to Parker."

Edgar stood up and hovered near the table for a few moments before saying, "Someday, you're going to need all the friends you can get. That's the day you'll remember doing this to me."

Without looking at him, Bosch said, "I know."

After Edgar had gone Bosch got the barmaid's attention and ordered another round. The quartet played "Rain Check" with some improvisational riffs that Bosch liked. The whiskey was beginning to warm his gut and he sat back and smoked and listened, trying not to think about anything to do with cops and killers.

But soon he felt a presence nearby and turned to see Bremmer standing there with his bottle of beer in hand.

"I take it by the look on Edgar's face when he left that he won't be coming back. Can I join you?"

"No, he won't be back and you can do whatever you want, but I'm off duty, off the record and off the road."

"In other words, you ain't saying shit."

"You got it."

The reporter sat down and lit a cigarette. His small but sharp green eyes squinted through the smoke.

"It's okay, 'cause I'm not working either."

"Bremmer, you're always working. Even now, I say the wrong word and you aren't going to forget about it."

"I suppose. But you forget the times we worked together. The stories that helped you, Harry. I write one story that doesn't go the way you want and all of that is forgotten. Now I'm just 'that damn reporter' who —"

"I haven't forgotten shit. You're sitting here, right? I remember what you did for me and I'll remember what you did against me. It all evens out in the end."

They sat in silence for a while and listened to the music. The set ended just as the barmaid was putting Bosch's third double Jack Black on the table.

"I'm not saying I would ever reveal it," Bremmer said, "but how come my source on the note story was so important?"

"It's not that important anymore. At the time I just wanted to know who was trying to nail me."

"You said that before. That someone was setting you up. You really think that?"

"It doesn't matter. What kind of story did you write for tomorrow?"

The reporter straightened up and and his eyes brightened.

"You'll see it. Pretty much a straight court story. Your testimony about someone else continuing the killings. It's going out front. It's a big story. That why I'm here. I always come in for a pop after I hit the front page."

"Party time, huh? What about my mother? Did you put that stuff in?"

"Harry, if that's what you are worried about, forget it. I didn't even mention that in the story. To be honest, it's of course vitally interesting to you, but as far as a newspaper story goes, I thought it was too much inside baseball. I left it out."

"Inside baseball?"

"Too arcane, like the stats those sports guys on TV throw around. You know, like how many fastballs Lefty So and So threw during the third inning of the fifth game of the 1956 World Series. I thought the stuff with your mother — Chandler's attempt to use it as your motivation for dropping this guy — was going too far inside."

Bosch just nodded. He was glad that part of his life would not be in the hands of a million newspaper buyers tomorrow, but he acted nonchalant about it.

"But," Bremmer said, "I gotta tell you, if we get a verdict back on this that goes against you and the jurors start saying they thought you did it to avenge your mother's death, then that is usable and I won't have a choice."

Bosch nodded again. It seemed fair enough. He looked at his watch and saw it was nearly ten. He knew he should call Sylvia and he knew he should get out of there before the next set started and he became entranced by the music again.

He finished his drink and said, "I'm gonna hit it."

"Yeah, me, too," Bremmer said. "I'll walk out with you."

Outside, the chilled night air cut through Bosch's whiskey daze. He said good-bye to Bremmer and put his hands in his pockets as he started down the sidewalk.

"Harry, you walking all the way back to Parker Center? Hop in. My car is right here."

Bosch watched Bremmer unlock the passenger door to his Le Sabre, which was parked right at the curb in front of the Wind. Bosch got in without a word of thanks and leaned over and unlocked the other side. When he was drunk he went through a stage where he said almost nothing, just vegetated in his own juices and listened.

Bremmer started the conversation during the four blocks to Parker Center.

"That Money Chandler is something else, isn't she? She really knows how to play a jury."

"You think she's got it, don't you?"

"It's going to be close, Harry. I think. But even if it's one of those statement verdicts that are popular these days against the LAPD, she'll get rich."

"Whaddaya mean?"

"You haven't been in federal court before have you?"

"No. I try not to make it a habit."

"Well, in a civil rights case, if the plaintiff wins — in this case, Chandler — then the defendant — in this case the city is paying your tab — has to pay the lawyer's fees. I guarantee you, Harry, that in her closing argument tomorrow Money will tell those jurors that all they need to do is make a statement that you acted wrongly. And even damages of a dollar make that statement. The jury will see that as the easy way out. They can say you were wrong and only give a dollar in damages. They won't know, because Belk is not allowed to tell them, that even if the plaintiff wins a dollar, Chandler bills the city. And that won't be a dollar. More like a couple hundred thousand of them. It's a scam."

"Shit."

"Yeah, that's the justice system."

Bremmer pulled into the lot and Bosch pointed out his Caprice in one of the front rows.

"You going to be all right to drive?" Bremmer asked.

"No problem."

Bosch was about to close the door when Bremmer stopped him.

"Hey, Harry, we both know I can't reveal my source. But I can tell you who it isn't. And I'll tell you it is not someone you'd expect. You know? Edgar and Pounds, if that's who you think it is, forget it. You'd never guess who it was, so don't bother. Okay?"

Bosch just nodded and shut the door.

21

After fumbling to find the right one, Bosch put the key in the ignition but didn't turn it. He briefly considered whether he should try to drive or whether he should go get coffee from the cafeteria first. He looked up through the windshield at the gray monolith that was Parker Center. Most of the lights were on but he knew the offices had emptied. The lights of the squad rooms were always left on to give the appearance that the fight against crime never sleeps. It was a lie.

He thought of the couch that was kept in one of the RHD interrogation rooms. That was also an alternative to driving. Unless, of course, it was already taken. But then he thought of Sylvia and how she had come to court despite what he had said about not wanting her there. He wanted to get home to her. Yes, he thought, home.

He put his hand on the key but then dropped it away again. He rubbed his eyes. They were tired and there were so many thoughts swimming in the whiskey. There was the sound of the tenor sax floating there, too. His own improvisational riff.

He tried to think of what Bremmer had just said, that Bosch would never guess who the source was. Why had he said it that way? He found that more tantalizing than wondering who his source actually was.

It didn't matter, he told himself. All would be over soon. He leaned his head against the side window, thinking about the trial and his testimony. He wondered how he had looked up there, all eyes on him. He never wanted to be in that position again. Ever. To have Honey Chandler cornering him with words.

Whoever fights monsters, he thought. What had she told the jury? About the abyss? Yes, where monsters dwell. Is that where I dwell? In the black place? The black heart, he remembered then. Locke had called it that. The black heart does not beat alone. In his mind he replayed the vision of Norman Church being knocked upright by the bullet and then flopping helplessly naked on the bed. The look in the dying man's eyes stayed with him. Four years later and the vision was as clear as yesterday. Why was that, he wanted to know. Why did he remember Norman Church's face and not his own mother's? Do I have the black heart, Bosch asked himself. Do I?

The darkness came up on him then like a wave and pulled him down. He was there with the monsters.

There was a sharp rap on the glass. Bosch abruptly opened his eyes and saw the patrolman next to the car holding his baton and flashlight. Harry quickly looked around and grabbed the wheel and put his foot on the brake. He didn't think he had been driving that badly, then he realized he hadn't been driving at all. He was still in the Parker Center lot. He reached over and rolled the window down.

The kid in the uniform was the lot cop. The lowest-rated cadet in each academy class was first assigned to watch the Parker Center lot during P.M. watch. It was a tradition but it also served a purpose. If the cops couldn't prevent car break-ins and other crime in the parking lot of their own headquarters, then it begged the question, where could they stop crime?

"Detective, are you all right?" he said as he slid his baton back into the ring on his belt. "I saw you get dropped off and get in your car. Then when you didn't leave I wanted to check."

"Yes," Bosch managed to say. "I'm, uh, fine. Thanks. I musta dozed off there. Been a long day."

"Yes, they all are. Be careful now."

"Yes."

"Are you okay driving?"

"Fine. Thank you."

"You sure?"

"I'm sure."

He waited until the cop walked away before starting the car. Bosch looked at his watch and figured he had slept for no more than thirty minutes. But the nap, and the sudden waking, had refreshed him. He lit a cigarette and pulled the car out onto Los Angeles Street and took it to the Hollywood Freeway entrance.

As he drove north on the freeway he rolled the window down so the cool air would keep him alert. It was a clear night. Ahead of him, the lights of the Hollywood Hills ascended into the sky where spotlights from two different locations behind the mountains cut through the darkness. He thought it was a beautiful scene, yet it made him feel melancholy.

Los Angeles had changed in the last few years, but then there was nothing new about that. It was always changing and that was why he loved it. But riot and recession had left a particularly harsh mark on the landscape, the landscape of memory. Bosch believed he would never forget the pall of smoke that hung over the city like some kind of supersmog that could not be lifted by the evening winds. The TV pictures of burning buildings and looters unchecked by the police. It had been the department's darkest hour and it still had not recovered.

And neither had the city. Many of the ills that led to such volcanic rage were still left untended. The city offered so much beauty and yet it offered so much danger and hate. It was a city of shaken confidence, living solely on its stores of hope. In Bosch's mind he saw the polarization of the haves and have-nots as a scene in which a ferry was leaving the dock. An overloaded ferry leaving an overloaded dock, with some people with a foot on the boat and a foot on the dock. The boat was pulling further away and it would only be so long before those in the middle would fall in. Meanwhile, the ferry was still too crowded and it would capsize at the first wave. Those left on the dock would certainly cheer this. They prayed for the wave.

He thought of Edgar and what he had done. He was one of those about to fall in. Nothing could be done about it. He and his wife, whom Edgar could not bring himself to tell about their precarious position. Bosch wondered if he had done the right thing. Edgar had spoken of the time that would come when Bosch would need every friend he could get. Would it have been wiser to bank this one, to let Edgar go, no harm no foul? He didn't know, but there was still time. He would have to decide.

As he drove through the Cahuenga Pass he rolled the window back up. It was getting cold. He looked up into the hills to the west and tried to spot the unlighted area where his dark house sat. He felt glad that he wasn't going up there tonight, that he was going to Sylvia.

He got there at 11:30 and used his own key to get in. There was a light on in the kitchen but the rest of the place was dark. Sylvia was asleep. It was too late for the news and the late-night talk shows never held his interest. He took his shoes off in the living room so as to not make any noise and went down the hall to her bedroom.

He stood still in the complete darkness, letting his eyes adjust.

"Hi," she said from the bed, though he could not yet see her.

"'Lo."

"Where have you been, Harry?"

She said it sweetly and with sleep still in her voice. It was not a challenge or a demand.

"I had to do a few things, then I had a few drinks."

"Hear any good music?"

"Yeah, they had a quartet. Not bad. Played a lot of Billy Strayhorn."

"Do you want me to fix you something?"

"Nah, go to sleep. You have school tomorrow. I'm not that hungry anyway and I can get something if I want it."

"C'mere."

He made his way to the bed and crawled across the down quilt. Her hand came up and around his neck and she pulled him down into a kiss.

"Yes, you did have a few drinks."

He laughed and then so did she.

"Let me go brush my teeth."

"Wait a minute."

She pulled him down again and he kissed her mouth and neck. She had a milky sweet smell of sleep and perfume about her that he liked. He noticed that she was not wearing a nightgown, though she usually did. He put his hand under the covers and traced the flatness of her stomach. He brought it up and caressed her breasts and then her neck. He kissed her again and then pushed his face into her hair and neck.

"Sylvia, thank you," he whispered.

"For what?"

"For coming today and being there. I know what I said before but it meant something to see you when I looked out there. It meant a lot."

That was all he could say about it. He got up then and went into the bathroom. He stripped off his clothes and carefully hung them on hooks on the back of the door. He would have to wear them again in the morning.

He took a quick shower, then shaved and brushed his teeth with the second set of toiletries he kept in her bathroom. He looked in the mirror as he brushed his damp hair back with his hands. And he smiled. It might have been the residue of the whiskey and beer, he knew. But he doubted it. It was because he felt lucky. He felt that he was neither on the ferry with the mad crowd nor left behind on the dock with the angry crowd. He was in his own boat. With just Sylvia.

They made love the way lonely people do, silently, with each trying too hard in the dark to please the other until they were almost clumsy about it. Still, there was a healing sense about it for Bosch. Afterward, she lay next to him, her finger tracing the outline of his tattoo.

"What are you thinking about?" she asked.

"Nothing. Just stuff."

"Tell me."

He waited a few moments before answering.

"Tonight I found out somebody betrayed me. Somebody close. And, well, I was just thinking that maybe I'd had it wrong. That it really wasn't me who was betrayed. It was himself. He had betrayed himself. And maybe living with that is punishment enough. I don't think I need to add to it."

He thought about what he had said to Edgar at the Red Wind and decided he would have to stop him from going to Pounds for the transfer.

"Betrayed how?"

"Uh, consorting with the enemy, I guess you'd call it."

"Honey Chandler?"

"Yeah."

"How bad is it?"

"Not too bad, I guess. It's just that he did it that matters. It hurts, I guess."

"Is there anything you can do? Not to him, I mean. I mean to limit the damage."

"No. Whatever damage there is, it's already done. I only figured out it was him tonight. It was by accident, otherwise I probably would have never even thought of him. Anyway, don't worry about it."

She caressed his chest with the tips of her fingernails.

"If you're not worried, I'm not."

He loved her knowing the boundaries of how much she could ask him, and that she didn't even think to ask him who it was he was talking about. He felt totally comfortable with her. No worries, no anxieties. It was home to him.

He was just beginning to fall off when she spoke again.

"Harry?"

"Uh huh."

"Are you worried about the trial, how the closing arguments will go?"

"Not really. I don't like being in the fishbowl, sitting at that table while everybody gets their chance to explain why they think I did what I did. But I'm not worried about the outcome, if that's what you mean. It doesn't mean anything. I just want it to be over and I don't really care anymore what they do. No jury can sanction what I did or didn't do. No jury can tell me I was right or wrong. You know? This trial could last a year and it wouldn't tell them everything about that night."

"What about the department? Will they care?"

He told her what Irving had told him that afternoon about what effect the trial's outcome would have. He didn't say anything about what the assistant chief had said about knowing his mother. But Irving's story crossed through his mind and for the first time since he had been in bed he felt the need for a cigarette.

But he didn't get up. He put the urge out of his mind and they lay quietly for a while after that. Bosch kept his eyes open in the dark. His thoughts were now about Edgar and then they segued to Mora. He wondered what the vice cop was doing at the same moment. Was he alone in the dark? Was he out looking?

"I meant what I said earlier today, Harry," Sylvia said.

"What's that?"

"That I want to know all about you, your past, the good and the bad. And I want you to know about me. . . . Don't ignore this. It could hurt us."

Her voice had lost some of its sleepy sweetness. He was silent and closed his eyes. He knew this one thing was more important to her than anything. She had been the loser in a past relationship where the stories of the past were not used as the building blocks of the future. He brought his hand up and rubbed his thumb along the back of her neck. She always smelled powdery after sex, he thought, yet she had not even gotten up to go into the bathroom. This was a mystery to him. It took him a while to answer her.

"You have to take me without a past. . . . I've let it go and don't want to go back to examine it, to tell it, to even think about it. I've spent my whole life getting away from my past. You understand? Just because a lawyer can throw it at me in a courtroom doesn't mean I have to . . ."

"What, tell me?"

He didn't answer. He turned his body into her and kissed and embraced her. He just wanted to hold her, to pull back away from this cliff.

"I love you," she said.

"I love you," he said.

She pulled herself closer to him and put her face in the crook of his neck. Her arms held him tightly, as if maybe she was scared.

It was the first time he had said it to her. It was the first time he had said it to anyone as far back as he could remember. Maybe he had never said it. It felt good to him, almost like a palpable presence, a warm flower of deep red opening in his chest. And he realized he was the one who was a little bit scared. As if by simply saying the words he had taken on a great responsibility. It was scary yet exciting. He thought of himself in the mirror, smiling.

She held herself pressed against him and he could feel her breath against his neck. In a short while her breathing became more measured as she fell asleep.

Lying awake, Bosch held her like that until well into the night. Now sleep would not come to him and with the insomnia came realities that robbed him of the good feelings he had only minutes before. He had thought about what she had said about betrayal and trust. And he knew that the pledges they spoke to each other this night would founder if built on deception. He knew what she had said was true. He would have to tell her who he was, what he was, if the words he had spoken were ever to be more than words. He thought about what Judge Keyes had said about words being beautiful and ugly on their own. Bosch had spoken the word love. He knew now that he must make it either ugly or beautiful.

The bedroom's windows were on the east side of the house and the light of dawn was just beginning to cling to the edges of the blinds when Bosch finally closed his eyes and slept.

Bosch looked rumpled and worn-out when he entered the courtroom Friday morning. Belk was already there, scribbling on his yellow pad. He looked up and appraised him as Bosch sat down.

"You look like shit and smell like an ashtray. And the jury will know that's the same suit and tie you wore yesterday."

"A clear sign I'm guilty."

"Don't be such a smartass. You never know what may turn a juror one way or the other."

"I don't really care. Besides, you're the one who has to look good today, right, Belk?"

This was not an encouraging thing to say to a man at least eighty pounds overweight who broke out in flop sweat every time the judge looked at him.

"What the hell do you mean you don't care? Everything is on the line today and you waltz in looking like you slept in your car and say you don't care."

"I'm relaxed, Belk. I call it Zen and the art of not giving a shit."

"Why now, Bosch, when I could have settled this for five figures two weeks ago?"

"Because I realize now that there are things more important than what twelve of my so-called peers think. Even if, as peers, they wouldn't give me the time of day on the street."

Belk looked at his watch and said, "Leave me alone, Bosch. We start in ten minutes and I want to be ready. I'm still working on my argument. I'm going to go shorter than even Keyes demanded."

Earlier in the trial, the judge had determined that closing arguments would be no longer than a half hour for each side. This was to be divided, with the plaintiff — in the person of Chandler — arguing for twenty minutes followed by the defendant's lawyer — Belk — delivering his entire thirty-minute argument. The plaintiff would then be allowed the last ten minutes. Chandler would have first and last word, another sign, Bosch believed, that the system was stacked against him.

Bosch looked over at the plaintiff's table and saw Deborah Church sitting there by herself, eyes focused straight ahead. The two daughters were in the first row of the gallery behind her. Chandler was not there but there were files and yellow pads laid out on the table. She was around.

"You work on your speech," he said to Belk. "I'll leave you alone."

"Don't be late coming back. Not again, please."

As he had hoped, Chandler was outside smoking by the statue. She gave him a cold glance, said nothing and then took a few steps away from the ash can in order to ignore him. She had on her blue suit — it was probably her lucky suit — and the one tress of blonde hair was loose from the braid at the back of her neck.

"Rehearsing?" Bosch asked.

"I don't need to rehearse. This is the easy part."

"I suppose."

"What's that mean?"

"I don't know. I suppose you're freer from the constraints of law during the arguments. Not as many rules of what you can and can't say. I think that's when you'd be in your element."

"Very perceptive."

That was all she said. There was no indication that she knew her arrangement with Edgar had been discovered. Bosch had been counting on that when he rehearsed what he was going to say to her. After waking from his brief sleep, he had looked at the events of the night before with a fresh mind and eyes and had seen something that was missed before. It was now his intention to play her. He had thrown her the soft pitch. Now he had a curve.

"When this is over," he said, "I'd like the note."

"What note?"

"The note the follower sent you."

A look of shock hit her face but was then quickly erased with the indifferent look she normally gave him. But she had not been quick enough. He had seen the look in her eyes, she sensed danger. He knew then he had her.

"It's evidence," he said.

"I don't know what you're talking about, Detective Bosch. I need to get back inside."

She stubbed a half-smoked cigarette with a lipstick print on the butt into the ash can, then took two steps toward the door.

"I know about Edgar. I saw you with him last night."

That stopped her. She turned around and looked at him.

"The Hung Jury. A Bloody Mary at the bar."

She weighed her response and then said, "Whatever he told you, I'm sure it was designed to place him in the best light. I would be careful if you are planning to go public with it."

"I'm not going public with anything . . . unless you don't give me the note. Withholding evidence of a crime is a crime in itself. But I don't need to tell you that."

"Whatever Edgar told you about a note is a lie. I told him noth —"

"And he told me nothing about a note. He didn't need to. I figured it out. You called him Monday after the body was found because you already knew about it and knew it was connected to the Dollmaker. I wondered how, and then it was clear. We got a note but that was secret until the next day. The only one who found out was Bremmer but his story said you couldn't be reached for comment. That was because you were out meeting Edgar. He said you called that afternoon asking about the body. You asked if we got a note. That was because you got a note, Counselor. And I need to see it. If it is different from the one we got, it could be helpful."

She looked at her watch and quickly lit another cigarette.

"I can get a warrant," he said.

She laughed a fake sort of laugh.

"I'd like to see you get a warrant. I'd like to see the judge in this town who would sign a warrant allowing the LAPD to search my house with this case in the papers every day. Judges are political animals, Detective, nobody's going to sign a warrant and then possibly come out on the wrong end of this."

"I was thinking more along the lines of your office. But thanks for at least telling me where it is."

The look came back into her face for a split second. She had slipped and maybe that was as big a shock to her as anything he had said. She put the cigarette into the sand after two puffs. Tommy Faraway would cherish it when he found it later.

"We convene in one minute. Detective, I don't know anything about a note. Understand? Nothing at all. There is no note. If you try to make any trouble over this, I will make even more for you."

"I haven't told Belk and I'm not going to. I just want the note. It's got nothing to do with the case at trial."

"That's easy for . . ."

"For me to say because I haven't read it? You're slipping, Counselor. Better be more careful than that."

She ignored that and went on to other business.

"Another thing, if you think my ... uh, arrangement with Edgar is grounds for a mistrial motion or a misconduct complaint, you will find that you are dead wrong. Edgar agreed to our relationship without any provocation. He suggested it, in fact. If you make any complaint I will sue you for slander and send out press releases when I do it."

He doubted anything that happened was at Edgar's suggestion but let it go. She gave him her best dead-eyed, killer look, then opened the door and disappeared through it.

Bosch finished his smoke, hoping his play might at least knock her off speed a little bit during her closing argument. But most of all he was pleased that he had gotten tacit confirmation of his theory. The follower had sent her a note.

The silence that descended over the courtroom as Chandler walked to the lectern was the kind of tension-filled quiet that accompanies the moment before a verdict is read. Bosch felt that this was because the verdict was a foregone conclusion in many of the minds in the courtroom and Chandler's words here would serve as his coup de grâce. The final, deadly blow.

She began with the perfunctory thank-yous to the jury for their patience and close attention to the case. She said she was fully confident that they would fairly deliberate a verdict.

In the trials Bosch had attended as an investigator, this was always stated by both lawyers to the jury, and he always thought it was a crock. Most juries have members who are there simply to avoid going to work at the factory or office. But once there, the issues are either too complicated or scary or boring and they spend their days in the box just trying to stay awake between the breaks, when they can fortify themselves with sugar, caffeine and nicotine.

After that opening salutation, Chandler quickly got to the heart of the matter. She said, "You will recall that on Monday I stood before you and gave you the road map. I told you what I would set out to prove, what I needed to prove and now it is your job to decide if I have done that. I think when you consider the week's testimony, you will have no doubt that I have.

"And speaking of doubt, the judge will instruct you but I would like to take a moment to explain to you once again that this is a civil matter. It is not a criminal case. It is not like Perry Mason or like anything else you have seen on TV or at the movies. In a civil trial, in order for you to find for the plaintiff, it requires only that a preponderance of the evidence be in favor of the plaintiff's case. A preponderance, what does that mean? It means the evidence for the plaintiff's case outweighs the evidence against it. A majority. It can be a simple majority, just fifty percent, plus one."

She spent a lot of time on this subject because this would be where the case was won or lost. She had to take twelve legally inept people — this was guaranteed by the juror selection process — and relieve them of media-conditioned beliefs or perceptions that cases were decided by reasonable doubts or beyond the shadow of doubt. That was for criminal cases. This was civil. In civil, the defendant lost the edge he got in criminal.

"Think of it as a set of scales. The scales of justice. And each piece of evidence or testimony introduced has a certain weight, depending on the validity you give it. One side of the scales is the plaintiff's case and the other, the defendant's. I think that when you have gone into the jury room to deliberate and have properly weighed the evidence of the case, there will be no doubt that the scales are tipped in the plaintiff's favor. If you find that is indeed the case, then you must find for Mrs. Church."

With the preliminaries out of the way, Bosch knew that she now had to finesse the rest, because the plaintiff was essentially presenting a two-part case, hoping to win at least one of them. One being that maybe Norman Church was the Dollmaker, a monstrous serial killer, but even if so, Bosch's actions behind the badge were equally heinous and should not be forgiven. The second part, the one that would surely bring untold riches if the jury bought it, was that Norman Church was an innocent and that Bosch had cut him down in cold blood, depriving his family of a loving husband and father.

"The evidence presented this week points to two possible findings by you," Chandler told the jury. "And this will be the most difficult task you have, to determine the level of Detective Bosch's culpability. Without a doubt it is clear that he acted rashly, recklessly and with wanton disregard for life and safety on the night Norman Church was killed. His actions were inexcusable and a man paid for it with his life. A family paid for it with its husband and father.

"But you must look beyond that at the man who was killed. The evidence –– from the videotape that is a clear alibi for one killing attributed to Norman Church, if not all of them, to the testimony of loved ones — should convince you that the police had the wrong man. If not, then Detective Bosch's own acknowledgments on the witness stand make it clear that the killings did not stop, that he killed the wrong man.

Bosch saw that Belk was scribbling on his pad. Hopefully, he was making note of all the things about Bosch's testimony and others that Chandler was conveniently leaving out of her argument.

"Lastly," she was saying, "you must look beyond the man who was killed and look at the killer."

Killer, Bosch thought. It sounded so awful when applied to him. He said the word over and over in his mind. Yes, he had killed. He had killed before and after Church, yet being called simply a killer without the explanations attached somehow seemed horrible. In that moment he realized that he did care after all. Despite what he had said earlier to Belk, he wanted the jury to sanction what he had done. He needed to be told he had done the right thing.

"You have a man," she said, "who has repeatedly shown the taste for blood. A cowboy who killed before and since the episode with the unarmed Mr. Church. A man who shoots first and looks for evidence later. You have a man with a deep-seated motive for killing a man who he thought might be a serial killer of women, of women from the street . . . like his own mother."

She let that float out there for a while as she pretended to be checking a point or two in the notes on her pad.

"When you go back into that room, you will have to decide if this is the kind of police officer you want in your city. The police force is supposed to mirror the society it protects. Its officers should exemplify the best in us. Ask yourself while you deliberate, who does Harry Bosch exemplify? What segment of our society does he present the mirror image of? If the answers to those questions don't trouble you, then return with a verdict in the defendant's favor. If they do trouble you, if you think our society deserves better than the cold-blooded killing of a potential suspect, then you have no choice but to return a verdict finding for the plaintiff."

Chandler paused here to go to the plaintiff's table and pour a glass of water. Belk leaned close to Bosch and whispered, "Not bad but I've seen her do better. . . . I've also seen her do worse."

"The time she did worse," Bosch whispered back, "did she win?"

Belk looked down at his pad, making the answer clear. As Chandler was returning to the lectern he leaned back to Bosch.

"This is her routine. Now she'll talk about money. After getting the water, Money always talks about money."

Chandler cleared her throat and began again.

"You twelve people are in a rare position. You have the ability to make societal change. Not many people ever get that chance. If you feel Detective Bosch was wrong, to whatever degree, and find for the plaintiff, you will be making change because you will be sending a clear signal, a message to every police officer in this city. From the chief and the administrators inside Parker Center two blocks from here to every rookie patrol officer on the street, the message will be that we do not want you to act this way. We will not accept it. Now, if you return such a verdict you must also set monetary damages. This is not a complicated task. The complicated part is the first part, deciding whether Detective Bosch was right or wrong. The damages can be anything, from one dollar to one million dollars or more. It doesn't matter. What is important is the message. For with the message, you will bring justice for Norman Church. You will bring justice to his family."

Bosch looked around behind himself and saw Bremmer in the gallery with the other reporters. Bremmer smiled slyly and Bosch turned back around. The reporter had been right on the money about Money.

Chandler walked back to the plaintiff's table, picked up a book and took it back to the lectern. It was old and without a dust jacket, its green cloth binding cracking. Bosch thought he could see a mark, probably a library stamp, on the top edge of its pages.

"In closing now," she said, "I would like to address a concern you might have. I know it is one I might have if I were in your place. And that is, how is it that we have come to have men like Detective Bosch as our police? Well, I don't think we can hope to answer that and it is not at point in this case. But if you recall, I quoted to you the philosopher Nietzsche at the beginning of the week. I read his words about the black place he called the abyss. To paraphrase him, he said we must take care that whoever fights monsters for us does not also become a monster. In today's society it is not hard to accept that there are monsters out there, many of them. And so it is not hard, then, to believe that a police officer could become a monster himself.

"After we finished here yesterday, I spent the evening at the library."

She glanced over at Bosch as she said this, flaunting the lie. He stared back at her and refused the impulse to look away.

"And I'd like to finish by reading something I found that Nathaniel Hawthorne wrote about the same subject we are dealing with today. That chasm of darkness where it can be easy for a person to cross over to the wrong side. In his book *The Marble Faun*, Hawthorne wrote, 'The chasm was merely one of the orifices of that pit of blackness that lies beneath us . . . everywhere.'

"Ladies and gentlemen, be careful in your deliberations and be true to yourselves. Thank you."

It was so quiet that Bosch could hear her heels on the rug as she walked back to her seat.

"Folks," Judge Keyes said, "we're gonna take a fifteen minute break and then Mr. Belk gets his turn."

As they were standing for the jury, Belk whispered, "I can't believe she used the word orifice in her closing argument."

Bosch looked at him. Belk seemed gleeful but Bosch recognized that he was just latching on to something, anything, so that he could pump himself up and get ready for his own turn behind the lectern. For Bosch knew that whatever words Chandler had used, she had been awfully good. Appraising the sweating fat man next to him, he felt not one bit of confidence.

Bosch went out to the justice statue and smoked two cigarettes during the break but Honey Chandler never came out. Tommy Faraway swung by, however, and clicked his tongue approvingly when he found the nearly whole cigarette she had put in the ash can before. He moved on without saying anything else. It occurred to Bosch that he had never seen Tommy Faraway smoke one of the stubs he culled from the sand.

Belk surprised Bosch with his closing. It wasn't half bad. It was just that he wasn't in the same league as Chandler. His closing was more a reaction to Chandler's than a stand-alone treatise on Bosch's innocence and the unfairness of the accusations against him. He said things like, "In all of Ms. Chandler's talk about the two possible findings you can come up with, she completely forgot about a third, that being that Detective Bosch acted properly and wisely. Correctly."

It scored points for the defense but it was also a backhanded confirmation by the defense that there were two possible findings for the plaintiff. Belk did not see this but Bosch did. The assistant city attorney was giving the jury three choices now, instead of two, and still only one choice absolved Bosch. At times he wanted to pull Belk back to the table and rewrite his script. But he couldn't. He had to hunker down as he had in the tunnels of Vietnam when the bombs would be hitting above ground, and hope that there were no cave-ins.

The middle of Belk's argument was largely centered on the evidence linking Church to the nine murders. He repeatedly hammered home that Church was the monster in this story, not Bosch, and the evidence clearly backed that up. He warned the jurors that the fact that similar murders apparently continued was unrelated to what Church had done and how Bosch reacted in the apartment on Hyperion.

He finally hit what Bosch figured to be his stride near the end. An inflection of true anger entered his voice when he criticized Chandler's description of Bosch as having acted recklessly and with wanton disregard for life.

"The truth is that life was all Detective Bosch had on his mind when he went through that door. His actions were predicated on the belief that another woman, another victim, was there. Detective Bosch had only one choice. That was to go through that door, secure the situation and deal with the consequences. Norman Church was killed when he refused repeated orders from a police officer and made the move to the pillow. It was a hand he dealt, not Bosch, and he paid the ultimate price.

"But think of Bosch in that situation. Can you imagine being there? Alone? Afraid? It is a unique individual who faces that kind of situation without flinching. It is what our society calls a hero. I think when you return to the jury room and carefully weigh the facts, not the accusations, of this case you will come to that same conclusion. Thank you very much."

Bosch couldn't believe Belk had used the word hero in a closing argument but decided not to bring that up with the portly lawyer as he returned to the defense table.

Instead, he whispered, "You did good. Thanks."

Chandler went to the lectern for her last shot and promised to be brief. She was.

"You can easily see the disparity of the beliefs the lawyers have in this case. The same disparity between the meanings of the words hero and monster. I suspect, as we all probably do, that the truth of this case and Detective Bosch is somewhere in between.

"Two last things before you begin deliberations. First, I want you to remember that both sides had the opportunity here to present full and complete cases. In Norman Church's behalf, we had a wife, a coworker, a friend, stand up and testify to his character, to what kind of man he was. Yet, the defense chose to have only one witness testify before you. Detective Bosch. No one else stood up for Detective —"

"Objection!" Belk yelled.

"— Bosch."

"Hold it right there, Ms. Chandler," Judge Keyes boomed.

The judge's face became very red as he thought about how to proceed.

"I should clear the jury out of here to do what I am going to do but I think if you're going to play with fire you have to accept the burns. Ms. Chandler, I'm holding you in contempt of this court for that grievous display of poor judgment. We'll talk about sanctions at a later date. But I guarantee that it won't be a pleasant date to look forward to."

The judge then swiveled in his chair toward the jury and leaned forward.

"Folks, this lady should never have said that. You see, the defense is not obligated to put anybody up as a witness and whether they do or don't, that cannot be seen as a reflection on their guilt or innocence on the matter before you. Ms. Chandler darn well knew this. She's an experienced trial lawyer and you better believe she knew this. The fact that she went and said it anyway, knowing Mr. Belk over there and myself would practically hit the ceiling, I think shows a cunning on her behalf that I find very distasteful and troubling in a court of law. I'm going to complain about that to the state law board but —"

"Your Honor," Chandler cut in. "I object to you tell —"

"Don't interrupt, Counselor. You stand there and keep quiet until I am through."

"Yes, Your Honor."

"I said keep quiet." He turned back to the jury. "As I was saying, what happens to Ms. Chandler is not for you to worry about. See, she's taking a gamble that no matter what I say to you now, you will still think about what she said about Detective Bosch not bringing any supporters to testify. I tell you now with the sternest admonition I can offer, do not think about that. What she said means nothing. In fact, I suspect that if he wanted to, Detective Bosch and Mr. Belk could muster a line of police officers ready to testify that would stretch out that door all the way to Parker Center if they thought they wanted it. But they don't. That's the strategy they chose and it is not your duty to question it in any way. Any way at all. Any questions?"

No one in the jury box even moved. The judge turned his chair back and looked at Belk.

"Anything you want to say, Mr. Belk?"

"One moment, Your Honor."

Belk turned to Bosch and whispered, "What do you think? He's primed to grant a mistrial. I've never seen him so mad. We'd get a new trial, maybe by then this copycat thing will be wrapped up."

Bosch thought a moment. He wanted this over and did not like the prospect of going through another trial with Chandler.

"Mr. Belk?" the judge said.

"I think we go with what we've got," Bosch whispered. "What do you think?"

Belk nodded and said, "I think he might have just given us the verdict."

Then he stood in his place and said, "Nothing at this time, Your Honor."

"You sure now?"

"Yes, Your Honor."

"Okay, Ms. Chandler, like I said, we'll deal with this at a later time but we will deal with it. You can proceed now, but be very careful."

"Your Honor, thank you. I want to say before going on that I apologize for my line of argument. I meant no disrespect to you. I, uh, was speaking extemporaneously and got carried away."

"You did. Apology accepted, but we will still deal with the contempt order later. Let's proceed. I want the jury to begin their work right after lunch."

Chandler adjusted her position at the lectern so that she was looking at the jury.

"Ladies and gentlemen, you heard Detective Bosch on the stand yourself. I ask you, lastly, to remember what he said. He said Norman Church got what he deserved. Think about that statement coming from a police officer and what it means. 'Norman Church got what he deserved.' We have seen in this courtroom how the justice system works. The checks and balances. The judge to referee, the jury to decide. By his own admission, Detective Bosch decided that was not necessary. He decided there was no need for a judge. No need for a jury. He robbed Norman Church of his chance for justice. And so, ultimately, he robbed you. Think about that."

She picked her yellow pad up off the lectern and sat down.

23

The jury began its deliberations at 11:15 and Judge Keyes ordered the federal marshals to arrange for lunch to be sent in. He said the twelve would not be interrupted until 4:30, unless they came up with a verdict first.

After the jury had filed out, the judge ordered that all parties be able to appear for a reading of the verdict within fifteen minutes of notification by the clerk. That meant Chandler and Belk could go back to their respective offices to wait. Norman Church's family was from Burbank so the wife and two daughters opted to go to Chandler's office. For Bosch, the Hollywood station would have been more than a fifteen-minute commute, but Parker Center was a five-minute walk. He gave the clerk his pager number and told her he'd be there.

The last piece of business the judge brought up was the contempt order against Chandler. He set a hearing for it to be discussed for two weeks later and then banged his gavel down.

Before leaving the courtroom, Belk took Bosch aside and said, "I think we're in pretty good shape but I'm nervous. You want to spin the dice?"

"What are you talking about?"

"I could try to low-ball Chandler one last time."

"Offer to settle?"

"Yeah. I have carte blanche from the office for anything up to fifty. After that, I'd have to get approval. But I could throw the fifty at her and see if they'd take it to walk away now."

"What about legal fees?"

"On a settlement, she'd have to take the cut from the fifty. Someone like her, she's probably going forty percent. That'd be twenty grand for a week in trial and a week picking a jury. Not bad."

"You think we're going to lose?"

"I don't know. I'm just thinking of all the angles. You never know what a jury will do. Fifty grand would be a cheap way out. She might take it, the way the judge came down on her there at the end. She's the one who's probably scared of losing now."

Belk didn't get it, Bosch knew. Maybe it had been too subtle for him. The whole contempt thing had been Chandler's last scam. She had purposely committed the infraction so the jury would see her being slapped down by the judge. She was showing them the justice system at work: a bad deed met with stern enforcement and punishment. She was saying to them, do you see? This is what Bosch escaped. This is what Norman Church faced, but Bosch decided to take the judge and jury's role instead.

It was clever, maybe too clever. The more Bosch thought about it, the more he wondered how much the judge had been a willing and knowing player in it. He looked at Belk and saw the young assistant city attorney apparently suspected none of this. Instead, he thought of it as a stroke on his side of the page. Probably in two weeks, when Keyes lets her go with a hundred-dollar fine and a lecture during the contempt hearing, he'll get it.

"You can do whatever you want," he told Belk. "But she isn't going to take it. She's in on this one until the end."

At Parker Center Bosch went into Irving's conference room through the door that opened directly off the hallway. Irving had decided the day before that the now-called Follower Task Force would work out of the conference room so the assistant chief could be kept up on developments to the minute. What wasn't said about the move but was known was that keeping the group out of one of the squad rooms improved the chance that word of what was happening would remain secure — for at least a few days.

When Bosch walked in only Rollenberger and Edgar were in the room. Bosch noticed that four phones had been installed and were on the round meeting table. There were also six rovers — Motorola two-way radios — and a main communications console on the table, ready to be used as needed. When Edgar looked up and saw Bosch he immediately looked away and picked up a phone to make a call.

"Bosch," Rollenberger said. "Welcome to our operations center. Are you free from the trial? No smoking in here, by the way."

"I'm free until a verdict but I've got a fifteen-minute leash on me. Anything going on? What's Mora doing?"

"Not much is happening. Been quiet. Mora spent the morning in the Valley. Went to an attorney's office in Sherman Oaks and then to a couple of casting agencies, also in Sherman Oaks."

Rollenberger was looking at a logbook in front of him on the table.

"After that he went to a couple houses in Studio City. There were vans outside of these houses and Sheehan and Opelt said they thought they might be making movies at these locations. He didn't stay long at either place. Anyway, he's back over at Ad-Vice now. Sheehan called in a couple minutes ago."

"Did we get the extra people?"

"Yeah, Mayfield and Yde will take the watch at four from the first team. Then we've got two other teams after that."

"Two?"

"Chief Irving changed his mind and wants an around-the-clock watch. So we'll be on him through the night, even if he just stays at home and sleeps. Personally, I think it's a good idea that we go 'round the clock."

Yeah, especially since Irving decided to do it, Bosch thought but didn't say. He looked at the radios on the table.

"What's our freek?"

"Uh, we're on . . . frequency, frequency — oh, yeah, we're on five. Symplex five. It's a DWP communications freek that they only use during a public emergency. Earthquake, flooding, stuff like that. Chief thought it be best to keep off our own freeks. If Mora is our man, then he might be keeping an ear to the radio."

Bosch thought Rollenberger probably thought it was a good idea, but didn't ask him.

"I think it's a good idea to play it safe this way," the lieutenant said.

"Right. Anything else I should know?" He looked at Edgar, who was still on the phone. "What's Edgar got?"

"Still trying to locate the survivor from four years ago. He already pulled a copy of Mora's divorce file. It was uncontested."

Edgar hung up, finished writing something in a notebook and then stood up without looking at Bosch. He said, "I'm going down to get a cup."

"Okay," Rollenberger said. "We should have our own coffeemaker in here by this afternoon. I talked it over with the chief and he was going to requisition one."

Bosch said, "Good idea. I think I'm going down with Edgar."

Edgar walked quickly down the hallway so that he could stay ahead of Bosch. At the elevator he pushed the button but then without breaking stride walked past the elevator and into the stairwell to go down. Bosch followed and after they had gone down one floor, Edgar stopped and whipped around.

"What are you following me for?"

"Coffee."

"Oh, bullshit."

"Did —"

"No, I didn't talk to Pounds yet. I've been busy, remember?"

"Good, then don't."

"What are you talking about?"

"If you haven't talked to Pounds about it, then don't. Forget about it."

"Serious?"

"Yeah."

He stood there looking at Bosch, still skeptical.

"Learn from it. So will I. I already have. Okay?"

"Thanks, Harry."

"No, don't 'Thanks, Harry' me. Just say 'okay.'"

"Okay."

They walked down to the next floor and to the cafeteria. Rather than sit in front of Rollenberger and talk, Bosch suggested they take their coffee to one of the tables.

"Hans Off, what a trip, man," Edgar said. "I keep picturing this cuckoo clock, only it's him that comes out and says, 'Great idea, Chief! Great idea, Chief!'"

Bosch smiled and Edgar laughed. Harry could tell a great burden had been lifted off the man and so he was heartened by what he had done. He felt good about it.

"So, nothing on the survivor yet?" he said.

"She's out there somewhere. But the four years since she escaped from the Follower have not been good to Georgia Stern."

"What happened?"

"Well, by reading her sheet and talking to some guys in street vice, it looks like she got on the needle. After that, she probably got too skaggy-looking to make movies. I mean, who wants to watch a film like that and the girl's got track marks up her arms or her thighs or her neck. That's the problem with the porno business if you're a hype. You're naked, man, you can't hide that shit.

"Anyway, I talked to Mora, just to make a routine contact and to tell him I was looking for her. He kinda gave me that rundown on how needle marks are the quickest way out of the business. But he had nothing else. You think that was cool, talking to him?"

Bosch considered it a few moments and then said, "Yeah, I do. Best way to keep him from being suspicious is to act like he knows as much as we do. If you hadn't asked him and then he heard from a source or somebody else in vice that you were looking for her, then he'd probably tumble to us."

"Yeah, that's the way I figured it, so I called him this morning and asked a few questions and then went on. Far as he knows, you and me are the only ones working this new case. He doesn't know anything about our task force. So far."

"Only problem with asking him about the survivor is that if he knows you're looking, he may go looking for her. We'll have to be careful about that. Let the surveillance teams know."

"Yeah, I will. Maybe Hans Off can tell 'em. You ought to hear this guy on the rovers, sounds like a fuckin' Eagle Scout."

Bosch smiled. He imagined Hans Off cut no slack in the use of radio code designations.

"Anyway, so that's why she isn't in the porno biz anymore," Edgar said, getting back to the survivor. "In the last three years, we got check charges, a couple of possessions, a couple prostitution rousts and many, many under-the-influence beefs. She's been in and out. Always time served, never anything serious. Two, three days at a time. Not enough to help her kick, either."

"So where's she work?"

"The Valley. I've been on the phone with Valley Vice all morning. They say she usually works the Sepulveda corridor with the other street pros."

Bosch remembered the young women he had seen the other afternoon while tracing down Cerrone, Rebecca Kaminski's manager/pimp. He wondered if he had seen or even talked to Georgia Stern and not known it.

"What is it?"

"Nothing. I was out there the other day and was wondering if I'd seen her. You know, not knowing who she was. Did the vice guys say whether she had protection?"

"Nah, no pimp that they know of. I got the idea she's bottom drawer stuff. Most pimps have better ponies."

"So, is Vice up there looking for her?"

"Not yet," Edgar said. "They have training today, but they'll be out on Sepulveda tomorrow night."

"Any recent photos?"

"Yeah."

Edgar reached into his sport coat and pulled out a stack of photos. They were copies of a booking photo. Georgia Stern certainly looked used up. Her bleached-blonde hair showed at least an inch of dark roots. There were circles under her eyes so deep they looked as though they had been cut into her face with a knife. Her cheeks were gaunt and she was glassy-eyed. Lucky for her she had fixed before she was busted. It meant less time in the cage hurting, waiting and craving the next fix.

"This is three months old. Under the influence. She did two in Sybil and out."

Sybil Brand Institute was the county's holding jail for women. Half of it was equipped to handle narcotics addicts.

"Get this," Edgar said. "I forgot about this. This guy Dean up in Valley Vice says he was the one who made this bust on her and when he was booking her he found a bottle of powder and was just about ready to run her ticket up to possession when he realized the bottle was a legit scrip. He said the powder was AZT. You know, for AIDS. She's got the virus, man, and she's out there on the street. On Sepulveda. He asked her if she makes 'em use rubbers and her answer was, 'Not if they don't want to.'"

Bosch just nodded. The story was not unusual. It had been Bosch's experience that most prostitutes despised the men they waved down and serviced for money. Those who became sick got it either from their customers or from dirty needles, which also sometimes came from customers. Either way, he believed it was part of the psychology to not care about passing it on to the population that may have given it to you. It was the belief that what goes around comes around.

"Not if they don't want to," Edgar said again, shaking his head. "I mean, man, that's cold."

Bosch finished his coffee and pushed his chair back. There was no smoking in the cafeteria so he wanted to go down to the lobby and out by the fallen-officers memorial to smoke. As long as Rollenberger was camped out in the conference room, smoking there was out.

"So —"

Bosch's pager went off and he visibly flinched. He had always subscribed to the theory that a quick verdict was a bad verdict was a stupid verdict. Hadn't they given the evidence careful consideration? He pulled it off his belt and looked at the number on the display. He breathed easier. It was an LAPD exchange.

"I think Mora is calling me."

"Better be careful. What were you going to say?"

"Uh, oh, yeah, I was just wondering if Stern will be any good to us if we find her. It's been four years. She's on the spike and sick. I wonder if she'll even remember the Follower."

"Yeah, I was thinking that, too. But my only alternatives are to go back to Hollywood and report to Pounds or volunteer for one of the surveillance shifts on Mora. I'm sticking on this. I'm going up there to Sepulveda tonight."

Bosch nodded.

"Hans Off said you pulled the divorce. Nothing there?"

"Not really. She filed but then Mora didn't contest it. File's about ten pages, that's it. Only one thing of note in it, and I don't know if it means anything or not."

"What?"

"She filed on the usual grounds. Irreconcilable differences, mental cruelty. But in the records, she also mentions the loss of consortium. You know what that is?"

"No sex."

"Yeah. What do you think that means?"

Bosch thought for a few moments and said, "I don't know. They split just before the Dollmaker stuff. Maybe he was into some strange stuff, building up to the killings. I can ask Locke."

"Yeah, that's what I was thinking. Anyway, I had DMV run the wife and she's still alive. But I was thinking we shouldn't approach her. Too dangerous. She might tip him."

"Yeah, don't go near her. Did DMV fax her DL?"

"Yeah. She's blonde. Five-foot-four, hundred and ten. It was only a face shot on the driver's license but I'd say she fits."

Bosch nodded and stood up.

After taking one of the rovers from the conference room, Bosch drove over to Central Division and parked in the back lot. He was still within the fifteen-minute radius of the federal courthouse. He left the rover in the car and walked out to the sidewalk and around front to the public entrance. He did this so he could see if he could spot Sheehan and Opelt. He assumed they would have to be parked within sight of the lot's exit so they would see Mora leaving, but he did not see them or any car that looked suspicious.

A pair of headlights briefly flashed from a parking lot behind an old gas station that was now a taco stand, featuring a sign that said HOME OF THE KOSHER BURRITO — PASTRAMI! He saw two figures in the car, which was a gray Eldorado, and just looked away.

Mora was at his desk eating a burrito that looked disgusting to Bosch because he could see it was filled with pastrami. It looked unnatural.

"Harry," he said with his mouth full.

"How is it?"

"It's okay. I'll go back to plain beef after this. I just tried it 'cause I saw a couple guys from RHD over across the street. One of 'em said they come all the way over from Parker to get these kosher things there. Thought I'd give it a try."

"Yeah, I think I've heard of that place."

"Well, you ask me, it ain't worth coming over from Parker Center for."

He wrapped what was left in the oil-stained paper it came in and then got up and walked out of the squad room. Bosch heard the package hit the bottom of a trash can in the hallway and then Mora was back.

"Don't want it to stink up my trash can."

"So, you buzzed?"

"Yeah, that was me. How's the trial?"

"Waiting on a verdict."

"Shit, that's scary."

Bosch knew from experience that if Mora wanted to tell you something, he would tell you in his own time. It would do him no good to keep asking the vice cop why he beeped him.

Back in his chair, Mora swiveled around to the filing cabinets behind him and began opening drawers. Over his shoulder, he said, "Hang on, Harry. I gotta get some stuff together for you here."

It took him two minutes during which Bosch saw him open several different files, take out photos and create a short stack. Then he turned back around.

"Four," he said. "I've come up with four more actresses that dropped out under what might be termed suspicious circumstances."

"Only four."

"Yeah. Actually, there were more than four chicks that people mentioned. But only four fit that profile we talked about. Blonde and built. There is also Gallery, who we already knew about, and your concrete blonde. So we've got six altogether. Here are the new ones."

He handed the group of photos across the desk to Bosch. Harry slowly looked through them. They were color publicity glossies with each woman's name printed in the white border at the bottom of the photo. Two of the women were naked and posing indoors on chairs, their legs apart. The other two were photographed at the beach and were wearing bikinis that would probably be illegal on most public beaches. To Bosch, the women in the photos almost looked interchangeable. Their bodies were similar. Their faces had the same fake pouts that were intended to show mystery and sexual abandonment at the same time. Each of the women had hair so blonde it was nearly white.

"All Snow Whites," Mora said, an unneeded commentary that made Bosch look up from the photos to look at him. The vice cop just stared back and said, "You know, the hair. That's what a producer calls them when he's casting movies. He says he wants a Snow White for this part 'cause he already has a red or whatever. Snow White. It's like the model name. These chicks are all interchangeable."

Bosch looked back down at the photos, not trusting that his eyes would not give his suspicions away.

He realized, though, that much of what Mora had just said was true. The main physical differences between the women in the photos were the tattoos and their locations on each body. Each woman had a small tattoo of a heart or a rose or a cartoon character. Candi Cummings had a heart just to the left of her carefully trimmed triangle of pubic hair. Mood Indigo had some kind of cartoon just above her left ankle but Bosch couldn't make it out because of the angle the photograph had been taken from. Dee Anne Dozit had a heart wrapped in a vine of barbed wire about six inches above the left nipple, which was pierced with a gold ring. And TeXXXas Rose had a red rose on the soft part of her right hand between the thumb and first finger.

Bosch realized they might all be dead now.

"No one's heard from them?"

"No one in the biz, at least."

"You're right. Physically, they fit."

"Yeah."

"They did outcall?"

"I assume they did, but I'm not sure yet. The people I talked to dealt with them in the film biz so they didn't know what these girls did when the cameras stopped rolling, so to speak. Or, so they said. My next step was to get some back issues of the sex rags and look for ads."

"Any dates? You know, when they disappeared, stuff like that?"

"Just generally speaking. These people, the agents and the moviemakers, they don't have minds for dates. We're dealing with memories, so I've only got a general picture. If I find out they ran outcall ads, I'll narrow it down pretty close to exact dates when I find out when they last ran. Anyway, let me give you what I got. You got your notebook?"

Mora told him what he had. No specific dates, just months and years. Adding in the approximate dates when Rebecca Kaminski, the concrete blonde, Constance Calvin, who became Gallery on film, and the seventh and eleventh victims originally attributed to Church had disappeared, there was a rough pattern of disappearances of the porno starlets about every six to seven months. The last disappearance was Mood Indigo, eight months earlier.

"See the pattern? He's due. He's out there hunting."

Bosch nodded and looked up from his notebook at Mora and thought he saw a gleam in his dark eyes. He thought he could see through them into a black emptiness inside. In that one chilling moment Bosch thought he saw the confirmation of evil in the other man. It was as if Mora was challenging him to come farther into the dark with him.

24

Bosch knew he was stretching his leash by going down to USC, but it was two o'clock and his choice was to hang around the conference room with Rollenberger and wait for a verdict or do something useful with his time. He decided on the latter and got on the Harbor Freeway going south. Depending on how northbound traffic on the freeway was, he could conceivably get back to downtown in fifteen minutes if a verdict came in. Getting a parking space at Parker Center and walking over to the courthouse would be another matter.

The University of Southern California was located in the tough neighborhoods that surround the Coliseum. But once through the gate and into the general campus, it seemed as bucolic as Catalina, though Bosch knew this peace had been interrupted with a quickening frequency in recent years, to the point that even Trojan football practice could be dangerous. A couple of seasons back a stray bullet from one of the daily drive-by shootings in the nearby neighborhoods had struck a gifted freshman linebacker while he stood with teammates on the practice field. It was incidents like that that had administrators complaining on a routine basis to the LAPD and students longingly thinking about UCLA, which was cheaper and located in the relatively crime-free suburban milieu of Westwood.

Bosch easily found the psychology building with a map given to him at the entry gate, but once he was inside the four-story brick building there was no directory to help him find Dr. John Locke or the psychohormonal studies lab. He walked down one lengthy hallway and then took stairs to the second floor. The first female student he asked for directions to the lab laughed, apparently believing his question was a come-on, and walked away without answering. He finally was directed to the basement of the building.

He read the signs on the doors as he walked along the dimly lit corridor and finally found the lab at the second-to-last doorway at the end of the hall. A blonde student sat behind a desk in the entry. She was reading a thick textbook. She looked up and smiled and Bosch asked for Locke.

"I'll call. Does he expect you?"

"You never know with a shrink."

He smiled but she didn't get it, then he wondered if it was even a joke.

"No, I didn't say I was coming."

"Well, Dr. Locke has student labs running all day. I shouldn't disturb him if —"

She finally looked up and saw the badge he was holding.

"I'll call right away."

"Just tell him it's Bosch and I need a few minutes if he can spare them."

She spoke briefly on the phone to someone, reiterating what Bosch had just said. She then waited silently for a few moments, said "Okay" and hung up.

"The grad assistant said Dr. Locke said he will come get you. It should only be a few minutes."

He thanked her and sat in one of the chairs by the door. He looked around the entry room. There was a bulletin board with handprinted announcements pinned to the cork. Mostly they were the roommate-wanted type of posting. There was an announcement of a party for psych undergrads this coming Saturday.

There was one other desk in the room in addition to the one the student occupied. But this one was empty at the moment.

"This part of the curriculum?" he asked. "You have to put in time here as the receptionist?"

She looked up from the textbook.

"No, it's just a job. I'm in child psych but jobs in the lab there are hard to come by. Nobody likes working down here in the basement. So this was open."

"How come?"

"All the creepy psychology is down here. Psychohormonal at this end. There is —"

The door opened on the other side of the room and Locke stepped through. He was wearing blue jeans and a tie-dyed T-shirt. He stuck his hand out to Bosch and Harry noticed the leather thong tied around his wrist.

"Harry, how goes it?"

"Fine. I'm fine. How're you? I'm sorry to barge in on you like this but I was wondering if you have a few minutes. I have some new information on that thing I bothered you with the other night."

"No bother at all. Believe me, it's great to get my fingers on a real case. Student labs can be boring."

He told Bosch to follow him and they went back through the door, down a hallway and into a suite of offices. Locke led him to the room in the back which was his office. Rows of textbooks and what Bosch guessed were collected theses lined shelves on the wall behind his desk. Locke dropped into a padded chair and put a foot up on the desk. A green banker's light on the table was lit, and the only other light came from a small casement window set high on the wall to the right. Every now and then the light from the window would flicker as someone up on the ground level walked by and briefly blocked its path, a human eclipse.

Looking up at the window, Locke said, "Sometimes I feel like I'm working in a dungeon down here."

"I think the student out front thinks so, too."

"Melissa? Well, what do you expect? She's chosen child psychology as her major and I can't seem to convince her to cross to my side of the road.

Anyway, I doubt you came to campus to hear stories about pretty young students, though I don't suppose it could hurt."

"Maybe some other time."

Bosch could smell that someone had smoked in the room, though he saw no ashtray. He took his cigarettes out without asking.

"You know, Harry, I could hypnotize you and alleviate that problem for you."

"No thanks, Doc, I hypnotized myself once and it didn't work."

"Really, are you one of the last of the dying breed of LAPD hypnotists? I heard about that experiment. Courts shot it down, right?"

"Yeah, wouldn't accept hypnotized witnesses in court. I'm the last one they taught who's still in the department. I think."

"Interesting."

"Anyway, there've been some developments since we last talked and I thought it would be good to touch base with you, see what you think. I think you steered us right with that porno angle and maybe you'll come up with something now."

"What have you got?"

"We have —"

"First off, do you want some coffee?"

"Are you having any?"

"Never touch it."

"Then I'm fine. We've come up with a suspect."

"Really?"

He dropped his foot off the desk and leaned forward. He seemed genuinely interested.

"And he had a foot in both camps, like you said. He was on the task force and his beat, uh, his area of expertise is the pornography business. I don't think I should identify him at this time because —"

"Of course not. I understand. He's a suspect, hasn't been charged with anything. Detective, don't worry, this entire conversation is off the record. Speak freely."

Bosch used a trash can next to Locke's desk as an ashtray.

"I appreciate it. So, we are watching him, seeing what he is doing. But it gets tricky here. See, because he is probably the department's top man on the porno industry, it is natural we go to him for advice and information."

"Naturally, if you didn't, he would most assuredly become suspicious of the fact that you are suspicious of him. Oh what a wonderful web we weave, Harry."

"Tangled."

"What?"

"Nothing."

Locke got up and started pacing around the room. He put his hands in his pockets and then took them out. He was staring at nothing, just thinking the whole time.

"Go on, this is great. What'd I tell you? Two independent actors playing the same role. The black heart does not beat alone. Go on."

"Well, like I said, it was natural to go to him and we did. We suspected that, with the discovery of the body this week and what you said, that there might be others. Other women who disappeared who were in that business."

"So you asked him to check it out? Excellent."

"Yes, I asked him yesterday. And today he gave me four more names. We already had the name of the concrete blonde found this week and one other that the suspect provided the other day. So you add the first two — Dollmaker victims seven and eleven — and now we have a total of eight. The suspect was under surveillance all day so we know he did the legwork needed to come up with these new names. He didn't just give me four names. He went through the motions."

"Of course he would do that. He would keep up the appearance of normal routine life whether he knew he was being followed or not. He would already know these names, you understand, but he would still go out and get them by doing the routine legwork. It's one of the signs of how smart he —"

He stopped, put his hands in his pockets and frowned while seemingly staring at the floor between his feet.

"You said six new names plus the first two?"

"Right."

"Eight kills in almost five years. Any chance there are others?"

"I was going to ask you that. This information comes from the suspect. Would he lie? Would he tell us less, give us fewer names than there actually were to screw with us, to mess up the investigation?"

"Ah." He continued pacing but didn't continue speaking for a half minute. "My gut instinct is to say no. No, he would not screw with you, as you say. He would do his job in earnest. I think if all he has given you are five new names, then that's all there are. You have to remember that this man thinks he is superior to you, the police, in every aspect. It would not be unusual for him to be perfectly honest with you about some aspects of the case."

"We have a rough idea of the times. The times of the killings. What it looks like is that he slowed his pace after the Dollmaker was killed. When he started hiding them, burying them, because he couldn't blend in any longer with the Dollmaker, the intervals lengthened. It looks like he went from less than two months between kills during the Dollmaker period to seven months. Maybe even longer. The last disappearance was almost eight months ago."

Locke looked up from the floor at Bosch.

"And all this recent activity," he said. "The trial in the papers. His sending the note. His involvement as a detective in the case. The high activity will speed the end of the cycle. Don't lose him, Harry. It could be time."

He turned and looked at the calendar that hung on the wall next to the door. There was some kind of maze-like design above the chart of the month's days. Locke started laughing. Bosch didn't get it.

"What?" he asked.

"Jeez, this weekend is a full moon, too." He spun around to look at Bosch. "Can you take me on the surveillance?"

"What?"

"Take me along. It would be the rarest of opportunities in the field of psychosexual studies. To observe the stalking pattern of a sexual sadist as it is actually taking place. Unbelievable. Harry, this could get me a grant from Hopkins. It could . . . it could" — his eyes lit up as he looked at the casement window — "get me out of this fucking dungeon!"

Bosch stood up. He was thinking he had made a mistake. Locke's vision of his own future was obscuring everything else. He had come for help, not to make Locke shrink of the year.

"Look, we're talking about a killer here. Real people. Real blood. I'm not going to do anything that might compromise the investigation. A surveillance is a delicate operation. When you add that it is a cop we are watching, then it makes it even harder. I can't bring you along. Don't even ask. I can tell you things here and fill you in whenever I can but there is no way I or my commander on this would approve bringing a civilian along for the ride."

Locke's eyes dropped and he looked like a chastised boy. He took a quick glance at the window again and walked around behind the desk. He sat down and his shoulders dropped.

"Yes, of course," he said quietly. "I completely understand, Harry. I got carried away there. The important thing is that we stop this man. We'll worry about studying him later. Now, a seven-month cycle. Wow, that's impressive."

Bosch flicked his ashes and sat back down.

"Well, we don't know for sure, considering the source. There still could be others."

"I doubt it."

Locke pinched the bridge of his nose and leaned back in his chair. He closed his eyes. He did not move for several seconds.

"Harry, I'm not sleeping. Just concentrating. Just thinking."

Bosch watched him for a few moments. It was weird. He then noticed that lined on a shelf just above Locke's head were the books the psychologist had written. There were several, all with his name on the spine. There were several duplicates, too. Maybe, Bosch thought, so he could give them away. He saw five copies of *Black Hearts*, the book Locke had mentioned during his testimony, and three copies of a book called *The Private Sex Life of the Public Porn Princess*.

"You wrote about the porno business?"

He opened his eyes.

"Why, yes. That was the book I did before *Black Hearts*. Did you read it?"

"Uh, no."

He closed his eyes again.

"Of course not. Despite the sexy title it really is a textbook. Used at the university level. Last I checked with my publisher, it was being sold in the bookstores at a hundred and forty-six universities, including Hopkins. It's been out two years, fourth printing, still haven't seen a royalty check. Would you like to read it?"

"I would."

"Well, if you go by the student union on your way out of here, they sell it there. It's steep, I should warn you. Thirty bucks. But I'm sure you can expense it. I should also warn you, it's quite explicit."

Bosch was annoyed that Locke didn't give him one of the extra copies on the shelf. Perhaps, it was Locke's childlike way of getting back at him for nixing the surveillance ride-along. He wondered what Melissa, the child-psych major, would make of such behavior.

"There is something else about this suspect. I don't know what it means."

Locke opened his eyes but didn't move.

"He was divorced about a year before the Dollmaker killings began. In the divorce record there's mention by the wife that there was a loss of consortium. Would that still fit?"

"They stopped doing it, huh?"

"I guess. It was in the court file."

"It could fit. But to be honest, we shrinks could find a way to make any activity fit into any prognosis we make. That's the field for you. But it could be a case where your suspect simply became impotent with his wife. He was moving toward the erotic mold, and she had no part in it. In effect, he was leaving her behind."

"So it is not seen by you to be a cause for rethinking our suspicions of this man?"

"On the contrary. My view is that it is more evidence that he has gone through major psychological changes. His sexual persona is evolving."

Bosch gave this some thought while trying to envision Mora. The vice cop spent every day in the tawdry milieu of pornography. After a while, he couldn't get it up for his own wife.

"Is there anything else you can tell me? Anything about this suspect that might help us? We don't have anything on him. No probable cause. We can't arrest him. All we can do is watch. And that gets dangerous. If we lose him —"

"He could kill."

"Right."

"And then you are still left with no probable cause, no evidence."

"What about trophies? What do I look for?"

"Where?"

"In his home."

"Ah, I see. You plan to continue your professional interaction with him, to visit him at home. On a ruse, perhaps. But you won't be able to move about freely."

"I might be able to, if someone else keeps him occupied. I'll go with somebody else."

Locke leaned forward in his chair, his eyes wide. It was starting again, his excitement.

"What if you kept him busy and I had a look around? I am the expert on this, Harry. You would be better at keeping him busy. You could talk detective talk, I'd ask to use the bathroom. I would have a better grasp of —"

"Forget it, Dr. Locke. Listen to me, there is no way it's going to happen that way. Okay? It's too dangerous. Now, do you want to help me here or not?"

"Okay, okay. Again, I'm sorry. The reason I am so excited by the prospect of being inside this man's house and mind is that I think that this man, who is on a killing cycle of seven months plus, would almost certainly have trophies that would help him feed into his fantasy and recreate his kills, thereby dulling urges to physically act out."

"I understand."

"You've got a man with an unusually long cycle. Believe me, during those seven months the impulses to act out, to go out and kill, do not lie dormant. They are there. They are always there. Remember the erotic mold? I testified about it?"

"I remember."

"Okay, well, he is going to need to satisfy that erotic mold. To fulfill it. How does he do it? How does he last six or seven or eight months? The answer is, he has trophies. These are reminders of past conquests. By conquests I mean kills. He has things that remind him and help bring the fantasy alive. It's not the real thing by a long shot but he can still use the reminders to widen the cycle, to stave off the impulse to act. He knows the less he kills, the less chance there is that he will be caught.

"If you're right about him, he is now nearly eight months into a cycle. It means he is pushing the edge of the envelope, all the while trying to maintain his control. Yet at the same time we have this note and his strange compulsion to not be overlooked. To stand up and say, I'm better than the Dollmaker. I go on! And if you don't believe me, check out what I left in the concrete at such and such a place. The note shows severe disassembling at the same time he is locked in this tremendous battle to control the impulses. He has gone seven months plus!"

Bosch pressed his cigarette against the side of the trash can and dropped it in. He took out his notebook. He said, "The clothing of the victims, both the Dollmaker's and the Follower's, was never found. These could be the trophies he uses?"

"They could be, but put the notebook away, Harry. It's easier than that. Remember, what you have here is a man who chose his victims after seeing them in videos. So what better way to keep his fantasies alive than through videos. If you get free of him in the house, look for videos, Harry. And a camera."

"He videotaped the killings," Bosch said.

It wasn't a question. He was just repeating Locke, preparing himself for what was ahead with Mora.

"Of course, we can't say for sure," Locke said. "Who knows? But I'd put my money on it. You remember Westley Dodd?"

Bosch shook his head no.

"He was the one they executed a couple of years ago in Washington. Hanged him — a perfect example of what goes around comes around. He was a child-killer. Liked to hang kids in his closet, on coat hangers. And he also had a Polaroid camera he liked to use. After his arrest the police found a carefully kept photo album, complete with Polaroids of the little boys he killed — hanging in the closet. He had taken the time to carefully label each picture with a caption. Very sick stuff. But as sick as it was, I guarantee you that that photo album saved the lives of other little boys. Absolutely. Because he could use it to indulge his fantasy and not act it out."

Bosch nodded his understanding. Somewhere in Mora's house he would find a video or maybe a photographic gallery that would turn most people's stomachs. But for Mora it was what kept him out of the black place for as long as eight months at a time.

"What about Jeffrey Dahmer?" Locke said. "Remember him, in Milwaukee? He was a cameraman, too. Liked taking pictures of corpses, parts of corpses. Helped him go undetected by the police for years and years. Then he started keeping the corpses. That was his mistake."

They were silent for a few moments after that. Bosch's head filled with horrible images of the dead he had seen. He rubbed his eyes as if that might erase them.

"What's that they say about photos?" Locke asked then. "On the TV commercials? Something like 'the gift that keeps on giving.' Then what's that make videotape to a serial killer?"

Before leaving campus, Bosch dropped by the student union and went into the bookstore. He found a stack of copies of Locke's book on the porno business in the section on psychology and social studies. The top one on the stack was well worn around the edges from being thumbed through. Bosch took the one below it.

When the girl at the register opened the book to get the price it flopped open to a black-and-white photo of a woman performing fellatio on a man. The girl's face turned red but not as scarlet as Bosch's.

"Sorry," was all he could think to say.

"That's okay, I've seen it before. The book, I mean."

"Yeah."

"Are you teaching a class with it next semester?"

Bosch realized that since he was too old to look like a student, seemingly the only valid reason for him to be buying the book was if he was a teacher. He thought that explaining that his interest was as a police officer would sound phony and get him more attention than he wanted.

"Yes," he lied.

"Really, what's it called? Maybe I'll take it."

"Uh, well, I haven't decided yet. I'm still formulating a —"

"Well, what's your name? I'll look for it in the catalog."

"Uh . . . Locke. Dr. John Locke, psychology."

"Oh, you wrote the book. Yeah, I've heard of you. I'll look the class up. Thanks and have a good day."

She gave him his change. He thanked her and left with the book in a bag.

25

Bosch was back in the federal courthouse shortly after four. While they waited for Judge Keyes to come out and dismiss the jury for the weekend, Belk whispered that he had called Chandler's office during the afternoon and offered the plaintiff fifty grand to walk away from the case.

"She told you to shove it."

"She wasn't that polite, actually."

Bosch smiled and looked over at Chandler. She was whispering something to Church's wife but must have felt Bosch's stare. She stopped speaking and looked over at him. For nearly half a minute they engaged in an adolescent stare-down contest, with neither backing down until the door to the judge's chambers opened and Judge Keyes bounded out and up to his place on the bench.

He had the clerk buzz in the jury. He asked if there was anything anybody needed to talk about and, when there wasn't, he instructed the jurors to avoid reading newspaper accounts of the case or watching the local TV news.

He then ordered the jurors and all other parties to the case to be back by 9:30 A.M., Monday, when deliberations would begin again.

Bosch stepped on the escalator right behind Chandler to go down to the lobby exit. She was standing about two steps up from Deborah Church.

"Counselor?" he said in a low voice so the widow would not hear. Chandler turned around on the step, grabbing the handrail for balance.

"The jury is out, there is nothing that can change the case now," he said. "Norman Church himself could be waiting for us in the lobby and we wouldn't be able to tell the jury. So, why don't you give me the note? This case might be over, but there is still an investigation."

Chandler said nothing the rest of the way down. But in the lobby she told Deborah Church to go on out to the sidewalk and she'd be along soon. Then she turned to Bosch.

"Again, I deny there is a note, okay?"

Bosch smiled.

"We're already past that, remember? You slipped up yesterday. You said —"

"I don't care what I said or you said. Look, if the guy sent me a note, it would've just been a copy of what you already got. He wouldn't waste his time writing a new one."

"I appreciate you at least telling me that, but even a copy could be helpful. There could be fingerprints. The copy paper might be traceable."

"Detective Bosch, how many times did you pull prints from the other letters he sent?"

Bosch didn't answer.

"That's what I figured," she said. "Have a good weekend."

She turned and pushed her way through the exit door. Bosch waited a few seconds, put a cigarette in his mouth and went out himself.

Sheehan and Opelt were in the conference room filling in Rollenberger on their surveillance shift. Edgar was also sitting at the round table listening. Bosch saw he had a photo of Mora on the table in front of him. It was a face shot, like the one the department takes of every cop every year when they reissue ID cards.

"If it happens, it's not going to happen during the day anyway," Sheehan was saying. "So maybe tonight they'll have good luck."

"All right," Rollenberger said. "Just type something up for the chron log and you guys can call it a day. I'll need it because I have a briefing with Chief Irving at five. But remember, you're both on call tonight. It's going to be all hands. If Mora starts acting hinky I want you to get back out there with Mayfield and Yde."

"Right," Opelt said.

While Opelt sat down at the lone typewriter Rollenberger had requisitioned, Sheehan poured them cups of coffee from the Mr. Coffee that had appeared on the counter behind the round table sometime during the afternoon. Hans Off wasn't much of a cop but he could sure set up an Ops Center, Bosch thought. He poured himself a cup and joined Sheehan and Edgar at the table.

"I missed most of that," he said to Sheehan. "Sounds like nothing happened."

"Right. After you dropped by, he went back out to the Valley in the afternoon and stopped by a bunch of different offices and warehouses in Canoga Park and Northridge. We've got the addresses if you want 'em. They were all porno distributors. Never stayed more than a half hour at any of them but we don't know what he was doing. Then he came back, did a little office work and went home."

Bosch assumed Mora was checking with other producers, trying to hunt down more victims, maybe asking about the mystery man Gallery had described four years ago. He asked Sheehan where Mora lived and wrote down the Sierra Bonita Avenue address in his notebook. He wanted to warn Sheehan about how close he had come to blowing the operation at the taco stand but didn't want to do so in front of Rollenberger. He'd mention it later.

"Anything new?" he asked Edgar.

"Nothing on the survivor, yet," Edgar answered. "I'm leaving in five minutes to go up to Sepulveda. The girls do a lot of rush-hour work up there, maybe I'll see her, pick her up."

Having gotten the updates from everyone else, Bosch told the detectives in the room about the information he had gotten from Mora and what Locke thought of it. At the end, Rollenberger whistled at the information as if it were a beautiful woman.

"Man, the chief should know this pronto. He might want to double up on the surveillance."

"Mora's a cop," Bosch said. "The more bodies you put on the watch, the better chance he has of making them. If he knows we're watching him, you can forget the whole thing."

Rollenberger thought about this and nodded, but said, "Well, we still have to let the man know what's developing. Tell you what, nobody go anywhere for a few minutes. I'll see if I can get with him a little early and we'll see where we go from there."

He stood up with some papers in his hand and knocked on the door leading to Irving's office. He then opened it and disappeared through.

"Dipshit," Sheehan said after the door was closed. "Goin' in for a little mouth-to-ass resuscitation."

Everybody laughed.

"Hey, you two," Bosch said to Sheehan and Opelt. "Mora mentioned your little meeting at the taco stand."

"Shit!" Opelt exclaimed.

"I think he bought the kosher burrito line," Bosch said and started laughing. "Until he tasted one! He couldn't get why you guys'd come all the way over from Parker for one of those shitty things. He threw half of his out. So if he sees you again out there, he'll put it together. Watch your ass."

"We will," Sheehan said. "That was Opelt's idea, that kosher burrito shit. He —"

"What? What'd you want me to say? The guy we're watching suddenly walks up to the car and says, 'What's happening, boys?' I had to think of —"

The door opened and Rollenberger came back in. He went to his place but didn't sit down. Instead, he put both hands on the table and sternly leaned forward as if he had just been given orders from God.

"I've brought the chief up to date. He's very pleased with everything we've come up with in just twenty-four hours. He is concerned about losing Mora, especially with the shrink saying we are at the end of the cycle, but he doesn't want to change the surveillance. Adding another team doubles the chance Mora will see something. I think he's right. It's a very good idea to maintain status quo. We —"

Edgar tried to hold back a laugh but couldn't. It sounded more like a sneeze.

"Detective Edgar, something funny?"

"No, I think I'm getting a cold or something. Go on, please."

"Well, that's it. Proceed as planned. I will inform the other surveillance teams of what Bosch has come up with. We have Rector and Heikes taking the midnight shift, then the presidents tomorrow morning at eight."

The presidents were a pair of RHD partners named Johnson and Nixon. They didn't like being called the presidents, especially Nixon.

"Sheehan, Opelt, you are back on tomorrow at four. You've got Saturday night, so be bright. Bosch, Edgar, still freelancing. See what you can come up with. Keep your pagers on and the rovers handy. We might need to pull everybody together on short notice."

"OT approved?" Edgar asked.

"All weekend. But if you're on the clock, I want to see the work. Only humps on this job, no freeloading. All right, that's it."

Rollenberger sat down then and pulled his chair close to the table. Bosch figured it was to cover up an erection, he seemed to get off so much on being the taskmaster here. All of them but Hans Off pushed into the hallway then and headed to the elevator.

"Who's drinking tonight?" Sheehan asked.

"More like, who isn't," Opelt answered.

Bosch got to his house by seven, after having only one beer at the Code Seven and finding that the alcohol was a turn-off after the overindulgence of the night before. He called Sylvia and told her there was no verdict yet. He said he was going to shower and change clothes and he would be up to see her by eight.

His hair was still damp when she opened her door. She grabbed him as soon as he stepped in and they held each other and kissed in the entry of her house for a long time. It was only when she stepped back that he saw she was wearing a black dress with a neckline that cut deeply between her breasts and a hemline about four inches over her knees.

"How'd it go today, the closing arguments and all?"

"Fine. What are you all dressed up for?"

"Because I am taking you out to dinner. I made reservations."

She leaned into him and kissed him on the mouth.

"Harry, last night was the best night we've ever had together. It was the best night I can remember with anyone. And not because of the sex. Actually, you and I have done better."

"Always room for improvement. How 'bout a little practice before dinner?"

She smiled and told him there was no time.

They drove down through the Valley and into Malibu Canyon to the Saddle Peak Lodge. It was an old hunting lodge and the menu featured a vegetarian's nightmare. It was all meat, from venison to buffalo. They each had a steak and Sylvia ordered a bottle of Merlot. Bosch sipped his slowly. He thought the meal and the evening were wonderful. They talked little about the case or anything else. They did a lot of looking at each other.

When they returned to her house, Sylvia turned down the air-conditioner thermostat and built a fire in the living room fireplace. He just watched her; he had never been good at building fires that lasted. Even with the AC on sixty it got very warm. They made love on a blanket she spread out in front of the fireplace. They were perfectly relaxed and moved smoothly together.

Afterward, he watched the fire reflect on the light sheen of sweat on her chest. He kissed her there and put his head down to listen to her heart. The rhythm was strong and it beat counterpoint to his own. He closed his eyes and started thinking of ways to guard against ever losing this woman.

The fire was nothing but a few glowing embers when he woke up in the darkness. There was a shrill sound and he was very cold.

"Your beeper," Sylvia said.

He crawled to the pile of clothes near the couch, traced the sound and cut it off.

"God, what time is it?" she said.

"I don't know."

"That's scary. I remember when —"

She stopped herself. Bosch knew it was a story about her husband that she was about to tell. She must have decided not to let his memory intrude here. But it was too late. Bosch found himself wondering if Sylvia and her husband had ever turned down the thermostat on a summer night and made love in front of the fireplace on that same blanket.

"Aren't you going to call?"

"Huh? Oh. Yeah. I'm, uh, just trying to wake up."

He pulled his pants on and went into the kitchen. He slid the door closed so the light would not bother her. After flicking the switch he looked at the clock on the wall. It was a plate and where the numbers should be were different vegetables. It was half past the carrot, meaning one-thirty. He realized he and Sylvia had been asleep only about an hour. It had seemed like days.

The number had an 818 area code and he didn't recognize it. Jerry Edgar picked up after a half ring.

"Harry?"

"Yeah."

"Sorry to bother you, man, especially since you're not home."

"It's okay. What's up?"

"I'm on Sepulveda just south of Roscoe. I got her, man."

Bosch knew he was talking about the survivor.

"What'd she say? She look at Mora's picture?"

"No. No, man, I don't really have her. I'm watching her. She's on the stroll here."

"Well, why don't you pick her up?"

"Because I'm alone. I think I could use some backup. I try to take her alone she might bite or something. You know, she's got AIDS."

Bosch was silent. Through the phone he could hear cars passing Edgar.

"Hey, man, I'm sorry. I shouldn't've called. I thought you might want to get in on this. I'll call the Van Nuys watch commander and get a couple uniforms out here. Have a good —"

"Forget it, I'll be there. Give me half an hour. You been out there all night?"

"Yeah. Went home for dinner. I've been looking all over. Didn't see her till now."

Bosch hung up wondering if Edgar had really missed her until now or if he was just filling his overtime envelope. He walked back into the living room. The light was on and Sylvia was not on the blanket.

She was in her bed, under the covers.

"I gotta go out," he said.

"I thought that's what it sounded like, so I decided to come in here. Nothing romantic about sleeping on the floor in front of a dead fireplace by yourself."

"Are you mad?"

"Of course not, Harry."

He leaned over the bed and kissed her and she put her hand on the back of his neck.

"I'll try to get back."

"Okay. Can you turn the thermostat back up on your way out? I forgot."

Edgar was parked in front of a Winchell's Donuts store, apparently not realizing the comic implications of this. Bosch parked behind him and then got in his car.

"Whereyat, Harry?"

"Where's she at?"

Edgar pointed across the street and up a block and a half. At the intersection of Roscoe and Sepulveda there was a bus bench with two women sitting on it and three standing nearby.

"She's the one in red shorts."

"You sure?"

"Yeah, I drove up to the light and eyeballed her. It's her. Problem is, we might have a cat fight if we go over there and try to take her. All them girls are working. The Sepulveda bus line stops running at one."

Bosch saw the one in the red shorts and tank top lift her shirt as a car drove by on Sepulveda. The car braked but then, after a moment of driver hesitation, went on.

"She had any business?"

"A few hours ago she had one guy. Walked him into that alley behind the mini-mall, did him there. Other than that it's been dry. She's too skaggy for your discerning john."

Edgar laughed. Bosch thought about how Edgar had just slipped up by saying he had been watching her for a few hours. Well, he thought, at least he didn't beep me while the fire was going.

"So if you don't want a cat fight, what's the plan?"

"I was thinking you'd drive up to Roscoe and take a left. Then come into the alley from the back way. You wait there and get down low. I'll walk over and tell her I want the nasty and she'll walk me back. Then we take her. But watch her mouth. She might be a spitter, too."

"Okay, let's get it over with."

Ten minutes later Bosch was slouched behind the wheel and parked in the alley, when Edgar came walking in from the street. Alone.

"What?"

"She made me."

"Well, shit, why didn't you just take her? If she made you there's nothing else we can do, she'll know I'm a cop if I try her again five minutes later."

"All right, she didn't make me."

"What's going on?"

"She wouldn't go with me. She asked if I had some brown sugar to trade and when I said no, no drugs, she said she doesn't do colored dick. You believe that shit? I haven't been called colored since I grew up in Chicago."

"Don't worry about it. Wait here and I'll go."

"Goddam whore."

Bosch got out of the car and over the roof said, "Edgar, cool it. She's a whore and a hype, for Chrissake. You care about that?"

"Harry, you have no idea what it's like. You see the way Rollenberger looks at me? I bet he counts the rovers every time I walk out of the room. German fuck."

"Hey, you're right, I don't know what it's like."

He took his jacket off and threw it in the car. Then he unbuttoned the top three buttons of his shirt and walked off toward the street.

"Be right back. You better hide. If she sees a colored guy she might not come into the alley with me."

They borrowed an interview room in the Van Nuys detective bureau. Bosch knew his way around the place because he had worked on the robbery table here after first getting his detective's badge.

What became immediately clear from the start was that the man Edgar had seen Georgia Stern go into the alley with earlier was not a john. He was a dealer and she had probably fixed in the alley. She might have paid for the shot with sex, but that still didn't make the dealer a john.

Regardless of who he was and what she did, she was on the nod when Bosch and Edgar brought her in and, therefore, was almost totally useless. Her eyes were droopy and dilated and would become fixed on objects in the distance. Even in the ten-by-ten interview room she looked as though she was staring at something a mile away.

Her hair was rumpled and the black roots were longer than in the photo Edgar had. She had a sore on the skin below her left ear, the kind of sore addicts get from nervously rubbing the same spot over and over. Her upper arms were as thin as the legs of the chair she sat on. Her deteriorated state was heightened by the T-shirt, which was several sizes too big. The neckline drooped to expose her upper chest and Bosch could see that she used the veins in her neck when she was banging heroin from a needle. Bosch could also see that despite her emaciated condition, she still had large, full breasts. Implants, he guessed, and for a moment a vision of the concrete blonde's desiccated body flashed to him.

"Miss Stern?" Bosch began. "Georgia? Do you know why you're here? Do you remember what I told you in the car?"

"I mem'er."

"Now, do you remember the night the man tried to kill you? More than four years ago? A night like this? June seventeenth. Remember?"

She nodded dreamily and Bosch wondered if she knew what he was talking about.

"The Dollmaker, remember?"

"He's dead."

"That's right, but we need to ask you some questions about the man anyway. You helped us draw this picture, remember?"

Bosch unfolded the composite drawing he had taken from the Dollmaker files. The drawing looked like neither Church nor Mora, but the Dollmaker was known to wear disguises so it was reasonable to believe the Follower did as well. Even so, there was always the chance a physical feature, like maybe Mora's penetrating eyes, would poke through the memory.

She looked at the composite for a long time.

"He was killed by the cops," she said. "He deserved it."

Even coming from her, it felt reassuring to Bosch to hear someone say the Dollmaker got what he deserved. But he knew what she didn't, that they weren't dealing with the Dollmaker here.

"We're going to show you some pictures. You got the six-pack, Jerry?"

She looked up abruptly and Bosch realized his mistake. She thought he was referring to beer, but a six-pack in cop terminology was a package of six mugshots which are shown to victims and witnesses. They usually contain photos of five cops and one suspect with the hope that the wit will point to the suspect and say that's the one. This time the six-pack contained photos of six cops. Mora's was the second one.

Bosch lined them up on the table in front of her and she looked for a long time. She laughed.

"What?" Bosch asked.

She pointed to the fourth photo.

"I think I fucked him once. But I thought he was a cop."

Bosch saw Edgar shake his head. The photo she had pointed to was of an undercover Hollywood Division narcotics officer named Arb Danforth. If her memory was correct, then Danforth was probably venturing off his beat into the Valley to extort sex from prostitutes. Bosch guessed that he was probably paying them with heroin stolen from evidence envelopes or suspects. What she had just said should be forwarded in a report to Internal Affairs, but both Edgar and Bosch knew without saying a word that neither of them would do that. It would be like committing suicide in the department. No street cop would ever trust them again. Still, Bosch knew Danforth was married and that the prostitute carried the AIDS virus. He decided he would drop Danforth an anonymous note telling him to get a blood test.

"What about the others, Georgia?" Bosch said. "Look at their eyes. Eyes don't change when somebody's in a disguise. Look at the eyes."

While she bent down to look closer at the pictures Bosch looked at Edgar, who shook his head. This was going nowhere, he was saying, and Bosch nodded that he knew. After a minute or so, her head jerked as she stopped herself from nodding off.

"Okay, Georgia, nothing there, right?"

"No."

"You don't see him?"

"No. He's dead."

"Okay, he's dead. You stay here. We're going out into the hall to talk for a minute. We'll be right back."

Outside, they decided it might be worth booking her on an under-the-influence charge into Sybil Brand and trying her again when she came off the high. Bosch noted that Edgar was eager to do this and volunteered to drive her downtown to Sybil. Bosch knew this was because it would make

Edgar's OT envelope thicker, not because he wanted to get the woman into the narco unit at Sybil and get her straightened out for a while. Compassion had nothing to do with it.

26

Sylvia had pulled the bedroom's heavy curtains across the blinds and the room stayed dark until well after the sun was up on Saturday morning. When Bosch awoke alone in her bed, he pulled his watch off the nightstand and saw it was already eleven. He had dreamed but when he woke the dream receded into the darkness and he couldn't reach back to grasp it. He lay there for nearly fifteen minutes trying to bring it back, but it was gone.

Every few minutes he would hear Sylvia make some kind of household noise. Sweeping the kitchen floor, emptying the dishwasher. He could tell she was trying to be quiet but he heard it anyway. There was the back door being opened and the splashing of water in the potted plants that lined the porch. It hadn't rained in at least seven weeks.

At 11:20 the phone rang and Sylvia got to it after one ring. But Bosch knew it was for him. His muscles tensed as he waited for the bedroom door to open and for her to summon him to the call. He had given Sylvia's phone number to Edgar when they were leaving the Van Nuys Division seven hours earlier.

But Sylvia never came and when he relaxed again he could hear parts of her conversation on the phone. It sounded like maybe she was counseling a student. After a while it sounded like she was crying.

Bosch got up, pulled on his clothes and walked out of the bedroom while trying to smooth his hair. She was at the table in the kitchen, holding the cordless phone to her ear. She was drawing circles on the tabletop with her finger and he had been right, she was crying.

"What?" he whispered.

She held her hand up, signaling him not to interrupt. He didn't. He just watched her on the phone.

"I'll be there, Mrs. Fontenot, just call me with the time and address . . . yes . . . yes, I will. Once again, I am so very sorry. Beatrice was such a fine young woman and student. I was very proud of her. Oh, my gosh . . ."

A strong gush of tears came as she hung up. Bosch came to her and put his hand on her neck.

"A student?"

"Beatrice Fontenot."

"What happened?"

"She's dead."

He leaned down and held her. She cried.

"This city . . . ," she began but didn't finish. "She's the one who wrote what I read to you the other night about *Day of the Locust.*"

Bosch remembered. Sylvia had said she worried about the girl. He wanted to say something but he knew there was nothing to say. This city. It seemed to say it all.

They spent the day around the house, doing odd jobs, cleaning up. Bosch cleared the charred logs out of the fireplace and then joined Sylvia in the backyard, where she was working in the garden, pulling weeds and cutting flowers for a bouquet she was going to take to Mrs. Fontenot.

They worked side by side but Sylvia spoke very little. Every now and then she would offer a sentence. She said it had been a drive-by shooting on Normandie. She said it happened the night before and that the girl was taken to Martin Luther King, Jr., Hospital, where she was determined to be brain-dead. They turned the machine off in the morning and harvested the organs for donating.

"That's weird, that they call it harvesting," she said. "Sounds like a farm or people growing on trees or something."

In the midafternoon she went into the kitchen and made an egg salad sandwich and a tuna fish sandwich. She cut them in half and they each had a half of both sandwiches. He made iced tea with slices of orange in the glass. She said that after the huge steaks they'd eaten the night before, she never wanted beef again. It was the day's only attempt at humor, but nobody smiled. She put the dishes in the sink afterward but didn't bother to rinse them. She turned and leaned on the counter and stared down at the floor.

"Mrs. Fontenot said the funeral would be sometime next week, probably Wednesday. I think I'm going to bring the class down. Get a bus."

"I think that'd be nice. Her family would appreciate it."

"Her two older brothers are dealers. She told me they sell crack."

He didn't say anything. He knew that was probably the reason the girl was dead. Since the Bloods-Crips gang truce, the street dealing in South Central had lost its command structure. There was a lot of infringement of turfs. A lot of drive-bys, a lot of innocents left dead.

"I think I'll ask her mother if I could read her book report. At the service. Or after. Maybe they'd know then what a loss this was."

"They probably know already."

"Yes."

"You want to take a nap, try to sleep?"

"Yes, I think I will. What are you going to do?"

"I have some stuff to do. Make some calls. Sylvia, I'm going to have to go out tonight. Hopefully, not for long. I'll get back as soon as I can."

"I'll be all right, Harry."

"Good."

Bosch looked in on her at about four and she was sleeping soundly. He could see where the pillow was wet from her crying.

He went down the hall to a bedroom that was used as a study. There was a desk with a phone on it. He closed the door so as not to disturb her.

The first call he made was to Seventy-seventh Street Division detectives. He asked for the homicide table and got a detective named Hanks. He didn't give a first name and Bosch didn't know him. Bosch identified himself and asked about the Fontenot case.

"What's your angle, Bosch? Hollywood, you said?"

"Yeah, Hollywood, but there's no angle. It's private. Mrs. Fontenot called the girl's teacher this morning. The teacher's a friend of mine. She's upset and I was, you know, just trying to find out what happened."

"Look, I don't have time to be holding people's hands. I'm working a case."

"In other words, you've got nothing."

"You've never worked the seven-seven, have you?"

"No. This the part where you tell me how tough it is?"

"Hey, fuck you, Bosch. What I'm gonna tell you is that there is no such thing as a witness south of Pico. Only way we clear a case is we get lucky and pull some prints, or we get luckier and the dude walks in and says, 'I's sorry, I did it.' You wanna guess how many times that happens?"

Bosch didn't say anything.

"Look, the teacher ain't the only one upset, okay? This is a bad one. They're all bad but some are bad on bad. This is one of those. Sixteen-year-old girl home reading a book, babysittin' her younger brother."

"Drive-by?"

"Yeah, you got it. Twelve holes in the walls. It was an AK. Twelve holes in the walls and one round in the back of her head."

"She never knew, did she?"

"No, she never knew what hit her. She must've caught the first one. She never ducked."

"It was a round meant for one of the older brothers, right?"

Hanks was quiet for a couple of seconds. Bosch could hear a radio squawking in the background of the squad room.

"How you know that, the teacher?"

"The girl told her the brothers sell crack."

"Yeah? They were walking around MLK this morning boo-hooing like they was altar boys. I'll check it out, Bosch. Anything else I can do you for?"

"Yeah. The book. What was she reading?"

"The book?"

"Yeah."

"It was called *The Big Sleep*. And that's what she got, man."

"You can do me a favor, Hanks."

"What's that?"

"If you talk to any reporters about this, leave the part about the book out."

"What do you mean?"

"Just leave it out."

Bosch hung up. He sat at the desk and felt ashamed that when Sylvia had first talked of the girl, he had been suspicious of her fine school work.

After a few minutes thinking about that, he picked the phone up again and called Irving's office. The phone was picked up on half a ring.

"Hello, this is Los Angeles Police Department Assistant Chief Irvin Irving's office, Lieutenant Hans Rollenberger speaking, how can I help you?"

Bosch figured Hans Off must be expecting Irving himself to call in and therefore trotted out the full-count official telephone greeting that was in the officer's manual but was roundly ignored by most of the people who answered phones in the department.

Bosch hung up without saying anything and redialed so the lieutenant could go through the whole spiel again.

"It's Bosch. I'm just checking in."

"Bosch, did you just call a few moments ago?"

"No, why?"

"Nothing. I'm here with Nixon and Johnson. They just came in and Sheehan and Opelt are with Mora now."

Bosch noticed how Rollenberger didn't dare call them the presidents when they were in the same room with him.

"Anything happen today?"

"No. The subject spent the morning at home, then a little while ago he went up to the Valley, visited a few more warehouses. Nothing suspicious."

"Where is he now?"

"At home."

"What about Edgar?"

"Edgar was here. He went over to Sybil to interview the survivor. He found her last night but she apparently was too dopey to talk to. He's giving it another try, now."

Then in a lower voice, he said, "If she confirms an ID of Mora, do we move?"

"I don't think it would be a good idea. It's not enough. And we'd tip our hand."

"My thoughts exactly," he said louder now, so the presidents would know he was clearly in command here. "We stick to him like glue and we'll be there when he makes his move."

"Hopefully. How're you working this with the surveillance teams? They giving you blow by blow?"

"Absolutely. They're on rovers and I'm listening here. I know every move the subject makes. I'm staying on late tonight. I have a feeling."

"About what?"

"I think t'night's the night, Bosch."

Bosch woke Sylvia at five but then sat on the bed and rubbed her back and neck for a half hour. After that, she got up and took a shower. Her eyes still looked sleepy when she came out to the living room. She wore her gray cotton T-shirt dress. Her blonde hair was tied in a tail behind her head.

"When do you have to go?"

"A little while."

She didn't ask where he was going or what for. He didn't offer to tell her.

"You want me to make you some soup or something?" he asked.

"No, I'm fine. I don't think I'm going to be hungry tonight."

The phone rang and Harry answered it in the kitchen. It was a reporter from the *Times* who had gotten the number from Mrs. Fontenot. The reporter wanted to speak with Sylvia about Beatrice.

"About what?" Bosch asked.

"Well, Mrs. Fontenot said Mrs. Moore said several nice things about her daughter. We are doing a major story on this because Beatrice was such a good kid. I thought Mrs. Moore would want to say something."

Bosch told her to hold on and went to find Sylvia. He told her about the reporter and Sylvia quickly said she wanted to talk about the girl.

She stayed on the phone fifteen minutes. While she was talking, Bosch went out to his car, turned on the rover and switched it to Symplex five, the DWP frequency. He heard nothing.

He pressed the transmit button and said, "Team One?"

A few seconds passed and he was about to try again when Sheehan's voice came back on the rover.

"Who's that?"

"Bosch."

"What it be?"

"How's our subject?"

The next voice was Rollenberger's coming in over Sheehan.

"This is Team Leader, please use your code designations when on the air."

Bosch smirked. The guy was an ass.

"Leader of the team, what's my designation?"

"You are Team Six, this is Team Leader, out."

"Rrrrrogaaahhhh that, dream leader."

"Say again?"

"Say again?"

"Your last transmission, Team Five, what was that?"

Rollenberger's voice had a frustrated quality to it. Bosch was smiling. He could hear a clicking sound over the radio and he knew it was Sheehan punching his transmit button, showing his approval.

"I asked who was on my team."

"Team Six, you are solo at this time."

"Then should I have another code, Team Leader? Perhaps, Solo Six?"

"Bo — uh, Team Six, please keep off the air unless you need or are giving information."

"Rrrogaahhh!"

Bosch put the radio down for a moment and laughed. He had tears in his eyes and he realized he was laughing too hard at something that was mildly humorous at best. He figured it was the release of some of the tension of the day. He picked up the radio again and called Sheehan back.

"Team One, is the subject moving?"

"That's affirmative, Solo — I mean, Team Six."

"Where is he?"

"He is code seven at the Ling's Wings at Hollywood and Cherokee."

Mora was eating at a fast-food restaurant. Bosch knew that would not give him enough time to do what he planned, especially since he was a half hour's drive from Hollywood.

"Team One, how's he look? Is he staying out tonight?"

"Looking good. Looks like he is going cruising."

"Talk to you later."

"Rrrrrogah!"

He could tell Sylvia had been crying again when he came inside but her spirits seemed improved. Maybe it was past her, he thought, the initial pain and anger. She was sitting in the kitchen drinking a cup of hot tea.

"Do you want a cup, Harry?"

"No, I'm fine. I'm going to have to go."

"Okay."

"What'd you tell her, the reporter?"

"I told her everything I could think of. I hope she does a good story."

"They usually do."

It appeared that Hanks hadn't told the reporter about the book the girl had been reading. If he had, the reporter would definitely have told Sylvia to get her reaction. He realized that Sylvia's returning strength was due to her having talked about the girl. He had always marveled about how women wanted to talk, to maybe set the record straight about someone they knew or loved who had died. It had happened to him countless times while making next-of-kin notifications. The women were hurt, yes, but they wanted to talk. Standing in Sylvia's kitchen, he realized that the first time he had met her was on such a mission. He had told her about her husband's death and they had stood in the same room they were in now, and she had talked. Almost from the start, Bosch had been hooked deeply in the heart by her.

"You going to be all right while I'm gone?"

"I'll be fine, Harry. I'm feeling better."

"I'll try to get back as soon as I can, but I can't be sure when that will be. Get something to eat."

"Okay."

At the door, they hugged and kissed and Bosch had an overwhelming urge not to go, to stay with her and hold her. He finally broke away.

"You are a good woman, Sylvia. Better than I deserve."

She reached up and put her hand on his mouth.

"Don't say that, Harry."

27

Mora's house was on Sierra Linda, near Sunset. Bosch pulled to the curb a half block away and watched the house as it grew dark outside. The street was mostly lined with Craftsman bungalows with full porches and dormer windows projecting from the sloping roofs. Bosch guessed it had been at least a decade since the street was as pretty as its name sounded. Many of the houses on the block were in disrepair. The one next to Mora's was abandoned and boarded. On other properties it was clear the owners had opted for chain-link fences instead of paint the last time they had the money to make a choice. Almost all had bars over their windows, even the dormers up top. There was a car sitting on cinderblocks in one of the driveways. It was the kind of neighborhood where you could find at least one yard sale every weekend.

Bosch had the rover on low on the seat next to him. The last report he had heard was that Mora was in a bar near the Boulevard called the Bullet. Bosch had been there before and pictured it in his mind, with Mora sitting at the bar. It was a dark place with a couple of neon beer signs, two pool tables, and a TV bolted to the ceiling over the bar. It wasn't a place to go for a quick one. There was no such thing as one drink at the Bullet. Bosch figured Mora was digging in for the evening.

As the sky turned deep purple, he watched the windows of Mora's house but no light came on behind any of them. Bosch knew Mora was divorced but he didn't know if he now had a roommate. Looking at the dark place from the Caprice, he doubted it.

"Team One?" Bosch said into the rover.

"Team One."

"This is Six, how's our boy?"

"Still bending the elbow. What are you up to tonight, Six?"

"Just hanging around the house. Let me know if you need anything, or if he starts to move."

"Will do."

He wondered if Sheehan and Opelt understood what he was saying and he hoped Rollenberger did not. He leaned over to the glove compartment and got his bag of picks out. He reached inside his blue plastic raid jacket and put them in the left pocket. Then he turned the rover's volume control knob to its lowest setting and put it inside the windbreaker in the other pocket. Because it said LAPD in bright yellow letters across the back of the jacket, he wore it inside out.

He got out, locked the car and was ready to cross the street when he heard a transmission from the radio. He got his keys back out, unlocked the car and got back in. He turned the radio up.

"What's that, One? I missed it."

"Subject is moving. Westbound on Hollywood."

"On foot?"

"Negative."

Shit, Bosch thought. He sat in the car for another forty-five minutes while Sheehan radioed reports of Mora's seemingly aimless cruising up and down Hollywood Boulevard. He wondered what Mora was doing. The cruising was not part of the profile of the second killer. The Follower, as far as they knew, worked exclusively out of hotels. That's where he lured his victims. The cruising didn't fit.

The radio was quiet for ten minutes and then Sheehan came up on the air again.

"He's dropping down to the strip."

The Sunset Strip was another problem altogether. The strip was in L.A. but directly south of it was West Hollywood, sheriff's department jurisdiction. If Mora dropped down south and started to make some kind of move, it could result in jurisdictional problems. A guy like Hans Off was completely frightened of jurisdictional problems.

"He's down to Santa Monica Boulevard now."

That was West Hollywood. Bosch expected Rollenberger to come up soon on the radio. He wasn't wrong.

"Team One, this is Team Leader. What is the subject doing?"

"If I didn't know what this guy was into, I'd say he was cruising Boys-town."

"All right, Team One, keep an eye on him but we don't want any contact. We're out of bounds here. I'll contact the sheriff's watch office and inform."

"We're not planning any contact."

Five minutes passed. Bosch watched a man walking his guard dog down Sierra Linda. He stopped to let the animal relieve itself on the burned-out lawn in front of the abandoned house.

"We're cool," Sheehan's voice said. "We're back in the country."

Meaning back inside the boundaries of Los Angeles.

"One, what's your twenty?" Bosch asked.

"Still Santa Monica, going east. Past La Brea — no, he's northbound now on La Brea. He might be going home."

Bosch slid low in his seat in case Mora came down the street. He listened as Sheehan reported that the vice cop was now eastbound on Sunset.

"Just passed Sierra Linda."

Mora was staying out. Bosch sat back up. He listened to five minutes of silence.

"He's going to the Dome," Sheehan finally said.

"The Dome?" Bosch responded.

"Movie theater on Sunset just past Wilcox. He's parked. He's paying for a ticket and is going in. Musta just been driving around till showtime."

Bosch tried to picture the area in his mind. The huge geodesic dome was one of Hollywood's landmark theaters.

"Team One, this is Team Leader. I want to split you up here. One of you goes in with the subject, one stays on the car, out."

"Roger that. Team One, out."

The Dome was ten minutes away from Sierra Linda. Bosch figured that meant that at maximum he had an hour and a half inside the house unless Mora left the movie early.

He quickly got out of the car again, crossed the street and moved up the block to Mora's house. The wide porch completely cloaked the front door in shadows. Bosch knocked on it and while he waited he turned to look at the house across the street. There were lights on downstairs and he could see the bluish glow of a TV on the curtains behind one of the upstairs rooms.

Nobody answered. He stepped back and appraised the front windows. He saw no warnings about security systems, no alarm tape on the glass. He looked between the bars and through the glass into what he believed was the living room. He looked up into the corners of the ceiling, searching for the dull glow of a motion detector. As he expected, there was nothing. Every cop knew the best defense was a good lock or a mean dog. Or both.

He went back to the door, opened the pouch and took out the penlight. There was black electrical tape over the end so that when he switched it on only a narrow beam of light was emitted. He knelt down and looked at the locks on the door. Mora had a dead bolt and a common key-entry knob. Bosch put the penlight in his mouth and aimed the beam at the dead bolt. With two picks, a tension wrench and a hook, he began working. It was a good lock with twelve teeth, not a Medeco but a cheaper knockoff. It took Bosch ten minutes to turn it. By then sweat had come down out of his hair and was stinging his eyes.

He pulled his shirt out of his pants and wiped his face. He also wiped the picks, which had become slippery with sweat, and took a quick look at the house across the street. Nothing seemed changed, nothing seemed amiss. The TV was still on upstairs. He turned back and put the beam on the knob. Then he heard a car coming. He cut the light and crawled behind the porch riser until it had passed.

Back at the door he palmed the knob and was working the hook in when he realized there was no pressure on the knob. He turned it and the door opened. The knob hadn't been locked. It made sense, Bosch knew. The dead bolt was the deterrent. If a burglar got by that, the knob lock was a gimme. Why bother locking it?

He stood in the darkness of the entrance without moving, letting his eyes adjust. When he was in Vietnam he could drop into one of Charlie's tunnels and he would have night eyes in fifteen seconds. Now it took him longer. Out of practice, he guessed. Or getting old. He stood in the entry for nearly a minute. When the shapes and shadows filled in, he called out, "Hey, Ray? You here? You left your door unlocked. Hello?"

There was no answer. He knew Mora wouldn't have a dog, not living alone and working a cop's hours.

Bosch took a few steps farther into the house and looked at the dark shapes of the furniture in the living room. He had creeped places before, even a cop's house, but the feeling always seemed new, that feeling of exhilaration, jagged fear and panic, all in one. It felt as though his center of gravity had dropped into his balls. He felt a strange power that he knew he could never describe to anyone.

For a brief moment the panic rose and threatened the delicate balance of his thoughts and feelings. The headline flashed in his mind — COP ON TRIAL CAUGHT IN BREAK-IN — but he quickly dismissed it. To think about failure was to invite failure. He saw the stairs and immediately moved toward them. His thought was that Mora would keep his trophies either in his bedroom or near a TV, which also could mean both. Rather than work his way toward the bedroom, he would start there.

The second floor was divided into two bedrooms with a bathroom in between them. The bedroom to the right had been converted to a carpeted gym. There was an assortment of chrome-plated equipment, a rowing machine, a stationary bike and a contraption Bosch didn't recognize. There was a rack of free weights and a bench press with a chest bar across it. On one wall of the room was a floor-to-ceiling mirror. It was spidered by a shatter point about face high in the center. For a moment Bosch looked at himself and studied his shattered reflection. He thought of Mora studying his own face there.

Bosch looked at his watch. It had already been thirty minutes since Mora had gone into the theater. He took out the radio.

"One, how's he doin'?"

"He's still inside. How're you doing?"

"Just hanging around. Call if you need me."

"Anything interesting on TV?"

"Not yet."

Then Rollenberger's voice came up.

"Teams One and Six, let's drop the banter and use the radio for pertinent transmissions only. Team Leader, out."

Neither Bosch nor Sheehan acknowledged him.

Bosch moved across the hallway into the other bedroom. This was where Mora slept. The bed was unmade and clothing was draped over a chair by the window. Bosch peeled some of the tape off his light to give him a wider swath of vision.

On the wall over the bed he saw a portrait of Jesus, his eyes cast downward, his sacred heart visible in his chest. Bosch moved to the bed table and held the light briefly on a framed photo that stood next to the alarm clock. It was a young blonde woman and Mora. His ex-wife, he assumed. Her hair was bleached and Bosch recognized that she fit into the physical archetype of the victims. Was Mora killing his ex-wife over and over? he wondered again. That would be one for Locke and the other headshrinkers to decide. On the table behind the photo was a religious holy card. Bosch picked it up and put the light on it. It was a picture of the Infant of Prague, a golden halo shooting up from behind the little king's head.

The night table's drawer contained mostly innocuous junk: playing cards, aspirin bottles, reading glasses, condoms — not the brand favored by the Dollmaker — and a small telephone book. Bosch sat on the bed and leafed through the phone book. There were several women listed by first names but he was not surprised to find none of the names of the women associated with the Follower or Dollmaker cases listed.

He closed the drawer and put the light on the shelf beneath it. There he found a foot-high stack of explicit pornography magazines. Bosch guessed there were more than fifty, their covers featuring glossy photos of couplings of all equations: male-female, male-male, female-female, male-female-male, and so on. He flipped through a handful of them and saw a check mark made with a Magic Marker on the top right corner of each cover, as he had seen Mora do with the magazines at his office. Mora was taking his work home. Or had he brought the magazines here for another reason?

Looking at the magazines, Bosch felt a tightening in his crotch and some strange feeling of guilt descended on him. What about me? he wondered. Am I doing more than my job here? Am I the voyeur? He put the stack back in place. He knew there were too many magazines for him to go through to try to find victims of the Follower. And if he found any, what would that prove?

There was a tall oak armoire against the wall opposite the bed. Bosch opened its doors and found a television and videocassette recorder inside. There were three videotape cassettes stacked on top of the TV. They were

120-minute tapes. He opened the two drawers in the cabinet and found one more cassette in the top drawer. The bottom drawer contained a collection of store-bought porno tapes. He slid a couple of these tapes out, but again there were too many of them and not enough time. His attention was drawn to the four tapes used for home recording.

He turned on the TV and VCR and checked to see if there was another tape already inserted. There wasn't. He put in one of the tapes that had been stacked on top of the TV. It only showed static. He hit the fast-forward play button and watched as the static continued until the end of the tape. It took him fifteen minutes to run through the three tapes that had been on top of the television. Each was blank.

A curious thing, Bosch thought. He had to assume that the tapes had been used at one time because they were no longer in the cardboard jackets and plastic wrap they came from the store in. Though he did not own a VCR, he was familiar with them and it occurred to him that people usually did not erase their home tapes. They just taped new programs over the old ones. Why had Mora taken the time to erase what had been on these tapes? He was tempted to take one of the blank tapes to have it analyzed but decided it would be too risky. It would probably be missed by Mora.

The last home tape, the one from the top drawer, wasn't blank. It contained scenes of an interior of a house. A child was playing with a stuffed animal on the floor. Through the window behind the girl Bosch could see a snow-covered yard. Then a man entered the video frame and hugged the girl. At first Bosch thought it was Mora. Then the man said, "Gabrielle, show Uncle Ray how much you like the horsie."

The girl hugged the stuffed horse and yelled, "Fankoo Uggle Way."

Bosch turned the tape off, returned it to the armoire's top drawer once again and then pulled both drawers out and looked below them. Nothing else. He stepped up onto the bed so he could see on top of the armoire and there was nothing there, either. He turned the equipment off and returned the armoire to the condition it was in when he opened it. He looked at his watch. Nearly an hour had gone by now.

The walk-in closet was neatly lined on both sides with clothes on hangers. The floor had eight pairs of shoes parked toe-in against the back wall. He found nothing else of interest and retreated into the bedroom. He took a quick look under the bed and through the drawers of the bureau but found nothing of interest. He moved back down the stairs and quickly looked into the living room but there was no TV. There was none in the kitchen or dining room either.

Bosch followed a hallway off the kitchen into the back of the house. There were three doors off the hallway and this area appeared to be either a converted garage or an addition that was constructed in recent years. There were air-conditioning vents in the ceiling of the hallway and the white pine flooring was much newer than the scarred and browned oak floors throughout the rest of the first floor.

The first door opened into a laundry room. Bosch quickly opened the cabinets above the washer and dryer and found nothing of interest. The next door was to a bathroom with newer fixtures than those he had seen in the bathroom upstairs.

The last door opened into a bedroom with a four-poster bed as its centerpiece. The coverlet was pink and it had the feel of a woman's room. It was the perfume, Bosch realized. But, still, the room did not have a lived-in feeling. It seemed more like a room waiting for its occupant's return. Bosch wondered if Mora might have a daughter away at college, or was this the room his ex-wife used before she finally ended the marriage and left?

There was a TV and VCR on a cart in the corner. He went to it and opened the video storage drawer below the VCR but it was empty except for a round metal object the size of a hockey puck. Bosch picked it up and looked at it but could not tell what it was. He thought it might be from the weight set upstairs. He put it back and closed the drawer.

He opened the drawers of the white dresser but found nothing but women's underwear in the top drawer. The second drawer held a box containing a palette of varying colors of eye makeup and several brushes. There was also a round plastic container of beige facial powder. The makeup containers were for home use, too large to carry in a purse and therefore could not have come from any of the Follower's victims. They belonged to whoever used this room.

There was nothing at all in the bottom three drawers. He looked at himself in the mirror above the bureau and saw he was sweating again. He knew he was using too much time. He looked at his watch; sixty minutes had gone by now.

Bosch opened the closet door and immediately launched himself backward as a jolt of fear punched into his chest. He took cover to the side of the door while drawing his gun.

"Ray! That you?"

No one answered. He realized he was leaning against the light switch for the deep, walk-in closet. He flicked it on and swung into the doorway in a low crouch, his gun pointing at the man he had seen when he opened the door.

He quickly reached outside the door and killed the light. On the shelf above the clothes bar was a round Styrofoam ball on which sat a wig of long black hair. Bosch caught his breath and stepped all the way into the closet. He studied the wig without touching it. How does this fit? he wondered. He turned to his right and found more pieces of women's sheer lingerie and a few thin silk dresses on hangers. On the floor beneath them, parked toe-in to the wall, was a pair of red shoes with stiletto heels.

On the other side of the closet, behind some clothes in dry-cleaner bags, stood a camera tripod. Bosch's adrenaline began flowing again at a quicker pace. He quickly raised his eyes and began looking among the boxes on the shelves above the clothing bar. One box was marked with Japanese writing and he carefully pulled it down, finding it surprisingly heavy. Opening it, he found a video camera and cassette recorder.

The camera was large and he recognized that it was not a department store–bought piece of equipment. It was more like the kind of camera Bosch had seen used by TV news crews. It had a detachable industrial battery and a strobe. It was connected by an eight-foot coaxial cable to the recorder. The recorder had a playback screen and editing controls.

He thought that Mora's having such obviously expensive equipment was curious but he did not know what to make of it. He wondered if the vice cop had seized it from a porno producer and never turned it in to the evidence lockup. He pressed a button that opened the cassette housing on the recorder but it was empty. He repacked the equipment in the box and replaced it on the shelf, all the while wondering why a man with such a camera would have only blank tapes. He realized, as he took another quick look around the closet, that the tapes he had found so far might have recently been erased. He knew if that was the case, Mora might have tumbled to the surveillance.

He looked at his watch. Seventy minutes. He was pushing the envelope.

As he closed the closet door and turned around, he caught his own image in the mirror over the bureau. He quickly turned to the door to go. That was when he saw the rack of lights on a track running high on the wall above the bedroom door. There were five lights and he did not need to turn them on to be able to tell they focused on the bed.

He focused on the bed himself for a moment as he began to put it together. He took another glance at his watch, though he already knew it was time to go, and headed for the door.

As he crossed the room he looked at the TV and VCR again and realized that he had forgotten something. He quickly dropped to his knees in front of the machines and turned the VCR on. He hit the eject button and a video-cassette popped out. He pushed it back in and hit the rewind button. He turned the TV on and pulled out the rover.

"One, how we doing?"

"Movie's getting out now. I'm watching for him."

That wasn't right, Bosch knew. No general release movie was that short. And he knew the Dome was a single theater. One movie shown at a time. So Mora had gone into the theater after the movie had started. If he had really gone in. An adrenaline-charged alert swept over him.

"You sure it's over, One? He's barely been in there an hour."

"We're going in!"

There was panic in Sheehan's voice. Then Bosch understood. We're going in. Opelt had not followed Mora into the theater. They had clicked off on Rollenberger's order to split up but they hadn't followed the order. They couldn't. Mora had seen Sheehan and Opelt the day before at the burrito stand by Central Division. There was no way one of them could go into a dark theater looking for Mora and risk being seen by the vice cop first. If that happened, Mora would instantly tumble to the setup. He would know. Sheehan had rogered the order from Rollenberger because the alternative was to tell the lieutenant that they had fucked up the day before.

The VCR rewind clicked off. Bosch sat there motionless, his finger poised in front of the VCR. He knew they had been made. Mora was a cop. He had made the tail. The theater stop had been a scam.

He hit the play button.

This tape had not been erased. The quality of the image on it was better than Bosch had seen in the video booth at X Marks the Spot four nights earlier. The tape had all the production values of a feature-length porno tape. Framed in the TV picture was the four-poster bed on which two men were engaged in sex with a woman. Bosch watched for a moment and hit the fast forward button while the picture was still on the screen. The players in the video began a quick jerking motion that was almost comedic. Bosch watched as they changed couplings over and over. Every conceivable coupling in fast speed. Finally, he returned it to normal speed and studied the players.

The woman did not fit the Follower's mold. She wore the black wig. She was also rail-thin and young. In fact, she wasn't a woman — legally, at least. Bosch doubted she was more than sixteen years old. One of her partners was young, too, perhaps he was her age or less. Bosch couldn't be sure. He was sure, however, that the third participant was Ray Mora. His face was turned away from the camera but Bosch could tell. And he could see the gold medal, the Holy Spirit, bouncing on his chest. He turned the tape off.

"I forgot about that tape, didn't I?"

Still on his knees in front of the television, Bosch turned. Ray Mora was standing there with a gun pointed at his face.

"Hey, Ray."

"Thanks for reminding me."

"Don't worry about it. Look, Ray, why don't you put —"

"Don't look at me."

"What?"

"I don't want you to look at me! Turn around, look at the screen."

Bosch obediently looked at the blank screen.

"You're a leftie, right? With your right hand take out your gun and slide it across the floor this way."

Bosch carefully followed the orders. He thought he heard Mora pick the gun up off the floor.

"You fucks think I'm the Follower."

"Look, I'm not going to lie to you, Ray, we were checking you out, that's all. . . . I know now, I know we're wrong. You —"

"The kosher burrito boys. Somebody ought to teach them how to follow a fucking suspect. They don't know shit . . . took me a while but I figured something was going down after I saw them."

"So we're wrong about you, right, Ray?"

"You have to ask, Bosch? After what you just saw? The answer is, yeah, you got your head up your ass. Whose idea was it to check me out? Eyman? Leiby?"

Eyman and Leiby were the co-commanders of Administrative Vice.

"No. It came from me. It was my call."

A long moment of silence followed this confession.

"Then maybe I ought to just blow your head off right here. Be within my rights, wouldn't it?"

"Look, Ray —"

"Don't!"

Bosch stopped from turning all the way and looked back at the television.

"You do that, Ray, and your life unalterably changes. You know that."

"It did that as soon as you broke in, Bosch. Why shouldn't I just take it to the logical conclusion? Cap you and just disappear."

"'Cause you're a cop, Ray."

"Am I? Am I still going to be a cop if I let you go? You going to kneel there and tell me you'll make it right for me?"

"Ray, I don't know what to tell you. Those kids on the video are underage. But I only know that because of an illegal search. You end this now and put away the gun, we can work something out."

"Yeah, Harry? Can everything go back to the way it was? The badge is all I've got. I can't give —"

"Ray. I —"

"Shut up! Just shut up! I'm trying to think."

Bosch felt the anger hitting him in the back like rain.

"You know my secret, Bosch. How the fuck does that make you feel?"

Bosch had no answer. His mind was tumbling, trying to come up with the next move, the next sentence, when he flinched at the sound of Sheehan's voice coming over the rover in his pocket.

"We lost him. He's not in the theater."

There was a sharp degree of urgency in Sheehan's voice.

Bosch and Mora were silent, listening.

"What do you mean, Team One?" Rollenberger's voice said.

"Who's that?" Mora asked.

"Rollenberger, RHD," Bosch answered.

Sheehan's voice said, "The movie got out ten minutes ago. People came out but he didn't. I went in, he's gone. His car is still here but he's gone."

"I thought one of you went in?" Rollenberger barked, his own voice tightening with panic.

"We did, but we lost him," Sheehan said.

"Liar," Mora said. A long moment of silence followed before he said, "Now, they'll probably start hitting the hotels, looking for me. Because to them, I'm the Follower."

"Yes," Bosch said. "But they know I'm here, Ray. I should call in."

As if on cue, Sheehan's voice came from the rover.

"Team Six?"

"That's Sheehan, Ray. I'm Six."

"Call him. Be careful, Harry."

Bosch slowly took the radio out of his pocket with his right hand and held it up to his mouth. He pressed the transmitter.

"One, did you find him?"

"Negative. In the wind. What's on TV?"

"Nothing. There's nothing on tonight."

"Then you ought to leave the house and help us out."

"Already on the way," Bosch said quickly. "Where are you at?"

"Bo — uh, Team Six, this is Team Leader, we need you to come in. We're bringing in the task force to help locate the suspect. All units will meet at the Dome parking lot."

"Be there in ten. Out."

He dropped his arm back to his side.

"A whole task force, huh?" Mora asked.

Bosch looked down and nodded.

"Look, Ray, that was all code. They know I went to your house. If I don't show up at the Dome in ten minutes they'll come looking for me here. What do you want to do?"

"I don't know . . . but I guess that gives me at least fifteen minutes to decide, doesn't it?"

"Sure, Ray. Take your time. Don't make a mistake."

"Too late for that," he said, almost wistfully. Then he added, "Tell you what. Take out the tape."

Bosch ejected the tape and held it up over his left shoulder to Mora.

"No, no, I want you to do this for me, Harry. Open the bottom drawer and take out the magnet."

That's what the hockey puck was. Bosch put the tape on top of the stand next to the TV and reached down for the magnet. Feeling its heaviness as he lifted it, he wondered if he'd have a chance, if he could maybe turn and hurl it at Mora before the vice cop got off a shot.

"You'd be dead before you tried," Mora said, knowing his thoughts. "You know what to do with it."

Bosch ran the magnet over the top side of the tape.

"Let's put it in and see how we did," Mora instructed.

"Okay, Ray. Whatever you say."

Bosch put the tape into the VCR and pushed the play button. The screen filled with the static of a dead channel. It cast a grayish shroud of dull light over Bosch. He hit the fast forward button and the static continued. The tape had been wiped clean.

"Good," Mora said. "That ought to do it. That was the last tape."

"No evidence, Ray. You're in the clear."

"But you'll always know. And you'll tell them, won't you, Harry? You'll tell IAD. You'll tell the world. I'll never be clear, so don't fuckin' say I'll be clear. Everyone will know."

Bosch didn't answer. After a moment, he thought he heard the creaking of the wood floor. When Mora spoke, he was very close behind.

"Let me give you a tip, Harry. . . . Nobody in this world is who they say they are. Nobody. Not when they're in their own room with the door shut and locked. And nobody knows anybody, no matter what they think. . . . The best you can hope for is to know yourself. And sometimes when you do, when you see your true self, you have to turn away."

Bosch heard nothing for several seconds. He kept his eyes on the television screen and thought he could see ghosts forming and disintegrating in the static. He felt the grayish-blue glow burning behind his eyes and the start of a headache. He hoped he was going to live long enough to get it.

"You were always a good guy to me, Harry. I —"

There was a sound from the hallway, then a shout.

"Mora!"

It was Sheehan's voice. Immediately it was followed by light that flooded the room. Bosch heard the pounding of several feet on the wood floor, then there was a shout from Mora and the sound of impact as he was tackled. Bosch took his thumb off the rover's transmit button and began to throw himself to the right, out of harm's way. And in that moment, a gunshot cracked across the room, echoing, it seemed, as loudly as anything he had ever heard.

28

Once Bosch had cleared the rover channel, Rollenberger came up almost immediately.

"Bosch! Sheehan — Team One! What is happening there. What is — report immediately."

After a long moment went by, Bosch answered calmly.

"This is Six. Team Leader, be advised you should proceed to the subject's twenty."

"His home? What — did we have shots fired?"

"Team Leader, be advised to keep the channel open. And all task force units, disregard the callout. All units are ten-seven until further notice. Unit Five, are you up?"

"Five," Edgar responded.

"Five, could you meet me at our subject's twenty?"

"On my way."

"Six out."

Bosch turned off the rover before Rollenberger could get back on the channel.

It took the lieutenant a half hour to get from the Parker Center operations post to the house on Sierra Linda. By the time he arrived, Edgar was already there and a plan was in place. Bosch opened the front door just as Rollenberger reached it. The lieutenant strode through the entrance with a face turned red with equal parts of anger and befuddlement.

"Okay, Bosch, what the hell is going on here? You had no authority to cancel the call out, to countermand my order."

"I thought the less people that know, the better, Lieutenant. I called out Edgar. I thought that would be enough to handle it and that way not too many would —"

"Know what, Bosch? Handle what? What is going on here?"

Bosch looked at him a moment before answering, then in an even voice said, "One of the men in your command conducted an illegal search of the suspect's residence. He was caught in the act when the suspect eluded the surveillance you were supervising. That's what happened."

Rollenberger reacted as if he had been slapped.

"Are you crazy, Bosch? Where's the phone? I want —"

"You call Chief Irving and you can forget about ever running a task force again. You can forget about a lot of things."

"Bullshit! I had nothing to do with this. You went freelancing on your own and got your fingers caught in the jar. Where's Mora?"

"He's upstairs in the room to the right, handcuffed to the Nautilus machine."

Rollenberger looked around at the others standing in the living room. Sheehan, Opelt, Edgar. They all gave him deadpan looks. Bosch said, "If you knew nothing about it, *Lieutenant*, you'll have to prove that. Everything said on Symplex five tonight is on the reel-to-reel down at the city com center. I said I was in the house, you were listening. You even spoke to me a few times."

"Bosch, you were talking in codes, I didn't — I knew nuh —"

Rollenberger suddenly sprang wildly at Bosch, his hands up and going for his neck. Bosch was ready and reacted more aggressively. He pounded both palms into the other man's chest and slammed him back against a hallway wall. A picture two feet to his side slid off the wall and clattered to the floor.

"Bosch, you fool, the bust is ruined now," he said while slumped against the wall. "It was all il —"

"There's no bust. He's the wrong man. I think. But we have to be sure. You want to help us search the place and think about how to contain this, or do you want to call out the chief and explain how badly you handled your command?"

Bosch stepped away, adding, "The phone's in the kitchen."

The search of the house took more than four hours. The five of them, working methodically and silently, searched every room, every drawer, every cabinet. What little evidence they gathered of Detective Ray Mora's secret life they put on the dining room table. All the while, their host remained in the upstairs gym room, cuffed to one of the chrome bars of the weight machine. He was accorded fewer rights than a murderer would have received had he been arrested in his home. No phone call. No lawyer. No rights. This was always the case when cops investigated cops. Every cop knew the most flagrant abuses of police power occurred when cops turned on their own.

Occasionally, as they began the initial work, they would hear Mora call out. He called for Bosch most often, sometimes Rollenberger. But no one came to him until finally Sheehan and Opelt — concerned that the neighbors would hear and maybe call the police — went into the room and gagged him with a bathroom towel and black electrical tape.

The silence of the searchers was not in deference to the neighbors, however. The detectives worked quietly because of the tensions among them. Though Rollenberger was visibly angry with Bosch, most of the tension was derived from Sheehan and Opelt having blown the surveillance, which directly led to Mora's discovery of Bosch inside his house. No one except Rollenberger was upset by Bosch's illegal entry of the house. Bosch's own home had been similarly violated at least twice that he knew about during times when he had been the focus of internal investigations. Just like the badge, it came with the job.

When they completed the search the dining room table was stacked with the porno magazines and store-bought tapes, the video equipment, the wig, the women's clothing and Mora's personal phone book. The television that had been hit by Mora's stray shot was also there. By then Rollenberger had cooled somewhat, having apparently used the hours to consider his situation as well as to search.

"All right," he said as the other four convened around the table and surveyed its contents. "What have we got? Number one, are we confident Mora is not our man?"

Rollenberger looked around the room and his eyes stopped on Bosch.

"What do you think, Bosch?"

"You heard my story. He denied it and what was on the last tape before he made me erase it doesn't fit with the Follower. Looked completely consensual, though the boy and girl with him were obviously underage. He isn't the Follower."

"Then what is he?"

"Somebody with problems. I think he got bent by staying too long in vice and started making his own flicks."

"Was he selling them?"

"I don't know. I doubt it. No evidence of that here. He didn't go very far in hiding himself in the tape I saw. I think it was just his own stuff. He wasn't in it for money. It was something deeper."

No one said anything, so Bosch continued.

"My guess is that he made our tail sometime after we set up on him and began getting rid of the evidence. Tonight he was probably playing around with the tail, trying to figure what we were on him for. He got rid of most of the evidence, but if you put somebody on that phone book, my bet is you'll put it together. Some of those listings with only a first name. You track them and you'll probably find some of the kids he used in his videos."

Sheehan made a move to pick up the phone book.

"Leave it," Rollenberger said. "If anybody continues this it will be Internal Affairs."

"How they going to do that?" Bosch asked.

"What do you mean?"

"It's all fruit of the poison tree. The search, everything. All of it's illegal. We can't move against Mora."

"And we can't let him carry a badge, either," Rollenberger said testily. "The man should be in jail."

The following silence was broken by the sound of Mora's hoarse but loud voice from upstairs. He had somehow slipped the gag.

"Bosch! Bosch! I wanna deal, Bosch. I'll give —" he began coughing "— I'll give him to you, Bosch. You hear me! You hear me!"

Sheehan headed toward the stairs, which began in the alcove outside the dining room. He said, "This time I'll make it so tight the fuck will strangle."

"Wait a minute," Rollenberger ordered.

Sheehan stopped at the archway leading to the alcove.

"What's he saying?" Rollenberger said. "Who will he give?"

He looked at Bosch, who shrugged his shoulders. They waited, Rollenberger looking up at the ceiling, but Mora was silent.

Bosch stepped over to the table and picked up the phone book. He said, "I think I've got an idea."

The odor of Mora's sweat filled the room. He sat on the floor, his hands cuffed behind him and to the work-out machine. The towel that had been wrapped around his mouth and taped had slipped down to his neck so that it looked like a cervical collar. The front of it was damp with spittle and Bosch guessed that Mora had loosened it by working his jaw up and down.

"Bosch, unhook me."

"Not yet."

Rollenberger stepped forward.

"Detective Mora, you have problems. You've —"

"You've got problems. You're the one. All of this is illegal. How you going to explain this? Know what I'm going to do? I'm going to hire that bitch Money Chandler and sue the department for a million dollars. Yeah, I'll —"

"Can't spend a million dollars in jail, Ray," Bosch said.

He held up Mora's phone book so that the vice cop could see it.

"This gets dropped off at Internal Affairs and they'll make a case. All those names and numbers, there's gotta be somebody that would talk about you. Somebody underage probably. Think we're giving you a hard time? Wait until IAD takes over. They'll make a case, Ray. And they'll make it without tonight's search. That will just be your word against ours."

Bosch saw a quick movement in Mora's eyes and he knew he had struck bone. Mora was afraid of the names in the book.

"So," Bosch said, "what deal did you have in mind, Ray?"

Mora looked away from the book, first to Rollenberger and then to Bosch and then back to Rollenberger.

"You can make a deal?"

"I have to hear it first," Rollenberger said.

"Okay, this is the deal. I walk and I give you the Follower. I know who it is."

Bosch was immediately skeptical but said nothing. Rollenberger looked at him and Bosch shook his head once.

"I know," Mora said. "The Peeping Tom I told you about. That was no bullshit. I got the ID today. It fits. I know who it is."

Now Bosch took him more seriously. He folded his arms in front of his body, threw a quick glance at Rollenberger.

"Who?" Rollenberger said.

"What's the deal first?"

Rollenberger stepped to the window and parted the curtains. He was turning it over to Bosch, who took a step forward and squatted like a baseball catcher in front of Mora.

"This is the deal. It is offered only this one time. Take it or let the chips fall where they may. You give the name to me and your badge to Lieutenant Rollenberger. You resign immediately from the department. You agree not to sue the department or any of us individually. In exchange, you walk."

"How do I know you'll —"

"You don't. And how do we know that you'll keep your end? I hang on to the phone book, Ray. You try to fuck us and it goes to IAD. Do we have a deal?"

Mora stared at him without speaking a long moment. Finally, Bosch got up and turned to the door. Rollenberger headed that way, too, and said, "Unhook him, Bosch. Take him to Parker and book him on assault on a police officer, unlawful sex with a minor, pandering, anything you can think —"

"We gotta deal," Mora blurted. "But I've got no insurance."

Bosch turned back to look at him.

"That's right, you don't. The name?"

Mora looked from Bosch to Rollenberger.

"Unhook me."

"The name, Mora," Rollenberger said. "This is it."

"It's Locke. The fucking shrink. You assholes, you put the finger on me and the whole time he's the one pushing the buttons."

Bosch was jolted but in that same moment he began immediately to see how it could be. Locke knew the Dollmaker's program, he fit the Follower's profile.

"He was the Tom?"

"Yeah, it was him. Got'm ID'd by a producer today. He went around saying he was writin' a book so he could get close to the girls. Then he killed them, Bosch. The whole time he's been playing doctor with you, Bosch, he's been out there . . . killing."

Rollenberger turned to Bosch and said, "What do you think?"

Bosch left the room without answering. He went down the stairs and trotted out the door to his car. Locke's book was on the back seat where Bosch had left it the day he bought it. As he headed back into the house with it he noticed that the first etchings of dawn's light were in the sky.

On Mora's dining room table, Bosch opened the book and began leafing through it until he came to a page marked Author's Note. In the second paragraph, Locke wrote, "The material for this book was gathered over the course of three years from interviews with countless adult film performers, many of whom requested that they remain anonymous or be identified only by their stage names. The author wishes to thank them and the film producers who granted him access to the sets and production offices at which these interviews were conducted."

The mystery man. Bosch realized Mora could be right that Locke was the man whom the video performer Gallery had reported as a suspect when she called the original task force tip number four years earlier. Bosch next flipped to the index of the book and ran his fingers down the names. Velvet Box was listed. So were Holly Lere and Magna Cum Loudly.

Bosch quickly reviewed in his mind Locke's involvement in the case. He would definitely fit as a suspect for the same reasons Mora had fit. He had had a foot in both camps, as Locke himself had described it. He had access to all information about the Dollmaker deaths and, at the same time, was conducting research for a book on the psychology of female performers in the pornography industry.

Bosch became excited, but more so he was angry. Mora had been right. Locke had punched his buttons, to the point that he had helped set the cops on the path to the wrong man. If Locke was the Follower, he had played Bosch perfectly.

*　　　*　　　*

Rollenberger dispatched Sheehan and Opelt to Locke's house to put him under immediate surveillance. "This time don't fuck it up," he said as he recovered some of his command presence.

Next he announced there would be a meeting of the task force at noon Sunday, little more than six hours away. He said they would then discuss seeking a search warrant for Locke's home and office and decide what moves to make. As he headed to the door, Rollenberger looked at Bosch and said, "Go cut him loose. Then, Bosch, you better go get some sleep. You're going to need it."

"What about you? How're you going to handle Irving on this?"

Rollenberger was looking down at the gold detective's shield he held in his hand. It was Mora's. He closed his hand over it and put it in his sport coat pocket. Then he looked at Bosch.

"That's my business, isn't it, Bosch? Don't worry about it."

After the others had left, Bosch and Edgar went up the stairs to the gym room. Mora was silent and refused to look at them as they removed the handcuffs. They said nothing and left him there, the towel still around his neck like a noose, staring at his fractured image in the wall mirror.

Bosch lit a cigarette and looked at his watch when he got to his car. It was 6:20 and he was too wired to go home to sleep. He got in the car and pulled the rover from his pocket.

"Frankie, you up?"

"Yo," Sheehan responded.

"Anything?"

"Just got here. No life showing. Don't know whether he's here or not. Garage door is down."

"Okay, then."

Bosch thought of an idea. He picked up Locke's book and took the cover off it. He folded it and put it in his pocket, then he started the car.

After stopping for coffee at a Winchell's, Bosch got to the Sybil Brand Institute by seven. Because of the early hour, he had to get the watch commander's approval to interview Georgia Stern.

He could see she was sick as soon as she was brought into the interview room. She sat hunched over with her arms folded in front of her, as if she were carrying a bag of groceries that had broken and was guarding against losing anything.

"Remember me?" he asked.

"Man, you gotta get me out."

"Can't do that. But I can get them to take you into the clinic. You can get methadone in your orange juice."

"I wanna get out."

"I'll get you in the clinic."

She dropped her head in defeat. She started a slight rocking motion, back and forth. She seemed pitiful to Bosch. But he knew he had to let it go. There were more important things, and she couldn't be saved.

"You remember me?" he asked again. "From the other night?"

She nodded.

"We showed you pictures? I've got another."

He put the dust jacket from the book on the table. She looked at Locke's photo for a long while.

"Well?"

"What? I seen him. He talked to me once."

"About what?"

"Making movies. He was — I think he's an interviewer."

"Interviewer?"

"I mean like a writer. He said it was for a book. I told him don't use any of my names but I never checked."

"Georgia, think back. Hard. This is very important. Could he also be the one who attacked you?"

"You mean the Dollmaker? The Dollmaker's dead."

"I know that. I think it was someone else who attacked you. Look at the photo. Was it him?"

She looked at the photo and shook her head.

"I don't know. They told me it was the Dollmaker, so I forgot what he looked like after he was killed."

Bosch leaned back in his chair. It was useless.

"You still going to get me in the clinic?" she asked timidly after seeing his change in mood.

"Yeah. You want for me to tell them you've got the virus?"

"What virus?"

"AIDS."

"What for?"

"To get you whatever medicine you need."

"I don't have AIDS."

"Look, I know the last time Van Nuys Vice put the bust on you you had AZT in your purse."

"That's for protection. I got that from a friend-a-mine who's sick. He gave me the bottle and I put cornstarch in it."

"Protection?"

"I don't want to work for no pimp. Some asshole comes up and says he's now your man, I show 'em the shit and say I got the virus, you know, and he splits. They don't want girls with AIDS. Bad for their business."

She smiled slyly and Bosch changed his mind about her. She might be saved after all. She had the instincts of a survivor.

The Hollywood Station detective bureau was completely deserted, which was not unusual for nine on a Sunday morning. After stealing a cup of coffee from the watch office while the sergeant was busy at the wall map, Bosch went to the homicide table and called Sylvia but got no answer. He wondered if she was gardening out back and hadn't heard the phone or had gone out, maybe to get the Sunday paper to read the story about Beatrice Fontenot.

Bosch leaned back in his chair. He didn't know what his next move was. He used the rover to check with Sheehan and once again was told that there had been no movement at Locke's house.

"Think we should go up and knock?" Sheehan asked.

He wasn't expecting an answer and Bosch didn't give one. But he started thinking about it. It gave him another idea. He decided he would go to Locke's house to finesse him. To run the story about Mora by him and see how Locke reacted and if he would say the vice cop was probably the Follower.

He threw the empty coffee cup in the trash can and looked over at his slot in the memo and mail box on the wall. He saw he had something in there. He got up and took three pink phone message forms and a white envelope back to his desk. He looked at the messages and one by one dismissed them as unimportant and put them on his message spike to be considered later. Two were from TV reporters and one was from a prosecutor asking about evidence in one of his other cases. All the calls had come in Friday.

Then he looked at the envelope and felt a chill, like a cold steel ball rolling down the back of his neck. It had only his name on the outside but the distinctive printing style could mean it was from nobody else. He dropped the envelope on the table, opened his drawer and dug around in the notebooks, pens and paper clips until he found a pair of rubber gloves. Then he carefully opened the Follower's message.

> Long aft' the body stops stinking
> Of me you'll be thinking
> For taking your precious blonde
> Oft' your bloody hands
>
> I'll make her my dolly
> Aft' I've had my sweet jolly
> And maybe to leave then
> For other soft lands
>
> No air for her to swallow
> Aft' me dare you not follow
> Her last word, my gosh!
> A sound like Boschhhhhh

As he left the station, he ran through the watch commander's office, almost knocked down the startled duty sergeant and yelled: "Get hold of Detective Jerry Edgar! Tell'm to come up on the rover. He'll know what I mean."

29

Getting to the freeway was so frustrating that Bosch believed he could actually feel his blood pressure rising. His skin began to feel tight around his eyes, his face grew warm. There was some kind of Sunday morning performance at the Hollywood Bowl and traffic on Highland was backed up to Fountain. Bosch tried taking some side streets but so were many of the people going to the Bowl. He was deep into this quagmire before he cursed himself for not remembering that he had the bubble and siren. Working homicide, it had been so long since he had to race to get anywhere that he had forgotten.

After he slid the bubble onto the roof and hit the siren, the cars began to part in front of him and he remembered how easy it could be. He had just gotten onto the Hollywood Freeway and was speeding north through the Cahuenga Pass when Jerry Edgar's voice came up on the rover on the seat next to him.

"Harry Bosch?"

"Yeah, Edgar, listen. I want you to call the sheriff's department, Valencia station, and tell them to get a car to Sylvia's house code three. Tell them to make sure she's okay."

Code three meant lights and siren, an emergency. He gave Edgar her address.

"Make the call now and then come back up."

"Okay, Harry. What's going on?"

"Make the call now!"

Three minutes later Edgar was back on the radio.

"They're on the way. What've you got?"

"I'm on my way, too. What I want you to do is go in to the division. I left a note on my desk. It's from the Follower. Secure it and then call Rollenberger and Irving and tell 'em what's happening."

"What is happening?"

Bosch had to swerve into the median to avoid hitting a car that pulled into the lane in front of him. The driver hadn't seen Bosch coming and Bosch knew he was going too fast — a steady ninety-three — for the siren to give much of a warning to the cars ahead of him.

"The note's another poem. He says he is going to take the blonde off my hands. Sylvia. There's no answer at her house but there still may be time. I don't think I was supposed to find the note until Monday, when I came in for work."

"On my way. Be careful, buddy. Stay cool."

Stay cool, Bosch thought. Right. He thought of what Locke had told him about the Follower being angry, wanting to get back at him for putting down the Dollmaker. Not Sylvia, he hoped. He wouldn't be able to live with it.

He picked the radio back up.

"Team One?"

"Yo," Sheehan replied.

"Go get him. If he's there, bring him in."

"You sure?"

"Bring him in."

There was a lone sheriff's car in front of Sylvia's house. When Bosch pulled to a stop, he saw a uniform deputy standing on the front step, back to the door. It looked as if he was guarding the place. As if he was protecting a crime scene.

As he started to get out, Bosch felt a sharp stabbing pain on the left side of his chest. He held still for a moment and it eased. He ran around the car and across the lawn, working his badge out of his pocket as he went.

"LAPD, what've you got?"

"It's locked. I walked around, all windows and doors secured. No answer. Looks like nobody's —"

Bosch pushed past him and used his key to open the door. He ran from room to room, making a quick search for obvious signs of foul play. There were none. The deputy had been right. Nobody was home. Bosch looked in the garage and Sylvia's Cherokee was not there.

Still, Bosch made a second sweep of the house, opening closets, looking under beds, looking for any indication that something was amiss. The deputy was standing in the living room when Bosch finally came out of the bedroom wing.

"Can I go now? I was pulled off a call that seems a little more important than this."

Bosch noted the annoyance in the deputy's voice and nodded for him to go. He followed him out and got the rover out of the Caprice.

"Edgar, you up?"

"What do you have there, Harry?"

There was the sound of genuine dread in his voice.

"Nothing here. No sign of her or anything else."

"I'm at the station, you want me to put a BOLO out?"

Bosch described Sylvia and her Cherokee for the Be On Look Out dispatch that would go out to all patrol cars.

"I'll put it out. We got the task force coming in. Irving, too. We'll be meeting here. There's nothing else to do but wait."

"I'm going to wait here a while. Keep me posted. . . . Team One, you up?"

"Team One," Sheehan said. "We went up to the door. Nobody home. We're standing by. If he shows, we'll bring him in."

Bosch sat in the living room, his arms folded in front of him, for more than an hour. He now knew why Georgia Stern had held herself this way at Sybil Brand. There was comfort in it. Still, the silence of the house was nerve-racking. He was staring at the portable phone he had put on the coffee table, waiting for it to ring, when he heard a key hit the lock on the front door. He jumped up and was moving toward the entry when the door opened and a man stepped in. It wasn't Locke. It wasn't anyone Bosch knew, but he had a key.

Without hesitating Bosch moved into the entrance and slammed the man up against the door as he turned to close it.

"Where is she?" he shouted.

"What? What?" the man cried out.

"Where is she?"

"She couldn't come. I'm going to watch it for her. She's got another open in Newhall. Please!"

Bosch realized what was happening just as the pager on his belt sounded its shrill tone. He stepped away from the man.

"You're the Realtor?"

"I work for her. What are you doing? Nobody's supposed to be here."

Bosch pulled the pager off his belt and saw the readout was his home phone number.

"I have to make a call."

He went back to the living room. Over his shoulder he heard the real estate man say, "Yeah, you do that! What the hell is going on here?"

Bosch punched the number into the phone and Sylvia picked up after one ring.

"Are you okay?"

"Yes, Harry, where are you?"

"At your place. Where have you been?"

"I picked up a pie at Marie Callendar's and took it and the flowers I cut to the Fontenots. I just felt like doing —"

"Sylvia, listen to me. Is the door locked?"

"What? I don't know."

"Put the phone down and go make sure. Make sure the sliding door to the porch is locked, too. And the door to the carport. I'll wait."

"Harry, what is —"

"Go do it now!"

She was back in a minute. Her voice sounded very timid.

"Okay, everything's locked."

"Okay, good. Now listen, I'm coming there right now and it will only take me half an hour. In the meantime, no matter who comes to the door, don't answer it and don't make any sound. Understand?"

"You're scaring me, Harry."

"I know that. Do you understand what I said?"

"Yes."

"Good."

Bosch thought for a moment. What else could he tell her?

"Sylvia, after we are done here. I want you to go to the closet near the front door. On the shelf there is a white box. Take it down and take out the gun. There are bullets in the red box in the cabinet over the sink. The red box, not the blue. Load the gun."

"I can't do — what are you telling me?"

"Yes, you can, Sylvia. Load the gun. Then wait for me. If anybody comes through the door and it's not me, protect yourself."

She didn't say anything.

"I'm on my way. I love you."

While Bosch was on the freeway going south, Edgar came up on the radio and told him Sheehan and Opelt still had made no sighting of Locke. The presidents had been dispatched to USC but Locke was not at his office, either.

"They're going to sit on both locations. I'm working on a warrant for the house now. But I don't think the PC is there."

Bosch knew he was probably right. Mora's identification of Locke as the man hanging around porno sets and the names of three of the victims in his book were not probable cause to search his house.

He told Edgar that he had located Sylvia and was headed to her now. After signing off, he realized that her trip to the Fontenot house might have saved her life. He saw a symbiotic grace in that. A life taken, a life saved.

Before opening the door to his house he loudly announced he was there, then turned the key and walked into Sylvia's trembling arms. He held her to his chest and said into the radio, "We're all safe here," then turned it off.

They sat down on the couch and Bosch told her everything that had happened since they had last been together. He could tell by her eyes that it scared her more knowing what was going on than not.

She, in turn, explained that she had to get out of the house because the Realtor was holding an open house. That was why she had gone to Bosch's house after visiting the Fontenots. He explained that he had forgotten about the open house.

"You might need to get a new Realtor after today," he said.

They laughed together to let some of the tension go.

"I'm sorry," he said. "This should never have involved you."

They sat in silence for a while after that. She leaned against him as if she was weary of everything.

"Why do you do this, Harry? You deal with so much — the most awful people and the things they do. Why do you keep going?"

He thought about that but knew there was no real answer and that she wasn't expecting one.

"I don't want to stay here," he said after a while.

"We can go back to my house at four."

"No, let's just get out of here."

The two-room suite at the Loews Hotel in Santa Monica gave them a sweeping view of the ocean across a wide beach. It was the kind of room that came with two full-length terrycloth robes and gold foil–wrapped chocolates left on the pillow. The suite's front door was off the fourth landing of a five-story atrium with a wall of glass that faced the ocean and would capture the entire arc of the sunset.

There was a porch with two chaise lounges and a table and they had lunch delivered by room service there. Bosch had brought the rover in with him but it was turned off. He would keep in touch as the search for Locke went on, but he was out of it for the day.

He had called in and talked to Edgar and then Irving. He told them he would stay with Sylvia, though it seemed unlikely that the Follower would make a move now. He was not needed anyway because the task force was in a holding pattern, waiting for Locke to turn up or something else to break.

Irving had said the presidents had contacted the dean of the psychology department at USC who, in turn, contacted one of Locke's graduate assistants. She reported that Locke had mentioned on Friday that he would be in Las Vegas for the weekend, staying at the Stardust. He taught no classes on Mondays, so he would not be back at the school until Tuesday.

"But we checked the Stardust," Irving said. "Locke had a reservation but never checked in."

"What about the warrant?"

"We've had three turn-downs from three judges. You know it's pretty weak when a judge won't rubber-stamp a search warrant for us. We're going to have to let that jell for a while. In the meantime, we'll be watching his house and his office. I'd like to leave it that way until he surfaces and we can talk to him."

Bosch heard the doubt in Irving's voice. He wondered how Rollenberger had explained the leap in the investigation from Mora to Locke as the suspect.

"You think we're wrong?"

He realized there was a quiver of doubt in his own voice.

"I don't know. We traced the note. Partially. It was left at the front desk sometime Saturday night. The deskman went back for coffee about nine, got sidetracked by the watch commander and when he came back out it was there on the counter. He had an Explorer put it in your slot. The only thing it means for sure is that we were wrong about Mora. Anyway, the point is, we could be wrong again. Right now all we have are hunches. Good hunches, mind you, but that's all. I want to proceed a little more carefully this time."

The translation was, you screwed us up with your hunch on Mora. We are going to be more skeptical this time. Bosch understood this.

"What if the Vegas trip was a cover? The note says something about moving on. Maybe Locke's running."

"Maybe."

"Should we put out a BOLO, get an arrest warrant?"

"I think we're going to wait until at least Tuesday, Detective. Give him a chance to come back. Just two more days."

It was clear Irving wanted to sit tight. He was going to wait for events to control what he would do next.

"Okay, I'll check in later."

They napped in the king-size bed until it was dark and then Bosch turned on the news to see if any of what had happened in the last twenty-four hours had leaked.

It hadn't, but midway through the newscast on 2, Bosch stopped flipping through the channels with the selector. The story that stopped him was an update on the Beatrice Fontenot killing. A photo of the girl, her hair in cornrows, appeared on the right side of the screen.

The blonde anchor said, "Police announced today that they have identified a suspected gunman in the death of sixteen-year-old Beatrice Fontenot. The man they are looking for is an alleged drug dealer who was a rival of Beatrice's older brothers, Detective Stanley Hanks said. He said the shots fired at the Fontenot house were in all probability meant for the brothers. Instead, a bullet struck Beatrice, an honor student at Grant High in the Valley, in the head. Her funeral is scheduled for later this week."

Bosch turned off the television and looked back at Sylvia, who was propped up on two pillows against the wall. They didn't say anything.

After a room service dinner, which they ate with almost no conversation in the front room of the suite, they took turns in the shower. Bosch went second and as the coarse water stung his scalp, he decided that it was time for him to lose all his baggage, to come clean. He trusted his faith in her, in her desire to know all of him. And he knew that if he did nothing, he was risking what they had each day he kept the secrets of his life inside. Somehow, he knew facing her was facing himself. He had to accept what he was, where he had come from and what he had become if he was to be accepted by her.

They were in their bleached white bathrobes, she in the chair by the sliding door, he standing near the bed. Beyond her through the door, he could see the full moon casting a shifting reflection on the Pacific. He didn't know how to start.

She had been leafing through a hotel magazine filled with suggestions for tourists on what to do in the city. None of them were things that people who lived here ever did. She closed it and put it on the table. She looked at him and then looked away. She started before he could say a word.

"Harry, I want you to go home."

He sat on the edge of the bed, put his elbows on his knees and ran his hands through his hair. He had no idea what was going on.

"What do you mean?"

"Too much death."

"Sylvia?"

"Harry, I've done so much thinking this weekend that I can't think anymore. But I know this, we have to be apart for a while. I have to sort things out. Your life, it's . . ."

"Two days ago you said our problem was that I held things back from you. Now you're saying you don't want to know about me. Your —"

"I'm not talking about you. I'm talking about what you do."

He shook his head.

"Same thing, Sylvia. You should know that."

"Look, it's been a rough couple of days. I just need some time to decide if this is right for me. For us. Believe me, I'm thinking about you, too. I'm not sure I'm the right one for you."

"I am, Sylvia."

"Please don't say that. Don't make it any more difficult. I —"

"I don't want to go back to being without you, Sylvia. That's all I know right now. I don't want to be alone."

"Harry, I don't want to hurt you and I would never ever ask you to change for me. I know you and I don't think you could change even if you wanted to. So . . . what I have to decide is whether I can live with that and live with you. . . . I do love you, Harry, but I need some time . . ."

She was crying now. Bosch could see it in the mirror. He wanted to get up to hold her but he knew it was the wrong move. He was the cause of her tears. There was a long silence, both of them sitting in private pain. She was looking down into her lap where her hands held each other. He looked out at the ocean and saw a drift-fishing boat cut across the reflected path of the moon on its way toward the Channel Islands.

"Say something to me," she finally said.

"I'll do whatever you want," he said. "You know that."

"I'll go into the bathroom until you get dressed and leave."

"Sylvia, I want to know that you are safe. I would like to ask you to let me sleep in the other room. In the morning, we'll figure something out. I'll leave then."

"No. We both know nothing will happen. That man, Locke, he's probably far away, running from you, Harry. I'll be safe. I'll take a taxi to school tomorrow and I'll be safe. Just give me some time."

"Time to decide."

"Yes. To decide."

She got up and walked quickly by him to the bathroom. He put his arm out but she brushed by it. After the door closed he could hear her pull tissues from the dispenser. Then he could hear her crying.

"Please leave, Harry," she said after a while. "Please."

He heard her turn the water on, so she wouldn't hear him if he said anything. Bosch felt like a fool to be sitting there in his luxury bathrobe. It ripped when he pulled it off.

That night he took a blanket from the trunk of the Caprice and made a bed on the sand about a hundred yards from the hotel. But he didn't sleep. He sat with his back to the ocean and his eyes on the curtained sliding door on the fourth-floor balcony next to the atrium. Through the glass wall of the atrium he could also see her front door and would know if anyone approached. It was cold on the beach but he didn't need the sea wind's chill to stay awake.

30

Bosch was ten minutes late coming into the courtroom Monday morning. He had waited to make sure Sylvia got a cab and was safely off to school before going home and changing into the same suit he had worn Friday. But as he hurried in, he saw that Judge Keyes wasn't on the bench and Chandler wasn't at the plaintiff's table. Church's widow sat alone, looking straight forward in a prayerful pose.

Harry sat down next to Belk and said, "What's up?"

"We were waiting for you and Chandler. Now we're just waiting for her. The judge was not happy about it."

Bosch saw the judge's clerk get up from her desk and knock on the chambers door. She then poked her head in and he could hear her say, "Detective Bosch is here. Ms. Chandler's secretary still hasn't located her."

The constricting feeling in his chest began then. Bosch felt himself immediately begin to sweat. How could he have missed it? He leaned forward and put his face into his hands.

"I gotta make a call," he said and stood up.

Belk turned, probably to tell him not to go anywhere, but was silenced by the opening of the chambers door. Judge Keyes strode out and said, "Remain seated."

He took his place on the bench and told the clerk to buzz the jury in. Bosch sat down.

"We're going to go ahead and get them started again without Ms. Chandler being here. We'll deal with her tardiness at a later date."

The jury filed in and the judge asked them if anybody had anything they wanted to bring up, a scheduling problem or anything else. No one said a word.

"All right then, we're going to send you back in to continue deliberations. The marshal will come speak to you later about lunch. By the way, Ms. Chandler had a scheduling conflict this morning and that's why you don't see her there at the plaintiff's table. You are to pay no mind to that. Thank you very much."

They filed back out. The judge instructed the parties who were present to stay within fifteen minutes of the courtroom again, then told the clerk to keep trying to find Chandler. With that, he stood up and walked back to his chambers.

Bosch was up quickly and out the door of the courtroom. He went to the pay phones and dialed the communications center. After giving his name and badge number, he asked the phone clerk to run a code-three DMV search on the name Honey Chandler. He said he needed the address and would hold.

The rover would not work until he was out of the courthouse underground garage. Once he was out on Los Angeles Street he tried again and got hold of Edgar, who had his rover on. He gave him the Carmelina Street address in Brentwood he had gotten for Chandler.

"Meet me there."

"On my way."

He drove down to Third and took it up through the tunnel and onto the Harbor Freeway. He was just hitting the Santa Monica Freeway when his pager sounded. He looked at the number while driving and didn't recognize it. He exited the freeway and pulled over at a Korea Town grocery store with a phone on the wall out front.

"Courtroom four," said the woman who answered his call.

"It's Detective Bosch, did someone beep me?"

"Yes, we did. We have a verdict. You need to get back here right away."

"What do you mean? I was just there. How'd they —"

"It's not unusual, Detective Bosch. They probably came to an agreement Friday and decided to take the weekend to see if they wanted to change their minds. Look, it gets them out of another day of work."

Back in the car, he picked up the rover again.

"Edgar, you there?"

"Uh, not quite. You?"

"I gotta turn around. Got a verdict. Can you check this out?"

"No problem. What am I checking out?"

"It's Chandler's house. She's blonde. She didn't show up in court today."

"I get the picture."

Bosch had never thought he would hope to see Honey Chandler in court at the table opposite his but he did. She wasn't there, though. A man Harry didn't recognize was sitting with the plaintiff.

As he walked to the defense table, Bosch saw that a couple of reporters, including Bremmer, were already in the courtroom.

"Who's that?" he asked Belk about the man next to the widow.

"Dan Daly. Keyes grabbed him out of the hallway to sit with the woman during the verdict. Chandler is apparently incommunicado. They can't find her."

"Anybody go to her house?"

"I don't know. I assume they called. What do you care? You should be worried about this verdict."

Judge Keyes came out then and took his place. He nodded to the clerk, who buzzed the jury. As the twelve filed in, none of them looked at Bosch but almost all of them eyed the man sitting next to Deborah Church.

"Again, folks," the judge began, "a scheduling conflict has prevented Ms. Chandler from being here. Mr. Daly, a fine lawyer, has agreed to sit in her stead. I understand from the marshal that you have reached a verdict."

Several of the twelve heads nodded. Bosch finally saw one man look at him. But then he looked away. Bosch could feel his heart pounding and he was unsure if it was because of the impending verdict or the disappearance of Honey Chandler. Or both.

"Can I have the verdict forms, please?"

The jury foreman handed a thin stack of papers to the marshal who handed them to the clerk who handed them to the judge. It was excruciating to watch. The judge had to put on a pair of reading glasses and then took his time studying the papers. Finally, he handed the papers back to the clerk and said, "Publish the verdict."

The clerk did a rehearsal reading in her head first and then began.

"In the above entitled matter on the question of whether defendant Hieronymus Bosch did deprive Norman Church of his civil rights to protection against unlawful search and seizure, we find for the plaintiff."

Bosch didn't move. He looked across the room and saw that now all the jurors were looking at him. His eyes turned to Deborah Church and he saw her grab the arm of the man next to her, even though she didn't know him, and smile. She was turning that smile triumphantly toward Bosch when Belk grabbed his arm.

"Don't worry," he whispered. "It's the damages that count."

The clerk continued.

"The jury hereby awards to the plaintiff in compensatory damages the amount of one dollar."

Bosch heard Belk whisper a gleeful "Yes!" under his breath.

"In the matter of punitive damages, the jury awards the plaintiff the amount of one dollar."

Belk whispered it again, only this time loud enough to be heard in the gallery. Bosch looked at Deborah Church just as the triumph dropped out of her smile and her eyes turned dead. It all seemed surrealistic to Bosch, as if he were observing a play but was actually on the stage with the actors. The verdict meant nothing to him. He just watched everybody.

Judge Keyes began his thank-you speech to the jury, telling them how they had performed their Constitutional duties and should be proud to have served and to be Americans. Bosch tuned it out and just sat there. Sylvia came to mind and he wished he could tell her.

The judge banged down the gavel and the jury filed out for the last time. Then he left the bench and Bosch thought he might have had an annoyed look on his face.

"Harry," Belk said. "It's a damn good verdict."

"Is it? I don't know."

"Well, it's a mixed verdict. But essentially the jury found what we already admitted to. We said you made mistakes going in like you did but you already had been reprimanded by your department for that. The jury found as a matter of law that you should not have kicked down the door like that. But in awarding only two dollars they were saying they believed you. Church made the furtive move. And Church was the Dollmaker."

He patted Bosch's back. He was probably waiting for Harry to thank him but it didn't come.

"What about Chandler?"

"Well, there's the rub, so to speak. The jury found for the plaintiff so we are going to have to pick up her tab. She'll probably ask for about one-eighty, maybe two hundred. We'll probably settle it for ninety. It's not bad, Harry. Not at all."

"I gotta go."

Bosch stood up and waded through a clot of people and reporters to get out of the courtroom. He moved quickly to the escalator and once on started fumbling to get the last cigarette out of his pack. Bremmer jumped on the step behind him, his notebook out and ready.

"Congrats, Harry," he said.

Bosch looked at him. The reporter seemed sincere.

"For what? They said I'm some kind of a Constitutional goon."

"Yeah, but you walk away two bucks light. That ain't bad."

"Yeah, well . . ."

"Well, any comment on the record? I take it 'Constitutional goon' was off, right?"

"Yeah, I'd appreciate that. Uh, tell you what, let me think for a while. I've gotta go but I'll call you later. Why don't you go back up and talk to Belk. He needs to see his name in the paper."

Outside he lit the cigarette and pulled the rover out of his pocket.

"Edgar, you up?"

"Here."

"How is it?"

"Better come on out, Harry. Everybody's rolling on it."

Bosch threw the cigarette in the ash can.

They had done a bad job of keeping it contained. By the time Bosch got to the house on Carmelina, there was already one news copter circling over-head and two other channels were there on the ground. It would not be long until it was a circus. The case would have two big draws: the Follower and Honey Chandler.

Bosch had to park two houses away because of the glut of official cars and vans lining both sides of the street. Parking control officers were just begin-ning to put down flares and close the street to traffic.

The property had been preserved by yellow plastic police lines. Bosch signed an attendance log held by a uniform officer at the tape and slipped underneath. It was a two-story Bauhaus-style home set on a hillside. Stand-ing outside, Bosch knew the floor-to-ceiling windows of the upstairs rooms would offer sweeping views of the flats below. He counted two chimneys. It was a nice house in a nice neighborhood filled with nice lawyers and UCLA professors. Not anymore, he thought. He wished he had a cigarette as he headed in.

Edgar was standing just inside the door in a tiled entryway. He was talking on a mobile phone and it sounded as if he was telling the media relations unit to send people out to handle this. He saw Bosch and pointed up the stairs.

The staircase was right off the entry and Bosch went up. There was a wide hallway that passed four doorways upstairs. A group of detectives milled about outside the farthest door and occasionally they looked inside at something. Bosch walked over.

In a way, Bosch knew, he had trained his mind to be almost like that of a psychopath. He practiced the psychology of objectification when at a death scene. Dead people weren't people, they were objects. He had to look at bodies as corpses, as evidence. It was the only way to deal with it and get the job done. It was the only way to survive. But this, of course, was always easier said or thought about than done. Often Bosch stumbled.

As a member of the original Dollmaker task force, he had seen the last six of the victims attributed to the serial killer. He saw them "in situ," as it was called — in the situation in which they were found. None of them was easy. There was something that seemed so helpless about these victims that it overwhelmed his best efforts at objectification. And knowing that they came from street backgrounds had made it all the worse. It was as if the torture visited upon each one by her killer was only the last in a life of indignities.

Now he looked down at the naked and tortured body of Honey Chandler and no manner of mental tricks or deception could prevent the horror he saw from burning into his soul. For the first time in his years as a homicide investigator, he wanted to close his eyes and just go away.

But he didn't. Instead, he stood with the other men who looked down with dead eyes and nonchalant poses. Like a gathering of serial killers. Something made him think of the bridge game at San Quentin that Locke had mentioned. A foursome of psychopaths sitting around the table, more killings to their credit than cards on the table.

Chandler was faceup, her arms outstretched at her sides. Her face was garishly painted with makeup. It hid much of the purplish discoloration which spread from her neck up. A leather strap, cut from a purse which lay spilled on the floor, was tied tightly around her neck, knotted on the right side as if pulled closed with a left hand. In keeping with the prior cases, whatever restraints and gag the killer used had been taken away with him.

But there was something outside of the program. Bosch saw that the Follower was improvising, now that he was no longer operating under the camouflage of the Dollmaker. Chandler's body was riddled with cigarette burns and bite marks. Some of them had bled and some were purplish with bruising, meaning the torture had taken place while she was still alive.

Rollenberger was in the room and was giving orders, even telling the photographer what angles he wanted. Nixon and Johnson were also in the room. Bosch realized, as probably Chandler had, that the final indignity was that her uncovered body would be left on display for hours in view of men who had despised her in life. Nixon looked up and saw Bosch in the hallway and stepped out of the room.

"Harry, what made you tumble to her?"

"She didn't show up for court today. Thought it was worth checking out. Guess she was the blonde. Too bad I didn't see it right away."

"Yeah."

"Got a TOD yet?"

"Yeah, an estimate. Coroner's tech says time of death was at least forty-eight hours ago."

Bosch nodded. It meant she was dead before he even found the note. It made it a little easier.

"Hear anything on Locke?"

"Nada."

"You and Johnson on point on this one?"

"Yeah, Hans Off put us on it. Edgar discovered it but he's primary on last week's case. I know it was your tumble but I guess Hans Off figured with court and —"

"Don't worry about it. What do you need me to do?"

"You tell me. What do you want to do?"

"I want to stay out of there. I didn't like her but I liked her, you know what I mean?"

"I think so. Yeah, this one's bad. You notice he's changing? He's biting now. Burning."

"Yeah, I noticed. Anything else new?"

"Not that we can tell."

"I'm going to have a look around the rest of the house. Is it clean?"

"We haven't had time to dust. Just a quick look through. Use gloves and let me know what you find."

Bosch went to one of the equipment boxes lined along the wall in the hallway and pulled a pair of plastic gloves from a dispenser that looked like a Kleenex box.

Irving passed by him wordlessly on the staircase, their eyes barely holding each other's for a second. When he got down to the entry, he saw two deputy chiefs standing out on the front steps. They weren't doing anything, just standing where they would be sure to be seen on the TV footage looking serious and concerned. Bosch could see that a growing number of reporters and cameramen were gathering at the plastic line.

He looked around and found Chandler's home office in a small room off the living room. Two of the walls contained built-in shelves that were lined with books. The room had one window that looked out onto the commotion just beyond the front lawn. He pulled on the gloves and began looking through the drawers of the desk. He didn't find what he was looking for but he could tell the desk had been rifled by someone else. Things were scattered in the drawers, papers from files were outside of files. It wasn't as neat as Chandler had kept her things on the plaintiff's table.

He checked underneath the blotter. The note from the Follower wasn't there. There were two books on the desk, *Black's Law Dictionary* and the *California Penal Code*. He fanned the pages of both but there was no note. He leaned back in the leather desk chair and looked up at the two walls of books.

He figured it would take two hours to go through all the books and he still might not find the note. Then he noticed the cracked green spine of a book on the second-to-the-top shelf nearest the window. He recognized the book. It was the one Chandler had read from during closing arguments. *The Marble Faun*. He got up and pulled the book out of its slot.

The note was there, folded into the center of the book. So was the envelope it came in. And Bosch quickly learned he had guessed correctly about her. The note was a photocopy of the page dropped at the police station last Monday, the day of opening statements. What was different about this one was the envelope. It hadn't been dropped off. It had been mailed. The envelope was stamped and then canceled in Van Nuys on the Saturday before opening statements.

Bosch looked at the postmark and knew it would be impossible to try any kind of trace on it. There would also be numerous prints on it from the many postal employees who handled it. He decided the note would be of little evidentiary value.

He left the office, carrying the note and envelope by the corners with his gloved hands. He had to go upstairs to find a tech with plastic evidence bags to place them in. He looked through the doorway into the bedroom and saw the coroner's tech and two body movers spreading open a plastic bag on a gurney. The public display of Honey Chandler was about to end. Bosch stepped back so he did not have to watch. Edgar walked over after reading the note, which the tech was labeling.

"He sent the same note to her? How come?"

"Guess he wanted to make sure we didn't sit on the one he dropped off for us. If we did, he could count on her bringing it up."

"If she had the note all along, how come she wanted to subpoena ours? She could've just taken this one into court."

"I think maybe she thought she'd get more mileage out of ours. Making the police turn it over gave it more legitimacy in the eyes of the jury. If she had just presented her own, my lawyer could've gotten it shot down. I don't know. It's just a guess."

Edgar nodded.

"By the way," Bosch said, "how'd you get in when you got here?"

"Front door was unlocked. No scratches on the lock or other signs of break-in."

"The Follower came here and was let in. . . . She wasn't lured to him. Something's going on. He's changing. He's biting and burning. He's making mistakes. He's letting something get to him. Why'd he go for her, rather than stick to his pattern of ordering victims from the sex tabs?"

"Too bad Locke's the fucking suspect. It'd be nice to ask him what all this means."

"Detective Harry Bosch!" a voice called from downstairs. "Harry Bosch!"

Bosch walked to the top of the stairs and looked down. A young patrolman, the one who was keeping the scene attendance log at the tape, stood in the entry area looking up.

"Guy at the tape wants to come in. Said he's a shrink who's been working with you."

Bosch looked over at Edgar. Their eyes locked. He looked back down at the patrolman.

"What's his name?"

The patrolman looked down at his clipboard and read off, "John Locke, from USC."

"Send him in."

Bosch started down the stairs and beckoned to Edgar with his hand. He said, "I'm taking him into her office. Tell Hans Off and then come down."

Bosch told Locke to sit in the chair behind the desk while he chose to stay standing. Through the window behind the psychologist, Bosch saw the press gathering into a tight group in preparation for a briefing by someone from media relations.

"Don't touch anything," Bosch said. "What're you doing here?"

"I came as soon as I heard," Locke said. "But I thought you said you had the suspect under surveillance."

"We did. It was the wrong guy. How did you hear?"

"It's all over the radio. I heard it while I was driving in and came right here. They didn't put out the exact address but once I got to Carmelina this wasn't hard to find. Just follow the helicopters."

Edgar slipped into the room then and closed the door.

"Detective Jerry Edgar, meet Dr. John Locke."

Edgar nodded but made no move to shake his hand. He stayed back, leaning against the door.

"Where've you been? We've been trying to find you since yesterday."

"Vegas."

"Vegas? Why'd you go to Vegas?"

"Why else, to gamble. I'm also thinking about a book project on the legal prostitutes that work in the towns north of — look, aren't we wasting time here? I'd like to view the body in situ. Then I could give you a read on it."

"Body's already moved, Doc," Edgar said.

"It is? Shit. Maybe I could survey the scene and —"

"We've already got too many people up there right now," Bosch said. "Maybe later. What do you make of bite marks? Cigarette burns?"

"Are you saying that's what you've found this time?"

"Plus, it wasn't a bimbo from the sex tabs," Edgar added. "He came here, she didn't come to him."

"He is changing quickly. It appears to be complete disassembling. Or some unknown force or reason compelling his actions."

"Such as?" Bosch asked.

"I don't know."

"We tried to call you in Vegas. You never checked in."

"Oh, the Stardust? Well, coming in I saw the new MGM had just opened and decided to see if they had a room. They did. I was there."

"Anyone with you?" Bosch asked.

"The whole time?" Edgar added.

A puzzled look came over Locke's face.

"What is going —"

He understood now. He shook his head.

"Harry, are you kidding?"

"No. Are you, coming here like this?"

"I think you —"

"No, don't answer that. Tell you what, it would probably be best for all of us if you know your rights before we go any further. Jerry, you got a card?"

Edgar pulled out his wallet and from it took a white plastic card with the Miranda warning printed on it. He started reading it to Locke. Both Bosch and Edgar knew the warning by heart but a departmental memo that was distributed with the plastic card said it was best practice to read directly from a card. This made it difficult for a defense attorney to later attack in court how the police administered the rights warning to a client.

As Edgar read the card, Bosch looked out the window at the huge clot of reporters standing around one of the deputy chiefs. He saw that Bremmer was there now. But the deputy chief's words must not have meant much; the reporter was not writing anything down. He was just standing to the side of the pack and smoking. He was probably waiting for the real info from the real guns, Irving and Rollenberger.

"Am I under arrest?" Locke asked when Edgar was done.

"Not yet," said Edgar.

"We just need to clear some things up," Bosch said.

"I resent the hell out of this."

"I understand. Now, do you want to clear this trip to Vegas up? Was there anyone with you?"

"From six o'clock Friday until I got out of my car down the block ten minutes ago, there has been a person with me every minute of every day except when I was in the bathroom. This is ridic —"

"And that is who, this person?"

"It's a friend of mine. Her name is Melissa Mencken."

Bosch remembered the young woman named Melissa who was in Locke's front office.

"The child-psych major? From your office? The blonde?"

"That's right," Locke answered reluctantly.

"And she will tell us you were together the whole time? Same room, same hotel, same everything, right?"

"Yes. She'll confirm it all. We were just coming back when we heard about this on the radio. KFWB. She's out there waiting for me in the car. Go talk to her."

"What kind of car?"

"It's the blue Jag. Look, Harry, you go talk to her and clear this up. If you don't make noise about me being with a student, I won't make a sound about this . . . this interrogation."

"This is no interrogation, Doctor. Believe me, if we interrogate you, you'll know it."

He nodded to Edgar, who slipped out the door to go find the Jag. When they were alone, Bosch pulled a high-backed chair away from the wall and sat down in front of the desk to wait.

"What happened to the suspect you were following, Harry?"

"We did."

"What's that supposed to —"

"Never mind."

They sat in silence for nearly five minutes until Edgar stuck his head in the door and signaled Bosch to come out.

"Checks out, Harry. I talked to the girl and her story is the same. There also were credit card receipts in the car. They checked into the MGM Saturday at three. There was a gas receipt in Victorville, had the time on it. Nine o'clock in the morning Saturday. Victorville's what, an hour away. Looks like they were on the road when Chandler got it. Besides, the girl says they also spent Friday night together at his house in the hills. We can do some more checking but I think he's being legit with us."

"Well . . . ," Bosch said, not completing the thought. "Why don't you go up and spread the word that he looks clear. I want to take him up to look around, if he still wants to."

"Will do."

Bosch went back into the study. He sat in the chair that was in front of the desk. Locke studied him.

"Well?"

"She's too scared, Locke. She isn't going along. She's telling us the truth."

"What the fuck are you talking about?" Locke yelled.

Now Bosch studied him. The surprise on his face, the utter fright, was too genuine. Bosch was sure now. He was sorry, yet felt some perverse feeling of power, having run Locke through the scam.

"You're clear, Dr. Locke. Just had to be sure. I guess the criminal only comes back to the scene of the crime in movies."

Locke took a deep breath and looked down into his lap. Bosch thought he looked like a driver who had just pulled to the side of the road to collect himself after missing a head-on collision with a truck by a matter of inches.

"Goddammit, Bosch, for a minute there, I had bad dreams, you know?"

Bosch nodded. He knew about bad dreams.

"Edgar's going up to smooth the way. He's going to ask the lieutenant if you can go up and give a read on the scene. If you still want to."

"Excellent," he said, but there wasn't much excitement left in him.

They sat in silence after that. Bosch took out his cigarettes and found the pack empty. But he put the pack back in his pocket so as not to leave false evidence in the trash can.

He didn't feel like talking to Locke anymore. Instead, he looked past him and out the window at the activity on the street. The media pack had dispersed after the briefing. Now some of the TV reporters were taping their reports with the "death house" behind them. Bosch could see Bremmer interviewing the neighbors across the street and writing feverishly in his notebook.

Edgar came in then and said, "We're ready for him upstairs."

Staring out the window, Bosch said, "Jerry, can you take him up? I just thought of something I need to do."

Locke stood up and looked at the two detectives.

"Fuck you," he said. "Both of you. Fuck you. . . . There, I just had to say that. Now, let's forget about it and go to work."

He crossed the room to Edgar. Bosch stopped him at the door.

"Dr. Locke?"

He turned back to Bosch.

"When we catch this guy, he'll want to gloat, won't he?"

Locke thought for a while and said, "Yes, he'll be very pleased with himself, his accomplishments. That might be the hardest part for him, keeping quiet when he knows he should. He'll want to gloat."

They left then and Bosch looked out the window for a few more minutes before getting up.

Some of the reporters who knew who he was pressed against the yellow tape and began shouting questions as he came out. He ducked under the tape and said he could make no comment and that Chief Irving was coming out soon. That seemed to mollify them temporarily and he started walking down the street to his car.

He knew Bremmer was the master of the anti-pack. He always let the pack move in and do their thing, then he came in after, by himself, to get what he wanted. Bosch wasn't mistaken. Bremmer showed up at the car.

"Pullin' out already, Harry?"

"No, I just need to get something."

"Pretty bad in there?"

"Is this on or off the record?"

"Whatever you like."

Bosch opened the car door.

"Off the record, yes, it's pretty bad in there. On the record, no comment."

He leaned in and made a show of looking in the glove compartment and not finding what he wanted.

"What are you guys calling this one? I mean, you know, since the Dollmaker was already taken."

Bosch got back out.

"The Follower. That's off the record, too. Ask Irving."

"Catchy."

"Yeah, I thought you reporters would like that."

Bosch pulled the empty cigarette pack out of his pocket, crumpled it and threw it into the car and closed the door.

"Give me a smoke, will you?"

"Sure."

Bremmer pulled a soft pack of Marlboros out of his sport coat and shook one out for Bosch. Then he lit it for him with a Zippo. With his left hand.

"Hell of a city we live in, Harry, isn't it."
"Yeah. This city . . ."

31

At 7:30 that night, Bosch was sitting in the Caprice in the back parking lot of St. Vibiana's in downtown. From his angle, he could look a half block up Second Street to the corner at Spring. But he couldn't see the *Times* building. That didn't matter, though. He knew that every *Times* employee without parking privileges in the executive garage would have to cross the corner of Spring and Second to get to one of the employee garages a half block down Spring. He was waiting for Bremmer.

After leaving the scene at Honey Chandler's house, Bosch had gone home and slept for two hours. Then he had paced in his house on the hill, thinking about Bremmer and seeing how perfectly he fit the mold. He called Locke and asked a few more general questions about the psychology of the Follower. But he did not tell Locke about Bremmer. He told no one about this, thinking three strikes and you're out. He came up with a plan, then dropped by Hollywood Division to gas up the Caprice and get the equipment he would need.

And now he waited. He watched a steady procession of homeless people walking down Second. As if heeding a siren's call, they were heading toward the Los Angeles Mission a few blocks away for a meal and a bed. Many carried with them or pushed in shopping carts their life's belongings.

Bosch never took his eyes off the corner but his mind drifted far from there. He thought of Sylvia and wondered what she was doing at that moment and what she was thinking. He hoped she didn't take too long to decide, because he knew his mind's instinctual protective devices and responses had begun to react. He was already looking at the positives that would come if she didn't come back. He told himself she made him weak. Hadn't he thought of her immediately when he found the note from the Follower? Yes, she had made him vulnerable. He told himself she might not be good for his life's mission, let her go.

His heartbeat jacked up a notch when he saw Bremmer step onto the corner and then walk in the direction of the parking garages. A building blocked Bosch's view after that. He quickly started the car and pulled out onto Second and up to Spring.

Down the block Bremmer entered the newer garage with a card key and Bosch watched the auto door and waited. In five minutes a blue Toyota Celica came out of the garage and slowed while the driver checked for traffic on Spring. Bosch could see clearly it was Bremmer. The Celica pulled onto Spring and so did Bosch.

Bremmer headed west on Beverly and into Hollywood. He made one stop at a Vons and came out fifteen minutes later with a single bag of groceries. He then proceeded to a neighborhood of single-family homes just north of the Paramount studio. He drove down the side of a small stuccoed house and parked in the detached garage in the back. Bosch pulled to the curb one house away and waited.

All the houses in the neighborhood were one of three basic designs. It was one of the cookie-cutter victory neighborhoods that had sprung up after World War II in the city, with affordable homes for returning servicemen. Now you'd probably need to be making a general's pay to buy in. The '80s did that. The occupation army of yuppies had the place now.

Each lawn had a little tin sign planted in it. They were from three or four different home-security companies but they all said the same thing. ARMED RESPONSE. It was the epitaph of the city. Sometimes Bosch thought the Hollywood sign should be taken down off the hill and replaced with those two words.

Bosch waited for Bremmer to either come around to the front to check his mail or to put lights on inside the house. When neither happened after five minutes, he got out and approached the driveway, his hand unconsciously tapping his sport coat on the side, making sure he had his Smith & Wesson. It was there, but he kept it holstered.

The driveway was unlit and in the recessed darkness of the open garage Bosch could only see the faint reflection of the red lenses of the taillights of Bremmer's car. But there was no sign of Bremmer.

A six-foot wooden-plank fence ran along the right side of the drive, separating Bremmer's property from his neighbor's. Branches of bougainvillea in bloom hung over and Bosch could hear faint television sounds from the house next door.

As he walked between the fence and Bremmer's house toward the garage, Bosch knew he was completely vulnerable. But he also knew that drawing his weapon couldn't help him here. Favoring the side of the drive nearest the house, he walked to the garage and stopped before its darkness. Standing beneath an old basketball goal with a bent rim, he said, "Bremmer?"

There was no sound save for the ticking of the engine of the car in the garage. Then, from behind, Bosch heard the light scraping of a shoe on concrete. He turned. Bremmer stood there, grocery bag in hand.

"What are you doing?" Bosch asked.

"That's what I should ask."

Bosch watched his hands as he spoke.

"You never called. So I came by."

"Called about what?"

"You wanted a comment about the verdict."

"You were supposed to call me. Remember? Doesn't matter, the story's been put to bed now. Besides, the verdict kind of took a back seat to the other developments of the day, if you know what I mean. The story on the Follower — and Irving did use that name on the record — is going out front."

Bosch took a few steps toward him.

"Then how come you're not at the Red Wind? I thought you said you always go for a pop when you hit the front page."

Holding the bag in his right arm, Bremmer reached into the pocket of his coat but Bosch heard the sound of keys.

"I didn't feel like it tonight. I kind've liked Honey Chandler, you know? What are you really doing here, Harry? I saw you following me."

"You going to ask me in? Maybe we can have that beer, toast your front-page story. One-A is what you reporters call it, right?"

"Yeah. This one's going above the fold."

"Above the fold, I like that."

They stared at each other in the darkness.

"Whaddaya say? About the beer."

"Sure," Bremmer said. He turned and went to the house's back door and unlocked it. He reached in and hit switches that turned on lights over the door and in the kitchen beyond. Then he stepped back and held out his arm for Bosch to go in first.

"After you. Go into the living room and have a seat. I'll get a couple bottles and be right there."

Bosch walked through the kitchen and down a short hall to the living room and dining room. He didn't sit down but rather stood near the curtain drawn across one of the front windows. He parted it and looked into the street and at the houses across. There was no one. No one had seen him come here. He wondered if he had made a mistake.

He looked down at the old-style radiator beneath the window, touched it with his hand. It was cold. Its iron coils had been painted black.

He stood there for a few more moments and then turned and looked around at the rest of the room. It was nicely furnished with blacks and grays. Bosch sat on a black leather couch. He knew if he arrested Bremmer in the house, he would be able to make a quick cursory search of the premises. If he found anything of an incriminating nature all he had to do was come back with a warrant. Bremmer, being a police and courts reporter, would know that, too. Why'd he let me in? Bosch wondered. Have I made a mistake? He began to lose confidence in his plan.

Bremmer brought out two bottles, no glasses, and sat in a matching chair to Bosch's right. Bosch studied his bottle for a long moment. There was a bubble pushing up from the top. It burst and he held the bottle up and said, "Above the fold."

"Above the fold," Bremmer toasted back. He didn't smile. He took a pull from his bottle and put it down on the coffee table.

Bosch took a large gulp from his bottle and held it in his mouth. It was ice cold and hurt some of his teeth. There was no known history of the Doll-maker or the Follower using drugs on their victims. He looked at Bremmer, their eyes locked for a moment, and he swallowed. It felt good going down.

Leaning forward, elbows on his knees, he held the bottle in his right hand and looked at Bremmer looking back at him. He knew from talking with Locke that the Follower would not be driven by conscience to admit anything. He had no conscience. The only way was trickery, to play on the killer's pride. He felt his confidence coming back. He stared at Bremmer with a glare that burned right through him.

"What is it?" the reporter asked quietly.

"Tell me you did it for the stories, or the book. To get above the fold, to have a bestseller, whatever. But don't tell me you're the sick fuck the shrink says you are."

"What are you talking about?"

"Skip the bullshit, Bremmer. It's you and you know I know it's you. Why else would I waste my time being here?"

"The Dol — the Follower? You're saying I'm the Follower? Are you crazy?"

"Are you? That's what I want to know."

Bremmer was silent for a long time. He seemed to retreat into himself, like a computer running a long equation, the Please Wait sign flashing. The answer finally registered and his eyes focused again on Bosch.

"I think you should go, Harry." He stood up. "It's very plain to see you've been under a lot of pressure with this case and I think —"

"You're the one coming apart, Bremmer. You've made mistakes. A lot of them."

Bremmer suddenly dove into Bosch, rolling so that his left shoulder slammed into Bosch's chest, pinning him to the couch. Bosch felt air burst from his lungs and sat helplessly as Bremmer worked his hands under Harry's sport coat and got to the gun. Bremmer then pulled away, switching off the safety and pointing the weapon at Bosch's face.

After nearly a minute of silence during which both men simply stared at each other, Bremmer said, "I admit only one thing: You have me intrigued, Harry. But before we go any further with this discussion, there is something I have to do."

A sense of relief and anticipation flooded Bosch's body. He tried not to show it. Instead he tried to put a look of terror on his face. He stared wide-eyed at the gun. Bremmer bent over him and ran his heavy hand down Bosch's chest and into his crotch, then around his sides. He found no wire.

"Sorry to get so personal," he said. "But you don't trust me and I don't trust you, right?"

Bremmer straightened and stepped back and sat down.

"Now, I don't need to remind you, but I will. I have the advantage here. So answer my questions. What mistakes? What mistakes have I made? Tell me what I did wrong, Harry, or I'll kneecap you with the first bullet."

Bosch tantalized him with silence for a few moments as he thought about how to proceed.

"Well," he finally began. "Let's go back to the basics first. Four years ago you were all over the Dollmaker case. As a reporter. From the start. It was your stories about the early cases that made the department form the task force. As a reporter you had access to the suspect intelligence, you probably had the autopsy reports. You also had sources like me and probably half the dicks on the task force and in the coroner's office. What I am saying is you knew what the Dollmaker did. Right down to the cross on the toenail, you knew. Later, after the Dollmaker was dead, you used it in your book."

"Yeah, I knew. It means nothing, Bosch. A lot of people knew."

"Oh, it's Bosch now. No more Harry? Have I suddenly become contemptible in your eyes? Or does the gun give you that sense that we are no longer equals?"

"Fuck you, Bosch. You're stupid. You've got nothing. What else you got? You know, this is great. It will definitely be worth a chapter in the book I do on the Follower."

"What else've I got? I've got the concrete blonde. And I've got the concrete. Did you know you dropped your cigarettes when you were pouring the concrete? Remember that? You were driving home, wanted a smoke and you reached into your pocket and there was nothing there.

"See, just like Becky Kaminski, they were in there waiting for us. Marlboro soft pack. That's your brand, Bremmer. That's mistake number one."

"A lot of people smoke them. Good luck taking this to the DA."

"A lot of people are left-handed, too, like you and the Follower. And me. But there's more. You want to hear it?"

Bremmer looked away from him, toward the window, and said nothing. Maybe it was a trick, Bosch thought, that he wanted Bosch to go for the gun.

"Hey, Bremmer!" he almost yelled. "There's more."

Bremmer's face snapped back into a stare at Bosch.

"Today after the verdict you said I should be happy because the verdict would leave the city only two bucks light. But when we had a drink the other night, remember, you gave me the big rundown on how Chandler would be able to charge the city a hundred grand or so if she won even a dollar judgment from the jury. Remember? So it makes me think that when you told me this morning the verdict was only going to cost two dollars, you knew it was only going to cost two dollars because you knew Chandler was dead and couldn't collect. You knew that because you killed her. Mistake number two."

Bremmer shook his head as if he were dealing with a child. His aim with the gun drooped to Bosch's midsection.

"Look, man, I was trying to make you feel good when I said that today, okay? I didn't know if she was alive or dead. No jury is going to make that leap of faith."

Bosch smiled brilliantly at him.

"So now at least you have me past the DA's office and to a jury. I guess my story is improving, isn't it?"

Bremmer coldly smiled back, raised the gun.

"Is that it, Bosch? Is that all you have?"

"I saved the best stuff for last."

He lit a cigarette, never taking his eyes off Bremmer.

"You remember before you killed Chandler, how you tortured her? You must remember that. You bit her. And burned her. Well, everyone was standing around in that house today wondering why the Follower was changing, doing all this new stuff — changing the mold. Locke, the shrink, he was the most puzzled of all. You really fucked with his mind, man. I kinda like that about you, Bremmer. But, you see, he didn't know what I knew."

He let that sit out there for a while. He knew Bremmer would bite.

"And what did you know, Sherlock?"

Bosch smiled. He was in complete control now.

"I knew why you did that to her. It was simple. You wanted your note back, didn't you? But she wouldn't tell you where it was. See, she knew she was dead whether she gave it to you or not, so she took it — everything you did to her, she took — and she didn't tell you. That woman had a lot of guts and in the end she beat you, Bremmer. She's the one who got you. Not me."

"What note?" Bremmer said weakly after a long moment.

"The one you fucked up with. You missed it. It's a big house to search, especially when you've got a dead woman lying in the bed. That'd be hard to explain if somebody happened to drop by. But don't worry, I found it. I've got it. Too bad you don't read Hawthorne. It was sitting there in his book. Too bad. But like I said, she beat you. Maybe there is justice sometimes."

Bremmer had no snappy comeback. Bosch looked at him and thought that he was doing well. He was almost there.

"She kept the envelope, too, in case you were wondering. I found that, too. And so I started wondering, why would he torture her for this note when it was the same one he dropped off for me? It was just a photocopy. Then I figured it out. You didn't want the note. You wanted the envelope."

Bremmer looked down at his hands.

"How am I doing? Am I losing you?"

"I have no idea," Bremmer said, looking back up. "You're fucking delirious as far as I'm concerned."

"Well, I only have to worry about making sense to the DA, don't I? And what I'm going to explain to him is that the poem on the note was in response to the story you wrote that appeared in the paper on Monday, the day the trial started. But the postmark on the envelope was the Saturday before. See, there's the puzzle. How would the Follower know to write a poem making reference to the newspaper article two days before it was in the newspaper? The answer is, of course, that he, the Follower, had prior knowledge of the article. He wrote that article. That also explains how you knew about the note in the next day's story. You were your own source, Bremmer. And that is mistake number three. Three strikes and you're out."

The silence that followed was so complete that Bosch could hear the low hiss coming from Bremmer's bottle of beer.

"You're forgetting something, Bosch," Bremmer finally said. "I'm holding the gun. Now, who else have you told this crazy story to?"

"Just to finish the housekeeping," Bosch said, "the new poem you dropped off for me this past weekend was just a front. You wanted the shrink and everybody else to make it look like you killed Chandler as a favor to me or some psycho bullshit, right?"

Bremmer said nothing.

"That way nobody would see the true reason you went after her. To get the note and the envelope back. . . . Shit, you being a reporter she was familiar with, she probably invited you in when you knocked on her door. Kind of like you inviting me in here. Familiarity breeds danger, Bremmer."

Bremmer said nothing.

"Answer a question for me, Bremmer. I'm curious why you dropped one note off and mailed the other. I know, being a reporter, you could blend in at the station, drop it on the desk and nobody would remember. But why mail it to her? Obviously, it was a mistake — that's why you went back and killed her. But why'd you make it?"

The reporter looked at Bosch for a long moment. Then he glanced down at the gun as if to reassure himself that he was in control and would get out of this. The gun was powerful bait. Bosch knew he had him.

"The story was supposed to run that Saturday, that's what it was scheduled for. But some dumb-ass editor held it, ran it Monday. I had mailed the letter before I looked at the paper that Saturday. That was my only mistake. But you're the one who made the big mistake."

"Oh, yeah? What's that?"

"Coming here alone . . ."

Now it was Bosch who was silent.

"Why come here alone, Bosch? Is this how you did it with the Dollmaker? You went alone so you could kill him in cold blood?"

Bosch thought a moment.

"That's a good question."

"Well, that was your second mistake. Thinking I was as unworthy an opponent as him. He was nothing. You killed him and therefore he deserved to die. But now it is you who deserve to die."

"Give me the gun, Bremmer."

He laughed as if Bosch had asked a crazy question.

"You think —"

"How many were there? How many women are buried out there?"

Bremmer's eyes lit with pride.

"Enough. Enough to fulfill my special needs."

"How many? Where are they?"

"You'll never know, Bosch. That will be your pain, your last pain. Never knowing. And losing."

Bremmer raised the gun so that its muzzle pointed to Bosch's heart. He pulled the trigger.

Bosch watched his eyes as the metallic click sounded. Bremmer pulled the trigger again and again. The same result, the growing terror in his eyes.

Bosch reached into his sock and pulled the extra clip, the one that was loaded with fifteen XTP bullets. He wrapped his fist around the cartridge and in one swift motion came off the couch and swung his fist into Bremmer's jaw. The impact of the blow knocked the reporter backward in his chair. His weight made the chair crash backward and he spilled to the floor. He dropped the Smith and Bosch quickly gathered it up, ejected the empty clip and put in the live ammunition.

"Get up! Get the fuck up!"

Bremmer did as he was told.

"Are you going to kill me now? Is that it, another kill for the gunslinger?"

"That's up to you, Bremmer."

"What are you talking about?"

"I'm talking about how I want to blow your head off, but for me to do that you have to make the first move, Bremmer. Just like with the Dollmaker. It was his play. Now it's yours."

"Look, Bosch, I don't want to die. Everything I said — I was just playing a game. You're making a mistake here. I just want to get it cleared up. Please, just take me to county and it will all get cleared up. Please."

"Did they plead like that when you had the strap around their necks? Did they? Did you make them plead for their lives, or for their deaths? What about Chandler? At the end, did she beg you to kill her?"

"Take me to county. Arrest me and take me to county."

"Then get against that wall, you fat fuck, and put your hands behind your back."

Bremmer obeyed. Bosch dropped his cigarette into an ashtray on the table and followed Bremmer to the wall. When he closed the handcuffs over the reporter's wrists, Bremmer's shoulders dropped as he apparently felt safe. He started squirming his arms, chafing his wrists on the cuffs.

"See that?" he said. "You see that, Bosch? I'm making marks on my wrists. You kill me now, they'll see the marks and know it was an execution. I'm not some dumb fuck like Church that you can slaughter like an animal."

"No, that's right, you know all the angles, don't you?"

"All of them. Now take me down to county. I'll be out before you wake up tomorrow. Know what all this is, what you've got? Just the wild speculation of a rogue cop. Even a federal jury agreed you go too far, Bosch. This won't work. You've got no evidence."

Bosch turned him away from the wall so that their faces were no more than two feet apart, their beer breath mixing.

"You did it, didn't you? And you think you're going to walk, don't you?"

Bremmer stared at him and Bosch saw the gleam of pride in his eyes again. Locke had been right about him. He was gloating. And he couldn't shut up even though he knew his life might depend on it.

"Yes," he said in a low, strange voice. "I did it. I'm the man. And, yes, I will walk. You wait and see. And when I'm out there you'll think of me every night for the rest of your life."

Bosch nodded.

"But I never said that, Bosch. It will be your word against mine. A rogue cop — it will never get to court. They couldn't afford to put you on the stand against me."

Bosch leaned closer to him and smiled.

"Then I suppose it's a good thing I taped it."

Bosch walked over to the radiator and pulled the microrecorder from between two of the iron coils. He held it up on his palm for Bremmer to see. Bremmer's eyes became enraged. He had been tricked. He had been cheated.

"Bosch, that tape is inadmissible. That's entrapment. I have not been advised. I have not been advised!"

"I'm advising you of your rights now. You weren't under arrest until now. I wasn't going to advise you until I arrested you. You know police procedure."

Bosch was smiling at him, digging it in.

"Let's go, Bremmer," he said when he got tired of the victory.

32

≈≈≈

It was an irony that Bosch savored Tuesday morning when he read Bremmer's above-the-fold story on the killing of Honey Chandler. He had booked the reporter into county jail on a no-bail hold shortly before midnight and had not alerted media relations. The word had not gotten out by the last deadline and now the paper had a front-page story about a murder that was written by the murderer. Bosch liked that. He smiled as he read it.

The one person Bosch had told was Irving. He had the com center patch him through on a phone line and in a half-hour-long conversation he told the assistant chief every step he had taken and described every building block of evidence that led to the arrest. Irving said nothing congratulatory, nor did he chastise Bosch for making the arrest alone. Either or both would come later, after it was seen whether the arrest would stick. Both men knew this.

At 9 A.M. Bosch was seated in front of a filing deputy's desk at the district attorney's office in the downtown criminal courts building. For the second time in eight hours he carefully went over the details of what happened and then played the tape of his conversation with Bremmer. The deputy DA, whose name was Chap Newell, made notations on a yellow pad while listening to the tape. He often furrowed his brow or shook his head because the sound was not good. The voices in Bremmer's living room had bounced through the iron radiator coils and had a tinny echo on the tape. Still, the words that were most important were audible.

Bosch just watched without saying a word. Newell looked as if he could be no more than three years out of law school. Because the arrest had not made a splash in the papers or on TV yet, it had not received the attention of one of the senior attorneys in the filings division. It had gone to Newell on the routine rotation.

When the tape was done, Newell made a few more notes to look as if he knew what he was doing and then looked up at Bosch.

"You haven't said anything about what was in his house."

"I didn't find anything on the quick search I made last night. There are others there now, with a warrant, doing a more thorough job."

"Well, I hope they find something."

"Why, you've got the case right there."

"And it is a good case, Bosch. Really good work."

"Coming from you, that means a lot."

Newell looked at him and narrowed his eyes. He wasn't sure what to make of that.

"But, uh . . ."

"But what?"

"Well, there's no question we can file with this. There is a lot here."

"But what?"

"I'm looking at it from a defense lawyer's perspective. What really do we have here? A lot of coincidences. He's left-handed, he smokes, he knew details about the Dollmaker. But those things are not hard evidence. They can apply to a lot of people."

Bosch started lighting a cigarette.

"Please don't do —"

He exhaled and blew the smoke across the desk.

"— never mind."

"What about the note and the postmark?"

"That's good but it is complicated and difficult to grasp. A good lawyer could make a jury see it as just another coincidence. He could confuse the issue, is what I'm trying to say."

"What about the tape, Newell? We have him confessing on tape. What more do you —"

"But during the confession he disavows the confession."

"Not at the end."

"Look, I'm not planning on using the tape."

"What are you talking about?"

"You know what I'm talking about. He confessed before you advised him. It brings up the specter of entrapment."

"There is no entrapment. He knew I was a cop and he knew his rights whether I advised him or not. He had a fucking gun on *me*. He freely made those statements. When he was formally arrested, I advised him."

"But he searched you for a wire. That is a clear indication of his desire not to be taped. Plus, he dropped the bomb — his most damaging statement — after you cuffed him but before you advised him. That could be dicey."

"You're going to use the tape."

Newell looked at him a long time. A red blotchiness appeared on his young cheeks.

"You are not in a position to tell me what I'm going to use, Bosch. Besides, if that's all we go with it will probably be up to the state court of appeals if we use it, because if Bremmer has any kind of a lawyer at all that's where he'll take it. We'll win the question here in superior because half the judges on those benches worked in the DA's office at one time or another. But when it gets up to appeals or to the state supreme court in San Francisco, it's anybody's guess. Is that what you want? To wait a couple years and have it blown out then? Or do you want to get it done correctly right from the get go?"

Bosch leaned forward and looked angrily at the young lawyer.

"Look, we're still working other angles. We're not done. There will be more evidence accumulated. But we have to charge this guy or let him go. We've got forty-eight hours from last night to file. But if we don't file right now with no bail, he'll grab a lawyer and get a bail hearing. The judge won't honor the no-bail arrest if you haven't even filed a single charge yet. So file on him now. We'll get all the evidence you need to back it up."

Newell nodded as if he agreed but said, "Thing is, I like to have the whole package, everything we can get, when I file a case. That way we know how we are going to work the prosecution, right from the start. We know if we are going to go with a plea bargain or go balls to the wall."

Bosch got up and walked to the office's open door. He stepped into the hall and looked at the plastic name plate affixed to the wall outside. Then he came back in.

"Bosch, what are you doing?"

"It's funny. I thought you were a filing deputy. I didn't know you were a trial deputy, too."

Newell dropped his pencil on his pad. His face got redder, the blotches spreading to his forehead.

"Look, I am a filing deputy. But it is part of my responsibility to make sure we have the best case possible from the get go. Every case that comes through that door I could file on, but that's not the point. The point is to have good, credible evidence and a lot of it. Cases that don't backfire. So I push, Bosch. I —"

"How old are you?"

"What?"

"How old?"

"Twenty-six. What's that got to —"

"Listen to me, you little prick. Don't you ever call me by my last name again. I was making cases like this before you cracked your first law book and I'll be making them long after you move your convertible Saab and your self-centered white-bread show to Century City. You can call me Detective or Detective Bosch, you can even call me Harry. But don't you ever call me just Bosch again, understand?"

Newell's mouth had dropped open.

"Do you understand?"

"Sure."

"Another thing, we're going to get more evidence and we're going to get it as soon as we can. But, in the meantime, you're going to file one charge of first-degree murder on Bremmer with a no-bail hold because we are going to make sure — from the get go, Mr. Newell — that this scumbag never sees the light of day again.

"Then, when we have more evidence, if you are still attached to this case, you will file multiple counts under theories of linkage between the deaths. At no time will you worry about the so-called package you will hand off to the trial attorney. The trial attorney will make those decisions. Because we both know that you are really just a clerk, a clerk who files what is brought to him. If you knew enough to even sit in court next to a trial attorney you would not be here. Do you have any questions?"

"No," he said quickly.

"No, what?"

"No ques — No, Detective Bosch."

Bosch went back to Irving's conference room and used the rest of the morning to work up an application for a search warrant to collect hair, blood and saliva specimens along with a dental mold from Bremmer.

Before taking it to the courthouse, he attended a brief meeting of the task force where they all reported on their respective assignments.

Edgar said he had been to Sybil Brand and had shown Georgia Stern, who was still being held there, a photo of Bremmer but she could not identify him as her attacker. She could not rule him out, either.

Sheehan said he and Opelt had shown the mug shot of Bremmer to the manager of the storage facility at Bing's and the man said Bremmer might have been one of the renters of the storage rooms two years earlier but he couldn't be sure. He said it was too long ago to remember well enough to send a man to the gas chamber.

"The guy's a wimp," Sheehan said. "My feeling was he recognized Bremmer but was too scared to stick it in all the way. We're going to hit him again tomorrow."

Rollenberger called the presidents up on the rover and they reported from Bremmer's house that there was nothing yet. No tapes, no bodies, nothing.

"I say we go for a warrant to dig up the yard, under the foundation," Nixon said.

"We might go to that," Rollenberger radioed back. "Meantime, keep at it."

Lastly, Yde reported by rover that he and Mayfield were getting the runaround from the *Times* lawyers and had not yet been able to so much as approach Bremmer's desk in the newsroom.

Rollenberger reported that Heikes and Rector were out of pocket, running down background on Bremmer. After that, he said that Irving had scheduled a five o'clock press conference to discuss the case with the media. If anything new was discovered, let Rollenberger know before then.

"That's it," Rollenberger said.

Bosch got up to head out.

The medical clinic on the high-power floor of the county jail reminded Bosch of Frankenstein's laboratory. There were chains on every bed and rings bolted to the tile walls to tether patients to. The pull-down lights over each bed were caged in steel so patients couldn't get to the light bulbs and use them as weapons. The tile was supposed to be white but over the years had surrendered to a depressing off-yellow.

Bosch and Edgar stood in the doorway to one of the bays where there were six beds and watched as Bremmer, who was lying in the sixth bed, was given a shot of sodium pentothal to make him more cooperative, more malleable. He had refused to give the court-ordered dental mold and samples of blood, saliva and hair.

After the drug began to take effect, the doctor pulled open the reporter's mouth, put two clamps in to hold it open and pushed a little square block of clay over the front upper teeth. He then followed the same procedure with the lower front teeth. When he was done, he relaxed the clamps and Bremmer appeared to be asleep.

"If we asked him something now, he'd tell the truth, right?" Edgar asked. "That's truth serum they're givin' him, right?"

"Supposedly," Bosch said. "But it'd prob'ly get the case thrown out of court."

The little gray blocks with teeth indentations were slid into plastic cases. The doctor closed them and handed them to Edgar. He then drew blood, wiped a cotton swab in Bremmer's mouth and cut snippets of hair from the suspect's head, chest and pubic area. He put these in envelopes which went into a small cardboard box like the kind chicken nuggets come in at fast-food restaurants.

Bosch took the box and they left then, Bosch going to the coroner's office to see Amado, the analyst, and Edgar going to Cal State Northridge to see the forensic archaeologist who had helped with the concrete blonde reconstruction.

By quarter to five, everyone was back in the conference room but Edgar. They were all milling about, waiting to watch Irving's press conference. There had been no other progress since noon.

"Where do you think he stashed everything, Harry?" Nixon asked as he was pouring coffee.

"I don't know. Probably has a storage locker somewhere. If he has tapes, I doubt he'd part with them. He probably has a drop somewhere. We'll find them."

"What about the other women?"

"They're out there somewhere, under the city. Only way they'll come up is by luck."

"Or if Bremmer talks," Irving said. He had just come in.

There was a good feeling in the room. Despite the day's slow progress, everyone to a man had no doubt they finally had the right man. And that certainty validated what they were about. So they wanted to drink coffee and hang out. Even Irving.

At five minutes before five, when Irving was going over some of the reports typed during the day for the last time before facing the media, Edgar came up on the rover. Rollenberger quickly picked up a radio and answered back.

"What do you have, Team Five?"

"Is Harry there?"

"Yes, Team Five, Team Six is present. What have you got?"

"I've got the package. Definite match between the suspect's teeth and the impressions on the victim."

"Roger that, Team Five."

There was a whoop in the conference room and a lot of backslapping and high fives. "He is going down," Nixon exclaimed.

Irving picked up his papers and headed for the hallway door. He wanted to be on time. At the doorway he passed close to Bosch.

"We're gold, Bosch. Thanks."

Bosch just nodded.

* * *

A few hours later Bosch was back at the county jail. It was after lock-down so the deputies wouldn't bring Bremmer out to see him. Instead, he had to go into the high-power module, the deputies watching him on remote cameras. He walked along the row of cells to 6–36 and looked through the wired one-foot-square window in the single-piece steel door.

Bremmer was on "keep away" status, so he was in there alone. He didn't notice Bosch watching. He lay on the bottom bunk on his back, his hands laced behind his head. His eyes were open and staring straight up. Bosch recognized the withdrawal state he had seen for a moment the night before. It was as if he wasn't there. Bosch leaned his mouth to the screen.

"Bremmer, you play bridge?"

Bremmer looked over at him, only moving his eyes.

"What?"

"I said, do you play bridge? You know, the card game?"

"What the fuck do you want, Bosch?"

"I just dropped by to tell you a little while ago they added three more to the one this morning. Linkage. You just got the concrete blonde and the two from before, the ones we first gave to the Dollmaker. You also got an attempted murder on the survivor."

"Oh, well, what's the difference? You got one, you got 'em all. All I need to do is beat the Chandler case and the others fall like dominoes."

"Except that isn't going to happen. We got your teeth, Bremmer, just as good as fingerprints. And we got the rest. I just came from the coroner's. They matched your pubic hair to samples found on victims seven and eleven — the ones we gave the Dollmaker credit for. You ought to think about dealing, Bremmer. Tell where the others are and they'll probably let you live. That's why I asked about bridge."

"What about it?"

"Well, I hear there's some guys up at Q play a good bridge game. They're always looking for new blood. You'll probably like 'em, have a lot in common."

"Why don't you leave me alone, Bosch?"

"I will. I will. But just so you know it, man, they're on death row. But don't worry about that, when you get there you'll get a lot of card playing in. What's the average lead time? Eight, ten years before they gas somebody? That's not bad. Unless, of course, you talk a deal."

"There is no deal, Bosch. Get out of here."

"I'm going. Believe me, it's nice to be able to walk out of this place. I'll see you then, okay? You know, in eight or ten years. I'm going to be there, Bremmer. When they strap you in. I'm going to be watching through the glass when the gas comes up. And then I'll come out and tell the reporters how you died. I'll tell them you went screaming, that you weren't much of a man."

"Fuck you, Bosch."

"Yeah, fuck me. See you then, Bremmer."

33

After Bremmer's arraignment Tuesday morning, Bosch got permission to take the rest of the week off in lieu of receiving all of the overtime he had built up on the case.

He spent the time hanging around the house, doing odd jobs and taking it easy. He replaced the wood railing on the back porch with new lengths of weather-treated oak. And while he was at Home Depot getting the wood, he also picked up new cushions for the chairs and the chaise lounge on the porch.

He began reading the *Times* sports pages again, noting the statistical changes in team ranks and player performances.

And, occasionally, he'd read one of the many stories the *Times* ran in the Metro section about what was becoming known nationwide as the Follower case. But it didn't really hold his fascination. He knew too much about the case already. The one interest he had in the stories was in the details about Bremmer that were coming out. The *Times* had sent a staffer to Texas, where Bremmer had been raised in an Austin suburb, and the reporter had returned with a story culled from old children's-court files and neighborhood gossip. He'd been raised by his mother in a single-parent home; his father, an itinerant blues musician, he saw once or twice a year at the most. The mother was described by former neighbors as a disciplinarian and plain mean-spirited when it came to her son.

The worst thing that the reporter came up with on Bremmer was that he was suspected but never charged in the arson of a neighbor's toolshed when he was thirteen. It was said by neighbors that his mother punished him as if he had committed the crime anyway, not allowing him to leave their tiny house the rest of the summer. The neighbors said that around the same time the neighborhood began to experience a problem with pets disappearing but this was never attributed to young Bremmer. At least until now. Now the neighbors seemed engaged in blaming Bremmer for any malady that beset their street that year.

A year after the fire Bremmer's mother died of alcoholism and the boy was raised after that on a state boys' farm, where the young charges wore white shirts and blue ties and blazers to classes, even when the thermometer went off the chart. The story said he worked as a reporter on one of the farm's student newspapers, thus beginning a journalism career that would eventually take him to Los Angeles.

His history was all grist for people like Locke to consider, to use as fuel for speculation on how the child Bremmer made the adult Bremmer do the things he did. It just made Bosch feel sad. He couldn't help, however, but stare for a long time at the photo of the mother the *Times* had dug up somewhere. In the picture she stood in front of the door to a sun-burned ranch-style house with her hand on a young Bremmer's shoulder. She had bleached-blonde hair and a provocative figure and large chest. She wore too much makeup, Bosch thought as he stared at the picture.

Aside from the Bremmer articles, the story he read and reread several times was in the Metro section of Thursday's paper. It was about the burial of Beatrice Fontenot. Sylvia was quoted in the article and it described how the Grant High teacher had read some of the girl's schoolwork at the memorial service. There was a photo from the service but Sylvia wasn't in it. It was of Beatrice's mother's stoic, tear-lined face at the funeral. Bosch kept the Metro page on the table next to the chaise lounge and read the story again every time he sat down there.

When he grew restless around the house he would drive. Down out of the hills, he'd head across the Valley with no place in particular to go. He'd drive forty minutes to have a hamburger at an In 'N' Out stand. Having grown up in the city, he liked to drive it, to know every one of its streets and corners. Once on Thursday and again on Friday morning his drives took him past Grant High but he never saw Sylvia through the windows of the classrooms as he went by. He felt sick at heart when he thought of her but he knew the closest he could come to her was to drive by the school. It was her move and he must wait for her to make it.

On Friday afternoon, when he came back from his drive, he saw the message light flashing on his phone machine and his hopes rushed into his throat. He thought maybe she had seen his car and was calling because she knew how his heart hurt. But when he played the message it was just Edgar asking him to call.

Eventually, he did.

"Harry, you're missing everything?"

"Yeah, what?"

"Well, we had *People* magazine in here yesterday."

"I'll watch for you on the cover."

"Just kidding. Actually, we've got big developments."

"Yeah, what?"

"All this publicity was bound to do us good. Some lady over in Culver City called up and said she recognized Bremmer, that he had a storage locker at her place, but under the name Woodward. We got a warrant and popped it first thing this morning."

"Yeah."

"Locke was right. He videotaped. We found the tapes. His trophies."

"Jesus."

"Yeah. If there was ever a doubt there ain't now. Got seven tapes and the camera. He must not have taped the first two, the ones we thought were the Dollmaker's. But we got tapes of seven others including Chandler and Maggie Cum Loudly. Bastard taped everything. Just horrible stuff. They're working up formal IDs on the other five victims on the tapes, but it looks like it's going to be the ones on the list Mora came up with. Gallery and the other four porno chicks."

"What else was in the locker?"

"Everything. We've got everything. We've got cuffs, belts, gags, a knife and a Glock nine. His whole killing kit. He must've used the gun to control them. That's why there was no sign of a struggle at Chandler's. He used the gun. We figure he'd hold it on them until he could cuff 'em and gag 'em. From the tapes, it looks like all the kills took place in Bremmer's house, the rear bedroom. Except Chandler, of course. She got it at home. . . . Those tapes, Harry, I couldn't watch."

Bosch could imagine. He envisioned the scenes and felt an unexpected flutter in his heart, as if it had torn loose inside of him and was banging against his ribs like a bird trying to break out of its cage.

"Anyway, the DA's got it and the big development is Bremmer's going to talk."

"He is?"

"Yeah, he heard we had the tapes and everything else. I guess he told his lawyer to deal. He's going to get life without the possibility of parole in exchange for leading us to the bodies and letting the shrinks have at him, study what makes him tick. My vote is they squash him like a fly, but I guess they are considering the families and science."

Bosch was silent. Bremmer would live. At first he didn't know what to think. Then he realized he could live with the deal. It had bothered him that those women might never be found. That was why he had visited Bremmer at the jail the day charges were first filed. Whether the victims had families who cared or not, he didn't want to leave them down there in the black chasm of the unknown.

It wasn't a bad deal, Bosch decided. Bremmer would be alive, but he wouldn't be living. It might even be worse for him than the gas chamber. And that would be justice, he thought.

"Anyway," Edgar said, "thought you'd want to know."

"Yeah."

"It's a weird fuckin' thing, you know? It being Bremmer. It's weirder than if it was Mora, man. A reporter! And, man, I knew the guy, too."

"Yeah, well, a lot of us did. I guess nobody knows anybody like they think."

"Yeah. Seeya, Harry."

Late that afternoon, he stood on the back deck, leaning forward on his new oak railing, looking out into the pass and thinking about the black heart. Its rhythm was so strong it could set the beat of a whole city. He knew it would always be the background beat, the cadence, of his own life. Bremmer would be banished now, hidden away forever, but he knew there would be another after him. And another after him. The black heart does not beat alone.

He lit a cigarette and thought about Honey Chandler, crowding his last view of her from his mind with the vision of her holding forth in court. That would always be her place in his mind. There had been something so pure and distilled about her fury — like the blue flame on a match before it burns out on its own. Even directed at him he could appreciate it.

His mind wandered to the statue at the courthouse steps. He still couldn't think of her name. A concrete blonde, Chandler had called her. Bosch wondered what Chandler had thought about justice at the end. At her end. He knew there was no justice without hope. Did she still have any hope left at the end? He believed that she did. Like the pure blue flame dimming to nothing, it was still there. Still hot. It was what allowed her to beat Bremmer.

He did not hear Sylvia until she stepped out onto the porch. He looked up and saw her there and wanted to go to her immediately, but held back. She was wearing blue jeans and a dark blue denim shirt. He'd bought the shirt for her birthday and he took that as a good sign. He guessed she had probably come from school, it having recessed for the weekend only an hour earlier.

"I called your office and they told me you were off. I thought I would come by to see how you were. I've been reading all about the case."

"I'm okay, Sylvia. How are you?"

"I'm fine."

"How are we?"

She smiled a little at that.

"Sounds like one of those bumper stickers you see. 'How'm I driving?' . . . Harry, I don't know how we are. I guess that's why I'm here."

There was an uneasy silence as she looked around the porch and out into the pass. Bosch crushed his cigarette out and dropped it in an old coffee can he kept by the door.

"Hey, new cushions."

"Yeah."

"Harry, you have to understand why I needed some time. It's —"

"I do."

"Let me finish. I rehearsed this enough times, I'd like to get a chance to actually say it to you. I just wanted to say that it is going to be very hard for me, for us, if we go on. It is going to be hard to deal with our pasts, our secrets, and most of all what you do, what you bring home with you . . ."

Bosch waited for her to continue. He knew she wasn't done.

"I know I don't have to remind you, but I've been through it before with a man I loved. And I saw it all go bad and — you know how it ended. There was a lot of pain for both of us. So you have to understand why I needed to take a step back and take a look at this. At us."

He nodded but she wasn't looking at him. Her not looking concerned him more than her words. He couldn't bring himself to speak, though. He didn't know what he could say.

"You live a very hard struggle, Harry. Your life, I mean. A cop. Yet with all your baggage I see and know there are still very noble things about you."

Now she looked at him.

"I do love you, Harry. I want to try to keep that alive because it's one of the best things about my life. One of the best things I know. I know it will be hard. But that might make it all the better. Who knows?"

He went to her then.

"Who knows?" he said.

And they held each other for a long time, his face next to hers, smelling her hair and skin. He held the back of her neck as though it was as fragile as a porcelain vase.

After a while they broke apart but only long enough to get on the chaise lounge together. They sat silently, just holding each other, for the longest time — until the sky started to dim and turn red and purple over the San Gabriels. Bosch knew there were still the secrets he carried, but they would keep for now. And he would avoid that black place of loneliness for just a while longer.

"Do you want to go away this weekend?" he asked. "Get away from the city? We could take that trip up to Lone Pine. Stay in a cabin tomorrow night."

"That would be wonderful. I could — We could use it."

A few minutes later she added, "We might not be able to get a cabin, Harry. There's so few of them and they're usually booked by Friday."

"I already have one on reserve."

She turned around so she could face him. She smiled slyly and said, "Oh, so you knew all the time. You were just hanging around waiting for me to come back. No sleepless nights, no surprise."

He didn't smile. He shook his head and for a few moments he looked out at the dying light reflected on the west wall of the San Gabriels.

"I didn't know, Sylvia," he said. "I hoped."